EVERYMAN,
I WILL GO WITH THEE,
AND BE THY GUIDE,
IN THY MOST NEED
TO GO BY THY SIDE

HENRY JAMES

Collected Stories

Volume 2 (1892–1910)
Selected and introduced by John Bayley

EVERYMAN'S LIBRARY

244

This book is one of 250 volumes in Everyman's Library
which have been distributed to 4500 state schools
throughout the United Kingdom.
The project has been supported by a grant of £4 million
from the Millennium Commission.

First included in Everyman's Library, 1999
Selection © David Campbell Publishers Ltd., 1999
Introduction, Bibliography and Chronology © David Campbell
Publishers Ltd., 1999
Typography by Peter B. Willberg

ISBN 1-85715-786-9

A CIP catalogue record for this book is available from the
British Library

Published by David Campbell Publishers Ltd.,
Gloucester Mansions, 140A Shaftesbury Avenue,
London WC2H 8HD

Distributed by Random House (UK) Ltd.,
20 Vauxhall Bridge Road, London SW1V 2SA

HENRY JAMES

CONTENTS

CONTENTS

INTRODUCTION

Early in this selection from the second half of James's treasure trove of stories comes the unexpectedly memorable tale he wrote for the Christmas issue of an illustrated magazine. As I remarked in the introduction to the first volume, James drew a distinction between what he called 'potboilers', written to order and for money, and the stories with which he was pleased, and which later he wished to preserve. 'Owen Wingrave' started life as one of the former, but ended in the second category. James recognized this by putting it in the New York edition of his tales, some years after its composition in 1892.

It is a tale which harks back to his own memories of the American Civil War, in which James had taken the same path as his young hero, following his own destiny as an aspirant of literature instead of responding to the national call and becoming a soldier. I doubt James felt guilt about this choice, then or later, but it must have made him extremely aware of the issues and the pressures involved; and this awareness makes the tale so memorable.

Ghost stories were becoming fashionable in the 1890s, and James found them a source of profit with magazines that had a large circulation and paid well. In the middle years of the decade three of his stories appeared in the *Yellow Book*, the new aesthetic quarterly which also featured the notorious drawings of Aubrey Beardsley. James, who carefully guarded his own reputation and distrusted anything overtly *louche*, had misgivings about this, but the *Yellow Book*'s editor Henry Harland would publish what he wanted, and at any length, and this offered a strong inducement to an author who as time went by was feeling, as he remarked, increasingly 'out of it'. James's play, *Guy Domville*, by means of which he had hoped not merely for fortune but for a new era of fame, had failed on the West End stage: the fans of his lengthier fiction, though still devoted, were a dwindling band. Even the loyal *Atlantic Review*, which had published so many of his tales, had shocked him by turning down 'The Pupil', ironically enough one of his best stories.

As one would expect, James handled the ghost story very much in his own way. He ignored its more vulgar and sensational appeal – not for him the all too physical spectres of his namesake and contemporary M. R. James – but he perceived in the form new methods of exploring dramatic situation and character. In 'Owen Wingrave' the supernatural is, as it were, on the side of those powerful and threatening forces of family and tradition which seek to prevent the young man from following his own inclinations and leading his own life. Death is the price he pays for the victory over them. When discovered in the haunted room 'He looked like a young soldier on a battle-field.' It is of some interest that James changed this last sentence when he revised his stories for the New York edition of his works to read, 'He was all the young soldier on the gained field.' That makes an elegant ending, but it also blurs the quiet pathos of the original, whose tone is so much more in keeping with the character of the hero and the nature of the tale. It imparts a distancing touch of irony, as the elaboration of James's late style is apt to do. Such afterthoughts and changes for the New York edition are occasionally felicitous but not often, and the stories in these two selected volumes are based, rightly in my view, on the text of their original publication in book form.

A further interest in the history of 'Owen Wingrave' is Bernard Shaw's remonstrance to James after he had seen as a theatre critic a one-act play called *The Saloon*, based by James on his story. Like almost all James's modest theatrical undertakings the play was not a success, but as a Socialist, and a believer in the capacity of human beings to help themselves and make their own future, Shaw was struck by what he felt to be James's pessimistic determinism. He urged James to change the play into something like a satiric comedy, in which the young hero would defeat those ghostly forces of tradition and family authority which sapped his own will as an individual. James naturally declined. Although the twentieth century had begun when the play appeared, he believed from his own past experience in the strength old powers of darkness still had to evoke irrational obedience, and the Great War that was to come in a few years showed him to be by no means wrong.

INTRODUCTION

'Daisy Miller', James's classic study of the All-American girl, had been by far the most successful story of his own earlier years. It is ironical that the one which became most well-known after his death should be 'The Turn of the Screw', the long ghost story which, like 'Owen Wingrave', had been originally conceived as a potboiler for magazine publication. It acquired fame too in his own lifetime, although James himself always professed that he could not see why, or understand what all the fuss was about. To him it was just another exercise in what had become a profitable genre, but for baffled and yet fascinated admirers it was to become the most enigmatic of all his tales.

And so it remains today, after the literary critics and the psychoanalysts who came after James have done, as it were, their worst. There have been many explanations of what happens in the tale, and numerous theories about it, some questioning the governess's own veracity and suggesting the ghosts did not exist for the two children, but were only present in her own neurotic imagination. As Leon Edel, the definitive biographer who had written so well on James, wisely observed, the factor of key importance is that James has deliberately left the reader 'the widest margin' of speculation. The reader, in other words, can draw his own conclusions about what happens in the tale: James did not come to any himself. He teased one inquisitive critic who asked him why evil in the story seemed to take an obscurely sexual form by saying that he himself had no notions in the story about either evil or sex. 'You have allowed yourself to get *ideas* about such things,' James is alleged to have said demurely, 'and I never do that'.

What is certain is that the story contains some of the author's best and most evocative writing. Whether or not we believe that the governess saw the ghosts, or whether there were in fact any ghosts to see, James's words etch the vision as sharply on the reader's mind as the vision itself did on that of the governess. The moment is so compelling that it suspends all disbelief.

I can hear again, as I write, the intense hush in which the sounds of evening dropped. The rooks stopped cawing in the golden sky and the friendly hour lost, for the minute, all its voice. But there was no other change in nature, unless indeed it were a change that I saw with a stranger sharpness. The gold was still in the sky, the clearness in the air, and the man who looked at me over the battlements was as definite as a picture in a frame.

The dead valet Quint appears on the top of a tower, as if James were deliberately borrowing the Gothic trappings of his predecessors in the ghost story business, like Mrs Radcliffe or the Brontës. 'Was there a "secret" at Bly', wonders the appalled governess – 'a mystery of Udolpho or an insane, unmentionable relative kept in unsuspected confinement?' As if for his own secret amusement James even hints here that the governess herself has read too many ghost stories. Is he, in the discreetest way possible, 'sending up' the genre? He certainly begins the story in the most traditional way possible, with assembled guests listening to a ghost story, a ghost story, moreover, that concerns what is spoken of as the worst imaginable kind of haunting – that of a young child – and not of one child only but two! Whether or not they are present in James's approach to the tale, such elements of parody make a perfect contrast with the reality his prose imposes upon the setting. There is nothing Gothic about its hallucinatory detail – that is pure James – down to the way in which the ghost's hand, as the apparition moves round the tower and seems to keep its eye on the governess, passes from one crenellation of the battlement to another.

Indeed, James's great strength as a writer of uncanny tales was precisely his sense of place, the same sense that had evoked for his reader London and Venice, the coast of New England and the English countryside. Bly, the gracious country home in 'The Turn of the Screw', is not a 'haunted house' – it is a tranquil place where dead persons have inexplicably come to appear – on the tower, at the edge of the wood across an ornamental water, outside the drawing-room window in the quiet of a calm afternoon. It is an incongruously peaceful setting for the two figures who have taken possession of it, as of the children who are its rightful inhabitants. The tale ends when little Miles's own heart, dispossessed of the ghostly pain, has stopped. Has the governess saved him? – or has her well-meaning persecution harassed him to death? The way James has handled the tale is so complete and so satisfying that at the end of it the query hardly seems to matter.

James contrives to make death itself a comforting topic and the solution in such stories. 'The Altar of the Dead' is one of his oddest yet most memorable tales. There are no ghosts in it, visible or invisible, but James himself archly classed it among his stories of a 'gruesome' variety, placing it in that category when he came to make a retrospective appraisal for the New York edition. Clearly the story meant much to him; the strange idea in it might appeal to an ageing man who has seen his friends drop off and die one by one, and who cherishes them in his memory as if he were lighting candles for them at an altar. Stransom actually does light such candles, and creates for himself a real chapel, unless the reader feels, as he well may, that altar and chapel and candles seem so real in the cadences of James's prose – here particularly reverberant – just because they are symbolical. There is, by coincidence, even an echo of a memorable little poem by Hardy, in which the poet sees his dead friend like a candle, burning lower and lower in the memory until it is no more than 'a spark, dying amid the dark'. Both James and Hardy seem to take refuge in the metaphor, as if it were the source of comfort that the candles and 'his dead' were to Stransom.

As Edel points out, James's imagination in the tale is purely secular: he does not connect his altar with any established religion, just as, in the different context of 'The Turn of the Screw', he does not connect what occurs with any conventional idea of ghosts, or with stories of the supernatural. Stransom's worship of the dead is a wholly subjective one, just as the governess's version of the things that happened at Bly may be. It is, so to speak, 'deadness' itself which is the inspiration of 'The Altar of the Dead', just as the unknowable secretive world of the child is possibly what inspired James's imagination in 'The Turn of the Screw'. James himself – his own moderately secret sense of humour much in evidence – claimed that the idea for 'The Altar of the Dead' came to him as he stopped in the street to watch a funeral procession with one of his French friends. Seeing the concourse 'bound merrily by' the friend remarked: *'Mourir à Londres, c'est être bien mort.'*

Edel is disposed to think, none the less, that there was something more deeply personal for James in the nature of the story, and he may well be right. James had never forgotten his friend Constance Fenimore Woolson, an American lady who had become very much attached to him, so much so indeed that James had taken fright and withdrawn himself from her, 'renouncing', like Stransom in his story, 'the friendship that was once so charming and comforting'. Poor Fenimore, as James always referred to her, retired to a lonely flat in Venice and died there in circumstances that pointed to suicide. It was probably one of the most traumatic events in James's life, and the shadow of it, embedded deep in memory and consciousness, is to be found in more than one of the stories, most notably in 'The Aspern Papers'. All great artists are egoists in their own style, and it was second nature to James to make use of whatever experience came his way, however painful and deep-seated it might be.

Such seems to be the case in 'The Altar of the Dead', where Stransom's friend Acton Hague has betrayed the woman who loved him as the narrator of 'The Aspern Papers' deceives the two women he seeks to make use of, and as James must have felt in gloomier moments that he had himself let down poor Fenimore. The story, like 'The Turn of the Screw', depends on atmosphere – the hypnotic, cumulative effect of style – rather than explanation or solution of a mystery. Whatever is going on, it is the going-on itself that matters. Whatever is 'rum' in life, as James would say, or in the psychology of the individual, can be presented, ruminated, pondered, but never definitively explained. James's later tales are the exact opposite not only of the genre of ghost story that was in vogue at the time, but also, and more obviously, the detective mystery or adventure tale, as exemplified by the Conan Doyle series featuring Sherlock Holmes. There is never any simple solution to the puzzles in the James casebook.

Melodrama and adventure, as James ironically perceived, depend on the nature of the interest we take in life. In 'The Story in It' he reflects on the significance of an invisible event, on the thing that might have happened, or happened only in the mind: in what was dreamed of or wished for rather than what occurred. What are considered the proper ingredients of a 'story', things that are dramatic and sensational, are precisely

the things that don't happen in the lives of ladies and gentlemen who have any respect for themselves. But what *does*
happen is of no less importance. In fact to the discerning
enquirer what does happen to such people in such a society is
of much greater and more absorbing interest than mere vulgar
adventure could be. The spectator who knows what to look
for can always find 'the story in it'.

The same sort of message is conveyed in a different form
through the narrative of the young searcher's quest for 'the
Figure in the Carpet'. Irony here is contained in the suggestion
that criticism, however well disposed, is looking the wrong
way if it is looking for the key that explains a writer's work,
and plucks out the heart of his mystery. The august author
Hugh Vereker, who might be seen as having a good deal in
common with James himself, frequently gives the impression,
throughout the richness of his writings, that some recurrent
motif there will afford an explanation of the whole. But the
quest is illusory: the idea itself provides an illusion of suspense,
of waiting for some coming revelation. But such a revelation,
for James as for his imaginary author, can only be in the mind
of the beholder, as much as in the creator's art. When the two
are, as James put it, 'wonderingly' in communion, the riches
of the carpet have been fully displayed. What an author needs
is the fullest sympathy from his reader with what his style
presents, and his sentences construct: the effect of the whole
less like the patterning of a carpet than it is like an Impressionist painting or a study by James's fellow-countryman Whistler.

Indeed, if there is a motif more or less common to James's
later tales it may lie in his muffled insistence that clarity of
explanation is not one of an author's duties or goals. What
matters most is what happens in the mind and the imagination,
the illusions and inner discoveries by which we live. 'We *know*
nothing on earth', as the Colonel observes in *The Golden Bowl*,
James's late, long and difficult masterpiece of a novel. This
is 'the soldier's watchword at night'. The times he was living
in now did feel like night to the elderly James: he felt neglected, ignored, and out of it. But he retained a tremendous
innate confidence in his own chosen method and approach;
and it is this approach itself which is explored, hinted at or

meditated in so many of the stories which he continued always to write.

Imagination is common to us all, whatever our circumstances and walk of life. James is as fully in sympathy with the inner life of the young telegraphist 'in the cage' as he is with the consciousness of a more privileged and liberated society. The girl of 'In the Cage' is nameless, like the governess in 'The Turn of the Screw', and the story may turn, once again, not on what is banally 'going on' but on what the young woman's imagination hopes and fears, wishes for and feeds upon. The telegrams that flash to and fro in cryptic fashion between exotic persons who live in high society and pursue its intrigues are for the girl the stuff of reality, because they are the stuff of dreams, the true interest of life. It would be unthinkable for James to reveal at the close of his tale what has actually been going on between the ladies and gentlemen of the telegrams. He does not know it: any more than his heroine does as she prepares to abandon all these glimpses of romance for the tedium of real life and a humdrum marriage. The interest has been all in the situation, and its promptings to the life of a curious mind.

'The Beast in the Jungle' is James's most sensational rendering of this theme, pushing, as it were, the non-existent to the point of melodrama. John Marcher is a man who lives in a state of permanent suspense, sure that something dire and tremendous is one day to happen to him, to spring out on his life like a crouching beast from its jungle lair. The revelation, as full of hidden irony as anything in James, is that nothing can or will happen because Marcher – appropriate name – is not the sort of man to whom things do happen. He marches unaware and in vain, accompanied by the ghost of what might have happened, the uncomplaining presence of the woman he might have loved. But the denouement of the tale is in its own Jamesian way as sensational, by reason of style and effect, as any melodramatic climax in Edgar Allan Poe. James indeed transposed the same underlying idea into an American setting when he wrote 'The Jolly Corner', a story prompted by his dislike of the crude new America he found when he revisited his native land in the new century. It is the story of a double, a Jekyll and Hyde situation with the appropriately Jamesian twist that the other half of the double does not exist – only *might* have existed, as the dreadful person that the Jamesian Spencer Brydon might have become, had he stayed on and worked for vulgar advancement in New York. Such an outcome, given James's temperament and personality, was unlikely to say the least of it: but once again such possibilities owe their truth, as art, to being 'all in the mind'.

And the mind can haunt itself to more than sufficient effect, just as memory may produce the most enduring of ghostly visitations. 'The Beast in the Jungle' has been hailed as a forerunner of Kafka and of his story *The Trial*, where the hero is accused of some crime he can hardly have committed, because it is not even specified. James's hero lives in the modern condition of *angst* and has been called an early example of Existential Man. James himself was certainly familiar with the loneliness which produces not only unmotivated guilt feelings but indefinite cravings for the life never lived. Leon Edel was no doubt right to sense yet again, in 'The Beast in the Jungle', the haunting presence of poor Constance Fenimore, who like May Bartram in the story may have loved a man with no love to give her in return. James, like Marcher, had, as Edel says, 'never allowed himself to know her feelings'; he was incapable of imagining in the woman to whom his own selfishness was attached a feeling that went beyond friendship.

In his declining years he had begun to see such things with penitential clarity, and as usual they went into his art. In 'The Bench of Desolation' it is the man who has been wronged, rather than the woman; but by coming together they are joined not so much in reconciliation and forgiveness as in a mutual recognition of their weakness and need. They are at least in that state together, a state that produces its own supportive feelings. These are the feelings and, ironically, the sense of living, that John Marcher can only have by clinging at the end to his own pain and bereavement, and to the shedding of his own tears – tears that at least, however 'belated and bitter, had something of the taste of life'.

As these examples indicate, there is a note of desperation

in James's last stories, even though it is a desperation overcome by the protagonists in a full and bitter knowledge of their plight; and for the author, as one may also feel, in the comfort of his mastery of the medium, the sombre joy of his own prose. As a critic observed of the earliest of James's stories in the *Atlantic Monthly*, it was a pleasure in itself, irrespective of plot, to read sentences so satisfying in themselves, 'so redolent of the completest shades of meaning'. Nevertheless there is an overwhelming sense of disillusionment – with society, with personal relationships, with his own self and its destiny – which was unknown among the enthusiasms and the abounding zest for life and experience to be found in earlier James. Many characters have become vessels full of hatred and revenge, like Mrs Grantham in 'The Two Faces', who makes a doll of her poor all-unknowing young rival in order to get her own back on the man who has jilted her. In 'The Beldonald Holbein' the cruelty that women in a high social position can wreak on other women makes a small intense and secret drama. As Edel observes, there now exist for James the most dully ferocious of beasts in the once for him alluring and intriguing social jungle, and he is all too horribly aware of them.

When he went to America things seemed even worse. The once cosy provincial town of New York dazed him with its savage glitter: its new skyscrapers, as James despondently remarked, looking like a lot of pins casually stuck into a pin cushion. And its denizens were made to match. Like the hero of a very late story, who has his money embezzled by a once trusted friend, James experiences here a sense of personal betrayal. His loneliness in the crowd and the big city desolates him and robs him of identity. And there is a new and meaningless malice and cruelty, on an appropriately grand scale. 'Crapy Cornelia' is a savage tale, full of James's rage against the brutal and fatuous vulgarity of the new smart class. James detests in particular the stifling *knowingness* of this new class. When he was younger he himself had loved in his own unique way to be in the know; but the leading theme in his last stories – and his last novels too, *The Golden Bowl* in particular – is the real stupidity of those who are sure they belong, as it were, to the 'knowing' élite, who can do no wrong.

INTRODUCTION

This was clearly going to be the music of the future – that if people were … made 'knowing' enough … all they had to do for civility was to take the amused ironic view of those who might be less initiated. In *his* time, when he was young or even when he was only but a little less middle-aged, the best manners had been the best kindness … concealing … for common humanity, if not for common decency, a part at least of the intensity and ferocity with which one might be 'in the know'.

Poor 'crapy Cornelia' is the victim of this new knowing and heartless unmannerliness, as James too increasingly felt himself to be.

But his work was done, and a great work it was. Even more than the majestic bulk of his novels his stories afford us a uniquely living record. They follow him throughout his life; they illustrate its purposes and its progress – where he lived, what he thought and experienced, what countries and towns he visited, what he tasted or rejected, what he hated and loved. The stories reveal the man, and in their own fascinating way demonstrate how he changed. Just as he was a sensitive instrument, far more sensitive even than other writers when it came to registering what was happening to him, so James continues to surprise and delight the reader of his stories with a sense of his own continuous growth and development. He is never a static being – always the same James – far from it. The stories are like a continuous frieze, almost a tapestry story, graphically displaying the author in the full emotional spectrum of his life and work, from youth to age.

John Bayley

About the Introducer

John Bayley is former Thomas Warton Professor of English Literature at the University of Oxford. His many books include *The Short Story: Henry James to Elizabeth Bowen*; *An Essay on Hardy, Shakespeare and Tragedy*; *Tolstoy and the Novel*; *Pushkin: A Comparative Commentary* and a detailed study of A. E. Housman's poems. He has also written several novels.

SELECT BIBLIOGRAPHY

───

Biographically, the five-volume *Life* by Leon Edel, Hart-Davis, 1953–72, is unchallenged in comprehensiveness. F. W. Dupee's *Henry James: His Life and Writings*, Methuen, 1951, rev. ed. 1965, remains an excellent short biography. Miranda Seymour's *A Ring of Foreign Correspondents: Henry James and his English Circle 1897–1916*, Hodder & Stoughton, 1988, offers a charming account of the writer's domestic life and friendships.

There are various collections of letters, including four volumes edited by Edel and published by Harvard University Press in the US and Macmillan in the UK, 1974–84. James's *Complete Notebooks*, edited by Edel and L. H. Powers, Oxford University Press, 1987, throw light on the fiction, including many of the longer tales.

There is a vast quantity of James criticism, much of it excellent. Complete listings can be found in the *Bibliography of Henry James* by Edel and D. H. Laurence, Hart-Davis, 1961, though this is probably only of use to the advanced student. Among accessible short surveys of James's fictions are Dupee (see above), D. W. Jefferson, *Henry James*, Oliver and Boyd, 1960, and Tony Tanner, *Henry James: The Writer and his Work*, University of Massachusetts Press, 1985, which includes a helpful brief bibliography and a chronological listing of James's books. While there are no good studies devoted specifically to the short stories, John Bayley's *The Short Story: Henry James to Elizabeth Bowen*, Harvester Press, 1988, is a useful starting point.

CHRONOLOGY

DATE	AUTHOR'S LIFE	LITERARY CONTEXT
1842	Birth of William James.	
1843	Henry James born in New York City.	
1848		
1851		Melville: *Moby-Dick*.
1852		
1854–6		
1855–9	Extensive travels and education abroad.	
1856		Flaubert: *Madame Bovary*. Turgenev: *Rudin*.
1857		
1859		Eliot: *Adam Bede*.
1860	Return to America.	Eliot: *The Mill on the Floss*. Turgenev: *On the Eve*. Hawthorne: *The Marble Faun*.
1861		Dickens: *Great Expectations*. Turgenev: *Fathers and Children*.
1861–5		
1862–3	Harvard Law School.	Flaubert: *Salammbô*.
1864	First story ('A Tragedy of Error') published anonymously.	Trollope: *Can You Forgive Her?*
1865	First signed story ('The Story of a Year') published in *Atlantic Monthly*.	Dickens: *Our Mutual Friend*.
1867		Zola: *Thérèse Raquin*.
1869	First adult travels in Europe (to 1870).	Flaubert: *L'Education sentimentale*. Tolstoy: *War and Peace*.
1870	Death of Minny Temple. *Watch and Ward* – first novel – serialized in *Atlantic Monthly*.	
1871		Eliot: *Middlemarch* (to 1872). Zola: *La Fortune des Rougon*.
1872–4	Further travels in Europe.	
1874–5	Returns to America on completion of his first large novel, *Roderick Hudson*.	Hardy: *Far from the Madding Crowd*.
1875	*Transatlantic Sketches*, *A Passionate Pilgrim* (first collection of stories) and *Roderick Hudson* published.	Trollope: *The Way We Live Now*.

European revolutions. Californian Gold Rush.
Great Exhibition.
Louis Napoleon proclaimed Emperor of France.
Crimean War.

Indian Mutiny.
Darwin: *The Origin of Species*.

Ten states secede from Union. American Civil war begins.

Presidency of Lincoln.

End of Civil War. Assassination of Lincoln.

Marx: *Das Kapital* I.

Franco-Prussian War.

First Impressionist exhibition in Paris (1874).

DATE	AUTHOR'S LIFE	LITERARY CONTEXT
1875–6	Visits Paris, where he meets Turgenev, Zola and Flaubert. Settles in London.	Eliot: *Daniel Deronda*. Twain: *Tom Sawyer*.
1877	*The American.*	
1878	'Daisy Miller' establishes his international reputation. Publishes first volume of essays (*French Poets and Novelists*).	Hardy: *The Return of the Native*.
1879	*Hawthorne.*	Ibsen: *A Doll's House*.
1880		Dostoevsky: *The Brothers Karamazov*. Death of George Eliot and Flaubert.
1881	*Washington Square. The Portrait of a Lady.*	
1882–3	Visits America. Death of his parents.	
1883		Maupassant: *Une Vie*.
1884	Returns to London with his sister Alice.	Mark Twain: *The Adventures of Huckleberry Finn*.
1885		Howells: *The Rise of Silas Lapham*. Zola: *Germinal*. Maupassant: *Bel Ami*.
1886	*The Bostonians. The Princess Casamassima.*	Stevenson: *Dr Jekyll and Mr Hyde*. Chekhov: 'The Kiss'.
1887	Living in Italy. Friendship with Constance Fenimore Woolson.	
1888	'The Aspern Papers'.	Kipling: *Plain Tales from the Hills*.
1890	*The Tragic Muse.* Dramatizes *The American*, which has a short run.	William James: *Principles of Psychology*. Kipling: *Soldiers Three*.
1891	Writing for the theatre.	Hardy: *Tess of the d'Urbervilles*. Gissing: *New Grub Street*.
1892	Death of Alice James.	Wilde: *Lady Windermere's Fan*.
1895	Booed off stage at première of *Guy Domville*. Gives up writing for theatre.	Crane: *The Red Badge of Courage*. Hardy: *Jude the Obscure*. Wells: *The Time Machine*. Wilde: *The Importance of Being Earnest*.
1896		
1897	Settles at Lamb House, Rye. *The Spoils of Pynton. What Maisie Knew.*	Conrad: *The Nigger of the 'Narcissus'*. Wells: *The Invisible Man*.
1898	'In the Cage'. 'The Turn of the Screw'.	Shaw: *Plays Pleasant and Unpleasant*.

CHRONOLOGY

HISTORICAL EVENTS

Invention of telephone (1876).

Gladstone becomes Prime Minister.

Irish Land Act.

Married Women's Property Act (1882).

Year of the 'Great Upheaval' (USA): 700,000 on strike; demand for eight-hour day.
Victoria's Golden Jubilee.

Klondike Gold Rush.

DATE	AUTHOR'S LIFE	LITERARY CONTEXT
1899	*The Awkward Age.* Friendship with Conrad and Wells.	Chopin: *The Awakening.* Norris: *McTeague.*
1900		Dreiser: *Sister Carrie.* Conrad: *Lord Jim.*
1901	*The Sacred Fount.*	Kipling: *Kim.*
1901–9		
1902	*The Wings of the Dove.*	William James: *Varieties of Religious Experience.*
1903	*The Ambassadors.* 'The Beast in the Jungle'. First meeting with Edith Wharton.	Butler: *The Way of All Flesh.* Chekhov: *The Cherry Orchard.*
1904	*The Golden Bowl.*	Conrad: *Nostromo.*
1905	Visits America for the first time in 20 years.	Wells: *Kipps.* Wharton: *The House of Mirth.*
1906	*The American Scene.*	Sinclair: *The Jungle.*
1906–10	Prepares 'New York Edition' of his work in 24 volumes.	
1907		Adams: *The Education of Henry Adams.* Conrad: *The Secret Agent.* William James: *Pragmatism.*
1908		Forster: *A Room with a View.* Bennett: *The Old Wives' Tale.*
1909		Wells: *Ann Veronica; Tono Bungay.*
1910	Last story, 'A Round of Visits', published. Death of brother, William.	Wells: *Mr Polly.* Forster: *Howards End.*
1911		Conrad: *Under Western Eyes.*
1912		Wharton: *Ethan Frome.* Mann: *Death in Venice.*
1913	*A Small Boy and Others* (autobiography).	Lawrence: *Sons and Lovers.* Wharton: *The Custom of the Country.* Proust: *Swann's Way.*
1914	*Notes of a Son and Brother* (autobiography).	Joyce: *Dubliners.* Conrad: *Chance.*
1915	Becomes British subject.	Lawrence: *The Rainbow.* Ford: *The Good Soldier.* Conrad: *Victory.* Woolf: *The Voyage Out.*
1916	Dies in London, 28 February.	Joyce: *A Portrait of the Artist as a Young Man.*
1917	*The Ivory Tower* and *The Sense of the Past* (unfinished novels). *The Middle Years* (autobiography).	

CHRONOLOGY

A NOTE ON THE TEXT

———

The texts of the stories in this collection are taken from their original publications in various sources, and not from the amended versions James prepared for the New York edition of his works.

HENRY JAMES
COLLECTED STORIES

VOLUME 2 (1892–1910)

THE PRIVATE LIFE

WE talked of London, face to face with a great bristling, prim-
eval glacier. The hour and the scene were one of those
impressions which make up a little, in Switzerland, for the
modern indignity of travel – the promiscuities and vulgarities,
the station and the hotel, the gregarious patience, the struggle
for a scrappy attention, the reduction to a numbered state. The
high valley was pink with the mountain rose, the cool air as
fresh as if the world were young. There was a faint flush of
afternoon on undiminished snows, and the fraternising tinkle
of the unseen cattle came to us with a cropped and sun-warmed
odour. The balconied inn stood on the very neck of the sweetest
pass in the Oberland, and for a week we had had company and
weather. This was felt to be great luck, for one would have
made up for the other had either been bad.

The weather certainly would have made up for the company; but it was not subjected to this tax, for we had by a happy
chance the *fleur des pois*: Lord and Lady Mellifont, Clare Vawdrey, the greatest (in the opinion of many) of our literary
glories, and Blanche Adney, the greatest (in the opinion of
all) of our theatrical. I mention these first, because they were
just the people whom in London, at that time, people tried to
'get'. People endeavoured to 'book' them six weeks ahead, yet
on this occasion we had come in for them, we had all come in
for each other, without the least wire-pulling. A turn of the
game had pitched us together, the last of August, and
we recognised our luck by remaining so, under protection of
the barometer. When the golden days were over – that would
come soon enough – we should wind down opposite sides of
the pass and disappear over the crest of surrounding heights.
We were of the same general communion, we participated in
the same miscellaneous publicity. We met, in London, with
irregular frequency; we were more or less governed by the
laws and the language, the traditions and the shibboleths of

the same dense social state. I think all of us, even the ladies, 'did' something, though we pretended we didn't when it was mentioned. Such things are not mentioned indeed in London, but it was our innocent pleasure to be different here. There had to be some way to show the difference, inasmuch as we were under the impression that this was our annual holiday. We felt at any rate that the conditions were more human than in London, or that at least we ourselves were. We were frank about this, we talked about it: it was what we were talking about as we looked at the flushing glacier, just as some one called attention to the prolonged absence of Lord Mellifont and Mrs Adney. We were seated on the terrace of the inn, where there were benches and little tables, and those of us who were most bent on proving that we had returned to nature were, in the queer Germanic fashion, having coffee before meat.

The remark about the absence of our two companions was not taken up, not even by Lady Mellifont, not even by little Adney, the fond composer; for it had been dropped only in the briefest intermission of Clare Vawdrey's talk. (This celebrity was 'Clarence' only on the title-page.) It was just that revelation of our being after all human that was his theme. He asked the company whether, candidly, every one hadn't been tempted to say to every one else: 'I had no idea you were really so nice.' I had had, for my part, an idea that *he* was, and even a good deal nicer, but that was too complicated to go into then; besides it is exactly my story. There was a general understanding among us that when Vawdrey talked we should be silent, and not, oddly enough, because he at all expected it. He didn't, for of all abundant talkers he was the most unconscious, the least greedy and professional. It was rather the religion of the host, of the hostess, that prevailed among us: it was their own idea, but they always looked for a listening circle when the great novelist dined with them. On the occasion I allude to there was probably no one present with whom, in London, he had not dined, and we felt the force of this habit. He had dined even with me; and on the evening of that dinner, as on this Alpine afternoon, I had been at no pains to hold my tongue, absorbed as I inveterately was in a study of the question which always rose before me, to such a height, in his fair, square, strong stature.

This question was all the more tormenting that he never suspected himself (I am sure) of imposing it, any more than he had ever observed that every day of his life every one listened to him at dinner. He used to be called 'subjective' in the weekly papers, but in society no distinguished man could have been less so. He never talked about himself; and this was a topic on which, though it would have been tremendously worthy of him, he apparently never even reflected. He had his hours and his habits, his tailor and his hatter, his hygiene and his particular wine, but all these things together never made up an attitude. Yet they constituted the only attitude he ever adopted, and it was easy for him to refer to our being 'nicer' abroad than at home. *He* was exempt from variations, and not a shade either less or more nice in one place than in another. He differed from other people, but never from himself (save in the extraordinary sense which I will presently explain), and struck me as having neither moods nor sensibilities nor preferences. He might have been always in the same company, so far as he recognised any influence from age or condition or sex: he addressed himself to women exactly as he addressed himself to men, and gossiped with all men alike, talking no better to clever folk than to dull. I used to feel a despair at his way of liking one subject – so far as I could tell – precisely as much as another: there were some I hated so myself. I never found him anything but loud and cheerful and copious, and I never heard him utter a paradox or express a shade or play with an idea. That fancy about our being 'human' was, in his conversation, quite an exceptional flight. His opinions were sound and second-rate, and of his perceptions it was too mystifying to think. I envied him his magnificent health.

Vawdrey had marched, with his even pace and his perfectly good conscience, into the flat country of anecdote, where stories are visible from afar like windmills and signposts; but I observed after a little that Lady Mellifont's attention wandered. I happened to be sitting next her. I noticed that her eyes rambled a little anxiously over the lower slopes of the

mountains. At last, after looking at her watch, she said to me:
'Do you know where they went?'

'Do you mean Mrs Adney and Lord Mellifont?'

'Lord Mellifont and Mrs Adney.' Her ladyship's speech
seemed – unconsciously indeed – to correct me, but it didn't
occur to me that this was because she was jealous. I imputed to
her no such vulgar sentiment: in the first place, because I liked
her, and in the second because it would always occur to one
quickly that it was right, in any connection, to put Lord Mellifont first. He *was* first – extraordinarily first. I don't say greatest
or wisest or most renowned, but essentially at the top of the list
and the head of the table. That is a position by itself, and his
wife was naturally accustomed to see him in it. My phrase had
sounded as if Mrs Adney had taken him; but it was not possible
for him to be taken – he only took. No one, in the nature of
things, could know this better than Lady Mellifont. I had
originally been rather afraid of her, thinking her, with her stiff
silences and the extreme blackness of almost everything that
made up her person, somewhat hard, even a little saturnine.
Her paleness seemed slightly grey, and her glossy black hair
metallic, like the brooches and bands and combs with which it
was inveterately adorned. She was in perpetual mourning, and
wore numberless ornaments of jet and onyx, a thousand click-
ing chains and bugles and beads. I had heard Mrs Adney call
her the queen of night, and the term was descriptive if you
understood that the night was cloudy. She had a secret, and if
you didn't find it out as you knew her better you at least
perceived that she was gentle and unaffected and limited, and
also rather submissively sad. She was like a woman with a
painless malady. I told her that I had merely seen her husband
and his companion stroll down the glen together about an hour
before, and suggested that Mr Adney would perhaps know
something of their intentions.

Vincent Adney, who, though he was fifty years old, looked
like a good little boy on whom it had been impressed that
children should not talk before company, acquitted himself
with remarkable simplicity and taste of the position of husband
of a great exponent of comedy. When all was said about her

making it easy for him, one couldn't help admiring the charmed affection with which he took everything for granted. It is difficult for a husband who is not on the stage, or at least in the theatre, to be graceful about a wife who is; but Adney was more than graceful – he was exquisite, he was inspired. He set his beloved to music; and you remember how genuine his music could be – the only English compositions I ever saw a foreigner take an interest in. His wife was in them, somewhere, always; they were like a free, rich translation of the impression she produced. She seemed, as one listened, to pass laughing, with loosened hair, across the scene. He had been only a little fiddler at her theatre, always in his place during the acts; but she had made him something rare and misunderstood. Their superiority had become a kind of partnership, and their happiness was a part of the happiness of their friends. Adney's one discomfort was that he couldn't write a play for his wife, and the only way he meddled with her affairs was by asking impossible people if *they* couldn't.

Lady Mellifont, after looking across at him a moment, remarked to me that she would rather not put any question to him. She added the next minute: 'I had rather people shouldn't see I'm nervous.'

'*Are* you nervous?'

'I always become so if my husband is away from me for any time.'

'Do you imagine something has happened to him?'

'Yes, always. Of course I'm used to it.'

'Do you mean his tumbling over precipices – that sort of thing?'

'I don't know exactly what it is: it's the general sense that he'll never come back.'

She said so much and kept back so much that the only way to treat the condition she referred to seemed the jocular. 'Surely he'll never forsake you!' I laughed.

She looked at the ground a moment. 'Oh, at bottom I'm easy.'

'Nothing can ever happen to a man so accomplished, so infallible, so armed at all points,' I went on, encouragingly.

'Oh, you don't know how he's armed!' she exclaimed, with such an odd quaver that I could account for it only by her being nervous. This idea was confirmed by her moving just afterwards, changing her seat rather pointlessly, not as if to cut our conversation short, but because she was in a fidget. I couldn't know what was the matter with her, but I was presently relieved to see Mrs Adney come toward us. She had in her hand a big bunch of wild flowers, but she was not closely attended by Lord Mellifont. I quickly saw, however, that she had no disaster to announce; yet as I knew there was a question Lady Mellifont would like to hear answered, but did not wish to ask, I expressed to her immediately the hope that his lordship had not remained in a crevasse.

'Oh, no; he left me but three minutes ago. He has gone into the house.' Blanche Adney rested her eyes on mine an instant – a mode of intercourse to which no man, for himself, could ever object. The interest, on this occasion, was quickened by the particular thing the eyes happened to say. What they usually said was only: 'Oh, yes I'm charming, I know, but don't make a fuss about it. I only want a new part – I do, I do!' At present they added, dimly, surreptitiously, and of course sweetly – for that was the way they did everything: 'It's all right, but something did happen. Perhaps I'll tell you later.' She turned to Lady Mellifont, and the transition to simple gaiety suggested her mastery of her profession. 'I've brought him safe. We had a charming walk.'

'I'm so very glad,' returned Lady Mellifont, with her faint smile; continuing vaguely, as she got up: 'He must have gone to dress for dinner. Isn't it rather near?' She moved away, to the hotel, in her leave-taking, simplifying fashion, and the rest of us, at the mention of dinner, looked at each other's watches, as if to shift the responsibility of such grossness. The head-waiter, essentially, like all head-waiters, a man of the world, allowed us hours and places of our own, so that in the evening, apart under the lamp, we formed a compact, an indulged little circle. But it was only the Mellifonts who 'dressed' and as to whom it was recognised that they naturally *would* dress: she in exactly the same manner as on any other evening of her ceremonious existence (she was not a woman whose habits could take account of anything so mutable as fitness); and he, on the other hand, with remarkable adjustment and suitability. He was almost as much a man of the world as the head-waiter, and spoke almost as many languages; but he abstained from courting a comparison of dress-coats and white waistcoats, analysing the occasion in a much finer way – into black velvet and blue velvet and brown velvet, for instance, into delicate harmonies of necktie and subtle informalities of shirt. He had a costume for every function and a moral for every costume; and his functions and costumes and morals were ever a part of the amusement of life – a part at any rate of its beauty and romance – for an immense circle of spectators. For his particular friends indeed these things were more than an amusement; they were a topic, a social support and of course, in addition, a subject of perpetual suspense. If his wife had not been present before dinner they were what the rest of us probably would have been putting our heads together about.

Clare Vawdrey had a fund of anecdote on the whole question: he had known Lord Mellifont almost from the beginning. It was a peculiarity of this nobleman that there could be no conversation about him that didn't instantly take the form of anecdote, and a still further distinction that there could apparently be no anecdote that was not on the whole to his honour. If he had come into a room at any moment, people might have said frankly: 'Of course we were telling stories about you!' As consciences go, in London, the general conscience would have been good. Moreover it would have been impossible to imagine his taking such a tribute otherwise than amiably, for he was always as unperturbed as an actor with the right cue. He had never in his life needed the prompter – his very embarrassments had been rehearsed. For myself, when he was talked about I always had an odd impression that we were speaking of the dead – it was with that peculiar accumulation of relish. His reputation was a kind of gilded obelisk, as if he had been buried beneath it; the body of legend and reminiscence of which he was to be the subject had crystallised in advance.

This ambiguity sprang, I suppose, from the fact that the mere sound of his name and air of his person, the general expectation he created, were, somehow, too exalted to be verified. The experience of his urbanity always came later; the prefigurement, the legend paled before the reality. I remember that on the evening I refer to the reality was particularly operative. The handsomest man of his period could never have looked better, and he sat among us like a bland conductor controlling by an harmonious play of arm an orchestra still a little rough. He directed the conversation by gestures as irresistible as they were vague; one felt as if without him it wouldn't have had anything to call a tone. This was essentially what he contributed to any occasion – what he contributed above all to English public life. He pervaded it, he coloured it, he embellished it, and without him it would scarcely have had a vocabulary. Certainly it would not have had a style; for a style was what it had in having Lord Mellifont. He *was* a style. I was freshly struck with it as, in the *salle à manger* of the little Swiss inn, we resigned ourselves to inevitable veal. Confronted with his form (I must parenthesise that it was not confronted much), Clare Vawdrey's talk suggested the reporter contrasted with the bard. It was interesting to watch the shock of characters from which, of an evening, so much would be expected. There was however no concussion – it was all muffled and minimised in Lord Mellifont's tact. It was rudimentary with him to find the solution of such a problem in playing the host, assuming responsibilities which carried with them their sacrifice. He had indeed never been a guest in his life; he was the host, the patron, the moderator at every board. If there was a defect in his manner (and I suggest it under my breath), it was that he had a little more art than any conjunction – even the most complicated – could possibly require. At any rate one made one's reflections in noticing how the accomplished peer handled the situation and how the sturdy man of letters was unconscious that the situation (and least of all he himself as part of it) was handled. Lord Mellifont poured forth treasures of tact, and Clare Vawdrey never dreamed he was doing it.

Vawdrey had no suspicion of any such precaution even when Blanche Adney asked him if he saw yet their third act – an inquiry into which she introduced a subtlety of her own. She had a theory that he was to write her a play and that the heroine, if he would only do his duty, would be the part for which she had immemorially longed. She was forty years old (this could be no secret to those who had admired her from the first), and she could now reach out her hand and touch her uttermost goal. This gave a kind of tragic passion – perfect actress of comedy as she was – to her desire not to miss the great thing. The years had passed, and still she had missed it; none of the things she had done was the thing she had dreamed of, so that at present there was no more time to lose. This was the canker in the rose, the ache beneath the smile. It made her touching – made her sadness even sweeter than her laughter. She had done the old English and the new French, and had charmed her generation; but she was haunted by the vision of a bigger chance, of something truer to the conditions that lay near her. She was tired of Sheridan and she hated Bowdler; she called for a canvas of a finer grain. The worst of it, to my sense, was that she would never extract her modern comedy from the great mature novelist, who was as incapable of producing it as he was of threading a needle. She coddled him, she talked to him, she made love to him, as she frankly proclaimed; but she dwelt in illusions – she would have to live and die with Bowdler.

It is difficult to be cursory over this charming woman, who was beautiful without beauty and complete with a dozen deficiencies. The perspective of the stage made her over, and in society she was like the model off the pedestal. She was the picture walking about, which to the artless social mind was a perpetual surprise – a miracle. People thought she told them the secrets of the pictorial nature, in return for which they gave her relaxation and tea. She told them nothing and she drank the tea; but they had, all the same, the best of the bargain. Vawdrey was really at work on a play; but if he had begun it because he liked her I think he let it drag for the same reason. He secretly felt the atrocious difficulty – knew that from his hand the finished piece would have received no active life. At the same time nothing could be more agreeable than to have such a question open with Blanche Adney, and from time to time he put something very good into the play. If he deceived Mrs Adney it was only because in her despair she was determined to be deceived. To her question about their third act he replied that, before dinner, he had written a magnificent passage.

'Before dinner?' I said. 'Why, *cher maître*, before dinner you were holding us all spellbound on the terrace.'

My words were a joke, because I thought his had been; but for the first time that I could remember I perceived a certain confusion in his face. He looked at me hard, throwing back his head quickly, the least bit like a horse who has been pulled up short. 'Oh, it was before that,' he replied, naturally enough.

'Before that you were playing billiards with *me*,' Lord Mellifont intimated.

'Then it must have been yesterday,' said Vawdrey.

But he was in a tight place. 'You told me this morning you did nothing yesterday,' the actress objected.

'I don't think I really know when I do things.' Vawdrey looked vaguely, without helping himself, at a dish that was offered him.

'It's enough if *we* know,' smiled Lord Mellifont.

'I don't believe you've written a line,' said Blanche Adney.

'I think I could repeat you the scene.' Vawdrey helped himself to *haricots verts*.

'Oh, do – oh, do!' two or three of us cried.

'After dinner, in the salon; it will be an immense *régal*,' Lord Mellifont declared.

'I'm not sure, but I'll try,' Vawdrey went on.

'Oh, you lovely man!' exclaimed the actress, who was practising Americanisms, being resigned even to an American comedy.

'But there must be this condition,' said Vawdrey: 'you must make your husband play.'

'Play while you're reading? Never!'

'I've too much vanity,' said Adney.

Lord Mellifont distinguished him. 'You must give us the overture, before the curtain rises. That's a peculiarly delightful moment.'

'I sha'n't read – I shall just speak,' said Vawdrey.

'Better still, let me go and get your manuscript,' the actress suggested.

Vawdrey replied that the manuscript didn't matter; but an hour later, in the salon, we wished he might have had it. We sat expectant, still under the spell of Adney's violin. His wife, in the foreground, on an ottoman, was all impatience and profile, and Lord Mellifont, in the chair – it was always *the* chair, Lord Mellifont's – made our grateful little group feel like a social science congress or a distribution of prizes. Suddenly, instead of beginning, our tame lion began to roar out of tune – he had clean forgotten every word. He was very sorry, but the lines absolutely wouldn't come to him; he was utterly ashamed, but his memory was a blank. He didn't look in the least ashamed – Vawdrey had never looked ashamed in his life; he was only imperturbably and merrily natural. He protested that he had never expected to make such a fool of himself, but we felt that this wouldn't prevent the incident from taking its place among his jolliest reminiscences. It was only *we* who were humiliated, as if he had played us a premeditated trick. This was an occasion, if ever, for Lord Mellifont's tact, which descended on us all like balm: he told us, in his charming artistic way, his way of bridging over arid intervals (he had a *débit* – there was nothing to approach it in England – like the actors of the Comédie Française), of his own collapse on a momentous occasion, the delivery of an address to a mighty multitude, when, finding he had forgotten his memoranda, he fumbled, on the terrible platform, the cynosure of every eye, fumbled vainly in irreproachable pockets for indispensable notes. But the point of his story was finer than that of Vawdrey's pleasantry; for he sketched with a few light gestures the brilliancy of a performance which had risen superior to embarrassment, had resolved itself, we were left to divine, into an effort recognised at the moment as not absolutely a blot on what the public was so good as to call his reputation.

'Play up – play up!' cried Blanche Adney, tapping her husband and remembering how, on the stage, a *contretemps* is always drowned in music. Adney threw himself upon his fiddle, and I said to Clare Vawdrey that his mistake could easily be corrected by his sending for the manuscript. If he would tell me where it was I would immediately fetch it from his room. To this he replied: 'My dear fellow, I'm afraid there *is* no manuscript.'

'Then you've not written anything?'

'I'll write it to-morrow.'

'Ah, you trifle with us,' I said, in much mystification.

Vawdrey hesitated an instant. 'If there *is* anything, you'll find it on my table.'

At this moment one of the others spoke to him, and Lady Mellifont remarked audibly, as if to correct gently our want of consideration, that Mr Adney was playing something very beautiful. I had noticed before that she appeared extremely fond of music; she always listened to it in a hushed transport. Vawdrey's attention was drawn away, but it didn't seem to me that the words he had just dropped constituted a definite permission to go to his room. Moreover I wanted to speak to Blanche Adney; I had something to ask her. I had to await my chance, however, as we remained silent awhile for her husband, after which the conversation became general. It was our habit to go to bed early, but there was still a little of the evening left. Before it quite waned I found an opportunity to tell the actress that Vawdrey had given me leave to put my hand on his manuscript. She adjured me, by all I held sacred, to bring it immediately, to give it to her; and her insistence was proof against my suggestion that it would now be too late for him to begin to read; besides which the charm was broken – the others wouldn't care. It was not too late for *her* to begin; therefore I was to possess myself, without more delay, of the precious pages. I told her she should be obeyed in a moment, but I wanted her first to satisfy my just curiosity. What had happened before dinner, while she was on the hills with Lord Mellifont?

'How do you know anything happened?'

'I saw it in your face when you came back.'

'And they call me an actress!' cried Mrs Adney.

'What do they call *me*?' I inquired.

'You're a searcher of hearts – that frivolous thing an observer.'

'I wish you'd let an observer write you a play!' I broke out.

'People don't care for what you write: you'd break any run of luck.'

'Well, I see plays all round me,' I declared; 'the air is full of them to-night.'

'The air? Thank you for nothing! I only wish my table-drawers were.'

'Did he make love to you on the glacier?' I went on.

She stared; then broke into the graduated ecstasy of her laugh. 'Lord Mellifont, poor dear? What a funny place! It would indeed be the place for *our* love!'

'Did he fall into a crevasse?' I continued.

Blanche Adney looked at me again as she had done for an instant when she came up, before dinner, with her hands full of flowers. 'I don't know into what he fell. I'll tell you to-morrow.'

'He did come down, then?'

'Perhaps he went up,' she laughed. 'It's really strange.'

'All the more reason you should tell me to-night.'

'I must think it over; I must puzzle it out.'

'Oh, if you want conundrums I'll throw in another,' I said. 'What's the matter with the master?'

'The master of what?'

'Of every form of dissimulation. Vawdrey hasn't written a line.'

'Go and get his papers and we'll see.'

'I don't like to expose him,' I said.

'Why not, if I expose Lord Mellifont?'

'Oh, I'd do anything for that,' I conceded. 'But why should Vawdrey have made a false statement? It's very curious.'

'It's very curious,' Blanche Adney repeated, with a musing air and her eyes on Lord Mellifont. Then, rousing herself, she added: 'Go and look in his room.'

'In Lord Mellifont's?'

She turned to me quickly. '*That* would be a way!'

'A way to what?'

'To find out – to find out!' She spoke gaily and excitedly, but suddenly checked herself. 'We're talking nonsense,' she said.

'We're mixing things up, but I'm struck with your idea. Get Lady Mellifont to let you.'

'Oh, *she* has looked!' Mrs Adney murmured, with the oddest dramatic expression. Then, after a movement of her beautiful uplifted hand, as if to brush away a fantastic vision, she exclaimed imperiously: 'Bring me the scene – bring me the scene!'

'I go for it,' I answered; 'but don't tell me I can't write a play.'

She left me, but my errand was arrested by the approach of a lady who had produced a birthday-book – we had been threatened with it for several evenings – and who did me the honour to solicit my autograph. She had been asking the others, and she couldn't decently leave me out. I could usually remember my name, but it always took me some time to recall my date, and even when I had done so I was never very sure. I hesitated between two days and I remarked to my petitioner that I would sign on both if it would give her any satisfaction. She said that surely I had been born only once; and I replied of course that on the day I made her acquaintance I had been born again. I mention the feeble joke only to show that, with the obligatory inspection of the other autographs, we gave some minutes to this transaction. The lady departed with her book, and then I became aware that the company had dispersed. I was alone in the little salon that had been appropriated to our use. My first impression was one of disappointment: if Vawdrey had gone to bed I didn't wish to disturb him. While I hesitated, however, I recognised that Vawdrey had not gone to bed. A window was open, and the sound of voices outside came in to me: Blanche was on the terrace with her dramatist, and they were talking about the stars. I went to the window for a glimpse – the Alpine night was splendid. My friends had stepped out together; the actress had picked up a cloak; she looked as I had seen her look in the wing of the theatre. They were silent awhile, and I heard the roar of a neighbouring torrent. I turned back into the room, and its quiet lamplight gave me an idea. Our companions had dispersed – it was late for a pastoral country – and we three should have the place to ourselves. Clare Vawdrey had written his scene – it was magnificent; and his reading it to us there, at such an hour, would be an episode intensely memorable. I would bring down his manuscript and meet the two with it as they came in.

I quitted the salon for this purpose; I had been in Vawdrey's room and knew it was on the second floor, the last in a long corridor. A minute later my hand was on the knob of his door, which I naturally pushed open without knocking. It was equally natural that in the absence of its occupant the room should be dark; the more so as, the end of the corridor being at that hour unlighted, the obscurity was not immediately diminished by the opening of the door. I was only aware at first that I had made no mistake and that, the window-curtains not being drawn, I was confronted with a couple of vague starlighted apertures. Their aid, however, was not sufficient to enable me to find what I had come for, and my hand, in my pocket, was already on the little box of matches that I always carried for cigarettes. Suddenly I withdrew it with a start, uttering an ejaculation, an apology. I had entered the wrong room; a glance prolonged for three seconds showed me a figure seated at a table near one of the windows – a figure I had at first taken for a travelling-rug thrown over a chair. I retreated, with a sense of intrusion; but as I did so I became aware, more rapidly than it takes me to express it, in the first place that this was Vawdrey's room and in the second that, most singularly, Vawdrey himself sat before me. Checking myself on the threshold I had a momentary feeling of bewilderment, but before I knew it I had exclaimed: 'Hullo! is that you, Vawdrey?'

He neither turned nor answered me, but my question received an immediate and practical reply in the opening of a door on the other side of the passage. A servant, with a candle, had come out of the opposite room, and in this flitting illumination I definitely recognised the man whom, an instant before, I had to the best of my belief left below in conversation with Mrs Adney. His back was half turned to me, and he bent over the table in the attitude of writing, but I was conscious that I was in no sort of error about his identity. 'I beg your pardon – I thought you were downstairs,' I said; and as the personage gave no sign of hearing me I added: 'If you're busy I won't disturb you.' I backed out, closing the door – I had been in the place, I suppose, less than a minute. I had a sense of mystification, which however deepened infinitely the next instant. I stood there with my hand still on the knob of the door, overtaken by the oddest impression of my life. Vawdrey was at his table, writing, and it was a very natural place for him to be; but why was he writing in the dark and why hadn't he answered me? I waited a few seconds for the sound of some movement, to see if he wouldn't rouse himself from his abstraction – a fit conceivable in a great writer – and call out: 'Oh, my dear fellow, is it you?' But I heard only the stillness, I felt only the starlighted dusk of the room, with the unexpected presence it enclosed. I turned away, slowly retracing my steps, and came confusedly downstairs. The lamp was still burning in the salon, but the room was empty. I passed round to the door of the hotel and stepped out. Empty too was the terrace. Blanche Adney and the gentleman with her had apparently come in. I hung about five minutes; then I went to bed.

I slept badly, for I was agitated. On looking back at these queer occurrences (you will see presently that they were queer), I perhaps suppose myself more agitated than I was; for great anomalies are never so great at first as after we have reflected upon them. It takes us some time to exhaust explanations. I was vaguely nervous – I had been sharply startled; but there was nothing I could not clear up by asking Blanche Adney, the first thing in the morning, who had been with her on the terrace. Oddly enough, however, when the morning dawned – it dawned admirably – I felt less desire to satisfy myself on this point than to escape, to brush away the shadow of my stupefaction. I saw the day would be splendid, and the fancy took me to spend it, as I had spent happy days of youth, in a lonely mountain ramble. I dressed early, partook of conventional coffee, put a big roll into one pocket and a small flask into the other, and, with a stout stick in my hand, went forth into the high places. My story is not closely concerned with the charming hours I passed there – hours of the kind that make intense memories. If I roamed away half of them on the shoulders of the hills, I lay on the sloping grass for the other half and, with my cap pulled over my eyes (save a peep for immensities of view), listened, in the bright stillness, to the mountain bee and felt most things sink and dwindle. Clare Vawdrey grew small, Blanche Adney grew dim, Lord Mellifont grew old, and before the day was over I forgot that I had ever been puzzled. When in the late afternoon I made my way down to the inn there was nothing I wanted so much to find out as whether dinner would not soon be ready. To-night I dressed, in a manner, and by the time I was presentable they were all at table.

In their company again my little problem came back to me, so that I was curious to see if Vawdrey wouldn't look at me the least bit queerly. But he didn't look at me at all; which gave me a chance both to be patient and to wonder why I should hesitate to ask him my question across the table. I did hesitate, and with the consciousness of doing so came back a little of the agitation I had left behind me, or below me, during the day. I wasn't ashamed of my scruple, however: it was only a fine discretion. What I vaguely felt was that a public inquiry wouldn't have been fair. Lord Mellifont was there, of course, to mitigate with his perfect manner all consequences; but I think it was present to me that with these particular elements his lordship would not be at home. The moment we got up, therefore, I approached Mrs Adney, asking her whether, as the evening was lovely, she wouldn't take a turn with me outside.

'You've walked a hundred miles; had you not better be quiet?' she replied.

'I'd walk a hundred miles more to get you to tell me something.'

She looked at me an instant, with a little of the queerness that I had sought, but had not found, in Clare Vawdrey's eyes. 'Do you mean what became of Lord Mellifont?'

'Of Lord Mellifont?' With my new speculation I had lost that thread.

'Where's your memory, foolish man? We talked of it last evening.'

'Ah, yes!' I cried, recalling; 'we shall have lots to discuss.' I drew her out to the terrace, and before we had gone three steps I said to her: 'Who was with you here last night?'

'Last night?' she repeated, as wide of the mark as I had been.

'At ten o'clock – just after our company broke up. You came out here with a gentleman; you talked about the stars.'

She stared a moment; then she gave her laugh. 'Are you jealous of dear Vawdrey?'

'Then it was he?'

'Certainly it was.'

'And how long did he stay?'

'You have it badly. He stayed about a quarter of an hour – perhaps rather more. We walked some distance; he talked about his play. There you have it all; that is the only witchcraft I have used.'

'And what did Vawdrey do afterwards?'

'I haven't the least idea. I left him and went to bed.'

'At what time did you go to bed?'

'At what time did *you*? I happen to remember that I parted from Mr Vawdrey at ten twenty-five,' said Mrs Adney. 'I came back into the salon to pick up a book, and I noticed the clock.'

'In other words you and Vawdrey distinctly lingered here from about five minutes past ten till the hour you mention?'

'I don't know how distinct we were, but we were very jolly. *Où voulez-vous en venir?*' Blanche Adney asked.

'Simply to this, dear lady: that at the time your companion was occupied in the manner you describe, he was also engaged in literary composition in his own room.'

She stopped short at this, and her eyes had an expression in the darkness. She wanted to know if I challenged her veracity; and I replied that, on the contrary, I backed it up – it made the case so interesting. She returned that this would only be if she should back up mine; which, however, I had no difficulty in persuading her to do, after I had related to her circumstantially the incident of my quest of the manuscript – the manuscript which, at the time, for a reason I could now understand, appeared to have passed so completely out of her own head.

'His talk made me forget it – I forgot I sent you for it. He made up for his fiasco in the salon: he declaimed me the scene,' said my companion. She had dropped on a bench to listen to me and, as we sat there, had briefly cross-examined me. Then she broke out into fresh laughter 'Oh, the eccentricities of genius!'

'They seem greater even than I supposed.'

'Oh, the mysteries of greatness!'

'You ought to know all about them, but they take me by surprise.'

'Are you absolutely certain it was Mr Vawdrey?' my companion asked.

'If it wasn't he, who in the world was it? That a strange gentleman, looking exactly like him, should be sitting in his room at that hour of the night and writing at his table *in the dark*,' I insisted, 'would be practically as wonderful as my own contention.'

'Yes, why in the dark?' mused Mrs Adney.

'Cats can see in the dark,' I said.

She smiled at me dimly. 'Did it look like a cat?'

'No, dear lady, but I'll tell you what it did look like – it looked like the author of Vawdrey's admirable works. It looked infinitely more like him than our friend does himself,' I declared.

'Do you mean it was somebody he gets to do them?'

'Yes, while he dines out and disappoints you.'

'Disappoints me?' murmured Mrs Adney artlessly.

'Disappoints *me* – disappoints every one who looks in him for the genius that created the pages they adore. Where is it in his talk?'

'Ah, last night he was splendid,' said the actress.

'He's always splendid, as your morning bath is splendid, or a sirloin of beef, or the railway service to Brighton. But he's never rare.'

'I see what you mean.'

'That's what makes you such a comfort to talk to. I've often wondered – now I know. There are two of them.'

'What a delightful idea!'

'One goes out, the other stays at home. One is the genius, the other's the bourgeois, and it's only the bourgeois whom we personally know. He talks, he circulates, he's awfully popular, he flirts with you –'

'Whereas it's the genius *you* are privileged to see!' Mrs Adney broke in. 'I'm much obliged to you for the distinction.'

I laid my hand on her arm. 'See him yourself. Try it, test it, go to his room.'

'Go to his room? It wouldn't be proper!' she exclaimed, in the tone of her best comedy.

'Anything is proper in such an inquiry. If you see him, it settles it.'

'How charming – to settle it!' She thought a moment, then she sprang up. 'Do you mean *now*?'

'Whenever you like.'

'But suppose I should find the wrong one?' said Blanche Adney, with an exquisite effect.

'The wrong one? Which one do you call the right?'

'The wrong one for a lady to go and see. Suppose I shouldn't find – the genius?'

'Oh, I'll look after the other,' I replied. Then, as I had happened to glance about me, I added: 'Take care – here comes Lord Mellifont.'

'I wish you'd look after *him*,' my interlocutress murmured.

'What's the matter with him?'

'That's just what I was going to tell you.'

'Tell me now; he's not coming.'

Blanche Adney looked a moment. Lord Mellifont, who appeared to have emerged from the hotel to smoke a meditative cigar, had paused, at a distance from us, and stood admiring the wonders of the prospect, discernible even in the dusk. We strolled slowly in another direction, and she presently said: 'My idea is almost as droll as yours.'

'I don't call mine droll: it's beautiful.'

'There's nothing so beautiful as the droll,' Mrs Adney declared.

'You take a professional view. But I'm all ears.' My curiosity was indeed alive again.

'Well then, my dear friend, if Clare Vawdrey is double (and I'm bound to say I think that the more of him the better), his lordship there has the opposite complaint: he isn't even whole.'

We stopped once more, simultaneously. 'I don't understand.'

'No more do I. But I have a fancy that if there are two of Mr Vawdrey, there isn't so much as one, all told, of Lord Mellifont.'

I considered a moment, then I laughed out. 'I think I see what you mean!'

'That's what makes *you* a comfort. Did you ever see him alone?'

I tried to remember. 'Oh, yes; he has been to see me.'

'Ah, then he wasn't alone.'

'And I've been to see him, in his study.'

'Did he know you were there?'

'Naturally – I was announced.'

Blanche Adney glanced at me like a lovely conspirator. 'You mustn't be announced!' With this she walked on.

I rejoined her, breathless. 'Do you mean one must come upon him when he doesn't know it?'

'You must take him unawares. You must go to his room – that's what you must do.'

If I was elated by the way our mystery opened out, I was also, pardonably, a little confused. 'When I know he's not there?'

'When you know he *is*.'

'And what shall I see?'

'You won't see anything!' Mrs Adney cried as we turned round.

We had reached the end of the terrace, and our movement brought us face to face with Lord Mellifont, who, resuming his walk, had now, without indiscretion, overtaken us. The sight of him at that moment was illuminating, and it kindled a great backward train, connecting itself with one's general impression of the personage. As he stood there smiling at us and waving a practised hand into the transparent night (he introduced the view as if it had been a candidate and 'supported' the very Alps), as he rose before us in the delicate fragrance of his cigar and all his other delicacies and fragrances, with more perfections, somehow, heaped upon his handsome head than one had ever seen accumulated before, he struck me as so essentially, so conspicuously and uniformly the public character that I read in a flash the answer to Blanche Adney's riddle. He was all public and had no corresponding private life, just as Clare Vawdrey was all private and had no corresponding public one. I had heard only half my companion's story, yet as we joined Lord Mellifont (he had followed us – he liked Mrs Adney; but it was always to be conceived of him that he accepted society rather than sought it), as we participated for half an hour in the distributed wealth of his conversation, I felt with unabashed duplicity that we had, as it were, found him out. I was even more deeply diverted by that whisk of the curtain to which the actress had just treated me than I had been by my own discovery; and if I was not ashamed of my share of her secret any more than of having divided my own with her (though my own was, of the two mysteries, the more glorious for the personage involved), this was because there was no cruelty in my advantage, but on the contrary an extreme tenderness and a positive compassion. Oh, he was safe with me, and I felt moreover rich and enlightened, as if I had suddenly put the universe into my pocket. I had learned what an affair of the spot and the moment a great appearance may be. It would doubtless be too much to say that I had always suspected the possibility, in the background of his lordship's being, of some such beautiful instance; but it is at least a fact that, patronising as it sounds, I had been conscious of a certain reserve of indulgence for him. I had secretly pitied him for the perfection of his performance, had wondered what blank face such a mask had to cover, what was left to him for the immitigable hours in which a man sits down with himself, or, more serious still, with that intenser self, his lawful wife. How was he at home and what did he do when he was alone? There was something in Lady Mellifont that gave a point to these researches – something that suggested that even to her he was still the public character and that she was haunted by similar questionings. She had never cleared them up: that was her eternal trouble. We therefore knew more than she did, Blanche Adney and I; but we wouldn't tell her for the world, nor would she probably thank us for doing so. She preferred the relative grandeur of uncertainty. She was not at home with him, so she couldn't say; and with her he was not alone, so he couldn't show her. He represented to his wife and he was a hero to his servants, and what one wanted to arrive at was what really became of him when no eye could see. He rested, presumably; but what form of rest could repair such a plenitude of presence? Lady Mellifont was too proud to pry, and as she had never looked through a keyhole she remained dignified and unassuaged.

It may have been a fancy of mine that Blanche Adney drew out our companion, or it may be that the practical irony of our relation to him at such a moment made me see him more vividly: at any rate he never had struck me as so dissimilar from what he would have been if we had not offered him a reflection of his image. We were only a concourse of two, but he had never been more public. His perfect manner had never been more perfect, his remarkable tact had never been more remarkable. I had a tacit sense that it would all be in the morning papers, with a leader, and also a secretly exhilarating one that I knew something that wouldn't be, that never could be, though any enterprising journal would give one a fortune for it. I must add, however, that in spite of my enjoyment – it was almost sensual, like that of a consummate dish – I was eager to be alone again with Mrs Adney, who owed me an anecdote. It proved impossible, that evening, for some of the others came out to see what we found so absorbing; and then Lord Mellifont bespoke a little music from the fiddler, who produced his violin and played to us divinely, on our platform of echoes, face to face with the ghosts of the mountains. Before the concert was over I missed our actress and, glancing into the window of the salon, saw that she was established with Vawdrey, who was reading to her from a manuscript. The great scene had apparently been achieved and was doubtless the more interesting to Blanche from the new lights she had gathered about its author. I judged it discreet not to disturb them, and I went to bed without seeing her again. I looked out for her betimes the next morning and, as the promise of the day was fair, proposed to her that we should take to the hills, reminding her of the high obligation she had incurred. She recognised the obligation and gratified me with her company; but before we had strolled ten yards up the pass she broke out with intensity: 'My dear friend, you've no idea how it works in me! I can think of nothing else.'

'Than your theory about Lord Mellifont?'

'Oh, bother Lord Mellifont! I allude to yours about Mr Vawdrey, who is much the more interesting person of the two. I'm fascinated by that vision of his – what-do-you-call-it?'

'His alternative identity?'

'His other self: that's easier to say.'

'You accept it, then, you adopt it?'

'Adopt it? I rejoice in it! It became tremendously vivid to me last evening.'

'While he read to you there?'

'Yes, as I listened to him, watched him. It simplified everything, explained everything.'

'That's indeed the blessing of it. Is the scene very fine?'

'Magnificent, and he reads beautifully.'

'Almost as well as the other one writes!' I laughed.

This made my companion stop a moment, laying her hand on my arm. 'You utter my very impression. I felt that he was reading me the work of another man.'

'What a service to the other man!'

'Such a totally different person,' said Mrs Adney. We talked of this difference as we went on, and of what a wealth it constituted, what a resource for life, such a duplication of character.

'It ought to make him live twice as long as other people,' I observed.

'Ought to make which of them?'

'Well, both; for after all they're members of a firm, and one of them couldn't carry on the business without the other. Moreover mere survival would be dreadful for either.'

Blanche Adney was silent a little; then she exclaimed: 'I don't know – I wish he *would* survive!'

'May I, on my side, inquire which?'

'If you can't guess I won't tell you.'

'I know the heart of woman. You always prefer the other.'

She halted again, looking round her. 'Off here, away from my husband, I *can* tell you. I'm in love with him!'

'Unhappy woman, he has no passions,' I answered.

'That's exactly why I adore him. Doesn't a woman with my history know that the passions of others are insupportable? An actress, poor thing, can't care for any love that's not all on *her* side; she can't afford to be repaid. My marriage proves that: marriage is ruinous. Do you know what was in my mind last night, all the while Mr Vawdrey was reading me those beautiful speeches? An insane desire to see the author.' And dramatically, as if to hide her shame, Blanche Adney passed on.

'We'll manage that,' I returned. 'I want another glimpse of him myself. But meanwhile please remember that I've been waiting more than forty-eight hours for the evidence that supports your sketch, intensely suggestive and plausible, of Lord Mellifont's private life.'

'Oh, Lord Mellifont doesn't interest me.'

'He did yesterday,' I said.

'Yes, but that was before I fell in love. You blotted him out with your story.'

'You'll make me sorry I told it. Come,' I pleaded, 'if you don't let me know how your idea came into your head I shall imagine you simply made it up.'

'Let me recollect then, while we wander in this grassy valley.'

We stood at the entrance of a charming crooked gorge, a portion of whose level floor formed the bed of a stream that was smooth with swiftness. We turned into it, and the soft walk beside the clear torrent drew us on and on; till suddenly, as we continued and I waited for my companion to remember, a bend of the valley showed us Lady Mellifont coming toward us. She was alone, under the canopy of her parasol, drawing her sable train over the turf; and in this form, on the devious ways, she was a sufficiently rare apparition. She usually took a footman, who marched behind her on the highroads and whose livery was strange to the mountaineers. She blushed on seeing us, as if she ought somehow to justify herself; she laughed vaguely and said she had come out for a little early stroll. We stood together a moment, exchanging platitudes, and then she remarked that she had thought she might find her husband.

'Is he in this quarter?' I inquired.

'I supposed he would be. He came out an hour ago to sketch.'

'Have you been looking for him?' Mrs Adney asked.

'A little; not very much,' said Lady Mellifont.

Each of the women rested her eyes with some intensity, as it seemed to me, on the eyes of the other.

'We'll look for him *for* you, if you like,' said Mrs Adney.

'Oh, it doesn't matter. I thought I'd join him.'

'He won't make his sketch if you don't,' my companion hinted.

'Perhaps he will if *you* do,' said Lady Mellifont.

'Oh, I daresay he'll turn up,' I interposed.

'He certainly will if he knows we're here!' Blanche Adney retorted.

'Will you wait while we search?' I asked of Lady Mellifont.

She repeated that it was of no consequence; upon which Mrs Adney went on: 'We'll go into the matter for our own pleasure.'

'I wish you a pleasant expedition,' said her ladyship, and was turning away when I sought to know if we should inform her husband that she had followed him. She hesitated a moment; then she jerked out oddly: 'I think you had better not.' With this she took leave of us, floating a little stiffly down the gorge.

My companion and I watched her retreat, then we exchanged a stare, while a light ghost of a laugh rippled from the actress's lips. 'She might be walking in the shrubberies at Mellifont!'

'She suspects it, you know,' I replied.

'And she doesn't want him to know it. There won't be any sketch.'

'Unless we overtake him,' I subjoined. 'In that case we shall find him producing one, in the most graceful attitude, and the queer thing is that it will be brilliant.'

'Let us leave him alone – he'll have to come home without it.'

'He'd rather never come home. Oh, he'll find a public!'

'Perhaps he'll do it for the cows,' Blanche Adney suggested; and as I was on the point of rebuking her profanity she went on: 'That's simply what I happened to discover.'

'What are you speaking of?'

'The incident of the day before yesterday.'

'Ah, let's have it at last!'

'That's all it was – that I was like Lady Mellifont: I couldn't find him.'

'Did you lose him?'

'He lost *me* – that appears to be the way of it. He thought I was gone.'

'But you did find him, since you came home with him.'

'It was he who found *me*. That again is what must happen. He's there from the moment he knows somebody else is.'

'I understand his intermissions,' I said after a short reflection, 'but I don't quite seize the law that governs them.'

'Oh, it's a fine shade, but I caught it at that moment. I had started to come home. I was tired, and I had insisted on his not coming back with me. We had found some rare flowers – those I brought home – and it was he who had discovered almost all of them. It amused him very much, and I knew he wanted to get more; but I was weary and I quitted him. He let me go – where else would have been his tact? – and I was too stupid then to have guessed that from the moment I was not there no flower would be gathered. I started homeward, but at the end of three minutes I found I had brought away his penknife – he had lent it to me to trim a branch – and I knew he would need it. I turned back a few steps, to call him, but before I spoke I looked about for him. You can't understand what happened then without having the place before you.'

'You must take me there,' I said.

'We may see the wonder here. The place was simply one that offered no chance for concealment – a great gradual hillside, without obstructions or trees. There were some rocks below me, behind which I myself had disappeared, but from which on coming back I immediately emerged again.'

'Then he must have seen you.'

'He was too utterly gone, for some reason best known to himself. It was probably some moment of fatigue – he's getting on, you know, so that, with the sense of returning solitude, the reaction had been proportionately great, the extinction proportionately complete. At any rate the stage was as bare as your hand.'

'Could he have been somewhere else?'

'He couldn't have been, in the time, anywhere but where I had left him. Yet the place was utterly empty – as empty as this stretch of valley before us. He had vanished – he had ceased to be. But as soon as my voice rang out (I uttered his name), he rose before me like the rising sun.'

'And where did the sun rise?'

'Just where it ought to – just where he would have been and where I should have seen him had he been like other people.'

I had listened with the deepest interest, but it was my duty to think of objections. 'How long a time elapsed between the moment you perceived his absence and the moment you called?'

'Oh, only an instant. I don't pretend it was long.'

'Long enough for you to be sure?' I said.

'Sure he wasn't there?'

'Yes, and that you were not mistaken, not the victim of some hocus-pocus of your eyesight.'

'I may have been mistaken, but I don't believe it. At any rate, that's just why I want you to look in his room.'

I thought a moment. 'How can I, when even his wife doesn't dare to?'

'She wants to; propose it to her. It wouldn't take much to make her. She does suspect.'

I thought another moment. 'Did he seem to know?'

'That I had missed him? So it struck me, but he thought he had been quick enough.'

'Did you speak of his disappearance?'

'Heaven forbid! It seemed to me too strange.'

'Quite right. And how did he look?'

Trying to think it out again and reconstitute her miracle, Blanche Adney gazed abstractedly up the valley. Suddenly she exclaimed: 'Just as he looks now!' and I saw Lord Mellifont stand before us with his sketch-block. I perceived, as we met him, that he looked neither suspicious nor blank: he looked simply, as he did always, everywhere, the principal feature of the scene. Naturally he had no sketch to show us, but nothing could better have rounded off our actual conception of him than the way he fell into position as we approached. He had been selecting his point of view; he took possession of it with a flourish of the pencil. He leaned against a rock; his beautiful little box of water-colours reposed on a natural table beside him, a ledge of the bank which showed how inveterately nature ministered to his convenience. He painted while he talked and he talked while he painted; and if the painting was as miscellaneous as the talk, the talk would equally have graced an album. We waited while the exhibition went on, and it seemed indeed as if the conscious profiles of the peaks were interested in his success. They grew as black as silhouettes in paper, sharp against a livid sky from which, however, there would be nothing to fear till Lord Mellifont's sketch should be finished. Blanche Adney communed with me dumbly, and I could read the language of her eyes: 'Oh, if *we* could only do it as well as that! He fills the stage in a way that beats us.' We could no more have left him than we could have quitted the theatre till the play was over; but in due time we turned round with him and strolled back to the inn, before the door of which his lordship, glancing again at his picture, tore the fresh leaf from the block and presented it with a few happy words to Mrs Adney. Then he went into the house; and a moment later, looking up from where we stood, we saw him, above, at the window of his sitting-room (he had the best apartments), watching the signs of the weather.

'He'll have to rest after this,' Blanche said, dropping her eyes on her water-colour.

'Indeed he will!' I raised mine to the window: Lord Mellifont had vanished. 'He's already reabsorbed.'

'Reabsorbed?' I could see the actress was now thinking of something else.

'Into the immensity of things. He has lapsed again; there's an *entr'acte*.'

'It ought to be long.' Mrs Adney looked up and down the terrace, and at that moment the head-waiter appeared in the doorway. Suddenly she turned to this functionary with the question: 'Have you seen Mr Vawdrey lately?'

The man immediately approached. 'He left the house five minutes ago – for a walk, I think. He went down the pass; he had a book.'

I was watching the ominous clouds. 'He had better have had an umbrella.'

The waiter smiled. 'I recommended him to take one.'

'Thank you,' said Mrs Adney; and the Oberkellner withdrew. Then she went on, abruptly: 'Will you do me a favour?'

'Yes, if you'll do *me* one. Let me see if your picture is signed.'

She glanced at the sketch before giving it to me. 'For a wonder it isn't.'

'It ought to be, for full value. May I keep it awhile?'

'Yes, if you'll do what I ask. Take an umbrella and go after Mr Vawdrey.'

'To bring him to Mrs Adney?'

'To keep him out – as long as you can.'

'I'll keep him as long as the rain holds off.'

'Oh, never mind the rain!' my companion exclaimed.

'Would you have us drenched?'

'Without remorse.' Then with a strange light in her eyes she added: 'I'm going to try.'

'To try?'

'To see the real one. Oh, if I can get at him!' she broke out with passion.

'Try, try!' I replied. 'I'll keep our friend all day.'

'If I can get at the one who does it' – and she paused, with shining eyes – 'if I can have it out with him I shall get my part!'

'I'll keep Vawdrey for ever!' I called after her as she passed quickly into the house.

Her audacity was communicative, and I stood there in a glow of excitement. I looked at Lord Mellifont's water-colour and I looked at the gathering storm; I turned my eyes again to his lordship's windows and then I bent them on my watch. Vawdrey had so little the start of me that I should have time to overtake him – time even if I should take five minutes to go up to Lord Mellifont's sitting-room (where we had all been hospitably received), and say to him, as a messenger, that Mrs Adney begged he would bestow upon his sketch the high consecration of his signature. As I again considered this work of art I perceived there was something it certainly did lack: what else then but so noble an autograph? It was my duty to supply the deficiency without delay, and in accordance with this conviction I instantly re-entered the hotel. I went up to Lord Mellifont's apartments; I reached the door of his salon. Here, however, I was met by a difficulty of which my extravagance had not taken account. If I were to knock I should spoil everything; yet was I prepared to dispense with this ceremony? I asked myself the question, and it embarrassed me; I turned my little picture round and round, but it didn't give me the answer I wanted. I wanted it to say: 'Open the door gently, gently, without a sound, yet very quickly: then you will see what you will see.' I had gone so far as to lay my hand upon the knob when I became aware (having my wits so about me), that exactly in the manner I was thinking of – gently, gently, without a sound – another door had moved, on the opposite side of the hall. At the same instant I found myself smiling rather constrainedly upon Lady Mellifont, who, on seeing me, had checked herself on the threshold of her room. For a moment, as she stood there, we exchanged two or three ideas that were the more singular for being unspoken. We had caught each other hovering, and we understood each other; but as I stepped over to her (so that we were separated from the sitting-room by the width of the hall), her lips formed the almost soundless entreaty: 'Don't!' I could see in her conscious eyes everything that the word expressed – the confession of her own curiosity and the dread of the consequences of mine. '*Don't!*' she repeated, as I stood before her. From the moment my experiment could strike her as an act of violence I was ready to renounce it; yet I thought I detected in her frightened face a still deeper betrayal – a possibility of disappointment if I should give way. It was as if she had said: 'I'll let you do it if you'll take the responsibility. Yes, with some one else I'd surprise him. But it would never do for him to think it was I.'

'We soon found Lord Mellifont,' I observed, in allusion to our encounter with her an hour before, 'and he was so good as to give this lovely sketch to Mrs Adney, who has asked me to come up and beg him to put in the omitted signature.'

Lady Mellifont took the drawing from me, and I could guess the struggle that went on in her while she looked at it. She was silent for some time; then I felt that all her delicacies and dignities, all her old timidities and pieties were fighting against her opportunity. She turned away from me and, with the drawing, went back to her room. She was absent for a couple of minutes, and when she reappeared I could see that she had vanquished her temptation; that even, with a kind of resurgent horror, she had shrunk from it. She had deposited the sketch in the room. 'If you will kindly leave the picture with me, I will see that Mrs Adney's request is attended to,' she said, with great courtesy and sweetness, but in a manner that put an end to our colloquy.

I assented, with a somewhat artificial enthusiasm perhaps, and then, to ease off our separation, remarked that we were going to have a change of weather.

'In that case we shall go – we shall go immediately,' said Lady Mellifont. I was amused at the eagerness with which she made this declaration: it appeared to represent a coveted flight into safety, an escape with her threatened secret. I was the more surprised therefore when, as I was turning away, she put out her hand to take mine. She had the pretext of bidding me farewell, but as I shook hands with her on this supposition I felt that what the movement really conveyed was: 'I thank you for the help you would have given me, but it's better as it is. If I should know, who would help me then?' As I went to my room to get my umbrella I said to myself: 'She's sure, but she won't put it to the proof.'

A quarter of an hour later I had overtaken Clare Vawdrey in the pass, and shortly after this we found ourselves looking for refuge. The storm had not only completely gathered, but it had broken at the last with extraordinary rapidity. We scrambled up a hillside to an empty cabin, a rough structure that was hardly more than a shed for the protection of cattle. It was a tolerable shelter however, and it had fissures through which we could watch the splendid spectacle of the tempest. This entertainment lasted an hour – an hour that has remained with me as full of odd disparities. While the lightning played with the thunder and the rain gushed in on our umbrellas, I said to myself that Clare Vawdrey was disappointing. I don't know exactly what I should have predicated of a great author exposed to the fury of the elements, I can't say what particular Manfred attitude I should have expected my companion to assume, but it seemed to me somehow that I shouldn't have looked to him to regale me in such a situation with stories (which I had already heard) about the celebrated Lady Ringrose. Her ladyship formed the subject of Vawdrey's conversation during this prodigious scene, though before it was quite over he had launched out on Mr Chafer, the scarcely less notorious reviewer. It broke my heart to hear a man like Vawdrey talk of reviewers. The lightning projected a hard clearness upon the truth, familiar to me for years, to which the last day or two had added transcendent support – the irritating certitude that for personal relations this admirable genius thought his second-best good enough. It *was*, no doubt, as society was made, but there was a contempt in the distinction which could not fail to be galling to an admirer. The world was vulgar and stupid, and the real man would have been a fool to come out for it when he could gossip and dine by deputy. None the less my heart sank as I felt my companion practise this economy. I don't know exactly what I wanted; I suppose I wanted him to make an exception for *me*. I almost believed he would, if he had known how I worshipped his talent. But I had never been able to translate this to him, and his application of his principle was relentless. At any rate I was more than ever sure that at such an hour his chair at home was not empty: *there* was the Manfred attitude, *there* were the responsive flashes. I could only envy Mrs Adney her presumable enjoyment of them.

The weather drew off at last, and the rain abated sufficiently to allow us to emerge from our asylum and make our way back to the inn, where we found on our arrival that our prolonged absence had produced some agitation. It was judged apparently that the fury of the elements might have placed us in a predicament. Several of our friends were at the door, and they seemed a little disconcerted when it was perceived that we were only drenched. Clare Vawdrey, for some reason, was wetter than I, and he took his course to his room. Blanche Adney was among the persons collected to look out for us, but as Vawdrey came toward her she shrank from him, without a greeting; with a movement that I observed as almost one of estrangement she turned her back on him and went quickly into the salon. Wet as I was I went in after her; on which she immediately flung round and faced me. The first thing I saw was that she had never been so beautiful. There was a light of inspiration in her face, and she broke out to me in the quickest whisper, which was at the same time the loudest cry, I have ever heard: 'I've got my *part*!'

'You went to his room – I was right?'

'Right?' Blanche Adney repeated. 'Ah, my dear fellow!' she murmured.

'He was there – you saw him?'

'He saw me. It was the hour of my life!'

'It must have been the hour of his, if you were half as lovely as you are at this moment.'

'He's splendid,' she pursued, as if she didn't hear me. 'He *is* the one who does it!' I listened, immensely impressed, and she added: 'We understood each other.'

'By flashes of lightning?'

'Oh, I didn't see the lightning then!'

'How long were you there?' I asked with admiration.

'Long enough to tell him I adore him.'

'Ah, that's what I've never been able to tell him!' I exclaimed ruefully.

'I shall have my part – I shall have my part!' she continued, with triumphant indifference; and she flung round the room with the joy of a girl, only checking herself to say: 'Go and change your clothes.'

'You shall have Lord Mellifont's signature,' I said.

'Oh, bother Lord Mellifont's signature! He's far nicer than Mr Vawdrey,' she went on irrelevantly.

'Lord Mellifont?' I pretended to inquire.

'Confound Lord Mellifont!' And Blanche Adney, in her elation, brushed by me, whisking again through the open door. Just outside of it she came upon her husband; whereupon, with a charming cry of 'We're talking of you, my love!' she threw herself upon him and kissed him.

I went to my room and changed my clothes, but I remained there till the evening. The violence of the storm had passed over us, but the rain had settled down to a drizzle. On descending to dinner I found that the change in the weather had already broken up our party. The Mellifonts had departed in a carriage and four, they had been followed by others, and several vehicles had been bespoken for the morning. Blanche Adney's was one of them, and on the pretext that she had preparations to make she quitted us directly after dinner. Clare Vawdrey asked me what was the matter with her – she suddenly appeared to dislike him. I forget what answer I gave, but I did my best to comfort him by driving away with him the next day. Mrs Adney had vanished when we came down; but they made up their quarrel in London, for he finished his play, which she produced. I must add that she is still, nevertheless, in want of the great part. I have a beautiful one in my head, but she doesn't come to see me to stir me up about it. Lady Mellifont always drops me a kind word when we meet, but that doesn't console me.

THE REAL THING

I

WHEN the porter's wife (she used to answer the house-bell) announced 'A gentleman – with a lady, sir,' I had, as I often had in those days, for the wish was father to the thought, an immediate vision of sitters. Sitters my visitors in this case proved to be; but not in the sense I should have preferred. However, there was nothing at first to indicate that they might not have come for a portrait. The gentleman, a man of fifty, very high and very straight, with a moustache slightly grizzled and a dark grey walking-coat admirably fitted, both of which I noted professionally – I don't mean as a barber or yet as a tailor – would have struck me as a celebrity if celebrities often were striking. It was a truth of which I had for some time been conscious that a figure with a good deal of frontage was, as one might say, almost never a public institution. A glance at the lady helped to remind me of this paradoxical law: she also looked too distinguished to be a 'personality'. Moreover one would scarcely come across two variations together.

Neither of the pair spoke immediately – they only prolonged the preliminary gaze which suggested that each wished to give the other a chance. They were visibly shy; they stood there letting me take them in – which, as I afterwards perceived, was the most practical thing they could have done. In this way their embarrassment served their cause. I had seen people painfully reluctant to mention that they desired anything so gross as to be represented on canvas; but the scruples of my new friends appeared almost insurmountable. Yet the gentleman might have said 'I should like a portrait of my wife,' and the lady might have said 'I should like a portrait of my husband.' Perhaps they were not husband and wife – this naturally would make the matter more delicate. Perhaps they wished to be done together – in which case they ought to have brought a third person to break the news.

39

'We come from Mr Rivet,' the lady said at last, with a dim smile which had the effect of a moist sponge passed over a 'sunk' piece of painting, as well as of a vague allusion to vanished beauty. She was as tall and straight, in her degree, as her companion, and with ten years less to carry. She looked as sad as a woman could look whose face was not charged with expression; that is her tinted oval mask showed friction as an exposed surface shows it. The hand of time had played over her freely, but only to simplify. She was slim and stiff, and so well-dressed, in dark blue cloth, with lappets and pockets and buttons, that it was clear she employed the same tailor as her husband. The couple had an indefinable air of prosperous thrift – they evidently got a good deal of luxury for their money. If I was to be one of their luxuries it would behove me to consider my terms.

'Ah, Claude Rivet recommended me?' I inquired; and I added that it was very kind of him, though I could reflect that, as he only painted landscape, this was not a sacrifice.

The lady looked very hard at the gentleman, and the gentleman looked round the room. Then staring at the floor a moment and stroking his moustache, he rested his pleasant eyes on me with the remark: 'He said you were the right one.'

'I try to be, when people want to sit.'

'Yes, we should like to,' said the lady anxiously.

'Do you mean together?'

My visitors exchanged a glance. 'If you could do anything with *me*, I suppose it would be double,' the gentleman stammered.

'Oh yes, there's naturally a higher charge for two figures than for one.'

'We should like to make it pay,' the husband confessed.

'That's very good of you,' I returned, appreciating so unwonted a sympathy – for I supposed he meant pay the artist.

A sense of strangeness seemed to dawn on the lady. 'We mean for the illustrations – Mr Rivet said you might put one in.'

'Put one in – an illustration?' I was equally confused.

'Sketch her off, you know,' said the gentleman, colouring.

It was only then that I understood the service Claude Rivet had rendered me; he had told them that I worked in black and white, for magazines, for story-books, for sketches of contemporary life, and consequently had frequent employment for models. These things were true, but it was not less true (I may confess it now – whether because the aspiration was to lead to everything or to nothing I leave the reader to guess), that I couldn't get the honours, to say nothing of the emoluments, of a great painter of portraits out of my head. My 'illustrations' were my pot-boilers; I looked to a different branch of art (far and away the most interesting it had always seemed to me) to perpetuate my fame. There was no shame in looking to it also to make my fortune; but that fortune was by so much further from being made from the moment my visitors wished to be 'done' for nothing. I was disappointed; for in the pictorial sense I had immediately *seen* them. I had seized their type – I had already settled what I would do with it. Something that wouldn't absolutely have pleased them, I afterwards reflected.

'Ah, you're – you're – a –?' I began, as soon as I had mastered my surprise. I couldn't bring out the dingy word 'models'; it seemed to fit the case so little.

'We haven't had much practice,' said the lady.

'We've got to *do* something, and we've thought that an artist in your line might perhaps make something of us,' her husband threw off. He further mentioned that they didn't know many artists and that they had gone first, on the off-chance (he painted views of course, but sometimes put in figures – perhaps I remembered), to Mr Rivet, whom they had met a few years before at a place in Norfolk where he was sketching.

'We used to sketch a little ourselves,' the lady hinted.

'It's very awkward, but we absolutely *must* do something,' her husband went on.

'Of course, we're not so *very* young,' she admitted, with a wan smile.

With the remark that I might as well know something more about them, the husband had handed me a card extracted from a neat new pocket-book (their appurtenances were all of the freshest) and inscribed with the words 'Major Monarch'.

Impressive as these words were they didn't carry my knowledge much further; but my visitor presently added: 'I've left the army, and we've had the misfortune to lose our money. In fact our means are dreadfully small.'

'It's an awful bore,' said Mrs Monarch.

They evidently wished to be discreet – to take care not to swagger because they were gentlefolks. I perceived they would have been willing to recognise this as something of a drawback, at the same time that I guessed at an underlying sense – their consolation in adversity – that they *had* their points. They certainly had; but these advantages struck me as preponderantly social; such for instance as would help to make a drawing-room look well. However, a drawing-room was always, or ought to be, a picture.

In consequence of his wife's allusion to their age Major Monarch observed: 'Naturally, it's more for the figure that we thought of going in. We can still hold ourselves up.' On the instant I saw that the figure was indeed their strong point. His 'naturally' didn't sound vain, but it lighted up the question. '*She* has got the best,' he continued, nodding at his wife, with a pleasant after-dinner absence of circumlocution. I could only reply, as if we were in fact sitting over our wine, that this didn't prevent his own from being very good; which led him in turn to rejoin: 'We thought that if you ever have to do people like us, we might be something like it. *She*, particularly – for a lady in a book, you know.'

I was so amused by them that, to get more of it, I did my best to take their point of view; and though it was an embarrassment to find myself appraising physically, as if they were animals on hire or useful blacks, a pair whom I should have expected to meet only in one of the relations in which criticism is tacit, I looked at Mrs Monarch judicially enough to be able to exclaim, after a moment, with conviction: 'Oh yes, a lady in a book!' She was singularly like a bad illustration.

'We'll stand up, if you like,' said the Major; and he raised himself before me with a really grand air.

I could take his measure at a glance – he was six feet two and a perfect gentleman. It would have paid any club in process of

formation and in want of a stamp to engage him at a salary to
stand in the principal window. What struck me immediately
was that in coming to me they had rather missed their vocation;
they could surely have been turned to better account for advertising purposes. I couldn't of course see the thing in detail, but
I could see them make someone's fortune – I don't mean their
own. There was something in them for a waistcoat-maker, an
hotel-keeper or a soap-vendor. I could imagine 'We always use
it' pinned on their bosoms with the greatest effect; I had a vision
of the promptitude with which they would launch a *table d'hôte*.

Mrs Monarch sat still, not from pride but from shyness, and
presently her husband said to her: 'Get up my dear and show
how smart you are.' She obeyed, but she had no need to get up
to show it. She walked to the end of the studio, and then she
came back blushing, with her fluttered eyes on her husband. I
was reminded of an incident I had accidentally had a glimpse of
in Paris – being with a friend there, a dramatist about to
produce a play – when an actress came to him to ask to be
entrusted with a part. She went through her paces before him,
walked up and down as Mrs Monarch was doing. Mrs Monarch did it quite as well, but I abstained from applauding. It was
very odd to see such people apply for such poor pay. She looked
as if she had ten thousand a year. Her husband had used the
word that described her: she was, in the London current jargon,
essentially and typically 'smart'. Her figure was, in the same
order of ideas, conspicuously and irreproachably 'good'. For a
woman of her age her waist was surprisingly small; her elbow
moreover had the orthodox crook. She held her head at the
conventional angle; but why did she come to *me*? She ought to
have tried on jackets at a big shop. I feared my visitors were not
only destitute, but 'artistic' – which would be a great complication. When she sat down again I thanked her, observing that
what a draughtsman most valued in his model was the faculty of
keeping quiet.

'Oh, *she* can keep quiet,' said Major Monarch. Then he
added, jocosely: 'I've always kept her quiet.'

'I'm not a nasty fidget, am I?' Mrs Monarch appealed to her
husband.

He addressed his answer to me. 'Perhaps it isn't out of place to mention – because we ought to be quite business-like, oughtn't we? – that when I married her she was known as the Beautiful Statue.'

'Oh dear!' said Mrs Monarch, ruefully.

'Of course I should want a certain amount of expression,' I rejoined.

'Of *course*!' they both exclaimed.

'And then I suppose you know that you'll get awfully tired.'

'Oh, we *never* get tired!' they eagerly cried.

'Have you had any kind of practice?'

They hesitated – they looked at each other. 'We've been photographed, *immensely*,' said Mrs Monarch.

'She means the fellows have asked us,' added the Major.

'I see – because you're so good-looking.'

'I don't know what they thought, but they were always after us.'

'We always got our photographs for nothing,' smiled Mrs Monarch.

'We might have brought some, my dear,' her husband remarked.

'I'm not sure we have any left. We've given quantities away,' she explained to me.

'With our autographs and that sort of thing,' said the Major.

'Are they to be got in the shops?' I inquired, as a harmless pleasantry.

'Oh, yes; *hers* – they used to be.'

'Not now,' said Mrs Monarch, with her eyes on the floor.

II

I COULD fancy the 'sort of thing' they put on the presentation-copies of their photographs, and I was sure they wrote a beautiful hand. It was odd how quickly I was sure of everything that concerned them. If they were now so poor as to have to earn shillings and pence, they never had had much of a margin. Their good looks had been their capital, and they had good-humouredly made the most of the career that this resource marked out for them. It was in their faces, the blankness, the deep intellectual repose of the twenty years of country-house visiting which had given them pleasant intonations. I could see the sunny drawing-rooms, sprinkled with periodicals she didn't read, in which Mrs Monarch had continuously sat; I could see the wet shrubberies in which she had walked, equipped to admiration for either exercise. I could see the rich covers the Major had helped to shoot and the wonderful garments in which, late at night, he repaired to the smoking-room to talk about them. I could imagine their leggings and waterproofs, their knowing tweeds and rugs, their rolls of sticks and cases of tackle and neat umbrellas; and I could evoke the exact appearance of their servants and the compact variety of their luggage on the platforms of country stations.

They gave small tips, but they were liked; they didn't do anything themselves, but they were welcome. They looked so well everywhere; they gratified the general relish for stature, complexion and 'form'. They knew it without fatuity or vulgarity, and they respected themselves in consequence. They were not superficial; they were thorough and kept themselves up – it had been their line. People with such a taste for activity had to have some line. I could feel how, even in a dull house, they could have been counted upon for cheerfulness. At present something had happened – it didn't matter what, their little income had grown less, it had grown least – and they had to do something for pocket-money. Their friends liked them, but didn't like to support them. There was something about them that represented credit – their clothes, their manners, their type; but if credit is a large empty pocket in which an occasional chink reverberates, the chink at least must be audible. What they wanted of me was to help to make it so. Fortunately they had no children – I soon divined that. They would also perhaps wish our relations to be kept secret: this was why it was 'for the figure' – the reproduction of the face would betray them.

I liked them – they were so simple; and I had no objection to them if they would suit. But, somehow, with all their perfections I didn't easily believe in them. After all they were amateurs, and the ruling passion of my life was the detestation of the amateur. Combined with this was another perversity – an innate preference for the represented subject over the real one: the defect of the real one was so apt to be a lack of representation. I liked things that appeared; then one was sure. Whether they *were* or not was a subordinate and almost always a profitless question. There were other considerations, the first of which was that I already had two or three people in use, notably a young person with big feet, in alpaca, from Kilburn, who for a couple of years had come to me regularly for my illustrations and with whom I was still – perhaps ignobly – satisfied. I frankly explained to my visitors how the case stood; but they had taken more precautions than I supposed. They had reasoned out their opportunity, for Claude Rivet had told them of the projected *édition de luxe* of one of the writers of our day – the rarest of the novelists – who, long neglected by the multitudinous vulgar and dearly prized by the attentive (need I mention Philip Vincent?) had had the happy fortune of seeing, late in life, the dawn and then the full light of a higher criticism – an estimate in which, on the part of the public, there was something really of expiation. The edition in question, planned by a publisher of taste, was practically an act of high reparation; the woodcuts with which it was to be enriched were the homage of English art to one of the most independent representatives of English letters. Major and Mrs Monarch confessed to me that they had hoped I might be able to work *them* into my share of the enterprise. They knew I was to do the first of the books, 'Rutland Ramsay', but I had to make clear to them that my participation in the rest of the affair – this first book was to be a test – was to depend on the satisfaction I should give. If this should be limited my employers would drop me without a scruple. It was therefore a crisis for me, and naturally I was making special preparations, looking about for new people, if they should be necessary, and securing the best types. I admitted however that I should like to settle down to two or three good models who would do for everything.

'Should we have often to – a – put on special clothes?' Mrs Monarch timidly demanded.

'Dear, yes – that's half the business.'

'And should we be expected to supply our own costumes?'

'Oh, no; I've got a lot of things. A painter's models put on – or put off – anything he likes.'

'And do you mean – a – the same?'

'The same?'

Mrs Monarch looked at her husband again.

'Oh, she was just wondering,' he explained, 'if the costumes are in *general* use.' I had to confess that they were, and I mentioned further that some of them (I had a lot of genuine, greasy last-century things) had served their time, a hundred years ago, on living, world-stained men and women. 'We'll put on anything that *fits*,' said the Major.

'Oh, I arrange that – they fit in the pictures.'

'I'm afraid I should do better for the modern books. I would come as you like,' said Mrs Monarch.

'She has got a lot of clothes at home: they might do for contemporary life,' her husband continued.

'Oh, I can fancy scenes in which you'd be quite natural.' And indeed I could see the slipshod rearrangements of stale properties – the stories I tried to produce pictures for without the exasperation of reading them – whose sandy tracts the good lady might help to people. But I had to return to the fact that for this sort of work – the daily mechanical grind – I was already equipped; the people I was working with were fully adequate.

'We only thought we might be more like *some* characters,' said Mrs Monarch mildly, getting up.

Her husband also rose; he stood looking at me with a dim wistfulness that was touching in so fine a man. 'Wouldn't it be rather a pull sometimes to have – a – to have –?' He hung fire; he wanted me to help him by phrasing what he meant. But I couldn't – I didn't know. So he brought it out, awkwardly: 'The *real* thing; a gentleman, you know, or a lady.' I was quite ready to give a general assent – I admitted that there was a great deal in that. This encouraged Major Monarch to say, following up his appeal with an unacted gulp: 'It's awfully hard – we've tried everything.' The gulp was communicative; it proved too much for his wife. Before I knew it Mrs Monarch had dropped again upon a divan and burst into tears. Her husband sat down beside her, holding one of her hands; whereupon she quickly dried her eyes with the other, while I felt embarrassed as she looked up at me. 'There isn't a confounded job I haven't applied for – waited for – prayed for. You can fancy we'd be pretty bad first. Secretaryships and that sort of thing? You might as well ask for a peerage. I'd be *anything* – I'm strong; a messenger or a coalheaver. I'd put on a gold-laced cap and open carriage-doors in front of the haberdasher's; I'd hang about a station, to carry portmanteaus; I'd be a postman. But they won't *look* at you; there are thousands, as good as yourself, already on the ground. *Gentlemen*, poor beggars, who have drunk their wine, who have kept their hunters!'

I was as reassuring as I knew how to be, and my visitors were presently on their feet again while, for the experiment, we agreed on an hour. We were discussing it when the door opened and Miss Churm came in with a wet umbrella. Miss Churm had to take the omnibus to Maida Vale and then walk half-a-mile. She looked a trifle blowsy and slightly splashed. I scarcely ever saw her come in without thinking afresh how odd it was that, being so little in herself, she should yet be so much in others. She was a meagre little Miss Churm, but she was an ample heroine of romance. She was only a freckled cockney, but she could represent everything, from a fine lady to a shepherdess; she had the faculty, as she might have had a fine voice or long hair. She couldn't spell, and she loved beer, but she had two or three 'points', and practice, and a knack, and mother-wit, and a kind of whimsical sensibility, and a love of the theatre, and seven sisters, and not an ounce of respect, especially for the *h*. The first thing my visitors saw was that her umbrella was wet, and in their spotless perfection they visibly winced at it. The rain had come on since their arrival.

'I'm all in a soak; there *was* a mess of people in the 'bus. I wish you lived near a stytion,' said Miss Churm. I requested her to get ready as quickly as possible, and she passed into the room in which she always changed her dress. But before going out she asked me what she was to get into this time.

'It's the Russian princess, don't you know?' I answered; 'the one with the "golden eyes", in black velvet, for the long thing in the *Cheapside*.'

'Golden eyes? I *say*!' cried Miss Churm, while my companions watched her with intensity as she withdrew. She always arranged herself, when she was late, before I could turn round; and I kept my visitors a little, on purpose, so that they might get an idea, from seeing her, what would be expected of themselves. I mentioned that she was quite my notion of an excellent model – she was really very clever.

'Do you think she looks like a Russian princess?' Major Monarch asked, with lurking alarm.

'When I make her, yes.'

'Oh, if you have to *make* her –!' he reasoned, acutely.

'That's the most you can ask. There are so many that are not makeable.'

'Well now, *here's* a lady' – and with a persuasive smile he passed his arm into his wife's – 'who's already made!'

'Oh, I'm not a Russian princess,' Mrs Monarch protested, a little coldly. I could see that she had known some and didn't like them. There, immediately, was a complication of a kind that I never had to fear with Miss Churm.

This young lady came back in black velvet – the gown was rather rusty and very low on her lean shoulders – and with a Japanese fan in her red hands. I reminded her that in the scene I was doing she had to look over someone's head. 'I forget whose it is; but it doesn't matter. Just look over a head.'

'I'd rather look over a stove,' said Miss Churm; and she took her station near the fire. She fell into position, settled herself into a tall attitude, gave a certain backward inclination to her head and a certain forward droop to her fan, and looked, at least to my prejudiced sense, distinguished and charming, foreign and dangerous. We left her looking so, while I went downstairs with Major and Mrs Monarch.

'I think I could come about as near it as that,' said Mrs Monarch.

'Oh, you think she's shabby, but you must allow for the alchemy of art.'

However, they went off with an evident increase of comfort, founded on their demonstrable advantage in being the real thing. I could fancy them shuddering over Miss Churm. She was very droll about them when I went back, for I told her what they wanted.

'Well, if *she* can sit I'll tyke to bookkeeping,' said my model.

'She's very lady-like,' I replied, as an innocent form of aggravation.

'So much the worse for *you*. That means she can't turn round.'

'She'll do for the fashionable novels.'

'Oh yes, she'll *do* for them!' my model humorously declared. 'Ain't they bad enough without her?' I had often sociably denounced them to Miss Churm.

III

IT was for the elucidation of a mystery in one of these works that I first tried Mrs Monarch. Her husband came with her, to be useful if necessary – it was sufficiently clear that as a general thing he would prefer to come with her. At first I wondered if this were for 'propriety's' sake – if he were going to be jealous and meddling. The idea was too tiresome, and if it had been confirmed it would speedily have brought our acquaintance to a close. But I soon saw there was nothing in it and that if he accompanied Mrs Monarch it was (in addition to the chance of being wanted), simply because he had nothing else to do. When she was away from him his occupation was gone – she never *had* been away from him. I judged, rightly, that in their awkward situation their close union was their main comfort and that this union had no weak spot. It was a real marriage, an encouragement to the hesitating, a nut for pessimists to crack. Their address was humble (I remember afterwards thinking it had been the only thing about them that was really professional), and I could fancy the lamentable lodgings in which the Major would have been left alone. He could bear them with his wife – he couldn't bear them without her.

He had too much tact to try and make himself agreeable when he couldn't be useful; so he simply sat and waited, when I was too absorbed in my work to talk. But I liked to make him talk – it made my work, when it didn't interrupt it, less sordid, less special. To listen to him was to combine the excitement of going out with the economy of staying at home. There was only one hindrance: that I seemed not to know any of the people he and his wife had known. I think he wondered extremely, during the term of our intercourse, whom the deuce I *did* know. He hadn't a stray sixpence of an idea to fumble for; so we didn't spin it very fine – we confined ourselves to questions of leather and even of liquor (saddlers and breeches-makers and how to get good claret cheap), and matters like 'good trains' and the habits of small game. His lore on these last subjects was astonishing, he managed to interweave the stationmaster with the ornithologist. When he couldn't talk about greater things he could talk cheerfully about smaller, and since I couldn't accompany him into reminiscences of the fashionable world he could lower the conversation without a visible effort to my level.

So earnest a desire to please was touching in a man who could so easily have knocked one down. He looked after the fire and had an opinion on the draught of the stove, without my asking him, and I could see that he thought many of my arrangements not half clever enough. I remember telling him that if I were only rich I would offer him a salary to come and teach me how to live. Sometimes he gave a random sigh, of which the essence was: 'Give me even such a bare old barrack as *this*, and I'd do something with it!' When I wanted to use him he came alone; which was an illustration of the superior courage of women. His wife could bear her solitary second floor, and she was in general more discreet; showing by various small reserves that she was alive to the propriety of keeping our relations markedly professional – not letting them slide into sociability. She wished it to remain clear that she and the Major were employed, not cultivated, and if she approved of me as a superior, who could be kept in his place, she never thought me quite good enough for an equal.

She sat with great intensity, giving the whole of her mind to it, and was capable of remaining for an hour almost as motionless as if she were before a photographer's lens. I could see she had been photographed often, but somehow the very habit that made her good for that purpose unfitted her for mine. At first I was extremely pleased with her lady-like air, and it was a satisfaction, on coming to follow her lines, to see how good they were and how far they could lead the pencil. But after a few times I began to find her too insurmountably stiff; do what I would with it my drawing looked like a photograph or a copy of a photograph. Her figure had no variety of expression – she herself had no sense of variety. You may say that this was my business, was only a question of placing her. I placed her in every conceivable position, but she managed to obliterate their differences. She was always a lady certainly, and into the bargain was always the same lady. She was the real thing, but always the same thing. There were moments when I was oppressed by the serenity of her confidence that she *was* the real thing. All her dealings with me and all her husband's were an implication that this was lucky for *me*. Meanwhile I found myself trying to invent types that approached her own, instead of making her own transform itself – in the clever way that was not impossible, for instance, to poor Miss Churm. Arrange as I would and take the precautions I would, she always, in my pictures, came out too tall – landing me in the dilemma of having represented a fascinating woman as seven feet high, which, out of respect perhaps to my own very much scantier inches, was far from my idea of such a personage.

The case was worse with the Major – nothing I could do would keep *him* down, so that he became useful only for the representation of brawny giants. I adored variety and range, I cherished human accidents, the illustrative note; I wanted to characterise closely, and the thing in the world I most hated was the danger of being ridden by a type. I had quarrelled with some of my friends about it – I had parted company with them for maintaining that one *had* to be, and that if the type was beautiful (witness Raphael and Leonardo), the servitude was only a gain. I was neither Leonardo nor Raphael; I might only be

a presumptuous young modern searcher, but I held that everything was to be sacrificed sooner than character. When they
averred that the haunting type in question could easily *be*
character, I retorted, perhaps superficially: 'Whose?' It
couldn't be everybody's – it might end in being nobody's.

After I had drawn Mrs Monarch a dozen times I perceived
more clearly than before that the value of such a model as Miss
Churm resided precisely in the fact that she had no positive
stamp, combined of course with the other fact that what she did
have was a curious and inexplicable talent for imitation. Her
usual appearance was like a curtain which she could draw up at
request for a capital performance. This performance was
simply suggestive; but it was a word to the wise – it was vivid
and pretty. Sometimes, even, I thought it, though she was plain
herself, too insipidly pretty; I made it a reproach to her that the
figures drawn from her were monotonously (*bêtement*, as we
used to say) graceful. Nothing made her more angry; it was so
much her pride to feel that she could sit for characters that had
nothing in common with each other. She would accuse me at
such moments of taking away her 'reputytion'.

It suffered a certain shrinkage, this queer quantity, from the
repeated visits of my new friends. Miss Churm was greatly in
demand, never in want of employment, so I had no scruple in
putting her off occasionally, to try them more at my ease. It was
certainly amusing at first to do the real thing – it was amusing to
do Major Monarch's trousers. They *were* the real thing, even if
he did come out colossal. It was amusing to do his wife's back
hair (it was so mathematically neat) and the particular 'smart'
tension of her tight stays. She lent herself especially to positions
in which the face was somewhat averted or blurred; she
abounded in lady-like back views and *profils perdus*. When she
stood erect she took naturally one of the attitudes in which
court-painters represent queens and princesses; so that I
found myself wondering whether, to draw out this accomplishment, I couldn't get the editor of the *Cheapside* to publish a
really royal romance, 'A Tale of Buckingham Palace'. Sometimes, however, the real thing and the make-believe came into
contact; by which I mean that Miss Churm, keeping an

appointment or coming to make one on days when I had much work in hand, encountered her invidious rivals. The encounter was not on their part, for they noticed her no more than if she had been the housemaid; not from intentional loftiness, but simply because, as yet, professionally, they didn't know how to fraternise, as I could guess that they would have liked – or at least that the Major would. They couldn't talk about the omnibus – they always walked; and they didn't know what else to try – she wasn't interested in good trains or cheap claret. Besides, they must have felt – in the air – that she was amused at them, secretly derisive of their ever knowing how. She was not a person to conceal her scepticism if she had had a chance to show it. On the other hand Mrs Monarch didn't think her tidy; for why else did she take pains to say to me (it was going out of the way, for Mrs Monarch) that she didn't like dirty women?

One day when my young lady happened to be present with my other sitters (she even dropped in, when it was convenient, for a chat), I asked her to be so good as to lend a hand in getting tea – a service with which she was familiar and which was one of a class that, living as I did in a small way, with slender domestic resources, I often appealed to my models to render. They liked to lay hands on my property, to break the sitting, and sometimes the china – I made them feel Bohemian. The next time I saw Miss Churm after this incident she surprised me greatly by making a scene about it – she accused me of having wished to humiliate her. She had not resented the outrage at the time, but had seemed obliging and amused, enjoying the comedy of asking Mrs Monarch, who sat vague and silent, whether she would have cream and sugar, and putting an exaggerated simper into the question. She had tried intonations – as if she too wished to pass for the real thing; till I was afraid my other visitors would take offence.

Oh, *they* were determined not to do this; and their touching patience was the measure of their great need. They would sit by the hour, uncomplaining, till I was ready to use them; they would come back on the chance of being wanted and would walk away cheerfully if they were not. I used to go to the door with them to see in what magnificent order they retreated.

I tried to find other employment for them – I introduced them to several artists. But they didn't 'take', for reasons I could appreciate, and I became conscious, rather anxiously, that after such disappointments they fell back upon me with a heavier weight. They did me the honour to think that it was I who was most *their* form. They were not picturesque enough for the painters, and in those days there were not so many serious workers in black and white. Besides, they had an eye to the great job I had mentioned to them – they had secretly set their hearts on supplying the right essence for my pictorial vindication of our fine novelist. They knew that for this under-taking I should want no costume-effects, none of the frippery of past ages – that it was a case in which everything would be contemporary and satirical and, presumably, genteel. If I could work them into it their future would be assured, for the labour would of course be long and the occupation steady.

One day Mrs Monarch came without her husband – she explained his absence by his having had to go to the City. While she sat there in her usual anxious stiffness there came, at the door, a knock which I immediately recognised as the subdued appeal of a model out of work. It was followed by the entrance of a young man whom I easily perceived to be a foreigner and who proved in fact an Italian acquainted with no English word but my name, which he uttered in a way that made it seem to include all others. I had not then visited his country, nor was I proficient in his tongue; but as he was not so meanly consti-tuted – what Italian is? – as to depend only on that member for expression he conveyed to me, in familiar but graceful mimicry, that he was in search of exactly the employment in which the lady before me was engaged. I was not struck with him at first, and while I continued to draw I emitted rough sounds of discouragement and dismissal. He stood his ground, however, not importunately, but with a dumb, dog-like fidelity in his eyes which amounted to innocent impudence – the manner of a devoted servant (he might have been in the house for years), unjustly suspected. Suddenly I saw that this very attitude and expression made a picture, whereupon I told him to sit down and wait till I should be free. There was another picture in the way he obeyed me, and I observed as I worked that there were others still in the way he looked wonderingly, with his head thrown back, about the high studio. He might have been crossing himself in St Peter's. Before I finished I said to myself: 'The fellow's a bankrupt orange-monger, but he's a treasure.'

When Mrs Monarch withdrew he passed across the room like a flash to open the door for her, standing there with the rapt, pure gaze of the young Dante spellbound by the young Beatrice. As I never insisted, in such situations, on the blankness of the British domestic, I reflected that he had the making of a servant (and I needed one, but couldn't pay him to be only that), as well as of a model; in short I made up my mind to adopt my bright adventurer if he would agree to officiate in the double capacity. He jumped at my offer, and in the event my rashness (for I had known nothing about him), was not brought home to me. He proved a sympathetic though a desultory ministrant, and had in a wonderful degree the *sentiment de la pose*. It was uncultivated, instinctive; a part of the happy instinct which had guided him to my door and helped him to spell out my name on the card nailed to it. He had had no other introduction to me than a guess, from the shape of my high north window, seen outside, that my place was a studio, and that as a studio it would contain an artist. He had wandered to England in search of fortune, like other itinerants, and had embarked, with a partner and a small green handcart, on the sale of penny ices. The ices had melted away and the partner had dissolved in their train. My young man wore tight yellow trousers with reddish stripes and his name was Oronte. He was sallow but fair, and when I put him into some old clothes of my own he looked like an Englishman. He was as good as Miss Churm, who could look, when required, like an Italian.

IV

I THOUGHT Mrs Monarch's face slightly convulsed when, on her coming back with her husband, she found Oronte installed. It was strange to have to recognise in a scrap of a lazzarone a competitor to her magnificent Major. It was she who scented danger first, for the Major was anecdotically unconscious. But Oronte gave us tea, with a hundred eager confusions (he had never seen such a queer process), and I think she thought better of me for having at last an 'establishment'. They saw a couple of drawings that I had made of the establishment, and Mrs Monarch hinted that it never would have struck her that he had sat for them. 'Now the drawings you make from *us*, they look exactly like us,' she reminded me, smiling in triumph; and I recognised that this was indeed just their defect. When I drew the Monarchs I couldn't, somehow, get away from them – get into the character I wanted to represent; and I had not the least desire my model should be discoverable in my picture. Miss Churm never was, and Mrs Monarch thought I hid her, very properly, because she was vulgar; whereas if she was lost it was only as the dead who go to heaven are lost – in the gain of an angel the more.

By this time I had got a certain start with 'Rutland Ramsay', the first novel in the great projected series; that is I had produced a dozen drawings, several with the help of the Major and his wife, and I had sent them in for approval. My understanding with the publishers, as I have already hinted, had been that I was to be left to do my work, in this particular case, as I liked, with the whole book committed to me; but my connection with the rest of the series was only contingent. There were moments when, frankly, it *was* a comfort to have the real thing under one's hand; for there were characters in 'Rutland Ramsay' that were very much like it. There were people presumably as straight as the Major and women of as good a fashion as Mrs Monarch. There was a great deal of country-house life – treated, it is true, in a fine, fanciful, ironical, generalised way – and there was a considerable implication of knickerbockers and kilts. There were certain things I had to settle at the outset; such things for instance as the exact appearance of the hero, the particular bloom of the heroine. The author of course gave me a lead, but there was a margin for interpretation. I took the Monarchs into my confidence, I told them frankly what I was about, I mentioned my embarrassments and alternatives. 'Oh, take *him*!' Mrs Monarch murmured sweetly, looking at her husband; and 'What could you want better than my wife?' the Major inquired, with the comfortable candour that now prevailed between us.

I was not obliged to answer these remarks – I was only obliged to place my sitters. I was not easy in mind, and I postponed, a little timidly perhaps, the solution of the question. The book was a large canvas, the other figures were numerous, and I worked off at first some of the episodes in which the hero and the heroine were not concerned. When once I had set *them* up I should have to stick to them – I couldn't make my young man seven feet high in one place and five feet nine in another. I inclined on the whole to the latter measurement, though the Major more than once reminded me that *he* looked about as young as anyone. It was indeed quite possible to arrange him, for the figure, so that it would have been difficult to detect his age. After the spontaneous Oronte had been with me a month, and after I had given him to understand several different times that his native exuberance would presently constitute an insurmountable barrier to our further intercourse, I waked to a sense of his heroic capacity. He was only five feet seven, but the remaining inches were latent. I tried him almost secretly at first, for I was really rather afraid of the judgement my other models would pass on such a choice. If they regarded Miss Churm as little better than a snare, what would they think of the representation by a person so little the real thing as an Italian street-vendor of a protagonist formed by a public school?

If I went a little in fear of them it was not because they bullied me, because they had got an oppressive foothold, but because in their really pathetic decorum and mysteriously permanent newness they counted on me so intensely. I was therefore very glad when Jack Hawley came home: he was always of such good counsel. He painted badly himself, but there was no one like him for putting his finger on the place. He had been absent from England for a year; he had been somewhere – I don't remember where – to get a fresh eye. I was in a good deal of dread of any such organ, but we were old friends; he had been away for months and a sense of emptiness was creeping into my life. I hadn't dodged a missile for a year.

He came back with a fresh eye, but with the same old black velvet blouse, and the first evening he spent in my studio we smoked cigarettes till the small hours. He had done no work himself, he had only got the eye; so the field was clear for the production of my little things. He wanted to see what I had done for the *Cheapside*, but he was disappointed in the exhibition. That at least seemed the meaning of two or three comprehensive groans which, as he lounged on my big divan, on a folded leg, looking at my latest drawings, issued from his lips with the smoke of the cigarette.

'What's the matter with you?' I asked.

'What's the matter with *you*?'

'Nothing save that I'm mystified.'

'You are indeed. You're quite off the hinge. What's the meaning of this new fad?' And he tossed me, with visible irreverence, a drawing in which I happened to have depicted both my majestic models. I asked if he didn't think it good, and he replied that it struck him as execrable, given the sort of thing I had always represented myself to him as wishing to arrive at; but I let that pass, I was so anxious to see exactly what he meant. The two figures in the picture looked colossal, but I supposed this was *not* what he meant, inasmuch as, for aught he knew to the contrary, I might have been trying for that. I maintained that I was working exactly in the same way as when he last had done me the honour to commend me. 'Well, there's a big hole somewhere,' he answered; 'wait a bit and I'll discover it.' I depended upon him to do so: where else was the fresh eye? But he produced at last nothing more luminous than 'I don't know – I don't like your types.' This was lame, for a critic who had never consented to discuss with me anything but the question of execution, the direction of strokes and the mystery of values.

'In the drawings you've been looking at I think my types are very handsome.'

'Oh, they won't do!'

'I've had a couple of new models.'

'I see you have. *They* won't do.'

'Are you very sure of that?'

'Absolutely – they're stupid.'

'You mean *I* am – for I ought to get round that.'

'You *can't* – with such people. Who are they?'

I told him, as far as was necessary, and he declared, heartlessly: '*Ce sont des gens qu'il faut mettre à la porte.*'

'You've never seen them; they're awfully good,' I compassionately objected.

'Not seen them? Why, all this recent work of yours drops to pieces with them. It's all I want to see of them.'

'No one else has said anything against it – the *Cheapside* people are pleased.'

'Everyone else is an ass, and the *Cheapside* people the biggest asses of all. Come, don't pretend, at this time of day, to have pretty illusions about the public, especially about publishers and editors. It's not for *such* animals you work – it's for those who know, *coloro che sanno*; so keep straight for *me* if you can't keep straight for yourself. There's a certain sort of thing you tried for from the first – and a very good thing it is. But this twaddle isn't *in* it.' When I talked with Hawley later about 'Rutland Ramsay' and its possible successors he declared that I must get back into my boat again or I would go to the bottom. His voice in short was the voice of warning.

I noted the warning, but I didn't turn my friends out of doors. They bored me a good deal; but the very fact that they bored me admonished me not to sacrifice them – if there was anything to be done with them – simply to irritation. As I look back at this phase they seem to me to have pervaded my life not a little. I have a vision of them as most of the time in my studio, seated, against the wall, on an old velvet bench to be out of the way, and looking like a pair of patient courtiers in a royal antechamber. I am convinced that during the coldest weeks of the winter they held their ground because it saved them fire. Their newness was losing its gloss, and it was impossible not to feel that they were objects of charity. Whenever Miss Churm arrived they went away, and after I was fairly launched in 'Rutland Ramsay' Miss Churm arrived pretty often. They managed to express to me tacitly that they supposed I wanted her for the low life of the book, and I let them suppose it, since they had attempted to study the work – it was lying about the studio – without discovering that it dealt only with the highest circles. They had dipped into the most brilliant of our novelists without deciphering many passages. I still took an hour from them, now and again, in spite of Jack Hawley's warning: it would be time enough to dismiss them, if dismissal should be necessary, when the rigour of the season was over. Hawley had made their acquaintance – he had met them at my fireside – and thought them a ridiculous pair. Learning that he was a painter they tried to approach him, to show him too that they were the real thing; but he looked at them, across the big room, as if they were miles away: they were a compendium of everything that he most objected to in the social system of his country. Such people as that, all convention and patent-leather, with ejaculations that stopped conversation, had no business in a studio. A studio was a place to learn to see, and how could you see through a pair of feather beds?

The main inconvenience I suffered at their hands was that, at first, I was shy of letting them discover how my artful little servant had begun to sit to me for 'Rutland Ramsay'. They knew that I had been odd enough (they were prepared by this time to allow oddity to artists) to pick a foreign vagabond out of the streets, when I might have had a person with whiskers and credentials; but it was some time before they learned how high I rated his accomplishments. They found him in an attitude more than once, but they never doubted I was doing him as an organ-grinder. There were several things they never guessed, and one of them was that for a striking scene in the novel, in which a footman briefly figured, it occurred to me to make use of Major Monarch as the menial. I kept putting this off, I didn't like to ask him to don the livery – besides the difficulty of finding a livery to fit him. At last, one day late in the winter, when I was at work on the despised Oronte (he caught one's idea in an instant), and was in the glow of feeling that I was going very straight, they came in, the Major and his wife, with their society laugh about nothing (there was less and less to laugh at), like country-callers – they always reminded me of that – who have walked across the park after church and are presently persuaded to stay to luncheon. Luncheon was over, but they could stay to tea – I knew they wanted it. The fit was on me, however, and I couldn't let my ardour cool and my work wait, with the fading daylight, while my model prepared it. So I asked Mrs Monarch if she would mind laying it out – a request which, for an instant, brought all the blood to her face. Her eyes were on her husband's for a second, and some mute telegraphy passed between them. Their folly was over the next instant; his cheerful shrewdness put an end to it. So far from pitying their wounded pride, I must add, I was moved to give it as complete a lesson as I could. They bustled about together and got out the cups and saucers and made the kettle boil. I know they felt as if they were waiting on my servant, and when the tea was prepared I said: 'He'll have a cup, please – he's tired.' Mrs Monarch brought him one where he stood, and he took it from her as if he had been a gentleman at a party, squeezing a crush-hat with an elbow.

Then it came over me that she had made a great effort for me – made it with a kind of nobleness – and that I owed her a compensation. Each time I saw her after this I wondered what the compensation could be. I couldn't go on doing the wrong thing to oblige them. Oh, it *was* the wrong thing, the stamp of the work for which they sat – Hawley was not the only person to say it now. I sent in a large number of the drawings I had made for 'Rutland Ramsay', and I received a warning that was more to the point than Hawley's. The artistic adviser of the house for which I was working was of opinion that many of my illustrations were not what had been looked for. Most of these illustrations were the subjects in which the Monarchs had figured. Without going into the question of what *had* been looked for, I saw at this rate I shouldn't get the other books to do. I hurled myself in despair upon Miss Churm, I put her through all her paces. I not only adopted Oronte publicly as my hero, but one morning when the Major looked in to see if I didn't require him to finish a figure for the *Cheapside*, for which he had begun to sit the week before, I told him that I had changed my mind – I would do the drawing from my man. At this my visitor turned pale and stood looking at me. 'Is *he* your idea of an English gentleman?' he asked.

I was disappointed, I was nervous, I wanted to get on with my work; so I replied with irritation: 'Oh, my dear Major – I can't be ruined for *you*!'

He stood another moment; then, without a word, he quitted the studio. I drew a long breath when he was gone, for I said to myself that I shouldn't see him again. I had not told him definitely that I was in danger of having my work rejected, but I was vexed at his not having felt the catastrophe in the air, read with me the moral of our fruitless collaboration, the lesson that, in the deceptive atmosphere of art, even the highest respectability may fail of being plastic.

I didn't owe my friends money, but I did see them again. They reappeared together, three days later, and under the circumstances there was something tragic in the fact. It was a proof to me that they could find nothing else in life to do. They had threshed the matter out in a dismal conference – they had digested the bad news that they were not in for the series. If they were not useful to me even for the *Cheapside* their function seemed difficult to determine, and I could only judge at first that they had come, forgivingly, decorously, to take a last leave. This made me rejoice in secret that I had little leisure for a scene; for I had placed both my other models in position together and I was pegging away at a drawing from which I hoped to derive glory. It had been suggested by the passage in which Rutland Ramsay, drawing up a chair to Artemisia's piano-stool, says extraordinary things to her while she ostensibly fingers out a difficult piece of music. I had done Miss Churm at the piano before – it was an attitude in which she knew how to take on an absolutely poetic grace. I wished the two figures to 'compose' together, intensely, and my little Italian had entered perfectly into my conception. The pair were vividly before me, the piano had been pulled out; it was a charming picture of blended youth and murmured love, which I had only to catch and keep. My visitors stood and looked at it, and I was friendly to them over my shoulder.

They made no response, but I was used to silent company and went on with my work, only a little disconcerted (even though exhilarated by the sense that *this* was at least the ideal thing) at not having got rid of them after all. Presently I heard Mrs Monarch's sweet voice beside, or rather above me: 'I wish her hair was a little better done.' I looked up and she was staring with a strange fixedness at Miss Churm, whose back was turned to her. 'Do you mind my just touching it?' she went on – a question which made me spring up for an instant, as with the instinctive fear that she might do the young lady a harm. But she quieted me with a glance I shall never forget – I confess I should like to have been able to paint *that* – and went for a moment to my model. She spoke to her softly, laying a hand upon her shoulder and bending over her; and as the girl, under-standing, gratefully assented, she disposed her rough curls, with a few quick passes, in such a way as to make Miss Churm's head twice as charming. It was one of the most heroic personal services I have ever seen rendered. Then Mrs Monarch turned away with a low sigh and, looking about her as if for something to do, stooped to the floor with a noble humility and picked up a dirty rag that had dropped out of my paint-box.

The Major meanwhile had also been looking for something to do and, wandering to the other end of the studio, saw before him my breakfast things, neglected, unremoved. 'I say, can't I be useful *here*?' he called out to me with an irrepressible quaver. I assented with a laugh that I fear was awkward and for the next ten minutes, while I worked, I heard the light clatter of china and the tinkle of spoons and glass. Mrs Monarch assisted her husband – they washed up my crockery, they put it away. They wandered off into my little scullery, and I afterwards found that they had cleaned my knives and that my slender stock of plate had an unprecedented surface. When it came over me, the latent eloquence of what they were doing, I confess that my drawing was blurred for a moment – the picture swam. They had accepted their failure, but they couldn't accept their fate. They had bowed their heads in bewilderment to the perverse and cruel law in virtue of which the real thing could be so much less precious than the unreal; but they didn't want to starve. If my servants were my models, my models might be my servants. They would reverse the parts – the others would sit for the ladies and gentlemen, and *they* would do the work. They would still be in the studio – it was an intense dumb appeal to me not to turn them out. 'Take us on,' they wanted to say – 'we'll do *anything*.'

When all this hung before me the *afflatus* vanished – my pencil dropped from my hand. My sitting was spoiled and I got rid of my sitters, who were also evidently rather mystified and awestruck. Then, alone with the Major and his wife, I had a most uncomfortable moment. He put their prayer into a single sentence: 'I say, you know – just let *us* do for you, can't you?' I couldn't – it was dreadful to see them emptying my slops; but I pretended I could, to oblige them, for about a week. Then I gave them a sum of money to go away; and I never saw them again. I obtained the remaining books, but my friend Hawley repeats that Major and Mrs Monarch did me a permanent harm, got me into a second-rate trick. If it be true I am content to have paid the price – for the memory.

OWEN WINGRAVE

I

'UPON my honour you must be off your head!' cried Spencer Coyle, as the young man, with a white face, stood there panting a little and repeating 'Really, I've quite decided,' and 'I assure you I've thought it all out.' They were both pale, but Owen Wingrave smiled in a manner exasperating to his interlocutor, who however still discriminated sufficiently to see that his grimace (it was like an irrelevant leer) was the result of extreme and conceivable nervousness.

'It was certainly a mistake to have gone so far; but that is exactly why I feel I mustn't go further,' poor Owen said, waiting mechanically, almost humbly (he wished not to swagger, and indeed he had nothing to swagger about) and carrying through the window to the stupid opposite houses the dry glitter of his eyes.

'I'm unspeakably disgusted. You've made me dreadfully ill,' Mr Coyle went on, looking thoroughly upset.

'I'm very sorry. It was the fear of the effect on you that kept me from speaking sooner.'

'You should have spoken three months ago. Don't you know your mind from one day to the other?'

The young man for a moment said nothing. Then he replied with a little tremor: 'You're very angry with me, and I expected it. I'm awfully obliged to you for all you've done for me. I'll do anything else for you in return, but I can't do that. Everyone else will let me have it, of course. I'm prepared for it – I'm prepared for everything. That's what has taken the time: to be sure I was prepared. I think it's your displeasure I feel most and regret most. But little by little you'll get over it.'

'*You'll* get over it rather faster, I suppose!' Spencer Coyle satirically exclaimed. He was quite as agitated as his young friend, and they were evidently in no condition to prolong an encounter in which they each drew blood. Mr Coyle was a professional 'coach'; he prepared young men for the army,

67

taking only three or four at a time, to whom he applied the irresistible stimulus of which the possession was both his secret and his fortune. He had not a great establishment; he would have said himself that it was not a wholesale business. Neither his system, his health nor his temper could have accommodated itself to numbers; so he weighed and measured his pupils and turned away more applicants than he passed. He was an artist in his line, caring only for picked subjects and capable of sacrifices almost passionate for the individual. He liked ardent young men (there were kinds of capacity to which he was indifferent) and he had taken a particular fancy to Owen Wingrave. This young man's facility really fascinated him. His candidates usually did wonders, and he might have sent up a multitude. He was a person of exactly the stature of the great Napoleon, with a certain flicker of genius in his light blue eye: it had been said of him that he looked like a pianist. The tone of his favourite pupil now expressed, without intention indeed, a superior wisdom which irritated him. He had not especially suffered before from Wingrave's high opinion of himself, which had seemed justified by remarkable parts; but to-day it struck him as intolerable. He cut short the discussion, declining absolutely to regard their relations as terminated, and remarked to his pupil that he had better go off somewhere (down to Eastbourne, say; the sea would bring him round) and take a few days to find his feet and come to his senses. He could afford the time, he was so well up: when Spencer Coyle remembered how well up he was he could have boxed his ears. The tall, athletic young man was not physically a subject for simplified reasoning; but there was a troubled gentleness in his handsome face, the index of compunction mixed with pertinacity, which signified that if it could have done any good he would have turned both cheeks. He evidently didn't pretend that his wisdom was superior; he only presented it as his own. It was his own career after all that was in question. He couldn't refuse to go through the form of trying Eastbourne or at least of holding his tongue, though there was that in his manner which implied that if he should do so it would be really to give Mr Coyle a chance to recuperate. He didn't feel a bit overworked, but there was nothing more natural than that with their tremendous pressure Mr Coyle should be. Mr Coyle's own intellect would derive an advantage from his pupil's holiday. Mr Coyle saw what he meant, but he controlled himself; he only demanded, as his right, a truce of three days. Owen Wingrave granted it, though as fostering sad illusions this went visibly against his conscience; but before they separated the famous crammer remarked:

'All the same I feel as if I ought to see someone. I think you mentioned to me that your aunt had come to town?'

'Oh yes; she's in Baker Street. Do go and see her,' the boy said comfortingly.

Mr Coyle looked at him an instant. 'Have you broached this folly to her?'

'Not yet – to no one. I thought it right to speak to you first.'

'Oh, what you "think right"!' cried Spencer Coyle, outraged by his young friend's standards. He added that he would probably call on Miss Wingrave; after which the recreant youth got out of the house.

Owen Wingrave didn't however start punctually for Eastbourne; he only directed his steps to Kensington Gardens, from which Mr Coyle's desirable residence (he was terribly expensive and had a big house) was not far removed. The famous coach 'put up' his pupils, and Owen had mentioned to the butler that he would be back to dinner. The spring day was warm to his young blood, and he had a book in his pocket which, when he had passed into the gardens and, after a short stroll, dropped into a chair, he took out with the slow, soft sigh that finally ushers in a pleasure postponed. He stretched his long legs and began to read it; it was a volume of Goethe's poems. He had been for days in a state of the highest tension, and now that the cord had snapped the relief was proportionate; only it was characteristic of him that this deliverance should take the form of an intellectual pleasure. If he had thrown up the probability of a magnificent career it was not to dawdle along Bond Street nor parade his indifference in the window of a club. At any rate he had in a few moments forgotten everything – the tremendous pressure, Mr Coyle's disappointment, and even his formidable aunt in Baker Street. If these watchers had overtaken him there would surely have been some excuse for their exasperation. There was no doubt he was perverse, for his very choice of a pastime only showed how he had got up his German.

'What the devil's the matter with him, do *you* know?' Spencer Coyle asked that afternoon of young Lechmere, who had never before observed the head of the establishment to set a fellow such an example of bad language. Young Lechmere was not only Wingrave's fellow-pupil, he was supposed to be his intimate, indeed quite his best friend, and had unconsciously performed for Mr Coyle the office of making the promise of his great gifts more vivid by contrast. He was short and sturdy and as a general thing uninspired, and Mr Coyle, who found no amusement in believing in him, had never thought him less exciting than as he stared now out of a face from which you could never guess whether he had caught an idea. Young Lechmere concealed such achievements as if they had been youthful indiscretions. At any rate he could evidently conceive no reason why it should be thought there was anything more than usual the matter with the companion of his studies; so Mr Coyle had to continue:

'He declines to go up. He chucks the whole thing!'

The first thing that struck young Lechmere in the case was the freshness it had imparted to the governor's vocabulary.

'He doesn't want to go to Sandhurst?'

'He doesn't want to go anywhere. He gives up the army altogether. He objects,' said Mr Coyle, in a tone that made young Lechmere almost hold his breath, 'to the military profession.'

'Why, it has been the profession of all his family!'

'Their profession? It has been their religion! Do you know Miss Wingrave?'

'Oh, yes. Isn't she awful?' young Lechmere candidly ejaculated.

His instructor demurred.

'She's formidable, if you mean that, and it's right she should be; because somehow in her very person, good maiden lady as she is, she represents the might, she represents the traditions and the exploits of the British army. She represents the expansive property of the English name. I think his family can be trusted to come down on him, but every influence should be set in motion. I want to know what yours is. Can *you* do anything in the matter?'

'I can try a couple of rounds with him,' said young Lechmere reflectively. 'But he knows a fearful lot. He has the most extraordinary ideas.'

'Then he has told you some of them – he has taken you into his confidence?'

'I've heard him jaw by the yard,' smiled the honest youth. 'He has told me he despises it.'

'What *is* it he despises? I can't make out.'

The most consecutive of Mr Coyle's nurslings considered a moment, as if he were conscious of a responsibility.

'Why, I think, military glory. He says we take the wrong view of it.'

'He oughtn't to talk to *you* that way. It's corrupting the youth of Athens. It's sowing sedition.'

'Oh, I'm all right!' said young Lechmere. 'And he never told me he meant to chuck it. I always thought he meant to see it through, simply because he had to. He'll argue on any side you like. It's a tremendous pity – I'm sure he'd have a big career.'

'Tell him so, then; plead with him; struggle with him – for God's sake.'

'I'll do what I can – I'll tell him it's a regular shame.'

'Yes, strike *that* note – insist on the disgrace of it.'

The young man gave Mr Coyle a more perceptive glance. 'I'm sure he wouldn't do anything dishonourable.'

'Well – it won't look right. He must be made to feel *that* – work it up. Give him a comrade's point of view – that of a brother-in-arms.'

'That's what I thought we were going to be!' young Lechmere mused romantically, much uplifted by the nature of the mission imposed on him. 'He's an awfully good sort.'

'No one will think so if he backs out!' said Spencer Coyle.

'They mustn't say it to *me*!' his pupil rejoined with a flush.

Mr Coyle hesitated a moment, noting his tone and aware that in the perversity of things, though this young man was a born soldier, no excitement would ever attach to *his* alternatives save perhaps on the part of the nice girl to whom at an early day he was sure to be placidly united. 'Do you like him very much – do you believe in him?'

Young Lechmere's life in these days was spent in answering terrible questions; but he had never been subjected to so queer an interrogation as this. 'Believe in him? Rather!'

'Then *save* him!'

The poor boy was puzzled, as if it were forced upon him by this intensity that there was more in such an appeal than could appear on the surface; and he doubtless felt that he was only entering into a complex situation when after another moment, with his hands in his pockets, he replied hopefully but not pompously: 'I daresay I can bring him round!'

II

BEFORE seeing young Lechmere Mr Coyle had determined to telegraph an inquiry to Miss Wingrave. He had prepaid the answer, which, being promptly put into his hand, brought the interview we have just related to a close. He immediately drove off to Baker Street, where the lady had said she awaited him, and five minutes after he got there, as he sat with Owen Wingrave's remarkable aunt, he repeated over several times, in his angry sadness and with the infallibility of his experience: 'He's so intelligent – he's so intelligent!' He had declared it had been a luxury to put such a fellow through.

'Of course he's intelligent, what else could he be? We've never, that I know of, had but *one* idiot in the family!' said Jane Wingrave. This was an allusion that Mr Coyle could understand, and it brought home to him another of the reasons for the disappointment, the humiliation as it were, of the good people at Paramore, at the same time that it gave an example of the conscientious coarseness he had on former occasions observed in his interlocutress. Poor Philip Wingrave, her late brother's eldest son, was literally imbecile and banished from view; deformed, unsocial, irretrievable, he had been relegated to a private asylum and had become among the friends of the family only a little hushed lugubrious legend. All the hopes of the house, picturesque Paramore, now unintermittently old Sir Philip's rather melancholy home (his infirmities would keep him there to the last) were therefore collected on the second boy's head, which nature, as if in compunction for her previous botch, had, in addition to making it strikingly handsome, filled with marked originalities and talents. These two had been the only children of the old man's only son, who, like so many of his ancestors, had given up a gallant young life to the service of his country. Owen Wingrave the elder had received his death-cut, in close-quarters, from an Afghan sabre; the blow had come crashing across his skull. His wife, at that time in India, was about to give birth to her third child; and when the event took place, in darkness and anguish, the baby came lifeless into the world and the mother sank under the multiplication of her woes. The second of the little boys in England, who was at Paramore with his grandfather, became the peculiar charge of his aunt, the only unmarried one, and during the interesting Sunday that, by urgent invitation, Spencer Coyle, busy as he was, had, after consenting to put Owen through, spent under that roof, the celebrated crammer received a vivid impression of the influence exerted at least in intention by Miss Wingrave. Indeed the picture of this short visit remained with the observant little man a curious one – the vision of an impoverished Jacobean house, shabby and remarkably 'creepy', but full of character still and full of felicity as a setting for the distinguished figure of the peaceful old soldier. Sir Philip Wingrave, a relic rather than a celebrity, was a small brown, erect octogenarian, with smouldering eyes and a studied courtesy. He liked to do the diminished honours of his house, but even when with a shaky hand he lighted a bedroom candle for a deprecating guest it was impossible not to feel that beneath the surface he was a merciless old warrior. The eye of the imagination could glance back into his crowded Eastern past – back at episodes in which his scrupulous forms would only have made him more terrible.

Mr Coyle remembered also two other figures – a faded in-offensive Mrs Julian, domesticated there by a system of frequent visits as the widow of an officer and a particular friend of Miss Wingrave, and a remarkably clever little girl of eighteen, who was this lady's daughter and who struck the speculative visitor as already formed for other relations. She was very impertinent to Owen, and in the course of a long walk that he had taken with the young man and the effect of which, in much talk, had been to clinch his high opinion of him, he had learned (for Owen chattered confidentially) that Mrs Julian was the sister of a very gallant gentleman, Captain Hume-Walker, of the Artillery, who had fallen in the Indian Mutiny and between whom and Miss Wingrave (it had been that lady's one known concession) a passage of some delicacy, taking a tragic turn, was believed to have been enacted. They had been engaged to be married, but she had given way to the jealousy of her nature – had broken with him and sent him off to his fate, which had been horrible. A passionate sense of having wronged him, a hard eternal remorse had thereupon taken possession of her, and when his poor sister, linked also to a soldier, had by a still heavier blow been left almost without resources, she had devoted herself charitably to a long expiation. She had sought comfort in taking Mrs Julian to live much of the time at Paramore, where she became an unremun-erated though not uncriticised housekeeper, and Spencer Coyle suspected that it was a part of this comfort that she could at her leisure trample on her. The impression of Jane Wingrave was not the faintest he had gathered on that intensifying Sunday – an occasion singularly tinged for him with the sense of bereavement and mourning and memory, of names never mentioned, of the far-away plaint of widows and the echoes of battles and bad news. It was all military indeed, and Mr Coyle was made to shudder a little at the profession of which he helped to open the door to harmless young men. Miss Wingrave moreover might have made such a bad conscience worse – so cold and clear a good one looked at him out of her hard, fine eyes and trumpeted in her sonorous voice.

She was a high, distinguished person; angular but not awk-ward, with a large forehead and abundant black hair, arranged like that of a woman conceiving perhaps excusably of her head as 'noble', and irregularly streaked to-day with white. If however she represented for Spencer Coyle the genius of a military race it was not that she had the step of a grenadier or the vocabulary of a camp-follower; it was only that such sympathies were vividly implied in the general fact to which her very presence and each of her actions and glances and tones were a constant and direct allusion – the paramount valour of her family. If she was military it was because she sprang from a military house and because she wouldn't for the world have been anything but what the Wingraves had been. She was almost vulgar about her ancestors, and if one had been tempted to quarrel with her one would have found a fair pretext in her defective sense of proportion. This temptation however said nothing to Spencer Coyle, for whom as a strong character revealing itself in colour and sound she was a spectacle and who was glad to regard her as a force exerted on his own side. He wished her nephew had more of her narrowness instead of being almost cursed with the tendency to look at things in their relations. He wondered why when she came up to town she always resorted to Baker Street for lodgings. He had never known nor heard of Baker Street as a residence – he associated it only with bazaars and photographers. He divined in her a rigid indifference to everything that was not the passion of her life. Nothing really mattered to her but that, and she would have occupied apartments in Whitechapel if they had been a feature in her tactics. She had received her visitor in a large cold, faded room, furnished with slippery seats and decorated with alabaster vases and wax-flowers. The only little personal comfort for which she appeared to have looked out was a fat catalogue of the Army and Navy Stores, which reposed on a vast, desolate table-cover of false blue. Her clear forehead – it was like a porcelain slate, a receptacle for addresses and sums – had flushed when her nephew's crammer told her the extraordinary news; but he saw she was fortunately more angry than frightened. She had essentially, she would always have, too little imagination for fear, and the healthy habit moreover of facing everything had taught her that the occasion usually found her a quantity to reckon with. Mr Coyle saw that her only fear at present could have been that of not being able to prevent her nephew from being absurd and that to such an apprehension as this she was in fact inaccessible. Practically too she was not troubled by surprise; she recognised none of the futile, none of the subtle sentiments. If Philip had for an hour made a fool of himself she was angry; disconcerted as she would have been on learning that he had confessed to debts or fallen in love with a low girl. But there remained in any annoyance the saving fact that no one could make a fool of *her*.

'I don't know when I've taken such an interest in a young man – I think I never have, since I began to handle them,' Mr Coyle said. 'I like him, I believe in him – it's been a delight to see how he was going.'

'Oh, I know how they go!' Miss Wingrave threw back her head with a familiar briskness, as if a rapid procession of the generations had flashed before her, rattling their scabbards and spurs. Spencer Coyle recognised the intimation that she had nothing to learn from anybody about the natural carriage of a Wingrave, and he even felt convicted by her next words of being, in her eyes, with the troubled story of his check, his weak complaint of his pupil, rather a poor creature. 'If you like him,' she exclaimed, 'for mercy's sake keep him quiet!'

Mr Coyle began to explain to her that this was less easy than she appeared to imagine; but he perceived that she understood very little of what he said. The more he insisted that the boy had a kind of intellectual independence, the more this struck her as a conclusive proof that her nephew was a Wingrave and a soldier. It was not till he mentioned to her that Owen had spoken of the profession of arms as of something that would be 'beneath' him, it was not till her attention was arrested by this intenser light on the complexity of the problem that Miss Wingrave broke out after a moment's stupefied reflection: 'Send him to see me immediately!'

'That's exactly what I wanted to ask your leave to do. But I've wanted also to prepare you for the worst, to make you understand that he strikes me as really obstinate and to suggest to you that the most powerful arguments at your command –

especially if you should be able to put your hand on some intensely practical one – will be none too effective.'

'I think I've got a powerful argument.' Miss Wingrave looked very hard at her visitor. He didn't know in the least what it was, but he begged her to put it forward without delay. He promised that their young man should come to Baker Street that evening, mentioning however that he had already urged him to spend without delay a couple of days at Eastbourne. This led Jane Wingrave to inquire with surprise what virtue there might be in *that* expensive remedy, and to reply with decision when Mr Coyle had said 'The virtue of a little rest, a little change, a little relief to overwrought nerves,' 'Ah, don't coddle him – he's costing us a great deal of money! I'll talk to him and I'll take him down to Paramore; then I'll send him back to you straightened out.'

Spencer Coyle hailed this pledge superficially with satisfaction, but before he quitted Miss Wingrave he became conscious that he had really taken on a new anxiety – a restlessness that made him say to himself, groaning inwardly: 'Oh, she *is* a grenadier at bottom, and she'll have no tact. I don't know what her powerful argument is; I'm only afraid she'll be stupid and make him worse. The old man's better – *he's* capable of tact, though he's not quite an extinct volcano. Owen will probably put him in a rage. In short the difficulty is that the boy's the best of them.'

Spencer Coyle felt afresh that evening at dinner that the boy was the best of them. Young Wingrave (who, he was pleased to observe, had not yet proceeded to the seaside) appeared at the repast as usual, looking inevitably a little self-conscious, but not too original for Bayswater. He talked very naturally to Mrs Coyle, who had thought him from the first the most beautiful young man they had ever received; so that the person most ill at ease was poor Lechmere, who took great trouble, as if from the deepest delicacy, not to meet the eye of his misguided mate. Spencer Coyle however paid the penalty of his own profundity in feeling more and more worried; he could so easily see that there were all sorts of things in his young friend that the people of Paramore wouldn't understand. He began even already to react against the notion of his being harassed – to reflect that after all he had a right to his ideas – to remember that he was of a substance too fine to be in fairness roughly used. It was in this way that the ardent little crammer, with his whimsical perceptions and complicated sympathies, was generally condemned not to settle down comfortably either into his displeasures or into his enthusiasms. His love of the real truth never gave him a chance to enjoy them. He mentioned to Wingrave after dinner the propriety of an immediate visit to Baker Street, and the young man, looking 'queer', as he thought – that is smiling again with the exaggerated glory he had shown in their recent interview – went off to face the ordeal. Spencer Coyle noted that he was scared – he was afraid of his aunt; but somehow this didn't strike him as a sign of pusillanimity. *He* should have been scared, he was well aware, in the poor boy's place, and the sight of his pupil marching up to the battery in spite of his terrors was a positive suggestion of the temperament of the soldier. Many a plucky youth would have shirked this particular peril.

'He *has* got ideas!' young Lechmere broke out to his instructor after his comrade had quitted the house. He was evidently bewildered and agitated – he had an emotion to work off. He had before dinner gone straight at his friend, as Mr Coyle had requested, and had elicited from him that his scruples were founded on an overwhelming conviction of the stupidity – the 'crass barbarism' he called it – of war. His great complaint was that people hadn't invented anything cleverer, and he was determined to show, the only way he could, that *he* wasn't such an ass.

'And he thinks all the great generals ought to have been shot, and that Napoleon Bonaparte in particular, the greatest, was a criminal, a monster for whom language has no adequate name!' Mr Coyle rejoined, completing young Lechmere's picture. 'He favoured you, I see, with exactly the same pearls of wisdom that he produced for me. But I want to know what *you* said.'

'I said they were awful rot!' Young Lechmere spoke with emphasis, and he was slightly surprised to hear Mr Coyle laugh incongruously at this just declaration and then after a moment continue:

'It's all very curious – I daresay there's something in it. But it's a pity!'

'He told me when it was that the question began to strike him in that light. Four or five years ago, when he did a lot of reading about all the great swells and their campaigns – Hannibal and Julius Caesar, Marlborough and Frederick and Bonaparte. He *has* done a lot of reading, and he says it opened his eyes. He says that a wave of disgust rolled over him. He talked about the "immeasurable misery" of wars, and asked me why nations don't tear to pieces the governments, the rulers that go in for them. He hates poor old Bonaparte worst of all.'

'Well, poor old Bonaparte *was* a brute. He was a frightful ruffian,' Mr Coyle unexpectedly declared. 'But I suppose you didn't admit that.'

'Oh, I daresay he was objectionable, and I'm very glad we laid him on his back. But the point I made to Wingrave was that his own behaviour would excite no end of remark.' Young Lechmere hesitated an instant, then he added: 'I told him he must be prepared for the worst.'

'Of course he asked you what you meant by the "worst",' said Spencer Coyle.

'Yes, he asked me that, and do you know what I said? I said people would say that his conscientious scruples and his wave of disgust are only a pretext. Then he asked "A pretext for what?"'

'Ah, he rather had you there!' Mr Coyle exclaimed with a little laugh that was mystifying to his pupil.

'Not a bit – for I told him.'

'What did you tell him?'

Once more, for a few seconds, with his conscious eyes in his instructor's, the young man hung fire.

'Why, what we spoke of a few hours ago. The appearance he'd present of not having —' The honest youth faltered a moment, then brought it out: 'The military temperament, don't you know? But do you know what he said to that?' young Lechmere went on.

'Damn the military temperament!' the crammer promptly replied.

Young Lechmere stared. Mr Coyle's tone left him uncertain if he were attributing the phrase to Wingrave or uttering his own opinion, but he exclaimed:

'Those were exactly his words!'

'He doesn't care,' said Mr Coyle.

'Perhaps not. But it isn't fair for him to abuse *us* fellows. I told him it's the finest temperament in the world, and that there's nothing so splendid as pluck and heroism.'

'Ah! there you had *him*.'

'I told him it was unworthy of him to abuse a gallant, a magnificent profession. I told him there's no type so fine as that of the soldier doing his duty.'

'That's essentially *your* type, my dear boy.' Young Lechmere blushed; he couldn't make out (and the danger was naturally unexpected to him) whether at that moment he didn't exist mainly for the recreation of his friend. But he was partly reassured by the genial way this friend continued, laying a hand on his shoulder: 'Keep *at* him that way! we may do something. I'm extremely obliged to you.' Another doubt however remained unassuaged – a doubt which led him to exclaim to Mr Coyle before they dropped the painful subject:

'He *doesn't* care! But it's awfully odd he shouldn't!'

'So it is, but remember what you said this afternoon – I mean about your not advising people to make insinuations to *you*.'

'I believe I should knock a fellow down!' said young Lechmere. Mr Coyle had got up; the conversation had taken place while they sat together after Mrs Coyle's withdrawal from the dinner-table and the head of the establishment administered to his disciple, on principles that were a part of his thoroughness, a glass of excellent claret. The disciple, also on his feet, lingered an instant, not for another 'go', as he would have called it, at the decanter, but to wipe his microscopic moustache with prolonged and unusual care. His companion saw he had something to bring out which required a final effort, and waited for him an instant with a hand on the knob of the door. Then as young Lechmere approached him Spencer Coyle grew conscious of an unwonted intensity in the round and ingenuous face. The boy was nervous, but he tried to behave like a man of the world. 'Of course, it's between ourselves,' he stammered, 'and I wouldn't breathe such a word to any one who wasn't interested in poor Wingrave as you are. But do you think he funks it?'

Mr Coyle looked at him so hard for an instant that he was visibly frightened at what he had said.

'Funks it! Funks what?'

'Why, what we're talking about – the service.' Young Lechmere gave a little gulp and added with a *naïveté* almost pathetic to Spencer Coyle: 'The dangers, you know!'

'Do you mean he's thinking of his skin?'

Young Lechmere's eyes expanded appealingly, and what his instructor saw in his pink face – he even thought he saw a tear – was the dread of a disappointment shocking in the degree in which the loyalty of admiration had been great.

'Is he – is he *afraid*?' repeated the honest lad, with a quaver of suspense.

'Dear no!' said Spencer Coyle, turning his back.

Young Lechmere felt a little snubbed and even a little ashamed; but he felt still more relieved.

III

LESS than a week after this Spencer Coyle received a note from Miss Wingrave, who had immediately quitted London with her nephew. She proposed that he should come down to Paramore for the following Sunday – Owen was really so tiresome. On the spot, in that house of examples and memories and in combination with her poor dear father, who was 'dreadfully annoyed', it might be worth their while to make a last stand. Mr Coyle read between the lines of this letter that the party at Paramore had got over a good deal of ground since Miss Wingrave, in Baker Street, had treated his despair as superficial. She was not an insinuating woman, but she went so far as to put the question on the ground of his conferring a particular favour on an afflicted family; and she expressed the pleasure it would give them if he should be accompanied by Mrs Coyle, for whom she inclosed a separate invitation. She mentioned that she was also writing, subject to Mr Coyle's approval, to young Lechmere. She thought such a nice manly boy might do her wretched nephew some good. The celebrated crammer determined to embrace this opportunity; and now it was the case not so much that he was angry as that he was anxious. As he directed his answer to Miss Wingrave's letter he caught himself smiling at the thought that at bottom he was going to defend his young friend rather than to attack him. He said to his wife, who was a fair, fresh, slow woman – a person of much more presence than himself – that she had better take Miss Wingrave at her word: it was such an extraordinary, such a fascinating specimen of an old English home. This last allusion was amicably sarcastic – he had already accused the good lady more than once of being in love with Owen Wingrave. She admitted that she was, she even gloried in her passion; which shows that the subject, between them, was treated in a liberal spirit. She carried out the joke by accepting the invitation with eagerness. Young Lechmere was delighted to do the same; his instructor had good-naturedly taken the view that the little break would freshen him up for his last spurt.

It was the fact that the occupants of Paramore did indeed take their trouble hard that struck Spencer Coyle after he had been an hour or two in that fine old house. This very short second visit, beginning on the Saturday evening, was to constitute the strangest episode of his life. As soon as he found himself in private with his wife – they had retired to dress for dinner – they called each other's attention with effusion and almost with alarm to the sinister gloom that was stamped on the place. The house was admirable with its old grey front which came forward in wings so as to form three sides of a square, but Mrs Coyle made no scruple to declare that if she had known in advance the sort of impression she was going to receive she would never have put her foot in it. She characterised it as 'uncanny', she accused her husband of not having warned her properly. He had mentioned to her in advance certain facts, but while she almost feverishly dressed she had innumerable questions to ask. He hadn't told her about the girl, the extraordinary girl, Miss Julian – that is, he hadn't told her that this young lady, who in plain terms was a mere dependant, would be in effect, and as a consequence of the way she carried herself, the most important person in the house. Mrs Coyle was already prepared to announce that she hated Miss Julian's affectations. Her husband above all hadn't told her that they should find their young charge looking five years older.

'I couldn't imagine that,' said Mr Coyle, 'nor that the character of the crisis here would be quite so perceptible. But I suggested to Miss Wingrave the other day that they should press her nephew in real earnest, and she has taken me at my word. They've cut off his supplies – they're trying to starve him out. That's not what I meant – but indeed I don't quite *know* today what I meant. Owen feels the pressure, but he won't yield.' The strange thing was that, now that he was there, the versatile little coach felt still more that his own spirit had been caught up by a wave of reaction. If he was there it was because he was on poor Owen's side. His whole impression, his whole apprehension, had on the spot become much deeper. There was something in the dear boy's very resistance that began to charm him. When his wife, in the intimacy of the conference I have mentioned, threw off the mask and commended even with extravagance the stand his pupil had taken (he was too good to be a horrid soldier and it was noble of him to suffer for his convictions – wasn't he as upright as a young hero, even though as pale as a Christian martyr?) the good lady only expressed the sympathy which, under cover of regarding his young friend as a rare exception, he had already recognised in his own soul.

For, half an hour ago, after they had had superficial tea in the brown old hall of the house, his young friend had proposed to him, before going to dress, to take a turn outside, and had even, on the terrace, as they walked together to one of the far ends of it, passed his hand entreatingly into his companion's arm, permitting himself thus a familiarity unusual between pupil and master and calculated to show that he had guessed whom he could most depend on to be kind to him. Spencer Coyle on his own side had guessed something, so that he was not surprised at the boy's having a particular confidence to make. He had felt on arriving that each member of the party had wished to get hold of him first, and he knew that at that moment Jane Wingrave was peering through the ancient blur of one of the windows (the house had been modernised so little that the thick dim panes were three centuries old) to see if her nephew looked as if he were poisoning the visitor's mind. Mr Coyle lost no time therefore in reminding the youth (and he took care to laugh as he did so) that he had not come down to Paramore to be corrupted. He had come down to make, face to face, a last appeal to him – he hoped it wouldn't be utterly vain. Owen smiled sadly as they went, asking him if he thought he had the general air of a fellow who was going to knock under.

'I think you look strange – I think you look ill,' Spencer Coyle said very honestly. They had paused at the end of the terrace.

'I've had to exercise a great power of resistance, and it rather takes it out of one.'

'Ah, my dear boy, I wish your great power – for you evidently possess it – were exerted in a better cause!'

Owen Wingrave smiled down at his small instructor. 'I don't believe that!' Then he added, to explain why: 'Isn't what you want, if you're so good as to think well of my character, to see me exert *most* power, in whatever direction? Well, *this* is the way I exert most.' Owen Wingrave went on to relate that he had had some terrible hours with his grandfather, who had denounced him in a way to make one's hair stand up on one's head. He had expected them not to like it, not a bit, but he had had no idea they would make such a row. His aunt was different, but she was equally insulting. Oh, they had made him feel they were ashamed of him; they accused him of putting a public dis-honour on their name. He was the only one who had ever backed out – he was the first for three hundred years. Every one had known he was to go up, and now every one would know he was a young hypocrite who suddenly pretended to have scruples. They talked of his scruples as you wouldn't talk of a cannibal's god. His grandfather had called him outrageous names. 'He called me – he called me— ' Here the young man faltered, his voice failed him. He looked as haggard as was possible to a young man in such magnificent health.

'I probably know!' said Spencer Coyle, with a nervous laugh.

Owen Wingrave's clouded eyes, as if they were following the far-off consequences of things, rested for an instant on a distant object. Then they met his companion's and for another moment sounded them deeply. 'It isn't true. No, it isn't. It's not *that*!'

'I don't suppose it is! But what *do* you propose instead of it?'

'Instead of what?'

'Instead of the stupid solution of war. If you take that away you should suggest at least a substitute.'

'That's for the people in charge, for governments and cabinets,' said Owen Wingrave. '*They*'ll arrive soon enough at a substitute, in the particular case, if they're made to understand that they'll be hung if they don't find one. Make it a capital crime – that'll quicken the wits of ministers!' His eyes brightened as he spoke, and he looked assured and exalted. Mr Coyle gave a sigh of perplexed resignation – it was a mono-mania. He fancied after this for a moment that Owen was going to ask him if he too thought he was a coward; but he was relieved to observe that he either didn't suspect him of it or shrank uncomfortably from putting the question to the test. Spencer Coyle wished to show confidence, but somehow a direct assurance that he didn't doubt of his courage appeared too gross a compliment – it would be like saying he didn't doubt of his honesty. The difficulty was presently averted by Owen's continuing: 'My grandfather can't break the entail, but I shall have nothing but this place, which, as you know, is small and, with the way rents are going, has quite ceased to yield an income. He has some money – not much, but such as it is he cuts me off. My aunt does the same – she has let me know her intentions. She was to have left me her six hundred a year. It was all settled; but now what's settled is that I don't get a penny of it if I give up the army. I must add in fairness that I have from my mother three hundred a year of my own. And I tell you the simple truth when I say that I don't care a rap for the loss of the money.' The young man drew a long, slow breath, like a creature in pain; then he subjoined: '*That's* not what worries me!'

'What are you going to do?' asked Spencer Coyle.

'I don't know; perhaps nothing. Nothing great, at all events. Only something peaceful!'

Owen gave a weary smile, as if, worried as he was, he could yet appreciate the humorous effect of such a declaration from a Wingrave; but what it suggested to his companion, who looked up at him with a sense that he was after all not a Wingrave for nothing and had a military steadiness under fire, was the exasperation that such a programme, uttered in such a way and striking them as the last word of the inglorious, might well have engendered on the part of his grandfather and his aunt. 'Perhaps nothing' – when he might carry on the great tradition! Yes, he wasn't weak, and he was interesting; but there *was* a point of view from which he was provoking. 'What *is* it then that worries you?' Mr Coyle demanded.

'Oh, the house – the very air and feeling of it. There are strange voices in it that seem to mutter at me – to say dreadful things as I pass. I mean the general consciousness and responsibility of what I'm doing. Of course it hasn't been easy for me – not a bit. I assure you I don't enjoy it.' With a light in them that was like a longing for justice Owen again bent his eyes on those of the little coach; then he pursued: 'I've started up all the old ghosts. The very portraits glower at me on the walls. There's one of my great-great-grandfather (the one the extraordinary story you know is about – the old fellow who hangs on the second landing of the big staircase) that fairly stirs on the canvas – just heaves a little – when I come near it. I have to go up and down stairs – it's rather awkward! It's what my aunt calls the family circle. It's all constituted here, it's a kind of indestructible presence, it stretches away into the past, and when I came back with her the other day Miss Wingrave told me I wouldn't have the impudence to stand in the midst of it and say such things. I *had* to say them to my grandfather; but now that I've said them it seems to me that the question's ended. I want to go away – I don't care if I never come back again.'

'Oh, you *are* a soldier; you must fight it out!' Mr Coyle laughed.

The young man seemed discouraged at his levity, but as they turned round, strolling back in the direction from which they had come, he himself smiled faintly after an instant and replied:

'Ah, we're tainted – all!'

They walked in silence part of the way to the old portico; then Spencer Coyle, stopping short after having assured himself that he was at a sufficient distance from the house not to be heard, suddenly put the question: 'What does Miss Julian say?'

'Miss Julian?' Owen had perceptibly coloured.

'I'm sure *she* hasn't concealed her opinion.'

'Oh, it's the opinion of the family circle, for she's a member of it of course. And then she has her own as well.'

'Her own opinion?'

'Her own family circle.'

'Do you mean her mother – that patient lady?'

'I mean more particularly her father, who fell in battle. And her grandfather, and *his* father, and her uncles and great-uncles – they all fell in battle.'

'Hasn't the sacrifice of so many lives been sufficient? Why should she sacrifice *you*?'

'Oh, she *hates* me!' Owen declared, as they resumed their walk.

'Ah, the hatred of pretty girls for fine young men!' exclaimed Spencer Coyle.

He didn't believe in it, but his wife did, it appeared perfectly, when he mentioned this conversation while, in the fashion that has been described, the visitors dressed for dinner. Mrs Coyle had already discovered that nothing could have been nastier than Miss Julian's manner to the disgraced youth during the half-hour the party had spent in the hall; and it was this lady's judgement that one must have had no eyes in one's head not to see that she was already trying outrageously to flirt with young Lechmere. It was a pity they had brought that silly boy: he was down in the hall with her at that moment. Spencer Coyle's version was different; he thought there were finer elements involved. The girl's footing in the house was inexplicable on any ground save that of her being predestined to Miss Wingrave's nephew. As the niece of Miss Wingrave's own unhappy intended she had been dedicated early by this lady to the office of healing by a union with Owen the tragic breach that had separated their elders; and if in reply to this it was to be said that a girl of spirit couldn't enjoy in such a matter having her duty cut out for her, Owen's enlightened friend was ready with the argument that a young person in Miss Julian's position would never be such a fool as really to quarrel with a capital chance. She was familiar at Paramore and she felt safe; therefore she might trust herself to the amusement of pretending that she had her option. But it was all innocent coquetry. She had a curious charm, and it was vain to pretend that the heir of that house wouldn't seem good enough to a girl, clever as she might be, of eighteen. Mrs Coyle reminded her husband that the poor young man was precisely now *not* of that house: this problem was among the questions that exercised their wits after the two men had taken the turn on the terrace. Spencer Coyle told his wife that Owen was afraid of the portrait of his great-great-grandfather. He would show it to her, since she hadn't noticed it, on their way down stairs.

'Why of his great-great-grandfather more than of any of the others?'

'Oh, because he's the most formidable. He's the one who's sometimes seen.'

'Seen where?' Mrs Coyle had turned round with a jerk.

'In the room he was found dead in – the White Room they've always called it.'

'Do you mean to say the house has a *ghost*?' Mrs Coyle almost shrieked. 'You brought me here without telling me?'

'Didn't I mention it after my other visit?'

'Not a word. You only talked about Miss Wingrave.'

'Oh, I was full of the story – you have simply forgotten.'

'Then you should have reminded me!'

'If I had thought of it I would have held my peace, for you wouldn't have come.'

'I wish, indeed, I hadn't!' cried Mrs Coyle. 'What *is* the story?'

'Oh, a deed of violence that took place here ages ago. I think it was in George the First's time. Colonel Wingrave, one of their ancestors, struck in a fit of passion one of his children, a lad just growing up, a blow on the head of which the unhappy child died. The matter was hushed up for the hour – some other explanation was put about. The poor boy was laid out in one of those rooms on the other side of the house, and amid strange smothered rumours the funeral was hurried on. The next morning, when the household assembled, Colonel Wingrave was missing; he was looked for vainly, and at last it occurred to some one that he might perhaps be in the room from which his child had been carried to burial. The seeker knocked without an answer – then opened the door. Colonel Wingrave lay dead on the floor, in his clothes, as if he had reeled and fallen back, without a wound, without a mark, without anything in his appearance to indicate that he had either struggled or suffered. He was a strong, sound man – there was nothing to account for such a catastrophe. He is supposed to have gone to the room during the night, just before going to bed, in some fit of compunction or some fascination of dread. It was only after this that the truth about the boy came out. But no one ever sleeps in the room.'

Mrs Coyle had fairly turned pale. 'I hope not! Thank heaven they haven't put *us* there!'

'We're at a comfortable distance; but I've seen the gruesome chamber.'

'Do you mean you've been *in* it?'

'For a few moments. They're rather proud of it and my young friend showed it to me when I was here before.'

Mrs Coyle stared. 'And what is it like?'

'Simply like an empty, dull, old-fashioned bedroom, rather big, with the things of the "period" in it. It's panelled from floor to ceiling, and the panels evidently, years and years ago, were painted white. But the paint has darkened with time and there are three or four quaint little ancient "samplers", framed and glazed, hung on the walls.'

Mrs Coyle looked round with a shudder. 'I'm glad there are no samplers here! I never heard anything so jumpy! Come down to dinner.'

On the staircase as they went down her husband showed her the portrait of Colonel Wingrave – rather a vigorous representation, for the place and period, of a gentleman with a hard, handsome face, in a red coat and a peruke. Mrs Coyle declared that his descendant Sir Philip was wonderfully like him; and her husband could fancy, though he kept it to himself, that if one should have the courage to walk about the old corridors of Paramore at night one might meet a figure that resembled him roaming, with the restlessness of a ghost, hand in hand with the figure of a tall boy. As he proceeded to the drawing-room with his wife he found himself suddenly wishing that he had made more of a point of his pupil's going to East-bourne. The evening however seemed to have taken upon itself to dissipate any such whimsical forebodings, for the grimness of the family circle, as Spencer Coyle had preconceived its com-position, was mitigated by an infusion of the 'neighbourhood'. The company at dinner was recruited by two cheerful couples – one of them the vicar and his wife, and by a silent young man who had come down to fish. This was a relief to Mr Coyle, who had begun to wonder what was after all expected of him and why he had been such a fool as to come, and who now felt that for the first hours at least the situation would not have directly to be dealt with. Indeed he found, as he had found before, sufficient occupation for his ingenuity in reading the various symptoms of which the picture before him was an expression. He should probably have an irritating day on the morrow: he foresaw the difficulty of the long decorous Sunday and how dry Jane Wingrave's ideas, elicited in a strenuous conference, would taste. She and her father would make him feel that they depended upon him for the impossible, and if they should try to associate him with a merely stupid policy he might end by telling them what he thought of it – an accident not required to make his visit a sensible mistake. The old man's actual design was evidently to let their friends see in it a positive mark of their being all right. The presence of the great London coach was tantamount to a profession of faith in the results of the impend-ing examination. It had clearly been obtained from Owen, rather to Spencer Coyle's surprise, that he would do nothing to interfere with the apparent harmony. He let the allusions to his hard work pass and, holding his tongue about his affairs,

talked to the ladies as amicably as if he had not been 'cut off'.
When Spencer Coyle looked at him once or twice across the
table, catching his eye, which showed an indefinable passion,
he saw a puzzling pathos in his laughing face: one couldn't
resist a pang for a young lamb so visibly marked for sacrifice.
'Hang him – what a pity he's such a fighter!' he privately sighed,
with a want of logic that was only superficial.

This idea however would have absorbed him more if so
much of his attention had not been given to Kate Julian, who
now that he had her well before him struck him as a remarkable
and even as a possibly fascinating young woman. The fascination resided not in any extraordinary prettiness, for if she was
handsome, with her long Eastern eyes, her magnificent hair
and her general unabashed originality, he had seen complex-
ions rosier and features that pleased him more: it resided in a
strange impression that she gave of being exactly the sort of
person whom, in her position, common considerations, those
of prudence and perhaps even a little those of decorum, would
have enjoined on her not to be. She was what was vulgarly
termed a dependant – penniless, patronised, tolerated; but
something in her aspect and manner signified that if her situation was inferior, her spirit, to make up for it, was above precautions or submissions. It was not in the least that she was
aggressive, she was too indifferent for that; it was only as if,
having nothing either to gain or to lose, she could afford to do as
she liked. It occurred to Spencer Coyle that she might really
have had more at stake than her imagination appeared to take
account of; whatever it was at any rate he had never seen a
young woman at less pains to be on the safe side. He wondered
inevitably how the peace was kept between Jane Wingrave and
such an inmate as this; but those questions of course were
unfathomable deeps. Perhaps Kate Julian lorded it even over
her protectress. The other time he was at Paramore he had
received an impression that, with Sir Philip beside her, the girl
could fight with her back to the wall. She amused Sir Philip, she
charmed him, and he liked people who weren't afraid; between
him and his daughter moreover there was no doubt which was
the higher in command. Miss Wingrave took many things for

granted, and most of all the rigour of discipline and the fate of the vanquished and the captive.

But between their clever boy and so original a companion of his childhood what odd relation would have grown up? It couldn't be indifference, and yet on the part of happy, handsome, youthful creatures it was still less likely to be aversion. They weren't Paul and Virginia, but they must have had their common summer and their idyll: no nice girl could have disliked such a nice fellow for anything but not liking *her*, and no nice fellow could have resisted such propinquity. Mr Coyle remembered indeed that Mrs Julian had spoken to him as if the propinquity had been by no means constant, owing to her daughter's absences at school, to say nothing of Owen's; her visits to a few friends who were so kind as to 'take her' from time to time; her sojourns in London – so difficult to manage, but still managed by God's help – for 'advantages', for drawing and singing, especially drawing or rather painting, in oils, in which she had had immense success. But the good lady had also mentioned that the young people were quite brother and sister, which *was* a little, after all, like Paul and Virginia. Mrs Coyle had been right, and it was apparent that Virginia was doing her best to make the time pass agreeably for young Lechmere. There was no such whirl of conversation as to render it an effort for Mr Coyle to reflect on these things, for the tone of the occasion, thanks principally to the other guests, was not disposed to stray – it tended to the repetition of anecdote and the discussion of rents, topics that huddled together like uneasy animals. He could judge how intensely his hosts wished the evening to pass off as if nothing had happened; and this gave him the measure of their private resentment. Before dinner was over he found himself fidgety about his second pupil. Young Lechmere, since he began to cram, had done all that might have been expected of him; but this couldn't blind his instructor to a present perception of his being in moments of relaxation as innocent as a babe. Mr Coyle had considered that the amusements of Paramore would probably give him a fillip, and the poor fellow's manner testified to the soundness of the forecast. The fillip had been unmistakably administered; it had come in the form of a revelation. The light on young Lechmere's brow announced with a candour that was almost an appeal for compassion, or at least a deprecation of ridicule, that he had never seen anything like Miss Julian.

IV

IN the drawing-room after dinner the girl found an occasion to approach Spencer Coyle. She stood before him a moment, smiling while she opened and shut her fan, and then she said abruptly, raising her strange eyes: 'I know what you've come for, but it isn't any use.'

'I've come to look after *you* a little. Isn't *that* any use?'

'It's very kind. But I'm not the question of the hour. You won't do anything with Owen.'

Spencer Coyle hesitated a moment. 'What will *you* do with his young friend?'

She stared, looked round her.

'Mr Lechmere? Oh, poor little lad! We've been talking about Owen. He admires him so.'

'So do I. I should tell you that.'

'So do we all. That's why we're in such despair.'

'Personally then you'd *like* him to be a soldier?' Spencer Coyle inquired.

'I've quite set my heart on it. I adore the army and I'm awfully fond of my old playmate,' said Miss Julian.

Her interlocutor remembered the young man's own different version of her attitude; but he judged it loyal not to challenge the girl.

'It's not conceivable that your old playmate shouldn't be fond of you. He must therefore wish to please you; and I don't see why – between you – you don't set the matter right.'

'Wish to please me!' Miss Julian exclaimed. 'I'm sorry to say he shows no such desire. He thinks me an impudent wretch. I've told him what I think of *him*, and he simply hates me.'

'But you think so highly! You just told me you admire him.'

'His talents, his possibilities, yes; even his appearance, if I may allude to such a matter. But I don't admire his present behaviour.'

'Have you had the question out with him?' Spencer Coyle asked.

'Oh, yes, I've ventured to be frank – the occasion seemed to excuse it. He couldn't like what I said.'

'What did you say?'

Miss Julian, thinking a moment, opened and shut her fan again.

'Why, that such conduct isn't that of a gentleman!'

After she had spoken her eyes met Spencer Coyle's, who looked into their charming depths.

'Do you want then so much to send him off to be killed?'

'How odd for *you* to ask that – in such a way!' she replied with a laugh. 'I don't understand your position: I thought your line was to *make* soldiers!'

'You should take my little joke. But, as regards Owen Wingrave, there's no "making" needed,' Mr Coyle added. 'To my sense' – the little crammer paused a moment, as if with a consciousness of responsibility for his paradox – 'to my sense he *is*, in a high sense of the term, a fighting man.'

'Ah, let him prove it!' the girl exclaimed, turning away.

Spencer Coyle let her go; there was something in her tone that annoyed and even a little shocked him. There had evidently been a violent passage between these young people, and the reflection that such a matter was after all none of his business only made him more sore. It was indeed a military house, and she was at any rate a person who placed her ideal of manhood (young persons doubtless always had their ideals of manhood) in the type of the belted warrior. It was a taste like another; but, even a quarter of an hour later, finding himself near young Lechmere, in whom this type was embodied, Spencer Coyle was still so ruffled that he addressed the innocent lad with a certain magisterial dryness. 'You're not to sit up late, you know. That's not what I brought you down for.' The dinner-guests were taking leave and the bedroom candles twinkled in a monitory row. Young Lechmere however was too agreeably agitated to be accessible to a snub: he had a happy preoccupation which almost engendered a grin.

'I'm only too eager for bedtime. Do you know there's an awfully jolly room?'

'Surely they haven't put you there?'

'No indeed: no one has passed a night in it for ages. But that's exactly what I want to do – it would be tremendous fun.'

'And have you been trying to get Miss Julian's permission?'

'Oh, *she* can't give leave, she says. But she believes in it, and she maintains that no man dare.'

'No man *shall*! A man in your critical position in particular must have a quiet night,' said Spencer Coyle.

Young Lechmere gave a disappointed but reasonable sigh.

'Oh, all right. But mayn't I sit up for a little go at Wingrave? I haven't had any yet.'

Mr Coyle looked at his watch.

'You may smoke *one* cigarette.'

He felt a hand on his shoulder, and he turned round to see his wife tilting candle-grease upon his coat. The ladies were going to bed and it was Sir Philip's inveterate hour; but Mrs Coyle confided to her husband that after the dreadful things he had told her she positively declined to be left alone, for no matter how short an interval, in any part of the house. He promised to follow her within three minutes, and after the orthodox handshakes the ladies rustled away. The forms were kept up at Paramore as bravely as if the old house had no present heartache. The only one of which Spencer Coyle noticed the omission was some salutation to himself from Kate Julian. She gave him neither a word nor a glance, but he saw her look hard at Owen Wingrave. Her mother, timid and pitying, was apparently the only person from whom this young man caught an inclination of the head. Miss Wingrave marshalled the three ladies – her little procession of twinkling tapers – up the wide oaken stairs and past the watching portrait of her ill-fated ancestor. Sir Philip's servant appeared and offered his arm to the old man, who turned a perpendicular back on poor Owen when the boy made a vague movement to anticipate this office. Spencer Coyle learned afterwards that before Owen had forfeited favour it had always, when he was at home, been his privilege at bedtime to conduct his grandfather ceremoniously to rest. Sir Philip's habits were contemptuously different now. His apartments were on the lower floor and he shuffled stiffly off to them with his valet's help, after fixing for a moment significantly on the most responsible of his visitors the thick red ray, like the glow of stirred embers, that always made his eyes conflict oddly with his mild manners. They seemed to say to Spencer Coyle 'We'll let the young scoundrel have it to-morrow!' One might have gathered from them that the young scoundrel, who had now strolled to the other end of the hall, had at least forged a cheque. Mr Coyle watched him an instant, saw him drop nervously into a chair and then with a restless movement get up. The same movement brought him back to where his late instructor stood addressing a last injunction to young Lechmere.

'I'm going to bed and I should like you particularly to conform to what I said to you a short time ago. Smoke a single cigarette with your friend here and then go to your room. You'll have me down on you if I hear of your having, during the night, tried any preposterous games.' Young Lechmere, looking down with his hands in his pockets, said nothing – he only poked at the corner of a rug with his toe; so that Spencer Coyle, dissatisfied with so tacit a pledge, presently went on, to Owen: 'I must request you, Wingrave, not to keep this sensitive subject sitting up – and indeed to put him to bed and turn his key in the door.' As Owen stared an instant, apparently not understanding the motive of so much solicitude, he added: 'Lechmere has a morbid curiosity about one of your legends – of your historic rooms. Nip it in the bud.'

'Oh, the legend's rather good, but I'm afraid the room's an awful sell!' Owen laughed.

'You know you don't *believe* that, my boy!' young Lechmere exclaimed.

'I don't think he does,' said Mr Coyle, noticing Owen's mottled flush.

'He wouldn't try a night there himself!' young Lechmere pursued.

'I know who told you that,' rejoined Owen, lighting a cigarette in an embarrassed way at the candle, without offering one to either of his companions.

'Well, what if she did?' asked the younger of these gentlemen, rather red. 'Do you want them *all* yourself?' he continued facetiously, fumbling in the cigarette-box.

Owen Wingrave only smoked quietly; then he exclaimed: 'Yes – what if she did? But she doesn't know,' he added.

'She doesn't know what?'

'She doesn't know anything! – I'll tuck him in!' Owen went on gaily to Mr Coyle, who saw that his presence, now that a certain note had been struck, made the young men uncomfortable. He was curious, but there was a kind of discretion, with his pupils, that he had always pretended to practise; a discretion that however didn't prevent him as he took his way upstairs from recommending them not to be donkeys.

At the top of the staircase, to his surprise, he met Miss Julian, who was apparently going down again. She had not begun to undress, nor was she perceptibly disconcerted at seeing him. She nevertheless, in a manner slightly at variance with the rigour with which she had overlooked him ten minutes before, dropped the words: 'I'm going down to look for something. I've lost a jewel.'

'A jewel?'

'A rather good turquoise, out of my locket. As it's the only ornament I have the honour to possess—!' And she passed down.

'Shall I go with you and help you?' asked Spencer Coyle.

The girl paused a few steps below him, looking back with her Oriental eyes.

'Don't I hear voices in the hall?'

'Those remarkable young men are there.'

'*They'll* help me.' And Kate Julian descended.

Spencer Coyle was tempted to follow her, but remembering his standard of tact he rejoined his wife in their apartment. He delayed however to go to bed, and though he went into his dressing-room he couldn't bring himself even to take off his coat. He pretended for half an hour to read a novel; after which, quietly, or perhaps I should say agitatedly, he passed from the dressing-room into the corridor. He followed this passage to the door of the room which he knew to have been assigned to young Lechmere and was comforted to see that it was closed. Half an hour earlier he had seen it standing open; therefore he could take for granted that the bewildered boy had come to bed. It was of this he had wished to assure himself, and having done so he was on the point of retreating. But at the same instant he heard a sound in the room – the occupant was doing, at the window, something which showed him that he might knock without the reproach of waking his pupil up. Young Lechmere came in fact to the door in his shirt and trousers. He admitted his visitor in some surprise, and when the door was closed again Spencer Coyle said:

'I don't want to make your life a burden to you, but I had it on my conscience to see for myself that you're not exposed to undue excitement.'

'Oh, there's plenty of that!' said the ingenuous youth. 'Miss Julian came down again.'

'To look for a turquoise?'

'So she said.'

'Did she find it?'

'I don't know. I came up. I left her with poor Wingrave.'

'Quite the right thing,' said Spencer Coyle.

'I don't know,' young Lechmere repeated uneasily. 'I left them quarrelling.'

'What about?'

'I don't understand. They're a quaint pair!'

Spencer Coyle hesitated. He had, fundamentally, principles and scruples, but what he had in particular just now was a curiosity, or rather, to recognise it for what it was, a sympathy, which brushed them away.

'Does it strike you that *she's* down on him?' he permitted himself to inquire.

'Rather! – when she tells him he lies!'

'What do you mean?'

'Why, before *me*. It made me leave them; it was getting too hot. I stupidly brought up the question of the haunted room again, and said how sorry I was that I had had to promise you not to try my luck with it.'

'You can't pry about in that gross way in other people's houses – you can't take such liberties, you know!' Mr Coyle interjected.

'I'm all right – see how good I am. I don't want to go *near* the place!' said young Lechmere, confidingly. 'Miss Julian said to me "Oh, I daresay *you'd* risk it, but" – and she turned and laughed at poor Owen – "that's more than we can expect of a gentleman who has taken *his* extraordinary line." I could see that something had already passed between them on the subject – some teasing or challenging of hers. It may have been only chaff, but his chucking the profession had evidently brought up the question of his pluck.'

'And what did Owen say?'

'Nothing at first; but presently he brought out very quietly: "I spent all last night in the confounded place." We both stared and cried out at this and I asked him what he had seen there. He said he had seen nothing, and Miss Julian replied that he ought to tell his story better than that – he ought to make something good of it. "It's not a story – it's a simple fact," said he; on which she jeered at him and wanted to know why, if he had done it, he hadn't told her in the morning, since he knew what she thought of him. "I know, but I don't care," said Wingrave. This made her angry, and she asked him quite seriously whether he would care if he should know she believed him to be trying to deceive us.'

'Ah, what a brute!' cried Spencer Coyle.

'She's a most extraordinary girl – I don't know what she's up to.'

'Extraordinary indeed – to be romping and bandying words at that hour of the night with fast young men!'

Young Lechmere reflected a moment. 'I mean because I think she likes him.'

Spencer Coyle was so struck with this unwonted symptom of subtlety that he flashed out: 'And do you think he likes *her*?'

But his interlocutor only replied with a puzzled sigh and a plaintive 'I don't know – I give it up! – I'm sure he *did* see something or hear something,' young Lechmere added.

'In that ridiculous place? What makes you sure?'

'I don't know – he looks as if he had. He behaves as if he had.'

'Why then shouldn't he mention it?'

Young Lechmere thought a moment. 'Perhaps it's too gruesome!'

Spencer Coyle gave a laugh. 'Aren't you glad then *you're* not in it?'

'Uncommonly!'

'Go to bed, you goose,' said Spencer Coyle, with another laugh. 'But before you go tell me what he said when she told him he was trying to deceive you.'

' "Take me there yourself, then, and lock me in!" '

'And *did* she take him?'

'I don't know – I came up.'

Spencer Coyle exchanged a long look with his pupil.

'I don't think they're in the hall now. Where's Owen's own room?'

'I haven't the least idea.'

Mr Coyle was perplexed; he was in equal ignorance, and he couldn't go about trying doors. He bade young Lechmere sink to slumber, and came out into the passage. He asked himself if he should be able to find his way to the room Owen had formerly shown him, remembering that in common with many of the others it had its ancient name painted upon it. But the corridors of Paramore were intricate; moreover some of the servants would still be up, and he didn't wish to have the appearance of roaming over the house. He went back to his own quarters, where Mrs Coyle soon perceived that his inability to rest had not subsided. As she confessed for her own part, in the dreadful place, to an increased sense of 'creepiness', they spent the early part of the night in conversation, so that a portion of their vigil was inevitably beguiled by her husband's account of his colloquy with little Lechmere and by their exchange of opinions upon it. Toward two o'clock Mrs Coyle became so nervous about their persecuted young friend, and so possessed by the fear that that wicked girl had availed herself of his invitation to put him to an abominable test, that she begged her husband to go and look into the matter at whatever cost to his own equilibrium. But Spencer Coyle, perversely, had ended, as the perfect stillness of the night settled upon them, by charming himself into a tremulous acquiescence in Owen's readiness to face a formidable ordeal – an ordeal the more formidable to an excited imagination as the poor boy now knew from the experience of the previous night how resolute an effort he should have to make. 'I hope he *is* there,' he said to his wife: 'it puts them all so in the wrong!' At any rate he couldn't take upon himself to explore a house he knew so little. He was inconsequent – he didn't prepare for bed. He sat in the dressing-room with his light and his novel, waiting to find himself nodding. At last however Mrs Coyle turned over and ceased to talk, and at last too he fell asleep in his chair. How long he slept he only knew afterwards by computation; what he knew to begin with was that he had started up, in confusion, with the sense of a sudden appalling sound. His sense cleared itself quickly, helped doubtless by a confirmatory cry of horror from his wife's room. But he gave no heed to his wife; he had already bounded into the passage. There the sound was repeated – it was the 'Help! help!' of a woman in agonised terror. It came from a distant quarter of the house, but the quarter was sufficiently indicated. Spencer Coyle rushed straight before him, with the sound of opening doors and alarmed voices in his ears and the faintness of the early dawn in his eyes. At a turn of one of the passages he came upon the white figure of a girl in a swoon on a bench, and in the vividness of the revelation he read as he went that Kate Julian, stricken in her pride too late with a chill of compunction for what she had mockingly done, had, after coming to release the victim of her derision, reeled away, overwhelmed, from the catastrophe that was her work – the catastrophe that the next moment he found himself aghast at on the threshold of an open door. Owen Wingrave, dressed as he had last seen him, lay dead on the spot on which his ancestor had been found. He looked like a young soldier on a battle-field.

THE MIDDLE YEARS

I

THE April day was soft and bright, and poor Dencombe, happy in the conceit of reasserted strength, stood in the garden of the hotel, comparing, with a deliberation in which, however, there was still something of languor, the attractions of easy strolls. He liked the feeling of the south, so far as you could have it in the north, he liked the sandy cliffs and the clustered pines, he liked even the colourless sea. 'Bournemouth as a health-resort' had sounded like a mere advertisement, but now he was reconciled to the prosaic. The sociable country postman, passing through the garden, had just given him a small parcel, which he took out with him, leaving the hotel to the right and creeping to a convenient bench that he knew of, a safe recess in the cliff. It looked to the south, to the tinted walls of the Island, and was protected behind by the sloping shoulder of the down. He was tired enough when he reached it, and for a moment he was disappointed; he was better, of course, but better, after all, than what? He should never again, as at one or two great moments of the past, be better than himself. The infinite of life had gone, and what was left of the dose was a small glass engraved like a thermometer by the apothecary. He sat and stared at the sea, which appeared all surface and twinkle, far shallower than the spirit of man. It was the abyss of human illusion that was the real, the tideless deep. He held his packet, which had come by book-post, unopened on his knee, liking, in the lapse of so many joys (his illness had made him feel his age), to know that it was there, but taking for granted there could be no complete renewal of the pleasure, dear to young experience, of seeing one's self 'just out'. Dencombe, who had a reputation, had come out too often and knew too well in advance how he should look.

His postponement associated itself vaguely, after a little, with a group of three persons, two ladies and a young man, whom, beneath him, straggling and seemingly silent, he could see move slowly together along the sands. The gentleman had his head bent over a book and was occasionally brought to a stop by the charm of this volume, which, as Dencombe could perceive even at a distance, had a cover alluringly red. Then his companions, going a little further, waited for him to come up, poking their parasols into the beach, looking around them at the sea and sky and clearly sensible of the beauty of the day. To these things the young man with the book was still more clearly indifferent; lingering, credulous, absorbed, he was an object of envy to an observer from whose connection with literature all such artlessness had faded. One of the ladies was large and mature; the other had the spareness of comparative youth and of a social situation possibly inferior. The large lady carried back Dencombe's imagination to the age of crinoline; she wore a hat of the shape of a mushroom, decorated with a blue veil, and had the air, in her aggressive amplitude, of clinging to a vanished fashion or even a lost cause. Presently her companion produced from under the folds of a mantle a limp, portable chair which she stiffened out and of which the large lady took possession. This act, and something in the movement of either party, instantly characterised the performers – they performed for Dencombe's recreation – as opulent matron and humble dependant. What, moreover, was the use of being an approved novelist if one couldn't establish a relation between such figures; the clever theory, for instance, that the young man was the son of the opulent matron, and that the humble dependant, the daughter of a clergyman or an officer, nourished a secret passion for him? Was that not visible from the way she stole behind her protectress to look back at him? – back to where he had let himself come to a full stop when his mother sat down to rest. His book was a novel; it had the catchpenny cover, and while the romance of life stood neglected at his side he lost himself in that of the circulating library. He moved mechanically to where the sand was softer, and ended by plumping down in it to finish his chapter at his ease. The humble dependant, discouraged by his remoteness, wandered, with a martyred droop of the head, in another direction, and the exorbitant lady, watching the waves, offered a confused resemblance to a flying-machine that had broken down.

When his drama began to fail Dencombe remembered that he had, after all, another pastime. Though such promptitude on the part of the publisher was rare, he was already able to draw from its wrapper his 'latest', perhaps his last. The cover of 'The Middle Years' was duly meretricious, the smell of the fresh pages the very odour of sanctity; but for the moment he went no further – he had become conscious of a strange alienation. He had forgotten what his book was about. Had the assault of his old ailment, which he had so fallaciously come to Bournemouth to ward off, interposed utter blankness as to what had preceded it? He had finished the revision of proof before quitting London, but his subsequent fortnight in bed had passed the sponge over colour. He couldn't have chanted to himself a single sentence, couldn't have turned with curiosity or confidence to any particular page. His subject had already gone from him, leaving scarcely a superstition behind. He uttered a low moan as he breathed the chill of this dark void, so desperately it seemed to represent the completion of a sinister process. The tears filled his mild eyes; something precious had passed away. This was the pang that had been sharpest during the last few years – the sense of ebbing time, of shrinking opportunity; and now he felt not so much that his last chance was going as that it was gone indeed. He had done all that he should ever do, and yet he had not done what he wanted. This was the laceration – that practically his career was over: it was as violent as a rough hand at his throat. He rose from his seat nervously, like a creature hunted by a dread; then he fell back in his weakness and nervously opened his book. It was a single volume; he preferred single volumes and aimed at a rare compression. He began to read, and little by little, in this occupation, he was pacified and reassured. Everything came back to him, but came back with a wonder, came back, above all, with a high and magnificent beauty. He read his own prose, he turned his own leaves, and had, as he sat there with the spring sunshine on the page, an emotion peculiar and intense. His career was over, no doubt, but it was over, after all, with *that*.

He had forgotten during his illness the work of the previous year; but what he had chiefly forgotten was that it was extra-ordinarily good. He dived once more into his story and was drawn down, as by a siren's hand, to where, in the dim under-world of fiction, the great glazed tank of art, strange silent subjects float. He recognised his motive and surrendered to his talent. Never, probably, had that talent, such as it was, been so fine. His difficulties were still there, but what was also there, to his perception, though probably, alas! to nobody's else, was the art that in most cases had surmounted them. In his sur-prised enjoyment of this ability he had a glimpse of a possible reprieve. Surely its force was not spent – there was life and service in it yet. It had not come to him easily, it had been backward and roundabout. It was the child of time, the nurs-ling of delay; he had struggled and suffered for it, making sacrifices not to be counted, and now that it was really mature was it to cease to yield, to confess itself brutally beaten? There was an infinite charm for Dencombe in feeling as he had never felt before that diligence *vincit omnia*. The result produced in his little book was somehow a result beyond his conscious intention: it was as if he had planted his genius, had trusted his method, and they had grown up and flowered with this sweetness. If the achievement had been real, however, the process had been painful enough. What he saw so intensely to-day, what he felt as a nail driven in, was that only now, at the very last, had he come into possession. His development had been abnormally slow, almost grotesquely gradual. He had been hindered and retarded by experience, and for long periods had only groped his way. It had taken too much of his life to produce too little of his art. The art had come, but it had come after everything else. At such a rate a first existence was too short – long enough only to collect material; so that to fructify, to use the material, one must have a second age, an extension. This extension was what poor Dencombe sighed for. As he turned the last leaves of his volume he murmured: 'Ah for another go! – ah for a better chance!'

The three persons he had observed on the sands had van-ished and then reappeared; they had now wandered up a path, an artificial and easy ascent, which led to the top of the cliff. Dencombe's bench was half-way down, on a sheltered ledge, and the large lady, a massive, heterogeneous person, with bold black eyes and kind red cheeks, now took a few moments to rest. She wore dirty gauntlets and immense diamond ear-rings; at first she looked vulgar, but she contradicted this announcement in an agreeable off-hand tone. While her companions stood waiting for her she spread her skirts on the end of Dencombe's seat. The young man had gold spectacles, through which, with his finger still in his red-covered book, he glanced at the volume, bound in the same shade of the same colour, lying on the lap of the original occupant of the bench. After an instant, Dencombe understood that he was struck with a resemblance, had recognised the gilt stamp on the crimson cloth, was reading 'The Middle Years', and now perceived that somebody else had kept pace with him. The stranger was startled, possibly even a little ruffled, to find that he was not the only person who had been favoured with an early copy. The eyes of the two proprietors met for a moment, and Dencombe borrowed amusement from the expression of those of his competitor, those, it might even be inferred, of his admirer. They confessed to some resentment – they seemed to say: 'Hang it, has he got it *already*? – Of course he's a brute of a reviewer!' Dencombe shuffled his copy out of sight while the opulent matron, rising from her repose, broke out: 'I feel already the good of this air!'

'I can't say I do,' said the angular lady. 'I find myself quite let down.'

'I find myself horribly hungry. At what time did you order lunch?' her protectress pursued.

The young person put the question by. 'Doctor Hugh always orders it.'

'I ordered nothing to-day – I'm going to make you diet,' said their comrade.

'Then I shall go home and sleep. *Qui dort dine!*'

'Can I trust you to Miss Vernham?' asked Doctor Hugh of his elder companion.

'Don't I trust *you*?' she archly inquired.

'Not too much!' Miss Vernham, with her eyes on the ground, permitted herself to declare. 'You must come with us at least to the house,' she went on, while the personage on whom they appeared to be in attendance began to mount higher. She had got a little out of ear-shot; nevertheless Miss Vernham became, so far as Dencombe was concerned, less distinctly audible to murmur to the young man: 'I don't think you realise all you owe the Countess!'

Absently, a moment, Doctor Hugh caused his gold-rimmed spectacles to shine at her.

'Is that the way I strike you? I see – I see!'

'She's awfully good to us,' continued Miss Vernham, compelled by her interlocutor's immovability to stand there in spite of his discussion of private matters. Of what use would it have been that Dencombe should be sensitive to shades had he not detected in that immovability a strange influence from the quiet old convalescent in the great tweed cape? Miss Vernham appeared suddenly to become aware of some such connection, for she added in a moment: 'If you want to sun yourself here you can come back after you've seen us home.'

Doctor Hugh, at this, hesitated, and Dencombe, in spite of a desire to pass for unconscious, risked a covert glance at him. What his eyes met this time, as it happened, was on the part of the young lady a queer stare, naturally vitreous, which made her aspect remind him of some figure (he couldn't name it) in a play or a novel, some sinister governess or tragic old maid. She seemed to scrutinise him, to challenge him, to say, from general spite: 'What have you got to do with us?' At the same instant the rich humour of the Countess reached them from above: 'Come, come, my little lambs, you should follow your old *bergère*!' Miss Vernham turned away at this, pursuing the ascent, and Doctor Hugh, after another mute appeal to Dencombe and a moment's evident demur, deposited his book on the bench, as if to keep his place or even as a sign that he would return, and bounded without difficulty up the rougher part of the cliff.

Equally innocent and infinite are the pleasures of observation and the resources engendered by the habit of analysing life.

It amused poor Dencombe, as he dawdled in his tepid air-bath, to think that he was waiting for a revelation of something at the back of a fine young mind. He looked hard at the book on the end of the bench, but he wouldn't have touched it for the world. It served his purpose to have a theory which should not be exposed to refutation. He already felt better of his melancholy; he had, according to his old formula, put his head at the window. A passing Countess could draw off the fancy when, like the elder of the ladies who had just retreated, she was as obvious as the giantess of a caravan. It was indeed general views that were terrible; short ones, contrary to an opinion sometimes expressed, were the refuge, were the remedy. Doctor Hugh couldn't possibly be anything but a reviewer who had understandings for early copies with publishers or with newspapers. He reappeared in a quarter of an hour, with visible relief at finding Dencombe on the spot, and the gleam of white teeth in an embarrassed but generous smile. He was perceptibly disappointed at the eclipse of the other copy of the book; it was a pretext the less for speaking to the stranger. But he spoke notwithstanding; he held up his own copy and broke out pleadingly:

'*Do* say, if you have occasion to speak of it, that it's the best thing he has done yet!'

Dencombe responded with a laugh: 'Done yet' was so amusing to him, made such a grand avenue of the future. Better still, the young man took *him* for a reviewer. He pulled out 'The Middle Years' from under his cape, but instinctively concealed any tell-tale look of fatherhood. This was partly because a person was always a fool for calling attention to his work. 'Is that what you're going to say yourself?' he inquired of his visitor.

'I'm not quite sure I shall write anything. I don't, as a regular thing – I enjoy in peace. But it's awfully fine.'

Dencombe debated a moment. If his interlocutor had begun to abuse him he would have confessed on the spot to his identity, but there was no harm in drawing him on a little to praise. He drew him on with such success that in a few moments his new acquaintance, seated by his side, was confessing candidly that Dencombe's novels were the only ones he could read a second time. He had come the day before from London, where a friend of his, a journalist, had lent him his copy of the last – the copy sent to the office of the journal and already the subject of a 'notice' which, as was pretended there (but one had to allow for 'swagger') it had taken a full quarter of an hour to prepare. He intimated that he was ashamed for his friend, and in the case of a work demanding and repaying study, of such inferior manners; and, with his fresh appreciation and inexplicable wish to express it, he speedily became for poor Dencombe a remarkable, a delightful apparition. Chance had brought the weary man of letters face to face with the greatest admirer in the new generation whom it was supposable he possessed. The admirer, in truth, was mystifying, so rare a case was it to find a bristling young doctor – he looked like a German physiologist – enamoured of literary form. It was an accident, but happier than most accidents, so that Dencombe, exhilarated as well as confounded, spent half an hour in making his visitor talk while he kept himself quiet. He explained his premature possession of 'The Middle Years' by an allusion to the friendship of the publisher, who, knowing he was at Bournemouth for his health, had paid him this graceful attention. He admitted that he had been ill, for Doctor Hugh would infallibly have guessed it; he even went so far as to wonder whether he mightn't look for some hygienic 'tip' from a personage combining so bright an enthusiasm with a presumable knowledge of the remedies now in vogue. It would shake his faith a little perhaps to have to take a doctor seriously who could take *him* so seriously, but he enjoyed this gushing modern youth and he felt with an acute pang that there would still be work to do in a world in which such odd combinations were presented. It was not true, what he had tried for renunciation's sake to believe, that all the combinations were exhausted. They were not, they were not – they were infinite: the exhaustion was in the miserable artist.

Doctor Hugh was an ardent physiologist, saturated with the spirit of the age – in other words he had just taken his degree; but he was independent and various, he talked like a man who would have preferred to love literature best. He would fain have made fine phrases, but nature had denied him the trick. Some of the finest in 'The Middle Years' had struck him inordinately, and he took the liberty of reading them to Dencombe in support of his plea. He grew vivid, in the balmy air, to his companion, for whose deep refreshment he seemed to have been sent; and was particularly ingenuous in describing how recently he had become acquainted, and how instantly infatuated, with the only man who had put flesh between the ribs of an art that was starving on superstitions. He had not yet written to him – he was deterred by a sentiment of respect. Dencombe at this moment felicitated himself more than ever on having never answered the photographers. His visitor's attitude promised him a luxury of intercourse, but he surmised that a certain security in it, for Doctor Hugh, would depend not a little on the Countess. He learned without delay with what variety of Countess they were concerned, as well as the nature of the tie that united the curious trio. The large lady, an Englishwoman by birth and the daughter of a celebrated baritone, whose taste, without his talent, she had inherited, was the widow of a French nobleman and mistress of all that remained of the handsome fortune, the fruit of her father's earnings, that had constituted her dower. Miss Vernham, an odd creature but an accomplished pianist, was attached to her person at a salary. The Countess was generous, independent, eccentric; she travelled with her minstrel and her medical man. Ignorant and passionate, she had nevertheless moments in which she was almost irresistible. Dencombe saw her sit for her portrait in Doctor Hugh's free sketch, and felt the picture of his young friend's relation to her frame itself in his mind. This young friend, for a representative of the new psychology, was himself easily hypnotised, and if he became abnormally communicative it was only a sign of his real subjection. Dencombe did accordingly what he wanted with him, even without being known as Dencombe.

Taken ill on a journey in Switzerland the Countess had picked him up at an hotel, and the accident of his happening to please her had made her offer him, with her imperious liberality, terms that couldn't fail to dazzle a practitioner without patients and whose resources had been drained dry by his studies. It was not the way he would have elected to spend his time, but it was time that would pass quickly, and meanwhile she was wonderfully kind. She exacted perpetual attention, but it was impossible not to like her. He gave details about his queer patient, a 'type' if there ever was one, who had in connection with her flushed obesity and in addition to the morbid strain of a violent and aimless will a grave organic disorder; but he came back to his loved novelist, whom he was so good as to pronounce more essentially a poet than many of those who went in for verse, with a zeal excited, as all his indiscretion had been excited, by the happy chance of Dencombe's sympathy and the coincidence of their occupation. Dencombe had confessed to a slight personal acquaintance with the author of 'The Middle Years', but had not felt himself as ready as he could have wished when his companion, who had never yet encountered a being so privileged, began to be eager for particulars. He even thought that Doctor Hugh's eye at that moment emitted a glimmer of suspicion. But the young man was too inflamed to be shrewd and repeatedly caught up the book to exclaim: 'Did you notice this?' or 'Weren't you immensely struck with that?' 'There's a beautiful passage toward the end,' he broke out; and again he laid his hand upon the volume. As he turned the pages he came upon something else, while Dencombe saw him suddenly change colour. He had taken up, as it lay on the bench, Dencombe's copy instead of his own, and his neighbour immediately guessed the reason of his start. Doctor Hugh looked grave an instant; then he said: 'I see you've been altering the text!' Dencombe was a passionate corrector, a fingerer of style; the last thing he ever arrived at was a form final for himself. His ideal would have been to publish secretly, and then, on the published text, treat himself to the terrified revise, sacrificing always a first edition and beginning for posterity and even for the collectors, poor dears, with a second. This morning, in 'The Middle Years', his pencil had pricked a dozen lights. He was amused at the effect of the young man's reproach; for an instant it made him change colour. He stammered, at any rate, ambiguously; then, through a blur of ebbing consciousness, saw Doctor Hugh's mystified eyes. He only had time to feel he was about to be ill again – that emotion, excitement, fatigue, the heat of the sun, the solicitation of the air, had combined to play him a trick, before, stretching out a hand to his visitor with a plaintive cry, he lost his senses altogether.

Later he knew that he had fainted and that Doctor Hugh had got him home in a bath-chair, the conductor of which, prowling within hail for custom, had happened to remember seeing him in the garden of the hotel. He had recovered his perception in the transit, and had, in bed, that afternoon, a vague recollection of Doctor Hugh's young face, as they went together, bent over him in a comforting laugh and expressive of something more than a suspicion of his identity. That identity was ineffaceable now, and all the more that he was disappointed, disgusted. He had been rash, been stupid, had gone out too soon, stayed out too long. He oughtn't to have exposed himself to strangers, he ought to have taken his servant. He felt as if he had fallen into a hole too deep to descry any little patch of heaven. He was confused about the time that had elapsed – he pieced the fragments together. He had seen his doctor, the real one, the one who had treated him from the first and who had again been very kind. His servant was in and out on tiptoe, looking very wise after the fact. He said more than once something about the sharp young gentleman. The rest was vagueness, in so far as it wasn't despair. The vagueness, however, justified itself by dreams, dozing anxieties from which he finally emerged to the consciousness of a dark room and a shaded candle.

'You'll be all right again – I know all about you now,' said a voice near him that he knew to be young. Then his meeting with Doctor Hugh came back. He was too discouraged to joke about it yet, but he was able to perceive, after a little, that the interest of it was intense for his visitor. 'Of course I can't attend you professionally – you've got your own man; with whom I've talked and who's excellent,' Doctor Hugh went on. 'But you must let me come to see you as a good friend. I've just looked in before going to bed. You're doing beautifully, but it's a good job

I was with you on the cliff. I shall come in early to-morrow. I want to do something for you. I want to do everything. You've done a tremendous lot for me.' The young man held his hand, hanging over him, and poor Dencombe, weakly aware of this living pressure, simply lay there and accepted his devotion. He couldn't do anything less – he needed help too much.

The idea of the help he needed was very present to him that night, which he spent in a lucid stillness, an intensity of thought that constituted a reaction from his hours of stupor. He was lost, he was lost – he was lost if he couldn't be saved. He was not afraid of suffering, of death; he was not even in love with life; but he had had a deep demonstration of desire. It came over him in the long, quiet hours that only with 'The Middle Years' had he taken his flight; only on that day, visited by soundless processions, had he recognised his kingdom. He had had a revelation of his range. What he dreaded was the idea that his reputation should stand on the unfinished. It was not with his past but with his future that it should properly be concerned. Illness and age rose before him like spectres with pitiless eyes: how was he to bribe such fates to give him the second chance? He had had the one chance that all men have – he had had the chance of life. He went to sleep again very late, and when he awoke Doctor Hugh was sitting by his head. There was already, by this time, something beautifully familiar in him.

'Don't think I've turned out your physician,' he said; 'I'm acting with his consent. He has been here and seen you. Somehow he seems to trust me. I told him how we happened to come together yesterday, and he recognises that I've a peculiar right.'

Dencombe looked at him with a calculating earnestness. 'How have you squared the Countess?'

The young man blushed a little, but he laughed. 'Oh, never mind the Countess!'

'You told me she was very exacting.'

Doctor Hugh was silent a moment. 'So she is.'

'And Miss Vernham's an *intrigante*.'

'How do you know that?'

'I know everything. One *has* to, to write decently!'

'I think she's mad,' said limpid Doctor Hugh.

'Well, don't quarrel with the Countess – she's a present help to you.'

'I don't quarrel,' Doctor Hugh replied. 'But I don't get on with silly women.' Presently he added: 'You seem very much alone.'

'That often happens at my age. I've outlived, I've lost by the way.'

Doctor Hugh hesitated; then surmounting a soft scruple: 'Whom have you lost?'

'Every one.'

'Ah, no,' the young man murmured, laying a hand on his arm.

'I once had a wife – I once had a son. My wife died when my child was born, and my boy, at school, was carried off by typhoid.'

'I wish I'd been there!' said Doctor Hugh simply.

'Well – if you're here!' Dencombe answered, with a smile that, in spite of dimness, showed how much he liked to be sure of his companion's whereabouts.

'You talk strangely of your age. You're not old.'

'Hypocrite – so early!'

'I speak physiologically.'

'That's the way I've been speaking for the last five years, and it's exactly what I've been saying to myself. It isn't till we *are* old that we begin to tell ourselves we're not!'

'Yet I know I myself am young,' Doctor Hugh declared.

'Not so well as I!' laughed his patient, whose visitor indeed would have established the truth in question by the honesty with which he changed the point of view, remarking that it must be one of the charms of age – at any rate in the case of high distinction – to feel that one has laboured and achieved. Doctor Hugh employed the common phrase about earning one's rest, and it made poor Dencombe, for an instant, almost angry. He recovered himself, however, to explain, lucidly enough, that if he, ungraciously, knew nothing of such a balm, it was doubtless because he had wasted inestimable years. He had followed literature from the first, but he had taken a lifetime to get alongside of her. Only to-day, at last, had he begun to *see*, so that what he had hitherto done was a movement without a direction. He had ripened too late and was so clumsily constituted that he had had to teach himself by mistakes.

'I prefer your flowers, then, to other people's fruit, and your mistakes to other people's successes,' said gallant Doctor Hugh. 'It's for your mistakes I admire you.'

'You're happy – you don't know,' Dencombe answered.

Looking at his watch the young man had got up; he named the hour of the afternoon at which he would return. Dencombe warned him against committing himself too deeply, and expressed again all his dread of making him neglect the Countess – perhaps incur her displeasure.

'I want to be like you – I want to learn by mistakes!' Doctor Hugh laughed.

'Take care you don't make too grave a one! But do come back,' Dencombe added, with the glimmer of a new idea.

'You should have had more vanity!' Doctor Hugh spoke as if he knew the exact amount required to make a man of letters normal.

'No, no – I only should have had more time. I want another go.'

'Another go?'

'I want an extension.'

'An extension?' Again Doctor Hugh repeated Dencombe's words, with which he seemed to have been struck.

'Don't you know? – I want to what they call "live".'

The young man, for good-bye, had taken his hand, which closed with a certain force. They looked at each other hard a moment. 'You *will* live,' said Doctor Hugh.

'Don't be superficial. It's too serious!'

'You *shall* live!' Dencombe's visitor declared, turning pale.

'Ah, that's better!' And as he retired the invalid, with a troubled laugh, sank gratefully back.

All that day and all the following night he wondered if it mightn't be arranged. His doctor came again, his servant was attentive, but it was to his confident young friend that he found himself mentally appealing. His collapse on the cliff was plausibly explained, and his liberation, on a better basis, promised

for the morrow; meanwhile, however, the intensity of his meditations kept him tranquil and made him indifferent. The idea
that occupied him was none the less absorbing because it was a
morbid fancy. Here was a clever son of the age, ingenious and
ardent, who happened to have set him up for connoisseurs to
worship. This servant of his altar had all the new learning in
science and all the old reverence in faith; wouldn't he therefore
put his knowledge at the disposal of his sympathy, his craft at
the disposal of his love? Couldn't he be trusted to invent a
remedy for a poor artist to whose art he had paid a tribute? If
he couldn't, the alternative was hard: Dencombe would have to
surrender to silence, unvindicated and undivined. The rest of
the day and all the next he toyed in secret with this sweet
futility. Who would work the miracle for him but the young
man who could combine such lucidity with such passion? He
thought of the fairy-tales of science and charmed himself into
forgetting that he looked for a magic that was not of this world.
Doctor Hugh was an apparition, and that placed him above the
law. He came and went while his patient, who sat up, followed
him with supplicating eyes. The interest of knowing the great
author had made the young man begin 'The Middle Years'
afresh, and would help him to find a deeper meaning in its
pages. Dencombe had told him what he 'tried for'; with all his
intelligence, on a first perusal, Doctor Hugh had failed to guess
it. The baffled celebrity wondered then who in the world *would*
guess it: he was amused once more at the fine, full way with
which an intention could be missed. Yet he wouldn't rail at the
general mind to-day – consoling as that ever had been: the
revelation of his own slowness had seemed to make all stupidity
sacred.

Doctor Hugh, after a little, was visibly worried, confessing,
on inquiry, to a source of embarrassment at home. 'Stick to the
Countess – don't mind me,' Dencombe said, repeatedly; for his
companion was frank enough about the large lady's attitude.
She was so jealous that she had fallen ill – she resented such a
breach of allegiance. She paid so much for his fidelity that she
must have it all: she refused him the right to other sympathies,
charged him with scheming to make her die alone, for it was

needless to point out how little Miss Vernham was a resource in trouble. When Doctor Hugh mentioned that the Countess would already have left Bournemouth if he hadn't kept her in bed, poor Dencombe held his arm tighter and said with decision: 'Take her straight away.' They had gone out together, walking back to the sheltered nook in which, the other day, they had met. The young man, who had given his companion a personal support, declared with emphasis that his conscience was clear – he could ride two horses at once. Didn't he dream, for his future, of a time when he should have to ride five hundred? Longing equally for virtue, Dencombe replied that in that golden age no patient would pretend to have contracted with him for his whole attention. On the part of the Countess was not such an avidity lawful? Doctor Hugh denied it, said there was no contract but only a free understanding, and that a sordid servitude was impossible to a generous spirit; he liked moreover to talk about art, and that was the subject on which, this time, as they sat together on the sunny bench, he tried most to engage the author of 'The Middle Years'. Dencombe, soaring again a little on the weak wings of convalescence and still haunted by that happy notion of an organised rescue, found another strain of eloquence to plead the cause of a certain splendid 'last manner', the very citadel, as it would prove, of his reputation, the stronghold into which his real treasure would be gathered. While his listener gave up the morning and the great still sea appeared to wait, he had a wonderful explanatory hour. Even for himself he was inspired as he told of what his treasure would consist – the precious metals he would dig from the mine, the jewels rare, strings of pearls, he would hang between the columns of his temple. He was wonderful for himself, so thick his convictions crowded; but he was still more wonderful for Doctor Hugh, who assured him, none the less, that the very pages he had just published were already encrusted with gems. The young man, however, panted for the combinations to come, and, before the face of the beautiful day, renewed to Dencombe his guarantee that his profession would hold itself responsible for such a life. Then he suddenly clapped his hand upon his watch-pocket and asked leave to absent himself for half an hour. Dencombe waited there for his return, but was at last recalled to the actual by the fall of a shadow across the ground. The shadow darkened into that of Miss Vernham, the young lady in attendance on the Countess; whom Dencombe, recognising her, perceived so clearly to have come to speak to him that he rose from his bench to acknowledge the civility. Miss Vernham indeed proved not particularly civil; she looked strangely agitated, and her type was now unmistakable.

'Excuse me if I inquire,' she said, 'whether it's too much to hope that you may be induced to leave Doctor Hugh alone.' Then, before Dencombe, greatly disconcerted, could protest: 'You ought to be informed that you stand in his light; that you may do him a terrible injury.'

'Do you mean by causing the Countess to dispense with his services?'

'By causing her to disinherit him.' Dencombe stared at this, and Miss Vernham pursued, in the gratification of seeing she could produce an impression: 'It has depended on himself to come into something very handsome. He has had a magnificent prospect, but I think you've succeeded in spoiling it.'

'Not intentionally, I assure you. Is there no hope the accident may be repaired?' Dencombe asked.

'She was ready to do anything for him. She takes great fancies, she lets herself go – it's her way. She has no relations, she's free to dispose of her money, and she's very ill.'

'I'm very sorry to hear it,' Dencombe stammered.

'Wouldn't it be possible for you to leave Bournemouth? That's what I've come to ask of you.'

Poor Dencombe sank down on his bench. 'I'm very ill myself, but I'll try!'

Miss Vernham still stood there with her colourless eyes and the brutality of her good conscience. 'Before it's too late, please!' she said; and with this she turned her back, in order, quickly, as if it had been a business to which she could spare but a precious moment, to pass out of his sight.

Oh, yes, after this Dencombe was certainly very ill. Miss Vernham had upset him with her rough, fierce news; it was the

sharpest shock to him to discover what was at stake for a
penniless young man of fine parts. He sat trembling on his
bench, staring at the waste of waters, feeling sick with the
directness of the blow. He was indeed too weak, too unsteady,
too alarmed; but he would make the effort to get away, for he
couldn't accept the guilt of interference, and his honour was
really involved. He would hobble home, at any rate, and then
he would think what was to be done. He made his way back to
the hotel and, as he went, had a characteristic vision of Miss
Vernham's great motive. The Countess hated women, of
course; Dencombe was lucid about that; so the hungry pianist
had no personal hopes and could only console herself with the
bold conception of helping Doctor Hugh in order either to
marry him after he should get his money or to induce him to
recognise her title to compensation and buy her off. If she had
befriended him at a fruitful crisis he would really, as a man of
delicacy, and she knew what to think of that point, have to
reckon with her.

At the hotel Dencombe's servant insisted on his going back
to bed. The invalid had talked about catching a train and had
begun with orders to pack; after which his humming nerves had
yielded to a sense of sickness. He consented to see his physician, who immediately was sent for, but he wished it to be
understood that his door was irrevocably closed to Doctor
Hugh. He had his plan, which was so fine that he rejoiced in
it after getting back to bed. Doctor Hugh, suddenly finding
himself snubbed without mercy, would, in natural disgust and
to the joy of Miss Vernham, renew his allegiance to the Countess. When his physician arrived Dencombe learned that he was
feverish and that this was very wrong: he was to cultivate calmness and try, if possible, not to think. For the rest of the day he
wooed stupidity; but there was an ache that kept him sentient,
the probable sacrifice of his 'extension', the limit of his course.
His medical adviser was anything but pleased; his successive
relapses were ominous. He charged this personage to put out a
strong hand and take Doctor Hugh off his mind – it would
contribute so much to his being quiet. The agitating name, in
his room, was not mentioned again, but his security was a

smothered fear, and it was not confirmed by the receipt, at ten o'clock that evening, of a telegram which his servant opened and read for him and to which, with an address in London, the signature of Miss Vernham was attached. 'Beseech you to use all influence to make our friend join us here in the morning. Countess much the worse for dreadful journey, but everything may still be saved.' The two ladies had gathered themselves up and had been capable in the afternoon of a spiteful revolution. They had started for the capital, and if the elder one, as Miss Vernham had announced, was very ill, she had wished to make it clear that she was proportionately reckless. Poor Dencombe, who was not reckless and who only desired that everything should indeed be 'saved', sent this missive straight off to the young man's lodging and had on the morrow the pleasure of knowing that he had quitted Bournemouth by an early train.

Two days later he pressed in with a copy of a literary journal in his hand. He had returned because he was anxious and for the pleasure of flourishing the great review of 'The Middle Years'. Here at least was something adequate – it rose to the occasion; it was an acclamation, a reparation, a critical attempt to place the author in the niche he had fairly won. Dencombe accepted and submitted; he made neither objection nor inquiry, for old complications had returned and he had had two atrocious days. He was convinced not only that he should never again leave his bed, so that his young friend might pardonably remain, but that the demand he should make on the patience of beholders would be very moderate indeed. Doctor Hugh had been to town, and he tried to find in his eyes some confession that the Countess was pacified and his legacy clinched; but all he could see there was the light of his juvenile joy in two or three of the phrases of the newspaper. Dencombe couldn't read them, but when his visitor had insisted on repeating them more than once he was able to shake an unintoxicated head. 'Ah, no; but they would have been true of what I *could* have done!'

'What people "could have done" is mainly what they've in fact done,' Doctor Hugh contended.

'Mainly, yes; but I've been an idiot!' said Dencombe.

Doctor Hugh did remain; the end was coming fast. Two days later Dencombe observed to him, by way of the feeblest of jokes, that there would now be no question whatever of a second chance. At this the young man stared; then he exclaimed: 'Why, it has come to pass – it has come to pass! The second chance has been the public's – the chance to find the point of view, to pick up the pearl!'

'Oh, the pearl!' poor Dencombe uneasily sighed. A smile as cold as a winter sunset flickered on his drawn lips as he added: 'The pearl is the unwritten – the pearl is the unalloyed, the *rest*, the lost!'

From that moment he was less and less present, heedless to all appearance of what went on around him. His disease was definitely mortal, of an action as relentless, after the short arrest that had enabled him to fall in with Doctor Hugh, as a leak in a great ship. Sinking steadily, though this visitor, a man of rare resources, now cordially approved by his physician, showed endless art in guarding him from pain, poor Dencombe kept no reckoning of favour or neglect, betrayed no symptom of regret or speculation. Yet toward the last he gave a sign of having noticed that for two days Doctor Hugh had not been in his room, a sign that consisted of his suddenly opening his eyes to ask of him if he had spent the interval with the Countess.

'The Countess is dead,' said Doctor Hugh. 'I knew that in a particular contingency she wouldn't resist. I went to her grave.'

Dencombe's eyes opened wider. 'She left you "something handsome"?'

The young man gave a laugh almost too light for a chamber of woe. 'Never a penny. She roundly cursed me.'

'Cursed you?' Dencombe murmured.

'For giving her up. I gave her up for *you*. I had to choose,' his companion explained.

'You chose to let a fortune go?'

'I chose to accept, whatever they might be, the consequences of my infatuation,' smiled Doctor Hugh. Then, as a larger pleasantry: 'A fortune be hanged! It's your own fault if I can't get your things out of my head.'

The immediate tribute to his humour was a long, bewildered moan; after which, for many hours, many days, Dencombe lay motionless and absent. A response so absolute, such a glimpse of a definite result and such a sense of credit worked together in his mind and, producing a strange commotion, slowly altered and transfigured his despair. The sense of cold submersion left him – he seemed to float without an effort. The incident was extraordinary as evidence, and it shed an intenser light. At the last he signed to Doctor Hugh to listen, and, when he was down on his knees by the pillow, brought him very near.

'You've made me think it all a delusion.'

'Not your glory, my dear friend,' stammered the young man.

'Not my glory – what there is of it! It *is* glory – to have been tested, to have had our little quality and cast our little spell. The thing is to have made somebody care. You happen to be crazy, of course, but that doesn't affect the law.'

'You're a great success!' said Doctor Hugh, putting into his young voice the ring of a marriage-bell.

Dencombe lay taking this in; then he gathered strength to speak once more. 'A second chance – *that's* the delusion. There never was to be but one. We work in the dark – we do what we can – we give what we have. Our doubt is our passion and our passion is our task. The rest is the madness of art.'

'If you've doubted, if you've despaired, you've always "done" it,' his visitor subtly argued.

'We've done something or other,' Dencombe conceded.

'Something or other is everything. It's the feasible. It's *you*!'

'Comforter!' poor Dencombe ironically sighed.

'But it's true,' insisted his friend.

'It's true. It's frustration that doesn't count.'

'Frustration's only life,' said Doctor Hugh.

'Yes, it's what passes.' Poor Dencombe was barely audible, but he had marked with the words the virtual end of his first and only chance.

THE DEATH OF THE LION

I

I HAD simply, I suppose, a change of heart, and it must have begun when I received my manuscript back from Mr Pinhorn. Mr Pinhorn was my 'chief', as he was called in the office: he had accepted the high mission of bringing the paper up. This was a weekly periodical, and had been supposed to be almost past redemption when he took hold of it. It was Mr Deedy who had let it down so dreadfully: he was never mentioned in the office now save in connection with that misdemeanour. Young as I was I had been in a manner taken over from Mr Deedy, who had been owner as well as editor; forming part of a promiscuous lot, mainly plant and office-furniture, which poor Mrs Deedy, in her bereavement and depression, parted with at a rough valuation. I could account for my continuity only on the supposition that I had been cheap. I rather resented the practice of fathering all flatness on my late protector, who was in his unhonoured grave; but as I had my way to make I found matter enough for complacency in being on a 'staff'. At the same time I was aware that I was exposed to suspicion as a product of the old lowering system. This made me feel that I was doubly bound to have ideas, and had doubtless been at the bottom of my proposing to Mr Pinhorn that I should lay my lean hands on Neil Paraday. I remember that he looked at me first as if he had never heard of this celebrity, who indeed at that moment was by no means in the centre of the heavens; and even when I had knowingly explained he expressed but little confidence in the demand for any such matter. When I had reminded him that the great principle on which we were supposed to work was just to create the demand we required, he considered a moment and then rejoined: 'I see; you want to write him up.'

'Call it that if you like.'

'And what's your inducement?'

'Bless my soul – my admiration!'

Mr Pinhorn pursed up his mouth. 'Is there much to be done with him?'

'Whatever there is, we should have it all to ourselves, for he hasn't been touched.'

This argument was effective, and Mr Pinhorn responded: 'Very well, touch him.' Then he added: 'But where can you do it?'

'Under the fifth rib!'

Mr Pinhorn stared. 'Where's that?'

'You want me to go down and see him?' I inquired when I had enjoyed his visible search for this obscure suburb.

'I don't "want" anything – the proposal's your own. But you must remember that that's the way we do things *now*,' said Mr Pinhorn, with another dig at Mr Deedy.

Unregenerate as I was, I could read the queer implications of this speech. The present owner's superior virtue as well as his deeper craft spoke in his reference to the late editor as one of that baser sort who deal in false representations. Mr Deedy would as soon have sent me to call on Neil Paraday as he would have published a 'holiday-number'; but such scruples presented themselves as mere ignoble thrift to his successor, whose own sincerity took the form of ringing door-bells and whose definition of genius was the art of finding people at home. It was as if Mr Deedy had published reports without his young men's having, as Pinhorn would have said, really been there. I was unregenerate, as I have hinted, and I was not concerned to straighten out the journalistic morals of my chief, feeling them indeed to be an abyss over the edge of which it was better not to peer. Really to be there this time moreover was a vision that made the idea of writing something subtle about Neil Paraday only the more inspiring. I would be as considerate as even Mr Deedy could have wished, and yet I should be as present as only Mr Pinhorn could conceive. My allusion to the sequestered manner in which Mr Paraday lived (which had formed part of my explanation, though I knew of it only by hearsay) was, I could divine, very much what had made Mr Pinhorn nibble. It struck him as inconsistent with the success of his paper that any one should be so sequestered as that. And then was not an immediate exposure of everything just what the public wanted? Mr Pinhorn effectually called me to order by reminding me of the promptness with which I had met Miss Braby at Liverpool on her return from her fiasco in the States. Hadn't we published, while its freshness and flavour were unimpaired, Miss Braby's own version of that great international episode? I felt somewhat uneasy at this lumping of the actress and the author, and I confess that after having enlisted Mr Pinhorn's sympathies I procrastinated a little. I had succeeded better than I wished, and I had, as it happened, work nearer at hand. A few days later I called on Lord Crouchley and carried off in triumph the most unintelligible statement that had yet appeared of his lordship's reasons for his change of front. I thus set in motion in the daily papers columns of virtuous verbiage. The following week I ran down to Brighton for a chat, as Mr Pinhorn called it, with Mrs Bounder, who gave me, on the subject of her divorce, many curious particulars that had not been articulated in court. If ever an article flowed from the primal fount it was that article on Mrs Bounder. By this time, however, I became aware that Neil Paraday's new book was on the point of appearing and that its approach had been the ground of my original appeal to Mr Pinhorn, who was now annoyed with me for having lost so many days. He bundled me off – we would at least not lose another. I have always thought his sudden alertness a remarkable example of the journalistic instinct. Nothing had occurred, since I first spoke to him, to create a visible urgency, and no enlightenment could possibly have reached him. It was a pure case of professional *flair* – he had smelt the coming glory as an animal smells its distant prey.

II

I MAY as well say at once that this little record pretends in no degree to be a picture either of my introduction to Mr Paraday or of certain proximate steps and stages. The scheme of my narrative allows no space for these things, and in any case a prohibitory sentiment would be attached to my recollection of so rare an hour. These meagre notes are essentially private, so that if they see the light the insidious forces that, as my story itself shows, make at present for publicity will simply have overmastered my precautions. The curtain fell lately enough on the lamentable drama. My memory of the day I alighted at Mr Paraday's door is a fresh memory of kindness, hospitality, compassion, and of the wonderful illuminating talk in which the welcome was conveyed. Some voice of the air had taught me the right moment, the moment of his life at which an act of unexpected young allegiance might most come home. He had recently recovered from a long, grave illness. I had gone to the neighbouring inn for the night, but I spent the evening in his company, and he insisted the next day on my sleeping under his roof. I had not an indefinite leave: Mr Pinhorn supposed us to put our victims through on the gallop. It was later, in the office, that the dance was set to music. I fortified myself, however, as my training had taught me to do, by the conviction that nothing could be more advantageous for my article than to be written in the very atmosphere. I said nothing to Mr Paraday about it, but in the morning, after my removal from the inn, while he was occupied in his study, as he had notified me that he should need to be, I committed to paper the quintessence of my impressions. Then thinking to commend myself to Mr Pinhorn by my celerity, I walked out and posted my little packet before luncheon. Once my paper was written I was free to stay on, and if it was designed to divert attention from my frivolity in so doing I could reflect with satisfaction that I had never been so clever. I don't mean to deny of course that I was aware it was much too good for Mr Pinhorn; but I was equally conscious that Mr Pinhorn had the supreme shrewdness of recognising from time to time the cases in which an article was not too bad only because it was too good. There was nothing he loved so much as to print on the right occasion a thing he hated. I had begun my visit to Mr Paraday on a Monday, and on the Wednesday his book came out. A copy of it arrived by the first post, and he let me go out into the garden with it immediately after breakfast. I read it from beginning to end that day, and in the evening he asked me to remain with him the rest of the week and over the Sunday.

That night my manuscript came back from Mr Pinhorn, accompanied with a letter, of which the gist was the desire to know what I meant by sending him such stuff. That was the meaning of the question, if not exactly its form, and it made my mistake immense to me. Such as this mistake was I could now only look it in the face and accept it. I knew where I had failed, but it was exactly where I couldn't have succeeded. I had been sent down there to be personal, and in point of fact I hadn't been personal at all: what I had sent up to London was just a little finicking, feverish study of my author's talent. Anything less relevant to Mr Pinhorn's purpose couldn't well be imagined, and he was visibly angry at my having (at his expense, with a second-class ticket) approached the object of our arrangement only to be so deucedly distant. For myself, I knew but too well what had happened, and how a miracle – as pretty as some old miracle of legend – had been wrought on the spot to save me. There had been a big brush of wings, the flash of an opaline robe, and then, with a great cool stir of the air, the sense of an angel's having swooped down and caught me to his bosom. He held me only till the danger was over, and it all took place in a minute. With my manuscript back on my hands I understood the phenomenon better, and the reflections I made on it are what I meant, at the beginning of this anecdote, by my change of heart. Mr Pinhorn's note was not only a rebuke decidedly stern, but an invitation immediately to send him (it was the case to say so) the genuine article, the revealing and reverberating sketch to the promise of which – and of which alone – I owed my squandered privilege. A week or two later I recast my peccant paper, and giving it a particular application to Mr Paraday's new book, obtained for it the hospitality of another journal, where, I must admit, Mr Pinhorn was so far justified that it attracted not the least attention.

III

I was frankly, at the end of three days, a very prejudiced critic, so that one morning when, in the garden, Neil Paraday had offered to read me something I quite held my breath as

I listened. It was the written scheme of another book – something he had put aside long ago, before his illness, and lately taken out again to reconsider. He had been turning it round when I came down upon him, and it had grown magnificently under this second hand. Loose, liberal, confident, it might have passed for a great gossiping, eloquent letter – the overflow into talk of an artist's amorous plan. The subject I thought singularly rich, quite the strongest he had yet treated; and this familiar statement of it, full too of fine maturities, was really, in summarised splendour, a mine of gold, a precious, independent work. I remember rather profanely wondering whether the ultimate production could possibly be so happy. His reading of the epistle, at any rate, made me feel as if I were, for the advantage of posterity, in close correspondence with him – were the distinguished person to whom it had been affectionately addressed. It was high distinction simply to be told such things. The idea he now communicated had all the freshness, the flushed fairness of the conception untouched and untried: it was Venus rising from the sea, before the airs had blown upon her. I had never been so throbbingly present at such an unveiling. But when he had tossed the last bright word after the others, as I had seen cashiers in banks, weighing mounds of coin, drop a final sovereign into the tray, I became conscious of a sudden prudent alarm.

'My dear master, how, after all, are you going to do it?' I asked. 'It's infinitely noble, but what time it will take, what patience and independence, what assured, what perfect conditions it will demand! Oh for a lone isle in a tepid sea!'

'Isn't this practically a lone isle, and aren't you, as an encircling medium, tepid enough?' he replied, alluding with a laugh to the wonder of my young admiration and the narrow limits of his little provincial home. 'Time isn't what I've lacked hitherto: the question hasn't been to find it, but to use it. Of course my illness made a great hole, but I daresay there would have been a hole at any rate. The earth we tread has more pockets than a billiard-table. The great thing is now to keep on my feet.'

'That's exactly what I mean.'

Neil Paraday looked at me with eyes – such pleasant eyes as he had – in which, as I now recall their expression, I seem to have seen a dim imagination of his fate. He was fifty years old, and his illness had been cruel, his convalescence slow. 'It isn't as if I weren't all right.'

'Oh, if you weren't all right I wouldn't look at you!' I tenderly said.

We had both got up, quickened by the full sound of it all, and he had lighted a cigarette. I had taken a fresh one, and, with an intenser smile, by way of answer to my exclamation, he touched it with the flame of his match. 'If I weren't better I shouldn't have thought of *that*!' He flourished his epistle in his hand.

'I don't want to be discouraging, but that's not true,' I returned. 'I'm sure that during the months you lay here in pain you had visitations sublime. You thought of a thousand things. You think of more and more all the while. That's what makes you, if you will pardon my familiarity, so respectable. At a time when so many people are spent you come into your second wind. But, thank God, all the same, you're better! Thank God, too, you're not, as you were telling me yesterday, "successful". If *you* weren't a failure, what would be the use of trying? That's my one reserve on the subject of your recovery – that it makes you "score", as the newspapers say. It looks well in the newspapers, and almost anything that does that is horrible. "We are happy to announce that Mr Paraday, the celebrated author, is again in the enjoyment of excellent health." Somehow I shouldn't like to see it.'

'You won't see it; I'm not in the least celebrated – my obscurity protects me. But couldn't you bear even to see I was dying or dead?' my companion asked.

'Dead – *passe encore*; there's nothing so safe. One never knows what a living artist may do – one has mourned so many. However, one must make the worst of it; you must be as dead as you can.'

'Don't I meet that condition in having just published a book?'

'Adequately, let us hope; for the book is verily a masterpiece.'

At this moment the parlour-maid appeared in the door that opened into the garden: Paraday lived at no great cost, and the frisk of petticoats, with a timorous 'Sherry, sir?' was about his modest mahogany. He allowed half his income to his wife, from whom he had succeeded in separating without redundancy of legend. I had a general faith in his having behaved well, and I had once, in London, taken Mrs Paraday down to dinner. He now turned to speak to the maid, who offered him, on a tray, some card or note, while agitated, excited, I wandered to the end of the garden. The idea of his security became supremely dear to me, and I asked myself if I were the same young man who had come down a few days before to scatter him to the four winds. When I retraced my steps he had gone into the house, and the woman (the second London post had come in) had placed my letters and a newspaper on a bench. I sat down there to the letters, which were a brief business, and then, without heeding the address, took the paper from its envelope. It was the journal of highest renown, *The Empire* of that morning. It regularly came to Paraday, but I remembered that neither of us had yet looked at the copy already delivered. This one had a great mark on the 'editorial' page, and, uncrumpling the wrapper, I saw it to be directed to my host and stamped with the name of his publishers. I instantly divined that *The Empire* had spoken of him, and I have not forgotten the odd little shock of the circumstance. It checked all eagerness and made me drop the paper a moment. As I sat there conscious of a palpitation I think I had a vision of what was to be. I had also a vision of the letter I would presently address to Mr Pinhorn, breaking as it were with Mr Pinhorn. Of course, however, the next minute the voice of *The Empire* was in my ears.

The article was not, I thanked heaven, a review; it was a 'leader', the last of three, presenting Neil Paraday to the human race. His new book, the fifth from his hand, had been but a day or two out, and *The Empire*, already aware of it, fired, as if on the birth of a prince, a salute of a whole column. The guns had been booming these three hours in the house without our suspecting them. The big blundering newspaper had discovered him, and now he was proclaimed and anointed and crowned. His place was assigned him as publicly as if a fat usher with a wand had pointed to the topmost chair; he was to pass up and still up, higher and higher, between the watching faces and the envious sounds – away up to the daïs and the throne. The article was a date; he had taken rank at a bound – waked up a national glory. A national glory was needed, and it was an immense convenience he was there. What all this meant rolled over me, and I fear I grew a little faint – it meant so much more than I could say 'yea' to on the spot. In a flash, somehow, all was different; the tremendous wave I speak of had swept something away. It had knocked down, I suppose, my little customary altar, my twinkling tapers and my flowers, and had reared itself into the likeness of a temple vast and bare. When Neil Paraday should come out of the house he would come out a contemporary. That was what had happened: the poor man was to be squeezed into his horrible age. I felt as if he had been overtaken on the crest of the hill and brought back to the city. A little more and he would have dipped down the short cut to posterity and escaped.

IV

WHEN he came out it was exactly as if he had been in custody, for beside him walked a stout man with a big black beard, who, save that he wore spectacles, might have been a policeman, and in whom at a second glance I recognised the highest contemporary enterprise.

'This is Mr Morrow,' said Paraday, looking, I thought, rather white: 'he wants to publish heaven knows what about me.'

I winced as I remembered that this was exactly what I myself had wanted. 'Already?' I exclaimed, with a sort of sense that my friend had fled to me for protection.

Mr Morrow glared, agreeably, through his glasses: they suggested the electric headlights of some monstrous modern ship, and I felt as if Paraday and I were tossing terrified under his bows. I saw that his momentum was irresistible. 'I was confident that I should be the first in the field,' he declared. 'A great interest is naturally felt in Mr Paraday's surroundings.'

'I hadn't the least idea of it,' said Paraday, as if he had been told he had been snoring.

'I find he has not read the article in *The Empire*,' Mr Morrow remarked to me. 'That's so very interesting – it's something to start with,' he smiled. He had begun to pull off his gloves, which were violently new, and to look encouragingly round the little garden. As a 'surrounding' I felt that I myself had already been taken in; I was a little fish in the stomach of a bigger one. 'I represent,' our visitor continued, 'a syndicate of influential journals, no less than thirty-seven, whose public – whose publics, I may say – are in peculiar sympathy with Mr Paraday's line of thought. They would greatly appreciate any expression of his views on the subject of the art he so brilliantly practises. Besides my connection with the syndicate just mentioned, I hold a particular commission from *The Tatler*, whose most prominent department, "Smatter and Chatter" – I daresay you've often enjoyed it – attracts such attention. I was honoured only last week, as a representative of *The Tatler*, with the confidence of Guy Walsingham, the author of "Obsessions". She expressed herself thoroughly pleased with my sketch of her method; she went so far as to say that I had made her genius more comprehensible even to herself.'

Neil Paraday had dropped upon the garden-bench and sat there at once detached and confused; he looked hard at a bare spot in the lawn, as if with an anxiety that had suddenly made him grave. His movement had been interpreted by his visitor as an invitation to sink sympathetically into a wicker chair that stood hard by, and as Mr Morrow so settled himself I felt that he had taken official possession and that there was no undoing it. One had heard of unfortunate people's having 'a man in the house', and this was just what we had. There was a silence of a moment, during which we seemed to acknowledge in the only way that was possible the presence of universal fate; the sunny stillness took no pity, and my thought, as I was sure Paraday's was doing, performed within the minute a great distant revolution. I saw just how emphatic I should make my rejoinder to

Mr Pinhorn, and that having come, like Mr Morrow, to betray, I must remain as long as possible to save. Not because I had brought my mind back, but because our visitor's last words were in my ear, I presently inquired with gloomy irrelevance if Guy Walsingham were a woman.

'Oh yes, a mere pseudonym; but convenient, you know, for a lady who goes in for the larger latitude. "Obsessions, by Miss So-and-so", would look a little odd, but men are more naturally indelicate. Have you peeped into "Obsessions"?' Mr Morrow continued sociably to our companion.

Paraday, still absent, remote, made no answer, as if he had not heard the question: a manifestation that appeared to suit the cheerful Mr Morrow as well as any other. Imperturbably bland, he was a man of resources – he only needed to be on the spot. He had pocketed the whole poor place while Paraday and I were woolgathering, and I could imagine that he had already got his 'heads'. His system, at any rate, was justified by the inevitability with which I replied, to save my friend the trouble: 'Dear, no; he hasn't read it. He doesn't read such things!' I unwarily added.

'Things that are *too* far over the fence, eh?' I was indeed a godsend to Mr Morrow. It was the psychological moment; it determined the appearance of his notebook, which, however, he at first kept slightly behind him, even as the dentist, approaching his victim, keeps the horrible forceps. 'Mr Paraday holds with the good old proprieties – I see!' And thinking of the thirty-seven influential journals, I found myself, as I found poor Paraday, helplessly gazing at the promulgation of this ineptitude. 'There's no point on which distinguished views are so acceptable as on this question – raised perhaps more strikingly than ever by Guy Walsingham – of the permissibility of the larger latitude. I have an appointment, precisely in connection with it, next week, with Dora Forbes, the author of "The Other Way Round", which everybody is talking about. Has Mr Paraday glanced at "The Other Way Round"?' Mr Morrow now frankly appealed to me. I took upon myself to repudiate the supposition, while our companion, still silent, got up nervously and walked away. His visitor paid no heed to his withdrawal; he only opened out the notebook with a more motherly pat. 'Dora Forbes, I gather, takes the ground, the same as Guy Walsingham's, that the larger latitude has simply got to come. He holds that it has got to be squarely faced. Of course his sex makes him a less prejudiced witness. But an authoritative word from Mr Paraday – from the point of view of *his* sex, you know – would go right round the globe. He takes the line that we *haven't* got to face it?'

I was bewildered: it sounded somehow as if there were three sexes. My interlocutor's pencil was poised, my private responsibility great. I simply sat staring, however, and only found presence of mind to say: 'Is this Miss Forbes a gentle-man?'

Mr Morrow hesitated an instant, smiling. 'It wouldn't be "Miss" – there's a wife!'

'I mean is she a man?'

'The wife?' – Mr Morrow, for a moment, was as confused as myself. But when I explained that I alluded to Dora Forbes in person he informed me, with visible amusement at my being so out of it, that this was the 'pen-name' of an indubitable male – he had a big red moustache. 'He only assumes a feminine personality because the ladies are such popular favourites. A great deal of interest is felt in this assumption, and there's every prospect of its being widely imitated.' Our host at this moment joined us again, and Mr Morrow remarked invitingly that he should be happy to make a note of any observation the move-ment in question, the bid for success under a lady's name, might suggest to Mr Paraday. But the poor man, without catching the allusion, excused himself, pleading that, though he was greatly honoured by his visitor's interest, he suddenly felt unwell and should have to take leave of him – have to go and lie down and keep quiet. His young friend might be trusted to answer for him, but he hoped Mr Morrow didn't expect great things even of his young friend. His young friend, at this moment, looked at Neil Paraday with an anxious eye, greatly wondering if he were doomed to be ill again; but Paraday's own kind face met his question reassuringly, seemed to say in a glance intelligible enough: 'Oh, I'm not ill, but I'm scared: get him out of the house as quietly as possible.' Getting newspaper-men out of the house was odd business for an emissary of Mr Pinhorn, and I was so exhilarated by the idea of it that I called after him as he left us:

'Read the article in *The Empire*, and you'll soon be all right!'

V

'DELICIOUS my having come down to tell him of it!' Mr Morrow ejaculated. 'My cab was at the door twenty minutes after *The Empire* had been laid upon my breakfast-table. Now what have you got for me?' he continued, dropping again into his chair, from which, however, the next moment he quickly rose. 'I was shown into the drawing-room, but there must be more to see – his study, his literary sanctum, the little things he has about, or other domestic objects or features. He wouldn't be lying down on his study-table? There's a great interest always felt in the scene of an author's labours. Sometimes we're favoured with very delightful peeps. Dora Forbes showed me all his table-drawers, and almost jammed my hand into one into which I made a dash! I don't ask that of you, but if we could talk things over right there where he sits I feel as if I should get the keynote.'

I had no wish whatever to be rude to Mr Morrow, I was much too initiated not to prefer the safety of other ways; but I had a quick inspiration and I entertained an insurmountable, an almost superstitious objection to his crossing the threshold of my friend's little lonely, shabby, consecrated workshop. 'No, no – we sha'n't get at his life that way,' I said. 'The way to get at his life is to – But wait a moment!' I broke off and went quickly into the house; then, in three minutes, I reappeared before Mr Morrow with the two volumes of Paraday's new book. 'His life's here,' I went on, 'and I'm so full of this admirable thing that I can't talk of anything else. The artist's life's his work, and this is the place to observe him. What he has to tell us he tells us with *this* perfection. My dear sir, the best interviewer's the best reader.'

Mr Morrow good-humouredly protested. 'Do you mean to say that no other source of information should be open to us?'

'None other till this particular one – by far the most copious – has been quite exhausted. Have you exhausted it, my dear sir? Had you exhausted it when you came down here? It seems to me in our time almost wholly neglected, and something should surely be done to restore its ruined credit. It's the course to which the artist himself at every step, and with such pathetic confidence, refers us. This last book of Mr Paraday's is full of revelations.'

'Revelations?' panted Mr Morrow, whom I had forced again into his chair.

'The only kind that count. It tells you with a perfection that seems to me quite final all the author thinks, for instance, about the advent of the "larger latitude".'

'Where does it do that?' asked Mr Morrow, who had picked up the second volume and was insincerely thumbing it.

'Everywhere – in the whole treatment of his case. Extract the opinion, disengage the answer – those are the real acts of homage.'

Mr Morrow, after a minute, tossed the book away. 'Ah, but you mustn't take me for a reviewer.'

'Heaven forbid I should take you for anything so dreadful! You came down to perform a little act of sympathy, and so, I may confide to you, did I. Let us perform our little act together. These pages overflow with the testimony we want: let us read them and taste them and interpret them. You will of course have perceived for yourself that one scarcely does read Neil Paraday till one reads him aloud; he gives out to the ear an extraordinary quality, and it's only when you expose it confidently to that test that you really get near his style. Take up your book again and let me listen, while you pay it out, to that wonderful fifteenth chapter. If you feel that you can't do it justice, compose yourself to attention while I produce for you – I think I can! – this scarcely less admirable ninth.'

Mr Morrow gave me a straight glance which was as hard as a blow between the eyes; he had turned rather red, and a question had formed itself in his mind which reached my sense as distinctly as if he had uttered it: 'What sort of a damned fool are *you*?' Then he got up, gathering together his hat and gloves, buttoning his coat, projecting hungrily all over the place the big transparency of his mask. It seemed to flare over Fleet Street and somehow made the actual spot distressingly humble: there was so little for it to feed on unless he counted the blisters of our stucco or saw his way to do something with the roses. Even the poor roses were common kinds. Presently his eyes fell upon the manuscript from which Paraday had been reading to me and which still lay on the bench. As my own followed them I saw that it looked promising, looked pregnant, as if it gently throbbed with the life the reader had given it. Mr Morrow indulged in a nod toward it and a vague thrust of his umbrella. 'What's that?'

'Oh, it's a plan – a secret.'

'A secret!' There was an instant's silence, and then Mr Morrow made another movement. I may have been mistaken, but it affected me as the translated impulse of the desire to lay hands on the manuscript, and this led me to indulge in a quick anticipatory grab which may very well have seemed ungraceful, or even impertinent, and which at any rate left Mr Paraday's two admirers very erect, glaring at each other while one of them held a bundle of papers well behind him. An instant later Mr Morrow quitted me abruptly, as if he had really carried something off with him. To reassure myself, watching his broad back recede, I only grasped my manuscript the tighter. He went to the back-door of the house, the one he had come out from, but on trying the handle he appeared to find it fastened. So he passed round into the front garden, and by listening intently enough I could presently hear the outer gate close behind him with a bang. I thought again of the thirty-seven influential journals and wondered what would be his revenge. I hasten to add that he was magnanimous: which was just the most dreadful thing he could have been. *The Tatler* published a charming, chatty, familiar account of Mr Paraday's 'Home-life', and on the wings of the thirty-seven influential journals it went, to use Mr Morrow's own expression, right round the globe.

VI

A WEEK later, early in May, my glorified friend came up to
town, where, it may be veraciously recorded, he was the king of
the beasts of the year. No advancement was ever more rapid, no
exaltation more complete, no bewilderment more teachable.
His book sold but moderately, though the article in *The Empire*
had done unwonted wonders for it; but he circulated in person
in a manner that the libraries might well have envied. His
formula had been found – he was a 'revelation'. His momentary
terror had been real, just as mine had been – the overclouding
of his passionate desire to be left to finish his work. He was far
from unsociable, but he had the finest conception of being let
alone that I have ever met. For the time, however, he took his
profit where it seemed most to crowd upon him, having in his
pocket the portable sophistries about the nature of the artist's
task. Observation too was a kind of work and experience a kind
of success; London dinners were all material and London
ladies were fruitful toil. 'No one has the faintest conception of
what I'm trying for,' he said to me, 'and not many have read
three pages that I've written; but I must dine with them first –
they'll find out why when they've time.' It was rather rude
justice, perhaps; but the fatigue had the merit of being a new
sort, and the phantasmagoric town was probably after all less of
a battlefield than the haunted study. He once told me that he
had had no personal life to speak of since his fortieth year, but
had had more than was good for him before. London closed the
parenthesis and exhibited him in relations; one of the most
inevitable of these being that in which he found himself to
Mrs Weeks Wimbush, wife of the boundless brewer and pro-
prietress of the universal menagerie. In this establishment, as
everybody knows, on occasions when the crush is great, the
animals rub shoulders freely with the spectators and the lions
sit down for whole evenings with the lambs.

It had been ominously clear to me from the first that in Neil
Paraday this lady, who, as all the world agreed, was tremendous
fun, considered that she had secured a prime attraction, a
creature of almost heraldic oddity. Nothing could exceed her

enthusiasm over her capture, and nothing could exceed the confused apprehensions it excited in me. I had an instinctive fear of her which I tried without effect to conceal from her victim, but which I let her perceive with perfect impunity. Paraday heeded it, but she never did, for her conscience was that of a romping child. She was a blind, violent force, to which I could attach no more idea of responsibility than to the creaking of a sign in the wind. It was difficult to say what she conduced to but to circulation. She was constructed of steel and leather, and all I asked of her for our tractable friend was not to do him to death. He had consented for a time to be of india-rubber, but my thoughts were fixed on the day he should resume his shape or at least get back into his box. It was evidently all right, but I should be glad when it was well over. I had a special fear – the impression was ineffaceable of the hour when, after Mr Morrow's departure, I had found him on the sofa in his study. That pretext of indisposition had not in the least been meant as a snub to the envoy of *The Tatler* – he had gone to lie down in very truth. He had felt a pang of his old pain, the result of the agitation wrought in him by this forcing open of a new period. His old programme, his old ideal even had to be changed. Say what one would, success was a complication and recognition had to be reciprocal. The monastic life, the pious illumination of the missal in the convent cell were things of the gathered past. It didn't engender despair, but it at least required adjustment. Before I left him on that occasion we had passed a bargain, my part of which was that I should make it my business to take care of him. Let whoever would represent the interest in his presence (I had a mystical prevision of Mrs Weeks Wimbush) I should represent the interest in his work – in other words in his absence. These two interests were in their essence opposed; and I doubt, as youth is fleeting, if I shall ever again know the intensity of joy with which I felt that in so good a cause I was willing to make myself odious.

One day, in Sloane Street, I found myself questioning Paraday's landlord, who had come to the door in answer to my knock. Two vehicles, a barouche and a smart hansom, were drawn up before the house.

'In the drawing-room, sir? Mrs Weeks Wimbush.'

'And in the dining-room?'

'A young lady, sir – waiting: I think a foreigner.'

It was three o'clock, and on days when Paraday didn't lunch out he attached a value to these subjugated hours. On which days, however, didn't the dear man lunch out? Mrs Wimbush, at such a crisis, would have rushed round immediately after her own repast. I went into the dining-room first, postponing the pleasure of seeing how, upstairs, the lady of the barouche would, on my arrival, point the moral of my sweet solicitude. No one took such an interest as herself in his doing only what was good for him, and she was always on the spot to see that he did it. She made appointments with him to discuss the best means of economising his time and protecting his privacy. She further made his health her special business, and had so much sympathy with my own zeal for it that she was the author of pleasing fictions on the subject of what my devotion had led me to give up. I gave up nothing (I don't count Mr Pinhorn) because I had nothing, and all I had as yet achieved was to find myself also in the menagerie. I had dashed in to save my friend, but I had only got domesticated and wedged; so that I could do nothing for him but exchange with him over people's heads looks of intense but futile intelligence.

VII

THE young lady in the dining-room had a brave face, black hair, blue eyes, and in her lap a big volume. 'I've come for his autograph,' she said when I had explained to her that I was under bonds to see people for him when he was occupied. 'I've been waiting half an hour, but I'm prepared to wait all day.' I don't know whether it was this that told me she was American, for the propensity to wait all day is not in general characteristic of her race. I was enlightened probably not so much by the spirit of the utterance as by some quality of its sound. At any rate I saw she had an individual patience and a lovely frock, together with an expression that played among her pretty features like a breeze among flowers. Putting her book upon the table, she showed me a massive album, showily bound and full of autographs of price. The collection of faded notes, of still more faded 'thoughts', of quotations, platitudes, signatures, represented a formidable purpose.

'Most people apply to Mr Paraday by letter, you know,' I said.

'Yes, but he doesn't answer. I've written three times.'

'Very true,' I reflected; 'the sort of letter you mean goes straight into the fire.'

'How do you know the sort I mean?' My interlocutress had blushed and smiled, and in a moment she added: 'I don't believe he gets many like them!'

'I'm sure they're beautiful, but he burns without reading.' I didn't add that I had told him he ought to.

'Isn't he then in danger of burning things of importance?'

'He would be, if distinguished men hadn't an infallible nose for nonsense.'

She looked at me a moment – her face was sweet and gay. 'Do *you* burn without reading, too?' she asked; in answer to which I assured her that if she would trust me with her repository I would see that Mr Paraday should write his name in it.

She considered a little. 'That's very well, but it wouldn't make me see him.'

'Do you want very much to see him?' It seemed ungracious to catechise so charming a creature, but somehow I had never yet taken my duty to the great author so seriously.

'Enough to have come from America for the purpose.'

I stared. 'All alone?'

'I don't see that that's exactly your business; but if it will make me more appealing I'll confess that I'm quite by myself. I had to come alone or not come at all.'

She was interesting; I could imagine that she had lost parents, natural protectors – could conceive even that she had inherited money. I was in a phase of my own fortune when keeping hansoms at doors seemed to me pure swagger. As a trick of this bold and sensitive girl, however, it became romantic – a part of the general romance of her freedom, her errand, her innocence. The confidence of young Americans

was notorious, and I speedily arrived at a conviction that no
impulse could have been more generous than the impulse that
had operated here. I foresaw at that moment that it would make
her my peculiar charge, just as circumstances had made Neil
Paraday. She would be another person to look after, and one's
honour would be concerned in guiding her straight. These
things became clearer to me later; at the instant I had scepticism enough to observe to her, as I turned the pages of her
volume, that her net had, all the same, caught many a big
fish. She appeared to have had fruitful access to the great
ones of the earth; there were people moreover whose signatures
she had presumably secured without a personal interview. She
couldn't have worried George Washington and Friedrich Schil-
ler and Hannah More. She met this argument, to my surprise,
by throwing up the album without a pang. It wasn't even her
own; she was responsible for none of its treasures. It belonged
to a girl-friend in America, a young lady in a western city. This
young lady had insisted on her bringing it, to pick up more
autographs: she thought they might like to see, in Europe, in
what company they would be. The 'girl-friend', the western
city, the immortal names, the curious errand, the idyllic faith,
all made a story as strange to me, and as beguiling, as some tale
in the Arabian Nights. Thus it was that my informant had
encumbered herself with the ponderous tome; but she
hastened to assure me that this was the first time she had
brought it out. For her visit to Mr Paraday it had simply been
a pretext. She didn't really care a straw that he should write his
name; what she did want was to look straight into his face.

I demurred a little. 'And why do you require to do that?'

'Because I just love him!' Before I could recover from the
agitating effect of this crystal ring my companion had continued: 'Hasn't there ever been any face that you've wanted to
look into?'

How could I tell her so soon how much I appreciated the
opportunity of looking into hers? I could only assent in general
to the proposition that there were certainly for every one such
hankerings, and even such faces; and I felt that the crisis
demanded all my lucidity, all my wisdom. 'Oh, yes, I'm a

student of physiognomy. Do you mean,' I pursued, 'that you've a passion for Mr Paraday's books?'

'They've been everything to me and a little more beside – I know them by heart. They've completely taken hold of me. There's no author about whom I feel as I do about Neil Paraday.'

'Permit me to remark then,' I presently rejoined, 'that you're one of the right sort.'

'One of the enthusiasts? Of course I am!'

'Oh, there are enthusiasts who are quite of the wrong. I mean you're one of those to whom an appeal can be made.'

'An appeal?' Her face lighted as if with the chance of some great sacrifice.

If she was ready for one it was only waiting for her, and in a moment I mentioned it. 'Give up this crude purpose of seeing him. Go away without it. That will be far better.'

She looked mystified; then she turned visibly pale. 'Why, hasn't he any personal charm?' The girl was terrible and laughable in her bright directness.

'Ah, that dreadful word "personal"!' I exclaimed; 'we're dying of it, and you women bring it out with murderous effect. When you encounter a genius as fine as this idol of ours, let him off the dreary duty of being a personality as well. Know him only by what's best in him, and spare him for the same sweet sake.'

My young lady continued to look at me in confusion and mistrust, and the result of her reflection on what I had just said was to make her suddenly break out: 'Look here, sir – what's the matter with him?'

'The matter with him is that, if he doesn't look out, people will eat a great hole in his life.'

She considered a moment. 'He hasn't any disfigurement?'

'Nothing to speak of !'

'Do you mean that social engagements interfere with his occupations?'

'That but feebly expresses it.'

'So that he can't give himself up to his beautiful imagination?'

'He's badgered, bothered, overwhelmed, on the pretext of being applauded. People expect him to give them his time, his golden time, who wouldn't themselves give five shillings for one of his books.'

'Five? I'd give five thousand!'

'Give your sympathy – give your forbearance. Two-thirds of those who approach him only do it to advertise themselves.'

'Why, it's too bad!' the girl exclaimed with the face of an angel. 'It's the first time I was ever called crude!' she laughed.

I followed up my advantage. 'There's a lady with him now who's a terrible complication, and who yet hasn't read, I am sure, ten pages that he ever wrote.'

My visitor's wide eyes grew tenderer. 'Then how does she talk—?'

'Without ceasing. I only mention her as a single case. Do you want to know how to show a superlative consideration? Simply avoid him.'

'Avoid him?' she softly wailed.

'Don't force him to have to take account of you; admire him in silence, cultivate him at a distance and secretly appropriate his message. Do you want to know,' I continued, warming to my idea, 'how to perform an act of homage really sublime?' Then as she hung on my words: 'Succeed in never seeing him at all!'

'Never at all?' she pathetically gasped.

'The more you get into his writings the less you'll want to; and you'll be immensely sustained by the thought of the good you're doing him.'

She looked at me without resentment or spite, and at the truth I had put before her with candour, credulity, pity. I was afterwards happy to remember that she must have recognised in my face the liveliness of my interest in herself. 'I think I see what you mean.'

'Oh, I express it badly; but I should be delighted if you would let me come to see you – to explain it better.'

She made no response to this, and her thoughtful eyes fell on the big album, on which she presently laid her hands as if to take it away. 'I did use to say out West that they might write a little less for autographs (to all the great poets, you know) and study the thoughts and style a little more.'

'What do they care for the thoughts and style? They didn't even understand you. I'm not sure,' I added, 'that I do myself, and I daresay that you by no means make me out.' She had got up to go, and though I wanted her to succeed in not seeing Neil Paraday I wanted her also, inconsequently, to remain in the house. I was at any rate far from desiring to hustle her off. As Mrs Weeks Wimbush, upstairs, was still saving our friend in her own way, I asked my young lady to let me briefly relate, in illustration of my point, the little incident of my having gone down into the country for a profane purpose and been converted on the spot to holiness. Sinking again into her chair to listen, she showed a deep interest in the anecdote. Then thinking it over gravely, she exclaimed with her odd intonation:

'Yes, but you do see him!' I had to admit that this was the case; and I was not so prepared with an effective attenuation as I could have wished. She eased the situation off, however, by the charming quaintness with which she finally said: 'Well, I wouldn't want him to be lonely!' This time she rose in earnest, but I persuaded her to let me keep the album to show to Mr Paraday. I assured her I would bring it back to her myself. 'Well, you'll find my address somewhere in it, on a paper!' she sighed resignedly, at the door.

VIII

I BLUSH to confess it, but I invited Mr Paraday that very day to transcribe into the album one of his most characteristic passages. I told him how I had got rid of the strange girl who had brought it – her ominous name was Miss Hurter, and she lived at an hotel; quite agreeing with him moreover as to the wisdom of getting rid with equal promptitude of the book itself. This was why I carried it to Albemarle Street no later than on the morrow. I failed to find her at home, but she wrote to me and I went again: she wanted so much to hear more about Neil Paraday. I returned repeatedly, I may briefly declare, to supply her with this information. She had been immensely taken, the more she thought of it, with that idea of mine about the act of homage: it had ended by filling her with a generous rapture. She positively desired to do something sublime for him, though indeed I could see that, as this particular flight was difficult, she appreciated the fact that my visits kept her up. I had it on my conscience to keep her up; I neglected nothing that would contribute to it, and her conception of our cherished author's independence became at last as fine as his own conception. 'Read him, read him,' I constantly repeated; while, seeking him in his works, she represented herself as convinced that, according to my assurance, this was the system that had, as she expressed it, weaned her. We read him together when I could find time, and the generous creature's sacrifice was fed by our conversation. There were twenty selfish women, about whom I told her, who stirred her with a beautiful rage. Immediately after my first visit her sister, Mrs Milsom, came over from Paris, and the two ladies began to present, as they called it, their letters. I thanked our stars that none had been presented to Mr Paraday. They received invitations and dined out, and some of these occasions enabled Fanny Hurter to perform, for consistency's sake, touching feats of submission. Nothing indeed would now have induced her even to look at the object of her admiration. Once, hearing his name announced at a party, she instantly left the room by another door and then straightway quitted the house. At another time, when I was at the opera with them (Mrs Milsom had invited me to their box) I attempted to point Mr Paraday out to her in the stalls. On this she asked her sister to change places with her, and while that lady devoured the great man through a powerful glass, presented, all the rest of the evening, her inspired back to the house. To torment her tenderly I pressed the glass upon her, telling her how wonderfully near it brought our friend's handsome head. By way of answer she simply looked at me in charged silence, letting me see that tears had gathered in her eyes. These tears, I may remark, produced an effect on me of which the end is not yet. There was a moment when I felt it my duty to mention them to Neil Paraday; but I was deterred by the reflection that there were questions more relevant to his happiness.

These questions indeed, by the end of the season, were reduced to a single one – the question of reconstituting, so far as might be possible, the conditions under which he had produced his best work. Such conditions could never all come back, for there was a new one that took up too much place; but some perhaps were not beyond recall. I wanted above all things to see him sit down to the subject of which, on my making his acquaintance, he had read me that admirable sketch. Something told me there was no security but in his doing so before the new factor, as we used to say at Mr Pinhorn's, should render the problem incalculable. It only half reassured me that the sketch itself was so copious and so eloquent that even at the worst there would be the making of a small but complete book, a tiny volume which, for the faithful, might well become an object of adoration. There would even not be wanting critics to declare, I foresaw, that the plan was a thing to be more thankful for than the structure to have been reared on it. My impatience for the structure, none the less, grew and grew with the interruptions. He had, on coming up to town, begun to sit for his portrait to a young painter, Mr Rumble, whose little game, as we also used to say at Mr Pinhorn's, was to be the first to perch on the shoulders of renown. Mr Rumble's studio was a circus in which the man of the hour, and still more the woman, leaped through the hoops of his showy frames almost as electrically as they burst into telegrams and 'specials'. He pranced into the exhibitions on their back; he was the reporter on canvas, the Vandyke up to date, and there was one roaring year in which Mrs Bounder and Miss Braby, Guy Walsingham and Dora Forbes proclaimed in chorus from the same pictured walls that no one had yet got ahead of him.

Paraday had been promptly caught and saddled, accepting with characteristic good-humour his confidential hint that to figure in his show was not so much a consequence as a cause of immortality. From Mrs Wimbush to the last 'representative' who called to ascertain his twelve favourite dishes, it was the same ingenuous assumption that he would rejoice in the repercussion. There were moments when I fancied I might have had more patience with them if they had not been so fatally benevolent. I hated, at all events, Mr Rumble's picture, and had my bottled resentment ready when, later on, I found my distracted friend had been stuffed by Mrs Wimbush into the mouth of another cannon. A young artist in whom she was intensely interested, and who had no connection with Mr Rumble, was to show how far he could make him go. Poor Paraday, in return, was naturally to write something somewhere about the young artist. She played her victims against each other with admirable ingenuity, and her establishment was a huge machine in which the tiniest and the biggest wheels went round to the same treadle. I had a scene with her in which I tried to express that the function of such a man was to exercise his genius – not to serve as a hoarding for pictorial posters. The people I was perhaps angriest with were the editors of magazines who had introduced what they called new features, so aware were they that the newest feature of all would be to make him grind their axes by contributing his views on vital topics and taking part in the periodical prattle about the future of fiction. I made sure that before I should have done with him there would scarcely be a current form of words left me to be sick of; but meanwhile I could make surer still of my animosity to bustling ladies for whom he drew the water that irrigated their social flower-beds.

I had a battle with Mrs Wimbush over the artist she protected, and another over the question of a certain week, at the end of July, that Mr Paraday appeared to have contracted to spend with her in the country. I protested against this visit; I intimated that he was too unwell for hospitality without a *nuance*, for caresses without imagination; I begged he might rather take the time in some restorative way. A sultry air of promises, of ponderous parties, hung over his August, and he would greatly profit by the interval of rest. He had not told me he was ill again – that he had had a warning; but I had not needed this, and I found his reticence his worst symptom. The only thing he said to me was that he believed a comfortable attack of something or other would set him up; it would put out of the question everything but the exemptions he prized. I am afraid I shall have presented him as a martyr in a very small cause if I fail to explain that he surrendered himself much more liberally than I surrendered him. He filled his lungs, for the most part, with the comedy of his queer fate: the tragedy was in the spectacles through which I chose to look. He was conscious of inconvenience, and above all of a great renouncement; but how could he have heard a mere dirge in the bells of his accession? The sagacity and the jealousy were mine, and his the impressions and the anecdotes. Of course, as regards Mrs Wimbush, I was worsted in my encounters, for was not the state of his health the very reason for his coming to her at Prestidge? Wasn't it precisely at Prestidge that he was to be coddled, and wasn't the dear Princess coming to help her to coddle him? The dear Princess, now on a visit to England, was of a famous foreign house, and, in her gilded cage, with her retinue of keepers and feeders, was the most expensive specimen in the good lady's collection. I don't think her august presence had had to do with Paraday's consenting to go, but it is not imposs-ible that he had operated as a bait to the illustrious stranger. The party had been made up for him, Mrs Wimbush averred, and every one was counting on it, the dear Princess most of all. If he was well enough he was to read them something absolutely fresh, and it was on that particular prospect the Princess had set her heart. She was so fond of genius, in *any* walk of life, and she was so used to it, and understood it so well; she was the greatest of Mr Paraday's admirers, she devoured everything he wrote. And then he read like an angel. Mrs Wimbush reminded me that he had again and again given her, Mrs Wimbush, the privilege of listening to him.

I looked at her a moment. 'What has he read to you?' I crudely inquired.

For a moment too she met my eyes, and for the fraction of a moment she hesitated and coloured. 'Oh, all sorts of things!'

I wondered whether this were an imperfect recollection or only a perfect fib, and she quite understood my unuttered comment on her perception of such things. But if she could forget Neil Paraday's beauties she could of course forget my rudeness, and three days later she invited me, by telegraph, to join the party at Prestidge. This time she might indeed have had a story about what I had given up to be near the master. I addressed from that fine residence several communications to a young lady in London, a young lady whom, I confess, I quitted with reluctance and whom the reminder of what she herself could give up was required to make me quit at all. It adds to the gratitude I owe her on other grounds that she kindly allows me to transcribe from my letters a few of the passages in which that hateful sojourn is candidly commemorated.

IX

'I SUPPOSE I ought to enjoy the joke of what's going on here,' I wrote, 'but somehow it doesn't amuse me. Pessimism on the contrary possesses me and cynicism solicits. I positively feel my own flesh sore from the brass nails in Neil Paraday's social harness. The house is full of people who like him, as they mention, awfully, and with whom his talent for talking nonsense has prodigious success. I delight in his nonsense myself; why is it therefore that I grudge these happy folk their artless satisfaction? Mystery of the human heart – abyss of the critical spirit! Mrs Wimbush thinks she can answer that question, and as my want of gaiety has at last worn out her patience she has given me a glimpse of her shrewd guess. I am made restless by the selfishness of the insincere friend – I want to monopolise Paraday in order that he may push me on. To be intimate with him is a feather in my cap; it gives me an importance that I couldn't naturally pretend to, and I seek to deprive him of social refreshment because I fear that meeting more disinterested people may enlighten him as to my real motive. All the disinterested people here are his particular admirers and have been carefully selected as such. There is supposed to be a copy of his last book in the house, and in the hall I come upon ladies, in attitudes, bending gracefully over the first volume. I discreetly avert my eyes, and when I next look round the precarious joy has been superseded by the book of life. There is a sociable circle or a confidential couple, and the relinquished volume lies open on its face, as if it had been dropped under extreme coercion. Somebody else presently finds it and transfers it, with its air of momentary desolation, to another piece of furniture. Every one is asking every one about it all day, and every one is telling every one where they put it last. I'm sure it's rather smudgy about the twentieth page. I have a strong impression too that the second volume is lost – has been packed in the bag of some departing guest; and yet everybody has the impression that somebody else has read to the end. You see therefore that the beautiful book plays a great part in our conversation. Why should I take the occasion of such distinguished honours to say that I begin to see deeper into Gustave Flaubert's doleful refrain about the hatred of literature? I refer you again to the perverse constitution of man.

'The Princess is a massive lady with the organisation of an athlete and the confusion of tongues of a *valet de place*. She contrives to commit herself extraordinarily little in a great many languages, and is entertained and conversed with in detachments and relays, like an institution which goes on from generation to generation or a big building contracted for under a forfeit. She can't have a personal taste any more than, when her husband succeeds, she can have a personal crown, and her opinion on any matter is rusty and heavy and plain – made, in the night of ages, to last and be transmitted. I feel as if I ought to pay some one a fee for my glimpse of it. She has been told everything in the world and has never perceived anything, and the echoes of her education respond awfully to the rash footfall – I mean the casual remark – in the cold Valhalla of her memory. Mrs Wimbush delights in her wit and says there is nothing so charming as to hear Mr Paraday draw it out. He is perpetually detailed for this job, and he tells me it has a peculiarly exhausting effect. Every one is beginning – at the end of two days – to sidle obsequiously away from her, and Mrs Wimbush pushes him again and again into the breach. None of the uses I have yet seen him put to irritate me quite so much. He looks very fagged, and has at last confessed to me that his condition makes him uneasy – has even promised me that he will go straight home instead of returning to his final engagements in town. Last night I had some talk with him about going to-day, cutting his visit short; so sure am I that he will be better as soon as he is shut up in his lighthouse. He told me that this is what he would like to do; reminding me, however, that the first lesson of his greatness has been precisely that he can't do what he likes. Mrs Wimbush would never forgive him if he should leave her before the Princess has received the last hand. When I say that a violent rupture with our hostess would be the best thing in the world for him he gives me to understand that if his reason assents to the proposition his courage hangs woefully back. He makes no secret of being mortally afraid of her, and when I ask what harm she can do him that she hasn't already done he simply repeats: "I'm afraid, I'm afraid! Don't inquire too closely," he said last night; "only believe that I feel a sort of terror. It's strange, when she's so kind! At any rate, I would as soon overturn that piece of priceless Sèvres as tell her that I must go before my date." It sounds dreadfully weak, but he has some reason, and he pays for his imagination, which puts him (I should hate it) in the place of others and makes him feel, even against himself, their feelings, their appetites, their motives. It's indeed inveterately against himself that he makes his imagination act. What a pity he has such a lot of it! He's too beastly intelligent. Besides, the famous reading is still to come off, and it has been postponed a day, to allow Guy Walsingham to arrive. It appears that this eminent lady is staying at a house a few miles off, which means of course that Mrs Wimbush has forcibly annexed her. She's to come over in a day or two – Mrs Wimbush wants her to hear Mr Paraday.

'To-day's wet and cold, and several of the company, at the invitation of the Duke, have driven over to luncheon at Big-wood. I saw poor Paraday wedge himself, by command, into the little supplementary seat of a brougham in which the Prin-cess and our hostess were already ensconced. If the front glass isn't open on his dear old back perhaps he'll survive. Bigwood, I believe, is very grand and frigid, all marble and precedence, and I wish him well out of the adventure. I can't tell you how much more and more *your* attitude to him, in the midst of all this, shines out by contrast. I never willingly talk to these people about him, but see what a comfort I find it to scribble to you! I appreciate it – it keeps me warm; there are no fires in the house. Mrs Wimbush goes by the calendar, the temperature goes by the weather, the weather goes by God knows what, and the Princess is easily heated. I have nothing but my acrimony to warm me, and have been out under an umbrella to restore my circulation. Coming in an hour ago, I found Lady Augusta Minch rummaging about the hall. When I asked her what she was looking for she said she had mislaid something that Mr Paraday had lent her. I ascertained in a moment that the article in question is a manuscript, and I have a foreboding that it's the noble morsel he read me six weeks ago. When I expressed my surprise that he should have bandied about anything so precious (I happen to know it's his only copy – in the most beautiful hand in all the world) Lady Augusta confessed to me that she had not had it from himself, but from Mrs Wimbush, who had wished to give her a glimpse of it as a salve for her not being able to stay and hear it read.

' "Is that the piece he's to read," I asked, "when Guy Walsingham arrives?"

' "It's not for Guy Walsingham they're waiting now, it's for Dora Forbes," Lady Augusta said. "She's coming, I believe, early to-morrow. Meanwhile Mrs Wimbush has found out about *him*, and is actively wiring to him. She says he also must hear him."

' "You bewilder me a little," I replied; "in the age we live in one gets lost among the genders and the pronouns. The clear thing is that Mrs Wimbush doesn't guard such a treasure as jealously as she might."

' "Poor dear, she has the Princess to guard! Mr Paraday lent her the manuscript to look over."

' "Did she speak as if it were the morning paper?"

'Lady Augusta stared – my irony was lost upon her. "She didn't have time, so she gave me a chance first; because unfortunately I go to-morrow to Bigwood."

' "And your chance has only proved a chance to lose it?"

' "I haven't lost it. I remember now – it was very stupid of me to have forgotten. I told my maid to give it to Lord Dorimont – or at least to his man." '

' "And Lord Dorimont went away directly after luncheon." '

' "Of course he gave it back to my maid – or else his man did," said Lady Augusta. "I daresay it's all right." '

'The conscience of these people is like a summer sea. They haven't time to "look over" a priceless composition; they've only time to kick it about the house. I suggested that the "man", fired with a noble emulation, had perhaps kept the work for his own perusal; and her ladyship wanted to know whether, if the thing didn't turn up again in time for the session appointed by our hostess, the author wouldn't have something else to read that would do just as well. Their questions are too delightful! I declared to Lady Augusta briefly that nothing in the world can ever do so well as the thing that does best; and at this she looked a little confused and scared. But I added that if the manuscript had gone astray our little circle would have the less of an effort of attention to make. The piece in question was very long – it would keep them three hours.

' "Three hours! Oh, the Princess will get up!" said Lady Augusta.

' "I thought she was Mr Paraday's greatest admirer." '

' "I daresay she is – she's so awfully clever. But what's the use of being a Princess—" '

' "If you can't dissemble your love?" I asked, as Lady Augusta was vague. She said, at any rate, that she would question her maid; and I am hoping that when I go down to dinner I shall find the manuscript has been recovered.'

X

'IT has not been recovered,' I wrote early the next day, 'and I am moreover much troubled about our friend. He came back from Bigwood with a chill and, being allowed to have a fire in his room, lay down awhile before dinner. I tried to send him to bed, and indeed thought I had put him in the way of it; but after I had gone to dress Mrs Wimbush came up to see him, with the inevitable result that when I returned I found him under arms and flushed and feverish, though decorated with the rare flower she had brought him for his button-hole. He came down to dinner, but Lady Augusta Minch was very shy of him. To-day he's in great pain, and the advent of *ces dames* – I mean of Guy Walsingham and Dora Forbes – doesn't at all console me. It does Mrs Wimbush however, for she has consented to his remaining in bed, so that he may be all right to-morrow for the listening circle. Guy Walsingham is already on the scene, and the doctor, for Paraday, also arrived early. I haven't yet seen the author of "Obsessions", but of course I've had a moment by myself with the doctor. I tried to get him to say that our invalid must go straight home – I mean to-morrow or next day; but he quite refuses to talk about the future. Absolute quiet and warmth and the regular administration of an important remedy are the points he mainly insists on. He returns this afternoon, and I'm to go back to see the patient at one o'clock, when he next takes his medicine. It consoles me a little that he certainly won't be able to read – an exertion he was already more than unfit for. Lady Augusta went off after breakfast, assuring me that her first care would be to follow up the lost manuscript. I can see she thinks me a shocking busybody and doesn't understand my alarm, but she will do what she can, for she's a good-natured woman. "So are they all honourable men." That was precisely what made her give the thing to Lord Dorimont and made Lord Dorimont bag it. What use *he* has for it God only knows. I have the worst forebodings, but somehow I'm strangely without passion – desperately calm. As I consider the unconscious, the well-meaning ravages of our appreciative circle I bow my head in submission to some great natural, some universal accident; I'm rendered almost indifferent, in fact quite gay (ha-ha!) by the sense of immitigable fate. Lady Augusta promises me to trace the precious object and let me have it, through the post, by the time Paraday is well enough to play his part with it. The last evidence is that her maid did give it to his lordship's valet. One would think it was some thrilling number of *The Family Budget*. Mrs Wimbush, who is aware of the accident, is much less agitated by it than she would doubtless be were she not for the hour inevitably engrossed with Guy Walsingham.'

Later in the day I informed my correspondent, for whom indeed I kept a sort of diary of the situation, that I had made the acquaintance of this celebrity and that she was a pretty little girl who wore her hair in what used to be called a crop. She looked so juvenile and so innocent that if, as Mr Morrow had announced, she was resigned to the larger latitude, her superiority to prejudice must have come to her early. I spent most of the day hovering about Neil Paraday's room, but it was communicated to me from below that Guy Walsingham, at Prestidge, was a success. Towards evening I became conscious somehow that her superiority was contagious, and by the time the company separated for the night I was sure that the larger latitude had been generally accepted. I thought of Dora Forbes and felt that he had no time to lose. Before dinner I received a telegram from Lady Augusta Minch. 'Lord Dorimont thinks he must have left bundle in train – inquire.' How could I inquire – if I was to take the word as command? I was too worried and now too alarmed about Neil Paraday. The doctor came back, and it was an immense satisfaction to me to feel that he was wise and interested. He was proud of being called to so distinguished a patient, but he admitted to me that night that my friend was gravely ill. It was really a relapse, a recrudescence of his old malady. There could be no question of moving him: we must at any rate see first, on the spot, what turn his condition would take. Meanwhile, on the morrow, he was to have a nurse. On the morrow the dear man was easier, and my spirits rose to such cheerfulness that I could almost laugh over Lady Augusta's second telegram: 'Lord Dorimont's servant been to station – nothing found. Push inquiries.' I did laugh, I am sure, as I remembered this to be the mystic scroll I had scarcely allowed poor Mr Morrow to point his umbrella at. Fool that I had been: the thirty-seven influential journals wouldn't have destroyed it, they would only have printed it. Of course I said nothing to Paraday.

When the nurse arrived she turned me out of the room, on which I went downstairs. I should premise that at breakfast the news that our brilliant friend was doing well excited universal complacency, and the Princess graciously remarked that he was only to be commiserated for missing the society of Miss Collop. Mrs Wimbush, whose social gift never shone brighter than in the dry decorum with which she accepted this fizzle in her fireworks, mentioned to me that Guy Walsingham had made a very favourable impression on her Imperial Highness. Indeed I think every one did so, and that, like the money-market or the national honour, her Imperial Highness was constitutionally sensitive. There was a certain gladness, a perceptible bustle in the air, however, which I thought slightly anomalous in a house where a great author lay critically ill. '*Le roy est mort – vive le roy*': I was reminded that another great author had already stepped into his shoes. When I came down again after the nurse had taken possession I found a strange gentleman hanging about the hall and pacing to and fro by the closed door of the drawing-room. This personage was florid and bald; he had a big red moustache and wore showy knickerbockers – characteristics all that fitted into my conception of the identity of Dora Forbes. In a moment I saw what had happened: the author of 'The Other Way Round' had just alighted at the portals of Prestidge, but had suffered a scruple to restrain him from penetrating further. I recognised his scruple when, pausing to listen at his gesture of caution, I heard a shrill voice lifted in a sort of rhythmic, uncanny chant. The famous reading had begun, only it was the author of 'Obsessions' who now furnished the sacrifice. The new visitor whispered to me that he judged something was going on that he oughtn't to interrupt.

'Miss Collop arrived last night,' I smiled, 'and the Princess has a thirst for the *inédit*.'

Dora Forbes lifted his bushy brows. 'Miss Collop?'

'Guy Walsingham, your distinguished *confrère* – or shall I say your formidable rival?'

'Oh!' growled Dora Forbes. Then he added: 'Shall I spoil it if I go in?'

'I should think nothing could spoil it!' I ambiguously laughed.

Dora Forbes evidently felt the dilemma; he gave an irritated crook to his moustache. '*Shall* I go in?' he presently asked.

We looked at each other hard a moment; then I expressed something bitter that was in me, expressed it in an infernal 'Do!' After this I got out into the air, but not so fast as not to hear, when the door of the drawing-room opened, the disconcerted drop of Miss Collop's public manner: she must have been in the midst of the larger latitude. Producing with extreme rapidity, Guy Walsingham has just published a work in which amiable people who are not initiated have been pained to see the genius of a sister-novelist held up to unmistakable ridicule; so fresh an exhibition does it seem to them of the dreadful way men have always treated women. Dora Forbes, it is true, at the present hour, is immensely pushed by Mrs Wimbush, and has sat for his portrait to the young artists she protects, sat for it not only in oils but in monumental alabaster.

What happened at Prestidge later in the day is of course contemporary history. If the interruption I had whimsically sanctioned was almost a scandal, what is to be said of that general dispersal of the company which, under the doctor's rule, began to take place in the evening? His rule was soothing to behold, small comfort as I was to have at the end. He decreed in the interest of his patient an absolutely soundless house and a consequent break-up of the party. Little country practitioner as he was, he literally packed off the Princess. She departed as promptly as if a revolution had broken out, and Guy Walsingham emigrated with her. I was kindly permitted to remain, and this was not denied even to Mrs Wimbush. The privilege was withheld indeed from Dora Forbes; so Mrs Wimbush kept her latest capture temporarily concealed. This was so little, however, her usual way of dealing with her eminent friends that a couple of days of it exhausted her patience, and she went up to town with him in great publicity. The sudden turn for the worse her afflicted guest had, after a brief improvement, taken on the third night raised an obstacle to her seeing him before her retreat; a fortunate circumstance doubtless, for she was fundamentally disappointed in him. This was not the kind of performance for which she had invited him to Prestidge, or invited the Princess. Let me hasten to add that none of the generous acts which have characterised her patronage of intellectual and

other merit have done so much for her reputation as her lending
Neil Paraday the most beautiful of her numerous homes to die
in. He took advantage to the utmost of the singular favour.
Day by day I saw him sink, and I roamed alone about the
empty terraces and gardens. His wife never came near him,
but I scarcely noticed it: as I paced there with rage in my heart
I was too full of another wrong. In the event of his death it
would fall to me perhaps to bring out in some charming
form, with notes, with the tenderest editorial care, that precious heritage of his written project. But where *was* that
precious heritage, and were both the author and the book to
have been snatched from us? Lady Augusta wrote me that she
had done all she could and that poor Lord Dorimont, who had
really been worried to death, was extremely sorry. I couldn't
have the matter out with Mrs Wimbush, for I didn't want to be
taunted by her with desiring to aggrandise myself by a public
connection with Mr Paraday's sweepings. She had signified her
willingness to meet the expense of all advertising, as indeed she
was always ready to do. The last night of the horrible series, the
night before he died, I put my ear closer to his pillow.

'That thing I read you that morning, you know.'

'In your garden that dreadful day? Yes!'

'Won't it do as it is?'

'It would have been a glorious book.'

'It *is* a glorious book,' Neil Paraday murmured. 'Print it as it
stands – beautifully.'

'Beautifully!' I passionately promised.

It may be imagined whether, now that he is gone, the promise seems to me less sacred. I am convinced that if such pages
had appeared in his lifetime the Abbey would hold him to-day. I
have kept the advertising in my own hands, but the manuscript
has not been recovered. It's impossible, and at any rate intolerable, to suppose it can have been wantonly destroyed. Perhaps some hazard of a blind hand, some brutal ignorance has
lighted kitchen-fires with it. Every stupid and hideous accident
haunts my meditations. My undiscourageable search for the
lost treasure would make a long chapter. Fortunately I have a
devoted associate in the person of a young lady who has every

day a fresh indignation and a fresh idea, and who maintains
with intensity that the prize will still turn up. Sometimes
I believe her, but I have quite ceased to believe myself. The
only thing for us, at all events, is to go on seeking and hoping
together; and we should be closely united by this firm tie even
were we not at present by another.

THE COXON FUND

I

'THEY'VE got him for life!' I said to myself that evening on my way back to the station; but later, alone in the compartment (from Wimbledon to Waterloo, before the glory of the District Railway) I amended this declaration in the light of the sense that my friends would probably after all not enjoy a monopoly of Mr Saltram. I won't pretend to have taken his vast measure on that first occasion, but I think I had achieved a glimpse of what the privilege of his acquaintance might mean for many persons in the way of charges accepted. He had been a great experience, and it was this perhaps that had put me into the frame of foreseeing how we should all, sooner or later, have the honour of dealing with him as a whole. Whatever impression I then received of the amount of this total, I had a full enough vision of the patience of the Mulvilles. He was staying with them all the winter: Adelaide dropped it in a tone which drew the sting from the temporary. These excellent people might indeed have been content to give the circle of hospitality a diameter of six months; but if they didn't say that he was staying for the summer as well it was only because this was more than they ventured to hope. I remember that at dinner that evening he wore slippers, new and predominantly purple, of some queer carpet-stuff; but the Mulvilles were still in the stage of supposing that he might be snatched from them by higher bidders. At a later time they grew, poor dears, to fear no snatching; but theirs was a fidelity which needed no help from competition to make them proud. Wonderful indeed as, when all was said, you inevitably pronounced Frank Saltram, it was not to be overlooked that the Kent Mulvilles were in their way still more extraordinary: as striking an instance as could easily be encountered of the familiar truth that remarkable men find remarkable conveniences.

They had sent for me from Wimbledon to come out and dine, and there had been an implication in Adelaide's note

163

(judged by her notes alone she might have been thought silly) that it was a case in which something momentous was to be determined or done. I had never known them not be in a 'state' about somebody, and I daresay I tried to be droll on this point in accepting their invitation. On finding myself in the presence of their latest revelation I had not at first felt irreverence droop – and, thank heaven, I have never been absolutely deprived of that alternative in Mr Saltram's company. I saw, however (I hasten to declare it), that compared to this specimen their other phoenixes had been birds of inconsiderable feather, and I afterwards took credit to myself for not having even in primal bewilderments made a mistake about the essence of the man. He had an incomparable gift; I never was blind to it – it dazzles me at present. It dazzles me perhaps even more in remembrance than in fact, for I'm not unaware that for a subject so magnificent the imagination goes to some expense, inserting a jewel here and there or giving a twist to a plume. How the art of portraiture would rejoice in this figure if the art of portraiture had only the canvas! Nature, in truth, had largely rounded it, and if memory, hovering about it, sometimes holds her breath, this is because the voice that comes back was really golden.

Though the great man was an inmate and didn't dress, he kept dinner on this occasion waiting, and the first words he uttered on coming into the room were a triumphant announcement to Mulville that he had found out something. Not catching the allusion and gaping doubtless a little at his face, I privately asked Adelaide what he had found out. I shall never forget the look she gave me as she replied: 'Everything!' She really believed it. At that moment, at any rate, he had found out that the mercy of the Mulvilles was infinite. He had previously of course discovered, as I had myself for that matter, that their dinners were *soignés*. Let me not indeed, in saying this, neglect to declare that I shall falsify my counterfeit if I seem to hint that there was in his nature any ounce of calculation. He took whatever came, but he never plotted for it, and no man who was so much of an absorbent can ever have been so little of a parasite. He had a system of the universe, but he had no system of sponging – that was quite hand-to-mouth. He had

fine, gross, easy senses, but it was not his good-natured appetite
that wrought confusion. If he had loved us for our dinners we
could have paid with our dinners, and it would have been a
great economy of finer matter. I make free in these connections
with the plural possessive because if I was never able to do what
the Mulvilles did, and people with still bigger houses and
simpler charities, I met, first and last, every demand of reflection, of emotion – particularly perhaps those of gratitude and of
resentment. No one, I think, paid the tribute of giving him up
so often, and if it's rendering honour to borrow wisdom I have a
right to talk of my sacrifices. He yielded lessons as the sea yields
fish – I lived for a while on this diet. Sometimes it almost
appeared to me that his massive, monstrous failure – if failure
after all it was – had been intended for my private recreation.
He fairly pampered my curiosity; but the history of that experience would take me too far. This is not the large canvas I just
now spoke of, and I would not have approached him with my
present hand had it been a question of all the features. Frank
Saltram's features, for artistic purposes, are verily the anecdotes that are to be gathered. Their name is legion, and this is
only one, of which the interest is that it concerns even more
closely several other persons. Such episodes, as one looks back,
are the little dramas that made up the innumerable facets of the
big drama – which is yet to be reported.

II

IT is furthermore remarkable that though the two stories are
distinct – my own, as it were, and this other – they equally
began, in a manner, the first night of my acquaintance with
Frank Saltram, the night I came back from Wimbledon so
agitated with a new sense of life that, in London, for the very
thrill of it, I could only walk home. Walking and swinging my
stick, I overtook, at Buckingham Gate, George Gravener, and
George Gravener's story may be said to have begun with my
making him, as our paths lay together, come home with me for a
talk. I duly remember, let me parenthesise, that it was still more
that of another person, and also that several years were to elapse

before it was to extend to a second chapter. I had much to say to him, none the less, about my visit to the Mulvilles, whom he more indifferently knew, and I was at any rate so amusing that for long afterwards he never encountered me without asking for news of the old man of the sea. I hadn't said Mr Saltram was old, and it was to be seen that he was of an age to outweather George Gravener. I had at that time a lodging in Ebury Street, and Gravener was staying at his brother's empty house in Eaton Square. At Cambridge, five years before, even in our devastating set, his intellectual power had seemed to me almost awful. Some one had once asked me privately, with blanched cheeks, what it was then that after all such a mind as that left standing. 'It leaves itself!' I could recollect devoutly replying. I could smile at present at this reminiscence, for even before we got to Ebury Street I was struck with the fact that, save in the sense of being well set up on his legs, George Gravener had actually ceased to tower. The universe he laid low had somehow bloomed again – the usual eminences were visible. I wondered whether he had lost his humour, or only, dreadful thought, had never had any – not even when I had fancied him most Aristophanesque. What was the need of appealing to laughter, however, I could enviously inquire, where you might appeal so confidently to measurement? Mr Saltram's queer figure, his thick nose and hanging lip, were fresh to me: in the light of my old friend's fine cold symmetry they presented mere success in amusing as the refuge of conscious ugliness. Already, at hungry twenty-six, Gravener looked as blank and parliamentary as if he were fifty and popular. In my scrap of a residence (he had a worldling's eye for its futile conveniences, but never a comrade's joke) I sounded Frank Saltram in his ears; a circumstance I mention in order to note that even then I was surprised at his impatience of my enlivenment. As he had never before heard of the personage, it took indeed the form of impatience of the preposterous Mulvilles, his relation to whom, like mine, had had its origin in an early, a childish intimacy with the young Adelaide, the fruit of multiplied ties in the previous generation. When she married Kent Mulville, who was older than Gravener and I and much more amiable, I gained a friend, but

Gravener practically lost one. We were affected in different ways by the form taken by what he called their deplorable social action – the form (the term was also his) of nasty second-rate gush. I may have held in my *for intérieur* that the good people at Wimbledon were beautiful fools, but when he sniffed at them I couldn't help taking the opposite line, for I already felt that even should we happen to agree it would always be for reasons that differed. It came home to me that he was admirably British as, without so much as a sociable sneer at my bookbinder, he turned away from the serried rows of my little French library.

'Of course I've never seen the fellow, but it's clear enough he's a humbug.'

'Clear "enough" is just what it isn't,' I replied; 'if it only were!' That ejaculation on my part must have been the beginning of what was to be later a long ache for final frivolous rest. Gravener was profound enough to remark after a moment that in the first place he couldn't be anything but a Dissenter, and when I answered that the very note of his fascination was his extraordinary speculative breadth, my friend retorted that there was no cad like your cultivated cad and that I might depend upon discovering (since I had had the levity not already to have inquired) that my shining light proceeded, a generation back, from a Methodist cheesemonger. I confess I was struck with his insistence, and I said, after reflection: 'It may be – I admit it may be; but why on earth are you so sure?' – asking the question mainly to lay him the trap of saying that it was because the poor man didn't dress for dinner. He took an instant to circumvent my trap and come blandly out the other side.

'Because the Kent Mulvilles have invented him. They've an infallible hand for frauds. All their geese are swans. They were born to be duped, they like it, they cry for it, they don't know anything from anything, and they disgust one (luckily perhaps!) with Christian charity.' His vehemence was doubtless an accident, but it might have been a strange foreknowledge. I forget what protest I dropped; it was at any rate something which led him to go on after a moment: 'I only ask one thing – it's perfectly simple. Is a man, in a given case, a real gentleman?'

'A real gentleman, my dear fellow – that's so soon said!'

'Not so soon when he isn't! If they've got hold of one this time he must be a great rascal!'

'I might feel injured,' I answered, 'if I didn't reflect that they don't rave about *me*.'

'Don't be too sure! I'll grant that he's a gentleman,' Gravener presently added, 'if you'll admit that he's a scamp.'

'I don't know which to admire most, your logic or your benevolence.'

My friend coloured at this, but he didn't change the subject. 'Where did they pick him up?'

'I think they were struck with something he had published.'

'I can fancy the dreary thing!'

'I believe they found out he had all sorts of worries and difficulties.'

'That, of course, was not to be endured, and they jumped at the privilege of paying his debts!' I replied that I knew nothing about his debts, and I reminded my visitor that though the dear Mulvilles were angels they were neither idiots nor millionaires. What they mainly aimed at was reuniting Mr Saltram to his wife. 'I was expecting to hear that he has basely abandoned her,' Gravener went on, at this, 'and I'm too glad you don't disappoint me.'

I tried to recall exactly what Mrs Mulville had told me. 'He didn't leave her – no. It's she who has left him.'

'Left him to *us*?' Gravener asked. 'The monster – many thanks! I decline to take him.'

'You'll hear more about him in spite of yourself. I can't, no, I really can't resist the impression that he's a big man.' I was already learning – to my shame perhaps be it said – just the tone that my old friend least liked.

'It's doubtless only a trifle,' he returned, 'but you haven't happened to mention what his reputation's to rest on.'

'Why, on what I began by boring you with – his extraordinary mind.'

'As exhibited in his writings?'

'Possibly in his writings, but certainly in his talk, which is far and away the richest I ever listened to.'

'And what is it all about?'

'My dear fellow, don't ask me! About everything!' I pursued, reminding myself of poor Adelaide. 'About his ideas of things,' I then more charitably added. 'You must have heard him to know what I mean – it's unlike anything that ever *was* heard.' I coloured, I admit, I overcharged a little, for such a picture was an anticipation of Saltram's later development and still more of my fuller acquaintance with him. However, I really expressed, a little lyrically perhaps, my actual imagination of him when I proceeded to declare that, in a cloud of tradition, of legend, he might very well go down to posterity as the greatest of all great talkers. Before we parted George Gravener demanded why such a row should be made about a chatterbox the more and why he should be pampered and pensioned. The greater the wind-bag the greater the calamity. Out of proportion to everything else on earth had come to be this wagging of the tongue. We were drenched with talk – our wretched age was dying of it. I differed from him here sincerely, only going so far as to concede, and gladly, that we were drenched with sound. It was not however the mere speakers who were killing us – it was the mere stammerers. Fine talk was as rare as it was refreshing – the gift of the gods themselves, the one starry spangle on the ragged cloak of humanity. How many men were there who rose to this privilege, of how many masters of conversation could he boast the acquaintance? Dying of talk? – why, we were dying of the lack of it! Bad writing wasn't talk, as many people seemed to think, and even good wasn't always to be compared to it. From the best talk indeed the best writing had something to learn. I fancifully added that we too should peradventure be gilded by the legend, should be pointed at for having listened, for having actually heard. Gravener, who had glanced at his watch and discovered it was midnight, found to all this a response beautifully characteristic of him.

'There is one little fact to be borne in mind in the presence equally of the best talk and of the worst.' He looked, in saying this, as if he meant so much that I thought he could only mean once more that neither of them mattered if a man wasn't a real gentleman. Perhaps it was what he did mean; he deprived me however of the exultation of being right by putting the truth in a slightly different way. 'The only thing that really counts for one's estimate of a person is his conduct.' He had his watch still in his hand, and I reproached him with unfair play in having ascertained beforehand that it was now the hour at which I always gave in. My pleasantry so far failed to mollify him that he promptly added that to the rule he had just enunciated there was absolutely no exception.

'None whatever?'

'None whatever.'

'Trust me then to try to be good at any price!' I laughed as I went with him to the door. 'I declare I will be, if I have to be horrible!'

III

IF that first night was one of the liveliest, or at any rate was the freshest, of my exaltations, there was another, four years later, that was one of my great discomposures. Repetition, I well knew by this time, was the secret of Saltram's power to alienate, and of course one would never have seen him at his finest if one hadn't seen him in his remorses. They set in mainly at this season and were magnificent, orchestral. I was perfectly aware that something of the sort was now due; but none the less, in our arduous attempt to set him on his feet as a lecturer, it was impossible not to feel that two failures were a large order, as we said, for a short course of five. This was the second time, and it was past nine o'clock; the audience, a muster unprecedented and really encouraging, had fortunately the attitude of bland-ness that might have been looked for in persons whom the promise (if I am not mistaken) of an Analysis of Primary Ideas had drawn to the neighbourhood of Upper Baker Street. There was in those days in that region a petty lecture-hall to be secured on terms as moderate as the funds left at our disposal by the irrepressible question of the maintenance of five small Saltrams (I include the mother) and one large one. By the time the Salt-rams, of different sizes, were all maintained, we had pretty well poured out the oil that might have lubricated the machinery for enabling the most original of men to appear to maintain them.

It was I, the other time, who had been forced into the
breach, standing up there for an odious lamplit moment to
explain to half a dozen thin benches, where the earnest brows
were virtuously void of anything so cynical as a suspicion, that
we couldn't put so much as a finger on Mr Saltram. There was
nothing to plead but that our scouts had been out from the early
hours and that we were afraid that on one of his walks abroad –
he took one, for meditation, whenever he was to address such a
company – some accident had disabled or delayed him. The
meditative walks were a fiction, for he never, that any one could
discover, prepared anything but a magnificent prospectus; so
that his circulars and programmes, of which I possess an almost
complete collection, are the solemn ghosts of generations never
born. I put the case, as it seemed to me, at the best; but I admit
I had been angry, and Kent Mulville was shocked at my want of
public optimism. This time therefore I left the excuses to his
more practised patience, only relieving myself in response to a
direct appeal from a young lady next whom, in the hall, I found
myself sitting. My position was an accident, but if it had been
calculated the reason would scarcely have eluded an observer of
the fact that no one else in the room had an approach to an
appearance. Our philosopher's 'tail' was deplorably limp. This
visitor was the only person who looked at her ease, who had
come a little in the spirit of adventure. She seemed to carry
amusement in her handsome young head, and her presence
quite gave me the sense of a sudden extension of Saltram's
sphere of influence. He was doing better than we hoped, and
he had chosen such an occasion, of all occasions, to succumb to
heaven knew which of his infirmities. The young lady produced
an impression of auburn hair and black velvet, and had on her
other hand a companion of obscurer type, presumably a wait-
ing-maid. She herself might perhaps have been a foreign countess, and before she spoke to me I had beguiled our sorry
interval by thinking that she brought vaguely back the first
page of some novel of Madame Sand. It didn't make her
more fathomable to perceive in a few minutes that she could
only be an American; it simply engendered depressing reflections as to the possible check to contributions from Boston. She

asked me if, as a person apparently more initiated, I would recommend further waiting, and I replied that if she considered I was on my honour I would privately deprecate it. Perhaps she didn't; at any rate something passed between us that led us to talk until she became aware that we were almost the only people left. I presently discovered that she knew Mrs Saltram, and this explained in a manner the miracle. The brotherhood of the friends of the husband was as nothing to the brotherhood, or perhaps I should say the sisterhood, of the friends of the wife. Like the Kent Mulvilles I belonged to both fraternities, and even better than they I think I had sounded the abyss of Mrs Saltram's wrongs. She bored me to extinction, and I knew but too well how she had bored her husband; but she had those who stood by her, the most efficient of whom were indeed the handful of poor Saltram's backers. They did her liberal justice, whereas her mere patrons and partisans had nothing but hatred for our philosopher. I am bound to say it was we, however – we of both camps, as it were – who had always done most for her.

I thought my young lady looked rich – I scarcely knew why; and I hoped she had put her hand in her pocket. But I soon discovered that she was not a fine fanatic – she was only a generous, irresponsible inquirer. She had come to England to see her aunt, and it was at her aunt's she had met the dreary lady we had all so much on our mind. I saw she would help to pass the time when she observed that it was a pity this lady wasn't intrinsically more interesting. That was refreshing, for it was an article of faith in Mrs Saltram's circle – at least among those who scorned to know her horrid husband – that she was attractive on her merits. She was really a very common person, as Saltram himself would have been if he hadn't been a prodigy. The question of vulgarity had no application to him, but it was a measure that his wife kept challenging you to apply. I hasten to add that the consequences of your doing so were no sufficient reason for his having left her to starve. 'He doesn't seem to have much force of character,' said my young lady; at which I laughed out so loud that my departing friends looked back at me over their shoulders as if I were making a joke of their discomfiture. My joke probably cost Saltram a subscription or two, but it helped me on with my interlocutress. 'She says he drinks like a fish,' she sociably continued, 'and yet she admits that his mind is wonderfully clear.' It was amusing to converse with a pretty girl who could talk of the clearness of Saltram's mind. I expected her next to say that she had been assured he was awfully clever. I tried to tell her – I had it almost on my conscience – what was the proper way to regard him; an effort attended perhaps more than ever on this occasion with the usual effect of my feeling that I wasn't after all very sure of it. She had come to-night out of high curiosity – she had wanted to find out this proper way for herself. She had read some of his papers and hadn't understood them; but it was at home, at her aunt's, that her curiosity had been kindled – kindled mainly by his wife's remarkable stories of his want of virtue. 'I suppose they ought to have kept me away,' my companion dropped, 'and I suppose they would have done so if I hadn't somehow got an idea that he's fascinating. In fact Mrs Saltram herself says he is.'

'So you came to see where the fascination resides? Well, you've seen!'

My young lady raised her fine eyebrows. 'Do you mean in his bad faith?'

'In the extraordinary effects of it; his possession, that is, of some quality or other that condemns us in advance to forgive him the humiliation, as I may call it, to which he has subjected us.'

'The humiliation?'

'Why mine, for instance, as one of his guarantors, before you as the purchaser of a ticket.'

'You don't look humiliated a bit, and if you did I should let you off, disappointed as I am; for the mysterious quality you speak of is just the quality I came to see.'

'Oh, you can't "see" it!' I exclaimed.

'How then do you get at it?'

'You don't! You mustn't suppose he's good-looking,' I added.

'Why, his wife says he's lovely!'

My hilarity may have struck my interlocutress as excessive, but I confess it broke out afresh. Had she acted only in obedience to this singular plea, so characteristic, on Mrs Saltram's part, of what was irritating in the narrowness of that lady's point of view? 'Mrs Saltram,' I explained, 'undervalues him where he is strongest, so that, to make up for it perhaps, she overpraises him where he's weak. He's not, assuredly, superficially attractive; he's middle-aged, fat, featureless save for his great eyes.'

'Yes, his great eyes,' said my young lady attentively. She had evidently heard all about his great eyes – the *beaux yeux* for which alone we had really done it all.

'They're tragic and splendid – lights on a dangerous coast. But he moves badly and dresses worse, and altogether he's anything but smart.'

My companion appeared to reflect on this, and after a moment she inquired: 'Do you call him a real gentleman?'

I started slightly at the question, for I had a sense of recognising it: George Gravener, years before, that first flushed night, had put me face to face with it. It had embarrassed me then, but it didn't embarrass me now, for I had lived with it and overcome it and disposed of it. 'A real gentleman? Emphatically not!'

My promptitude surprised her a little, but I quickly felt that it was not to Gravener I was now talking. 'Do you say that because he's – what do you call it in England? – of humble extraction?'

'Not a bit. His father was a country schoolmaster and his mother the widow of a sexton, but that has nothing to do with it. I say it simply because I know him well.'

'But isn't it an awful drawback?'

'Awful – quite awful.'

'I mean isn't it positively fatal?'

'Fatal to what? Not to his magnificent vitality.'

Again there was a meditative moment. 'And is his magnificent vitality the cause of his vices?'

'Your questions are formidable, but I'm glad you put them. I was thinking of his noble intellect. His vices, as you say, have been much exaggerated: they consist mainly after all in one comprehensive defect.'

'A want of will?'

'A want of dignity.'

'He doesn't recognise his obligations?'

'On the contrary, he recognises them with effusion, especially in public: he smiles and bows and beckons across the street to them. But when they pass over he turns away, and he speedily loses them in the crowd. The recognition is purely spiritual – it isn't in the least social. So he leaves all his belongings to other people to take care of. He accepts favours, loans, sacrifices, with nothing more deterrent than an agony of shame. Fortunately we're a little faithful band, and we do what we can.' I held my tongue about the natural children, engendered, to the number of three, in the wantonness of his youth. I only remarked that he did make efforts – often tremendous ones. 'But the efforts,' I said, 'never come to much: the only things that come to much are the abandonments, the surrenders.'

'And how much do they come to?'

'You're right to put it as if we had a big bill to pay, but, as I've told you before, your questions are rather terrible. They come, these mere exercises of genius, to a great sum total of poetry, of philosophy, a mighty mass of speculation, of notation. The genius is there, you see, to meet the surrender; but there's no genius to support the defence.'

'But what is there, after all, at his age, to show?'

'In the way of achievement recognised and reputation established?' I interrupted. 'To "show" if you will, there isn't much, for his writing, mostly, isn't as fine, isn't certainly as showy, as his talk. Moreover two-thirds of his work are merely colossal projects and announcements. "Showing" Frank Saltram is often a poor business: we endeavoured, you will have observed, to show him to-night! However, if he *had* lectured, he would have lectured divinely. It would just have been his talk.'

'And what would his talk just have been?'

I was conscious of some ineffectiveness as well perhaps as of a little impatience as I replied: 'The exhibition of a splendid intellect.' My young lady looked not quite satisfied at this, but as I was not prepared for another question I hastily pursued: 'The sight of a great suspended, swinging crystal, huge, lucid, lustrous, a block of light, flashing back every impression of life and every possibility of thought!' This gave her something to think about till we had passed out to the dusky porch of the hall, in front of which the lamps of a quiet brougham were almost the only thing Saltram's treachery hadn't extinguished. I went with her to the door of her carriage, out of which she leaned a moment after she had thanked me and taken her seat. Her smile even in the darkness was pretty. 'I do want to see that crystal!'

'You've only to come to the next lecture.'

'I go abroad in a day or two with my aunt.'

'Wait over till next week,' I suggested. 'It's quite worth it.'

She became grave. 'Not unless he really comes!' At which the brougham started off, carrying her away too fast, fortunately for my manners, to allow me to exclaim 'Ingratitude!'

IV

MRS SALTRAM made a great affair of her right to be informed where her husband had been the second evening he failed to meet his audience. She came to me to ascertain, but I couldn't satisfy her, for in spite of my ingenuity I remained in ignorance. It was not till much later that I found this had not been the case with Kent Mulville, whose hope for the best never twirled his thumbs more placidly than when he happened to know the worst. He had known it on the occasion I speak of – that is immediately after. He was impenetrable then, but he ultimately confessed. What he confessed was more than I shall venture to confess to-day. It was of course familiar to me that Saltram was incapable of keeping the engagements which, after their separation, he had entered into with regard to his wife, a deeply wronged, justly resentful, quite irreproachable and insufferable person. She often appeared at my chambers to talk over his lapses, for if, as she declared, she had washed her hands of him, she had carefully preserved the water of this ablution and she handed it about for inspection. She had arts of her own of exciting one's impatience, the most infallible of which was perhaps her assumption that we were kind to her because we liked her. In reality her personal fall had been a sort of social rise, for there had been a moment when, in our little conscientious circle, her desolation almost made her the fashion. Her voice was grating and her children ugly; moreover she hated the good Mulvilles, whom I more and more loved. They were the people who by doing most for her husband had in the long run done most for herself; and the warm confidence with which he had laid his length upon them was a pressure gentle compared with her stiffer persuadability. I am bound to say he didn't criticise his benefactors, though practically he got tired of them; she, however, had the highest standards about ele- mosynary forms. She offered the odd spectacle of a spirit puffed up by dependence, and indeed it had introduced her to some excellent society. She pitied me for not knowing certain people who aided her and whom she doubtless patronised in turn for their luck in not knowing me. I daresay I should have got on with her better if she had had a ray of imagination – if it had occasionally seemed to occur to her to regard Saltram's mani- festations in any other manner than as separate subjects of woe. They were all flowers of his nature, pearls strung on an endless thread; but she had a stubborn little way of challenging them one after the other, as if she never suspected that he *had* a nature, such as it was, or that deficiencies might be organic; the irritating effect of a mind incapable of a generalisation. One might doubtless have overdone the idea that there was a general exemption for such a man; but if this had happened it would have been through one's feeling that there could be none for such a woman.

I recognised her superiority when I asked her about the aunt of the disappointed young lady: it sounded like a sentence from a phrase-book. She triumphed in what she told me and she may have triumphed still more in what she withheld. My friend of the other evening, Miss Anvoy, had but lately come to England; Lady Coxon, the aunt, had been established here for years in consequence of her marriage with the late Sir Gregory of that ilk. She had a house in the Regent's Park, a Bath-chair and a fernery; and above all she had sympathy. Mrs Saltram had made her acquaintance through mutual friends.

This vagueness caused me to feel how much I was out of it and how large an independent circle Mrs Saltram had at her command. I should have been glad to know more about the disappointed young lady, but I felt that I should know most by not depriving her of her advantage, as she might have mysterious means of depriving me of my knowledge. For the present, moreover, this experience was arrested, Lady Coxon having in fact gone abroad, accompanied by her niece. The niece, besides being immensely clever, was an heiress, Mrs Saltram said; the only daughter and the light of the eyes of some great American merchant, a man, over there, of endless indulgences and dollars. She had pretty clothes and pretty manners, and she had, what was prettier still, the great thing of all. The great thing of all for Mrs Saltram was always sympathy, and she spoke as if during the absence of these ladies she might not know where to turn for it. A few months later indeed, when they had come back, her tone perceptibly changed: she alluded to them, on my leading her up to it, rather as to persons in her debt for favours received. What had happened I didn't know, but I saw it would take only a little more or a little less to make her speak of them as thankless subjects of social countenance – people for whom she had vainly tried to do something. I confess I saw that it would not be in a mere week or two that I should rid myself of the image of Ruth Anvoy, in whose very name, when I learnt it, I found something secretly to like. I should probably neither see her nor hear of her again: the knight's widow (he had been mayor of Clockborough) would pass away and the heiress would return to her inheritance. I gathered with surprise that she had not communicated to his wife the story of her attempt to hear Mr Saltram, and I founded this reticence on the easy supposition that Mrs Saltram had fatigued by overpressure the spring of the sympathy of which she boasted. The girl at any rate would forget the small adventure, be distracted, take a husband; besides which she would lack opportunity to repeat her experiment.

We clung to the idea of the brilliant course, delivered without an accident, that, as a lecturer, would still make the paying public aware of our great mind; but the fact remained that in the case of an inspiration so unequal there was treachery, there was fallacy at least, in the very conception of a series. In our scrutiny of ways and means we were inevitably subject to the old convention of the synopsis, the syllabus, partly of course not to lose the advantage of his grand free hand in drawing up such things; but for myself I laughed at our play-bills even while I stickled for them. It was indeed amusing work to be scrupulous for Frank Saltram, who also at moments laughed about it, so far as the comfort of a sigh so unstudied as to be cheerful might pass for such a sound. He admitted with a candour all his own that he was in truth only to be depended on in the Mulvilles' drawing-room. 'Yes,' he suggestively conceded, 'it's there, I think, that I am at my best; quite late, when it gets toward eleven – and if I've not been too much worried.' We all knew what too much worry meant; it meant too enslaved for the hour to the superstition of sobriety. On the Saturdays I used to bring my portmanteau, so as not to have to think of eleven o'clock trains. I had a bold theory that as regards this temple of talk and its altars of cushioned chintz, its pictures and its flowers, its large fireside and clear lamplight, we might really arrive at something if the Mulvilles would only charge for admission. But here it was that the Mulvilles shamelessly broke down; as there is a flaw in every perfection, this was the inexpugnable refuge of their egotism. They declined to make their saloon a market, so that Saltram's golden words continued to be the only coin that rang there. It can have happened to no man, however, to be paid a greater price than such an enchanted hush as surrounded him on his greatest nights. The most profane, on these occasions, felt a presence; all minor eloquence grew dumb. Adelaide Mulville, for the pride of her hospitality, anxiously watched the door or stealthily poked the fire. I used to call it the music-room, for we had anticipated Bayreuth. The very gates of the kingdom of light seemed to open and the horizon of thought of flash with the beauty of a sunrise at sea.

In the consideration of ways and means, the sittings of our little board, we were always conscious of the creak of Mrs Saltram's shoes. She hovered, she interrupted, she almost presided, the state of affairs being mostly such as to supply her with every incentive for inquiring what was to be done next. It was the pressing pursuit of this knowledge that, in concatenations of omnibuses and usually in very wet weather, led her so often to my door. She thought us spiritless creatures with editors and publishers; but she carried matters to no great effect when she personally pushed into back-shops. She wanted all moneys to be paid to herself: they were otherwise liable to such strange adventures. They trickled away into the desert, and they were mainly at best, alas, but a slender stream. The editors and the publishers were the last people to take this remarkable thinker at the valuation that has now pretty well come to be established. The former were half distraught between the desire to 'cut' him and the difficulty of finding a crevice for their shears; and when a volume on this or that portentous subject was proposed to the latter they suggested alternative titles which, as reported to our friend, brought into his face the noble blank melancholy that sometimes made it handsome. The title of an unwritten book didn't after all much matter, but some masterpiece of Saltram's may have died in his bosom of the shudder with which it was then convulsed. The ideal solution, failing the fee at Kent Mulville's door, would have been some system of subscription to projected treatises with their non-appearance provided for – provided for, I mean, by the indulgence of subscribers. The author's real misfortune was that subscribers were so wretchedly literal. When they tastelessly inquired why publication had not ensued I was tempted to ask who in the world had ever been so published. Nature herself had brought him out in voluminous form, and the money was simply a deposit on borrowing the work.

V

I WAS doubtless often a nuisance to my friends in those years; but there were sacrifices I declined to make, and I never passed the hat to George Gravener. I never forgot our little discussion in Ebury Street, and I think it stuck in my throat to have to make to him the admission I had made so easily to Miss Anvoy.

It had cost me nothing to confide to this charming girl, but it would have cost me much to confide to the friend of my youth, that the character of the 'real gentleman' was not an attribute of the man I took such pains for. Was this because I had already generalised to the point of perceiving that women are really the unfastidious sex? I knew at any rate that Gravener, already quite in view but still hungry and frugal, had naturally enough more ambition than charity. He had sharp aims for stray sovereigns, being in view most from the tall steeple of Clockborough. His immediate ambition was to wholly occupy the field of vision of that smokily-seeing city, and all his movements and postures were calculated for this angle. The movement of the hand to the pocket had thus to alternate gracefully with the posture of the hand on the heart. He talked to Clockborough in short only less beguilingly than Frank Saltram talked to his electors; with the difference in our favour, however, that we had already voted and that our candidate had no antagonist but himself. He had more than once been at Wimbledon – it was Mrs Mulville's work, not mine – and, by the time the claret was served, had seen the god descend. He took more pains to swing his censer than I had expected, but on our way back to town he forestalled any little triumph I might have been so artless as to express by the observation that such a man was – a hundred times! – a man to use and never a man to be used by. I remember that this neat remark humiliated me almost as much as if virtually, in the fever of broken slumbers, I hadn't often made it myself. The difference was that on Gravener's part a force attached to it that could never attach to it on mine. He was able to use people – he had the machinery; and the irony of Saltram's being made showy at Clockborough came out to me when he said, as if he had no memory of our original talk and the idea were quite fresh to him: 'I hate his type, you know, but I'll be hanged if I don't put some of those things in. I can find a place for them: we might even find a place for the fellow himself.' I myself should have had some fear, not, I need scarcely say, for the 'things' themselves, but for some other things very near them – in fine for the rest of my eloquence.

Later on I could see that the oracle of Wimbledon was not in this case so appropriate as he would have been had the politics of the gods only coincided more exactly with those of the party. There was a distinct moment when, without saying anything more definite to me, Gravener entertained the idea of annexing Mr Saltram. Such a project was delusive, for the discovery of analogies between his body of doctrine and that pressed from headquarters upon Clockborough – the bottling, in a word, of the air of those lungs for convenient public uncorking in corn-exchanges – was an experiment for which no one had the leisure. The only thing would have been to carry him massively about, paid, caged, clipped; to turn him on for a particular occasion in a particular channel. Frank Saltram's channel, however, was essentially not calculable, and there was no knowing what disastrous floods might have ensued. For what there would have been to do *The Empire*, the great newspaper, was there to look to; but it was no new misfortune that there were delicate situations in which *The Empire* broke down. In fine there was an instinctive apprehension that a clever young journalist commissioned to report upon Mr Saltram might never come back from the errand. No one knew better than George Gravener that that was a time when prompt returns counted double. If he therefore found our friend an exasperating waste of orthodoxy it was because he was, as he said, up in the clouds, not because he was down in the dust. He would have been a real enough gentleman if he could have helped to put in a real gentleman. Gravener's great objection to the actual member was that he was not one.

Lady Coxon had a fine old house, a house with 'grounds', at Clockborough, which she had let; but after she returned from abroad I learned from Mrs Saltram that the lease had fallen in and that she had gone down to resume possession. I could see the faded red livery, the big square shoulders, the high-walled garden of this decent abode. As the rumble of dissolution grew louder the suitor would have pressed his suit, and I found myself hoping that the politics of the late Mayor's widow would not be such as to enjoin upon her to ask him to dinner; perhaps indeed I went so far as to hope that they would be such as to put all countenance out of the question. I tried to focus the page, in the daily airing, as he perhaps even pushed the Bath-chair over somebody's toes. I was destined to hear, however, through Mrs Saltram (who, I afterwards learned, was in cor-respondence with Lady Coxon's housekeeper) that Gravener was known to have spoken of the habitation I had in my eye as the pleasantest thing at Clockborough. On his part, I was sure, this was the voice not of envy but of experience. The vivid scene was now peopled, and I could see him in the old-time garden with Miss Anvoy, who would be certain, and very justly, to think him good-looking. It would be too much to say that I was troubled by this evocation; but I seem to remember the relief, singular enough, of feeling it suddenly brushed away by an annoyance really much greater; an annoyance the result of its happening to come over me about that time with a rush that I was simply ashamed of Frank Saltram. There were limits after all, and my mark at last had been reached.

I had had my disgusts, if I may allow myself to-day such an expression; but this was a supreme revolt. Certain things cleared up in my mind, certain values stood out. It was all very well to have an unfortunate temperament; there was noth-ing so unfortunate as to have, for practical purposes, nothing else. I avoided George Gravener at this moment and reflected that at such a time I should do so most effectually by leaving England. I wanted to forget Frank Saltram – that was all. I didn't want to do anything in the world to him but that. Indignation had withered on the stalk, and I felt that one could pity him as much as one ought only by never thinking of him again. It wasn't for anything he had done to me; it was for something he had done to the Mulvilles. Adelaide cried about it for a week, and her husband, profiting by the example so signally given him of the fatal effect of a want of character, left the letter unanswered. The letter, an incredible one, addressed by Saltram to Wimbledon during a stay with the Pudneys at Ramsgate, was the central feature of the incident, which, however, had many features, each more painful than whichever other we compared it with. The Pudneys had behaved shockingly, but that was no excuse. Base ingratitude, gross indecency – one had one's choice only of such formulas as that the more they fitted the less they gave one rest. These are dead aches now, and I am under no obligation, thank heaven, to be definite about the business. There are things which if I had had to tell them – well, I wouldn't have told my story.

I went abroad for the general election, and if I don't know how much, on the Continent, I forgot, I at least know how much I missed, him. At a distance, in a foreign land, ignoring, abjuring, unlearning him, I discovered what he had done for me. I owed him, oh unmistakably, certain noble conceptions; I had lighted my little taper at his smoky lamp, and lo, it continued to twinkle. But the light it gave me just showed me how much more I wanted. I was pursued of course by letters from Mrs Saltram, which I didn't scruple not to read, though I was duly conscious that her embarrassments would now be of the gravest. I sacrificed to propriety by simply putting them away, and this is how, one day as my absence drew to an end, my eye, as I rummaged in my desk for another paper, was caught by a name on a leaf that had detached itself from the packet. The allusion was to Miss Anvoy, who, it appeared, was engaged to be married to Mr George Gravener; and the news was two months old. A direct question of Mrs Saltram's had thus remained unanswered – she had inquired of me in a post-script what sort of man this Mr Gravener might be. This Mr Gravener had been triumphantly returned for Clockborough, in the interest of the party that had swept the country, so that I might easily have referred Mrs Saltram to the journals of the day. But when I at last wrote to her that I was coming home and would discharge my accumulated burden by seeing her, I remarked in regard to her question that she must really put it to Miss Anvoy.

VI

I HAD almost avoided the general election, but some of its consequences, on my return, had smartly to be faced. The season, in London, began to breathe again and to flap its folded wings. Confidence, under the new Ministry, was understood to be reviving, and one of the symptoms, in the social body, was a recovery of appetite. People once more fed together, and it happened that, one Saturday night, at somebody's house, I fed with George Gravener. When the ladies left the room I moved up to where he sat and offered him my congratulation. 'On my election?' he asked after a moment; whereupon I feigned, jocosely, not to have heard of his election and to be alluding to something much more important, the rumour of his engagement. I daresay I coloured, however, for his political victory had momentarily passed out of my mind. What was present to it was that he was to marry that beautiful girl; and yet his question made me conscious of some discomposure – I had not intended to put that before everything. He himself indeed ought gracefully to have done so, and I remember thinking the whole man was in this assumption that in expressing my sense of what he had won I had fixed my thoughts on his 'seat'. We straightened the matter out, and he was so much lighter in hand than I had lately seen him that his spirits might well have been fed from a double source. He was so good as to say that he hoped I should soon make the acquaintance of Miss Anvoy, who, with her aunt, was presently coming up to town. Lady Coxon, in the country, had been seriously unwell, and this had delayed their arrival. I told him I had heard the marriage would be a splendid one; on which, brightened and humanised by his luck, he laughed and said: 'Do you mean for *her*?' When I had again explained what I meant he went on: 'Oh, she's an American, but you'd scarcely know it; unless, perhaps,' he added, 'by her being used to more money than most girls in England, even the daughters of rich men. That wouldn't in the least do for a fellow like me, you know, if it wasn't for the great liberality of her father. He really has been most kind, and everything is quite satisfactory.' He added that his eldest brother had taken a tremendous fancy to her and that during a recent visit at Coldfield she had nearly won over Lady Maddock. I gathered from something he dropped later that the free-handed gentleman beyond the seas had not made a settlement, but had given a handsome present and was apparently to be looked to, across the water, for other favours. People are simplified alike by great

contentments and great yearnings, and whether or no it was
Gravener's directness that begot my own I seem to recall that in
some turn taken by our talk he almost imposed it on me as an
act of decorum to ask if Miss Anvoy had also by chance
expectations from her aunt. My inquiry drew out that Lady
Coxon, who was the oddest of women, would have in any
contingency to act under her late husband's will, which was
odder still, saddling her with a mass of queer obligations complicated with queer loopholes. There were several dreary
people, Coxon cousins, old maids, to whom she would have
more or less to minister. Gravener laughed, without saying no,
when I suggested that the young lady might come in through a
loophole; then suddenly, as if he suspected that I had turned
a lantern on him, he exclaimed quite dryly: 'That's all rot – one
is moved by other springs!'

A fortnight later, at Lady Coxon's own house, I understood
well enough the springs one was moved by. Gravener had
spoken of me there as an old friend, and I received a gracious
invitation to dine. The knight's widow was again indisposed –
she had succumbed at the eleventh hour; so that I found Miss
Anvoy bravely playing hostess, without even Gravener's help,
inasmuch as, to make matters worse, he had just sent up word
that the House, the insatiable House, with which he supposed
he had contracted for easier terms, positively declined to
release him. I was struck with the courage, the grace and gaiety
of the young lady left to deal unaided with the possibilities of
the Regent's Park. I did what I could to help her to keep them
down, or up, after I had recovered from the confusion of seeing
her slightly disconcerted at perceiving in the guest introduced
by her intended the gentleman with whom she had had that talk
about Frank Saltram. I had at that moment my first glimpse of
the fact that she was a person who could carry a responsibility;
but I leave the reader to judge of my sense of the aggravation,
for either of us, of such a burden when I heard the servant
announce Mrs Saltram. From what immediately passed
between the two ladies I gathered that the latter had been
sent for post-haste to fill the gap created by the absence of the
mistress of the house. 'Good!' I exclaimed, 'she will be put by

me'; and my apprehension was promptly justified. Mrs Saltram taken in to dinner, and taken in as a consequence of an appeal to her amiability, was Mrs Saltram with a vengeance. I asked myself what Miss Anvoy meant by doing such things, but the only answer I arrived at was that Gravener was verily fortunate. She had not happened to tell him of her visit to Upper Baker Street, but she would certainly tell him to-morrow; not indeed that this would make him like any better her having had the simplicity to invite such a person as Mrs Saltram on such an occasion. I reflected that I had never seen a young woman put such ignorance into her cleverness, such freedom into her modesty; this, I think, was when, after dinner, she said to me frankly, with almost jubilant mirth: 'Oh, you don't admire Mrs Saltram?' Why should I? This was truly an innocent maiden. I had briefly to consider before I could reply that my objection to the lady in question was the objection often formulated in regard to persons met at the social board – I knew all her stories. Then, as Miss Anvoy remained momentarily vague, I added: 'About her husband.'

'Oh yes, but there are some new ones.'

'None for me. Oh, novelty would be pleasant!'

'Doesn't it appear that of late he has been particularly horrid?'

'His fluctuations don't matter,' I replied, 'for at night all cats are grey. You saw the shade of this one the night we waited for him together. What will you have? He has no dignity.'

Miss Anvoy, who had been introducing with her American distinctness, looked encouragingly round at some of the combinations she had risked. 'It's too bad I can't see him.'

'You mean Gravener won't let you?'

'I haven't asked him. He lets me do everything.'

'But you know he knows him and wonders what some of us see in him.'

'We haven't happened to talk of him,' the girl said.

'Get him to take you some day out to see the Mulvilles.'

'I thought Mr Saltram had thrown the Mulvilles over.'

'Utterly. But that won't prevent his being planted there again, to bloom like a rose, within a month or two.'

Miss Anvoy thought a moment. Then, 'I should like to see them,' she said with her fostering smile.

'They're tremendously worth it. You mustn't miss them.'

'I'll make George take me,' she went on as Mrs Saltram came up to interrupt us. The girl smiled at her as kindly as she had smiled at me and, addressing the question to her, continued: 'But the chance of a lecture – one of the wonderful lectures? Isn't there another course announced?'

'Another? There are about thirty!' I exclaimed, turning away and feeling Mrs Saltram's little eyes in my back. A few days after this I heard that Gravener's marriage was near at hand – was settled for Whitsuntide; but as I had received no invitation I doubted it, and presently there came to me in fact the report of a postponement. Something was the matter; what was the matter was supposed to be that Lady Coxon was now critically ill. I had called on her after my dinner in the Regent's Park, but I had neither seen her nor seen Miss Anvoy. I forget to-day the exact order in which, at this period, certain incidents occurred and the particular stage at which it suddenly struck me, making me catch my breath a little, that the progression, the acceleration was for all the world that of a drama. This was probably rather late in the day, and the exact order doesn't matter. What had already occurred was some accident determining a more patient wait. George Gravener, whom I met again, in fact told me as much, but without signs of perturbation. Lady Coxon had to be constantly attended to, and there were other good reasons as well. Lady Coxon had to be so constantly attended to that on the occasion of a second attempt in the Regent's Park I equally failed to obtain a sight of her niece. I judged it discreet under the circumstances not to make a third; but this didn't matter, for it was through Adelaide Mulville that the side-wind of the comedy, though I was at first unwitting, began to reach me. I went to Wimbledon at times because Saltram was there, and I went at others because he was not. The Pudneys, who had taken him to Birmingham, had already got rid of him, and we had a horrible consciousness of his wandering roofless, in dishonour, about the smoky Midlands, almost as the injured Lear wandered on the storm-lashed heath. His room, upstairs, had been lately done up (I could hear the crackle of the new chintz) and the difference only made his smirches and bruises, his splendid tainted genius, the more tragic. If he wasn't barefoot in the mire he was sure to be unconventionally shod. These were the things Adelaide and I, who were old enough friends to stare at each other in silence, talked about when we didn't speak. When we spoke it was only about the brilliant girl George Gravener was to marry, whom he had brought out the other Sunday. I could see that this presentation had been happy, for Mrs Mulville commemorated it in the only way in which she ever expressed her confidence in a new relation. 'She likes me – she likes me': her native humility exulted in that measure of success. We all knew for ourselves how she liked those who liked her, and as regards Ruth Anvoy she was more easily won over than Lady Maddock.

VII

ONE of the consequences, for the Mulvilles, of the sacrifices they made for Frank Saltram was that they had to give up their carriage. Adelaide drove gently into London in a one-horse greenish thing, an early Victorian landau, hired, near at hand, imaginatively, from a broken-down jobmaster whose wife was in consumption – a vehicle that made people turn round all the more when her pensioner sat beside her in a soft white hat and a shawl, one of her own. This was his position and I daresay his costume when on an afternoon in July she went to return Miss Anvoy's visit. The wheel of fate had now revolved, and amid silences deep and exhaustive, compunctions and condonations alike unutterable, Saltram was reinstated. Was it in pride or in penance that Mrs Mulville began immediately to drive him about? If he was ashamed of his ingratitude she might have been ashamed of her forgiveness; but she was incorrigibly cap-able of liking him to be seen strikingly seated in the landau while she was in shops or with her acquaintance. However, if he was in the pillory for twenty minutes in the Regent's Park (I mean at Lady Coxon's door, while her companion paid her call) it was not for the further humiliation of any one concerned

that she presently came out for him in person, not even to show
either of them what a fool she was that she drew him in to be
introduced to the clever young American. Her account of the
introduction I had in its order, but before that, very late in the
season, under Gravener's auspices, I met Miss Anvoy at tea at
the House of Commons. The member for Clockborough had
gathered a group of pretty ladies, and the Mulvilles were not of
the party. On the great terrace, as I strolled off a little with her,
the guest of honour immediately exclaimed to me: 'I've seen
him, you know – I've seen him!' She told me about Saltram's
call.

'And how did you find him?'

'Oh, so strange!'

'You didn't like him?'

'I can't tell till I see him again.'

'You want to do that?'

She was silent a moment. 'Immensely.'

We stopped; I fancied she had become aware Gravener was
looking at us. She turned back toward the knot of the others,
and I said: 'Dislike him as much as you will – I see you are
bitten.'

'Bitten?' I thought she coloured a little.

'Oh, it doesn't matter!' I laughed; 'one doesn't die of it.'

'I hope I shan't die of anything before I've seen more of Mrs
Mulville.' I rejoiced with her over plain Adelaide, whom she
pronounced the loveliest woman she had met in England; but
before we separated I remarked to her that it was an act of mere
humanity to warn her that if she should see more of Frank
Saltram (which would be likely to follow on any increase of
acquaintance with Mrs Mulville) she might find herself flatten-
ing her nose against the clear, hard pane of an eternal question –
that of the relative importance of virtue. She replied that this
was surely a subject on which one took everything for granted;
whereupon I admitted that I had perhaps expressed myself ill.
What I referred to was what I had referred to the night we met
in Upper Baker Street – the importance relative (relative to
virtue) of other gifts. She asked me if I called virtue a gift – as
if it were handed to us in a parcel on our birthday; and I declared

that this very inquiry showed me the problem had already caught her by the skirt. She would have help, however, help that I myself had once had, in resisting its tendency to make one cross.

'What help do you mean?'

'That of the member for Clockborough.'

She stared, smiled, then exclaimed: 'Why, my idea has been to help *him*!'

She *had* helped him – I had his own word for it that at Clockborough her bedevilment of the voters had really put him in. She would do so doubtless again and again, but I heard the very next month that this fine faculty had undergone a temporary eclipse. News of the catastrophe first came to me from Mrs Saltram, and it was afterwards confirmed at Wimbledon: poor Miss Anvoy was in trouble – great disasters in America had suddenly summoned her home. Her father, in New York, had had reverses – lost so much money that it was really provoking as showing how much he had had. It was Adelaide who told me that she had gone off alone at less than a week's notice.

'Alone? Gravener has permitted that?'

'What will you have? The House of Commons!'

I'm afraid I cursed the House of Commons: I was so much interested. Of course he would follow her as soon as he was free to make her his wife; only she mightn't now be able to bring him anything like the marriage-portion of which he had begun by having the virtual promise. Mrs Mulville let me know what was already said: she was charming, this American girl, but really these American fathers! What was a man to do? Mr Saltram, according to Mrs Mulville, was of opinion that a man was never to suffer his relation to money to become a spiritual relation, but was to keep it wholesomely mechanical. '*Moi pas comprendre!*' I commented on this; in rejoinder to which Adelaide, with her beautiful sympathy, explained that she supposed he simply meant that the thing was to use it, don't you know? but not to think too much about it. 'To take it, but not to thank you for it?' I still more profanely inquired. For a quarter of an hour afterwards she wouldn't look at me, but this didn't prevent my asking her what had been the result, that afternoon in the Regent's Park, of her taking our friend to see Miss Anvoy.

'Oh, so charming!' she answered, brightening. 'He said he recognised in her a nature he could absolutely trust.'

'Yes, but I'm speaking of the effect on herself.'

Mrs Mulville was silent an instant. 'It was everything one could wish.'

Something in her tone made me laugh. 'Do you mean she gave him something?'

'Well, since you ask me!'

'Right there – on the spot?'

Again poor Adelaide faltered. 'It was to me of course she gave it.'

I stared; somehow I couldn't see the scene. 'Do you mean a sum of money?'

'It was very handsome.' Now at last she met my eyes, though I could see it was with an effort. 'Thirty pounds.'

'Straight out of her pocket?'

'Out of the drawer of a table at which she had been writing. She just slipped the folded notes into my hand. He wasn't looking; it was while he was going back to the carriage. Oh,' said Adelaide reassuringly, 'I dole it out!' The dear practical soul thought my agitation, for I confess I was agitated, had reference to the administration of the money. Her disclosure made me for a moment muse violently, and I daresay that during that moment I wondered if anything else in the world makes people so indelicate as unselfishness. I uttered, I suppose, some vague synthetic cry, for she went on as if she had had a glimpse of my inward amaze at such episodes. 'I assure you, my dear friend, he was in one of his happy hours.'

But I wasn't thinking of that. 'Truly, indeed, these Americans!' I said. 'With her father in the very act, as it were, of swindling her betrothed!'

Mrs Mulville stared. 'Oh, I suppose Mr Anvoy has scarcely failed on purpose. Very likely they won't be able to keep it up, but there it was, and it was a very beautiful impulse.'

'You say Saltram was very fine?'

'Beyond everything. He surprised even me.'

'And I know what *you've* heard.' After a moment I added: 'Had he peradventure caught a glimpse of the money in the table-drawer?'

At this my companion honestly flushed. 'How can you be so cruel when you know how little he calculates?'

'Forgive me, I do know it. But you tell me things that act on my nerves. I'm sure he hadn't caught a glimpse of anything but some splendid idea.'

Mrs Mulville brightly concurred. 'And perhaps even of her beautiful listening face.'

'Perhaps even! And what was it all about?'

'His talk? It was *à propos* of her engagement, which I had told him about: the idea of marriage, the philosophy, the poetry, the sublimity of it.' It was impossible wholly to restrain one's mirth at this, and some rude ripple that I emitted again caused my companion to admonish me. 'It sounds a little stale, but you know his freshness.'

'Of illustration? Indeed I do!'

'And how he has always been right on that great question.'

'On what great question, dear lady, hasn't he been right?'

'Of what other great men can you equally say it? I mean that he has never, but *never*, had a deviation?' Mrs Mulville exultantly demanded.

I tried to think of some other great man, but I had to give it up. 'Didn't Miss Anvoy express her satisfaction in any less diffident way than by her charming present?' I was reduced to inquiring instead.

'Oh yes, she overflowed to me on the steps while he was getting into the carriage.' These words somehow brushed up a picture of Saltram's big shawled back as he hoisted himself into the green landau. 'She said she was not disappointed,' Adelaide pursued.

I meditated a moment. 'Did he wear his shawl?'

'His shawl?' She had not even noticed.

'I mean yours.'

'He looked very nice, and you know he's really clean. Miss Anvoy used such a remarkable expression – she said his mind is like a crystal!'

I pricked up my ears. 'A crystal?'

'Suspended in the moral world – swinging and shining and flashing there. She's monstrously clever, you know.'

I reflected again. 'Monstrously!'

VIII

GEORGE GRAVENER didn't follow her, for late in September, after the House had risen, I met him in a railway-carriage. He was coming up from Scotland, and I had just quitted the abode of a relation who lived near Durham. The current of travel back to London was not yet strong; at any rate on entering the compartment I found he had had it for some time to himself. We fared in company, and though he had a blue-book in his lap and the open jaws of his bag threatened me with the white teeth of confused papers, we inevitably, we even at last sociably conversed. I saw that things were not well with him, but I asked no question until something dropped by himself made, as it had made on another occasion, an absence of curiosity invidious. He mentioned that he was worried about his good old friend Lady Coxon, who, with her niece likely to be detained some time in America, lay seriously ill at Clock-borough, much on his mind and on his hands.

'Ah, Miss Anvoy's in America?'

'Her father has got into a horrid hole, lost no end of money.'

I hesitated, after expressing due concern, but I presently said: 'I hope that raises no objection to your marriage.'

'None whatever; moreover it's my trade to meet objections. But it may create tiresome delays, of which there have been too many, from various causes, already. Lady Coxon got very bad, then she got much better. Then Mr Anvoy suddenly began to totter, and now he seems quite on his back. I'm afraid he's really in for some big reverse. Lady Coxon is worse again, awfully upset by the news from America, and she sends me word that she *must* have Ruth. How can I give her Ruth? I haven't got Ruth myself!'

'Surely you haven't lost her?' I smiled.

'She's everything to her wretched father. She writes me every post – telling me to smooth her aunt's pillow. I've other things to smooth; but the old lady, save for her servants, is really alone. She won't receive her Coxon relations, because she's angry at so much of her money going to them. Besides, she's hopelessly mad,' said Gravener very frankly.

I don't remember whether it was this, or what it was, that made me ask if she had not such an appreciation of Mrs Saltram as might render that active person of some use.

He gave me a cold glance, asking me what had put Mrs Saltram into my head, and I replied that she was unfortunately never out of it. I happened to remember the wonderful accounts she had given me of the kindness Lady Coxon had shown her. Gravener declared this to be false; Lady Coxon, who didn't care for her, hadn't seen her three times. The only foundation for it was that Miss Anvoy, who used, poor girl, to chuck money about in a manner she must now regret, had for an hour seen in the miserable woman (you could never know what she would see in people) an interesting pretext for the liberality with which her nature overflowed. But even Miss Anvoy was now quite tired of her. Gravener told me more about the crash in New York and the annoyance it had been to him, and we also glanced here and there in other directions; but by the time we got to Doncaster the principal thing he had communicated was that he was keeping something back. We stopped at that station, and, at the carriage-door, some one made a movement to get in. Gravener uttered a sound of impatience, and I said to myself that but for this I should have had the secret. Then the intruder, for some reason, spared us his company; we started afresh, and my hope of the secret returned. Gravener remained silent, however, and I pretended to go to sleep; in fact, in discouragement, I really dozed. When I opened my eyes I found he was looking at me with an injured air. He tossed away with some vivacity the remnant of a cigarette and then he said: 'If you're not too sleepy I want to put you a case.' I answered that I would make every effort to attend, and I felt it was going to be interesting when he went on: 'As I told you a while ago, Lady Coxon, poor dear, is a maniac.' His tone had much behind it – was full of promise. I inquired if her ladyship's misfortune were a feature of her malady or only of her character, and he replied that it was a product of both. The case he wanted to put to me was a matter on which it would interest him to have the impression – the judgement, he might also say – of another person. 'I mean of the average intelligent man,' he said; 'but you see I take what I can get.' There would be the technical, the strictly legal view; then there would be the way the question would strike a man of the world. He had lighted another cigarette while he talked, and I saw he was glad to have it to handle when he brought out at last, with a laugh slightly artificial: 'In fact it's a subject on which Miss Anvoy and I are pulling different ways.'

'And you want me to pronounce between you? I pronounce in advance for Miss Anvoy.'

'In advance – that's quite right. That's how I pronounced when I asked her to marry me. But my story will interest you only so far as your mind is not made up.' Gravener puffed his cigarette a minute and then continued: 'Are you familiar with the idea of the Endowment of Research?'

'Of Research?' I was at sea for a moment.

'I give you Lady Coxon's phrase. She has it on the brain.'

'She wishes to endow—?'

'Some earnest and disinterested seeker,' Gravener said. 'It was a sketchy design of her late husband's, and he handed it on to her; setting apart in his will a sum of money of which she was to enjoy the interest for life, but of which, should she eventually see her opportunity – the matter was left largely to her discretion – she would best honour his memory by determining the exemplary public use. This sum of money, no less than thirteen thousand pounds, was to be called the Coxon Fund; and poor Sir Gregory evidently proposed to himself that the Coxon Fund should cover his name with glory – be universally desired and admired. He left his wife a full declaration of his views, so far at least as that term may be applied to views vitiated by a vagueness really infantine. A little learning is a dangerous thing, and a good citizen who happens to have been an ass is worse for a community than bad sewerage. He's worst of all when he's dead, because then he can't be stopped. However, such as they were, the poor man's aspirations are now in his wife's bosom, or fermenting rather in her foolish brain: it lies with her to carry them out. But of course she must first catch her hare.'

'Her earnest, disinterested seeker?'

'The flower that blushes unseen for want of the pecuniary independence necessary to cause the light that is in it to shine upon the human race. The individual, in a word, who, having the rest of the machinery, the spiritual, the intellectual, is most hampered in his search.'

'His search for what?'

'For Moral Truth. That's what Sir Gregory calls it.'

I burst out laughing. 'Delightful, munificent Sir Gregory! It's a charming idea.'

'So Miss Anvoy thinks.'

'Has she a candidate for the Fund?'

'Not that I know of; and she's perfectly reasonable about it. But Lady Coxon has put the matter before her, and we've naturally had a lot of talk.'

'Talk that, as you've so interestingly intimated, has landed you in a disagreement.'

'She considers there's something in it,' Gravener said.

'And you consider there's nothing?'

'It seems to me a puerility fraught with consequences inevitably grotesque and possibly immoral. To begin with, fancy the idea of constituting an endowment without establishing a tribunal – a bench of competent people, of judges.'

'The sole tribunal is Lady Coxon?'

'And any one she chooses to invite.'

'But she has invited you.'

'I'm not competent – I hate the thing. Besides, she hasn't. The real history of the matter, I take it, is that the inspiration was originally Lady Coxon's own, that she infected him with it, and that the flattering option left her is simply his tribute to her beautiful, her aboriginal enthusiasm. She came to England forty years ago, a thin transcendental Bostonian, and even her odd, happy, frumpy Clockborough marriage never really

materialised her. She feels indeed that she has become very
British – as if that, as a process, as a *Werden*, were conceivable;
but it's precisely what makes her cling to the notion of the
"Fund" – cling to it as to a link with the ideal.'

'How can she cling if she's dying?'

'Do you mean how can she act in the matter?' my companion asked. 'That's precisely the question. She can't! As she has
never yet caught her hare, never spied out her lucky impostor
(how should she, with the life she has led?), her husband's
intention has come very near lapsing. His idea, to do him
justice, was that it *should* lapse if exactly the right person, the
perfect mixture of genius and chill penury, should fail to turn
up. Ah! Lady Coxon's very particular – she says there must be
no mistake.'

I found all this quite thrilling – I took it in with avidity. 'If she
dies without doing anything, what becomes of the money?'
I demanded.

'It goes back to his family, if she hasn't made some other
disposition of it.'

'She may do that, then – she may divert it?'

'Her hands are not tied. The proof is that three months ago
she offered to make it over to her niece.'

'For Miss Anvoy's own use?'

'For Miss Anvoy's own use – on the occasion of her prospective marriage. She was discouraged – the earnest seeker
required so earnest a search. She was afraid of making a mistake; every one she could think of seemed either not earnest
enough or not poor enough. On the receipt of the first bad news
about Mr Anvoy's affairs she proposed to Ruth to make the
sacrifice for her. As the situation in New York got worse she
repeated her proposal.'

'Which Miss Anvoy declined?'

'Except as a formal trust.'

'You mean except as committing herself legally to place the
money?'

'On the head of the deserving object, the great man
frustrated,' said Gravener. 'She only consents to act in the spirit
of Sir Gregory's scheme.'

'And you blame her for that?' I asked with an excited smile.

My tone was not harsh, but he coloured a little and there was a queer light in his eye. 'My dear fellow, if I "blamed" the young lady I'm engaged to, I shouldn't immediately say so even to so old a friend as you.' I saw that some deep discomfort, some restless desire to be sided with, reassuringly, approvingly mirrored, had been at the bottom of his drifting so far, and I was genuinely touched by his confidence. It was inconsistent with his habits; but being troubled about a woman was not, for him, a habit: that itself was an inconsistency. George Gravener could stand straight enough before any other combination of forces. It amused me to think that the combination he had succumbed to had an American accent, a transcendental aunt and an insolvent father; but all my old loyalty to him mustered to meet this unexpected hint that I could help him. I saw that I could from the insincere tone in which he pursued: 'I've criticised her of course, I've contended with her, and it has been great fun.' It clearly couldn't have been such great fun as to make it improper for me presently to ask if Miss Anvoy had nothing at all settled upon herself. To this he replied that she had only a trifle from her mother – a mere four hundred a year, which was exactly why it would be convenient to him that she shouldn't decline, in the face of this total change in her prospects, an accession of income which would distinctly help them to marry. When I inquired if there were no other way in which so rich and so affectionate an aunt could cause the weight of her benevolence to be felt, he answered that Lady Coxon was affectionate indeed, but was scarcely to be called rich. She could let her project of the Fund lapse for her niece's benefit, but she couldn't do anything else. She had been accustomed to regard her as tremendously provided for, and she was up to her eyes in promises to anxious Coxons. She was a woman of an inordinate conscience, and her conscience was now a distress to her, hovering round her bed in irreconcilable forms of resentful husbands, portionless nieces and undiscoverable philosophers.

We were by this time getting into the whirr of fleeting platforms, the multiplication of lights. 'I think you'll find,' I said

with a laugh, 'that your predicament will disappear in the very
fact that the philosopher *is* undiscoverable.'

He began to gather up his papers. 'Who can set a limit to the
ingenuity of an extravagant woman?'

'Yes, after all, who indeed?' I echoed, as I recalled the extravagance commemorated in Mrs Mulville's anecdote of Miss
Anvoy and the thirty pounds.

IX

THE thing I had been most sensible of in that talk with George
Gravener was the way Saltram's name kept out of it. It seemed
to me at the time that we were quite pointedly silent about him;
but afterwards it appeared more probable there had been on my
companion's part no conscious avoidance. Later on I was sure
of this, and for the best of reasons – the simple reason of my
perceiving more completely that, for evil as well as for good, he
said nothing to Gravener's imagination. Gravener was not
afraid of him; he was too much disgusted with him. No more
was I, doubtless, and for very much the same reason. I treated
my friend's story as an absolute confidence; but when before
Christmas, by Mrs Saltram, I was informed of Lady Coxon's
death without having had news of Miss Anvoy's return, I found
myself taking for granted that we should hear no more of these
nuptials, in which I now recognised an element incongruous
from the first. I began to ask myself how people who suited each
other so little could please each other so much. The charm was
some material charm, some affinity exquisite doubtless, yet
superficial; some surrender to youth and beauty and passion,
to force and grace and fortune, happy accidents and easy contacts. They might dote on each other's persons, but how could
they know each other's souls? How could they have the same
prejudices, how could they have the same horizon? Such questions, I confess, seemed quenched but not answered when, one
day in February, going out to Wimbledon, I found our young
lady in the house. A passion that had brought her back across
the wintry ocean was as much of a passion as was necessary. No
impulse equally strong indeed had drawn George Gravener to

America; a circumstance on which, however, I reflected only long enough to remind myself that it was none of my business. Ruth Anvoy was distinctly different, and I felt that the difference was not simply that of her being in mourning. Mrs Mulville told me soon enough what it was: it was the difference between a handsome girl with large expectations and a handsome girl with only four hundred a year. This explanation indeed did not wholly content me, not even when I learned that her mourning had a double cause – learned that poor Mr Anvoy, giving way altogether, buried under the ruins of his fortune and leaving next to nothing, had died a few weeks before.

'So she has come out to marry George Gravener?' I demanded. 'Wouldn't it have been prettier of him to have saved her the trouble?'

'Hasn't the House just met?' said Adelaide. Then she added: 'I gather that her having come is exactly a sign that the marriage is a little shaky. If it were certain, a self-respecting girl like Ruth would have waited for him over there.'

I noted that they were already Ruth and Adelaide, but what I said was: 'Do you mean that she has returned to make it a certainty?'

'No, I mean that I figure she has come out for some reason independent of it.' Adelaide could only figure as yet, and there was more, as we found, to be revealed. Mrs Mulville, on hearing of her arrival, had brought the young lady out in the green landau for the Sunday. The Coxons were in possession of the house in Regent's Park, and Miss Anvoy was in dreary lodgings. George Gravener was with her when Adelaide called, but he had assented graciously enough to the little visit at Wimbledon. The carriage, with Mr Saltram in it but not mentioned, had been sent off on some errand from which it was to return and pick the ladies up. Gravener left them together, and at the end of an hour, on the Saturday afternoon, the party of three drove out to Wimbledon. This was the girl's second glimpse of our great man, and I was interested in asking Mrs Mulville if the impression made by the first appeared to have been confirmed. On her replying, after consideration, that of course with time and opportunity it couldn't fail to be, but as yet she was disappointed, I was sufficiently struck with her use of this last word to question her further.

'Do you mean that you're disappointed because you judge that Miss Anvoy is?'

'Yes; I hoped for a greater effect last evening. We had two or three people, but he scarcely opened his mouth.'

'He'll be all the better this evening,' I added after a moment. 'What particular importance do you attach to the idea of her being impressed?'

Adelaide turned her mild, pale eyes on me as if she were amazed at my levity. 'Why, the importance of her being as happy as *we* are!'

I'm afraid that at this my levity increased. 'Oh, that's a happiness almost too great to wish a person!' I saw she had not yet in her mind what I had in mine, and at any rate the visitor's actual bliss was limited to a walk in the garden with Kent Mulville. Later in the afternoon I also took one, and I saw nothing of Miss Anvoy till dinner, at which we were without the company of Saltram, who had caused it to be reported that he was indisposed, lying down. This made us, most of us – for there were other friends present – convey to each other in silence some of the unutterable things which in those years our eyes had inevitably acquired the art of expressing. If an American inquirer had not been there we would have expressed them otherwise, and Adelaide would have pretended not to hear. I had seen her, before the very fact, abstract herself nobly; and I knew that more than once, to keep it from the servants, managing, dissimulating cleverly, she had helped her husband to carry him bodily to his room. Just recently he had been so wise and so deep and so high that I had begun to get nervous – to wonder if by chance there was something behind it, if he were kept straight for instance by the knowledge that the hated Pudneys would have more to tell us if they chose. He was lying low, but unfortunately it was common wisdom with us that the biggest splashes took place in the quietest pools. We should have had a merry life indeed if all the splashes had sprinkled us as refreshingly as the waters we were even then to feel about our ears. Kent Mulville had been up to his room, but had come back with a face that told as few tales as I had seen it succeed in telling on the evening I waited in the lecture-room with Miss Anvoy. I said to myself that our friend had gone out, but I was glad that the presence of a comparative stranger deprived us of the dreary duty of suggesting to each other, in respect of his errand, edifying possibilities in which we didn't ourselves believe. At ten o'clock he came into the drawing-room with his waistcoat much awry but his eyes sending out great signals. It was precisely with his entrance that I ceased to be vividly conscious of him. I saw that the crystal, as I had called it, had begun to swing, and I had need of my immediate attention for Miss Anvoy.

Even when I was told afterwards that he had, as we might have said to-day, broken the record, the manner in which that attention had been rewarded relieved me of a sense of loss. I had of course a perfect general consciousness that something great was going on: it was a little like having been etherised to hear Herr Joachim play. The old music was in the air; I felt the strong pulse of thought, the sink and swell, the flight, the poise, the plunge; but I knew something about one of the listeners that nobody else knew, and Saltram's monologue could reach me only through that medium. To this hour I'm of no use when, as a witness, I'm appealed to (for they still absurdly contend about it) as to whether or no on that historic night he was drunk; and my position is slightly ridiculous, for I have never cared to tell them what it really was I was taken up with. What I got out of it is the only morsel of the total experience that is quite my own. The others were shared, but this is incommunicable. I feel that now, I'm bound to say, in even thus roughly evoking the occasion, and it takes something from my pride of clearness. However, I shall perhaps be as clear as is absolutely necessary if I remark that she was too much given up to her own intensity of observation to be sensible of mine. It was plainly not the question of her marriage that had brought her back. I greatly enjoyed this discovery and was sure that had that question alone been involved she would have remained away. In this case doubtless Gravener would, in spite of the House of

Commons, have found means to rejoin her. It afterwards made me uncomfortable for her that, alone in the lodging Mrs Mulville had put before me as dreary, she should have in any degree the air of waiting for her fate; so that I was presently relieved at hearing of her having gone to stay at Coldfield. If she was in England at all while the engagement stood the only proper place for her was under Lady Maddock's wing. Now that she was unfortunate and relatively poor, perhaps her prospective sister-in-law would be wholly won over. There would be much to say, if I had space, about the way her behaviour, as I caught gleams of it, ministered to the image that had taken birth in my mind, to my private amusement, as I listened to George Gravener in the railway-carriage. I watched her in the light of this queer possibility – a formidable thing certainly to meet – and I was aware that it coloured, extravagantly perhaps, my interpretation of her very looks and tones. At Wimbledon for instance it had seemed to me that she was literally afraid of Saltram, in dread of a coercion that she had begun already to feel. I had come up to town with her the next day and had been convinced that, though deeply interested, she was immensely on her guard. She would show as little as possible before she should be ready to show everything. What this final exhibition might be on the part of a girl perceptibly so able to think things out I found it great sport to forecast. It would have been exciting to be approached by her, appealed to by her for advice; but I prayed to heaven I mightn't find myself in such a predicament. If there was really a present rigour in the situation of which Gravener had sketched for me the elements she would have to get out of her difficulty by herself. It was not I who had launched her and it was not I who could help her. I didn't fail to ask myself why, since I couldn't help her, I should think so much about her. It was in part my suspense that was responsible for this; I waited impatiently to see whether she wouldn't have told Mrs Mulville a portion at least of what I had learned from Gravener. But I saw Mrs Mulville was still reduced to wonder what she had come out again for if she hadn't come as a conciliatory bride. That she had come in some other character was the only thing that fitted all the appearances. Having for family reasons to spend some time that spring in the west of England, I was in a manner out of earshot of the great oceanic rumble (I mean of the continuous hum of Saltram's thought) and my uneasiness tended to keep me quiet. There was something I wanted so little to have to say that my prudence surmounted my curiosity. I only wondered if Ruth Anvoy talked over the idea of the Coxon Fund with Lady Maddock, and also somewhat why I didn't hear from Wimbledon. I had a reproachful note about something or other from Mrs Saltram, but it contained no mention of Lady Coxon's niece, on whom her eyes had been much less fixed since the recent untoward events.

X

ADELAIDE's silence was fully explained later; it was practically explained when in June, returning to London, I was honoured by this admirable woman with an early visit. As soon as she appeared I guessed everything, and as soon as she told me that darling Ruth had been in her house nearly a month I exclaimed: 'What in the name of maidenly modesty is she staying in England for?'

'Because she loves me so!' cried Adelaide gaily. But she had not come to see me only to tell me Miss Anvoy loved her: that was now sufficiently established, and what was much more to the point was that Mr Gravener had now raised an objection to it. That is he had protested against her being at Wimbledon, where in the innocence of his heart he had originally brought her himself; in short he wanted her to put an end to their engagement in the only proper, the only happy manner.

'And why in the world doesn't she do so?' I inquired.

Adelaide hesitated. 'She says you know.' Then on my also hesitating she added: 'A condition he makes.'

'The Coxon Fund?' I cried.

'He has mentioned to her his having told you about it.'

'Ah, but so little! Do you mean she has accepted the trust?'

'In the most splendid spirit – as a duty about which there can be no two opinions.' Then said Adelaide after an instant: 'Of course she's thinking of Mr Saltram.'

I gave a quick cry at this, which, in its violence, made my visitor turn pale. 'How very awful!'

'Awful?'

'Why, to have anything to do with such an idea oneself.'

'I'm sure you needn't!' Mrs Mulville gave a slight toss of her head.

'He isn't good enough!' I went on; to which she responded with an ejaculation almost as lively as mine had been. This made me, with genuine, immediate horror, exclaim: 'You haven't influenced her, I hope!' and my emphasis brought back the blood with a rush to poor Adelaide's face. She declared while she blushed (for I had frightened her again) that she had never influenced anybody and that the girl had only seen and heard and judged for herself. *He* had influenced her, if I would, as he did every one who had a soul: that word, as we knew, even expressed feebly the power of the things he said to haunt the mind. How could she, Adelaide, help it if Miss Anvoy's mind was haunted? I demanded with a groan what right a pretty girl engaged to a rising M.P. had to *have* a mind; but the only explanation my bewildered friend could give me was that she was so clever. She regarded Mr Saltram naturally as a tremendous force for good. She was intelligent enough to understand him and generous enough to admire.

'She's many things enough, but is she, among them, rich enough?' I demanded. 'Rich enough, I mean, to sacrifice such a lot of good money?'

'That's for herself to judge. Besides, it's not her own money; she doesn't in the least consider it so.'

'And Gravener does, if not *his* own; and that's the whole difficulty?'

'The difficulty that brought her back, yes: she had absolutely to see her poor aunt's solicitor. It's clear that by Lady Coxon's will she may have the money, but it's still clearer to her conscience that the original condition, definite, intensely implied on her uncle's part, is attached to the use of it. She can only take one view of it. It's for the Endowment or it's for nothing.'

'The Endowment is a conception superficially sublime, but fundamentally ridiculous.'

'Are you repeating Mr Gravener's words?' Adelaide asked.

'Possibly, though I've not seen him for months. It's simply the way it strikes me too. It's an old wife's tale. Gravener made some reference to the legal aspect, but such an absurdly loose arrangement has no legal aspect.'

'Ruth doesn't insist on that,' said Mrs Mulville; 'and it's, for her, exactly this technical weakness that constitutes the force of the moral obligation.'

'Are you repeating her words?' I inquired. I forget what else Adelaide said, but she said she was magnificent. I thought of George Gravener confronted with such magnificence as that, and I asked what could have made two such people ever suppose they understood each other. Mrs Mulville assured me the girl loved him as such a woman could love and that she suffered as such a woman could suffer. Nevertheless she wanted to see me. At this I sprang up with a groan. 'Oh, I'm so sorry! – when?' Small though her sense of humour, I think Adelaide laughed at my tone. We discussed the day, the nearest it would be convenient I should come out; but before she went I asked my visitor how long she had been acquainted with these prodigies.

'For several weeks, but I was pledged to secrecy.'

'And that's why you didn't write?'

'I couldn't very well tell you she was with me without telling you that no time had even yet been fixed for her marriage. And I couldn't very well tell you as much as that without telling you what I knew of the reason of it. It was not till a day or two ago,' Mrs Mulville went on, 'that she asked me to ask you if you wouldn't come and see her. Then at last she said that you knew about the idea of the Endowment.'

I considered a little. 'Why on earth does she want to see me?'

'To talk with you, naturally, about Mr Saltram.'

'As a subject for the prize?' This was hugely obvious, and I presently exclaimed: 'I think I'll sail to-morrow for Australia.'

'Well then – sail!' said Mrs Mulville, getting up.

'On Thursday at five, we said?' I frivolously continued. The appointment was made definite and I inquired how, all this time, the unconscious candidate had carried himself.

'In perfection, really, by the happiest of chances: he has been a dear. And then, as to what we revere him for, in the most wonderful form. His very highest – pure celestial light. You *won't* do him an ill turn?' Adelaide pleaded at the door.

'What danger can equal for him the danger to which he is exposed from himself?' I asked. 'Look out sharp, if he has lately been decorous. He'll presently take a day off, treat us to some exhibition that will make an Endowment a scandal.'

'A scandal?' Mrs Mulville dolorously echoed.

'Is Miss Anvoy prepared for that?'

My visitor, for a moment, screwed her parasol into my carpet. 'He grows bigger every day.'

'So do you!' I laughed as she went off.

That girl at Wimbledon, on the Thursday afternoon, more than justified my apprehensions. I recognised fully now the cause of the agitation she had produced in me from the first – the faint foreknowledge that there was something very stiff I should have to do for her. I felt more than ever committed to my fate as, standing before her in the big drawing-room where they had tactfully left us to ourselves, I tried with a smile to string together the pearls of lucidity which, from her chair, she successively tossed me. Pale and bright, in her monotonous mourning, she was an image of intelligent purpose, of the passion of duty; but I asked myself whether any girl had ever had so charming an instinct as that which permitted her to laugh out, as if in the joy of her difficulty, into the priggish old room. This remarkable young woman could be earnest without being solemn, and at moments when I ought doubtless to have cursed her obstinacy I found myself watching the unstudied play of her eyebrows or the recurrence of a singularly intense whiteness produced by the parting of her lips. These aberrations, I hasten to add, didn't prevent my learning soon enough why she had wished to see me. Her reason for this was as distinct as her beauty: it was to make me explain what I had meant, on the occasion of our first meeting, by Mr Saltram's want of dignity. It wasn't that she couldn't imagine, but she desired it there from my lips. What she really desired of course was to know whether there was worse about him than what she had found out for herself. She hadn't been a month in the house with him, that way, without discovering that he wasn't a man of monumental bronze. He was like a jelly without a mould, he had to be embanked; and that was precisely the source of her interest in him and the ground of her project. She put her project boldly before me: there it stood in its preposterous beauty. She was as willing to take the humorous view of it as I could be: the only difference was that for her the humorous view of a thing was not necessarily prohibitive, was not paralysing.

Moreover she professed that she couldn't discuss with me the primary question – the moral obligation: that was in her own breast. There were things she couldn't go into – injunctions, impressions she had received. They were a part of the closest intimacy of her intercourse with her aunt, they were absolutely clear to her; and on questions of delicacy, the interpretation of a fidelity, of a promise, one had always in the last resort to make up one's mind for oneself. It was the idea of the application to the particular case, such a splendid one at last, that troubled her, and she admitted that it stirred very deep things. She didn't pretend that such a responsibility was a simple matter; if it had been she wouldn't have attempted to saddle me with any portion of it. The Mulvilles were sympathy itself; but were they absolutely candid? Could they indeed be, in their position – would it even have been to be desired? Yes, she had sent for me to ask no less than that of me – whether there was anything dreadful kept back. She made no allusion whatever to George Gravener – I thought her silence the only good taste and her gaiety perhaps a part of the very anxiety of that discretion, the effect of a determination that people shouldn't know from herself that her relations with the man she was to marry were strained. All the weight, however, that she left me to throw was a sufficient implication of the weight that he had thrown in vain. Oh, she knew the question of character was immense, and that one couldn't entertain any plan for making merit comfortable without running the gauntlet of that terrible procession of interrogation-points which, like a young ladies' school out for a walk, hooked their uniform

noses at the tail of governess Conduct. But were we absolutely
to hold that there was never, never, never an exception, never,
never, never an occasion for liberal acceptance, for clever charity, for suspended pedantry – for letting one side, in short,
outbalance another? When Miss Anvoy threw off this inquiry
I could have embraced her for so delightfully emphasising
her unlikeness to Mrs Saltram. 'Why not have the courage of
one's forgiveness,' she asked, 'as well as the enthusiasm of one's
adhesion?'

'Seeing how wonderfully you have threshed the whole thing
out,' I evasively replied, 'gives me an extraordinary notion of
the point your enthusiasm has reached.'

She considered this remark an instant with her eyes on mine,
and I divined that it struck her I might possibly intend it as a
reference to some personal subjection to our fat philosopher, to
some aberration of sensibility, some perversion of taste. At least
I couldn't interpret otherwise the sudden flush that came into
her face. Such a manifestation, as the result of any word of
mine, embarrassed me; but while I was thinking how to reassure her the flush passed away in a smile of exquisite good-
nature. 'Oh, you see, one forgets so wonderfully how one
dislikes him!' she said; and if her tone simply extinguished his
strange figure with the brush of its compassion, it also rings in
my ear to-day as the purest of all our praises. But with what
quick response of compassion such a relegation of the man
himself made me privately sigh, 'Ah, poor Saltram!' She
instantly, with this, took the measure of all I didn't believe,
and it enabled her to go on: 'What can one do when a person
has given such a lift to one's interest in life?'

'Yes, what can one do?' If I struck her as a little vague it was
because I was thinking of another person. I indulged in another
inarticulate murmur – 'Poor George Gravener!' What had
become of the lift *he* had given that interest? Later on I made
up my mind that she was sore and stricken at the appearance he
presented of wanting the miserable money. This was the hidden reason of her alienation. The probable sincerity, in spite of
the illiberality, of his scruples about the particular use of it
under discussion didn't efface the ugliness of his demand that

they should buy a good house with it. Then, as for *his* alienation, he didn't, pardonably enough, grasp the lift Frank Saltram had given her interest in life. If a mere spectator could ask
that last question, with what rage in his heart the man himself
might! He was not, like her, I was to see, too proud to show me
why he was disappointed.

XI

I WAS unable, this time, to stay to dinner: such, at any rate, was
the plea on which I took leave. I desired in truth to get away
from my young lady, for that obviously helped me not to pretend to satisfy her. How *could* I satisfy her? I asked myself – how
could I tell her how much had been kept back? I didn't even
know, and I certainly didn't desire to know. My own policy had
ever been to learn the least about poor Saltram's weaknesses –
not to learn the most. A great deal that I had in fact learned had
been forced upon me by his wife. There was something even
irritating in Miss Anvoy's crude conscientiousness, and I wondered why, after all, she couldn't have let him alone and been
content to entrust George Gravener with the purchase of the
good house. I was sure he would have driven a bargain, got
something excellent and cheap. I laughed louder even than she,
I temporised, I failed her; I told her I must think over her case.
I professed a horror of responsibilities and twitted her with her
own extravagant passion for them. It was not really that I was
afraid of the scandal, the moral discredit for the Fund; what
troubled me most was a feeling of a different order. Of course, as
the beneficiary of the Fund was to enjoy a simple life-interest,
as it was hoped that new beneficiaries would arise and come up
to new standards, it would not be a trifle that the first of these
worthies should not have been a striking example of the domestic virtues. The Fund would start badly, as it were, and the
laurel would, in some respects at least, scarcely be greener from
the brows of the original wearer. That idea, however, was at that
hour, as I have hinted, not the source of anxiety it ought
perhaps to have been, for I felt less the irregularity of Saltram's
getting the money than that of this exalted young woman's

giving it up. I wanted her to have it for herself, and I told her so before I went away. She looked graver at this than she had looked at all, saying she hoped such a preference wouldn't make me dishonest.

It made me, to begin with, very restless – made me, instead of going straight to the station, fidget a little about that many coloured Common which gives Wimbledon horizons. There was a worry for me to work off, or rather keep at a distance, for I declined even to admit to myself that I had, in Miss Anvoy's phrase, been saddled with it. What could have been clearer indeed than the attitude of recognising perfectly what a world of trouble the Coxon Fund would in future save us, and of yet liking better to face a continuance of that trouble than see, and in fact contribute to, a deviation from attainable bliss in the life of two other persons in whom I was deeply interested? Suddenly, at the end of twenty minutes, there was projected across this clearness the image of a massive, middle-aged man seated on a bench, under a tree, with sad, far-wandering eyes and plump white hands folded on the head of a stick – a stick I recognised, a stout gold-headed staff that I had given him in throbbing days. I stopped short as he turned his face to me, and it happened that for some reason or other I took in as I had perhaps never done before the beauty of his rich blank gaze. It was charged with experience as the sky is charged with light, and I felt on the instant as if we had been overspanned and conjoined by the great arch of a bridge or the great dome of a temple. Doubtless I was rendered peculiarly sensitive to it by something in the way I had been giving him up and sinking him. While I met it I stood there smitten, and I felt myself responding to it with a sort of guilty grimace. This brought back his attention in a smile which expressed for me a cheerful, weary patience, a bruised, noble gentleness. I had told Miss Anvoy that he had no dignity, but what did he seem to me, all unbuttoned and fatigued as he waited for me to come up, if he didn't seem unconcerned with small things, didn't seem in short majestic? There was majesty in his mere unconsciousness of our little conferences and puzzlements over his maintenance and his reward.

After I had sat by him a few minutes I passed my arm over his big soft shoulder (wherever you touched him you found equally little firmness) and said in a tone of which the suppliance fell oddly on my own ear: 'Come back to town with me, old friend – come back and spend the evening.' I wanted to hold him, I wanted to keep him, and at Waterloo, an hour later, I tele-graphed possessively to the Mulvilles. When he objected, as regards staying all night, that he had no things, I asked him if he hadn't everything of mine. I had abstained from ordering din-ner, and it was too late for preliminaries at a club; so we were reduced to tea and fried fish at my rooms – reduced also to the transcendent. Something had come up which made me want him to feel at peace with me, which was all the dear man himself wanted on any occasion. I had too often had to press upon him considerations irrelevant, but it gives me pleasure now to think that on that particular evening I didn't even mention Mrs Salt-ram and the children. Late into the night we smoked and talked; old shames and old rigours fell away from us; I only let him see that I was conscious of what I owed him. He was as mild as contrition and as abundant as faith; he was never so fine as on a shy return, and even better at forgiving than at being forgiven. I daresay it was a smaller matter than that famous night at Wimbledon, the night of the problematical sobriety and of Miss Anvoy's initiation; but I was as much in it on this occasion as I had been out of it then. At about 1.30 he was sublime.

He never, under any circumstances, rose till all other risings were over, and his breakfasts, at Wimbledon, had always been the principal reason mentioned by departing cooks. The coast was therefore clear for me to receive her when, early the next morning, to my surprise, it was announced to me that his wife had called. I hesitated, after she had come up, about telling her Saltram was in the house, but she herself settled the question, kept me reticent by drawing forth a sealed letter which, looking at me very hard in the eyes, she placed, with a pregnant absence of comment, in my hand. For a single moment there glimmered before me the fond hope that Mrs Saltram had tendered me, as it were, her resignation and desired to embody the act in an unsparing form. To bring this about I would have feigned any humiliation; but after my eyes had caught the superscription I heard myself say with a flatness that betrayed a sense of something very different from relief: 'Oh, the Pudneys!' I knew their envelopes though they didn't know mine. They always used the kind sold at post-offices with the stamp affixed, and as this letter had not been posted they had wasted a penny on me. I had seen their horrid missives to the Mulvilles, but had not been in direct correspondence with them.

'They enclosed it to me, to be delivered. They doubtless explain to you that they hadn't your address.'

I turned the thing over without opening it. 'Why in the world should they write to me?'

'Because they have something to tell you. The worst,' Mrs Saltram dryly added.

It was another chapter, I felt, of the history of their lamentable quarrel with her husband, the episode in which, vindictively, disingenuously as they themselves had behaved, one had to admit that he had put himself more grossly in the wrong than at any moment of his life. He had begun by insulting the matchless Mulvilles for these more specious protectors, and then, according to his wont at the end of a few months, had dug a still deeper ditch for his aberration than the chasm left yawning behind. The chasm at Wimbledon was now blessedly closed; but the Pudneys, across their persistent gulf, kept up the nastiest fire. I never doubted they had a strong case, and I had been from the first for not defending him – reasoning that if they were not contradicted they would perhaps subside. This was above all what I wanted, and I so far prevailed that I did arrest the correspondence in time to save our little circle an infliction heavier than it perhaps would have borne. I knew, that is I divined, that their allegations had gone as yet only as far as their courage, conscious as they were in their own virtue of an exposed place in which Saltram could have planted a blow. It was a question with them whether a man who had himself so much to cover up would dare his blow; so that these vessels of rancour were in a manner afraid of each other. I judged that on the day the Pudneys should cease for some reason or other to be afraid they would treat us to some revelation more disconcerting than any of its predecessors. As I held Mr Pudney's letter in my hand it was distinctly communicated to me that the day had come – they had ceased to be afraid. 'I don't want to know the worst,' I presently declared.

'You'll have to open the letter. It also contains an enclosure.'

I felt it – it was fat and uncanny. 'Wheels within wheels!' I exclaimed. 'There is something for me too to deliver.'

'So they tell me – to Miss Anvoy.'

I stared; I felt a certain thrill. 'Why don't they send it to her directly?'

Mrs Saltram hesitated. 'Because she's staying with Mr and Mrs Mulville.'

'And why should that prevent?'

Again my visitor faltered, and I began to reflect on the grotesque, the unconscious perversity of her action. I was the only person save George Gravener and the Mulvilles who was aware of Sir Gregory Coxon's and of Miss Anvoy's strange bounty. Where could there have been a more signal illustration of the clumsiness of human affairs than her having complacently selected this moment to fly in the face of it? 'There's the chance of their seeing her letters. They know Mr Pudney's hand.'

Still I didn't understand; then it flashed upon me. 'You mean they might intercept it? How can you imply anything so base?' I indignantly demanded.

'It's not I; it's Mr Pudney!' cried Mrs Saltram with a flush. 'It's his own idea.'

'Then why couldn't he send the letter to *you* to be delivered?'

Mrs Saltram's embarrassment increased; she gave me another hard look. 'You must make that out for yourself.'

I made it out quickly enough. 'It's a denunciation?'

'A real lady doesn't betray her husband!' this virtuous woman exclaimed.

I burst out laughing, and I fear my laugh may have had an effect of impertinence.

'Especially to Miss Anvoy, who's so easily shocked? Why do such things concern *her*?' I asked, much at a loss.

'Because she's there, exposed to all his craft. Mr and Mrs Pudney have been watching this: they feel she may be taken in.'

'Thank you for all the rest of us! What difference can it make when she has lost her power to contribute?'

Again Mrs Saltram considered; then very nobly, 'There are other things in the world than money,' she remarked. This hadn't occurred to her so long as the young lady had any; but she now added, with a glance at my letter, that Mr and Mrs Pudney doubtless explained their motives. 'It's all in kindness,' she continued as she got up.

'Kindness to Miss Anvoy? You took, on the whole, another view of kindness before her reverses.'

My companion smiled with some acidity. 'Perhaps you're no safer than the Mulvilles!'

I didn't want her to think that, nor that she should report to the Pudneys that they had not been happy in their agent; and I well remember that this was the moment at which I began, with considerable emotion, to promise myself to enjoin upon Miss Anvoy never to open any letter that should come to her in one of those penny envelopes. My emotion and I fear I must add my confusion quickly deepened; I presently should have been as glad to frighten Mrs Saltram as to think I might by some diplomacy restore the Pudneys to a quieter vigilance.

'It's best you should take *my* view of my safety,' I at any rate soon responded. When I saw she didn't know what I meant by this I added: 'You may turn out to have done, in bringing me this letter, a thing you will profoundly regret.' My tone had a significance which, I could see, did make her uneasy, and there was a moment, after I had made two or three more remarks of studiously bewildering effect, at which her eyes followed so hungrily the little flourish of the letter with which I emphasised them that I instinctively slipped Mr Pudney's communication into my pocket. She looked, in her embarrassed annoyance, as if she might grab it and send it back to him. I felt, after she had gone, as if I had almost given her my word I wouldn't deliver the enclosure. The passionate movement, at any rate, with which, in solitude, I transferred the whole thing, unopened, from my pocket to a drawer which I double-locked would have amounted for an initiated observer to some such promise.

XII

MRS SALTRAM left me drawing my breath more quickly and indeed almost in pain – as if I had just perilously grazed the loss of something precious. I didn't quite know what it was – it had a shocking resemblance to my honour. The emotion was the livelier doubtless in that my pulses were still shaken with the rejoicing with which, the night before, I had rallied to the rare analyst, the great intellectual adventurer and pathfinder. What had dropped from me like a cumbersome garment as Saltram appeared before me in the afternoon on the heath was the disposition to haggle over his value. Hang it, one had to choose, one had to put that value somewhere; so I would put it really high and have done with it. Mrs Mulville drove in for him at a discreet hour – the earliest she could suppose him to have got up; and I learned that Miss Anvoy would also have come had she not been expecting a visit from Mr Gravener. I was perfectly mindful that I was under bonds to see this young lady, and also that I had a letter to deliver to her; but I took my time, I waited from day to day. I left Mrs Saltram to deal as her apprehensions should prompt with the Pudneys. I knew at last what I meant – I had ceased to wince at my responsibility. I gave this supreme impression of Saltram time to fade if it would; but it didn't fade, and, individually, it has not faded even now. During the month that I thus invited myself to stiffen again, Adelaide Mulville, perplexed by my absence, wrote to me to ask why I *was* so stiff. At that season of the year I was usually oftener with them. She also wrote that she feared a real estrangement had set in between Mr Gravener and her sweet young friend – a state of things only partly satisfactory to her so long as the advantage accruing to Mr Saltram failed to disengage itself from the merely nebulous state. She intimated that her sweet young friend was, if anything, a trifle too reserved; she also intimated that there might now be an opening for another clever young man. There never was the slightest opening, I may here parenthesise, and of course the question can't come up to-day. These are old frustrations now. Ruth Anvoy has not married, I hear, and neither have I. During the month, toward the end, I wrote to George Gravener to ask if, on a special errand, I might come to see him, and his answer was to knock the very next day at my door. I saw he had immediately connected my inquiry with the talk we had had in the railway-carriage, and his promptitude showed that the ashes of his eagerness were not yet cold. I told him there was something I thought I ought in candour to let him know – I recognised the obligation his friendly confidence had laid upon me.

'You mean that Miss Anvoy has talked to you? She has told me so herself,' he said.

'It was not to tell you so that I wanted to see you,' I replied; 'for it seemed to me that such a communication would rest wholly with herself. If however she did speak to you of our conversation she probably told you I was discouraging.'

'Discouraging?'

'On the subject of a present application of the Coxon Fund.'

'To the case of Mr Saltram? My dear fellow, I don't know what you call discouraging!' Gravener exclaimed.

'Well I thought I was, and I thought she thought I was.'

'I believe she did, but such a thing is measured by the effect. She's not discouraged.'

'That's her own affair. The reason I asked you to see me was that it appeared to me I ought to tell you frankly that decidedly I can't undertake to produce that effect. In fact I don't want to!'

'It's very good of you, damn you!' my visitor laughed, red and really grave. Then he said: 'You would like to see that fellow publicly glorified – perched on the pedestal of a great complimentary fortune?'

'Taking one form of public recognition with another, it seems to me on the whole I could bear it. When I see the compliments that *are* paid right and left, I ask myself why this one shouldn't take its course. This therefore is what you're entitled to have looked to me to mention to you. I have some evidence that perhaps would be really dissuasive, but I propose to invite Miss Anvoy to remain in ignorance of it.'

'And to invite me to do the same?'

'Oh, you don't require it – you've evidence enough. I speak of a sealed letter which I've been requested to deliver to her.'

'And you don't mean to?'

'There's only one consideration that would make me.'

Gravener's clear, handsome eyes plunged into mine a minute, but evidently without fishing up a clue to this motive – a failure by which I was almost wounded. 'What does the letter contain?'

'It's sealed, as I tell you, and I don't know what it contains.'

'Why is it sent through you?'

'Rather than you?' I hesitated a moment. 'The only explanation I can think of is that the person sending it may have imagined your relations with Miss Anvoy to be at an end – may have been told this is the case by Mrs Saltram.'

'My relations with Miss Anvoy are not at an end,' poor Gravener stammered.

Again, for an instant, I deliberated. 'The offer I propose to make you gives me the right to put you a question remarkably direct. Are you still engaged to Miss Anvoy?'

'No, I'm not,' he slowly brought out. 'But we're perfectly good friends.'

'Such good friends that you will again become prospective husband and wife if the obstacle in your path be removed?'

'Removed?' Gravener anxiously repeated.

'If I give Miss Anvoy the letter I speak of she may drop her project.'

'Then for God's sake give it!'

'I'll do so if you're ready to assure me that her dropping it would now presumably bring about your marriage.'

'I'd marry her the next day!' my visitor cried.

'Yes, but would she marry you? What I ask of you of course is nothing less than your word of honour as to your conviction of this. If you give it me,' I said, 'I'll engage to hand her the letter before night.'

Gravener took up his hat; turning it mechanically round, he stood looking a moment hard at its unruffled perfection. Then, very angrily, honestly and gallantly: 'Hand it to the devil!'

he broke out; with which he clapped the hat on his head and left me.

'Will you read it or not?' I said to Ruth Anvoy, at Wimbledon, when I had told her the story of Mrs Saltram's visit.

She reflected for a period which was probably of the briefest, but which was long enough to make me nervous. 'Have you brought it with you?'

'No indeed. It's at home, locked up.'

There was another great silence, and then she said: 'Go back and destroy it.'

I went back, but I didn't destroy it till after Saltram's death, when I burnt it unread. The Pudneys approached her again pressingly, but, prompt as they were, the Coxon Fund had already become an operative benefit and a general amaze: Mr Saltram, while we gathered about, as it were, to watch the manna descend, was already drawing the magnificent income. He drew it as he had always drawn everything, with a grand abstracted gesture. Its magnificence, alas, as all the world now knows, quite quenched him; it was the beginning of his decline. It was also naturally a new grievance for his wife, who began to believe in him as soon as he was blighted, and who at this hour accuses us of having bribed him, on the whim of a meddlesome American, to renounce his glorious office, to become, as she says, like everybody else. The very day he found himself able to publish he wholly ceased to produce. This deprived us, as may easily be imagined, of much of our occupation, and especially deprived the Mulvilles, whose want of self-support I never measured till they lost their great inmate. They have no one to live on now. Adelaide's most frequent reference to their destitution is embodied in the remark that dear far-away Ruth's intentions were doubtless good. She and Kent are even yet looking for another prop, but no one presents a true sphere of usefulness. They complain that people are self-sufficing. With Saltram the fine type of the child of adoption was scattered, the grander, the elder style. They have got their carriage back, but what's an empty carriage? In short I think we were all happier as well as poorer before; even including George Gravener, who, by the deaths of his brother and his nephew, has lately become

Lord Maddock. His wife, whose fortune clears the property, is criminally dull; he hates being in the upper House, and he has not yet had high office. But what are these accidents, which I should perhaps apologise for mentioning, in the light of the great eventual boon promised the patient by the rate at which the Coxon Fund must be rolling up?

THE NEXT TIME

MRS HIGHMORE'S errand this morning was odd enough to deserve commemoration: she came to ask me to write a notice of her great forthcoming work. Her great works have come forth so frequently without my assistance that I was sufficiently entitled on this occasion to open my eyes; but what really made me stare was the ground on which her request reposed, and what leads me to record the incident is the train of memory lighted by that explanation. Poor Ray Limbert, while we talked, seemed to sit there between us: she reminded me that my acquaintance with him had begun, eighteen years ago, with her having come in precisely as she came in this morning to bespeak my charity for him. If she didn't know then how little my charity was worth she is at least enlightened about it to-day, and this is just the circumstance that makes the drollery of her visit. As I hold up the torch to the dusky years – by which I mean as I cipher up with a pen that stumbles and stops the figured column of my reminiscences – I see that Limbert's public hour, or at least my small apprehension of it, is rounded by those two occasions. It was *finis*, with a little moralising flourish, that Mrs Highmore seemed to trace to-day at the bottom of the page. 'One of the most voluminous writers of the time,' she has often repeated this sign; but never, I daresay, in spite of her professional command of appropriate emotion, with an equal sense of that mystery and that sadness of things which to people of imagination generally hover over the close of human histories. This romance at any rate is bracketed by her early and her late appeal; and when its melancholy protrusions had caught the declining light again from my half-hour's talk with her I took a private vow to recover while that light still lingers something of the delicate flush, to pick out with a brief patience the perplexing lesson.

It was wonderful to observe how for herself Mrs Highmore had already done so: she wouldn't have hesitated to announce

223

to me what was the matter with Ralph Limbert, or at all events to give me a glimpse of the high admonition she had read in his career. There could have been no better proof of the vividness of this parable, which we were really in our pleasant sympathy quite at one about, than that Mrs Highmore, of all hardened sinners, should have been converted. This indeed was not news to me: she impressed upon me that for the last ten years she had wanted to do something artistic, something as to which she was prepared not to care a rap whether or no it should sell. She brought home to me further that it had been mainly seeing what her brother-in-law did and how he did it that had wedded her to this perversity. As *he* didn't sell dear soul, and as several persons, of whom I was one, thought highly of that, the fancy had taken her – taken her even quite early in her prolific course – of reaching, if only once, the same heroic eminence. She yearned to be, like Limbert, but of course only once, an exquisite failure. There was something a failure was, a failure in the market, that a success somehow wasn't. A success was as prosaic as a good dinner: there was nothing more to be said about it than that you had had it. Who but vulgar people, in such a case, made gloating remarks about the courses? It was often by such vulgar people that a success was attested. It made if you came to look at it nothing but money; that is it made so much that any other result showed small in comparison. A failure now could make – oh, with the aid of immense talent of course, for there were failures and failures – such a reputation! She did me the honour – she had often done it – to intimate that what she meant by reputation was seeing *me* toss a flower. If it took a failure to catch a failure I was by my own admission well qualified to place the laurel. It was because she had made so much money and Mr Highmore had taken such care of it that she could treat herself to an hour of pure glory. She perfectly remembered that as often as I had heard her heave that sigh I had been prompt with my declaration that a book sold might easily be as glorious as a book unsold. Of course she knew this, but she knew also that it was the age of trash triumphant and that she had never heard me speak of anything that had 'done well' exactly as she had sometimes heard me speak of something that hadn't – with just two or three words of respect which, when I used them, seemed to convey more than they commonly stood for, seemed to hush up the discussion a little, as if for the very beauty of the secret.

I may declare in regard to these allusions that, whatever I then thought of myself as a holder of the scales I had never scrupled to laugh out at the humour of Mrs Highmore's pursuit of quality at any price. It had never rescued her even for a day from the hard doom of popularity, and though I never gave her my word for it there was no reason at all why it should. The public *would* have her, as her husband used roguishly to remark; not indeed that, making her bargains, standing up to her publishers and even, in his higher flights, to her reviewers, he ever had a glimpse of her attempted conspiracy against her genius, or rather as I may say against mine. It was not that when she tried to be what she called subtle (for wasn't Limbert subtle, and wasn't I?) her fond consumers, bless them, didn't suspect the trick nor show what they thought of it: they straightway rose on the contrary to the morsel she had hoped to hold too high, and, making but a big, cheerful bite of it, wagged their great collective tail artlessly for more. It was not given to her not to please, nor granted even to her best refinements to affright. I have always respected the mystery of those humiliations, but I was fully aware this morning that they were practically the reason why she had come to me. Therefore when she said with the flush of a bold joke in her kind, coarse face, 'What I feel is, you know, that *you* could settle me if you only would,' I knew quite well what she meant. She meant that of old it had always appeared to be the fine blade, as some one had hyperbolically called it, of my particular opinion that snapped the silken thread by which Limbert's chance in the market was wont to hang. She meant that my favour was compromising, that my praise indeed was fatal. I had made myself a little speciality of seeing nothing in certain celebrities, of seeing overmuch in an occasional nobody, and of judging from a point of view that, say what I would for it (and I had a monstrous deal to say) remained perverse and obscure. Mine was in short the love that killed, for my subtlety, unlike Mrs Highmore's, produced

no tremor of the public tail. She had not forgotten how, toward
the end, when his case was worst, Limbert would absolutely
come to me with a funny, shy pathos in his eyes and say: 'My
dear fellow, I think I've done it this time, if you'll only keep
quiet.' If my keeping quiet in those days was to help him to
appear to have hit the usual taste, for the want of which he was
starving, so now my breaking out was to help Mrs Highmore to
appear to have hit the unusual.

The moral of all this was that I had frightened the public too
much for our late friend, but that as she was not starving this was
exactly what her grosser reputation required. And then, she
good-naturedly and delicately intimated, there would always
be, if further reasons were wanting, the price of my clever little
article. I think she gave that hint with a flattering impression –
spoiled child of the booksellers as she is – that the price of my
clever little articles is high. Whatever it is, at any rate, she had
evidently reflected that poor Limbert's anxiety for his own profit
used to involve my sacrificing mine. Any inconvenience that my
obliging her might entail would not in fine be pecuniary. Her
appeal, her motive, her fantastic thirst for quality and her ingenious theory of my influence struck me all as excellent comedy,
and when I consented contingently to oblige her she left me the
sheets of her new novel. I could plead no inconvenience and have
been looking them over; but I am frankly appalled at what she
expects of me. What is she thinking of, poor dear, and what has
put it into her head that 'quality' has descended upon her? Why
does she suppose that she has been 'artistic'? She hasn't been
anything whatever, I surmise, that she has not inveterately been.
What does she imagine she has left out? What does she conceive
she has put in? She has neither left out nor put in anything. I shall
have to write her an embarrassed note. The book doesn't exist,
and there's nothing in life to say about it. How can there be
anything but the same old faithful rush for it?

I

THIS rush had already begun when, early in the seventies, in
the interest of her prospective brother-in-law, she approached

me on the singular ground of the unencouraged sentiment I had entertained for her sister. Pretty pink Maud had cast me out, but I appear to have passed in the flurried little circle for a magnanimous youth. Pretty pink Maud, so lovely then, before her troubles, that dusky Jane was gratefully conscious of all she made up for, Maud Stannace, very literary too, very languishing and extremely bullied by her mother, had yielded, invidiously as it might have struck me, to Ray Limbert's suit, which Mrs Stannace was not the woman to stomach. Mrs Stannace was seldom the woman to do anything: she had been shocked at the way her children, with the grubby taint of their father's blood (he had published pale Remains or flat Conversations of *his* father) breathed the alien air of authorship. If not the daughter, nor even the niece, she was, if I am not mistaken, the second cousin of a hundred earls and a great stickler for relationship, so that she had other views for her brilliant child, especially after her quiet one (such had been her original discreet forecast of the producer of eighty volumes) became the second wife of an ex-army-surgeon, already the father of four children. Mrs Stannace had too manifestly dreamed it would be given to pretty pink Maud to detach some one of the hundred, who wouldn't be missed, from the cluster. It was because she cared only for cousins that I unlearnt the way to her house, which she had once reminded me was one of the few paths of gentility I could hope to tread. Ralph Limbert, who belonged to nobody and had done nothing – nothing even at Cambridge – had only the uncanny spell he had cast upon her younger daughter to recommend him; but if her younger daughter had a spark of filial feeling she wouldn't commit the indecency of deserting for his sake a deeply dependent and intensely aggravated mother.

These things I learned from Jane Highmore, who, as if her books had been babies (they remained her only ones), had waited till after marriage to show what she could do and now bade fair to surround her satisfied spouse (he took, for some mysterious reason, a part of the credit) with a little family, in sets of triplets, which properly handled would be the support of his declining years. The young couple, neither of whom had a

penny, were now virtually engaged: the thing was subject to
Ralph's putting his hand on some regular employment. People
more enamoured couldn't be conceived, and Mrs Highmore,
honest woman, who had moreover a professional sense for a
love-story, was eager to take them under her wing. What was
wanted was a decent opening for Limbert, which it had
occurred to her I might assist her to find, though indeed I had
not yet found any such matter for myself. But it was well known
that I was too particular, whereas poor Ralph, with the easy
manners of genius, was ready to accept almost anything to
which a salary, even a small one, was attached. If he could
only for instance get a place on a newspaper the rest of his
maintenance would come freely enough. It was true that his
two novels, one of which she had brought to leave with me, had
passed unperceived and that to her, Mrs Highmore personally,
they didn't irresistibly appeal; but she could all the same assure
me that I should have only to spend ten minutes with him (and
our encounter must speedily take place) to receive an impression of latent power.

Our encounter took place soon after I had read the volumes
Mrs Highmore had left with me, in which I recognised an
intention of a sort that I had then pretty well given up the
hope of meeting. I daresay that without knowing it I had been
looking out rather hungrily for an altar of sacrifice: however
that may be I submitted when I came across Ralph Limbert to
one of the rarest emotions of my literary life, the sense of an
activity in which I could critically rest. The rest was deep and
salutary, and it has not been disturbed to this hour. It has been a
long, large surrender, the luxury of dropped discriminations.
He couldn't trouble me, whatever he did, for I practically
enjoyed him as much when he was worse as when he was better.
It was a case, I suppose, of natural prearrangement, in which,
I hasten to add, I keep excellent company. We are a numerous
band, partakers of the same repose, who sit together in the
shade of the tree, by the plash of the fountain, with the glare
of the desert around us and no great vice that I know of but the
habit perhaps of estimating people a little too much by what
they think of a certain style. If it had been laid upon these few

pages, none the less, to be the history of an enthusiasm, I should not have undertaken them: they are concerned with Ralph Limbert in relations to which I was a stranger or in which I participated only by sympathy. I used to talk about his work, but I seldom talk now: the brotherhood of the faith have become, like the Trappists, a silent order. If to the day of his death, after mortal disenchantments, the impression he first produced always evoked the word 'ingenuous', those to whom his face was familiar can easily imagine what it must have been when it still had the light of youth. I had never seen a man of genius look so passive, a man of experience so off his guard. At the period I made his acquaintance this freshness was all unbrushed. His foot had begun to stumble, but he was full of big intentions and of sweet Maud Stannace. Black-haired and pale, deceptively languid, he had the eyes of a clever child and the voice of a bronze bell. He saw more even than I had done in the girl he was engaged to; as time went on I became conscious that we had both, properly enough, seen rather more than there was. Our odd situation, that of the three of us, became perfectly possible from the moment I observed that he had more patience with her than I should have had. I was happy at not having to supply this quantity, and she, on her side, found pleasure in being able to be impertinent to me without incurring the reproach of a bad wife.

Limbert's novels appeared to have brought him no money: they had only brought him, so far as I could then make out, tributes that took up his time. These indeed brought him from several quarters some other things, and on my part at the end of three months *The Blackport Beacon*. I don't to-day remember how I obtained for him the London correspondence of the great northern organ, unless it was through somebody's having obtained it for myself. I seem to recall that I got rid of it in Limbert's interest, persuaded the editor that he was much the better man. The better man was naturally the man who had pledged himself to support a charming wife. We were neither of us good, as the event proved, but he had a finer sort of badness. *The Blackport Beacon* had two London correspondents – one a supposed haunter of political circles, the other a votary of

questions sketchily classified as literary. They were both
expected to be lively, and what was held out to each was that
it was honourably open to him to be livelier than the other.
I recollect the political correspondent of that period and how
the problem offered to Ray Limbert was to try to be livelier than
Pat Moyle. He had not yet seemed to me so candid as when he
undertook this exploit, which brought matters to a head with
Mrs Stannace, inasmuch as her opposition to the marriage now
logically fell to the ground. It's all tears and laughter as I look
back upon that admirable time, in which nothing was so
romantic as our intense vision of the real. No fool's paradise
ever rustled such a cradle-song. It was anything but Bohemia –
it was the very temple of Mrs Grundy. We knew we were too
critical, and that made us sublimely indulgent; we believed we
did our duty or wanted to, and that made us free to dream. But
we dreamed over the multiplication-table; we were nothing if
not practical. Oh, the long smokes and sudden ideas, the knowing hints and banished scruples! The great thing was for Limbert to bring out his next book, which was just what his
delightful engagement with the *Beacon* would give him leisure
and liberty to do. The kind of work, all human and elastic and
suggestive, was capital experience: in picking up things for his
bi-weekly letter he would pick up life as well, he would pick up
literature. The new publications, the new pictures, the new
people – there would be nothing too novel for us and nobody
too sacred. We introduced everything and everybody into Mrs
Stannace's drawing-room, of which I again became a familiar.

Mrs Stannace, it was true, thought herself in strange company; she didn't particularly mind the new books, though some
of them seemed queer enough, but to the new people she had
decided objections. It was notorious however that poor Lady
Robeck secretly wrote for one of the papers, and the thing had
certainly, in its glance at the doings of the great world, a side
that might be made attractive. But we were going to make every
side attractive and we had everything to say about the sort of
thing a paper like the *Beacon* would want. To give it what it
would want and to give it nothing else was not doubtless an
inspiring, but it was a perfectly respectable task, especially for a

man with an appealing bride and a contentious mother-in-law.
I thought Limbert's first letters as charming as the type
allowed, though I won't deny that in spite of my sense of the
importance of concessions I was just a trifle disconcerted at
the way he had caught the tone. The tone was of course to be
caught, but need it have been caught so in the act? The creature
was even cleverer, as Maud Stannace said, than she had ventured to hope. Verily it was a good thing to have a dose of the
wisdom of the serpent. If it had to be journalism – well, it *was*
journalism. If he had to be 'chatty' – well, he *was* chatty. Now
and then he made a hit that – it was stupid of me – brought the
blood to my face. I hated him to be so personal; but still, if it
would make his fortune—! It wouldn't of course directly, but
the book would, practically and in the sense to which our pure
ideas of fortune were confined; and these things were all for the
book. The daily balm meanwhile was in what one knew of
the book – there were exquisite things to know; in the quiet
monthly cheques from Blackport and in the deeper rose of
Maud's little preparations, which were as dainty, on their tiny
scale, as if she had been a humming-bird building a nest. When
at the end of three months her betrothed had fairly settled down
to his correspondence – in which Mrs Highmore was the only
person, so far as we could discover, disappointed, even she
moreover being in this particular tortuous and possibly jealous;
when the situation had assumed such a comfortable shape it
was quite time to prepare. I published at that moment my first
volume, mere faded ink to-day, a little collection of literary
impressions, odds and ends of criticism contributed to a journal less remunerative but also less chatty than the *Beacon*, small
ironies and ecstasies, great phrases and mistakes; and the very
week it came out poor Limbert devoted half of one of his letters
to it, with the happy sense this time of gratifying both himself
and me as well as the Blackport breakfast-tables. I remember
his saying it wasn't literature, the stuff, superficial stuff, he had
to write about me; but what did that matter if it came back, as
we knew, to the making for literature in the round-about way?
I sold the thing, I remember, for ten pounds, and with the
money I bought in Vigo Street a quaint piece of old silver for

Maud Stannace, which I carried to her with my own hand as a wedding-gift. In her mother's small drawing-room, a faded bower of photography fenced in and bedimmed by folding screens out of which sallow persons of fashion with dashing signatures looked at you from retouched eyes and little windows of plush, I was left to wait long enough to feel in the air of the house a hushed vibration of disaster. When our young lady came in she was very pale and her eyes too had been retouched.

'Something horrid has happened,' I immediately said; and having really all along but half believed in her mother's meagre permission I risked with an unguarded groan the introduction of Mrs Stannace's name.

'Yes, she has made a dreadful scene; she insists on our putting it off again. We're very unhappy: poor Ray has been turned off.' Her tears began to flow again.

I had such a good conscience that I stared. 'Turned off what?'

'Why, his paper of course. The *Beacon* has given him what he calls the sack. They don't like his letters: they're not the style of thing they want.'

My blankness could only deepen. 'Then what style of thing *do* they want?'

'Something more chatty.'

'More?' I cried, aghast.

'More gossipy, more personal. They want "journalism". They want tremendous trash.'

'Why, that's just what his letters have *been*!' I broke out.

This was strong, and I caught myself up, but the girl offered me the pardon of a beautiful wan smile. 'So Ray himself declares. He says he has stooped so low.'

'Very well – he must stoop lower. He *must* keep the place.'

'He can't!' poor Maud wailed. 'He says he has tried all he knows, has been abject, has gone on all fours, and that if they don't like that—'

'He accepts his dismissal?' I interposed in dismay.

She gave a tragic shrug. 'What other course is open to him? He wrote to them that such work as he has done is the very worst he can do for the money.'

'Therefore,' I inquired with a flash of hope, 'they'll offer him more for worse?'

'No indeed,' she answered, 'they haven't even offered him to go on at a reduction. He isn't funny enough.'

I reflected a moment. 'But surely such a thing as his notice of my book—!'

'It was your wretched book that was the last straw! He should have treated it superficially.'

'Well, if he didn't—!' I began. Then I checked myself. '*Je vous porte malheur.*'

She didn't deny this; she only went on: 'What on earth is he to do?'

'He's to do better than the monkeys! He's to write!'

'But what on earth are we to marry on?'

I considered once more. 'You're to marry on *The Major Key.*'

II

The Major Key was the new novel, and the great thing accordingly was to finish it; a consummation for which three months of the *Beacon* had in some degree prepared the way. The action of that journal was indeed a shock, but I didn't know then the worst, didn't know that in addition to being a shock it was also a symptom. It was the first hint of the difficulty to which poor Limbert was eventually to succumb. His state was the happier of a truth for his not immediately seeing all that it meant. Difficulty was the law of life, but one could thank heaven it was exceptionally present in that horrid quarter. There was the difficulty that inspired, the difficulty of *The Major Key* to wit, which it was after all base to sacrifice to the turning of somersaults for pennies. These convictions Ray Limbert beguiled his fresh wait by blandly entertaining: not indeed, I think, that the failure of his attempt to be chatty didn't leave him slightly humiliated. If it was bad enough to have grinned through a horse-collar it was very bad indeed to have grinned in vain. Well, he would try no more grinning or at least no more horse-collars. The only success worth one's powder was success in the line of one's idiosyncrasy.

Consistency was in itself distinction, and what was talent but the art of being completely whatever it was that one happened to be? One's things were characteristic or they were nothing. I look back rather fondly on our having exchanged in those days these admirable remarks and many others; on our having been very happy too, in spite of postponements and obscurities, in spite also of such occasional hauntings as could spring from our lurid glimpse of the fact that even twaddle cunningly calculated was far above people's heads. It was easy to wave away spectres by the reflection that all one had to do was not to write for people; it was certainly not for people that Limbert wrote while he hammered at *The Major Key*. The taint of literature was fatal only in a certain kind of air, which was precisely the kind against which we had now closed our window. Mrs Stannace rose from her crumpled cushions as soon as she had obtained an adjournment, and Maud looked pale and proud, quite victorious and superior, at her having obtained nothing more. Maud behaved well, I thought, to her mother, and well indeed for a girl who had mainly been taught to be flowerlike to every one. What she gave Ray Limbert her fine abundant needs made him then and ever pay for; but the gift was liberal, almost wonderful – an assertion I make even while remembering to how many clever women, early and late, his work has been dear. It was not only that the woman he was to marry was in love with him, but that (this was the strangeness) she had really seen almost better than any one what he could do. The greatest strangeness was that she didn't want him to do something different. This boundless belief was indeed the main way of her devotion; and as an act of faith it naturally asked for miracles. She was a rare wife for a poet if she was not perhaps the best who could have been picked out for a poor man.

Well, we were to have the miracles at all events and we were in a perfect state of mind to receive them. There were more of us every day, and we thought highly even of our friend's odd jobs and pot-boilers. The *Beacon* had had no successor, but he found some quiet corners and stray chances. Perpetually poking the fire and looking out of the window, he was certainly not a monster of facility, but he was, thanks perhaps to a certain method in that madness, a monster of certainty. It wasn't every one however who knew him for this: many editors printed him but once. He was getting a small reputation as a man it was well to have the first time; he created obscure apprehensions as to what might happen the second. He was good for making an impression, but no one seemed exactly to know what the impression was good for when made. The reason was simply that they had not seen yet *The Major Key*, that fiery-hearted rose as to which we watched in private the formation of petal after petal and flame after flame. Nothing mattered but this, for it had already elicited a splendid bid, much talked about in Mrs Highmore's drawing-room, where at this point my reminiscences grow particularly thick. *Her* roses bloomed all the year and her sociability increased with her row of prizes. We had an idea that we 'met every one' there – so we naturally thought when we met each other. Between our hostess and Ray Limbert flourished the happiest relation, the only cloud on which was that her husband eyed him rather askance. When he was called clever this personage wanted to know what he had to 'show'; and it was certain that he showed nothing that could compare with Jane Highmore. Mr Highmore took his stand on accomplished work and, turning up his coat-tails, warmed his rear with a good conscience at the neat bookcase in which the generations of triplets were chronologically arranged. The harmony between his companions rested on the fact that, as I have already hinted, each would have liked so much to be the other. Limbert couldn't but have a feeling about a woman who in addition to being the best creature and her sister's backer would have made, could she have condescended, such a success with the *Beacon*. On the other hand Mrs Highmore used freely to say: 'Do you know, he'll do exactly the thing that *I* want to do? I shall never do it myself, but he'll do it instead. Yes, he'll do *my* thing, and I shall hate him for it – the wretch.' Hating him was her pleasant humour, for the wretch was personally to her taste.

She prevailed on her own publisher to promise to take *The Major Key* and to engage to pay a considerable sum down, as the phrase is, on the presumption of its attracting attention. This was good news for the evening's end at Mrs Highmore's when there were only four or five left and cigarettes ran low; but there was better news to come, and I have never forgotten how, as it was I who had the good fortune to bring it, I kept it back on one of those occasions, for the sake of my effect, till only the right people remained. The right people were now more and more numerous, but this was a revelation addressed only to a choice residuum – a residuum including of course Limbert himself, with whom I haggled for another cigarette before I announced that as a consequence of an interview I had had with him that afternoon, and of a subtle argument I had brought to bear, Mrs Highmore's pearl of publishers had agreed to put forth the new book as a serial. He was to 'run' it in his magazine and he was to pay ever so much more for the privilege. I produced a fine gasp which presently found a more articulate relief, but poor Limbert's voice failed him once for all (he knew he was to walk away with me) and it was some one else who asked me in what my subtle argument had resided. I forget what florid description I then gave of it: today I have no reason not to confess that it had resided in the simple plea that the book was exquisite. I had said: 'Come, my dear friend, be original; just risk it for that!' My dear friend seemed to rise to the chance, and I followed up my advantage, permitting him honestly no illusion as to the quality of the work. He clutched interrogatively at two or three attenuations, but I dashed them aside, leaving him face to face with the formidable truth. It was just a pure gem: was he the man not to flinch? His danger appeared to have acted upon him as the anaconda acts upon the rabbit; fascinated and paralysed, he had been engulfed in the long pink throat. When a week before, at my request, Limbert had let me possess for a day the complete manuscript, beautifully copied out by Maud Stannace, I had flushed with indignation at its having to be said of the author of such pages that he hadn't the common means to marry. I had taken the field in a great glow to repair this scandal, and it was therefore quite directly my fault if three months later, when *The Major Key* began to run, Mrs Stannace was driven to the wall. She had made a condition of a fixed income; and at last a fixed income was achieved.

She had to recognise it, and after much prostration among the photographs she recognised it to the extent of accepting some of the convenience of it in the form of a project for a common household, to the expenses of which each party should proportionately contribute. Jane Highmore made a great point of her not being left alone, but Mrs Stannace herself determined the proportion, which on Limbert's side at least and in spite of many other fluctuations was never altered. His income had been 'fixed' with a vengeance: having painfully stooped to the comprehension of it Mrs Stannace rested on this effort to the end and asked no further question on the subject. *The Major Key* in other words ran ever so long, and before it was half out Limbert and Maud had been married and the common household set up. These first months were probably the happiest in the family annals, with wedding-bells and budding laurels, the quiet, assured course of the book and the friendly, familiar note, round the corner, of Mrs Highmore's big guns. They gave Ralph time to block in another picture as well as to let me know after a while that he had the happy prospect of becoming a father. We had at times some dispute as to whether *The Major Key* was making an impression, but our contention could only be futile so long as we were not agreed as to what an impression consisted of. Several persons wrote to the author and several others asked to be introduced to him: wasn't that an impression? One of the lively 'weeklies', snapping at the deadly 'monthlies', said the whole thing was 'grossly inartistic' – wasn't that? It was somewhere else proclaimed 'a wonderfully subtle character-study' – wasn't that too? The strongest effect doubtless was produced on the publisher when, in its lemon-coloured volumes, like a little dish of three custards, the book was at last served cold: he never got his money back and so far as I know has never got it back to this day. *The Major Key* was rather a great performance than a great success. It converted readers into friends and friends into lovers; it placed the author, as the phrase is – placed him all too definitely; but it shrank to obscurity in the account of sales eventually rendered. It was in short an exquisite thing, but it was scarcely a thing to have published and certainly not a thing

to have married on. I heard all about the matter, for my intervention had much exposed me. Mrs Highmore said the second
volume had given her ideas, and the ideas are probably to be
found in some of her works, to the circulation of which they
have even perhaps contributed. This was not absolutely yet the
very thing she wanted to do, but it was on the way to it. So
much, she informed me, she particularly perceived in the light
of a critical study which I put forth in a little magazine; which
the publisher in his advertisements quoted from profusely; and
as to which there sprang up some absurd story that Limbert
himself had written it. I remember that on my asking some one
why such an idiotic thing had been said my interlocutor replied:
'Oh, because, you know, it's just the way he *would* have written!' My spirit sank a little perhaps as I reflected that with such
analogies in our manner there might prove to be some in our
fate.

It was during the next four or five years that our eyes were
open to what, unless something could be done, that fate, at
least on Limbert's part, might be. The thing to be done was of
course to write the book, the book that would make the difference, really justify the burden he had accepted and consummately express his power. For the works that followed upon *The
Major Key* he had inevitably to accept conditions the reverse of
brilliant, at a time too when the strain upon his resources had
begun to show sharpness. With three babies in due course, an
ailing wife and a complication still greater than these, it became
highly important that a man should do only his best. Whatever
Limbert did was his best; so at least each time I thought and so
I unfailingly said somewhere, though it was not my saying it,
heaven knows, that made the desired difference. Every one else
indeed said it, and there was among multiplied worries always
the comfort that his position was quite assured. The two books
that followed *The Major Key* did more than anything else to
assure it, and Jane Highmore was always crying out: 'You stand
alone, dear Ray; you stand absolutely alone!' Dear Ray used to
tell me that he felt the truth of this in feebly-attempted discussions with his bookseller. His sister-in-law gave him good
advice into the bargain; she was a repository of knowing hints,

of esoteric learning. These things were doubtless not the less valuable to him for bearing wholly on the question of how a reputation might be with a little gumption, as Mrs Highmore said, 'worked'. Save when she occasionally bore testimony to her desire to do, as Limbert did, something some day for her own very self, I never heard her speak of the literary motive as if it were distinguishable from the pecuniary. She cocked up his hat, she pricked up his prudence for him, reminding him that as one seemed to take one's self so the silly world was ready to take one. It was a fatal mistake to be too candid even with those who were all right – not to look and to talk prosperous, not at least to pretend that one had beautiful sales. To listen to her you would have thought the profession of letters a wonderful game of bluff. Wherever one's idea began it ended somehow in inspired paragraphs in the newspapers. '*I* pretend, I assure you, that you are going off like wildfire – I can at least do that for you!' she often declared, prevented as she was from doing much else by Mr Highmore's insurmountable objection to *their* taking Mrs Stannace.

I couldn't help regarding the presence of this latter lady in Limbert's life as the major complication: whatever he attempted it appeared given to him to achieve as best he could in the mere margin of the space in which she swung her petticoats. I may err in the belief that she practically lived on him, for though it was not in him to follow adequately Mrs Highmore's counsel there were exasperated confessions he never made, scanty domestic curtains he rattled on their rings. I may exaggerate in the retrospect his apparent anxieties, for these after all were the years when his talent was freshest and when as a writer he most laid down his line. It wasn't of Mrs Stannace nor even as time went on of Mrs Limbert that we mainly talked when I got at longer intervals a smokier hour in the little grey den from which we could step out, as we used to say, to the lawn. The lawn was the back-garden, and Limbert's study was behind the dining-room, with folding doors not impervious to the clatter of the children's tea. We sometimes took refuge from it in the depths – a bush and a half deep – of the shrubbery, where was a bench that gave us a view while we gossiped of Mrs Stannace's tiara-like headdress nodding at an upper window. Within doors and without Limbert's life was overhung by an awful region that figured in his conversation, comprehensively and with unpremeditated art, as Upstairs. It was Upstairs that the thunder gathered, that Mrs Stannace kept her accounts and her state, that Mrs Limbert had her babies and her headaches, that the bells for ever jangled at the maids, that everything imperative in short took place – everything that he had somehow, pen in hand, to meet and dispose of in the little room on the garden-level. I don't think he liked to go Upstairs, but no special burst of confidence was needed to make me feel that a terrible deal of service went. It was the habit of the ladies of the Stannace family to be extremely waited on, and I've never been in a house where three maids and a nursery-governess gave such an impression of a retinue. 'Oh, they're so deucedly, so hereditarily fine!' – I remember how that dropped from him in some worried hour. Well, it was because Maud was so universally fine that we had both been in love with her. It was not an air moreover for the plaintive note: no private inconvenience could long outweigh for him the great happiness of these years – the happiness that sat with us when we talked and that made it always amusing to talk, the sense of his being on the heels of success, coming closer and closer, touching it at last, knowing that he should touch it again and hold it fast and hold it high. Of course when we said success we didn't mean exactly what Mrs Highmore for instance meant. He used to quote at me as a definition something from a nameless page of my own, some stray dictum to the effect that the man of his craft had achieved it when of a beautiful subject his expression was complete. Well, wasn't Limbert's in all conscience complete?

III

IT was bang upon this completeness all the same that the turn arrived, the turn I can't say of his fortune – for what was that? – but of his confidence, of his spirits and, what was more to the point, of his system. The whole occasion on which the first

symptom flared out is before me as I write. I had met them both
at dinner: they were diners who had reached the penultimate
stage – the stage which in theory is a rigid selection and in
practice a wan submission. It was late in the season and
stronger spirits than theirs were broken; the night was close
and the air of the banquet such as to restrict conversation to the
refusal of dishes and consumption to the sniffing of a flower. It
struck me all the more that Mrs Limbert was flying her flag. As
vivid as a page of her husband's prose, she had one of those
flickers of freshness that are the miracle of her sex and one of
those expensive dresses that are the miracle of ours. She had
also a neat brougham in which she had offered to rescue an old
lady from the possibilities of a queer cab-horse; so that when
she had rolled away with her charge I proposed a walk home
with her husband, whom I had overtaken on the door-step.
Before I had gone far with him he told me he had news for me –
he had accepted, of all people and of all things, an 'editorial
position'. It had come to pass that very day, from one hour to
another, without time for appeals or ponderations: Mr Bousefield, the proprietor of a 'high-class monthly', making, as they
said, a sudden change, had dropped on him heavily out of the
blue. It was all right – there was a salary and an idea, and both of
them, as such things went, rather high. We took our way slowly
through the vacant streets, and in the explanations and revelations that as we lingered under lamp-posts I drew from him
I found with an apprehension that I tried to gulp down a
foretaste of the bitter end. He told me more than he had ever
told me yet. He couldn't balance accounts – that was the
trouble: his expenses were too rising a tide. It was absolutely
necessary that he should at last make money, and now he must
work only for that. The need this last year had gathered the
force of a crusher: it had rolled over him and laid him on his
back. He had his scheme; this time he knew what he was about;
on some good occasion, with leisure to talk it over, he would tell
me the blessed whole. His editorship would help him, and for
the rest he must help himself. If he couldn't they would have to
do something fundamental – change their life altogether, give
up London, move into the country, take a house at thirty

pounds a year, send their children to the Board-school. I saw that he was excited, and he admitted that he was: he had waked out of a trance. He had been on the wrong tack; he had piled mistake on mistake. It was the vision of his remedy that now excited him: ineffably, grotesquely simple, it had yet come to him only within a day or two. No, he wouldn't tell me what it was; he would give me the night to guess, and if I shouldn't guess it would be because I was as big an ass as himself. However, a lone man might be an ass: he had room in his life for his ears. Ray had a burden that demanded a back: the back must therefore now be properly instituted. As to the editorship, it was simply heaven-sent, being not at all another case of *The Blackport Beacon* but a case of the very opposite. The proprietor, the great Mr Bousefield, had approached him precisely because his name, which was to be on the cover, *didn't* represent the chatty. The whole thing was to be – oh, on fiddling little lines of course – a protest against the chatty. Bousefield wanted him to be himself; it was for himself Bousefield had picked him out. Wasn't it beautiful and brave of Bousefield? He wanted literature, he saw the great reaction coming, the way the cat was going to jump. 'Where will you get literature?' I woefully asked; to which he replied with a laugh that what he had to get was not literature but only what Bousefield would take for it.

In that single phrase without more ado I discovered his famous remedy. What was before him for the future was not to do his work but to do what somebody else would take for it. I had the question out with him on the next opportunity, and of all the lively discussions into which we had been destined to drift it lingers in my mind as the liveliest. This was not, I hasten to add, because I disputed his conclusions: it was an effect of the very force with which, when I had fathomed his wretched premises, I took them to my soul. It was very well to talk with Jane Highmore about his standing alone: the eminent relief of this position had brought him to the verge of ruin. Several persons admired his books – nothing was less contestable; but they appeared to have a mortal objection to acquiring them by subscription or by purchase: they begged or borrowed or stole, they delegated one of the party perhaps to commit the volumes to memory and repeat them, like the bards of old, to listening multitudes. Some ingenious theory was required at any rate to account for the inexorable limits of his circulation. It wasn't a thing for five people to live on; therefore either the objects circulated must change their nature or the organisms to be nourished must. The former change was perhaps the easier to consider first. Limbert considered it with extraordinary ingenuity from that time on, and the ingenuity, greater even than any I had yet had occasion to admire in him, made the whole next stage of his career rich in curiosity and suspense.

'I have been butting my skull against a wall,' he had said in those hours of confidence; 'and, to be as sublime a blockhead, if you'll allow me the word, you, my dear fellow, have kept sounding the charge. We've sat prating here of "success", heaven help us, like chanting monks in a cloister, hugging the sweet delusion that it lies somewhere in the work itself, in the expression, as you said, of one's subject or the intensification, as somebody else somewhere says, of one's note. One has been going on in short as if the only thing to do were to accept the law of one's talent and thinking that if certain consequences didn't follow it was only because one wasn't logical enough. My disaster has served me right – I mean for using that ignoble word at all. It's a mere distributor's, a mere hawker's word. What *is* "success" anyhow? When a book's right, it's right – shame to it surely if it isn't. When it sells it sells – it brings money like potatoes or beer. If there's dishonour one way and inconvenience the other, it certainly is comfortable, but it as certainly isn't glorious to have escaped them. People of delicacy don't brag either about their probity or about their luck. Success be hanged! – I want to sell. It's a question of life and death. I must study the way. I've studied too much the other way – I know the other way now, every inch of it. I must cultivate the market – it's a science like another. I must go in for an infernal cunning. It will be very amusing, I foresee that; I shall lead a dashing life and drive a roaring trade. I haven't been obvious – I must *be* obvious. I haven't been popular – I must *be* popular. It's another art – or perhaps it isn't an art at all. It's something else; one must find out *what* it is. Is it something awfully queer?

– you blush! – something barely decent? All the greater incentive to curiosity! Curiosity's an immense motive; we shall have
tremendous sport. They all do it; it's only a question of how. Of
course I've everything to unlearn; but what is life, as Jane
Highmore says, but a lesson? I must get all I can, all she can
give me, from Jane. She can't explain herself much; she's all
intuition; her processes are obscure; it's the spirit that swoops
down and catches her up. But I must study her reverently in her
works. Yes, you've defied me before, but now my loins are
girded: I declare I'll read one of them – I really will: I'll put it
through if I perish!'

I won't pretend that he made all these remarks at once; but
there wasn't one that he didn't make at one time or another, for
suggestion and occasion were plentiful enough, his life being
now given up altogether to his new necessity. It wasn't a question of his having or not having, as they say, my intellectual
sympathy: the brute force of the pressure left no room for
judgement; it made all emotion a mere recourse to the spy-
glass. I watched him as I should have watched a long race or a
long chase, irresistibly siding with him but much occupied with
the calculation of odds. I confess indeed that my heart, for the
endless stretch that he covered so fast, was often in my throat.
I saw him peg away over the sun-dappled plain, I saw him
double and wind and gain and lose; and all the while I secretly
entertained a conviction. I wanted him to feed his many
mouths, but at the bottom of all things was my sense that if
he should succeed in doing so in this particular way I should
think less well of him. Now I had an absolute terror of that.
Meanwhile so far as I could I backed him up, I helped him: all
the more that I had warned him immensely at first, smiled with
a compassion it was very good of him not to have found exasperating over the complacency of his assumption that a man
could escape from himself. Ray Limbert at all events would
certainly never escape; but one could make believe for him,
make believe very hard – an undertaking in which at first Mr
Bousefield was visibly a blessing. Limbert was delightful on the
business of this being at last my chance too – my chance, so
miraculously vouchsafed, to appear with a certain luxuriance.

He didn't care how often he printed me, for wasn't it exactly in my direction Mr Bousefield held that the cat was going to jump? This was the least he could do for me. I might write on anything I liked – on anything at least but Mr Limbert's second manner. He didn't wish attention strikingly called to his second manner; it was to operate insidiously; people were to be left to believe they had discovered it long ago. 'Ralph Limbert? Why, when did we ever live without him?' – that's what he wanted them to say. Besides, they hated manners – let sleeping dogs lie. His understanding with Mr Bousefield – on which he had had not at all to insist; it was the excellent man who insisted – was that he should run one of his beautiful stories in the magazine. As to the beauty of his story however Limbert was going to be less admirably straight than as to the beauty of everything else. That was another reason why I mustn't write about his new line: Mr Bousefield was not to be too definitely warned that such a periodical was exposed to prostitution. By the time he should find it out for himself the public – *le gros public* – would have bitten, and then perhaps he would be conciliated and forgive. Everything else would be literary in short, and above all *I* would be; only Ralph Limbert wouldn't – he'd chuck up the whole thing sooner. He'd be vulgar, he'd be rudimentary, he'd be atrocious: he'd be elaborately what he hadn't been before.

I duly noticed that he had more trouble in making 'everything else' literary than he had at first allowed for; but this was largely counteracted by the ease with which he was able to obtain that his mark should not be overshot. He had taken well to heart the old lesson of the *Beacon*; he remembered that he was after all there to keep his contributors down much rather than to keep them up. I thought at times that he kept them down a trifle too far, but he assured me that I needn't be nervous: he had his limit – his limit was inexorable. He would reserve pure vulgarity for his serial, over which he was sweating blood and water; elsewhere it should be qualified by the prime qualification, the mediocrity that attaches, that endears. Bousefield, he allowed, was proud, was difficult: nothing was really good enough for him but the middling good; but he himself was prepared for adverse comment, resolute for his noble course. Hadn't Limbert moreover in the event of a charge of laxity from headquarters the great strength of being able to point to my contributions? Therefore I must let myself go, I must abound in my peculiar sense, I must be a resource in case of accidents. Limbert's vision of accidents hovered mainly over the sudden awakening of Mr Bousefield to the stuff that in the department of fiction his editor was palming off. He would then have to confess in all humility that this was not what the good old man wanted, but I should be all the more there as a salutary specimen. I would cross the scent with something showily impossible, splendidly unpopular – I must be sure to have something on hand. I always had plenty on hand – poor Limbert needn't have worried: the magazine was forearmed each month by my care with a retort to any possible accusation of trifling with Mr Bousefield's standard. He had admitted to Limbert, after much consideration indeed, that he was prepared to be perfectly human; but he had added that he was not prepared for an abuse of this admission. The thing in the world I think I least felt myself was an abuse, even though (as I had never mentioned to my friendly editor) I too had my project for a bigger reverberation. I daresay I trusted mine more than I trusted Limbert's; at all events the golden mean in which in the special case he saw his salvation as an editor was something I should be most sure of if I were to exhibit it myself. I exhibited it month after month in the form of a monstrous levity, only praying heaven that my editor might now not tell me, as he had so often told me, that my result was awfully good. I knew what that would signify – it would signify, sketchily speaking, disaster. What he did tell me heartily was that it was just what his game required: his new line had brought with it an earnest assumption – earnest save when we privately laughed about it – of the locutions proper to real bold enterprise. If I tried to keep him in the dark even as he kept Mr Bousefield there was nothing to show that I was not tolerably successful: each case therefore presented a promising analogy for the other. He never noticed my descent, and it was accordingly possible that Mr Bousefield would never notice his. But would nobody notice it at all? – that was a question that added a prospective zest to one's possession of a critical sense. So much depended upon it that I was rather relieved than otherwise not to know the answer too soon. I waited in fact a year – the year for which Limbert had cannily engaged on trial with Mr Bousefield; the year as to which through the same sharpened shrewdness it had been conveyed in the agreement between them that Mr Bousefield was not to intermeddle. It had been Limbert's general prayer that we would during this period let him quite alone. His terror of my direct rays was a droll, dreadful force that always operated: he explained it by the fact that I understood him too well, expressed too much of his intention, saved him too little from himself. The less he was saved the more he didn't sell: I literally interpreted, and that was simply fatal.

I held my breath accordingly; I did more – I closed my eyes, I guarded my treacherous ears. He induced several of us to do that (of such devotions we were capable) so that not even glancing at the thing from month to month, and having nothing but his shamed, anxious silence to go by, I participated only vaguely in the little hum that surrounded his act of sacrifice. It was blown about the town that the public would be surprised; it was hinted, it was printed that he was making a desperate bid. His new work was spoken of as 'more calculated for general acceptance'. These tidings produced in some quarters much reprobation, and nowhere more, I think, than on the part of certain persons who had never read a word of him, or assuredly had never spent a shilling on him, and who hung for hours over the other attractions of the newspaper that announced his abasement. So much asperity cheered me a little – seemed to signify that he might really be doing something. On the other hand I had a distinct alarm; some one sent me for some alien reason an American journal (containing frankly more than that source of affliction) in which was quoted a passage from our friend's last instalment. The passage – I couldn't for my life help reading it – was simply superb. Ah, he *would* have to move to the country if that was the worst he could do! It gave me a pang to see how little after all he had improved since the days of his competition with Pat Moyle. There was nothing in the passage quoted in the American paper that Pat would for a moment have owned. During the last weeks, as the opportunity of reading the complete thing drew near, one's suspense was barely endurable, and I shall never forget the July evening on which I put it to rout. Coming home to dinner I found the two volumes on my table, and I sat up with them half the night, dazed, bewildered, rubbing my eyes, wondering at the monstrous joke. *Was* it a monstrous joke, his second manner – was *this* the new line, the desperate bid, the scheme for more general acceptance and the remedy for material failure? Had he made a fool of all his following, or had he most injuriously made a still bigger fool of himself? Obvious? – where the deuce was it obvious? Popular? – how on earth could it be popular? The thing was charming with all his charm and powerful with all his power: it was an unscrupulous, an unsparing, a shameless, merciless masterpiece. It was, no doubt, like the old letters to the *Beacon*, the worst he could do; but the perversity of the effort, even though heroic, had been frustrated by the purity of the gift. Under what illusion had he laboured, with what wavering, treacherous compass had he steered? His honour was inviolable, his measurements were all wrong. I was thrilled with the whole impression and with all that came crowding in its train. It was too grand a collapse – it was too hideous a triumph; I exulted almost with tears – I lamented with a strange delight. Indeed as the short night waned and, threshing about in my emotion, I fidgeted to my high-perched window for a glimpse of the summer dawn, I became at last aware that I was staring at it out of eyes that had compassionately and admiringly filled. The eastern sky, over the London housetops, had a wonderful tragic crimson. That was the colour of his magnificent mistake.

IV

IF something less had depended on my impression I daresay I should have communicated it as soon as I had swallowed my breakfast; but the case was so embarrassing that I spent the first half of the day in reconsidering it, dipping into the book again, almost feverishly turning its leaves and trying to extract from them, for my friend's benefit, some symptom of reassurance, some ground for felicitation. This rash challenge had consequences merely dreadful; the wretched volumes, imperturbable and impeccable, with their shyer secrets and their second line of defence, were like a beautiful woman more denuded or a great symphony on a new hearing. There was something quite sinister in the way they stood up to me. I couldn't however be dumb – that was to give the wrong tinge to my disappointment; so that later in the afternoon, taking my courage in both hands, I approached with a vain tortuosity poor Limbert's door. A smart victoria waited before it in which from the bottom of the street I saw that a lady who had apparently just issued from the house was settling herself. I recognised Jane Highmore and instantly paused till she should drive down to me. She presently met me half-way and as soon as she saw me stopped her carriage in agitation. This was a relief – it postponed a moment the sight of that pale, fine face of our friend's fronting me for the right verdict. I gathered from the flushed eagerness with which Mrs Highmore asked me if I had heard the news that a verdict of some sort had already been rendered.

'What news? – about the book?'

'About that horrid magazine. They're shockingly upset. He has lost his position – he has had a fearful flare-up with Mr Bousefield.'

I stood there blank, but not unaware in my blankness of how history repeats itself. There came to me across the years Maud's announcement of their ejection from the *Beacon*, and dimly, confusedly the same explanation was in the air. This time however I had been on my guard; I had had my suspicion. 'He has made it too flippant?' I found breath after an instant to inquire.

Mrs Highmore's vacuity exceeded my own. 'Too "flippant"? He has made it too oracular. Mr Bousefield says he has killed it.' Then perceiving my stupefaction: 'Don't you know what has happened?' she pursued; 'isn't it because in his trouble, poor love, he has sent for you that you've come? You've heard nothing at all? Then you had better know before you see them. Get in here with me – I'll take you a turn and tell you.' We were close to the Park, the Regent's, and when with extreme alacrity I had placed myself beside her and the carriage had begun to enter it she went on: 'It was what I feared, you know. It reeked with culture. He keyed it up too high.'

I felt myself sinking in the general collapse. 'What are you talking about?'

'Why, about that beastly magazine. They're all on the streets. I shall have to take mamma.'

I pulled myself together. 'What on earth then did Bousefield want? He said he wanted intellectual power.'

'Yes, but Ray overdid it.'

'Why, Bousefield said it was a thing he *couldn't* overdo.'

'Well, Ray managed: he took Mr Bousefield too literally. It appears the thing has been doing dreadfully, but the proprietor couldn't say anything, because he had covenanted to leave the editor quite free. He describes himself as having stood there in a fever and seen his ship go down. A day or two ago the year was up, so he could at last break out. Maud says he did break out quite fearfully; he came to the house and let poor Ray have it. Ray gave it to him back; he reminded him of his own idea of the way the cat was going to jump.'

I gasped with dismay. 'Has Bousefield abandoned that idea? Isn't the cat going to jump?'

Mrs Highmore hesitated. 'It appears that she doesn't seem in a hurry. Ray at any rate has jumped too far ahead of her. He should have temporised a little, Mr Bousefield says; but I'm beginning to think, you know,' said my companion, 'that Ray *can't* temporise.' Fresh from my emotions of the previous twenty-four hours I was scarcely in a position to disagree with her. 'He published too much pure thought.'

'Pure thought?' I cried. 'Why, it struck me so often – certainly in a due proportion of cases – as pure drivel!'

'Oh, you're more keyed up than he! Mr Bousefield says that of course he wanted things that were suggestive and clever, things that he could point to with pride. But he contends that

Ray didn't allow for human weakness. He gave everything in too stiff doses.'

Sensibly, I fear, to my neighbour I winced at her words; I felt a prick that made me meditate. Then I said: 'Is that, by chance, the way he gave *me*?' Mrs Highmore remained silent so long that I had somehow the sense of a fresh pang; and after a minute, turning in my seat, I laid my hand on her arm, fixed my eyes upon her face and pursued pressingly: 'Do you suppose it to be to my "Occasional Remarks" that Mr Bousefield refers?'

At last she met my look. 'Can you bear to hear it?'

'I think I can bear anything now.'

'Well then, it was really what I wanted to give you an inkling of. It's largely over you that they've quarrelled. Mr Bousefield wants him to chuck you.'

I grabbed her arm again. 'And Limbert *won't*?'

'He seems to cling to you. Mr Bousefield says no magazine can afford you.'

I gave a laugh that agitated the very coachman. 'Why, my dear lady, has he any idea of my price?'

'It isn't your price – he says you're dear at any price; you do so much to sink the ship. Your "Remarks" are called "Occasional", but nothing could be more deadly regular: you're there month after month and you're never anywhere else. And you supply no public want.'

'I supply the most delicious irony.'

'So Ray appears to have declared. Mr Bousefield says that's not in the least a public want. No one can make out what you're talking about and no one would care if he could. I'm only quoting *him*, mind.'

'Quote, quote – if Limbert holds out. I think I must leave you now, please: I must rush back to express to him what I feel.'

'I'll drive you to his door. That isn't all,' said Mrs Highmore. And on the way, when the carriage had turned, she communicated the rest. 'Mr Bousefield really arrived with an ultimatum: it had the form of something or other by Minnie Meadows.'

'Minnie Meadows?' I was stupefied.

'The new lady-humourist every one is talking about. It's the first of a series of screaming sketches for which poor Ray was to find a place.'

'Is *that* Mr Bousefield's idea of literature?'

'No, but he says it's the public's, and you've got to take *some* account of the public. *Aux grands maux les grands remèdes*. They had a tremendous lot of ground to make up, and no one would make it up like Minnie. She would be the best concession they could make to human weakness; she would strike at least this note of showing that it was not going to be quite all – well, all *you*. Now Ray draws the line at Minnie; he won't stoop to Minnie; he declines to touch, to look at Minnie. When Mr Bousefield – rather imperiously, I believe – made Minnie a *sine quâ non* of his retention of his post he said something rather violent, told him to go to some unmentionable place and take Minnie with him. That of course put the fat on the fire. They had really a considerable scene.'

'So had he with the *Beacon* man,' I musingly replied. 'Poor dear, he seems born for considerable scenes! It's on Minnie, then, that they've really split?' Mrs Highmore exhaled her despair in a sound which I took for an assent, and when we had rolled a little further I rather inconsequently and to her visible surprise broke out of my reverie. 'It will never do in the world – he *must* stoop to Minnie!'

'It's too late – and what I've told you still isn't all. Mr Bousefield raises another objection.'

'What other, pray?'

'Can't you guess?'

I wondered. 'No more of Ray's fiction?'

'Not a line. That's something else no magazine can stand. Now that his novel has run its course Mr Bousefield is distinctly disappointed.'

I fairly bounded in my place. 'Then it may do?'

Mrs Highmore looked bewildered. 'Why so, if he finds it too dull?'

'Dull? Ralph Limbert? He's as fine as a needle!'

'It comes to the same thing – he won't penetrate leather. Mr Bousefield had counted on something that *would*, on something that would have a wider acceptance. Ray says he wants iron pegs.' I collapsed again; my flicker of elation dropped to a throb of quieter comfort; and after a moment's silence I asked my neighbour if she had herself read the work our friend had just put forth. 'No,' she replied, 'I gave him my word at the beginning, on his urgent request, that I wouldn't.'

'Not even as a book?'

'He begged me never to look at it at all. He said he was trying a low experiment. Of course I knew what he meant and I entreated him to let me just for curiosity take a peep. But he was firm, he declared he couldn't bear the thought that a woman like me should see him in the depths.'

'He's only, thank God, in the depths of distress,' I replied. 'His experiment's nothing worse than a failure.'

'Then Bousefield *is* right – his circulation won't budge?'

'It won't move one, as they say in Fleet Street. The book has extraordinary beauty.'

'Poor duck – after trying so hard!' Jane Highmore sighed with real tenderness. 'What *will* then become of them?'

I was silent an instant. 'You must take your mother.'

She was silent too. 'I must speak of it to Cecil!' she presently said. Cecil is Mr Highmore, who then entertained, I knew, strong views on the inadjustability of circumstances in general to the idiosyncrasies of Mrs Stannace. He held it supremely happy that in an important relation she should have met her match. Her match was Ray Limbert – not much of a writer but a practical man. 'The dear things still think, you know,' my companion continued, 'that the book will be the beginning of their fortune. Their illusion, if you're right, will be rudely dispelled.'

'That's what makes me dread to face them. I've just spent with his volumes an unforgettable night. His illusion has lasted because so many of us have been pledged till this moment to turn our faces the other way. We haven't known the truth and have therefore had nothing to say. Now that we do know it indeed we have practically quite as little. I hang back from the threshold. How can I follow up with a burst of enthusiasm such a catastrophe as Mr Bousefield's visit?'

As I turned uneasily about my neighbour more comfortably snuggled. 'Well, I'm glad then I haven't read him and have nothing unpleasant to say!' We had come back to Limbert's door, and I made the coachman stop short of it. 'But he'll try again, with that determination of his: he'll build his hopes on the next time.'

'On what else has he built them from the very first? It's never the present for him that bears the fruit; that's always postponed and for somebody else: there has always to be another try. I admit that his idea of a "new line" has made him try harder than ever. It makes no difference,' I brooded, still timorously lingering; 'his achievement of his necessity, his hope of a market will continue to attach themselves to the future. But the next time will disappoint him as each last time has done – and then the next and the next and the next!'

I found myself seeing it all with a clearness almost inspired: it evidently cast a chill on Mrs Highmore. 'Then what on earth will become of him?' she plaintively asked.

'I don't think I particularly care what may become of *him*,' I returned with a conscious, reckless increase of my exaltation; 'I feel it almost enough to be concerned with what may become of one's enjoyment of him. I don't know in short what will become of his circulation; I am only quite at my ease as to what will become of his work. It will simply keep all its quality. He'll try again for the common with what he'll believe to be a still more infernal cunning, and again the common will fatally elude him, for his infernal cunning will have been only his genius in an ineffectual disguise.' We sat drawn up by the pavement, facing poor Limbert's future as I saw it. It relieved me in a manner to know the worst, and I prophesied with an assurance which as I look back upon it strikes me as rather remarkable. '*Que voulez-vous?*' I went on; 'you can't make a sow's ear of a silk purse! It's grievous indeed if you like – there are people who can't be vulgar for trying. *He* can't – it wouldn't come off, I promise you, even once. It takes more than trying – it comes by grace. It happens not to be given to Limbert to fall. He belongs to the heights – he breathes there, he lives there, and it's accordingly to the heights I must ascend,' I said as I took leave of my conductress, 'to carry him this wretched news from where *we* move!'

V

A FEW months were sufficient to show how right I had been about his circulation. It didn't move on, as I had said; it stopped short in the same place, fell off in a sheer descent, like some precipice gaped up at by tourists. The public in other words drew the line for him as sharply as he had drawn it for Minnie Meadows. Minnie has skipped with a flouncing caper over his line, however; whereas the mark traced by a lustier cudgel has been a barrier insurmountable to Limbert. Those next times I had spoken of to Jane Highmore, I see them simplified by retrocession. Again and again he made his desperate bid – again and again he tried to. His rupture with Mr Bousefield caused him, I fear, in professional circles to be thought impracticable, and I am perfectly aware, to speak candidly, that no sordid advantage ever accrued to him from such public patronage of my performances as he had occasionally been in a position to offer. I reflect for my comfort that any injury I may have done him by untimely application of a faculty of analysis which could point to no converts gained by honourable exercise was at least equalled by the injury he did himself. More than once, as I have hinted, I held my tongue at his request, but my frequent plea that such favours weren't politic never found him, when in other connections there was an opportunity to give me a lift, anything but indifferent to the danger of the association. He let them have me in a word whenever he could; sometimes in periodicals in which he had credit, sometimes only at dinner. He talked about me when he couldn't get me in, but it was always part of the bargain that I shouldn't make him a topic. 'How can I successfully serve you if you do?' he used to ask: he was more afraid than I thought he ought to have been of the charge of tit for tat. I didn't care, for I never could distinguish tat from tit; but as I have intimated I dropped into silence really more than anything else because there was a certain fascinated observation of his course which was quite testimony enough and to which in this huddled conclusion of it he practically reduced me.

I see it all foreshortened, his wonderful remainder – see it from the end backward, with the direction widening toward me as if on a level with the eye. The migration to the country promised him at first great things – smaller expenses, larger leisure, conditions eminently conducive on each occasion to the possible triumph of the next time. Mrs Stannace, who altogether disapproved of it, gave as one of her reasons that her son-in-law, living mainly in a village on the edge of a goose-green, would be deprived of that contact with the great world which was indispensable to the painter of manners. She had the showiest arguments for keeping him in touch, as she called it, with good society; wishing to know with some force where, from the moment he ceased to represent it from observation, the novelist could be said to be. In London fortunately a clever man was just a clever man; there were charming houses in which a person of Ray's undoubted ability, even though without the knack of making the best use of it, could always be sure of a quiet corner for watching decorously the social kaleidoscope. But the kaleidoscope of the goose-green, what in the world was that, and what such delusive thrift as drives about the land (with a fearful account for flys from the inn) to leave cards on the country magnates? This solicitude for Limbert's subject-matter was the specious colour with which, deeply determined not to affront mere tolerance in a cottage, Mrs Stannace over-laid her indisposition to place herself under the heel of Cecil Highmore. She knew that he ruled Upstairs as well as down, and she clung to the fable of the association of interests in the north of London. The Highmores had a better address – they lived now in Stanhope Gardens; but Cecil was fearfully artful – he wouldn't hear of an association of interests nor treat with his mother-in-law save as a visitor. She didn't like false positions; but on the other hand she didn't like the sacrifice of everything she was accustomed to. Her universe at all events was a universe full of card-leavings and charming houses, and it was fortunate that she couldn't Upstairs catch the sound of the doom to which, in his little grey den, describing to me his diplomacy, Limbert consigned alike the country magnates and the opportunities of London. Despoiled of every guarantee she went to Stanhope Gardens like a mere maidservant, with restrictions on her very luggage, while during the year that followed this upheaval Limbert, strolling with me on the goose-green, to which I often ran down, played extravagantly over the theme that with what he was now going in for it was a positive comfort not to have the social kaleidoscope. With a cold-blooded trick in view what had life or manners or the best society or flys from the inn to say to the question? It was as good a place as another to play his new game. He had found a quieter corner than any corner of the great world, and a damp old house at sixpence a year, which, beside leaving him all his margin to educate his children, would allow of the supreme luxury of his frankly presenting himself as a poor man. This was a convenience that *ces dames*, as he called them, had never yet fully permitted him.

It rankled in me at first to see his reward so meagre, his conquest so mean; but the simplification effected had a charm that I finally felt: it was a forcing-house for the three or four other fine miscarriages to which his scheme was evidently condemned. I limited him to three or four, having had my sharp impression, in spite of the perpetual broad joke of the thing, that a spring had really snapped in him on the occasion of that deeply disconcerting sequel to the episode of his editorship. He never lost his sense of the grotesque want, in the difference made, of adequate relation to the effort that had been the intensest of his life. He had from that moment a charge of shot in him, and it slowly worked its way to a vital part. As he met his embarrassments each year with his punctual false remedy I wondered periodically where he found the energy to return to the attack. He did it every time with a rage more blanched, but it was clear to me that the tension must finally snap the cord. We got again and again the irrepressible work of art, but what did *he* get, poor man, who wanted something so different? There were likewise odder questions than this in the matter, phenomena more curious and mysteries more puzzling, which often for sympathy if not for illumination I intimately discussed with Mrs Limbert. She had her burdens, dear lady: after the removal from London and a considerable interval she twice again became a mother. Mrs Stannace too, in a more restricted sense, exhibited afresh, in relation to the home she had abandoned, the same exemplary character. In her poverty of guarantees at Stanhope Gardens there had been least of all, it appeared, a proviso that she shouldn't resentfully revert again from Goneril to Regan. She came down to the goose-green like Lear himself, with fewer knights, or at least baronets, and the joint household was at last patched up. It fell to pieces and was put together on various occasions before Ray Limbert died. He was ridden to the end by the superstition that he had broken up Mrs Stannace's original home on pretences that had proved hollow and that if he hadn't given Maud what she might have had he could at least give her back her mother. I was always sure that a sense of the compensations he owed was half the motive of the dogged pride with which he tried to wake up the libraries. I believed Mrs Stannace still had money, though she pretended that, called upon at every turn to retrieve deficits, she had long since poured it into the general fund. This conviction haunted me; I suspected her of secret hoards, and I said to myself that she couldn't be so infamous as not some day on her deathbed to leave everything to her less opulent daughter. My compassion for the Limberts led me to hover perhaps indiscreetly round that closing scene, to dream of some happy time when such an accession of means would make up a little for their present penury.

This however was crude comfort, as in the first place I had nothing definite to go by and in the second I held it for more and more indicated that Ray wouldn't outlive her. I never ventured to sound him as to what in this particular he hoped or feared, for after the crisis marked by his leaving London I had new scruples about suffering him to be reminded of where he fell short. The poor man was in truth humiliated, and there were things as to which that kept us both silent. In proportion as he tried more fiercely for the market the old plaintive arithmetic, fertile in jokes, dropped from our conversation. We joked immensely still about the process, but our treatment of the results became sparing and superficial. He talked as much as ever, with monstrous arts and borrowed hints, of the traps he kept setting, but we all agreed to take merely for granted that the animal was caught. This propriety had really dawned upon me the day that after Mr Bousefield's visit Mrs Highmore put me down at his door. Mr Bousefield in that juncture had been served up to me anew, but after we had disposed of him we came to the book, which I was obliged to confess I had already rushed through. It was from this moment – the moment at which my terrible impression of it had blinked out at his anxious query – that the image of his scared face was to abide with me. I couldn't attenuate then – the cat was out of the bag; but later, each of the next times, I did, I acknowledge, attenuate. We all did religiously, so far as was possible; we cast ingenious ambiguities over the strong places, the beauties that betrayed him most, and found ourselves in the queer position of admirers banded to mislead a confiding artist. If we stifled our cheers however and dissimulated our joy our fond hypocrisy accomplished little, for Limbert's finger was on a pulse that told a plainer story. It was a satisfaction to have secured a greater freedom with his wife, who at last, much to her honour, entered into the conspiracy and whose sense of responsibility was flattered by the frequency of our united appeal to her for some answer to the marvellous riddle. We had all turned it over till we were tired of it, threshing out the question why the note he strained every chord to pitch for common ears should invariably insist on addressing itself to the angels. Being, as it were, ourselves the angels we had only a limited quarrel in each case with the event; but its inconsequent character, given the forces set in motion, was peculiarly baffling. It was like an interminable sum that wouldn't come straight; nobody had the time to handle so many figures. Limbert gathered, to make his pudding, dry bones and dead husks; how then was one to formulate the law that made the dish prove a feast? What was the cerebral treachery that defied his own vigilance? There was some obscure interference of taste, some obsession of the exquisite. All one could say was that genius was a fatal disturber or that the unhappy man had no effectual *flair*. When he went abroad to gather garlic he came home with heliotrope.

I hasten to add that if Mrs Limbert was not directly illuminating she was yet rich in anecdote and example, having found a refuge from mystification exactly where the rest of us had found it, in a more devoted embrace and the sense of a finer glory. Her disappointments and eventually her privations had been many, her discipline severe; but she had ended by accepting the long grind of life and was now quite willing to take her turn at the mill. She was essentially one of us – she always understood. Touching and admirable at the last, when through the unmistakable change in Limbert's health her troubles were thickest, was the spectacle of the particular pride that she wouldn't have exchanged for prosperity. She had said to me once – only once, in a gloomy hour in London days when things were not going at all – that one really had to think him a very great man because if one didn't one would be rather ashamed of him. She had distinctly felt it at first – and in a very tender place – that almost every one passed him on the road; but I believe that in these final years she would almost have been ashamed of him if he had suddenly gone into editions. It is certain indeed that her complacency was not subjected to that shock. She would have liked the money immensely, but she would have missed something she had taught herself to regard as rather rare. There is another remark I remember her making, a remark to the effect that of course if she could have chosen she would have liked him to be Shakespeare or Scott, but that failing this she was very glad he wasn't – well, she named the two gentlemen, but I won't. I daresay she sometimes laughed out to escape an alternative. She contributed passionately to the capture of the second manner, foraging for him further afield than he could conveniently go, gleaning in the barest stubble, picking up shreds to build the nest and in particular in the study of the great secret of how, as we always said, they all did it laying waste the circulating libraries. If Limbert had a weakness he rather broke down in his reading. It was fortunately not till after the appearance of *The Hidden Heart* that he broke down in everything else. He had had rheumatic fever in the spring, when the book was but half finished, and this ordeal in addition to interrupting his work had enfeebled his powers of resistance and greatly reduced his vitality. He recovered from the fever and was able to take up the book again, but the organ of life was pronounced ominously weak and it was enjoined upon him with some sharpness that he should lend himself to no worries. It might have struck me as on the cards that his worries would now be surmountable, for when he began to mend he expressed to me a conviction almost contagious that he had never yet made so adroit a bid as in the idea of *The Hidden Heart*. It is grimly droll to reflect that this superb little composition, the shortest of his novels but perhaps the love-liest, was planned from the first as an 'adventure-story' on approved lines. It was the way they all did the adventure-story that he tried most dauntlessly to emulate. I wonder how many readers ever divined to which of their bookshelves *The Hidden Heart* was so exclusively addressed. High medical advice early in the summer had been quite viciously clear as to the incon-venience that might ensue to him should he neglect to spend the winter in Egypt. He was not a man to neglect anything; but Egypt seemed to us all then as unattainable as a second edition. He finished *The Hidden Heart* with the energy of apprehension and desire, for if the book should happen to do what 'books of that class', as the publisher said, sometimes did he might well have a fund to draw on. As soon as I read the deep and delicate thing I knew, as I had known in each case before, exactly how well it would do. Poor Limbert in this long business always figured to me an undiscourageable parent to whom only girls kept being born. A bouncing boy, a son and heir was devoutly prayed for and almanacks and old wives consulted; but the spell was inveterate, incurable, and *The Hidden Heart* proved, so to speak, but another female child. When the winter arrived accordingly Egypt was out of the question. Jane Highmore, to my knowledge, wanted to lend him money, and there were even greater devotees who did their best to induce him to lean on them. There was so marked a 'movement' among his friends that a very considerable sum would have been at his disposal; but his stiffness was invincible: it had its root, I think, in his sense, on his own side, of sacrifices already made. He had sacrificed honour and pride, and he had sacrificed them precisely to the question of money. He would evidently, should he be able to go on, have to continue to sacrifice them, but it must be all in the way to which he had now, as he considered, hardened himself. He had spent years in plotting for favour, and since on favour he must live it could only be as a bargain and a price.

He got through the early part of the season better than we feared, and I went down in great elation to spend Christmas on the goose-green. He told me late on Christmas eve, after our simple domestic revels had sunk to rest and we sat together by the fire, that he had been visited the night before in wakeful hours by the finest fancy for a really good thing that he had ever felt descend in the darkness. 'It's just the vision of a situation that contains, upon my honour, everything,' he said, 'and I wonder that I've never thought of it before.' He didn't describe it further, contrary to his common practice, and I only knew later, by Mrs Limbert, that he had begun *Derogation* and that he was completely full of his subject. It was a subject however that he was not to live to treat. The work went on for a couple of months in happy mystery, without revelations even to his wife. He had not invited her to help him to get up his case – she had not taken the field with him as on his previous campaigns. We only knew he was at it again but that less even than ever had been said about the impression to be made on the market. I saw him in February and thought him sufficiently at ease. The great thing was that he was immensely interested and was pleased with the omens. I got a strange, stirring sense that he had not consulted the usual ones and indeed that he had floated away into a grand indifference, into a reckless consciousness of art. The voice of the market had suddenly grown faint and far: he had come back at the last, as people so often do, to one of the moods, the sincerities of his prime. Was he really with a blurred sense of the urgent doing something now only for himself? We wondered and waited – we felt that he was a little confused. What had happened, I was afterwards satisfied, was that he had quite forgotten whether he generally sold or not. He had merely waked up one morning again in the country of the blue and had stayed there with a good conscience and a great idea. He stayed till death knocked at the gate, for the pen dropped from his hand only at the moment when from sudden failure of the heart his eyes, as he sank back in his chair, closed for ever. *Derogation* is a splendid fragment; it evidently would have been one of his high successes. I am not prepared to say it would have waked up the libraries.

THE ALTAR OF THE DEAD

I

HE had a mortal dislike, poor Stransom, to lean anniversaries, and he disliked them still more when they made a pretence of a figure. Celebrations and suppressions were equally painful to him, and there was only one of the former that found a place in his life. Again and again he had kept in his own fashion the day of the year on which Mary Antrim died. It would be more to the point perhaps to say that the day kept *him*: it kept him at least, effectually, from doing anything else. It took hold of him year after year with a hand of which time had softened but had never loosened the touch. He waked up to this feast of memory as consciously as he would have waked up to his marriage-morn. Marriage had had, of old, but too little to say to the matter: for the girl who was to have been his bride there had been no bridal embrace. She had died of a malignant fever after the wedding-day had been fixed, and he had lost, before fairly tasting it, an affection that promised to fill his life to the brim.

Of that benediction, however, it would have been false to say this life could really be emptied: it was still ruled by a pale ghost, it was still ordered by a sovereign presence. He had not been a man of numerous passions, and even in all these years no sense had grown stronger with him than the sense of being bereft. He had needed no priest and no altar to make him for ever widowed. He had done many things in the world – he had done almost all things but one: he had never forgotten. He had tried to put into his existence whatever else might take up room in it, but he had never made it anything but a house of which the mistress was eternally absent. She was most absent of all on the recurrent December day that his tenacity set apart. He had no designed observance of it, but his nerves made it all their own. They always drove him forth on a long walk, for the goal of his pilgrimage was far. She had been buried in a London suburb, in a place then almost natural, but which he had seen lose one after another every feature of freshness. It was in truth during the moments he stood there that his eyes beheld the place least. They looked at another image, they opened to another light. Was it a credible future? Was it an incredible past? Whatever it was, it was an immense escape from the actual.

It is true that if there were not other dates than this there were other memories; and by the time George Stransom was fifty-five such memories had greatly multiplied. There were other ghosts in his life than the ghost of Mary Antrim. He had perhaps not had more losses than most men, but he had counted his losses more; he had not seen death more closely, but he had, in a manner, felt it more deeply. He had formed little by little the habit of numbering his Dead: it had come to him tolerably early in life that there was something one had to do for them. They were there in their simplified, intensified essence, their conscious absence and expressive patience, as personally there as if they had only been stricken dumb. When all sense of them failed, all sound of them ceased, it was as if their purgatory were really still on earth: they asked so little that they got, poor things, even less, and died again, died every day, of the hard usage of life. They had no organised service, no reserved place, no honour, no shelter, no safety. Even ungenerous people provided for the living, but even those who were called most generous did nothing for the others. So, on George Stransom's part, there grew up with the years a determination that he at least would do something, do it, that is, for his own, and perform the great charity without reproach. Every man had his own, and every man had, to meet this charity, the ample resources of the soul.

It was doubtless the voice of Mary Antrim that spoke for them best; at any rate, as the years went on, he found himself in regular communion with these alternative associates, with those whom indeed he always called in his thoughts the Others. He spared them the moments, he organised the charity. How it grew up he probably never could have told you, but what came to pass was that an altar, such as was after all within everybody's compass, lighted with perpetual candles and dedicated to these secret rites, reared itself in his spiritual spaces. He had wondered of old, in some embarrassment, whether he had a religion; being very sure, and not a little content, that he had not at all events the religion some of the people he had known wanted him to have. Gradually this question was straightened out for him: it became clear to him that the religion instilled by his earliest consciousness had been simply the religion of the Dead. It suited his inclination, it satisfied his spirit, it gave employment to his piety. It answered his love of great offices, of a solemn and splendid ritual, for no shrine could be more bedecked and no ceremonial more stately than those to which his worship was attached. He had no imagination about these things save that they were accessible to every one who should ever feel the need of them. The poorest could build such temples of the spirit – could make them blaze with candles and smoke with incense, make them flash with pictures and flowers. The cost, in the common phrase, of keeping them up fell entirely on the liberal heart.

II

HE had this year, on the eve of his anniversary, as it happened, an emotion not unconnected with that range of feeling. Walking home at the close of a busy day, he was arrested in the London street by the particular effect of a shop-front which lighted the dull brown air with its mercenary grin and before which several persons were gathered. It was the window of a jeweller whose diamonds and sapphires seemed to laugh, in flashes like high notes of sound, with the mere joy of knowing how much more they were 'worth' than most of the dingy pedestrians staring at them from the other side of the pane. Stransom lingered long enough to suspend, in a vision, a string of pearls about the white neck of Mary Antrim, and then was kept an instant longer by the sound of a voice he knew. Next him was a mumbling old woman, and beyond the old woman a gentleman with a lady on his arm. It was from him, from Paul Creston, the voice had proceeded: he was talking with the lady of some precious object in the window. Stransom had no sooner recognised him than the old woman turned away; but simultaneously with this increase of opportunity he became aware of a strangeness which stayed him in the very act of laying his hand on his friend's arm. It lasted only a few seconds, but a few seconds were long enough for the flash of a wild question. Was *not* Mrs Creston dead? – the ambiguity met him there in the short drop of her husband's voice, the drop conjugal, if it ever was, and in the way the two figures leaned to each other. Creston, making a step to look at something else, came nearer, glanced at him, started and exclaimed – a circumstance the effect of which was at first only to leave Stransom staring, staring back across the months at the different face, the wholly other face the poor man had shown him last, the blurred, ravaged mask bent over the open grave by which they had stood together. Creston was not in mourning now; he detached his arm from his companion's to grasp the hand of the older friend. He coloured as well as smiled in the strong light of the shop when Stransom raised a tentative hat to the lady. Stransom had just time to see that she was pretty before he found himself gaping at a fact more portentous. 'My dear fellow, let me make you acquainted with my wife.'

Creston had blushed and stammered over it, but in half a minute, at the rate we live in polite society, it had practically become, for Stransom, the mere memory of a shock. They stood there and laughed and talked; Stransom had instantly whisked the shock out of the way, to keep it for private consumption. He felt himself grimacing, he heard himself exaggerating the usual, but he was conscious that he had turned slightly faint. That new woman, that hired performer, Mrs Creston? Mrs Creston had been more living for him than any woman but one. This lady had a face that shone as publicly as the jeweller's window, and in the happy candour with which she wore her monstrous character there was an effect of gross immodesty. The character of Paul Creston's wife thus attributed to her was monstrous for reasons which Stransom could see that his friend perfectly knew that he knew. The happy pair had just arrived from America, and Stransom had not needed to be told this to divine the nationality of the lady. Somehow it deepened the foolish air that her husband's confused cordiality was unable to conceal. Stransom recalled that he had heard of poor Creston's having, while his bereavement was still fresh, gone to the United States for what people in such predicaments call a little change. He had found the little change indeed, he had brought the little change back; it was the little change that stood there and that, do what he would, he couldn't, while he showed those high front-teeth of his, look like anything but a conscious ass about. They were going into the shop Mrs Creston said, and she begged Mr Stransom to come with them and help to decide. He thanked her, opening his watch and pleading an engagement for which he was already late, and they parted while she shrieked into the fog, 'Mind now you come to see me right away!' Creston had had the delicacy not to suggest that, and Stransom hoped it hurt him somewhere to hear her scream it to all the echoes.

He felt quite determined, as he walked away, never in his life to go near her. She was perhaps a human being, but Creston oughtn't to have shown her without precautions, oughtn't indeed to have shown her at all. His precautions should have been those of a forger or a murderer, and the people at home would never have mentioned extradition. This was a wife for foreign service or purely external use; a decent consideration would have spared her the injury of comparisons. Such were the first reflections of George Stransom's amazement; but as he sat alone that night – there were particular hours that he always passed alone – the harshness dropped from them and left only the pity. *He* could spend an evening with Kate Creston, if the man to whom she had given everything couldn't. He had known her twenty years, and she was the only woman for whom he might perhaps have been unfaithful. She was all cleverness and sympathy and charm; her house had been the very easiest in all the world and her friendship the very firmest. Without accidents he had loved her, without accidents every one had loved her: she had made the passions about her as regular as the moon makes the tides. She had been also of course far too good for her husband, but he never suspected it, and in nothing had she been more admirable than in the exquisite art with which she tried to keep every one else (keeping Creston was no trouble) from finding it out. Here was a man to whom she had devoted her life and for whom she had given it up – dying to bring into the world a child of his bed; and she had had only to submit to her fate to have, ere the grass was green on her grave, no more existence for him than a domestic servant he had replaced. The frivolity, the indecency of it made Stransom's eyes fill; and he had that evening a rich, almost happy sense that he alone, in a world without delicacy, had a right to hold up his head. While he smoked, after dinner, he had a book in his lap, but he had no eyes for his page: his eyes, in the swarming void of things, seemed to have caught Kate Creston's, and it was into their sad silences he looked. It was to him her sentient spirit had turned, knowing that it was of her he would think. He thought, for a long time, of how the closed eyes of dead women could still live – how they could open again, in a quiet lamplit room, long after they had looked their last. They had looks that remained, as great poets had quoted lines.

The newspaper lay by his chair – the thing that came in the afternoon and the servants thought one wanted; without sense for what was in it he had mechanically unfolded and then dropped it. Before he went to bed he took it up, and this time, at the top of a paragraph, he was caught by five words that made him start. He stood staring, before the fire, at the 'Death of Sir Acton Hague, K.C.B.', the man who, ten years earlier, had been the nearest of his friends and whose deposition from this eminence had practically left it without an occupant. He had seen him after that catastrophe, but he had not seen him for years. Standing there before the fire he turned cold as he read what had befallen him. Promoted a short time previous to the governorship of the Westward Islands, Acton Hague had died, in the bleak honour of this exile, of an illness consequent on the bite of a poisonous snake. His career was compressed by the newspaper into a dozen lines, the perusal of which excited on George Stransom's part no warmer feeling than one of relief at the absence of any mention of their quarrel, an incident accidentally tainted at the time, thanks to their joint immersion in large affairs, with a horrible publicity. Public indeed was the wrong Stransom had, to his own sense, suffered, the insult he had blankly taken from the only man with whom he had ever been intimate; the friend, almost adored, of his University years, the subject, later, of his passionate loyalty: so public that he had never spoken of it to a human creature, so public that he had completely overlooked it. It had made the difference for him that friendship too was all over, but it had only made just that one. The shock of interests had been private, intensely so; but the action taken by Hague had been in the face of men. To-day it all seemed to have occurred merely to the end that George Stransom should think of him as 'Hague' and measure exactly how much he himself could feel like a stone. He went cold, suddenly and horribly cold, to bed.

III

THE next day, in the afternoon, in the great grey suburb, he felt that his long walk had tired him. In the dreadful cemetery alone he had been on his feet an hour. Instinctively, coming back, they had taken him a devious course, and it was a desert in which no circling cabman hovered over possible prey. He paused on a corner and measured the dreariness; then he became aware in the gathered dusk that he was in one of those tracts of London which are less gloomy by night than by day, because, in the former case, of the civil gift of light. By day there was nothing, but by night there were lamps, and George Stransom was in a mood which made lamps good in themselves. It wasn't that they could show him anything; it was only that they could burn clear. To his surprise, however, after a while, they did show him something: the arch of a high doorway approached by a low terrace of steps, in the depth of which – it formed a dim vestibule – the raising of a curtain, at the moment he passed, gave him a glimpse of an avenue of gloom with a glow of tapers at the end. He stopped and looked up, making out that the place was a church. The thought quickly came to him that since he was tired he might rest there; so that after a moment he had in turn pushed up the leathern curtain and gone in. It was a temple of the old persuasion, and there had evidently been a function – perhaps a service for the dead; the high altar was still a blaze of candles. This was an exhibition he always liked, and he dropped into a seat with relief. More than it had ever yet come home to him it struck him as good that there should be churches.

This one was almost empty and the other altars were dim; a verger shuffled about, an old woman coughed, but it seemed to Stransom there was hospitality in the thick sweet air. Was it only the savour of the incense, or was it something larger and more guaranteed? He had at any rate quitted the great grey suburb and come nearer to the warm centre. He presently ceased to feel an intruder – he gained at last even a sense of community with the only worshipper in his neighbourhood, the sombre presence of a woman, in mourning unrelieved, whose back was all he could see of her and who had sunk deep into prayer at no great distance from him. He wished he could sink, like her, to the very bottom, be as motionless, as rapt in prostration. After a few moments he shifted his seat; it was almost indelicate to be so aware of her. But Stransom subsequently lost himself altogether; he floated away on the sea of light. If occasions like this had been more frequent in his life he would have been more frequently conscious of the great original type, set up in a myriad temples, of the unapproachable shrine he had erected in his mind. That shrine had begun as a reflection of ecclesiastical pomps, but the echo had ended by growing more distinct than the sound. The sound now rang out, the type blazed at him with all its fires and with a mystery of radiance in which endless meanings could glow. The thing became, as he sat there, his appropriate altar, and each starry candle an appropriate vow. He numbered them, he named them, he grouped them – it was the silent roll-call of his Dead. They made together a brightness vast and intense, a brightness in which the mere chapel of his thoughts grew so dim that as it faded away he asked himself if he shouldn't find his real comfort in some material act, some outward worship.

This idea took possession of him while, at a distance, the black-robed lady continued prostrate; he was quietly thrilled with his conception, which at last brought him to his feet in the sudden excitement of a plan. He wandered softly about the church, pausing in the different chapels, which were all, save one, applied to a special devotion. It was in this one, dark and ungarnished, that he stood longest – the length of time it took him fully to grasp the conception of gilding it with his bounty. He should snatch it from no other rites and associate it with nothing profane; he would simply take it as it should be given up to him and make it a masterpiece of splendour and a mountain of fire. Tended sacredly all the year, with the sanctifying church around it, it would always be ready for his offices. There would be difficulties, but from the first they presented themselves only as difficulties surmounted. Even for a person so little affiliated the thing would be a matter of arrangement. He saw it all in advance, and how bright in especial the place would become to him in the intermissions of toil and the dusk of afternoons; how rich in assurance at all times, but especially in the indifferent world. Before withdrawing he drew nearer again to the spot where he had first sat down, and in the movement he met the lady whom he had seen praying and who was now on her way to the door. She passed him quickly, and he had only a glimpse of her pale face and her unconscious, almost sightless eyes. For that instant she looked faded and handsome.

This was the origin of the rites more public, yet certainly esoteric, that he at last found himself able to establish. It took a long time, it took a year, and both the process and the result would have been – for any who knew – a vivid picture of his good faith. No one did know, in fact – no one but the bland ecclesiastics whose acquaintance he had promptly sought, whose objections he had softly overridden, whose curiosity and sympathy he had artfully charmed, whose assent to his eccentric munificence he had eventually won, and who had asked for concessions in exchange for indulgences. Stransom had of course at an early stage of his inquiry been referred to the Bishop, and the Bishop had been delightfully human, the Bishop had been almost amused. Success was within sight, at any rate, from the moment the attitude of those whom it concerned became liberal in response to liberality. The altar and the small chapel that enclosed it, consecrated to an ostensible and customary worship, were to be splendidly maintained; all that Stransom reserved to himself was the number of his lights and the free enjoyment of his intention. When the intention had taken complete effect the enjoyment became even greater than he had ventured to hope. He liked to think of this effect when he was far from it – he liked to convince himself of it yet again when he was near. He was not often, indeed, so near as that a visit to it had not perforce something of the patience of a pilgrimage; but the time he gave to his devotion came to seem to him more a contribution to his other interests than a betrayal of them. Even a loaded life might be easier when one had added a new necessity to it.

How much easier was probably never guessed by those who simply knew that there were hours when he disappeared and for many of whom there was a vulgar reading of what they used to call his plunges. These plunges were into depths quieter than the deep sea-caves, and the habit, at the end of a year or two, had become the one it would have cost him most to relinquish. Now they had really, his Dead, something that was indefeasibly theirs; and he liked to think that they might, in cases, be the Dead of others, as well as that the Dead of others might be invoked there under the protection of what he had done. Whoever bent a knee on the carpet he had laid down appeared to him to act in the spirit of his intention. Each of his lights had a name for him, and from time to time a new light was kindled. This was what he had fundamentally agreed for, that there should always be room for them all. What those who passed or lingered saw was simply the most resplendent of the altars, called suddenly into vivid usefulness, with a quiet elderly man, for whom it evidently had a fascination, often seated there in a maze or a doze; but half the satisfaction of the spot for this mysterious and fitful worshipper was that he found the years of his life there, and the ties, the affections, the struggles, the submissions, the conquests, if there had been such, a record of that adventurous journey in which the beginnings and the endings of human relations are the lettered mile-stones. He had in general little taste for the past as a part of his own history; at other times and in other places it mostly seemed to him pitiful to consider and impossible to repair; but on these occasions he accepted it with something of that positive gladness with which one adjusts one's self to an ache that is beginning to succumb to treatment. To the treatment of time the malady of life begins at a given moment to succumb; and these were doubtless the hours at which that truth most came home to him. The day was written for him there on which he had first become acquainted with death, and the successive phases of the acquaintance were each marked with a flame.

The flames were gathering thick at present, for Stransom had entered that dark defile of our earthly descent in which some one dies every day. It was only yesterday that Kate Creston had flashed out her white fire; yet already there were younger stars ablaze on the tips of the tapers. Various persons in whom his interest had not been intense drew closer to him by entering this company. He went over it, head by head, till he felt like the shepherd of a huddled flock, with all a shepherd's vision of differences imperceptible. He knew his candles apart, up to the colour of the flame, and would still have known them had their positions all been changed. To other imaginations they might stand for other things – that they should stand for something to be hushed before was all he desired; but he was intensely conscious of the personal note of each and of the distinguishable way it contributed to the concert. There were hours at which he almost caught himself wishing that certain of his friends would now die, that he might establish with them in this manner a connection more charming than, as it happened, it was possible to enjoy with them in life. In regard to those from whom one was separated by the long curves of the globe such a connection could only be an improvement: it brought them instantly within reach. Of course there were gaps in the constellation, for Stransom knew he could only pretend to act for his own, and it was not every figure passing before his eyes into the great obscure that was entitled to a memorial. There was a strange sanctification in death, but some characters were more sanctified by being forgotten than by being remembered. The greatest blank in the shining page was the memory of Acton Hague, of which he inveterately tried to rid himself. For Acton Hague no flame could ever rise on any altar of his.

IV

EVERY year, the day he walked back from the great graveyard, he went to church as he had done the day his idea was born. It was on this occasion, as it happened, after a year had passed, that he began to observe his altar to be haunted by a worshipper at least as frequent as himself. Others of the faithful, and in the rest of the church, came and went, appealing sometimes, when they disappeared, to a vague or to a particular recognition; but this unfailing presence was always to be observed when he arrived and still in possession when he departed. He was surprised, the first time, at the promptitude with which it assumed an identity for him – the identity of the lady whom, two years before, on his anniversary, he had seen so intensely bowed, and of whose tragic face he had had so flitting a vision. Given the time that had elapsed, his recollection of her was fresh enough to make him wonder. Of himself she had of course no impression, or rather she had none at first: the time came when her manner of transacting her business suggested to him that she had gradually guessed his call to be of the same order. She used his altar for her own purpose – he could only hope that, sad and solitary as she always struck him, she used it for her own Dead. There were interruptions, infidelities, all on his part, calls to other associations and duties; but as the months went on he found her whenever he returned, and he ended by taking pleasure in the thought that he had given her almost the contentment he had given himself. They worshipped side by side so often that there were moments when he wished he might be sure, so straight did their prospect stretch away of growing old together in their rites. She was younger than he, but she looked as if her Dead were at least as numerous as his candles. She had no colour, no sound, no fault, and another of the things about which he had made up his mind was that she had no fortune. She was always black-robed, as if she had had a succession of sorrows. People were not poor, after all, whom so many losses could overtake; they were positively rich when they had so much to give up. But the air of this devoted and indifferent woman, who always made, in any attitude, a beautiful, accidental line, conveyed somehow to Stransom that she had known more kinds of trouble than one.

He had a great love of music and little time for the joy of it; but occasionally, when workaday noises were muffled by Saturday afternoons, it used to come back to him that there were glories. There were moreover friends who reminded him of this and side by side with whom he found himself sitting out concerts. On one of these winter evenings, in St James's Hall, he became aware after he had seated himself that the lady he had so often seen at church was in the place next him and was evidently alone, as he also this time happened to be. She was at first too absorbed in the consideration of the programme to heed him, but when she at last glanced at him he took advantage of the movement to speak to her, greeting her with the remark that he felt as if he already knew her. She smiled as she said 'Oh yes, I recognise you'; yet in spite of this admission of their long acquaintance it was the first time he had ever seen her smile. The effect of it was suddenly to contribute more to that acquaintance than all the previous meetings had done. He hadn't 'taken in', he said to himself, that she was so pretty. Later, that evening (it was while he rolled along in a hansom on his way to dine out) he added that he hadn't taken in that she was so interesting. The next morning, in the midst of his work, he quite suddenly and irrelevantly reflected that his impression of her, beginning so far back, was like a winding river that had at last reached the sea.

His work was indeed blurred a little, all that day, by the sense of what had now passed between them. It wasn't much, but it had just made the difference. They had listened together to Beethoven and Schumann; they had talked in the pauses and at the end, when at the door, to which they moved together, he had asked her if he could help her in the matter of getting away. She had thanked him and put up her umbrella, slipping into the crowd without an allusion to their meeting yet again and leaving him to remember at leisure that not a word had been exchanged about the place in which they frequently met. This circumstance seemed to him at one moment natural enough and at another perverse. She mightn't in the least have recognised his warrant for speaking to her; and yet if she hadn't he would have judged her an underbred woman. It was odd that when nothing had really ever brought them together he should have been able successfully to assume that they were in a manner old friends – that this negative quantity was somehow more than they could express. His success, it was true, had been qualified by her quick escape, so that there grew up in him an absurd desire to put it to some better test. Save in so far as some other improbable accident might assist him, such a test could be only to meet her afresh at church. Left to himself he would have gone to church the very next afternoon, just for the curiosity of seeing if he should find her there. But he was not left to himself, a fact he discovered quite at the last, after he had virtually made up his mind to go. The influence that kept him away really revealed to him how little to himself his Dead ever left him. They reminded him that he went only for them – for nothing else in the world.

The force of this reminder kept him away ten days: he hated to connect the place with anything but his offices or to give a glimpse of the curiosity that had been on the point of moving him. It was absurd to weave a tangle about a matter so simple as a custom of devotion that might so easily have been daily or hourly; yet the tangle got itself woven. He was sorry, he was disappointed: it was as if a long, happy spell had been broken and he had lost a familiar security. At the last, however, he asked himself if he was to stay away for ever from the fear of this muddle about motives. After an interval neither longer nor shorter than usual he re-entered the church with a clear con-viction that he should scarcely heed the presence or the absence of the lady of the concert. This indifference didn't prevent his instantly perceiving that for the only time since he had first seen her she was not on the spot. He had now no scruple about giving her time to arrive, but she didn't arrive, and when he went away still missing her he was quite profanely and consent-ingly sorry. If her absence made the tangle more intricate, that was only her fault. By the end of another year it was very intricate indeed; but by that time he didn't in the least care, and it was only his cultivated consciousness that had given him scruples. Three times in three months he had gone to church without finding her, and he felt that he had not needed these occasions to show him that his suspense had quite dropped. Yet it was, incongruously, not indifference, but a refinement of delicacy that had kept him from asking the sacristan, who would of course immediately have recognised his description of her, whether she had been seen at other hours. His delicacy had kept him from asking any question about her at any time, and it was exactly the same virtue that had left him so free to be decently civil to her at the concert.

This happy advantage now served him anew, enabling him when she finally met his eyes – it was after a fourth trial – to determine without hesitation to wait till she should retire. He joined her in the street as soon as she had done so, and asked her if he might accompany her a certain distance. With her placid permission he went as far as a house in the neighbour-hood at which she had business: she let him know it was not where she lived. She lived, as she said, in a mere slum, with an old aunt, a person in connection with whom she spoke of the engrossment of humdrum duties and regular occupations. She was not, the mourning niece, in her first youth, and her van-ished freshness had left something behind which, for Stransom, represented the proof that it had been tragically sacrificed. Whatever she gave him the assurance of she gave it without references. She might in fact have been a divorced duchess, and she might have been an old maid who taught the harp.

V

THEY fell at last into the way of walking together almost every time they met, though, for a long time, they never met any-where save at church. He couldn't ask her to come and see him, and, as if she had not a proper place to receive him, she never invited him. As much as himself she knew the world of London, but from an undiscussed instinct of privacy they haunted the region not mapped on the social chart. On the return she always made him leave her at the same corner. She looked with him, as a pretext for a pause, at the depressed things in

suburban shop-fronts; and there was never a word he had said
to her that she had not beautifully understood. For long ages he
never knew her name, any more than she had ever pronounced
his own; but it was not their names that mattered, it was only
their perfect practice and their common need.

These things made their whole relation so impersonal that
they had not the rules or reasons people found in ordinary
friendships. They didn't care for the things it was supposed
necessary to care for in the intercourse of the world. They
ended one day (they never knew which of them expressed it
first) by throwing out the idea that they didn't care for each
other. Over this idea they grew quite intimate; they rallied to it
in a way that marked a fresh start in their confidence. If to feel
deeply together about certain things wholly distinct from themselves didn't constitute a safety, where was safety to be looked
for? Not lightly nor often, not without occasion nor without
emotion, any more than in any other reference by serious
people to a mystery of their faith; but when something had
happened to warm, as it were, the air for it, they came as near
as they could come to calling their Dead by name. They felt it
was coming very near to utter their thought at all. The word
'they' expressed enough; it limited the mention, it had a dignity
of its own, and if, in their talk, you had heard our friends use it,
you might have taken them for a pair of pagans of old alluding
decently to the domesticated gods. They never knew – at least
Stransom never knew – how they had learned to be sure about
each other. If it had been with each a question of what the other
was there for, the certitude had come in some fine way of its
own. Any faith, after all, has the instinct of propagation, and it
was as natural as it was beautiful that they should have taken
pleasure on the spot in the imagination of a following. If the
following was for each but a following of one, it had proved in
the event to be sufficient. Her debt, however, of course, was
much greater than his, because while she had only given him a
worshipper he had given her a magnificent temple. Once she
said she pitied him for the length of his list (she had counted his
candles almost as often as himself) and this made him wonder
what could have been the length of hers. He had wondered

before at the coincidence of their losses, especially as from time to time a new candle was set up. On one occasion some accident led him to express this curiosity, and she answered as if she was surprised that he hadn't already understood. 'Oh, for me, you know, the more there are the better – there could never be too many. I should like hundreds and hundreds – I should like thousands; I should like a perfect mountain of light.'

Then of course, in a flash, he understood. 'Your Dead are only One?'

She hesitated as she had never hesitated. 'Only One,' she answered, colouring as if now he knew her innermost secret. It really made him feel that he knew less than before, so difficult was it for him to reconstitute a life in which a single experience had reduced all others to nought. His own life, round its central hollow, had been packed close enough. After this she appeared to have regretted her confession, though at the moment she spoke there had been pride in her very embarrassment. She declared to him that his own was the larger, the dearer possession – the portion one would have chosen if one had been able to choose; she assured him she could perfectly imagine some of the echoes with which his silences were peopled. He knew she couldn't: one's relation to what one had loved and hated had been a relation too distinct from the relations of others. But this didn't affect the fact that they were growing old together in their piety. She was a feature of that piety, but even at the ripe stage of acquaintance in which they occasionally arranged to meet at a concert or to go together to an exhibition she was not a feature of anything else. The most that happened was that his worship became paramount. Friend by friend dropped away till at last there were more emblems on his altar than houses left him to enter. She was more than any other the friend who remained, but she was unknown to all the rest. Once when she had discovered, as they called it, a new star, she used the expression that the chapel at last was full.

'Oh no,' Stransom replied, 'there is a great thing wanting for that! The chapel will never be full till a candle is set up before which all the others will pale. It will be the tallest candle of all.'

Her mild wonder rested on him. 'What candle do you mean?'

'I mean, dear lady, my own.'

He had learned after a long time that she earned money by her pen, writing under a designation that she never told him in magazines that he never saw. She knew too well what he couldn't read and what she couldn't write, and she taught him to cultivate indifference with a success that did much for their good relations. Her invisible industry was a convenience to him; it helped his contented thought of her, the thought that rested in the dignity of her proud, obscure life, her little remunerated art and her little impenetrable home. Lost, with her obscure relative, in her dim suburban world, she came to the surface for him in distant places. She was really the priestess of his altar, and whenever he quitted England he committed it to her keeping. She proved to him afresh that women have more of the spirit of religion than men; he felt his fidelity pale and faint in comparison with hers. He often said to her that since he had so little time to live he rejoiced in her having so much; so glad was he to think she would guard the temple when he should have ceased. He had a great plan for that, which of course he told her too, a bequest of money to keep it up in undiminished state. Of the administration of this fund he would appoint her superintendent, and if the spirit should move her she might kindle a taper even for him.

'And who will kindle one even for me?' she gravely inquired.

VI

SHE was always in mourning, yet the day he came back from the longest absence he had yet made her appearance immediately told him she had lately had a bereavement. They met on this occasion as she was leaving the church, so that postponing his own entrance he instantly offered to turn round and walk away with her. She considered, then she said: 'Go in now, but come and see me in an hour.' He knew the small vista of her street, closed at the end and as dreary as an empty pocket, where the pairs of shabby little houses, semi-detached but indissolubly united, were like married couples on bad terms. Often, however, as he had gone to the beginning, he had never gone beyond. Her aunt was dead – that he immediately guessed, as well as that it made a difference; but when she had for the first time mentioned her number he found himself, on her leaving him, not a little agitated by this sudden liberality. She was not a person with whom, after all, one got on so very fast: it had taken him months and months to learn her name, years and years to learn her address. If she had looked, on this reunion, so much older to him, how in the world did he look to her? She had reached the period of life that he had long since reached, when, after separations, the dreadful clockface of the friend we meet announces the hour we have tried to forget. He couldn't have said what he expected as, at the end of his waiting, he turned the corner at which, for years, he had always paused; simply not to pause was a sufficient cause for emotion. It was an event, somehow; and in all their long acquaintance there had never been such a thing. The event grew larger when, five minutes later, in the faint elegance of her little drawing-room, she quavered out some greeting which showed the measure she took of it. He had a strange sense of having come for something in particular; strange because, literally, there was nothing particular between them, nothing save that they were at one on their great point, which had long ago become a magnificent matter of course. It was true that after she had said 'You can always come now, you know,' the thing he was there for seemed already to have happened. He asked her if it was the death of her aunt that made the difference; to which she replied: 'She never knew I knew you. I wished her not to.' The beautiful clearness of her candour – her faded beauty was like a summer twilight – disconnected the words from any image of deceit. They might have struck him as the record of a deep dissimulation; but she had always given him a sense of noble reasons. The vanished aunt was present, as he looked about him, in the small complacencies of the room, the beaded velvet and the fluted moreen; and though, as we know, he had the worship of the Dead, he found himself not definitely regretting this lady. If she was not in his long list, however, she was in her niece's short one, and Stransom presently observed to his friend that now, at least, in the place they haunted together, she would have another object of devotion.

'Yes, I shall have another. She was very kind to me. It's that that makes the difference.'

He judged, wondering a good deal before he made any motion to leave her, that the difference would somehow be very great and would consist of still other things than her having let him come in. It rather chilled him, for they had been happy together as they were. He extracted from her at any rate an intimation that she should now have larger means, that her aunt's tiny fortune had come to her, so that there was henceforth only one to consume what had formerly been made to suffice for two. This was a joy to Stransom, because it had hitherto been equally impossible for him either to offer her presents or to find contentment in not doing so. It was too ugly to be at her side that way, abounding himself and yet not able to overflow – a demonstration that would have been a signally false note. Even her better situation too seemed only to draw out in a sense the loneliness of her future. It would merely help her to live more and more for their small ceremonial, at a time when he himself had begun wearily to feel that, having set it in motion, he might depart. When they had sat a while in the pale parlour she got up and said: 'This isn't *my* room: let us go into mine.' They had only to cross the narrow hall, as he found, to pass into quite another air. When she had closed the door of the second room, as she called it, he felt that he had at last real possession of her. The place had the flush of life – it was expressive; its dark red walls were articulate with memories and relics. These were simple things – photographs and water-colours, scraps of writing framed and ghosts of flowers embalmed; but only a moment was needed to show him they had a common meaning. It was here that she had lived and worked; and she had already told him she would make no change of scene. He saw that the objects about her mainly had reference to certain places and times; but after a minute he distinguished among them a small portrait of a gentleman. At a distance and without their glasses his eyes were only caught by

it enough to feel a vague curiosity. Presently this impulse
carried him nearer, and in another moment he was staring at
the picture in stupefaction and with the sense that some sound
had broken from him. He was further conscious that he showed
his companion a white face when he turned round on her with
the exclamation: 'Acton Hague!'

She gave him back his astonishment. 'Did you know him?'

'He was the friend of all my youth – my early manhood. And
you knew him?'

She coloured at this, and for a moment her answer failed;
her eyes took in everything in the place, and a strange irony
reached her lips as she echoed: 'Knew him?'

Then Stransom understood, while the room heaved like the
cabin of a ship, that its whole contents cried out with him, that
it was a museum in his honour, that all her later years had been
addressed to him and that the shrine he himself had reared had
been passionately converted to this use. It was all for Acton
Hague that she had kneeled every day at his altar. What need
had there been for a consecrated candle when he was present in
the whole array? The revelation seemed to smite our friend in
the face, and he dropped into a seat and sat silent. He had
quickly become aware that she was shocked at the vision of his
own shock, but as she sank on the sofa beside him and laid her
hand on his arm he perceived almost as soon that she was
unable to resent it as much as she would have liked.

VII

HE learned in that instant two things: one of them was that
even in so long a time she had gathered no knowledge of his
great intimacy and his great quarrel; the other was that in spite
of this ignorance, strangely enough, she supplied on the spot a
reason for his confusion. 'How extraordinary,' he presently
exclaimed, 'that we should never have known!'

She gave a wan smile which seemed to Stransom stranger
even than the fact itself. 'I never, never spoke of him.'

Stransom looked about the room again. 'Why then, if your
life had been so full of him?'

'Mayn't I put you that question as well? Hadn't your life also been full of him?'

'Any one's, every one's life was who had the wonderful experience of knowing him. I never spoke of him,' Stransom added in a moment, 'because he did me – years ago – an unforgettable wrong.' She was silent, and with the full effect of his presence all about them it almost startled her visitor to hear no protest escape from her. She accepted his words; he turned his eyes to her again to see in what manner she accepted them. It was with rising tears and an extraordinary sweetness in the movement of putting out her hand to take his own. Nothing more wonderful had ever appeared to Stransom than, in that little chamber of remembrance and homage, to see her convey with such exquisite mildness that as from Acton Hague any injury was credible. The clock ticked in the stillness – Hague had probably given it to her – and while he let her hold his hand with a tenderness that was almost an assumption of responsibility for his old pain as well as his new, Stransom after a minute broke out: 'Good God, how he must have used *you*!'

She dropped his hand at this, got up and, moving across the room, made straight a small picture to which, on examining it, he had given a slight push. Then turning round on him with her pale gaiety recovered: 'I've forgiven him!' she declared.

'I know what you've done,' said Stransom; 'I know what you've done for years.' For a moment they looked at each other across the room, with their long community of service in their eyes. This short passage made, to Stransom's sense, for the woman before him, an immense, an absolutely naked confession; which was presently, suddenly blushing red and changing her place again, what she appeared to become aware that he perceived in it. He got up. 'How you must have loved him!' he cried.

'Women are not like men. They can love even where they've suffered.'

'Women are wonderful,' said Stransom. 'But I assure you I've forgiven him too.'

'If I had known of anything so strange I wouldn't have brought you here.'

'So that we might have gone on in our ignorance to the last?'

'What do you call the last?' she asked, smiling still.

At this he could smile back at her. 'You'll see – when it comes.'

She reflected a moment. 'This is better perhaps; but as we were – it was good.'

'Did it never happen that he spoke of me?' Stransom inquired.

Considering more intently, she made no answer, and he quickly recognised that he would have been adequately answered by her asking how often he himself had spoken of their terrible friend. Suddenly a brighter light broke in her face, and an excited idea sprang to her lips in the question: 'You *have* forgiven him?'

'How, if I hadn't, could I linger here?'

She winced, for an instant, at the deep but unintended irony of this; but even while she did so she panted quickly: 'Then in the lights on your altar—?'

'There's never a light for Acton Hague!'

She stared, with a great visible fall. 'But if he's one of your Dead?'

'He's one of the world's, if you like – he's one of yours. But he's not one of mine. Mine are only the Dead who died possessed of me. They're mine in death because they were mine in life.'

'*He* was yours in life then, even if for a while he ceased to be. If you forgave him you went back to him. Those whom we've once loved—'

'Are those who can hurt us most,' Stransom broke in.

'Ah, it's not true – you've *not* forgiven him!' she wailed with a passion that startled him.

He looked at her a moment. 'What was it he did to you?'

'Everything!' Then abruptly she put out her hand in farewell. 'Good-bye.'

He turned as cold as he had turned that night he read of the death of Acton Hague. 'You mean that we meet no more?'

'Not as we have met – not *there*!'

He stood aghast at this snap of their great bond, at the renouncement that rang out in the word she so passionately emphasised. 'But what's changed – for you?'

She hesitated, in all the vividness of a trouble that, for the first time since he had known her, made her splendidly stern. 'How can you understand now when you didn't understand before?'

'I didn't understand before only because I didn't know. Now that I know, I see what I've been living with for years,' Stransom went on very gently.

She looked at him with a larger allowance, as if she appreciated his good-nature. 'How can I, then, with this new knowledge of my own, ask you to continue to live with it?'

'I set up my altar, with its multiplied meanings,' Stransom began; but she quickly interrupted him.

'You set up your altar, and when I wanted one most I found it magnificently ready. I used it, with the gratitude I've always shown you, for I knew from of old that it was dedicated to Death. I told you, long ago, that my Dead were not many. Yours were, but all you had done for them was none too much for *my* worship! You had placed a great light for Each – I gathered them together for One!'

'We had simply different intentions,' Stransom replied. 'That, as you say, I perfectly knew, and I don't see why your intention shouldn't still sustain you.'

'That's because you're generous – you can imagine and think. But the spell is broken.'

It seemed to poor Stransom, in spite of his resistance, that it really was, and the prospect stretched grey and void before him. All, however, that he could say was: 'I hope you'll try before you give up.'

'If I had known you had ever known him I should have taken for granted he had his candle,' she presently rejoined. 'What's changed, as you say, is that on making the discovery I find he never has had it. That makes *my* attitude –' she paused a moment, as if thinking how to express it, then said simply – 'all wrong.'

'Come once again,' Stransom pleaded.

'Will you give him his candle?' she asked.

He hesitated, but only because it would sound ungracious; not because he had a doubt of his feeling. 'I can't do that!' he declared at last.

'Then good-bye.' And she gave him her hand again.

He had got his dismissal; besides which, in the agitation of everything that had opened out to him, he felt the need to recover himself as he could only do in solitude. Yet he lingered – lingered to see if she had no compromise to express, no attenuation to propose. But he only met her great lamenting eyes, in which indeed he read that she was as sorry for him as for any one else. This made him say: 'At least, at any rate, I may see you here.'

'Oh, yes, come if you like. But I don't think it will do.'

Stransom looked round the room once more; he felt in truth by no means sure it would do. He felt also stricken and more and more cold, and his chill was like an ague in which he had to make an effort not to shake. 'I must try on my side, if you can't try on yours,' he dolefully rejoined. She came out with him to the hall and into the doorway, and here he put to her the question that seemed to him the one he could least answer from his own wit. 'Why have you never let me come before?'

'Because my aunt would have seen you, and I should have had to tell her how I came to know you.'

'And what would have been the objection to that?'

'It would have entailed other explanations; there would at any rate have been that danger.'

'Surely she knew you went every day to church,' Stransom objected.

'She didn't know what I went for.'

'Of me then she never even heard?'

'You'll think I was deceitful. But I didn't need to be!'

Stransom was now on the lower doorstep, and his hostess held the door half-closed behind him. Through what remained of the opening he saw her framed face. He made a supreme appeal. 'What *did* he do to you?'

'It would have come out – *she* would have told you. That fear, at my heart – that was my reason!' And she closed the door, shutting him out.

VIII

HE had ruthlessly abandoned her – that, of course, was what he had done. Stransom made it all out in solitude, at leisure, fitting the unmatched pieces gradually together and dealing one by one with a hundred obscure points. She had known Hague only after her present friend's relations with him had wholly terminated; obviously indeed a good while after; and it was natural enough that of his previous life she should have ascertained only what he had judged good to communicate. There were passages it was quite conceivable that even in moments of the tenderest expansion he should have withheld. Of many facts in the career of a man so in the eye of the world there was of course a common knowledge; but this lady lived apart from public affairs, and the only period perfectly clear to her would have been the period following the dawn of her own drama. A man, in her place, would have 'looked up' the past – would even have consulted old newspapers. It remained singular indeed that in her long contact with the partner of her retrospect no accident had lighted a train; but there was no arguing about that; the accident had in fact come: it had simply been that security had prevailed. She had taken what Hague had given her, and her blankness in respect of his other connections was only a touch in the picture of that plasticity Stransom had supreme reason to know so great a master could have been trusted to produce.

This picture, for a while, was all that our friend saw: he caught his breath again and again as it came over him that the woman with whom he had had for years so fine a point of contact was a woman whom Acton Hague, of all men in the world, had more or less fashioned. Such as she sat there to-day, she was ineffaceably stamped with him. Beneficent, blameless as Stransom held her, he couldn't rid himself of the sense that he had been the victim of a fraud. She had imposed upon him hugely, though she had known it as little as he. All this later past came back to him as a time grotesquely misspent. Such at least were his first reflections; after a while he found himself more divided and only, as the end of it, more troubled. He imagined, recalled, reconstituted, figured out for himself the truth she had refused to give him; the effect of which was to make her seem to him only more saturated with her fate. He felt her spirit, in the strange business, to be finer than his own in the very degree in which she might have been, in which she certainly had been, more wronged. A woman, when she was wronged, was always more wronged than a man, and there were conditions when the least she could have got off with was more than the most he could have to endure. He was sure this rare creature wouldn't have got off with the least. He was awestruck at the thought of such a surrender – such a prostration. Moulded indeed she had been by powerful hands, to have converted her injury into an exaltation so sublime. The fellow had only had to die for everything that was ugly in him to be washed out in a torrent. It was vain to try to guess what had taken place, but nothing could be clearer than that she had ended by accusing herself. She absolved him at every point, she adored her very wounds. The passion by which he had profited had rushed back after its ebb, and now the tide of tenderness, arrested for ever at flood, was too deep even to fathom. Stransom sincerely considered that he had forgiven him; but how little he had achieved the miracle that she had achieved! His forgiveness was silence, but hers was mere unuttered sound. The light she had demanded for his altar would have broken his silence with a blare; whereas all the lights in the church were for her too great a hush.

She had been right about the difference – she had spoken the truth about the change: Stransom felt before long that he was perversely but definitely jealous. *His* tide had ebbed, not flowed; if he had 'forgiven' Acton Hague, that forgiveness was a motive with a broken spring. The very fact of her appeal for a material sign, a sign that should make her dead lover equal there with the others, presented the concession to Stransom as too handsome for the case. He had never thought of himself as hard, but an exorbitant article might easily render him so. He moved round and round this one, but only in widening circles – the more he looked at it the less acceptable it appeared. At the same time he had no illusion about the effect of his refusal; he perfectly saw that it was the beginning of a separation. He left her alone for many days; but when at last he called upon her again this conviction acquired a depressing force. In the interval he had kept away from the church, and he needed no fresh assurance from her to know she had not entered it. The change was complete enough: it had broken up her life. Indeed it had broken up his, for all the fires of his shrine seemed to him suddenly to have been quenched. A great indifference fell upon him, the weight of which was in itself a pain; and he never knew what his devotion had been for him till, in that shock, it stopped like a dropped watch. Neither did he know with how large a confidence he had counted on the final service that had now failed: the mortal deception was that in this abandonment the whole future gave way.

These days of her absence proved to him of what she was capable; all the more that he never dreamed she was vindictive or even resentful. It was not in anger she had forsaken him; it was in absolute submission to hard reality, to crude destiny. This came home to him when he sat with her again in the room in which her late aunt's conversation lingered like the tone of a cracked piano. She tried to make him forget how much they were estranged; but in the very presence of what they had given up it was impossible not to be sorry for her. He had taken from her so much more than she had taken from him. He argued with her again, told her she could now have the altar to herself; but she only shook her head with pleading sadness, begging him not to waste his breath on the impossible, the extinct. Couldn't he see that in relation to her private need the rites he had established were practically an elaborate exclusion? She regretted nothing that had happened; it had all been right so long as she didn't know, and it was only that now she knew too much and that from the moment their eyes were open they would simply have to conform. It had doubtless been happiness enough for them to go on together so long. She was gentle, grateful, resigned; but this was only the form of a deep immutability. He saw that he should never more cross the threshold of the second room, and he felt how much this alone would make a stranger of him and give a conscious stiffness to his visits. He would have hated to plunge again into that well of reminders, but he enjoyed quite as little the vacant alternative.

After he had been with her three or four times it seemed to him that to have come at last into her house had had the horrid effect of diminishing their intimacy. He had known her better, had liked her in greater freedom, when they merely walked together or kneeled together. Now they only pretended; before they had been nobly sincere. They began to try their walks again, but it proved a lame imitation, for these things, from the first, beginning or ending, had been connected with their visits to the church. They had either strolled away as they came out or gone in to rest on the return. Besides, Stransom now grew weary; he couldn't walk as of old. The omission made everything false; it was a horrible mutilation of their lives. Our friend was frank and monotonous; he made no mystery of his remonstrance and no secret of his predicament. Her response, whatever it was, always came to the same thing – an implied invitation to him to judge, if he spoke of predica-ments, of how much comfort she had in hers. For him indeed there was no comfort even in complaint, for every allusion to what had befallen them only made the author of their trouble more present. Acton Hague was between them, that was the essence of the matter; and he was never so much between them as when they were face to face. Stransom, even while he wanted to banish him, had the strangest sense of desiring a satisfaction that could come only from having accepted him. Deeply disconcerted by what he knew, he was still worse tormented by really not knowing. Perfectly aware that it would have been horribly vulgar to abuse his old friend or to tell his companion the story of their quarrel, it yet vexed him that her depth of reserve should give him no opening and should have the effect of a magnanimity greater even than his own.

He challenged himself, denounced himself, asked himself if he were in love with her that he should care so much what adventures she had had. He had never for a moment admitted that he was in love with her; therefore nothing could have surprised him more than to discover that he was jealous. What but jealousy could give a man that sore, contentious wish to have the detail of what would make him suffer? Well enough he knew indeed that he should never have it from the only person who, to-day, could give it to him. She let him press her with his sombre eyes, only smiling at him with an exquisite mercy and breathing equally little the word that would expose her secret and the word that would appear to deny his literal right to bitterness. She told nothing, she judged nothing; she accepted everything but the possibility of her return to the old symbols. Stransom divined that for her too they had been vividly individual, had stood for particular hours or particular attributes – particular links in her chain. He made it clear to himself, as he believed, that his difficulty lay in the fact that the very nature of the plea for his faithless friend constituted a prohibition; that it happened to have come from *her* was precisely the vice that attached to it. To the voice of impersonal generosity he felt sure he would have listened; he would have deferred to an advocate who, speaking from abstract justice, knowing of his omission without having known Hague, should have had the imagination to say: 'Oh, remember only the best of him; pity him; provide for him.' To provide for him on the very ground of having discovered another of his turpitudes was not to pity him, but to glorify him. The more Stransom thought the more he made it out that this relation of Hague's, whatever it was, could only have been a deception finely practised. Where had it come into the life that all men saw? Why had he never heard of it, if it had had the frankness of an attitude honourable? Stransom knew enough of his other ties, of his obligations and appearances, not to say enough of his general character, to be sure there had been some infamy. In one way or another the poor woman had been coldly sacrificed. That was why, at the last as well as the first, he must still leave him out.

IX

AND yet this was no solution, especially after he had talked again to his friend of all it had been his plan that she should finally do for him. He had talked in the other days, and she had responded with a frankness qualified only by a courteous reluctance, a reluctance that touched him, to linger on the question of his death. She had then practically accepted the charge, suffered him to feel that he could depend upon her to be the eventual guardian of his shrine; and it was in the name of what had so passed between them that he appealed to her not to forsake him in his old age. She listened to him now with a sort of shining coldness and all her habitual forbearance to insist on her terms; her deprecation was even still tenderer, for it expressed the compassion of her own sense that he was abandoned. Her terms, however, remained the same, and scarcely the less audible for not being uttered; although he was sure that, secretly, even more than he, she felt bereft of the satisfaction his solemn trust was to have provided for her. They both missed the rich future, but she missed it most, because after all it was to have been entirely hers; and it was her acceptance of the loss that gave him the full measure of her preference for the thought of Acton Hague over any other thought whatever. He had humour enough to laugh rather grimly when he said to himself: 'Why the deuce does she like him so much more than she likes me?' – the reasons being really so conceivable. But even his faculty of analysis left the irritation standing, and this irritation proved perhaps the greatest misfortune that had ever overtaken him. There had been nothing yet that made him so much want to give up. He had of course by this time well reached the age of renouncement; but it had not hitherto been vivid to him that it was time to give up everything.

Practically, at the end of six months, he had renounced the friendship that was once so charming and comforting. His privation had two faces, and the face it had turned to him on the occasion of his last attempt to cultivate that friendship was the one he could look at least. This was the privation he inflicted; the other was the privation he bore. The conditions she never phrased he used to murmur to himself in solitude: 'One more, one more – only just one.' Certainly he was going down; he often felt it when he caught himself, over his work, staring at vacancy and giving voice to that inanity. There was proof enough besides in his being so weak and so ill. His irritation took the form of melancholy, and his melancholy that of the conviction that his health had quite failed. His altar moreover had ceased to exist; his chapel, in his dreams, was a great dark cavern. All the lights had gone out – all his Dead had died again. He couldn't exactly see at first how it had been in the power of his late companion to extinguish them, since it was neither for her nor by her that they had been called into being. Then he understood that it was essentially in his own soul the revival had taken place, and that in the air of this soul they were now unable to breathe. The candles might mechanically burn, but each of them had lost its lustre. The church had become a void; it was his presence, her presence, their common presence, that had made the indispensable medium. If anything was wrong everything was – her silence spoiled the tune.

Then when three months were gone he felt so lonely that he went back; reflecting that as they had been his best society for years his Dead perhaps wouldn't let him forsake them without doing something more for him. They stood there, as he had left them, in their tall radiance, the bright cluster that had already made him, on occasions when he was willing to compare small things with great, liken them to a group of sea-lights on the edge of the ocean of life. It was a relief to him, after a while, as he sat there, to feel that they had still a virtue. He was more and more easily tired, and he always drove now; the action of his heart was weak and gave him none of the reassurance conferred by the action of his fancy. None the less he returned yet again, returned several times, and finally, during six months, haunted the place with a renewal of frequency and a strain of impatience. In winter the church was unwarmed, and exposure to cold was forbidden him, but the glow of his shrine was an influence in which he could almost bask. He sat and wondered to what he had reduced his absent associate and what she now did with the hours of her absence. There were other churches, there were other altars, there were other candles; in one way or another her piety would still operate; he couldn't absolutely have deprived her of her rites. So he argued, but without contentment; for he well enough knew there was no other such rare semblance of the mountain of light she had once mentioned to him as the satisfaction of her need. As this semblance again gradually grew great to him and his pious practice more regular, there was a sharper and sharper pang for him in the imagination of her darkness; for never so much as in these weeks had his rites been real, never had his gathered company seemed so to respond and even to invite. He lost himself in the large lustre, which was more and more what he had from the first wished it to be – as dazzling as the vision of heaven in the mind of a child. He wandered in the fields of light; he passed, among the tall tapers, from tier to tier, from fire to fire, from name to name, from the white intensity of one clear emblem, of one saved soul, to another. It was in the quiet sense of having saved his souls that his deep, strange instinct rejoiced. This was no dim theological rescue, no boon of a contingent world; they were saved better than faith or works could save them, saved for the warm world they had shrunk from dying to, for actuality, for continuity, for the certainty of human remembrance.

By this time he had survived all his friends; the last straight flame was three years old, there was no one to add to the list. Over and over he called his roll, and it appeared to him compact and complete. Where should he put in another, where, if there were no other objection, would it stand in its place in the rank? He reflected, with a want of sincerity of which he was quite conscious, that it would be difficult to determine that place. More and more, besides, face to face with his little legion, reading over endless histories, handling the empty shells and playing with the silence – more and more he could see that he had never introduced an alien. He had had his great compassions, his indulgences – there were cases in which they had been immense; but what had his devotion after all been if it hadn't been fundamentally a respect? He was, however, himself surprised at his stiffness; by the end of the winter the responsibility of it was what was uppermost in his thoughts. The refrain had grown old to them, the plea for just one more. There came a day when, for simple exhaustion, if symmetry should really demand just one more he was ready to take symmetry into account. Symmetry was harmony, and the idea of harmony began to haunt him; he said to himself that harmony was of course everything. He took, in fancy, his composition to pieces, redistributing it into other lines, making other juxtapositions and contrasts. He shifted this and that candle, he made the spaces different, he effaced the disfigurement of a possible gap. There were subtle and complex relations, a scheme of cross-reference, and moments in which he seemed to catch a glimpse of the void so sensible to the woman who wandered in exile or sat where he had seen her with the portrait of Acton Hague. Finally, in this way, he arrived at a conception of the total, the ideal, which left a clear opportunity for just another figure. 'Just one more – to round it off; just one more, just one,' continued to hum itself in his head. There was a strange confusion in the thought, for he felt the day to be near when he too should be one of the Others. What, in this case, would the Others matter to him, since they only mattered to the living? Even as one of the Dead, what would his altar matter to him, since his particular dream of keeping it up had melted away? What had harmony to do with the case if his lights were all to be quenched? What he had hoped for was an instituted thing. He might perpetuate it on some other pretext, but his special meaning would have dropped. This meaning was to have lasted with the life of the one other person who understood it.

In March he had an illness during which he spent a fortnight in bed, and when he revived a little he was told of two things that had happened. One was that a lady, whose name was not known to the servants (she left none) had been three times to ask about him; the other was that in his sleep, and on an occasion when his mind evidently wandered, he was heard to murmur again and again: 'Just one more – just one.' As soon as he found himself able to go out, and before the doctor in attendance had pronounced him so, he drove to see the lady who had come to ask about him. She was not at home; but this gave him the opportunity, before his strength should fail again, to take his way to the church. He entered the church alone; he had declined, in a happy manner he possessed of being able to decline effectively, the company of his servant or of a nurse. He knew now perfectly what these good people thought; they had discovered his clandestine connection, the magnet that had drawn him for so many years, and doubtless attached a significance of their own to the odd words they had repeated to him. The nameless lady was the clandestine connection – a fact nothing could have made clearer than his indecent haste to rejoin her. He sank on his knees before his altar, and his head fell over on his hands. His weakness, his life's weariness overtook him. It seemed to him he had come for the great surrender. At first he asked himself how he should get away; then, with the failing belief in the power, the very desire to move gradually left him. He had come, as he always came, to lose himself; the fields of light were still there to stray in; only this time, in straying, he would never come back. He had given himself to his Dead, and it was good: this time his Dead would keep him. He couldn't rise from his knees; he believed he should never rise again; all he could do was to lift his face and fix his eyes upon his lights. They looked unusually, strangely splendid, but the one that always drew him most had an unprecedented lustre. It was the central voice of the choir, the glowing heart of the brightness, and on this occasion it seemed to expand, to spread great wings of flame. The whole altar flared – it dazzled and blinded; but the source of the vast radiance burned clearer than the rest, it gathered itself into form, and the form was human beauty and human charity – it was the far-off face of Mary Antrim. She smiled at him from the glory of heaven – she brought the glory down with her to take him. He bowed his head in submission, and at the same moment another wave rolled over him. Was it the quickening of joy to pain? In the midst of his joy at any rate he felt his buried face grow hot as with some communicated knowledge that had the force of a reproach. It suddenly made him contrast that very rapture with the bliss he had refused to another. This breath of the passion immortal was all that other had asked; the descent of Mary Antrim opened his spirit with a great compunctious throb for the descent of Acton Hague. It was as if Stransom had read what her eyes said to him.

After a moment he looked round him in a despair which made him feel as if the source of life were ebbing. The church had been empty – he was alone; but he wanted to have something done, to make a last appeal. This idea gave him strength for an effort; he rose to his feet with a movement that made him turn, supporting himself by the back of a bench. Behind him was a prostrate figure, a figure he had seen before; a woman in deep mourning, bowed in grief or in prayer. He had seen her in other days – the first time he came into the church, and he slightly wavered there, looking at her again till she seemed to become aware he had noticed her. She raised her head and met his eyes: the partner of his long worship was there. She looked across at him an instant with a face wondering and scared; he saw that he had given her an alarm. Then quickly rising, she came straight to him with both hands out.

'Then you *could* come? God sent you!' he murmured with a happy smile.

'You're very ill – you shouldn't be here,' she urged in anxious reply.

'God sent me too, I think. I was ill when I came, but the sight of you does wonders.' He held her hands, and they steadied and quickened him. 'I've something to tell you.'

'Don't tell me!' she tenderly pleaded; 'let me tell you. This afternoon, by a miracle, the sweetest of miracles, the sense of our difference left me. I was out – I was near, thinking, wandering alone, when, on the spot, something changed in my heart. It's my confession – there it is. To come back, to come back on the instant – the idea gave me wings. It was as if I suddenly saw something – as if it all became possible. I could come for what you yourself came for: that was enough. So here I am. It's not for my own – that's over. But I'm here for *them*.' And breathless, infinitely relieved by her low, precipitate explanation, she looked with eyes that reflected all its splendour at the magnificence of their altar.

'They're here for you,' Stransom said, 'they're present tonight as they've never been. They speak for you – don't you see? – in a passion of light – they sing out like a choir of angels. Don't you hear what they say? – they offer the very thing you asked of me.'

'Don't talk of it – don't think of it; forget it!' She spoke in hushed supplication, and while the apprehension deepened in her eyes she disengaged one of her hands and passed an arm round him, to support him better, to help him to sink into a seat.

He let himself go, resting on her; he dropped upon the bench, and she fell on her knees beside him with his arm on her shoulder. So he remained an instant, staring up at his shrine. 'They say there's a gap in the array – they say it's not full, complete. Just one more,' he went on, softly – 'isn't that what you wanted? Yes, one more, one more.'

'Ah, no more – no more!' she wailed, as if with a quick, new horror of it, under her breath.

'Yes, one more,' he repeated, simply; 'just one!' And with this his head dropped on her shoulder; she felt that in his weakness he had fainted. But alone with him in the dusky church a great dread was on her of what might still happen, for his face had the whiteness of death.

THE FIGURE IN THE CARPET

I

I HAD done a few things and earned a few pence – I had perhaps even had time to begin to think I was finer than was perceived by the patronising; but when I take the little measure of my course (a fidgety habit, for it's none of the longest yet) I count my real start from the evening George Corvick, breathless and worried, came in to ask me a service. He had done more things than I, and earned more pence, though there were chances for cleverness I thought he sometimes missed. I could only however that evening declare to him that he never missed one for kindness. There was almost rapture in hearing it proposed to me to prepare for *The Middle*, the organ of our lucubrations, so called from the position in the week of its day of appearance, an article for which he had made himself responsible and of which, tied up with a stout string, he laid on my table the subject. I pounced upon my opportunity – that is on the first volume of it – and paid scant attention to my friend's explanation of his appeal. What explanation could be more to the point than my obvious fitness for the task? I had written on Hugh Vereker, but never a word in *The Middle*, where my dealings were mainly with the ladies and the minor poets. This was his new novel, an advance copy, and whatever much or little it should do for his reputation I was clear on the spot as to what it should do for mine. Moreover if I always read him as soon as I could get hold of him I had a particular reason for wishing to read him now: I had accepted an invitation to Bridges for the following Sunday, and it had been mentioned in Lady Jane's note that Mr Vereker was to be there. I was young enough to have an emotion about meeting a man of his renown and innocent enough to believe the occasion would demand the display of an acquaintance with his 'last'.

Corvick, who had promised a review of it, had not even had time to read it; he had gone to pieces in consequence of news requiring – as on precipitate reflection he judged – that he should catch the night-mail to Paris. He had had a telegram from Gwendolen Erme in answer to his letter offering to fly to her aid. I knew already about Gwendolen Erme; I had never seen her, but I had my ideas, which were mainly to the effect that Corvick would marry her if her mother would only die. That lady seemed now in a fair way to oblige him; after some dreadful mistake about some climate or some waters she had suddenly collapsed on the return from abroad. Her daughter, unsupported and alarmed, desiring to make a rush for home but hesitating at the risk, had accepted our friend's assistance, and it was my secret belief that at the sight of him Mrs Erme would pull round. His own belief was scarcely to be called secret; it discernibly at any rate differed from mine. He had showed me Gwendolen's photograph with the remark that she wasn't pretty but was awfully interesting; she had published at the age of nineteen a novel in three volumes, 'Deep Down', about which, in *The Middle*, he had been really splendid. He appreciated my present eagerness and undertook that the periodical in question should do no less; then at the last, with his hand on the door, he said to me: 'Of course you'll be all right, you know.' Seeing I was a trifle vague he added: 'I mean you won't be silly.'

'Silly – about Vereker! Why, what do I ever find him but awfully clever?'

'Well, what's that but silly? What on earth does "awfully clever" mean? For God's sake try to get *at* him. Don't let him suffer by our arrangement. Speak of him, you know, if you can, as *I* should have spoken of him.'

I wondered an instant. 'You mean as far and away the biggest of the lot – that sort of thing?'

Corvick almost groaned. 'Oh, you know, I don't put them back to back that way; it's the infancy of art! But he gives me a pleasure so rare; the sense of' – he mused a little – 'something or other.'

I wondered again. 'The sense, pray, of what?'

'My dear man, that's just what I want *you* to say!'

Even before Corvick had banged the door I had begun, book in hand, to prepare myself to say it. I sat up with Vereker half the night; Corvick couldn't have done more than that. He was awfully clever – I stuck to that, but he wasn't a bit the biggest of the lot. I didn't allude to the lot, however; I flattered myself that I emerged on this occasion from the infancy of art. 'It's all right,' they declared vividly at the office; and when the number appeared I felt there was a basis on which I could meet the great man. It gave me confidence for a day or two, and then that confidence dropped. I had fancied him reading it with relish, but if Corvick was not satisfied how could Vereker himself be? I reflected indeed that the heat of the admirer was sometimes grosser even than the appetite of the scribe. Corvick at all events wrote me from Paris a little ill-humouredly. Mrs Erme was pulling round, and I hadn't at all said what Vereker gave him the sense of.

II

THE effect of my visit to Bridges was to turn me out for more profundity. Hugh Vereker, as I saw him there, was of a contact so void of angles that I blushed for the poverty of imagination involved in my small precautions. If he was in spirits it was not because he had read my review; in fact on the Sunday morning I felt sure he hadn't read it, though *The Middle* had been out three days and bloomed, I assured myself, in the stiff garden of periodicals which gave one of the ormolu tables the air of a stand at a station. The impression he made on me personally was such that I wished him to read it, and I corrected to this end with a surreptitious hand what might be wanting in the careless conspicuity of the sheet. I am afraid I even watched the result of my manoeuvre, but up to luncheon I watched in vain.

When afterwards, in the course of our gregarious walk, I found myself for half an hour, not perhaps without another manoeuvre, at the great man's side, the result of his affability was a still livelier desire that he should not remain in ignorance of the peculiar justice I had done him. It was not that he seemed to thirst for justice; on the contrary I had not yet caught in his talk the faintest grunt of a grudge – a note for which my young experience had already given me an ear. Of late he had had more recognition, and it was pleasant, as we used to say in *The Middle*, to see that it drew him out. He wasn't of course popular, but I judged one of the sources of his good humour to be precisely that his success was independent of that. He had none the less become in a manner the fashion; the critics at least had put on a spurt and caught up with him. We had found out at last how clever he was, and he had had to make the best of the loss of his mystery. I was strongly tempted, as I walked beside him, to let him know how much of that unveiling was my act; and there was a moment when I probably should have done so had not one of the ladies of our party, snatching a place at his other elbow, just then appealed to him in a spirit comparatively self-ish. It was very discouraging: I almost felt the liberty had been taken with myself.

I had had on my tongue's end, for my own part, a phrase or two about the right word at the right time; but later on I was glad not to have spoken, for when on our return we clustered at tea I perceived Lady Jane, who had not been out with us, brandishing *The Middle* with her longest arm. She had taken it up at her leisure; she was delighted with what she had found, and I saw that, as a mistake in a man may often be a felicity in a woman, she would practically do for me what I hadn't been able to do for myself. 'Some sweet little truths that needed to be spoken,' I heard her declare, thrusting the paper at rather a bewildered couple by the fireplace. She grabbed it away from them again on the reappearance of Hugh Vereker, who after our walk had been upstairs to change something. 'I know you don't in general look at this kind of thing, but it's an occasion really for doing so. You *haven't* seen it? Then you must. The man has actually got *at* you, at what *I* always feel, you know.' Lady Jane threw into her eyes a look evidently intended to give an idea of what she always felt; but she added that she couldn't have expressed it. The man in the paper expressed it in a striking manner. 'Just see there, and there, where I've dashed it, how he brings it out.' She had literally marked for him the brightest patches of my prose, and if I was a little amused Vereker himself may well have been. He showed how much he was when before us all Lady Jane wanted to read something aloud. I liked at any

rate the way he defeated her purpose by jerking the paper
affectionately out of her clutch. He would take it upstairs with
him, would look at it on going to dress. He did this half an hour
later – I saw it in his hand when he repaired to his room. That
was the moment at which, thinking to give her pleasure,
I mentioned to Lady Jane that I was the author of the review.
I did give her pleasure, I judged, but perhaps not quite so much
as I had expected. If the author was 'only me' the thing didn't
seem quite so remarkable. Hadn't I had the effect rather of
diminishing the lustre of the article than of adding to my own?
Her ladyship was subject to the most extraordinary drops. It
didn't matter; the only effect I cared about was the one it would
have on Vereker up there by his bedroom fire.

At dinner I watched for the signs of this impression, tried to
fancy there was some happier light in his eyes; but to my
disappointment Lady Jane gave me no chance to make sure. I
had hoped she would call triumphantly down the table, publicly demand if she hadn't been right. The party was large –
there were people from outside as well, but I had never seen a
table long enough to deprive Lady Jane of a triumph. I was just
reflecting in truth that this interminable board would deprive
me of one when the guest next me, dear woman – she was Miss
Poyle, the vicar's sister, a robust, unmodulated person – had
the happy inspiration and the unusual courage to address herself across it to Vereker, who was opposite, but not directly, so
that when he replied they were both leaning forward. She
inquired, artless body, what he thought of Lady Jane's 'pane-
gyric', which she had read – not connecting it however with her
right-hand neighbour; and while I strained my ear for his reply I
heard him, to my stupefaction, call back gaily, with his mouth
full of bread: 'Oh, it's all right – it's the usual twaddle!'

I had caught Vereker's glance as he spoke, but Miss Poyle's
surprise was a fortunate cover for my own. 'You mean he
doesn't do you justice?' said the excellent woman.

Vereker laughed out, and I was happy to be able to do the
same. 'It's a charming article,' he tossed us.

Miss Poyle thrust her chin half across the cloth. 'Oh you're
so deep!' she drove home.

'As deep as the ocean! All I pretend is, the author doesn't see—'

A dish was at this point passed over his shoulder, and we had to wait while he helped himself.

'Doesn't see what?' my neighbour continued.

'Doesn't see anything.'

'Dear me – how very stupid!'

'Not a bit,' Vereker laughed again. 'Nobody does.'

The lady on his further side appealed to him, and Miss Poyle sank back to me. 'Nobody sees anything!' she cheerfully announced; to which I replied that I had often thought so too, but had somehow taken the thought for a proof on my own part of a tremendous eye. I didn't tell her the article was mine; and I observed that Lady Jane, occupied at the end of the table, had not caught Vereker's words.

I rather avoided him after dinner, for I confess he struck me as cruelly conceited, and the revelation was a pain. 'The usual twaddle' – my acute little study! That one's admiration should have had a reserve or two could gall him to that point? I had thought him placid, and he was placid enough; such a surface was the hard, polished glass that encased the bauble of his vanity. I was really ruffled, and the only comfort was that if nobody saw anything George Corvick was quite as much out of it as I. This comfort however was not sufficient, after the ladies had dispersed, to carry me in the proper manner – I mean in a spotted jacket and humming an air – into the smoking-room. I took my way in some dejection to bed; but in the passage I encountered Mr Vereker, who had been up once more to change, coming out of his room. *He* was humming an air and had on a spotted jacket, and as soon as he saw me his gaiety gave a start.

'My dear young man,' he exclaimed, 'I'm so glad to lay hands on you! I'm afraid I most unwittingly wounded you by those words of mine at dinner to Miss Poyle. I learned but half an hour ago from Lady Jane that you wrote the little notice in *The Middle*.'

I protested that no bones were broken; but he moved with me to my own door, his hand, on my shoulder, kindly feeling for a fracture; and on hearing that I had come up to bed he asked leave to cross my threshold and just tell me in three words what his qualification of my remarks had represented. It was plain he really feared I was hurt, and the sense of his solicitude suddenly made all the difference to me. My cheap review fluttered off into space, and the best things I had said in it became flat enough beside the brilliancy of his being there. I can see him there still, on my rug, in the firelight and his spotted jacket, his fine, clear face all bright with the desire to be tender to my youth. I don't know what he had at first meant to say, but I think the sight of my relief touched him, excited him, brought up words to his lips from far within. It was so these words presently conveyed to me something that, as I afterwards knew, he had never uttered to any one. I have always done justice to the generous impulse that made him speak; it was simply compunction for a snub unconsciously administered to a man of letters in a position inferior to his own, a man of letters moreover in the very act of praising him. To make the thing right he talked to me exactly as an equal and on the ground of what we both loved best. The hour, the place, the unexpectedness deepened the impression: he couldn't have done anything more exquisitely successful.

III

'I DON'T quite know how to explain it to you,' he said, 'but it was the very fact that your notice of my book had a spice of intelligence, it was just your exceptional sharpness that produced the feeling – a very old story with me, I beg you to believe – under the momentary influence of which I used in speaking to that good lady the words you so naturally resent. I don't read the things in the newspapers unless they're thrust upon me as that one was – it's always one's best friend that does it! But I used to read them sometimes – ten years ago. I daresay they were in general rather stupider then; at any rate it always seemed to me that they missed my little point with a perfection exactly as admirable when they patted me on the back as when they kicked me in the shins. Whenever since I've happened to have a glimpse of them they were still blazing away – still missing it, I mean, deliciously. *You* miss it, my dear fellow, with inimitable assurance; the fact of your being awfully clever and your article's being awfully nice doesn't make a hair's breadth of difference. It's quite with you rising young men,' Vereker laughed, 'that I feel most what a failure I am!'

I listened with intense interest; it grew intenser as he talked. '*You* a failure – heavens! What then may your "little point" happen to be?'

'Have I got to *tell* you, after all these years and labours?' There was something in the friendly reproach of this – jocosely exaggerated – that made me, as an ardent young seeker for truth, blush to the roots of my hair. I'm as much in the dark as ever, though I've grown used in a sense to my obtuseness; at that moment, however, Vereker's happy accent made me appear to myself, and probably to him, a rare donkey. I was on the point of exclaiming 'Ah, yes, don't tell me: for my honour, for that of the craft, don't!' when he went on in a manner that showed he had read my thought and had his own idea of the probability of our some day redeeming ourselves. 'By my little point I mean – what shall I call it? – the particular thing I've written my books most *for.* Isn't there for every writer a particular thing of that sort, the thing that most makes him apply himself, the thing without the effort to achieve which he wouldn't write at all, the very passion of his passion, the part of the business in which, for him, the flame of art burns most intensely? Well, it's *that!*'

I considered a moment. I was fascinated – easily, you'll say; but I wasn't going after all to be put off my guard. 'Your description's certainly beautiful, but it doesn't make what you describe very distinct.'

'I promise you it would be distinct if it should dawn on you at all.' I saw that the charm of our topic overflowed for my companion into an emotion as lively as my own. 'At any rate,' he went on, 'I can speak for myself: there's an idea in my work without which I wouldn't have given a straw for the whole job. It's the finest, fullest intention of the lot, and the application of it has been, I think, a triumph of patience, of ingenuity. I ought to leave that to somebody else to say; but that nobody does say it is precisely what we're talking about. It stretches, this little trick of mine, from book to book, and everything else, comparatively, plays over the surface of it. The order, the form, the texture of my books will perhaps some day constitute for the initiated a complete representation of it. So it's naturally the thing for the critic to look for. It strikes me,' my visitor added, smiling, 'even as the thing for the critic to find.'

This seemed a responsibility indeed. 'You call it a little trick?'

'That's only my little modesty. It's really an exquisite scheme.'

'And you hold that you've carried the scheme out?'

'The way I've carried it out is the thing in life I think a bit well of myself for.'

I was silent a moment. 'Don't you think you ought – just a trifle – to assist the critic?'

'Assist him? What else have I done with every stroke of my pen? I've shouted my intention in his great blank face!' At this, laughing out again, Vereker laid his hand on my shoulder to show that the allusion was not to my personal appearance.

'But you talk about the initiated. There must therefore, you see, be initiation.'

'What else in heaven's name is criticism supposed to be?' I'm afraid I coloured at this too; but I took refuge in repeating that his account of his silver lining was poor in something or other that a plain man knows things by. 'That's only because you've never had a glimpse of it,' he replied. 'If you had had one the element in question would soon have become practically all you'd see. To me it's exactly as palpable as the marble of this chimney. Besides, the critic just *isn't* a plain man: if he were, pray, what would he be doing in his neighbour's garden? You're anything but a plain man yourself, and the very *raison d'être* of you all is that you're little demons of subtlety. If my great affair's a secret, that's only because it's a secret in spite of itself – the amazing event has made it one. I not only never took the smallest precaution to do so, but never dreamed of any such accident. If I had I shouldn't in advance have had the heart to

go on. As it was I only became aware little by little, and meanwhile I had done my work.'

'And now you quite like it?' I risked.

'My work?'

'Your secret. It's the same thing.'

'Your guessing that,' Vereker replied, 'is a proof that you're
as clever as I say!' I was encouraged by this to remark that he
would clearly be pained to part with it, and he confessed that it
was indeed with him now the great amusement of life. 'I live
almost to see if it will ever be detected.' He looked at me for a
jesting challenge; something at the back of his eyes seemed to
peep out. 'But I needn't worry – it won't!'

'You fire me as I've never been fired,' I returned; 'you make
me determined to do or die.' Then I asked: 'Is it a kind of
esoteric message?'

His countenance fell at this – he put out his hand as if to bid
me good-night. 'Ah, my dear fellow, it can't be described in
cheap journalese!'

I knew of course he would be awfully fastidious, but our talk
had made me feel how much his nerves were exposed. I was
unsatisfied – I kept hold of his hand. 'I won't make use of the
expression then,' I said, 'in the article in which I shall eventually
announce my discovery, though I daresay I shall have hard
work to do without it. But meanwhile, just to hasten that
difficult birth, can't you give a fellow a clue?' I felt much more
at my ease.

'My whole lucid effort gives him the clue – every page and
line and letter. The thing's as concrete there as a bird in a cage,
a bait on a hook, a piece of cheese in a mouse-trap. It's stuck
into every volume as your foot is stuck into your shoe. It
governs every line, it chooses every word, it dots every i, it
places every comma.'

I scratched my head. 'Is it something in the style or something in the thought? An element of form or an element of
feeling?'

He indulgently shook my hand again, and I felt my questions to be crude and my distinctions pitiful. 'Good-night, my
dear boy – don't bother about it. After all, you do like a fellow.'

'And a little intelligence might spoil it?' I still detained him.

He hesitated. 'Well, you've got a heart in your body. Is that an element of form or an element of feeling? What I contend that nobody has ever mentioned in my work is the organ of life.'

'I see – it's some idea about life, some sort of philosophy. Unless it be,' I added with the eagerness of a thought perhaps still happier, 'some kind of game you're up to with your style, something you're after in the language. Perhaps it's a preference for the letter P!' I ventured profanely to break out. 'Papa, potatoes, prunes – that sort of thing?' He was suitably indulgent: he only said I hadn't got the right letter. But his amusement was over; I could see he was bored. There was nevertheless something else I had absolutely to learn. 'Should you be able, pen in hand, to state it clearly yourself – to name it, phrase it, formulate it?'

'Oh,' he almost passionately sighed, 'if I were only, pen in hand, one of *you* chaps!'

'That would be a great chance for you of course. But why should you despise us chaps for not doing what you can't do yourself?'

'Can't do?' He opened his eyes. 'Haven't I done it in twenty volumes? I do it in my way,' he continued. 'You don't do it in yours.'

'Ours is so devilish difficult,' I weakly observed.

'So is mine. We each choose our own. There's no compulsion. You won't come down and smoke?'

'No. I want to think this thing out.'

'You'll tell me then in the morning that you've laid me bare?'

'I'll see what I can do; I'll sleep on it. But just one word more,' I added. We had left the room – I walked again with him a few steps along the passage. 'This extraordinary "general intention", as you call it – for that's the most vivid description I can induce you to make of it – is then generally a sort of buried treasure?'

His face lighted. 'Yes, call it that, though it's perhaps not for me to do so.'

'Nonsense!' I laughed. 'You know you're hugely proud of it.'

'Well, I didn't propose to tell you so; but it *is* the joy of my soul!'

'You mean it's a beauty so rare, so great?'

He hesitated a moment. 'The loveliest thing in the world!' We had stopped, and on these words he left me; but at the end of the corridor, while I looked after him rather yearningly, he turned and caught sight of my puzzled face. It made him earnestly, indeed I thought quite anxiously, shake his head and wave his finger. 'Give it up – give it up!'

This wasn't a challenge – it was fatherly advice. If I had had one of his books at hand I would have repeated my recent act of faith – I would have spent half the night with him. At three o'clock in the morning, not sleeping, remembering moreover how indispensable he was to Lady Jane, I stole down to the library with a candle. There wasn't, so far as I could discover, a line of his writing in the house.

IV

RETURNING to town I feverishly collected them all; I picked out each in its order and held it up to the light. This gave me a maddening month, in the course of which several things took place. One of these, the last, I may as well immediately mention, was that I acted on Vereker's advice: I renounced my ridiculous attempt. I could really make nothing of the business; it proved a dead loss. After all, before, as he had himself observed, I liked him; and what now occurred was simply that my new intelligence and vain preoccupation damaged my liking. I not only failed to find his general intention – I found myself missing the subordinate intentions I had formerly found. His books didn't even remain the charming things they had been for me; the exasperation of my search put me out of conceit of them. Instead of being a pleasure the more they became a resource the less; for from the moment I was unable to follow up the author's hint I of course felt it a point of honour not to make use professionally of my knowledge of them. I *had* no knowledge – nobody had any. It was humiliating, but I could bear it – they only annoyed me now. At last they even bored me, and I accounted for my confusion – perversely, I confess – by the idea that Vereker had made a fool of me. The buried treasure was a bad joke, the general intention a monstrous *pose*.

The great incident of the time however was that I told George Corvick all about the matter and that my information had an immense effect upon him. He had at last come back, but so, unfortunately, had Mrs Erme, and there was as yet, I could see, no question of his nuptials. He was immensely stirred up by the anecdote I had brought from Bridges; it fell in so completely with the sense he had had from the first that there was more in Vereker than met the eye. When I remarked that the eye seemed what the printed page had been expressly invented to meet he immediately accused me of being spiteful because I had been foiled. Our commerce had always that pleasant latitude. The thing Vereker had mentioned to me was exactly the thing he, Corvick, had wanted me to speak of in my review. On my suggesting at last that with the assistance I had now given him he would doubtless be prepared to speak of it himself he admitted freely that before doing this there was more he must understand. What he would have said, had he reviewed the new book, was that there was evidently in the writer's inmost art something to *be* understood. I hadn't so much as hinted at that: no wonder the writer hadn't been flattered! I asked Corvick what he really considered he meant by his own supersubtlety, and, unmistakably kindled, he replied: 'It isn't for the vulgar – it isn't for the vulgar!' He had hold of the tail of something; he would pull hard, pull it right out. He pumped me dry on Vereker's strange confidence and, pronouncing me the luckiest of mortals, mentioned half a dozen questions he wished to goodness I had had the gumption to put. Yet on the other hand he didn't want to be told too much – it would spoil the fun of seeing what would come. The failure of my fun was at the moment of our meeting not complete, but I saw it ahead, and Corvick saw that I saw it. I, on my side, saw likewise that one of the first things he would do would be to rush off with my story to Gwendolen.

On the very day after my talk with him I was surprised by the receipt of a note from Hugh Vereker, to whom our encounter at Bridges had been recalled, as he mentioned, by his falling, in a magazine, on some article to which my signature was appended. 'I read it with great pleasure,' he wrote, 'and remembered under its influence our lively conversation by your bedroom fire. The consequence of this has been that I begin to measure the temerity of my having saddled you with a knowledge that you may find something of a burden. Now that the fit's over I can't imagine how I came to be moved so much beyond my wont. I had never before related, no matter in what expansion, the history of my little secret, and I shall never speak of the business again. I was accidentally so much more explicit with you than it had ever entered into my game to be, that I find this game – I mean the pleasure of playing it – suffers considerably. In short, if you can understand it, I've spoiled a part of my fun. I really don't want to give anybody what I believe you clever young men call the tip. That's of course a selfish solicitude, and I name it to you for what it may be worth to you. If you're disposed to humour me don't repeat my revelation. Think me demented – it's your right; but don't tell anybody why.'

The sequel to this communication was that as early on the morrow as I dared I drove straight to Mr Vereker's door. He occupied in those years one of the honest old houses in Kensington-square. He received me immediately, and as soon as I came in I saw I had not lost my power to minister to his mirth. He laughed out at the sight of my face, which doubtless expressed my perturbation. I had been indiscreet – my compunction was great. 'I *have* told somebody,' I panted, 'and I'm sure that person will by this time have told somebody else! It's a woman, into the bargain.'

'The person you've told?'

'No, the other person. I'm quite sure he must have told her.'

'For all the good it will do her – or do *me*! A woman will never find out.'

'No, but she'll talk all over the place: she'll do just what you don't want.'

Vereker thought a moment, but he was not so disconcerted as I had feared: he felt that if the harm was done it only served him right. 'It doesn't matter – don't worry.'

'I'll do my best, I promise you, that your talk with me shall go no further.'

'Very good; do what you can.'

'In the meantime,' I pursued, 'George Corvick's possession of the tip may, on his part, really lead to something.'

'That will be a brave day.'

I told him about Corvick's cleverness, his admiration, the intensity of his interest in my anecdote; and without making too much of the divergence of our respective estimates mentioned that my friend was already of opinion that he saw much further into a certain affair than most people. He was quite as fired as I had been at Bridges. He was moreover in love with the young lady: perhaps the two together would puzzle something out.

Vereker seemed struck with this. 'Do you mean they're to be married?'

'I daresay that's what it will come to.'

'That may help them,' he conceded, 'but we must give them time!'

I spoke of my own renewed assault and confessed my difficulties; whereupon he repeated his former advice: 'Give it up, give it up!' He evidently didn't think me intellectually equipped for the adventure. I stayed half an hour, and he was most good-natured, but I couldn't help pronouncing him a man of shifting moods. He had been free with me in a mood, he had repented in a mood, and now in a mood he had turned indifferent. This general levity helped me to believe that, so far as the subject of the tip went, there wasn't much in it. I contrived however to make him answer a few more questions about it, though he did so with visible impatience. For himself, beyond doubt, the thing we were all so blank about was vividly there. It was something, I guessed, in the primal plan, something like a complex figure in a Persian carpet. He highly approved of this image when I used it, and he used another himself. 'It's the very string,' he said, 'that my pearls are strung on!' The reason of his note to me had been that he really didn't want to give us a grain of succour – our density was a thing too perfect in its way to touch. He had formed the habit of depending upon it, and if the spell was to break it must break by some force of its own. He comes back to me from that last occasion – for I was never to speak to him again – as a man with some safe secret for enjoyment. I wondered as I walked away where he had got *his* tip.

V

WHEN I spoke to George Corvick of the caution I had received he made me feel that any doubt of his delicacy would be almost an insult. He had instantly told Gwendolen, but Gwendolen's ardent response was in itself a pledge of discretion. The question would now absorb them, and they would enjoy their fun too much to wish to share it with the crowd. They appeared to have caught instinctively Vereker's peculiar notion of fun. Their intellectual pride, however, was not such as to make them indifferent to any further light I might throw on the affair they had in hand. They were indeed of the 'artistic temperament', and I was freshly struck with my colleague's power to excite himself over a question of art. He called it letters, he called it life – it was all one thing. In what he said I now seemed to understand that he spoke equally for Gwendolen, to whom, as soon as Mrs Erme was sufficiently better to allow her a little leisure, he made a point of introducing me. I remember our calling together one Sunday in August at a huddled house in Chelsea, and my renewed envy of Corvick's possession of a friend who had some light to mingle with his own. He could say things to her that I could never say to him. She had indeed no sense of humour and, with her pretty way of holding her head on one side, was one of those persons whom you want, as the phrase is, to shake, but who have learnt Hungarian by themselves. She conversed perhaps in Hungarian with Corvick; she had remarkably little English for his friend. Corvick afterwards told me that I had chilled her by my apparent indisposition to oblige her with the detail of what Vereker had said to me. I admitted that I felt I had given thought enough to this exposure: hadn't I even made up my mind that it was hollow, wouldn't stand the test? The importance they attached to it was irritating – it rather envenomed my dissent.

That statement looks unamiable, and what probably happened was that I felt humiliated at seeing other persons derive a daily joy from an experiment which had brought me only chagrin. I was out in the cold while, by the evening fire, under the lamp, they followed the chase for which I myself had sounded the horn. They did as I had done, only more deliberately and sociably – they went over their author from the beginning. There was no hurry, Corvick said – the future was before them and the fascination could only grow; they would take him page by page, as they would take one of the classics, inhale him in slow draughts and let him sink deep in. I doubt whether they would have got so wound up if they had not been in love: poor Vereker's secret gave them endless occasion to put their young heads together. None the less it represented the kind of problem for which Corvick had a special aptitude, drew out the particular pointed patience of which, had he lived, he would have given more striking and, it is to be hoped, more fruitful examples. He at least was, in Vereker's words, a little demon of subtlety. We had begun by disputing, but I soon saw that without my stirring a finger his infatuation would have its bad hours. He would bound off on false scents as I had done – he would clap his hands over new lights and see them blown out by the wind of the turned page. He was like nothing, I told him, but the maniacs who embrace some bedlamitical theory of the cryptic character of Shakespeare. To this he replied that if we had had Shakespeare's own word for his being cryptic he would immediately have accepted it. The case there was altogether different – we had nothing but the word of Mr Snooks. I rejoined that I was stupefied to see him attach such importance even to the word of Mr Vereker. He inquired thereupon whether I treated Mr Vereker's word as a lie. I wasn't perhaps prepared, in my unhappy rebound, to go as far as that, but I insisted that till the contrary was proved I should view it as too fond an imagination. I didn't, I confess, say – I didn't at that time quite know – all I felt. Deep down, as Miss Erme would have said, I was uneasy, I was expectant. At the core of my personal confusion – for my curiosity lived in its ashes – was the sharpness of a sense that Corvick would at last probably come out somewhere. He made, in defence of his credulity, a great point of the fact that from of old, in his study of this genius, he had caught whiffs and hints of he didn't know what, faint wandering notes of a hidden music. That was just the rarity, that was the charm: it fitted so perfectly into what I reported.

If I returned on several occasions to the little house in Chelsea I daresay it was as much for news of Vereker as for news of Miss Erme's mamma. The hours spent there by Corvick were present to my fancy as those of a chessplayer bent with a silent scowl, all the lamplit winter, over his board and his moves. As my imagination filled it out the picture held me fast. On the other side of the table was a ghostlier form, the faint figure of an antagonist good-humouredly but a little wearily secure – an antagonist who leaned back in his chair with his hands in his pockets and a smile on his fine clear face. Close to Corvick, behind him, was a girl who had begun to strike me as pale and wasted and even, on more familiar view, as rather handsome, and who rested on his shoulder and hung upon his moves. He would take up a chessman and hold it poised a while over one of the little squares, and then he would put it back in its place with a long sigh of disappointment. The young lady, at this, would slightly but uneasily shift her position and look across, very hard, very long, very strangely, at their dim participant. I had asked them at an early stage of the business if it mightn't contribute to their success to have some closer communication with him. The special circumstances would surely be held to have given me a right to introduce them. Corvick immediately replied that he had no wish to approach the altar before he had prepared the sacrifice. He quite agreed with our friend both as to the sport and as to the honour – he would bring down the animal with his own rifle. When I asked him if Miss Erme were as keen a shot he said after a hesitation: 'No; I'm ashamed to say she wants to set a trap. She'd give anything to see him; she says she requires another tip. She's really quite morbid about it. But she must play fair – she *shan't* see him!' he emphatically added. I had a suspicion that they had even quarrelled a little on the subject – a suspicion not corrected by the way he more than once exclaimed to me: 'She's quite incredibly literary, you know – quite fantastically!' I remember his saying of her that she felt in italics and thought in capitals. 'Oh, when I've run him to earth,' he also said, 'then, you know, I shall knock at his door. Rather – I beg you to believe. I'll have it from his own lips: "Right you are, my boy; you've done it this time!" He shall crown me victor – with the critical laurel.'

Meanwhile he really avoided the chances London life might have given him of meeting the distinguished novelist; a danger however that disappeared with Vereker's leaving England for an indefinite absence, as the newspapers announced – going to the south for motives connected with the health of his wife, which had long kept her in retirement. A year – more than a year – had elapsed since the incident at Bridges, but I had not encountered him again. I think at bottom I was rather ashamed – I hated to remind him that though I had irremediably missed his point a reputation for acuteness was rapidly overtaking me. This scruple led me a dance; kept me out of Lady Jane's house, made me even decline, when in spite of my bad manners she was a second time so good as to make me a sign, an invitation to her beautiful seat. I once saw her with Vereker at a concert and was sure I was seen by them, but I slipped out without being caught. I felt, as on that occasion I splashed along in the rain, that I couldn't have done anything else; and yet I remember saying to myself that it was hard, was even cruel. Not only had I lost the books, but I had lost the man himself: they and their author had been alike spoiled for me. I knew too which was the loss I most regretted. I had liked the man still better than I had liked the books.

VI

SIX months after Vereker had left England George Corvick, who made his living by his pen, contracted for a piece of work which imposed on him an absence of some length and a journey of some difficulty, and his undertaking of which was much of a surprise to me. His brother-in-law had become editor of a great provincial paper, and the great provincial paper, in a fine flight of fancy, had conceived the idea of sending a 'special commissioner' to India. Special commissioners had begun, in the 'metropolitan press', to be the fashion, and the journal in question felt that it had passed too long for a mere country cousin. Corvick had no hand, I knew, for the big brush of the correspondent, but that was his brother-in-law's affair, and the fact that a particular task was not in his line was apt to be with himself exactly a reason for accepting it. He was prepared to out-Herod the metropolitan press; he took solemn precautions against priggishness, he exquisitely outraged taste. Nobody ever knew it – the taste was all his own. In addition to his expenses he was to be conveniently paid, and I found myself able to help him, for the usual fat book, to a plausible arrangement with the usual fat publisher. I naturally inferred that his obvious desire to make a little money was not unconnected with the prospect of a union with Gwendolen Erme. I was aware that her mother's opposition was largely addressed to his want of means and of lucrative abilities, but it so happened that, on my saying the last time I saw him something that bore on the question of his separation from our young lady, he exclaimed with an emphasis that startled me: 'Ah, I'm not a bit engaged to her, you know!'

'Not overtly,' I answered, 'because her mother doesn't like you. But I've always taken for granted a private understanding.'

'Well, there *was* one. But there isn't now.' That was all he said, except something about Mrs Erme's having got on her feet again in the most extraordinary way – a remark from which I gathered he wished me to think he meant that private understandings were of little use when the doctor didn't share them. What I took the liberty of really thinking was that the girl might in some way have estranged him. Well, if he had taken the turn of jealousy for instance it could scarcely be jealousy of me. In that case (besides the absurdity of it) he wouldn't have gone away to leave us together. For some time before his departure we had indulged in no allusion to the buried treasure, and from his silence, of which mine was the consequence, I had drawn a sharp conclusion. His courage had dropped, his ardour had gone the way of mine – this inference at least he left me to enjoy. More than that he couldn't do; he couldn't face the triumph with which I might have greeted an explicit admission. He needn't have been afraid, poor dear, for I had by this time lost all need to triumph. In fact I considered that I showed magnanimity in not reproaching him with his collapse, for the sense of his having thrown up the game made me feel more than ever how much I at last depended on him. If Corvick had broken down I should never know; no one would be of any use if *he* wasn't. It wasn't a bit true that I had ceased to care for knowledge; little by little my curiosity had not only begun to ache again, but had become the familiar torment of my consciousness. There are doubtless people to whom torments of such an order appear hardly more natural than the contortions of disease; but I don't know after all why I should in this connection so much as mention them. For the few persons, at any rate, abnormal or not, with whom my anecdote is concerned, literature was a game of skill, and skill meant courage, and courage meant honour, and honour meant passion, meant life. The stake on the table was of a different substance, and our roulette was the revolving mind, but we sat round the green board as intently as the grim gamblers at Monte Carlo. Gwendolen Erme, for that matter, with her white face and her fixed eyes, was of the very type of the lean ladies one had met in the temples of chance. I recognised in Corvick's absence that she made this analogy vivid. It was extravagant, I admit, the way she lived for the art of the pen. Her passion visibly preyed upon her, and in her presence I felt almost tepid. I got hold of 'Deep Down' again: it was a desert in which she had lost herself, but in which too she had dug a wonderful hole in the sand – a cavity out of which Corvick had still more remarkably pulled her.

Early in March I had a telegram from her, in consequence of which I repaired immediately to Chelsea, where the first thing she said to me was: 'He has got it, he has got it!'

She was moved, as I could see, to such depths that she must mean the great thing. 'Vereker's idea?'

'His general intention. George has cabled from Bombay.'

She had the missive open there; it was emphatic, but it was brief. 'Eureka. Immense.' That was all – he had saved the money of the signature. I shared her emotion, but I was disappointed. 'He doesn't say what it is.'

'How could he – in a telegram? He'll write it.'

'But how does he know?'

'Know it's the real thing? Oh, I'm sure when you see it you do know. *Vera incessu patuit dea!*'

'It's you, Miss Erme, who are a dear for bringing me such news!' – I went all lengths in my high spirits. 'But fancy finding our goddess in the temple of Vishnu! How strange of George to have been able to go into the thing again in the midst of such different and such powerful solicitations!'

'He hasn't gone into it, I know; it's the thing itself, let severely alone for six months, that has simply sprung out at him like a tigress out of the jungle. He didn't take a book with him – on purpose; indeed he wouldn't have needed to – he knows every page, as I do, by heart. They all worked in him together, and some day somewhere, when he wasn't thinking, they fell, in all their superb intricacy, into the one right combination. The figure in the carpet came out. That's the way he knew it would come and the real reason – you didn't in the least understand, but I suppose I may tell you now – why he went and why I consented to his going. We knew the change would do it, the difference of thought, of scene, would give the needed touch, the magic shake. We had perfectly, we had admirably calculated. The elements were all in his mind, and in the *secousse* of a new and intense experience they just struck light.' She positively struck light herself – she was literally, facially luminous. I stammered something about unconscious cerebration, and she continued: 'He'll come right home – this will bring him.'

'To see Vereker, you mean?'

'To see Vereker – and to see *me*. Think what he'll have to tell me!'

I hesitated. 'About India?'

'About fiddlesticks! About Vereker – about the figure in the carpet.'

'But, as you say, we shall surely have that in a letter.'

She thought like one inspired, and I remembered how Corvick had told me long before that her face was interesting. 'Perhaps it won't go in a letter if it's "immense".'

'Perhaps not if it's immense bosh. If he has got something that won't go in a letter he hasn't got *the* thing. Vereker's own statement to me was exactly that the "figure" *would* go in a letter.'

'Well, I cabled to George an hour ago – two words,' said Gwendolen.

'Is it indiscreet of me to inquire what they were?'

She hung fire, but at last she brought them out. ' "Angel, write." '

'Good!' I exclaimed. 'I'll make it sure – I'll send him the same.'

VII

MY words however were not absolutely the same – I put something instead of 'angel'; and in the sequel my epithet seemed the more apt, for when eventually we heard from Corvick it was merely, it was thoroughly to be tantalised. He was magnificent in his triumph, he described his discovery as stupendous; but his ecstasy only obscured it – there were to be no particulars till he should have submitted his conception to the supreme authority. He had thrown up his commission, he had thrown up his book, he had thrown up everything but the instant need to hurry to Rapallo, on the Genoese shore, where Vereker was making a stay. I wrote him a letter which was to await him at Aden – I besought him to relieve my suspense. That he found my letter was indicated by a telegram which, reaching me after weary days and without my having received an answer to my laconic dispatch at Bombay, was evidently intended as a reply to both communications. Those few words were in familiar French, the French of the day, which Corvick often made use of to show he wasn't a prig. It had for some persons the opposite effect, but his message may fairly be paraphrased. 'Have patience; I want to see, as it breaks on you, the face you'll make!' '*Tellement envie de voir ta tête!*' – that was what I had to sit down with. I can certainly not be said to have sat down, for I seem to remember myself at this time as rushing constantly between the little house in Chelsea and my own. Our impatience, Gwendolen's and mine, was equal, but I kept hoping her light would be greater. We all spent during this episode, for people of our means, a great deal of money in telegrams, and I counted on the receipt of news from Rapallo immediately after the junction of the discoverer with the discovered. The interval seemed an age, but late one day I heard a hansom rattle up to my door with the crash engendered by a hint of liberality. I lived with my heart in my mouth and I bounded to the window – a movement which gave me a view of a young lady erect on the footboard of the vehicle and eagerly looking up at my house. At sight of me she flourished a paper with a movement that brought me straight down, the movement with which, in melo-dramas, handkerchiefs and reprieves are flourished at the foot of the scaffold.

'Just seen Vereker – not a note wrong. Pressed me to bosom – keeps me a month.' So much I read on her paper while the cabby dropped a grin from his perch. In my excitement I paid him profusely and in hers she suffered it; then as he drove away we started to walk about and talk. We had talked, heaven knows, enough before, but this was a wondrous lift. We pictured the whole scene at Rapallo, where he would have written, mention-ing my name, for permission to call; that is *I* pictured it, having more material than my companion, whom I felt hang on my lips as we stopped on purpose before shop-windows we didn't look into. About one thing we were clear: if he was staying on for fuller communication we should at least have a letter from him that would help us through the dregs of delay. We understood his staying on, and yet each of us saw, I think, that the other hated it. The letter we were clear about arrived; it was for Gwendolen, and I called upon her in time to save her the trouble of bringing it to me. She didn't read it out, as was natural enough; but she repeated to me what it chiefly embodied. This consisted of the remarkable statement that he would tell her when they were married exactly what she wanted to know.

'Only when we're married – not before,' she explained. 'It's tantamount to saying – isn't it? – that I must marry him straight off!' She smiled at me while I flushed with disappointment, a vision of fresh delay that made me at first unconscious of my surprise. It seemed more than a hint that on me as well he would impose some tiresome condition. Suddenly, while she reported several more things from his letter, I remembered what he had told me before going away. He found Mr Vereker deliriously interesting and his own possession of the secret a kind of intoxication. The buried treasure was all gold and gems. Now that it was there it seemed to grow and grow before him; it was in all time, in all tongues, one of the most wonderful flowers of art. Nothing, above all, when once one was face to face with it, had been more consummately done. When once it came out it came out, was there with a splendour that made you ashamed; and there had not been, save in the bottomless vulgarity of the age, with every one tasteless and tainted, every sense stopped, the smallest reason why it should have been overlooked. It was immense, but it was simple – it was simple, but it was immense, and the final knowledge of it was an experience quite apart. He intimated that the charm of such an experience, the desire to drain it, in its freshness, to the last drop, was what kept him there close to the source. Gwendolen, frankly radiant as she tossed me these fragments, showed the elation of a prospect more assured than my own. That brought me back to the question of her marriage, prompted me to ask her if what she meant by what she had just surprised me with was that she was under an engagement.

'Of course I am!' she answered. 'Didn't you know it?' She appeared astonished; but I was still more so, for Corvick had told me the exact contrary. I didn't mention this, however; I only reminded her that I had not been to that degree in her confidence, or even in Corvick's, and that moreover I was not in ignorance of her mother's interdict. At bottom I was troubled by the disparity of the two assertions; but after a moment I felt that Corvick's was the one I least doubted. This simply reduced me to asking myself if the girl had on the spot improvised an engagement – vamped up an old one or dashed off a new – in order to arrive at the satisfaction she desired. I reflected that she had resources of which I was destitute; but she made her case slightly more intelligible by rejoining presently: 'What the state of things has been is that we felt of course bound to do nothing in mamma's lifetime.'

'But now you think you'll just dispense with your mother's consent?'

'Ah, it may not come to that!' I wondered what it might come to, and she went on: 'Poor dear, she may swallow the dose. In fact, you know,' she added with a laugh, 'she really *must*!' – a proposition of which, on behalf of every one concerned, I fully acknowledged the force.

VIII

NOTHING more annoying had ever happened to me than to become aware before Corvick's arrival in England that I should not be there to put him through. I found myself abruptly called to Germany by the alarming illness of my younger brother, who, against my advice, had gone to Munich to study, at the feet indeed of a great master, the art of portraiture in oils. The near relative who made him an allowance had threatened to withdraw it if he should, under specious pretexts, turn for superior truth to Paris – Paris being somehow, for a Cheltenham aunt, the school of evil, the abyss. I deplored this prejudice at the time, and the deep injury of it was now visible – first in the fact that it had not saved the poor boy, who was clever, frail and foolish, from congestion of the lungs, and second in the greater remoteness from London to which the event condemned me. I am afraid that what was uppermost in my mind during several anxious weeks was the sense that if we had only been in Paris I might have run over to see Corvick. This was actually out of the question from every point of view: my brother, whose recovery gave us both plenty to do, was ill for three months, during which I never left him and at the end of which we had to face the absolute prohibition of a return to England. The consideration of climate imposed itself, and he was in no state to meet it alone. I took him to Meran and there spent the summer with him, trying to show him by example how to get back to work and nursing a rage of another sort that I tried not to show him.

The whole business proved the first of a series of phenomena so strangely combined that, taken together (which was how I had to take them) they form as good an illustration as I can recall of the manner in which, for the good of his soul doubtless, fate sometimes deals with a man's avidity. These incidents certainly had larger bearings than the comparatively meagre consequence we are here concerned with – though I feel that consequence also to be a thing to speak of with some respect. It's mainly in such a light, I confess, at any rate, that at this hour the ugly fruit of my exile is present to me. Even at first indeed the spirit in which my avidity, as I have called it, made me regard this term owed no element of ease to the fact that before coming back from Rapallo George Corvick addressed me in a way I didn't like. His letter had none of the sedative action that I must to-day profess myself sure he had wished to give it, and the march of occurrences was not so ordered as to make up for what it lacked. He had begun on the spot, for one of the quarterlies, a great last word on Vereker's writings, and this exhaustive study, the only one that would have counted, have existed, was to turn on the new light, to utter – oh, so quietly! – the unimagined truth. It was in other words to trace the figure in the carpet through every convolution, to reproduce it in every tint. The result, said Corvick, was to be the greatest literary portrait ever painted, and what he asked of me was just to be so good as not to trouble him with questions till he should hang up his masterpiece before me. He did me the honour to declare that, putting aside the great sitter himself, all aloft in his indifference, I was individually the connoisseur he was most working for. I was therefore to be a good boy and not try to peep under the curtain before the show was ready: I should enjoy it all the more if I sat very still.

I did my best to sit very still, but I couldn't help giving a jump on seeing in *The Times*, after I had been a week or two in Munich and before, as I knew, Corvick had reached London, the announcement of the sudden death of poor Mrs Erme. I instantly wrote to Gwendolen for particulars, and she replied

that her mother had succumbed to long-threatened failure of
the heart. She didn't say, but I took the liberty of reading into
her words, that from the point of view of her marriage and also
of her eagerness, which was quite a match for mine, this was a
solution more prompt than could have been expected and more
radical than waiting for the old lady to swallow the dose.
I candidly admit indeed that at the time – for I heard from her
repeatedly – I read some singular things into Gwendolen's
words and some still more extraordinary ones into her silences.
Pen in hand, this way, I live the time over, and it brings back the
oddest sense of my having been for months and in spite of
myself a kind of coerced spectator. All my life had taken refuge
in my eyes, which the procession of events appeared to have
committed itself to keep astare. There were days when I
thought of writing to Hugh Vereker and simply throwing myself
on his charity. But I felt more deeply that I hadn't fallen quite so
low, besides which, quite properly, he would send me about my
business. Mrs Erme's death brought Corvick straight home,
and within the month he was united 'very quietly' – as quietly I
suppose as he meant in his article to bring out his *trouvaille* – to
the young lady he had loved and quitted. I use this last term, I
may parenthetically say, because I subsequently grew sure that
at the time he went to India, at the time of his great news from
Bombay, there was no engagement whatever. There was none
at the moment she affirmed the opposite. On the other hand he
certainly became engaged the day he returned. The happy pair
went down to Torquay for their honeymoon, and there, in a
reckless hour, it occurred to poor Corvick to take his young
bride a drive. He had no command of that business: this had
been brought home to me of old in a little tour we had once
made together in a dogcart. In a dogcart he perched his companion for a rattle over Devonshire hills, on one of the likeliest
of which he brought his horse, who, it was true, had bolted,
down with such violence that the occupants of the cart were
hurled forward and that he fell horribly on his head. He was
killed on the spot; Gwendolen escaped unhurt.

I pass rapidly over the question of this unmitigated tragedy,
of what the loss of my best friend meant for me, and I complete

my little history of my patience and my pain by the frank statement of my having, in a postscript to my very first letter to her after the receipt of the hideous news, asked Mrs Corvick whether her husband had not at least finished the great article on Vereker. Her answer was as prompt as my inquiry: the article, which had been barely begun, was a mere heart-breaking scrap. She explained that Corvick had just settled down to it when he was interrupted by her mother's death; then, on his return, he had been kept from work by the engrossments into which that calamity plunged them. The opening pages were all that existed; they were striking, they were promising, but they didn't unveil the idol. That great intellectual feat was obviously to have formed his climax. She said nothing more, nothing to enlighten me as to the state of her own knowledge – the knowledge for the acquisition of which I had conceived her doing prodigious things. This was above all what I wanted to know: had *she* seen the idol unveiled? Had there been a private ceremony for a palpitating audience of one? For what else but that ceremony had the previous ceremony been enacted? I didn't like as yet to press her, though when I thought of what had passed between us on the subject in Corvick's absence her reticence surprised me. It was therefore not till much later, from Meran, that I risked another appeal, risked it in some trepidation, for she continued to tell me nothing. 'Did you hear in those few days of your blighted bliss,' I wrote, 'what we desired so to hear?' I said, 'we' as a little hint; and she showed me she could take a little hint. 'I heard everything,' she replied, 'and I mean to keep it to myself!'

IX

IT was impossible not to be moved with the strongest sympathy for her, and on my return to England I showed her every kindness in my power. Her mother's death had made her means sufficient, and she had gone to live in a more convenient quarter. But her loss had been great and her visitation cruel; it never would have occurred to me moreover to suppose she could come to regard the enjoyment of a technical tip, of a piece of literary experience, as a counterpoise to her grief. Strange to say, none the less, I couldn't help fancying after I had seen her a few times that I caught a glimpse of some such oddity. I hasten to add that there had been other things I couldn't help fancying; and as I never felt I was really clear about these, so, as to the point I here touch on, I give her memory the benefit of every doubt. Stricken and solitary, highly accomplished and now, in her deep mourning, her maturer grace and her uncomplaining sorrow incontestably handsome, she presented herself as leading a life of singular dignity and beauty. I had at first found a way to believe that I should soon get the better of the reserve formulated the week after the catastrophe in her reply to an appeal as to which I was not unconscious that it might strike her as mistimed. Certainly that reserve was something of a shock to me – certainly it puzzled me the more I thought of it, though I tried to explain it, with moments of success, by the supposition of exalted sentiments, of superstitious scruples, of a refinement of loyalty. Certainly it added at the same time hugely to the price of Vereker's secret, precious as that mystery already appeared. I may as well confess abjectly that Mrs Corvick's unexpected attitude was the final tap on the nail that was to fix, as they say, my luckless idea, convert it into the obsession of which I am for ever conscious.

But this only helped me the more to be artful, to be adroit, to allow time to elapse before renewing my suit. There were plenty of speculations for the interval, and one of them was deeply absorbing. Corvick had kept his information from his young friend till after the removal of the last barriers to their intimacy; then he had let the cat out of the bag. Was it Gwendolen's idea, taking a hint from him, to liberate this animal only on the basis of the renewal of such a relation? Was the figure in the carpet traceable or describable only for husbands and wives – for lovers supremely united? It came back to me in a mystifying manner that in Kensington Square, when I told him that Corvick would have told the girl he loved, some word had dropped from Vereker that gave colour to this possibility. There might be little in it, but there was enough to make me

wonder if I should have to marry Mrs Corvick to get what I
wanted. Was I prepared to offer her this price for the blessing of
her knowledge? Ah! that way madness lay – so I said to myself at
least in bewildered hours. I could see meanwhile the torch she
refused to pass on flame away in her chamber of memory – pour
through her eyes a light that made a glow in her lonely house. At
the end of six months I was fully sure of what this warm
presence made up to her for. We had talked again and again
of the man who had brought us together, of his talent, his
character, his personal charm, his certain career, his dreadful
doom, and even of his clear purpose in that great study which
was to have been a supreme literary portrait, a kind of critical
Vandyke or Velázquez. She had conveyed to me in abundance
that she was tongue-tied by her perversity, by her piety, that she
would never break the silence it had not been given to the 'right
person', as she said, to break. The hour however finally arrived.
One evening when I had been sitting with her longer than usual
I laid my hand firmly on her arm.

'Now, at last, what *is* it?'

She had been expecting me; she was ready. She gave a long,
slow, soundless headshake, merciful only in being inarticulate.
This mercy didn't prevent its hurling at me the largest, finest,
coldest 'Never!' I had yet, in the course of a life that had known
denials, had to take full in the face. I took it and was aware that
with the hard blow the tears had come into my eyes. So for a
while we sat and looked at each other; after which I slowly rose.
I was wondering if some day she would accept me; but this was
not what I brought out. I said as I smoothed down my hat:
'I know what to think then; it's nothing!'

A remote, disdainful pity for me shone out of her dim smile;
then she exclaimed in a voice that I hear at this moment: 'It's
my *life*!' As I stood at the door she added: 'You've insulted him!'

'Do you mean Vereker?'

'I mean – the Dead!'

I recognised when I reached the street the justice of her
charge. Yes, it was her life – I recognised that too; but her life
none the less made room with the lapse of time for another
interest. A year and a half after Corvick's death she published in

a single volume her second novel, 'Overmastered', which I pounced on in the hope of finding in it some tell-tale echo or some peeping face. All I found was a much better book than her younger performance, showing I thought the better company she had kept. As a tissue tolerably intricate it was a carpet with a figure of its own; but the figure was not the figure I was looking for. On sending a review of it to *The Middle* I was surprised to learn from the office that a notice was already in type. When the paper came out I had no hesitation in attributing this article, which I thought rather vulgarly overdone, to Drayton Deane, who in the old days had been something of a friend of Corvick's, yet had only within a few weeks made the acquaintance of his widow. I had had an early copy of the book, but Deane had evidently had an earlier. He lacked all the same the light hand with which Corvick had gilded the gingerbread – he laid on the tinsel in splotches.

X

SIX months later appeared 'The Right of Way', the last chance, though we didn't know it, that we were to have to redeem ourselves. Written wholly during Vereker's absence, the book had been heralded, in a hundred paragraphs, by the usual ineptitudes. I carried it, as early a copy as any, I this time flattered myself, straightway to Mrs Corvick. This was the only use I had for it; I left the inevitable tribute of *The Middle* to some more ingenious mind and some less irritated temper. 'But I already have it,' Gwendolen said. 'Drayton Deane was so good as to bring it to me yesterday, and I've just finished it.'

'Yesterday? How did he get it so soon?'

'He gets everything soon. He's to review it in *The Middle*.'

'He – Drayton Deane – review Vereker?' I couldn't believe my ears.

'Why not? One fine ignorance is as good as another.'

I winced, but I presently said: 'You ought to review him yourself!'

'I don't "review",' she laughed. 'I'm reviewed!'

Just then the door was thrown open. 'Ah yes, here's your reviewer!' Drayton Deane was there with his long legs and his tall forehead: he had come to see what she thought of 'The Right of Way', and to bring news which was singularly relevant. The evening papers were just out with a telegram on the author of that work, who, in Rome, had been ill for some days with an attack of malarial fever. It had at first not been thought grave, but had taken in consequence of complications a turn that might give rise to anxiety. Anxiety had indeed at the latest hour begun to be felt.

I was struck in the presence of these tidings with the fundamental detachment that Mrs Corvick's public regret quite failed to conceal: it gave me the measure of her consummate independence. That independence rested on her knowledge, the knowledge which nothing now could destroy and which nothing could make different. The figure in the carpet might take on another twist or two, but the sentence had virtually been written. The writer might go down to his grave: she was the person in the world to whom – as if she had been his favoured heir – his continued existence was least of a need. This reminded me how I had observed at a particular moment – after Corvick's death – the drop of her desire to see him face to face. She had got what she wanted without that. I had been sure that if she hadn't got it she wouldn't have been restrained from the endeavour to sound him personally by those superior reflections, more conceivable on a man's part than on a woman's, which in my case had served as a deterrent. It wasn't however, I hasten to add, that my case, in spite of this invidious comparison, wasn't ambiguous enough. At the thought that Vereker was perhaps at that moment dying there rolled over me a wave of anguish – a poignant sense of how inconsistently I still depended on him. A delicacy that it was my one compensation to suffer to rule me had left the Alps and the Apennines between us, but the vision of the waning opportunity made me feel as if I might in my despair at last have gone to him. Of course I would really have done nothing of the sort. I remained five minutes, while my companions talked of the new book, and when Drayton Deane appealed to me for my opinion of it

I replied, getting up, that I detested Hugh Vereker – simply couldn't read him. I went away with the moral certainty that as the door closed behind me Deane would remark that I was awfully superficial. His hostess wouldn't contradict him.

I continue to trace with a briefer touch our intensely odd concatenation. Three weeks after this came Vereker's death, and before the year was out the death of his wife. That poor lady I had never seen, but I had had a futile theory that, should she survive him long enough to be decorously accessible, I might approach her with the feeble flicker of my petition. Did she know and if she knew would she speak? It was much to be presumed that for more reasons than one she would have nothing to say; but when she passed out of all reach I felt that renouncement was indeed my appointed lot. I was shut up in my obsession for ever – my gaolers had gone off with the key. I find myself quite as vague as a captive in a dungeon about the time that further elapsed before Mrs Corvick became the wife of Drayton Deane. I had foreseen, through my bars, this end of the business, though there was no indecent haste and our friendship had rather fallen off. They were both so 'awfully intellectual' that it struck people as a suitable match, but I knew better than any one the wealth of understanding the bride would contribute to the partnership. Never, for a marriage in literary circles – so the newspapers described the alliance – had a bride been so handsomely dowered. I began with due promptness to look for the fruit of their union – that fruit, I mean, of which the premonitory symptoms would be peculiarly visible in the husband. Taking for granted the splendour of the lady's nuptial gift, I expected to see him make a show commensurate with his increase of means. I knew what his means had been – his article on 'The Right of Way' had distinctly given one the figure. As he was now exactly in the position in which still more exactly I was not I watched from month to month, in the likely periodicals, for the heavy message poor Corvick had been unable to deliver and the responsibility of which would have fallen on his successor. The widow and wife would have broken by the rekindled hearth the silence that only a widow and wife might break, and Deane would be as aflame with the knowledge as Corvick in his own hour, as Gwendolen in hers had been. Well, he was aflame doubtless, but the fire was apparently not to become a public blaze. I scanned the periodicals in vain: Drayton Deane filled them with exuberant pages, but he withheld the page I most feverishly sought. He wrote on a thousand subjects, but never on the subject of Vereker. His special line was to tell truths that other people either 'funked', as he said, or overlooked, but he never told the only truth that seemed to me in these days to signify. I met the couple in those literary circles referred to in the papers: I have sufficiently intimated that it was only in such circles we were all constructed to revolve. Gwendolen was more than ever committed to them by the publication of her third novel, and I myself definitely classed by holding the opinion that this work was inferior to its immediate predecessor. Was it worse because she had been keeping worse company? If her secret was, as she had told me, her life – a fact discernible in her increasing bloom, an air of conscious privilege that, cleverly corrected by pretty charities, gave distinction to her appearance – it had yet not a direct influence on her work. That only made – everything only made – one yearn the more for it, rounded it off with a mystery finer and subtler.

XI

IT was therefore from her husband I could never remove my eyes: I hovered about him in a manner that might have made him uneasy. I went even so far as to engage him in conversation. *Didn't* he know, hadn't he come into it as a matter of course? – that question hummed in my brain. Of course he knew; otherwise he wouldn't return my stare so queerly. His wife had told him what I wanted, and he was amiably amused at my impotence. He didn't laugh – he was not a laugher: his system was to present to my irritation, so that I should crudely expose myself, a conversational blank as vast as his big bare brow. It always happened that I turned away with a settled conviction from these unpeopled expanses, which seemed to complete each other geographically and to symbolise together Drayton

Deane's want of voice, want of form. He simply hadn't the art
to use what he knew; he literally was incompetent to take up the
duty where Corvick had left it. I went still further – it was
the only glimpse of happiness I had. I made up my mind that
the duty didn't appeal to him. He wasn't interested, he didn't
care. Yes, it quite comforted me to believe him too stupid to
have joy of the thing I lacked. He was as stupid after as before,
and that deepened for me the golden glory in which the mystery
was wrapped. I had of course however to recollect that his wife
might have imposed her conditions and exactions. I had above
all to recollect that with Vereker's death the major incentive
dropped. He was still there to be honoured by what might be
done – he was no longer there to give it his sanction. Who, alas,
but he had the authority?

Two children were born to the pair, but the second cost the
mother her life. After this calamity I seemed to see another
ghost of a chance. I jumped at it in thought, but I waited a
certain time for manners, and at last my opportunity arrived in
a remunerative way. His wife had been dead a year when I met
Drayton Deane in the smoking-room of a small club of which
we both were members, but where for months – perhaps
because I rarely entered it – I had not seen him. The room
was empty and the occasion propitious. I deliberately offered
him, to have done with the matter for ever, that advantage for
which I felt he had long been looking.

'As an older acquaintance of your late wife's than even you
were,' I began, 'you must let me say to you something I have on
my mind. I shall be glad to make any terms with you that you
see fit to name for the information she had from George Corvick – the information, you know, that he, poor fellow, in one of
the happiest hours of his life, had straight from Hugh Vereker.'

He looked at me like a dim phrenological bust. 'The information—?'

'Vereker's secret, my dear man – the general intention of his
books: the string the pearls were strung on, the buried treasure,
the figure in the carpet.'

He began to flush – the numbers on his bumps to come out.
'Vereker's books had a general intention?'

I stared in my turn. 'You don't mean to say you don't know it?' I thought for a moment he was playing with me. 'Mrs Deane knew it; she had it, as I say, straight from Corvick, who had, after infinite search and to Vereker's own delight, found the very mouth of the cave. Where *is* the mouth? He told after their marriage – and told alone – the person who, when the circumstances were reproduced, must have told you. Have I been wrong in taking for granted that she admitted you, as one of the highest privileges of the relation in which you stood to her, to the knowledge of which she was after Corvick's death the sole depositary? All *I* know is that that knowledge is infinitely precious, and what I want you to understand is that if you will in your turn admit *me* to it you will do me a kindness for which I shall be everlastingly grateful.'

He had turned at last very red; I daresay he had begun by thinking I had lost my wits. Little by little he followed me; on my own side I stared with a livelier surprise. 'I don't know what you're talking about,' he said.

He wasn't acting – it was the absurd truth. 'She *didn't* tell you—?'

'Nothing about Hugh Vereker.'

I was stupefied; the room went round. It had been too good even for that! 'Upon your honour?'

'Upon my honour. What the devil's the matter with you?' he demanded.

'I'm astounded – I'm disappointed. I wanted to get it out of you.'

'It isn't *in* me!' he awkwardly laughed. 'And even if it were—'

'If it were you'd let me have it – oh yes, in common humanity. But I believe you. I see – I see!' I went on, conscious, with the full turn of the wheel, of my great delusion, my false view of the poor man's attitude. What I saw, though I couldn't say it, was that his wife hadn't thought him worth enlightening. This struck me as strange for a woman who had thought him worth marrying. At last I explained it by the reflection that she couldn't possibly have married him for his understanding. She had married him for something else. He was to some extent

enlightened now, but he was even more astonished, more disconcerted: he took a moment to compare my story with his
quickened memories. The result of his meditation was his
presently saying with a good deal of rather feeble form:

'This is the first I hear of what you allude to. I think you must
be mistaken as to Mrs Drayton Deane's having had any
unmentioned, and still less any unmentionable, knowledge
about Hugh Vereker. She would certainly have wished it – if it
bore on his literary character – to be used.'

'It *was* used. She used it herself. She told me with her own
lips that she "lived" on it.'

I had no sooner spoken than I repented of my words; he
grew so pale that I felt as if I had struck him. 'Ah, "lived"—!' he
murmured, turning short away from me.

My compunction was real; I laid my hand on his shoulder. 'I
beg you to forgive me – I've made a mistake. You *don't* know
what I thought you knew. You could, if I had been right, have
rendered me a service; and I had my reasons for assuming that
you would be in a position to meet me.'

'Your reasons?' he asked. 'What were your reasons?'

I looked at him well; I hesitated; I considered. 'Come and sit
down with me here, and I'll tell you.' I drew him to a sofa, I
lighted another cigarette and, beginning with the anecdote of
Vereker's one descent from the clouds, I gave him an account of
the extraordinary chain of accidents that had in spite of it kept
me till that hour in the dark. I told him in a word just what I've
written out here. He listened with deepening attention, and I
became aware, to my surprise, by his ejaculations, by his questions, that he would have been after all not unworthy to have
been trusted by his wife. So abrupt an experience of her want of
trust had an agitating effect on him, but I saw that immediate
shock throb away little by little and then gather again into waves
of wonder and curiosity – waves that promised, I could perfectly judge, to break in the end with the fury of my own highest
tides. I may say that to-day as victims of unappeased desire
there isn't a pin to choose between us. The poor man's state is
almost my consolation; there are indeed moments when I feel it
to be almost my revenge.

THE TURN OF THE SCREW

THE story had held us, round the fire, sufficiently breathless, but except the obvious remark that it was gruesome, as, on Christmas eve in an old house, a strange tale should essentially be, I remember no comment uttered till somebody happened to say that it was the only case he had met in which such a visitation had fallen on a child. The case, I may mention, was that of an apparition in just such an old house as had gathered us for the occasion – an appearance, of a dreadful kind, to a little boy sleeping in the room with his mother and waking her up in the terror of it; waking her not to dissipate his dread and soothe him to sleep again, but to encounter also, herself, before she had succeeded in doing so, the same sight that had shaken him. It was this observation that drew from Douglas – not immediately, but later in the evening – a reply that had the interesting consequence to which I call attention. Someone else told a story not particularly effective, which I saw he was not following. This I took for a sign that he had himself something to produce and that we should only have to wait. We waited in fact till two nights later; but that same evening, before we scattered, he brought out what was in his mind.

'I quite agree – in regard to Griffin's ghost, or whatever it was – that its appearing first to the little boy, at so tender an age, adds a particular touch. But it's not the first occurrence of its charming kind that I know to have involved a child. If the child gives the effect another turn of the screw, what do you say to *two* children—?'

'We say, of course,' somebody exclaimed, 'that they give two turns! Also that we want to hear about them.'

I can see Douglas there before the fire, to which he had got up to present his back, looking down at his interlocutor with his hands in his pockets. 'Nobody but me, till now, has ever heard. It's quite too horrible.' This, naturally, was declared by several voices to give the thing the utmost price, and our friend, with quiet art, prepared his triumph by turning his eyes over the rest of us and going on: 'It's beyond everything. Nothing at all that I know touches it.'

'For sheer terror?' I remember asking.

He seemed to say it was not so simple as that; to be really at a loss how to qualify it. He passed his hand over his eyes, made a little wincing grimace. 'For dreadful – dreadfulness!'

'Oh, how delicious!' cried one of the women.

He took no notice of her; he looked at me, but as if, instead of me, he saw what he spoke of. 'For general uncanny ugliness and horror and pain.'

'Well then,' I said, 'just sit right down and begin.'

He turned round to the fire, gave a kick to a log, watched it an instant. Then as he faced us again: 'I can't begin. I shall have to send to town.' There was a unanimous groan at this, and much reproach; after which, in his preoccupied way, he explained. 'The story's written. It's in a locked drawer – it has not been out for years. I could write to my man and enclose the key; he could send down the packet as he finds it.' It was to me in particular that he appeared to propound this – appeared almost to appeal for aid not to hesitate. He had broken a thickness of ice, the formation of many a winter; had had his reasons for a long silence. The others resented postponement, but it was just his scruples that charmed me. I adjured him to write by the first post and to agree with us for an early hearing; then I asked him if the experience in question had been his own. To this his answer was prompt. 'Oh, thank God, no!'

'And is the record yours? You took the thing down?'

'Nothing but the impression. I took that *here*' – he tapped his heart. 'I've never lost it.'

'Then your manuscript—?'

'Is in old, faded ink, and in the most beautiful hand.' He hung fire again. 'A woman's. She has been dead these twenty years. She sent me the pages in question before she died.' They were all listening now, and of course there was somebody to be arch, or at any rate to draw the inference. But if he put the inference by without a smile it was also without irritation. 'She was a most charming person, but she was ten years older than I.

She was my sister's governess,' he quietly said. 'She was the most agreeable woman I've ever known in her position; she would have been worthy of any whatever. It was long ago, and this episode was long before. I was at Trinity, and I found her at home on my coming down the second summer. I was much there that year – it was a beautiful one; and we had, in her off-hours, some strolls and talks in the garden – talks in which she struck me as awfully clever and nice. Oh yes; don't grin: I liked her extremely and am glad to this day to think she liked me too. If she hadn't she wouldn't have told me. She had never told anyone. It wasn't simply that she said so, but that I knew she hadn't. I was sure; I could see. You'll easily judge why when you hear.'

'Because the thing had been such a scare?'

He continued to fix me. 'You'll easily judge,' he repeated: '*you* will.'

I fixed him too. 'I see. She was in love.'

He laughed for the first time. 'You *are* acute. Yes, she was in love. That is she had been. That came out – she couldn't tell her story without its coming out. I saw it, and she saw I saw it; but neither of us spoke of it. I remember the time and the place – the corner of the lawn, the shade of the great beeches and the long, hot summer afternoon. It wasn't a scene for a shudder; but oh – !' He quitted the fire and dropped back into his chair.

'You'll receive the packet Thursday morning?' I inquired.

'Probably not till the second post.'

'Well then; after dinner – '

'You'll all meet me here?' He looked us round again. 'Isn't anybody going?' It was almost the tone of hope.

'Everybody will stay!'

'*I* will – and *I* will!' cried the ladies whose departure had been fixed. Mrs Griffin, however, expressed the need for a little more light. 'Who was it she was in love with?'

'The story will tell,' I took upon myself to reply.

'Oh, I can't wait for the story!'

'The story *won't* tell,' said Douglas; 'not in any literal, vulgar way.'

'More's the pity then. That's the only way I ever understand.'

'Won't *you* tell, Douglas?' somebody else inquired.

He sprang to his feet again. 'Yes – to-morrow. Now I must go to bed. Good night.' And, quickly, catching up a candlestick, he left us slightly bewildered. From our end of the great brown hall we heard his step on the stair; whereupon Mrs Griffin spoke. 'Well, if I don't know who she was in love with, I know who *he* was.'

'She was ten years older,' said her husband.

'*Raison de plus* – at that age! But it's rather nice, his long reticence.'

'Forty years!' Griffin put in.

'With this outbreak at last.'

'The outbreak,' I returned, 'will make a tremendous occasion of Thursday night;' and everyone so agreed with me that, in the light of it, we lost all attention for everything else. The last story, however incomplete and like the mere opening of a serial, had been told; we handshook and 'candle-stuck', as somebody said, and went to bed.

I knew the next day that a letter containing the key had, by the first post, gone off to his London apartments; but in spite of – or perhaps just on account of – the eventual diffusion of this knowledge we quite let him alone till after dinner, till such an hour of the evening, in fact, as might best accord with the kind of emotion on which our hopes were fixed. Then he became as communicative as we could desire and indeed gave us his best reason for being so. We had it from him again before the fire in the hall, as we had had our mild wonders of the previous night. It appeared that the narrative he had promised to read us really required for a proper intelligence a few words of prologue. Let me say here distinctly, to have done with it, that this narrative, from an exact transcript of my own made much later, is what I shall presently give. Poor Douglas, before his death – when it was in sight – committed to me the manuscript that reached him on the third of these days and that, on the same spot, with immense effect, he began to read to our hushed little circle on the night of the fourth. The departing ladies who had said they would stay didn't, of course, thank heaven, stay: they departed, in consequence of arrangements made, in a rage of curiosity, as they professed, produced by the touches with which he had already worked us up. But that only made his little final auditory more compact and select, kept it, round the hearth, subject to a common thrill.

The first of these touches conveyed that the written statement took up the tale at a point after it had, in a manner, begun. The fact to be in possession of was therefore that his old friend, the youngest of several daughters of a poor country parson, had, at the age of twenty, on taking service for the first time in the schoolroom, come up to London, in trepidation, to answer in person an advertisement that had already placed her in brief correspondence with the advertiser. This person proved, on her presenting herself, for judgment, at a house, in Harley Street, that impressed her as vast and imposing – this prospective patron proved a gentleman, a bachelor in the prime of life, such a figure as had never risen, save in a dream or an old novel, before a fluttered, anxious girl out of a Hampshire vicarage. One could easily fix his type; it never, happily, dies out. He was handsome and bold and pleasant, off-hand and gay and kind. He struck her, inevitably, as gallant and splendid, but what took her most of all and gave her the courage she afterwards showed was that he put the whole thing to her as a kind of favour, an obligation he should gratefully incur. She conceived him as rich, but as fearfully extravagant – saw him all in a glow of high fashion, of good looks, of expensive habits, of charming ways with women. He had for his town residence a big house filled with the spoils of travel and the trophies of the chase; but it was to his country home, an old family place in Essex, that he wished her immediately to proceed.

He had been left, by the death of their parents in India, guardian to a small nephew and a small niece, children of a younger, a military brother, whom he had lost two years before. These children were, by the strangest of chances for a man in his position – a lone man without the right sort of experience or a grain of patience – very heavily on his hands. It had all been a great worry and, on his own part doubtless, a series of blunders,

but he immensely pitied the poor chicks and had done all he
could; had in particular sent them down to his other house, the
proper place for them being of course the country, and kept
them there, from the first, with the best people he could find to
look after them, parting even with his own servants to wait on
them and going down himself, whenever he might, to see how
they were doing. The awkward thing was that they had practically no other relations and that his own affairs took up all his
time. He had put them in possession of Bly, which was healthy
and secure, and had placed at the head of their little establishment – but below stairs only – an excellent woman, Mrs Grose,
whom he was sure his visitor would like and who had formerly
been maid to his mother. She was now housekeeper and was
also acting for the time as superintendent to the little girl, of
whom, without children of her own, she was, by good luck,
extremely fond. There were plenty of people to help, but of
course the young lady who should go down as governess would
be in supreme authority. She would also have, in holidays, to
look after the small boy, who had been for a term at school –
young as he was to be sent, but what else could be done? – and
who, as the holidays were about to begin, would be back from
one day to the other. There had been for the two children at first
a young lady whom they had had the misfortune to lose. She
had done for them quite beautifully – she was a most respectable person – till her death, the great awkwardness of which
had, precisely, left no alternative but the school for little Miles.
Mrs Grose, since then, in the way of manners and things, had
done as she could for Flora; and there were, further, a cook, a
housemaid, a dairywoman, an old pony, an old groom and an
old gardener, all likewise thoroughly respectable.

So far had Douglas presented his picture when someone put
a question. 'And what did the former governess die of? – of so
much respectability?'

Our friend's answer was prompt. 'That will come out. I don't
anticipate.'

'Excuse me – I thought that was just what you *are* doing.'

'In her successor's place,' I suggested, 'I should have wished
to learn if the office brought with it—'

'Necessary danger to life?' Douglas completed my thought. 'She did wish to learn, and she did learn. You shall hear to-morrow what she learnt. Meanwhile, of course, the prospect struck her as slightly grim. She was young, untried, nervous: it was a vision of serious duties and little company, of really great loneliness. She hesitated – took a couple of days to consult and consider. But the salary offered much exceeded her modest measure, and on a second interview she faced the music, she engaged.' And Douglas, with this, made a pause that, for the benefit of the company, moved me to throw in –

'The moral of which was of course the seduction exercised by the splendid young man. She succumbed to it.'

He got up and, as he had done the night before, went to the fire, gave a stir to a log with his foot, then stood a moment with his back to us. 'She saw him only twice.'

'Yes, but that's just the beauty of her passion.'

A little to my surprise, on this, Douglas turned round to me. 'It *was* the beauty of it. There were others,' he went on, 'who hadn't succumbed. He told her frankly all his difficulty – that for several applicants the conditions had been prohibitive. They were, somehow, simply afraid. It sounded dull – it sounded strange; and all the more so because of his main condition.'

'Which was—?'

'That she should never trouble him – but never, never: neither appeal nor complain nor write about anything; only meet all questions herself, receive all moneys from his solicitor, take the whole thing over and let him alone. She promised to do this, and she mentioned to me that when, for a moment, dis-burdened, delighted, he held her hand, thanking her for the sacrifice, she already felt rewarded.'

'But was that all her reward?' one of the ladies asked.

'She never saw him again.'

'Oh!' said the lady; which, as our friend immediately left us again, was the only other word of importance contributed to the subject till, the next night, by the corner of the hearth, in the best chair, he opened the faded red cover of a thin old-fashioned gilt-edged album. The whole thing took indeed more nights than one, but on the first occasion the same lady put another question. 'What is your title?'

'I haven't one.'

'Oh, *I* have!' I said. But Douglas, without heeding me, had begun to read with a fine clearness that was like a rendering to the ear of the beauty of his author's hand.

I

I REMEMBER the whole beginning as a succession of flights and drops, a little see-saw of the right throbs and the wrong. After rising, in town, to meet his appeal, I had at all events a couple of very bad days – found myself doubtful again, felt indeed sure I had made a mistake. In this state of mind I spent the long hours of bumping, swinging coach that carried me to the stopping-place at which I was to be met by a vehicle from the house. This convenience, I was told, had been ordered, and I found, toward the close of the June afternoon, a commodious fly in waiting for me. Driving at that hour, on a lovely day, through a country to which the summer sweetness seemed to offer me a friendly welcome, my fortitude mounted afresh and, as we turned into the avenue, encountered a reprieve that was probably but a proof of the point to which it had sunk. I suppose I had expected, or had dreaded, something so melancholy that what greeted me was a good surprise. I remember as a most pleasant impression the broad, clear front, its open windows and fresh curtains and the pair of maids looking out; I remember the lawn and the bright flowers and the crunch of my wheels on the gravel and the clustered tree-tops over which the rooks circled and cawed in the golden sky. The scene had a greatness that made it a different affair from my own scant home, and there immediately appeared at the door, with a little girl in her hand, a civil person who dropped me as decent a curtsey as if I had been the mistress or a distinguished visitor. I had received in Harley Street a narrower notion of the place, and that, as I recalled it, made me think the proprietor still more of a gentleman, suggested that what I was to enjoy might be something beyond his promise.

I had no drop again till the next day, for I was carried triumphantly through the following hours by my introduction to the younger of my pupils. The little girl who accompanied Mrs Grose appeared to me on the spot a creature so charming as to make it a great fortune to have to do with her. She was the most beautiful child I had ever seen, and I afterwards wondered that my employer had not told me more of her. I slept little that night – I was too much excited; and this astonished me too, I recollect, remained with me, adding to my sense of the liberality with which I was treated. The large, impressive room, one of the best in the house, the great state bed, as I almost felt it, the full, figured draperies, the long glasses in which, for the first time, I could see myself from head to foot, all struck me – like the extraordinary charm of my small charge – as so many things thrown in. It was thrown in as well, from the first moment, that I should get on with Mrs Grose in a relation over which, on my way, in the coach, I fear I had rather brooded. The only thing indeed that in this early outlook might have made me shrink again was the clear circumstance of her being so glad to see me. I perceived within half an hour that she was so glad – stout, simple, plain, clean, wholesome woman – as to be positively on her guard against showing it too much. I wondered even then a little why she should wish not to show it, and that, with reflection, with suspicion, might of course have made me uneasy.

But it was a comfort that there could be no uneasiness in a connection with anything so beatific as the radiant image of my little girl, the vision of whose angelic beauty had probably more than anything else to do with the restlessness that, before morning, made me several times rise and wander about my room to take in the whole picture and prospect; to watch, from my open window, the faint summer dawn, to look at such portions of the rest of the house as I could catch, and to listen, while, in the fading dusk, the first birds began to twitter, for the possible recurrence of a sound or two, less natural and not without, but within, that I had fancied I heard. There had been a moment when I believed I recognised, faint and far, the cry of a child; there had been another when I found myself just consciously starting as at the passage, before my door, of a light footstep. But these fancies were not marked enough not to be thrown off, and it is only in the light, or the gloom, I should rather say, of other and subsequent matters that they now come back to me. To watch, teach, 'form' little Flora would too evidently be the making of a happy and useful life. It had been agreed between us downstairs that after this first occasion I should have her as a matter of course at night, her small white bed being already arranged, to that end, in my room. What I had undertaken was the whole care of her, and she had remained, just this last time, with Mrs Grose only as an effect of our consideration for my inevitable strangeness and her natural timidity. In spite of this timidity – which the child herself, in the oddest way in the world, had been perfectly frank and brave about, allowing it, without a sign of uncomfortable consciousness, with the deep, sweet serenity indeed of one of Raphael's holy infants, to be discussed, to be imputed to her and to determine us – I felt quite sure she would presently like me. It was part of what I already liked Mrs Grose herself for, the pleasure I could see her feel in my admiration and wonder as I sat at supper with four tall candles and with my pupil, in a high chair and a bib, brightly facing me, between them, over bread and milk. There were naturally things that in Flora's presence could pass between us only as prodigious and gratified looks, obscure and roundabout allusions.

'And the little boy – does he look like her? Is he too so very remarkable?'

One wouldn't flatter a child. 'Oh Miss, *most* remarkable. If you think well of this one!' – and she stood there with a plate in her hand, beaming at our companion, who looked from one of us to the other with placid heavenly eyes that contained nothing to check us.

'Yes; if I do—?'

'You *will* be carried away by the little gentleman!'

'Well, that, I think, is what I came for – to be carried away. I'm afraid, however,' I remember feeling the impulse to add, 'I'm rather easily carried away. I was carried away in London!'

I can still see Mrs Grose's broad face as she took this in. 'In Harley Street?'

'In Harley Street.'

'Well, Miss, you're not the first – and you won't be the last.'

'Oh, I've no pretension,' I could laugh, 'to being the only one. My other pupil, at any rate, as I understand, comes back tomorrow?'

'Not tomorrow – Friday, Miss. He arrives, as you did, by the coach, under care of the guard, and is to be met by the same carriage.'

I forthwith expressed that the proper as well as the pleasant and friendly thing would be therefore that on the arrival of the public conveyance I should be in waiting for him with his little sister; an idea in which Mrs Grose concurred so heartily that I somehow took her manner as a kind of comforting pledge – never falsified, thank heaven! – that we should on every question be quite at one. Oh, she was glad I was there!

What I felt the next day was, I suppose, nothing that could be fairly called a reaction from the cheer of my arrival; it was probably at the most only a slight oppression produced by a fuller measure of the scale, as I walked round them, gazed up at them, took them in, of my new circumstances. They had, as it were, an extent and mass for which I had not been prepared and in the presence of which I found myself, freshly, a little scared as well as a little proud. Lessons, in this agitation, certainly suffered some delay; I reflected that my first duty was, by the gentlest arts I could contrive, to win the child into the sense of knowing me. I spent the day with her out of doors; I arranged with her, to her great satisfaction, that it should be she, she only, who might show me the place. She showed it step by step and room by room and secret by secret, with droll, delightful, childish talk about it and with the result, in half an hour, of our becoming immense friends. Young as she was, I was struck, throughout our little tour, with her confidence and courage with the way, in empty chambers and dull corridors, on crooked staircases that made me pause and even on the summit of an old machicolated square tower that made me dizzy, her morning music, her disposition to tell me so many more things than she asked, rang out and led me on. I have not seen Bly since the day I left it, and I daresay that to my older and more informed eyes it would now appear sufficiently contracted. But as my little conductress, with her hair of gold and her frock of blue, danced before me round corners and pattered down passages, I had the view of a castle of romance inhabited by a rosy sprite, such a place as would somehow, for diversion of the young idea, take all colour out of storybooks and fairy-tales. Wasn't it just a storybook over which I had fallen a-doze and a-dream? No; it was a big, ugly, antique, but convenient house, embodying a few features of a building still older, half replaced and half utilised, in which I had the fancy of our being almost as lost as a handful of passengers in a great drifting ship. Well, I was, strangely, at the helm!

II

THIS came home to me when, two days later, I drove over with Flora to meet, as Mrs Grose said, the little gentleman; and all the more for an incident that, presenting itself the second evening, had deeply disconcerted me. The first day had been, on the whole, as I have expressed, reassuring; but I was to see it wind up in keen apprehension. The postbag, that evening – it came late – contained a letter for me, which, however, in the hand of my employer, I found to be composed but of a few words enclosing another, addressed to himself, with a seal still unbroken. 'This, I recognise, is from the head-master, and the head-master's an awful bore. Read him, please; deal with him; but mind you don't report. Not a word. I'm off!' I broke the seal with a great effort – so great a one that I was a long time coming to it; took the unopened missive at last up to my room and only attacked it just before going to bed. I had better have let it wait till morning, for it gave me a second sleepless night. With no counsel to take, the next day, I was full of distress; and it finally got so the better of me that I determined to open myself at least to Mrs Grose.

'What does it mean? The child's dismissed his school.'

She gave me a look that I remarked at the moment; then, visibly, with a quick blankness, seemed to try to take it back. 'But aren't they all—?'

'Sent home – yes. But only for the holidays. Miles may never go back at all.'

Consciously, under my attention, she reddened. 'They won't take him?'

'They absolutely decline.'

At this she raised her eyes, which she had turned from me; I saw them fill with good tears. 'What has he done?'

I hesitated; then I judged it best simply to hand her my letter – which, however, had the effect of making her, without taking it, simply put her hands behind her. She shook her head sadly. 'Such things are not for me, Miss.'

My counsellor couldn't read! I winced at my mistake, which I attenuated as I could, and opened my letter again to repeat it to her; then, faltering in the act and folding it up once more, I put it back in my pocket. 'Is he really *bad*?'

The tears were still in her eyes. 'Do the gentlemen say so?'

'They go into no particulars. They simply express their regret that it should be impossible to keep him. That can have only one meaning.' Mrs Grose listened with dumb emotion; she forbore to ask me what this meaning might be; so that, presently, to put the thing with some coherence and with the mere aid of her presence to my own mind, I went on: 'That he's an injury to the others.'

At this, with one of the quick turns of simple folk, she suddenly flamed up. 'Master Miles! – *him* an injury?'

There was such a flood of good faith in it that, though I had not yet seen the child, my very fears made me jump to the absurdity of the idea. I found myself, to meet my friend the better, offering it, on the spot, sarcastically. 'To his poor little innocent mates!'

'It's too dreadful,' cried Mrs Grose, 'to say such cruel things! Why, he's scarce ten years old.'

'Yes, yes; it would be incredible.'

She was evidently grateful for such a profession. 'See him, Miss, first. *Then* believe it!' I felt forthwith a new impatience to see him; it was the beginning of a curiosity that, for all the next hours, was to deepen almost to pain. Mrs Grose was aware, I could judge, of what she had produced in me, and she followed it up with assurance. 'You might as well believe it of the little lady. Bless her,' she added the next moment – '*look* at her!'

I turned and saw that Flora, whom, ten minutes before, I had established in the schoolroom with a sheet of white paper, a pencil and a copy of nice 'round O's', now presented herself to view at the open door. She expressed in her little way an extra-ordinary detachment from disagreeable duties, looking to me, however, with a great childish light that seemed to offer it as a mere result of the affection she had conceived for my person, which had rendered necessary that she should follow me. I needed nothing more than this to feel the full force of Mrs Grose's comparison, and, catching my pupil in my arms, covered her with kisses in which there was a sob of atonement.

None the less, the rest of the day, I watched for further occasion to approach my colleague, especially as, toward evening, I began to fancy she rather sought to avoid me. I overtook her, I remember, on the staircase; we went down together, and at the bottom I detained her, holding her there with a hand on her arm. 'I take what you said to me at noon as a declaration that *you've* never known him to be bad.'

She threw back her head; she had clearly, by this time, and very honestly, adopted an attitude. 'Oh, never known him – I don't pretend *that!*'

I was upset again. 'Then you *have* known him—?'

'Yes indeed, Miss, thank God!'

On reflection I accepted this. 'You mean that a boy who never is—?'

'Is no boy for *me!*'

I held her tighter. 'You like them with the spirit to be naughty?' Then, keeping pace with her answer, 'So do I!' I eagerly brought out. 'But not to the degree to contaminate—'

'To contaminate?' – my big word left her at a loss.

I explained it. 'To corrupt.'

She stared, taking my meaning in; but it produced in her an odd laugh. 'Are you afraid he'll corrupt *you*?' She put the question with such a fine bold humour that, with a laugh, a little silly doubtless, to match her own, I gave way for the time to the apprehension of ridicule.

But the next day, as the hour for my drive approached, I cropped up in another place. 'What was the lady who was here before?'

'The last governess? She was also young and pretty – almost as young and almost as pretty, Miss, even as you.'

'Ah, then, I hope her youth and her beauty helped her!' I recollect throwing off. 'He seems to like us young and pretty!'

'Oh, he *did*,' Mrs Grose assented: 'it was the way he liked everyone!' She had no sooner spoken indeed than she caught herself up. 'I mean that's *his* way – the master's.'

I was struck. 'But of whom did you speak first?'

She look blank, but she coloured. 'Why, of *him*.'

'Of the master?'

'Of who else?'

There was so obviously no one else that the next moment I had lost my impression of her having accidentally said more than she meant; and I merely asked what I wanted to know. 'Did *she* see anything in the boy—?'

'That wasn't right? She never told me.'

I had a scruple, but I overcame it. 'Was she careful – particular?'

Mrs Grose appeared to try to be conscientious. 'About some things – yes.'

'But not about all?'

Again she considered. 'Well, Miss – she's gone. I won't tell tales.'

'I quite understand your feeling,' I hastened to reply; but I thought it, after an instant, not opposed to this concession to pursue: 'Did she die here?'

'No – she went off.'

I don't know what there was in this brevity of Mrs Grose's that struck me as ambiguous. 'Went off to die?' Mrs Grose looked straight out of the window, but I felt that, hypothetically, I had a right to know what young persons engaged for Bly were expected to do. 'She was taken ill, you mean, and went home?'

'She was not taken ill, so far as appeared, in this house. She left it, at the end of the year, to go home, as she said, for a short holiday, to which the time she had put in had certainly given her a right. We had then a young woman – a nursemaid who had stayed on and who was a good girl and clever; and *she* took the children altogether for the interval. But our young lady never came back, and at the very moment I was expecting her I heard from the master that she was dead.'

I turned this over. 'But of what?'

'He never told me! But please, Miss,' said Mrs Grose, 'I must get to my work.'

III

HER thus turning her back on me was fortunately not, for my just preoccupations, a snub that could check the growth of our mutual esteem. We met, after I had brought home little Miles, more intimately than ever on the ground of my stupefaction, my general emotion: so monstrous was I then ready to pronounce it that such a child as had now been revealed to me should be under an interdict. I was a little late on the scene, and I felt, as he stood wistfully looking out for me before the door of the inn at which the coach had put him down, that I had seen him, on the instant, without and within, in the great glow of freshness, the same positive fragrance of purity, in which I had, from the first moment, seen his little sister. He was incredibly beautiful, and Mrs Grose had put her finger on it: everything but a sort of passion of tenderness for him was swept away by his presence. What I then and there took him to my heart for was something divine that I have never found to the same degree in any child – his indescribable little air of knowing nothing in the world but love. It would have been impossible to carry a bad name with a greater sweetness of innocence, and by the time I had got back to Bly with him I remained merely bewildered – so far, that is, as I was not outraged – by the sense of the horrible letter locked up in my room, in a drawer. As soon as I could compass a private word with Mrs Grose I declared to her that it was grotesque.

She promptly understood me. 'You mean the cruel charge—?'

'It doesn't live an instant. My dear woman, *look* at him!'

She smiled at my pretension to have discovered his charm. 'I assure you, Miss, I do nothing else! What will you say, then?' she immediately added.

'In answer to the letter?' I had made up my mind. 'Nothing.'

'And to his uncle?'

I was incisive. 'Nothing.'

'And to the boy himself?'

I was wonderful. 'Nothing.'

She gave with her apron a great wipe to her mouth. 'Then I'll stand by you. We'll see it out.'

'We'll see it out!' I ardently echoed, giving her my hand to make it a vow.

She held me there a moment, then whisked up her apron again with her detached hand. 'Would you mind, Miss, if I used the freedom—'

'To kiss me? No!' I took the good creature in my arms and, after we had embraced like sisters, felt still more fortified and indignant.

This, at all events, was for the time: a time so full that, as I recall the way it went, it reminds me of all the art I now need to make it a little distinct. What I look back at with amazement is the situation I accepted. I had undertaken, with my companion, to see it out, and I was under a charm, apparently, that could smooth away the extent and the far and difficult connections of such an effort. I was lifted aloft on a great wave of infatuation and pity. I found it simple, in my ignorance, my confusion, and perhaps my conceit, to assume that I could deal with a boy whose education for the world was all on the point of beginning. I am unable even to remember at this day what proposal I framed for the end of his holidays and the resumption of his studies. Lessons with me indeed, that charming summer, we all had a theory that he was to have; but I now feel that, for weeks, the lessons must have been rather my own. I learnt something – at first certainly – that had not been one of the teachings of my small, smothered life; learnt to be amused, and even amusing, and not to think for the morrow. It was the first time, in a manner, that I had known space and air and freedom, all the music of summer and all the mystery of nature. And then there was consideration – and consideration was sweet. Oh, it was a trap – not designed, but deep – to my imagination, to my delicacy, perhaps to my vanity; to whatever, in me, was most excitable. The best way to picture it all is to say that I was off my guard. They gave me so little trouble – they were of a gentleness so extraordinary. I used to speculate – but even this with a dim disconnectedness – as to how the rough future (for all futures are rough!) would handle them and might bruise them. They had the bloom of health and happiness; and yet, as if I had been in charge of a pair of little grandees, of princes of the blood, for whom everything, to be right, would have to be enclosed and protected, the only form that, in my fancy, the after-years could take for them was that of a romantic, a really royal extension of the garden and the park. It may be, of course, above all, that what suddenly broke into this gives the previous time a charm of stillness – that hush in which something gathers or crouches. The change was actually like the spring of a beast.

In the first weeks the days were long; they often, at their finest, gave me what I used to call my own hour, the hour when, for my pupils, tea-time and bed-time having come and gone, I had, before my final retirement, a small interval alone. Much as I liked my companions, this hour was the thing in the day I liked most; and I liked it best of all when, as the light faded – or rather, I should say, the day lingered and the last calls of the last birds sounded, in a flushed sky, from the old trees – I could take a turn into the grounds and enjoy, almost with a sense of property that amused and flattered me, the beauty and dignity of the place. It was a pleasure at these moments to feel myself tranquil and justified; doubtless, perhaps, also to reflect that by my discretion, my quiet good sense and general high propriety, I was giving pleasure – if he ever thought of it! – to the person to whose pressure I had responded. What I was doing was what he had earnestly hoped and directly asked of me, and that I *could*, after all, do it proved even a greater joy than I had expected. I daresay I fancied myself, in short, a remarkable young woman and took comfort in the faith that this would more publicly appear. Well, I needed to be remarkable to offer a front to the remarkable things that presently gave their first sign.

It was plump, one afternoon, in the middle of my very hour: the children were tucked away and I had come out for my stroll. One of the thoughts that, as I don't in the least shrink now from noting, used to be with me in these wanderings was that it would be as charming as a charming story suddenly to meet someone. Someone would appear there at the turn of a path and would stand before me and smile and approve. I didn't ask more than that – I only asked that he should *know*; and the only way to be sure he knew would be to see it, and the kind light of it, in his handsome face. That was exactly present to me – by which I mean the face was – when, on the first of these occasions, at the end of a long June day, I stopped short on emerging from one of the plantations and coming into view of the house. What arrested me on the spot – and with a shock much greater than any vision had allowed for – was the sense that my imagination had, in a flash, turned real. He did stand there! – but high up, beyond the lawn and at the very top of the tower to which, on that first morning, little Flora had conducted me. This tower was one of a pair – square, incongruous, crenelated structures – that were distinguished, for some reason, though I could see little difference, as the new and the old. They flanked opposite ends of the house and were probably architectural absurdities, redeemed in a measure indeed by not being wholly disengaged nor of a height too pretentious, dating, in their gingerbread antiquity, from a romantic revival that was already a respectable past. I admired them, had fancies about them, for we could all profit in a degree, especially when they loomed through the dusk, by the grandeur of their actual battlements; yet it was not at such an elevation that the figure I had so often invoked seemed most in place.

It produced in me, this figure, in the clear twilight, I remember, two distinct gasps of emotion, which were, sharply, the shock of my first and that of my second surprise. My second was a violent perception of the mistake of my first: the man who met my eyes was not the person I had precipitately supposed. There came to me thus a bewilderment of vision of which, after these years, there is no living view that I can hope to give. An unknown man in a lonely place is a permitted object of fear to a young woman privately bred; and the figure that faced me was – a few more seconds assured me – as little any one else I knew as it was the image that had been in my mind. I had not seen it in Harley Street – I had not seen it anywhere. The place, more-over, in the strangest way in the world, had, on the instant, and by the very fact of its appearance, become a solitude. To me at least, making my statement here with a deliberation with which I have never made it, the whole feeling of the moment returns. It was as if, while I took in – what I did take in – all the rest of the scene had been stricken with death. I can hear again, as I write, the intense hush in which the sounds of evening dropped. The rooks stopped cawing in the golden sky and the friendly hour lost, for the minute, all its voice. But there was no other change in nature, unless indeed it were a change that I saw with a stranger sharpness. The gold was still in the sky, the clearness in the air, and the man who looked at me over the battlements was as definite as a picture in a frame. That's how I thought, with extraordinary quickness, of each person that he might have been and that he was not. We were confronted across our distance quite long enough for me to ask myself with intensity who then he was and to feel, as an effect of my inability to say, a wonder that in a few instants more became intense.

The great question, or one of these, is, afterwards, I know, with regard to certain matters, the question of how long they have lasted. Well, this matter of mine, think what you will of it, lasted while I caught at a dozen possibilities, none of which made a difference for the better, that I could see, in there having been in the house – and for how long, above all? – a person of whom I was in ignorance. It lasted while I just bridled a little with the sense that my office demanded that there should be no such ignorance and no such person. It lasted while this visitant, at all events – and there was a touch of the strange freedom, as I remember, in the sign of familiarity of his wearing no hat – seemed to fix me, from his position, with just the question, just the scrutiny through the fading light, that his own presence provoked. We were too far apart to call to each other, but there was a moment at which, at shorter range, some challenge between us, breaking the hush, would have been the right result of our straight mutual stare. He was in one of the angles, the one away from the house, very erect, as it struck me, and with both hands on the ledge. So I saw him as I see the letters I form on this page; then, exactly, after a minute, as if to add to the spectacle, he slowly changed his place – passed, looking at me hard all the while, to the opposite corner of the platform. Yes, I had the sharpest sense that during this transit he never took his eyes from me, and I can see at this moment the way his hand, as he went, passed from one of the crenelations to the next. He stopped at the other corner, but less long, and even as he turned away still markedly fixed me. He turned away; that was all I knew.

IV

IT was not that I didn't wait, on this occasion, for more, for I was rooted as deeply as I was shaken. Was there a 'secret' at Bly – a mystery of Udolpho or an insane, an unmentionable relative kept in unsuspected confinement? I can't say how long I turned it over, or how long, in a confusion of curiosity and dread, I remained where I had had my collision; I only recall that when I re-entered the house darkness had quite closed in. Agitation, in the interval, certainly had held me and driven me, for I must, in circling about the place, have walked three miles; but I was to be, later on, so much more overwhelmed that this mere dawn of alarm was a comparatively human chill. The most singular part of it in fact – singular as the rest had been – was the part I became, in the hall, aware of in meeting Mrs Grose. This picture comes back to me in the general train – the impression, as I received it on my return, of the wide white panelled space, bright in the lamplight and with its portraits and red carpet, and of the good surprised look of my friend, which immediately told me she had missed me. It came to me straightway, under her contact, that, with plain heartiness, mere relieved anxiety at my appearance, she knew nothing whatever that could bear upon the incident I had there ready for her. I had not suspected in advance that her comfortable face would pull me up, and I somehow measured the importance of what I had seen by my thus finding myself hesitate to mention it. Scarce anything in the whole history seems to me so odd as this fact that my real beginning of fear was one, as I may say, with the instinct of sparing my companion. On the spot, accordingly, in the pleasant hall and with her eyes on me, I, for a reason that I couldn't then have phrased, achieved an inward revolution – offered a vague pretext for my lateness and, with the plea of the beauty of the night and of the heavy dew and wet feet, went as soon as possible to my room.

Here it was another affair; here, for many days after, it was a queer affair enough. There were hours, from day to day – or at least there were moments, snatched even from clear duties – when I had to shut myself up to think. It was not so much yet that I was more nervous than I could bear to be as that I was remarkably afraid of becoming so; for the truth I had now to turn over was, simply and clearly, the truth that I could arrive at no account whatever of the visitor with whom I had been so inexplicably and yet, as it seemed to me, so intimately concerned. It took little time to see that I could sound without forms of inquiry and without exciting remark any domestic complication. The shock I had suffered must have sharpened all my senses; I felt sure, at the end of three days and as the result of mere closer attention, that I had not been practised upon by the servants nor made the object of any 'game'. Of whatever it was that I knew nothing was known around me. There was but one sane inference: someone had taken a liberty rather gross. That was what, repeatedly, I dipped into my room and locked the door to say to myself. We had been, collectively, subject to an intrusion; some unscrupulous traveller, curious in old houses, had made his way in unobserved, enjoyed the prospect from the best point of view and then stolen out as he came. If he had given me such a bold hard stare, that was but a part of his indiscretion. The good thing, after all, was that we should surely see no more of him.

This was not so good a thing, I admit, as not to leave me to judge that what, essentially, made nothing else much signify was simply my charming work. My charming work was just my life with Miles and Flora, and through nothing could I so like it as through feeling that I could throw myself into it in trouble. The attraction of my small charges was a constant joy, leading me to wonder afresh at the vanity of my original fears, the distaste I had begun by entertaining for the probable grey prose of my office. There was to be no grey prose, it appeared, and no long grind; so how could work not be charming that presented itself as daily beauty? It was all the romance of the nursery and the poetry of the schoolroom. I don't mean by this, of course, that we studied only fiction and verse; I mean I can express no otherwise the sort of interest my companions inspired. How can I describe that except by saying that instead of growing used to them – and it's a marvel for a governess: I call the sisterhood to witness! – I made constant fresh discoveries. There was one direction, assuredly, in which these discoveries stopped: deep obscurity continued to cover the region of the boy's conduct at school. It had been promptly given me, I have noted, to face that mystery without a pang. Perhaps even it would be nearer the truth to say that – without a word – he himself had cleared it up. He had made the whole charge absurd. My conclusion bloomed there with the real rose-flush of his innocence: he was only too fine and fair for the little horrid, unclean school-world, and he had paid a price for it. I reflected acutely that the sense of such differences, such superiorities of quality, always, on the part of the majority – which could include even stupid, sordid head-masters – turns infallibly to the vindictive.

Both the children had a gentleness (it was their only fault, and it never made Miles a muff) that kept them – how shall I express it? – almost impersonal and certainly quite unpunishable. They were like the cherubs of the anecdote, who had – morally, at any rate – nothing to whack! I remember feeling with Miles in especial as if he had had, as it were, no history. We expect of a small child a scant one, but there was in this beautiful little boy something extraordinarily sensitive, yet extraordinarily happy, that, more than in any creature of his age I have seen, struck me as beginning anew each day. He had never for a second suffered. I took this as a direct disproof of his having really been chastised. If he had been wicked he would have 'caught' it, and I should have caught it by the rebound – I should have found the trace. I found nothing at all, and he was therefore an angel. He never spoke of his school, never mentioned a comrade or a master; and I, for my part, was quite too much disgusted to allude to them. Of course I was under the spell, and the wonderful part is that, even at the time, I perfectly knew I was. But I gave myself up to it; it was an antidote to any pain, and I had more pains than one. I was in receipt in these days of disturbing letters from home, where things were not going well. But with my children, what things in the world mattered? That was the question I used to put to my scrappy retirements. I was dazzled by their loveliness.

There was a Sunday – to get on – when it rained with such force and for so many hours that there could be no procession to church; in consequence of which, as the day declined, I had arranged with Mrs Grose that, should the evening show improvement, we would attend together the late service. The rain happily stopped, and I prepared for our walk, which, through the park and by the good road to the village, would be a matter of twenty minutes. Coming down stairs to meet my colleague in the hall, I remembered a pair of gloves that had required three stitches and that had received them – with a publicity perhaps not edifying – while I sat with the children at their tea, served on Sundays, by exception, in that cold, clean temple of mahogany and brass, the 'grown-up' dining-room. The gloves had been dropped there, and I turned in to recover them. The day was grey enough, but the afternoon light still lingered, and it enabled me, on crossing the threshold, not only to recognise, on a chair near the wide window, then closed, the articles I wanted, but to become aware of a person on the other side of the window and looking straight in. One step into the room had sufficed; my vision was instantaneous; it was all there. The person looking straight in was the person who had already appeared to me. He appeared thus again with I won't say greater distinctness, for that was impossible, but with a nearness that represented a forward stride in our intercourse and made me, as I met him, catch my breath and turn cold. He was the same – he was the same, and seen, this time, as he had been seen before, from the waist up, the window, though the dining-room was on the ground-floor, not going down to the terrace on which he stood. His face was close to the glass, yet the effect of this better view was, strangely, only to show me how intense the former had been. He remained but a few seconds – long enough to convince me he also saw and recognised; but it was as if I had been looking at him for years and had known him always. Something, however, happened this time that had not happened before; his stare into my face, through the glass and across the room, was as deep and hard as then, but it quitted me for a moment during which I could still watch it, see it fix successively several other things. On the spot there came to me the added shock of a certitude that it was not for me he had come there. He had come for someone else.

The flash of this knowledge – for it was knowledge in the midst of dread – produced in me the most extraordinary effect, started, as I stood there, a sudden vibration of duty and courage. I say courage because I was beyond all doubt already far gone. I bounded straight out of the door again, reached that of the house, got, in an instant, upon the drive, and, passing along the terrace as fast as I could rush, turned a corner and came full in sight. But it was in sight of nothing now – my visitor had vanished. I stopped, I almost dropped, with the real relief of this; but I took in the whole scene – I gave him time to reappear. I call it time, but how long was it? I can't speak to the purpose to-day of the duration of these things. That kind of measure must have left me: they couldn't have lasted as they actually appeared to me to last. The terrace and the whole place, the lawn and the garden beyond it, all I could see of the park, were empty with a great emptiness. There were shrubberies and big trees, but I remember the clear assurance I felt that none of them concealed him. He was there or was not there: not there if I didn't see him. I got hold of this; then, instinctively, instead of returning as I had come, went to the window. It was confusedly present to me that I ought to place myself where he had stood. I did so; I applied my face to the pane and looked, as he had looked, into the room. As if, at this moment, to show me exactly what his range had been, Mrs Grose, as I had done for himself just before, came in from the hall. With this I had the full image of a repetition of what had already occurred. She saw me as I had seen my own visitant; she pulled up short as I had done; I gave her something of the shock that I had received. She turned white, and this made me ask myself if I had blanched as much. She stared, in short, and retreated on just *my* lines, and I knew she had then passed out and come round to me and that I should presently meet her. I remained where I was, and while I waited I thought of more things than one. But there's only one I take space to mention. I wondered why *she* should be scared.

V

OH, she let me know as soon as, round the corner of the house, she loomed again into view. 'What in the name of goodness is the matter—?' She was now flushed and out of breath.

I said nothing till she came quite near. 'With me?' I must have made a wonderful face. 'Do I show it?'

'You're as white as a sheet. You look awful.'

I considered; I could meet on this, without scruple, any innocence. My need to respect the bloom of Mrs Grose's had dropped, without a rustle, from my shoulders, and if I wavered for the instant it was not with what I kept back. I put out my hand to her and she took it; I held her hard a little, liking to feel her close to me. There was a kind of support in the shy heave of her surprise. 'You came for me for church, of course, but I can't go.'

'Has anything happened?'

'Yes. You must know now. Did I look very queer?'

'Through this window? Dreadful!'

'Well,' I said, 'I've been frightened.' Mrs Grose's eyes expressed plainly that *she* had no wish to be, yet also that she knew too well her place not to be ready to share with me any marked inconvenience. Oh, it was quite settled that she *must* share! 'Just what you saw from the dining-room a minute ago was the effect of that. What *I* saw – just before – was much worse.'

Her hand tightened. 'What was it?'

'An extraordinary man. Looking in.'

'What extraordinary man?'

'I haven't the least idea.'

Mrs Grose gazed round us in vain. 'Then where is he gone?'

'I know still less.'

'Have you seen him before?'

'Yes – once. On the old tower.'

She could only look at me harder. 'Do you mean he's a stranger?'

'Oh, very much!'

'Yet you didn't tell me?'

'No – for reasons. But now that you've guessed—'

Mrs Grose's round eyes encountered this charge. 'Ah, I haven't guessed!' she said very simply. 'How can I if *you* don't imagine?'

'I don't in the very least.'

'You've seen him nowhere but on the tower?'

'And on this spot just now.'

Mrs Grose looked round again. 'What was he doing on the tower?'

'Only standing there and looking down at me.'

She thought a minute. 'Was he a gentleman?'

I found I had no need to think. 'No.' She gazed in deeper wonder. 'No.'

'Then nobody about the place? Nobody from the village?'

'Nobody – nobody. I didn't tell you, but I made sure.'

She breathed a vague relief: this was, oddly, so much to the good. It only went indeed a little way. 'But if he isn't a gentleman—'

'What *is* he? He's a horror.'

'A horror?'

'He's – God help me if I know *what* he is!'

Mrs Grose looked round once more; she fixed her eyes on the duskier distance, then, pulling herself together, turned to me with abrupt inconsequence. 'It's time we should be at church.'

'Oh, I'm not fit for church!'

'Won't it do you good?'

'It won't do *them*—!' I nodded at the house.

'The children?'

'I can't leave them now.'

'You're afraid—?'

I spoke boldly. 'I'm afraid of *him*.'

Mrs Grose's large face showed me, at this, for the first time, the far-away faint glimmer of a consciousness more acute: I somehow made out in it the delayed dawn of an idea I myself had not given her and that was as yet quite obscure to me. It comes back to me that I thought instantly of this as something I could get from her; and I felt it to be connected with the desire she presently showed to know more. 'When was it – on the tower?'

'About the middle of the month. At this same hour.'

'Almost at dark,' said Mrs Grose.

'Oh no, not nearly. I saw him as I see you.'

'Then how did he get in?'

'And how did he get out?' I laughed. 'I had no opportunity to ask him! This evening, you see,' I pursued, 'he has not been able to get in.'

'He only peeps?'

'I hope it will be confined to that!' She had now let go my hand; she turned away a little. I waited an instant; then I brought out: 'Go to church. Good-bye. I must watch.'

Slowly she faced me again. 'Do you fear for them?'

We met in another long look. 'Don't *you*?' Instead of answering she came nearer to the window and, for a minute, applied her face to the glass. 'You see how he could see,' I meanwhile went on.

She didn't move. 'How long was he here?'

'Till I came out. I came to meet him.'

Mrs Grose at last turned round, and there was still more in her face. '*I* couldn't have come out.'

'Neither could I!' I laughed again. 'But I did come. I have my duty.'

'So have I mine,' she replied; after which she added: 'What is he like?'

'I've been dying to tell you. But he's like nobody.'

'Nobody?' she echoed.

'He has no hat.' Then seeing in her face that she already, in this, with a deeper dismay, found a touch of picture, I quickly added stroke to stroke. 'He has red hair, very red, close-curling, and a pale face, long in shape, with straight, good features and little, rather queer whiskers that are as red as his hair. His eyebrows are, somehow, darker; they look particularly arched and as if they might move a good deal. His eyes are sharp, strange – awfully; but I only know clearly that they're rather small and very fixed. His mouth's wide, and his lips are thin, and except for his little whiskers he's quite clean-shaven. He gives me a sort of sense of looking like an actor.'

'An actor!' It was impossible to resemble one less, at least, than Mrs Grose at that moment.

'I've never seen one, but so I suppose them. He's tall, active, erect,' I continued, 'but never – no, never! – a gentleman.'

My companion's face had blanched as I went on; her round eyes started and her mild mouth gaped. 'A gentleman?' she gasped, confounded, stupefied: 'a gentleman *he*?'

'You know him then?'

She visibly tried to hold herself. 'But he *is* handsome?'

I saw the way to help her. 'Remarkably!'

'And dressed—?'

'In somebody's clothes. They're smart, but they're not his own.'

She broke into a breathless affirmative groan. 'They're the master's!'

I caught it up. 'You *do* know him?'

She faltered but a second. 'Quint!' she cried.

'Quint?'

'Peter Quint – his own man, his valet, when he was here!'

'When the master was?'

Gaping still, but meeting me, she pieced it all together. 'He never wore his hat, but he did wear – well, there were waistcoats missed! They were both here – last year. Then the master went, and Quint was alone.'

I followed, but halting a little. 'Alone?'

'Alone with *us*.' Then, as from a deeper depth, 'In charge,' she added.

'And what became of him?'

She hung fire so long that I was still more mystified. 'He went too,' she brought out at last.

'Went where?'

Her expression, at this, became extraordinary. 'God knows where! He died.'

'Died?' I almost shrieked.

She seemed fairly to square herself, plant herself more firmly to utter the wonder of it. 'Yes. Mr Quint is dead.'

VI

It took of course more than that particular passage to place us together in presence of what we had now to live with as we could – my dreadful liability to impressions of the order so vividly exemplified, and my companion's knowledge, hence- forth – a knowledge half consternation and half compassion – of that liability. There had been, this evening, after the revela- tion that left me, for an hour, so prostrate – there had been, for either of us, no attendance on any service but a little service of tears and vows, of prayers and promises, a climax to the series of mutual challenges and pledges that had straightway ensued on our retreating together to the schoolroom and shutting ourselves up there to have everything out. The result of our having everything out was simply to reduce our situation to the last rigour of its elements. She herself had seen nothing, not the shadow of a shadow, and nobody in the house but the govern- ess was in the governess's plight; yet she accepted without directly impugning my sanity the truth as I gave it to her, and ended by showing me, on this ground, an awe-stricken tender- ness, an expression of the sense of my more than questionable privilege, of which the very breath has remained with me as that of the sweetest of human charities.

What was settled between us, accordingly, that night, was that we thought we might bear things together; and I was not even sure that, in spite of her exemption, it was she who had the best of the burden. I knew at this hour, I think, as well as I knew later what I was capable of meeting to shelter my pupils; but it took me some time to be wholly sure of what my honest ally was prepared for to keep terms with so compromising a contract. I was queer company enough – quite as queer as the company I received; but as I trace over what we went through I see how much common ground we must have found in the one idea that, by good fortune, *could* steady us. It was the idea, the second movement, that led me straight out, as I may say, of the inner chamber of my dread. I could take the air in the court, at least, and there Mrs Grose could join me. Perfectly can I recall now the particular way strength came to me before we separated for the night. We had gone over and over every feature of what I had seen.

'He was looking for someone else, you say – someone who was not you?'

'He was looking for little Miles.' A portentous clearness now possessed me. '*That's* whom he was looking for.'

'But how do you know?'

'I know, I know, I know!' My exaltation grew. 'And *you* know, my dear!'

She didn't deny this, but I required, I felt, not even so much telling as that. She resumed in a moment, at any rate: 'What if *he* should see him?'

'Little Miles? That's what he wants!'

She looked immensely scared again. 'The child?'

'Heaven forbid! The man. He wants to appear to *them*.' That he might was an awful conception, and yet, some-how, I could keep it at bay; which, moreover, as we lingered there, was what I succeeded in practically proving. I had an absolute certainty that I should see again what I had already seen, but something within me said that by offering myself bravely as the sole subject of such experience, by accepting, by inviting, by surmounting it all, I should serve as an expiatory victim and guard the tranquillity of my companions. The children, in especial, I should thus fence about and absolutely save. I recall one of the last things I said that night to Mrs Grose.

'It does strike me that my pupils have never mentioned—'

She looked at me hard as I musingly pulled up. 'His having been here and the time they were with him?'

'The time they were with him, and his name, his presence, his history, in any way.'

'Oh, the little lady doesn't remember. She never heard or knew.'

'The circumstances of his death?' I thought with some intensity. 'Perhaps not. But Miles would remember – Miles would know.'

'Ah, don't try him!' broke from Mrs Grose.

I returned her the look she had given me. 'Don't be afraid.' I continued to think. 'It *is* rather odd.'

'That he has never spoken of him?'

'Never by the least allusion. And you tell me they were "great friends"?'

'Oh, it wasn't *him*!' Mrs Grose with emphasis declared. 'It was Quint's own fancy. To play with him, I mean – to spoil him.' She paused a moment; then she added: 'Quint was much too free.'

This gave me, straight from my vision of his face – *such* a face! – a sudden sickness of disgust. 'Too free with *my* boy?'

'Too free with everyone!'

I forbore, for the moment, to analyse this description further than by the reflection that a part of it applied to several of the members of the household, of the half-dozen maids and men who were still of our small colony. But there was everything, for our apprehension, in the lucky fact that no discomfortable legend, no perturbation of scullions, had ever, within anyone's memory, attached to the kind old place. It had neither bad name nor ill fame, and Mrs Grose, most apparently, only desired to cling to me and to quake in silence. I even put her, the very last thing of all, to the test. It was when, at midnight, she had her hand on the schoolroom door to take leave. 'I have it from you then – for it's of great importance – that he was definitely and admittedly bad?'

'Oh, not admittedly. *I* knew it – but the master didn't.'

'And you never told him?'

'Well, he didn't like tale-bearing – he hated complaints. He was terribly short with anything of that kind, and if people were all right to *him*—'

'He wouldn't be bothered with more?' This squared well enough with my impression of him: he was not a trouble-loving gentleman, nor so very particular perhaps about some of the company *he* kept. All the same, I pressed my interlocutress. 'I promise you *I* would have told!'

She felt my discrimination. 'I daresay I was wrong. But, really, I was afraid.'

'Afraid of what?'

'Of things that man could do. Quint was so clever – he was so deep.'

I took this in still more than, probably, I showed. 'You weren't afraid of anything else? Not of his effect—?'

'His effect?' she repeated with a face of anguish and waiting while I faltered.

'On innocent little precious lives. They were in your charge.'

'No, they were not in mine!' she roundly and distressfully returned. 'The master believed in him and placed him here because he was supposed not to be well and the country air so good for him. So he had everything to say. Yes' – she let me have it – 'even about *them*.'

'Them – that creature?' I had to smother a kind of howl. 'And you could bear it?'

'No. I couldn't – and I can't now!' And the poor woman burst into tears.

A rigid control, from the next day, was, as I have said, to follow them; yet how often and how passionately, for a week, we came back together to the subject! Much as we had discussed it that Sunday night, I was, in the immediate later hours in especial – for it may be imagined whether I slept – still haunted with the shadow of something she had not told me. I myself had kept back nothing, but there was a word Mrs Grose had kept back. I was sure, moreover, by morning, that this was not from a failure of frankness, but because on every side there were fears. It seems to me indeed, in retrospect, that by the time the morrow's sun was high I had restlessly read into the facts before us almost all the meaning they were to receive from subsequent and more cruel occurrences. What they gave me above all was just the sinister figure of the living man – the dead one would keep a while! – and of the months he had continuously passed at Bly, which, added up, made a formidable stretch. The limit of this evil time had arrived only when, on the dawn of a winter's morning, Peter Quint was found, by a labourer going to early work, stone dead on the road from the village: a catastrophe explained – superficially at least – by a visible wound to his head; such a wound as might have been produced – and as, on the final evidence, *had* been – by a fatal slip, in the dark and after leaving the public house, on the steepish icy slope, a wrong path altogether, at the bottom of which he lay. The icy slope, the turn mistaken at night and in liquor, accounted for much – practically, in the end and after the inquest and boundless chatter, for everything; but there had been matters in his life – strange passages and perils, secret disorders, vices more than suspected – that would have accounted for a good deal more.

I scarce know how to put my story into words that shall be a credible picture of my state of mind; but I was in these days literally able to find a joy in the extraordinary flight of heroism the occasion demanded of me. I now saw that I had been asked for a service admirable and difficult; and there would be a greatness in letting it be seen – oh, in the right quarter! – that I could succeed where many another girl might have failed. It was an immense help to me – I confess I rather applaud myself as I look back! – that I saw my service so strongly and so simply. I was there to protect and defend the little creatures in the world the most bereaved and the most loveable, the appeal of whose helplessness had suddenly become only too explicit, a deep, constant ache of one's own committed heart. We were cut off, really, together; we were united in our danger. They had nothing but me, and I – well, I had *them*. It was in short a magnificent chance. This chance presented itself to me in an image richly material. I was a screen – I was to stand before them. The more I saw, the less they would. I began to watch them in a stifled suspense, a disguised excitement that might well, had it continued too long, have turned to something like madness. What saved me, as I now see, was that it turned to something else altogether. It didn't last as suspense – it was superseded by horrible proofs. Proofs, I say, yes – from the moment I really took hold.

This moment dated from an afternoon hour that I happened to spend in the grounds with the younger of my pupils alone. We had left Miles indoors, on the red cushion of a deep window-seat; he had wished to finish a book, and I had been glad to encourage a purpose so laudable in a young man whose only defect was an occasional excess of the restless. His sister, on the contrary, had been alert to come out, and I strolled with her half an hour, seeking the shade, for the sun was still high and the day exceptionally warm. I was aware afresh, with her, as we went, of how, like her brother, she contrived – it was the charming thing in both children – to let me alone without appearing to drop me and to accompany me without appearing to surround. They were never importunate and yet never listless. My attention to them all really went to seeing them amuse themselves immensely without me: this was a spectacle they seemed actively to prepare and that engaged me as an active admirer. I walked in a world of their invention – they had no occasion whatever to draw upon mine; so that my time was taken only with being, for them, some remarkable person or thing that the game of the moment required and that was merely, thanks to my superior, my exalted stamp, a happy and highly distinguished sinecure. I forget what I was on the present occasion; I only remember that I was something very important and very quiet and that Flora was playing very hard. We were on the edge of the lake, and, as we had lately begun geography, the lake was the Sea of Azof.

Suddenly, in these circumstances, I became aware that, on the other side of the Sea of Azof, we had an interested spectator. The way this knowledge gathered in me was the strangest thing in the world – the strangest, that is, except the very much stranger in which it quickly merged itself. I had sat down with a piece of work – for I was something or other that could sit – on the old stone bench which overlooked the pond; and in this position I began to take in with certitude, and yet without direct vision, the presence, at a distance, of a third person. The old trees, the thick shrubbery, made a great and pleasant shade, but it was all suffused with the brightness of the hot, still hour. There was no ambiguity in anything; none whatever, at least, in the conviction I from one moment to another found myself forming as to what I should see straight before me and across the lake as a consequence of raising my eyes. They were attached at this juncture to the stitching in which I was engaged, and I can feel once more the spasm of my effort not to move them till I should so have steadied myself as to be able to make up my mind what to do. There was an alien object in view – a figure whose right of presence I instantly, passionately questioned. I recollect counting over perfectly the possibilities, reminding myself that nothing was more natural, for instance, than the appearance of one of the men about the place, or even of a messenger, a postman or a tradesman's boy, from the village. That reminder had as little effect on my practical certitude as I was conscious – still even without looking – of its having upon the character and attitude of our visitor. Nothing was more natural than that these things should be the other things that they absolutely were not.

Of the positive identity of the apparition I would assure myself as soon as the small clock of my courage should have ticked out the right second; meanwhile, with an effort that was already sharp enough, I transferred my eyes straight to little Flora, who, at the moment, was about ten yards away. My heart had stood still for an instant with the wonder and terror of the question whether she too would see; and I held my breath while I waited for what a cry from her, what some sudden innocent sign either of interest or of alarm, would tell me. I waited, but nothing came; then, in the first place – and there is something more dire in this, I feel, than in anything I have to relate – I was determined by a sense that, within a minute, all sounds from her had previously dropped; and, in the second, by the circumstance that, also within the minute, she had, in her play, turned her back to the water. This was her attitude when I at last looked at her – looked with the confirmed conviction that we were still, together, under direct personal notice. She had picked up a small flat piece of wood, which happened to have in it a little hole that had evidently suggested to her the idea of sticking in another fragment that might figure as a mast and make the thing a boat. This second morsel, as I watched her, she was very markedly and intently attempting to tighten in its place. My apprehension of what she was doing sustained me so that after some seconds I felt I was ready for more. Then I again shifted my eyes – I faced what I had to face.

VII

I GOT hold of Mrs Grose as soon after this as I could; and I can give no intelligible account of how I fought out the interval. Yet I still hear myself cry as I fairly threw myself into her arms: 'They *know* – it's too monstrous: they know, they know!'

'And what on earth—?' I felt her incredulity as she held me.

'Why, all that *we* know – and heaven knows what else besides!' Then, as she released me, I made it out to her, made it out perhaps only now with full coherency even to myself. 'Two hours ago, in the garden' – I could scarce articulate – 'Flora *saw*!'

Mrs Grose took it as she might have taken a blow in the stomach. 'She has told you?' she panted.

'Not a word – that's the horror. She kept it to herself! The child of eight, *that* child!' Unutterable still, for me, was the stupefaction of it.

Mrs Grose, of course, could only gape the wider. 'Then how do you know?'

'I was there – I saw with my eyes: saw that she was perfectly aware.'

'Do you mean aware of *him*?'

'No – of *her*.' I was conscious as I spoke that I looked prodigious things, for I got the slow reflection of them in my companion's face. 'Another person – this time; but a figure of quite as unmistakeable horror and evil: a woman in black, pale and dreadful – with such an air also, and such a face! – on the other side of the lake. I was there with the child – quiet for the hour; and in the midst of it she came.'

'Came how – from where?'

'From where they come from! She just appeared and stood there – but not so near.'

'And without coming nearer?'

'Oh, for the effect and the feeling, she might have been as close as you!'

My friend, with an odd impulse, fell back a step. 'Was she someone you've never seen?'

'Yes. But someone the child has. Someone *you* have.' Then, to show how I had thought it all out: 'My predecessor – the one who died.'

'Miss Jessel?'

'Miss Jessel. You don't believe me?' I pressed.

She turned right and left in her distress. 'How can you be sure?'

This drew from me, in the state of my nerves, a flash of impatience. 'Then ask Flora – *she's* sure!' But I had no sooner spoken than I caught myself up. 'No, for God's sake, *don't*! She'll say she isn't – she'll lie!'

Mrs Grose was not too bewildered instinctively to protest. 'Ah, how *can* you?'

'Because I'm clear. Flora doesn't want me to know.'

'It's only then to spare you.'

'No, no – there are depths, depths! The more I go over it, the more I see in it, and the more I see in it the more I fear. I don't know what I *don't* see – what I *don't* fear!'

Mrs Grose tried to keep up with me. 'You mean you're afraid of seeing her again?'

'Oh no; that's nothing – now!' Then I explained. 'It's of *not* seeing her.'

But my companion only looked wan. 'I don't understand you.'

'Why, it's that the child may keep it up – and that the child assuredly *will* – without my knowing it.'

At the image of this possibility Mrs Grose for a moment collapsed, yet presently pulled herself together again, as if from the positive force of the sense of what, should we yield an inch, there would really be to give way to. 'Dear, dear – we must keep our heads! And after all, if she doesn't mind it—!' She even tried a grim joke. 'Perhaps she likes it!'

'Likes *such* things – a scrap of an infant!'

'Isn't it just a proof of her blessed innocence?' my friend bravely inquired.

She brought me, for the instant, almost round. 'Oh, we must clutch at *that* – we must cling to it! If it isn't a proof of what you say, it's a proof of – God knows what! For the woman's a horror of horrors.'

Mrs Grose, at this, fixed her eyes a minute on the ground; then at last raising them, 'Tell me how you know,' she said.

'Then you admit it's what she was?' I cried.

'Tell me how you know,' my friend simply repeated.

'Know? By seeing her! By the way she looked.'

'At you, do you mean – so wickedly?'

'Dear me, no – I could have borne that. She gave me never a glance. She only fixed the child.'

Mrs Grose tried to see it. 'Fixed her?'

'Ah, with such awful eyes!'

She stared at mine as if they might really have resembled them. 'Do you mean of dislike?'

'God help us, no. Of something much worse.'

'Worse than dislike?' – this left her indeed at a loss.

'With a determination – indescribable. With a kind of fury of intention.'

I made her turn pale. 'Intention?'

'To get hold of her.' Mrs Grose – her eyes just lingering on mine – gave a shudder and walked to the window; and while she stood there looking out I completed my statement. '*That's* what Flora knows.'

After a little she turned round. 'The person was in black, you say?'

'In mourning – rather poor, almost shabby. But – yes – with extraordinary beauty.' I now recognised to what I had at last, stroke by stroke, brought the victim of my confidence, for she quite visibly weighed this. 'Oh, handsome – very, very,' I insisted; 'wonderfully handsome. But infamous.'

She slowly came back to me. 'Miss Jessel – *was* infamous.' She once more took my hand in both her own, holding it as tight as if to fortify me against the increase of alarm I might draw from this disclosure. 'They were both infamous,' she finally said.

So, for a little, we faced it once more together; and I found absolutely a degree of help in seeing it now so straight. 'I appreciate,' I said, 'the great decency of your not having hitherto spoken; but the time has certainly come to give me the whole thing.' She appeared to assent to this, but still only in silence; seeing which I went on: 'I must have it now. Of what did she die? Come, there was something between them.'

'There was everything.'

'In spite of the difference—?'

'Oh, of their rank, their condition' – she brought it woefully out. '*She* was a lady.'

I turned it over; I again saw. 'Yes – she was a lady.'

'And he so dreadfully below,' said Mrs Grose.

I felt that I doubtless needn't press too hard, in such company, on the place of a servant in the scale; but there was nothing to prevent an acceptance of my companion's own measure of my predecessor's abasement. There was a way to deal with that, and I dealt; the more readily for my full vision – on the evidence – of our employer's late clever, good-looking 'own' man; impudent, assured, spoiled, depraved. 'The fellow was a hound.'

Mrs Grose considered as if it were perhaps a little a case for a sense of shades. 'I've never seen one like him. He did what he wished.'

'With *her*?'

'With them all.'

It was as if now in my friend's own eyes Miss Jessel had again appeared. I seemed at any rate, for an instant, to see their evocation of her as distinctly as I had seen her by the pond; and I brought out with decision: 'It must have been also what *she* wished!'

Mrs Grose's face signified that it had been indeed, but she said at the same time: 'Poor woman – she paid for it!'

'Then you do know what she died of?' I asked.

'No – I know nothing. I wanted not to know; I was glad enough I didn't; and I thanked heaven she was well out of this!'

'Yet you had, then, your idea—'

'Of her real reason for leaving? Oh yes – as to that. She couldn't have stayed. Fancy it here – for a governess! And afterwards I imagined – and I still imagine. And what I imagine is dreadful.'

'Not so dreadful as what *I* do,' I replied; on which I must have shown her – as I was indeed but too conscious – a front of miserable defeat. It brought out again all her compassion for me, and at the renewed touch of her kindness my power to resist broke down. I burst, as I had, the other time, made her burst, into tears; she took me to her motherly breast, and my lamentation overflowed. 'I don't do it!' I sobbed in despair; 'I don't save or shield them! It's far worse than I dreamed – they're lost!'

VIII

WHAT I had said to Mrs Grose was true enough: there were in the matter I had put before her depths and possibilities that I lacked resolution to sound; so that when we met once more in the wonder of it we were of a common mind about the duty of resistance to extravagant fancies. We were to keep our heads if we should keep nothing else – difficult indeed as that might be in the face of what, in our prodigious experience, was least to be questioned. Late that night, while the house slept, we had another talk in my room; when she went all the way with me as to its being beyond doubt that I had seen exactly what I had seen. To hold her perfectly in the pinch of that, I found, I had only to ask her how, if I had 'made it up', I came to be able to give, of each of the persons appearing to me, a picture disclosing, to the last detail, their special marks – a portrait on the exhibition of which she had instantly recognised and named them. She wished, of course – small blame to her! – to sink the whole subject; and I was quick to assure her that my own interest in it had now violently taken the form of a search for the way to escape from it. I encountered her on the ground of a probability that with recurrence – for recurrence we took for granted – I should get used to my danger; distinctly professing that my personal exposure had suddenly become the least of my discomforts. It was my new suspicion that was intolerable; and yet even to this complication the later hours of the day had brought a little ease.

On leaving her, after my first outbreak, I had of course returned to my pupils, associating the right remedy for my dismay with that sense of their charm which I had already found to be a thing I could positively cultivate and which had never failed me yet. I had simply, in other words, plunged afresh into Flora's special society and there become aware – it was almost a luxury! – that she could put her little conscious hand straight upon the spot that ached. She had looked at me in sweet speculation and then had accused me to my face of having 'cried'. I had supposed I had brushed away the ugly signs; but I could literally – for the time, at all events – rejoice, under this fathomless charity, that they had not entirely disappeared. To gaze into the depths of blue of the child's eyes and pronounce their loveliness a trick of premature cunning was to be guilty of a cynicism in preference to which I naturally preferred to abjure my judgement and, so far as might be, my agitation. I couldn't abjure for merely wanting to, but I could repeat to Mrs Grose – as I did there, over and over, in the small hours – that with their voices in the air, their pressure on one's heart and their fragrant faces against one's cheek, everything fell to the ground but their incapacity and their beauty. It was a pity that, somehow, to settle this once for all, I had equally to re-enumerate the signs of subtlety that, in the afternoon, by the lake, had made a miracle of my show of self-possession. It was a pity to be obliged to reinvestigate the certitude of the moment itself and repeat how it had come to me as a revelation that the inconceivable communion I then surprised was a matter, for either party, of habit. It was a pity that I should have had to quaver out again the reasons for my not having, in my delusion, so much as questioned that the little girl saw our visitant even as I actually saw Mrs Grose herself, and that she wanted, by just so much as she did thus see, to make me suppose she didn't, and at the same time, without showing anything, arrive at a guess as to whether I myself did! It was a pity that I needed once more to describe the portentous little activity by which she sought to divert my attention – the perceptible increase of movement, the greater intensity of play, the singing, the gabbling, of nonsense and the invitation to romp.

Yet if I had not indulged, to prove there was nothing in it, in this review, I should have missed the two or three dim elements of comfort that still remained to me. I should not for instance have been able to asseverate to my friend that I was certain – which was so much to the good – that *I* at least had not betrayed myself. I should not have been prompted, by stress of need, by desperation of mind – I scarce know what to call it – to invoke such further aid to intelligence as might spring from pushing my colleague fairly to the wall. She had told me, bit by bit, under pressure, a great deal; but a small shifty spot on the wrong side of it all still sometimes brushed my brow like the wing of a bat; and I remember how on this occasion – for the sleeping house and the concentration alike of our danger and our watch seemed to help – I felt the importance of giving the last jerk to the curtain. 'I don't believe anything so horrible,' I recollect saying; 'no, let us put it definitely, my dear, that I don't. But if I did, you know, there's a thing I should require now, just without sparing you the least bit more – oh, not a scrap, come! – to get out of you. What was it you had in mind when, in our distress, before Miles came back, over the letter from his school, you said, under my insistence, that you didn't pretend for him that he had not literally *ever* been "bad"? He has *not* literally "ever", in these weeks that I myself have lived with him and so closely watched him; he has been an imperturbable little prodigy of delightful, loveable goodness. Therefore you might perfectly have made the claim for him if you had not, as it happened, seen an exception to take. What was your exception, and to what passage in your personal observation of him did you refer?'

It was a dreadfully austere inquiry, but levity was not our note, and, at any rate, before the grey dawn admonished us to separate I had got my answer. What my friend had had in mind proved to be immensely to the purpose. It was neither more nor less than the circumstance that for a period of several months Quint and the boy had been perpetually together. It was in fact the very appropriate truth that she had ventured to criticise the propriety, to hint at the incongruity, of so close an alliance, and even to go so far on the subject as a frank overture to Miss Jessel. Miss Jessel had, with a most strange manner, requested her to mind her business, and the good woman had, on this, directly approached little Miles. What she had said to him, since I pressed, was that *she* liked to see young gentlemen not forget their station.

I pressed again, of course, at this. 'You reminded him that Quint was only a base menial?'

'As you might say! And it was his answer, for one thing, that was bad.'

'And for another thing?' I waited. 'He repeated your words to Quint?'

'No, not that. It's just what he *wouldn't*!' she could still impress upon me. 'I was sure, at any rate,' she added, 'that he didn't. But he denied certain occasions.'

'What occasions?'

'When they had been about together quite as if Quint were his tutor – and a very grand one – and Miss Jessel only for the little lady. When he had gone off with the fellow, I mean, and spent hours with him.'

'He then prevaricated about it – he said he hadn't?' Her assent was clear enough to cause me to add in a moment: 'I see. He lied.'

'Oh!' Mrs Grose mumbled. This was a suggestion that it didn't matter; which indeed she backed up by a further remark. 'You see, after all, Miss Jessel didn't mind. She didn't forbid him.'

I considered. 'Did he put that to you as a justification?'

At this she dropped again. 'No, he never spoke of it.'

'Never mentioned her in connection with Quint?'

She saw, visibly flushing, where I was coming out. 'Well, he didn't show anything. He denied,' she repeated; 'he denied.'

Lord, how I pressed her now! 'So that you could see he knew what was between the two wretches?'

'I don't know – I don't know!' the poor woman groaned.

'You do know, you dear thing,' I replied; 'only you haven't my dreadful boldness of mind, and you keep back, out of timidity and modesty and delicacy, even the impression that, in the past, when you had, without my aid, to flounder about in silence, most of all made you miserable. But I shall get it out of you yet! There was something in the boy that suggested to you,' I continued, 'that he covered and concealed their relation.'

'Oh, he couldn't prevent—'

'Your learning the truth? I daresay! But, heavens,' I fell, with vehemence, a-thinking, 'what it shows that they must, to that extent, have succeeded in making of him!'

'Ah, nothing that's not nice *now*!' Mrs Grose lugubriously pleaded.

'I don't wonder you looked queer,' I persisted, 'when I mentioned to you the letter from his school!'

'I doubt if I looked as queer as you!' she retorted with homely force. 'And if he was so bad then as that comes to, how is he such an angel now?'

'Yes indeed – and if he was a fiend at school! How, how, how? Well,' I said in my torment, 'you must put it to me again, but I shall not be able to tell you for some days. Only, put it to me again!' I cried in a way that made my friend stare. 'There are directions in which I must not for the present let myself go.' Meanwhile I returned to her first example – the one to which she had just previously referred – of the boy's happy capacity for an occasional slip. 'If Quint – on your remonstrance at the time you speak of – was a base menial, one of the things Miles said to you, I find myself guessing, was that you were another.' Again her admission was so adequate that I continued: 'And you forgave him that?'

'Wouldn't *you*?'

'Oh yes!' And we exchanged there, in the stillness, a sound of the oddest amusement. Then I went on: 'At all events, while he was with the man—'

'Miss Flora was with the woman. It suited them all!'

It suited me too, I felt, only too well; by which I mean that it suited exactly the particular deadly view I was in the very act of forbidding myself to entertain. But I so far succeeded in checking the expression of this view that I will throw, just here, no further light on it than may be offered by the mention of my final observation to Mrs Grose. 'His having lied and been impudent are, I confess, less engaging specimens than I had hoped to have from you of the outbreak in him of the little natural man. Still,' I mused, 'they must do, for they make me feel more than ever that I must watch.'

It made me blush, the next minute, to see in my friend's face how much more unreservedly she had forgiven him than her anecdote struck me as presenting to my own tenderness an occasion for doing. This came out when, at the schoolroom door, she quitted me. 'Surely you don't accuse *him*—'

'Of carrying on an intercourse that he conceals from me? Ah, remember that, until further evidence, I now accuse nobody.' Then, before shutting her out to go, by another passage, to her own place, 'I must just wait,' I wound up.

IX

I WAITED and waited, and the days, as they elapsed, took something from my consternation. A very few of them, in fact, passing, in constant sight of my pupils, without a fresh incident, sufficed to give to grievous fancies and even to odious memories a kind of brush of the sponge. I have spoken of the surrender to their extraordinary childish grace as a thing I could actively cultivate, and it may be imagined if I neglected now to address myself to this source for whatever it would yield. Stranger than I can express, certainly, was the effort to struggle against my new lights; it would doubtless have been, however, a greater tension still had it not been so frequently successful. I used to wonder how my little charges could help guessing that I thought strange things about them; and the circumstance that these things only made them more interesting was not by itself a direct aid to keeping them in the dark. I trembled lest they should see that they *were* so immensely more interesting. Putting things at the worst, at all events, as in meditation I so often did, any clouding of their innocence could only be – blameless and foredoomed as they were – a reason the more for taking risks. There were moments when, by an irresistible impulse, I found myself catching them up and pressing them to my heart. As soon as I had done so I used to say to myself: 'What will they think of that? Doesn't it betray too much?' It would have been easy to get into a sad, wild tangle about how much I might betray; but the real account, I feel, of the hours of peace that I could still enjoy was that the immediate charm of my companions was a beguilement still effective even under the shadow of the possibility that it was studied. For if it occurred to me that I might occasionally excite suspicion by the little outbreaks of my sharper passion for them, so too I remember wondering if I mightn't see a queerness in the traceable increase of their own demonstrations.

They were at this period extravagantly and preternaturally fond of me; which, after all, I could reflect, was no more than a graceful response in children perpetually bowed over and hugged. The homage of which they were so lavish succeeded, in truth, for my nerves, quite as well as if I never appeared to myself, as I may say, literally to catch them at a purpose in it. They had never, I think, wanted to do so many things for their poor protectress; I mean – though they got their lessons better and better, which was naturally what would please her most – in the way of diverting, entertaining, surprising her; reading her passages, telling her stories, acting her charades, pouncing out at her, in disguises, as animals and historical characters, and above all astonishing her by the 'pieces' they had secretly got by heart and could interminably recite. I should never get to the bottom – were I to let myself go even now – of the prodigious private commentary, all under still more private correction, with which, in these days, I overscored their full hours. They had shown me from the first a facility for everything, a general faculty which, taking a fresh start, achieved remarkable flights. They got their little tasks as if they loved them, and indulged, from the mere exuberance of the gift, in the most unimposed little miracles of memory. They not only popped out at me as tigers and as Romans, but as Shakespeareans, astronomers and navigators. This was so singularly the case that it had presumably much to do with the fact as to which, at the present day, I am at a loss for a different explanation: I allude to my unnatural composure on the subject of another school for Miles. What I remember is that I was content not, for the time, to open the question, and that contentment must have sprung from the sense of his perpetually striking show of cleverness. He was too clever for a bad governess, for a parson's daughter, to spoil; and the strangest if not the brightest thread in the pensive embroidery I just spoke of was the impression I might have got, if I had dared to work it out, that he was under some influence operating in his small intellectual life as a tremendous incitement.

If it was easy to reflect, however, that such a boy could postpone school, it was at least as marked that for such a boy to have been 'kicked out' by a schoolmaster was a mystification without end. Let me add that in their company now – and I was careful almost never to be out of it – I could follow no scent very far. We lived in a cloud of music and love and success and private theatricals. The musical sense in each of the children was of the quickest, but the elder in especial had a marvellous knack of catching and repeating. The schoolroom piano broke into all gruesome fancies; and when that failed there were confabulations in corners, with a sequel of one of them going out in the highest spirits in order to 'come in' as something new. I had had brothers myself, and it was no revelation to me that little girls could be slavish idolaters of little boys. What surpassed everything was that there was a little boy in the world who could have for the inferior age, sex and intelligence so fine a consideration. They were extraordinarily at one, and to say that they never either quarrelled or complained is to make the note of praise coarse for their quality of sweetness. Sometimes indeed, when I dropped into coarseness, I perhaps came across traces of little understandings between them by which one of them should keep me occupied while the other slipped away. There is a *naïf* side, I suppose, in all diplomacy; but if my pupils practised upon me it was surely with the minimum of grossness. It was all in the other quarter that, after a lull, the grossness broke out.

I find that I really hang back; but I must take my plunge. In going on with the record of what was hideous at Bly I not only challenge the most liberal faith – for which I little care; but – and this is another matter – I renew what I myself suffered, I again push my way through it to the end. There came suddenly an hour after which, as I look back, the affair seems to me to have been all pure suffering; but I have at least reached the heart of it, and the straightest road out is doubtless to advance. One evening – with nothing to lead up or to prepare it – I felt the cold touch of the impression that had breathed on me the night of my arrival and which, much lighter then, as I have mentioned, I should probably have made little of in memory had my subsequent sojourn been less agitated. I had not gone to bed; I sat reading by a couple of candles. There was a roomful of old books at Bly – last-century fiction, some of it, which, to the extent of a distinctly deprecated renown, but never to so much as that of a stray specimen, had reached the sequestered home and appealed to the unavowed curiosity of my youth. I remember that the book I had in my hand was Fielding's *Amelia*; also that I was wholly awake. I recall further both a general conviction that it was horribly late and a particular objection to looking at my watch. I figure, finally, that the white curtain draping, in the fashion of those days, the head of Flora's little bed, shrouded, as I had assured myself long before, the perfection of childish rest. I recollect in short that, though I was deeply interested in my author, I found myself, at the turn of a page and with his spell all scattered, looking straight up from him and hard at the door of my room. There was a moment during which I listened, reminded of the faint sense I had had, the first night, of there being something undefinably astir in the house, and noted the soft breath of the open casement just move the half-drawn blind. Then, with all the marks of a deliberation that must have seemed magnificent had there been anyone to admire it, I laid down my book, rose to my feet and, taking a candle, went straight out of the room and, from the passage, on which my light made little impression, noiselessly closed and locked the door.

I can say now neither what determined nor what guided me, but I went straight along the lobby, holding my candle high, till I came within sight of the tall window that presided over the great turn of the staircase. At this point I precipitately found myself aware of three things. They were practically simultaneous, yet they had flashes of succession. My candle, under a bold flourish, went out, and I perceived, by the uncovered window, that the yielding dusk of earliest morning rendered it unnecessary. Without it, the next instant, I saw that there was someone on the stair. I speak of sequences, but I required no lapse of seconds to stiffen myself for a third encounter with Quint. The apparition had reached the landing half way up and was therefore on the spot nearest the window, where, at sight of me, it stopped short and fixed me exactly as it had fixed me from the tower and from the garden. He knew me as well as I knew him; and so, in the cold, faint twilight, with a glimmer in the high glass and another on the polish of the oak stair below, we faced each other in our common intensity. He was absolutely, on this occasion, a living, detestable, dangerous presence. But that was not the wonder of wonders; I reserve this distinction for quite another circumstance: the circumstance that dread had unmistakeably quitted me and that there was nothing in me there that didn't meet and measure him.

I had plenty of anguish after that extraordinary moment, but I had, thank God, no terror. And he knew I had not – I found myself at the end of an instant magnificently aware of this. I felt, in a fierce rigour of confidence, that if I stood my ground a minute I should cease – for the time, at least – to have him to reckon with; and during the minute, accordingly, the thing was as human and hideous as a real interview: hideous just because it *was* human, as human as to have met alone, in the small hours, in a sleeping house, some enemy, some adventurer, some criminal. It was the dead silence of our long gaze at such close quarters that gave the whole horror, huge as it was, its only note of the unnatural. If I had met a murderer in such a place and at such an hour we still at least would have spoken. Something would have passed, in life, between us; if nothing had passed one of us would have moved. The moment was so prolonged that it would have taken but little more to make me doubt if even *I* were in life. I can't express what followed it save by saying that the silence itself – which was indeed in a manner an attestation of my strength – became the element into which I saw the figure disappear; in which I definitely saw it turn, as I might have seen the low wretch to which it had once belonged turn on receipt of an order, and pass, with my eyes on the villainous back that no hunch could have more disfigured, straight down the staircase and into the darkness in which the next bend was lost.

X

I REMAINED a while at the top of the stair, but with the effect presently of understanding that when my visitor had gone, he had gone: then I returned to my room. The foremost thing I saw there by the light of the candle I had left burning was that Flora's little bed was empty; and on this I caught my breath with all the terror that, five minutes before, I had been able to resist. I dashed at the place in which I had left her lying and over which (for the small silk counterpane and the sheets were disarranged) the white curtains had been deceivingly pulled forward; then my step, to my unutterable relief, produced an answering sound: I perceived an agitation of the window-blind, and the child, ducking down, emerged rosily from the other side of it. She stood there in so much of her candour and so little of her nightgown, with her pink bare feet and the golden glow of her curls. She looked intensely grave, and I had never had such a sense of losing an advantage acquired (the thrill of which had just been so prodigious) as on my consciousness that she addressed me with a reproach. 'You naughty: where *have* you been?' – instead of challenging her own irregularity I found myself arraigned and explaining. She herself explained, for that matter, with the loveliest, eagerest simplicity. She had known suddenly, as she lay there, that I was out of the room, and had jumped up to see what had become of me. I had dropped, with the joy of her reappearance, back into my chair – feeling then, and then only, a little faint; and she had pattered straight over to me, thrown herself upon my knee, given herself to be held with the flame of the candle full in the wonderful little face that was still flushed with sleep. I remember closing my eyes an instant, yieldingly, consciously, as before the excess of something beautiful that shone out of the blue of her own. 'You were looking for me out of the window?' I said. 'You thought I might be walking in the grounds?'

'Well, you know, I thought someone was' – she never blanched as she smiled out that at me.

Oh, how I looked at her now! 'And did you see anyone?'

'Ah, *no*!' she returned, almost, with the full privilege of childish inconsequence, resentfully, though with a long sweetness in her little drawl of the negative.

At that moment, in the state of my nerves, I absolutely believed she lied; and if I once more closed my eyes it was before the dazzle of the three or four possible ways in which I might take this up. One of these, for a moment, tempted me with such singular intensity that, to withstand it, I must have gripped my little girl with a spasm that, wonderfully, she submitted to without a cry or a sign of fright. Why not break out at her on the spot and have it all over? – give it to her straight in her lovely little lighted face? 'You see, you see, you *know* that you do and that you already quite suspect I believe it; therefore why not frankly confess it to me, so that we may at least live with it together and learn perhaps, in the strangeness of our fate, where we are and what it means?' This solicitation dropped, alas, as it came: if I could immediately have succumbed to it I might have spared myself—well, you'll see what. Instead of succumbing I sprang again to my feet, looked at her bed and took a helpless middle way. 'Why did you pull the curtain over the place to make me think you were still there?'

Flora luminously considered; after which, with her little divine smile: 'Because I don't like to frighten you!'

'But if I had, by your idea, gone out—?'

She absolutely declined to be puzzled; she turned her eyes to the flame of the candle as if the question were as irrelevant, or at any rate as impersonal, as Mrs Marcet or nine-times-nine. 'Oh, but you know,' she quite adequately answered, 'that you might come back, you dear, and that you *have*!' And after a little, when she had got into bed, I had, for a long time, by almost sitting on her to hold her hand, to prove that I recognised the pertinence of my return.

You may imagine the general complexion, from that moment, of my nights. I repeatedly sat up till I didn't know when; I selected moments when my room-mate unmistakeably slept, and, stealing out, took noiseless turns in the passage and even pushed as far as to where I had last met Quint. But I never met him there again; and I may as well say at once that I on no other occasion saw him in the house. I just missed, on the staircase, on the other hand, a different adventure. Looking down it from the top I once recognised the presence of a woman seated on one of the lower steps with her back presented to me, her body half bowed and her head, in an attitude of woe, in her hands. I had been there but an instant, however, when she vanished without looking round at me. I knew, none the less, exactly what dreadful face she had to show; and I wondered whether, if instead of being above I had been below, I should have had, for going up, the same nerve I had lately shown Quint. Well, there continued to be plenty of chance for nerve. On the eleventh night after my latest encounter with that gentleman – they were all numbered now – I had an alarm that perilously skirted it and that indeed, from the particular quality of its unexpectedness, proved quite my sharpest shock. It was precisely the first night during this series that, weary with watching, I had felt that I might again without laxity lay myself down at my old hour. I slept immediately and, as I afterwards knew, till about one o'clock; but when I woke it was to sit straight up, as completely roused as if a hand had shook me. I had left a light burning, but it was now out, and I felt an instant certainty that Flora had extinguished it. This brought me to my feet and straight, in the darkness, to her bed, which I found she had left. A glance at the window enlightened me further, and the striking of a match completed the picture.

The child had again got up – this time blowing out the taper, and had again, for some purpose of observation or response, squeezed in behind the blind and was peering out into the night. That she now saw – as she had not, I had satisfied myself, the previous time – was proved to me by the fact that she was disturbed neither by my re-illumination nor by the haste I made to get into slippers and into a wrap. Hidden, protected, absorbed, she evidently rested on the sill – the casement opened forward – and gave herself up. There was a great still moon to help her, and this fact had counted in my quick decision. She was face to face with the apparition we had met at the lake, and could now communicate with it as she had not then been able to do. What I, on my side, had to care for was, without disturbing her, to reach, from the corridor, some other window in the same quarter. I got to the door without her hearing me; I got out of it, closed it and listened, from the other side, for some sound from her. While I stood in the passage I had my eyes on her brother's door, which was but ten steps off and which, indescribably, produced in me a renewal of the strange impulse that I lately spoke of as my temptation. What if I should go straight in and march to *his* window? – what if, by risking to his boyish bewilderment a revelation of my motive, I should throw across the rest of the mystery the long halter of my boldness?

This thought held me sufficiently to make me cross to his threshold and pause again. I preternaturally listened; I figured to myself what might portentously be; I wondered if his bed were also empty and he too were secretly at watch. It was a deep, soundless minute, at the end of which my impulse failed. He was quiet; he might be innocent; the risk was hideous; I turned away. There was a figure in the grounds – a figure prowling for a sight, the visitor with whom Flora was engaged; but it was not the visitor most concerned with my boy. I hesitated afresh, but on other grounds and only a few seconds; then I had made my choice. There were empty rooms at Bly, and it was only a question of choosing the right one. The right one suddenly presented itself to me as the lower one – though high above the gardens – in the solid corner of the house that I have spoken of as the old tower. This was a large, square chamber, arranged with some state as a bedroom, the extravagant size of which made it so inconvenient that it had not for years, though kept by Mrs Grose in exemplary order, been occupied. I had often admired it and I knew my way about in it; I had only, after just faltering at the first chill gloom of its disuse, to pass across it and unbolt as quietly as I could one of the shutters. Achieving this transit, I uncovered the glass without a sound and, applying my face to the pane, was able, the darkness without being much less than within, to see that I commanded the right direction. Then I saw something more. The moon made the night extraordinarily penetrable and showed me on the lawn a person, diminished by distance, who stood there motionless and as if fascinated, looking up to where I had appeared – looking, that is, not so much straight at me as at something that was apparently above me. There was clearly another person above me – there was a person on the tower; but the presence on the lawn was not in the least what I had conceived and had confidently hurried to meet. The presence on the lawn – I felt sick as I made it out – was poor little Miles himself.

XI

IT was not till late next day that I spoke to Mrs Grose; the rigour with which I kept my pupils in sight making it often difficult to meet her privately, and the more as we each felt the importance of not provoking – on the part of the servants quite as much as on that of the children – any suspicion of a secret flurry or of a discussion of mysteries. I drew a great security in this particular from her mere smooth aspect. There was nothing in her fresh face to pass on to others my horrible confidences. She believed me, I was sure, absolutely: if she hadn't I don't know what would have become of me, for I couldn't have borne the business alone. But she was a magnificent monument to the blessing of a want of imagination, and

if she could see in our little charges nothing but their beauty and
amiability, their happiness and cleverness, she had no direct
communication with the sources of my trouble. If they had
been at all visibly blighted or battered she would doubtless
have grown, on tracing it back, haggard enough to match
them; as matters stood, however, I could feel her, when she
surveyed them with her large white arms folded and the habit of
serenity in all her look, thank the Lord's mercy that if they were
ruined the pieces would still serve. Flights of fancy gave place,
in her mind, to a steady fireside glow, and I had already begun
to perceive how, with the development of the conviction that –
as time went on without a public accident – our young things
could, after all, look out for themselves, she addressed her
greatest solicitude to the sad case presented by their instruc-
tress. That, for myself, was a sound simplification: I could
engage that, to the world, my face should tell no tales, but it
would have been, in the conditions, an immense added strain
to find myself anxious about hers.

At the hour I now speak of she had joined me, under pressure, on the terrace, where, with the lapse of the season, the
afternoon sun was now agreeable; and we sat there together
while, before us, at a distance, but within call if we wished, the
children strolled to and fro in one of their most manageable
moods. They moved slowly, in unison, below us, over the lawn,
the boy, as they went, reading aloud from a storybook and
passing his arm round his sister to keep her quite in touch.
Mrs Grose watched them with positive placidity; then I caught
the suppressed intellectual creak with which she conscientiously turned to take from me a view of the back of the tapestry.
I had made her a receptacle of lurid things, but there was an
odd recognition of my superiority – my accomplishments and
my function – in her patience under my pain. She offered her
mind to my disclosures as, had I wished to mix a witch's broth
and proposed it with assurance, she would have held out a large
clean saucepan. This had become thoroughly her attitude by
the time that, in my recital of the events of the night, I reached
the point of what Miles had said to me when, after seeing him,
at such a monstrous hour, almost on the very spot where he

happened now to be, I had gone down to bring him in; choosing then, at the window, with a concentrated need of not alarming the house, rather that method than a signal more resonant. I had left her meanwhile in little doubt of my small hope of representing with success even to her actual sympathy my sense of the real splendour of the little inspiration with which, after I had got him into the house, the boy met my final articulate challenge. As soon as I appeared in the moonlight on the terrace he had come to me as straight as possible; on which I had taken his hand without a word and led him, through the dark spaces, up the staircase where Quint had so hungrily hovered for him, along the lobby where I had listened and trembled, and so to his forsaken room.

Not a sound, on the way, had passed between us, and I had wondered – oh, *how* I had wondered! – if he were groping about in his little mind for something plausible and not too grotesque. It would tax his invention, certainly, and I felt, this time, over his real embarrassment, a curious thrill of triumph. It was a sharp trap for the inscrutable! He couldn't play any longer at innocence; so how the deuce would he get out of it? There beat in me indeed, with the passionate throb of this question, an equal dumb appeal as to how the deuce *I* should. I was confronted at last, as never yet, with all the risk attached even now to sounding my own horrid note. I remember in fact that as we pushed into his little chamber, where the bed had not been slept in at all and the window, uncovered to the moonlight, made the place so clear that there was no need of striking a match – I remember how I suddenly dropped, sank upon the edge of the bed from the force of the idea that he must know how he really, as they say, 'had' me. He could do what he liked, with all his cleverness to help him, so long as I should continue to defer to the old tradition of the criminality of those caretakers of the young who minister to superstitions and fears. He 'had' me indeed, and in a cleft stick; for who would ever absolve me, who would consent that I should go unhung, if, by the faintest tremor of an overture, I were the first to introduce into our perfect intercourse an element so dire? No, no: it was useless to attempt to convey to Mrs Grose, just as it is scarcely less so to attempt to suggest here, how, in our short, stiff brush in the dark, he fairly shook me with admiration. I was of course thoroughly kind and merciful; never, never yet had I placed on his little shoulders hands of such tenderness as those with which, while I rested against the bed, I held him there well under fire. I had no alternative but, in form at least, to put it to him.

'You must tell me now – and all the truth. What did you go out for? What were you doing there?'

I can still see his wonderful smile, the whites of his beautiful eyes and the uncovering of his little teeth, shine to me in the dusk. 'If I tell you why, will you understand?' My heart, at this, leaped into my mouth. *Would* he tell me why? I found no sound on my lips to press it, and I was aware of replying only with a vague, repeated, grimacing nod. He was gentleness itself, and while I wagged my head at him he stood there more than ever a little fairy prince. It was his brightness indeed that gave me a respite. Would it be so great if he were really going to tell me? 'Well,' he said at last, 'just exactly in order that you should do this.'

'Do what?'

'Think me – for a change – *bad*!' I shall never forget the sweetness and gaiety with which he brought out the word, nor how, on top of it, he bent forward and kissed me. It was practically the end of everything. I met his kiss and I had to make, while I folded him for a minute in my arms, the most stupendous effort not to cry. He had given exactly the account of himself that permitted least of my going behind it, and it was only with the effect of confirming my acceptance of it that, as I presently glanced about the room, I could say –

'Then you didn't undress at all?'

He fairly glittered in the gloom. 'Not at all. I sat up and read.'

'And when did you go down?'

'At midnight. When I'm bad I *am* bad!'

'I see, I see – it's charming. But how could you be sure I would know it?'

'Oh, I arranged that with Flora.' His answers rang out with a readiness! 'She was to get up and look out.'

'Which is what she did do.' It was I who fell into the trap!

'So she disturbed you, and, to see what she was looking at, you also looked – you saw.'

'While you,' I concurred, 'caught your death in the night air!'

He literally bloomed so from this exploit that he could afford radiantly to assent. 'How otherwise should I have been bad enough?' he asked. Then, after another embrace, the incident and our interview closed on my recognition of all the reserves of goodness that, for his joke, he had been able to draw upon.

XII

THE particular impression I had received proved in the morning light, I repeat, not quite successfully presentable to Mrs Grose, though I reinforced it with the mention of still another remark that he had made before we separated. 'It all lies in half-a-dozen words,' I said to her, 'words that really settle the matter. "Think, you know, what I *might* do!" He threw that off to show me how good he is. He knows down to the ground what he "might" do. That's what he gave them a taste of at school.'

'Lord, you do change!' cried my friend.

'I don't change – I simply make it out. The four, depend upon it, perpetually meet. If on either of these last nights you had been with either child you would clearly have understood. The more I've watched and waited the more I've felt that if there were nothing else to make it sure it would be made so by the systematic silence of each. *Never*, by a slip of the tongue, have they so much as alluded to either of their old friends, any more than Miles has alluded to his expulsion. Oh yes, we may sit here and look at them, and they may show off to us there to their fill; but even while they pretend to be lost in their fairy-tale they're steeped in their vision of the dead restored. He's not reading to her,' I declared; 'they're talking of *them* – they're talking horrors! I go on, I know, as if I were crazy; and it's a wonder I'm not. What I've seen would have made *you* so; but it has only made me more lucid, made me get hold of still other things.'

My lucidity must have seemed awful, but the charming creatures who were victims of it, passing and repassing in their interlocked sweetness, gave my colleague something to hold on by; and I felt how tight she held as, without stirring in the breath of my passion, she covered them still with her eyes. 'Of what other things have you got hold?'

'Why, of the very things that have delighted, fascinated and yet, at bottom, as I now so strangely see, mystified and troubled me. Their more than earthly beauty, their absolutely unnatural goodness. It's a game,' I went on; 'it's a policy and a fraud!'

'On the part of little darlings—?'

'As yet mere lovely babies? Yes, mad as that seems!' The very act of bringing it out really helped me to trace it – follow it all up and piece it all together. 'They haven't been good – they've only been absent. It has been easy to live with them, because they're simply leading a life of their own. They're not mine – they're not ours. They're his and they're hers!'

'Quint's and that woman's?'

'Quint's and that woman's. They want to get to them.'

Oh, how, at this, poor Mrs Grose appeared to study them! 'But for what?'

'For the love of all the evil that, in those dreadful days, the pair put into them. And to ply them with that evil still, to keep up the work of demons, is what brings the others back.'

'Laws!' said my friend under her breath. The exclamation was homely, but it revealed a real acceptance of my further proof of what, in the bad time – for there had been a worse even than this! – must have occurred. There could have been no such justification for me as the plain assent of her experience to whatever depth of depravity I found credible in our brace of scoundrels. It was in obvious submission of memory that she brought out after a moment: 'They *were* rascals! But what can they now do?' she pursued.

'Do?' I echoed so loud that Miles and Flora, as they passed at their distance, paused an instant in their walk and looked at us. 'Don't they do enough?' I demanded in a lower tone, while the children, having smiled and nodded and kissed hands to us, resumed their exhibition. We were held by it a minute; then I answered: 'They can destroy them!' At this my companion did turn, but the inquiry she launched was a silent one, the effect of which was to make me more explicit. 'They don't know, as yet, quite how – but they're trying hard. They're seen only across, as it were, and beyond – in strange places and on high places, the top of towers, the roof of houses, the outside of windows, the further edge of pools; but there's a deep design, on either side, to shorten the distance and overcome the obstacle; and the success of the tempters is only a question of time. They've only to keep to their suggestions of danger.'

'For the children to come?'

'And perish in the attempt!' Mrs Grose slowly got up, and I scrupulously added: 'Unless, of course, we can prevent!'

Standing there before me while I kept my seat, she visibly turned things over. 'Their uncle must do the preventing. He must take them away.'

'And who's to make him?'

She had been scanning the distance, but she now dropped on me a foolish face. 'You, Miss.'

'By writing to him that his house is poisoned and his little nephew and niece mad?'

'But if they *are*, Miss?'

'And if I am myself, you mean? That's charming news to be sent him by a governess whose prime undertaking was to give him no worry.'

Mrs Grose considered, following the children again. 'Yes, he do hate worry. That was the great reason—'

'Why those fiends took him in so long? No doubt, though his indifference must have been awful. As I'm not a fiend, at any rate, I shouldn't take him in.'

My companion, after an instant and for all answer, sat down again and grasped my arm. 'Make him at any rate come to you.'

I stared. 'To *me*?' I had a sudden fear of what she might do. ' "Him"?'

'He ought to *be* here – he ought to help.'

I quickly rose, and I think I must have shown her a queerer face than ever yet. 'You see me asking him for a visit?' No, with her eyes on my face she evidently couldn't. Instead of it even – as a woman reads another – she could see what I myself saw: his derision, his amusement, his contempt for the break-down of my resignation at being left alone and for the fine machinery I had set in motion to attract his attention to my slighted charms. She didn't know – no one knew – how proud I had been to serve him and to stick to our terms; yet she none the less took the measure, I think, of the warning I now gave her. 'If you should so lose your head as to appeal to him for me—'

She was really frightened. 'Yes, Miss?'

'I would leave, on the spot, both him and you.'

XIII

IT was all very well to join them, but speaking to them proved quite as much as ever an effort beyond my strength – offered, in close quarters, difficulties as insurmountable as before. This situation continued a month, and with new aggravations and particular notes, the note above all, sharper and sharper, of the small ironic consciousness on the part of my pupils. It was not, I am as sure to-day as I was sure then, my mere infernal imagina-tion: it was absolutely traceable that they were aware of my predicament and that this strange relation made, in a manner, for a long time, the air in which we moved. I don't mean that they had their tongues in their cheeks or did anything vulgar, for that was not one of their dangers: I do mean, on the other hand, that the element of the unnamed and untouched became, between us, greater than any other, and that so much avoidance could not have been so successfully effected without a great deal of tacit arrangement. It was as if, at moments, we were perpetually coming into sight of subjects before which we must stop short, turning suddenly out of alleys that we perceived to be blind, closing with a little bang that made us look at each other – for, like all bangs, it was something louder than we had intended – the doors we had indiscreetly opened. All roads lead to Rome, and there were times when it might have struck us that almost every branch of study or subject of conversation skirted forbidden ground. Forbidden ground was the question of the return of the dead in general and of whatever, in especial, might survive, in memory, of the friends little children had lost. There were days when I could have sworn that one of them had, with a small invisible nudge, said to the other: 'She thinks she'll do it this time – but she *won't*!' To 'do it' would have been to indulge for instance – and for once in a way – in some direct reference to the lady who had prepared them for my discipline. They had a delightful endless appetite for passages in my own history, to which I had again and again treated them; they were in possession of everything that had ever happened to me, had had, with every circumstance, the story of my smallest adventures and of those of my brothers and sisters and of the cat and the dog at home, as well as many particulars of the eccentric nature of my father, of the furniture and arrangement of our house and of the conversation of the old women of our village. There were things enough, taking one with another, to chatter about, if one went very fast and knew by instinct when to go round. They pulled with an art of their own the strings of my invention and my memory; and nothing else perhaps, when I thought of such occasions afterwards, gave me so the suspicion of being watched from under cover. It was in any case over *my* life, *my* past and *my* friends alone that we could take anything like our ease; a state of affairs that led them sometimes without the least pertinence to break out into sociable reminders. I was invited – with no visible connection – to repeat afresh Goody Gosling's celebrated *mot* or to confirm the details already supplied as to the cleverness of the vicarage pony.

It was partly at such junctures as these and partly at quite different ones that, with the turn my matters had now taken, my predicament, as I have called it, grew most sensible. The fact that the days passed for me without another encounter ought, it would have appeared, to have done something toward soothing my nerves. Since the light brush, that second night on the upper landing, of the presence of a woman at the foot of the stair, I had seen nothing, whether in or out of the house, that one had better not have seen. There was many a corner round which I expected to come upon Quint, and many a situation that, in a merely sinister way, would have favoured the appearance of

Miss Jessel. The summer had turned, the summer had gone; the autumn had dropped upon Bly and had blown out half our lights. The place, with its grey sky and withered garlands, its bared spaces and scattered dead leaves, was like a theatre after the performance – all strewn with crumpled playbills. There were exactly states of the air, conditions of sound and of still-ness, unspeakable impressions of the *kind* of ministering moment, that brought back to me, long enough to catch it, the feeling of the medium in which, that June evening out-of-doors, I had had my first sight of Quint, and in which, too, at those other instants, I had, after seeing him through the win-dow, looked for him in vain in the circle of shrubbery. I recog-nised the signs, the portents – I recognised the moment, the spot. But they remained unaccompanied and empty, and I continued unmolested; if unmolested one could call a young woman whose sensibility had, in the most extraordinary fash-ion, not declined but deepened. I had said in my talk with Mrs Grose on that horrid scene of Flora's by the lake – and had perplexed her by so saying – that it would from that moment distress me much more to lose my power than to keep it. I had then expressed what was vividly in my mind: the truth that, whether the children really saw or not – since, that is, it was not yet definitely proved – I greatly preferred, as a safeguard, the fulness of my own exposure. I was ready to know the very worst that was to be known. What I had then had an ugly glimpse of was that my eyes might be sealed just while theirs were most opened. Well, my eyes *were* sealed, it appeared, at present – a consummation for which it seemed blasphemous not to thank God. There was, alas, a difficulty about that: I would have thanked him with all my soul had I not had in a proportionate measure this conviction of the secret of my pupils.

How can I retrace to-day the strange steps of my obsession? There were times of our being together when I would have been ready to swear that, literally, in my presence, but with my direct sense of it closed, they had visitors who were known and were welcome. Then it was that, had I not been deterred by the very chance that such an injury might prove greater than the injury to be averted, my exaltation would have broken out. 'They're here, they're here, you little wretches,' I would have cried, 'and you can't deny it now!' The little wretches denied it with all the added volume of their sociability and their tenderness, in just the crystal depths of which – like the flash of a fish in a stream – the mockery of their advantage peeped up. The shock, in truth, had sunk into me still deeper than I knew on the night when, looking out to see either Quint or Miss Jessel under the stars, I had beheld the boy over whose rest I watched and who had immediately brought in with him – had straightway, there, turned it on me – the lovely upward look with which, from the battlements above me, the hideous apparition of Quint had played. If it was a question of a scare, my discovery on this occasion had scared me more than any other, and it was in the condition of nerves produced by it that I made my actual inductions. They harassed me so that sometimes, at odd moments, I shut myself up audibly to rehearse – it was at once a fantastic relief and a renewed despair – the manner in which I might come to the point. I approached it from one side and the other while, in my room, I flung myself about, but I always broke down in the monstrous utterance of names. As they died away on my lips I said to myself that I should indeed help them to represent something infamous if, by pronouncing them, I should violate as rare a little case of instinctive delicacy as any schoolroom, probably, had ever known. When I said to myself: '*They* have the manners to be silent, and you, trusted as you are, the baseness to speak!' I felt myself crimson and I covered my face with my hands. After these secret scenes I chattered more than ever, going on volubly enough till one of our prodigious, palpable hushes occurred – I can call them nothing else – the strange, dizzy lift or swim (I try for terms!) into a stillness, a pause of all life, that had nothing to do with the more or less noise that at the moment we might be engaged in making and that I could hear through any deepened exhilaration or quickened recitation or louder strum of the piano. Then it was that the others, the outsiders, were there. Though they were not angels, they 'passed', as the French say, causing me, while they stayed, to tremble with the fear of their addressing to their younger victims some yet more infernal message or more vivid image than they had thought good enough for myself.

What it was most impossible to get rid of was the cruel idea that, whatever I had seen, Miles and Flora saw *more* – things terrible and unguessable and that sprang from dreadful passages of intercourse in the past. Such things naturally left on the surface, for the time, a chill which we vociferously denied that we felt; and we had, all three, with repetition, got into such splendid training that we went, each time, almost automatically, to mark the close of the incident, through the very same movements. It was striking of the children, at all events, to kiss me inveterately with a kind of wild irrelevance and never to fail – one or the other – of the precious question that has helped us through many a peril. 'When do you think he *will* come? Don't you think we *ought* to write?' – there was nothing like that inquiry, we found by experience, for carrying off an awkwardness. 'He' of course was their uncle in Harley Street; and we lived in much profusion of theory that he might at any moment arrive to mingle in our circle. It was impossible to have given less encouragement than he had done to such a doctrine, but if we had not had the doctrine to fall back upon we should have deprived each other of some of our finest exhibitions. He never wrote to them – that may have been selfish, but it was a part of the flattery of his trust of me; for the way in which a man pays his highest tribute to a woman is apt to be but by the more festal celebration of one of the sacred laws of his comfort; and I held that I carried out the spirit of the pledge given not to appeal to him when I let my charges understand that their own letters were but charming literary exercises. They were too beautiful to be posted; I kept them myself; I have them all to this hour. This was a rule indeed which only added to the satiric effect of my being plied with the supposition that he might at any moment be among us. It was exactly as if my charges knew how almost more awkward than anything else that might be for me. There appears to me, moreover, as I look back, no note in all this more extraordinary than the mere fact that, in spite of my tension and of their triumph, I never lost patience with them. Adorable they must in truth have been, I now reflect, that I didn't in these days hate them! Would exasperation, however, if relief had longer been postponed, finally have betrayed me? It little matters, for relief arrived. I call it relief though it was only the relief that a snap brings to a strain or the burst of a thunderstorm to a day of suffocation. It was at least change, and it came with a rush.

XIV

WALKING to church a certain Sunday morning, I had little Miles at my side and his sister, in advance of us and at Mrs Grose's, well in sight. It was a crisp, clear day, the first of its order for some time; the night had brought a touch of frost, and the autumn air, bright and sharp, made the church-bells almost gay. It was an odd accident of thought that I should have happened at such a moment to be particularly and very gratefully struck with the obedience of my little charges. Why did they never resent my inexorable, my perpetual society? Something or other had brought nearer home to me that I had all but pinned the boy to my shawl and that, in the way our companions were marshalled before me, I might have appeared to provide against some danger of rebellion. I was like a gaoler with an eye to possible surprises and escapes. But all this belonged – I mean their magnificent little surrender – just to the special array of the facts that were most abysmal. Turned out for Sunday by his uncle's tailor, who had had a free hand and a notion of pretty waistcoats and of his grand little air, Miles's whole title to independence, the rights of his sex and situation, were so stamped upon him that if he had suddenly struck for freedom I should have had nothing to say. I was by the strangest of chances wondering how I should meet him when the revolution unmistakeably occurred. I call it a revolution because I now see how, with the word he spoke, the curtain rose on the last act of my dreadful drama and the catastrophe was precipitated. 'Look here, my dear, you know,' he charmingly said, 'when in the world, please, am I going back to school?'

Transcribed here the speech sounds harmless enough, particularly as uttered in the sweet, high, casual pipe with which, at all interlocutors, but above all at his eternal governess, he threw off intonations as if he were tossing roses. There was something in them that always made one 'catch', and I caught, at any rate, now so effectually that I stopped as short as if one of the trees of the park had fallen across the road. There was something new, on the spot, between us, and he was perfectly aware that I recognised it, though, to enable me to do so, he had no need to look a whit less candid and charming than usual. I could feel in him how he already, from my at first finding nothing to reply, perceived the advantage he had gained. I was so slow to find anything that he had plenty of time, after a minute, to continue with his suggestive but inconclusive smile: 'You know, my dear, that for a fellow to be with a lady *always*—!' His 'my dear' was constantly on his lips for me, and nothing could have expressed more the exact shade of the sentiment with which I desired to inspire my pupils than its fond familiarity. It was so respectfully easy.

But, oh, how I felt that at present I must pick my own phrases! I remember that, to gain time, I tried to laugh, and I seemed to see in the beautiful face with which he watched me how ugly and queer I looked. 'And always with the same lady?' I returned.

He neither blenched nor winked. The whole thing was virtually out between us. 'Ah, of course she's a jolly, "perfect" lady; but, after all, I'm a fellow, don't you see? that's – well, getting on.'

I lingered there with him an instant ever so kindly. 'Yes, you're getting on.' Oh, but I felt helpless!

I have kept to this day the heartbreaking little idea of how he seemed to know that and to play with it. 'And you can't say I've not been awfully good, can you?'

I laid my hand on his shoulder, for, though I felt how much better it would have been to walk on, I was not yet quite able. 'No, I can't say that, Miles.'

'Except just that one night, you know—!'

'That one night?' I couldn't look as straight as he.

'Why, when I went down – went out of the house.'

'Oh yes. But I forget what you did it for.'

'You forget?' – he spoke with the sweet extravagance of childish reproach. 'Why, it was to show you I could!'

'Oh yes, you could.'

'And I can again.'

I felt that I might, perhaps, after all, succeed in keeping my wits about me. 'Certainly. But you won't.'

'No, not *that* again. It was nothing.'

'It was nothing,' I said. 'But we must go on.'

He resumed our walk with me, passing his hand into my arm. 'Then when *am* I going back?'

I wore, in turning it over, my most responsible air. 'Were you very happy at school?'

He just considered. 'Oh, I'm happy enough anywhere!'

'Well then,' I quavered, 'if you're just as happy here—!'

'Ah, but that isn't everything! Of course *you* know a lot—'

'But you hint that you know almost as much?' I risked as he paused.

'Not half I want to!' Miles honestly professed. 'But it isn't so much that.'

'What is it then?'

'Well – I want to see more life.'

'I see; I see.' We had arrived within sight of the church and of various persons, including several of the household of Bly, on their way to it and clustered about the door to see us go in. I quickened our step; I wanted to get there before the question between us opened up much further; I reflected hungrily that, for more than an hour, he would have to be silent; and I thought with envy of the comparative dusk of the pew and of the almost spiritual help of the hassock on which I might bend my knees. I seemed literally to be running a race with some confusion to which he was about to reduce me, but I felt that he had got in first when, before we had even entered the churchyard, he threw out –

'I want my own sort!'

It literally made me bound forward. 'There are not many of your own sort, Miles!' I laughed. 'Unless perhaps dear little Flora!'

'You really compare me to a baby girl?'

This found me singularly weak. 'Don't you, then, *love* our sweet Flora?'

'If I didn't – and you too; if I didn't—!' he repeated as if retreating for a jump, yet leaving his thought so unfinished that, after we had come into the gate, another stop, which he imposed on me by the pressure of his arm, had become inevitable. Mrs Grose and Flora had passed into the church, the other worshippers had followed, and we were, for the minute, alone among the old, thick graves. We had paused, on the path from the gate, by a low, oblong, table-like tomb.

'Yes, if you didn't—?'

He looked, while I waited, about at the graves. 'Well, you know what!' But he didn't move, and he presently produced something that made me drop straight down on the stone slab, as if suddenly to rest. 'Does my uncle think what *you* think?'

I markedly rested. 'How do you know what I think?'

'Ah well, of course I don't; for it strikes me you never tell me. But I mean does *he* know?'

'Know what, Miles?'

'Why, the way I'm going on.'

I perceived quickly enough that I could make, to this inquiry, no answer that would not involve something of a sacrifice of my employer. Yet it appeared to me that we were all, at Bly, sufficiently sacrificed to make that venial. 'I don't think your uncle much cares.'

Miles, on this, stood looking at me. 'Then don't you think he can be made to?'

'In what way?'

'Why, by his coming down.'

'But who'll get him to come down?'

'*I* will!' the boy said with extraordinary brightness and emphasis. He gave me another look charged with that expression and then marched off alone into church.

XV

THE business was practically settled from the moment I never followed him. It was a pitiful surrender to agitation, but my being aware of this had somehow no power to restore me. I only sat there on my tomb and read into what my little friend had said to me the fulness of its meaning; by the time I had grasped the whole of which I had also embraced, for absence, the pretext that I was ashamed to offer my pupils and the rest of the congregation such an example of delay. What I said to myself above all was that Miles had got something out of me and that the proof of it, for him, would be just this awkward collapse. He had got out of me that there was something I was much afraid of and that he should probably be able to make use of my fear to gain, for his own purpose, more freedom. My fear was of having to deal with the intolerable question of the grounds of his dismissal from school, for that was really but the question of the horrors gathered behind. That his uncle should arrive to treat with me of these things was a solution that, strictly speaking, I ought now to have desired to bring on; but I could so little face the ugliness and the pain of it that I simply procrastinated and lived from hand to mouth. The boy, to my deep discomposure, was immensely in the right, was in a position to say to me: 'Either you clear up with my guardian the mystery of this interruption of my studies, or you cease to expect me to lead with you a life that's so unnatural for a boy.' What was so unnatural for the particular boy I was concerned with was this sudden revelation of a consciousness and a plan.

That was what really overcame me, what prevented my going in. I walked round the church, hesitating, hovering; I reflected that I had already, with him, hurt myself beyond repair. Therefore I could patch up nothing, and it was too extreme an effort to squeeze beside him into the pew: he would be so much more sure than ever to pass his arm into mine and make me sit there for an hour in close, silent contact with his commentary on our talk. For the first minute since his arrival I wanted to get away from him. As I paused beneath the high east window and listened to the sounds of worship I was taken with an impulse that might master me, I felt, completely should I give it the least encouragement. I might easily put an end to my predicament by getting away altogether. Here was my chance; there was no one to stop me; I could give the whole thing up – turn my back and retreat. It was only a question of hurrying again, for a few preparations, to the house which the attendance at church of so many of the servants would practically have left unoccupied. No one, in short, could blame me if I should just drive desperately off. What was it to get away if I got away only till dinner? That would be in a couple of hours, at the end of which – I had the acute prevision – my little pupils would play at innocent wonder about my non-appearance in their train.

'What *did* you do, you naughty, bad thing? Why in the world, to worry us so – and take our thoughts off too, don't you know? – did you desert us at the very door?' I couldn't meet such questions nor, as they asked them, their false little lovely eyes; yet it was all so exactly what I should have to meet that, as the prospect grew sharp to me, I at last let myself go.

I got, so far as the immediate moment was concerned, away; I came straight out of the churchyard and, thinking hard, retraced my steps through the park. It seemed to me that by the time I reached the house I had made up my mind I would fly. The Sunday stillness both of the approaches and of the interior, in which I met no one, fairly excited me with a sense of opportunity. Were I to get off quickly, this way, I should get off without a scene, without a word. My quickness would have to be remarkable, however, and the question of a conveyance was the great one to settle. Tormented, in the hall, with difficulties and obstacles, I remember sinking down at the foot of the staircase – suddenly collapsing there on the lowest step and then, with a revulsion, recalling that it was exactly where, more than a month before, in the darkness of night and just so bowed with evil things, I had seen the spectre of the most horrible of women. At this I was able to straighten myself; I went the rest of the way up; I made, in my bewilderment, for the schoolroom, where there were objects belonging to me that I should have to take. But I opened the door to find again, in a flash, my eyes unsealed. In the presence of what I saw I reeled straight back upon my resistance.

Seated at my own table in the clear noonday light I saw a person whom, without my previous experience, I should have taken at the first blush for some housemaid who might have stayed at home to look after the place and who, availing herself of rare relief from observation and of the schoolroom table and my pens, ink and paper, had applied herself to the considerable effort of a letter to her sweetheart. There was an effort in the way that, while her arms rested on the table, her hands, with evident weariness, supported her head; but at the moment I took this in I had already become aware that, in spite of my entrance, her attitude strangely persisted. Then it was – with the very act of its announcing itself – that her identity flared up in a change of posture. She rose, not as if she had heard me, but with an indescribable grand melancholy of indifference and detachment, and, within a dozen feet of me, stood there as my vile predecessor. Dishonoured and tragic, she was all before me; but even as I fixed and, for memory, secured it, the awful image passed away. Dark as midnight in her black dress, her haggard beauty and her unutterable woe, she had looked at me long enough to appear to say that her right to sit at my table was as good as mine to sit at hers. While these instants lasted indeed I had the extraordinary chill of a feeling that it was I who was the intruder. It was as a wild protest against it that, actually addressing her – 'You terrible, miserable woman!' – I heard myself break into a sound that, by the open door, rang through the long passage and the empty house. She looked at me as if she heard me, but I had recovered myself and cleared the air. There was nothing in the room the next minute but the sunshine and a sense that I must stay.

XVI

I HAD so perfectly expected that the return of my pupils would be marked by a demonstration that I was freshly upset at having to take into account that they were dumb about my absence. Instead of gaily denouncing and caressing me they made no allusion to my having failed them, and I was left, for the time, on perceiving that she too said nothing, to study Mrs Grose's odd face. I did this to such purpose that I made sure they had in some way bribed her to silence; a silence that, however, I would engage to break down on the first private opportunity. This opportunity came before tea: I secured five minutes with her in the housekeeper's room, where, in the twilight, amid a smell of lately-baked bread, but with the place all swept and garnished, I found her sitting in pained placidity before the fire. So I see her still, so I see her best: facing the flame from her straight chair in the dusky, shining room, a large clean image of the 'put away' – of drawers closed and locked and rest without a remedy.

'Oh yes, they asked me to say nothing; and to please them – so long as they were there – of course I promised. But what had happened to you?'

'I only went with you for the walk,' I said. 'I had then to come back to meet a friend.'

She showed her surprise. 'A friend – *you*?'

'Oh yes, I have a couple!' I laughed. 'But did the children give you a reason?'

'For not alluding to your leaving us? Yes; they said you would like it better. Do you like it better?'

My face had made her rueful. 'No, I like it worse!' But after an instant I added: 'Did they say why I should like it better?'

'No; Master Miles only said "We must do nothing but what she likes!"'

'I wish indeed he would! And what did Flora say?'

'Miss Flora was too sweet. She said "Oh, of course, of course!" – and I said the same.'

I thought a moment. 'You were too sweet too – I can hear you all. But none the less, between Miles and me, it's now all out.'

'All out?' My companion stared. 'But what, Miss?'

'Everything. It doesn't matter. I've made up my mind. I came home, my dear,' I went on, 'for a talk with Miss Jessel.'

I had by this time formed the habit of having Mrs Grose literally well in hand in advance of my sounding that note; so that even now, as she bravely blinked under the signal of my word, I could keep her comparatively firm. 'A talk! Do you mean she spoke?'

'It came to that. I found her, on my return, in the schoolroom.'

'And what did she say?' I can hear the good woman still, and the candour of her stupefaction.

'That she suffers the torments—!'

It was this, of a truth, that made her, as she filled out my picture, gape. 'Do you mean,' she faltered ' – of the lost?'

'Of the lost. Of the damned. And that's why, to share them—' I faltered myself with the horror of it.

But my companion, with less imagination, kept me up. 'To share them—?'

'She wants Flora.' Mrs Grose might, as I gave it to her, fairly have fallen away from me had I not been prepared. I still held her there, to show I was. 'As I've told you, however, it doesn't matter.'

'Because you've made up your mind? But to what?'

'To everything.'

'And what do you call "everything"?'

'Why, sending for their uncle.'

'Oh Miss, in pity do,' my friend broke out.

'Ah, but I will, I *will*! I see it's the only way. What's "out", as I told you, with Miles is that if he thinks I'm afraid to – and has ideas of what he gains by that – he shall see he's mistaken. Yes, yes; his uncle shall have it here from me on the spot (and before the boy himself if necessary) that if I'm to be reproached with having done nothing again about more school—'

'Yes, Miss—' my companion pressed me.

'Well, there's that awful reason.'

There were now clearly so many of these for my poor colleague that she was excusable for being vague. 'But – a – which?'

'Why, the letter from his old place.'

'You'll show it to the master?'

'I ought to have done so on the instant.'

'Oh no!' said Mrs Grose with decision.

'I'll put it before him,' I went on inexorably, 'that I can't undertake to work the question on behalf of a child who has been expelled—'

'For we've never in the least known what!' Mrs Grose declared.

'For wickedness. For what else – when he's so clever and beautiful and perfect? Is he stupid? Is he untidy? Is he infirm? Is he ill-natured? He's exquisite – so it can be only *that*; and that would open up the whole thing. After all,' I said, 'it's their uncle's fault. If he left here such people—!'

'He didn't really in the least know them. The fault's mine.' She had turned quite pale.

'Well, you shan't suffer,' I answered.

'The children shan't!' she emphatically returned.

I was silent a while; we looked at each other. 'Then what am I to tell him?'

'You needn't tell him anything. *I'll* tell him.'

I measured this. 'Do you mean you'll write –?' Remembering she couldn't, I caught myself up. 'How do you communicate?'

'I tell the bailiff. *He* writes.'

'And should you like him to write our story?'

My question had a sarcastic force that I had not fully intended, and it made her, after a moment, inconsequently break down. The tears were again in her eyes. 'Ah, Miss, *you* write!'

'Well – to-night,' I at last answered; and on this we separated.

XVII

I WENT so far, in the evening, as to make a beginning. The weather had changed back, a great wind was abroad, and beneath the lamp, in my room, with Flora at peace beside me, I sat for a long time before a blank sheet of paper and listened to the lash of the rain and the batter of the gusts. Finally I went out, taking a candle; I crossed the passage and listened a minute at Miles's door. What, under my endless obsession, I had been impelled to listen for was some betrayal of his not being at rest, and I presently caught one, but not in the form I had expected. His voice tinkled out. 'I say, you there – come in.' It was a gaiety in the gloom!

I went in with my light and found him, in bed, very wide awake, but very much at his ease. 'Well, what are *you* up to?' he asked with a grace of sociability in which it occurred to me that Mrs Grose, had she been present, might have looked in vain for proof that anything was 'out'.

I stood over him with my candle. 'How did you know I was there?'

'Why, of course I heard you. Did you fancy you made no noise? You're like a troop of cavalry!' he beautifully laughed.

'Then you weren't asleep?'

'Not much! I lie awake and think.'

I had put my candle, designedly, a short way off, and then, as he held out his friendly old hand to me, had sat down on the edge of his bed. 'What is it,' I asked, 'that you think of?'

'What in the world, my dear, but *you*?'

'Ah, the pride I take in your appreciation doesn't insist on that! I had so far rather you slept.'

'Well, I think also, you know, of this queer business of ours.'

I marked the coolness of his firm little hand. 'Of what queer business, Miles?'

'Why, the way you bring me up. And all the rest!'

I fairly held my breath a minute, and even from my glimmering taper there was light enough to show how he smiled up at me from his pillow. 'What do you mean by all the rest?'

'Oh, you know, you know!'

I could say nothing for a minute, though I felt, as I held his hand and our eyes continued to meet, that my silence had all the air of admitting his charge and that nothing in the whole world of reality was perhaps at that moment so fabulous as our actual relation. 'Certainly you shall go back to school,' I said, 'if it be that that troubles you. But not to the old place – we must find another, a better. How could I know it did trouble you, this question, when you never told me so, never spoke of it at all?' His clear, listening face, framed in its smooth whiteness, made him for the minute as appealing as some wistful patient in a children's hospital; and I would have given, as the resemblance came to me, all I possessed on earth really to be the nurse or the sister of charity who might have helped to cure him. Well, even as it was, I perhaps might help! 'Do you know you've never said a word to me about your school – I mean the old one; never mentioned it in any way?'

He seemed to wonder; he smiled with the same loveliness. But he clearly gained time; he waited, he called for guidance. 'Haven't I?' It wasn't for *me* to help him – it was for the thing I had met!

Something in his tone and the expression of his face, as I got this from him, set my heart aching with such a pang as it had never yet known; so unutterably touching was it to see his little brain puzzled and his little resources taxed to play, under the spell laid on him, a part of innocence and consistency. 'No, never – from the hour you came back. You've never mentioned to me one of your masters, one of your comrades, nor the least little thing that ever happened to you at school. Never, little Miles – no never – have you given me an inkling of anything that *may* have happened there. Therefore you can fancy how much I'm in the dark. Until you came out, that way, this morning, you had, since the first hour I saw you, scarce even made a reference to anything in your previous life. You seemed so perfectly to accept the present.' It was extraordinary how my absolute conviction of his secret precocity (or whatever I might call the poison of an influence that I dared but half to phrase) made him, in spite of the faint breath of his inward trouble, appear as accessible as an older person – imposed him almost as an intellectual equal. 'I thought you wanted to go on as you are.'

It struck me that at this he just faintly coloured. He gave, at any rate, like a convalescent slightly fatigued, a languid shake of his head. 'I don't – I don't. I want to get away.'

'You're tired of Bly?'

'Oh no, I like Bly.'

'Well, then—?'

'Oh, *you* know what a boy wants!'

I felt that I didn't know so well as Miles, and I took temporary refuge. 'You want to go to your uncle?'

Again, at this, with his sweet ironic face, he made a movement on the pillow. 'Ah, you can't get off with that!'

I was silent a little, and it was I, now, I think, who changed colour. 'My dear, I don't want to get off!'

'You can't, even if you do. You can't, you can't!' – he lay beautifully staring. 'My uncle must come down, and you must completely settle things.'

'If we do,' I returned with some spirit, 'you may be sure it will be to take you quite away.'

'Well, don't you understand that that's exactly what I'm working for? You'll have to tell him – about the way you've let it all drop: you'll have to tell him a tremendous lot!'

The exultation with which he uttered this helped me somehow, for the instant, to meet him rather more. 'And how much will *you*, Miles, have to tell him? There are things he'll ask you!'

He turned it over. 'Very likely. But what things?'

'The things you've never told me. To make up his mind what to do with you. He can't send you back—'

'Oh, I don't want to go back!' he broke in. 'I want a new field.'

He said it with admirable serenity, with positive unimpeachable gaiety; and doubtless it was that very note that most evoked for me the poignancy, the unnatural childish tragedy, of his probable reappearance at the end of three months with all this bravado and still more dishonour. It overwhelmed me now that I should never be able to bear that, and it made me let myself go. I threw myself upon him and in the tenderness of my pity I embraced him. 'Dear little Miles, dear little Miles—!'

My face was close to his, and he let me kiss him, simply taking it with indulgent good humour. 'Well, old lady?'

'Is there nothing – nothing at all that you want to tell me?'

He turned off a little, facing round toward the wall and holding up his hand to look at as one had seen sick children look. 'I've told you – I told you this morning.'

Oh, I was sorry for him! 'That you just want me not to worry you?'

He looked round at me now, as if in recognition of my understanding him; then ever so gently, 'To let me alone,' he replied.

There was even a singular little dignity in it, something that made me release him, yet, when I had slowly risen, linger beside him. God knows I never wished to harass him, but I felt that merely, at this, to turn my back on him was to abandon or, to put it more truly, to lose him. 'I've just begun a letter to your uncle,' I said.

'Well then, finish it!'

I waited a minute. 'What happened before?'

He gazed up at me again. 'Before what?'

'Before you came back. And before you went away.'

For some time he was silent, but he continued to meet my eyes. 'What happened?'

It made me, the sound of the words, in which it seemed to me that I caught for the very first time a small faint quaver of consenting consciousness – it made me drop on my knees beside the bed and seize once more the chance of possessing him. 'Dear little Miles, dear little Miles, if you *knew* how I want to help you! It's only that, it's nothing but that, and I'd rather die than give you a pain or do you a wrong – I'd rather die than hurt a hair of you. Dear little Miles' – oh, I brought it out now even if I *should* go too far – 'I just want you to help me to save you!' But I knew in a moment after this that I had gone too far. The answer to my appeal was instantaneous, but it came in the form of an extraordinary blast and chill, a gust of frozen air and a shake of the room as great as if, in the wild wind, the casement had crashed in. The boy gave a loud, high shriek which, lost in the rest of the shock of sound, might have seemed, indistinctly, though I was so close to him, a note either of jubilation or of terror. I jumped to my feet again and was conscious of darkness. So for a moment we remained, while I stared about me and saw that the drawn curtains were unstirred and the window tight. 'Why, the candle's out!' I then cried.

'It was I who blew it, dear!' said Miles.

XVIII

THE next day, after lessons, Mrs Grose found a moment to say to me quietly: 'Have you written, Miss?'

'Yes – I've written.' But I didn't add – for the hour – that my letter, sealed and directed, was still in my pocket. There would be time enough to send it before the messenger should go to the village. Meanwhile there had been, on the part of my pupils, no more brilliant, more exemplary morning. It was exactly as if they had both had at heart to gloss over any recent little friction. They performed the dizziest feats of arithmetic, soaring quite out of *my* feeble range, and perpetrated, in higher spirits than ever, geographical and historical jokes. It was conspicuous of course in Miles in particular that he appeared to wish to show how easily he could let me down. This child, to my memory, really lives in a setting of beauty and misery that no words can translate; there was a distinction all his own in every impulse he revealed; never was a small natural creature, to the uninitiated eye all frankness and freedom, a more ingenious, a more extraordinary little gentleman. I had perpetually to guard against the wonder of contemplation into which my initiated view betrayed me; to check the irrelevant gaze and discouraged sigh in which I constantly both attacked and renounced the enigma of what such a little gentleman could have done that deserved a penalty. Say that, by the dark prodigy I knew, the imagination of all evil *had* been opened up to him: all the justice within me ached for the proof that it could ever have flowered into an act.

He had never, at any rate, been such a little gentleman as when, after our early dinner on this dreadful day, he came round to me and asked if I shouldn't like him, for half an hour, to play to me. David playing to Saul could never have shown a finer sense of the occasion. It was literally a charming exhibition of tact, of magnanimity, and quite tantamount to his saying outright: 'The true knights we love to read about never push an advantage too far. I know what you mean now: you mean that – to be let alone yourself and not followed up – you'll cease to worry and spy upon me, won't keep me so close to you, will let me go and come. Well, I "come", you see – but I don't go! There'll be plenty of time for that. I do really delight in your society, and I only want to show you that I contended for a principle.' It may be imagined whether I resisted this appeal or failed to accompany him again, hand in hand, to the schoolroom. He sat down at the old piano and played as he had never played; and if there are those who think he had better have been kicking a football I can only say that I wholly agree with them. For at the end of a time that, under his influence, I had quite ceased to measure, I started up with a strange sense of having literally slept at my post. It was after luncheon, and by the schoolroom fire, and yet I hadn't really, in the least, slept: I had only done something much worse – I had forgotten. Where, all this time, was Flora? When I put the question to Miles he played on a minute before answering, and then could only say: 'Why, my dear, how do *I* know?' – breaking moreover into a happy laugh which, immediately after, as if it were a vocal accompaniment, he prolonged into incoherent, extravagant song.

I went straight to my room, but his sister was not there; then, before going downstairs, I looked into several others. As she was nowhere about she would surely be with Mrs Grose, whom, in the comfort of that theory, I accordingly proceeded in quest of. I found her where I had found her the evening before, but she met my quick challenge with blank, scared ignorance. She had only supposed that, after the repast, I had carried off both the children; as to which she was quite in her right, for it was the very first time I had allowed the little girl out of my sight without some special provision. Of course now indeed she might be with the maids, so that the immediate thing was to look for her without an air of alarm. This we promptly arranged between us; but when, ten minutes later and in pursuance of our arrangement, we met in the hall, it was only to report on either side that after guarded inquiries we had altogether failed to trace her. For a minute there, apart from observation, we exchanged mute alarms, and I could feel with what high interest my friend returned me all those I had from the first given her.

'She'll be above,' she presently said – 'in one of the rooms you haven't searched.'

'No; she's at a distance.' I had made up my mind. 'She has gone out.'

Mrs Grose stared. 'Without a hat?'

I naturally also looked volumes. 'Isn't that woman always without one?'

'She's with *her*?'

'She's with *her*!' I declared. 'We must find them.'

My hand was on my friend's arm, but she failed for the moment, confronted with such an account of the matter, to respond to my pressure. She communed, on the contrary, on the spot, with her uneasiness. 'And where's Master Miles?'

'Oh, *he's* with Quint. They're in the schoolroom.'

'Lord, Miss!' My view, I was myself aware – and therefore I suppose my tone – had never yet reached so calm an assurance.

'The trick's played,' I went on; 'they've successfully worked their plan. He found the most divine little way to keep me quiet while she went off.'

' "Divine"?' Mrs Grose bewilderedly echoed.

'Infernal, then!' I almost cheerfully rejoined. 'He has provided for himself as well. But come!'

She had helplessly gloomed at the upper regions. 'You leave him—?'

'So long with Quint? Yes – I don't mind that now.'

She always ended, at these moments, by getting possession of my hand, and in this manner she could at present still stay me. But after gasping an instant at my sudden resignation, 'Because of your letter?' she eagerly brought out.

I quickly, by way of answer, felt for my letter, drew it forth, held it up, and then, freeing myself, went and laid it on the great hall-table. 'Luke will take it,' I said as I came back. I reached the house-door and opened it; I was already on the steps.

My companion still demurred: the storm of the night and the early morning had dropped, but the afternoon was damp and grey. I came down to the drive while she stood in the doorway. 'You go with nothing on?'

'What do I care when the child has nothing? I can't wait to dress,' I cried, 'and if you must do so I leave you. Try meanwhile, yourself, upstairs.'

'With *them*?' Oh, on this, the poor woman promptly joined me!

XIX

WE went straight to the lake, as it was called at Bly, and I daresay rightly called, though I reflect that it may in fact have

been a sheet of water less remarkable than it appeared to my
untravelled eyes. My acquaintance with sheets of water was
small, and the pool of Bly, at all events on the few occasions of
my consenting, under the protection of my pupils, to affront its
surface in the old flat-bottomed boat moored there for our use,
had impressed me both with its extent and its agitation. The
usual place of embarkation was half a mile from the house, but I
had an intimate conviction that, wherever Flora might be, she
was not near home. She had not given me the slip for any small
adventure, and, since the day of the very great one that I had
shared with her by the pond, I had been aware, in our walks, of
the quarter to which she most inclined. This was why I had now
given to Mrs Grose's steps so marked a direction – a direction
that made her, when she perceived it, oppose a resistance that
showed me she was freshly mystified. 'You're going to the
water, Miss?—you think she's *in*—?'

'She may be, though the depth is, I believe, nowhere very
great. But what I judge most likely is that she's on the spot from
which, the other day, we saw together what I told you.'

'When she pretended not to see—?'

'With that astounding self-possession! I've always been sure
she wanted to go back alone. And now her brother has managed it for her.'

Mrs Grose still stood where she had stopped. 'You suppose
they really *talk* of them?'

I could meet this with a confidence! 'They say things that, if
we heard them, would simply appal us.'

'And if she *is* there—?'

'Yes?'

'Then Miss Jessel is?'

'Beyond a doubt. You shall see.'

'Oh, thank you!' my friend cried, planted so firm that, taking
it in, I went straight on without her. By the time I reached the
pool, however, she was close behind me, and I knew that,
whatever, to her apprehension, might befall me, the exposure
of my society struck her as her least danger. She exhaled a moan
of relief as we at last came in sight of the greater part of the water
without a sight of the child. There was no trace of Flora on that

nearer side of the bank where my observation of her had been most startling, and none on the opposite edge, where, save for a margin of some twenty yards, a thick copse came down to the water. The pond, oblong in shape, had a width so scant compared to its length that, with its ends out of view, it might have been taken for a scant river. We looked at the empty expanse, and then I felt the suggestion of my friend's eyes. I knew what she meant and I replied with a negative headshake.

'No, no; wait! She has taken the boat.'

My companion stared at the vacant mooring-place and then again across the lake. 'Then where is it?'

'Our not seeing it is the strongest of proofs. She has used it to go over, and then has managed to hide it.'

'All alone – that child?'

'She's not alone, and at such times she's not a child: she's an old, old woman.' I scanned all the visible shore while Mrs Grose took again, into the queer element I offered her, one of her plunges of submission; then I pointed out that the boat might perfectly be in a small refuge formed by one of the recesses of the pool, an indentation masked, for the hither side, by a projection of the bank and by a clump of trees growing close to the water.

'But if the boat's there, where on earth's *she*?' my colleague anxiously asked.

'That's exactly what we must learn.' And I started to walk further.

'By going all the way round?'

'Certainly, far as it is. It will take us but ten minutes, but it's far enough to have made the child prefer not to walk. She went straight over.'

'Laws!' cried my friend again; the chain of my logic was ever too much for her. It dragged her at my heels even now, and when we had got half way round – a devious, tiresome process, on ground much broken and by a path choked with overgrowth – I paused to give her breath. I sustained her with a grateful arm, assuring her that she might hugely help me; and this started us afresh, so that in the course of but few minutes more we reached a point from which we found the boat to be where I had supposed it. It had been intentionally left as much as possible out of sight and was tied to one of the stakes of a fence that came, just there, down to the brink and that had been an assistance to disembarking. I recognised, as I looked at the pair of short, thick oars, quite safely drawn up, the prodigious character of the feat for a little girl; but I had lived, by this time, too long among wonders and had panted to too many livelier measures. There was a gate in the fence, through which we passed, and that brought us, after a trifling interval, more into the open. Then 'There she is!' we both exclaimed at once.

Flora, a short way off, stood before us on the grass and smiled as if her performance was now complete. The next thing she did, however, was to stoop straight down and pluck – quite as if it were all she was there for – a big, ugly spray of withered fern. I instantly became sure she had just come out of the copse. She waited for us, not herself taking a step, and I was conscious of the rare solemnity with which we presently approached her. She smiled and smiled, and we met; but it was all done in a silence by this time flagrantly ominous. Mrs Grose was the first to break the spell: she threw herself on her knees and, drawing the child to her breast, clasped in a long embrace the little tender, yielding body. While this dumb convulsion lasted I could only watch it – which I did the more intently when I saw Flora's face peep at me over our companion's shoulder. It was serious now – the flicker had left it; but it strengthened the pang with which I at that moment envied Mrs Grose the simplicity of *her* relation. Still, all this while, nothing more passed between us save that Flora had let her foolish fern again drop to the ground. What she and I had virtually said to each other was that pretexts were useless now. When Mrs Grose finally got up she kept the child's hand, so that the two were still before me; and the singular reticence of our communion was even more marked in the frank look she launched me. 'I'll be hanged,' it said, 'if *I'll* speak!'

It was Flora who, gazing all over me in candid wonder, was the first. She was struck with our bareheaded aspect. 'Why, where are your things?'

'Where yours are, my dear!' I promptly returned.

She had already got back her gaiety and appeared to take this as an answer quite sufficient. 'And where's Miles?' she went on.

There was something in the small valour of it that quite finished me: these three words from her were, in a flash like the glitter of a drawn blade, the jostle of the cup that my hand, for weeks and weeks, had held high and full to the brim and that now, even before speaking, I felt overflow in a deluge. 'I'll tell you if you'll tell *me*—' I heard myself say, then heard the tremor in which it broke.

'Well, what?'

Mrs Grose's suspense blazed at me, but it was too late now, and I brought the thing out handsomely. 'Where, my pet, is Miss Jessel?'

XX

JUST as in the churchyard with Miles, the whole thing was upon us. Much as I had made of the fact that this name had never once, between us, been sounded, the quick, smitten glare with which the child's face now received it fairly likened my breach of the silence to the smash of a pane of glass. It added to the interposing cry, as if to stay the blow, that Mrs Grose, at the same instant, uttered over my violence – the shriek of a creature scared, or rather wounded, which, in turn, within a few seconds, was completed by a gasp of my own. I seized my colleague's arm. 'She's there, she's there!'

Miss Jessel stood before us on the opposite bank exactly as she had stood the other time, and I remember, strangely, as the first feeling now produced in me, my thrill of joy at having brought on a proof. She was there, and I was justified; she was there, and I was neither cruel nor mad. She was there for poor scared Mrs Grose, but she was there most for Flora; and no moment of my monstrous time was perhaps so extraordinary as that in which I consciously threw out to her, with the sense that – pale and ravenous demon as she was, she would catch and understand it – an inarticulate message of gratitude. She rose erect on the spot my friend and I had lately quitted, and there was not, in all the long reach of her desire, an inch of her evil that fell short. This first vividness of vision and emotion were things of a few seconds, during which Mrs Grose's dazed blink across to where I pointed struck me as a sovereign sign that she too at last saw, just as it carried my own eyes precipitately to the child. The revelation then of the manner in which Flora was affected startled me, in truth, far more than it would have done to find her also merely agitated, for direct dismay was of course not what I had expected. Prepared and on her guard as our pursuit had actually made her, she would repress every betrayal; and I was therefore shaken, on the spot, by my first glimpse of the particular one for which I had not allowed. To see her, without a convulsion of her small pink face, not even feign to glance in the direction of the prodigy I announced, but only, instead of that, turn at *me* an expression of hard, still gravity, an expression absolutely new and unprecedented and that appeared to read and accuse and judge me – this was a stroke that somehow converted the little girl herself into the very presence that could make me quail. I quailed even though my certitude that she thoroughly saw was never greater than at that instant, and in the immediate need to defend myself I called it passionately to witness. 'She's there, you little unhappy thing – there, there, *there*, and you see her as well as you see me!' I had said shortly before to Mrs Grose that she was not at these times a child, but an old, old woman, and that description of her could not have been more strikingly confirmed than in the way in which, for all answer to this, she simply showed me, without a concession, an admission, of her eyes, a countenance of deeper and deeper, of indeed suddenly quite fixed reprobation. I was by this time – if I can put the whole thing at all together – more appalled at what I may properly call her manner than at anything else, though it was simultaneously with this that I became aware of having Mrs Grose also, and very formidably, to reckon with. My elder companion, the next moment, at any rate, blotted out everything but her own flushed face and her loud, shocked protest, a burst of high disapproval. 'What a dreadful turn, to be sure, Miss! Where on earth do you see anything?'

I could only grasp her more quickly yet, for even while she spoke the hideous plain presence stood undimmed and undaunted. It had already lasted a minute, and it lasted while I continued, seizing my colleague, quite thrusting her at it and presenting her to it, to insist with my pointing hand. 'You don't see her exactly as *we* see? – you mean to say you don't now – *now*? She's as big as a blazing fire! Only look, dearest woman, *look*—!' She looked, even as I did, and gave me, with her deep groan of negation, repulsion, compassion – the mixture with her pity of her relief at her exemption – a sense, touching to me even then, that she would have backed me up if she could. I might well have needed that, for with this hard blow of the proof that her eyes were hopelessly sealed I felt my own situation horribly crumble, I felt – I saw – my livid predecessor press, from her position, on my defeat, and I was conscious, more than all, of what I should have from this instant to deal with in the astounding little attitude of Flora. Into this attitude Mrs Grose immediately and violently entered, breaking, even while there pierced through my sense of ruin a prodigious private triumph, into breathless reassurance.

'She isn't there, little lady, and nobody's there – and you never see nothing, my sweet! How can poor Miss Jessel – when poor Miss Jessel's dead and buried? *We* know, don't we, love?' – and she appealed, blundering in, to the child. 'It's all a mere mistake and a worry and a joke – and we'll go home as fast as we can!'

Our companion, on this, had responded with a strange, quick primness of propriety, and they were again, with Mrs Grose on her feet, united, as it were, in pained opposition to me. Flora continued to fix me with her small mask of reprobation, and even at that minute I prayed God to forgive me for seeming to see that, as she stood there holding tight to our friend's dress, her incomparable childish beauty had suddenly failed, had quite vanished. I've said it already – she was literally, she was hideously hard; she had turned common and almost ugly. 'I don't know what you mean. I see nobody. I see nothing. I never *have*. I think you're cruel. I don't like you!' Then, after this deliverance, which might have been that of a vulgarly pert little girl in the street, she hugged Mrs Grose more closely and buried in her skirts the dreadful little face. In this position she produced an almost furious wail. 'Take me away, take me away – oh, take me away from *her*!'

'From *me*?' I panted.

'From you – from you!' she cried.

Even Mrs Grose looked across at me dismayed; while I had nothing to do but communicate again with the figure that, on the opposite bank, without a movement, as rigidly still as if catching, beyond the interval, our voices, was as vividly there for my disaster as it was not there for my service. The wretched child had spoken exactly as if she had got from some outside source each of her stabbing little words, and I could therefore, in the full despair of all I had to accept, but sadly shake my head at her. 'If I had ever doubted, all my doubt would at present have gone. I've been living with the miserable truth, and now it has only too much closed round me. Of course I've lost you: I've interfered, and you've seen – under *her* dictation' – with which I faced, over the pool again, our infernal witness – 'the easy and perfect way to meet it. I've done my best, but I've lost you. Good-bye.' For Mrs Grose I had an imperative, an almost frantic 'Go, go!' before which, in infinite distress, but mutely possessed of the little girl and clearly convinced, in spite of her blindness, that something awful had occurred and some collapse engulfed us, she retreated, by the way we had come, as fast as she could move.

Of what first happened when I was left alone I had no subsequent memory. I only knew that at the end of, I suppose, a quarter of an hour, an odorous dampness and roughness, chilling and piercing my trouble, had made me understand that I must have thrown myself, on my face, on the ground and given way to a wildness of grief. I must have lain there long and cried and sobbed, for when I raised my head the day was almost done. I got up and looked a moment, through the twilight, at the grey pool and its blank, haunted edge, and then I took, back to the house, my dreary and difficult course. When I reached the gate in the fence the boat, to my surprise, was gone, so that I had a fresh reflection to make on Flora's extraordinary command of the situation. She passed that night, by the most tacit, and I should add, were not the word so grotesque a false note, the happiest of arrangements, with Mrs Grose. I saw neither of them on my return, but, on the other hand, as by an ambiguous compensation, I saw a great deal of Miles. I saw – I can use no other phrase – so much of him that it was as if it were more than it had ever been. No evening I had passed at Bly had the portentous quality of this one; in spite of which – and in spite also of the deeper depths of consternation that had opened beneath my feet – there was literally, in the ebbing actual, an extraordinarily sweet sadness. On reaching the house I had never so much as looked for the boy; I had simply gone straight to my room to change what I was wearing and to take in, at a glance, much material testimony to Flora's rupture. Her little belongings had all been removed. When later, by the schoolroom fire, I was served with tea by the usual maid, I indulged, on the article of my other pupil, in no inquiry whatever. He had his freedom now – he might have it to the end! Well, he did have it; and it consisted – in part at least – of his coming in at about eight o'clock and sitting down with me in silence. On the removal of the tea-things I had blown out the candles and drawn my chair closer: I was conscious of a mortal coldness and felt as if I should never again be warm. So, when he appeared, I was sitting in the glow with my thoughts. He paused a moment by the door as if to look at me; then – as if to share them – came to the other side of the hearth and sank into a chair. We sat there in absolute stillness; yet he wanted, I felt, to be with me.

XXI

BEFORE a new day, in my room, had fully broken, my eyes opened to Mrs Grose, who had come to my bedside with worse news. Flora was so markedly feverish that an illness was perhaps at hand; she had passed a night of extreme unrest, a night agitated above all by fears that had for their subject not in the least her former, but wholly her present governess. It was not against the possible re-entrance of Miss Jessel on the scene that she protested – it was conspicuously and passionately against mine. I was promptly on my feet of course, and with an immense deal to ask; the more that my friend had discernibly now girded her loins to meet me once more. This I felt as soon as I had put to her the question of her sense of the child's sincerity as against my own. 'She persists in denying to you that she saw, or has ever seen, anything?'

My visitor's trouble, truly, was great. 'Ah, Miss, it isn't a matter on which I can push her! Yet it isn't either, I must say, as if I much needed to. It has made her, every inch of her, quite old.'

'Oh, I see her perfectly from here. She resents, for all the world like some high little personage, the imputation on her truthfulness and, as it were, her respectability. "Miss Jessel indeed – *she*!" Ah, she's "respectable", the chit! The impression she gave me there yesterday was, I assure you, the very strangest of all; it was quite beyond any of the others. I *did* put my foot in it! She'll never speak to me again.'

Hideous and obscure as it all was, it held Mrs Grose briefly silent; then she granted my point with a frankness which, I made sure, had more behind it. 'I think indeed, Miss, she never will. She do have a grand manner about it!'

'And that manner' – I summed it up – 'is practically what's the matter with her now.'

Oh, that manner, I could see in my visitor's face, and not a little else besides! 'She asks me every three minutes if I think you're coming in.'

'I see – I see.' I too, on my side, had so much more than worked it out. 'Has she said to you since yesterday – except to repudiate her familiarity with anything so dreadful – a single other word about Miss Jessel?'

'Not one, Miss. And of course you know,' my friend added, 'I took it from her, by the lake that, just then and there at least, there *was* nobody.'

'Rather! And, naturally, you take it from her still.'

'I don't contradict her. What else can I do?'

'Nothing in the world! You've the cleverest little person to deal with. They've made them – their two friends, I mean – still cleverer even than nature did; for it was wondrous material to play on! Flora has now her grievance, and she'll work it to the end.'

'Yes, Miss; but to *what* end?'

'Why, that of dealing with me to her uncle. She'll make me out to him the lowest creature—!'

I winced at the fair show of the scene in Mrs Grose's face; she looked for a minute as if she sharply saw them together. 'And him who thinks so well of you!'

'He has an odd way – it comes over me now,' I laughed, '– of proving it! But that doesn't matter. What Flora wants, of course, is to get rid of me.'

My companion bravely concurred. 'Never again to so much as look at you.'

'So that what you've come to me now for,' I asked, 'is to speed me on my way?' Before she had time to reply, however, I had her in check. 'I've a better idea – the result of my reflections. My going *would* seem the right thing, and on Sunday I was terribly near it. Yet that won't do. It's *you* who must go. You must take Flora.'

My visitor, at this, did speculate. 'But where in the world—?'

'Away from here. Away from *them*. Away, even most of all, now, from me. Straight to her uncle.'

'Only to tell on you—?'

'No, not "only"! To leave me, in addition, with my remedy.'

She was still vague. 'And what *is* your remedy?'

'Your loyalty, to begin with. And then Miles's.'

She looked at me hard. 'Do you think he—?'

'Won't, if he has the chance, turn on me? Yes, I venture still to think it. At all events, I want to try. Get off with his sister as soon as possible and leave me with him alone.' I was amazed, myself, at the spirit I had still in reserve, and therefore perhaps a trifle the more disconcerted at the way in which, in spite of this fine example of it, she hesitated. 'There's one thing, of course,' I went on: 'they mustn't, before she goes, see each other for three seconds.' Then it came over me that, in spite of Flora's presumable sequestration from the instant of her return from the pool, it might already be too late. 'Do you mean,' I anxiously asked, 'that they *have* met?'

At this she quite flushed. 'Ah, Miss, I'm not such a fool as that! If I've been obliged to leave her three or four times, it has been each time with one of the maids, and at present, though she's alone, she's locked in safe. And yet – and yet!' There were too many things.

'And yet what?'

'Well, are you so sure of the little gentleman?'

'I'm not sure of anything but *you*. But I have, since last evening, a new hope. I think he wants to give me an opening. I do believe that – poor little exquisite wretch! – he wants to speak. Last evening, in the firelight and the silence, he sat with me for two hours as if it were just coming.'

Mrs Grose looked hard, through the window, at the grey, gathering day. 'And did it come?'

'No, though I waited and waited, I confess it didn't, and it was without a breach of the silence or so much as a faint allusion to his sister's condition and absence that we at last kissed for good night. All the same,' I continued, 'I can't, if her uncle sees her, consent to his seeing her brother without my having given the boy – and most of all because things have got so bad – a little more time.'

My friend appeared on this ground more reluctant than I could quite understand. 'What do you mean by more time?'

'Well, a day or two – really to bring it out. He'll then be on *my* side – of which you see the importance. If nothing comes, I shall only fail, and you will, at the worst, have helped me by doing, on your arrival in town, whatever you may have found possible.' So I put it before her, but she continued for a little so inscrutably embarrassed that I came again to her aid. 'Unless indeed,' I wound up, 'you really want *not* to go.'

I could see it, in her face, at last clear itself; she put out her hand to me as a pledge. 'I'll go – I'll go. I'll go this morning.'

I wanted to be very just. 'If you *should* wish still to wait, I would engage she shouldn't see me.'

'No, no: it's the place itself. She must leave it.' She held me a moment with heavy eyes, then brought out the rest. 'Your idea's the right one. I myself, Miss—'

'Well?'

'I can't stay.'

The look she gave me with it made me jump at possibilities. 'You mean that, since yesterday, you *have* seen—?'

She shook her head with dignity. 'I've *heard*—!'

'Heard?'

'From that child – horrors! There!' she sighed with tragic relief. 'On my honour, Miss, she says things—!' But at this evocation she broke down; she dropped, with a sudden sob, upon my sofa and, as I had seen her do before, gave way to all the grief of it.

It was quite in another manner that I, for my part, let myself go. 'Oh, thank God!'

She sprang up again at this, drying her eyes with a groan. '"Thank God"?'

'It so justifies me!'

'It does that, Miss!'

I couldn't have desired more emphasis, but I just hesitated. 'She's so horrible?'

I saw my colleague scarce knew how to put it. 'Really shocking.'

'And about me?'

'About you, Miss – since you must have it. It's beyond everything, for a young lady; and I can't think wherever she must have picked up—'

'The appalling language she applied to me? I can, then!' I broke in with a laugh that was doubtless significant enough.

It only, in truth, left my friend still more grave. 'Well, perhaps I ought to also – since I've heard some of it before! Yet I can't bear it,' the poor woman went on while, with the same movement, she glanced, on my dressing-table, at the face of my watch. 'But I must go back.'

I kept her, however. 'Ah, if you can't bear it—!'

'How can I stop with her, you mean? Why, just *for* that: to get her away. Far from this,' she pursued, 'far from *them*—'

'She may be different? she may be free?' I seized her almost with joy. 'Then, in spite of yesterday, you *believe*—'

'In such doings?' Her simple description of them required, in the light of her expression, to be carried no further, and she gave me the whole thing as she had never done. 'I believe.'

Yes, it was a joy, and we were still shoulder to shoulder: if I might continue sure of that I should care but little what else happened. My support in the presence of disaster would be the same as it had been in my early need of confidence, and if my friend would answer for my honesty I would answer for all the rest. On the point of taking leave of her, none the less, I was to some extent embarrassed. 'There's one thing of course – it occurs to me – to remember. My letter, giving the alarm, will have reached town before you.'

I now perceived still more how she had been beating about the bush and how weary at last it had made her. 'Your letter won't have got there. Your letter never went.'

'What then became of it?'

'Goodness knows! Master Miles—'

'Do you mean *he* took it?' I gasped.

She hung fire, but she overcame her reluctance. 'I mean that I saw yesterday, when I came back with Miss Flora, that it wasn't where you had put it. Later in the evening I had the chance to question Luke, and he declared that he had neither noticed nor touched it.' We could only exchange, on this, one of our deeper mutual soundings, and it was Mrs Grose who first brought up the plumb with an almost elate 'You see!'

'Yes, I see that if Miles took it instead he probably will have read it and destroyed it.'

'And don't you see anything else?'

I faced her a moment with a sad smile. 'It strikes me that by this time your eyes are open even wider than mine.'

They proved to be so indeed, but she could still blush, almost, to show it. 'I make out now what he must have done at school.' And she gave, in her simple sharpness, an almost droll disillusioned nod. 'He stole!'

I turned it over – I tried to be more judicial. 'Well – perhaps.'

She looked as if she found me unexpectedly calm. 'He stole *letters!*'

She couldn't know my reasons for a calmness after all pretty shallow; so I showed them off as I might. 'I hope then it was to more purpose than in this case! The note, at any rate, that I put on the table yesterday,' I pursued, 'will have given him so scant an advantage – for it contained only the bare demand for an interview – that he is already much ashamed of having gone so far for so little, and that what he had on his mind last evening was precisely the need of confession.' I seemed to myself, for the instant, to have mastered it, to see it all. 'Leave us, leave us' – I was already, at the door, hurrying her off. 'I'll get it out of him. He'll meet me – he'll confess. If he confesses, he's saved. And if he's saved—'

'Then *you* are?' The dear woman kissed me on this, and I took her farewell. 'I'll save you without him!' she cried as she went.

XXII

YET it was when she had got off – and I missed her on the spot – that the great pinch really came. If I had counted on what it would give me to find myself alone with Miles I speedily perceived, at least, that it would give me a measure. No hour of my stay in fact was so assailed with apprehensions as that of my coming down to learn that the carriage containing Mrs Grose and my younger pupil had already rolled out of the gates. Now I *was*, I said to myself, face to face with the elements, and for much of the rest of the day, while I fought my weakness, I could consider that I had been supremely rash. It was a tighter place still than I had yet turned round in; all the more that, for the first time, I could see in the aspect of others a confused reflection of the crisis. What had happened naturally caused them all to stare; there was too little of the explained, throw out whatever we might, in the suddenness of my colleague's act. The maids and the men looked blank; the effect of which on my nerves was an aggravation until I saw the necessity of making it a positive aid. It was precisely, in short, by just clutching the helm that I avoided total wreck; and I daresay that, to bear up at all, I became, that morning, very grand and very dry. I welcomed the consciousness that I was charged with much to do, and I caused it to be known as well that, left thus to myself, I was quite remarkably firm. I wandered with that manner, for the next hour or two, all over the place and looked, I have no doubt, as if I were ready for any onset. So, for the benefit of whom it might concern, I paraded with a sick heart.

The person it appeared least to concern proved to be, till dinner, little Miles himself. My perambulations had given me, meanwhile, no glimpse of him, but they had tended to make more public the change taking place in our relation as a consequence of his having at the piano, the day before, kept me, in Flora's interest, so beguiled and befooled. The stamp of publicity had of course been fully given by her confinement and departure, and the change itself was now ushered in by our non-observance of the regular custom of the schoolroom. He had already disappeared when, on my way down, I pushed open his door, and I learned below that he had breakfasted – in the presence of a couple of the maids – with Mrs Grose and his sister. He had then gone out, as he said, for a stroll; than which nothing, I reflected, could better have expressed his frank view of the abrupt transformation of my office. What he would now permit this office to consist of was yet to be settled: there was a queer relief, at all events – I mean for myself in especial – in the renouncement of one pretension. If so much had sprung to the surface I scarce put it too strongly in saying that what had perhaps sprung highest was the absurdity of our prolonging the fiction that I had anything more to teach him. It sufficiently stuck out that, by tacit little tricks in which even more than myself he carried out the care for my dignity, I had had to appeal to him to let me off straining to meet him on the ground of his true capacity. He had at any rate his freedom now; I was never to touch it again; as I had amply shown, moreover, when, on his joining me in the schoolroom the previous night, I had uttered, on the subject of the interval just concluded, neither challenge nor hint. I had too much, from this moment, my other ideas. Yet when he at last arrived the difficulty of applying them, the accumulations of my problem, were brought straight home to me by the beautiful little presence on which what had occurred had as yet, for the eye, dropped neither stain nor shadow.

To mark, for the house, the high state I cultivated I decreed that my meals with the boy should be served, as we called it, downstairs; so that I had been awaiting him in the ponderous pomp of the room outside of the window of which I had had from Mrs Grose, that first scared Sunday, my flash of something it would scarce have done to call light. Here at present I felt afresh – for I had felt it again and again – how my equilibrium depended on the success of my rigid will, the will to shut my eyes as tight as possible to the truth that what I had to deal with was, revoltingly, against nature. I could only get on at all by taking 'nature' into my confidence and my account, by treating my monstrous ordeal as a push in a direction unusual, of course, and unpleasant, but demanding, after all, for a fair front, only another turn of the screw of ordinary human virtue. No attempt, none the less, could well require more tact than just this attempt to supply, one's self, *all* the nature. How could I put even a little of that article into a suppression of reference to what had occurred? How, on the other hand, could I make a reference without a new plunge into the hideous obscure? Well, a sort of answer, after a time, had come to me, and it was so far confirmed as that I was met, incontestably, by the quickened vision of what was rare in my little companion. It was indeed as if he had found even now – as he had so often found at lessons – still some other delicate way to ease me off. Wasn't there light in the fact which, as we shared our solitude, broke out with a specious glitter it had never yet quite worn? – the fact that (opportunity aiding, precious opportunity which had now come) it would be pre-posterous, with a child so endowed, to forgo the help one might wrest from absolute intelligence? What had his intelligence been given him for but to save him? Mightn't one, to reach his mind, risk the stretch of an angular arm over his character? It was as if, when we were face to face in the dining-room, he had literally shown me the way. The roast mutton was on the table, and I had dispensed with attendance. Miles, before he sat down, stood a moment with his hands in his pockets and looked at the joint, on which he seemed on the point of passing some humorous judgement. But what he presently produced was: 'I say, my dear, is she really very awfully ill?'

'Little Flora? Not so bad but that she'll presently be better. London will set her up. Bly had ceased to agree with her. Come here and take your mutton.'

He alertly obeyed me, carried the plate carefully to his seat and, when he was established, went on. 'Did Bly disagree with her so terribly suddenly?'

'Not so suddenly as you might think. One had seen it coming on.'

'Then why didn't you get her off before?'

'Before what?'

'Before she became too ill to travel.'

I found myself prompt. 'She's *not* too ill to travel: she only might have become so if she had stayed. This was just the moment to seize. The journey will dissipate the influence' – oh, I was grand! – 'and carry it off.'

'I see, I see' – Miles, for that matter, was grand too. He settled to his repast with the charming little 'table manner' that, from the day of his arrival, had relieved me of all grossness of admonition. Whatever he had been driven from school for, it was not for ugly feeding. He was irreproachable, as always, to-day; but he was unmistakeably more conscious. He was discernibly trying to take for granted more things than he found, without assistance, quite easy; and he dropped into peaceful silence while he felt his situation. Our meal was of the briefest – mine a vain pretence, and I had the things immediately removed. While this was done Miles stood again with his hands in his little pockets and his back to me – stood and looked out of the wide window through which, that other day, I had seen what pulled me up. We continued silent while the maid was with us – as silent, it whimsically occurred to me, as some young couple who, on their wedding-journey, at the inn, feel shy in the presence of the waiter. He turned round only when the waiter had left us. 'Well – so we're alone!'

XXIII

'Oh, more or less.' I fancy my smile was pale. 'Not absolutely. We shouldn't like that!' I went on.

'No – I suppose we shouldn't. Of course we have the others.'

'We have the others – we have indeed the others,' I concurred.

'Yet even though we have them,' he returned, still with his hands in his pockets and planted there in front of me, 'they don't much count, do they?'

I made the best of it, but I felt wan. 'It depends on what you call "much"!'

'Yes' – with all accommodation – 'everything depends!' On this, however, he faced to the window again and presently reached it with his vague, restless, cogitating step. He remained there a while, with his forehead against the glass, in contemplation of the stupid shrubs I knew and the dull things of November. I had always my hypocrisy of 'work', behind which, now, I gained the sofa. Steadying myself with it there as I had repeatedly done at those moments of torment that I have described as the moments of my knowing the children to be given to something from which I was barred, I sufficiently obeyed my habit of being prepared for the worst. But an extraordinary impression dropped on me as I extracted a meaning from the boy's embarrassed back – none other than the impression that I was not barred now. This inference grew in a few minutes to sharp intensity and seemed bound up with the direct perception that it was positively *he* who was. The frames and squares of the great window were a kind of image, for him, of a kind of failure. I felt that I saw him, at any rate, shut in or shut out. He was admirable, but not comfortable: I took it in with a throb of hope. Wasn't he looking, through the haunted pane, for something he couldn't see? – and wasn't it the first time in the whole business that he had known such a lapse? The first, the very first: I found it a splendid portent. It made him anxious, though he watched himself; he had been anxious all day and, even while in his usual sweet little manner he sat at table, had needed all his small strange genius to give it a gloss. When he at last turned round to meet me it was almost as if this genius had succumbed. 'Well, I think I'm glad Bly agrees with *me*!'

'You would certainly seem to have seen, these twenty-four hours, a good deal more of it than for some time before. I hope,' I went on bravely, 'that you've been enjoying yourself.'

'Oh yes, I've been ever so far; all round about – miles and miles away. I've never been so free.'

He had really a manner of his own, and I could only try to keep up with him. 'Well, do you like it?'

He stood there smiling; then at last he put into two words – 'Do *you*?' – more discrimination than I had ever heard two words contain. Before I had time to deal with that, however, he continued as if with the sense that this was an impertinence to be softened. 'Nothing could be more charming than the way you take it, for of course if we're alone together now it's you that are alone most. But I hope,' he threw in, 'you don't particularly mind!'

'Having to do with you?' I asked. 'My dear child, how can I help minding? Though I've renounced all claim to your company – you're so beyond me – I at least greatly enjoy it. What else should I stay on for?'

He looked at me more directly, and the expression of his face, graver now, struck me as the most beautiful I had ever found in it. 'You stay on just for *that*?'

'Certainly. I stay on as your friend and from the tremendous interest I take in you till something can be done for you that may be more worth your while. That needn't surprise you.' My voice trembled so that I felt it impossible to suppress the shake. 'Don't you remember how I told you, when I came and sat on your bed the night of the storm, that there was nothing in the world I wouldn't do for you?'

'Yes, yes!' He, on his side, more and more visibly nervous, had a tone to master; but he was so much more successful than I that, laughing out through his gravity, he could pretend we were pleasantly jesting. 'Only that, I think, was to get me to do something for *you*!'

'It was partly to get you to do something,' I conceded. 'But, you know, you didn't do it.'

'Oh yes,' he said with the brightest superficial eagerness, 'you wanted me to tell you something.'

'That's it. Out, straight out. What you have on your mind, you know.'

'Ah then, is *that* what you've stayed over for?'

He spoke with a gaiety through which I could still catch the finest little quiver of resentful passion; but I can't begin to express the effect upon me of an implication of surrender even so faint. It was as if what I had yearned for had come at last only to astonish me. 'Well, yes – I may as well make a clean breast of it. It was precisely for that.'

He waited so long that I supposed it for the purpose of repudiating the assumption on which my action had been founded; but what he finally said was: 'Do you mean now – here?'

'There couldn't be a better place or time.' He looked round him uneasily, and I had the rare – oh, the queer! – impression of the very first symptom I had seen in him of the approach of immediate fear. It was as if he were suddenly afraid of me – which struck me indeed as perhaps the best thing to make him. Yet in the very pang of the effort I felt it vain to try sternness, and I heard myself the next instant so gentle as to be almost grotesque. 'You want so to go out again?'

'Awfully!' He smiled at me heroically, and the touching little bravery of it was enhanced by his actually flushing with pain. He had picked up his hat, which he had brought in, and stood twirling it in a way that gave me, even as I was just nearly reaching port, a perverse horror of what I was doing. To do it in *any* way was an act of violence, for what did it consist of but the obtrusion of the idea of grossness and guilt on a small helpless creature who had been for me a revelation of the possibilities of beautiful intercourse? Wasn't it base to create for a being so exquisite a mere alien awkwardness? I suppose I now read into our situation a clearness it couldn't have had at the time, for I seem to see our poor eyes already lighted with some spark of a prevision of the anguish that was to come. So we circled about, with terrors and scruples, like fighters not daring to close. But it was for each other we feared! That kept us a little longer suspended and unbruised. 'I'll tell you everything,' Miles said – 'I mean I'll tell you anything you like. You'll stay on with me, and we shall both be all right and I *will* tell you – I *will*. But not now.'

'Why not now?'

My insistence turned him from me and kept him once more at his window in a silence during which, between us, you might have heard a pin drop. Then he was before me again with the air of a person for whom, outside, someone who had frankly to be reckoned with was waiting. 'I have to see Luke.'

I had not yet reduced him to quite so vulgar a lie, and I felt proportionately ashamed. But, horrible as it was, his lies made up my truth. I achieved thoughtfully a few loops of my knitting. 'Well then, go to Luke, and I'll wait for what you promise. Only, in return for that, satisfy, before you leave me, one very much smaller request.'

He looked as if he felt he had succeeded enough to be able still a little to bargain. 'Very much smaller—?'

'Yes, a mere fraction of the whole. Tell me' – oh, my work preoccupied me, and I was off-hand! – 'if, yesterday afternoon, from the table in the hall, you took, you know, my letter.'

XXIV

MY sense of how he received this suffered for a minute from something that I can describe only as a fierce split of my attention – a stroke that at first, as I sprang straight up, reduced me to the mere blind movement of getting hold of him, drawing him close and, while I just fell for support against the nearest piece of furniture, instinctively keeping him with his back to the window. The appearance was full upon us that I had already had to deal with here: Peter Quint had come into view like a sentinel before a prison. The next thing I saw was that, from outside, he had reached the window, and then I knew that, close to the glass and glaring in through it, he offered once more to the room his white face of damnation. It represents but grossly what took place within me at the sight to say that on the second my decision was made; yet I believe that no woman so overwhelmed ever in so short a time recovered her grasp of the *act*. It came to me in the very horror of the immediate presence that the act would be, seeing and facing what I saw and faced, to keep the boy himself unaware. The inspiration – I can call it by no other name – was that I felt how voluntarily, how transcendently, I *might*. It was like fighting with a demon for a human soul, and when I had fairly so appraised it I saw how the human soul – held out, in the tremor of my hands, at arms' length – had a perfect dew of sweat on a lovely childish forehead. The face that was close to mine was as white as the face against the glass, and out of it presently came a sound, not low nor weak, but as if from much further away, that I drank like a waft of fragrance.

'Yes – I took it.'

At this, with a moan of joy, I enfolded, I drew him close; and while I held him to my breast, where I could feel in the sudden fever of his little body the tremendous pulse of his little heart, I kept my eyes on the thing at the window and saw it move and shift its posture. I have likened it to a sentinel, but its slow wheel, for a moment, was rather the prowl of a baffled beast. My present quickened courage, however, was such that, not too much to let it through, I had to shade, as it were, my flame. Meanwhile the glare of the face was again at the window, the scoundrel fixed as if to watch and wait. It was the very confidence that I might now defy him, as well as the positive certitude, by this time, of the child's unconsciousness, that made me go on. 'What did you take it for?'

'To see what you said about me.'

'You opened the letter?'

'I opened it.'

My eyes were now, as I held him off a little again, on Miles's own face, in which the collapse of mockery showed me how complete was the ravage of uneasiness. What was prodigious was that at last, by my success, his sense was sealed and his communication stopped: he knew that he was in presence, but knew not of what, and knew still less that I also was and that I did know. And what did this strain of trouble matter when my eyes went back to the window only to see that the air was clear again and – by my personal triumph – the influence quenched? There was nothing there. I felt that the cause was mine and that I should surely get *all*. 'And you found nothing!' – I let my elation out.

He gave the most mournful, thoughtful little headshake. 'Nothing.'

'Nothing, nothing!' I almost shouted in my joy.

'Nothing, nothing,' he sadly repeated.

I kissed his forehead; it was drenched. 'So what have you done with it?'

'I've burnt it.'

'Burnt it?' It was now or never. 'Is that what you did at school?'

Oh, what this brought up! 'At school?'

'Did you take letters? – or other things?'

'Other things?' He appeared now to be thinking of something far off and that reached him only through the pressure of his anxiety. Yet it did reach him. 'Did I *steal*?'

I felt myself redden to the roots of my hair as well as wonder if it were more strange to put to a gentleman such a question or to see him take it with allowances that gave the very distance of his fall in the world. 'Was it for that you mightn't go back?'

The only thing he felt was rather a dreary little surprise. 'Did you know I mightn't go back?'

'I know everything.'

He gave me at this the longest and strangest look. 'Everything?'

'Everything. Therefore *did* you—?' But I couldn't say it again.

Miles could, very simply. 'No. I didn't steal.'

My face must have shown him I believed him utterly; yet my hands – but it was for pure tenderness – shook him as if to ask him why, if it was all for nothing, he had condemned me to months of torment. 'What then did you do?'

He looked in vague pain all round the top of the room and drew his breath, two or three times over, as if with difficulty. He might have been standing at the bottom of the sea and raising his eyes to some faint green twilight. 'Well – I said things.'

'Only that?'

'They thought it was enough!'

'To turn you out for?'

Never, truly, had a person 'turned out' shown so little to explain it as this little person! He appeared to weigh my question, but in a manner quite detached and almost helpless. 'Well, I suppose I oughtn't.'

'But to whom did you say them?'

He evidently tried to remember, but it dropped – he had lost it. 'I don't know!'

He almost smiled at me in the desolation of his surrender, which was indeed practically, by this time, so complete that I ought to have left it there. But I was infatuated – I was blind with victory, though even then the very effect that was to have brought him so much nearer was already that of added separation. 'Was it to everyone?' I asked.

'No; it was only to—' But he gave a sick little headshake. 'I don't remember their names.'

'Were they then so many?'

'No – only a few. Those I liked.'

Those he liked? I seemed to float not into clearness, but into a darker obscure, and within a minute there had come to me out of my very pity the appalling alarm of his being perhaps innocent. It was for the instant confounding and bottomless, for if he *were* innocent, what then on earth was *I*? Paralysed, while it lasted, by the mere brush of the question, I let him go a little, so that, with a deep-drawn sigh, he turned away from me again; which, as he faced toward the clear window, I suffered, feeling that I had nothing now there to keep him from. 'And did they repeat what you said?' I went on after a moment.

He was soon at some distance from me, still breathing hard and again with the air, though now without anger for it, of being confined against his will. Once more, as he had done before, he looked up at the dim day as if, of what had hitherto sustained him, nothing was left but an unspeakable anxiety. 'Oh yes,' he nevertheless replied – 'they must have repeated them. To those *they* liked,' he added.

There was, somehow, less of it than I had expected; but I turned it over. 'And these things came round—?'

'To the masters? Oh yes!' he answered very simply. 'But I didn't know they'd tell.'

'The masters? They didn't – they've never told. That's why I ask you.'

He turned to me again his little beautiful fevered face. 'Yes, it was too bad.'

'Too bad?'

'What I suppose I sometimes said. To write home.'

I can't name the exquisite pathos of the contradiction given to such a speech by such a speaker; I only know that the next instant I heard myself throw off with homely force: 'Stuff and nonsense!' But the next after that I must have sounded stern enough. 'What *were* these things?'

My sternness was all for his judge, his executioner; yet it made him avert himself again, and that movement made *me*, with a single bound and an irrepressible cry, spring straight upon him. For there again, against the glass, as if to blight his confession and stay his answer, was the hideous author of our woe – the white face of damnation. I felt a sick swim at the drop of my victory and all the return of my battle, so that the wildness of my veritable leap only served as a great betrayal. I saw him, from the midst of my act, meet it with a divination, and on the perception that even now he only guessed, and that the window was still to his own eyes free, I let the impulse flame up to convert the climax of his dismay into the very proof of his liberation. 'No more, no more, no more!' I shrieked, as I tried to press him against me, to my visitant.

'Is she *here*?' Miles panted as he caught with his sealed eyes the direction of my words. Then as his strange 'she' staggered me and, with a gasp, I echoed it, 'Miss Jessel, Miss Jessel!' he with a sudden fury gave me back.

I seized, stupefied, his supposition – some sequel to what we had done to Flora, but this made me only want to show him that it was better still than that. 'It's not Miss Jessel! But it's at the window – straight before us. It's *there* – the coward horror, there for the last time!'

At this, after a second in which his head made the movement of a baffled dog's on a scent and then gave a frantic little shake for air and light, he was at me in a white rage, bewildered, glaring vainly over the place and missing wholly, though it now, to my sense, filled the room like the taste of poison, the wide, overwhelming presence. 'It's *he*?'

I was so determined to have all my proof that I flashed into ice to challenge him. 'Whom do you mean by "he"?'

'Peter Quint – you devil!' His face gave again, round the room, its convulsed supplication. '*Where?*'

They are in my ears still, his supreme surrender of the name and his tribute to my devotion. 'What does he matter now, my own? – what will he *ever* matter? *I* have you,' I launched at the beast, 'but he has lost you for ever!' Then, for the demonstration of my work, 'There, *there*!' I said to Miles.

But he had already jerked straight round, stared, glared again, and seen but the quiet day. With the stroke of the loss I was so proud of he uttered the cry of a creature hurled over an abyss, and the grasp with which I recovered him might have been that of catching him in his fall. I caught him, yes, I held him – it may be imagined with what a passion; but at the end of a minute I began to feel what it truly was that I held. We were alone with the quiet day, and his little heart, dispossessed, had stopped.

IN THE CAGE

I

It had occurred to her early that in her position – that of a young person spending, in framed and wired confinement, the life of a guinea-pig or a magpie – she should know a great many persons without their recognising the acquaintance. That made it an emotion the more lively – though singularly rare and always, even then, with opportunity still very much smothered – to see any one come in whom she knew, as she called it, outside, and who could add something to the poor identity of her function. Her function was to sit there with two young men – the other telegraphist and the counter-clerk; to mind the 'sounder', which was always going, to dole out stamps and postal-orders, weigh letters, answer stupid questions, give difficult change and, more than anything else, count words as numberless as the sands of the sea, the words of the telegrams thrust, from morning to night, through the gap left in the high lattice, across the encumbered shelf that her forearm ached with rubbing. This transparent screen fenced out or fenced in, according to the side of the narrow counter on which the human lot was cast, the duskiest corner of a shop pervaded not a little, in winter, by the poison of perpetual gas, and at all times by the presence of hams, cheese, dried fish, soap, varnish, paraffin, and other solids and fluids that she came to know perfectly by their smells without consenting to know them by their names.

The barrier that divided the little post-and-telegraph-office from the grocery was a frail structure of wood and wire; but the social, the professional separation was a gulf that fortune, by a stroke quite remarkable, had spared her the necessity of contributing at all publicly to bridge. When Mr Cocker's young men stepped over from behind the other counter to change a five-pound note – and Mr Cocker's situation, with the cream of the 'Court Guide' and the dearest furnished apartments, Simpkin's, Ladle's, Thrupp's, just round the corner, was so select

451

that his place was quite pervaded by the crisp rustle of these emblems – she pushed out the sovereigns as if the applicant were no more to her than one of the momentary appearances in the great procession; and this perhaps all the more from the very fact of the connection – only recognised outside indeed – to which she had lent herself with ridiculous inconsequence. She recognised the others the less because she had at last so unreservedly, so irredeemably, recognised Mr Mudge. But she was a little ashamed, none the less, of having to admit to herself that Mr Mudge's removal to a higher sphere – to a more commanding position, that is, though to a much lower neighbourhood – would have been described still better as a luxury than as the simplification that she contented herself with calling it. He had, at any rate, ceased to be all day long in her eyes, and this left something a little fresh for them to rest on of a Sunday. During the three months that he had remained at Cocker's after her consent to their engagement, she had often asked herself what it was that marriage would be able to add to a familiarity so final. Opposite there, behind the counter of which his superior stature, his whiter apron, his more clustering curls and more present, too present, h's had been for a couple of years the principal ornament, he had moved to and fro before her as on the small sanded floor of their contracted future. She was conscious now of the improvement of not having to take her present and her future at once. They were about as much as she could manage when taken separate.

She had, none the less, to give her mind steadily to what Mr Mudge had again written her about, the idea of her applying for a transfer to an office quite similar – she couldn't yet hope for a place in a bigger – under the very roof where he was foreman, so that, dangled before her every minute of the day, he should see her, as he called it, 'hourly', and in a part, the far N. W. district, where, with her mother, she would save, on their two rooms alone, nearly three shillings. It would be far from dazzling to exchange Mayfair for Chalk Farm, and it was something of a predicament that he so kept at her; still, it was nothing to the old predicaments, those of the early times of their great misery, her own, her mother's, and her elder sister's – the last of whom had succumbed to all but absolute want when, as conscious, incredulous ladies, suddenly bereaved, betrayed, overwhelmed, they had slipped faster and faster down the steep slope at the bottom of which she alone had rebounded. Her mother had never rebounded any more at the bottom than on the way; had only rumbled and grumbled down and down, making, in respect of caps and conversation, no effort whatever, and too often, alas! smelling of whisky.

II

IT was always rather quiet at Cocker's while the contingent from Ladle's and Thrupp's and all the other great places were at luncheon, or, as the young men used vulgarly to say, while the animals were feeding. She had forty minutes in advance of this to go home for her own dinner; and when she came back, and one of the young men took his turn, there was often half an hour during which she could pull out a bit of work or a book – a book from the place where she borrowed novels, very greasy, in fine print and all about fine folks, at a ha'penny a day. This sacred pause was one of the numerous ways in which the establishment kept its finger on the pulse of fashion and fell into the rhythm of the larger life. It had something to do, one day, with the particular vividness marking the advent of a lady whose meals were apparently irregular, yet whom she was destined, she afterwards found, not to forget. The girl was *blasée*; nothing could belong more, as she perfectly knew, to the intense publicity of her profession; but she had a whimsical mind and wonderful nerves; she was subject, in short, to sudden flickers of antipathy and sympathy, red gleams in the grey, fitful awakings and followings, odd caprices of curiosity. She had a friend who had invented a new career for women – that of being in and out of people's houses to look after the flowers. Mrs Jordan had a manner of her own of sounding this allusion; 'the flowers', on her lips, were, in happy homes, as usual as the coals or the daily papers. She took charge of them, at any rate, in all the rooms, at so much a month, and people were quickly finding out what it was to make over this delicate duty to the widow of a clergyman. The widow, on her side, dilating on the initiations thus opened up to her, had been splendid to her young friend over the way she was made free of the greatest houses – the way, especially when she did the dinner-tables, set out so often for twenty, she felt that a single step more would socially, would absolutely, introduce her. On its being asked of her, then, if she circulated only in a sort of tropical solitude, with the upper servants for picturesque natives, and on her having to assent to this glance at her limitations, she had found a reply to the girl's invidious question. 'You've no imagination, my dear!' – that was because the social door might at any moment open so wide.

Our young lady had not taken up the charge, had dealt with it good-humouredly, just because she knew so well what to think of it. It was at once one of her most cherished complaints and most secret supports that people didn't understand her, and it was accordingly a matter of indifference to her that Mrs Jordan shouldn't; even though Mrs Jordan, handed down from their early twilight of gentility and also the victim of reverses, was the only member of her circle in whom she recognised an equal. She was perfectly aware that her imaginative life was the life in which she spent most of her time; and she would have been ready, had it been at all worth while, to contend that, since her outward occupation didn't kill it, it must be strong indeed. Combinations of flowers and greenstuff, forsooth! What *she* could handle freely, she said to herself, was combinations of men and women. The only weakness in her faculty came from the positive abundance of her contact with the human herd; this was so constant, had the effect of becoming so cheap, that there were long stretches in which inspiration, divination and interest, quite dropped. The great thing was the flashes, the quick revivals, absolute accidents all, and neither to be counted on nor to be resisted. Some one had only sometimes to put in a penny for a stamp, and the whole thing was upon her. She was so absurdly constructed that these were literally the moments that made up – made up for the long stiffness of sitting there in the stocks, made up for the cunning hostility of Mr Buckton and the importunate sympathy of the counter-clerk, made up for the daily, deadly, flourishy letter from Mr Mudge, made up even for the most haunting of her worries, the rage at moments of not knowing how her mother did 'get it'.

She had surrendered herself moreover, of late, to a certain expansion of her consciousness; something that seemed perhaps vulgarly accounted for by the fact that, as the blast of the season roared louder and the waves of fashion tossed their spray further over the counter, there were more impressions to be gathered and really – for it came to that – more life to be led. Definite, at any rate, it was that by the time May was well started the kind of company she kept at Cocker's had begun to strike her as a reason – a reason she might almost put forward for a policy of procrastination. It sounded silly, of course, as yet, to plead such a motive, especially as the fascination of the place was, after all, a sort of torment. But she liked her torment; it was a torment she should miss at Chalk Farm. She was ingenious and uncandid, therefore, about leaving the breadth of London a little longer between herself and that austerity. If she had not quite the courage, in short, to say to Mr Mudge that her actual chance for a play of mind was worth, any week, the three shillings he desired to help her to save, she yet saw something happen in the course of the month that, in her heart of hearts at least, answered the subtle question. This was connected precisely with the appearance of the memorable lady.

III

SHE pushed in three bescribbled forms which the girl's hand was quick to appropriate, Mr Buckton having so frequent a perverse instinct for catching first any eye that promised the sort of entertainment with which she had her peculiar affinity. The amusements of captives are full of a desperate contrivance, and one of our young friend's ha'pennyworths had been the charming tale of *Picciola*. It was of course the law of the place that they were never to take no notice, as Mr Buckton said, whom they served; but this also never prevented, certainly on the same gentleman's own part, what he was fond of describing as the underhand game. Both her companions, for that matter, made no secret of the number of favourites they had among the ladies; sweet familiarities in spite of which she had repeatedly caught each of them in stupidities and mistakes, confusions of identity and lapses of observation that never failed to remind her how the cleverness of men ended where the cleverness of women began. 'Marguerite, Regent Street. Try on at six. All Spanish lace. Pearls. The full length.' That was the first; it had no signature. 'Lady Agnes Orme, Hyde Park Place. Impossible to-night, dining Haddon. Opera to-morrow, promised Fritz, but could do play Wednesday. Will try Haddon for Savoy, and anything in the world you like, if you can get Gussy. Sunday, Montenero. Sit Mason Monday, Tuesday. Marguerite awful. Cissy.' That was the second. The third, the girl noted when she took it, was on a foreign form: 'Everard, Hôtel Brighton, Paris. Only understand and believe. 22nd to 26th, and certainly 8th and 9th. Perhaps others. Come. Mary.'

Mary was very handsome, the handsomest woman, she felt in a moment, she had ever seen – or perhaps it was only Cissy. Perhaps it was both, for she had seen stranger things than that – ladies wiring to different persons under different names. She had seen all sorts of things and pieced together all sorts of mysteries. There had once been one – not long before – who, without winking, sent off five over five different signatures. Perhaps these represented five different friends who had asked her – all women, just as perhaps now Mary and Cissy, or one or other of them, were wiring by deputy. Sometimes she put in too much – too much of her own sense; sometimes she put in too little; and in either case this often came round to her afterwards, for she had an extraordinary way of keeping clues. When she noticed, she noticed; that was what it came to. There were days and days, there were weeks sometimes, of vacancy. This arose often from Mr Buckton's devilish and successful subterfuges for keeping her at the sounder whenever it looked as if anything might amuse; the sounder, which it was equally his business to mind, being the innermost cell of cap-tivity, a cage within the cage, fenced off from the rest by a frame of ground glass. The counter-clerk would have played into her hands; but the counter-clerk was really reduced to idiocy by the effect of his passion for her. She flattered herself moreover, nobly, that with the unpleasant conspicuity of this passion she would never have consented to be obliged to him. The most she would ever do would be always to shove off on him whenever she could the registration of letters, a job she happened particularly to loathe. After the long stupors, at all events, there almost always suddenly would come a sharp taste of something; it was in her mouth before she knew it; it was in her mouth now.

To Cissy, to Mary, whichever it was, she found her curiosity going out with a rush, a mute effusion that floated back to her, like a returning tide, the living colour and splendour of the beautiful head, the light of eyes that seemed to reflect such utterly other things than the mean things actually before them; and, above all, the high, curt consideration of a manner that, even at bad moments, was a magnificent habit and of the very essence of the innumerable things – her beauty, her birth, her father and mother, her cousins, and all her ancestors – that its possessor couldn't have got rid of if she had wished. How did our obscure little public servant know that, for the lady of the telegrams, this was a bad moment? How did she guess all sorts of impossible things, such as, almost on the very spot, the presence of drama, at a critical stage, and the nature of the tie with the gentleman at the Hôtel Brighton? More than ever before it floated to her through the bars of the cage that this at last was the high reality, the bristling truth that she had hitherto only patched up and eked out – one of the creatures, in fine, in whom all the conditions for happiness actually met, and who, in the air they made, bloomed with an unwitting insolence. What came home to the girl was the way the insolence was tempered by something that was equally a part of the distinguished life, the custom of a flowerlike bend to the less fortunate – a dropped fragrance, a mere quick breath, but which in fact pervaded and lingered. The apparition was very young, but certainly married, and our fatigued friend had a sufficient store of mythological comparison to recognise the port of Juno. Marguerite might be 'awful', but she knew how to dress a goddess.

Pearls and Spanish lace – she herself, with assurance, could see them, and the 'full length' too, and also red velvet bows, which, disposed on the lace in a particular manner (she could have placed them with the turn of a hand), were of course to adorn the front of a black brocade that would be like a dress in a picture. However, neither Marguerite, nor Lady Agnes, nor Haddon, nor Fritz, nor Gussy was what the wearer of this garment had really come in for. She had come in for Everard – and that was doubtless not *his* true name either. If our young lady had never taken such jumps before, it was simply that she had never before been so affected. She went all the way. Mary and Cissy had been round together, in their single superb person, to see him – he must live round the corner; they had found that, in consequence of something they had come, precisely, to make up for or to have another scene about, he had gone off – gone off just on purpose to make them feel it; on which they had come together to Cocker's as to the nearest place; where they had put in the three forms partly in order not to put in the one alone. The two others, in a manner, covered it, muffled it, passed it off. Oh yes, she went all the way, and this was a specimen of how she often went. She would know the hand again any time. It was as handsome and as everything else as the woman herself. The woman herself had, on learning his flight, pushed past Everard's servant and into his room; she had written her missive at his table and with his pen. All this, every inch of it, came in the waft that she blew through and left behind her, the influence that, as I have said, lingered. And among the things the girl was sure of, happily, was that she should see her again.

IV

SHE saw her, in fact, and only ten days later; but this time she was not alone, and that was exactly a part of the luck of it. Being clever enough to know through what possibilities it could range, our young lady had ever since had in her mind a dozen conflicting theories about Everard's type; as to which, the instant they came into the place, she felt the point settled with a thump that seemed somehow addressed straight to her heart. That organ literally beat faster at the approach of the gentleman who was this time with Cissy, and who, as seen from within the cage, became on the spot the happiest of the happy circumstances with which her mind had invested the friend of Fritz and Gussy. He was a very happy circumstance indeed as, with his cigarette in his lips and his broken familiar talk caught by his companion, he put down the half-dozen telegrams which it would take them together some minutes to despatch. And here it occurred, oddly enough, that if, shortly before, the girl's interest in his companion had sharpened her sense for the messages then transmitted, her immediate vision of himself had the effect, while she counted his seventy words, of preventing intelligibility. *His* words were mere numbers, they told her nothing whatever; and after he had gone she was in possession of no name, of no address, of no meaning, of nothing but a vague, sweet sound and an immense impression. He had been there but five minutes, he had smoked in her face, and, busy with his telegrams, with the tapping pencil and the conscious danger, the odious betrayal that would come from a mistake, she had had no wandering glances nor roundabout arts to spare. Yet she had taken him in; she knew everything; she had made up her mind.

He had come back from Paris; everything was rearranged; the pair were again shoulder to shoulder in their high encounter with life, their large and complicated game. The fine, soundless pulse of this game was in the air for our young woman while they remained in the shop. While they remained? They remained all day; their presence continued and abode with her, was in everything she did till nightfall, in the thousands of other words she counted, she transmitted, in all the stamps she detached and the letters she weighed and the change she gave, equally unconscious and unerring in each of these particulars, and not, as the run on the little office thickened with the afternoon hours, looking up at a single ugly face in the long sequence, nor really hearing the stupid questions that she patiently and perfectly answered. All patience was possible now, and all questions stupid after his – all faces ugly. She had been sure she should see the lady again; and even now she should perhaps, she should probably, see her often. But for him it was totally different; she should never, never see him. She wanted it too much. There was a kind of wanting that helped – she had arrived, with her rich experience, at that generalisation; and there was another kind that was fatal. It was this time the fatal kind; it would prevent.

Well, she saw him the very next day, and on this second occasion it was quite different; the sense of every syllable he despatched was fiercely distinct; she indeed felt her progressive pencil, dabbing as if with a quick caress the marks of his own, put life into every stroke. He was there a long time – had not brought his forms filled out, but worked them off in a nook on the counter; and there were other people as well – a changing, pushing cluster, with every one to mind at once and endless right change to make and information to produce. But she kept hold of him throughout; she continued, for herself, in a relation with him as close as that in which, behind the hated ground glass, Mr Buckton luckily continued with the sounder. This morning everything changed, but with a kind of dreariness too; she had to swallow the rebuff to her theory about fatal desires, which she did without confusion and indeed with absolute levity; yet if it was now flagrant that he did live close at hand – at Park Chambers – and belonged supremely to the class that wired everything, even their expensive feelings (so that, as he never wrote, his correspondence cost him weekly pounds and pounds, and he might be in and out five times a day), there was, all the same, involved in the prospect, and by reason of its positive excess of light, a perverse melancholy, almost a misery. This was rapidly to give it a place in an order of feelings on which I shall presently touch.

Meanwhile, for a month, he was very constant. Cissy, Mary, never reappeared with him; he was always either alone or accompanied only by some gentleman who was lost in the blaze of his glory. There was another sense, however – and indeed there was more than one – in which she mostly found herself counting in the splendid creature with whom she had originally connected him. He addressed this correspondent neither as Mary nor as Cissy; but the girl was sure of whom it was, in Eaton Square, that he was perpetually wiring to – and so irreproachably! – as Lady Bradeen. Lady Bradeen was Cissy, Lady Bradeen was Mary, Lady Bradeen was the friend of Fritz and of Gussy, the customer of Marguerite, and the close ally, in short (as was ideally right, only the girl had not yet found a descriptive term that was), of the most magnificent of men. Nothing could equal the frequency and variety of his communications to her ladyship but their extraordinary, their abysmal propriety. It was just the talk – so profuse sometimes that she wondered what was left for their real meetings – of the happiest people in the world. Their real meetings must have been constant, for half of it was appointments and allusions, all swimming in a sea of other allusions still, tangled in a complexity of questions that gave a wondrous image of their life. If Lady Bradeen was Juno, it was all certainly Olympian. If the girl, missing the answers, her ladyship's own outpourings, sometimes wished that Cocker's had only been one of the bigger offices where telegrams arrived as well as departed, there were yet ways in which, on the whole, she pressed the romance closer by reason of the very quantity of imagination that it demanded. The days and hours of this new friend, as she came to account him, were at all events unrolled, and however much more she might have known she would still have wished to go beyond. In fact she did go beyond; she went quite far enough.

But she could none the less, even after a month, scarce have told if the gentlemen who came in with him recurred or changed; and this in spite of the fact that they too were always posting and wiring, smoking in her face and signing or not signing. The gentlemen who came in with him were nothing, at any rate, when he was there. They turned up alone at other times – then only perhaps with a dim richness of reference. He himself, absent as well as present, was all. He was very tall, very fair, and had, in spite of his thick preoccupations, a good-humour that was exquisite, particularly as it so often had the effect of keeping him on. He could have reached over anybody, and anybody – no matter who – would have let him; but he was so extraordinarily kind that he quite pathetically waited, never waggling things at her out of his turn or saying 'Here!' with horrid sharpness. He waited for pottering old ladies, for gaping slaveys, for the perpetual Buttonses from Thrupp's; and the thing in all this that she would have liked most unspeakably to put to the test was the possibility of her having for him a personal identity that might in a particular way appeal. There were moments when he actually struck her as on her side, arranging to help, to support, to spare her.

But such was the singular spirit of our young friend, that she could remind herself with a sort of rage that when people had awfully good manners – people of that class, – you couldn't tell. These manners were for everybody, and it might be drearily unavailing for any poor particular body to be overworked and unusual. What he did take for granted was all sorts of facility; and his high pleasantness, his relighting of cigarettes while he waited, his unconscious bestowal of opportunities, of boons, of blessings, were all a part of his magnificent security, the instinct that told him there was nothing such an existence as his could ever lose by. He was, somehow, at once very bright and very grave, very young and immensely complete; and whatever he was at any moment, it was always as much as all the rest the mere bloom of his beatitude. He was sometimes Everard, as he had been at the Hôtel Brighton, and he was sometimes Captain Everard. He was sometimes Philip with his surname and sometimes Philip without it. In some directions he was merely Phil, in others he was merely Captain. There were relations in which he was none of these things, but a quite different person – 'the Count'. There were several friends for whom he was William. There were several for whom, in allusion perhaps to his complexion, he was 'the Pink 'Un'. Once, once only by good luck, he had, coinciding comically, quite miraculously, with another person also near to her, been 'Mudge'. Yes, whatever he was, it was a part of his happiness – whatever he was and probably whatever he wasn't. And his happiness was a part – it became so little by little – of something that, almost from the first of her being at Cocker's, had been deeply with the girl.

V

THIS was neither more nor less than the queer extension of her experience, the double life that, in the cage, she grew at last to lead. As the weeks went on there she lived more and more into the world of whiffs and glimpses, and found her divinations work faster and stretch further. It was a prodigious view as the pressure heightened, a panorama fed with facts and figures, flushed with a torrent of colour and accompanied with wondrous world-music. What it mainly came to at this period was a picture of how London could amuse itself; and that, with the running commentary of a witness so exclusively a witness, turned for the most part to a hardening of the heart. The nose of this observer was brushed by the bouquet, yet she could never really pluck even a daisy. What could still remain fresh in her daily grind was the immense disparity, the difference and contrast, from class to class, of every instant and every motion. There were times when all the wires in the country seemed to start from the little hole-and-corner where she plied for a livelihood, and where, in the shuffle of feet, the flutter of 'forms', the straying of stamps and the ring of change over the counter, the people she had fallen into the habit of remembering and fitting together with others, and of having her theories and interpretations of, kept up before her their long procession and rotation. What twisted the knife in her vitals was the way the profligate rich scattered about them, in extravagant chatter over their extravagant pleasures and sins, an amount of money that would have held the stricken household of her frightened childhood, her poor pinched mother and tormented father and lost brother and starved sister, together for a lifetime. During her first weeks she had often gasped at the sums people were willing to pay for the stuff they transmitted – the 'much love's, the 'awful' regrets, the compliments and wonderments and vain, vague gestures that cost the price of a new pair of boots. She had had a way then of glancing at the people's faces, but she had early learned that if you became a telegraphist you soon ceased to be astonished. Her eye for types amounted nevertheless to genius, and there were those she liked and those she hated, her feeling for the latter of which grew to a positive possession, an instinct of observation and detection. There were the brazen women, as she called them, of the higher and the lower fashion, whose squanderings and graspings, whose struggles and secrets and love-affairs and lies, she tracked and stored up against them, till she had at moments, in private, a triumphant, vicious feeling of mastery and power, a sense of having their silly, guilty secrets in her pocket, her small retentive brain, and thereby knowing so much more about them than they suspected or would care to think. There were those she would have liked to betray, to trip up, to bring down with words altered and fatal; and all through a personal hostility provoked by the lightest signs, by their accidents of tone and manner, by the particular kind of relation she always happened instantly to feel.

There were impulses of various kinds, alternately soft and severe, to which she was constitutionally accessible and which were determined by the smallest accidents. She was rigid, in general, on the article of making the public itself affix its stamps, and found a special enjoyment in dealing, to that end, with some of the ladies who were too grand to touch them. She had thus a play of refinement and subtlety greater, she flattered herself, than any of which she could be made the subject; and though most people were too stupid to be conscious of this, it brought her endless little consolations and revenges. She recognised quite as much those of her sex whom she would have liked to help, to warn, to rescue, to see more of; and that alternative as well operated exactly through the hazard of personal sympathy, her vision for silver threads and moonbeams and her gift for keeping the clues and finding her way in the tangle. The moonbeams and silver threads presented at moments all the vision of what poor *she* might have made of happiness. Blurred and blank as the whole thing often inevitably, or mercifully, became, she could still, through crevices and crannies, be stupefied, especially by what, in spite of all seasoning, touched the sorest place in her consciousness, the revelation of the golden shower flying about without a gleam of gold for herself. It remained prodigious to the end, the money her fine friends were able to spend to get still more, or even to complain to fine friends of their own that they were in want. The pleasures they proposed were equalled only by those they declined, and they made their appointments often so expensively that she was left wondering at the nature of the delights to which the mere approaches were so paved with shillings. She quivered on occasion into the perception of this and that one whom she would, at all events, have just simply liked to *be*. Her conceit, her baffled vanity were possibly monstrous; she certainly often threw herself into a defiant conviction that she would have done the whole thing much better. But her greatest comfort, on the whole, was her comparative vision of the men; by whom I mean the unmistakable gentlemen, for she had no interest in the spurious or the shabby, and no mercy at all for the poor. She could have found a sixpence, outside, for an appearance of want; but her fancy, in some directions so alert, had never a throb of response for any sign of the sordid. The men she did follow, moreover, she followed mainly in one relation, the relation as to which the cage convinced her, she believed, more than anything else could have done, that it was quite the most diffused.

She found her ladies, in short, almost always in communication with her gentlemen, and her gentlemen with her ladies, and she read into the immensity of their intercourse stories and meanings without end. Incontestably she grew to think that the men cut the best figure; and in this particular, as in many others, she arrived at a philosophy of her own, all made up of her private notations and cynicisms. It was a striking part of the business, for example, that it was much more the women, on the whole, who were after the men than the men who were after the women: it was literally visible that the general attitude of the one sex was that of the object pursued and defensive, apologetic and attenuating, while the light of her own nature helped her more or less to conclude as to the attitude of the other. Perhaps she herself a little even fell into the custom of pursuit in occasionally deviating only for gentlemen from her high rigour about the stamps. She had early in the day made up her mind, in fine, that they had the best manners; and if there were none of them she noticed when Captain Everard was there, there were plenty she could place and trace and name at other times, plenty who, with their way of being 'nice' to her, and of handling, as if their pockets were private tills, loose, mixed masses of silver and gold, were such pleasant appearances that she could envy them without dislike. *They* never had to give change – they only had to get it. They ranged through every suggestion, every shade of fortune, which evidently included indeed lots of bad luck as well as of good, declining even toward Mr Mudge and his bland, firm thrift, and ascending, in wild signals and rocket-flights, almost to within hail of her highest standard. So, from month to month, she went on with them all, through a thousand ups and downs and a thousand pangs and indifferences. What virtually happened was that in the shuffling herd that passed before her by far the greater part only passed – a proportion but just appreciable stayed. Most of the elements swam straight away, lost themselves in the bottomless common, and by so doing really kept the page clear. On the clearness, therefore, what she did retain stood sharply out; she nipped and caught it, turned it over and interwove it.

VI

SHE met Mrs Jordan whenever she could, and learned from her more and more how the great people, under her gentle shake, and after going through everything with the mere shops, were waking up to the gain of putting into the hands of a person of real refinement the question that the shop-people spoke of so vulgarly as that of the floral decorations. The regular dealers in these decorations were all very well; but there was a peculiar magic in the play of taste of a lady who had only to remember, through whatever intervening dusk, all her own little tables, little bowls and little jars and little other arrangements, and the wonderful thing she had made of the garden of the vicarage. This small domain, which her young friend had never seen, bloomed in Mrs Jordan's discourse like a new Eden, and she converted the past into a bank of violets by the tone in which she said, 'Of course you always knew my one passion!' She obviously met now, at any rate, a big contemporary need, measured what it was rapidly becoming for people to feel they could trust her without a tremor. It brought them a peace that – during the quarter of an hour before dinner in especial – was worth more to them than mere payment could express. Mere payment, none the less, was tolerably prompt; she engaged by the month, taking over the whole thing; and there was an evening on which, in respect to our heroine, she at last returned to the charge. 'It's growing and growing, and I see that I must really divide the work. One wants an associate – of one's own kind, don't you know? You know the look they want it all to have? – of having come, not from a florist, but from one of themselves. Well, I'm sure *you* could give it – because you *are* one. Then we *should* win. Therefore just come in with me.'

'And leave the P.O.?'

'Let the P.O. simply bring you your letters. It would bring you lots, you'd see: orders, after a bit, by the dozen.' It was on this, in due course, that the great advantage again came up: 'One seems to live again with one's own people.' It had taken some little time (after their having parted company in the tempest of their troubles and then, in the glimmering dawn, finally sighted each other again) for each to admit that the other was, in her private circle, her only equal; but the admission came, when it did come, with an honest groan; and since equality *was* named, each found much personal profit in exaggerating the other's original grandeur. Mrs Jordan was ten years the older, but her young friend was struck with the smaller difference this now made: it had counted otherwise at the time when, much more as a friend of her mother's, the bereaved lady, without a penny of provision, and with stop-gaps, like their own, all gone, had, across the sordid landing on which the opposite doors of the pair of scared miseries opened and to which they were bewilderedly bolted, borrowed coals and umbrellas that were repaid in potatoes and postage-stamps. It had been a questionable help, at that time, to ladies submerged, floundering, panting, swimming for their lives, that they *were* ladies; but such an advantage could come up again in proportion as others vanished, and it had grown very great by the time it was the only ghost of one they possessed. They had literally watched it take to itself a portion of the substance of each that had departed; and it became prodigious now, when they could talk of it together, when they could look back at it across a desert of accepted derogation, and when, above all, they could draw from each other a credulity about it that they could draw from no one else. Nothing was really so marked as that they felt the need to cultivate this legend much more after having found their feet and stayed their stomachs in the ultimate obscure than they had done in the upper air of mere frequent shocks. The thing they could now oftenest say to each other was that they knew what they meant; and the sentiment with which, all round, they knew it was known had been a kind of promise to stick well together again.

Mrs Jordan was at present fairly dazzling on the subject of the way that, in the practice of her beautiful art, she more than peeped in – she penetrated. There was not a house of the great kind – and it was, of course, only a question of those, real homes of luxury – in which she was not, at the rate such people now had things, all over the place. The girl felt before the picture the cold breath of disinheritance as much as she had ever felt it in the cage; she knew, moreover, how much she betrayed this, for the experience of poverty had begun, in her life, too early, and her ignorance of the requirements of homes of luxury had grown, with other active knowledge, a depth of simplification. She had accordingly at first often found that in these colloquies she could only pretend she understood. Educated as she had rapidly been by her chances at Cocker's, there were still strange gaps in her learning – she could never, like Mrs Jordan, have found her way about one of the 'homes'. Little by little, however, she had caught on, above all in the light of what Mrs Jordan's redemption had materially made of that lady, giving her, though the years and the struggles had naturally not straightened a feature, an almost super-eminent air. There were women in and out of Cocker's who were quite nice and who yet didn't look well; whereas Mrs Jordan looked well and yet, with her extraordinarily protrusive teeth, was by no means quite nice. It would seem, mystifyingly, that it might really come from all the greatness she could live with. It was fine to hear her talk so often of dinners of twenty and of her doing, as she said, exactly as she liked with them. She spoke as if, for that matter, she invited the company. 'They simply *give* me the table – all the rest, all the other effects, come afterwards.'

VII

'THEN you *do* see them?' the girl again asked.

Mrs Jordan hesitated, and indeed the point had been ambiguous before. 'Do you mean the guests?'

Her young friend, cautious about an undue exposure of innocence, was not quite sure. 'Well – the people who live there.'

'Lady Ventnor? Mrs Bubb? Lord Rye? Dear, yes. Why, they *like* one.'

'But does one personally *know* them?' our young lady went on, since that was the way to speak. 'I mean socially, don't you know? – as you know *me*.'

'They're not so nice as you!' Mrs Jordan charmingly cried. 'But I *shall* see more and more of them.'

Ah, this was the old story. 'But how soon?'

'Why, almost any day. Of course,' Mrs Jordan honestly added, 'they're nearly always out.'

'Then why do they want flowers all over?'

'Oh, that doesn't make any difference.' Mrs Jordan was not philosophic; she was only evidently determined it shouldn't make any. 'They're awfully interested in my ideas, and it's inevitable they should meet me over them.'

Her interlocutress was sturdy enough. 'What do you call your ideas?'

Mrs Jordan's reply was fine. 'If you were to see me some day with a thousand tulips, you'd soon discover.'

'A thousand?' – the girl gaped at such a revelation of the scale of it; she felt, for the instant, fairly planted out. 'Well, but if in fact they never do meet you?' she none the less pessimistically insisted.

'Never? They *often* do – and evidently quite on purpose. We have grand long talks.'

There was something in our young lady that could still stay her from asking for a personal description of these apparitions; that showed too starved a state. But while she considered, she took in afresh the whole of the clergyman's widow. Mrs Jordan couldn't help her teeth, and her sleeves were a distinct rise in the world. A thousand tulips at a shilling clearly took one further than a thousand words at a penny; and the betrothed of Mr Mudge, in whom the sense of the race for life was always acute, found herself wondering, with a twinge of her easy jealousy, if it mightn't after all then, for *her* also, be better – better than where she was – to follow some such scent. Where she was was where Mr Buckton's elbow could freely enter her right side and the counter-clerk's breathing – he had something the matter with his nose – pervade her left ear. It was something to fill an office under Government, and she knew but too well there were places commoner still than Cocker's; but it never required much of a chance to bring back to her the picture of servitude and promiscuity that she must present to the eye of comparative freedom. She was so boxed up with her young men, and anything like a margin so absent, that it needed more art than she should ever possess to pretend in the least to compass, with any one in the nature of an acquaintance – say with Mrs Jordan herself, flying in, as it might happen, to wire sympathetically to Mrs Bubb – an approach to a relation of elegant privacy. She remembered the day when Mrs Jordan *had*, in fact, by the greatest chance, come in with fifty-three words for Lord Rye and a five-pound note to change. This had been the dramatic manner of their reunion – their mutual recognition was so great an event. The girl could at first only see her from the waist up, besides making but little of her long telegram to his lordship. It was a strange whirligig that had converted the clergyman's widow into such a specimen of the class that went beyond the sixpence.

Nothing of the occasion, all the more, had ever become dim; least of all the way that, as her recovered friend looked up from counting, Mrs Jordan had just blown, in explanation, through her teeth and through the bars of the cage: 'I *do* flowers, you know.' Our young woman had always, with her little finger crooked out, a pretty movement for counting; and she had not forgotten the small secret advantage, a sharpness of triumph it might even have been called, that fell upon her at this moment and avenged her for the incoherence of the message, an unintelligible enumeration of numbers, colours, days, hours. The correspondence of people she didn't know was one thing; but the correspondence of people she did had an aspect of its own for her, even when she couldn't understand it. The speech in which Mrs Jordan had defined a position and announced a profession was like a tinkle of bluebells; but, for herself, her one idea about flowers was that people had them at funerals, and her present sole gleam of light was that lords probably had them most. When she watched, a minute later, through the cage, the swing of her visitor's departing petticoats, she saw the sight from the waist down; and when the counter-clerk, after a mere male glance, remarked, with an intention unmistakably low, 'Handsome woman!' she had for him the finest of her chills: 'She's the widow of a bishop.' She always felt, with the counter-clerk, that it was impossible sufficiently to put it on; for what she wished to express to him was the maximum of her contempt, and that element in her nature was confusedly stored. 'A bishop' *was* putting it on, but the counter-clerk's approaches were vile. The night, after this, when, in the fulness of time, Mrs Jordan mentioned the grand long talks, the girl at last brought out: 'Should *I* see them? – I mean if I *were* to give up everything for you.'

Mrs Jordan at this became most arch. 'I'd send you to all the bachelors!'

Our young lady could be reminded by such a remark that she usually struck her friend as pretty. 'Do *they* have their flowers?'

'Oceans. And they're the most particular.' Oh, it was a wonderful world. 'You should see Lord Rye's.'

'His flowers?'

'Yes, and his letters. He writes me pages on pages – with the most adorable little drawings and plans. You should see his diagrams!'

VIII

THE girl had in course of time every opportunity to inspect these documents, and they a little disappointed her; but in the meanwhile there had been more talk, and it had led to her saying, as if her friend's guarantee of a life of elegance were not quite definite: 'Well, I see every one at *my* place.'

'Every one?'

'Lots of swells. They flock. They live, you know, all round, and the place is filled with all the smart people, all the fast people, those whose names are in the papers – mamma has still the *Morning Post* – and who come up for the season.'

Mrs Jordan took this in with complete intelligence. 'Yes, and I daresay it's some of your people that *I* do.'

Her companion assented, but discriminated. 'I doubt if you "do" them as much as I! Their affairs, their appointments and arrangements, their little games and secrets and vices – those things all pass before me.'

This was a picture that could impose on a clergyman's widow a certain strain; it was in intention, moreover, something of a retort to the thousand tulips. 'Their vices? Have they got vices?'

Our young critic even more remarkably stared; then with a touch of contempt in her amusement: 'Haven't you found *that* out?' The homes of luxury, then, hadn't so much to give. '*I* find out everything,' she continued.

Mrs Jordan, at bottom a very meek person, was visibly struck. 'I see. You do "have" them.'

'Oh, I don't care! Much good does it do me!'

Mrs Jordan, after an instant, recovered her superiority. 'No – it doesn't lead to much.' Her own initiations so clearly did. Still – after all; and she was not jealous; 'There must be a charm.'

'In seeing them?' At this the girl suddenly let herself go. 'I hate them; there's that charm!'

Mrs Jordan gaped again. 'The *real* "smarts"?'

'Is that what you call Mrs Bubb? Yes – it comes to me; I've had Mrs Bubb. I don't think she has been in herself, but there are things her maid has brought. Well, my dear!' – and the young person from Cocker's, recalling these things and summing them up, seemed suddenly to have much to say. But she didn't say it; she checked it; she only brought out: 'Her maid, who's horrid – *she* must have her!' Then she went on with indifference: 'They're *too* real! They're selfish brutes.'

Mrs Jordan, turning it over, adopted at last the plan of treating it with a smile. She wished to be liberal. 'Well, of course, they do lay it out.'

'They bore me to death,' her companion pursued with slightly more temperance.

But this was going too far. 'Ah, that's because you've no sympathy!'

The girl gave an ironic laugh, only retorting that she wouldn't have any either if she had to count all day all the words in the dictionary; a contention Mrs Jordan quite granted, the more that she shuddered at the notion of ever failing of the very gift to which she owed the vogue – the rage she might call it – that had caught her up. Without sympathy – or without imagination, for it came back again to that – how should she get, for big dinners, down the middle and toward the far corners at all? It wasn't the combinations, which were easily managed: the strain was over the ineffable simplicities, those that the bachelors above all, and Lord Rye perhaps most of any, threw off – just blew off, like cigarette-puffs – such sketches of. The betrothed of Mr Mudge at all events accepted the explanation, which had the effect, as almost any turn of their talk was now apt to have, of bringing her round to the terrific question of that gentleman. She was tormented with the desire to get out of Mrs Jordan, on this subject, what she was sure was at the back of Mrs Jordan's head; and to get it out of her, queerly enough, if only to vent a certain irritation at it. She knew that what her friend would already have risked if she had not been timid and

tortuous was: 'Give him up – yes, give him up: you'll see that
with your sure chances you'll be able to do much better.'

Our young woman had a sense that if that view could only be
put before her with a particular sniff for poor Mr Mudge she
should hate it as much as she morally ought. She was conscious
of not, as yet, hating it quite so much as that. But she saw that
Mrs Jordan was conscious of something too, and that there was
a sort of assurance she was waiting little by little to gather. The
day came when the girl caught a glimpse of what was still
wanting to make her friend feel strong; which was nothing
less than the prospect of being able to announce the climax of
sundry private dreams. The associate of the aristocracy had
personal calculations – she pored over them in her lonely
lodgings. If she did the flowers for the bachelors, in short,
didn't she expect that to have consequences very different
from the outlook, at Cocker's, that she had described as leading
to nothing? There seemed in very truth something auspicious
in the mixture of bachelors and flowers, though, when looked
hard in the eye, Mrs Jordan was not quite prepared to say she
had expected a positive proposal from Lord Rye to pop out of it.
Our young woman arrived at last, none the less, at a definite
vision of what was in her mind. This was a vivid foreknowledge
that the betrothed of Mr Mudge would, unless conciliated in
advance by a successful rescue, almost hate her on the day she
should break a particular piece of news. How could that unfortunate otherwise endure to hear of what, under the protection of Lady Ventnor, was after all so possible?

IX

MEANWHILE, since irritation sometimes relieved her, the
betrothed of Mr Mudge drew straight from that admirer an
amount of it that was proportioned to her fidelity. She always
walked with him on Sundays, usually in the Regent's Park, and
quite often, once or twice a month, he took her, in the Strand or
thereabouts, to see a piece that was having a run. The produc-
tions he always preferred were the really good ones – Shakespeare, Thompson, or some funny American thing; which, as it

also happened that she hated vulgar plays, gave him ground for what was almost the fondest of his approaches, the theory that their tastes were, blissfully, just the same. He was for ever reminding her of that, rejoicing over it, and being affectionate and wise about it. There were times when she wondered how in the world she could bear him, how she could bear any man so smugly unconscious of the immensity of her difference. It was just for this difference that, if she was to be liked at all, she wanted to be liked, and if that was not the source of Mr Mudge's admiration, she asked herself, what on earth *could* be? She was not different only at one point, she was different all round; unless perhaps indeed in being practically human, which her mind just barely recognised that he also was. She would have made tremendous concessions in other quarters: there was no limit, for instance, to those she would have made to Captain Everard; but what I have named was the most she was prepared to do for Mr Mudge. It was because *he* was different that, in the oddest way, she liked as well as deplored him; which was after all a proof that the disparity, should they frankly recognise it, wouldn't necessarily be fatal. She felt that, oleaginous – too oleaginous – as he was, he was somehow comparatively primitive: she had once, during the portion of his time at Cocker's that had overlapped her own, seen him collar a drunken soldier, a big, violent man, who, having come in with a mate to get a postal-order cashed, had made a grab at the money before his friend could reach it and had so produced, among the hams and cheeses and the lodgers from Thrupp's, reprisals instantly ensuing, a scene of scandal and consternation. Mr Buckton and the counter-clerk had crouched within the cage, but Mr Mudge had, with a very quiet but very quick step round the counter, triumphantly interposed in the scrimmage, parted the combatants, and shaken the delinquent in his skin. She had been proud of him at that moment, and had felt that if their affair had not already been settled the neatness of his execution would have left her without resistance.

Their affair had been settled by other things: by the evident sincerity of his passion and by the sense that his high white apron resembled a front of many floors. It had gone a great way

with her that he would build up a business to his chin, which he
carried quite in the air. This could only be a question of time; he
would have all Piccadilly in the pen behind his ear. That was a
merit in itself for a girl who had known what she had known.
There were hours at which she even found him good-looking,
though, frankly, there could be no crown for her effort to
imagine, on the part of the tailor or the barber, some such
treatment of his appearance as would make him resemble
even remotely a gentleman. His very beauty was the beauty of
a grocer, and the finest future would offer it none too much
room to expand. She had engaged herself, in short, to the
perfection of a type, and perfection of anything was much for
a person who, out of early troubles, had just escaped with her
life. But it contributed hugely at present to carry on the two
parallel lines of her contacts in the cage and her contacts out of
it. After keeping quiet for some time about this opposition, she
suddenly – one Sunday afternoon on a penny chair in the
Regent's Park – broke, for him, capriciously, bewilderingly,
into an intimation of what it came to. He naturally pressed
more and more on the subject of her again placing herself
where he could see her hourly, and for her to recognise that as
she had as yet given him no sane reason for delay she had no
need to hear him say that he couldn't make out what she was up
to. As if, with her absurd bad reasons, she knew it herself!
Sometimes she thought it would be amusing to let him have
them full in the face, for she felt she should die of him unless she
once in a while stupefied him; and sometimes she thought it
would be disgusting and perhaps even fatal. She liked him,
however, to think her silly, for that gave her the margin which,
at the best, she would always require; and the only difficulty
about this was that he hadn't enough imagination to oblige her.
It produced, none the less, something of the desired effect – to
leave him simply wondering why, over the matter of their
reunion, she didn't yield to his arguments. Then at last, simply
as if by accident and out of mere boredom on a day that was
rather flat, she preposterously produced her own. 'Well, wait a
bit. Where I am I still see things.' And she talked to him even
worse, if possible, than she had talked to Mrs Jordan.

Little by little, to her own stupefaction, she caught that he was trying to take it as she meant it, and that he was neither astonished nor angry. Oh, the British tradesman – this gave her an idea of his resources! Mr Mudge would be angry only with a person who, like the drunken soldier in the shop, should have an unfavourable effect upon business. He seemed positively to enter, for the time and without the faintest flash of irony or ripple of laughter, into the whimsical grounds of her enjoyment of Cocker's custom, and instantly to be casting up whatever it might, as Mrs Jordan had said, lead to. What he had in mind was not, of course, what Mrs Jordan had had: it was obviously not a source of speculation with him that his sweetheart might pick up a husband. She could see perfectly that this was not, for a moment, even what he supposed she herself dreamed of. What she had done was simply to give his fancy another push into the dim vast of trade. In that direction it was all alert, and she had whisked before it the mild fragrance of a 'connection'. That was the most he could see in any picture of her keeping in with the gentry; and when, getting to the bottom of this, she quickly proceeded to show him the kind of eye she turned on such people and to give him a sketch of what that eye discovered, she reduced him to the particular confusion in which he could still be amusing to her.

X

'THEY´RE the most awful wretches, I assure you – the lot all about there.'

'Then why do you want to stay among them?'

'My dear man, just because they *are*. It makes me hate them so.'

'Hate them? I thought you liked them.'

'Don't be stupid. What I "like" is just to loathe them. You wouldn't believe what passes before my eyes.'

'Then why have you never told me? You didn't mention anything before I left.'

'Oh, I hadn't got into it then. It's the sort of thing you don't believe at first; you have to look round you a bit and then you understand. You work into it more and more. Besides,' the girl went on, 'this is the time of the year when the worst lot come up. They're simply packed together in those smart streets. Talk of the numbers of the poor! What *I* can vouch for is the numbers of the rich! There are new ones every day, and they seem to get richer and richer. Oh, they do come up!' she cried, imitating, for her private recreation – she was sure it wouldn't reach Mr Mudge – the low intonation of the counter-clerk.

'And where do they come from?' her companion candidly inquired.

She had to think a moment; then she found something. 'From the "spring meetings". They bet tremendously.'

'Well, they bet enough at Chalk Farm, if that's all.'

'It *isn't* all. It isn't a millionth part!' she replied with some sharpness. 'It's immense fun' – she would tantalise him. Then, as she had heard Mrs Jordan say, and as the ladies at Cocker's even sometimes wired, 'It's quite too dreadful!' She could fully feel how it was Mr Mudge's propriety, which was extreme – he had a horror of coarseness and attended a Wesleyan chapel – that prevented his asking for details. But she gave him some of the more innocuous in spite of himself, especially putting before him how, at Simpkin's and Ladle's, they all made the money fly. That was indeed what he liked to hear: the connection was not direct, but one was somehow more in the right place where the money was flying than where it was simply and meagrely nesting. It enlivened the air, he had to acknowledge, much less at Chalk Farm than in the district in which his beloved so oddly enjoyed her footing. She gave him, she could see, a restless sense that these might be familiarities not to be sacrificed; germs, possibilities, faint foreshowings – heaven knew what – of the initiation it would prove profitable to have arrived at when, in the fulness of time, he should have his own shop in some such paradise. What really touched him – that was discernible – was that she could feed him with so much mere vividness of reminder, keep before him, as by the play of a fan, the very wind of the swift bank-notes and the charm of the existence of a class that Providence had raised up to be the blessing of grocers. He liked to think that the class was there, that it was always there, and that she contributed in her slight but appreciable degree to keep it up to the mark. He couldn't have formulated his theory of the matter, but the exuberance of the aristocracy was the advantage of trade, and everything was knit together in a richness of pattern that it was good to follow with one's finger-tips. It was a comfort to him to be thus assured that there were no symptoms of a drop. What did the sounder, as she called it, nimbly worked, do but keep the ball going?

What it came to, therefore, for Mr Mudge, was that all enjoyments were, in short, interrelated, and that the more people had the more they wanted to have. The more flirtations, as he might roughly express it, the more cheese and pickles. He had even in his own small way been dimly struck with the concatenation between the tender passion and cheap champagne. What he would have liked to say had he been able to work out his thought to the end was: 'I see, I see. Lash them up then, lead them on, keep them going: some of it can't help, some time, coming *our* way.' Yet he was troubled by the suspicion of subtleties on his companion's part that spoiled the straight view. He couldn't understand people's hating what they liked or liking what they hated; above all it hurt him somewhere – for he had his private delicacies – to see anything *but* money made out of his betters. To be curious at the expense of the gentry was vaguely wrong; the only thing that was distinctly right was to be prosperous. Wasn't it just because they were up there aloft that they were lucrative? He concluded, at any rate, by saying to his young friend: 'If it's improper for you to remain at Cocker's, then that falls in exactly with the other reasons that I have put before you for your removal.'

'Improper?' – her smile became a long, wide look at him. 'My dear boy, there's no one like you!'

'I daresay,' he laughed; 'but that doesn't help the question.'

'Well,' she returned, 'I can't give up my friends. I'm making even more than Mrs Jordan.'

Mr Mudge considered. 'How much is *she* making?'

'Oh, you dear donkey!' – and, regardless of all the Regent's Park, she patted his cheek. This was the sort of moment at which she was absolutely tempted to tell him that she liked to be near Park Chambers. There was a fascination in the idea of seeing if, on a mention of Captain Everard, he wouldn't do what she thought he might; wouldn't weigh against the obvious objection the still more obvious advantage. The advantage, of course, could only strike him at the best as rather fantastic; but it was always to the good to keep hold when you *had* hold, and such an attitude would also after all involve a high tribute to her fidelity. Of one thing she absolutely never doubted: Mr Mudge believed in her with a belief—! She believed in herself too, for that matter: if there was a thing in the world no one could charge her with, it was being the kind of low barmaid person who rinsed tumblers and bandied slang. But she forbore as yet to speak; she had not spoken even to Mrs Jordan; and the hush that on her lips surrounded the Captain's name maintained itself as a kind of symbol of the success that, up to this time, had attended something or other – she couldn't have said what – that she humoured herself with calling, without words, her relation with him.

XI

SHE would have admitted indeed that it consisted of little more than the fact that his absences, however frequent and however long, always ended with his turning up again. It was nobody's business in the world but her own if that fact continued to be enough for her. It was of course not enough just in itself; what it had taken on to make it so was the extraordinary possession of the elements of his life that memory and attention had at last given her. There came a day when this possession, on the girl's part, actually seemed to enjoy, between them, while their eyes met, a tacit recognition that was half a joke and half a deep solemnity. He bade her good morning always now; he often quite raised his hat to her. He passed a remark when there was time or room, and once she went so far as to say to him that she had not seen him for 'ages'. 'Ages' was the word she consciously and carefully, though a trifle tremulously, used; 'ages' was exactly what she meant. To this he replied in terms doubtless less anxiously selected, but perhaps on that account not the less remarkable, 'Oh yes, hasn't it been awfully wet?' That was a specimen of their give and take; it fed her fancy that no form of intercourse so transcendent and distilled had ever been established on earth. Everything, so far as they chose to consider it so, might mean almost anything. The want of margin in the cage, when he peeped through the bars, wholly ceased to be appreciable. It was a drawback only in superficial commerce. With Captain Everard she had simply the margin of the universe. It may be imagined, therefore, how their unuttered reference to all she knew about him could, in this immensity, play at its ease. Every time he handed in a telegram it was an addition to her knowledge: what did his constant smile mean to mark if it didn't mean to mark that? He never came into the place without saying to her in this manner: 'Oh yes, you have me by this time so completely at your mercy that it doesn't in the least matter what I give you now. You've become a comfort, I assure you!'

She had only two torments; the greatest of which was that she couldn't, not even once or twice, touch with him on some individual fact. She would have given anything to have been able to allude to one of his friends by name, to one of his engagements by date, to one of his difficulties by the solution. She would have given almost as much for just the right chance – it would have to be tremendously right – to show him in some sharp, sweet way that she had perfectly penetrated the greatest of these last and now lived with it in a kind of heroism of sympathy. He was in love with a woman to whom, and to any view of whom, a lady-telegraphist, and especially one who passed a life among hams and cheeses, was as the sand on the floor; and what her dreams desired was the possibility of its somehow coming to him that her own interest in him could take a pure and noble account of such an infatuation and even of such an impropriety. As yet, however, she could only rub along with the hope that an accident, sooner or later, might give her a lift toward popping out with something that would surprise and perhaps even, some fine day, assist him. What could people mean, moreover – cheaply sarcastic people – by not feeling all that could be got out of the weather? *She* felt it all, and seemed literally to feel it most when she went quite wrong, speaking of the stuffy days as cold, of the cold ones as stuffy, and betraying how little she knew, in her cage, of whether it was foul or fair. It was, for that matter, always stuffy at Cocker's, and she finally settled down to the safe proposition that the outside element was 'changeable'. Anything seemed true that made him so radiantly assent.

This indeed is a small specimen of her cultivation of insidious ways of making things easy for him – ways to which of course she couldn't be at all sure that he did real justice. Real justice was not of this world: she had had too often to come back to that; yet, strangely, happiness was, and her traps had to be set for it in a manner to keep them unperceived by Mr Buckton and the counter-clerk. The most she could hope for apart from the question, which constantly flickered up and died down, of the divine chance of his consciously liking her, would be that, without analysing it, he should arrive at a vague sense that Cocker's was – well, attractive; easier, smoother, sociably brighter, slightly more picturesque, in short more propitious in general to his little affairs, than any other establishment just thereabouts. She was quite aware that they couldn't be, in so huddled a hole, particularly quick; but she found her account in the slowness – she certainly could bear it if *he* could. The great pang was that, just thereabouts, post-offices were so awfully thick. She was always seeing him, in imagination, in other places and with other girls. But she would defy any other girl to follow him as she followed. And though they weren't, for so many reasons, quick at Cocker's, she could hurry for him when, through an intimation light as air, she gathered that he was pressed.

When hurry was, better still, impossible, it was because of the pleasantest thing of all, the particular element of their contact – she would have called it their friendship – that consisted of an almost humorous treatment of the look of some of his words. They would never perhaps have grown half so intimate if he had not, by the blessing of heaven, formed some of his letters with a queerness—! It was positive that the queerness could scarce have been greater if he had practised it for the very purpose of bringing their heads together over it as far as was possible to heads on different sides of a cage. It had taken her in reality but once or twice to master these tricks, but, at the cost of striking him perhaps as stupid, she could still challenge them when circumstances favoured. The great circumstance that favoured was that she sometimes actually believed he knew she only feigned perplexity. If he knew it, therefore, he tolerated it; if he tolerated it he came back; and if he came back he liked her. This was her seventh heaven; and she didn't ask much of his liking – she only asked of it to reach the point of his not going away because of her own. He had at times to be away for weeks; he had to lead his life; he had to travel – there were places to which he was constantly wiring for 'rooms': all this she granted him, forgave him; in fact, in the long-run, literally blessed and thanked him for. If he had to lead his life, that precisely fostered his leading it so much by telegraph: therefore the benediction was to come in when he could. That was all she asked – that he shouldn't wholly deprive her.

Sometimes she almost felt that he couldn't have done so even had he been minded, on account of the web of revelation that was woven between them. She quite thrilled herself with thinking what, with such a lot of material, a bad girl would do. It would be a scene better than many in her ha'penny novels, this going to him in the dusk of evening at Park Chambers and letting him at last have it. 'I know too much about a certain person now not to put it to you – excuse my being so lurid – that it's quite worth your while to buy me off. Come, therefore; buy me!' There was a point indeed at which such flights had to drop again – the point of an unreadiness to name, when it came to that, the purchasing medium. It wouldn't, certainly, be any-thing so gross as money, and the matter accordingly remained rather vague, all the more that *she* was not a bad girl. It was not for any such reason as might have aggravated a mere minx that she often hoped he would again bring Cissy. The difficulty of this, however, was constantly present to her, for the kind of communion to which Cocker's so richly ministered rested on the fact that Cissy and he were so often in different places. She knew by this time all the places – Suchbury, Monkhouse, Whiteroy, Finches, – and even how the parties, on these occasions, were composed; but her subtlety found ways to make her knowledge fairly protect and promote their keeping, as she had heard Mrs Jordan say, in touch. So, when he actually sometimes smiled as if he really felt the awkwardness of giving her again one of the same old addresses, all her being went out in the desire – which her face must have expressed – that he should recognise her forbearance to criticise as one of the finest, tenderest sacrifices a woman had ever made for love.

XII

SHE was occasionally worried, all the same, by the impression that these sacrifices, great as they were, were nothing to those that his own passion had imposed; if indeed it was not rather the passion of his confederate, which had caught him up and was whirling him round like a great steam-wheel. He was at any rate in the strong grip of a dizzy, splendid fate; the wild wind of his life blew him straight before it. Didn't she catch in his face, at times, even through his smile and his happy habit, the gleam of that pale glare with which a bewildered victim appeals, as he passes, to some pair of pitying eyes? He perhaps didn't even himself know how scared he was; but *she* knew. They were in danger, they were in danger, Captain Everard and Lady Bradeen: it beat every novel in the shop. She thought of Mr Mudge and his safe sentiment; she thought of herself and blushed even more for her tepid response to it. It was a comfort to her at such moments to feel that in another relation – a relation supplying that affinity with her nature that Mr Mudge, deluded creature, would never supply – she should have been no more tepid than her ladyship. Her deepest sound- ings were on two or three occasions of finding herself almost sure that, if she dared, her ladyship's lover would have gathered relief from 'speaking' to her. She literally fancied once or twice that, projected as he was toward his doom, her own eyes struck him, while the air roared in his ears, as the one pitying pair in the crowd. But how could he speak to her while she sat sand-wiched there between the counter-clerk and the sounder?

She had long ago, in her comings and goings, made acquaintance with Park Chambers, and reflected, as she looked up at their luxurious front, that *they*, of course, would supply the ideal setting for the ideal speech. There was not a picture in London that, before the season was over, was more stamped upon her brain. She went round about to pass it, for it was not on the short way; she passed on the opposite side of the street and always looked up, though it had taken her a long time to be sure of the particular set of windows. She had made that out at last by an act of audacity that, at the time, had almost stopped her heart-beats and that, in retrospect, greatly quickened her blushes. One evening, late, she had lingered and watched – watched for some moment when the porter, who was in uni-form and often on the steps, had gone in with a visitor. Then she followed boldly, on the calculation that he would have taken the visitor up and that the hall would be free. The hall *was* free, and the electric light played over the gilded and lettered board that showed the names and numbers of the occupants of the different floors. What she wanted looked straight at her – Captain Everard was on the third. It was as if, in the immense intimacy of this, they were, for the instant and the first time, face to face outside the cage. Alas! they were face to face but a second or two: she was whirled out on the wings of a panic fear that he might just then be entering or issuing. This fear was indeed, in her shameless deflections, never very far from her, and was mixed in the oddest way with depressions and disappointments. It was dreadful, as she trembled by, to run the risk of looking to him as if she basely hung about; and yet it was dreadful to be obliged to pass only at such moments as put an encounter out of the question.

At the horrible hour of her first coming to Cocker's he was always – it was to be hoped – snug in bed; and at the hour of her final departure he was of course – she had such things all on her fingers'-ends – dressing for dinner. We may let it pass that if she could not bring herself to hover till he was dressed, this was simply because such a process for such a person could only be terribly prolonged. When she went in the middle of the day to her own dinner she had too little time to do anything but go straight, thought it must be added that for a real certainty she would joyously have omitted the repast. She had made up her mind as to there being on the whole no decent pretext to justify her flitting casually past at three o'clock in the morning. That was the hour at which, if the ha'penny novels were not all wrong, he probably came home for the night. She was therefore reduced to merely picturing that miraculous meeting toward which a hundred impossibilities would have to conspire. But if nothing was more impossible than the fact, nothing was more intense than the vision. What may not, we can only moralise, take place in the quickened, muffled perception of a girl of a certain kind of soul? All our young friend's native distinction, her refinement of personal grain, of heredity, of pride, took refuge in this small throbbing spot; for when she was most conscious of the abjection of her vanity and the pitifulness of her little flutters and manoeuvres, then the consolation and the redemption were most sure to shine before her in some just discernible sign. He did like her!

XIII

HE never brought Cissy back, but Cissy came one day without him, as fresh as before from the hands of Marguerite, or only, at the season's end, a trifle less fresh. She was, however, distinctly less serene. She had brought nothing with her, and looked about with some impatience for the forms and the place to write. The latter convenience, at Cocker's, was obscure and barely adequate, and her clear voice had the light note of disgust which her lover's never showed as she responded with a 'There?' of surprise to the gesture made by the counter-clerk in answer to her sharp inquiry. Our young friend was busy with half a dozen people, but she had despatched them in her most business-like manner by the time her ladyship flung through the bars the light of reappearance. Then the directness with which the girl managed to receive this missive was the result of the concentration that had caused her to make the stamps fly during the few minutes occupied by the production of it. This concentration, in turn, may be described as the effect of the apprehension of imminent relief. It was nineteen days, counted and checked off, since she had seen the object of her homage; and as, had he been in London, she should, with his habits, have been sure to see him often, she was now about to learn what other spot his presence might just then happen to sanctify. For she thought of them, the other spots, as ecstatically conscious of it, expressively happy in it.

But, gracious, how handsome *was* her ladyship, and what an added price it gave him that the air of intimacy he threw out should have flowed originally from such a source! The girl looked straight through the cage at the eyes and lips that must so often have been so near his own – looked at them with a strange passion that, for an instant, had the result of filling out some of the gaps, supplying the missing answers, in his correspondence. Then, as she made out that the features she thus scanned and associated were totally unaware of it, that they glowed only with the colour of quite other and not at all guessable thoughts, this directly added to their splendour, gave the girl the sharpest impression she had yet received of the uplifted, the unattainable plains of heaven, and yet at the same time caused her to thrill with a sense of the high company she did somehow keep. She was with the absent through her ladyship and with her ladyship through the absent. The only pang – but it didn't matter – was the proof in the admirable face, in the sightless preoccupation of its possessor, that the latter hadn't a notion of her. Her folly had gone to the point of half believing that the other party to the affair must sometimes mention in Eaton Square the extraordinary little person at the place from which he so often wired. Yet the perception of her visitor's blankness actually helped this extraordinary little person, the next instant, to take refuge in a reflection that could be as proud as it liked. 'How little she knows, how little she knows!' the girl cried to herself; for what did that show after all but that Captain Everard's telegraphic confidant was Captain Everard's charming secret? Our young friend's perusal of her ladyship's telegram was literally prolonged by a momentary daze: what swam between her and the words, making her see them as through rippled, shallow, sunshot water, was the great, the perpetual flood of 'How much *I* know – how much *I* know!' This produced a delay in her catching that, on the face, these words didn't give her what she wanted, though she was prompt enough with her remembrance that her grasp was, half the time, just of what was *not* on the face. 'Miss Dolman, Parade Lodge, Parade Terrace, Dover. Let him instantly know right one, Hôtel de France, Ostend. Make it seven nine four nine six one. Wire me alternative Burfield's.'

The girl slowly counted. Then he was at Ostend. This hooked on with so sharp a click that, not to feel she was as quickly letting it all slip from her, she had absolutely to hold it a minute longer and to do something to that end. Thus it was that she did on this occasion what she never did – threw off an 'Answer paid?' that sounded officious, but that she partly made up for by deliberately affixing the stamps and by waiting till she had done so to give change. She had, for so much coolness, the strength that she considered she knew all about Miss Dolman.

'Yes – paid.' She saw all sorts of things in this reply, even to a small, suppressed start of surprise at so correct an assumption; even to an attempt, the next minute, at a fresh air of detachment. 'How much, with the answer?' The calculation was not abstruse, but our intense observer required a moment more to make it, and this gave her ladyship time for a second thought. 'Oh, just wait!' The white, begemmed hand bared to write rose in sudden nervousness to the side of the wonderful face which, with eyes of anxiety for the paper on the counter, she brought closer to the bars of the cage. 'I think I must alter a word!' On this she recovered her telegram and looked over it again; but she had a new, obvious trouble, and studied it without deciding and with much of the effect of making our young woman watch her.

This personage, meanwhile, at the sight of her expression, had decided on the spot. If she had always been sure they were in danger, her ladyship's expression was the best possible sign of it. There was a word wrong, but she had lost the right one, and much, clearly, depended on her finding it again. The girl, therefore, sufficiently estimating the affluence of customers and the distraction of Mr Buckton and the counter-clerk, took the jump and gave it. 'Isn't it Cooper's?'

It was as if she had bodily leaped – cleared the top of the cage and alighted on her interlocutress. 'Cooper's?' – the stare was heightened by a blush. Yes, she had made Juno blush.

This was all the more reason for going on. 'I mean instead of Burfield's.'

Our young friend fairly pitied her; she had made her in an instant so helpless, and yet not a bit haughty nor outraged. She was only mystified and scared. 'Oh, you know—?'

'Yes, I know!' Our young friend smiled, meeting the other's eyes, and, having made Juno blush, proceeded to patronise her. '*I'll* do it' – she put out a competent hand. Her ladyship only submitted, confused and bewildered, all presence of mind quite gone; and the next moment the telegram was in the cage again and its author out of the shop. Then quickly, boldly, under all the eyes that might have witnessed her tampering, the extraordinary little person at Cocker's made the proper change. People were really too giddy, and if they *were*, in a certain case, to be caught, it shouldn't be the fault of her own grand memory. Hadn't it been settled weeks before? – for Miss Dolman it was always to be 'Cooper's'.

XIV

BUT the summer 'holidays' brought a marked difference; they were holidays for almost everyone but the animals in the cage. The August days were flat and dry, and, with so little to feed it, she was conscious of the ebb of her interest in the secrets of the refined. She was in a position to follow the refined to the extent of knowing – they had made so many of their arrangements with her aid – exactly where they were; yet she felt quite as if the panorama had ceased unrolling and the band stopped playing. A stray member of the latter occasionally turned up, but the communications that passed before her bore now largely on rooms at hotels, prices of furnished houses, hours of trains,

dates of sailings and arrangements for being 'met': she found
them for the most part prosaic and coarse. The only thing was
that they brought into her stuffy corner as straight a whiff of
Alpine meadows and Scotch moors as she might hope ever to
inhale; there were moreover, in especial, fat, hot, dull ladies
who had out with her, to exasperation, the terms for seaside
lodgings, which struck her as huge, and the matter of the
number of beds required, which was not less portentous: this
in reference to places of which the names – Eastbourne,
Folkestone, Cromer, Scarborough, Whitby – tormented her
with something of the sound of the plash of water that haunts
the traveller in the desert. She had not been out of London for a
dozen years, and the only thing to give a taste to the present
dead weeks was the spice of a chronic resentment. The sparse
customers, the people she did see, were the people who were
'just off' – off on the decks of fluttered yachts, off to the uttermost point of rocky headlands where the very breeze was then
playing for the want of which she said to herself that she
sickened.

There was accordingly a sense in which, at such a period, the
great differences of the human condition could press upon her
more than ever; a circumstance drawing fresh force, in truth,
from the very fact of the chance that at last, for a change, did
squarely meet her – the chance to be 'off', for a bit, almost as far
as anybody. They took their turns in the cage as they took them
both in the shop and at Chalk Farm, and she had known these
two months that time was to be allowed in September – no less
than eleven days – for her personal, private holiday. Much of
her recent intercourse with Mr Mudge had consisted of the
hopes and fears, expressed mainly by himself, involved in the
question of their getting the same dates – a question that, in
proportion as the delight seemed assured, spread into a sea of
speculation over the choice of where and how. All through July,
on the Sunday evenings and at such other odd times as he could
seize, he had flooded their talk with wild waves of calculation. It
was practically settled that, with her mother, somewhere 'on
the south coast' (a phrase of which she liked the sound) they
should put in their allowance together; but she already felt the

prospect quite weary and worn with the way he went round and round on it. It had become his sole topic, the theme alike of his most solemn prudences and most placid jests, to which every opening led for return and revision and in which every little flower of a foretaste was pulled up as soon as planted. He had announced at the earliest day – characterising the whole business, from that moment, as their 'plans', under which name he handled it as a syndicate handles a Chinese, or other, Loan – he had promptly declared that the question must be thoroughly studied, and he produced, on the whole subject, from day to day, an amount of information that excited her wonder and even, not a little, as she frankly let him know, her disdain. When she thought of the danger in which another pair of lovers rapturously lived, she inquired of him anew why he could leave nothing to chance. Then she got for answer that this profundity was just his pride, and he pitted Ramsgate against Bournemouth and even Boulogne against Jersey – for he had great ideas – with all the mastery of detail that was some day, professionally, to carry him far.

The longer the time since she had seen Captain Everard, the more she was booked, as she called it, to pass Park Chambers; and this was the sole amusement that, in the lingering August days and the long, sad twilights, it was left her to cultivate. She had long since learned to know it for a feeble one, though its feebleness was perhaps scarce the reason for her saying to herself each evening as her time for departure approached: 'No, no – not to-night.' She never failed of that silent remark, any more than she failed of feeling, in some deeper place than she had even yet fully sounded, that one's remarks were as weak as straws, and that, however one might indulge in them at eight o'clock, one's fate infallibly declared itself in absolute indifference to them at about eight-fifteen. Remarks were remarks, and very well for that; but fate was fate, and this young lady's was to pass Park Chambers every night in the working week. Out of the immensity of her knowledge of the life of the world there bloomed on these occasions a specific remembrance that it was regarded in that region, in August and September, as rather pleasant just to be caught for something or other in passing through town. Somebody was always passing and somebody might catch somebody else. It was in full cognisance of this subtle law that she adhered to the most ridiculous circuit she could have made to get home. One warm, dull, featureless Friday, when an accident had made her start from Cocker's a little later than usual, she became aware that something of which the infinite possibilities had for so long peopled her dreams was at last prodigiously upon her, though the perfection in which the conditions happened to present it was almost rich enough to be but the positive creation of a dream. She saw, straight before her, like a vista painted in a picture, the empty street and the lamps that burned pale in the dusk not yet established. It was into the convenience of this quiet twilight that a gentleman on the door-step of the Chambers gazed with a vagueness that our young lady's little figure violently trembled, in the approach, with the measure of its power to dissipate. Everything indeed grew in a flash terrific and distinct; her old uncertainties fell away from her, and since she was so familiar with fate, she felt as if the very nail that fixed it were driven in by the hard look with which, for a moment, Captain Everard awaited her.

The vestibule was open behind him and the porter as absent as on the day she had peeped in; he had just come out – was in town, in a tweed suit and a pot hat, but between two journeys – duly bored over his evening and at a loss what to do with it. Then it was that she was glad she had never met him in that way before: she reaped with such ecstasy the benefit of his not being able to think she passed often. She jumped in two seconds to the determination that he should even suppose it to be the first time and the queerest chance: this was while she still wondered if he would identify or notice her. His original attention had not, she instinctively knew, been for the young woman at Cocker's; it had only been for any young woman who might advance with an air of not upholding ugliness. Ah, but then, and just as she had reached the door, came his second observation, a long, light reach with which, visibly and quite amusedly, he recalled and placed her. They were on different sides, but the street, narrow and still, had only made more of a stage for the small momentary drama. It was not over, besides, it was far from over, even on his sending across the way, with the pleasantest laugh she had ever heard, a little lift of his hat and an 'Oh, good evening!' It was still less over on their meeting, the next minute, though rather indirectly and awkwardly, in the middle of the road – a situation to which three or four steps of her own had unmistakably contributed, – and then passing not again to the side on which she had arrived, but back toward the portal of Park Chambers.

'I didn't know you at first. Are you taking a walk?'

'Oh, I don't take walks at night! I'm going home after my work.'

'Oh!'

That was practically what they had meanwhile smiled out, and his exclamation, to which, for a minute, he appeared to have nothing to add, left them face to face and in just such an attitude as, for his part, he might have worn had he been wondering if he could properly ask her to come in. During this interval, in fact, she really felt his question to be just '*How* properly—?' It was simply a question of the degree of properness.

XV

SHE never knew afterwards quite what she had done to settle it, and at the time she only knew that they presently moved, with vagueness, but with continuity, away from the picture of the lighted vestibule and the quiet stairs and well up the street together. This also must have been in the absence of a definite permission, of anything vulgarly articulate, for that matter, on the part of either; and it was to be, later on, a thing of remembrance and reflection for her that the limit of what, just here, for a longish minute, passed between them was his taking in her thoroughly successful deprecation, though conveyed without pride or sound or touch, of the idea that she might be, out of the cage, the very shopgirl at large that she hugged the theory she was not. Yes, it was strange, she afterwards thought, that so much could have come and gone and yet not troubled the air either with impertinence or with resentment, with any of the horrid notes of that kind of acquaintance. He had taken no liberty, as she would have called it; and, through not having to betray the sense of one, she herself had, still more charmingly, taken none. Yet on the spot, nevertheless, she could speculate as to what it meant that, if his relation with Lady Bradeen continued to be what her mind had built it up to, he should feel free to proceed in any private direction. This was one of the questions he was to leave her to deal with – the question whether people of his sort still asked girls up to their rooms when they were so awfully in love with other women. Could people of his sort do that without what people of *her* sort would call being 'false to their love'? She had already a vision of how the true answer was that people of her sort didn't, in such cases, matter – didn't count as infidelity, counted only as something else: she might have been curious, since it came to that, to see exactly what.

Strolling together slowly in their summer twilight and their empty corner of Mayfair, they found themselves emerge at last opposite to one of the smaller gates of the Park; upon which, without any particular word about it – they were talking so of other things – they crossed the street and went in and sat down on a bench. She had gathered by this time one magnificent hope about him – the hope that he would say nothing vulgar. She knew what she meant by that; she meant something quite apart from any matter of his being 'false'. Their bench was not far within; it was near the Park Lane paling and the patchy lamplight and the rumbling cabs and 'buses. A strange emotion had come to her, and she felt indeed excitement within excitement; above all a conscious joy in testing him with chances he didn't take. She had an intense desire he should know the type she really was without her doing anything so low as tell him, and he had surely begun to know it from the moment he didn't seize the opportunities into which a common man would promptly have blundered. These were on the mere surface, and *their* relation was behind and below them. She had questioned so little on the way what they were doing, that as soon as they were seated she took straight hold of it. Her hours, her confinement, the many conditions of service in the post-office, had – with a glance at his own postal resources and alternatives – formed, up to this stage, the subject of their talk. 'Well, here we are, and it may be right enough; but this isn't the least, you know, where I was going.'

'You were going home?'

'Yes, and I was already rather late. I was going to my supper.'

'You haven't had it?'

'No, indeed!'

'Then you haven't eaten—?'

He looked, of a sudden, so extravagantly concerned that she laughed out. 'All day? Yes, we do feed once. But that was long ago. So I must presently say good-bye.'

'Oh, deary *me*!' he exclaimed, with an intonation so droll and yet a touch so light and a distress so marked – a confession of helplessness for such a case, in short, so unrelieved – that she felt sure, on the spot, she had made the great difference plain. He looked at her with the kindest eyes and still without saying what she had known he wouldn't. She had known he wouldn't say, 'Then sup with *me*!' but the proof of it made her feel as if she had feasted.

'I'm not a bit hungry,' she went on.

'Ah, you *must* be, awfully!' he made answer, but settling himself on the bench as if, after all, that needn't interfere with his spending his evening. 'I've always quite wanted the chance to thank you for the trouble you so often take for me.'

'Yes, I know,' she replied; uttering the words with a sense of the situation far deeper than any pretence of not fitting his allusion. She immediately saw that he was surprised and even a little puzzled at her frank assent; but, for herself, the trouble she had taken could only, in these fleeting minutes – they would probably never come back – be all there like a little hoard of gold in her lap. Certainly he might look at it, handle it, take up the pieces. Yet if he understood anything he must understand all. 'I consider you've already immensely thanked me.' The horror was back upon her of having seemed to hang about for some reward. 'It's awfully odd that you should have been there just the one time—!'

'The one time you've passed my place?'

'Yes; you can fancy I haven't many minutes to waste. There was a place to-night I had to stop at.'

'I see, I see' – he knew already so much about her work. 'It must be an awful grind – for a lady.'

'It is; but I don't think I groan over it any more than my companions – and you've seen *they're* not ladies!' She mildly jested, but with an intention. 'One gets used to things, and there are employments I should have hated much more.' She had the finest conception of the beauty of not, at least, boring him. To whine, to count up her wrongs, was what a barmaid or a shopgirl would do, and it was quite enough to sit there like one of these.

'If you had had another employment,' he remarked after a moment, 'we might never have become acquainted.'

'It's highly probable – and certainly not in the same way.' Then, still with her heap of gold in her lap and something of the pride of it in her manner of holding her head, she continued not to move – she only smiled at him. The evening had thickened now; the scattered lamps were red; the Park, all before them, was full of obscure and ambiguous life; there were other couples on other benches, whom it was impossible not to see, yet at whom it was impossible to look. 'But I've walked so much out of my way with you only just to show you that – that' – with this she paused; it was not, after all, so easy to express – 'that anything you may have thought is perfectly true.'

'Oh, I've thought a tremendous lot!' her companion laughed. 'Do you mind my smoking?'

'Why should I? You always smoke *there*.'

'At your place? Oh yes, but here it's different.'

'No,' she said, as he lighted a cigarette, 'that's just what it isn't. It's quite the same.'

'Well, then, that's because "there" it's so wonderful!'

'Then you're conscious of how wonderful it is?' she returned.

He jerked his handsome head in literal protest at a doubt. 'Why, that's exactly what I mean by my gratitude for all your trouble. It has been just as if you took a particular interest.' She only looked at him in answer to this, in such sudden, immediate embarrassment, as she was quite aware, that, while she remained silent, he showed he was at a loss to interpret her expression. 'You *have* – haven't you? – taken a particular interest?'

'Oh, a particular interest!' she quavered out, feeling the whole thing – her immediate embarrassment – get terribly the better of her, and wishing, with a sudden scare, all the more to keep her emotion down. She maintained her fixed smile a moment and turned her eyes over the peopled darkness, unconfused now, because there was something much more confusing. This, with a fatal great rush, was simply the fact that they were thus together. They were near, near, and all that she had imagined of that had only become more true, more dreadful and overwhelming. She stared straight away in silence till she felt that she looked like an idiot; then, to say something, to say nothing, she attempted a sound which ended in a flood of tears.

XVI

HER tears helped her really to dissimulate, for she had instantly, in so public a situation, to recover herself. They had come and gone in half a minute, and she immediately explained them. 'It's only because I'm tired. It's that – it's that!' Then she added a trifle incoherently: 'I shall never see you again.'

'Ah, but why not?' The mere tone in which her companion asked this satisfied her once for all as to the amount of imagination for which she could count on him. It was naturally not large: it had exhausted itself in having arrived at what he had already touched upon – the sense of an intention in her poor zeal at Cocker's. But any deficiency of this kind was no fault in him: *he* wasn't obliged to have an inferior cleverness – to have second-rate resources and virtues. It had been as if he almost really believed she had simply cried for fatigue, and he had accordingly put in some kind, confused plea – 'You ought really to take something: won't you have something or other *somewhere*?' – to which she had made no response but a headshake of a sharpness that settled it. 'Why shan't we all the more keep meeting?'

'I mean meeting this way – only this way. At my place there – *that* I've nothing to do with, and I hope of course you'll turn up, with your correspondence, when it suits you. Whether I stay or not, I mean; for I shall probably not stay.'

'You're going somewhere else?' – he put it with positive anxiety.

'Yes; ever so far away – to the other end of London. There are all sorts of reasons I can't tell you; and it's practically settled. It's better for me, much; and I've only kept on at Cocker's for you.'

'For me?'

Making out in the dusk that he fairly blushed, she now measured how far he had been from knowing too much. Too much, she called it at present; and that was easy, since it proved so abundantly enough for her that he should simply be where he was. 'As we shall never talk this way but to-night – never, never again! – here it all is; I'll say it; I don't care what you think; it doesn't matter; I only want to help you. Besides, you're kind – you're kind. I've been thinking, then, of leaving for ever so long. But you've come so often – at times, – and you've had so much to do, and it has been so pleasant and interesting, that I've remained, I've kept putting off any change. More than once, when I had nearly decided, you've turned up again and I've thought, "Oh no!" That's the simple fact!' She had by this time got her confusion down so completely that she could laugh. 'This is what I meant when I said to you just now that I "knew". I've known perfectly that you knew I took trouble for you; and that knowledge has been for me, and I seemed to see it was for you, as if there were something – I don't know what to call it! – between us. I mean something unusual and good – something not a bit horrid or vulgar.'

She had by this time, she could see, produced a great effect upon him; but she would have spoken the truth to herself if she had at the same moment declared that she didn't in the least care: all the more that the effect must be one of extreme perplexity. What, in it all, was visibly clear for him, none the less, was that he was tremendously glad he had met her. She held him, and he was astonished at the force of it; he was intent, immensely considerate. His elbow was on the back of the seat, and his head, with the pot-hat pushed quite back, in a boyish way, so that she really saw almost for the first time his forehead and hair, rested on the hand into which he had crumpled his gloves. 'Yes,' he assented, 'it's not a bit horrid or vulgar.'

She just hung fire a moment; then she brought out the whole truth. 'I'd do anything for you. I'd do anything for you.' Never in her life had she known anything so high and fine as this, just letting him have it and bravely and magnificently leaving it. Didn't the place, the associations and circumstances, perfectly make it sound what it was not? and wasn't that exactly the beauty?

So she bravely and magnificently left it, and little by little she felt him take it up, take it down, as if they had been on a satin sofa in a boudoir. She had never seen a boudoir, but there had been lots of boudoirs in the telegrams. What she had said, at all events, sank into him, so that after a minute he simply made a movement that had the result of placing his hand on her own – presently indeed that of her feeling herself firmly enough grasped. There was no pressure she need return, there was none she need decline; she just sat admirably still, satisfied, for the time, with the surprise and bewilderment of the impression she made on him. His agitation was even greater, on the whole, than she had at first allowed for. 'I say, you know, you mustn't think of leaving!' he at last broke out.

'Of leaving Cocker's, you mean?'

'Yes, you must stay on there, whatever happens, and help a fellow.'

She was silent a little, partly because it was so strange and exquisite to feel him watch her as if it really mattered to him and he were almost in suspense. 'Then you *have* quite recognised what I've tried to do?' she asked.

'Why, wasn't that exactly what I dashed over from my door just now to thank you for?'

'Yes; so you said.'

'And don't you believe it?'

She looked down a moment at his hand, which continued to cover her own; whereupon he presently drew it back, rather restlessly folding his arms. Without answering his question she went on: 'Have you ever spoken of me?'

'Spoken of you?'

'Of my being there – of my knowing, and that sort of thing.'

'Oh, never to a human creature!' he eagerly declared.

She had a small drop at this, which was expressed in another pause; after which she returned to what he had just asked her. 'Oh yes, I quite believe you like it – my always being there and our taking things up so familiarly and successfully: if not exactly where we left them,' she laughed, 'almost always, at least, in an interesting place!' He was about to say something in reply to this, but her friendly gaiety was quicker. 'You want a great many things in life, a great many comforts and helps and luxuries – you want everything as pleasant as possible. There-fore, so far as it's in the power of any particular person to contribute to all that—' She had turned her face to him smiling, just thinking.

'Oh, see here!' But he was highly amused. 'Well, what then?' he inquired, as if to humour her.

'Why, the particular person must never fail. We must man-age it for you somehow.'

He threw back his head, laughing out; he was really exhila-rated. 'Oh yes, somehow!'

'Well, I think we each do – don't we? – in one little way and another and according to our limited lights. I'm pleased, at any rate, for myself, that you are; for I assure you I've done my best.'

'You do better than any one!' He had struck a match for another cigarette, and the flame lighted an instant his respon-sive, finished face, magnifying into a pleasant grimace the kindness with which he paid her this tribute. 'You're awfully clever, you know; cleverer, cleverer, cleverer—!' He had appeared on the point of making some tremendous statement; then suddenly, puffing his cigarette and shifting almost with violence on his seat, let it altogether fall.

XVII

In spite of this drop, if not just by reason of it, she felt as if Lady Bradeen, all but named out, had popped straight up; and she practically betrayed her consciousness by waiting a little before she rejoined: 'Cleverer than who?'

'Well, if I wasn't afraid you'd think I swagger, I should say – than anybody! If you leave your place there, where shall you go?' he more gravely demanded.

'Oh, too far for you ever to find me!'

'I'd find you anywhere.'

The tone of this was so still more serious that she had but her one acknowledgement. 'I'd do anything for you – I'd do anything for you,' she repeated. She had already, she felt, said it all; so what did anything more, anything less, matter? That was the very reason indeed why she could, with a lighter note, ease him generously of any awkwardness produced by solemnity, either his own or hers. 'Of course it must be nice for you to be able to think there are people all about who feel in such a way.'

In immediate appreciation of this, however, he only smoked without looking at her. 'But you don't want to give up your present work?' he at last inquired. 'I mean you *will* stay in the post-office?'

'Oh yes; I think I've a genius for that.'

'Rather! No one can touch you.' With this he turned more to her again. 'But you can get, with a move, greater advantages?'

'I can get, in the suburbs, cheaper lodgings. I live with my mother. We need some space; and there's a particular place that has other inducements.'

He just hesitated. 'Where is it?'

'Oh, quite out of *your* way. You'd never have time.'

'But I tell you I'd go anywhere. Don't you believe it?'

'Yes, for once or twice. But you'd soon see it wouldn't do for you.'

He smoked and considered; seemed to stretch himself a little and, with his legs out, surrender himself comfortably. 'Well, well, well – I believe everything you say. I take it from you – anything you like – in the most extraordinary way.' It struck her certainly – and almost without bitterness – that the way in which she was already, as if she had been an old friend, arranging for him and preparing the only magnificence she could muster, was quite the most extraordinary. 'Don't, *don't* go!' he presently went on. 'I shall miss you too horribly!'

'So that you just put it to me as a definite request?' – oh, how she tried to divest this of all sound of the hardness of bargaining! That ought to have been easy enough, for what was she arranging to get? Before he could answer she had continued: 'To be perfectly fair, I should tell you I recognise at Cocker's certain strong attractions. All you people come. I like all the horrors.'

'The horrors?'

'Those you all – you know the set I mean, *your* set – show me with as good a conscience as if I had no more feeling than a letter-box.'

He looked quite excited at the way she put it. 'Oh, they don't know!'

'Don't know I'm not stupid? No, how should they?'

'Yes, how should they?' said the Captain sympathetically. 'But isn't "horrors" rather strong?'

'What you *do* is rather strong!' the girl promptly returned.

'What *I* do?'

'Your extravagance, your selfishness, your immorality, your crimes,' she pursued, without heeding his expression.

'I *say*!' – her companion showed the queerest stare.

'I like them, as I tell you – I revel in them. But we needn't go into that,' she quietly went on; 'for all I get out of it is the harmless pleasure of knowing. I know, I know, I know!' – she breathed it ever so gently.

'Yes; that's what has been between us,' he answered much more simply.

She could enjoy his simplicity in silence, and for a moment she did so. 'If I do stay because you want it – and I'm rather capable of that – there are two or three things I think you ought to remember. One is, you know, that I'm there sometimes for days and weeks together without your ever coming.'

'Oh, I'll come every day!' he exclaimed.

She was on the point, at this, of imitating with her hand his movement of shortly before; but she checked herself, and there was no want of effect in the tranquillising way in which she said: 'How can you? How can you?' He had, too manifestly, only to look at it there, in the vulgarly animated gloom, to see that he couldn't; and at this point, by the mere action of his silence, everything they had so definitely not named, the whole presence round which they had been circling became a part of their reference, settled solidly between them. It was as if then, for a minute, they sat and saw it all in each other's eyes, saw so much that there was no need of a transition for sounding it at last. 'Your danger, your danger—!' Her voice indeed trembled with it, and she could only, for the moment, again leave it so.

During this moment he leaned back on the bench, meeting her in silence and with a face that grew more strange. It grew so strange that, after a further instant, she got straight up. She stood there as if their talk were now over, and he just sat and watched her. It was as if now – owing to the third person they had brought in – they must be more careful; so that the most he could finally say was: 'That's where it is!'

'That's where it is!' the girl as guardedly replied. He sat still, and she added: 'I won't abandon you. Good-bye.'

'Good-bye?' – he appealed, but without moving.

'I don't quite see my way, but I won't abandon you,' she repeated. 'There. Good-bye.'

It brought him with a jerk to his feet, tossing away his cigarette. His poor face was flushed. 'See here – see here!'

'No, I won't; but I must leave you now,' she went on as if not hearing him.

'See here – see here!' He tried, from the bench, to take her hand again.

But that definitely settled it for her: this would, after all, be as bad as his asking her to supper. 'You mustn't come with me – no, no!'

He sank back, quite blank, as if she had pushed him. 'I mayn't see you home?'

'No, no; let me go.' He looked almost as if she had struck him, but she didn't care; and the manner in which she spoke – it was literally as if she were angry – had the force of a command. 'Stay where you are!'

'See here – see here!' he nevertheless pleaded.

'I won't abandon you!' she cried once more – this time quite with passion; on which she got away from him as fast as she could and left him staring after her.

XVIII

MR MUDGE had lately been so occupied with their famous 'plans' that he had neglected, for a while, the question of her transfer; but down at Bournemouth, which had found itself selected as the field of their recreation by a process consisting, it seemed, exclusively of innumerable pages of the neatest arithmetic in a very greasy but most orderly little pocket-book, the distracting possible melted away – the fleeting irremediable ruled the scene. The plans, hour by hour, were simply superseded, and it was much of a rest to the girl, as she sat on the pier and overlooked the sea and the company, to see them evaporate in rosy fumes and to feel that from moment to moment there was less left to cipher about. The week proved blissfully fine, and her mother, at their lodgings – partly to her embarrassment and partly to her relief – struck up with the landlady an alliance that left the younger couple a great deal of freedom. This relative took her pleasure of a week at Bournemouth in a stuffy back-kitchen and endless talks; to that degree even that Mr Mudge himself – habitually inclined indeed to a scrutiny of all mysteries and to seeing, as he sometimes admitted, too much in things – made remarks on it as he sat on the cliff with his betrothed, or on the decks of steamers that conveyed them, close-packed items in terrific totals of enjoyment, to the Isle of Wight and the Dorset coast.

He had a lodging in another house, where he had speedily learned the importance of keeping his eyes open, and he made no secret of his suspecting that sinister mutual connivances might spring, under the roof of his companions, from unnatural sociabilities. At the same time he fully recognised that, as a source of anxiety, not to say of expense, his future mother-in-law would have weighted them more in accompanying their steps than in giving her hostess, in the interest of the tendency they considered that they never mentioned, equivalent pledges as to the tea-caddy and the jam-pot. These were the questions – these indeed the familiar commodities – that he had now to put into the scales; and his betrothed had, in consequence, during her holiday, the odd, and yet pleasant and almost languid, sense of an anticlimax. She had become conscious of an extraordinary collapse, a surrender to stillness and to retrospect. She cared neither to walk nor to sail; it was enough for her to sit on benches and wonder at the sea and taste the air and not be at Cocker's and not see the counter-clerk. She still seemed to wait for something – something in the key of the immense discussions that had mapped out their little week of idleness on the scale of a world-atlas. Something came at last, but without perhaps appearing quite adequately to crown the monument.

Preparation and precaution were, however, the natural flowers of Mr Mudge's mind, and in proportion as these things declined in one quarter they inevitably bloomed elsewhere. He could always, at the worst, have on Tuesday the project of their taking the Swanage boat on Thursday, and on Thursday that of their ordering minced kidneys on Saturday. He had, moreover, a constant gift of inexorable inquiry as to where and what they should have gone and have done if they had not been exactly as they were. He had in short his resources, and his mistress had never been so conscious of them; on the other hand they had never interfered so little with her own. She liked to be as she was – if it could only have lasted. She could accept even without bitterness a rigour of economy so great that the little fee they paid for admission to the pier had to be balanced against other delights. The people at Ladle's and at Thrupp's had *their* ways of amusing themselves, whereas she had to sit and hear Mr Mudge talk of what he might do if he didn't take a bath, or of the bath he might take if he only hadn't taken something else. He was always with her now, of course, always beside her; she saw him more than 'hourly', more than ever yet, more even than he had planned she should do at Chalk Farm. She preferred to sit at the far end, away from the band and the crowd; as to which she had frequent differences with her friend, who reminded her often that they could have only in the thick of it the sense of the money they were getting back. That had little effect on her, for she got back her money by seeing many things, the things of the past year, fall together and connect themselves, undergo the happy relegation that transforms melancholy and misery, passion and effort, into experience and knowledge.

She liked having done with them, as she assured herself she had practically done, and the strange thing was that she neither missed the procession now nor wished to keep her place for it. It had become there, in the sun and the breeze and the sea-smell, a far-away story, a picture of another life. If Mr Mudge himself liked processions, liked them at Bournemouth and on the pier quite as much as at Chalk Farm or anywhere, she learned after a little not to be worried by his perpetual counting of the figures that made them up. There were dreadful women in particular, usually fat and in men's caps and white shoes, whom he could never let alone – not that *she* cared; it was not the great world, the world of Cocker's and Ladle's and Thrupp's, but it offered an endless field to his faculties of memory, philosophy, and frolic. She had never accepted him so much, never arranged so successfully for making him chatter while she carried on secret conversations. Her talks were with herself; and if they both practised a great thrift, she had quite mastered that of merely spending words enough to keep him imperturbably and continuously going.

He was charmed with the panorama, not knowing – or at any rate not at all showing that he knew – what far other images peopled her mind than the women in the navy caps and the shopboys in the blazers. His observations on these types, his general interpretation of the show, brought home to her the prospect of Chalk Farm. She wondered sometimes that he should have derived so little illumination, during his period, from the society at Cocker's. But one evening, as their holiday cloudlessly waned, he gave her such a proof of his quality as might have made her ashamed of her small reserves. He brought out something that, in all his overflow, he had been able to keep back till other matters were disposed of. It was the announcement that he was at last ready to marry – that he saw his way. A rise at Chalk Farm had been offered him; he was to be taken into the business, bringing with him a capital the estimation of which by other parties constituted the handsomest recognition yet made of the head on his shoulders. Therefore their waiting was over – it could be a question of a near date. They would settle this date before going back, and he meanwhile had his eye on a sweet little home. He would take her to see it on their first Sunday.

XIX

HIS having kept this great news for the last, having had such a card up his sleeve and not floated it out in the current of his chatter and the luxury of their leisure, was one of those incalculable strokes by which he could still affect her; the kind of thing that reminded her of the latent force that had ejected the drunken soldier – an example of the profundity of which his promotion was the proof. She listened a while in silence, on this occasion, to the wafted strains of the music; she took it in as she had not quite done before that her future was now constituted. Mr Mudge was distinctly her fate; yet at this moment she turned her face quite away from him, showing him so long a mere quarter of her cheek that she at last again heard his voice. He couldn't see a pair of tears that were partly the reason of her delay to give him the assurance he required; but he expressed at a venture the hope that she had had her fill of Cocker's.

She was finally able to turn back. 'Oh, quite. There's nothing going on. No one comes but the Americans at Thrupp's, and *they* don't do much. They don't seem to have a secret in the world.'

'Then the extraordinary reason you've been giving me for holding on there has ceased to work?'

She thought a moment. 'Yes, that one. I've seen the thing through – I've got them all in my pocket.'

'So you're ready to come?'

For a little, again, she made no answer. 'No, not yet, all the same. I've still got a reason – a different one.'

He looked her all over as if it might have been something she kept in her mouth or her glove or under her jacket – something she was even sitting upon. 'Well, I'll have it, please.'

'I went out the other night and sat in the Park with a gentleman,' she said at last.

Nothing was ever seen like his confidence in her; and she wondered a little now why it didn't irritate her. It only gave her ease and space, as she felt, for telling him the whole truth that no one knew. It had arrived at present at her really wanting to do that, and yet to do it not in the least for Mr Mudge, but altogether and only for herself. This truth filled out for her the whole experience she was about to relinquish, suffused and coloured it as a picture that she should keep and that, describe it as she might, no one but herself would ever really see. Moreover she had no desire whatever to make Mr Mudge jealous; there would be no amusement in it, for the amusement she had lately known had spoiled her for lower pleasures. There were even no materials for it. The odd thing was that she never doubted that, properly handled, his passion was poisonable; what had happened was that he had cannily selected a partner with no poison to distil. She read then and there that she should never interest herself in anybody as to whom some other sentiment, some superior view, wouldn't be sure to interfere, for him, with jealousy. 'And what did you get out of that?' he asked with a concern that was not in the least for his honour.

'Nothing but a good chance to promise him I wouldn't forsake him. He's one of my customers.'

'Then it's for him not to forsake *you*.'

'Well, he won't. It's all right. But I must just keep on as long as he may want me.'

'Want you to sit with him in the Park?'

'He may want me for that – but I shan't. I rather liked it, but once, under the circumstances, is enough. I can do better for him in another manner.'

'And what manner, pray?'

'Well, elsewhere.'

'Elsewhere? – I *say*!'

This was an ejaculation used also by Captain Everard, but, oh, with what a different sound! 'You needn't "say" – there's nothing to be said. And yet you ought perhaps to know.'

'Certainly I ought. But *what* – up to now?'

'Why, exactly what I told him. That I would do anything for him.'

'What do you mean by "anything"?'

'Everything.'

Mr Mudge's immediate comment on this statement was to draw from his pocket a crumpled paper containing the remains of half a pound of 'sundries'. These sundries had figured conspicuously in his prospective sketch of their tour, but it was only at the end of three days that they had defined themselves unmistakably as chocolate-creams. 'Have another? – *that* one,' he said. She had another, but not the one he indicated, and then he continued: 'What took place afterwards?'

'Afterwards?'

'What did you do when you had told him you would do everything?'

'I simply came away.'

'Out of the Park?'

'Yes, leaving him there. I didn't let him follow me.'

'Then what did you let him do?'

'I didn't let him do anything.'

Mr Mudge considered an instant. 'Then what did you go there for?' His tone was even slightly critical.

'I didn't quite know at the time. It was simply to be with him, I suppose – just once. He's in danger, and I wanted him to know I know it. It makes meeting him – at Cocker's, for it's that I want to stay on for – more interesting.'

'It makes it mighty interesting for *me*!' Mr Mudge freely declared. 'Yet he didn't follow you?' he asked. '*I* would!'

'Yes, of course. That was the way you began, you know. You're awfully inferior to him.'

'Well, my dear, you're not inferior to anybody. You've got a cheek! What is he in danger of?'

'Of being found out. He's in love with a lady – and it isn't right – and *I've* found him out.'

'That'll be a look-out for *me*!' Mr Mudge joked. 'You mean she has a husband?'

'Never mind what she has! They're in awful danger, but his is the worst, because he's in danger from her too.'

'Like me from you – the woman *I* love? If he's in the same funk as me—'

'He's in a worse one. He's not only afraid of the lady – he's afraid of other things.'

Mr Mudge selected another chocolate-cream. 'Well, I'm only afraid of one! But how in the world can you help this party?'

'I don't know – perhaps not at all. But so long as there's a chance—'

'You won't come away?'

'No, you've got to wait for me.'

Mr Mudge enjoyed what was in his mouth. 'And what will he give you?'

'Give me?'

'If you do help him.'

'Nothing. Nothing in all the wide world.'

'Then what will he give *me*?' Mr Mudge inquired. 'I mean for waiting.'

The girl thought a moment; then she got up to walk. 'He never heard of you,' she replied.

'You haven't mentioned me?'

'We never mention anything. What I've told you is just what I've found out.'

Mr Mudge, who had remained on the bench, looked up at her; she often preferred to be quiet when he proposed to walk, but now that he seemed to wish to sit she had a desire to move. 'But you haven't told me what *he* has found out.'

She considered her lover. 'He'd never find *you*, my dear!'

Her lover, still on his seat, appealed to her in something of the attitude in which she had last left Captain Everard, but the impression was not the same. 'Then where do I come in?'

'You don't come in at all. That's just the beauty of it!' – and with this she turned to mingle with the multitude collected round the band. Mr Mudge presently overtook her and drew her arm into his own with a quiet force that expressed the serenity of possession; in consonance with which it was only when they parted for the night at her door that he referred again to what she had told him.

'Have you seen him since?'

'Since the night in the Park? No, not once.'

'Oh, what a cad!' said Mr Mudge.

XX

IT was not till the end of October that she saw Captain Everard again, and on that occasion – the only one of all the series on which hindrance had been so utter – no communication with him proved possible. She had made out, even from the cage, that it was a charming golden day: a patch of hazy autumn sunlight lay across the sanded floor and also, higher up, quickened into brightness a row of ruddy bottled syrups. Work was slack and the place in general empty; the town, as they said in the cage, had not waked up, and the feeling of the day likened itself to something that in happier conditions she would have thought of romantically as St Martin's summer. The counter-clerk had gone to his dinner; she herself was busy with arrears of postal jobs, in the midst of which she became aware that Captain Everard had apparently been in the shop a minute and that Mr Buckton had already seized him.

He had, as usual, half a dozen telegrams; and when he saw that she saw him and their eyes met, he gave, on bowing to her, an exaggerated laugh in which she read a new consciousness. It was a confession of awkwardness; it seemed to tell her that of course he knew he ought better to have kept his head, ought to have been clever enough to wait, on some pretext, till he should have found her free. Mr Buckton was a long time with him, and her attention was soon demanded by other visitors; so that nothing passed between them but the fulness of their silence. The look she took from him was his greeting, and the other one a simple sign of the eyes sent her before going out. The only token they exchanged, therefore, was his tacit assent to her wish that, since they couldn't attempt a certain frankness, they should attempt nothing at all. This was her intense preference; she could be as still and cold as any one when that was the sole solution.

Yet, more than any contact hitherto achieved, these counted instants struck her as marking a step: they were built so – just in the mere flash – on the recognition of his now definitely knowing what it was she would do for him. The 'anything, anything' she had uttered in the Park went to and fro between them and under the poked-out chins that interposed. It had all at last even put on the air of their not needing now clumsily to manoeuvre to converse: their former little postal make-believes, the intense implications of questions and answers and change, had become in the light of the personal fact, of their having had their moment, a possibility comparatively poor. It was as if they had met for all time – it exerted on their being in presence again an influence so prodigious. When she watched herself, in the memory of that night, walk away from him as if she were making an end, she found something too pitiful in the primness of such a gait. Hadn't she precisely established on the part of each a consciousness that could end only with death?

It must be admitted that, in spite of this brave margin, an irritation, after he had gone, remained with her; a sense that presently became one with a still sharper hatred of Mr Buckton, who, on her friend's withdrawal, had retired with the telegrams to the sounder and left her the other work. She knew indeed she should have a chance to see them, when she would, on file; and she was divided, as the day went on, between the two impressions of all that was lost and all that was reasserted. What beset her above all, and as she had almost never known it before, was the desire to bound straight out, to overtake the autumn afternoon before it passed away for ever and hurry off to the Park and perhaps be with him there again on a bench. It became, for an hour, a fantastic vision with her that he might just have gone to sit and wait for her. She could almost hear him, through the tick of the sounder, scatter with his stick, in his impatience, the fallen leaves of October. Why should such a vision seize her at this particular moment with such a shake? There was a time – from four to five – when she could have cried with happiness and rage.

Business quickened, it seemed, toward five, as if the town did wake up; she had therefore more to do, and she went through it with little sharp stampings and jerkings: she made the crisp postal-orders fairly snap while she breathed to herself: 'It's the last day – the last day!' The last day of what? She couldn't have told. All she knew now was that if she *were* out of the cage she wouldn't in the least have minded, this time, its not yet being dark. She would have gone straight toward Park Chambers and have hung about there till no matter when. She would have waited, stayed, rung, asked, have gone in, sat on the stairs. What the day was the last of was probably, to her strained inner sense, the group of golden ones, of any occasion for seeing the hazy sunshine slant at that angle into the smelly shop, of any range of chances for his wishing still to repeat to her the two words that, in the Park, she had scarcely let him bring out. 'See here – see here!' – the sound of these two words had been with her perpetually; but it was in her ears to-day without mercy, with a loudness that grew and grew. What was it they then expressed? what was it he had wanted her to see? She seemed, whatever it was, perfectly to see it now – to see that if she should just chuck the whole thing, should have a great and beautiful courage, he would somehow make everything up to her. When the clock struck five she was on the very point of saying to Mr Buckton that she was deadly ill and rapidly getting worse. This announcement was on her lips, and she had quite composed the pale, hard face she would offer him: 'I can't stop – I must go home. If I feel better, later on, I'll come back. I'm very sorry, but I *must* go.' At that instant Captain Everard once more stood there, producing in her agitated spirit, by his real presence, the strangest, quickest revolution. He stopped her off without knowing it, and by the time he had been a minute in the shop she felt that she was saved.

That was from the first minute what she called it to herself. There were again other persons with whom she was occupied, and again the situation could only be expressed by their silence. It was expressed, in fact, in a larger phrase than ever yet, for her eyes now spoke to him with a kind of supplication. 'Be quiet, be quiet!' they pleaded; and they saw his own reply: 'I'll do whatever you say; I won't even look at you – see, see!' They kept conveying thus, with the friendliest liberality, that they wouldn't look, quite positively wouldn't. What she was to see was that he hovered at the other end of the counter, Mr Buckton's end, surrendered himself again to that frustration. It quickly proved so great indeed that what she was to see further was how he turned away before he was attended to, and hung off, waiting, smoking, looking about the shop; how he went over to Mr Cocker's own counter and appeared to price things, gave in fact presently two or three orders and put down money, stood there a long time with his back to her, considerately abstaining from any glance round to see if she were free. It at last came to pass in this way that he had remained in the shop longer than she had ever yet known him to do, and that, nevertheless, when he did turn about she could see him time himself – she was freshly taken up – and cross straight to her postal subordinate, whom some one else had released. He had in his hand all this while neither letters nor telegrams, and now that he was close to her – for she was close to the counter-clerk – it brought her heart into her mouth merely to see him look at her neighbour and open his lips. She was too nervous to bear it. He asked for a Post-Office Guide, and the young man whipped out a new one; whereupon he said that he wished not to purchase, but only to consult one a moment; with which, the copy kept on loan being produced, he once more wandered off.

What was he doing to her? What did he want of her? Well, it was just the aggravation of his 'See here!' She felt at this moment strangely and portentously afraid of him – had in her ears the hum of a sense that, should it come to that kind of tension, she must fly on the spot to Chalk Farm. Mixed with her dread and with her reflection was the idea that, if he wanted her so much as he seemed to show, it might be after all simply to do for him the 'anything' she had promised, the 'everything' she had thought it so fine to bring out to Mr Mudge. He might want her to help him, might have some particular appeal; though, of a truth, his manner didn't denote that – denoted, on the contrary, an embarrassment, an indecision, something of a desire not so much to be helped as to be treated rather more nicely than she had treated him the other time. Yes, he considered quite probably that he had help rather to offer than to ask for. Still, none the less, when he again saw her free he continued to keep away from her; when he came back with his *Guide* it was Mr Buckton he caught – it was from Mr Buckton he obtained half-a-crown's-worth of stamps.

After asking for the stamps he asked, quite as a second thought, for a postal-order for ten shillings. What did he want with so many stamps when he wrote so few letters? How could he enclose a postal-order in a telegram? She expected him, the next thing, to go into the corner and make up one of his telegrams – half a dozen of them – on purpose to prolong his presence. She had so completely stopped looking at him that she could only guess his movements – guess even where his eyes rested. Finally she saw him make a dash that might have been towards the nook where the forms were hung; and at this she suddenly felt that she couldn't keep it up. The counter-clerk had just taken a telegram from a slavey, and, to give herself something to cover her, she snatched it out of his hand. The gesture was so violent that he gave her an odd look, and she also perceived that Mr Buckton noticed it. The latter personage, with a quick stare at her, appeared for an instant to wonder whether his snatching it in *his* turn mightn't be the thing she would least like, and she anticipated this practical criticism by the frankest glare she had ever given him. It sufficed: this time it paralysed him; and she sought with her trophy the refuge of the sounder.

XXI

IT was repeated the next day; it went on for three days; and at the end of that time she knew what to think. When, at the beginning, she had emerged from her temporary shelter Captain Everard had quitted the shop; and he had not come again that evening, as it had struck her he possibly might – might all the more easily that there were numberless persons who came, morning and afternoon, numberless times, so that he wouldn't necessarily have attracted attention. The second day it was different and yet on the whole worse. His access to her had become possible – she felt herself even reaping the fruit of her yesterday's glare at Mr Buckton; but transacting his business with him didn't simplify – it could, in spite of the rigour of circumstance, feed so her new conviction. The rigour was tremendous, and his telegrams – not, now, mere pretexts for getting at her – were apparently genuine; yet the conviction had taken but a night to develop. It could be simply enough expressed; she had had the glimmer of it the day before in her idea that he needed no more help than she had already given; that it was help he himself was prepared to render. He had come up to town but for three or four days; he had been absolutely obliged to be absent after the other time; yet he would, now that he was face to face with her, stay on as much longer as she liked. Little by little it was thus clarified, though from the first flash of his reappearance she had read into it the real essence.

That was what the night before, at eight o'clock, her hour to go, had made her hang back and dawdle. She did last things or pretended to do them; to be in the cage had suddenly become her safety, and she was literally afraid of the alternate self who might be waiting outside. *He* might be waiting; it was he who was her alternate self, and of him she was afraid. The most extraordinary change had taken place in her from the moment of her catching the impression he seemed to have returned on purpose to give her. Just before she had done so, on that bewitched afternoon, she had seen herself approach, without a scruple, the porter at Park Chambers; then, as the effect of the rush of a consciousness quite altered, she had, on at last quitting Cocker's, gone straight home for the first time since her return from Bournemouth. She had passed his door every night for weeks, but nothing would have induced her to pass it now. This change was the tribute of her fear – the result of a change in himself as to which she needed no more explanation than his mere face vividly gave her; strange though it was to find an element of deterrence in the object that she regarded as the most beautiful in the world. He had taken it from her in the Park that night that she wanted him not to propose to her to sup; but he had put away the lesson by this time – he practically proposed supper every time he looked at her. This was what, for that matter, mainly filled the three days. He came in twice on each of these, and it was as if he came in to give her a chance to relent. That was, after all, she said to herself in the intervals, the most that he did. There were ways, she fully recognised, in which he spared her, and other particular ways as to which she meant that her silence should be full, to him, of exquisite pleading. The most particular of all was his not being outside, at the corner, when she quitted the place for the night. This he might so easily have been – so easily if he hadn't been so nice. She continued to recognise in his forbearance the fruit of her dumb supplication, and the only compensation he found for it was the harmless freedom of being able to appear to say: 'Yes, I'm in town only for three or four days, but, you know, I *would* stay on.' He struck her as calling attention each day, each hour, to the rapid ebb of time; he exaggerated to the point of putting it that there were only two days more, that there was at last, dreadfully, only one.

There were other things still that he struck her as doing with a special intention; as to the most marked of which – unless indeed it were the most obscure – she might well have marvelled that it didn't seem to her more horrid. It was either the frenzy of her imagination or the disorder of his baffled passion that gave her once or twice the vision of his putting down redundant money – sovereigns not concerned with the little payments he was perpetually making – so that she might give him some sign of helping him to slip them over to her. What was most extraordinary in this impression was the amount of excuse that, with some incoherence, she found for him. He wanted to pay her because there was nothing to pay her for. He wanted to offer her things that he knew she wouldn't take. He wanted to show her how much he respected her by giving her the supreme chance to show *him* she was respectable. Over the driest transactions, at any rate, their eyes had out these questions. On the third day he put in a telegram that had evidently something of the same point as the stray sovereigns – a message that was, in the first place, concocted, and that, on a second thought, he took back from her before she had stamped it. He had given her time to read it, and had only then bethought himself that he had better not send it. If it was not to Lady Bradeen at Twindle – where she knew her ladyship then to be – this was because an address to Doctor Buzzard at Brickwood was just as good, with the added merit of its not giving away quite so much a person whom he had still, after all, in a manner to consider. It was of course most complicated, only half lighted; but there was, discernibly enough, a scheme of communication in which Lady Bradeen at Twindle and Dr Buzzard at Brickwood were, within limits, one and the same person. The words he had shown her and then taken back consisted, at all events, of the brief but vivid phrase: 'Absolutely impossible.' The point was not that she should transmit it; the point was just that she should see it. What was absolutely impossible was that before he had settled something at Cocker's he should go either to Twindle or to Brickwood.

The logic of this, in turn, for herself, was that she could lend herself to no settlement so long as she so intensely knew. What she knew was that he was, almost under peril of life, clenched in a situation: therefore how could she also know where a poor girl in the P.O. might really stand? It was more and more between them that if he might convey to her that he was free, that everything she had seen so deep into was a closed chapter, her own case might become different for her, she might understand and meet him and listen. But he could convey nothing of the sort, and he only fidgeted and floundered in his want of power. The chapter wasn't in the least closed, not for the other party; and the other party had a pull, somehow and somewhere: this his whole attitude and expression confessed, at the same time that they entreated her not to remember and not to mind. So long as she did remember and did mind he could only circle about and go and come, doing futile things of which he was ashamed. He was ashamed of his two words to Dr Buzzard, and went out of the shop as soon as he had crumpled up the paper again and thrust it into his pocket. It had been an abject little exposure of dreadful, impossible passion. He appeared in fact to be too ashamed to come back. He had left town again, and a first week elapsed, and a second. He had had naturally to return to the real mistress of his fate; she had insisted – she knew how, and he couldn't put in another hour. There was always a day when she called time. It was known to our young friend more-over that he had now been despatching telegrams from other offices. She knew at last so much, that she had quite lost her earlier sense of merely guessing. There were no shades of dis-tinctness – it all bounced out.

XXII

EIGHTEEN days elapsed, and she had begun to think it prob-able she should never see him again. He too then understood now: he had made out that she had secrets and reasons and impediments, that even a poor girl at the P.O. might have her complications. With the charm she had cast on him lightened by distance he had suffered a final delicacy to speak to him, had made up his mind that it would be only decent to let her alone. Never so much as during these latter days had she felt the precariousness of their relation – the happy, beautiful, untroubled original one, if it could only have been restored, – in which the public servant and the casual public only were concerned. It hung at the best by the merest silken thread, which was at the mercy of any accident and might snap at any minute. She arrived by the end of the fortnight at the highest sense of actual fitness, never doubting that her decision was now complete. She would just give him a few days more to come back to her on a proper impersonal basis – for even to an embarrassing representative of the casual public a public ser-vant with a conscience did owe something, – and then would signify to Mr Mudge that she was ready for the little home. It had been visited, in the further talk she had had with him at Bournemouth, from garret to cellar, and they had especially lingered, with their respectively darkened brows, before the niche into which it was to be broached to her mother that she was to find means to fit.

He had put it to her more definitely than before that his calculations had allowed for that dingy presence, and he had thereby marked the greatest impression he had ever made on her. It was a stroke superior even again to his handling of the drunken soldier. What she considered that, in the face of it, she hung on at Cocker's for, was something that she could only have described as the common fairness of a last word. Her actual last word had been, till it should be superseded, that she wouldn't abandon her other friend, and it stuck to her, through thick and thin, that she was still at her post and on her honour. This other friend had shown so much beauty of conduct already that he would surely, after all, just reappear long enough to relieve her, to give her something she could take away. She saw it, caught it, at times, his parting present; and there were moments when she felt herself sitting like a beggar with a hand held out to an almsgiver who only fumbled. She hadn't taken the sovereigns, but she *would* take the penny. She heard, in imagination, on the counter, the ring of the copper. 'Don't put yourself out any longer,' he would say, 'for so bad a case. You've done all there is to be done. I thank and acquit and release you. Our lives take us. I don't know much – though I have really been interested – about yours; but I suppose you've got one. Mine, at any rate, will take *me* – and where it will. Heigh-ho! Good-bye.' And then once more, for the sweetest, faintest flower of all: 'Only, I say – see here!' She had framed the whole picture with a squareness that included also the image of how again she would decline to 'see there', decline, as she might say, to see anywhere or anything. Yet it befell that just in the fury of this escape she saw more than ever.

He came back one night with a rush, near the moment of their closing, and showed her a face so different and new, so upset and anxious, that almost anything seemed to look out of it but clear recognition. He poked in a telegram very much as if the simple sense of pressure, the distress of extreme haste, had blurred the remembrance of where in particular he was. But as she met his eyes a light came; it broke indeed on the spot into a positive, conscious glare. That made up for everything, for it was an instant proclamation of the celebrated 'danger'; it seemed to pour things out in a flood. 'Oh yes, here it is – it's upon me at last! Forget, for God's sake, my having worried or bored you, and just help me, just *save* me, by getting this off without the loss of a second!' Something grave had clearly occurred, a crisis declared itself. She recognised immediately the person to whom the telegram was addressed – the Miss Dolman, of Parade Lodge, to whom Lady Bradeen had wired, at Dover, on the last occasion, and whom she had then, with her recollection of previous arrangements, fitted into a particular setting. Miss Dolman had figured before and not figured since, but she was now the subject of an imperative appeal. 'Absolutely necessary to see you. Take last train Victoria if you can catch it. If not, earliest morning, and answer me direct either way.'

'Reply paid?' said the girl. Mr Buckton had just departed, and the counter-clerk was at the sounder. There was no other representative of the public, and she had never yet, as it seemed to her, not even in the street or in the Park, been so alone with him.

'Oh yes, reply paid, and as sharp as possible, please.'

She affixed the stamps in a flash. 'She'll catch the train!' she then declared to him breathlessly, as if she could absolutely guarantee it.

'I don't know – I hope so. It's awfully important. So kind of you. Awfully sharp, please.' It was wonderfully innocent now, his oblivion of all but his danger. Anything else that had ever passed between them was utterly out of it. Well, she had wanted him to be impersonal!

There was less of the same need therefore, happily, for herself; yet she only took time, before she flew to the sounder, to gasp at him: 'You're in trouble?'

'Horrid, horrid – there's a row!' But they parted, on it, in the next breath; and as she dashed at the sounder, almost pushing, in her violence, the counter-clerk off the stool, she caught the bang with which, at Cocker's door, in his further precipitation, he closed the apron of the cab into which he had leaped. As he rushed off to some other precaution suggested by his alarm, his appeal to Miss Dolman flashed straight away.

But she had not, on the morrow, been in the place five minutes before he was with her again, still more discomposed and quite, now, as she said to herself, like a frightened child coming to its mother. Her companions were there, and she felt it to be remarkable how, in the presence of his agitation, his mere scared, exposed nature, she suddenly ceased to mind. It came to her as it had never come to her before that with absolute directness and assurance they might carry almost anything off. He had nothing to send – she was sure he had been wiring all over, – and yet his business was evidently huge. There was nothing but that in his eyes – not a glimmer of reference or memory. He was almost haggard with anxiety, and had clearly not slept a wink. Her pity for him would have given her any courage, and she seemed to know at last why she had been such a fool. 'She didn't come?' she panted.

'Oh yes, she came; but there has been some mistake. We want a telegram.'

'A telegram?'

'One that was sent from here ever so long ago. There was something in it that has to be recovered. Something very, *very* important, please – we want it immediately.'

He really spoke to her as if she had been some strange young woman at Knightsbridge or Paddington; but it had no other effect on her than to give her the measure of his tremendous flurry. Then it was that, above all, she felt how much she had missed in the gaps and blanks and absent answers – how much she had had to dispense with: it was black darkness now, save for this little wild red flare. So much as that she saw and possessed. One of the lovers was quaking somewhere out of town, and the other was quaking just where he stood. This was vivid enough, and after an instant she knew it was all she wanted. She wanted no detail, no fact – she wanted no nearer vision of discovery or shame. 'When was your telegram? Do you mean you sent it from here?' She tried to do the young woman at Knightsbridge.

'Oh yes, from here – several weeks ago. Five, six, seven' – he was confused and impatient, – 'don't you remember?'

'Remember?' she could scarcely keep out of her face, at the word, the strangest of smiles.

But the way he didn't catch what it meant was perhaps even stranger still. 'I mean, don't you keep the old ones?'

'For a certain time.'

'But how long?'

She thought; she *must* do the young woman, and she knew exactly what the young woman would say and, still more, wouldn't. 'Can you give me the date?'

'Oh God, no! It was some time or other in August – toward the end. It was to the same address as the one I gave you last night.'

'Oh!' said the girl, knowing at this the deepest thrill she had ever felt. It came to her there, with her eyes on his face, that she held the whole thing in her hand, held it as she held her pencil, which might have broken at that instant in her tightened grip. This made her feel like the very fountain of fate, but the emotion was such a flood that she had to press it back with all her force. That was positively the reason, again, of her flute-like Paddington tone. 'You can't give us anything a little nearer?' Her 'little' and her 'us' came straight from Paddington. These things were no false note for him – his difficulty absorbed them all. The eyes with which he pressed her, and in the depths of which she read terror and rage and literal tears, were just the same he would have shown any other prim person.

'I don't know the date. I only know the thing went from here, and just about the time I speak of. It wasn't delivered, you see. We've got to recover it.'

XXIII

SHE was as struck with the beauty of his plural pronoun as she had judged he might be with that of her own; but she knew now so well what she was about that she could almost play with him and with her new-born joy. 'You say "about the time you speak of ". But I don't think you speak of an exact time – *do* you?'

He looked splendidly helpless. 'That's just what I want to find out. Don't you keep the old ones? – can't you look it up?'

Our young lady – still at Paddington – turned the question over. 'It wasn't delivered?'

'Yes, it *was*; yet, at the same time, don't you know? it wasn't.' He just hung back, but he brought it out. 'I mean it was intercepted, don't you know? and there was something in it.' He paused again and, as if to further his quest and woo and supplicate success and recovery, even smiled with an effort at the agreeable that was almost ghastly and that turned the knife in her tenderness. What must be the pain of it all, of the open gulf and the throbbing fever, when this was the mere hot breath? 'We want to get what was in it – to know what it was.'

'I see – I see.' She managed just the accent they had at Paddington when they stared like dead fish. 'And you have no clue?'

'Not at all – I've the clue I've just given you.'

'Oh, the last of August?' If she kept it up long enough she would make him really angry.

'Yes, and the address, as I've said.'

'Oh, the same as last night?'

He visibly quivered, as if with a gleam of hope; but it only poured oil on her quietude, and she was still deliberate. She ranged some papers. 'Won't you look?' he went on.

'I remember your coming,' she replied.

He blinked with a new uneasiness; it might have begun to come to him, through her difference, that he was somehow different himself. 'You were much quicker then, you know!'

'So were you – you must do me that justice,' she answered with a smile. 'But let me see. Wasn't it Dover?'

'Yes, Miss Dolman—'

'Parade Lodge, Parade Terrace?'

'Exactly – thank you so awfully much!' He began to hope again. 'Then you *have* it – the other one?'

She hesitated afresh; she quite dangled him. 'It was brought by a lady?'

'Yes; and she put in by mistake something wrong. That's what we've got to get hold of!'

Heavens! what was he going to say? – flooding poor Paddington with wild betrayals! She couldn't too much, for her joy,
dangle him, yet she couldn't either, for his dignity, warn or
control or check him. What she found herself doing was just
to treat herself to the middle way. 'It was intercepted?'

'It fell into the wrong hands. But there's something in it,' he
continued to blurt out, 'that *may* be all right. That is, if it's
wrong, don't you know? It's all right if it's wrong,' he remarkably explained.

What *was* he, on earth, going to say? Mr Buckton and the
counter-clerk were already interested; no one *would* have the
decency to come in; and she was divided between her particular
terror for him and her general curiosity. Yet she already saw
with what brilliancy she could add, to carry the thing off, a little
false knowledge to all her real. 'I quite understand,' she said
with benevolent, with almost patronising quickness. 'The lady
has forgotten what she did put.'

'Forgotten most wretchedly, and it's an immense inconvenience. It has only just been found that it didn't get there; so that
if we could immediately have it—'

'Immediately?'

'Every minute counts. You *have*,' he pleaded, 'surely got
them on file?'

'So that you can see it on the spot?'

'Yes, please – this very minute.' The counter rang with his
knuckles, with the knob of his stick, with his panic of alarm.
'Do, *do* hunt it up!' he repeated.

'I daresay we could get it for you,' the girl sweetly returned.

'Get it?' – he looked aghast. 'When?'

'Probably by to-morrow.'

'Then it isn't here?' – his face was pitiful.

She caught only the uncovered gleams that peeped out of
the blackness, and she wondered what complication, even
among the most supposable, the very worst, could be bad
enough to account for the degree of his terror. There were
twists and turns, there were places where the screw drew
blood, that she couldn't guess. She was more and more glad
she didn't want to. 'It has been sent on.'

'But how do you know if you don't look?'

She gave him a smile that was meant to be, in the absolute irony of its propriety, quite divine. 'It was August 23rd, and we have nothing later here than August 27th.'

Something leaped into his face. '27th – 23rd? Then you're sure? You know?'

She felt she scarce knew what – as if she might soon be pounced upon for some lurid connection with a scandal. It was the queerest of all sensations, for she had heard, she had read, of these things, and the wealth of her intimacy with them at Cocker's might be supposed to have schooled and seasoned her. This particular one that she had really quite lived with was, after all, an old story; yet what it had been before was dim and distant beside the touch under which she now winced. Scandal? – it had never been but a silly word. Now it was a great palpable surface, and the surface was, somehow, Captain Everard's wonderful face. Deep down in his eyes was a picture, the vision of a great place like a chamber of justice, where, before a watching crowd, a poor girl, exposed but heroic, swore with a quavering voice to a document, proved an *alibi*, supplied a link. In this picture she bravely took her place. 'It was the 23rd.'

'Then can't you get it this morning – or some time to-day?'

She considered, still holding him with her look, which she then turned on her two companions, who were by this time unreservedly enlisted. She didn't care – not a scrap, and she glanced about for a piece of paper. With this she had to recognise the rigour of official thrift – a morsel of blackened blotter was the only loose paper to be seen. 'Have you got a card?' she said to her visitor. He was quite away from Paddington now, and the next instant, with a pocket-book in his hand, he had whipped a card out. She gave no glance at the name on it – only turned it to the other side. She continued to hold him, she felt at present, as she had never held him; and her command of her colleagues was, for the moment, not less marked. She wrote something on the back of the card and pushed it across to him.

He fairly glared at it. 'Seven, nine, four—'

'Nine, six, one' – she obligingly completed the number. 'Is it right?' she smiled.

He took the whole thing in with a flushed intensity; then there broke out in him a visibility of relief that was simply a tremendous exposure. He shone at them all like a tall lighthouse, embracing even, for sympathy, the blinking young men. 'By all the powers – it's wrong!' And without another look, without a word of thanks, without time for anything or anybody, he turned on them the broad back of his great stature, straightened his triumphant shoulders, and strode out of the place.

She was left confronted with her habitual critics. ' "If it's wrong it's all right!" ' she extravagantly quoted to them.

The counter-clerk was really awe-stricken. 'But how did you know, dear?'

'I remembered, love!'

Mr Buckton, on the contrary, was rude. 'And what game is that, miss?'

No happiness she had ever known came within miles of it, and some minutes elapsed before she could recall herself sufficiently to reply that it was none of his business.

XXIV

IF life at Cocker's, with the dreadful drop of August, had lost something of its savour, she had not been slow to infer that a heavier blight had fallen on the graceful industry of Mrs Jordan. With Lord Rye and Lady Ventnor and Mrs Bubb all out of town, with the blinds down on all the homes of luxury, this ingenious woman might well have found her wonderful taste left quite on her hands. She bore up, however, in a way that began by exciting much of her young friend's esteem; they perhaps even more frequently met as the wine of life flowed less free from other sources, and each, in the lack of better diversion, carried on with more mystification for the other an intercourse that consisted not a little of peeping out and drawing back. Each waited for the other to commit herself, each profusely curtained for the other the limits of low horizons. Mrs Jordan was indeed probably the more reckless skirmisher; nothing could exceed her frequent incoherence unless it was indeed her occasional bursts of confidence. Her account of her private affairs rose and fell like a flame in the wind – sometimes the bravest bonfire and sometimes a handful of ashes. This our young woman took to be an effect of the position, at one moment and another, of the famous door of the great world. She had been struck in one of her ha'penny volumes with the translation of a French proverb according to which a door had to be either open or shut; and it seemed a part of the precariousness of Mrs Jordan's life that hers mostly managed to be neither. There had been occasions when it appeared to gape wide – fairly to woo her across its threshold; there had been others, of an order distinctly disconcerting, when it was all but banged in her face. On the whole, however, she had evidently not lost heart; these still belonged to the class of things in spite of which she looked well. She intimated that the profits of her trade had swollen so as to float her through any state of the tide, and she had, besides this, a hundred profundities and explanations.

She rose superior, above all, on the happy fact that there were always gentlemen in town and that gentlemen were her greatest admirers; gentlemen from the City in especial – as to whom she was full of information about the passion and pride excited in such breasts by the objects of her charming commerce. The City men *did*, in short, go in for flowers. There was a certain type of awfully smart stockbroker – Lord Rye called them Jews and 'bounders', but she didn't care – whose extravagance, she more than once threw out, had really, if one had any conscience, to be forcibly restrained. It was not perhaps a pure love of beauty: it was a matter of vanity and a sign of business; they wished to crush their rivals, and that was one of their weapons. Mrs Jordan's shrewdness was extreme; she knew, in any case, her customer – she dealt, as she said, with all sorts; and it was, at the worst, a race for her – a race even in the dull months – from one set of chambers to another. And then, after all, there were also still the ladies; the ladies of stockbroking circles were perpetually up and down. They were not quite perhaps Mrs Bubb or Lady Ventnor; but you couldn't tell the difference unless you quarrelled with them, and then you knew it only by their making-up sooner. These ladies formed the branch of her subject on which she most swayed in the breeze; to that degree that her confidant had ended with an inference or two tending to banish regret for opportunities not embraced. There were indeed tea-gowns that Mrs Jordan described – but tea-gowns were not the whole of respectability, and it was odd that a clergyman's widow should sometimes speak as if she almost thought so. She came back, it was true, unfailingly, to Lord Rye, never, evidently, quite losing sight of him even on the longest excursions. That he was kindness itself had become in fact the very moral it all pointed – pointed in strange flashes of the poor woman's nearsighted eyes. She launched at her young friend many portentous looks, solemn heralds of some extraordinary communication. The communication itself, from week to week, hung fire; but it was to the facts over which it hovered that she owed her power of going on. 'They *are*, in one way *and* another,' she often emphasised, 'a tower of strength'; and as the allusion was to the aristocracy, the girl could quite wonder why, if they were so in 'one' way, they should require to be so in two. She thoroughly knew, however, how many ways Mrs Jordan counted in. It all meant simply that her fate was pressing her close. If that fate was to be sealed at the matrimonial altar it was perhaps not remarkable that she shouldn't come all at once to the scratch of overwhelming a mere telegraphist. It would necessarily present to such a person a prospect of regretful sacrifice. Lord Rye – if it *was* Lord Rye – wouldn't be 'kind' to a nonentity of that sort, even though people quite as good had been.

One Sunday afternoon in November they went, by arrangement, to church together; after which – on the inspiration of the moment; the arrangement had not included it – they proceeded to Mrs Jordan's lodging in the region of Maida Vale. She had raved to her friend about her service of predilection; she was excessively 'high', and had more than once wished to introduce the girl to the same comfort and privilege. There was a thick brown fog, and Maida Vale tasted of acrid smoke; but they had been sitting among chants and incense and wonderful music,

during which, though the effect of such things on her mind was
great, our young lady had indulged in a series of reflections but
indirectly related to them. One of these was the result of Mrs
Jordan's having said to her on the way, and with a certain fine
significance, that Lord Rye had been for some time in town.
She had spoken as if it were a circumstance to which little
required to be added – as if the bearing of such an item on her
life might easily be grasped. Perhaps it was the wonder of
whether Lord Rye wished to marry her that made her guest,
with thoughts straying to that quarter, quite determine that
some other nuptials also should take place at St Julian's. Mr
Mudge was still an attendant at his Wesleyan chapel, but this
was the least of her worries – it had never even vexed her
enough for her to so much as name it to Mrs Jordan. Mr
Mudge's form of worship was one of several things – they
made up in superiority and beauty for what they wanted in
number – that she had long ago settled he should take from her,
and she had now moreover for the first time definitely established her own. Its principal feature was that it was to be the
same as that of Mrs Jordan and Lord Rye; which was indeed
very much what she said to her hostess as they sat together later
on. The brown fog was in this hostess's little parlour, where it
acted as a postponement of the question of there being,
besides, anything else than the teacups and a pewter pot, and
a very black little fire, and a paraffin lamp without a shade.
There was at any rate no sign of a flower; it was not for herself
Mrs Jordan gathered sweets. The girl waited till they had had a
cup of tea – waited for the announcement that she fairly
believed her friend had, this time, possessed herself of her
formally at last to make; but nothing came, after the interval,
save a little poke at the fire, which was like the clearing of a
throat for a speech.

XXV

'I THINK you must have heard me speak of Mr Drake?' Mrs
Jordan had never looked so queer, nor her smile so suggestive of
a large benevolent bite.

'Mr Drake? Oh yes; isn't he a friend of Lord Rye?'

'A great and trusted friend. Almost – I may say – a loved friend.'

Mrs Jordan's 'almost' had such an oddity that her companion was moved, rather flippantly perhaps, to take it up. 'Don't people as good as love their friends when they "trust" them?'

It pulled up a little the eulogist of Mr Drake. 'Well, my dear, I love *you*—'

'But you don't trust me?' the girl unmercifully asked.

Again Mrs Jordan paused – still she looked queer. 'Yes,' she replied with a certain austerity; 'that's exactly what I'm about to give you rather a remarkable proof of.' The sense of its being remarkable was already so strong that, while she bridled a little, this held her auditor in a momentary muteness of submission. 'Mr Drake has rendered his lordship, for several years, services that his lordship has highly appreciated and that make it all the more – a – unexpected that they should, perhaps a little suddenly, separate.'

'Separate?' Our young lady was mystified, but she tried to be interested; and she already saw that she had put the saddle on the wrong horse. She had heard something of Mr Drake, who was a member of his lordship's circle – the member with whom, apparently, Mrs Jordan's avocations had most happened to throw her. She was only a little puzzled at the 'separation'. 'Well, at any rate,' she smiled, 'if they separate as friends—!'

'Oh, his lordship takes the greatest interest in Mr Drake's future. He'll do anything for him; he has in fact just done a great deal. There *must*, you know, be changes—!'

'No one knows it better than I,' the girl said. She wished to draw her interlocutress out. 'There will be changes enough for me.'

'You're leaving Cocker's?'

The ornament of that establishment waited a moment to answer, and then it was indirect. 'Tell me what *you're* doing.'

'Well, what will you think of it?'

'Why, that you've found the opening you were always so sure of.'

Mrs Jordan, on this, appeared to muse with embarrassed intensity. 'I was always sure, yes – and yet I often wasn't!'

'Well, I hope you're sure now. Sure, I mean, of Mr Drake.'

'Yes, my dear, I think I may say I *am*. I kept him going till I was.'

'Then he's yours?'

'My very own.'

'How nice! And awfully rich?' our young woman went on.

Mrs Jordan showed promptly enough that she loved for higher things. 'Awfully handsome – six foot two. And he *has* put by.'

'Quite like Mr Mudge, then!' that gentleman's friend rather desperately exclaimed.

'Oh, not *quite*!' Mr Drake's was ambiguous about it, but the name of Mr Mudge had evidently given her some sort of stimulus. 'He'll have more opportunity now, at any rate. He's going to Lady Bradeen.'

'To Lady Bradeen?' This was bewilderment. ' "Going—"?'

The girl had seen, from the way Mrs Jordan looked at her, that the effect of the name had been to make her let something out. 'Do you know her?'

She hesitated; then she found her feet. 'Well, you'll remember I've often told you that if you have grand clients, I have them too.'

'Yes,' said Mrs Jordan; 'but the great difference is that you hate yours, whereas I really love mine. *Do* you know Lady Bradeen?' she pursued.

'Down to the ground! She's always in and out.'

Mrs Jordan's foolish eyes confessed, in fixing themselves on this sketch, to a degree of wonder and even of envy. But she bore up and, with a certain gaiety, 'Do you hate *her*?' she demanded.

Her visitor's reply was prompt. 'Dear no! – not nearly so much as some of them. She's too outrageously beautiful.'

Mrs Jordan continued to gaze. 'Outrageously?'

'Well, yes; deliciously.' What was really delicious was Mrs Jordan's vagueness. 'You don't know her – you've not seen her?' her guest lightly continued.

'No, but I've heard a great deal about her.'

'So have I!' our young lady exclaimed.

Mrs Jordan looked an instant as if she suspected her good faith, or at least her seriousness. 'You know some friend—?'

'Of Lady Bradeen's? Oh yes – I know one.'

'Only one?'

The girl laughed out. 'Only one – but he's so intimate.'

Mrs Jordan just hesitated. 'He's a gentleman?'

'Yes, he's not a lady.'

Her interlocutress appeared to muse. 'She's immensely surrounded.'

'She *will* be – with Mr Drake!'

Mrs Jordan's gaze became strangely fixed. 'Is she *very* good-looking?'

'The handsomest person I know.'

Mrs Jordan continued to contemplate. 'Well, *I* know some beauties.' Then, with her odd jerkiness, 'Do you think she looks *good*?' she inquired.

'Because that's not always the case with the good-looking?' – the other took it up. 'No, indeed, it isn't: that's one thing Cocker's has taught me. Still, there are some people who have everything. Lady Bradeen, at any rate, has enough: eyes and a nose and a mouth, a complexion, a figure—'

'A figure?' Mrs Jordan almost broke in.

'A figure, a head of hair!' The girl made a little conscious motion that seemed to let the hair all down, and her companion watched the wonderful show. 'But Mr Drake *is* another—?'

'Another?' – Mrs Jordan's thoughts had to come back from a distance.

'Of her ladyship's admirers. He's "going", you say, to her?'

At this Mrs Jordan really faltered. 'She has engaged him.'

'Engaged him?' – our young woman was quite at sea.

'In the same capacity as Lord Rye.'

'And was Lord Rye engaged?'

XXVI

MRS JORDAN looked away from her now – looked, she thought, rather injured and, as if trifled with, even a little angry. The mention of Lady Bradeen had frustrated for a while the convergence of our heroine's thoughts; but with this impression of her old friend's combined impatience and diffidence they began again to whirl round her, and continued it till one of them appeared to dart at her, out of the dance, as if with a sharp peck. It came to her with a lively shock, with a positive sting, that Mr Drake was – could it be possible? With the idea she found herself afresh on the edge of laughter, of a sudden and strange perversity of mirth. Mr Drake loomed, in a swift image, before her; such a figure as she had seen in open doorways of houses in Cocker's quarter – majestic, middle-aged, erect, flanked on either side by a footman and taking the name of a visitor. Mr Drake then verily *was* a person who opened the door! Before she had time, however, to recover from the effect of her evocation, she was offered a vision which quite engulfed it. It was communicated to her somehow that the face with which she had seen it rise prompted Mrs Jordan to dash, at a venture, at something that might attenuate criticism. 'Lady Bradeen is rearranging – she's going to be married.'

'Married?' The girl echoed it ever so softly, but there it was at last.

'Didn't you know it?'

She summoned all her sturdiness. 'No, she hasn't told me.'

'And her friends – haven't they?'

'I haven't seen any of them lately. I'm not so fortunate as *you*.'

Mrs Jordan gathered herself. 'Then you haven't even heard of Lord Bradeen's death?'

Her comrade, unable for a moment to speak, gave a slow headshake. 'You know it from Mr Drake?' It was better surely not to learn things at all than to learn them by the butler.

'She tells him everything.'

'And he tells *you* – I see.' Our young lady got up; recovering her muff and her gloves, she smiled. 'Well, I haven't, unfortunately, any Mr Drake. I congratulate you with all my heart. Even without your sort of assistance, however, there's a trifle here and there that I do pick up. I gather that if she's to marry any one, it must quite necessarily be my friend.'

Mrs Jordan was now also on her feet. 'Is Captain Everard your friend?'

The girl considered, drawing on a glove. 'I saw, at one time, an immense deal of him.'

Mrs Jordan looked hard at the glove, but she had not, after all, waited for that to be sorry it was not cleaner. 'What time was that?'

'It must have been the time you were seeing so much of Mr Drake.' She had now fairly taken it in: the distinguished person Mrs Jordan was to marry would answer bells and put on coals and superintend, at least, the cleaning of boots for the other distinguished person whom *she* might – well, whom she might have had, if she had wished, so much more to say to. 'Good-bye,' she added; 'good-bye.'

Mrs Jordan, however, again taking her muff from her, turned it over, brushed it off, and thoughtfully peeped into it. 'Tell me this before you go. You spoke just now of your own changes. Do you mean that Mr Mudge—?'

'Mr Mudge has had great patience with me – he has brought me at last to the point. We're to be married next month and have a nice little home. But he's only a grocer, you know' – the girl met her friend's intent eyes – 'so that I'm afraid that, with the set you've got into, you won't see your way to keep up our friendship.'

Mrs Jordan for a moment made no answer to this; she only held the muff up to her face, after which she gave it back. 'You don't like it. I see, I see.'

To her guest's astonishment there were tears now in her eyes. 'I don't like what?' the girl asked.

'Why, my engagement. Only, with your great cleverness,' the poor lady quavered out, 'you put it in your own way. I mean that you'll cool off. You already *have*—!' And on this, the next instant, her tears began to flow. She succumbed to them and collapsed; she sank down again, burying her face and trying to smother her sobs.

Her young friend stood there, still in some rigour, but taken much by surprise even if not yet fully moved to pity. 'I don't put anything in any "way", and I'm very glad you're suited. Only, you know, you did put to *me* so splendidly what, even for me, if I had listened to you, it might lead to.'

Mrs Jordan kept up a mild, thin, weak wail; then, drying her eyes, as feebly considered this reminder. 'It has led to my not starving!' she faintly gasped.

Our young lady, at this, dropped into the place beside her, and now, in a rush, the small, silly misery was clear. She took her hand as a sign of pitying it, then, after another instant, confirmed this expression with a consoling kiss. They sat there together; they looked out, hand in hand, into the damp, dusky, shabby little room and into the future, of no such very different suggestion, at last accepted by each. There was no definite utterance, on either side, of Mr Drake's position in the great world, but the temporary collapse of his prospective bride threw all further necessary light; and what our heroine saw and felt for in the whole business was the vivid reflection of her own dreams and delusions and her own return to reality. Reality, for the poor things they both were, could only be ugliness and obscurity, could never be the escape, the rise. She pressed her friend – she had tact enough for that – with no other personal question, brought on no need of further revelations, only just continued to hold and comfort her and to acknowledge by stiff little forbearances the common element in their fate. She felt indeed magnanimous in such matters; for if it was very well, for condolence or reassurance, to suppress just then invidious shrinkings, she yet by no means saw herself sitting down, as she might say, to the same table with Mr Drake. There would luckily, to all appearance, be little question of tables; and the circumstance that, on their peculiar lines, her friend's interests would still attach themselves to Mayfair flung over Chalk Farm the first radiance it had shown. Where was one's pride and one's passion when the real way to judge of one's luck was by making not the wrong, but the right, comparison? Before she had again gathered herself to go she felt very small and cautious and thankful. 'We shall have our own house,' she said, 'and you must come very soon and let me show it you.'

'*We* shall have our own too,' Mrs Jordan replied; 'for, don't you know, he makes it a condition that he sleeps out?'

'A condition?' – the girl felt out of it.

'For any new position. It was on that he parted with Lord Rye. His lordship can't meet it; so Mr Drake has given him up.'

'And all for you?' – our young woman put it as cheerfully as possible.

'For me and Lady Bradeen. Her ladyship's too glad to get him at any price. Lord Rye, out of interest in us, has in fact quite *made* her take him. So, as I tell you, he will have his own establishment.'

Mrs Jordan, in the elation of it, had begun to revive; but there was nevertheless between them rather a conscious pause – a pause in which neither visitor nor hostess brought out a hope or an invitation. It expressed in the last resort that, in spite of submission and sympathy, they could now, after all, only look at each other across the social gulf. They remained together as if it would be indeed their last chance, still sitting, though awkwardly, quite close, and feeling also – and this most unmistakably – that there was one thing more to go into. By the time it came to the surface, moreover, our young friend had recognised the whole of the main truth, from which she even drew again a slight irritation. It was not the main truth perhaps that most signified; but after her momentary effort, her embarrassment and her tears, Mrs Jordan had begun to sound afresh – and even without speaking – the note of a social connection. She hadn't really let go of it that she was marrying into society. Well, it was a harmless compensation, and it was all that the prospective bride of Mr Mudge had to leave with her.

XXVII

THIS young lady at last rose again, but she lingered before going. 'And has Captain Everard nothing to say to it?'

'To what, dear?'

'Why, to such questions – the domestic arrangements, things in the house.'

'How *can* he, with any authority, when nothing in the house is his?'

'Not his?' The girl wondered, perfectly conscious of the appearance she thus conferred on Mrs Jordan of knowing, in comparison with herself, so tremendously much about it. Well, there were things she wanted so to get at that she was willing at last, though it hurt her, to pay for them with humiliation. 'Why are they not his?'

'Don't you know, dear, that he has nothing?'

'Nothing?' It was hard to see him in such a light, but Mrs Jordan's power to answer for it had a superiority that began, on the spot, to grow. 'Isn't he rich?'

Mrs Jordan looked immensely, looked both generally and particularly, informed. 'It depends upon what you call—! Not, at any rate, in the least as *she* is. What does he bring? Think what she has. And then, my love, his debts.'

'His debts?' His young friend was fairly betrayed into help-less innocence. She could struggle a little, but she had to let herself go; and if she had spoken frankly she would have said: 'Do tell me, for I don't know so much about him as *that*!' As she didn't speak frankly she only said: 'His debts are nothing – when she so adores him.'

Mrs Jordan began to fix her again, and now she saw that she could only take it all. That was what it had come to: his having sat with her there, on the bench and under the trees, in the summer darkness, and put his hand on her, making her know what he would have said if permitted; his having returned to her afterwards, repeatedly, with supplicating eyes and a fever in his blood; and her having, on her side, hard and pedantic, helped by some miracle and with her impossible condition, only answered him, yet supplicating back, through the bars of the cage, – all simply that she might hear of him, now for ever lost, only through Mrs Jordan, who touched him through Mr Drake, who reached him through Lady Bradeen. 'She adores him – but of course that wasn't all there was about it.'

The girl met her eyes a minute, then quite surrendered. 'What was there else about it?'

'Why, don't you know?' – Mrs Jordan was almost compassionate.

Her interlocutress had, in the cage, sounded depths, but there was a suggestion here somehow of an abyss quite measureless. 'Of course I know that she would never let him alone.'

'How *could* she – fancy! – when he had so compromised her?'

The most artless cry they had ever uttered broke, at this, from the younger pair of lips. '*Had* he so—?'

'Why, don't you know the scandal?'

Our heroine thought, recollected; there was something, whatever it was, that she knew, after all, much more of than Mrs Jordan. She saw him again as she had seen him come that morning to recover the telegram – she saw him as she had seen him leave the shop. She perched herself a moment on this. 'Oh, there was nothing public.'

'Not exactly public – no. But there was an awful scare and an awful row. It was all on the very point of coming out. Something was lost – something was found.'

'Ah yes,' the girl replied, smiling as if with the revival of a blurred memory; 'something was found.'

'It all got about – and there was a point at which Lord Bradeen had to act.'

'Had to – yes. But he didn't.'

Mrs Jordan was obliged to admit it. 'No, he didn't. And then, luckily for them, he died.'

'I didn't know about his death,' her companion said.

'It was nine weeks ago, and most sudden. It has given them a prompt chance.'

'To get married' – this was a wonder – 'within nine weeks?'

'Oh, not immediately, but – in all the circumstances – very quietly and, I assure you, very soon. Every preparation's made. Above all, she holds him.'

'Oh yes, she holds him!' our young friend threw off. She had this before her again a minute; then she continued: 'You mean through his having made her talked about?'

'Yes, but not only that. She has still another pull.'

'Another?'

Mrs Jordan hesitated. 'Why, he was *in* something.'

Her comrade wondered. 'In what?'

'I don't know. Something bad. As I tell you, something was found.'

The girl stared. 'Well?'

'It would have been very bad for him. But she helped him some way – she recovered it, got hold of it. It's even said she stole it!'

Our young woman considered afresh. 'Why, it was what was found that precisely saved him.'

Mrs Jordan, however, was positive. 'I beg your pardon. I happen to know.'

Her disciple faltered but an instant. 'Do you mean through Mr Drake? Do they tell *him* these things?'

'A good servant,' said Mrs Jordan, now thoroughly superior and proportionately sententious, 'doesn't need to be told! Her ladyship saved – as a woman so often saves! – the man she loves.'

This time our heroine took longer to recover herself, but she found a voice at last. 'Ah well – of course I don't know! The great thing was that he got off. They seem then, in a manner,' she added, 'to have done a great deal for each other.'

'Well, it's she that has done most. She has him tight.'

'I see, I see. Good-bye.' The women had already embraced, and this was not repeated; but Mrs Jordan went down with her guest to the door of the house. Here again the younger lingered, reverting, though three or four other remarks had on the way passed between them, to Captain Everard and Lady Bradeen. 'Did you mean just now that if she hadn't saved him, as you call it, she wouldn't hold him so tight?'

'Well, I daresay.' Mrs Jordan, on the door-step, smiled with a reflection that had come to her; she took one of her big bites of the brown gloom. 'Men always dislike one when they have done one an injury.'

'But what injury had he done her?'

'The one I've mentioned. He *must* marry her, you know.'

'And didn't he want to?'

'Not before.'

'Not before she recovered the telegram?'

Mrs Jordan was pulled up a little. 'Was it a telegram?'

The girl hesitated. 'I thought you said so. I mean whatever it was.'

'Yes, whatever it was, I don't think she saw *that*.'

'So she just nailed him?'

'She just nailed him.' The departing friend was now at the bottom of the little flight of steps; the other was at the top, with a certain thickness of fog. 'And when am I to think of you in your little home? – next month?' asked the voice from the top.

'At the very latest. And when am I to think of you in yours?'

'Oh, even sooner. I feel, after so much talk with you about it, as if I were already there!' Then '*Good*-bye!' came out of the fog.

'Good-*bye*!' went into it. Our young lady went into it also, in the opposed quarter, and presently, after a few sightless turns, came out on the Paddington canal. Distinguishing vaguely what the low parapet enclosed, she stopped close to it and stood a while, very intently, but perhaps still sightlessly, looking down on it. A policeman, while she remained, strolled past her; then, going his way a little further and half lost in the atmosphere, paused and watched her. But she was quite unaware – she was full of her thoughts. They were too numerous to find a place just here, but two of the number may at least be mentioned. One of these was that, decidedly, her little home must be not for next month, but for next week; the other, which came indeed as she resumed her walk and went her way, was that it was strange such a matter should be at last settled for her by Mr Drake.

THE REAL RIGHT THING

I

WHEN, after the death of Ashton Doyne – but three months after – George Withermore was approached, as the phrase is, on the subject of a 'volume', the communication came straight from his publishers, who had been, and indeed much more, Doyne's own; but he was not surprised to learn, on the occurrence of the interview they next suggested, that a certain pressure as to the early issue of a Life had been brought to bear upon them by their late client's widow. Doyne's relations with his wife had been, to Withermore's knowledge, a very special chapter – which would present itself, by the way, as a delicate one for the biographer; but a sense of what she had lost, and even of what she had lacked, had betrayed itself, on the poor woman's part, from the first days of her bereavement, sufficiently to prepare an observer at all initiated for some attitude of reparation, some espousal even exaggerated of the interests of a distinguished name. George Withermore was, as he felt, initiated; yet what he had not expected was to hear that she had mentioned him as the person in whose hands she would most promptly place the materials for a book.

These materials – diaries, letters, memoranda, notes, documents of many sorts – were her property, and wholly in her control, no conditions at all attaching to any portion of her heritage; so that she was free at present to do as she liked – free, in particular, to do nothing. What Doyne would have arranged had he had time to arrange could be but supposition and guess. Death had taken him too soon and too suddenly, and there was all the pity that the only wishes he was known to have expressed were wishes that put it positively out of account. He had broken short off – that was the way of it; and the end was ragged and needed trimming. Withermore was conscious, abundantly, how close he had stood to him, but he was not less aware of his comparative obscurity. He was young, a journalist, a critic, a hand-to-mouth character, with little, as yet, as was vulgarly

543

said, to show. His writings were few and small, his relations scant and vague. Doyne, on the other hand, had lived long enough – above all had had talent enough – to become great, and among his many friends gilded also with greatness were several to whom his wife would have struck those who knew her as much more likely to appeal.

The preference she had, at all events, uttered – and uttered in a roundabout, considerate way that left him a measure of freedom – made our young man feel that he must at least see her and that there would be in any case a good deal to talk about. He immediately wrote to her, she as promptly named an hour, and they had it out. But he came away with his particular idea immensely strengthened. She was a strange woman, and he had never thought her an agreeable one; only there was something that touched him now in her bustling, blundering impatience. She wanted the book to make up, and the individual whom, of her husband's set, she probably believed she might most manipulate was in every way to help it to make up. She had not taken Doyne seriously enough in life, but the biography should be a solid reply to every imputation on herself. She had scantly known how such books were constructed, but she had been looking and had learned something. It alarmed Withermore a little from the first to see that she would wish to go in for quantity. She talked of 'volumes' – but he had his notion of that.

'My thought went straight to *you*, as his own would have done,' she had said almost as soon as she rose before him there in her large array of mourning – with her big black eyes, her big black wig, her big black fan and gloves, her general gaunt, ugly, tragic, but striking and, as might have been thought from a certain point of view, 'elegant' presence. 'You're the one he liked most; oh, *much*!' – and it had been quite enough to turn Withermore's head. It little mattered that he could afterward wonder if she had known Doyne enough, when it came to that, to be sure. He would have said for himself indeed that her testimony on such a point would scarcely have counted. Still, there was no smoke without fire; she knew at least what she meant, and he was not a person she could have an interest in flattering. They went up together, without delay, to the great man's vacant study, which was at the back of the house and looked over the large green garden – a beautiful and inspiring scene, to poor Withermore's view – common to the expensive row.

'You can perfectly work here, you know,' said Mrs Doyne: 'you shall have the place quite to yourself – I'll give it all up to you; so that in the evenings, in particular, don't you see? for quiet and privacy, it will be perfection.'

Perfection indeed, the young man felt as he looked about – having explained that, as his actual occupation was an evening paper and his earlier hours, for a long time yet, regularly taken up, he would have to come always at night. The place was full of their lost friend; everything in it had belonged to him; everything they touched had been part of his life. It was for the moment too much for Withermore – too great an honour and even too great a care; memories still recent came back to him, and, while his heart beat faster and his eyes filled with tears, the pressure of his loyalty seemed almost more than he could carry. At the sight of his tears Mrs Doyne's own rose to her lids, and the two, for a minute, only looked at each other. He half expected her to break out: 'Oh, help me to feel as I know you know I want to feel!' And after a little one of them said, with the other's deep assent – it didn't matter which: 'It's here that we're *with* him.' But it was definitely the young man who put it, before they left the room, that it was there he was with *them*.

The young man began to come as soon as he could arrange it, and then it was, on the spot, in the charmed stillness, between the lamp and the fire and with the curtains drawn, that a certain intenser consciousness crept over him. He turned in out of the black London November; he passed through the large, hushed house and up the red-carpeted staircase where he only found in his path the whisk of a soundless, trained maid, or the reach, out of a doorway, of Mrs Doyne's queenly weeds and approving tragic face; and then, by a mere touch of the well-made door that gave so sharp and pleasant a click, shut himself in for three or four warm hours with the spirit – as he had always distinctly declared it – of his master. He was not a little frightened when, even the first night, it came over him that he had really been most affected, in the whole matter, by the prospect, the privilege and the luxury, of this sensation. He had not, he could now reflect, definitely considered the question of the book – as to which there was here, even already, much to consider: he had simply let his affection and admiration – to say nothing of his gratified pride – meet, to the full, the temptation Mrs Doyne had offered them.

How did he know, without more thought, he might begin to ask himself, that the book was, on the whole, to be desired? What warrant had he ever received from Ashton Doyne himself for so direct and, as it were, so familiar an approach? Great was the art of biography, but there were lives and lives, there were subjects and subjects. He confusedly recalled, so far as that went, old words dropped by Doyne over contemporary compilations, suggestions of how he himself discriminated as to other heroes and other panoramas. He even remembered how his friend, at moments, would have seemed to show himself as holding that the 'literary' career might – save in the case of a Johnson and a Scott, with a Boswell and a Lockhart to help – best content itself to be represented. The artist was what he *did* – he was nothing else. Yet how, on the other hand, was not *he*, George Withermore, poor devil, to have jumped at the chance of spending his winter in an intimacy so rich? It had been simply dazzling – that was the fact. It hadn't been the 'terms', from the publishers – though these were, as they said at the office, all right; it had been Doyne himself, his company and contact and presence – it had been just what it was turning out, the possibility of an intercourse closer than that of life. Strange that death, of the two things, should have the fewer mysteries and secrets! The first night our young man was alone in the room it seemed to him that his master and he were really for the first time together.

II

MRS DOYNE had for the most part let him expressively alone, but she had on two or three occasions looked in to see if his needs had been met, and he had had the opportunity of thanking her on the spot for the judgement and zeal with which she had smoothed his way. She had to some extent herself been looking things over and had been able already to muster several groups of letters; all the keys of drawers and cabinets she had, moreover, from the first placed in his hands, with helpful information as to the apparent whereabouts of different matters. She had put him, in a word, in the fullest possible possession, and whether or no her husband had trusted her, she at least, it was clear, trusted her husband's friend. There grew upon Withermore, nevertheless, the impression that, in spite of all these offices, she was not yet at peace, and that a certain unappeasable anxiety continued even to keep step with her confidence. Though she was full of consideration, she was at the same time perceptibly *there*: he felt her, through a super-subtle sixth sense that the whole connection had already brought into play, hover, in the still hours, at the top of landings and on the other side of doors, gathered from the soundless brush of her skirts the hint of her watchings and waitings. One evening when, at his friend's table, he had lost himself in the depths of correspondence, he was made to start and turn by the suggestion that some one was behind him. Mrs Doyne had come in without his hearing the door, and she gave a strained smile as he sprang to his feet. 'I hope,' she said, 'I haven't frightened you.'

'Just a little – I was so absorbed. It was as if, for the instant,' the young man explained, 'it had been himself.'

The oddity of her face increased in her wonder. 'Ashton?'

'He does seem so near,' said Withermore.

'To you too?'

This naturally struck him. 'He does then to you?'

She hesitated, not moving from the spot where she had first stood, but looking round the room as if to penetrate its duskier angles. She had a way of raising to the level of her nose the big black fan which she apparently never laid aside and with which she thus covered the lower half of her face, her rather hard eyes, above it, becoming the more ambiguous. 'Sometimes.'

'Here,' Withermore went on, 'it's as if he might at any moment come in. That's why I jumped just now. The time is so short since he really used to – it only *was* yesterday. I sit in his chair, I turn his books, I use his pens, I stir his fire, exactly as if, learning he would presently be back from a walk, I had come up here contentedly to wait. It's delightful – but it's strange.'

Mrs Doyne, still with her fan up, listened with interest. 'Does it worry you?'

'No – I like it.'

She hesitated again. 'Do you ever feel as if he were – a – quite – a – personally in the room?'

'Well, as I said just now,' her companion laughed, 'on hearing you behind me I seemed to take it so. What do we want, after all,' he asked, 'but that he shall be with us?'

'Yes, as you said he would be – that first time.' She stared in full assent. 'He *is* with us.'

She was rather portentous, but Withermore took it smiling. 'Then we must keep him. We must do only what he would like.'

'Oh, only that, of course – only. But if he *is* here—?' And her sombre eyes seemed to throw it out, in vague distress, over her fan.

'It shows that he's pleased and wants only to help? Yes, surely; it must show that.'

She gave a light gasp and looked again round the room. 'Well,' she said as she took leave of him, 'remember that I too want only to help.' On which, when she had gone, he felt sufficiently – that she had come in simply to see he was all right.

He was all right more and more, it struck him after this, for as he began to get into his work he moved, as it appeared to him, but the closer to the idea of Doyne's personal presence. When once this fancy had begun to hang about him he welcomed it, persuaded it, encouraged it, quite cherished it, looking forward all day to feeling it renew itself in the evening, and waiting for the evening very much as one of a pair of lovers might wait for the hour of their appointment. The smallest accidents humoured and confirmed it, and by the end of three or four weeks he had come quite to regard it as the consecration of his enterprise. Wasn't it what settled the question of what Doyne would have thought of what they were doing? What they were doing was what he wanted done, and they could go on, from step to step, without scruple or doubt. Withermore rejoiced indeed at moments to feel this certitude: there were times of dipping deep into some of Doyne's secrets when it was particularly pleasant to be able to hold that Doyne desired him, as it were, to know them. He was learning many things that he had not suspected, drawing many curtains, forcing many doors, reading many riddles, going, in general, as they said, behind almost everything. It was at an occasional sharp turn of some of the duskier of these wanderings 'behind' that he really, of a sudden, most felt himself, in the intimate, sensible way, face to face with his friend; so that he could scarcely have told, for the instant, if their meeting occurred in the narrow passage and tight squeeze of the past, or at the hour and in the place that actually held him. Was it '67, or was it but the other side of the table?

Happily, at any rate, even in the vulgarest light publicity could ever shed, there would be the great fact of the way Doyne was 'coming out'. He was coming out too beautifully – better yet than such a partisan as Withermore could have supposed. Yet, all the while, as well, how would this partisan have represented to any one else the special state of his own consciousness? It wasn't a thing to talk about – it was only a thing to feel. There were moments, for instance, when, as he bent over his papers, the light breath of his dead host was as distinctly in his hair as his own elbows were on the table before him. There were moments when, had he been able to look up, the other side of the table would have shown him this companion as vividly as the shaded lamplight showed him his page. That he couldn't at such a juncture look up was his own affair, for the situation was ruled – that was but natural – by deep delicacies and fine timidities, the dread of too sudden or too rude an advance. What was intensely in the air was that if Doyne *was* there it was not nearly so much for himself as for the young priest of his altar. He hovered and lingered, he came and went, he might almost have been, among the books and the papers, a hushed, discreet librarian, doing the particular things, rendering the quiet aid, liked by men of letters.

Withermore himself, meanwhile, came and went, changed his place, wandered on quests either definite or vague; and more than once, when, taking a book down from a shelf and finding in it marks of Doyne's pencil, he got drawn on and lost, he had heard documents on the table behind him gently shifted and stirred, had literally, on his return, found some letter he had mislaid pushed again into view, some wilderness cleared by the opening of an old journal at the very date he wanted. How should he have gone so, on occasion, to the special box or drawer, out of fifty receptacles, that would help him, had not his mystic assistant happened, in fine prevision, to tilt its lid, or to pull it half open, in just the manner that would catch his eye? – in spite, after all, of the fact of lapses and intervals in which, *could* one have really looked, one would have seen somebody standing before the fire a trifle detached and over-erect – somebody fixing one the least bit harder than in life.

III

THAT this auspicious relation had in fact existed, had continued, for two or three weeks, was sufficiently proved by the dawn of the distress with which our young man found himself aware that he had, for some reason, from a certain evening, begun to miss it. The sign of that was an abrupt, surprised sense – on the occasion of his mislaying a marvellous unpublished page which, hunt where he would, remained stupidly, irrecoverably lost – that his protected state was, after all, exposed to some confusion and even to some depression. If, for the joy of the business, Doyne and he had, from the start, been together, the situation had, within a few days of his first new suspicion of it, suffered the odd change of their ceasing to be so. That was what was the matter, he said to himself, from the moment an impression of mere mass and quantity struck him as taking, in his happy outlook at his material, the place of his pleasant assumption of a clear course and a lively pace. For five nights he struggled; then, never at his table, wandering about the room, taking up his references only to lay them down, looking out of the window, poking the fire, thinking strange thoughts and listening for signs and sounds not as he suspected or imagined, but as he vainly desired and invoked them, he made up his mind that he was, for the time at least, forsaken.

The extraordinary thing thus became that it made him not only sad not to feel Doyne's presence, but in a high degree uneasy. It was stranger, somehow, that he shouldn't be there than it had ever been that he *was* – so strange indeed at last that Withermore's nerves found themselves quite inconsequently affected. They had taken kindly enough to what was of an order impossible to explain, perversely reserving their sharpest state for the return to the normal, the supersession of the false. They were remarkably beyond control when, finally, one night, after resisting an hour or two, he simply edged out of the room. It had only now, for the first time, become impossible to him to remain there. Without design, but panting a little and positively as a man scared, he passed along his usual corridor and reached the top of the staircase. From this point he saw Mrs Doyne looking up at him from the bottom quite as if she had known he would come; and the most singular thing of all was that, though he had been conscious of no notion to resort to her, had only been prompted to relieve himself by escape, the sight of her position made him recognise it as just, quickly feel it as a part of some monstrous oppression that was closing over both of them. It was wonderful how, in the mere modern London hall, between the Tottenham Court Road rugs and the electric light, it came up to him from the tall black lady, and went again from him down to her, that he knew what she meant by looking as if he would know. He descended straight, she turned into her own little lower room, and there, the next thing, with the door shut, they were, still in silence and with queer faces, confronted over confessions that had taken sudden life from these two or three movements. Withermore gasped as it came to him why he had lost his friend. 'He has been with *you*?'

With this it was all out – out so far that neither had to explain and that, when 'What do you suppose is the matter?' quickly passed between them, one appeared to have said it as much as the other. Withermore looked about at the small, bright room in which, night after night, she had been living her life as he had been living his own upstairs. It was pretty, cosy, rosy; but she had by turns felt in it what he had felt and heard in it what he had heard. Her effect there – fantastic black, plumed and extravagant, upon deep pink – was that of some 'decadent' coloured print, some poster of the newest school. 'You understood he had left me?' he asked.

She markedly wished to make it clear. 'This evening – yes. I've made things out.'

'You knew – before – that he was with me?'

She hesitated again. 'I felt he wasn't with *me*. But on the stairs—'

'Yes?'

'Well – he passed, more than once. He was in the house. And at your door—'

'Well?' he went on as she once more faltered.

'If I stopped I could sometimes tell. And from your face,' she added, 'to-night, at any rate, I knew your state.'

'And that was why you came out?'

'I thought you'd come to me.'

He put out to her, on this, his hand, and they thus, for a minute, in silence, held each other clasped. There was no peculiar presence for either, now – nothing more peculiar than that of each for the other. But the place had suddenly become as if consecrated, and Withermore turned over it again his anxiety. 'What *is* then the matter?'

'I only want to do the real right thing,' she replied after a moment.

'And are we not doing it?'

'I wonder. Are *you* not?'

He wondered too. 'To the best of my belief. But we must think.'

'We must think,' she echoed. And they did think – thought, with intensity, the rest of that evening together, and thought, independently – Withermore at least could answer for himself – during many days that followed. He intermitted for a little his visits and his work, trying, in meditation, to catch himself in the act of some mistake that might have accounted for their disturbance. Had he taken, on some important point – or looked as if he might take – some wrong line or wrong view? had he somewhere benightedly falsified or inadequately insisted? He went back at last with the idea of having guessed two or three questions he might have been on the way to muddle; after which he had, above stairs, another period of agitation, presently followed by another interview, below, with Mrs Doyne, who was still troubled and flushed.

'He's there?'

'He's there.'

'I knew it!' she returned in an odd gloom of triumph. Then as to make it clear: 'He has not been again with *me*.'

'Nor with me again to help,' said Withermore.

She considered. 'Not to help?'

'I can't make it out – I'm at sea. Do what I will, I feel I'm wrong.'

She covered him a moment with her pompous pain. 'How do you feel it?'

'Why, by things that happen. The strangest things. I can't describe them – and you wouldn't believe them.'

'Oh yes, I would!' Mrs Doyne murmured.

'Well, he intervenes.' Withermore tried to explain. 'However I turn, I find him.'

She earnestly followed. ' "Find" him?'

'I meet him. He seems to rise there before me.'

Mrs Doyne, staring, waited a little. 'Do you mean you see him?'

'I feel as if at any moment I may. I'm baffled. I'm checked.' Then he added: 'I'm afraid.'

'Of *him*?' asked Mrs Doyne.

He thought. 'Well – of what I'm doing.'

'Then what, that's so awful, *are* you doing?'

'What you proposed to me. Going into his life.'

She showed, in her gravity, now, a new alarm. 'And don't you *like* that?'

'Doesn't *he*? That's the question. We lay him bare. We serve him up. What is it called? We give him to the world.'

Poor Mrs Doyne, as if on a menace to her hard atonement, glared at this for an instant in deeper gloom. 'And why shouldn't we?'

'Because we don't know. There are natures, there are lives, that shrink. He mayn't wish it,' said Withermore. 'We never asked him.'

'How *could* we?'

He was silent a little. 'Well, we ask him now. That's, after all, what our start has, so far, represented. We've put it to him.'

'Then – if he has been with us – we've had his answer.'

Withermore spoke now as if he knew what to believe. 'He hasn't been "with" us – he has been against us.'

'Then why did you think—'

'What I *did* think, at first – that what he wishes to make us feel is his sympathy? Because, in my original simplicity, I was mistaken. I was – I don't know what to call it – so excited and charmed that I didn't understand. But I understand at last. He only wanted to communicate. He strains forward out of his darkness; he reaches toward us out of his mystery; he makes us dim signs out of his horror.'

'"Horror"?' Mrs Doyne gasped with her fan up to her mouth.

'At what we're doing.' He could by this time piece it all together. 'I see now that at first—'

'Well, what?'

'One had simply to feel he was there, and therefore not indifferent. And the beauty of that misled me. But he's there to be a protest.'

'Against *my* Life?' Mrs Doyne wailed.

'Against *any* Life. He's there to *save* his Life. He's there to be let alone.'

'So you give up?' she almost shrieked.

He could only meet her. 'He's there as a warning.'

For a moment, on this, they looked at each other deep. 'You *are* afraid!' she at last brought out.

It affected him, but he insisted. 'He's there as a curse!'

With that they parted, but only for two or three days; her last word to him continuing to sound so in his ears that, between his need really to satisfy her and another need presently to be noted, he felt that he might not yet take up his stake. He finally went back at his usual hour and found her in her usual place. 'Yes, I *am* afraid,' he announced as if he had turned that well over and knew now all it meant. 'But I gather that you're not.'

She faltered, reserving her word. 'What is it you fear?'

'Well, that if I go on I *shall* see him.'

'And then—?'

'Oh, then,' said George Withermore, 'I *should* give up!'

She weighed it with her lofty but earnest air. 'I think, you know, we must have a clear sign.'

'You wish me to try again?'

She hesitated. 'You see what it means – for me – to give up.'

'Ah, but *you* needn't,' Withermore said.

She seemed to wonder, but in a moment she went on. 'It would mean that he won't take from me—' But she dropped for despair.

'Well, what?'

'Anything,' said poor Mrs Doyne.

He faced her a moment more. 'I've thought myself of the clear sign. I'll try again.'

As he was leaving her, however, she remembered. 'I'm only afraid that to-night there's nothing ready – no lamp and no fire.'

'Never mind,' he said from the foot of the stairs; 'I'll find things.'

To which she answered that the door of the room would probably, at any rate, be open; and retired again as if to wait for him. She had not long to wait; though, with her own door wide and her attention fixed, she may not have taken the time quite as it appeared to her visitor. She heard him, after an interval, on the stair, and he presently stood at her entrance, where, if he had not been precipitate, but rather, as to step and sound, backward and vague, he showed at least as livid and blank.

'I give up.'

'Then you've seen him?'

'On the threshold – guarding it.'

'Guarding it?' She glowed over her fan. 'Distinct?'

'Immense. But dim. Dark. Dreadful,' said poor George Withermore.

She continued to wonder. 'You didn't go in?'

The young man turned away. 'He forbids!'

'You say *I* needn't,' she went on after a moment. 'Well then, need I?'

'See him?' George Withermore asked.

She waited an instant. 'Give up.'

'You must decide.' For himself he could at last but drop upon the sofa with his bent face in his hands. He was not quite to know afterwards how long he had sat so; it was enough that what he did next know was that he was alone among her favourite objects. Just as he gained his feet, however, with this sense and that of the door standing open to the hall, he found himself afresh confronted, in the light, the warmth, the rosy space, with her big black perfumed presence. He saw at a glance, as she offered him a huger, bleaker stare over the mask of her fan, that she had been above; and so it was that, for the last time, they faced together their strange question. 'You've seen him?' Withermore asked.

He was to infer later on from the extraordinary way she closed her eyes and, as if to steady herself, held them tight and long, in silence, that beside the unutterable vision of Ashton Doyne's wife his own might rank as an escape. He knew before she spoke that all was over. 'I give up.'

THE GREAT GOOD PLACE

I

GEORGE DANE had waked up to a bright new day, the face of nature well washed by last night's downpour and shining as with high spirits, good resolutions, lively intentions – the great glare of recommencement, in short, fixed in his patch of sky. He had sat up late to finish work – arrears overwhelming; then at last had gone to bed with the pile but little reduced. He was now to return to it after the pause of the night; but he could only look at it, for the time, over the bristling hedge of letters planted by the early postman an hour before and already, on the customary table by the chimney-piece, formally rounded and squared by his systematic servant. It was something too merciless, the domestic perfection of Brown. There were newspapers on another table, ranged with the same rigour of custom, newspapers too many – what could any creature want of so much news? – and each with its hand on the neck of the other, so that the row of their bodiless heads was like a series of decapitations. Other journals, other periodicals of every sort, folded and in wrappers, made a huddled mound that had been growing for several days and of which he had been wearily, helplessly aware. There were new books, also in wrappers as well as disenveloped and dropped again – books from publishers, books from authors, books from friends, books from enemies, books from his own bookseller, who took, it sometimes struck him, inconceivable things for granted. He touched nothing, approached nothing, only turned a heavy eye over the work, as it were, of the night – the fact, in his high, wide-windowed room, where the hard light of duty could penetrate every corner, of the unashamed admonition of the day. It was the old rising tide, and it rose and rose even under a minute's watching. It had been up to his shoulders last night – it was up to his chin now.

Nothing had passed while he slept – everything had stayed; nothing, that he could yet feel, had died – many things had been born. To let them alone, these things, the new things, let them utterly alone and see if that, by chance, wouldn't somehow prove the best way to deal with them: this fancy brushed his face for a moment as a possible solution, just giving it, as many a time before, a cool wave of air. Then he knew again as well as ever that leaving was difficult, leaving impossible – that the only remedy, the true, soft, effacing sponge, would be to *be* left, to be forgotten. There was no footing on which a man who had ever liked life – liked it, at any rate, as *he* had – could now escape from it. He must reap as he had sown. It was a thing of meshes; he had simply gone to sleep under the net and had simply waked up there. The net was too fine; the cords crossed each other at spots so near together, making at each a little tight, hard knot that tired fingers, this morning, were too limp and too tender to touch. Our poor friend's touched nothing – only stole significantly into his pockets as he wandered over to the window and faintly gasped at the energy of nature. What was most overwhelming was that she herself was so ready. She had soothed him rather, the night before, in the small hours by the lamp. From behind the drawn curtain of his study the rain had been audible and in a manner merciful; washing the window in a steady flood, it had seemed the right thing, the retarding, interrupting thing, the thing that, if it would only last, might clear the ground by floating out to a boundless sea the innumerable objects among which his feet stumbled and strayed. He had positively laid down his pen as on a sense of friendly pressure from it. The kind, full swash had been on the glass when he turned out his lamp; he had left his phrase unfinished and his papers lying quite as if for the flood to bear them away on its bosom. But there still, on the table, were the bare bones of the sentence – and not all of those; the single thing borne away and that he could never recover was the missing half that might have paired with it and begotten a figure.

Yet he could at last only turn back from the window; the world was everywhere, without and within, and, with the great staring egotism of its health and strength, was not to be trusted for tact or delicacy. He faced about precisely to meet his servant and the absurd solemnity of two telegrams on a tray. Brown ought to have kicked them into the room – then he himself might have kicked them out.

'And you told me to remind you, sir –'

George Dane was at last angry. 'Remind me of nothing!'

'But you insisted, sir, that I was to insist!'

He turned away in despair, speaking with a pathetic quaver at absurd variance with his words: 'If you insist, Brown, I'll kill you!' He found himself anew at the window, whence, looking down from his fourth floor, he could see the vast neighbourhood, under the trumpet-blare of the sky, beginning to rush about. There was a silence, but he knew Brown had not left him – knew exactly how straight and serious and stupid and faithful he stood there. After a minute he heard him again.

'It's only because, sir, you know, sir, you can't remember—'

At this Dane did flash round; it was more than at such a moment he could bear. 'Can't remember, Brown? I can't forget. That's what's the matter with me.'

Brown looked at him with the advantage of eighteen years of consistency. 'I'm afraid you're not well, sir.'

Brown's master thought. 'It's a shocking thing to say, but I wish to heaven I weren't! It would be perhaps an excuse.'

Brown's blankness spread like the desert. 'To put them off?'

'Ah!' The sound was a groan; the plural pronoun, *any* pronoun, so mistimed. 'Who is it?'

'Those ladies you spoke of – to lunch.'

'Oh!' The poor man dropped into the nearest chair and stared a while at the carpet. It was very complicated.

'How many will there be, sir?' Brown asked.

'Fifty!'

'Fifty, sir?'

Our friend, from his chair, looked vaguely about; under his hand were the telegrams, still unopened, one of which he now tore asunder. ' "Do hope you sweetly won't mind, to-day, 1.30, my bringing poor dear Lady Mullet, who is so awfully bent," ' he read to his companion.

His companion weighed it. 'How many does *she* make, sir?'

'Poor dear Lady Mullet? I haven't the least idea.'

'Is she – a – deformed, sir?' Brown inquired, as if in this case she might make more.

His master wondered, then saw he figured some personal curvature. 'No; she's only bent on coming!' Dane opened the other telegram and again read out: ' "So sorry it's at eleventh hour impossible, and count on you here, as very greatest favour, at two sharp instead." '

'How many does *that* make?' Brown imperturbably continued.

Dane crumpled up the two missives and walked with them to the waste-paper basket, into which he thoughtfully dropped them. 'I can't say. You must do it all yourself. I shan't be there.'

It was only on this that Brown showed an expression. 'You'll go instead—'

'I'll go instead!' Dane raved.

Brown, however, had had occasion to show before that *he* would never desert their post. 'Isn't that rather sacrificing the three?' Between respect and reproach he paused.

'*Are* there three?'

'I lay for four in all.'

His master had, at any rate, caught his thought. 'Sacrificing the three to the one, you mean? Oh, I'm not going to *her*!'

Brown's famous 'thoroughness' – his great virtue – had never been so dreadful. 'Then where *are* you going?'

Dane sat down to his table and stared at his ragged phrase. ' "There is a happy land – far, far away!" ' He chanted it like a sick child and knew that for a minute Brown never moved. During this minute he felt between his shoulders the gimlet of criticism.

'Are you quite sure you're all right?'

'It's my certainty that overwhelms me, Brown. Look about you and judge. Could anything be more "right", in the view of the envious world, than everything that surrounds us here; that immense array of letters, notes, circulars; that pile of printers' proofs, magazines and books; these perpetual telegrams, these impending guests; this retarded, unfinished and interminable work? What could a man want more?'

'Do you mean there's too much, sir?' – Brown had some-times these flashes.

'There's too much. There's too much. But *you* can't help it, Brown.'

'No, sir,' Brown assented. 'Can't *you*?'

'I'm thinking – I must see. There are hours –!' Yes, there were hours, and this was one of them: he jerked himself up for another turn in his labyrinth, but still not touching, not even again meeting, his interlocutor's eye. If he was a genius for any one he was a genius for Brown; but it was terrible what that meant, being a genius for Brown. There had been times when he had done full justice to the way it kept him up; now, how-ever, it was almost the worst of the avalanche. 'Don't trouble about me,' he went on insincerely and looking askance through his window again at the bright and beautiful world. 'Perhaps it will rain – that *may* not be over. I do love the rain,' he weakly pursued. 'Perhaps, better still, it will snow.'

Brown now had indeed a perceptible expression, and the expression was fear. 'Snow, sir – the end of May?' Without pressing this point he looked at his watch. 'You'll feel better when you've had breakfast.'

'I daresay,' said Dane, whom breakfast struck in fact as a pleasant alternative to opening letters. 'I'll come in immedi-ately.'

'But without waiting—?'

'Waiting for what?'

Brown had at last, under his apprehension, his first lapse from logic, which he betrayed by hesitating in the evident hope that his companion would, by a flash of remembrance, relieve him of an invidious duty. But the only flashes now were the good man's own. 'You say you can't forget, sir; but you do forget—'

'Is it anything very horrible?' Dane broke in.

Brown hung fire. 'Only the gentleman you told me you had asked—'

Dane again took him up; horrible or not, it came back – indeed its mere coming back classed it. 'To breakfast to-day? It *was* to-day; I see.' It came back, yes, came back; the

appointment with the young man – he supposed him young –
and whose letter, the letter about – what was it? – had struck
him. 'Yes, yes; wait, wait.'

'Perhaps he'll do you good, sir,' Brown suggested.

'Sure to – sure to. All right!' Whatever he might do, he
would at least prevent some other doing: that was present to
our friend as, on the vibration of the electric bell at the door of
the flat, Brown moved away. Two things, in the short interval
that followed, were present to Dane: his having utterly forgotten the connection, the whence, whither and why of his guest;
and his continued disposition not to touch – no, not with the
finger. Ah, if he might *never* again touch! All the unbroken seals
and neglected appeals lay there while, for a pause that he
couldn't measure, he stood before the chimney-piece with his
hands still in his pockets. He heard a brief exchange of words in
the hall, but never afterward recovered the time taken by
Brown to reappear, to precede and announce another person
– a person whose name, somehow, failed to reach Dane's ear.
Brown went off again to serve breakfast, leaving host and guest
confronted. The duration of this first stage also, later on, defied
measurement; but that little mattered, for in the train of what
happened came promptly the second, the third, the fourth, the
rich succession of the others. Yet what happened was but that
Dane took his hand from his pocket, held it straight out and felt
it taken. Thus indeed, if he had wanted never again to touch, it
was already done.

II

HE might have been a week in the place – the scene of his new
consciousness – before he spoke at all. The occasion of it then
was that one of the quiet figures he had been idly watching drew
at last nearer and showed him a face that was the highest
expression – to his pleased but as yet slightly confused perception – of the general charm. What *was* the general charm? He
couldn't, for that matter, easily have phrased it; it was such an
abyss of negatives, such an absence of everything. The oddity
was that, after a minute, he was struck as by the reflection of his

own very image in this first interlocutor seated with him, on the easy bench, under the high, clear portico and above the wide, far-reaching garden, where the things that most showed in the greenness were the surface of still water and the white note of old statues. The absence of everything was, in the aspect of the Brother who had thus informally joined him – a man of his own age, tired, distinguished, modest, kind – really, as he could soon see, but the absence of what he didn't want. He didn't want, for the time, anything but just to *be* there, to stay in the bath. He was in the bath yet, the broad, deep bath of stillness. They sat in it together now, with the water up to their chins. He had not had to talk, he had not had to think, he had scarce even had to feel. He had been sunk that way before, sunk – when and where? – in another flood; only a flood of rushing waters, in which bumping and gasping were all. This was a current so slow and so tepid that one floated practically without motion and without chill. The break of silence was not immediate, though Dane seemed indeed to feel it begin before a sound passed. It could pass quite sufficiently without words that he and his mate were Brothers, and what that meant.

Dane wondered, but with no want of ease – for want of ease was impossible – if his friend found in *him* the same likeness, the proof of peace, the gauge of what the place could do. The long afternoon crept to its end; the shadows fell further and the sky glowed deeper; but nothing changed – nothing *could* change – in the element itself. It was a conscious security. It was wonderful! Dane had lived into it, but he was still immensely aware. He would have been sorry to lose that, for just this fact, as yet, the blessed fact of consciousness, seemed the greatest thing of all. Its only fault was that, being in itself such an occupation, so fine an unrest in the heart of gratitude, the life of the day all went to it. But what even then was the harm? He had come only to come, to take what he found. This was the part where the great cloister, inclosed externally on three sides and probably the largest, lightest, fairest effect, to his charmed sense, that human hands could ever have expressed in dimensions of length and breadth, opened to the south its splendid fourth quarter, turned to the great view an outer gallery that combined with the rest of the portico to form a high, dry loggia, such as he a little pretended to himself he had, in Italy, in old days, seen in old cities, old convents, old villas. This recall of the disposition of some great abode of an Order, some mild Monte Cassino, some Grande Chartreuse more accessible, was his main term of comparison; but he knew he had really never anywhere beheld anything at once so calculated and so generous.

Three impressions in particular had been with him all the week, and he could only recognise in silence their happy effect on his nerves. How it was all managed he couldn't have told – he had been content moreover till now with his ignorance of cause and pretext; but whenever he chose to listen with a certain intentness he made out, as from a distance, the sound of slow, sweet bells. How could they be so far and yet so audible? How could they be so near and yet so faint? How, above all, could they, in such an arrest of life, be, to *time* things, so frequent? The very essence of the bliss of Dane's whole change had been precisely that there was nothing now to time. It was the same with the slow footsteps that always, within earshot, to the vague attention, marked the space and the leisure, seemed, in long, cool arcades, lightly to fall and perpetually to recede. This was the second impression, and it melted into the third, as, for that matter, every form of softness, in the great good place, was but a further turn, without jerk or gap, of the endless roll of serenity. The quiet footsteps were quiet figures; the quiet figures that, to the eye, kept the picture human and brought its perfection within reach. This perfection, he felt on the bench by his friend, was now more in reach that ever. His friend at last turned to him a look different from the looks of friends in London clubs.

'The thing was to find it out!'

It was extraordinary how this remark fitted into his thought. 'Ah, wasn't it? And when I think,' said Dane, 'of all the people who haven't and who never will!' He sighed over these unfortunates with a tenderness that, in its degree, was practically new to him, feeling, too, how well his companion would know the people he meant. He only meant some, but they were all who would want it; though of these, no doubt – well, for reasons, for things that, in the world, he had observed – there would never be too many. Not all perhaps who wanted would really find; but none at least would find who didn't really want. And then what the need would have to have been first! What it at first had to be for himself! He felt afresh, in the light of his companion's face, what it might still be even when deeply satisfied, as well as what communication was established by the mere mutual knowledge of it.

'Every man must arrive by himself and on his own feet – isn't that so? We're brothers here for the time, as in a great monastery, and we immediately think of each other and recognise each other as such; but we must have first got here as we can, and we meet after long journeys by complicated ways. Moreover we meet – don't we? – with closed eyes.'

'Ah, don't speak as if we were dead!' Dane laughed.

'I shan't mind death if it's like this,' his friend replied.

It was too obvious, as Dane gazed before him, that one wouldn't but after a moment he asked, with the first articulation, as yet, of his most elementary wonder: 'Where is it?'

'I shouldn't be surprised if it were much nearer than one ever suspected.'

'Nearer town, do you mean?'

'Nearer everything – nearer every one.'

George Dane thought. 'Somewhere, for instance, down in Surrey?'

His Brother met him on this with a shade of reluctance. 'Why should we call it names? It must have a climate, you see.'

'Yes,' Dane happily mused; 'without that – !' All it so securely did have overwhelmed him again, and he couldn't help breaking out: '*What* is it?'

'Oh, it's positively a part of our ease and our rest and our change, I think, that we don't at all know and that we may really call it, for that matter, anything in the world we like – the thing, for instance, we love it most for being.'

'I know what *I* call it,' said Dane after a moment. Then as his friend listened with interest: 'Just simply "The Great Good Place".'

'I see – what can you say more? I've put it to myself perhaps a little differently.' They sat there as innocently as small boys confiding to each other the names of toy animals. 'The Great Want Met.'

'Ah, yes, that's it!'

'Isn't it enough for us that it's a place carried on, for our benefit, so admirably that we strain our ears in vain for a creak of the machinery? Isn't it enough for us that it's simply a thorough hit?'

'Ah, a hit!' Dane benignantly murmured.

'It does for us what it pretends to do,' his companion went on; 'the mystery isn't deeper than that. The thing is probably simple enough in fact, and on a thoroughly practical basis; only it has had its origin in a splendid thought, in a real stroke of genius.'

'Yes,' Dane exclaimed, 'in a sense – on somebody or other's part – so exquisitely personal!'

'Precisely – it rests, like all good things, on experience. The "great want" comes home – that's the great thing it does! On the day it came home to the right mind this dear place was constituted. It always, moreover, in the long run, *has* been met – it always must be. How can it not require to be, more and more, as pressure of every sort grows?'

Dane, with his hands folded in his lap, took in these words of wisdom. 'Pressure of every sort *is* growing!' he placidly observed.

'I see well enough what that fact has done to *you*,' his Brother returned.

Dane smiled. 'I couldn't have borne it longer. I don't know what would have become of me.'

'I know what would have become of *me*.'

'Well, it's the same thing.'

'Yes,' said Dane's companion, 'it's doubtless the same thing.' On which they sat in silence a little, seeming pleasantly to follow, in the view of the green garden, the vague movements of the monster – madness, surrender, collapse – they had escaped. Their bench was like a box at the opera. 'And

I may perfectly, you know,' the Brother pursued, 'have seen you before. I may even have known you well. We don't know.'

They looked at each other again serenely enough, and at last Dane said: 'No, we don't know.'

'That's what I meant by our coming with our eyes closed. Yes – there's something out. There's a gap – a link missing, the great hiatus!' the Brother laughed. 'It's as simple a story as the old, old rupture – the break that lucky Catholics have always been able to make, that they are still, with their innumerable religious houses, able to make, by going into "retreat". I don't speak of the pious exercises; I speak only of the material simplification. I don't speak of the putting off of one's self; I speak only – if one has a self worth sixpence – of the getting it back. The place, the time, the way were, for those of the old persuasion, always there – are indeed practically there for them as much as ever. They can always get off – the blessed houses receive. So it was high time that we – we of the great Protestant peoples, still more, if possible, in the sensitive individual case, overscored and overwhelmed, still more congested with mere quantity and prostituted, through our "enterprise", to mere profanity – should learn how to get off, should find somewhere *our* retreat and remedy. There was such a huge chance for it!'

Dane laid his hand on his companion's arm. 'It's charming, how, when we speak for ourselves, we speak for each other. That was exactly what I said!' He had fallen to recalling from over the gulf the last occasion.

The Brother, as if it would do them both good, only desired to draw him out. 'What you said – ?'

'To *him* – that morning.' Dane caught a far bell again and heard a slow footstep. A quiet figure passed somewhere – neither of them turned to look. What was, little by little, more present to him was the perfect taste. It was supreme – it was everywhere. 'I just dropped my burden – and he received it.'

'And was it very great?'

'Oh, such a load!' Dane laughed.

'Trouble, sorrow, doubt?'

'Oh, no; worse than that!'

'Worse?'

' "Success" – the vulgarest kind!' And Dane laughed again.

'Ah, I know that, too! No one in future, as things are going, will be able to face success.'

'Without something of this sort – never. The better it is the worse – the greater the deadlier. But my one pain here,' Dane continued, 'is in thinking of my poor friend.'

'The person to whom you've already alluded?'

'My substitute in the world. Such an unutterable benefactor. He turned up that morning when everything had somehow got on my nerves, when the whole great globe indeed, nerves, or no nerves, seemed to have squeezed itself into my study. It wasn't a question of nerves, it was a mere question of the displacement of everything – of submersion by our eternal too much. I didn't know *où donner de la tête* – I couldn't have gone a step further.'

The intelligence with which the Brother listened kept them as children feeding from the same bowl. 'And then you got the tip?'

'I got the tip!' Dane happily sighed.

'Well, we all get it. But I daresay differently.'

'Then how did *you* – ?'

The Brother hesitated, smiling. 'You tell me first.'

III

'WELL,' said George Dane, 'it was a young man I had never seen – a man, at any rate, much younger than myself – who had written to me and sent me some article, some book. I read the stuff, was much struck with it, told him so and thanked him – on which, of course, I heard from him again. He asked me things – his questions were interesting; but to save time and writing I said to him: "Come to see me – we can talk a little; but all I can give you is half an hour at breakfast." He turned up at the hour on a day when, more than ever in my life before, I seemed, as it happened, in the endless press and stress, to have lost possession of my soul and to be surrounded only with the affairs of other people and the irrelevant, destructive, brutalising sides of life. It made me literally ill – made me feel as I had never felt that if I should once really, for an hour, lose hold of the thing itself, the thing I was trying for, I should never recover it again. The wild waters would close over me, and I should drop straight to the bottom where the vanquished dead lie.'

'I follow you every step of your way,' said the friendly Brother. 'The wild waters, you mean, of our horrible time.'

'Of our horrible time – precisely. Not, of course – as we sometimes dream – of any other.'

'Yes, any other is only a dream. We really know none but our own.'

'No, thank God – that's enough,' Dane said. 'Well, my young man turned up, and I hadn't been a minute in his presence before making out that practically it would be in him somehow or other to help me. He came to me with envy, envy extravagant – really passionate. I was, heaven save us, the great "success" for him; he himself was broken and beaten. How can I say what passed between us? – it was so strange, so swift, so much a matter, from one to the other, of instant perception and agreement. He was so clever and haggard and hungry!'

'Hungry?' the Brother asked.

'I don't mean for bread, though he had none too much, I think, even of that. I mean for – well, what *I* had and what I was a monument of to him as I stood there up to my neck in preposterous evidence. He, poor chap, had been for ten years serenading closed windows and had never yet caused a shutter to show that it stirred. My dim blind was the first to be raised an inch; my reading of his book, my impression of it, my note and my invitation, formed literally the only response ever dropped into his dark street. He saw in my littered room, my shattered day, my bored face and spoiled temper – it's embarrassing, but I must tell you – the very blaze of my glory. And he saw in the blaze of my glory – deluded innocent! – what he had yearned for in vain.'

'What he had yearned for was to *be* you,' said the Brother. Then he added: 'I see where you're coming out.'

'At my saying to him by the end of five minutes: "My dear fellow, I wish you'd just try it – wish you'd, for a while, just *be* me!" You go straight to the mark, and that was exactly what occurred – extraordinary though it was that we should both have understood. I saw what he could give, and he did too. He saw moreover what I could take; in fact what he saw was wonderful.'

'He must be very remarkable!' the Brother laughed.

'There's no doubt of it whatever – far more remarkable than I. That's just the reason why what I put to him in joke – with a fantastic, desperate irony – became, on his hands, with his vision of his chance, the blessed guarantee of my sitting on this spot in your company. "Oh, if I could just shift it all – make it straight over for an hour to other shoulders! If there only *were* a pair!" – that's the way I put it to him. And then at something in his face, "Would *you*, by a miracle, undertake it?" I asked. I let him know all it meant – how it meant that he should at that very moment step in. It meant that he should finish my work and open my letters and keep my engagements and be subject, for better or worse, to my contacts and complications. It meant that he should live with my life, and think with my brain, and write with my hand, and speak with my voice. It meant, above all, that I should get off. He accepted with magnificence – rose to it like a hero. Only he said: "What will become of *you*?"'

'There was the hitch!' the Brother admitted.

'Ah, but only for a minute. He came to my help again,' Dane pursued, 'when he saw I couldn't quite meet that, could at least only say that I wanted to think, wanted to cease, wanted to do the thing itself – the thing I was trying for, miserable me, and that thing only – and therefore wanted first of all really to *see* it again, planted out, crowded out, frozen out as it now so long had been. "I know what you want," he after a moment quietly remarked to me. "Ah, what I want doesn't exist!" "I know what you want," he repeated. At that I began to believe him.'

'Had you any idea yourself?' the Brother asked.

'Oh, yes,' said Dane, 'and it was just my idea that made me despair. There it was as sharp as possible in my imagination and my longing – there it was so utterly *not* in fact. We were sitting together on my sofa as we waited for breakfast. He presently laid his hand on my knee – showed me a face that the sudden great light in it had made, for me, indescribably beautiful. "It exists – it exists," he at last said. And so, I remember, we sat a while and looked at each other, with the final effect of my finding that I absolutely believed him. I remember we weren't at all solemn – we smiled with the joy of discoverers. He was as glad as I – he was tremendously glad. That came out in the whole manner of his reply to the appeal that broke from me: "Where is it, then, in God's name? Tell me without delay where it is!"'

The Brother had attended with a sympathy! 'He gave you the address?'

'He was thinking it out – feeling for it, catching it. He has a wonderful head of his own and must be making of the whole thing, while we sit here gossiping, something much better than ever *I* did. The mere sight of his face, the sense of his hand on my knee, made me, after a little, feel that he not only knew what I wanted, but was getting nearer to it than I could have got in ten years. He suddenly sprang up and went over to my study-table – sat straight down there as if to write me my passport. Then it was – at the mere sight of his back, which was turned to me – that I felt the spell work. I simply sat and watched him with the queerest, deepest, sweetest sense in the world – the sense of an ache that had stopped. All life was lifted; I myself at least was somehow off the ground. He was already where I had been.'

'And where were you?' the Brother amusedly inquired.

'Just on the sofa always, leaning back on the cushion and feeling a delicious ease. He was already me.'

'And who were you?' the Brother continued.

'Nobody. That was the fun.'

'That *is* the fun,' said the Brother, with a sigh like soft music.

Dane echoed the sigh, and, as nobody talking with nobody, they sat there together still and watched the sweet wide picture darken into tepid night.

IV

AT the end of three weeks – so far as time was distinct – Dane began to feel there was something he had recovered. It was the

thing they never named – partly for want of the need and partly
for lack of the word; for what indeed was the description that
would cover it all? The only real need was to know it, to see it, in
silence. Dane had a private, practical sign for it, which, however, he had appropriated by theft – 'the vision and the faculty
divine'. That, doubtless, was a flattering phrase for his idea of
his genius; the genius, at all events, was what he had been in
danger of losing and had at last held by a thread that might at
any moment have broken. The change was that, little by little,
his hold had grown firmer, so that he drew in the line – more
and more each day – with a pull that he was delighted to find it
would bear. The mere dream-sweetness of the place was superseded; it was more and more a world of reason and order, of
sensible, visible arrangement. It ceased to be strange – it was
high, triumphant clearness. He cultivated, however, but
vaguely, the question of where he was, finding it near enough
the mark to be almost sure that if he was not in Kent he was
probably in Hampshire. He paid for everything but that – that
wasn't one of the items. Payment, he had soon learned, was
definite; it consisted of sovereigns and shillings – just like those
of the world he had left, only parted with more ecstatically –
that he put, in his room, in a designated place and that were
taken away in his absence by one of the unobtrusive, effaced
agents – shadows projected on the hours like the noiseless
march of the sundial – that were always at work. The institution
had sides that had their recalls, and a pleased, resigned perception of these things was at once the effect and the cause of its
grace.

Dane picked out of his dim past a dozen halting similes. The
sacred, silent convent was one; another was the bright country-
house. He did the place no outrage to liken it to an hotel; he
permitted himself on occasion to trace its resemblance to a
club. Such images, however, but flickered and went out –
they lasted only long enough to light up the difference. An
hotel without noise, a club without newspapers – when he
turned his face to what it was 'without' the view opened wide.
The only approach to a real analogy was in himself and his
companions. They were brothers, guests, members; they were

even, if one liked – and they didn't in the least mind what they were called – 'regular boarders'. It was not they who made the conditions, it was the conditions that made them. These conditions found themselves accepted, clearly, with an appreciation, with a rapture, it was rather to be called, that had to do – as the very air that pervaded them and the force that sustained – with their quiet and noble assurance. They combined to form the large, simple idea of a general refuge – an image of embracing arms, of liberal accommodation. What was the effect, really, but the poetisation by perfect taste of a type common enough? There was no daily miracle; the perfect taste, with the aid of space, did the trick. What underlay and overhung it all, better yet, Dane mused, was some original inspiration, but confirmed, unquenched, some happy thought of an individual breast. It had been born somehow and somewhere – it had had to insist on being – the blessed conception. The author might remain in the obscure, for that was part of the perfection: personal service so hushed and regulated that you scarce caught it in the act and only knew it by its results. Yet the wise mind was everywhere – the whole thing, infallibly, centred, at the core, in a consciousness. And what a consciousness it had been, Dane thought, a consciousness how like his own! The wise mind had felt, the wise mind had suffered: then, for all the worried company of minds, the wise mind had seen a chance. Of the creation thus arrived at you could none the less never have said if it were the last echo of the old or the sharpest note of the modern.

Dane again and again, among the far bells and the soft footfalls, in cool cloister and warm garden, found himself wanting not to know more and yet liking not to know less. It was part of the general beauty that there was no personal publicity, much less any personal success. Those things were in the world – in what he had left; there was no vulgarity here of credit or claim or fame. The real exquisite was to be without the complication of an identity, and the greatest boon of all, doubtless, the solid security, the clear confidence one could feel in the keeping of the contract. That was what had been most in the wise mind – the importance of the absolute sense, on the part of its beneficiaries, that what was offered was guaranteed. They had no concern but to pay – the wise mind knew what they paid for. It was present to Dane each hour that he could never be overcharged. Oh, the deep, deep bath, the soft, cool plash in the stillness! – this, time after time, as if under regular treatment, a sublimated German 'cure', was the vivid name for his luxury. The inner life woke up again, and it was the inner life, for people of his generation, victims of the modern madness, mere maniacal extension and motion, that was returning health. He had talked of independence and written of it, but what a cold, flat word it had been! This was the wordless fact itself – the uncontested possession of the long, sweet, stupid day. The fragrance of flowers just wandered through the void, and the quiet recurrence of delicate, plain fare in a high, clean refectory where the soundless, simple service was the triumph of art. That, as he analysed, remained the constant explanation: all the sweetness and serenity were created, calculated things. He analysed, however, but in a desultory way and with a positive delight in the residuum of mystery that made for the great artist in the background the innermost shrine of the idol of a temple; there were odd moments for it, mild meditations when, in the broad cloister of peace or some garden-nook where the air was light, a special glimpse of beauty or reminder of felicity seemed, in passing, to hover and linger. In the mere ecstasy of change that had at first possessed him he had not discriminated – had only let himself sink, as I have mentioned, down to hushed depths. Then had come the slow, soft stages of intelligence and notation, more marked and more fruitful perhaps after that long talk with his mild mate in the twilight, and seeming to wind up the process by putting the key into his hand. This key, pure gold, was simply the cancelled list. Slowly and blissfully he read into the general wealth of his comfort all the particular absences of which it was composed. One by one he touched, as it were, all the things it was such rapture to be without.

It was the paradise of his own room that was most indebted to them – a great square, fair chamber, all beautified with omissions, from which, high up, he looked over a long valley to a far horizon, and in which he was vaguely and pleasantly reminded of some old Italian picture, some Carpaccio or some early Tuscan, the representation of a world without newspapers and letters, without telegrams and photographs, without the dreadful, fatal too much. There, for a blessing, he *could* read and write; there, above all, he could do nothing – he could live. And there were all sorts of freedoms – always, for the occasion, the particular right one. He could bring a book from the library – he could bring two, he could bring three. An effect produced by the charming place was that, for some reason, he never wanted to bring more. The library was a benediction – high and clear and plain, like everything else, but with something, in all its arched amplitude, unconfused and brave and gay. He should never forget, he knew, the throb of immediate perception with which he first stood there, a single glance round sufficing so to show him that it would give him what for years he had desired. He had not had detachment, but there was detachment here – the sense of a great silver bowl from which he could ladle up the melted hours. He strolled about from wall to wall, too pleasantly in tune on that occasion to sit down punctually or to choose; only recognising from shelf to shelf every dear old book that he had to take for lost and unheard. He came back, of course, soon, came back every day; enjoyed there, of all the rare, strange moments, those that were at once most quickened and most caught – moments in which every apprehension counted double and every act of the mind was a lover's embrace. It was the quarter he perhaps, as the days went on, liked best; though indeed it only shared with the rest of the place, with every aspect to which his face happened to be turned, the power to remind him of the masterly general control.

There were times when he looked up from his book to lose himself in the mere tone of the picture that never failed at any moment or at any angle. The picture was always there, yet was made up of things common enough. It was in the way an open window in a broad recess let in the pleasant morning; in the way the dry air pricked into faint freshness the gilt of old bindings; in the way an empty chair beside a table unlittered showed a volume just laid down; in the way a happy Brother – as detached as oneself and with his innocent back presented – lingered before a shelf with the slow sound of turned pages. It was a part of the whole impression that, by some extraordinary law, one's vision seemed less from the facts than the facts from one's vision; that the elements were determined at the moment by the moment's need or the moment's sympathy. What most prompted this reflection was the degree in which, after a while, Dane had a consciousness of company. After that talk with the good Brother on the bench there were other good Brothers in other places – always in cloister or garden some figure that stopped if he himself stopped and with which a greeting became, in the easiest way in the world, a sign of the diffused amenity. Always, always, however, in all contacts, was the balm of a happy ignorance. What he had felt the first time recurred: the friend was always new and yet at the same time – it was amusing, not disturbing – suggested the possibility that he might be but an old one altered. That was only delightful – as positively delightful in the particular, the actual conditions as it might have been the reverse in the conditions abolished. These others, the abolished, came back to Dane at last so easily that he could exactly measure each difference, but with what he had finally been hustled on to hate in them robbed of its terror in consequence of something that had happened. What had happened was that in tranquil walks and talks the deep spell had worked and he had got his soul again. He had drawn in by this time, with his lightened hand, the whole of the long line, and that fact just dangled at the end. He could put his other hand on it, he could unhook it, he was once more in possession. This, as it befell, was exactly what he supposed he must have said to a comrade beside whom, one afternoon in the cloister, he found himself measuring steps.

'Oh, it comes – comes of itself, doesn't it, thank goodness? – just by the simple fact of finding room and time!'

The comrade was possibly a novice or in a different stage from his own; there was at any rate a vague envy in the recognition that shone out of the fatigued, yet freshened face. 'It has come to *you* then? – you've got what you wanted?' That was the

gossip and interchange that could pass to and fro. Dane, years
before, had gone in for three months of hydropathy, and there
was a droll echo, in this scene, of the old questions of the water-
cure, the questions asked in the periodical pursuit of the 'reaction' – the ailment, the progress of each, the action of the skin
and the state of the appetite. Such memories worked in now –
all familiar reference, all easy play of mind; and among them
our friends, round and round, fraternised ever so softly,
until, suddenly stopping short, Dane, with a hand on his companion's arm, broke into the happiest laugh he had yet
sounded.

V

'WHY, it's raining!' And he stood and looked at the splash of
the shower and the shine of the wet leaves. It was one of the
summer sprinkles that bring out sweet smells.

'Yes – but why not?' his mate demanded.

'Well – because it's so charming. It's so exactly right.'

'But everything *is*. Isn't that just why we're here?'

'Just exactly,' Dane said; 'only I've been living in
the beguiled supposition that we've somehow or other a
climate.'

'So have I; so, I daresay, has every one. Isn't that the blessed
moral? – that we live in beguiled suppositions. They come so
easily here, and nothing contradicts them.' The good Brother
looked placidly forth – Dane could identify his phase. 'A
climate doesn't consist in its never raining, does it?'

'No, I daresay not. But somehow the good I've got has been
half the great, easy absence of all that friction of which the
question of weather mostly forms a part – has been indeed
largely the great, easy, perpetual air-bath.'

'Ah, yes – that's not a delusion; but perhaps the sense comes
a little from our breathing an emptier medium. There are fewer
things *in* it! Leave people alone, at all events, and the air is what
they take to. Into the closed and the stuffy they have to be
driven. I've had, too – I think we must all have – a fond sense
of the south.'

'But imagine it,' said Dane, laughing, 'in the beloved British islands and so near as we are to Bradford!'

His friend was ready enough to imagine. 'To Bradford?' he asked, quite unperturbed. 'How near?'

Dane's gaiety grew. 'Oh, it doesn't matter!'

His friend, quite unmystified, accepted it. 'There are things to puzzle out – otherwise it would be dull. It seems to me one can puzzle them.'

'It's because we're so well disposed,' Dane said.

'Precisely – we find good in everything.'

'In everything,' Dane went on. 'The conditions settle that – they determine us.'

They resumed their stroll, which evidently represented on the good Brother's part infinite agreement. 'Aren't they probably in fact very simple?' he presently inquired. 'Isn't simplification the secret?'

'Yes, but applied with a tact!'

'There it is. The thing's so perfect that it's open to as many interpretations as any other great work – a poem of Goethe, a dialogue of Plato, a symphony of Beethoven.'

'It simply stands quiet, you mean,' said Dane, 'and lets us call it names?'

'Yes, but all such loving ones. We're "staying" with some one – some delicious host or hostess who never shows.'

'It's liberty-hall – absolutely,' Dane assented.

'Yes – or a convalescent home.'

To this, however, Dane demurred. 'Ah, that, it seems to me, scarcely puts it. You weren't *ill* – were you? I'm very sure *I* really wasn't. I was only, as the world goes, too "beastly well"!'

The good Brother wondered. 'But if we couldn't keep it up—?'

'We couldn't keep it *down* – that was all the matter!'

'I see – I see.' The good Brother sighed contentedly; after which he brought out again with kindly humour: 'It's a sort of kindergarten!'

'The next thing you'll be saying that we're babes at the breast!'

'Of some great mild, invisible mother who stretches away into space and whose lap is the whole valley—?'

'And her bosom' – Dane completed the figure – 'the noble eminence of our hill? That will do; anything will do that covers the essential fact.'

'And what do you call the essential fact?'

'Why, that – as in old days on Swiss lake-sides – we're *en pension*.'

The good Brother took this gently up. 'I remember – I remember: seven francs a day without wine! But, alas, it's more than seven francs here.'

'Yes, it's considerably more,' Dane had to confess. 'Perhaps it isn't particularly cheap.'

'Yet should you call it particularly dear?' his friend after a moment inquired.

George Dane had to think. 'How do I know, after all? What practice has one ever had in estimating the inestimable? Particular cheapness certainly isn't the note that we feel struck all round; but don't we fall naturally into the view that there *must* be a price to anything so awfully sane?'

The good Brother in his turn reflected. 'We fall into the view that it must pay – that it does pay.'

'Oh, yes; it does pay!' Dane eagerly echoed. 'If it didn't it wouldn't last. It has *got* to last, of course!' he declared.

'So that we can come back?'

'Yes – think of knowing that we shall be able to!'

They pulled up again at this and, facing each other, thought of it, or at any rate pretended to; for what was really in their eyes was the dread of a loss of the clue. 'Oh, when we want it again we shall find it,' said the good Brother. 'If the place really pays, it will keep on.'

'Yes, that's the beauty; that it isn't, thank heaven, carried on only for love.'

'No doubt, no doubt; and yet, thank heaven, there's love in it too.' They had lingered as if, in the mild, moist air, they were charmed with the patter of the rain and the way the garden drank it. After a little, however, it did look rather as if they were trying to talk each other out of a faint, small fear. They saw the increasing rage of life and the recurrent need, and they wondered proportionately whether to return to the front when their hour should sharply strike would be the end of the dream. Was this a threshold perhaps, after all, that could only be crossed one way? They must return to the front sooner or later – that was certain: for each his hour would strike. The flower would have been gathered and the trick played – the sands, in short, would have run.

There, in its place, *was* life – with all its rage; the vague unrest of the need for action knew it again, the stir of the faculty that had been refreshed and reconsecrated. They seemed each, thus confronted, to close their eyes a moment for dizziness; then they were again at peace, and the Brother's confidence rang out. 'Oh, we shall meet!'

'Here, do you mean?'

'Yes – and I daresay in the world too.'

'But we shan't recognise or know,' said Dane.

'In the world, do you mean?'

'Neither in the world nor here.'

'Not a bit – not the least little bit, you think?'

Dane turned it over. 'Well, so it is that it seems to me all best to hang together. But we shall see.'

His friend happily concurred. 'We shall see.' And at this, for farewell, the Brother held out his hand.

'You're going?' Dane asked.

'No, but I thought *you* were.'

It was odd, but at this Dane's hour seemed to strike – his consciousness to crystallise. 'Well, I am. I've got it. You stay?' he went on.

'A little longer.'

Dane hesitated. 'You haven't yet got it?'

'Not altogether – but I think it's coming.'

'Good!' Dane kept his hand, giving it a final shake, and at that moment the sun glimmered again through the shower, but with the rain still falling on the hither side of it and seeming to patter even more in the brightness. 'Hallo – how charming!'

The Brother looked a moment from under the high arch – then again turned his face to our friend. He gave this time his longest, happiest sigh. 'Oh, it's all right!'

But why was it, Dane after a moment found himself wondering, that in the act of separation his own hand was so long retained? Why but through a queer phenomenon of change, on the spot, in his companion's face – change that gave it another, but an increasing and above all a much more familiar identity, an identity not beautiful, but more and more distinct, an identity with that of his servant, with the most conspicuous, the physiognomic seat of the public propriety of Brown? To this anomaly his eyes slowly opened; it was not his good Brother, it was verily Brown who possessed his hand. If his eyes had to open, it was because they had been closed and because Brown appeared to think he had better wake up. So much as this Dane took in, but the effect of his taking it was a relapse into darkness, a recontraction of the lids just prolonged enough to give Brown time, on a second thought, to withdraw his touch and move softly away. Dane's next consciousness was that of the desire to make sure he *was* away, and this desire had somehow the result of dissipating the obscurity. The obscurity was completely gone by the time he had made out that the back of a person writing at his study-table was presented to him. He recognised a portion of a figure that he had somewhere described to somebody – the intent shoulders of the unsuccessful young man who had come that bad morning to breakfast. It was strange, he at last reflected, but the young man was still there. How long had he stayed – days, weeks, months? He was exactly in the position in which Dane had last seen him. Everything – stranger still – was exactly in that position; everything, at least, but the light of the window, which came in from another quarter and showed a different hour. It wasn't after breakfast now; it was after – well, what? He suppressed a gasp – it was after everything. And yet – quite literally – there were but two other differences. One of these was that if he was still on the sofa he was now lying down; the other was the patter on the glass that showed him how the rain – the great rain of the night – had come back. It was the rain of the night, yet when had he last heard it? But two minutes before? Then how many were there before the young man at the table, who seemed intensely occupied, found a moment to look round at him and, on meeting his open eyes, get up and draw near?

'You've slept all day,' said the young man.

'All day?'

The young man looked at his watch. 'From ten to six. You were extraordinarily tired. I just, after a bit, let you alone, and you were soon off.' Yes, that was it; he had been 'off' – off, off, off. He began to fit it together; while he had been off the young man had been on. But there were still some few confusions; Dane lay looking up. 'Everything's done,' the young man continued.

'Everything?'

'Everything.'

Dane tried to take it all in, but was embarrassed and could only say weakly and quite apart from the matter: 'I've been so happy!'

'So have I,' said the young man. He positively looked so; seeing which George Dane wondered afresh, and then, in his wonder, read it indeed quite as another face, quite, in a puzzling way, as another person's. Every one was a little some one else. While he asked himself who else then the young man was, this benefactor, struck by his appealing stare, broke again into perfect cheer. 'It's all right!' That answered Dane's question; the face was the face turned to him by the good Brother there in the portico while they listened together to the rustle of the shower. It was all queer, but all pleasant and all distinct, so distinct that the last words in his ear – the same from both quarters – appeared the effect of a single voice. Dane rose and looked about his room, which seemed disencumbered, different, twice as large. It *was* all right.

MISS GUNTON OF POUGHKEEPSIE

'IT's astonishing what you take for granted!' Lady Champer had exclaimed to her young friend at an early stage; and this might have served as a sign that even then the little plot had begun to thicken. The reflection was uttered at the time the outlook of the charming American girl in whom she found herself so interested was still much in the rough. They had often met, with pleasure to each, during a winter spent in Rome; and Lily had come to her in London towards the end of May with further news of a situation the dawn of which, in March and April, by the Tiber, the Arno and the Seine, had considerably engaged her attention. The Prince had followed Miss Gunton to Florence and then with almost equal promptitude to Paris, where it was both clear and comical for Lady Champer that the rigour of his uncertainty as to parental commands and remittances now detained him. This shrewd woman promised herself not a little amusement from her view of the possibilities of the case. Lily was on the whole showing a wonder; therefore the drama would lose nothing from her character, her temper, her tone. She was waiting – this was the truth she had imparted to her clever protectress – to see if her Roman captive would find himself drawn to London. Should he really turn up there she would the next thing start for America, putting him to the test of that wider range and declining to place her confidence till he should have arrived in New York at her heels. If he remained in Paris or returned to Rome she would stay in London and, as she phrased it, have a good time by herself. Did he expect her to go back to Paris for him? Why not in that case just as well go back to Rome at once? The first thing for her, Lily intimated to her London adviser, was to show what, in her position, *she* expected.

Her position meanwhile was one that Lady Champer, try as she would, had as yet succeeded neither in understanding nor in resigning herself not to understand. It was that of being extraordinarily pretty, amazingly free and perplexingly good, and of presenting these advantages in a positively golden light. How was one to estimate a girl whose nearest approach to a drawback – that is to an encumbrance – appeared to be a grandfather carrying on a business in an American city her ladyship had never otherwise heard of, with whom communication was all by cable and on the subject of 'drawing'? Expression was on the old man's part moreover as concise as it was expensive, consisting as it inveterately did of but the single word 'Draw'. Lily drew, on every occasion in life, and it at least could not be said of the pair – when the 'family idea', as embodied in America, was exposed to criticism – that they were not in touch. Mr Gunton had given her further Mrs Brine, to come out with her, and with this provision and the perpetual pecuniary he plainly figured – to Lily's own mind – as solicitous to the point of anxiety. Mrs Brine's scheme of relations seemed in truth to be simpler still. There was a transatlantic 'Mr Brine', of whom she often spoke – and never in any other way; but she wrote for newspapers; she prowled in catacombs, visiting more than once even those of Paris; she haunted hotels; she picked up compatriots; she spoke above all a language that often baffled comprehension. She mattered, however, but little; she was mainly so occupied in having what Lily had likewise independently glanced at – a good time by herself. It was difficult enough indeed to Lady Champer to see the wonderful girl reduced to that, yet she was a little person who kept one somehow in presence of the incalculable. Old measures and familiar rules were of no use at all with her – she had so broken the moulds and so mixed the marks. What was confounding was her disparities – the juxtaposition in her of beautiful sun-flushed heights and deep dark holes. She had none of the things that the other things implied. She dangled in the air in a manner that made one dizzy; though one took comfort, at the worst, in feeling that one was there to catch her if she fell. Falling, at the same time, appeared scarce one of her properties, and it was positive for Lady Champer at moments that if one held out one's arms one might be, after all, much more likely to be pulled up. That was really a part of the excitement of the acquaintance.

'Well,' said this friend and critic on one of the first of the London days, 'say he does, on your return to your own country, go after you: how do you read, on that occurrence, the course of events?'

'Why, if he comes after me I'll have him.'

'And do you think it so easy to "have" him?'

Lily appeared, lovely and candid – and it was an air and a way she often had – to wonder what she thought. 'I don't know that I think it any easier than he seems to think it to have *me*. I know moreover that, though he wants awfully to see the country, he wouldn't just now come to America unless to marry me; and if I take him at all,' she pursued, 'I want first to be able to show him to the girls.'

'Why "first"?' Lady Champer asked. 'Wouldn't it do as well last?'

'Oh, I should want them to see me in Rome too,' said Lily. 'But, dear me, I'm afraid I want a good many things! What I most want of course is that he should show me unmistakably what *he* wants. Unless he wants me more than anything else in the world I don't want him. Besides, I hope he doesn't think I'm going to be married anywhere but in my own place.'

'I see,' said Lady Champer. 'It's for your wedding you want the girls. And it's for the girls you want the Prince.'

'Well, we're all bound by that promise. And of course *you'll* come!'

'Ah, my dear child—!' Lady Champer gasped.

'You can come with the old Princess. You'll be just the right company for her.'

The elder friend considered afresh, with depth, the younger's beauty and serenity. 'You *are*, love, beyond everything!'

The beauty and serenity took on for a moment a graver cast. 'Why do you so often say that to me?'

'Because you so often make it the only thing to say. But you'll some day find out why,' Lady Champer added with an intention of encouragement.

Lily Gunton, however, was a young person to whom encouragement looked queer; she had grown up without need of it, and it seemed indeed scarce required in her situation. 'Do you mean you believe his mother won't come?'

'Over mountains and seas to see you married? – and to be seen also of the girls? If she does, *I* will. But we had perhaps better,' Lady Champer wound up, 'not count our chickens before they're hatched.' To which, with one of the easy returns of gaiety that were irresistible in her, Lily made answer that neither of the ladies in question struck her quite as chickens.

The Prince at all events presented himself in London with a promptitude that contributed to make the warning gratuitous. Nothing could have exceeded, by this time, Lady Champer's appreciation of her young friend, whose merits 'town' at the beginning of June threw into renewed relief; but she had the imagination of greatness and, though she believed she tactfully kept it to herself, she thought what the young man had thus done a great deal for a Roman prince to do. Take him as he was, with the circumstances – and they were certainly peculiar, and he was charming – it was a far cry for him from Piazza Colonna to Clarges Street. If Lady Champer had the imagination of greatness, which the Prince in all sorts of ways gratified, Miss Gunton of Poughkeepsie – it was vain to pretend the contrary – was not great in any particular save one. She was great when she 'drew'. It was true that at the beginning of June she did draw with unprecedented energy and in a manner that, though Mrs Brine's remarkable nerve apparently could stand it, fairly made a poor baronet's widow, little as it was her business, hold her breath. It was none of her business at all, yet she talked of it even with the Prince himself – to whom it was indeed a favourite subject and whose greatness, oddly enough, never appeared to shrink in the effect it produced upon him. The line they took together was that of wondering if the scale of Lily's drafts made really most for the presumption that the capital at her disposal was rapidly dwindling, or for that of its being practically infinite. 'Many a fellow,' the young man smiled, 'would marry her to pull her up.' He was in any case of the opinion that it was an occasion for deciding – one way or the other – quickly. Well, he did decide – so quickly that within the week Lily communicated to her friend that he had offered her his hand, his heart, his fortune and all his titles, grandeurs and appurtenances. She had given him his answer, and he was in bliss; though nothing, as yet, was settled but that.

Tall, fair, active, educated, amiable, simple, carrying so naturally his great name and pronouncing so kindly Lily's small one, the happy youth, if he was one of the most ancient of princes, was one of the most modern of Romans. This second character it was his special aim and pride to cultivate. He would have been pained at feeling himself an hour behind his age; and he had a way – both touching and amusing to some observers – of constantly comparing his watch with the dial of the day's news. It was in fact easy to see that in deciding to ally himself with a young alien of vague origin, whose striking beauty was reinforced only by her presumptive money, he had even put forward a little the fine hands of his timepiece. No one else, however – not even Lady Champer, and least of all Lily herself – had quite taken the measure, in this connection, of his merit. The quick decision he had spoken of was really a flying leap. He desired incontestably to rescue Miss Gunton's remainder; but to rescue it he had to take it for granted, and taking it for granted was nothing less than – at whatever angle considered – a risk. He never, naturally, used the word to her, but he distinctly faced a peril. The sense of what he had staked on a vague return gave him, at the height of the London season, bad nights, or rather bad mornings – for he danced with his intended, as a usual thing, conspicuously, till dawn – besides obliging him to take, in the form of long explanatory, argumentative and persuasive letters to his mother and sisters, his uncles, aunts, cousins and preferred confidants, large measures of justification at home. The family sense was strong in his huge old house, just as the family array was numerous; he was dutifully conscious of the trust reposed in him, and moved from morning till night, he perfectly knew, as the observed of a phalanx of observers; whereby he the more admired himself for his passion, precipitation and courage. He had only a probability to go upon, but he was – and by the romantic tradition of his race – so in love that he should surely not be taken in.

His private agitation of course deepened when, to do honour to her engagement and as if she would have been ashamed to do less, Lily 'drew' again most gloriously; but he managed to smile beautifully on her asking him if he didn't want her to be splendid, and at his worst hours he went no further than to wish that he might be married on the morrow. Unless it were the next day, or at most the next month, it really at moments seemed best that it should never be at all. On the most favourable view – with the solidity of the residuum fully assumed – there were still minor questions and dangers. A vast America, arching over his nuptials, bristling with expectant bridesmaids and underlaying their feet with expensive flowers, stared him in the face and prompted him to the reflection that if she dipped so deep into the mere remote overflow her dive into the fount itself would verily be a header. If she drew at such a rate in London how wouldn't she draw at Poughkeepsie? he asked himself, and practically asked Lady Champer; yet bore the strain of the question, without an answer, so nobly that when, with small delay, Poughkeepsie seemed simply to heave with reassurances, he regarded the ground as firm and his tact as rewarded. 'And now at last, dearest,' he said, 'since everything's so satisfactory, you *will* write?' He put it appealingly, endearingly, yet as if he could scarce doubt.

'Write, love? Why,' she replied, 'I've done nothing *but* write! I've written ninety letters.'

'But not to mamma,' he smiled.

'Mamma?' – she stared. 'My dear boy, I've not at this time of day to remind you that I've the misfortune to have no mother. I lost mamma, you know, as you lost your father, in childhood. You may be sure,' said Lily Gunton, 'that I wouldn't otherwise have waited for you to prompt me.'

There came into his face a kind of amiable convulsion. 'Of course, darling, I remember – your beautiful mother (she *must* have been beautiful!) whom I should have been so glad to know. I was thinking of *my* mamma – who'll be so delighted to hear from you.' The Prince spoke English in perfection – had lived in it from the cradle and appeared, particularly when alluding to his home and family, to matters familiar and of fact, or to those of dress and sport, of general recreation, to draw such a comfort from it as made the girl think of him as scarce more a foreigner than a pleasant, auburn, slightly awkward, slightly slangy and extremely well-tailored young Briton would have been. He sounded 'mamma' like a rosy English schoolboy; yet just then, for the first time, the things with which he was connected struck her as in a manner strange and far-off. Everything in him, none the less – face and voice and tact, above all his deep desire – laboured to bring them near and make them natural. This was intensely the case as he went on: 'Such a little letter as you *might* send would really be awfully jolly.'

'My dear child,' Lily replied on quick reflection, 'I'll write to her with joy the minute I hear from her. Won't she write to *me*?'

The Prince just visibly flushed. 'In a moment if you'll only—'

'Write to her first?'

'Just pay her a little – no matter how little – your respects.'

His attenuation of the degree showed perhaps a sense of a weakness of position; yet it was no perception of this that made the girl immediately say: 'Oh, *caro*, I don't think I can begin. If you feel that *she* won't – as you evidently do – is it because you've asked her and she has refused?' The next moment, 'I see you *have*!' she exclaimed. His rejoinder to this was to catch her in his arms, to press his cheek to hers, to murmur a flood of tender words in which contradiction, confession, supplication and remonstrance were oddly confounded; but after he had sufficiently disengaged her to allow her to speak again his effusion was checked by what came. 'Do you really mean you can't induce her?' It renewed itself on the first return of ease; or it, more correctly perhaps, in order to renew itself, took this return – a trifle too soon – for granted. Singular, for the hour, was the quickness with which ease could leave them – so blissfully at one as they were; and, to be brief, it had not come back even when Lily spoke of the matter to Lady Champer. It is true that she waited but little to do so. She then went straight to the point. 'What would you do if his mother doesn't write?'

'The old Princess – to *you*?' Her ladyship had not had time to
mount guard in advance over the tone of this, which was doubtless (as she instantly, for that matter, herself became aware) a
little too much that of 'Have you really expected she would?'
What Lily had expected found itself therefore not unassisted to
come out – and came out indeed to such a tune that with all
kindness, but with a melancholy deeper than any she had ever
yet in the general connection used, Lady Champer was moved
to remark that the situation might have been found more
possible had a little more historic sense been brought to it.
'You're the dearest thing in the world, and I can't imagine a
girl's carrying herself in any way, in a difficult position, better
than you do; only I'm bound to say I think you ought to
remember that you're entering a very great house, of tremendous antiquity, fairly groaning under the weight of ancient
honours, the heads of which – through the tradition of the
great part they've played in the world – are accustomed to
a great deal of deference. The old Princess, my dear, you see'
– her ladyship gathered confidence a little as she went – 'is a
most prodigious personage.'

'Why, Lady Champer, of course she is, and that's just what
I like her for!' said Lily Gunton.

'She has never in her whole life made an advance, any more
than any one has ever dreamed of expecting it of her. It's a pity
that while you were there you didn't see her, for I think it would
have helped you to understand. However, as you did see his
sisters, the two Duchesses and dear little Donna Claudia, you
know how charming they all *can* be. They only want to be nice,
I know, and I daresay that on the smallest opportunity you'll
hear from the Duchesses.'

The plural had a sound of splendour, but Lily quite kept her
head. 'What do you call an opportunity? Am I not giving them,
by accepting their son and brother, the best – and in fact the
only – opportunity they could desire?'

'I like the way, darling,' Lady Champer smiled, 'you talk
about "accepting"!'

Lily thought of this – she thought of everything. 'Well, say it
would have been a better one still for them if I had refused him.'

Her friend caught her up. 'But you haven't.'

'Then they must make the most of the occasion as it is.' Lily was very sweet, but very lucid. 'The Duchesses may write or not, as they like; but I'm afraid the Princess simply *must*.' She hesitated, but after a moment went on: 'He oughtn't to be willing moreover that I shouldn't expect to be welcomed.'

'He isn't!' Lady Champer blurted out.

Lily jumped at it. 'Then he has told you? It's her attitude?'

She had spoken without passion, but her friend was scarce the less frightened. 'My poor child, what can he do?'

Lily saw perfectly. 'He can make her.'

Lady Champer turned it over, but her fears were what was clearest. 'And if he doesn't?'

'If he "doesn't"?' The girl ambiguously echoed it.

'I mean if he can't.'

Well, Lily, more cheerfully, declined, for the hour, to consider this. He would certainly do for her what was right; so that after all, though she had herself put the question, she disclaimed the idea that an answer was urgent. There was time, she conveyed – which Lady Champer only desired to believe; a faith moreover somewhat shaken in the latter when the Prince entered her room the next day with the information that there was none – none at least to leave everything in the air. Lady Champer had not yet made up her mind as to which of these young persons she liked most to draw into confidence, nor as to whether she most inclined to take the Roman side with the American or the American side with the Roman. But now in truth she was settled; she gave proof of it in the increased lucidity with which she spoke for Lily.

'Wouldn't the Princess depart – a – from her usual attitude for such a great occasion?'

The difficulty was a little that the young man so well understood his mother. 'The devil of it is, you see, that it's for Lily herself, so much more, she thinks the occasion great.'

Lady Champer mused. 'If you hadn't her consent I could understand it. But from the moment she thinks the girl good enough for you to marry—'

'Ah, she doesn't!' the Prince gloomily interposed. 'However,' he explained, 'she accepts her because there are reasons – my own feeling, now so my very life, don't you see? But it isn't quite open arms. All the same, as I tell Lily, the arms *would* open.'

'If she'd make the first step? Hum!' said Lady Champer, not without the note of grimness. 'She'll be obstinate.'

The young man, with a melancholy eye, quite coincided. 'She'll be obstinate.'

'So that I strongly recommend you to manage it,' his friend went on after a pause. 'It strikes me that if the Princess can't do it for Lily she might at least do it for you. Any girl you marry becomes thereby somebody.'

'Of course – doesn't she? She certainly ought to do it for *me*. I'm after all the head of the house.'

'Well then, make her!' said Lady Champer a little impatiently.

'I will. Mamma adores me, and I adore *her*.'

'And you adore Lily, and Lily adores you – therefore everybody adores everybody, especially as I adore you both. With so much adoration all round, therefore, things ought to march.'

'They shall!' the young man declared with spirit. 'I adore you too – you don't mention that; for you help me immensely. But what do you suppose she'll do if she doesn't?'

The agitation already visible in him ministered a little to vagueness; but his friend after an instant disembroiled it. 'What do I suppose Lily will do if your mother remains stiff?' Lady Champer faltered, but she let him have it. 'She'll break.'

His wondering eyes became strange. 'Just for that?'

'You may certainly say it isn't much – when people love as you do.'

'Ah, I'm afraid then Lily doesn't!' – and he turned away in his trouble.

She watched him while he moved, not speaking for a minute. 'My dear young man, are you afraid of your mamma?'

He faced short about again. 'I'm afraid of this – that if she does do it she won't forgive her. She *will* do it – yes. But Lily will be for her, in consequence, ever after, the person who has made her submit herself. She'll hate her for that – and then she'll hate me for being concerned in it.' The Prince presented it all with clearness – almost with charm. 'What do you say to that?'

His friend had to think. 'Well, only, I fear, that we belong, Lily and I, to a race unaccustomed to counting with such passions. Let her hate!' she, however, a trifle inconsistently wound up.

'But I love her so!'

'Which?' Lady Champer asked it almost ungraciously; in such a tone at any rate that, seated on the sofa with his elbows on his knees, his much-ringed hands nervously locked together and his eyes of distress wide open, he met her with visible surprise. What she met *him* with is perhaps best noted by the fact that after a minute of it his hands covered his bent face and she became aware she had drawn tears. This produced such regret in her that before they parted she did what she could to attenuate and explain – making a great point, at all events, of her rule, with Lily, of putting only his own side of the case. 'I insist awfully, you know, on your greatness!'

He jumped up, wincing. 'Oh, that's horrid.'

'I don't know. Whose fault is it then, at any rate, if trying to help you may have that side?' This was a question that, with the tangle he had already to unwind, only added a twist; yet she went on as if positively to add another. 'Why on earth don't you, all of you, leave them alone?'

'Leave them –?'

'All your Americans.'

'Don't you like them then – the women?'

She hesitated. 'No. Yes. They're an interest. But they're a nuisance. It's a question, very certainly, if they're worth the trouble they give.'

This at least it seemed he could take in. 'You mean that one should be quite sure first what they *are* worth?'

He made her laugh now. 'It would appear that you never *can* be. But also really that you can't keep your hands off.'

He fixed the social scene an instant with his heavy eye. 'Yes. Doesn't it?'

'However,' she pursued as if he again a little irritated her, 'Lily's position is quite simple.'

'Quite. She just loves me.'

'I mean simple for herself. She really makes no differences. It's only we – you and I – who make them all.'

The Prince wondered. 'But she tells me she delights in us; has, that is, such a sense of what we are supposed to "represent".'

'Oh, she *thinks* she has. Americans think they have all sorts of things; but they haven't. That's just *it*' – Lady Champer was philosophic. 'Nothing but their Americanism. If you marry anything you marry that; and if your mother accepts anything that's what she accepts.' Then, though the young man followed the demonstration with an apprehension almost pathetic, she gave him without mercy the whole of it. 'Lily's rigidly logical. A girl – as *she* knows girls – is "welcomed", on her engagement, before anything else can happen, by the family of her young man; and the motherless girl, alone in the world, more punctually than any other. His mother – if she's a "lady" – takes it upon herself. Then the girl goes and stays with them. But she does nothing before. *Tirez-vous de là.*'

The young man sought on the spot to obey this last injunction, and his effort presently produced a flash. 'Oh, if she'll come and *stay* with us' – all would, easily, be well! The flash went out, however, when Lady Champer returned: 'Then let the Princess invite her.'

Lily a fortnight later simply said to her, from one hour to the other, 'I'm going home,' and took her breath away by sailing on the morrow with the Bransbys. The tense cord had somehow snapped; the proof was in the fact that the Prince, dashing off to his good friend at this crisis an obscure, an ambiguous note, started the same night for Rome. Lady Champer, for the time, sat in darkness, but during the summer many things occurred; and one day in the autumn, quite unheralded and with the signs of some of them in his face, the Prince appeared again before her. He was not long in telling her his story, which was simply that he had come to her, all the way from Rome, for news of Lily and to talk of Lily. She was prepared, as it happened, to meet his impatience; yet her preparation was but little older than his arrival and was deficient moreover in an important particular. She was not prepared to knock him down, and she made him talk to gain time. She had however, to understand, put a primary question: 'She never wrote then?'

'Mamma? Oh yes – when she at last got frightened at Miss Gunton's having become so silent. She wrote in August; but Lily's own decisive letter – letter to me, I mean – crossed with it. It was too late – that put an end.'

'A *real* end?'

Everything in the young man showed how real. 'On the ground of her being willing no longer to keep up, by the stand she had taken, such a relation between mamma and *me*. But her rupture,' he wailed, 'keeps it up more than anything else.'

'And is it very bad?'

'Awful, I assure you. I've become for my mother a person who has made her make, all for nothing, an unprecedented advance, a humble submission; and she's so disgusted, all round, that it's no longer the same old charming thing for us to be together. It makes it worse for her that I'm still madly in love.'

'Well,' said Lady Champer after a moment, 'if you're still madly in love I can only be sorry for you.'

'You can *do* nothing for me? – don't advise me to go over?'

She had to take a longer pause. 'You don't at all know then what has happened? – that old Mr Gunton has died and left her everything?'

All his vacancy and curiosity came out in a wild echo. ' "Everything"?'

'She writes me that it's a great deal of money.'

'You've just heard from her then?'

'This morning. I seem to make out,' said Lady Champer, 'an extraordinary number of dollars.'

'Oh, I was sure it was!' the young man moaned.

'And she's engaged,' his friend went on, 'to Mr Bransby.'

He bounded, rising before her. 'Mr Bransby?'

' "Adam P." ' – the gentleman with whose mother and sisters she went home. *They*, she writes, have beautifully welcomed her.'

'*Dio mio!*' The Prince stared; he had flushed with the blow, and the tears had come into his eyes. 'And I believed she loved me!'

'*I* didn't!' said Lady Champer with some curtness.

He gazed about; he almost rocked; and, unconscious of her words, he appealed, inarticulate and stricken. At last, however, he found his voice. 'What on earth then shall I do? I can less than ever go back to mamma!'

She got up for him, she thought for him, pushing a better chair into her circle. 'Stay here with me, and I'll ring for tea. Sit there nearer the fire – you're cold.'

'Awfully!' he confessed as he sank. 'And I believed she loved me!' he repeated as he stared at the fire.

'*I* didn't!' Lady Champer once more declared. This time, visibly, he heard her, and she immediately met his wonder. 'No – it was all the rest; your great historic position, the glamour of your name and your past. Otherwise what she stood out for wouldn't be excusable. But she has the sense of such things, and *they* were what she loved.' So, by the fire, his hostess explained it, while he wondered the more.

'I thought that last summer you told me just the contrary.'

It seemed, to do her justice, to strike her. 'Did I? Oh, well, how does one know? With Americans one is lost!'

THE ABASEMENT OF THE
NORTHMORES

I

WHEN Lord Northmore died public reference to the event took for the most part rather a ponderous and embarrassed form. A great political figure had passed away. A great light of our time had been quenched in mid-career. A great usefulness had somewhat anticipated its term, though a great part, none the less, had been signally played. The note of greatness, all along the line, kept sounding, in short, by a force of its own, and the image of the departed evidently lent itself with ease to figures and flourishes, the poetry of the daily press. The newspapers and their purchasers equally did their duty by it – arranged it neatly and impressively, though perhaps with a hand a little violently expeditious, upon the funeral car, saw the conveyance properly down the avenue, and then, finding the subject suddenly quite exhausted, proceeded to the next item on their list. His lordship had been a person, in fact, in connection with whom there was almost nothing but the fine monotony of his success to mention. This success had been his profession, his means as well as his end; so that his career admitted of no other description and demanded, indeed suffered, no further analysis. He had made politics, he had made literature, he had made land, he had made a bad manner and a great many mistakes, he had made a gaunt, foolish wife, two extravagant sons and four awkward daughters – he had made everything, as he *could* have made almost anything, thoroughly pay. There had been something deep down in him that did it, and his old friend Warren Hope, the person knowing him earliest and probably, on the whole, best, had never, even to the last, for curiosity, quite made out what it was. The secret was one that this distinctly distanced competitor had in fact mastered as little for intellectual relief as for emulous use; and there was quite a kind of tribute to it in the way that, the night before the obsequies and addressing himself to his wife, he said after some silent thought: 'Hang it, you know, I must see the old boy through. I must go to the grave.'

Mrs Hope looked at her husband at first in anxious silence. 'I've no patience with you. You're much more ill than *he* ever was.'

'Ah, but if that qualifies me but for the funerals of others—!'

'It qualifies you to break my heart by your exaggerated chivalry, your renewed refusal to consider your interests. You sacrificed them to him, for thirty years, again and again, and from this supreme sacrifice – possibly that of your life – you might, in your condition, I think, be absolved.' She indeed lost patience. 'To the grave – in this weather – after his treatment of you!'

'My dear girl,' Hope replied, 'his treatment of me is a figment of your ingenious mind – your too-passionate, your beautiful loyalty. Loyalty, I mean, to *me*.'

'I certainly leave it to you,' she declared, 'to have any to *him*!'

'Well, he was, after all, one's oldest, one's earliest friend. I'm not in such bad case – I do go out; and I want to do the decent thing. The fact remains that we never broke – we always kept together.'

'Yes indeed,' she laughed in her bitterness, 'he always took care of that! He never recognised you, but he never let you go. You kept him up, and he kept you down. He used you, to the last drop he could squeeze, and left you the only one to wonder, in your incredible idealism and your incorrigible modesty, how on earth such an idiot made his way. He made his way on your back. You put it, candidly, to others – "What in the world was his gift?" And others are such gaping idiots that they too haven't the least idea. *You* were his gift!'

'And you're mine, my dear!' her husband, pressing her to him, more resignedly laughed. He went down the next day by 'special' to the interment, which took place on the great man's own property, in the great man's own church. But he went alone – that is in a numerous and distinguished party, the flower of the unanimous, gregarious demonstration; his wife had no wish to accompany him, though she was anxious while he was absent. She passed the time uneasily, watching the weather and fearing the cold; she roamed from room to room, pausing vaguely at dull windows, and before he came back she had thought of many things. It was as if, while he saw the great man buried, she also, by herself, in the contracted home of their later years, stood before an open grave. She lowered into it, with her weak hands, the heavy past and all their common dead dreams and accumulated ashes. The pomp surrounding Lord Northmore's extinction made her feel more than ever that it was not Warren who had made anything pay. He had been always what he was still, the cleverest man and the hardest worker she knew; but what was there, at fifty-seven, as the vulgar said, to 'show' for it all but his wasted genius, his ruined health and his paltry pension? It was the term of comparison conveniently given her by his happy rival's now foreshortened splendour that fixed these things in her eye. It was as happy rivals to their own flat union that she always had thought of the Northmore pair; the two men, at least, having started together, after the University, shoulder to shoulder and with – superficially speaking – much the same outfit of preparation, ambition and opportunity. They had begun at the same point and wanting the same things – only wanting them in such different ways. Well, the dead man had wanted them in the way that got them; had got too, in his peerage, for instance, those Warren had never wanted: there was nothing else to be said. There was nothing else, and yet, in her sombre, her strangely apprehensive solitude at this hour, she said much more than I can tell. It all came to this – that there had been, somewhere and somehow, a wrong. Warren was the one who should have succeeded. But she was the one person who knew it now, the single other person having descended, with *his* knowledge, to the tomb.

She sat there, she roamed there, in the waiting greyness of her small London house, with a deepened sense of the several odd knowledges that had flourished in their company of three. Warren had always known everything and, with his easy power – in nothing so high as for indifference – had never cared. John Northmore had known, for he had, years and years before, told her so; and thus had had a reason the more – in addition to not believing her stupid – for guessing at her view. She lived back; she lived it over; she had it all there in her hand. John North-more had known her first, and how he had wanted to marry her the fat little bundle of his love-letters still survived to tell. He had introduced Warren Hope to her – quite by accident and because, at the time they had chambers together, he couldn't help it: that was the one thing he *had* done for them. Thinking of it now, she perhaps saw how much he might conscientiously have considered that it disburdened him of more. Six months later she had accepted Warren, and for just the reason the absence of which had determined her treatment of his friend. She had believed in his future. She held that John Northmore had never afterwards remitted the effort to ascertain the degree in which she felt herself 'sold'. But, thank God, she had never shown him.

Her husband came home with a chill, and she put him straight to bed. For a week, as she hovered near him, they only looked deep things at each other; the point was too quickly passed at which she could bearably have said 'I told you so!' That his late patron should never have had difficulty in making *him* pay was certainly no marvel. But it was indeed a little too much, after all, that he should have made him pay with his life. This was what it had come to – she was sure, now, from the first. Congestion of the lungs, that night, declared itself, and on the morrow, sickeningly, she was face to face with pneumonia. It was more than – with all that had gone before – they could meet. Warren Hope ten days later succumbed. Tenderly, div-inely as he loved her, she felt his surrender, through all the anguish, as an unspeakable part of the sublimity of indifference into which his hapless history had finally flowered. 'His easy power, his easy power!' – her passion had never yet found such relief in that simple, secret phrase for him. He was so proud, so fine and so flexible, that to fail a little had been as bad for him as to fail much; therefore he had opened the flood-gates wide – had thrown, as the saying was, the helve after the hatchet. He had amused himself with seeing what the devouring world would take. Well, it had taken all.

II

But it was after he had gone that his name showed as written in water. What had he left? He had only left *her* and her grey desolation, her lonely piety and her sore, unresting rebellion. Sometimes, when a man died, it did something for him that life had not done; people, after a little, on one side or the other, discovered and named him, annexing him to their flag. But the sense of having lost Warren Hope appeared not in the least to have quickened the world's wit; the sharper pang for his widow indeed sprang just from the commonplace way in which he was spoken of as known. She received letters enough, when it came to that, for of course, personally, he had been liked; the newspapers were fairly copious and perfectly stupid; the three or four societies, 'learned' and other, to which he had belonged, passed resolutions of regret and condolence, and the three or four colleagues about whom he himself used to be most amusing stammered eulogies; but almost anything, really, would have been better for her than the general understanding that the occasion had been met. Two or three solemn noodles in 'administrative circles' wrote her that she must have been gratified at the unanimity of regret, the implication being clearly that she was ridiculous if she were not. Meanwhile what she felt was that she could have borne well enough his not being noticed at all; what she couldn't bear was this treatment of him as a minor celebrity. He was, in economics, in the higher politics, in philosophic history, a splendid unestimated genius, or he was nothing. He wasn't, at any rate – heaven forbid! – a 'notable figure'. The waters, none the less, closed over him as over Lord Northmore; which was precisely, as time went on, the fact she found it hardest to accept. That personage, the week after his death, without an hour of reprieve, the place swept as clean of him as a hall, lent for a charity, of the tables and booths of a three-days' bazaar – that personage had gone straight to the bottom, dropped like a crumpled circular into the waste-basket. Where then was the difference? – if the end *was* the end for each alike? For Warren it should have been properly the beginning.

During the first six months she wondered what she could herself do, and had much of the time the sense of walking by some swift stream on which an object dear to her was floating out to sea. All her instinct was to keep up with it, not to lose sight of it, to hurry along the bank and reach in advance some point from which she could stretch forth and catch and save it. Alas, it only floated and floated; she held it in sight, for the stream was long, but no convenient projection offered itself to the rescue. She ran, she watched, she lived with her great fear, and all the while, as the distance to the sea diminished, the current visibly increased. At the last, to do anything, she must hurry. She went into his papers, she ransacked his drawers; something of that sort, at least, she might do. But there were difficulties, the case was special; she lost herself in the labyrinth, and her competence was questioned; two or three friends to whose judgement she appealed struck her as tepid, even as cold, and publishers, when sounded – most of all in fact the house through which his three or four important volumes had been given to the world – showed an absence of eagerness for a collection of literary remains. It was only now that she fully understood how remarkably little the three or four important volumes had 'done'. He had successfully kept that from her, as he had kept other things she might have ached at: to handle his notes and memoranda was to come at every turn, in the wilderness, the wide desert, upon the footsteps of his scrupulous soul. But she had at last to accept the truth that it was only for herself, her own relief, she must follow him. His work, unencouraged and interrupted, failed of a final form: there would have been nothing to offer but fragments of fragments. She felt, all the same, in recognising this, that she abandoned him; he died for her at that hour over again.

The hour moreover happened to coincide with another hour, so that the two mingled their bitterness. She received a note from Lady Northmore, announcing a desire to gather in and publish his late lordship's letters, so numerous and so interesting, and inviting Mrs Hope, as a more than probable depositary, to be so good as to contribute to the project those addressed to her husband. This gave her a start of more kinds than one. The long comedy of his late lordship's greatness was *not* then over? The monument was to be built to him that she had but now schooled herself to regard as impossible for his defeated friend? Everything was to break out afresh, the comparisons, the contrasts, the conclusions so invidiously in his favour? – the business all cleverly managed to place him in the light and keep every one else in the shade? Letters? – had John Northmore indited three lines that could, at that time of day, be of the smallest consequence? Whose idea was such a publication, and what infatuated editorial patronage could the family have secured? She of course didn't know, but she should be surprised if there were material. Then it came to her, on reflection, that editors and publishers must of course have flocked – his star would still rule. Why shouldn't he make his letters pay in death as he had made them pay in life? Such as they were they *had* paid. They would be a tremendous success. She thought again of her husband's rich, confused relics – thought of the loose blocks of marble that could only lie now where they had fallen; after which, with one of her deep and frequent sighs, she took up anew Lady Northmore's communication.

His letters to Warren, kept or not kept, had never so much as occurred to her. Those to herself were buried and safe – she knew where her hand would find them; but those to herself her correspondent had carefully not asked for and was probably unaware of the existence of. They belonged moreover to that phase of the great man's career that was distinctly – as it could only be called – previous: previous to the greatness, to the proper subject of the volume, and, in especial, to Lady Northmore. The faded fat packet lurked still where it had lurked for years; but she could no more to-day have said why she had kept it than why – though he knew of the early episode – she had never mentioned her preservation of it to Warren. This last circumstance certainly absolved her from mentioning it to Lady Northmore, who, no doubt, knew of the episode too. The odd part of the matter was, at any rate, that her retention of these documents had not been an accident. She had obeyed a dim instinct or a vague calculation. A calculation of what? She couldn't have told: it had operated, at the back of her head, simply as a sense that, not destroyed, the complete little collection made for safety. But for whose, just heaven? Perhaps she should still see; though nothing, she trusted, would occur requiring her to touch the things or to read them over. She wouldn't have touched them or read them over for the world.

She had not as yet, at all events, overhauled those receptacles in which the letters Warren kept would have accumulated; and she had her doubts of their containing any of Lord Northmore's. Why should he have kept any? Even she herself had had more reasons. Was his lordship's later epistolary manner supposed to be good, or of the kind that, on any grounds, prohibited the waste-basket or the fire? Warren had lived in a deluge of documents, but these perhaps he might have regarded as contributions to contemporary history. None the less, surely, he wouldn't have stored up many. She began to look, in cupboards, boxes, drawers yet unvisited, and she had her surprises both as to what he had kept and as to what he hadn't. Every word of her own was there – every note that, in occasional absence, he had ever had from her. Well, that matched happily enough her knowing just where to put her finger on every note that, on such occasions, she herself had received. *Their* correspondence at least was complete. But so, in fine, on one side, it gradually appeared, was Lord Northmore's. The superabundance of these missives had not been sacrificed by her husband, evidently, to any passing convenience; she judged more and more that he had preserved every scrap; and she was unable to conceal from herself that she was – she scarce knew why – a trifle disappointed. She had not quite unhopefully, even though vaguely, seen herself writing to Lady Northmore that, to her great regret and after an exhausting search, she could find nothing at all.

She found, alas, in fact, everything. She was conscientious and she hunted to the end, by which time one of the tables quite groaned with the fruits of her quest. The letters appeared moreover to have been cared for and roughly classified – she should be able to consign them to the family in excellent order. She made sure, at the last, that she had overlooked nothing, and then, fatigued and distinctly irritated, she prepared to answer in a sense so different from the answer she had, as might have been said, planned. Face to face with her note, however, she found she couldn't write it; and, not to be alone longer with the pile on the table, she presently went out of the room. Late in the evening – just before going to bed – she came back, almost as if she hoped there might have been since the afternoon some pleasant intervention in the interest of her distaste. Mightn't it have magically happened that her discovery was a mistake? – that the letters were either not there or were, after all, somebody's else? Ah, they *were* there, and as she raised her lighted candle in the dusk the pile on the table squared itself with insolence. On this, poor lady, she had for an hour her temptation.

It was obscure, it was absurd; all that could be said of it was that it was, for the moment, extreme. She saw herself, as she circled round the table, writing with perfect impunity: 'Dear Lady Northmore, I have hunted high and low and have found nothing whatever. My husband evidently, before his death, destroyed everything. I'm *so* sorry – I should have liked so much to help you. Yours most truly.' She should have only, on the morrow, privately and resolutely to annihilate the heap, and those words would remain an account of the matter that nobody was in a position to challenge. What good would it do her? – was *that* the question? It would do her the good that it would make poor Warren seem to have been just a little less used and duped. This, in her mood, would ease her off. Well, the temptation was real; but so, she after a while felt, were other things. She sat down at midnight to her note. 'Dear Lady Northmore, I am happy to say I have found a great deal – my husband appears to have been so careful to keep everything. I have a mass at your disposition if you can conveniently send. So glad to be able to help your work. Yours most truly.' She stepped out as she was and dropped the letter into the nearest pillar-box. By noon the next day the table had, to her relief, been cleared. Her ladyship sent a responsible servant – her butler, in a four-wheeler, with a large japanned box.

III

AFTER this, for a twelvemonth, there were frequent announcements and allusions. They came to her from every side, and there were hours at which the air, to her imagination, contained almost nothing else. There had been, at an early stage, immediately after Lady Northmore's communication to her, an official appeal, a circular *urbi et orbi*, reproduced, applauded, commended in every newspaper, desiring all possessors of letters to remit them without delay to the family. The family, to do it justice, rewarded the sacrifice freely – so far as it was a reward to keep the world informed of the rapid progress of the work. Material had shown itself more copious than was to have been conceived. Interesting as the imminent volumes had naturally been expected to prove, those who had been favoured with a glimpse of their contents already felt warranted in promising the public an unprecedented treat. They would throw upon certain sides of the writer's mind and career lights hitherto unsuspected. Lady Northmore, deeply indebted for favours received, begged to renew her solicitation; gratifying as the response had been, it was believed that, particularly in connection with several dates, which were given, a residuum of buried treasure might still be looked for.

Mrs Hope saw, she felt, as time went on, fewer and fewer people; yet her circle was even now not too narrow for her to hear it blown about that Thompson and Johnson had 'been asked'. Conversation in the London world struck her for a time as almost confined to such questions and such answers. 'Have *you* been asked?' 'Oh yes – rather. Months ago. And you?' The whole place was under contribution, and the striking thing was that being asked had been clearly accompanied, in every case, with the ability to respond. The spring had but to be touched – millions of letters flew out. Ten volumes, at such a rate, Mrs Hope mused, would not exhaust the supply. She mused a great deal – did nothing but muse; and, strange as this may at first appear, it was inevitable that one of the final results of her musing should be a principle of doubt. It could only seem possible, in view of such unanimity, that she should, after all, have been mistaken. It *was* then, to the general sense, the great departed's, a reputation sound and safe. It wasn't he who had been at fault – it was her silly self, still burdened with the fallibility of Being. He had been a giant then, and the letters would triumphantly show it. She had looked only at the envelopes of those she had surrendered, but she was prepared for anything. There was the fact, not to be blinked, of Warren's own marked testimony. The attitude of others was but *his* attitude; and she sighed as she perceived him in this case, for the only time in his life, on the side of the chattering crowd.

She was perfectly aware that her obsession had run away with her, but as Lady Northmore's publication really loomed into view – it was now definitely announced for March, and they were in January – her pulses quickened so that she found herself, in the long nights, mostly lying awake. It was in one of these vigils that, suddenly, in the cold darkness, she felt the brush of almost the only thought that, for many a month, had not made her wince; the effect of which was that she bounded out of bed with a new felicity. Her impatience flashed, on the spot, up to its maximum – she could scarce wait for day to give herself to action. Her idea was neither more nor less than immediately to collect and put forth the letters of *her* hero. She would publish her husband's own – glory be to God! – and she even wasted none of her time in wondering why she had waited. She *had* waited – all too long; yet it was perhaps no more than natural that, for eyes sealed with tears and a heart heavy with injustice, there should not have been an instant vision of where her remedy lay. She thought of it already as her remedy – though she would probably have found an awkwardness in giving a name, publicly, to her wrong. It was a wrong to feel, but not, doubtless, to talk about. And lo, straightway, the balm had begun to drop: the balance would so soon be even. She spent all that day in reading over her own old letters, too intimate and too sacred – oh, unluckily! – to figure in her project, but pouring wind, nevertheless, into its sails and adding magnificence to her presumption. She had of course, with separation, all their years, never frequent and never prolonged, known her husband as a correspondent much less than others; still, these relics constituted a property – she was surprised at their number – and testified hugely to his inimitable gift.

He was a letter-writer if you liked – natural, witty, various, vivid, playing, with the idlest, lightest hand, up and down the whole scale. His easy power – his easy power: everything that brought him back brought back that. The most numerous were of course the earlier, and the series of those during their engagement, witnesses of their long probation, which were rich and unbroken; so full indeed and so wonderful that she fairly groaned at having to defer to the common measure of married modesty. There was discretion, there was usage, there was taste; but she would fain have flown in their face. If there were pages too intimate to publish, there were too many others too rare to suppress. Perhaps after her death –! It not only pulled her up, the happy thought of that liberation alike for herself and for her treasure, making her promise herself straightway to arrange: it quickened extremely her impatience for the term of her mortality, which would leave a free field to the justice she invoked. Her great resource, however, clearly, would be the friends, the colleagues, the private admirers to whom he had written for years, to whom she had known him to write, and many of whose own letters, by no means remarkable, she had come upon in her recent sortings and siftings. She drew up a list of these persons and immediately wrote to them or, in cases in which they had passed away, to their widows, children, representatives; reminding herself in the process not disagreeably, in fact quite inspiringly, of Lady Northmore. It had struck her that Lady Northmore took, somehow, a good deal for granted; but this idea failed, oddly enough, to occur to her in regard to Mrs Hope. It was indeed with her ladyship she began, addressing her exactly in the terms of this personage's own appeal, every word of which she remembered.

Then she waited, but she had not, in connection with that quarter, to wait long. 'Dear Mrs Hope, I have hunted high and low and have found nothing whatever. My husband evidently, before his death, destroyed everything. I'm so sorry – I should have liked so much to help you. Yours most truly.' This was all Lady Northmore wrote, without the grace of an allusion to the assistance she herself had received; though even in the first flush of amazement and resentment our friend recognised the odd identity of form between her note and another that had never been written. She was answered as she had, in the like case, in her one evil hour, dreamed of answering. But the answer was not over with this – it had still to flow in, day after day, from every other source reached by her question. And day after day, while amazement and resentment deepened, it consisted simply of three lines of regret. Everybody had looked, and everybody had looked in vain. Everybody would have been so glad, but everybody was reduced to being, like Lady Northmore, so sorry. Nobody could find anything, and nothing, it was therefore to be gathered, had been kept. Some of these informants were more prompt than others, but all replied in time, and the business went on for a month, at the end of which the poor woman, stricken, chilled to the heart, accepted perforce her situation and turned her face to the wall. In this position, as it were, she remained for days, taking heed of nothing and only feeling and nursing her wound. It was a wound the more cruel for having found her so unguarded. From the moment her remedy had been whispered to her, she had not had an hour of doubt, and the beautiful side of it had seemed that it was, above all, so easy. The strangeness of the issue was even greater than the pain. Truly it was a world *pour rire*, the world in which John Northmore's letters were classed and labelled for posterity and Warren Hope's kindled fires. All sense, all measure of anything, could only leave one – leave one indifferent and dumb. There was nothing to be done – the show was upside-down. John Northmore was immortal and Warren Hope was damned. And for herself, she was finished. She was beaten. She leaned thus, motionless, muffled, for a time of which, as I say, she took no account; then at last she was reached by a great sound that made her turn her veiled head. It was the report of the appearance of Lady Northmore's volumes.

IV

THIS was a great noise indeed, and all the papers, that day, were particularly loud with it. It met the reader on the threshold, and the work was everywhere the subject of a 'leader' as well as of a review. The reviews moreover, she saw at a glance, overflowed with quotation; it was enough to look at two or three sheets to judge of the enthusiasm. Mrs Hope looked at the two or three that, for confirmation of the single one she habitually received, she caused, while at breakfast, to be purchased; but her attention failed to penetrate further; she couldn't, she found, face the contrast between the pride of the Northmores on such a morning and her own humiliation. The papers brought it too sharply home; she pushed them away and, to get rid of them, not to feel their presence, left the house early. She found pretexts for remaining out; it was as if there had been a cup prescribed for her to drain, yet she could put off the hour of the ordeal. She filled the time as she might; bought things, in shops, for which she had no use, and called on friends for whom she had no taste. Most of her friends, at present, were reduced to that category, and she had to choose, for visits, the houses guiltless, as she might have said, of her husband's blood. She couldn't speak to the people who had answered in such dreadful terms her late circular; on the other hand the people out of its range were such as would also be stolidly unconscious of Lady Northmore's publication and from whom the sop of sympathy could be but circuitously extracted. As she had lunched at a pastrycook's, so she stopped out to tea, and the March dusk had fallen when she got home. The first thing she then saw in her lighted hall was a large neat package on the table; whereupon she knew before approaching it that Lady Northmore had sent her the book. It had arrived, she learned, just after her going out; so that, had she not done this, she might have spent the day with it. She now quite understood her prompt instinct of flight. Well, flight had helped her, and the touch of the great indifferent general life. She would at last face the music.

She faced it, after dinner, in her little closed drawing-room, unwrapping the two volumes – *The Public and Private*

Correspondence of the Right Honourable &c., &c. – and looking well, first, at the great escutcheon on the purple cover and at the various portraits within, so numerous that wherever she opened she came on one. It had not been present to her before that he was so perpetually 'sitting', but he figured in every phase and in every style, and the gallery was enriched with views of his successive residences, each one a little grander than the last. She had ever, in general, found that, in portraits, whether of the known or the unknown, the eyes seemed to seek and to meet her own; but John Northmore everywhere looked straight away from her, quite as if he had been in the room and were unconscious of acquaintance. The effect of this was, oddly enough, so sharp that at the end of ten minutes she found herself sinking into his text as if she had been a stranger and beholden, vulgarly and accidentally, to one of the libraries. She had been afraid to plunge, but from the moment she got in she was – to do every one, all round, justice – thoroughly held. She sat there late, and she made so many reflections and discoveries that – as the only way to put it – she passed from mystification to stupefaction. Her own contribution had been almost exhaustively used; she had counted Warren's letters before sending them and perceived now that scarce a dozen were not all there – a circumstance explaining to her Lady Northmore's present. It was to these pages she had turned first, and it was as she hung over them that her stupefaction dawned. It took, in truth, at the outset, a particular form – the form of a sharpened wonder at Warren's unnatural piety. Her original surprise had been keen – when she had tried to take reasons for granted; but her original surprise was as nothing to her actual bewilderment. The letters to Warren had been practically, she judged, for the family, the great card; yet if the great card made only that figure, what on earth was one to think of the rest of the pack?

She pressed on, at random, with a sense of rising fever; she trembled, almost panting, not to be sure too soon; but wherever she turned she found the prodigy spread. The letters to Warren were an abyss of inanity; the others followed suit as they could; the book was surely then a sandy desert, the publication

a theme for mirth. She so lost herself, as her perception of the
scale of the mistake deepened, in uplifting visions, that when
her parlour-maid, at eleven o'clock, opened the door she
almost gave the start of guilt surprised. The girl, withdrawing
for the night, had come but to say so, and her mistress, supremely wide-awake and with remembrance kindled, appealed
to her, after a blank stare, with intensity. 'What have you done
with the papers?'

'The papers, ma'am?'

'All those of this morning – don't tell me you've destroyed
them! Quick, quick – bring them back.' The young woman, by
a rare chance, had not destroyed them; she presently reappeared with them, neatly folded; and Mrs Hope, dismissing
her with benedictions, had at last, in a few minutes, taken the
time of day. She saw her impression portentously reflected in
the public prints. It was not then the illusion of her jealousy – it
was the triumph, unhoped for, of her justice. The reviewers
observed a decorum, but, frankly, when one came to look, their
stupefaction matched her own. What she had taken in the
morning for enthusiasm proved mere perfunctory attention,
unwarned in advance and seeking an issue for its mystification.
The question was, if one liked, asked civilly, but it was asked,
none the less, all round: 'What *could* have made Lord Northmore's family take him for a letter-writer?' Pompous and ponderous, yet loose and obscure, he managed, by a trick of his
own, to be both slipshod and stiff. Who, in such a case, had
been primarily responsible, and under what strangely belated
advice had a group of persons destitute of wit themselves been
thus deplorably led thus astray? With fewer accomplices in the
preparation, it might almost have been assumed that they had
been dealt with by practical jokers.

They had at all events committed an error of which the most
merciful thing to say was that, as founded on loyalty, it was
touching. These things, in the welcome offered, lay perhaps not
quite on the face, but they peeped between the lines and would
force their way through on the morrow. The long quotations
given were quotations marked Why? – 'Why,' in other words, as
interpreted by Mrs Hope, 'drag to light such helplessness of

expression? why give the text of his dullness and the proof of his fatuity?' The victim of the error had certainly been, in his way and day, a useful and remarkable person, but almost any other evidence of the fact might more happily have been adduced. It rolled over her, as she paced her room in the small hours, that the wheel had come full circle. There was after all a rough justice. The monument that had over-darkened her was reared, but it would be within a week the opportunity of every humourist, the derision of intelligent London. Her husband's strange share in it continued, that night, between dreams and vigils, to puzzle her, but light broke with her final waking, which was comfortably late. She opened her eyes to it, and, as it stared straight into them, she greeted it with the first laugh that had for a long time passed her lips. How could she, idiotically, not have guessed? Warren, playing insidiously the part of a guardian, had done what he had done on purpose! He had acted to an end long foretasted, and the end – the full taste – had come.

V

IT was after this, none the less – after the other organs of criticism, including the smoking-rooms of the clubs, the lobbies of the House and the dinner-tables of everywhere, had duly embodied their reserves and vented their irreverence, and the unfortunate two volumes had ranged themselves, beyond appeal, as a novelty insufficiently curious and prematurely stale – it was when this had come to pass that Mrs Hope really felt how beautiful her own chance would now have been and how sweet her revenge. The success of *her* volumes, for the inevitability of which nobody had had an instinct, would have been as great as the failure of Lady Northmore's, for the inevitability of which everybody had had one. She read over and over her letters and asked herself afresh if the confidence that had preserved *them* might not, at such a crisis, in spite of everything, justify itself. Did not the discredit to English wit, as it were, proceeding from the uncorrected attribution to an established public character of such mediocrity of thought and form, really demand, for that matter, some such redemptive stroke as

the appearance of a collection of masterpieces gathered from a
similar walk? To have such a collection under one's hand and
yet sit and see one's self not use it was a torment through which
she might well have feared to break down.

But there was another thing she might do, not redemptive
indeed, but perhaps, after all, as matters were going, apposite.
She fished out of their nook, after long years, the packet of John
Northmore's epistles to herself, and, reading them over in the
light of his later style, judged them to contain to the full
the promise of that inimitability; felt that they would deepen
the impression and that, in the way of the *inédit*, they constituted her supreme treasure. There was accordingly a terrible
week for her in which she itched to put them forth. She composed mentally the preface, brief, sweet, ironic, representing
her as prompted by an anxious sense of duty to a great reputation and acting upon the sight of laurels so lately gathered.
There would naturally be difficulties; the documents were her
own, but the family, bewildered, scared, suspicious, figured to
her fancy as a dog with a dust-pan tied to its tail and ready for
any dash to cover at the sound of the clatter of tin. They would
have, she surmised, to be consulted, or, if not consulted,
would put in an injunction; yet of the two courses, that of
scandal braved for the man she had rejected drew her on,
while the charm of this vision worked, still further than that of
delicacy over-ridden for the man she had married.

The vision closed round her and she lingered on the idea –
fed, as she handled again her faded fat packet, by re-perusals
more richly convinced. She even took opinions as to the interference open to her old friend's relatives; took, in fact, from this
time on, many opinions; went out anew, picked up old threads,
repaired old ruptures, resumed, as it was called, her place in
society. She had not been for years so seen of men as during the
few weeks that followed the abasement of the Northmores. She
called, in particular, on every one she had cast out after the
failure of her appeal. Many of these persons figured as Lady
Northmore's contributors, the unwitting agents of the unprecedented exposure; they having, it was sufficiently clear, acted
in dense good faith. Warren, foreseeing and calculating, might

have the benefit of such subtlety, but it was not for any one else. With every one else – for they did, on facing her, as she said to herself, look like fools – she made inordinately free; putting right and left the question of what, in the past years, they, or their progenitors, could have been thinking of. 'What on earth had you in mind, and where, among you, were the rudiments of intelligence, when you burnt up my husband's priceless letters and clung as if for salvation to Lord Northmore's? You see how you have been saved!' The weak explanations, the imbecility, as she judged it, of the reasons given, were so much balm to her wound. The great balm, however, she kept to the last: she would go to see Lady Northmore only when she had exhausted all other comfort. That resource would be as supreme as the treasure of the fat packet. She finally went and, by a happy chance, if chance could ever be happy in such a house, was received. She remained half an hour – there were other persons present, and, on rising to go, felt that she was satisfied. She had taken in what she desired, had sounded what she saw; only, unexpectedly, something had overtaken her more absolute than the hard need she had obeyed or the vindictive advantage she had cherished. She had counted on herself for almost anything but for pity of these people, yet it was in pity that, at the end of ten minutes, she felt everything else dissolve.

They were suddenly, on the spot, transformed for her by the depth of their misfortune, and she saw them, the great Northmores, as – of all things – consciously weak and flat. She neither made nor encountered an allusion to volumes published or frustrated; and so let her arranged inquiry die away that when, on separation, she kissed her wan sister in widowhood, it was not with the kiss of Judas. She had meant to ask lightly if she mightn't have *her* turn at editing; but the renunciation with which she re-entered her house had formed itself before she left the room. When she got home indeed she at first only wept – wept for the commonness of failure and the strangeness of life. Her tears perhaps brought her a sense of philosophy; it was all as broad as it was long. When they were spent, at all events, she took out for the last time the faded fat packet. Sitting down by a receptacle daily emptied for the benefit of the dustman, she destroyed, one by one, the gems of the collection in which each piece had been a gem. She tore up, to the last scrap, Lord Northmore's letters. It would never be known now, as regards this series, either that they had been hoarded or that they had been sacrificed. And she was content so to let it rest. On the following day she began another task. She took out her husband's and attacked the business of transcription. She copied them piously, tenderly, and, for the purpose to which she now found herself settled, judged almost no omissions imperative. By the time they should be published—! She shook her head, both knowingly and resignedly, as to criticism so remote. When her transcript was finished she sent it to a printer to set up, and then, after receiving and correcting proof, and with every precaution for secrecy, had a single copy struck off and the type, under her eyes, dispersed. Her last act but one — or rather perhaps but two – was to put these sheets, which, she was pleased to find, would form a volume of three hundred pages, carefully away. Her next was to add to her testamentary instrument a definite provision for the issue, after her death, of such a volume. Her last was to hope that death would come in time.

THE SPECIAL TYPE

I NOTE it as a wonderful case of its kind – the finest of all perhaps, in fact, that I have ever chanced to encounter. The kind, moreover, is the greatest kind, the roll recruited, for our high esteem and emulation, from history and fiction, legend and song. In the way of service and sacrifice for love I've really known nothing go beyond it. However, you can judge. My own sense of it happens just now to be remarkably rounded off by the sequel – more or less looked for on her part – of the legal step taken by Mrs Brivet. I hear from America that, a decent interval being held to have elapsed since her gain of her divorce, she is about to marry again – an event that will, it would seem, put an end to any question of the disclosure of the real story. It's this that's the real story, or will be, with nothing wanting, as soon as I shall have heard that her husband (who, on his side, has only been waiting for her to move first) has sanctified his union with Mrs Cavenham.

I

SHE was, of course, often in and out, Mrs Cavenham, three years ago, when I was painting her portrait; and the more so that I found her, I remember, one of those comparatively rare sitters who present themselves at odd hours, turn up without an appointment. The thing is to get most women to keep those they do make; but she used to pop in, as she called it, on the chance, letting me know that if I had a moment free she was quite at my service. When I hadn't the moment free she liked to stay to chatter, and she more than once expressed to me, I recollect, her theory that an artist really, for the time, could never see too much of his model. I must have shown her rather frankly that I understood her as meaning that a model could never see too much of her artist. I understood in fact every-thing, and especially that she was, in Brivet's absence, so unoccupied and restless that she didn't know what to do with herself. I was conscious in short that it was he who would pay for the picture, and that gives, I think, the measure of my enlightenment. If I took such pains and bore so with her folly, it was fundamentally for Brivet.

I was often at that time, as I had often been before, occupied – for various 'subjects' – with Mrs Dundene, in connection with which a certain occasion comes back to me as the first slide in the lantern. If I had invented my story I couldn't have made it begin better than with Mrs Cavenham's irruption during the presence one morning of that lady. My door, by some chance, had been unguarded, and she was upon us without a warning. This was the sort of thing my model hated – the one, I mean, who, after all, sat mainly to oblige; but I remember how well she behaved. She was not dressed for company, though indeed a dress was never strictly necessary to her best effect. I recall that I had a moment of uncertainty, but I must have dropped the name of each for the other, as it was Mrs Cavenham's line always, later on, that I had made them acquainted; and inevitably, though I wished her not to stay and got rid of her as soon as possible, the two women, of such different places in the scale, but of such almost equal beauty, were face to face for some minutes, of which I was not even at the moment unaware that they made an extraordinary use for mutual inspection. It was sufficient; they from that instant knew each other.

'Isn't she lovely?' I remember asking – and quite without the spirit of mischief – when I came back from restoring my visitor to her cab.

'Yes, awfully pretty. But I hate her.'

'Oh,' I laughed, 'she's not so bad as that.'

'Not so handsome as I, you mean?' And my sitter protested. 'It isn't fair of you to speak as if I were one of those who can't bear even at the worst – or the best – another woman's looks. I should hate her even if she were ugly.'

'But what have you to do with her?'

She hesitated; then with characteristic looseness: 'What have I to do with anyone?'

'Well, there's no one else I know of that you do hate.'

'That shows,' she replied, 'how good a reason there must be, even if I don't know it yet.'

She knew it in the course of time, but I have never seen a reason, I must say, operate so little for relief. As a history of the hatred of Alice Dundene my anecdote becomes wondrous indeed. Meanwhile, at any rate, I had Mrs Cavenham again with me for her regular sitting, and quite as curious as I had expected her to be about the person of the previous time.

'Do you mean she isn't, so to speak, a lady?' she asked after I had, for reasons of my own, fenced a little. 'Then if she's not "professional" either, what is she?'

'Well,' I returned as I got at work, 'she escapes, to my mind, any classification save as one of the most beautiful and good-natured of women.'

'I see her beauty,' Mrs Cavenham said. 'It's immense. Do you mean that her good-nature's as great?'

I had to think a little. 'On the whole, yes.'

'Then I understand. That represents a greater quantity than *I*, I think, should ever have occasion for.'

'Oh, the great thing's to be sure to have enough,' I growled.

But she laughed it off. 'Enough, certainly, is as good as a feast!'

It was – I forget how long, some months – after this that Frank Brivet, whom I had not seen for two years, knocked again at my door. I didn't at all object to him at my other work as I did to Mrs Cavenham, but it was not till he had been in and out several times that Alice – which is what most people still really call her – chanced to see him and received in such an extraordinary way the impression that was to be of such advantage to him. She had been obliged to leave me that day before he went – though he stayed but a few minutes later; and it was not till the next time we were alone together that I was struck with her sudden interest, which became frankly pressing. I had met her, to begin with, expansively enough.

'An American? But what *sort* – don't you know? There are so many.'

I didn't mean it as an offence, but in the matter of men, and though her acquaintance with them is so large, I always simplify with her. '*The* sort. He's rich.'

'And how rich?'

'Why, *as* an American. Disgustingly.'

I told her on this occasion more about him, but it was on that fact, I remember, that, after a short silence, she brought out with a sigh: 'Well, I'm sorry. I should have liked to love him for himself.'

II

QUITE apart from having been at school with him, I'm conscious – though at times he so puts me out – that I've a taste for Frank Brivet. I'm quite aware, by the same token – and even if when a man's so rich it's difficult to tell – that he's not everyone's affinity. I was struck, at all events, from the first of the affair, with the way he clung to me and seemed inclined to haunt my studio. He's fond of art, though he has some awful pictures, and more or less understands mine; but it wasn't this that brought him. Accustomed as I was to notice what his wealth everywhere does for him, I was rather struck with his being so much thrown upon me and not giving London – the big fish that rises so to the hook baited with gold – more of a chance to perform to him. I very soon, however, understood. He had his reasons for wishing not to be seen much with Mrs Cavenham, and, as he was in love with her, felt the want of some machinery for keeping temporarily away from her. I was his machinery, and, when once I perceived this, was willing enough to turn his wheel. His situation, moreover, became interesting from the moment I fairly grasped it, which he soon enabled me to do. His old reserve on the subject of Mrs Brivet went to the winds, and it's not my fault if I let him see how little I was shocked by his confidence. His marriage had originally seemed to me to require much more explanation than anyone could give, and indeed in the matter of women in general, I confess, I've never seized his point of view. His inclinations are strange, and strange, too, perhaps, his indifferences. Still, I can enter into some of his aversions, and I agreed with him that his wife was odious.

'She has hitherto, since we began practically to live apart,' he said, 'mortally hated the idea of doing anything so pleasant for me as to divorce me. But I've reason to believe she has now changed her mind. She'd like to get clear.'

I waited a moment. 'For a man?'

'Oh, such a jolly good one! Remson Sturch.'

I wondered. 'Do you call *him* good?'

'Good for *her*. If she only can be got to be – which it oughtn't to be difficult to make her – fool enough to marry him, he'll give her the real size of his foot, and I shall be avenged in a manner positively ideal.'

'Then will she institute proceedings?'

'She can't, as things stand. She has nothing to go upon. I've been,' said poor Brivet, 'I positively have, so blameless.' I thought of Mrs Cavenham, and, though I said nothing, he went on after an instant as if he knew it. 'They can't put a finger. I've been so d—d particular.'

I hesitated. 'And your idea is now not to be particular any more?'

'Oh, about *her*,' he eagerly replied, 'always!' On which I laughed out and he coloured. 'But my idea is nevertheless, at present,' he went on, 'to pave the way; that is, I mean, if I can keep the person you're thinking of so totally out of it that not a breath in the whole business can possibly touch her.'

'I see,' I reflected. 'She isn't willing?'

He stared. 'To be compromised? Why the devil *should* she be?'

'Why shouldn't she – for *you*? Doesn't she love you?'

'Yes, and it's because she does, dearly, that I don't feel the right way to repay her is by spattering her over.'

'Yet if she stands,' I argued, 'straight in the splash—!'

'She doesn't!' he interrupted me, with some curtness. 'She stands a thousand miles out of it; she stands on a pinnacle; she stands as she stands in your charming portrait – lovely, lonely, untouched. And so she must remain.'

'It's beautiful, it's doubtless inevitable,' I returned after a little, 'that you should feel so. Only, if your wife doesn't divorce you for a woman you love, I don't quite see how she can do it for the woman you don't.'

'Nothing is more simple,' he declared; on which I saw he had figured it out rather more than I thought. 'It will be quite enough if she *believes* I love her.'

'If the lady in question does – or Mrs Brivet?'

'Mrs Brivet – confound her! If she believes I love somebody else. I must have the appearance, and the appearance must of course be complete. All I've got to do is to take up—'

'To take up—?' I asked, as he paused.

'Well, publicly, with someone or other; someone who could easily be squared. One would undertake, after all, to produce the impression.'

'On your wife naturally, you mean?'

'On my wife, and on the person concerned.'

I turned it over and did justice to his ingenuity. 'But what impression would you undertake to produce on—?'

'Well?' he inquired as I just faltered.

'On the person *not* concerned. How would the lady you just accused me of having in mind be affected toward such a proceeding?'

He had to think a little, but he thought with success. 'Oh, I'd answer for her.'

'To the other lady?' I laughed.

He remained quite grave. 'To myself. She'd leave us alone. As it would be for her good, she'd understand.'

I was sorry for him, but he struck me as artless. 'Understand, in that interest, the "spattering" of another person?'

He coloured again, but he was sturdy. 'It must of course be exactly the right person – a special type. Someone who, in the first place,' he explained, 'wouldn't mind, and of whom, in the second, she wouldn't be jealous.'

I followed perfectly, but it struck me as important all round that we should be clear. 'But wouldn't the danger be great that any woman who shouldn't have that effect – the effect of jealousy – upon her wouldn't have it either on your wife?'

'Ah,' he acutely returned, 'my wife wouldn't be warned. She wouldn't be "in the know".'

'I see.' I quite caught up. 'The two other ladies distinctly would.'

But he seemed for an instant at a loss. 'Wouldn't it be indispensable only as regards one?'

'Then the other would be simply sacrificed?'

'She would be,' Brivet splendidly put it, 'remunerated.'

I was pleased even with the sense of financial power betrayed by the way he said it, and I at any rate so took the measure of his intention of generosity and his characteristically big view of the matter that this quickly suggested to me what at least might be his exposure. 'But suppose that, in spite of "remuneration", this secondary personage should perversely like you? She would have to be indeed, as you say, a special type, but even special types may have general feelings. Suppose she should like you too much.'

It had pulled him up a little. 'What do you mean by "too much"?'

'Well, more than enough to leave the case quite as simple as you'd require it.'

'Oh, money always simplifies. Besides, I should make a point of being a brute.' And on my laughing at this: 'I should pay her enough to keep her down, to make her easy. But the thing,' he went on with a drop back to the less mitigated real – 'the thing, hang it! is first to find her.'

'Surely,' I concurred; 'for she should have to lack, you see, no requirement whatever for plausibility. She must be, for instance, not only "squareable", but – before anything else even – awfully handsome.'

'Oh, "awfully"!' He could make light of *that*, which was what Mrs Cavenham was.

'It wouldn't do for her, at all events,' I maintained, 'to be a bit less attractive than—'

'Well, than who?' he broke in, not only with a comic effect of disputing my point, but also as if he knew whom I was thinking of.

Before I could answer him, however, the door opened,
and we were interrupted by a visitor – a visitor who, on
the spot, in a flash, primed me with a reply. But I had of
course for the moment to keep it to myself. 'Than Mrs Dundene!'

III

I HAD nothing more than that to do with it, but before I could
turn round it was done; by which I mean that Brivet, whose
previous impression of her had, for some sufficient reason,
failed of sharpness, now jumped straight to the perception
that here to his hand for the solution of his problem was the
missing quantity and the appointed aid. They were in presence
on this occasion, for the first time, half an hour, during which
he sufficiently showed me that he felt himself to have found the
special type. He was certainly to that extent right that nobody
could – in those days in particular – without a rapid sense that
she was indeed 'special', spend any such time in the company of
our extraordinary friend. I couldn't quarrel with his recognising
so quickly what I had myself instantly recognised, yet if it did in
truth appear almost at a glance that she would, through the
particular facts of situation, history, aspect, tone, temper,
beautifully 'do', I felt from the first so affected by the business
that I desired to wash my hands of it. There was something
I wished to say to him before it went further, but after that
I cared only to be out of it. I may as well say at once, however,
that I never *was* out of it; for a man habitually ridden by the twin
demons of imagination and observation is never – enough for
his peace – out of anything. But I wanted to be able to apply to
either, should anything happen, ' "Thou canst not say *I* did
it!" ' What might in particular happen was represented by what
I said to Brivet the first time he gave me a chance. It was what
I had wished before the affair went further, but it had then
already gone so far that he had been twice – as he immediately
let me know – to see her at home. He clearly desired me to keep
up with him, which I was eager to declare impossible; but he
came again to see me only after he had called. Then I instantly

made my point, which was that she was really, hang it! too good for his fell purpose.

'But, my dear man, my purpose is a sacred one. And if, moreover, she herself doesn't think she's too good—'

'Ah,' said I, 'she's in love with you, and so it isn't fair.'

He wondered. 'Fair to *me*?'

'Oh, I don't care a button for you! What I'm thinking of is her risk.'

'And what do you mean by her risk?'

'Why, her finding, of course, before you've done with her, that she can't do without you.'

He met me as if he had quite thought of that. 'Isn't it much more *my* risk?'

'Ah, but you take it deliberately, walk into it with your eyes open. What I want to be sure of, liking her as I do, is that she fully understands.'

He had been moving about my place with his hands in his pockets, and at this he stopped short. 'How much do you like her?'

'Oh, ten times more than she likes me; so *that* needn't trouble you. Does she understand that it can be only to help somebody else?'

'Why, my dear chap, she's as sharp as a steam-whistle.'

'So that she also already knows who the other person is?'

He took a turn again, then brought out, 'There's no other person for her but me. Of course, as yet, there are things one doesn't say; I haven't set straight to work to dot all my i's, and the beauty of her, as she's really charming – and would be charming in *any* relation – is just exactly that I don't expect to have to. We'll work it out all right, I think, so that what I most wanted just to make sure of from you was what you've been good enough to tell me. I mean that you don't object – for yourself.'

I could with philosophic mirth allay that scruple, but what I couldn't do was to let him see what really most worried me. It stuck, as they say, in my crop that a woman like – yes, when all was said and done – Alice Dundene should simply minister to the convenience of a woman like Rose Cavenham. 'But there's one thing more.' This was as far as I could go. 'I may take from you then that she not only knows it's for your divorce and remarriage, but can fit the shoe on the very person?'

He waited a moment. 'Well, you may take from me that I find her no more of a fool than, as I seem to see, many other fellows have found her.'

I too was silent a little, but with a superior sense of being able to think it all out further than he. 'She's magnificent!'

'Well, so am I!' said Brivet. And for months afterward there was much – in fact everything – in the whole picture to justify his claim. I remember how it struck me as a lively sign of this that Mrs Cavenham, at an early day, gave up her pretty house in Wilton Street and withdrew for a time to America. That was palpable design and diplomacy, but I'm afraid that I quite as much, and doubtless very vulgarly, read into it that she had had money from Brivet to go. I even promised myself, I confess, the entertainment of finally making out that, whether or no the marriage should come off, she would not have been the person to find the episode least lucrative.

She left the others, at all events, completely together, and so, as the plot, with this, might be said definitely to thicken, it came to me in all sorts of ways that the curtain had gone up on the drama. It came to me, I hasten to add, much less from the two actors themselves than from other quarters – the usual sources, which never fail, of chatter; for after my friends' direction was fairly taken they had the good taste on either side to handle it, in talk, with gloves, not to expose it to what I should have called the danger of definition. I even seemed to divine that, allowing for needful preliminaries, they dealt even with each other on this same unformulated plane, and that it well might be that no relation in London at that moment, between a remarkable man and a beautiful woman, had more of the general air of good manners. I saw for a long time, directly, but little of them, for they were naturally much taken up, and Mrs Dundene in particular intermitted, as she had never yet done in any complication of her chequered career, her calls at my studio. As the months went by I couldn't but feel – partly, perhaps, for this very reason – that their undertaking announced itself as likely not to fall short of its aim. I gathered from the voices of the air that nothing whatever was neglected that could make it a success, and just this vision it was that made me privately project wonders into it, caused anxiety and curiosity often again to revisit me, and led me in fine to say to myself that so rich an effect could be arrived at on either side only by a great deal of heroism. As the omens markedly developed I supposed the heroism had likewise done so, and that the march of the matter was logical I inferred from the fact that even though the ordeal, all round, was more protracted than might have been feared, Mrs Cavenham made no fresh appearance. This I took as a sign that she knew she was safe – took indeed as the feature not the least striking of the situation constituted in her interest. I held my tongue, naturally, about her interest, but I watched it from a distance with an attention that, had I been caught in the act, might have led to a mistake about the direction of my sympathy. I had to make it my proper secret that, while I lost as little as possible of what was being done for her, I felt more and more that I myself could never have begun to do it.

IV

SHE came back at last, however, and one of the first things she did on her arrival was to knock at my door and let me know immediately, to smooth the way, that she was there on particular business. I was not to be surprised – though even if I were she shouldn't mind – to hear that she wished to bespeak from me, on the smallest possible delay, a portrait, full-length for preference, of our delightful friend Mr Brivet. She brought this out with a light perfection of assurance of which the first effect – I couldn't help it – was to make me show myself almost too much amused for good manners. She first stared at my laughter, then wonderfully joined in it, looking meanwhile extraordinarily pretty and elegant – more completely handsome in fact, as well as more completely happy, than I had ever yet seen her. She was distinctly the better, I quickly saw, for what was being done for her, and it was an odd spectacle indeed that while, out of her sight and to the exclusion of her very name, the good work went on, it put roses in her cheeks and rings on her fingers and the sense of success in her heart. What had made me laugh, at all events, was the number of other ideas suddenly evoked by her request, two of which, the next moment, had disengaged themselves with particular brightness. She wanted, for all her confidence, to omit no precaution, to close up every issue, and she had acutely conceived that the possession of Brivet's picture – full-length, above all! – would constitute for her the strongest possible appearance of holding his supreme pledge. If that had been her foremost thought her second then had been that if I should paint him he would have to sit, and that in order to sit he would have to return. He had been at this time, as I knew, for many weeks in foreign cities – which helped moreover to explain to me that Mrs Cavenham had thought it compatible with her safety to reopen her London house. Everything accordingly seemed to make for a victory, but there *was* such a thing, her proceeding implied, as one's – at least as *her* – susceptibility and her nerves. This question of his return I of course immediately put to her; on which she immediately answered that it was expressed in her very proposal, inasmuch as this proposal was nothing but the offer that Brivet had himself made her. The thing was to be his gift; she had only, he had assured her, to choose her artist and arrange the time; and she had amiably chosen me – chosen me for the dates, as she called them, immediately before us. I doubtless – but I don't care – give the measure of my native cynicism in confessing that I didn't the least avoid showing her that I saw through her game. 'Well, I'll do him,' I said, 'if he'll come himself and ask me.'

She wanted to know, at this, of course, if I impugned her veracity. 'You don't believe what I tell you? You're afraid for your money?'

I took it in high good-humour. 'For my money not a bit.'

'For what then?'

I had to think first how much I could say, which seemed to me, naturally, as yet but little. 'I know perfectly that whatever happens Brivet always pays. But let him come; then we'll talk.'

'Ah, well,' she returned, 'you'll see if he doesn't come.' And come he did in fact – though without a word from myself directly – at the end of ten days; on which we immediately got to work, an idea highly favourable to it having meanwhile shaped itself in my own breast. Meanwhile too, however, before his arrival, Mrs Cavenham had been again to see me, and this it was precisely, I think, that determined my idea. My present explanation of what afresh passed between us is that she really felt the need to build up her security a little higher by borrowing from my own vision of what had been happening. I had not, she saw, been very near to that, but I had been at least, during her time in America, nearer than she. And I had doubt-less somehow 'aggravated' her by appearing to disbelieve in the guarantee she had come in such pride to parade to me. It had in any case befallen that, on the occasion of her second visit, what I least expected or desired – her avowal of being 'in the know' – suddenly went too far to stop. When she did speak she spoke with elation. 'Mrs Brivet has filed her petition.'

'For getting rid of him?'

'Yes, in order to marry again; which is exactly what he wants her to do. It's wonderful – and, in a manner, I think, quite splendid – the way he has made it easy for her. He has met her wishes handsomely – obliged her in every particular.'

As she preferred, subtly enough, to put it all as if it were for the sole benefit of his wife, I was quite ready for this tone; but I privately defied her to keep it up. 'Well, then, he hasn't laboured in vain.'

'Oh, it *couldn't* have been in vain. What has happened has been the sort of thing that she couldn't possibly fail to act upon.'

'Too great a scandal, eh?'

She but just paused at it. 'Nothing neglected, certainly, or omitted. He was not the man to undertake it—'

'And not put it through? No, I should say he wasn't the man. In any case he apparently hasn't been. But he must have found the job—'

'Rather a bore?' she asked as I had hesitated.

'Well, not so much a bore as a delicate matter.'

She seemed to demur. 'Delicate?'

'Why, your sex likes him so.'

'But isn't just that what has made it easy?'

'Easy for *him* – yes,' I after a moment admitted.

But it wasn't what she meant. 'And not difficult, also, for *them*.'

This was the nearest approach I was to have heard her make, since the day of the meeting of the two women at my studio, to naming Mrs Dundene. She never, to the end of the affair, came any closer to her in speech than by the collective and promiscuous plural pronoun. There might have been a dozen of them, and she took cognisance, in respect to them, only of quantity. It was as if it had been a way of showing how little of anything else she imputed. Quality, as distinguished from quantity, was what *she* had. 'Oh, I think,' I said, 'that we can scarcely speak for them.'

'Why not? They must certainly have had the most beautiful time. Operas, theatres, suppers, dinners, diamonds, carriages, journeys hither and yon with him, poor dear, telegrams sent by each from everywhere to everywhere and always lying about, elaborate arrivals and departures at stations for everyone to see, and, in fact, quite a crowd usually collected – as many witnesses as you like. Then,' she wound up, 'his brougham standing always – half the day and half the night – at their doors. He has had to keep a brougham, and the proper sort of man, just for that alone. In other words unlimited publicity.'

'I see. What more can they have wanted? Yes,' I pondered, 'they like, for the most part, we suppose, a studied, outrageous *affichage*, and they must have thoroughly enjoyed it.'

'Ah, but it was only that.'

I wondered. 'Only what?'

'Only *affiché*. Only outrageous. Only the *form* of – well, of what would definitely serve. He never saw them alone.'

I wondered – or at least appeared to – still more. 'Never?'

'Never. Never once.' She had a wonderful air of answering for it. 'I know.'

I saw that, after all, she really believed she knew, and I had indeed, for that matter, to recognise that I myself believed her knowledge to be sound. Only there went with it a complacency, an enjoyment of having really made me see what could be done for her, so little to my taste that for a minute or two I could scarce trust myself to speak: she looked somehow, as she sat there, so lovely, and yet, in spite of her loveliness – or perhaps even just because of it – so smugly selfish; she put it to me with so small a consciousness of anything but her personal triumph that, while she had kept her skirts clear, her name unuttered and her reputation untouched, 'they' had been in it even more than her success required. It was their skirts, their name and their reputation that, in the proceedings at hand, would bear the brunt. It was only after waiting a while that I could at last say: 'You're perfectly sure then of Mrs Brivet's intention?'

'Oh, we've had formal notice.'

'And he's himself satisfied of the sufficiency—?'

'Of the sufficiency—?'

'Of what he has done.'

She rectified. 'Of what he has *appeared* to do.'

'That *is* then enough?'

'Enough,' she laughed, 'to send him to the gallows!' To which I could only reply that all was well that ended well.

V

ALL for me, however, as it proved, had not ended yet. Brivet, as I have mentioned, duly reappeared to sit for me, and Mrs Cavenham, on his arrival, as consistently went abroad. He confirmed to me that lady's news of how he had 'fetched', as he called it, his wife – let me know, as decently owing to me after what had passed, on the subject, between us, that the forces set in motion had logically operated; but he made no other allusion to his late accomplice – for I now took for granted the close of the connection – than was conveyed in this intimation. He spoke – and the effect was almost droll – as if he had had, since our previous meeting, a busy and responsible year and wound up an affair (as he was accustomed to wind up affairs) involving a mass of detail; he even dropped into occasional reminiscence of what he had seen and enjoyed and disliked during a recent period of rather far-reaching adventure; but he stopped just as short as Mrs Cavenham had done – and, indeed, much shorter than she – of introducing Mrs Dundene by name into our talk. And what was singular in this, I soon saw, was – apart from a general discretion – that he abstained not at all because his mind was troubled, but just because, on the contrary, it was so much at ease. It was perhaps even more singular still, meanwhile, that, though I had scarce been able to bear Mrs Cavenham's manner in this particular, I found I could put up perfectly with that of her friend. She had annoyed me, but he didn't – I give the inconsistency for what it is worth. The obvious state of his conscience had always been a strong point in him and one that exactly irritated some people as much as it charmed others; so that if, in general, it was positively, and in fact quite aggressively approving, this monitor, it had never held its head so high as at the juncture of which I speak. I took all this in with eagerness, for I saw how it would play into my work. Seeking as I always do, instinctively, to represent sitters in the light of the thing, whatever it may be, that facially, least wittingly or responsibly, gives the pitch of their aspect, I felt immediately that I should have the clue for making a capital thing of Brivet were I to succeed in showing him in just this freshness of his cheer. His cheer was that of his being able to say to himself that he had got all he wanted precisely *as* he wanted: without having harmed a fly. He had arrived so neatly where most men arrive besmirched, and what he seemed to cry out as he stood before my canvas – wishing everyone well all round – was: 'See how clever and pleasant and practicable, how jolly and lucky and rich I've been!' I determined, at all events, that I would make some such characteristic words as these cross, at any cost, the footlights, as it were, of my frame.

Well, I can't but feel to this hour that I really hit my nail – that the man *is* fairly painted in the light and that the work remains as yet my high-water mark. He himself was delighted with it – and all the more, I think, that before it was finished he received from America the news of his liberation. He had not defended the suit – as to which judgment, therefore, had been expeditiously rendered; and he was accordingly free as air and with the added sweetness of every augmented appearance that his wife was herself blindly preparing to seek chastisement at the hands of destiny. There being at last no obstacle to his open association with Mrs Cavenham, he called her directly back to London to admire my achievement, over which, from the very first glance, she as amiably let herself go. It was the very view of him she had desired to possess; it was the dear man in his intimate essence for those who knew him; and for any one who should ever be deprived of him it would be the next best thing to the sound of his voice. We of course by no means lingered, however, on the contingency of privation, which was promptly swept away in the rush of Mrs Cavenham's vision of how straight also, above and beyond, I had, as she called it, attacked. I couldn't quite myself, I fear, tell how straight, but Mrs Cavenham perfectly could, and did, for everybody: she had at her fingers' ends all the reasons why the thing would be a treasure even for those who had never seen 'Frank'.

I had finished the picture, but was, according to my practice, keeping it near me a little, for afterthoughts, when I received from Mrs Dundene the first visit she had paid me for many a month. 'I've come,' she immediately said, 'to ask you a favour'; and she turned her eyes, for a minute, as if contentedly full of her thought, round the large workroom she already knew so well and in which her beauty had really rendered more services than could ever be repaid. There were studies of her yet on the walls; there were others thrust away in corners; others still had gone forth from where she stood and carried to far-away places the reach of her lingering look. I had greatly, almost inconveniently missed her, and I don't know why it was that she struck me now as more beautiful than ever. She had always, for that matter, had a way of seeming each time a little different and a little better. Dressed very simply in black materials, feathers and lace, that gave the impression of being light and fine, she had indeed the air of a special type, but quite as some great lady might have had it. She looked like a princess in Court mourning. Oh, she had been a case for the petitioner – was everything the other side wanted! 'Mr Brivet,' she went on to say, 'has kindly offered me a present. I'm to ask of him whatever in the world I most desire.'

I knew in an instant, on this, what was coming, but I was at first wholly taken up with the simplicity of her allusion to her late connection. Had I supposed that, like Brivet, she wouldn't allude to it at all? or had I stupidly assumed that if she did it would be with ribaldry and rancour? I hardly know; I only know that I suddenly found myself charmed to receive from her thus the key of my own freedom. There was something I wanted to say to her, and she had thus given me leave. But for the moment I only repeated as with amused interest: 'Whatever in the world—?'

'Whatever in all the world.'

'But that's immense, and in what way can poor *I* help—?'

'By painting him for me. I want a portrait of him.'

I looked at her a moment in silence. She was lovely. 'That's what – "in all the world" – you've chosen?'

'Yes – thinking it over: full-length. I want it for remembrance, and I want it as you will do it. It's the only thing I do want.'

'Nothing else?'

'Oh, it's enough.' I turned about – she was wonderful. I had whisked out of sight for a month the picture I had produced for Mrs Cavenham, and it was now completely covered with a large piece of stuff. I stood there a little, thinking of it, and she went on as if she feared I might be unwilling. '*Can't* you do it?'

It showed me that she had not heard from him of my having painted him, and this, further, was an indication that, his purpose effected, he had ceased to see her. 'I suppose you know,' I presently said, 'what you've done for him?'

'Oh yes; it was what I wanted.'

'It was what *he* wanted!' I laughed.

'Well, I want what he wants.'

'Even to his marrying Mrs Cavenham?'

She hesitated. 'As well her as anyone, from the moment he couldn't marry *me*.'

'It was beautiful of you to be so sure of that,' I returned.

'How could I be anything else but sure? He doesn't so much as *know* me!' said Alice Dundene.

'No,' I declared, 'I verily believe he doesn't. There's your picture,' I added, unveiling my work.

She was amazed and delighted. 'I may have *that*?'

'So far as I'm concerned – absolutely.'

'Then he had himself the beautiful thought of sitting for me?'

I faltered but an instant. 'Yes.'

Her pleasure in what I had done was a joy to me. 'Why, it's of a truth—! It's perfection.'

'I think it is.'

'It's the whole story. It's life.'

'That's what I tried for,' I said; and I added to myself: 'Why the deuce *do* we?'

'It will be *him* for me,' she meanwhile went on. 'I shall *live* with it, keep it all to myself, and – do you know what it will do? – it will seem to make up.'

'To make up?'

'I never saw him alone,' said Mrs Dundene.

I am still keeping the thing to send to her, punctually, on the day he's married; but I had of course, on my understanding with her, a tremendous bout with Mrs Cavenham, who protested with indignation against my 'base treachery' and made to Brivet an appeal for redress which, enlightened, face to face with the magnificent humility of his other friend's selection, he couldn't, for shame, entertain. All he was able to do was to suggest to me that I might for one or other of the ladies, at my choice, do him again; but I had no difficulty in replying that my best was my best and that what was done was done. He assented with the awkwardness of a man in dispute between women, and Mrs Cavenham remained furious. 'Can't "they" – of *all* possible things, think! – take something else?'

'Oh, they want *him*!'

'Him?' It was monstrous.

'To live with,' I explained – 'to make up.'

'To make up for what?'

'Why, you know, they never saw him alone.'

THE TONE OF TIME

I

I WAS too pleased with what it struck me that, as an old, old friend, I had done for her, not to go to her that very afternoon with the news. I knew she worked late, as in general I also did; but I sacrificed for her sake a good hour of the February daylight. She was in her studio, as I had believed she would be, where her card ('Mary J. Tredick' – not Mary Jane, but Mary Juliana) was manfully on the door; a little tired, a little old and a good deal spotted, but with her ugly spectacles taken off, as soon as I appeared, to greet me. She kept on, while she scraped her palette and wiped her brushes, the big stained apron that covered her from head to foot and that I have often enough before seen her retain in conditions giving the measure of her renunciation of her desire to dazzle. Every fresh reminder of this brought home to me that she had given up everything but her work, and that there had been in her history some reason. But I was as far from the reason as ever. She had given up too much; this was just why one wanted to lend her a hand. I told her, at any rate, that I had a lovely job for her.

'To copy something I do like?'

Her complaint, I knew, was that people only gave orders, if they gave them at all, for things she did not like. But this wasn't a case of copying – not at all, at least, in the common sense. 'It's for a portrait – quite in the air.'

'Ah, you do portraits yourself!'

'Yes, and you know how. My trick won't serve for this. What's wanted is a pretty picture.'

'Then of whom?'

'Of nobody. That is of anybody. Anybody you like.'

She naturally wondered. 'Do you mean I'm myself to choose my sitter?'

'Well, the oddity is that there is to *be* no sitter.'

'Whom then is the picture to represent?'

637

'Why, a handsome, distinguished, agreeable man, of not more than forty, clean-shaven, thoroughly well-dressed, and a perfect gentleman.'

She continued to stare. 'And I'm to find him myself?'

I laughed at the term she used. 'Yes, as you "find" the canvas, the colours and the frame.' After which I immediately explained. 'I've just had the "rummest" visit, the effect of which was to make me think of you. A lady, unknown to me and unintroduced, turned up at my place at three o'clock. She had come straight, she let me know, without preliminaries, on account of one's high reputation – the usual thing – and of her having admired one's work. Of course I instantly saw – I mean I saw it as soon as she named her affair – that she hadn't understood my work at all. What am I good for in the world but just the impression of the given, the presented case? I can do but the face I see.'

'And do you think I can do the face I don't?'

'No, but you see so many more. You see them in fancy and memory, and they come out, for you, from all the museums you've haunted and all the great things you've studied. I *know* you'll be able to see the one my visitor wants and to give it – what's the *crux* of the business – the tone of time.'

She turned the question over. 'What does she want it for?'

'Just *for* that – for the tone of time. And, except that it's to hang over her chimney, she didn't tell me. I've only my idea that it's to represent, to symbolise, as it were, her husband, who's not alive and who perhaps never was. This is exactly what will give you a free hand.'

'With nothing to go by – no photographs or other portraits?'

'Nothing.'

'She only proposes to describe him?'

'Not even; she wants the picture itself to do that. Her only condition is that he be a *très-bel homme*.'

She had begun at last, a little thoughtfully, to remove her apron. 'Is she French?'

'I don't know. I give it up. She calls herself Mrs Bridgenorth.'

Mary wondered. '*Connais pas!* I never heard of her.'

'You wouldn't.'

'You mean it's not her real name?'

I hesitated. 'I mean that she's a very downright fact, full of the implication that she'll pay a downright price. It's clear to me that you can ask what you like; and it's therefore a chance that I can't consent to your missing.' My friend gave no sign either way, and I told my story. 'She's a woman of fifty, perhaps of more, who has been pretty, and who still presents herself, with her grey hair a good deal powdered, as I judge, to carry it off, extraordinarily well. She was a little frightened and a little free; the latter because of the former. But she did uncommonly well, I thought, considering the oddity of her wish. This oddity she quite admits; she began indeed by insisting on it so in advance that I found myself expecting I didn't know what. She broke at moments into French, which was perfect, but no better than her English, which isn't vulgar; not more at least than that of everybody else. The things people *do* say, and the way they say them, to artists! She wanted immensely, I could see, not to fail of her errand, not to be treated as absurd; and she was extremely grateful to me for meeting her so far as I did. She was beautifully dressed and she came in a brougham.'

My listener took it in; then, very quietly, 'Is she respectable?' she inquired.

'Ah, there you are!' I laughed; 'and how you always pick the point right out, even when one has endeavoured to diffuse a specious glamour! She's extraordinary,' I pursued after an instant; 'and just what she wants of the picture, I think, is to make her a little less so.'

'Who is she, then? What is she?' my companion simply went on.

It threw me straightway back on one of my hobbies. 'Ah, my dear, what is so interesting as life? What is, above all, so stupendous as London? There's everything in it, everything in the world, and nothing too amazing not some day to pop out at you. What is a woman, faded, preserved, pretty, powdered, vague, odd, dropping on one without credentials, but with a carriage and very good lace? What is such a person but a person who *may* have had adventures, and have made them, in one way or another, pay? They're, however, none of one's business; it's scarcely on the cards that one should ask her. I should like, with Mrs Bridgenorth, to see a fellow ask! She goes in for propriety, the real thing. If I suspect her of being the creation of her own talents, she has clearly, on the other hand, seen a lot of life. Will you meet her?' I next demanded.

My hostess waited. 'No.'

'Then you won't try?'

'Need I meet her to try?' And the question made me guess that, so far as she had understood, she began to feel herself a little taken. 'It seems strange,' she none the less mused, 'to attempt to please her on such a basis. To attempt,' she presently added, 'to please her at all. It's your idea that she's not married?' she, with this, a trifle inconsequently asked.

'Well,' I replied, 'I've only had an hour to think of it, but I somehow already see the scene. Not immediately, not the day after, or even perhaps the year after the thing she desires is set up there, but in due process of time and on convenient opportunity, the transfiguration will occur. "Who is that awfully handsome man?" "That? Oh, that's an old sketch of my dear dead husband." Because I told her – insidiously sounding her – that she would want it to look old, and that the tone of time is exactly what you're full of.'

'I believe I am,' Mary sighed at last.

'Then put on your hat.' I had proposed to her on my arrival to come out to tea with me, and it was when left alone in the studio while she went to her room that I began to feel sure of the success of my errand. The vision that had an hour before determined me grew deeper and brighter for her while I moved about and looked at her things. There were more of them there on her hands than one liked to see; but at least they sharpened my confidence, which was pleasant for me in view of that of my visitor, who had accepted without reserve my plea for Miss Tredick. Four or five of her copies of famous portraits – ornaments of great public and private collections – were on the walls, and to see them again together was to feel at ease about my guarantee. The mellow manner of them was what I had had in my mind in saying, to excuse myself to Mrs Bridgenorth,

'Oh, my things, you know, look as if they had been painted to-morrow!' It made no difference that Mary's Vandykes and Gainsboroughs were reproductions and replicas, for I had known her more than once to amuse herself with doing the thing quite, as she called it, off her own bat. She had copied so bravely so many brave things that she had at the end of her brush an extraordinary bag of tricks. She had always replied to me that such things were mere clever humbug, but mere clever humbug was what our client happened to want. The thing was to let her have it – one could trust her for the rest. And at the same time that I mused in this way I observed to myself that there was already something more than, as the phrase is, met the eye in such response as I felt my friend had made. I had touched, without intention, more than one spring; I had set in motion more than one impulse. I found myself indeed quite certain of this after she had come back in her hat and her jacket. She was different – her idea had flowered; and she smiled at me from under her tense veil, while she drew over her firm, narrow hands a pair of fresh gloves, with a light distinctly new. 'Please tell your friend that I'm greatly obliged to both of you and that I take the order.'

'Good. And to give him all his good looks?'

'It's just to do *that* that I accept. I shall make him supremely beautiful – and supremely base.'

'Base?' I just demurred.

'The finest gentleman you'll ever have seen, and the worst friend.'

I wondered, as I was startled; but after an instant I laughed for joy. 'Ah well, so long as he's not mine! I see we *shall* have him,' I said as we went, for truly I had touched a spring. In fact I had touched *the* spring.

It rang, more or less, I was presently to find, all over the place. I went, as I had promised, to report to Mrs Bridgenorth on my mission, and though she declared herself much gratified at the success of it I could see she a little resented the apparent absence of any desire on Miss Tredick's part for a preliminary conference. 'I only thought she might have liked just to see me, and have imagined I might like to see *her*.'

But I was full of comfort. 'You'll see her when it's finished. You'll see her in time to thank her.'

'And to pay her, I suppose,' my hostess laughed, with an asperity that was, after all, not excessive. 'Will she take very long?'

I thought. 'She's so full of it that my impression would be that she'll do it off at a heat.'

'She *is* full of it then?' she asked; and on hearing to what tune, though I told her but half, she broke out with admiration. 'You artists are the most extraordinary people!' It was almost with a bad conscience that I confessed we indeed were, and while she said that what she meant was that we seemed to understand everything, and I rejoined that this was also what *I* meant, she took me into another room to see the place for the picture – a proceeding of which the effect was singularly to confirm the truth in question. The place for the picture – in her own room, as she called it, a boudoir at the back, over-looking the general garden of the approved modern row and, as she said, only just wanting that touch – proved exactly the place (the space of a large panel in the white woodwork over the mantel) that I had spoken of to my friend. She put it quite candidly, 'Don't you see what it will do?' and looked at me, wonderfully, as for a sign that I could sympathetically take from her what she didn't literally say. She said it, poor woman, so very nearly that I had no difficulty whatever. The portrait, tastefully enshrined there, of the finest gentleman one should ever have seen, would do even more for herself than it would do for the room.

I may as well mention at once that my observation of Mrs Bridgenorth was not in the least of a nature to unseat me from the hobby I have already named. In the light of the impression she made on me life seemed quite as prodigious and London quite as amazing as I had ever contended, and nothing could have been more in the key of that experience than the manner in which everything was vivid between us and nothing expressed. We remained on the surface with the tenacity of shipwrecked persons clinging to a plank. Our plank was our concentrated gaze at Mrs Bridgenorth's mere present. We allowed her past to exist for us only in the form of the prettiness that she had gallantly rescued from it and to which a few scraps of its identity still adhered. She was amiable, gentle, consistently proper. She gave me more than anything else the sense, simply, of waiting. She was like a house so freshly and successfully 'done up' that you were surprised it wasn't occupied. She was waiting for something to happen – for somebody to come. She was waiting, above all, for Mary Tredick's work. She clearly counted that it would help her.

I had foreseen the fact – the picture was produced at a heat; rapidly, directly, at all events, for the sort of thing it proved to be. I left my friend alone at first, left the ferment to work, troubling her with no questions and asking her for no news; two or three weeks passed, and I never went near her. Then at last, one afternoon as the light was failing, I looked in. She immediately knew what I wanted. 'Oh yes, I'm doing him.'

'Well,' I said, 'I've respected your intensity, but I *have* felt curious.'

I may not perhaps say that she was never so sad as when she laughed, but it's certain that she always laughed when she was sad. When, however, poor dear, for that matter, was she, secretly, not? Her little gasps of mirth were the mark of her worst moments. But why should she have one of these just now? 'Oh, I know your curiosity!' she replied to me; and the small chill of her amusement scarcely met it. 'He's coming out, but I can't show him to you yet. I must muddle it through in my own way. It has insisted on being, after all, a "likeness",' she added. 'But nobody will ever know.'

'Nobody?'

'Nobody *she* sees.'

'Ah, she doesn't, poor thing,' I returned, 'seem to see anybody!'

'So much the better. I'll risk it.' On which I felt I should have to wait, though I had suddenly grown impatient. But I still hung about, and while I did so she explained. 'If what I've done is really a portrait, the conditions itself prescribed it. If I was to do the most beautiful man in the world I could do but one.'

We looked at each other; then I laughed. 'It can scarcely be *me*! But you're getting,' I asked, 'the great thing?'

'The infamy? Oh yes, please God.'

It took away my breath a little, and I even for the moment scarce felt at liberty to press. But one could always be cheerful. 'What I meant is the tone of time.'

'Getting it, my dear man? Didn't I get it long ago? Don't I *show* it – the tone of time?' she suddenly, strangely sighed at me, with something in her face I had never yet seen. 'I can't give it to him more than – for all these years – he was to have given it to *me*.'

I scarce knew what smothered passion, what remembered wrong, what mixture of joy and pain my words had accidentally quickened. Such an effect of them could only become, for me, an instant pity, which, however, I brought out but indirectly. 'It's the tone,' I smiled, 'in which you're speaking now.'

This served, unfortunately, as something of a check. 'I didn't mean to speak now.' Then with her eyes on the picture, 'I've said everything there. Come back,' she added, 'in three days. He'll be all right.'

He was indeed when at last I saw him. She had produced an extraordinary thing – a thing wonderful, ideal, for the part it was to play. My only reserve, from the first, was that it was too fine for its part, that something much less 'sincere' would equally have served Mrs Bridgenorth's purpose, and that relegation to that lady's 'own room' – whatever charm it was to work there – might only mean for it cruel obscurity. The picture is before me now, so that I could describe it if description availed. It represents a man of about five-and-thirty, seen only as to the head and shoulders, but dressed, the observer gathers, in a fashion now almost antique and which was far from contemporaneous with the date of the work. His high, slightly narrow face, which would be perhaps too aquiline but for the beauty of the forehead and the sweetness of the mouth, has a charm that even, after all these years, still stirs my imagination. His type has altogether a distinction that you feel to have been firmly caught and yet not vulgarly emphasised. The eyes are just too near together, but they are, in a wondrous way, both careless and intense, while lip, cheek, and chin, smooth and clear, are admirably drawn. Youth is still, you see, in all his presence, the joy and pride of life, the perfection of a high spirit and the expectation of a great fortune, which he takes for granted with unconscious insolence. Nothing has ever happened to humiliate or disappoint him, and if my fancy doesn't run away with me the whole presentation of him is a guarantee that he will die without having suffered. He is so handsome, in short, that you can scarcely say what he means, and so happy that you can scarcely guess what he feels.

It is of course, I hasten to add, an appreciably feminine rendering, light, delicate, vague, imperfectly synthetic – insistent and evasive, above all, in the wrong places; but the composition, none the less, is beautiful and the suggestion infinite. The grandest air of the thing struck me in fact, when first I saw it, as coming from the high artistic impertinence with which it offered itself as painted about 1850. It would have been a rare flower of refinement for that dark day. The 'tone' – that of such a past as it pretended to – was there almost to excess, a brown bloom into which the image seemed mysteriously to retreat. The subject of it looks at me now across more years and more knowledge, but what I felt at the moment was that he managed to be at once a triumphant trick and a plausible evocation. He hushed me, I remember, with so many kinds of awe that I shouldn't have dreamt of asking who he was. All I said, after my first incoherences of wonder at my friend's practised skill, was: 'And you've arrived at this truth without documents?'

'It depends on what you call documents.'

'Without notes, sketches, studies?'

'I destroyed them years ago.'

'Then you once had them?'

She just hung fire. 'I once had everything.'

It told me both more and less than I had asked; enough at all events to make my next question, as I uttered it, sound even to myself a little foolish. 'So that it's all memory?'

From where she stood she looked once more at her work; after which she jerked away and, taking several steps, came back to me with something new – whatever it was I had already seen – in her air and answer. 'It's all *hate*!' she threw at me, and then went out of the room. It was not till she had gone that I quite understood why. Extremely affected by the impression visibly made on me, she had burst into tears but had wished me not to see them. She left me alone for some time with her wonderful subject, and I again, in her absence, made things out. He was dead – he had been dead for years; the sole humiliation, as I have called it, that he was to know had come to him in that form. The canvas held and cherished him, in any case, as it only holds the dead. She had suffered from him, it came to me, the worst that a woman can suffer, and the wound he had dealt her, though hidden, had never effectually healed. It had bled again while she worked. Yet when she at last re-appeared there was but one thing to say. 'The beauty, heaven knows, I see. But I don't see what you call the infamy.'

She gave him a last look – again she turned away. 'Oh, he was like that.'

'Well, whatever he was like,' I remember replying, 'I wonder you can bear to part with him. Isn't it better to let her see the picture first here?'

As to this she doubted. 'I don't think I want her to come.'

I wondered. 'You continue to object so to meet her?'

'What good will it do? It's quite impossible I should alter him for her.'

'Oh, she won't want *that*!' I laughed. 'She'll adore him as he is.'

'Are you quite sure of your idea?'

'That he's to figure as Mr Bridgenorth? Well, if I hadn't been from the first, my dear lady, I should be now. Fancy, with the chance, her *not* jumping at him! Yes, he'll figure as Mr Bridgenorth.'

'Mr Bridgenorth!' she echoed, making the sound, with her small, cold laugh, grotesquely poor for him. He might really have been a prince, and I wondered if he hadn't been. She had, at all events, a new notion. 'Do you mind my having it taken to your place and letting her come to see it there?' Which – as I immediately embraced her proposal, deferring to her reasons, whatever they were – was what was speedily arranged.

II

THE next day therefore I had the picture in charge, and on the following Mrs Bridgenorth, whom I had notified, arrived. I had placed it, framed and on an easel, well in evidence, and I have never forgotten the look and the cry that, as she became aware of it, leaped into her face and from her lips. It was an extra-ordinary moment, all the more that it found me quite unprepared – so extraordinary that I scarce knew at first what had happened. By the time I really perceived, moreover, more things had happened than one, so that when I pulled myself together it was to face the situation as a whole. She had recognised on the instant the subject; that came first and was irrepressibly vivid in her. Her recognition had, for the length of a flash, lighted for her the possibility that the stroke had been directed. That came second, and she flushed with it as with a blow in the face. What came third – and it was what was really most wondrous – was the quick instinct of getting both her strange recognition and her blind suspicion well in hand. She couldn't control, however, poor woman, the strong colour in her face and the quick tears in her eyes. She could only glare at the canvas, gasping, grimacing, and try to gain time. Whether in surprise or in resentment she intensely reflected, feeling more than anything else how little she might prudently show; and I was conscious even at the moment that nothing of its kind could have been finer than her effort to swallow her shock in ten seconds.

How many seconds she took I didn't measure; enough, assuredly, for me also to profit. I gained more time than she, and the greatest oddity doubtless was my own private man-oeuvre – the quickest calculation that, acting from a mere confused instinct, I had ever made. If she had known the great gentleman represented there and yet had determined on the spot to carry herself as ignorant, all my loyalty to Mary Tredick came to the surface in a prompt counter-move. What gave me opportunity was the red in her cheek. 'Why, you've known him!'

I saw her ask herself for an instant if she mightn't success-fully make her startled state pass as the mere glow of pleasure –

her natural greeting to her acquisition. She was pathetically, yet at the same time almost comically, divided. Her line was so to cover her tracks that every avowal of a past connection was a danger; but it also concerned her safety to learn, in the light of our astounding coincidence, how far she already stood exposed. She meanwhile begged the question. She smiled through her tears. 'He's too magnificent!'

But I gave her, as I say, all too little time. 'Who is he? Who *was* he?'

It must have been my look still more than my words that determined her. She wavered but an instant longer, panted, laughed, cried again, and then, dropping into the nearest seat, gave herself up so completely that I was almost ashamed. 'Do you think I'd tell you his *name*?' The burden of the backward years – all the effaced and ignored – lived again, almost like an accent unlearned but freshly breaking out at a touch, in the very sound of the words. These perceptions she, however, the next thing showed me, were a game at which two could play. She had to look at me but an instant. 'Why, you really *don't* know it!'

I judged best to be frank. 'I don't know it.'

'Then how does *she*?'

'How do you?' I laughed. 'I'm a different matter.'

She sat a minute turning things round, staring at the picture. 'The likeness, the likeness!' It was almost too much.

'It's so true?'

'Beyond everything.'

I considered. 'But a resemblance to a known individual – that wasn't what you wanted.'

She sprang up at this in eager protest. 'Ah, no one else would see it.'

I showed again, I fear, my amusement. 'No one but you and she?'

'It's her doing *him*!' She was held by her wonder. 'Doesn't she, on your honour, know?'

'That his is the very head you would have liked if you had dared? Not a bit. How *should* she? She knows nothing – on my honour.'

Mrs Bridgenorth continued to marvel. 'She just painted him for the kind of face—?'

'That corresponds with my description of what you wished? Precisely.'

'But *how* – after so long? From memory? As a friend?'

'As a reminiscence – yes. Visual memory, you see, in our uncanny race, is wonderful. As the ideal thing, simply, for your purpose. You *are* then suited?' I after an instant added.

She had again been gazing, and at this turned her eyes on me; but I saw she couldn't speak, couldn't do more at least than sound, unutterably, 'Suited!' so that I was positively not surprised when suddenly – just as Mary had done, the power to produce this effect seeming a property of the model – she burst into tears. I feel no harsher in relating it, however I may appear, than I did at the moment, but it is a fact that while she just wept I literally had a fresh inspiration on behalf of Miss Tredick's interests. I knew exactly, moreover, before my companion had recovered herself, what she would next ask me; and I consciously brought this appeal on in order to have it over. I explained that I had not the least idea of the identity of our artist's sitter, to which she had given me no clue. I had nothing but my impression that she had known him – known him well; and, from whatever material she had worked, the fact of his having also been known to Mrs Bridgenorth was a coincidence pure and simple. It partook of the nature of prodigy, but such prodigies did occur. My visitor listened with avidity and credulity. She was so far reassured. Then I saw her question come. 'Well, if she doesn't dream he was ever anything to me – or what he will be now – I'm going to ask you, as a very particular favour, never to tell her. She will want to know of course exactly how I've been struck. You'll naturally say that I'm delighted, but may I exact from you that you say nothing else?'

There was supplication in her face, but I had to think. 'There are conditions I must put to you first, and one of them is also a question, only more frank than yours. Was this mysterious personage – frustrated by death – to have married you?'

She met it bravely. 'Certainly, if he had lived.'

I was only amused at an artlessness in her 'certainly'. 'Very good. But why do you wish the coincidence—'

'Kept from her?' She knew exactly why. 'Because if she suspects it she won't let me have the picture. Therefore,' she added with decision, 'you must let me pay for it on the spot.'

'What do you mean by on the spot?'

'I'll send you a cheque as soon as I get home.'

'Oh,' I laughed, 'let us understand. Why do you consider she won't let you have the picture?'

She made me wait a little for this, but when it came it was perfectly lucid. 'Because she'll then see how much more I must want it.'

'How much less – wouldn't it be rather, since the bargain was, as the more convenient thing, not for a likeness?'

'Oh,' said Mrs Bridgenorth with impatience, 'the likeness will take care of itself. She'll put this and that together.' Then she brought out her real apprehension. 'She'll be jealous.'

'Oh!' I laughed. But I was startled.

'She'll hate me!'

I wondered. 'But I don't think she liked him.'

'Don't think?' She stared at me, with her echo, over all that might be in it, then seemed to find little enough. 'I *say*!'

It was almost comically the old Mrs Bridgenorth. 'But I gather from her that he was bad.'

'Then what was *she*?'

I barely hesitated. 'What were *you*?'

'That's my own business.' And she turned again to the picture. 'He was good enough for her to do *that* of him.'

I took it in once more. 'Artistically speaking, for the way it's done, it's one of the most curious things I've ever seen.'

'It's a grand treat!' said poor Mrs Bridgenorth more simply.

It was, it *is* really; which is exactly what made the case so interesting. 'Yet I feel somehow that, as I say, it wasn't done with love.'

It was wonderful how she understood. 'It was done with rage.'

'Then what have you to fear?'

She knew again perfectly. 'What happened when he made *me* jealous. So much,' she declared, 'that if you'll give me your word for silence—'

'Well?'

'Why, I'll double the money.'

'Oh,' I replied, taking a turn about in the excitement of our concurrence, 'that's exactly what – to do a still better stroke for her – it had just come to *me* to propose!'

'It's understood then, on your oath as a gentleman?' She was so eager that practically this settled it, though I moved to and fro a little while she watched me in suspense. It vibrated all round us that she had gone out to the thing in a stifled flare, that a whole close relation had in the few minutes revived. We know it of the truly amiable person that he will strain a point for another that he wouldn't strain for himself. The stroke to put in for Mary was positively prescribed. The work represented really much more than had been covenanted, and if the purchaser chose so to value it this was her own affair. I decided. 'If it's understood also on *your* word.'

We were so at one that we shook hands on it. 'And when may I send?'

'Well, I shall see her this evening. Say early to-morrow.'

'Early to-morrow.' And I went with her to her brougham, into which, I remember, as she took leave, she expressed regret that she mightn't then and there have introduced the canvas for removal. I consoled her with remarking that she couldn't have got it in – which was not quite true.

I saw Mary Tredick before dinner, and though I was not quite ideally sure of my present ground with her I instantly brought out my news. 'She's so delighted that I felt I must in conscience do something still better for you. She's not to have it on the original terms. I've put up the price.'

Mary wondered. 'But to what?'

'Well, to four hundred. If you say so I'll try even for five.'

'Oh, she'll never give that.'

'I beg your pardon.'

'After the agreement?' She looked grave. 'I don't like such leaps and bounds.'

'But, my dear child, they're yours. You contracted for a decorative trifle and you've produced a breathing masterpiece.'

She thought. 'Is that what she calls it?' Then, as having to think too, I hesitated, 'What does she know?' she pursued.

'She knows she wants it.'

'So much as that?'

At this I had to brace myself a little. 'So much that she'll send me the cheque this afternoon, and that you'll have mine by the first post in the morning.'

'Before she has even received the picture?'

'Oh, she'll send for it to-morrow.' And as I was dining out and had still to dress, my time was up. Mary came with me to the door, where I repeated my assurance. 'You shall receive my cheque by the first post.' To which I added: 'If it's little enough for a lady so much in need to pay for *any* husband, it isn't worth mentioning as the price of such a one as you've given her!'

I was in a hurry, but she held me. 'Then you've felt your idea confirmed?'

'My idea?'

'That that's what I *have* given her?'

I suddenly fancied I had perhaps gone too far; but I had kept my cab and was already in it. 'Well, put it,' I called with excess of humour over the front, 'that you've, at any rate, given *him* a wife!'

When on my return from dinner that night I let myself in, my first care, in my dusky studio, was to make light for another look at Mary's subject. I felt the impulse to bid him good night, but, to my astonishment, he was no longer there. His place was a void – he had already disappeared. I saw, however, after my first surprise, what had happened – saw it moreover, frankly, with some relief. As my servants were in bed I could ask no questions, but it was clear that Mrs Bridgenorth, whose note, containing its cheque, lay on my table, had been after all unable to wait. The note, I found, mentioned nothing but the enclosure; but it had come by hand, and it was her silence that told the tale. Her messenger had been instructed to 'act'; he had come with a vehicle, he had transferred to it canvas and frame. The prize was now therefore landed and the incident closed. I didn't

altogether, the next morning, know why, but I had slept the
better for the sense of these things, and as soon as my attendant
came in I asked for details. It was on this that his answer
surprised me. 'No, sir, there was no man; she came herself.
She had only a four-wheeler, but I helped her, and we got it in.
It was a squeeze, sir, but she *would* take it.'

I wondered. 'She had a four-wheeler? and not her servant?'

'No, no, sir. She came, as you may say, single-handed.'

'And not even in her brougham, which would have been
larger?'

My man, with his habit, weighed it. 'But *have* she a brougham, sir?'

'Why, the one she was here in yesterday.'

Then light broke. 'Oh, *that* lady! It wasn't her, sir. It was
Miss Tredick.'

Light broke, but darkness a little followed it – a darkness
that, after breakfast, guided my steps back to my friend. There,
in its own first place, I met her creation; but I saw it would be a
different thing meeting *her*. She immediately put down on a
table, as if she had expected me, the cheque I had sent her
overnight. 'Yes, I've brought it away. And I can't take the
money.'

I found myself in despair. 'You want to keep him?'

'I don't understand what has happened.'

'You just back out?'

'I don't understand,' she repeated, 'what has happened.'
But what I had already perceived was, on the contrary, that
she very nearly, that she in fact quite remarkably, did understand. It was as if in my zeal I had given away my case, and I felt
that my test was coming. She had been thinking all night with
intensity, and Mrs Bridgenorth's generosity, coupled with Mrs
Bridgenorth's promptitude, had kept her awake. Thence, for a
woman nervous and critical, imaginations, visions, questions.
'Why, in writing me last night, did you take for granted it was
she who had swooped down? Why,' asked Mary Tredick,
'should she swoop?'

Well, if I could drive a bargain for Mary I felt I could *a fortiori*
lie for her. 'Because it's her way. She does swoop. She's

impatient and uncontrolled. And it's affectation for you to pretend,' I said with diplomacy, 'that you see no reason for her falling in love—'

'Falling in love?' She took me straight up.

'With that gentleman. Certainly. What woman wouldn't? What woman didn't? I really don't see, you know, your right to back out.'

'I won't back out,' she presently returned, 'if you'll answer me a question. Does she know the man represented?' Then as I hung fire: 'It has come to me that she must. It would account for so much. For the strange way I feel,' she went on, 'and for the extraordinary sum you've been able to extract from her.'

It was a pity, and I flushed with it, besides wincing at the word she used. But Mrs Bridgenorth and I, between us, had clearly made the figure too high. 'You think that, if she *had* guessed, I would naturally work it to "extract" more?'

She turned away from me on this and, looking blank in her trouble, moved vaguely about. Then she stopped. 'I see him set up there. I hear her say it. What you said she would make him pass for.'

I believe I foolishly tried – though only for an instant – to look as if I didn't remember what I had said. 'Her husband?'

'He wasn't.'

The next minute I had risked it. 'Was he yours?'

I don't know what I had expected, but I found myself surprised at her mere pacific head-shake. 'No.'

'Then why mayn't he have been—?'

'Another woman's? Because he died, to my absolute knowledge, unmarried.' She spoke as quietly. 'He had known many women, and there was one in particular with whom he became – and too long remained – ruinously intimate. She tried to make him marry her, and he was very near it. Death, however, saved him. But she was the reason—'

'Yes?' I feared again from her a wave of pain, and I went on while she kept it back. 'Did you know her?'

'She was one I wouldn't.' Then she brought it out. 'She was the reason he failed me.' Her successful detachment somehow said all, reduced me to a flat, kind 'Oh!' that marked my sense of her telling me, against my expectation, more than I knew what to do with. But it was just while I wondered how to turn her confidence that she repeated, in a changed voice, her challenge of a moment before. 'Does she know the man represented?'

'I haven't the least idea.' And having so acquitted myself I added, with what strikes me now as futility: 'She certainly – yesterday – didn't name him.'

'Only recognised him?'

'If she did she brilliantly concealed it.'

'So that you got nothing from her?'

It was a question that offered me a certain advantage. 'I thought you accused me of getting too much.'

She gave me a long look, and I now saw everything in her face. 'It's very nice – what you're doing for me, and you do it handsomely. It's beautiful – beautiful, and I thank you with all my heart. But I know.'

'And what do you know?'

She went about now preparing her usual work. 'What he must have been to her.'

'You mean she was the person?'

'Well,' she said, putting on her old spectacles, 'she was one of them.'

'And you accept so easily the astounding coincidence—?'

'Of my finding myself, after years, in so extraordinary a relation with her? What do you call easily? I've passed a night of torment.'

'But what put it into your head—?'

'That I had so blindly and strangely given him back to her? *You* put it – yesterday.'

'And how?'

'I can't tell you. You didn't in the least mean to – on the contrary. But you dropped the seed. The plant, after you had gone,' she said with a business-like pull at her easel, 'the plant began to grow. I *saw* them there – in your studio – face to face.'

'You were jealous?' I laughed.

She gave me through her glasses another look, and they seemed, from this moment, in their queerness, to have placed her quite on the other side of the gulf of time. She was firm there; she was settled; I couldn't get at her now. 'I see she told you I *would* be.' I doubtless kept down too little my start at it, and she immediately pursued. 'You say I accept the coincidence, which is of course prodigious. But such things happen. Why shouldn't I accept it if you do?'

'*Do* I?' I smiled.

She began her work in silence, but she presently exclaimed: 'I'm glad I didn't meet her!'

'I don't yet see why you wouldn't.'

'Neither do I. It was an instinct.'

'Your instincts' – I tried to be ironic – 'are miraculous.'

'They *have* to be, to meet such accidents. I must ask you kindly to tell her, when you return her gift, that now I have done the picture I find I must after all keep it for myself.'

'Giving no reason?'

She painted away. 'She'll know the reason.'

Well, by this time I knew it too; I knew so many things that I fear my resistance was weak. If our wonderful client hadn't been his wife in fact, she was not to be helped to become his wife in fiction. I knew almost more than I can say, more at any rate than I could then betray. He had been bound in common mercy to stand by my friend, and he had basely forsaken her. This indeed brought up the obscure, into which I shyly gazed. 'Why, even granting your theory, should you grudge her the portrait? It was painted in bitterness.'

'Yes. Without that—!'

'It wouldn't have come? Precisely. Is it in bitterness, then, you'll keep it?'

She looked up from her canvas. 'In what would *you* keep it?'

It made me jump. 'Do you mean I *may*?' Then I had my idea. 'I'd give you her price for it!'

Her smile through her glasses was beautiful. 'And afterwards make it over to her? You shall have it when I die.' With which she came away from her easel, and I saw that I was staying her work and should properly go. So I put out my hand to her. 'It took – whatever you will! – to paint it,' she said, 'but I shall keep it in joy.' I could answer nothing now –

had to cease to pretend; the thing was in her hands. For a moment we stood there, and I had again the sense, melancholy and final, of her being, as it were, remotely glazed and fixed into what she had done. 'He's taken from me, and for all those years he's kept. Then she herself, by a prodigy—!' She lost herself again in the wonder of it.

'Unwittingly gives him back?'

She fairly, for an instant over the marvel, closed her eyes. 'Gives him back.'

Then it was I saw how he would be kept! But it was the end of my vision. I could only write, ruefully enough, to Mrs Bridgenorth, whom I never met again, but of whose death – preceding by a couple of years Mary Tredick's – I happened to hear. This is an old man's tale. I have inherited the picture, in the deep beauty of which, however, darkness still lurks. No one, strange to say, has ever recognised the model, but everyone asks his name. I don't even know it.

THE TWO FACES

I

THE servant, who, in spite of his sealed, stamped look, appeared to have his reasons, stood there for instruction, in a manner not quite usual, after announcing the name. Mrs Grantham, however, took it up – 'Lord Gwyther?' – with a quick surprise that for an instant justified him even to the small scintilla in the glance she gave her companion, which might have had exactly the sense of the butler's hesitation. This companion, a shortish, fairish, youngish man, clean-shaven and keen-eyed, had, with a promptitude that would have struck an observer – which the butler indeed was – sprung to his feet and moved to the chimney-piece, though his hostess herself, meanwhile, managed not otherwise to stir. 'Well?' she said, as for the visitor to advance; which she immediately followed with a sharper 'He's not there?'

'Shall I show him up, ma'am?'

'But of course!' The point of his doubt made her at last rise for impatience, and Bates, before leaving the room, might still have caught the achieved irony of her appeal to the gentleman into whose communion with her he had broken. 'Why in the world not—? What a way—!' she exclaimed, as Sutton felt beside his cheek the passage of her eyes to the glass behind him.

'He wasn't sure you'd see anyone.'

'I don't see "anyone", but I see individuals.'

'That's just it; and sometimes you don't see them.'

'Do you mean ever because of *you*?' she asked as she touched into place a tendril of hair. 'That's just his impertinence, as to which I shall speak to him.'

'Don't,' said Shirley Sutton. 'Never notice anything.'

'That's nice advice from you,' she laughed, 'who notice everything!'

'Ah, but I speak of nothing.'

She looked at him a moment. 'You're still more impertinent than Bates. You'll please not budge,' she went on.

'Really? I must sit him out?' he continued as, after a minute, she had not again spoken – only glancing about, while she changed her place, partly for another look at the glass and partly to see if she could improve her seat. What she felt was rather more than, clever and charming though she was, she could hide. 'If you're wondering how you seem, I can tell you. Awfully cool and easy.'

She gave him another stare. She was beautiful and conscious. 'And if you're wondering how *you* seem—'

'Oh, I'm not!' he laughed from before the fire; 'I always perfectly know.'

'How you seem,' she retorted, 'is as if you didn't!'

Once more for a little he watched her. 'You're looking lovely for him – extraordinarily lovely, within the marked limits of your range. But that's enough. Don't be clever.'

'Then who *will* be?'

'There you are!' he sighed with amusement.

'Do you know him?' she asked as, through the door left open by Bates, they heard steps on the landing.

Sutton had to think an instant, and produced a 'No' just as Lord Gwyther was again announced, which gave an unexpectedness to the greeting offered him a moment later by this personage – a young man, stout and smooth and fresh, but not at all shy, who, after the happiest rapid passage with Mrs Grantham, put out a hand with a frank, pleasant 'How d'ye do?'

'Mr Shirley Sutton,' Mrs Grantham explained.

'Oh yes,' said her second visitor, quite as if he knew; which, as he couldn't have known, had for her first the interest of confirming a perception that his lordship would be – no, not at all, in general, embarrassed, only was now exceptionally and especially agitated. As it is, for that matter, with Sutton's total impression that we are particularly and almost exclusively concerned, it may be further mentioned that he was not less clear as to the really handsome way in which the young man kept himself together and little by little – though with all proper aid indeed – finally found his feet. All sorts of things, for the twenty minutes, occurred to Sutton, though one of them was certainly not that it would, after all, be better he should go. One of them was that their hostess was doing it in perfection – simply, easily, kindly, yet with something the least bit queer in her wonderful eyes; another was that if he had been recognised without the least ground it was through a tension of nerves on the part of his fellow-guest that produced inconsequent motions; still another was that, even had departure been indicated, he would positively have felt dissuasion in the rare promise of the scene. This was in especial after Lord Gwyther not only had announced that he was now married, but had mentioned that he wished to bring his wife to Mrs Grantham for the benefit so certain to be derived. It was the passage immediately produced by that speech that provoked in Sutton the intensity, as it were, of his arrest. He already knew of the marriage as well as Mrs Grantham herself, and as well also as he knew of some other things; and this gave him, doubtless, the better measure of what took place before him and the keener consciousness of the quick look that, at a marked moment – though it was not absolutely meant for him any more than for his companion – Mrs Grantham let him catch.

She smiled, but it had a gravity. 'I think, you know, you ought to have told me before.'

'Do you mean when I first got engaged? Well, it all took place so far away, and we really told, at home, so few people.'

Oh, there might have been reasons; but it had not been quite right. 'You were married at Stuttgart? That wasn't too far for *my* interest, at least, to reach.'

'Awfully kind of you – and of course one knew you *would* be kind. But it wasn't at Stuttgart; it was over there, but quite in the country. We should have managed it in England but that her mother naturally wished to be present, yet was not in health to come. So it was really, you see, a sort of little hole-and-corner German affair.'

This didn't in the least check Mrs Grantham's claim, but it started a slight anxiety. 'Will she be – a, then, German?'

Sutton knew her to know perfectly what Lady Gwyther would 'be', but he had by this time, while their friend explained, his independent interest. 'Oh dear, no! My father-in-law has never parted with the proud birthright of a Briton. But his wife, you see, holds an estate in Würtemberg from *her* mother, Countess Kremnitz, on which, with the awful condition of his English property, you know, they've found it for years a tremendous saving to live. So that though Valda was luckily born at home she has practically spent her life over there.'

'Oh, I see.' Then, after a slight pause, 'Is Valda her pretty name?' Mrs Grantham asked.

'Well,' said the young man, only wishing, in his candour, it was clear, to be drawn out – 'well, she has, in the manner of her mother's people, about thirteen; but that's the one we generally use.'

Mrs Grantham hesitated but an instant. 'Then may *I* generally use it?'

'It would be too charming of you; and nothing would give her – as, I assure you, nothing would give *me*, greater pleasure.' Lord Gwyther quite glowed with the thought.

'Then I think that instead of coming alone you might have brought her to see me.'

'It's exactly what,' he instantly replied, 'I came to ask your leave to do.' He explained that for the moment Lady Gwyther was not in town, having as soon as she arrived gone down to Torquay to put in a few days with one of her aunts, also her godmother, to whom she was an object of great interest. She had seen no one yet, and no one – not that *that* mattered – had seen her; she knew nothing whatever of London and was awfully frightened at facing it and at what – however little – might be expected of her. 'She wants some one,' he said, 'some one who knows the whole thing, don't you see? and who's thoroughly kind and clever, as you would be, if I may say so, to take her by the hand.' It was at this point and on these words that the eyes of Lord Gwyther's two auditors inevitably and wonderfully met. But there was nothing in the way he kept it up to show that he caught the encounter. 'She wants, if I may tell you so, for the great labyrinth, a real friend; and asking myself what I could do to make things ready for her, and who would be absolutely the best woman in London—'

'You thought, naturally, of *me*?' Mrs Grantham had listened with no sign but the faint flash just noted; now, however, she gave him the full light of her expressive face – which immediately brought Shirley Sutton, looking at his watch, once more to his feet.

'She *is* the best woman in London!' He addressed himself with a laugh to the other visitor, but offered his hand in farewell to their hostess.

'You're going?'

'I must,' he said without scruple.

'Then we do meet at dinner?'

'I hope so.' On which, to take leave, he returned with interest to Lord Gwyther the friendly clutch he had a short time before received.

II

THEY did meet at dinner, and if they were not, as it happened, side by side, they made that up afterwards in the happiest angle of a drawing-room that offered both shine and shadow and that was positively much appreciated, in the circle in which they moved, for the favourable 'corners' created by its shrewd mistress. Her face, charged with something produced in it by Lord Gwyther's visit, had been with him so constantly for the previous hours that, when she instantly challenged him on his 'treatment' of her in the afternoon, he was on the point of naming it as his reason for not having remained with her. Something new had quickly come into her beauty; he couldn't as yet have said what, nor whether on the whole to its advantage or its loss. Till he could make up his mind about that, at any rate, he would say nothing; so that, with sufficient presence of mind, he found a better excuse. If in short he had in defiance of her particular request left her alone with Lord Gwyther, it was simply because the situation had suddenly turned so exciting that he had fairly feared the contagion of it – the temptation of its making him, most improperly, put in his word.

They could now talk of these things at their ease. Other couples, ensconced and scattered, enjoyed the same privilege,

and Sutton had more and more the profit, such as it was, of
feeling that his interest in Mrs Grantham had become – what
was the luxury of so high a social code – an acknowledged and
protected relation. He knew his London well enough to know
that he was on the way to be regarded as her main source of
consolation for the trick that, several months before, Lord
Gwyther had publicly played her. Many persons had not held
that, by the high social code in question, his lordship could
have 'reserved the right' to turn up in that way, from one day to
another, engaged. For himself London took, with its short cuts
and its cheap psychology, an immense deal for granted. To his
own sense he was never – could in the nature of things never be
– any man's 'successor'. Just what had constituted the pre-
decessorship of other men was apparently that they had been
able to make up their mind. He, worse luck, was at the mercy of
her face, and more than ever at the mercy of it now, which
meant, moreover, not that it made a slave of him, but that it
made, disconcertingly, a sceptic. It was the absolute perfection
of the handsome; but things had a way of coming into it. 'I felt,'
he said, 'that you were there together at a point at which you
had a right to the ease that the absence of a listener would give. I
reflected that when you made me promise to stay you hadn't
guessed—'

'That he could possibly have come to me on such an extraordinary errand? No, of course I hadn't guessed. Who *would*?
But didn't you see how little I was upset by it?'

Sutton demurred. Then with a smile, 'I think *he* saw how
little.'

'You yourself didn't, then?'

He again held back, but not, after all, to answer. 'He was
wonderful, wasn't he?'

'I think he was,' she replied after a moment. To which she
added: 'Why did he pretend that way he knew you?'

'He didn't pretend. He felt on the spot as if we were friends.'
Sutton had found this afterwards, and found truth in it. 'It was
an effusion of cheer and hope. He was so glad to see me there,
and to find you happy.'

'Happy?'

'Happy. Aren't you?'

'Because of *you*?'

'Well – according to the impression he received as he came in.'

'That was sudden then,' she asked, 'and unexpected?'

Her companion thought. 'Prepared in some degree, but confirmed by the sight of us, there together, so awfully jolly and sociable over your fire.'

Mrs Grantham turned this round. 'If he knew I was "happy" then – which, by the way, is none of his business, nor of yours either – why in the world did he come?'

'Well, for good manners, and for his idea,' said Sutton.

She took it in, appearing to have no hardness of rancour that could bar discussion. 'Do you mean by his idea his proposal that I should grandmother his wife? And, if you do, is the proposal your reason for calling him wonderful?'

Sutton laughed. 'Pray, what's yours?' As this was a question, however, that she took her time to answer or not to answer – only appearing interested for a moment in a combination that had formed itself on the other side of the room – he presently went on. 'What's *his*? – that would seem to be the point. His, I mean, for having decided on the extraordinary step of throwing his little wife, bound hands and feet, into your arms. Intelligent as you are, and with these three or four hours to have thought it over, I yet don't see how that can fail still to mystify you.'

She continued to watch their opposite neighbours. ' "Little", you call her. Is she so very small?'

'Tiny, tiny – she *must* be; as different as possible in every way – of necessity – from you. They always *are* the opposite pole, you know,' said Shirley Sutton.

She glanced at him now. 'You strike me as of an impudence—!'

'No, no. I only like to make it out with you.'

She looked away again and, after a little, went on. 'I'm sure she's charming, and only hope one isn't to gather that he's already tired of her.'

'Not a bit! He's tremendously in love, and he'll remain so.'

'So much the better. And if it's a question,' said Mrs Grantham, 'of one's doing what one can for her, he has only, as I told him when you had gone, to give me the chance.'

'Good! So he *is* to commit her to you?'

'You use extraordinary expressions, but it's settled that he brings her.'

'And you'll really and truly help her?'

'Really and truly?' said Mrs Grantham, with her eyes again upon him. 'Why not? For what do you take me?'

'Ah, isn't that just what I still have the discomfort, every day I live, of asking myself?'

She had made, as she spoke, a movement to rise, which, as if she was tired of his tone, his last words appeared to determine. But, also getting up, he held her, when they were on their feet, long enough to hear the rest of what he had to say. 'If you do help her, you know, you'll show him that you've understood.'

'Understood what?'

'Why, his idea – the deep, acute train of reasoning that has led him to take, as one may say, the bull by the horns; to reflect that as you might, as you probably *would*, in any case, get at her, he plays the wise game, as well as the bold one, by assuming your generosity and placing himself publicly under an obligation to you.'

Mrs Grantham showed not only that she had listened, but that she had for an instant considered. 'What is it you elegantly describe as my getting "at" her?'

'He takes his risk, but puts you, you see, on your honour.'

She thought a moment more. 'What profundities indeed then over the simplest of matters! And if your idea is,' she went on, 'that if I do help her I shall show him I've understood them, so it will be that if I don't—'

'You'll show him' – Sutton took her up – 'that you haven't? Precisely. But in spite of not wanting to appear to have understood *too* much—'

'I may still be depended on to do what I can? Quite certainly. You'll see what I may still be depended on to do.' And she moved away.

III

It was not, doubtless, that there had been anything in their rather sharp separation at that moment to sustain or prolong the interruption; yet it definitely befell that, circumstances aiding, they practically failed to meet again before the great party at Burbeck. This occasion was to gather in some thirty persons from a certain Friday to the following Monday, and it was on the Friday that Sutton went down. He had known in advance that Mrs Grantham was to be there, and this perhaps, during the interval of hindrance, had helped him a little to be patient. He had before him the certitude of a real full cup – two days brimming over with the sight of her. He found, however, on his arrival that she was not yet in the field, and presently learned that her place would be in a small contingent that was to join the party on the morrow. This knowledge he extracted from Miss Banker, who was always the first to present herself at any gathering that was to enjoy her, and whom, moreover – partly on that very account – the wary not less than the speculative were apt to hold themselves well-advised to engage with at as early as possible a stage of the business. She was stout, red, rich, mature, universal – a massive, much-fingered volume, alphabetical, wonderful, indexed, that opened of itself at the right place. She opened for Sutton instinctively at G—, which happened to be remarkably convenient. 'What she's really waiting over for is to bring down Lady Gwyther.'

'Ah, the Gwythers are coming?'

'Yes; caught, through Mrs Grantham, just in time. *She'll* be the feature – everyone wants to see her.'

Speculation and wariness met and combined at this moment in Shirley Sutton. 'Do you mean – a – Mrs Grantham?'

'Dear no! Poor little Lady Gwyther, who, but just arrived in England, appears now literally for the first time in her life in any society whatever, and whom (don't you know the extraordinary story? you ought to – *you*!) she, of all people, has so wonderfully taken up. It will be quite – here – as if she were "presenting" her.'

Sutton, of course, took in more things than even appeared. 'I never know what I ought to know; I only know, inveterately, what I oughtn't. So what *is* the extraordinary story?'

'You really haven't heard—?'

'Really!' he replied without winking.

'It happened, indeed, but the other day,' said Miss Banker, 'yet everyone is already wondering. Gwyther has thrown his wife on her mercy – but I won't believe you if you pretend to me you don't know why he shouldn't.'

Sutton asked himself then what he *could* pretend. 'Do you mean because she's merciless?'

She hesitated. 'If you don't know, perhaps I oughtn't to tell you.'

He liked Miss Banker, and found just the right tone to plead. '*Do* tell me.'

'Well,' she sighed, 'it will be your own fault—! They had been such friends that there could have been but one name for the crudity of his original *procédé*. When I was a girl we used to call it throwing over. They call it in French to *lâcher*. But I refer not so much to the act itself as to the manner of it, though you may say indeed, of course, that there is in such cases, after all, only one manner. Least said, soonest mended.'

Sutton seemed to wonder. 'Oh, he said too much?'

'He said nothing. That was it.'

Sutton kept it up. 'But was *what*?'

'Why, what she must, like any woman in her shoes, have felt to be his perfidy. He simply went and *did* it – took to himself this child, that is, without the preliminary of a scandal or a rupture – before she could turn round.'

'I follow you. But it would appear from what you say that she *has* turned round now.'

'Well,' Miss Banker laughed, 'we shall see for ourselves how far. It will be what everyone will try to see.'

'Oh, then we've work cut out!' And Sutton certainly felt that he himself had – an impression that lost nothing from a further talk with Miss Banker in the course of a short stroll in the grounds with her the next day. He spoke as one who had now considered many things.

'Did I understand from you yesterday that Lady Gwyther's a "child"?'

'Nobody knows. It's prodigious the way she has managed.'

'The way Lady Gwyther has—?'

'No; the way May Grantham has kept her till this hour in her pocket.'

He was quick at his watch. 'Do you mean by "this hour" that they're due now?'

'Not till tea. All the others arrive together in time for that.' Miss Banker had clearly, since the previous day, filled in gaps and become, as it were, revised and enlarged. 'She'll have kept a cat from seeing her, so as to produce her entirely herself.'

'Well,' Sutton mused, 'that will have been a very noble sort of return—'

'For Gwyther's behaviour? Very. Yet I feel creepy.'

'Creepy?'

'Because so much depends for the girl – in the way of the right start or the wrong start – on the signs and omens of this first appearance. It's a great house and a great occasion, and we're assembled here, it strikes me, very much as the Roman mob at the circus used to be to see the next Christian maiden brought out to the tigers.'

'Oh, if she *is* a Christian maiden—!' Sutton murmured. But he stopped at what his imagination called up.

It perhaps fed that faculty a little that Miss Banker had the effect of making out that Mrs Grantham might individually be, in any case, something of a Roman matron. 'She has kept her in the dark so that we may only take her from her hand. She will have formed her for us.'

'In so few days?'

'Well, she will have prepared her – decked her for the sacrifice with ribbons and flowers.'

'Ah, if you only mean that she will have taken her to her dressmaker—!' And it came to Sutton, at once as a new light and as a check, almost, to anxiety, that this was all poor Gwyther, mistrustful probably of a taste formed by Stuttgart, might have desired of their friend.

There were usually at Burbeck many things taking place at once; so that wherever else, on such occasions, tea might be served, it went forward with matchless pomp, weather permitting, on a shaded stretch of one of the terraces and in presence of one of the prospects. Shirley Sutton, moving, as the afternoon waned, more restlessly about and mingling in dispersed groups only to find they had nothing to keep him quiet, came upon it as he turned a corner of the house – saw it seated there in all its state. It might be said that at Burbeck it was, like everything else, made the most of. It constituted immediately, with multiplied tables and glittering plate, with rugs and cushions and ices and fruit and wonderful porcelain and beautiful women, a scene of splendour, almost an incident of grand opera. One of the beautiful women might quite have been expected to rise with a gold cup and a celebrated song.

One of them did rise, as it happened, while Sutton drew near, and he found himself a moment later seeing nothing and nobody but Mrs Grantham. They met on the terrace, just away from the others, and the movement in which he had the effect of arresting her might have been that of withdrawal. He quickly saw, however, that if she had been about to pass into the house it was only on some errand – to get something or to call someone – that would immediately have restored her to the public. It somehow struck him on the spot – and more than ever yet, though the impression was not wholly new to him – that she felt herself a figure for the forefront of the stage and indeed would have been recognised by anyone at a glance as the *prima donna assoluta*. She caused, in fact, during the few minutes he stood talking to her, an extraordinary series of waves to roll extraordinarily fast over his sense, not the least mark of the matter being that the appearance with which it ended was again the one with which it had begun. 'The face – the face,' as he kept dumbly repeating; that was at last, as at first, all he could clearly see. She had a perfection resplendent, but what in the world had it done, this perfection, to her beauty? It was her beauty, doubtless, that looked out at him, but it was into something else that, as their eyes met, he strangely found himself looking.

It was as if something had happened in consequence of which she had changed, and there was that in this swift perception that made him glance eagerly about for Lady Gwyther. But as he took in the recruited group – identities of the hour added to those of the previous twenty-four – he saw, among his recognitions, one of which was the husband of the person missing, that Lady Gwyther was not there. Nothing in the whole business was more singular than his consciousness that, as he came back to his interlocutress after the nods and smiles and hand-waves he had launched, she knew what had been his thought. She knew for whom he had looked without success; but why should this knowledge visibly have hardened and sharpened her, and precisely at a moment when she was unprecedentedly magnificent? The indefinable apprehension that had somewhat sunk after his second talk with Miss Banker and then had perversely risen again – this nameless anxiety now produced on him, with a sudden sharper pinch, the effect of a great suspense. The action of that, in turn, was to show him that he had not yet fully known how much he had at stake on a final view. It was revealed to him for the first time that he 'really cared' whether Mrs Grantham were a safe nature. It was too ridiculous by what a thread it hung, but something was cer--tainly in the air that would definitely tell him.

What was in the air descended the next moment to earth. He turned round as he caught the expression with which her eyes attached themselves to something that approached. A little person, very young and very much dressed, had come out of the house, and the expression in Mrs Grantham's eyes was that of the artist confronted with her work and interested, even to impatience, in the judgement of others. The little person drew nearer, and though Sutton's companion, without looking at him now, gave it a name and met it, he had jumped for himself at certitude. He saw many things – too many, and they appeared to be feathers, frills, excrescences of silk and lace – massed together and conflicting, and after a moment also saw struggling out of them a small face that struck him as either scared or sick. Then, with his eyes again returning to Mrs Grantham, he saw another.

He had no more talk with Miss Banker till late that evening – an evening during which he had felt himself too noticeably silent; but something had passed between this pair, across dinner-table and drawing-room, without speech, and when they at last found words it was in the needed ease of a quiet end of the long, lighted gallery, where she opened again at the very paragraph.

'You were right – that *was* it. She did the only thing that, at such short notice, she *could* do. She took her to her dressmaker.'

Sutton, with his back to the reach of the gallery, had, as if to banish a vision, buried his eyes for a minute in his hands. 'And oh, the face – the face!'

'Which?' Miss Banker asked.

'Whichever one looks at.'

'But May Grantham's glorious. She has turned herself out—'

'With a splendour of taste and a sense of effect, eh? Yes.' Sutton showed he saw far.

'She *has* the sense of effect. The sense of effect as exhibited in Lady Gwyther's clothes—!' was something Miss Banker failed of words to express. 'Everybody's overwhelmed. Here, you know, that sort of thing's grave. The poor creature's lost.'

'Lost?'

'Since on the first impression, as we said, so much depends. The first impression's made – oh, made! I defy her now ever to unmake it. Her husband, who's proud, won't like her the better for it. And I don't see,' Miss Banker went on, 'that her prettiness *was* enough – a mere little feverish, frightened freshness; what *did* he see in her? – to be so blasted. It has been done with an atrocity of art—'

'That supposes the dressmaker then also a devil?'

'Oh, your London women and their dressmakers!' Miss Banker laughed.

'But the face – the face!' Sutton woefully repeated.

'May's?'

'The little girl's. It's exquisite.'

'Exquisite?'

'For unimaginable pathos.'

'Oh!' Miss Banker dropped.

'She has at last begun to see.' Sutton showed again how far *he* saw. 'It glimmers upon her innocence, she makes it dimly out – what has been done with her. She's even worse this evening – the way, my eye, she looked at dinner! – than when she came. Yes' – he was confident – 'it has dawned (how couldn't it, out of all of you?) and she knows.'

'She ought to have known before!' Miss Banker intelligently sighed.

'No; she wouldn't in that case have been so beautiful.'

'Beautiful?' cried Miss Banker; 'overloaded like a monkey in a show!'

'The face, yes; which goes to the heart. It's that that makes it,' said Shirley Sutton. 'And it's that' – he thought it out – 'that makes the other.'

'I see. Conscious?'

'Horrible!'

'You take it hard,' said Miss Banker.

Lord Gwyther, just before she spoke, had come in sight and now was near them. Sutton on this, appearing to wish to avoid him, reached, before answering his companion's observation, a door that opened close at hand. 'So hard,' he replied from that point, 'that I shall be off to-morrow morning.'

'And not see the rest?' she called after him.

But he had already gone, and Lord Gwyther, arriving, amiably took up her question. 'The rest of what?'

Miss Banker looked him well in the eyes. 'Of Mrs Grantham's clothes.'

THE BELDONALD HOLBEIN

I

MRS MUNDEN had not yet been to my studio on so good a pretext as when she first put it to me that it would be quite open to me – should I only care, as she called it, to throw the handkerchief – to paint her beautiful sister-in-law. I needn't go here, more than is essential, into the question of Mrs Munden, who would really, by the way, be a story in herself. She has a manner of her own of putting things, and some of those she has put to me—! Her implication was that Lady Beldonald had not only seen and admired certain examples of my work, but had literally been prepossessed in favour of the painter's 'personality'. Had I been struck with this sketch I might easily have imagined that Lady Beldonald was throwing *me* the handkerchief. 'She hasn't done,' my visitor said, 'what she ought.'

'Do you mean she has done what she oughtn't?'

'Nothing horrid – oh dear, no.' And something in Mrs Munden's tone, with the way she appeared to muse a moment, even suggested to me that what she 'oughtn't' was perhaps what Lady Beldonald had too much neglected. 'She hasn't got on.'

'What's the matter with her?'

'Well, to begin with, she's American.'

'But I thought that was the way of ways to get on.'

'It's one of them. But it's one of the ways of being awfully out of it too. There are so many!'

'So many Americans?' I asked.

'Yes, plenty of *them*,' Mrs Munden sighed. 'So many ways, I mean, of being one.'

'But if your sister-in-law's way is to be beautiful—?'

'Oh, there are different ways of that too.'

'And she hasn't taken the right way?'

'Well,' my friend returned, as if it were rather difficult to express, 'she hasn't done with it—'

675

'I see,' I laughed; 'what she oughtn't!'

Mrs Munden in a manner corrected me, but it *was* difficult to express. 'My brother, at all events, was certainly selfish. Till he died she was almost never in London; they wintered, year after year, for what he supposed to be his health – which it didn't help, since he was so much too soon to meet his end – in the south of France and in the dullest holes he could pick out, and when they came back to England he always kept her in the country. I must say for her that she always behaved beautifully. Since his death she has been more in London, but on a stupidly unsuccessful footing. I don't think she quite understands. She hasn't what *I* should call a life. It may be, of course, that she doesn't want one. That's just what I can't exactly find out. I can't make out how much she knows.'

'I can easily make out,' I returned with hilarity, 'how much *you* do!'

'Well, you're very horrid. Perhaps she's too old.'

'Too old for what?' I persisted.

'For anything. Of course she's no longer even a little young; only preserved – oh, but preserved, like bottled fruit, in syrup! I want to help her, if only because she gets on my nerves, and I really think the way of it would be just the right thing of yours at the Academy and on the line.'

'But suppose,' I threw out, 'she should give on *my* nerves?'

'Oh, she will. But isn't that all in the day's work, and don't great beauties always—?'

'*You* don't,' I interrupted; but I at any rate saw Lady Beldonald later on – the day came when her kinswoman brought her, and then I understood that her life had its centre in her own idea of her appearance. Nothing else about her mattered – one knew her all when one knew that. She is indeed in one particular, I think, sole of her kind – a person whom vanity has had the odd effect of keeping positively safe and sound. This passion is supposed surely, for the most part, to be a principle of perversion and injury, leading astray those who listen to it and landing them, sooner or later, in this or that complication; but it has landed her ladyship nowhere whatever – it has kept her from the first moment of full consciousness, one feels, exactly in the same place. It has protected her from every danger, has made her absolutely proper and prim. If she is 'preserved', as Mrs Munden originally described her to me, it is her vanity that has beautifully done it – putting her years ago in a plate-glass case and closing up the receptacle against every breath of air. How shouldn't she be preserved, when you might smash your knuckles on this transparency before you could crack it? And she *is* – oh, amazingly! Preservation is scarce the word for the rare condition of her surface. She looks *naturally* new, as if she took out every night her large, lovely, varnished eyes and put them in water. The thing was to paint her, I perceived, *in* the glass case – a most tempting, attaching feat; render to the full the shining, interposing plate and the general show-window effect.

It was agreed, though it was not quite arranged, that she should sit to me. If it was not quite arranged, this was because, as I was made to understand from an early stage, the conditions for our start must be such as should exclude all elements of disturbance, such, in a word, as she herself should judge absolutely favourable. And it seemed that these conditions were easily imperilled. Suddenly, for instance, at a moment when I was expecting her to meet an appointment – the first – that I had proposed, I received a hurried visit from Mrs Munden, who came on her behalf to let me know that the season happened just not to be propitious and that our friend couldn't be quite sure, to the hour, when it would again become so. Nothing, she felt, would make it so but a total absence of worry.

'Oh, a "total absence",' I said, 'is a large order! We live in a worrying world.'

'Yes; and she feels exactly that – more than you'd think. It's in fact just why she mustn't have, as she has now, a particular distress on at the very moment. She wants to look, of course, her best, and such things tell on her appearance.'

I shook my head. 'Nothing tells on her appearance. Nothing reaches it in any way; nothing gets *at* it. However, I can understand her anxiety. But what's her particular distress?'

'Why, the illness of Miss Dadd.'

'And who in the world's Miss Dadd?'

'Her most intimate friend and constant companion – the lady who was with us here that first day.'

'Oh, the little round, black woman who gurgled with admiration?'

'None other. But she was taken ill last week, and it may very well be that she'll gurgle no more. She was very bad yesterday and is no better to-day, and Nina is much upset. If anything happens to Miss Dadd she'll have to get another, and, though she has had two or three before, that won't be so easy.'

'Two or three Miss Dadds? Is it possible? And still wanting another!' I recalled the poor lady completely now. 'No; I shouldn't indeed think it would be easy to get another. But why is a succession of them necessary to Lady Beldonald's existence?'

'Can't you guess?' Mrs Munden looked deep, yet impatient. 'They help.'

'Help what? Help whom?'

'Why, every one. You and me for instance. To do what? Why, to think Nina beautiful. She has them for that purpose; they serve as foils, as accents serve on syllables, as terms of comparison. They make her "stand out". It's an effect of contrast that must be familiar to you artists; it's what a woman does when she puts a band of black velvet under a pearl ornament that may require, as she thinks, a little showing off.'

I wondered. 'Do you mean she always has them black?'

'Dear no; I've seen them blue, green, yellow. They may be what they like, so long as they're always one other thing.'

'Hideous?'

Mrs Munden hesitated. 'Hideous is too much to say; she doesn't really require them as bad as that. But consistently, cheerfully, loyally plain. It's really a most happy relation. She loves them for it.'

'And for what do they love *her*?'

'Why, just for the amiability that they produce in her. Then, also, for their "home". It's a career for them.'

'I see. But if that's the case,' I asked, 'why are they so difficult to find?'

'Oh, they must be safe; it's all in that: her being able to depend on them to keep to the terms of the bargain and never have moments of rising – as even the ugliest woman will now and then (say when she's in love) – superior to themselves.'

I turned it over. 'Then if they can't inspire passions the poor things mayn't even at least feel them?'

'She distinctly deprecates it. That's why such a man as you may be, after all, a complication.'

I continued to muse. 'You're very sure Miss Dadd's ailment isn't an affection that, being smothered, has struck in?' My joke, however, was not well timed, for I afterwards learned that the unfortunate lady's state had been, even while I spoke, such as to forbid all hope. The worst symptoms had appeared; she was not destined to recover; and a week later I heard from Mrs Munden that she would in fact 'gurgle' no more.

II

ALL this, for Lady Beldonald, had been an agitation so great that access to her apartment was denied for a time even to her sister-in-law. It was much more out of the question, of course, that she should unveil her face to a person of my special business with it; so that the question of the portrait was, by common consent, postponed to that of the installation of a successor to her late companion. Such a successor, I gathered from Mrs Munden, widowed, childless, and lonely, as well as inapt for the minor offices, she had absolutely to have; a more or less humble *alter ego* to deal with the servants, keep the accounts, make the tea and arrange the light. Nothing seemed more natural than that she should marry again, and obviously that might come; yet the predecessors of Miss Dadd had been contemporaneous with a first husband, and others formed in her image might be contemporaneous with a second. I was much occupied in those months, at any rate, so that these questions and their ramifications lost themselves for a while to my view, and I was only brought back to them by Mrs Munden's coming to me one day with the news that we were all right again – her sister-in-law was once more 'suited'. A

certain Mrs Brash, an American relative whom she had not
seen for years, but with whom she had continued to communicate, was to come out to her immediately; and this person,
it appeared, could be quite trusted to meet the conditions. She
was ugly – ugly enough, without abuse of it, and she was
unlimitedly good. The position offered her by Lady Beldonald
was, moreover, exactly what she needed; widowed also, after
many troubles and reverses, with her fortune of the smallest
and her various children either buried or placed about, she had
never had time or means to come to England, and would really
be grateful in her declining years for the new experience and the
pleasant light work involved in her cousin's hospitality. They
had been much together early in life, and Lady Beldonald was
immensely fond of her – would have in fact tried to get hold of
her before had not Mrs Brash been always in bondage to family
duties, to the variety of her tribulations. I daresay I laughed at
my friend's use of the term 'position' – the position, one might
call it, of a candle-stick or a sign-post, and I daresay I must have
asked if the special service the poor lady was to render had been
made clear to her. Mrs Munden left me, at all events, with the
rather droll image of her faring forth, across the sea, quite
consciously and resignedly to perform it.

The point of the communication had, however, been that
my sitter was again looking up and would doubtless, on the
arrival and due initiation of Mrs Brash, be in form really to wait
on me. The situation must, further, to my knowledge, have
developed happily, for I arranged with Mrs Munden that our
friend, now all ready to begin, but wanting first just to see the
things I had most recently done, should come once more, as a
final preliminary, to my studio. A good foreign friend of mine, a
French painter, Paul Outreau, was at the moment in London,
and I had proposed, as he was much interested in types, to get
together for his amusement a small afternoon party. Everyone
came, my big room was full, there was music and a modest
spread; and I have not forgotten the light of admiration in
Outreau's expressive face as, at the end of half an hour, he
came up to me in his enthusiasm.

'*Bonté divine, mon cher – que cette vieille est donc belle!*'

I had tried to collect all the beauty I could, and also all the youth, so that for a moment I was at a loss. I had talked to many people and provided for the music, and there were figures in the crowd that were still lost to me. 'What old woman do you mean?'

'I don't know her name – she was over by the door a moment ago. I asked somebody and was told, I think, that she's American.'

I looked about and saw one of my guests attach a pair of fine eyes to Outreau very much as if she knew he must be talking of her. 'Oh, Lady Beldonald! Yes, she's handsome; but the great point about her is that she has been "put up", to keep, and that she wouldn't be flattered if she knew you spoke of her as old. A box of sardines is only "old" after it has been opened. Lady Beldonald never has yet been – but I'm going to do it.' I joked, but I was somehow disappointed. It was a type that, with his unerring sense for the *banal*, I shouldn't have expected Outreau to pick out.

'You're going to paint her? But, my dear man, she *is* painted – and as neither you nor I can do it. *Où est-elle donc?*' He had lost her, and I saw I had made a mistake. 'She's the greatest of all the great Holbeins.'

I was relieved. 'Ah, then, not Lady Beldonald! But do I possess a Holbein, of *any* price, unawares?'

'There she is – there she is! Dear, dear, dear, what a head!' And I saw whom he meant – and what: a small old lady in a black dress and a black bonnet, both relieved with a little white, who had evidently just changed her place to reach a corner from which more of the room and of the scene was presented to her. She appeared unnoticed and unknown, and I immediately recognised that some other guest must have brought her and, for want of opportunity, had as yet to call my attention to her. But two things, simultaneously with this and with each other, struck me with force; one of them the truth of Outreau's description of her, the other the fact that the person bringing her could only have been Lady Beldonald. She *was* a Holbein – of the first water; yet she was also Mrs Brash, the imported 'foil', the indispensable 'accent', the successor to the dreary

Miss Dadd! By the time I had put these things together – Outreau's 'American' having helped me – I was in just such full
possession of her face as I had found myself, on the other first
occasion, of that of her patroness. Only with so different a
consequence. I couldn't look at her enough, and I started and
stared till I became aware she might have fancied me challenging her as a person unpresented. 'All the same,' Outreau went
on, equally held, '*c'est une tête à faire*. If I were only staying long
enough for a crack at her! But I tell you what' – and he seized
my arm – 'bring her over!'

'Over?'

'To Paris. She'd have a *succès fou*.'

'Ah, thanks, my dear fellow,' I was now quite in a position to
say; 'she's the handsomest thing in London, and' – for what
I might do with her was already before me with intensity – 'I
propose to keep her to myself.' It was before me with intensity,
in the light of Mrs Brash's distant perfection of a little white old
face, in which every wrinkle was the touch of a master; but
something else, I suddenly felt, was not less so, for Lady Beldonald, in the other quarter, and though she couldn't have
made out the subject of our notice, continued to fix us, and
her eyes had the challenge of those of the woman of consequence who has missed something. A moment later I was
close to her, apologising first for not having been more on the
spot at her arrival, but saying in the next breath uncontrollably,
'Why, my dear lady, it's a Holbein!'

'A Holbein? What?'

'Why, the wonderful sharp old face – so extraordinarily,
consummately drawn – in the frame of black velvet. That of
Mrs Brash, I mean – isn't it her name? – your companion.'

This was the beginning of a most odd matter – the essence of
my anecdote; and I think the very first note of the oddity must
have sounded for me in the tone in which her ladyship spoke
after giving me a silent look. It seemed to come to me out of a
distance immeasurably removed from Holbein. 'Mrs Brash is
not my "companion" in the sense you appear to mean. She's
my rather near relation and a very dear old friend. I *love* her –
and you must know her.'

'Know her? Rather! Why, to see her is to want, on the spot, to "go" for her. She also must sit for me.'

'*She?* Louisa Brash?' If Lady Beldonald had the theory that her beauty directly showed it when things were not well with her, this impression, which the fixed sweetness of her serenity had hitherto struck me by no means as justifying, gave me now my first glimpse of its grounds. It was as if I had never before seen her face invaded by anything I should have called an expression. This expression, moreover, was of the faintest – was like the effect produced on a surface by an agitation both deep within and as yet much confused. 'Have you told her so?' she then quickly asked, as if to soften the sound of her surprise.

'Dear no, I've but just noticed her – Outreau a moment ago put me on her. But we're both so taken, and he also wants—'

'To *paint* her?' Lady Beldonald uncontrollably murmured.

'Don't be afraid we shall fight for her,' I returned with a laugh for this tone. Mrs Brash was still where I could see her without appearing to stare, and she mightn't have seen I was looking at her, though her protectress, I am afraid, could scarce have failed of this perception. 'We must each take our turn, and at any rate she's a wonderful thing, so that, if you'll take her to Paris, Outreau promises her there—'

'*There?*' my companion gasped.

'A career bigger still than among *us*, as he considers that we haven't half their eye. He guarantees her a *succès fou*.'

She couldn't get over it. 'Louisa Brash? In Paris?'

'They do see,' I exclaimed, 'more than we; and they live extraordinarily, don't you know, *in* that. But she'll do something here too.'

'And what will she do?'

If, frankly, now, I couldn't help giving Mrs Brash a longer look, so after it I could as little resist sounding my interlocutress. 'You'll see. Only give her time.'

She said nothing during the moment in which she met my eyes; but then: 'Time, it seems to me, is exactly what you and your friend want. If you haven't talked with her—'

'We haven't seen her? Oh, we see bang off – with a click like a
steel spring. It's our trade; it's our life; and we should be
donkeys if we made mistakes. That's the way I saw you
yourself, my lady, if I may say so; that's the way, with a long
pin straight through your body, I've got you. And just so I've
got *her*.'

All this, for reasons, had brought my guest to her feet; but
her eyes, while we talked, had never once followed the direction
of mine. 'You call her a Holbein?'

'Outreau did, and I of course immediately recognised it.
Don't *you*? She brings the old boy to life! It's just as I should
call you a Titian. You bring *him* to life.'

She couldn't be said to relax, because she couldn't be said to
have hardened; but something at any rate on this took place in
her – something indeed quite disconnected from what I would
have called her. 'Don't you understand that she has always
been supposed—?' It had the ring of impatience; nevertheless,
on a scruple, it stopped short.

I knew what it was, however, well enough to say it for her if
she preferred. 'To be nothing whatever to look at? To be
unfortunately plain – or even if you like repulsively ugly? Oh
yes, I understand it perfectly, just as I understand – I have to as
a part of my trade – many other forms of stupidity. It's nothing
new to one that ninety-nine people out of a hundred have no
eyes, no sense, no taste. There are whole communities
impenetrably sealed. I don't say your friend is a person to
make the men turn round in Regent Street. But it adds to the
joy of the few who do see that they have it so much to themselves. Where in the world can she have lived? You must tell me
all about that – or rather, if she'll be so good, *she* must.'

'You mean then to speak to her—?'

I wondered as she pulled up again. 'Of her beauty?'

'Her beauty!' cried Lady Beldonald so loud that two or three
persons looked round.

'Ah, with every precaution of respect!' I declared in a much
lower tone. But her back was by this time turned to me, and in
the movement, as it were, one of the strangest little dramas
I have ever known was well launched.

III

IT was a drama of small, smothered intensely private things, and I knew of but one other person in the secret; yet that person and I found it exquisitely susceptible of notation, followed it with an interest the mutual communication of which did much for our enjoyment, and were present with emotion at its touching catastrophe. The small case – for so small a case – had made a great stride even before my little party separated, and in fact within the next ten minutes.

In that space of time two things had happened; one of which was that I made the acquaintance of Mrs Brash, and the other that Mrs Munden reached me, cleaving the crowd, with one of her usual pieces of news. What she had to impart was that, on her having just before asked Nina if the conditions of our sitting had been arranged with me, Nina had replied, with something like perversity, that she didn't propose to arrange them, that the whole affair was 'off' again, and that she preferred not to be, for the present, further pressed. The question for Mrs Munden was naturally what had happened and whether I understood. Oh, I understood perfectly, and what I at first most understood was that even when I had brought in the name of Mrs Brash intelligence was not yet in Mrs Munden. She was quite as surprised as Lady Beldonald had been on hearing of the esteem in which I held Mrs Brash's appearance. She was stupefied at learning that I had just in my ardour proposed to the possessor of it to sit to me. Only she came round promptly – which Lady Beldonald really never did. Mrs Munden was in fact wonderful; for when I had given her quickly 'Why, she's a Holbein, you know,' she took it up, after a first fine vacancy, with an immediate abysmal 'Oh, *is* she?' that, as a piece of social gymnastics, did her the greatest honour; and she was in fact the first in London to spread the tidings. For a face-about it was magnificent. But she was also the first, I must add, to see what would really happen – though this she put before me only a week or two later.

'It will kill her, my dear – that's what it will do!'

She meant neither more nor less than that it would kill Lady Beldonald if I were to paint Mrs Brash; for at this lurid light had we arrived in so short a space of time. It was for me to decide whether my aesthetic need of giving life to my idea was such as to justify me in destroying it in a woman after all, in most eyes, so beautiful. The situation was, after all, sufficiently queer; for it remained to be seen what I should positively gain by giving up Mrs Brash. I appeared to have in any case lost Lady Beldonald, now too 'upset' – it was always Mrs Munden's word about her and, as I inferred, her own about herself – to meet me again on our previous footing. The only thing, I of course soon saw, was to temporise – to drop the whole question for the present and yet so far as possible keep each of the pair in view. I may as well say at once that this plan and this process gave their principal interest to the next several months. Mrs Brash had turned up, if I remember, early in the new year, and her little wonderful career was in our particular circle one of the features of the following season. It was at all events for myself the most attaching; it is not my fault if I am so put together as often to find more life in situations obscure and subject to interpretation than in the gross rattle of the foreground. And there were all sorts of things, things touching, amusing, mystifying – and above all such an instance as I had never yet met – in this funny little fortune of the useful American cousin. Mrs Munden was promptly at one with me as to the rarity and, to a near and human view, the beauty and interest of the position. We had neither of us ever before seen that degree and that special sort of personal success come to a woman for the first time so late in life. I found it an example of poetic, of absolutely retributive, justice; so that my desire grew great to work it, as we say, on those lines. I had seen it all from the original moment at my studio; the poor lady had never known an hour's appreciation – which, moreover, in perfect good faith, she had never missed. The very first thing I did after producing so unintentionally the resentful retreat of her protectress had been to go straight over to her and say almost without preliminaries that I should hold myself immeasurably obliged if she would give me a few sittings. What I thus came face to face with was, on the instant, her whole unenlightened past, and the full, if foreshortened, revelation of what among us all was now unfailingly in store for her. To turn the handle and start that tune came to me on the spot as a temptation. Here was a poor lady who had waited for the approach of old age to find out what she was worth. Here was a benighted being to whom it was to be disclosed in her fifty-seventh year (I was to make that out) that she had something that might pass for a face. She looked much more than her age, and was fairly frightened – as if I had been trying on her some possibly heartless London trick – when she had taken in my appeal. That showed me in what an air she had lived and – as I should have been tempted to put it had I spoken out – among what children of darkness. Later on I did them more justice; saw more that her wonderful points must have been points largely the fruit of time, and even that possibly she might never in all her life have looked so well as at this particular moment. It might have been that if her hour had struck I just happened to be present at the striking. What had occurred, all the same, was at the worst a sufficient comedy.

The famous 'irony of fate' takes many forms, but I had never yet seen it take quite this one. She had been 'had over' on an understanding, and she was not playing fair. She had broken the law of her ugliness and had turned beautiful on the hands of her employer. More interesting even perhaps than a view of the conscious triumph that this might prepare for her, and of which, had I doubted of my own judgement, I could still take Outreau's fine start as the full guarantee – more interesting was the question of the process by which such a history could get itself enacted. The curious thing was that, all the while, the reasons of her having passed for plain – the reasons for Lady Beldonald's fond calculation, which they quite justified – were written large in her face, so large that it was easy to understand them as the only ones she herself had ever read. What was it, then, that actually made the old stale sentence mean something so different? – into what new combinations, what extraordinary language, unknown but understood at a glance, had time and life translated it? The only thing to be said was that time and life

were artists who beat us all, working with recipes and secrets
that we could never find out. I really ought to have, like a
lecturer or a showman, a chart or a blackboard to present
properly the relation, in the wonderful old tender, battered,
blanched face, between the original elements and the
exquisite final 'style'. I could do it with chalks, but I can
scarcely do it thus. However, the thing was, for any artist who
respected himself, to *feel* it – which I abundantly did; and
then not to conceal from *her* that I felt it – which I neglected
as little. But she was really, to do her complete justice, the last
to understand; and I am not sure that, to the end – for there was
an end – she quite made it all out or knew where she was.
When you have been brought up for fifty years on black, it
must be hard to adjust your organism, at a day's notice, to
gold-colour. Her whole nature had been pitched in the key of
her supposed plainness. She had known how to be ugly – it was
the only thing she had learnt save, if possible, how not to mind
it. Being beautiful, at any rate, took a new set of muscles. It was
on the prior theory, literally, that she had developed her admirable dress, instinctively felicitous, always either black or white,
and a matter of rather severe squareness and studied line. She
was magnificently neat; everything she showed had a way of
looking both old and fresh; and there was on every occasion the
same picture in her draped head – draped in low-falling black –
and the fine white plaits (of a painter's white, somehow)
disposed on her chest. What had happened was that these
arrangements, determined by certain considerations, lent
themselves in effect much better to certain others. Adopted as
a kind of refuge, they had really only deepened her accent. It
was singular, moreover, that, so constituted, there was
nothing in her aspect of the ascetic or the nun. She was a
good, hard, sixteenth-century figure, not withered with
innocence, bleached rather by life in the open. She was, in
short, just what we had made of her, a Holbein for a great
museum; and our position, Mrs Munden's and mine, rapidly
became that of persons having such a treasure to dispose of.
The world – I speak of course mainly of the art-world – flocked
to see it.

IV

'BUT has she any idea herself, poor thing?' was the way I had put it to Mrs Munden on our next meeting after the incident at my studio; with the effect, however, only of leaving my friend at first to take me as alluding to Mrs Brash's possible prevision of the chatter she might create. I had my own sense of that – this prevision had been *nil*; the question was of her consciousness of the office for which Lady Beldonald had counted on her and for which we were so promptly proceeding to spoil her altogether.

'Oh, I think she arrived with a goodish notion,' Mrs Munden had replied when I had explained; 'for she's clever too, you know, as well as good-looking, and I don't see how, if she ever really *knew* Nina, she could have supposed for a moment that she was not wanted for whatever she might have left to give up. Hasn't she moreover always been made to feel that she's ugly enough for anything?' It was even at this point already wonderful how my friend had mastered the case, and what lights, alike for its past and its future, she was prepared to throw on it. 'If she has seen herself as ugly enough for anything, she has seen herself – and that was the only way – as ugly enough for Nina; and she has had her own manner of showing that she understands without making Nina commit herself to anything vulgar. Women are never without ways for doing such things – both for communicating and receiving knowledge – that I can't explain to you, and that you wouldn't understand if I could, as you must *be* a woman even to do that. I daresay they've expressed it all to each other simply in the language of kisses. But doesn't it, at any rate, make something rather beautiful of the relation between them as affected by our discovery?'

I had a laugh for her plural possessive. 'The point is, of course, that if there was a conscious bargain, and our action on Mrs Brash is to deprive her of the sense of keeping her side of it, various things may happen that won't be good either for her or for ourselves. She may conscientiously throw up the position.'

'Yes,' my companion mused – 'for she *is* conscientious. Or Nina, without waiting for that, may cast her forth.'

I faced it all. 'Then *we* should have to keep her.'

'As a regular model?' Mrs Munden was ready for anything. 'Oh, that would be lovely!'

But I further worked it out. 'The difficulty is that she's *not* a model, hang it – that she's too good for one, that she's the very thing herself. When Outreau and I have each had our go, that will be all; there'll be nothing left for anyone else. Therefore it behoves us quite to understand that our attitude's a responsibility. If we can't do for her positively more than Nina does—'

'We must let her alone?' My companion continued to muse. 'I see!'

'Yet don't,' I returned, 'see too much. We *can* do more.'

'Than Nina?' She was again on the spot. 'It wouldn't, after all, be difficult. We only want the directly opposite thing – and which is the only one the poor dear can give. Unless, indeed,' she suggested, 'we simply retract – we back out.'

I turned it over. 'It's too late for that. Whether Mrs Brash's peace is gone, I can't say. But Nina's is.'

'Yes, and there's no way to bring it back that won't sacrifice her friend. We can't turn round and say Mrs Brash *is* ugly, can we? But fancy Nina's not having *seen*!' Mrs Munden exclaimed.

'She doesn't see now,' I answered. 'She can't, I'm certain, make out what we mean. The woman, for *her* still, is just what she always was. But she has, nevertheless, had her stroke, and her blindness, while she wavers and gropes in the dark, only adds to her discomfort. Her blow was to see the attention of the world deviate.'

'All the same, I don't think, you know,' my interlocutress said, 'that Nina will have made her a scene, or that, whatever we do, she'll ever make her one. That isn't the way it will happen, for she's exactly as conscientious as Mrs Brash.'

'Then what *is* the way?' I asked.

'It will just happen in silence.'

'And what will "it", as you call it, be?'

'Isn't that what we want really to see?'

'Well,' I replied after a turn or two about, 'whether we want it or not, it's exactly what we *shall* see; which is a reason the more for fancying, between the pair there – in the quiet,

exquisite house, and full of superiorities and suppressions as
they both are – the extraordinary situation. If I said just now
that it's too late to do anything but accept, it's because I've
taken the full measure of what happened at my studio. It took
but a few moments – but she tasted of the tree.'

My companion wondered. 'Nina?'

'Mrs Brash.' And to have to put it so ministered, while I took
yet another turn, to a sort of agitation. Our attitude *was* a
responsibility.

But I had suggested something else to my friend, who
appeared for a moment detached. 'Should you say she'll hate
her worse if she *doesn't* see?'

'Lady Beldonald? Doesn't see what *we* see, you mean, than if
she does? Ah, I give *that* up!' I laughed. 'But what I can tell you
is why I hold that, as I said just now, we can do most. We can do
this: we can give to a harmless and sensitive creature hitherto
practically disinherited – and give with an unexpectedness that
will immensely add to its price – the pure joy of a deep draught
of the very pride of life, of an acclaimed personal triumph in our
superior, sophisticated world.'

Mrs Munden had a glow of response for my sudden eloquence. 'Oh, it will be beautiful!'

V

WELL, that is what, on the whole, and in spite of everything, it
really was. It has dropped into my memory a rich little gallery of
pictures, a regular panorama of those occasions that were the
proof of the privilege that had made me for a moment – in the
words I have just recorded – lyrical. I see Mrs Brash on each of
these occasions practically enthroned and surrounded and
more or less mobbed; see the hurrying and the nudging
and the pressing and the staring; see the people 'making up'
and introduced, and catch the word when they have had their
turn; hear it above all, the great one – 'Ah yes, the famous
Holbein!' – passed about with that perfection of promptitude
that makes the motions of the London mind so happy a mixture
of those of the parrot and the sheep. Nothing would be easier,

of course, than to tell the whole little tale with an eye only for
that silly side of it. Great was the silliness, but great also as to
this case of poor Mrs Brash, I will say for it, the good nature. Of
course, furthermore, it took in particular 'our set', with its
positive child-terror of the *banal*, to be either so foolish or so
wise; though indeed I've never quite known where our set
begins and ends, and have had to content myself on this score
with the indication once given me by a lady next whom I was
placed at dinner: 'Oh, it's bounded on the north by Ibsen and
on the south by Sargent!' Mrs Brash never sat to me; she
absolutely declined; and when she declared that it was quite
enough for her that I had with that fine precipitation invited
her, I quite took this as she meant it, for before we had gone very
far our understanding, hers and mine, was complete. Her
attitude was as happy as her success was prodigious. The
sacrifice of the portrait was a sacrifice to the true inwardness
of Lady Beldonald, and did much, for the time, I divined,
toward muffling their domestic tension. All that was thus in
her power to say – and I heard of a few cases of her having said it
– was that she was sure I would have painted her beautifully if
she hadn't prevented me. She couldn't even tell the truth,
which was that I certainly would have done so if Lady Beldonald hadn't; and she never could mention the subject at all
before that personage. I can only describe the affair, naturally,
from the outside, and heaven forbid indeed that I should try too
closely to reconstruct the possible strange intercourse of these
good friends at home.

My anecdote, however, would lose half such point as it may
possess were I to omit all mention of the charming turn that her
ladyship appeared gradually to have found herself able to give
to her deportment. She had made it impossible I should myself
bring up our old, our original question, but there was real
distinction in her manner of now accepting certain other possibilities. Let me do her that justice; her effort at magnanimity
must have been immense. There couldn't fail, of course, to be
ways in which poor Mrs Brash paid for it. How much she had to
pay we were, in fact, soon enough to see; and it is my intimate
conviction that, as a climax, her life at last was the price. But

while she lived, at least – and it was with an intensity, for those wondrous weeks, of which she had never dreamed – Lady Beldonald herself faced the music. This is what I mean by the possibilities, by the sharp actualities indeed, that she accepted. She took our friend out, she showed her at home, never attempted to hide or to betray her, played her no trick whatever so long as the ordeal lasted. She drank deep, on *her* side too, of the cup – the cup that for her own lips could only be bitterness. There was, I think, scarce a special success of her companion's at which she was not personally present. Mrs Munden's theory of the silence in which all this would be muffled for them was, none the less, and in abundance, confirmed by our observations. The whole thing was to be the death of one or the other of them, but they never spoke of it at tea. I remember even that Nina went so far as to say to me once, looking me full in the eyes, quite sublimely, 'I've made out what you mean – she *is* a picture.' The beauty of this, moreover, was that, as I am persuaded, she hadn't really made it out at all – the words were the mere hypocrisy of her reflective endeavour for virtue. She couldn't possibly have made it out; her friend was as much as ever 'dreadfully plain' to her; she must have wondered to the last what on earth possessed us. Wouldn't it in fact have been, after all, just this failure of vision, this supreme stupidity in short, that kept the catastrophe so long at bay? There was a certain sense of greatness for her in seeing so many of us so absurdly mistaken; and I recall that on various occasions, and in particular when she uttered the words just quoted, this high serenity, as a sign of the relief of her soreness, if not of the effort of her conscience, did something quite visible to my eyes, and also quite unprecedented, for the beauty of her face. She got a real lift from it – such a momentary discernible sublimity that I recollect coming out on the spot with a queer, crude, amused 'Do you know I believe I could paint you *now*?'

She was a fool not to have closed with me then and there; for what has happened since has altered everything – what was to happen a little later was so much more than I could swallow. This was the disappearance of the famous Holbein from one day to the other – producing a consternation among us all as great as if the Venus of Milo had suddenly vanished from the Louvre. 'She has simply shipped her straight back' – the explanation was given in that form by Mrs Munden, who added that any cord pulled tight enough would end at last by snapping. At the snap, in any case, we mightily jumped, for the masterpiece we had for three or four months been living with had made us feel its presence as a luminous lesson and a daily need. We recognised more than ever that it had been, for high finish, the gem of our collection – we found what a blank it left on the wall. Lady Beldonald might fill up the blank, but *we* couldn't. That she did soon fill it up – and, heaven help us, *how*? – was put before me after an interval of no great length, but during which I had not seen her. I dined on the Christmas of last year at Mrs Munden's, and Nina, with a 'scratch lot', as our hostess said, was there, and, the preliminary wait being longish, approached me very sweetly. 'I'll come to you to-morrow if you like,' she said; and the effect of it, after a first stare at her, was to make me look all round. I took in, in these two motions, two things; one of which was that, though now again so satisfied herself of her high state, she could give me nothing comparable to what I should have got had she taken me up at the moment of my meeting her on her distinguished concession; the other that she was 'suited' afresh, and that Mrs Brash's successor was fully installed. Mrs Brash's successor was at the other side of the room, and I became conscious that Mrs Munden was waiting to see my eyes seek her. I guessed the meaning of the wait; what *was* one, this time, to say? Oh, first and foremost, assuredly, that it was immensely droll, for this time, at least, there was no mistake. The lady I looked upon, and as to whom my friend, again quite at sea, appealed to me for a formula, was as little a Holbein, or a specimen of any other school, as she was, like Lady Beldonald herself, a Titian. The formula was easy to give, for the amusement was that her prettiness – yes, literally, prodigiously, her prettiness – was distinct. Lady Beldonald had been magnificent – had been almost intelligent. Miss What's-her-name continues pretty, continues even young, and doesn't matter a straw! She matters so ideally little that Lady Beldonald is practically safer, I judge, than she has ever been. There has not been a symptom of chatter about this person, and I believe her protectress is much surprised that we are not more struck.

It was, at any rate, strictly impossible to me to make an appointment for the day as to which I have just recorded Nina's proposal; and the turn of events since then has not quickened my eagerness. Mrs Munden remained in correspondence with Mrs Brash – to the extent, that is, of three letters, each of which she showed me. They so told, to our imagination, her terrible little story that we were quite prepared – or thought we were – for her going out like a snuffed candle. She resisted, on her return to her original conditions, less than a year; the taste of the tree, as I had called it, had been fatal to her; what she had contentedly enough lived without before for half a century she couldn't now live without for a day. I know nothing of her original conditions – some minor American city – save that for her to have gone back to them was clearly to have stepped out of her frame. We performed, Mrs Munden and I, a small funeral service for her by talking it all over and making it all out. It wasn't – the minor American city – a market for Holbeins, and what had occurred was that the poor old picture, banished from its museum and refreshed by the rise of no new movement to hang it, was capable of the miracle of a silent revolution, of itself turning, in its dire dishonour, its face to the wall. So it stood, without the intervention of the ghost of a critic, till they happened to pull it round again and find it mere dead paint. Well, it had had, if that is anything, its season of fame, its name on a thousand tongues and printed in capitals in the catalogue. *We* had not been at fault. I haven't, all the same, the least note of her – not a scratch. And I did her so in intention! Mrs Munden continues to remind me, however, that this is not the sort of rendering with which, on the other side, after all, Lady Beldonald proposes to content herself. She has come back to the question of her own portrait. Let me settle it then at last. Since she *will* have the real thing – well, hang it, she shall!

THE STORY IN IT

I

THE weather had turned so much worse that the rest of the day was certainly lost. The wind had risen and the storm gathered force; they gave from time to time a thump at the firm windows and dashed even against those protected by the verandah their vicious splotches of rain. Beyond the lawn, beyond the cliff, the great wet brush of the sky dipped deep into the sea. But the lawn, already vivid with the touch of May, showed a violence of watered green; the budding shrubs and trees repeated the note as they tossed their thick masses, and the cold, troubled light, filling the pretty drawing-room, marked the spring afternoon as sufficiently young. The two ladies seated there in silence could pursue without difficulty – as well as, clearly, without interruption – their respective tasks; a confidence expressed, when the noise of the wind allowed it to be heard, by the sharp scratch of Mrs Dyott's pen at the table where she was busy with letters.

Her visitor, settled on a small sofa that, with a palm-tree, a screen, a stool, a stand, a bowl of flowers and three photographs in silver frames, had been arranged near the light wood-fire as a choice 'corner' – Maud Blessingbourne, her guest, turned audibly, though at intervals neither brief nor regular, the leaves of a book covered in lemon-coloured paper and not yet despoiled of a certain fresh crispness. This effect of the volume, for the eye, would have made it, as presumably the newest French novel – and evidently, from the attitude of the reader, 'good' – consort happily with the special tone of the room, a consistent air of selection and suppression, one of the finer aesthetic evolutions. If Mrs Dyott was fond of ancient French furniture, and distinctly difficult about it, her inmates could be fond – with whatever critical cocks of charming dark-braided heads over slender sloping shoulders – of modern French authors. Nothing had passed for half an hour – nothing, at least, to be exact, but that each of the companions occasionally and covertly intermitted her pursuit in such a manner as to ascertain the degree of absorption of the other without turning round. What their silence was charged with, therefore, was not only a sense of the weather, but a sense, so to speak, of its own nature. Maud Blessingbourne, when she lowered her book into her lap, closed her eyes with a conscious patience that seemed to say she waited; but it was nevertheless she who at last made the movement representing a snap of their tension. She got up and stood by the fire, into which she looked a minute; then came round and approached the window as if to see what was really going on. At this Mrs Dyott wrote with refreshed intensity. Her little pile of letters had grown, and if a look of determination was compatible with her fair and slightly faded beauty, the habit of attending to her business could always keep pace with any excursion of her thought. Yet she was the first who spoke.

'I trust your book has been interesting.'

'Well enough; a little mild.'

A louder throb of the tempest had blurred the sound of the words. 'A little wild?'

'Dear, no – timid and tame; unless I've quite lost my sense.'

'Perhaps you have,' Mrs Dyott placidly suggested – 'reading so many.'

Her companion made a motion of feigned despair. 'Ah, you take away my courage for going to my room, as I was just meaning to, for another.'

'Another French one?'

'I'm afraid.'

'Do you carry them by the dozen—'

'Into innocent British homes?' Maud tried to remember. 'I believe I brought three – seeing them in a shop window as I passed through town. It never rains but it pours! But I've already read two.'

'And are they the only ones you do read?'

'French ones?' Maud considered. 'Oh, no. D'Annunzio.'

'And what's that?' Mrs Dyott asked as she affixed a stamp.

'Oh, you dear thing!' Her friend was amused, yet almost showed pity. 'I know you don't read,' Maud went on; 'but why should you? *You* live!'

'Yes – wretchedly enough,' Mrs Dyott returned, getting her letters together. She left her place, holding them as a neat, achieved handful, and came over to the fire, while Mrs Blessingbourne turned once more to the window, where she was met by another flurry.

Maud spoke then as if moved only by the elements. 'Do you expect him through all this?'

Mrs Dyott just waited, and it had the effect, indescribably, of making everything that had gone before seem to have led up to the question. This effect was even deepened by the way she then said, 'Whom do you mean?'

'Why, I thought you mentioned at luncheon that Colonel Voyt was to walk over. Surely he can't.'

'Do you care very much?' Mrs Dyott asked.

Her friend now hesitated. 'It depends on what you call "much". If you mean should I like to see him – then certainly.'

'Well, my dear, I think he understands you're here.'

'So that as he evidently isn't coming,' Maud laughed, 'it's particularly flattering! Or rather,' she added, giving up the prospect again, 'it would be, I think, quite extraordinarily flattering if he did. Except that, of course,' she subjoined, 'he might come partly for you.'

' "Partly" is charming. Thank you for "partly". If you *are* going upstairs, will you kindly,' Mrs Dyott pursued, 'put these into the box as you pass?'

The younger woman, taking the little pile of letters, considered them with envy. 'Nine! You *are* good. You're always a living reproach!'

Mrs Dyott gave a sigh. 'I don't do it on purpose. The only thing, this afternoon,' she went on, reverting to the other question, 'would be their not having come down.'

'And as to that you don't know.'

'No – I don't know.' But she caught even as she spoke a rat-tat-tat of the knocker, which struck her as a sign. 'Ah, there!'

'Then I go.' And Maud whisked out.

Mrs Dyott, left alone, moved with an air of selection to the window, and it was as so stationed, gazing out at the wild weather, that the visitor, whose delay to appear spoke of the wiping of boots and the disposal of drenched mackintosh and cap, finally found her. He was tall, lean, fine, with little in him, on the whole, to confirm the titular in the 'Colonel Voyt' by which he was announced. But he had left the army, and his reputation for gallantry mainly depended now on his fighting Liberalism in the House of Commons. Even these facts, however, his aspect scantly matched; partly, no doubt, because he looked, as was usually said, un-English. His black hair, cropped close, was lightly powdered with silver, and his dense glossy beard, that of an emir or a caliph, and grown for civil reasons, repeated its handsome colour and its somewhat foreign effect. His nose had a strong and shapely arch, and the dark grey of his eyes was tinted with blue. It had been said of him – in relation to these signs – that he would have struck you as a Jew had he not, in spite of his nose, struck you so much as an Irishman. Neither responsibility could in fact have been fixed upon him, and just now, at all events, he was only a pleasant, weather-washed, wind-battered Briton, who brought in from a struggle with the elements that he appeared quite to have enjoyed a certain amount of unremoved mud and an unusual quantity of easy expression. It was exactly the silence ensuing on the retreat of the servant and the closed door that marked between him and his hostess the degree of this ease. They met, as it were, twice: the first time while the servant was there and the second as soon as he was not. The difference was great between the two encounters, though we must add in justice to the second that its marks were at first mainly negative. This communion consisted only in their having drawn each other for a minute as close as possible – as possible, that is, with no help but the full clasp of hands. Thus they were mutually held, and the closeness was at any rate such that, for a little, though it took account of dangers, it did without words. When words presently came the pair were talking by the fire, and she had rung for tea. He had by this time asked if the note he had despatched to her after breakfast had been safely delivered.

'Yes, before luncheon. But I'm always in a state when – except for some extraordinary reason – you send such things by hand. I knew, without it, that you had come. It never fails. I'm sure when you're there – I'm sure when you're not.'

He wiped, before the glass, his wet moustache. 'I see. But this morning I had an impulse.'

'It was beautiful. But they make me as uneasy, sometimes, your impulses, as if they were calculations; make me wonder what you have in reserve.'

'Because when small children are too awfully good they die? Well, I *am* a small child compared to you – but I'm not dead yet. I cling to life.'

He had covered her with his smile, but she continued grave. 'I'm not half so much afraid when you're nasty.'

'Thank you! What then did you do,' he asked, 'with my note?'

'You deserve that I should have spread it out on my dressing-table – or left it, better still, in Maud Blessingbourne's room.'

He wondered while he laughed. 'Oh, but what does *she* deserve?'

It was her gravity that continued to answer. 'Yes – it would probably kill her.'

'She believes so in you?'

'She believes so in *you*. So don't be *too* nice to her.'

He was still looking, in the chimney-glass, at the state of his beard – brushing from it, with his handkerchief, the traces of wind and wet. 'If she also then prefers me when I'm nasty, it seems to me I ought to satisfy her. Shall I now, at any rate, see her?'

'She's so like a pea on a pan over the possibility of it that she's pulling herself together in her room.'

'Oh then, we must try and keep her together. But why, graceful, tender, pretty too – quite, or almost – as she is, doesn't she remarry?'

Mrs Dyott appeared – and as if the first time – to look for the reason. 'Because she likes too many men.'

It kept up his spirits. 'And how many *may* a lady like—?'

'In order not to like any of them too much? Ah, that, you know, I never found out – and it's too late now. When,' she presently pursued, 'did you last see her?'

He really had to think. 'Would it have been since last November or so? – somewhere or other where we spent three days.'

'Oh, at Surredge? I know all about that. I thought you also met afterwards.'

He had again to recall. 'So we did! Wouldn't it have been somewhere at Christmas? But it wasn't by arrangement!' he laughed, giving with his forefinger a little pleasant nick to his hostess's chin. Then as if something in the way she received this attention put him back to his question of a moment before, 'Have you kept my note?'

She held him with her pretty eyes. 'Do you want it back?'

'Ah, don't speak as if I did take things—!'

She dropped her gaze to the fire. 'No, you don't; not even the hard things a really generous nature often would.' She quitted, however, as if to forget that, the chimney-place. 'I put it *there*!'

'You've burnt it? Good!' It made him easier, but he noticed the next moment on a table the lemon-coloured volume left there by Mrs Blessingbourne, and, taking it up for a look, immediately put it down. 'You might, while you were about it, have burnt that too.'

'You've read it?'

'Dear, yes. And you?'

'No,' said Mrs Dyott; 'it wasn't for me Maud brought it.'

It pulled her visitor up. 'Mrs Blessingbourne brought it?'

'For such a day as this.' But she wondered. 'How you look! Is it so awful?'

'Oh, like his others.' Something had occurred to him; his thought was already far. 'Does she know?'

'Know what?'

'Why, anything.'

But the door opened too soon for Mrs Dyott, who could only murmur quickly –

'Take care!'

II

IT was in fact Mrs Blessingbourne, who had under her arm the book she had gone up for – a pair of covers that this time showed a pretty, a candid blue. She was followed next minute by the servant, who brought in tea, the consumption of which, with the passage of greetings, inquiries and other light civilities between the two visitors, occupied a quarter of an hour. Mrs Dyott meanwhile, as a contribution to so much amenity, mentioned to Maud that her fellow-guest wished to scold her for the books she read – a statement met by this friend with the remark that he must first be sure about them. But as soon as he had picked up the new volume he broke out into a frank 'Dear, dear!'

'Have you read that too?' Mrs Dyott inquired. 'How much you'll have to talk over together! The other one,' she explained to him, 'Maud speaks of as terribly tame.'

'Ah, I must have that out with her! You don't feel the extraordinary force of the fellow?' Voyt went on to Mrs Blessingbourne.

And so, round the hearth, they talked – talked soon, while they warmed their toes, with zest enough to make it seem as happy a chance as any of the quieter opportunities their imprisonment might have involved. Mrs Blessingbourne did feel, it then appeared, the force of the fellow, but she had her reserves and reactions, in which Voyt was much interested. Mrs Dyott rather detached herself, mainly gazing, as she leaned back, at the fire; she intervened, however, enough to relieve Maud of the sense of being listened to. That sense, with Maud, was too apt to convey that one was listened to for a fool. 'Yes, when I read a novel I mostly read a French one,' she had said to Voyt in answer to a question about her usual practice; 'for I seem with it to get hold more of the real thing – to get more life for my money. Only I'm not so infatuated with them but that sometimes for months and months on end I don't read any fiction at all.'

The two books were now together beside them. 'Then when you begin again you read a mass?'

'Dear, no. I only keep up with three or four authors.'

He laughed at this over the cigarette he had been allowed to light. 'I like your "keeping up", and keeping up in particular with "authors".'

'One must keep up with somebody,' Mrs Dyott threw off.

'I daresay I'm ridiculous,' Mrs Blessingbourne conceded without heeding it; 'but that's the way we express ourselves in my part of the country.'

'I only alluded,' said Voyt, 'to the tremendous conscience of your sex. It's more than mine can keep up with. You take everything too hard. But if you can't read the novel of British and American manufacture, heaven knows I'm at one with you. It seems really to show our sense of life as the sense of puppies and kittens.'

'Well,' Maud more patiently returned, 'I'm told all sorts of people are now doing wonderful things; but somehow I remain outside.'

'Ah, it's *they*, it's our poor twangers and twaddlers who remain outside. They pick up a living in the street. And who indeed would want them in?'

Mrs Blessingbourne seemed unable to say, and yet at the same time to have her idea. The subject, in truth, she evidently found, was not so easy to handle. 'People lend me things, and I try; but at the end of fifty pages—'

'There you are! Yes – heaven help us!'

'But what I mean,' she went on, 'isn't that I don't get woefully weary of the eternal French thing. What's *their* sense of life?'

'Ah, *voila*!' Mrs Dyott softly sounded.

'Oh, but it *is* one; you can make it out,' Voyt promptly declared. 'They do what they feel, and they feel more things than we. They strike so many more notes, and with so different a hand. When it comes to any account of a relation, say, between a man and a woman – I mean an intimate or a curious or a suggestive one – where are we compared to them? They don't exhaust the subject, no doubt,' he admitted; 'but we don't touch it, don't even skim it. It's as if we denied its existence, its possibility. You'll doubtless tell me, however,' he went on, 'that as all such relations *are* for us, at the most, much simpler, we can only have all round less to say about them.'

She met this imputation with the quickest amusement. 'I beg your pardon. I don't think I shall tell you anything of the sort. I don't know that I even agree with your premise.'

'About such relations?' He looked agreeably surprised. 'You think we make them larger? – or subtler?'

Mrs Blessingbourne leaned back, not looking, like Mrs Dyott, at the fire, but at the ceiling. 'I don't know what I think.'

'It's not that she doesn't know,' Mrs Dyott remarked. 'It's only that she doesn't say.'

But Voyt had this time no eye for their hostess. For a moment he watched Maud. 'It sticks out of you, you know, that you've yourself written something. Haven't you – and published? I've a notion I could read *you*.'

'When I do publish,' she said without moving, 'you'll be the last one I shall tell. I *have*,' she went on, 'a lovely subject, but it would take an amount of treatment—!'

'Tell us then at least what it is.'

At this she again met his eyes. 'Oh, to tell it would be to express it, and that's just what I can't do. What I meant to say just now,' she added, 'was that the French, to my sense, give us only again and again, for ever and ever, the same couple. There they are once more, as one has had them to satiety, in that yellow thing, and there I shall certainly again find them in the blue.'

'Then why do you keep reading about them?' Mrs Dyott demanded.

Maud hesitated. 'I don't!' she sighed. 'At all events, I sha'n't any more. I give it up.'

'You've been looking for something, I judge,' said Colonel Voyt, 'that you're not likely to find. It doesn't exist.'

'What is it?' Mrs Dyott inquired.

'I never look,' Maud remarked, 'for anything but an interest.'

'Naturally. But your interest,' Voyt replied, 'is in something different from life.'

'Ah, not a bit! I *love* life – in art, though I hate it anywhere else. It's the poverty of the life those people show, and the awful bounders, of both sexes, that they represent.'

'Oh, now we have you!' her interlocutor laughed. 'To me, when all's said and done, they seem to be – as near as art can come – in the truth of the truth. It can only take what life gives it, though it certainly may be a pity that that isn't better. Your complaint of their monotony is a complaint of their conditions. When you say we get always the same couple what do you mean but that we get always the same passion? Of course we do!' Voyt declared. 'If what you're looking for is another, that's what you won't anywhere find.'

Maud for a while said nothing, and Mrs Dyott seemed to wait. 'Well, I suppose I'm looking, more than anything else, for a decent woman.'

'Oh then, you mustn't look for her in pictures of passion. That's not her element nor her whereabouts.'

Mrs Blessingbourne weighed the objection. 'Doesn't it depend on what you mean by passion?'

'I think one can mean only one thing: the enemy to behaviour.'

'Oh, I can imagine passions that are, on the contrary, friends to it.'

Her interlocutor thought. 'Doesn't it depend perhaps on what you mean by behaviour?'

'Dear, no. Behaviour is just behaviour – the most definite thing in the world.'

'Then what do you mean by the "interest" you just now spoke of? The picture of that definite thing?'

'Yes – call it that. Women aren't *always* vicious, even when they're—'

'When they're what?' Voyt asked.

'When they're unhappy. They can be unhappy and good.'

'That one doesn't for a moment deny. But can they be "good" and interesting?'

'That must be Maud's subject!' Mrs Dyott explained. 'To show a woman who *is*. I'm afraid, my dear,' she continued, 'you could only show yourself.'

'You'd show then the most beautiful specimen conceivable' – and Voyt addressed himself to Maud. 'But doesn't it prove that life is, against your contention, more interesting than art? Life you embellish and elevate; but art would find itself able to do nothing with you, and, on such impossible terms, would ruin you.'

The colour in her faint consciousness gave beauty to her stare. ' "Ruin" me?'

'He means,' Mrs Dyott again indicated, 'that you would ruin "art".'

'Without, on the other hand' – Voyt seemed to assent – 'its giving at all a coherent impression of you.'

'She wants her romance cheap!' said Mrs Dyott.

'Oh, no – I should be willing to pay for it. I don't see why the romance – since you give it that name – should be all, as the French inveterately make it, for the women who are bad.'

'Oh, they pay for it!' said Mrs Dyott.

'*Do* they?'

'So, at least' – Mrs Dyott a little corrected herself – 'one has gathered (for I don't read your books, you know!) that they're usually shown as doing.'

Maud wondered, but looking at Voyt, 'They're shown often, no doubt, as paying for their badness. But are they shown as paying for their romance?'

'My dear lady,' said Voyt, 'their romance *is* their badness. There isn't any other. It's a hard law, if you will, and a strange, but goodness has to go without that luxury. Isn't to *be* good just exactly, all round, to go without?' He put it before her kindly and clearly – regretfully too, as if he were sorry the truth should be so sad. He and she, his pleasant eyes seemed to say, would, had they had the making of it, have made it better. 'One has heard it before – at least *I* have; one has heard your question put. But always, when put to a mind not merely muddled, for an inevitable answer. "Why don't you, *cher monsieur*, give us the drama of virtue?" "Because, *chère madame*, the high privilege of virtue is precisely to avoid drama." The adventures of the honest lady? The honest lady hasn't – can't possibly have – adventures.'

Mrs Blessingbourne only met his eyes at first, smiling with a certain intensity. 'Doesn't it depend a little on what you call adventures?'

'My poor Maud,' said Mrs Dyott, as if in compassion for sophistry so simple, 'adventures are just adventures. That's all you can make of them!'

But her friend went on, for their companion, as if without hearing. 'Doesn't it depend a good deal on what you call drama?' Maud spoke as one who had already thought it out. 'Doesn't it depend on what you call romance?'

Her listener gave these arguments his very best attention. 'Of course you may call things anything you like – speak of them as one thing and mean quite another. But why should it depend on anything? Behind these words we use – the adventure, the novel, the drama, the romance, the situation, in short, as we most comprehensively say – behind them all stands the same sharp fact that they all, in their different ways, represent.'

'Precisely!' Mrs Dyott was full of approval.

Maud, however, was full of vagueness. 'What great fact?'

'The fact of a relation. The adventure's a relation; the relation's an adventure. The romance, the novel, the drama are the picture of one. The subject the novelist treats is the rise, the formation, the development, the climax, and for the most part the decline, of one. And what is the honest lady doing on that side of the town?'

Mrs Dyott was more pointed. 'She doesn't so much as *form* a relation.'

But Maud bore up. 'Doesn't it depend, again, on what you call a relation?'

'Oh,' said Mrs Dyott, 'if a gentleman picks up her pocket-handkerchief—'

'Ah, even that's one,' their friend laughed, 'if she has thrown it to him. We can only deal with one that *is* one.'

'Surely,' Maud replied. 'But if it's an innocent one—?'

'Doesn't it depend a good deal,' Mrs Dyott asked, 'on what you call innocent?'

'You mean that the adventures of innocence have so often been the material of fiction? Yes,' Voyt replied; 'that's exactly what the bored reader complains of. He has asked for bread and been given a stone. What is it but, with absolute directness, a question of interest, or, as people say, of the story? What's a situation undeveloped but a subject lost? If a relation stops, where's the story? If it doesn't stop, where's the innocence? It seems to me you must choose. It would be very pretty if it were otherwise, but that's how we flounder. Art is our flounderings shown.'

Mrs Blessingbourne – and with an air of deference scarce supported perhaps by its sketchiness – kept her deep eyes on this definition. 'But sometimes we flounder out.'

It immediately touched in Colonel Voyt the spring of a genial derision. 'That's just where I expected *you* would! One always sees it come.'

'He has, you notice,' Mrs Dyott parenthesised to Maud, 'seen it come so often; and he has always waited for it and met it.'

'Met it, dear lady, simply enough! It's the old story, Mrs Blessingbourne. The relation is innocent that the heroine gets out of. The book is innocent that's the story of her getting out. But what the devil – in the name of innocence – was she doing *in*?'

Mrs Dyott promptly echoed the question. 'You have to be in, you know, to *get* out. So there you are already with your relation. It's the end of your goodness.'

'And the beginning,' said Voyt, 'of your play!'

'Aren't they all, for that matter, even the worst,' Mrs Dyott pursued, 'supposed *some* time or other to get out? But if, meanwhile, they've been in, however briefly, long enough to adorn a tale—'

'They've been in long enough to point a moral. That is to point ours!' With which, and as if a sudden flush of warmer light had moved him, Colonel Voyt got up. The veil of the storm had parted over a great red sunset.

Mrs Dyott also was on her feet, and they stood before his charming antagonist, who, with eyes lowered and a somewhat fixed smile, had not moved. 'We've spoiled her subject!' the elder lady sighed.

'Well,' said Voyt, 'it's better to spoil an artist's subject than to spoil his reputation. I mean,' he explained to Maud with his indulgent manner, 'his appearance of knowing what he has got hold of, for that, in the last resort, is his happiness.'

She slowly rose at this, facing him with an aspect as handsomely mild as his own. 'You can't spoil my happiness.'

He held her hand an instant as he took leave. 'I wish I could add to it!'

III

WHEN he had quitted them and Mrs Dyott had candidly asked if her friend had found him rude or crude, Maud replied – though not immediately – that she had feared showing only too much that she found him charming. But if Mrs Dyott took this, it was to weigh the sense. 'How could you show it too much?'

'Because I always feel that that's my only way of showing anything. It's absurd, if you like,' Mrs Blessingbourne pursued, 'but I never know, in such intense discussions, what strange impression I may give.'

Her companion looked amused. 'Was it intense?'

'*I* was,' Maud frankly confessed.

'Then it's a pity you were so wrong. Colonel Voyt, you know, is right.' Mrs Blessingbourne at this gave one of the slow, soft, silent headshakes to which she often resorted and which, mostly accompanied by the light of cheer, had somehow, in spite of the small obstinacy that smiled in them, a special grace. With this grace, for a moment, her friend, looking her up and down, appeared impressed, yet not too much so to take, the next minute, a decision. 'Oh, my dear, I'm sorry to differ from anyone so lovely – for you're awfully beautiful to-night, and your frock's the very nicest I've ever seen you wear. But he's as right as he can be.'

Maud repeated her motion. 'Not so right, at all events, as he thinks he is. Or perhaps I can say,' she went on, after an instant, 'that I'm not so wrong. I do know a little what I'm talking about.'

Mrs Dyott continued to study her. 'You *are* vexed. You naturally don't like it – such destruction.'

'Destruction?'

'Of your illusion.'

'I *have* no illusion. If I had, moreover, it wouldn't be destroyed. I have, on the whole, I think, my little decency.'

Mrs Dyott stared. 'Let us grant it for argument. What, then?'

'Well, I've also my little drama.'

'An attachment?'

'An attachment.'

'That you shouldn't have?'

'That I shouldn't have.'

'A passion?'

'A passion.'

'Shared?'

'Ah, thank goodness, no!'

Mrs Dyott continued to gaze. 'The object's unaware—?'

'Utterly.'

Mrs Dyott turned it over. 'Are you sure?'

'Sure.'

'That's what you call your decency? But isn't it,' Mrs Dyott asked, 'rather *his?*'

'Dear, no. It's only his good fortune.'

Mrs Dyott laughed. 'But yours, darling – your good fortune: where does *that* come in?'

'Why, in my sense of the romance of it.'

'The romance of what? Of his not knowing?'

'Of my not wanting him to. If I did' – Maud had touchingly worked it out – 'where would be my honesty?'

The inquiry, for an instant, held her friend; yet only, it seemed, for a stupefaction that was almost amusement. 'Can you want or not want as you like? Where in the world, if you don't want, is your romance?'

Mrs Blessingbourne still wore her smile, and she now, with a light gesture that matched it, just touched the region of her heart. 'There!'

Her companion admiringly marvelled. 'A lovely place for it, no doubt! – but not quite a place, that I can see, to make the sentiment a relation.'

'Why not? What more is required for a relation for *me*?'

'Oh, all sorts of things, I should say! And many more, added to those, to make it one for the person you mention.'

'Ah, that I don't pretend it either should be or *can* be. I only speak for myself.'

It was said in a manner that made Mrs Dyott, with a visible mixture of impressions, suddenly turn away. She indulged in a vague movement or two, as if to look for something, then again found herself near her friend, on whom with the same abruptness, in fact with a strange sharpness, she conferred a kiss that might have represented either her tribute to exalted consistency or her idea of a graceful close of the discussion. 'You deserve that one should speak *for* you!'

Her companion looked cheerful and secure. 'How *can* you, without knowing——?'

'Oh, by guessing! It's not——?'

But that was as far as Mrs Dyott could get. 'It's not,' said Maud, 'anyone you've ever seen.'

'Ah then, I give you up!'

And Mrs Dyott conformed, for the rest of Maud's stay, to the spirit of this speech. It was made on a Saturday night, and Mrs Blessingbourne remained till the Wednesday following, an interval during which, as the return of fine weather was confirmed by the Sunday, the two ladies found a wider range of action. There were drives to be taken, calls made, objects of interest seen, at a distance; with the effect of much easy talk and still more easy silence. There had been a question of Colonel Voyt's probable return on the Sunday, but the whole time passed without a sign from him, and it was merely mentioned by Mrs Dyott, in explanation, that he must have been suddenly called, as he was so liable to be, to town. That this in fact was what had happened he made clear to her on Thursday afternoon, when, walking over again late, he found her alone. The consequence of his Sunday letters had been his taking, that day, the 4.15. Mrs Voyt had gone back on Thursday, and he now, to settle on the spot the question of a piece of work begun at his place, had rushed down for a few hours in anticipation of the usual collective move for the week's end. He was to go up again by the late train, and had to count a little – a fact accepted by his hostess with the hard pliancy of practice – his present happy moments. Too few as these were, however, he found time to make of her an inquiry or two not directly bearing on their situation. The first was a recall of the question for which Mrs Blessingbourne's entrance on the previous Saturday had arrested her answer. Did that lady know of anything between them?

'No. I'm sure. There's one thing she does know,' Mrs Dyott went on; 'but it's quite different and not so very wonderful.'

'What, then, is it?'

'Well, that she's herself in love.'

Voyt showed his interest. 'You mean she told you?'

'I got it out of her.'

He showed his amusement. 'Poor thing! And with whom?'

'With you.'

His surprise, if the distinction might be made, was less than his wonder. 'You got that out of her too?'

'No – it remains in. Which is much the best way for it. For you to know it would be to end it.'

He looked rather cheerfully at sea. 'Is that then why you tell me?'

'I mean for her to know you know it. Therefore it's in your interest not to let her.'

'I see,' Voyt after a moment returned. 'Your real calculation is that my interest will be sacrificed to my vanity – so that, if your other idea is just, the flame will in fact, and thanks to her morbid conscience, expire by her taking fright at seeing me so pleased. But I promise you,' he declared, 'that she sha'n't see it. So there you are!' She kept her eyes on him and had evidently to admit, after a little, that there she was. Distinct as he had made the case, however, he was not yet quite satisfied. 'Why are you so sure that I'm the man?'

'From the way she denies you.'

'You put it to her?'

'Straight. If you hadn't been she would, of course, have confessed to you – to keep me in the dark about the real one.'

Poor Voyt laughed out again. 'Oh, you dear souls!'

'Besides,' his companion pursued, 'I was not in want of that evidence.'

'Then what other had you?'

'Her state before you came – which was what made me ask you how much you had seen her. And her state after it,' Mrs Dyott added. 'And her state,' she wound up, 'while you were here.'

'But her state while I was here was charming.'

'Charming. That's just what I say.'

She said it in a tone that placed the matter in its right light – a light in which they appeared kindly, quite tenderly, to watch Maud wander away into space with her lovely head bent under a theory rather too big for it. Voyt's last word, however, was that there was just enough in it – in the theory – for them to allow that she had not shown herself, on the occasion of their talk, wholly bereft of sense. Her consciousness, if they let it alone – as they of course after this mercifully must – *was*, in the last analysis, a kind of shy romance. Not a romance like their own, a thing to make the fortune of any author up to the mark – one who should have the invention or who *could* have the courage; but a small, scared, starved, subjective satisfaction that would do her no harm and nobody else any good. Who but a duffer – he stuck to his contention – would see the shadow of a 'story' in it?

FLICKERBRIDGE

I

FRANK GRANGER had arrived from Paris to paint a portrait – an order given him, as a young compatriot with a future, whose early work would some day have a price, by a lady from New York, a friend of his own people and also, as it happened, of Addie's, the young woman to whom it was publicly both affirmed and denied that he was engaged. Other young women in Paris – fellow-members there of the little tight transpontine world of art-study – professed to know that the pair had been 'several times' over so closely contracted. This, however, was their own affair; the last phase of the relation, the last time of the times, had passed into vagueness; there was perhaps even an impression that if they were inscrutable to their friends they were not wholly crystalline to each other and themselves. What had occurred for Granger, at all events, in connection with the portrait was that Mrs Bracken, his intending model, whose return to America was at hand, had suddenly been called to London by her husband, occupied there with pressing business, but had yet desired that her displacement should not interrupt her sittings. The young man, at her request, had followed her to England and profited by all she could give him, making shift with a small studio lent him by a London painter whom he had known and liked, a few years before, in the French *atelier* that then cradled, and that continued to cradle, so many of their kind.

The British capital was a strange, grey world to him, where people walked, in more ways than one, by a dim light; but he was happily of such a turn that the impression, just as it came, could nowhere ever fail him, and even the worst of these things was almost as much an occupation – putting it only at that – as the best. Mrs Bracken, moreover, passed him on, and while the darkness ebbed a little in the April days he found himself consolingly committed to a couple of fresh subjects. This cut him out work for more than another month, but meanwhile, as

715

he said, he saw a lot – a lot that, with frequency and with much expression, he wrote about to Addie. She also wrote to her absent friend, but in briefer snatches, a meagreness to her reasons for which he had long since assented. She had other play for her pen, as well as, fortunately, other remuneration; a regular correspondence for a 'prominent Boston paper,' fitful connections with public sheets perhaps also, in cases, fitful, and a mind, above all, engrossed at times, to the exclusion of everything else, with the study of the short story. This last was what she had mainly come out to go into, two or three years after he had found himself engulfed in the mystery of Carolus. She was indeed, on her own deep sea, more engulfed than he had ever been, and he had grown to accept the sense that, for progress too, she sailed under more canvas. It had not been particularly present to him till now that he had in the least got on, but the way in which Addie had – and evidently, still more, would – was the theme, as it were, of every tongue. She had thirty short stories out and nine descriptive articles. His three or four portraits of fat American ladies – they were all fat, all ladies and all American – were a poor show compared with these triumphs; especially as Addie had begun to throw out that it was about time they should go home. It kept perpetually coming up in Paris, in the transpontine world, that, as the phrase was, America had grown more interesting since they left. Addie was attentive to the rumour, and, as full of conscience as she was of taste, of patriotism as of curiosity, had often put it to him frankly, with what he, who was of New York, recognised as her New England emphasis: 'I'm not sure, you know, that we do *real* justice to our country.' Granger felt he would do it on the day – if the day ever came – he should irrevocably marry her. No other country could possibly have produced her.

II

BUT meanwhile it befell, in London, that he was stricken with influenza and with subsequent sorrow. The attack was short but sharp – had it lasted Addie would certainly have come to his aid; most of a blight, really, in its secondary stage. The good ladies his sitters – the ladies with the frizzled hair, with the diamond earrings, with the chins tending to the massive – left for him, at the door of his lodgings, flowers, soup and love, so that with their assistance he pulled through; but his convalescence was slow and his weakness out of proportion to the muffled shock. He came out, but he went about lame; it tired him to paint – he felt as if he had been ill for a month. He strolled in Kensington Gardens when he should have been at work; he sat long on penny chairs and helplessly mused and mooned. Addie desired him to return to Paris, but there were chances under his hand that he felt he had just wit enough left not to relinquish. He would have gone for a week to the sea – he would have gone to Brighton; but Mrs Bracken had to be finished – Mrs Bracken was so soon to sail. He just managed to finish her in time – the day before the date fixed for his breaking ground on a greater business still, the circumvallation of Mrs Dunn. Mrs Dunn duly waited on him, and he sat down before her, feeling, however, ere he rose, that he must take a long breath before the attack. While asking himself that night, therefore, where he should best replenish his lungs, he received from Addie, who had had from Mrs Bracken a poor report of him, a communication which, besides being of sudden and startling interest, applied directly to his case.

His friend wrote to him under the lively emotion of having from one day to another become aware of a new relative, an ancient cousin, a sequestered gentlewoman, the sole survival of 'the English branch of the family', still resident, at Flickerbridge, in the 'old family home', and with whom, that he might immediately betake himself to so auspicious a quarter for change of air, she had already done what was proper to place him, as she said, in touch. What came of it all, to be brief, was that Granger found himself so placed almost as he read: he was in touch with Miss Wenham of Flickerbridge, to the extent of being in correspondence with her, before twenty-four hours had sped. And on the second day he was in the train, settled for a five-hours' run to the door of this amiable woman, who had so abruptly and kindly taken him on trust and of whom but yesterday he had never so much as heard. This was an oddity – the whole incident was – of which, in the corner of his compartment, as he proceeded, he had time to take the size. But the surprise, the incongruity, as he felt, could but deepen as he went. It was a sufficiently queer note, in the light, or the absence of it, of his late experience, that so complex a product as Addie should have *any* simple insular tie; but it was a queerer note still that she should have had one so long only to remain unprofitably unconscious of it. Not to have done something with it, used it, worked it, talked about it at least, and perhaps even written – these things, at the rate she moved, represented a loss of opportunity under which, as he saw her, she was peculiarly formed to wince. She was at any rate, it was clear, doing something with it now; using it, working it, certainly, already talking – and, yes, quite possibly writing – about it. She was, in short, smartly making up what she had missed, and he could take such comfort from his own action as he had been helped to by the rest of the facts, succinctly reported from Paris on the very morning of his start.

It was the singular story of a sharp split – in a good English house – that dated now from years back. A worthy Briton, of the best middling stock, had, early in the forties, as a very young man, in Dresden, whither he had been despatched to qualify in German for a stool in an uncle's counting-house, met, admired, wooed and won an American girl, of due attractions, domiciled at that period with her parents and a sister, who was also attractive, in the Saxon capital. He had married her, taken her to England, and there, after some years of harmony and happiness, lost her. The sister in question had, after her death, come to him, and to his young child, on a visit, the effect of which, between the pair, eventually defined itself as a sentiment that was not to be resisted. The bereaved husband, yielding to a new attachment and a new response, and finding a new union thus prescribed, had yet been forced to reckon with the unaccommodating law of the land. Encompassed with frowns in his own country, however, marriages of this particular type were wreathed in smiles in his sister's-in-law, so that his remedy was not forbidden. Choosing between two allegiances he had let the one go that seemed the least close, and had, in brief, transplanted his possibilities to an easier air. The knot was tied for the couple in New York, where, to protect the legitimacy of such other children as might come to them, they settled and prospered. Children came, and one of the daughters, growing up and marrying in her turn, was, if Frank rightly followed, the mother of his own Addie, who had been deprived of the know-ledge of her indeed, in childhood, by death, and been brought up, though without undue tension, by a stepmother – a char-acter thus, in the connection, repeated.

The breach produced in England by the invidious action, as it was there held, of the girl's grandfather, had not failed to widen – all the more that nothing had been done on the American side to close it. Frigidity had settled, and hostility had only been arrested by indifference. Darkness, therefore, had fortunately supervened, and a cousinship completely divided. On either side of the impassable gulf, of the impenet-rable curtain, each branch had put forth its leaves – a foliage wanting, in the American quarter, it was distinct enough to Granger, in no sign or symptom of climate and environment. The graft in New York had taken, and Addie was a vivid, an unmistakeable flower. At Flickerbridge, or wherever, on the other hand, strange to say, the parent stem had had a fortune comparatively meagre. Fortune, it was true, in the vulgarest sense, had attended neither party. Addie's immediate belong-ings were as poor as they were numerous, and he gathered that Miss Wenham's pretensions to wealth were not so marked as to expose the claim of kinship to the imputation of motive. To this lady's single identity, at all events, the original stock had dwindled, and our young man was properly warned that he would find her shy and solitary. What was singular was that, in these conditions, she should desire, she should endure, to receive him. But that was all another story, lucid enough when mastered. He kept Addie's letters, exceptionally copious, in his lap; he conned them at intervals; he held the threads.

He looked out between whiles at the pleasant English land, an April *aquarelle* washed in with wondrous breadth. He knew the French thing, he knew the American, but he had known nothing of this. He saw it already as the remarkable Miss Wenham's setting. The doctor's daughter at Flickerbridge, with nippers on her nose, a palette on her thumb and innocence in her heart, had been the miraculous link. She had become aware, even there, in our world of wonders, that the current fashion for young women so equipped was to enter the Parisian lists. Addie had accordingly chanced upon her, on the slopes of Montparnasse, as one of the English girls in one of the thorough-going sets. They had met in some easy collocation and had fallen upon common ground; after which the young woman, restored to Flickerbridge for an interlude and retailing there her adventures and impressions, had mentioned to Miss Wenham, who had known and protected her from babyhood, that that lady's own name of Adelaide was, as well as the surname conjoined with it, borne, to her knowledge, in Paris, by an extraordinary American specimen. She had then recrossed the Channel with a wonderful message, a courteous challenge, to her friend's duplicate, who had in turn granted through her every satisfaction. The duplicate had, in other words, bravely let Miss Wenham know exactly who she was. Miss Wenham, in whose personal tradition the flame of resentment appeared to have been reduced by time to the palest ashes – for whom, indeed, the story of the great schism was now but a legend only needing a little less dimness to make it romantic – Miss Wenham had promptly responded by a letter fragrant with the hope that old threads might be taken up. It was a relationship that they must puzzle out together, and she had earnestly sounded the other party to it on the subject of a possible visit. Addie had met her with a definite promise; she would come soon, she would come when free, she would come in July; but meanwhile she sent her deputy. Frank asked himself by what name she had described, by what character introduced him to Flickerbridge. He felt mainly, on the whole, as if he were going there to find out if he were engaged to her. He was at sea, really, now, as to which of the various views Addie herself took of it. To Miss Wenham she must definitely have taken one, and perhaps Miss Wenham would reveal it. This expectation was really his excuse for a possible indiscretion.

III

HE was indeed to learn on arrival to what he had been committed; but that was for a while so much a part of his first general impression that the fact took time to detach itself, the first general impression demanding verily all his faculties of response. He almost felt, for a day or two, the victim of a practical joke, a gross abuse of confidence. He had presented himself with the moderate amount of flutter involved in a sense of due preparation; but he had then found that, however primed with prefaces and prompted with hints, he had not been prepared at all. How *could* he be, he asked himself, for anything so foreign to his experience, so alien to his proper world, so little to be preconceived in the sharp north light of the newest impressionism, and yet so recognised, after all, really, in the event, so noted and tasted and assimilated? It was a case he would scarce have known how to describe – could doubtless have described best with a full, clean brush, supplemented by a play of gesture; for it was always his habit to see an occasion, of whatever kind, primarily as a picture, so that he might get it, as he was wont to say, so that he might keep it, well together. He had been treated of a sudden, in this adventure, to one of the sweetest, fairest, coolest impressions of his life – one, moreover, visibly, from the start, complete and homogeneous. Oh, it was *there*, if that was all one wanted of a thing! It was so 'there' that, as had befallen him in Italy, in Spain, confronted at last, in dusky side-chapel or rich museum, with great things dreamed of or with greater ones unexpectedly presented, he had held his breath for fear of breaking the spell; had almost, from the quick impulse to respect, to prolong, lowered his voice and moved on tiptoe. Supreme beauty suddenly revealed is apt to strike us as a possible illusion, playing with our desire – instant freedom with it to strike us as a possible rashness.

This fortunately, however – and the more so as his freedom for the time quite left him – didn't prevent his hostess, the evening of his advent and while the vision was new, from being exactly as queer and rare and *impayable*, as improbable, as impossible, as delightful at dinner at eight (she appeared to keep these immense hours) as she had overwhelmingly been at tea at five. She was in the most natural way in the world one of the oddest apparitions, but that the particular means to such an end *could* be natural was an inference difficult to make. He failed in fact to make it for a couple of days; but then – though then only – he made it with confidence. By this time indeed he was sure of everything, including, luckily, himself. If we compare his impression, with slight extravagance, to some of the greatest he had ever received, this is simply because the image before him was so rounded and stamped. It expressed with pure perfection, it exhausted its character. It was so absolutely and so unconsciously what it was. He had been floated by the strangest of chances out of the rushing stream into a clear, still backwater – a deep and quiet pool in which objects were sharply mirrored. He had hitherto in life known nothing that was old except a few statues and pictures; but here everything was old, was immemorial, and nothing so much so as the very freshness itself. Vaguely to have supposed there were such nooks in the world had done little enough, he now saw, to temper the glare of their opposites. It was the fine touches that counted, and these had to be seen to be believed.

Miss Wenham, fifty-five years of age, and unappeasably timid, unaccountably strange, had, on her reduced scale, an almost Gothic grotesqueness; but the final effect of one's sense of it was an amenity that accompanied one's steps like wafted gratitude. More flurried, more spasmodic, more apologetic, more completely at a loss at one moment and more precipitately abounding at another, he had never before in all his days seen any maiden lady; yet for no maiden lady he had ever seen had he so promptly conceived a private enthusiasm. Her eyes protruded, her chin receded and her nose carried on in conversation a queer little independent motion. She wore on the top of her head an upright circular cap that made her resemble a caryatid disburdened, and on other parts of her person strange combinations of colours, stuffs, shapes, of metal, mineral and plant. The tones of her voice rose and fell, her facial convulsions, whether tending – one could scarce make out – to expression or *re*pression, succeeded each other by a law of their own; she was embarrassed at nothing and at everything, frightened at everything and at nothing, and she approached objects, subjects, the simplest questions and answers and the whole material of intercourse, either with the indirectness of terror or with the violence of despair. These things, none the less, her refinements of oddity and intensities of custom, her suggestion at once of conventions and simplicities, of ease and of agony, her roundabout, retarded suggestions and perceptions, still permitted her to strike her guest as irresistibly charming. He didn't know what to call it; she was a fruit of time. She had a queer distinction. She had been expensively produced, and there would be a good deal more of her to come.

The result of the whole quality of her welcome, at any rate, was that the first evening, in his room, before going to bed, he relieved his mind in a letter to Addie, which, if space allowed us to embody it in our text, would usefully perform the office of a 'plate'. It would enable us to present ourselves as profusely illustrated. But the process of reproduction, as we say, costs. He wished his friend to know how grandly their affair turned out. She had put him in the way of something absolutely special – an old house untouched, untouchable, indescribable, an old corner such as one didn't believe existed, and the holy calm of which made the chatter of studios, the smell of paint, the slang of critics, the whole sense and sound of Paris, come back as so many signs of a huge monkey-cage. He moved about, restless, while he wrote; he lighted cigarettes and, nervous and suddenly scrupulous, put them out again; the night was mild and one of the windows of his large high room, which stood over the garden, was up. He lost himself in the things about him, in the type of the room, the last century with not a chair moved, not a point stretched. He hung over the objects and ornaments, blissfully few and adorably good, perfect pieces all, and never one, for a change, French. The scene was as rare as some fine old print with the best bits down in the corners. Old books and old pictures, allusions remembered and aspects conjectured, reappeared to him; he knew now what anxious islanders had been trying for in their backward hunt for the homely. But the homely at Flickerbridge was all style, even as style at the same time was mere honesty. The larger, the smaller past – he scarce knew which to call it – was at all events so hushed to sleep round him as he wrote that he had almost a bad conscience about having come. How one might love it, but how one might spoil it! To look at it too hard was positively to make it conscious, and to make it conscious was positively to wake it up. Its only safety, of a truth, was to be left still to sleep – to sleep in its large, fair chambers, and under its high, clean canopies.

He added thus restlessly a line to his letter, maundered round the room again, noted and fingered something else, and then, dropping on the old flowered sofa, sustained by the tight cubes of its cushions, yielded afresh to the cigarette, hesitated, stared, wrote a few words more. He wanted Addie to know, that was what he most felt, unless he perhaps felt more how much she herself would want to. Yes, what he supremely saw was all that Addie would make of it. Up to his neck in it there he fairly turned cold at the sense of suppressed opportunity, of the outrage of privation, that his correspondent would retrospectively and, as he even divined with a vague shudder, almost vindictively nurse. Well, what had happened was that the acquaintance had been kept for her, like a packet enveloped and sealed for delivery, till her attention was free. He saw her there, heard her and felt her – felt how she would feel and how she would, as she usually said, 'rave'. Some of her young compatriots called it 'yell', and in the reference itself, alas! illustrated their meaning. She would understand the place, at any rate, down to the ground; there wasn't the slightest doubt of that. Her sense of it would be exactly like his own, and he could see, in anticipation, just the terms of recognition and rapture in which she would abound. He knew just what she would call quaint, just what she would call bland, just what she would call weird, just what she would call wild. She would take it all in with an intelligence much more fitted than his own, in fact, to deal with what he supposed he must regard as its literary relations. She would have read the obsolete, long-winded memoirs and novels that both the figures and the setting ought clearly to remind one of; she would know about the past generations – the lumbering county magnates and their turbaned wives and round-eyed daughters, who, in other days, had treated the ruddy, sturdy, tradeless town, the solid square houses and wide, walled gardens, the streets to-day all grass and gossip, as the scene of a local 'season'. She would have warrant for the assemblies, dinners, deep potations; for the smoked sconces in the dusky parlours; for the long, muddy century of family coaches, 'holsters', highwaymen. She would put a finger, in short, just as he had done, on the vital spot – the rich humility of the whole thing, the fact that neither Flicker-bridge in general nor Miss Wenham in particular, nor anything nor anyone concerned, had a suspicion of their character and their merit. Addie and he would have to come to let in light.

He let it in then, little by little, before going to bed, through the eight or ten pages he addressed to her; assured her that it was the happiest case in the world, a little picture – yet full of 'style' too – absolutely composed and transmitted, with tradition, and tradition only, in every stroke, tradition still noiselessly breathing and visibly flushing, marking strange hours in the tall mahogany clocks that were never wound up and that yet audibly ticked on. All the elements, he was sure he should see, would hang together with a charm, presenting his hostess – a strange iridescent fish for the glazed exposure of an aquarium – as floating in her native medium. He left his letter open on the table, but, looking it over next morning, felt of a sudden indisposed to send it. He would keep it to add more, for there would be more to know; yet when three days had elapsed he had still not sent it. He sent instead, after delay, a much briefer report, which he was moved to make different and, for some reason, less vivid. Meanwhile he learned from Miss Wenham how Addie had introduced him. It took time to arrive with her at that point, but after the Rubicon was crossed they went far afield.

IV

'OH yes, she said you were engaged. That was why – since I *had* broken out so – she thought I would like to see you; as I assure you I've been so delighted to. But *aren't* you?' the good lady asked as if she saw in his face some ground for doubt.

'Assuredly – if she says so. It may seem very odd to you, but I haven't known, and yet I've felt that, being nothing whatever to you directly, I need some warrant for consenting thus to be thrust on you. We *were*,' the young man explained, 'engaged a year ago; but since then (if you don't mind my telling you such things; I feel now as if I could tell you anything!) I haven't quite known how I stand. It hasn't seemed that we were in a position to marry. Things are better now, but I haven't quite known how she would see them. They were so bad six months ago that I understood her, I thought, as breaking off. I haven't broken; I've only accepted, for the time – because men must be easy with women – being treated as "the best of friends". Well, I try to be. I wouldn't have come here if I hadn't been. I thought it would be charming for her to know you – when I heard from her the extraordinary way you had dawned upon her, and charming therefore if I could help her to it. And if I'm helping you to know *her*,' he went on, 'isn't that charming too?'

'Oh, I so want to!' Miss Wenham murmured, in her unpractical, impersonal way. 'You're so different!' she wistfully declared.

'It's *you*, if I may respectfully, ecstatically say so, who are different. That's the point of it all. I'm not sure that anything so terrible really ought to happen to you as to know us.'

'Well,' said Miss Wenham, 'I do know you a little, by this time, don't I? And I don't find it terrible. It's a delightful change for me.'

'Oh, I'm not sure you ought to have a delightful change!'

'Why not – if you do?'

'Ah, I can bear it. I'm not sure that you can. I'm too bad to spoil – I *am* spoiled. I'm nobody, in short; I'm nothing. I've no type. You're *all* type. It has taken long, delicious years of security and monotony to produce you. You fit your frame with a perfection only equalled by the perfection with which your frame fits you. So this admirable old house, all time-softened white within and time-faded red without, so everything that surrounds you here and that has, by some extraordinary mercy, escaped the inevitable fate of exploitation: so it all, I say, is the sort of thing that, if it were the least bit to fall to pieces, could never, ah, never more, be put together again. I have, dear Miss Wenham,' Granger went on, happy himself in his extravagance, which was yet all sincere, and happier still in her deep, but altogether pleased, mystification – 'I've found, do you know, just the thing one has ever heard of that you most resemble. You're the Sleeping Beauty in the wood.'

He still had no compunction when he heard her bewilderedly sigh: 'Oh, you're too delightfully droll!'

'No, I only put things just as they are, and as I've also learned a little, thank heaven, to see them – which isn't, I quite agree with you, at all what anyone does. You're in the deep doze of the spell that has held you for long years, and it would be a shame, a crime, to wake you up. Indeed I already feel, with a thousand scruples, that I'm giving you the fatal shake. I say it even though it makes me sound a little as if I thought myself the fairy prince.'

She gazed at him with her queerest, kindest look, which he was getting used to, in spite of a faint fear, at the back of his head, of the strange things that sometimes occurred when lonely ladies, however mature, began to look at interesting young men from over the seas as if the young men desired to flirt. 'It's so wonderful,' she said, 'that you should be so very odd and yet so very good-natured.' Well, it all came to the same thing – it was so wonderful that *she* should be so simple and yet so little of a bore. He accepted with gratitude the theory of his languor – which moreover was real enough and partly perhaps why he was so sensitive; he let himself go as a convalescent, let her insist on the weakness that always remained after fever. It helped him to gain time, to preserve the spell even while he talked of breaking it; saw him through slow strolls and soft sessions, long gossips, fitful, hopeless questions – there was so much more to tell than, by any contortion, she *could* – and explanations addressed gallantly and patiently to her understanding, but not, by good fortune, really reaching it. They were perfectly at cross-purposes, and it was all the better, and they wandered together in the silver haze with all communication blurred.

When they sat in the sun in her formal garden he was quite aware that the tenderest consideration failed to disguise his treating her as the most exquisite of curiosities. The term of comparison most present to him was that of some obsolete musical instrument. The old-time order of her mind and her air had the stillness of a painted spinet that was duly dusted, gently rubbed, but never tuned nor played on. Her opinions were like dried rose-leaves; her attitudes like British sculpture; her voice was what he imagined of the possible tone of the old gilded, silver-stringed harp in one of the corners of the drawing-room. The lonely little decencies and modest dignities of her life, the fine grain of its conservatism, the innocence of its ignorance, all its monotony of stupidity and salubrity, its cold dullness and dim brightness, were there before him. Meanwhile, within him, strange things took place. It was literally true that his impression began again, after a lull, to make him nervous and anxious, and for reasons peculiarly confused, almost grotesquely mingled, or at least comically sharp. He was distinctly an agitation and a new taste – that he could see; and he saw quite as much therefore the excitement she already drew from the vision of Addie, an image intensified by the sense of closer kinship and presented to her, clearly, with various erratic enhancements, by her friend the doctor's daughter. At the end of a few days he said to her: 'Do you know she wants to come without waiting any longer? She wants to come while I'm here. I received this morning her letter proposing it, but I've been thinking it over and have waited to speak to you. The thing is, you see, that if she writes to *you* proposing it—'

'Oh, I shall be so particularly glad!'

V

THEY were, as usual, in the garden, and it had not yet been so present to him that if he were only a happy cad there would be a good way to protect her. As she wouldn't hear of his being yet beyond precautions she had gone into the house for a particular shawl that was just the thing for his knees, and, blinking in the watery sunshine, had come back with it across the fine little lawn. He was neither fatuous nor asinine, but he had almost to put it to himself as a small task to resist the sense of his absurd advantage with her. It filled him with horror and awkwardness, made him think of he didn't know what, recalled something of Maupassant's – the smitten 'Miss Harriet' and her tragic fate. There was a preposterous possibility – yes, he held the strings quite in his hands – of keeping the treasure for himself. That was the art of life – what the real artist would consistently do. He would close the door on his impression, treat it as a private museum. He would see that he could lounge and linger there, live with wonderful things there, lie up there to rest and refit. For himself he was sure that after a little he should be able to paint there – do things in a key he had never thought of before. When she brought him the rug he took it from her and made her sit down on the bench and resume her knitting; then, passing behind her with a laugh, he placed it over her own shoulders; after which he moved to and fro before her, his hands in his pockets and his cigarette in his teeth. He was ashamed of the cigarette – a villainous false note; but she allowed, liked, begged him to smoke, and what he said to her on it, in one of the pleasantries she benevolently missed, was that he did so for fear of doing worse. That only showed that the end was really in sight. 'I daresay it will strike you as quite awful, what I'm going to say to you, but I can't help it. I speak out of the depths of my respect for you. It will seem to you horrid disloyalty to poor Addie. Yes – there we are; there *I* am, at least, in my naked monstrosity.' He stopped and looked at her till she might have been almost frightened. 'Don't let her come. Tell her not to. I've tried to prevent it, but she suspects.'

The poor woman wondered. 'Suspects?'

'Well, I drew it, in writing to her, on reflection, as mild as I could – having been visited, in the watches of the night, by the instinct of what might happen. Something told me to keep back my first letter – in which, under the first impression, I myself rashly "raved"; and I concocted instead of it an insincere and guarded report. But guarded as I was I clearly didn't keep you "down", as we say, enough. The wonder of your colour – daub you over with grey as I might – must have come through and told the tale. She scents battle from afar – by which I mean she scents "quaintness". But keep her off. It's hideous, what I'm saying – but I owe it to you. I owe it to the world. She'll kill you.'

'You mean I shan't get on with her?'

'Oh, fatally! See how *I* have. She's intelligent, remarkably pretty, remarkably good. And she'll adore you.'

'Well then?'

'Why, that will be just how she'll do for you.'

'Oh, I can hold my own!' said Miss Wenham with the head-shake of a horse making his sleigh-bells rattle in frosty air.

'Ah, but you can't hold hers! She'll rave about you. She'll write about you. You're Niagara before the first white traveller – and you know, or rather you can't know, what Niagara became *after* that gentleman. Addie will have discovered Niagara. She will understand you in perfection; she will feel you down to the ground; not a delicate shade of you will she lose or let anyone else lose. You'll be too weird for words, but the words will nevertheless come. You'll be too exactly the real thing and to be left too utterly just as you are, and all Addie's friends and all Addie's editors and contributors and readers will cross the Atlantic and flock to Flickerbridge, so, unanimously, universally, vociferously, to leave you. You'll be in the magazines with illustrations; you'll be in the papers with headings; you'll be everywhere with everything. You don't understand – you think you do, but you don't. Heaven forbid you *should* understand! That's just your beauty – your "sleeping" beauty. But you needn't. You can take me on trust. Don't have her. Say, as a pretext, as a reason, anything in the world you like. Lie to her – scare her away. I'll go away and give you up – I'll sacrifice everything myself.' Granger pursued his exhortation, convincing himself more and more. 'If I saw my way out, my way completely through, *I* would pile up some fabric of fiction for her – I should only want to be sure of its not tumbling down. One would have, you see, to keep the thing up. But I would throw dust in her eyes. I would tell her that you don't do at all – that you're not, in fact, a desirable acquaintance. I'd tell her you're vulgar, improper, scandalous; I'd tell her you're mercenary, designing, dangerous; I'd tell her the only safe course is immediately to let you drop. I would thus surround you with an impenetrable legend of conscientious misrepresentation, a circle of pious fraud, and all the while privately keep you for myself.'

She had listened to him as if he were a band of music and she a small shy garden-party. 'I shouldn't like you to go away. I shouldn't in the least like you not to come again.'

'Ah, there it is!' he replied. 'How can I come again if Addie ruins you?'

'But how will she ruin me – even if she does what you say? I know I'm too old to change and really much too queer to please in any of the extraordinary ways you speak of. If it's a question of quizzing me I don't think my cousin, or anyone else, will have quite the hand for it that *you* seem to have. So that if *you* haven't ruined me—!'

'But I *have* – that's just the point!' Granger insisted. 'I've undermined you at least. I've left, after all, terribly little for Addie to do.'

She laughed in clear tones. 'Well, then, we'll admit that you've done everything but frighten me.'

He looked at her with surpassing gloom. 'No – that again is one of the most dreadful features. You'll positively like it – what's to come. You'll be caught up in a chariot of fire like the prophet – wasn't there, was there, one? – of old. That's exactly why – if one could but have done it – you would have been to be kept ignorant and helpless. There's something or other in Latin that says that it's the finest things that change the most easily for the worse. You already enjoy your dishonour and revel in your shame. It's too late – you're lost!'

VI

ALL this was as pleasant a manner of passing the time as any other, for it didn't prevent his old-world corner from closing round him more entirely, nor stand in the way of his making out, from day to day, some new source, as well as some new

effect, of its virtue. He was really scared at moments at some of
the liberties he took in talk – at finding himself so familiar; for
the great note of the place was just that a certain modern ease
had never crossed its threshold, that quick intimacies and quick
oblivions were a stranger to its air. It had known, in all its days,
no rude, no loud invasion. Serenely unconscious of most contemporary things, it had been so of nothing so much as of the
diffused social practice of running in and out. Granger held his
breath, on occasions, to think how Addie would run. There
were moments when, for some reason, more than at others,
he heard her step on the staircase and her cry in the hall. If he
played freely, none the less, with the idea with which we have
shown him as occupied, it was not that in every measurable way
he didn't sacrifice, to the utmost, to stillness. He only hovered,
ever so lightly, to take up again his thread. She wouldn't hear of
his leaving her, of his being in the least fit again, as she said, to
travel. She spoke of the journey to London – which was in fact a
matter of many hours – as an experiment fraught with lurking
complications. He added then day to day, yet only hereby, as he
reminded her, giving other complications a larger chance to
multiply. He kept it before her, when there was nothing else to
do, that she must consider; after which he had his times of fear
that she perhaps really would make for him this sacrifice.

He knew that she had written again to Paris, and knew that
he must himself again write – a situation abounding for each in
the elements of a quandary. If he stayed so long, why then he
wasn't better, and if he wasn't better Addie might take it into
her head—! They must make it clear that he *was* better, so that,
suspicious, alarmed at what was kept from her, she shouldn't
suddenly present herself to nurse him. If he was better, however, why did he stay so long? If he stayed only for the attraction
the sense of the attraction might be contagious. This was what
finally grew clearest for him, so that he had for his mild disciple
hours of still sharper prophecy. It consorted with his fancy to
represent to her that their young friend had been by this time
unsparingly warned; but nothing could be plainer than that this
was ineffectual so long as he himself resisted the ordeal. To
plead that he remained because he was too weak to move was

only to throw themselves back on the other horn of their dilemma. If he was too weak to move Addie would bring him her strength – of which, when she got there, she would give them specimens enough. One morning he broke out at breakfast with an intimate conviction. They would see that she was actually starting – they would receive a wire by noon. They didn't receive it, but by his theory the portent was only the stronger. It had, moreover, its grave as well as its gay side, for Granger's paradox and pleasantry were only the most convenient way for him of saying what he felt. He literally heard the knell sound, and in expressing this to Miss Wenham with the conversational freedom that seemed best to pay his way he the more vividly faced the contingency. He could never return, and though he announced it with a despair that did what might be to make it pass as a joke, he saw that, whether or no she at last understood, she quite at last believed him. On this, to his knowledge, she wrote again to Addie, and the contents of her letter excited his curiosity. But that sentiment, though not assuaged, quite dropped when, the day after, in the evening, she let him know that she had had, an hour before, a telegram.

'She comes Thursday.'

He showed not the least surprise. It was the deep calm of the fatalist. It *had* to be. 'I must leave you then to-morrow.'

She looked, on this, as he had never seen her; it would have been hard to say whether what was in her face was the last failure to follow or the first effort to meet. 'And really not to come back?'

'Never, never, dear lady. Why should I come back? You can never be again what you *have* been. I shall have seen the last of you.'

'Oh!' she touchingly urged.

'Yes, for I should next find you simply brought to self-consciousness. You'll be exactly what you are, I charitably admit – nothing more or less, nothing different. But you'll be it all in a different way. We live in an age of prodigious machinery, all organised to a single end. That end is publicity – a publicity as ferocious as the appetite of a cannibal. The thing therefore is not to have any illusions – fondly to flatter yourself,

in a muddled moment, that the cannibal will spare you. He
spares nobody. He spares nothing. It will be all right. You'll
have a lovely time. You'll be only just a public character – blown
about the world for all you are and proclaimed for all you are on
the housetops. It will be for *that*, mind, I quite recognise –
because Addie is superior – as well as for all you aren't. So
good-bye.'

He remained, however, till the next day, and noted at intervals the different stages of their friend's journey; the hour, this
time, she would really have started, the hour she would reach
Dover, the hour she would get to town, where she would alight
at Mrs Dunn's. Perhaps she would bring Mrs Dunn, for Mrs
Dunn would swell the chorus. At the last, on the morrow, as if
in anticipation of this, stillness settled between them; he
became as silent as his hostess. But before he went she brought
out, shyly and anxiously, as an appeal, the question that, for
hours, had clearly been giving her thought. 'Do you meet her
then to-night in London?'

'Dear, no. In what position am I, alas! to do that? When can I
ever meet her again?' He had turned it all over. 'If I could meet
Addie after this, you know, I could meet *you*. And if I do
meet Addie,' he lucidly pursued, 'what will happen, by the
same stroke, is that I *shall* meet you. And that's just what I've
explained to you that I dread.'

'You mean that she and I will be inseparable?'

He hesitated. 'I mean that she'll tell me all about you. I can
hear her, and her ravings, now.'

She gave again – and it was infinitely sad – her little whinny-
ing laugh. 'Oh, but if what you say is true, you'll know.'

'Ah, but Addie won't! Won't, I mean, know that *I* know – or
at least won't believe it. Won't believe that anyone knows.
Such,' he added, with a strange, smothered sigh, '*is* Addie.
Do you know,' he wound up, 'that what, after all, has most
definitely happened is that you've made me see her as I've never
done before?'

She blinked and gasped, she wondered and despaired. 'Oh,
no, it will be *you*. I've had nothing to do with it. Everything's
all you!'

But for all it mattered now! 'You'll see,' he said, 'that she's charming. I shall go, for to-night, to Oxford. I shall almost cross her on the way.'

'Then, if she's charming, what am I to tell her from you in explanation of such strange behaviour as your flying away just as she arrives?'

'Ah, you needn't mind about that – you needn't tell her anything.'

She fixed him as if as never again. 'It's none of my business, of course I feel; but isn't it a little cruel if you're engaged?'

Granger gave a laugh almost as odd as one of her own. 'Oh, you've cost me that!' and he put out his hand to her.

She wondered while she took it. 'Cost you—?'

'We're not engaged. Good-bye.'

THE BEAST IN THE JUNGLE

I

WHAT determined the speech that startled him in the course of their encounter scarcely matters, being probably but some words spoken by himself quite without intention – spoken as they lingered and slowly moved together after their renewal of acquaintance. He had been conveyed by friends, an hour or two before, to the house at which she was staying; the party of visitors at the other house, of whom he was one, and thanks to whom it was his theory, as always, that he was lost in the crowd, had been invited over to luncheon. There had been after luncheon much dispersal, all in the interest of the original motive, a view of Weatherend itself and the fine things, intrinsic features, pictures, heirlooms, treasures of all the arts, that made the place almost famous; and the great rooms were so numerous that guests could wander at their will, hang back from the principal group, and, in cases where they took such matters with the last seriousness, give themselves up to mysterious appreciations and measurements. There were persons to be observed, singly or in couples, bending toward objects in out-of-the-way corners with their hands on their knees and their heads nodding quite as with the emphasis of an excited sense of smell. When they were two they either mingled their sounds of ecstasy or melted into silences of even deeper import, so that there were aspects of the occasion that gave it for Marcher much the air of the 'look round', previous to a sale highly advertised, that excites or quenches, as may be, the dream of acquisition. The dream of acquisition at Weatherend would have had to be wild indeed, and John Marcher found himself, among such suggestions, disconcerted almost equally by the presence of those who knew too much and by that of those who knew nothing. The great rooms caused so much poetry and history to press upon him that he needed to wander apart to feel in a proper relation with them, though his doing so was not, as happened, like the gloating of some of his companions, to be compared to the movements of a dog sniffing a cupboard. It had an issue promptly enough in a direction that was not to have been calculated.

It led, in short, in the course of the October afternoon, to his closer meeting with May Bartram, whose face, a reminder, yet not quite a remembrance, as they sat, much separated, at a very long table, had begun merely by troubling him rather pleasantly. It affected him as the sequel of something of which he had lost the beginning. He knew it, and for the time quite welcomed it, as a continuation, but didn't know what it continued, which was an interest, or an amusement, the greater as he was also somehow aware – yet without a direct sign from her – that the young woman herself had not lost the thread. She had not lost it, but she wouldn't give it back to him, he saw, without some putting forth of his hand for it; and he not only saw that, but saw several things more, things odd enough in the light of the fact that at the moment some accident of grouping brought them face to face he was still merely fumbling with the idea that any contact between them in the past would have had no importance. If it had had no importance he scarcely knew why his actual impression of her should so seem to have so much; the answer to which, however, was that in such a life as they all appeared to be leading for the moment one could but take things as they came. He was satisfied, without in the least being able to say why, that this young lady might roughly have ranked in the house as a poor relation; satisfied also that she was not there on a brief visit, but was more or less a part of the establishment – almost a working, a remunerated part. Didn't she enjoy at periods a protection that she paid for by helping, among other services, to show the place and explain it, deal with the tiresome people, answer questions about the dates of the buildings, the styles of the furniture, the authorship of the pictures, the favourite haunts of the ghost? It wasn't that she looked as if you could have given her shillings – it was impossible to look less so. Yet when she finally drifted toward him, distinctly handsome, though ever so much older – older than when he had seen her before – it might have been as an effect of her guessing that he had, within the couple of hours, devoted more imagination to her than to all the others put together, and had thereby penetrated to a kind of truth that the others were too stupid for. She *was* there on harder terms than anyone; she was there as a consequence of things suffered, in one way and another, in the interval of years; and she remembered him very much as she was remembered – only a good deal better.

By the time they at last thus came to speech they were alone in one of the rooms – remarkable for a fine portrait over the chimney-place – out of which their friends had passed, and the charm of it was that even before they had spoken they had practically arranged with each other to stay behind for talk. The charm, happily, was in other things too; it was partly in there being scarce a spot at Weatherend without something to stay behind for. It was in the way the autumn day looked into the high windows as it waned; in the way the red light, breaking at the close from under a low, sombre sky, reached out in a long shaft and played over old wainscots, old tapestry, old gold, old colour. It was most of all perhaps in the way she came to him as if, since she had been turned on to deal with the simpler sort, he might, should he choose to keep the whole thing down, just take her mild attention for a part of her general business. As soon as he heard her voice, however, the gap was filled up and the missing link supplied; the slight irony he divined in her attitude lost its advantage. He almost jumped at it to get there before her. 'I met you years and years ago in Rome. I remember all about it.' She confessed to disappointment – she had been so sure he didn't; and to prove how well he did he began to pour forth the particular recollections that popped up as he called for them. Her face and her voice, all at his service now, worked the miracle – the impression operating like the torch of a lamplighter who touches into flame, one by one, a long row of gas jets. Marcher flattered himself that the illumination was brilliant, yet he was really still more pleased on her showing him, with amusement, that in his haste to make everything right he had got most things rather wrong. It hadn't been at Rome – it had been at Naples; and it hadn't been seven years before – it had been more nearly ten. She hadn't been either with her uncle and aunt, but with her mother and her brother; in addition to which it was not with the Pembles that *he* had been, but with the Boyers, coming down in their company from Rome – a point on which she insisted, a little to his confusion, and as to which she had her evidence in hand. The Boyers she had known, but she didn't know the Pembles, though she had heard of them, and it was the people he was with who had made them acquainted. The incident of the thunderstorm that had raged round them with such violence as to drive them for refuge into an excavation – this incident had not occurred at the Palace of the Caesars, but at Pompeii, on an occasion when they had been present there at an important find.

He accepted her amendments, he enjoyed her corrections, though the moral of them was, she pointed out, that he *really* didn't remember the least thing about her; and he only felt it as a drawback that when all was made conformable to the truth there didn't appear much of anything left. They lingered together still, she neglecting her office – for from the moment he was so clever she had no proper right to him – and both neglecting the house, just waiting as to see if a memory or two more wouldn't again breathe upon them. It had not taken them many minutes, after all, to put down on the table, like the cards of a pack, those that constituted their respective hands; only what came out was that the pack was unfortunately not perfect – that the past, invoked, invited, encouraged, could give them, naturally, no more than it had. It had made them meet – her at twenty, him at twenty-five; but nothing was so strange, they seemed to say to each other, as that, while so occupied, it hadn't done a little more for them. They looked at each other as with the feeling of an occasion missed; the present one would have been so much better if the other, in the far distance, in the foreign land, hadn't been so stupidly meagre. There weren't, apparently, all counted, more than a dozen little old things that had succeeded in coming to pass between them; trivialities of youth, simplicities of freshness, stupidities of ignorance, small possible germs, but too deeply buried – too deeply (didn't it seem?) to sprout after so many years. Marcher said to himself that he ought to have rendered her some service – saved her from a capsized boat in the Bay, or at least recovered her dressing-bag, filched from her cab, in the streets of Naples, by a lazzarone with a stiletto. Or it would have been nice if he could have been taken with fever, alone, at his hotel, and she could have come to look after him, to write to his people, to drive him out in convalescence. *Then* they would be in possession of the something or other that their actual show seemed to lack. It yet somehow presented itself, this show, as too good to be spoiled; so that they were reduced for a few minutes more to wondering a little helplessly why – since they seemed to know a certain number of the same people – their reunion had been so long averted. They didn't use that name for it, but their delay from minute to minute to join the others was a kind of confession that they didn't quite want it to be a failure. Their attempted supposition of reasons for their not having met but showed how little they knew of each other. There came in fact a moment when Marcher felt a positive pang. It was vain to pretend she was an old friend, for all the communities were wanting, in spite of which it was as an old friend that he saw she would have suited him. He had new ones enough – was surrounded with them, for instance, at that hour at the other house; as a new one he probably wouldn't have so much as noticed her. He would have liked to invent something, get her to make-believe with him that some passage of a romantic or critical kind *had* originally occurred. He was really almost reaching out in imagination – as against time – for something that would do, and saying to himself that if it didn't come this new incident would simply and rather awkwardly close. They would separate, and now for no second or for no third chance. They would have tried and not succeeded. Then it was, just at the turn, as he afterwards made it out to himself, that, everything else failing, she herself decided to take up the case and, as it were, save the situation. He felt as soon as she spoke that she had been consciously keeping back what she said and hoping to get on without it; a scruple in her that immensely touched him when, by the end of three or four minutes more, he was able to measure it. What she brought out, at any rate, quite cleared the air and supplied the link – the link it was such a mystery he should frivolously have managed to lose.

'You know you told me something that I've never forgotten and that again and again has made me think of you since; it was that tremendously hot day when we went to Sorrento, across the bay, for the breeze. What I allude to was what you said to me, on the way back, as we sat, under the awning of the boat, enjoying the cool. Have you forgotten?'

He had forgotten, and he was even more surprised than ashamed. But the great thing was that he saw it was no vulgar reminder of any 'sweet' speech. The vanity of women had long memories, but she was making no claim on him of a compliment or a mistake. With another woman, a totally different one, he might have feared the recall possibly even of some imbecile 'offer'. So, in having to say that he had indeed forgotten, he was conscious rather of a loss than of a gain; he already saw an interest in the matter of her reference. 'I try to think – but I give it up. Yet I remember the Sorrento day.'

'I'm not very sure you do,' May Bartram after a moment said; 'and I'm not very sure I ought to want you to. It's dreadful to bring a person back, at any time, to what he was ten years before. If you've lived away from it,' she smiled, 'so much the better.'

'Ah, if *you* haven't why should I?' he asked.

'Lived away, you mean, from what I myself was?'

'From what *I* was. I was of course an ass,' Marcher went on; 'but I would rather know from you just the sort of ass I was than – from the moment you have something in your mind – not know anything.'

Still, however, she hesitated. 'But if you've completely ceased to be that sort—?'

'Why, I can then just so all the more bear to know. Besides, perhaps I haven't.'

'Perhaps. Yet if you haven't,' she added, 'I should suppose you would remember. Not indeed that *I* in the least connect with my impression the invidious name you use. If I had only thought you foolish,' she explained, 'the thing I speak of wouldn't so have remained with me. It was about yourself.' She waited, as if it might come to him; but as, only meeting her eyes in wonder, he gave no sign, she burnt her ships. 'Has it ever happened?'

Then it was that, while he continued to stare, a light broke for him and the blood slowly came to his face, which began to burn with recognition. 'Do you mean I told you—?' But he faltered, lest what came to him shouldn't be right, lest he should only give himself away.

'It was something about yourself that it was natural one shouldn't forget – that is if one remembered you at all. That's why I ask you,' she smiled, 'if the thing you then spoke of has ever come to pass?'

Oh, then he saw, but he was lost in wonder and found himself embarrassed. This, he also saw, made her sorry for him, as if her allusion had been a mistake. It took him but a moment, however, to feel that it had not been, much as it had been a surprise. After the first little shock of it her knowledge on the contrary began, even if rather strangely, to taste sweet to him. She was the only other person in the world then who would have it, and she had had it all these years, while the fact of his having so breathed his secret had unaccountably faded from him. No wonder they couldn't have met as if nothing had happened. 'I judge,' he finally said, 'that I know what you mean. Only I had strangely enough lost the consciousness of having taken you so far into my confidence.'

'Is it because you've taken so many others as well?'

'I've taken nobody. Not a creature since then.'

'So that I'm the only person who knows?'

'The only person in the world.'

'Well,' she quickly replied, 'I myself have never spoken. I've never, never repeated of you what you told me.' She looked at him so that he perfectly believed her. Their eyes met over it in such a way that he was without a doubt. 'And I never will.'

She spoke with an earnestness that, as if almost excessive, put him at ease about her possible derision. Somehow the whole question was a new luxury to him – that is, from the moment she was in possession. If she didn't take the ironic view she clearly took the sympathetic, and that was what he had had, in all the long time, from no one whomsoever. What he felt was

that he couldn't at present have begun to tell her and yet could
profit perhaps exquisitely by the accident of having done so of
old. 'Please don't then. We're just right as it is.'

'Oh, I am,' she laughed, 'if you are!' To which she added:
'Then you do still feel in the same way?'

It was impossible to him not to take to himself that she was
really interested, and it all kept coming as a sort of revelation.
He had thought of himself so long as abominably alone, and, lo,
he wasn't alone a bit. He hadn't been, it appeared, for an hour –
since those moments on the Sorrento boat. It was *she* who had
been, he seemed to see as he looked at her – she who had been
made so by the graceless fact of his lapse of fidelity. To tell her
what he had told her – what had it been but to ask something of
her? something that she had given, in her charity, without his
having, by a remembrance, by a return of the spirit, failing
another encounter, so much as thanked her. What he had
asked of her had been simply at first not to laugh at him. She
had beautifully not done so for ten years, and she was not doing
so now. So he had endless gratitude to make up. Only for that
he must see just how he had figured to her. 'What, exactly, was
the account I gave—?'

'Of the way you did feel? Well, it was very simple. You said
you had had from your earliest time, as the deepest thing within
you, the sense of being kept for something rare and strange,
possibly prodigious and terrible, that was sooner or later to
happen to you, that you had in your bones the foreboding and
the conviction of, and that would perhaps overwhelm you.'

'Do you call that very simple?' John Marcher asked.

She thought a moment. 'It was perhaps because I seemed, as
you spoke, to understand it.'

'You do understand it?' he eagerly asked.

Again she kept her kind eyes on him. 'You still have the
belief?'

'Oh!' he exclaimed helplessly. There was too much to say.

'Whatever it is to be,' she clearly made out, 'it hasn't yet
come.'

He shook his head in complete surrender now. 'It hasn't yet
come. Only, you know, it isn't anything I'm to *do*, to achieve in

the world, to be distinguished or admired for. I'm not such an ass as *that*. It would be much better, no doubt, if I were.'

'It's to be something you're merely to suffer?'

'Well, say to wait for – to have to meet, to face, to see suddenly break out in my life; possibly destroying all further consciousness, possibly annihilating me; possibly, on the other hand, only altering everything, striking at the root of all my world and leaving me to the consequences, however they shape themselves.'

She took this in, but the light in her eyes continued for him not to be that of mockery. 'Isn't what you describe perhaps but the expectation – or, at any rate, the sense of danger, familiar to so many people – of falling in love?'

John Marcher thought. 'Did you ask me that before?'

'No – I wasn't so free-and-easy then. But it's what strikes me now.'

'Of course,' he said after a moment, 'it strikes you. Of course it strikes *me*. Of course what's in store for me may be no more than that. The only thing is,' he went on, 'that I think that if it had been that, I should by this time know.'

'Do you mean because you've *been* in love?' And then as he but looked at her in silence: 'You've been in love, and it hasn't meant such a cataclysm, hasn't proved the great affair?'

'Here I am, you see. It hasn't been overwhelming.'

'Then it hasn't been love,' said May Bartram.

'Well, I at least thought it was. I took it for that – I've taken it till now. It was agreeable, it was delightful, it was miserable,' he explained. 'But it wasn't strange. It wasn't what *my* affair's to be.'

'You want something all to yourself – something that nobody else knows or *has* known?'

'It isn't a question of what I "want" – God knows I don't want anything. It's only a question of the apprehension that haunts me – that I live with day by day.'

He said this so lucidly and consistently that, visibly, it further imposed itself. If she had not been interested before she would have been interested now. 'Is it a sense of coming violence?'

Evidently now too, again, he liked to talk of it. 'I don't think of it as – when it does come – necessarily violent. I only think of it as natural and as of course, above all, unmistakeable. I think of it simply as *the* thing. *The* thing will of itself appear natural.'

'Then how will it appear strange?'

Marcher bethought himself. 'It won't – to *me*.'

'To whom then?'

'Well,' he replied, smiling at last, 'say to you.'

'Oh then, I'm to be present?'

'Why, you *are* present – since you know.'

'I see.' She turned it over. 'But I mean at the catastrophe.'

At this, for a minute, their lightness gave way to their gravity; it was as if the long look they exchanged held them together. 'It will only depend on yourself – if you'll watch with me.'

'Are you afraid?' she asked.

'Don't leave me *now*,' he went on.

'Are you afraid?' she repeated.

'Do you think me simply out of my mind?' he pursued instead of answering. 'Do I merely strike you as a harmless lunatic?'

'No,' said May Bartram. 'I understand you. I believe you.'

'You mean you feel how my obsession – poor old thing! – may correspond to some possible reality?'

'To some possible reality.'

'Then you *will* watch with me?'

She hesitated, then for the third time put her question. 'Are you afraid?'

'Did I tell you I was – at Naples?'

'No, you said nothing about it.'

'Then I don't know. And I should *like* to know,' said John Marcher. 'You'll tell me yourself whether you think so. If you'll watch with me you'll see.'

'Very good then.' They had been moving by this time across the room, and at the door, before passing out, they paused as if for the full wind-up of their understanding. 'I'll watch with you,' said May Bartram.

II

THE fact that she 'knew' – knew and yet neither chaffed him nor betrayed him – had in a short time begun to constitute between them a sensible bond, which became more marked when, within the year that followed their afternoon at Weatherend, the opportunities for meeting multiplied. The event that thus promoted these occasions was the death of the ancient lady, her great-aunt, under whose wing, since losing her mother, she had to such an extent found shelter, and who, though but the widowed mother of the new successor to the property, had succeeded – thanks to a high tone and a high temper – in not forfeiting the supreme position at the great house. The deposition of this personage arrived but with her death, which, followed by many changes, made in particular a difference for the young woman in whom Marcher's expert attention had recognised from the first a dependant with a pride that might ache though it didn't bristle. Nothing for a long time had made him easier than the thought that the aching must have been much soothed by Miss Bartram's now finding herself able to set up a small home in London. She had acquired property, to an amount that made that luxury just possible, under her aunt's extremely complicated will, and when the whole matter began to be straightened out, which indeed took time, she let him know that the happy issue was at last in view. He had seen her again before that day, both because she had more than once accompanied the ancient lady to town and because he had paid another visit to the friends who so conveniently made of Weatherend one of the charms of their own hospitality. These friends had taken him back there; he had achieved there again with Miss Bartram some quiet detachment; and he had in London succeeded in persuading her to more than one brief absence from her aunt. They went together, on these latter occasions, to the National Gallery and the South Kensington Museum, where, among vivid reminders, they talked of Italy at large – not now attempting to recover, as at first, the taste of their youth and their ignorance. That recovery, the first day at Weatherend, had

served its purpose well, had given them quite enough; so that
they were, to Marcher's sense, no longer hovering about the
head-waters of their stream, but had felt their boat pushed
sharply off and down the current.

They were literally afloat together; for our gentleman this
was marked, quite as marked as that the fortunate cause of it
was just the buried treasure of her knowledge. He had with his
own hands dug up this little hoard, brought to light – that is to
within reach of the dim day constituted by their discretions and
privacies – the object of value the hiding-place of which he had,
after putting it into the ground himself, so strangely, so long
forgotten. The exquisite luck of having again just stumbled on
the spot made him indifferent to any other question; he would
doubtless have devoted more time to the odd accident of his
lapse of memory if he had not been moved to devote so much to
the sweetness, the comfort, as he felt, for the future, that this
accident itself had helped to keep fresh. It had never entered
into his plan that anyone should 'know', and mainly for the
reason that it was not in him to tell anyone. That would have
been impossible, since nothing but the amusement of a cold
world would have waited on it. Since, however, a mysterious
fate had opened his mouth in youth, in spite of him, he would
count that a compensation and profit by it to the utmost. That
the right person *should* know tempered the asperity of his secret
more even than his shyness had permitted him to imagine; and
May Bartram was clearly right, because – well, because there
she was. Her knowledge simply settled it; he would have been
sure enough by this time had she been wrong. There was that in
his situation, no doubt, that disposed him too much to see her
as a mere confidant, taking all her light for him from the fact –
the fact only – of her interest in his predicament, from her
mercy, sympathy, seriousness, her consent not to regard him
as the funniest of the funny. Aware, in fine, that her price for
him was just in her giving him this constant sense of his being
admirably spared, he was careful to remember that she had,
after all, also a life of her own, with things that might happen to
her, things that in friendship one should likewise take account
of. Something fairly remarkable came to pass with him, for that

matter, in this connection – something represented by a certain passage of his consciousness, in the suddenest way, from one extreme to the other.

He had thought himself, so long as nobody knew, the most disinterested person in the world, carrying his concentrated burden, his perpetual suspense, ever so quietly, holding his tongue about it, giving others no glimpse of it nor of its effect upon his life, asking of them no allowance and only making on his side all those that were asked. He had disturbed nobody with the queerness of having to know a haunted man, though he had had moments of rather special temptation on hearing people say that they were 'unsettled'. If they were as unsettled as he was – he who had never been settled for an hour in his life – they would know what it meant. Yet it wasn't, all the same, for him to make them, and he listened to them civilly enough. This was why he had such good – though possibly such rather colourless – manners; this was why, above all, he could regard himself, in a greedy world, as decently – as, in fact, perhaps even a little sublimely – unselfish. Our point is accordingly that he valued this character quite sufficiently to measure his present danger of letting it lapse, against which he promised himself to be much on his guard. He was quite ready, none the less, to be selfish just a little, since, surely, no more charming occasion for it had come to him. 'Just a little', in a word, was just as much as Miss Bartram, taking one day with another, would let him. He never would be in the least coercive, and he would keep well before him the lines on which consideration for her – the very highest – ought to proceed. He would thoroughly establish the heads under which her affairs, her requirements, her peculiarities – he went so far as to give them the latitude of that name – would come into their intercourse. All this naturally was a sign of how much he took the intercourse itself for granted. There was nothing more to be done about *that*. It simply existed; had sprung into being with her first penetrating question to him in the autumn light there at Weatherend. The real form it should have taken on the basis that stood out large was the form of their marrying. But the devil in this was that the very basis itself put marrying out of the question. His

conviction, his apprehension, his obsession, in short, was not a
condition he could invite a woman to share; and that consequence of it was precisely what was the matter with him.
Something or other lay in wait for him, amid the twists and
the turns of the months and the years, like a crouching beast in
the jungle. It signified little whether the crouching beast were
destined to slay him or to be slain. The definite point was the
inevitable spring of the creature; and the definite lesson from
that was that a man of feeling didn't cause himself to be accompanied by a lady on a tiger-hunt. Such was the image under
which he had ended by figuring his life.

They had at first, none the less, in the scattered hours spent
together, made no allusion to that view of it; which was a sign he
was handsomely ready to give that he didn't expect, that he in
fact didn't care always to be talking about it. Such a feature in
one's outlook was really like a hump on one's back. The difference it made every minute of the day existed quite independently of discussion. One discussed, of course, *like* a hunchback,
for there was always, if nothing else, the hunchback face. That
remained, and she was watching him; but people watched best,
as a general thing, in silence, so that such would be predominantly the manner of their vigil. Yet he didn't want, at the same
time, to be solemn; solemn was what he imagined he too much
tended to be with other people. The thing to be, with the one
person who knew, was easy and natural – to make the reference
rather than be seeming to avoid it, to avoid it rather than be
seeming to make it, and to keep it, in any case, familiar, facetious even, rather than pedantic and portentous. Some such
consideration as the latter was doubtless in his mind, for
instance, when he wrote pleasantly to Miss Bartram that perhaps the great thing he had so long felt as in the lap of the gods
was no more than this circumstance, which touched him so
nearly, of her acquiring a house in London. It was the first
allusion they had yet again made, needing any other hitherto
so little; but when she replied, after having given him the news,
that she was by no means satisfied with such a trifle, as the
climax to so special a suspense, she almost set him wondering if
she hadn't even a larger conception of singularity for him than

he had for himself. He was at all events destined to become aware little by little, as time went by, that she was all the while looking at his life, judging it, measuring it, in the light of the thing she knew, which grew to be at last, with the consecration of the years, never mentioned between them save as 'the real truth' about him. That had always been his own form of reference to it, but she adopted the form so quietly that, looking back at the end of a period, he knew there was no moment at which it was traceable that she had, as he might say, got inside his condition, or exchanged the attitude of beautifully indulging for that of still more beautifully believing him.

It was always open to him to accuse her of seeing him but as the most harmless of maniacs, and this, in the long run – since it covered so much ground – was his easiest description of their friendship. He had a screw loose for her, but she liked him in spite of it, and was practically, against the rest of the world, his kind, wise keeper, unremunerated, but fairly amused and, in the absence of other near ties, not disreputably occupied. The rest of the world of course thought him queer, but she, she only, knew how, and above all why, queer; which was precisely what enabled her to dispose the concealing veil in the right folds. She took his gaiety from him – since it had to pass with them for gaiety – as she took everything else; but she certainly so far justified by her unerring touch his finer sense of the degree to which he had ended by convincing her. *She* at least never spoke of the secret of his life except as 'the real truth about you', and she had in fact a wonderful way of making it seem, as such, the secret of her own life too. That was in fine how he so constantly felt her as allowing for him; he couldn't on the whole call it anything else. He allowed for himself, but she, exactly, allowed still more; partly because, better placed for a sight of the matter, she traced his unhappy perversion through portions of its course into which he could scarce follow it. He knew how he felt, but, besides knowing that, she knew how he *looked* as well; he knew each of the things of importance he was insidiously kept from doing, but she could add up the amount they made, understand how much, with a lighter weight on his spirit, he might have done, and thereby establish how, clever as he was,

he fell short. Above all she was in the secret of the difference
between the forms he went through – those of his little office
under Government, those of caring for his modest patrimony,
for his library, for his garden in the country, for the people in
London whose invitations he accepted and repaid – and the
detachment that reigned beneath them and that made of all
behaviour, all that could in the least be called behaviour, a long
act of dissimulation. What it had come to was that he wore a
mask painted with the social simper, out of the eye-holes of
which there looked eyes of an expression not in the least matching the other features. This the stupid world, even after years,
had never more than half discovered. It was only May Bartram
who had, and she achieved, by an art indescribable, the feat of
at once – or perhaps it was only alternately – meeting the eyes
from in front and mingling her own vision, as from over his
shoulder, with their peep through the apertures.

So, while they grew older together, she did watch with him,
and so she let this association give shape and colour to her own
existence. Beneath *her* forms as well detachment had learned to
sit, and behaviour had become for her, in the social sense, a
false account of herself. There was but one account of her that
would have been true all the while, and that she could give,
directly, to nobody, least of all to John Marcher. Her whole
attitude was a virtual statement, but the perception of that only
seemed destined to take its place for him as one of the many
things necessarily crowded out of his consciousness. If she had,
moreover, like himself, to make sacrifices to their real truth, it
was to be granted that her compensation might have affected
her as more prompt and more natural. They had long periods,
in this London time, during which, when they were together, a
stranger might have listened to them without in the least prick-
ing up his ears; on the other hand, the real truth was equally
liable at any moment to rise to the surface, and the auditor
would then have wondered indeed what they were talking
about. They had from an early time made up their mind that
society was, luckily, unintelligent, and the margin that this gave
them had fairly become one of their commonplaces. Yet there
were still moments when the situation turned almost fresh –

usually under the effect of some expression drawn from herself. Her expressions doubtless repeated themselves, but her intervals were generous. 'What saves us, you know, is that we answer so completely to so usual an appearance: that of the man and woman whose friendship has become such a daily habit, or almost, as to be at last indispensable.' That, for instance, was a remark she had frequently enough had occasion to make, though she had given it at different times different developments. What we are especially concerned with is the turn it happened to take from her one afternoon when he had come to see her in honour of her birthday. This anniversary had fallen on a Sunday, at a season of thick fog and general outward gloom; but he had brought her his customary offering, having known her now long enough to have established a hundred little customs. It was one of his proofs to himself, the present he made her on her birthday, that he had not sunk into real selfishness. It was mostly nothing more than a small trinket, but it was always fine of its kind, and he was regularly careful to pay for it more than he thought he could afford. 'Our habit saves you, at least, don't you see? because it makes you, after all, for the vulgar, indistinguishable from other men. What's the most inveterate mark of men in general? Why, the capacity to spend endless time with dull women – to spend it, I won't say without being bored, but without minding that they are, without being driven off at a tangent by it; which comes to the same thing. I'm your dull woman, a part of the daily bread for which you pray at church. That covers your tracks more than anything.'

'And what covers yours?' asked Marcher, whom his dull woman could mostly to this extent amuse. 'I see of course what you mean by your saving me, in one way and another, so far as other people are concerned – I've seen it all along. Only, what is it that saves *you*? I often think, you know, of that.'

She looked as if she sometimes thought of that too, but in rather a different way. 'Where other people, you mean, are concerned?'

'Well, you're really so in with me, you know – as a sort of result of my being so in with yourself. I mean of my having such an immense regard for you, being so tremendously grateful for all you've done for me. I sometimes ask myself if it's quite fair. Fair I mean to have so involved and – since one may say it – interested you. I almost feel as if you hadn't really had time to do anything else.'

'Anything else but be interested?' she asked. 'Ah, what else does one ever want to be? If I've been "watching" with you, as we long ago agreed that I was to do, watching is always in itself an absorption.'

'Oh, certainly,' John Marcher said, 'if you hadn't had your curiosity—! Only, doesn't it sometimes come to you, as time goes on, that your curiosity is not being particularly repaid?'

May Bartram had a pause. 'Do you ask that, by any chance, because you feel at all that yours isn't? I mean because you have to wait so long.'

Oh, he understood what she meant. 'For the thing to happen that never does happen? For the beast to jump out? No, I'm just where I was about it. It isn't a matter as to which I can *choose*, I can decide for a change. It isn't one as to which there *can* be a change. It's in the lap of the gods. One's in the hands of one's law – there one is. As to the form the law will take, the way it will operate, that's its own affair.'

'Yes,' Miss Bartram replied; 'of course one's fate is coming, of course it *has* come, in its own form and its own way, all the while. Only, you know, the form and the way in your case were to have been – well, something so exceptional and, as one may say, so particularly *your* own.'

Something in this made him look at her with suspicion. 'You say "were to *have* been", as if in your heart you had begun to doubt.'

'Oh!' she vaguely protested.

'As if you believed,' he went on, 'that nothing will now take place.'

She shook her head slowly, but rather inscrutably. 'You're far from my thought.'

He continued to look at her. 'What then is the matter with you?'

'Well,' she said after another wait, 'the matter with me is simply that I'm more sure than ever my curiosity, as you call it, will be but too well repaid.'

They were frankly grave now; he had got up from his seat, had turned once more about the little drawing-room to which, year after year, he brought his inevitable topic; in which he had, as he might have said, tasted their intimate community with every sauce, where every object was as familiar to him as the things of his own house and the very carpets were worn with his fitful walk very much as the desks in old counting-houses are worn by the elbows of generations of clerks. The generations of his nervous moods had been at work there, and the place was the written history of his whole middle life. Under the impression of what his friend had just said he knew himself, for some reason, more aware of these things, which made him, after a moment, stop again before her. 'Is it, possibly, that you've grown afraid?'

'Afraid?' He thought, as she repeated the word, that his question had made her, a little, change colour; so that, lest he should have touched on a truth, he explained very kindly, 'You remember that that was what you asked *me* long ago – that first day at Weatherend.'

'Oh yes, and you told me you didn't know – that I was to see for myself. We've said little about it since, even in so long a time.'

'Precisely,' Marcher interposed – 'quite as if it were too delicate a matter for us to make free with. Quite as if we might find, on pressure, that I *am* afraid. For then,' he said, 'we shouldn't, should we? quite know what to do.'

She had for the time no answer to this question. 'There have been days when I thought you were. Only, of course,' she added, 'there have been days when we have thought almost anything.'

'Everything. Oh!' Marcher softly groaned as with a gasp, half spent, at the face, more uncovered just then than it had been for a long while, of the imagination always with them. It had always had its incalculable moments of glaring out, quite as with the very eyes of the very Beast, and, used as he was to them, they could still draw from him the tribute of a sigh that rose from the depths of his being. All that they had thought, first and last, rolled over him; the past seemed to have been reduced to mere barren speculation. This in fact was what the place had just struck him as so full of – the simplification of everything but the state of suspense. That remained only by seeming to hang in the void surrounding it. Even his original fear, if fear it had been, had lost itself in the desert. 'I judge, however,' he continued, 'that you see I'm not afraid now.'

'What I see is, as I make it out, that you've achieved something almost unprecedented in the way of getting used to danger. Living with it so long and so closely, you've lost your sense of it; you know it's there, but you're indifferent, and you cease even, as of old, to have to whistle in the dark. Considering what the danger is,' May Bartram wound up, 'I'm bound to say that I don't think your attitude could well be surpassed.'

John Marcher faintly smiled. 'It's heroic?'

'Certainly – call it that.'

He considered. 'I *am*, then, a man of courage?'

'That's what you were to show me.'

He still, however, wondered. 'But doesn't the man of courage know what he's afraid of – or *not* afraid of? I don't know *that*, you see. I don't focus it. I can't name it. I only know I'm exposed.'

'Yes, but exposed – how shall I say? – so directly. So intimately. That's surely enough.'

'Enough to make you feel, then – as what we may call the end of our watch – that I'm not afraid?'

'You're not afraid. But it isn't,' she said, 'the end of our watch. That is, it isn't the end of yours. You've everything still to see.'

'Then why haven't you?' he asked. He had had, all along, today, the sense of her keeping something back, and he still had it. As this was his first impression of that, it made a kind of date. The case was the more marked as she didn't at first answer; which in turn made him go on. 'You know something I don't.' Then his voice, for that of a man of courage, trembled a little. 'You know what's to happen.' Her silence, with the face she showed, was almost a confession – it made him sure. 'You know, and you're afraid to tell me. It's so bad that you're afraid I'll find out.'

All this might be true, for she did look as if, unexpectedly to her, he had crossed some mystic line that she had secretly drawn round her. Yet she might, after all, not have worried; and the real upshot was that he himself, at all events, needn't. 'You'll never find out.'

III

IT was all to have made, none the less, as I have said, a date; as came out in the fact that again and again, even after long intervals, other things that passed between them wore, in relation to this hour, but the character of recalls and results. Its immediate effect had been indeed rather to lighten insistence – almost to provoke a reaction; as if their topic had dropped by its own weight and as if moreover, for that matter, Marcher had been visited by one of his occasional warnings against egotism. He had kept up, he felt, and very decently on the whole, his consciousness of the importance of not being selfish, and it was true that he had never sinned in that direction without promptly enough trying to press the scales the other way. He often repaired his fault, the season permitting, by inviting his friend to accompany him to the opera; and it not infrequently thus happened that, to show he didn't wish her to have but one sort of food for her mind, he was the cause of her appearing there with him a dozen nights in the month. It even happened that, seeing her home at such times, he occasionally went in with her to finish, as he called it, the evening, and, the better to make his point, sat down to the frugal but always careful little supper that awaited his pleasure. His point was made, he thought, by his not eternally insisting with her on himself; made for instance, at such hours, when it befell that, her piano at hand and each of them familiar with it, they went over passages of the opera together. It chanced to be on one of these occasions, however, that he reminded her of her not having answered a certain question he had put to her during the talk that had taken place between them on her last birthday. 'What is it that saves *you*?' – saved her, he meant, from that appearance of variation from the usual human type. If he had practically escaped remark, as she pretended, by doing, in the most important particular, what most men do – find the answer to life in patching up an alliance of a sort with a woman no better than himself – how had she escaped it, and how could the alliance, such as it was, since they must suppose it had been more or less noticed, have failed to make her rather positively talked about?

'I never said,' May Bartram replied, 'that it hadn't made me talked about.'

'Ah well then, you're not "saved".'

'It has not been a question for me. If you've had your woman, I've had,' she said, 'my man.'

'And you mean that makes you all right?'

She hesitated. 'I don't know why it shouldn't make me – humanly, which is what we're speaking of – as right as it makes you.'

'I see,' Marcher returned. ' "Humanly", no doubt, as showing that you're living for something. Not, that is, just for me and my secret.'

May Bartram smiled. 'I don't pretend it exactly shows that I'm not living for you. It's my intimacy with you that's in question.'

He laughed as he saw what she meant. 'Yes, but since, as you say, I'm only, so far as people make out, ordinary, you're – aren't you? – no more than ordinary either. You help me to pass for a man like another. So if I *am*, as I understand you, you're not compromised. Is that it?'

She had another hesitation, but she spoke clearly enough. 'That's it. It's all that concerns me – to help you to pass for a man like another.'

He was careful to acknowledge the remark handsomely. 'How kind, how beautiful, you are to me! How shall I ever repay you?'

She had her last grave pause, as if there might be a choice of ways. But she chose. 'By going on as you are.'

It was into this going on as he was that they relapsed, and really for so long a time that the day inevitably came for a further sounding of their depths. It was as if these depths, constantly bridged over by a structure that was firm enough in spite of its lightness and of its occasional oscillation in the somewhat vertiginous air, invited on occasion, in the interest of their nerves, a dropping of the plummet and a measurement of the abyss. A difference had been made moreover, once for all, by the fact that she had, all the while, not appeared to feel the need of rebutting his charge of an idea within her that she didn't dare to express, uttered just before one of the fullest of their later discussions ended. It had come up for him then that she 'knew' something and that what she knew was bad – too bad to tell him. When he had spoken of it as visibly so bad that she was afraid he might find it out, her reply had left the matter too equivocal to be let alone and yet, for Marcher's special sensibility, almost too formidable again to touch. He circled about it at a distance that alternately narrowed and widened and that yet was not much affected by the consciousness in him that there was nothing she could 'know', after all, any better than he did. She had no source of knowledge that he hadn't equally – except of course that she might have finer nerves. That was what women had where they were interested; they made out things, where people were concerned, that the people often couldn't have made out for themselves. Their nerves, their sensibility, their imagination, were conductors and revealers, and the beauty of May Bartram was in particular that she had given herself so to his case. He felt in these days what, oddly enough, he had never felt before, the growth of a dread of losing her by some catastrophe – some catastrophe that yet wouldn't at all be *the* catastrophe: partly because she had, almost of a sudden, begun to strike him as useful to him as never yet, and partly by reason of an appearance of uncertainty in her health, coincident and equally new. It was characteristic of the inner detachment he had hitherto so successfully cultivated and to which our whole account of him is a reference, it was characteristic that his complications, such as they were, had never yet seemed so as at this crisis to thicken about him, even to the point of making him ask himself if he were, by any chance, of a truth, within sight or sound, within touch or reach, within the immediate jurisdiction of the thing that waited.

When the day came, as come it had to, that his friend confessed to him her fear of a deep disorder in her blood, he felt somehow the shadow of a change and the chill of a shock. He immediately began to imagine aggravations and disasters, and above all to think of her peril as the direct menace for himself of personal privation. This indeed gave him one of those partial recoveries of equanimity that were agreeable to him – it showed him that what was still first in his mind was the loss she herself might suffer. 'What if she should have to die before knowing, before seeing—?' It would have been brutal, in the early stages of her trouble, to put that question to her; but it had immediately sounded for him to his own concern, and the possibility was what most made him sorry for her. If she did 'know', moreover, in the sense of her having had some – what should he think? – mystical, irresistible light, this would make the matter not better, but worse, inasmuch as her original adoption of his own curiosity had quite become the basis of her life. She had been living to see what would *be* to be seen, and it would be cruel to her to have to give up before the accomplishment of the vision. These reflections, as I say, refreshed his generosity; yet, make them as he might, he saw himself, with the lapse of the period, more and more disconcerted. It lapsed for him with a strange, steady sweep, and the oddest oddity was that it gave him, independently of the threat of much inconvenience, almost the only positive surprise his career, if career it could be called, had yet offered him. She kept the house as she had never done; he had to go to her to see her – she could meet him nowhere now, though there was scarce a corner of their loved old London in which she had not in the past, at one time or another, done so; and he found her always seated by her fire in the deep, old-fashioned chair she was less and less able to leave. He had been struck one day, after an absence exceeding his usual measure, with her suddenly looking much older to him than he had ever thought of her being; then he recognised that the suddenness was all on his side – he had just been suddenly struck. She looked older because inevitably, after so many years, she *was* old, or almost; which was of course true in still greater measure of her companion. If she was old, or almost, John Marcher assuredly was, and yet it was her showing of the lesson, not his own, that brought the truth home to him. His surprises began here; when once they had begun they multiplied; they came rather with a rush: it was as if, in the oddest way in the world, they had all been kept back, sown in a thick cluster, for the late afternoon of life, the time at which, for people in general, the unexpected has died out.

One of them was that he should have caught himself – for he *had* so done – *really* wondering if the great accident would take form now as nothing more than his being condemned to see this charming woman, this admirable friend, pass away from him. He had never so unreservedly qualified her as while confronted in thought with such a possibility; in spite of which there was small doubt for him that as an answer to his long riddle the mere effacement of even so fine a feature of his situation would be an abject anticlimax. It would represent, as connected with his past attitude, a drop of dignity under the shadow of which his existence could only become the most grotesque of failures. He had been far from holding it a failure – long as he had waited for the appearance that was to make it a success. He had waited for a quite other thing, not for such a one as that. The breath of his good faith came short, however, as he recognised how long he had waited, or how long, at least, his companion had. That she, at all events, might be recorded as having waited in vain – this affected him sharply, and all the more because of his at first having done little more than amuse himself with the idea. It grew more grave as the gravity of her condition grew, and the state of mind it produced in him, which he ended by watching, himself, as if it had been some definite disfigurement of his outer person, may pass for another of his surprises. This conjoined itself still with another, the really stupefying consciousness of a question that he would have allowed to shape itself had he dared. What did everything mean – what, that is, did *she* mean, she and her vain waiting and her probable death and the soundless admonition of it all –

unless that, at this time of day, it was simply, it was overwhelmingly too late? He had never, at any stage of his queer consciousness, admitted the whisper of such a correction; he had never, till within these last few months, been so false to his conviction as not to hold that what was to come to him had time, whether *he* struck himself as having it or not. That at last, at last, he certainly hadn't it, to speak of, or had it but in the scantiest measure – such, soon enough, as things went with him, became the inference with which his old obsession had to reckon: and this it was not helped to do by the more and more confirmed appearance that the great vagueness casting the long shadow in which he had lived had, to attest itself, almost no margin left. Since it was in Time that he was to have met his fate, so it was in Time that his fate was to have acted; and as he waked up to the sense of no longer being young, which was exactly the sense of being stale, just as that, in turn, was the sense of being weak, he waked up to another matter beside. It all hung together; they were subject, he and the great vagueness, to an equal and indivisible law. When the possibilities themselves had, accordingly, turned stale, when the secret of the gods had grown faint, had perhaps even quite evaporated, that, and that only, was failure. It wouldn't have been failure to be bankrupt, dishonoured, pilloried, hanged; it was failure not to be anything. And so, in the dark valley into which his path had taken its unlooked-for twist, he wondered not a little as he groped. He didn't care what awful crash might overtake him, with what ignominy or what monstrosity he might yet be associated – since he wasn't, after all, too utterly old to suffer – if it would only be decently proportionate to the posture he had kept, all his life, in the promised presence of it. He had but one desire left – that he shouldn't have been 'sold'.

IV

THEN it was that one afternoon, while the spring of the year was young and new, she met, all in her own way, his frankest betrayal of these alarms. He had gone in late to see her, but evening had not settled, and she was presented to him in that long, fresh light of waning April days which affects us often with a sadness sharper than the greyest hours of autumn. The week had been warm, the spring was supposed to have begun early, and May Bartram sat, for the first time in the year, without a fire, a fact that, to Marcher's sense, gave the scene of which she formed part a smooth and ultimate look, an air of knowing, in its immaculate order and its cold, meaningless cheer, that it would never see a fire again. Her own aspect – he could scarce have said why – intensified this note. Almost as white as wax, with the marks and signs in her face as numerous and as fine as if they had been etched by a needle, with soft white draperies relieved by a faded green scarf, the delicate tone of which had been consecrated by the years, she was the picture of a serene, exquisite, but impenetrable sphinx, whose head, or indeed all whose person, might have been powdered with silver. She was a sphinx, yet with her white petals and green fronds she might have been a lily too – only an artificial lily, wonderfully imitated and constantly kept, without dust or stain, though not exempt from a slight droop and a complexity of faint creases, under some clear glass bell. The perfection of household care, of high polish and finish, always reigned in her rooms, but they especially looked to Marcher at present as if everything had been wound up, tucked in, put away, so that she might sit with folded hands and with nothing more to do. She was 'out of it', to his vision; her work was over; she communicated with him as across some gulf, or from some island of rest that she had already reached, and it made him feel strangely abandoned. Was it – or, rather, wasn't it – that if for so long she had been watching with him the answer to their question had swum into her ken and taken on its name, so that her occupation was verily gone? He had as much as charged her with this in saying to her, many months before, that she even then knew something she was keeping from him. It was a point he had never since ventured to press, vaguely fearing, as he did, that it might become a difference, perhaps a disagreement, between them. He had in short, in this later time, turned nervous, which was what, in all the other years, he had never been; and the oddity was that his nervousness should have waited till he had begun to doubt, should have held off so long as he was sure. There was something, it seemed to him, that the wrong word would bring down on his head, something that would so at least put an end to his suspense. But he wanted not to speak the wrong word; that would make everything ugly. He wanted the knowledge he lacked to drop on him, if drop it could, by its own august weight. If she was to forsake him it was surely for her to take leave. This was why he didn't ask her again, directly, what she knew; but it was also why, approaching the matter from another side, he said to her in the course of his visit: 'What do you regard as the very worst that, at this time of day, *can* happen to me?'

He had asked her that in the past often enough; they had, with the odd, irregular rhythm of their intensities and avoidances, exchanged ideas about it and then had seen the ideas washed away by cool intervals, washed like figures traced in sea-sand. It had ever been the mark of their talk that the oldest allusions in it required but a little dismissal and reaction to come out again, sounding for the hour as new. She could thus at present meet his inquiry quite freshly and patiently. 'Oh yes, I've repeatedly thought, only it always seemed to me of old that I couldn't quite make up my mind. I thought of dreadful things, between which it was difficult to choose; and so must you have done.'

'Rather! I feel now as if I had scarce done anything else. I appear to myself to have spent my life in thinking of nothing *but* dreadful things. A great many of them I've at different times named to you, but there were others I couldn't name.'

'They were too, too dreadful?'

'Too, too dreadful – some of them.'

She looked at him a minute, and there came to him as he met it an inconsequent sense that her eyes, when one got their full clearness, were still as beautiful as they had been in youth, only beautiful with a strange, cold light – a light that somehow was a part of the effect, if it wasn't rather a part of the cause, of the pale, hard sweetness of the season and the hour. 'And yet,' she said at last, 'there are horrors we have mentioned.'

It deepened the strangeness to see her, as such a figure in such a picture, talk of 'horrors', but she was to do, in a few minutes, something stranger yet – though even of this he was to take the full measure but afterwards – and the note of it was already in the air. It was, for the matter of that, one of the signs that her eyes were having again such a high flicker of their prime. He had to admit, however, what she said. 'Oh yes, there were times when we did go far.' He caught himself in the act of speaking as if it all were over. Well, he wished it were; and the consummation depended, for him, clearly, more and more on his companion.

But she had now a soft smile. 'Oh, far—!'

It was oddly ironic. 'Do you mean you're prepared to go further?'

She was frail and ancient and charming as she continued to look at him, yet it was rather as if she had lost the thread. 'Do you consider that we went so far?'

'Why, I thought it the point you were just making – that we *had* looked most things in the face.'

'Including each other?' She still smiled. 'But you're quite right. We've had together great imaginations, often great fears; but some of them have been unspoken.'

'Then the worst – we haven't faced that. I *could* face it, I believe, if I knew what you think it. I feel,' he explained, 'as if I had lost my power to conceive such things.' And he wondered if he looked as blank as he sounded. 'It's spent.'

'Then why do you assume,' she asked, 'that mine isn't?'

'Because you've given me signs to the contrary. It isn't a question for you of conceiving, imagining, comparing. It isn't a question now of choosing.' At last he came out with it. 'You know something that I don't. You've shown me that before.'

These last words affected her, he could see in a moment, remarkably, and she spoke with firmness. 'I've shown you, my dear, nothing.'

He shook his head. 'You can't hide it.'

'Oh, oh!' May Bartram murmured over what she couldn't hide. It was almost a smothered groan.

'You admitted it months ago, when I spoke of it to you as of something you were afraid I would find out. Your answer was that I couldn't, that I wouldn't, and I don't pretend I have. But you had something therefore in mind, and I see now that it must have been, that it still is, the possibility that, of all possibilities, has settled itself for you as the worst. This,' he went on, 'is why I appeal to you. I'm only afraid of ignorance now – I'm not afraid of knowledge.' And then as for a while she said nothing: 'What makes me sure is that I see in your face and feel here, in this air and amid these appearances, that you're out of it. You've done. You've had your experience. You leave me to my fate.'

Well, she listened, motionless and white in her chair, as if she had in fact a decision to make, so that her whole manner was a virtual confession, though still with a small, fine, inner stiffness, an imperfect surrender. 'It *would* be the worst,' she finally let herself say. 'I mean the thing that I've never said.'

It hushed him a moment. 'More monstrous than all the monstrosities we've named?'

'More monstrous. Isn't that what you sufficiently express,' she asked, 'in calling it the worst?'

Marcher thought. 'Assuredly – if you mean, as I do, something that includes all the loss and all the shame that are thinkable.'

'It would if it *should* happen,' said May Bartram. 'What we're speaking of, remember, is only my idea.'

'It's your belief,' Marcher returned. 'That's enough for me. I feel your beliefs are right. Therefore if, having this one, you give me no more light on it, you abandon me.'

'No, no!' she repeated. 'I'm with you – don't you see? – still.' And as if to make it more vivid to him she rose from her chair – a movement she seldom made in these days – and showed herself, all draped and all soft, in her fairness and slimness. 'I haven't forsaken you.'

It was really, in its effort against weakness, a generous assurance, and had the success of the impulse not, happily, been great, it would have touched him to pain more than to pleasure. But the cold charm in her eyes had spread, as she hovered before him, to all the rest of her person, so that it was, for the minute, almost like a recovery of youth. He couldn't pity her for that; he could only take her as she showed – as capable still of helping him. It was as if, at the same time, her light might at any instant go out; wherefore he must make the most of it. There passed before him with intensity the three or four things he wanted most to know; but the question that came of itself to his lips really covered the others. 'Then tell me if I shall consciously suffer.'

She promptly shook her head. 'Never!'

It confirmed the authority he imputed to her, and it produced on him an extraordinary effect. 'Well, what's better than that? Do you call that the worst?'

'You think nothing is better?' she asked.

She seemed to mean something so special that he again sharply wondered, though still with the dawn of a prospect of relief. 'Why not, if one doesn't *know*?' After which, as their eyes, over his question, met in a silence, the dawn deepened and something to his purpose came, prodigiously, out of her very face. His own, as he took it in, suddenly flushed to the forehead, and he gasped with the force of a perception to which, on the instant, everything fitted. The sound of his gasp filled the air; then he became articulate. 'I see – if I don't suffer!'

In her own look, however, was doubt. 'You see what?'

'Why, what you mean – what you've always meant.'

She again shook her head. 'What I mean isn't what I've always meant. It's different.'

'It's something new?'

She hesitated. 'Something new. It's not what you think. I see what you think.'

His divination drew breath then; only her correction might be wrong. 'It isn't that I *am* a donkey?' he asked between faintness and grimness. 'It isn't that it's all a mistake?'

'A mistake?' she pityingly echoed. *That* possibility, for her, he saw, would be monstrous; and if she guaranteed him the immunity from pain it would accordingly not be what she had in mind. 'Oh, no,' she declared; 'it's nothing of that sort. You've been right.'

Yet he couldn't help asking himself if she weren't, thus pressed, speaking but to save him. It seemed to him he should be most lost if his history should prove all a platitude. 'Are you telling me the truth, so that I sha'n't have been a bigger idiot than I can bear to know? I *haven't* lived with a vain imagination, in the most besotted illusion? I haven't waited but to see the door shut in my face?'

She shook her head again. 'However the case stands *that* isn't the truth. Whatever the reality, it *is* a reality. The door isn't shut. The door's open,' said May Bartram.

'Then something's to come?'

She waited once again, always with her cold, sweet eyes on him. 'It's never too late.' She had, with her gliding step, diminished the distance between them, and she stood nearer to him, close to him, a minute, as if still full of the unspoken. Her movement might have been for some finer emphasis of what she was at once hesitating and deciding to say. He had been standing by the chimney-piece, fireless and sparely adorned, a small, perfect old French clock and two morsels of rosy Dresden constituting all its furniture; and her hand grasped the shelf while she kept him waiting, grasped it a little as for support and encouragement. She only kept him waiting, however; that is he only waited. It had become suddenly, from her movement and attitude, beautiful and vivid to him that she had something more to give him; her wasted face delicately shone with it, and it glittered, almost as with the white lustre of silver, in her expression. She was right, incontestably, for what he saw in her face was the truth, and strangely, without consequence, while their talk of it as dreadful was still in the air, she appeared to present it as inordinately soft. This, prompting bewilderment, made him but gape the more gratefully for her revelation, so that they continued for some minutes silent, her face shining at him, her contact imponderably pressing, and his stare all kind, but all expectant. The end, none the less, was that what he had expected failed to sound. Something else took place instead, which seemed to consist at first in the mere closing of her eyes. She gave way at the same instant to a slow, fine shudder, and though he remained staring – though he stared, in fact, but the harder – she turned off and regained her chair. It was the end of what she had been intending, but it left him thinking only of that.

'Well, you don't say—?'

She had touched in her passage a bell near the chimney and had sunk back, strangely pale. 'I'm afraid I'm too ill.'

'Too ill to tell me?' It sprang up sharp to him, and almost to his lips, the fear that she would die without giving him light. He checked himself in time from so expressing his question, but she answered as if she had heard the words.

'Don't you know – now?'

' "Now"—?' She had spoken as if something that had made a difference had come up within the moment. But her maid, quickly obedient to her bell, was already with them. 'I know nothing.' And he was afterwards to say to himself that he must have spoken with odious impatience, such an impatience as to show that, supremely disconcerted, he washed his hands of the whole question.

'Oh!' said May Bartram.

'Are you in pain?' he asked, as the woman went to her.

'No,' said May Bartram.

Her maid, who had put an arm round her as if to take her to her room, fixed on him eyes that appealingly contradicted her; in spite of which, however, he showed once more his mystification. 'What then has happened?'

She was once more, with her companion's help, on her feet, and, feeling withdrawal imposed on him, he had found, blankly, his hat and gloves and had reached the door. Yet he waited for her answer. 'What *was* to,' she said.

V

HE came back the next day, but she was then unable to see him, and as it was literally the first time this had occurred in the long stretch of their acquaintance he turned away, defeated and sore, almost angry – or feeling at least that such a break in their custom was really the beginning of the end – and wandered alone with his thoughts, especially with one of them that he was unable to keep down. She was dying, and he would lose her; she was dying, and his life would end. He stopped in the park, into which he had passed, and stared before him at his recurrent doubt. Away from her the doubt pressed again; in her presence he had believed her, but as he felt his forlornness he threw himself into the explanation that, nearest at hand, had most of a miserable warmth for him and least of a cold torment. She had deceived him to save him – to put him off with something in which he should be able to rest. What could the thing that was to happen to him be, after all, but just this thing that had begun to happen? Her dying, her death, his consequent solitude – *that* was what he had figured as the beast in the jungle, that was what had been in the lap of the gods. He had had her word for it as he left her; for what else, on earth, could she have meant? It wasn't a thing of a monstrous order; not a fate rare and distinguished; not a stroke of fortune that overwhelmed and immortalised; it had only the stamp of the common doom. But poor Marcher, at this hour, judged the common doom sufficient. It would serve his turn, and even as the consummation of infinite waiting he would bend his pride to accept it. He sat down on a bench in the twilight. He hadn't been a fool. Something had *been*, as she had said, to come. Before he rose indeed it had quite struck him that the final fact really matched with the long avenue through which he had had to reach it. As sharing his suspense, and as giving herself all, giving her life, to bring it to an end, she had come with him every step of the way. He had lived by her aid, and to leave her behind would be cruelly, damnably to miss her. What could be more overwhelming than that?

Well, he was to know within the week, for though she kept him a while at bay, left him restless and wretched during a series of days on each of which he asked about her only again to have to turn away, she ended his trial by receiving him where she had always received him. Yet she had been brought out at some hazard into the presence of so many of the things that were, consciously, vainly, half their past, and there was scant service left in the gentleness of her mere desire, all too visible, to check his obsession and wind up his long trouble. That was clearly what she wanted; the one thing more, for her own peace, while she could still put out her hand. He was so affected by her state that, once seated by her chair, he was moved to let everything go; it was she herself therefore who brought him back, took up again, before she dismissed him, her last word of the other time. She showed how she wished to leave their affair in order. 'I'm not sure you understood. You've nothing to wait for more. It *has* come.'

Oh, how he looked at her! 'Really?'

'Really.'

'The thing that, as you said, *was* to?'

'The thing that we began in our youth to watch for.'

Face to face with her once more he believed her; it was a claim to which he had so abjectly little to oppose. 'You mean that it has come as a positive, definite occurrence, with a name and a date?'

'Positive. Definite. I don't know about the "name", but, oh, with a date!'

He found himself again too helplessly at sea. 'But come in the night – come and passed me by?'

May Bartram had her strange, faint smile. 'Oh no, it hasn't passed you by!'

'But if I haven't been aware of it, and it hasn't touched me—?'

'Ah, your not being aware of it,' and she seemed to hesitate an instant to deal with this – 'your not being aware of it is the strangeness *in* the strangeness. It's the wonder *of* the wonder.' She spoke as with the softness almost of a sick child, yet now at last, at the end of all, with the perfect straightness of a sibyl. She visibly knew that she knew, and the effect on him was of something co-ordinate, in its high character, with the law that had ruled him. It was the true voice of the law; so on her lips would the law itself have sounded. 'It *has* touched you,' she went on. 'It has done its office. It has made you all its own.'

'So utterly without my knowing it?'

'So utterly without your knowing it.' His hand, as he leaned to her, was on the arm of her chair, and, dimly smiling always now, she placed her own on it. 'It's enough if *I* know it.'

'Oh!' he confusedly sounded, as she herself of late so often had done.

'What I long ago said is true. You'll never know now, and I think you ought to be content. You've *had* it,' said May Bartram.

'But had what?'

'Why, what was to have marked you out. The proof of your law. It has acted. I'm too glad,' she then bravely added, 'to have been able to see what it's *not*.'

He continued to attach his eyes to her, and with the sense that it was all beyond him, and that *she* was too, he would still have sharply challenged her, had he not felt it an abuse of her weakness to do more than take devoutly what she gave him, take it as hushed as to a revelation. If he did speak, it was out of the foreknowledge of his loneliness to come. 'If you're glad of what it's "not", it might then have been worse?'

She turned her eyes away, she looked straight before her with which, after a moment: 'Well, you know our fears.'

He wondered. 'It's something then we never feared?'

On this, slowly, she turned to him. 'Did we ever dream, with all our dreams, that we should sit and talk of it thus?'

He tried for a little to make out if they had; but it was as if their dreams, numberless enough, were in solution in some thick, cold mist, in which thought lost itself. 'It might have been that we couldn't talk?'

'Well' – she did her best for him – 'not from this side. This, you see,' she said, 'is the *other* side.'

'I think,' poor Marcher returned, 'that all sides are the same to me.' Then, however, as she softly shook her head in correction: 'We mightn't, as it were, have got across—?'

'To where we are – no. We're *here*' – she made her weak emphasis.

'And much good does it do us!' was her friend's frank comment.

'It does us the good it can. It does us the good that *it* isn't here. It's past. It's behind,' said May Bartram. 'Before—' but her voice dropped.

He had got up, not to tire her, but it was hard to combat his yearning. She after all told him nothing but that his light had failed – which he knew well enough without her. 'Before—?' he blankly echoed.

'Before, you see, it was always to *come*. That kept it present.'

'Oh, I don't care what comes now! Besides,' Marcher added, 'it seems to me I liked it better present, as you say, than I can like it absent with *your* absence.'

'Oh, mine!' – and her pale hands made light of it.

'With the absence of everything.' He had a dreadful sense of standing there before her for – so far as anything but this proved, this bottomless drop was concerned – the last time of their life. It rested on him with a weight he felt he could scarce bear, and this weight it apparently was that still pressed out what remained in him of speakable protest. 'I believe you; but I can't begin to pretend I understand. *Nothing*, for me, is past; nothing *will* pass until I pass myself, which I pray my stars may be as soon as possible. Say, however,' he added, 'that I've eaten my cake, as you contend, to the last crumb – how can the thing I've never felt at all be the thing I was marked out to feel?'

She met him, perhaps, less directly, but she met him unperturbed. 'You take your "feelings" for granted. You were to suffer your fate. That was not necessarily to know it.'

'How in the world – when what is such knowledge but suffering?'

She looked up at him a while, in silence. 'No – you don't understand.'

'I suffer,' said John Marcher.

'Don't, don't!'

'How can I help at least *that*?'

'*Don't!*' May Bartram repeated.

She spoke it in a tone so special, in spite of her weakness, that he stared an instant – stared as if some light, hitherto hidden, had shimmered across his vision. Darkness again closed over it, but the gleam had already become for him an idea. 'Because I haven't the right—?'

'Don't *know* – when you needn't,' she mercifully urged. 'You needn't – for we shouldn't.'

'Shouldn't?' If he could but know what she meant!

'No – it's too much.'

'Too much?' he still asked – but with a mystification that was the next moment, of a sudden, to give way. Her words, if they meant something, affected him in this light – the light also of her wasted face – as meaning *all*, and the sense of what knowledge had been for herself came over him with a rush which broke through into a question. 'Is it of that, then, you're dying?'

She but watched him, gravely at first, as if to see, with this, where he was, and she might have seen something, or feared something, that moved her sympathy. 'I would live for you still – if I could.' Her eyes closed for a little, as if, withdrawn into herself, she were, for a last time, trying. 'But I can't!' she said as she raised them again to take leave of him.

She couldn't indeed, as but too promptly and sharply appeared, and he had no vision of her after this that was anything but darkness and doom. They had parted forever in that strange talk; access to her chamber of pain, rigidly guarded, was almost wholly forbidden him; he was feeling now moreover, in the face of doctors, nurses, the two or three relatives attracted doubtless by the presumption of what she had to 'leave', how few were the rights, as they were called in such cases, that he had to put forward, and how odd it might even seem that their intimacy shouldn't have given him more of them. The stupidest fourth cousin had more, even though she had been nothing in such a person's life. She had been a feature of features in *his*, for what else was it to have been so indispensable? Strange beyond saying were the ways of existence, baffling for him the anomaly of his lack, as he felt it to be, of producible claim. A woman might have been, as it were, everything to him, and it might yet present him in no connection that anyone appeared obliged to recognise. If this was the case in these closing weeks it was the case more sharply on the occasion of the last offices rendered, in the great grey London cemetery, to what had been mortal, to what had been precious, in his friend. The concourse at her grave was not numerous, but he saw himself treated as scarce more nearly concerned with it than if there had been a thousand others. He was in short from this moment face to face with the fact that he was to profit extraordinarily little by the interest May Bartram had taken in him. He couldn't quite have said what he expected, but he had somehow not expected this approach to a double privation. Not only had her interest failed him, but he seemed to feel himself unattended – and for a reason he couldn't sound – by the distinction, the dignity, the propriety, if nothing else, of the man markedly bereaved. It was as if, in the view of society, he had not *been* markedly bereaved, as if there still failed some sign or proof of it, and as if, none the less, his character could never be affirmed, nor the deficiency ever made up. There were moments, as the weeks went by, when he would have liked, by some almost aggressive act, to take his stand on the intimacy of his loss, in order that it *might* be questioned and his retort, to the relief of his spirit, so recorded; but the moments of an irritation more helpless followed fast on these, the moments during which, turning things over with a good conscience but with a bare horizon, he found himself wondering if he oughtn't to have begun, so to speak, further back.

He found himself wondering indeed at many things, and this last speculation had others to keep it company. What could he have done, after all, in her lifetime, without giving them both, as it were, away? He couldn't have made it known she was watching him, for that would have published the superstition of the Beast. This was what closed his mouth now – now that the Jungle had been threshed to vacancy and that the Beast had stolen away. It sounded too foolish and too flat; the difference for him in this particular, the extinction in his life of the element of suspense, was such in fact as to surprise him. He could scarce have said what the effect resembled; the abrupt cessation, the positive prohibition, of music perhaps, more than anything else, in some place all adjusted and all accustomed to sonority and to attention. If he could at any rate have conceived lifting the veil from his image at some moment of the past (what had he done, after all, if not lift it to *her?*), so to do this to-day, to talk to people at large of the jungle cleared and confide to them that he now felt it as safe, would have been not only to see them listen as to a good-wife's tale, but really to hear himself tell one.

What it presently came to in truth was that poor Marcher waded through his beaten grass, where no life stirred, where no breath sounded, where no evil eye seemed to gleam from a possible lair, very much as if vaguely looking for the Beast, and still more as if missing it. He walked about in an existence that had grown strangely more spacious, and, stopping fitfully in places where the undergrowth of life struck him as closer, asked himself yearningly, wondered secretly, and sorely, if it would have lurked here or there. It would have at all events *sprung*; what was at least complete was his belief in the truth itself of the assurance given him. The change from his old sense to his new was absolute and final: what was to happen *had* so absolutely and finally happened that he was as little able to know a fear for his future as to know a hope; so absent in short was any question of anything still to come. He was to live entirely with the other question, that of his unidentified past, that of his having to see his fortune impenetrably muffled and masked.

The torment of this vision became then his occupation; he couldn't perhaps have consented to live but for the possibility of guessing. She had told him, his friend, not to guess; she had forbidden him, so far as he might, to know, and she had even in a sort denied the power in him to learn: which were so many things, precisely, to deprive him of rest. It wasn't that he wanted, he argued for fairness, that anything that had happened to him should happen over again; it was only that he shouldn't, as an anticlimax, have been taken sleeping so sound as not to be able to win back by an effort of thought the lost stuff of consciousness. He declared to himself at moments that he would either win it back or have done with consciousness for ever; he made this idea his one motive, in fine, made it so much his passion that none other, to compare with it, seemed ever to have touched him. The lost stuff of consciousness became thus for him as a strayed or stolen child to an unappeasable father; he hunted it up and down very much as if he were knocking at doors and inquiring of the police. This was the spirit in which, inevitably, he set himself to travel; he started on a journey that was to be as long as he could make it; it danced before him that, as the other side of the globe couldn't possibly have less to say to him, it might, by a possibility of suggestion, have more. Before he quitted London, however, he made a pilgrimage to May Bartram's grave, took his way to it through the endless avenues of the grim suburban necropolis, sought it out in the wilderness of tombs, and, though he had come but for the renewal of the act of farewell, found himself, when he had at last stood by it, beguiled into long intensities. He stood for an hour, powerless to turn away and yet powerless to penetrate the darkness of death; fixing with his eyes her inscribed name and date, beating his forehead against the fact of the secret they kept, drawing his breath, while he waited as if, in pity of him, some sense would rise from the stones. He kneeled on the stones, however, in vain; they kept what they concealed; and if the face of the tomb did become a face for him it was because her two names were like a pair of eyes that didn't know him. He gave them a last long look, but no palest light broke.

VI

HE stayed away, after this, for a year; he visited the depths of Asia, spending himself on scenes of romantic interest, of superlative sanctity; but what was present to him everywhere was that for a man who had known what *he* had known the world was vulgar and vain. The state of mind in which he had lived for so many years shone out to him, in reflection, as a light that coloured and refined, a light beside which the glow of the East was garish, cheap and thin. The terrible truth was that he had lost – with everything else – a distinction as well; the things he saw couldn't help being common when he had become common to look at them. He was simply now one of them himself – he was in the dust, without a peg for the sense of difference; and there were hours when, before the temples of gods and the sepulchres of kings, his spirit turned, for nobleness of association, to the barely discriminated slab in the London suburb. That had become for him, and more intensely with time and distance, his one witness of a past glory. It was all that was left to him for proof or pride, yet the past glories of Pharaohs were nothing to him as he thought of it. Small wonder then that he came back to it on the morrow of his return. He was drawn there this time as irresistibly as the other, yet with a confidence, almost, that was doubtless the effect of the many months that had elapsed. He had lived, in spite of himself, into his change of feeling, and in wandering over the earth had wandered, as might be said, from the circumference to the centre of his desert. He had settled to his safety and accepted perforce his extinction; figuring to himself, with some colour, in the likeness of certain little old men he remembered to have seen, of whom, all meagre and wizened as they might look, it was related that they had in their time fought twenty duels or been loved by ten princesses. They indeed had been wondrous for others, while he was but wondrous for himself; which, however, was exactly the cause of his haste to renew the wonder by getting back, as he might put it, into his own presence. That had quickened his steps and checked his delay. If his visit was prompt it was because he had been separated so long from the part of himself that alone he now valued.

It is accordingly not false to say that he reached his goal with a certain elation and stood there again with a certain assurance. The creature beneath the sod *knew* of his rare experience, so that, strangely now, the place had lost for him its mere blankness of expression. It met him in mildness – not, as before, in mockery; it wore for him the air of conscious greeting that we find, after absence, in things that have closely belonged to us and which seem to confess of themselves to the connection. The plot of ground, the graven tablet, the tended flowers affected him so as belonging to him that he quite felt for the hour like a contented landlord reviewing a piece of property. Whatever had happened – well, had happened. He had not come back this time with the vanity of that question, his former worrying, 'What, *what*?' now practically so spent. Yet he would, none the less, never again so cut himself off from the spot; he would come back to it every month, for if he did nothing else by its aid he at least held up his head. It thus grew for him, in the oddest way, a positive resource; he carried out his idea of periodical returns, which took their place at last among the most inveterate of his habits. What it all amounted to, oddly

enough, was that, in his now so simplified world, this garden of
death gave him the few square feet of earth on which he could
still most live. It was as if, being nothing anywhere else for
anyone, nothing even for himself, he were just everything
here, and if not for a crowd of witnesses, or indeed for any
witness but John Marcher, then by clear right of the register
that he could scan like an open page. The open page was the
tomb of his friend, and *there* were the facts of the past, there the
truth of his life, there the backward reaches in which he could
lose himself. He did this, from time to time, with such effect
that he seemed to wander through the old years with his hand in
the arm of a companion who was, in the most extraordinary
manner, his other, his younger self; and to wander, which was
more extraordinary yet, round and round a third presence – not
wandering she, but stationary, still, whose eyes, turning with
his revolution, never ceased to follow him, and whose seat was
his point, so to speak, of orientation. Thus in short he settled to
live – feeding only on the sense that he once *had* lived, and
dependent on it not only for a support but for an identity.

It sufficed him, in its way, for months, and the year elapsed;
it would doubtless even have carried him further but for an
accident, superficially slight, which moved him, in a quite other
direction, with a force beyond any of his impressions of Egypt
or of India. It was a thing of the merest chance – the turn, as he
afterwards felt, of a hair, though he was indeed to live to believe
that if light hadn't come to him in this particular fashion it
would still have come in another. He was to live to believe
this, I say, though he was not to live, I may not less definitely
mention, to do much else. We allow him at any rate the benefit
of the conviction, struggling up for him at the end, that, whatever might have happened or not happened, he would have
come round of himself to the light. The incident of an autumn
day had put the match to the train laid from of old by his misery.
With the light before him he knew that even of late his ache had
only been smothered. It was strangely drugged, but it
throbbed; at the touch it began to bleed. And the touch, in
the event, was the face of a fellow-mortal. This face, one grey
afternoon when the leaves were thick in the alleys, looked into

Marcher's own, at the cemetery, with an expression like the cut of a blade. He felt it, that is, so deep down that he winced at the steady thrust. The person who so mutely assaulted him was a figure he had noticed, on reaching his own goal, absorbed by a grave a short distance away, a grave apparently fresh, so that the emotion of the visitor would probably match it for frankness. This fact alone forbade further attention, though during the time he stayed he remained vaguely conscious of his neighbour, a middle-aged man apparently, in mourning, whose bowed back, among the clustered monuments and mortuary yews, was constantly presented. Marcher's theory that these were elements in contact with which he himself revived, had suffered, on this occasion, it may be granted, a sensible though inscrutable check. The autumn day was dire for him as none had recently been, and he rested with a heaviness he had not yet known on the low stone table that bore May Bartram's name. He rested without power to move, as if some spring in him, some spell vouchsafed, had suddenly been broken forever. If he could have done that moment as he wanted he would simply have stretched himself on the slab that was ready to take him, treating it as a place prepared to receive his last sleep. What in all the wide world had he now to keep awake for? He stared before him with the question, and it was then that, as one of the cemetery walks passed near him, he caught the shock of the face.

His neighbour at the other grave had withdrawn, as he himself, with force in him to move, would have done by now, and was advancing along the path on his way to one of the gates. This brought him near, and his pace was slow, so that – and all the more as there was a kind of hunger in his look – the two men were for a minute directly confronted. Marcher felt him on the spot as one of the deeply stricken – a perception so sharp that nothing else in the picture lived for it, neither his dress, his age, nor his presumable character and class; nothing lived but the deep ravage of the features that he showed. He *showed* them – that was the point; he was moved, as he passed, by some impulse that was either a signal for sympathy or, more possibly, a challenge to another sorrow. He might already have been aware of our friend, might, at some previous hour, have noticed in him the smooth habit of the scene, with which the state of his own senses so scantly consorted, and might thereby have been stirred as by a kind of overt discord. What Marcher was at all events conscious of was, in the first place, that the image of scarred passion presented to him was conscious too – of something that profaned the air; and, in the second, that, roused, startled, shocked, he was yet the next moment looking after it, as it went, with envy. The most extraordinary thing that had happened to him – though he had given that name to other matters as well – took place, after his immediate vague stare, as a consequence of this impression. The stranger passed, but the raw glare of his grief remained, making our friend wonder in pity what wrong, what wound it expressed, what injury not to be healed. What had the man *had* to make him, by the loss of it, so bleed and yet live?

Something – and this reached him with a pang – that *he*, John Marcher, hadn't; the proof of which was precisely John Marcher's arid end. No passion had ever touched him, for this was what passion meant; he had survived and maundered and pined, but where had been *his* deep ravage? The extraordinary thing we speak of was the sudden rush of the result of this question. The sight that had just met his eyes named to him, as in letters of quick flame, something he had utterly, insanely missed, and what he had missed made these things a train of fire, made them mark themselves in an anguish of inward throbs. He had seen *outside* of his life, not learned it within, the way a woman was mourned when she had been loved for herself; such was the force of his conviction of the meaning of the stranger's face, which still flared for him like a smoky torch. It had not come to him, the knowledge, on the wings of experience; it had brushed him, jostled him, upset him, with the disrespect of chance, the insolence of an accident. Now that the illumination had begun, however, it blazed to the zenith, and what he presently stood there gazing at was the sounded void of his life. He gazed, he drew breath, in pain; he turned in his dismay, and, turning, he had before him in sharper incision than ever the open page of his story. The name on the table smote him as the passage of his neighbour had done, and what it said to him, full in the face, was that *she* was what he had missed. This was the awful thought, the answer to all the past, the vision at the dread clearness of which he turned as cold as the stone beneath him. Everything fell together, confessed, explained, overwhelmed; leaving him most of all stupefied at the blindness he had cherished. The fate he had been marked for he had met with a vengeance – he had emptied the cup to the lees; he had been the man of his time, *the* man, to whom nothing on earth was to have happened. That was the rare stroke – that was his visitation. So he saw it, as we say, in pale horror, while the pieces fitted and fitted. So *she* had seen it, while he didn't, and so she served at this hour to drive the truth home. It was the truth, vivid and monstrous, that all the while he had waited the wait was itself his portion. This the companion of his vigil had at a given moment perceived, and she had then offered him the chance to baffle his doom. One's doom, however, was never baffled, and on the day she had told him that his own had come down she had seen him but stupidly stare at the escape she offered him.

The escape would have been to love her; then, *then* he would have lived. *She* had lived – who could say now with what passion? – since she had loved him for himself; whereas he had never thought of her (ah, how it hugely glared at him!) but in the chill of his egotism and the light of her use. Her spoken words came back to him, and the chain stretched and stretched. The beast had lurked indeed, and the beast, at its hour, had sprung; it had sprung in that twilight of the cold April when, pale, ill, wasted, but all beautiful, and perhaps even then recoverable, she had risen from her chair to stand before him and let him imaginably guess. It had sprung as he didn't guess; it had sprung as she hopelessly turned from him, and the mark, by the time he left her, had fallen where it *was* to fall. He had justified his fear and achieved his fate; he had failed, with the last exactitude, of all he was to fail of; and a moan now rose to his lips as he remembered she had prayed he mightn't know. This horror of waking – *this* was knowledge, knowledge under the breath of which the very tears in his eyes seemed to freeze.

Through them, none the less, he tried to fix it and hold it; he kept it there before him so that he might feel the pain. That at least, belated and bitter, had something of the taste of life. But the bitterness suddenly sickened him, and it was as if, horribly, he saw, in the truth, in the cruelty of his image, what had been appointed and done. He saw the Jungle of his life and saw the lurking Beast; then, while he looked, perceived it, as by a stir of the air, rise, huge and hideous, for the leap that was to settle him. His eyes darkened – it was close; and, instinctively turning, in his hallucination, to avoid it, he flung himself, on his face, on the tomb.

THE PAPERS

I

THERE was a longish period – the dense duration of a London winter, cheered, if cheered it could be called, with lurid electric, with fierce 'incandescent' flares and glares – when they repeatedly met, at feeding-time, in a small and not quite savoury pothouse a stone's-throw from the Strand. They talked always of pothouses, of feeding-time – by which they meant any hour between one and four of the afternoon; they talked of most things, even of some of the greatest, in a manner that gave, or that they desired to show as giving, in respect to the conditions of their life, the measure of their detachment, their contempt, their general irony. Their general irony, which they tried at the same time to keep gay and to make amusing at least to each other, was their refuge from the want of savour, the want of napkins, the want, too often, of shillings, and of many things besides that they would have liked to have. Almost all they had with any security was their youth, complete, admirable, very nearly invulnerable, or as yet inattackable; for they didn't count their talent, which they had originally taken for granted and had since then lacked freedom of mind, as well indeed as any offensive reason, to reappraise. They were taken up with other questions and other estimates – the remarkable limits, for instance, of their luck, the remarkable smallness of the talent of their friends. They were above all in that phase of youth and in that state of aspiration in which 'luck' is the subject of most frequent reference, as definite as the colour red, and in which it is the elegant name for money when people are as refined as they are poor. She was only a suburban young woman in a sailor hat, and he a young man destitute, in strictness, of occasion for a 'topper'; but they felt that they had in a peculiar way the freedom of the town, and the town, if it did nothing else, gave a range to the spirit. They sometimes went, on excursions that they groaned at as professional, far afield from the Strand, but the curiosity with which they came back

785

was mostly greater than any other, the Strand being for them, with its ampler alternative Fleet Street, overwhelmingly the Papers, and the Papers being, at a rough guess, all the furniture of their consciousness.

The Daily Press played for them the part played by the embowered nest on the swaying bough for the parent birds that scour the air. It was, as they mainly saw it, a receptacle, owing its form to the instinct more remarkable, as they held the journalistic, than that even of the most highly organised animal, into which, regularly, breathlessly, contributions had to be dropped – odds and ends, all grist to the mill, all somehow digestible and convertible, all conveyed with the promptest possible beak and the flutter, often, of dreadfully fatigued little wings. If there had been no Papers there would have been no young friends for us of the figure we hint at, no chance mates, innocent and weary, yet acute even to penetration, who were apt to push off their plates and rest their elbows on the table in the interval between the turn-over of the pint-pot and the call for the awful glibness of their score. Maud Blandy drank beer – and welcome, as one may say; and she smoked cigarettes when privacy permitted, though she drew the line at this in the right place, just as she flattered herself she knew how to draw it, journalistically, where other delicacies were concerned. She was fairly a product of the day – so fairly that she might have been born afresh each morning, to serve, after the fashion of certain agitated ephemeral insects, only till the morrow. It was as if a past had been wasted on her and a future were not to be fitted; she was really herself, so far at least as her great pre-occupation went, an edition, an 'extra special', coming out at the loud hours and living its life, amid the roar of vehicles, the hustle of pavements, the shriek of newsboys, according to the quantity of shock to be proclaimed and distributed, the quantity to be administered, thanks to the varying temper of Fleet Street, to the nerves of the nation. Maud was a shocker, in short, in petticoats, and alike for the thoroughfare, the club, the suburban train and the humble home; though it must honestly be added that petticoats were not of her essence. This was one of the reasons, in an age of 'emancipations', of her intense actuality, as well as, positively, of a good fortune to which, however impersonal she might have appeared, she was not herself in a position to do full justice; the felicity of her having about her naturally so much of the young bachelor that she was saved the disfigurement of any marked straddling or elbowing. It was literally true of her that she would have pleased less, or at least have offended more, had she been obliged, or been prompted, to assert – all too vainly, as it would have been sure to be – her superiority to sex. Nature, constitution, accident, whatever we happen to call it, had relieved her of this care; the struggle for life, the competition with men, the taste of the day, the fashion of the hour had *made* her superior, or had at any rate made her indifferent, and she had no difficulty in remaining so. The thing was therefore, with the aid of an extreme general flatness of person, directness of step and simplicity of motive, quietly enough done, without a grace, a weak inconsequence, a stray reminder to interfere with the success; and it is not too much to say that the success – by which I mean the plainness of the type – would probably never have struck you as so great as at the moments of our young lady's chance comradeship with Howard Bight. For the young man, though his personal signs had not, like his friend's, especially the effect of one of the stages of an evolution, might have been noted as not so fiercely or so freshly a male as to distance Maud in the show.

She presented him in truth, while they sat together, as comparatively girlish. She fell naturally into gestures, tones, expressions, resemblances, that he either suppressed, from sensibility to her personal predominance, or that were merely latent in him through much taking for granted. Mild, sensitive, none too solidly nourished, and condemned, perhaps by a deep delusion as to the final issue of it, to perpetual coming and going, he was so resigned to many things, and so disgusted even with many others, that the least of his cares was the cultivation of a bold front. What mainly concerned him was its being bold enough to get him his dinner, and it was never more void of aggression than when he solicited in person those scraps of information, snatched at those floating particles of news, on which his dinner depended. Had he had time a little more to try his case, he would have made out that if he liked Maud Blandy it was partly by the impression of what she could do for him: what she could do for herself had never entered into his head. The positive quantity, moreover, was vague to his mind; it existed, that is, for the present, but as the proof of how, in spite of the want of encouragement, a fellow could keep going. She struck him in fact as the only encouragement he had, and this altogether by example, since precept, frankly, was deterrent on her lips, as speech was free, judgement prompt, and accent not absolutely pure. The point was that, as the easiest thing to be with her, he was so passive that it almost made him graceful and so attentive that it almost made him distinguished. She was herself neither of these things, and they were not of course what a man had most to be; whereby she contributed to their common view the impatiences required by a proper reaction, forming thus for him a kind of protective hedge behind which he could wait. Much waiting, for either, was, I hasten to add, always in order, inasmuch as their novitiate seemed to them interminable and the steps of their ladder fearfully far apart. It rested – the ladder – against the great stony wall of the public attention – a sustaining mass which apparently wore somewhere, in the upper air, a big, thankless, expressionless face, a countenance equipped with eyes, ears, an uplifted nose and a gaping mouth – all convenient if they could only be reached. The ladder groaned meanwhile, swayed and shook with the weight of the close-pressed climbers, tier upon tier, occupying the upper, the middle, the nethermost rounds and quite preventing, for young persons placed as our young friends were placed, any view of the summit. It was meanwhile moreover only Howard Bight's perverse view – he was confessedly perverse – that Miss Blandy had arrived at a perch superior to his own.

She had hitherto recognised in herself indeed but a tighter clutch and a grimmer purpose; she had recognised, she believed, in keen moments, a vocation; she had recognised that there had been eleven of them at home, with herself as youngest, and distinctions by that time so blurred in her that she might as easily have been christened John. She had recognised truly, most of all, that if they came to talk they both were nowhere; yet this was compatible with her insisting that Howard had as yet comparatively had the luck. When he wrote to people they consented, or at least they answered; almost always, for that matter, they answered with greed, so that he was not without something of some sort to hawk about to buyers. Specimens indeed of human greed – *the* greed, the great one, the eagerness to figure, the snap at the bait of publicity, he had collected in such store as to stock, as to launch, a museum. In this museum the prize object, the high rare specimen, had been for some time established; a celebrity of the day enjoying, uncontested, a glass case all to himself, more conspicuous than any other, before which the arrested visitor might rebound from surprised recognition. Sir A. B. C. Beadel-Muffet K.C.B., M.P., stood forth there as large as life, owing indeed his particular place to the shade of direct acquaintance with him that Howard Bight could boast, yet with his eminent presence in such a collection but too generally and notoriously justified. He was universal and ubiquitous, commemorated, under some rank rubric, on every page of every public print every day in every year, and as inveterate a feature of each issue of any self-respecting sheet as the name, the date, the tariffed advertisements. He had always done something, or was about to do something, round which the honours of announcement clustered, and indeed, as he had inevitably thus become a subject of fallacious report, one half of his chronicle appeared to consist of official contradiction of the other half. His activity – if it had not better been called his passivity – was beyond any other that figured in the public eye, for no other assuredly knew so few or such brief intermittences. Yet, as there was the inside as well as the outside view of his current history, the quantity of it was easy to analyse for the possessor of the proper crucible. Howard Bight, with his arms on the table, took it apart and put it together again most days in the year, so that an amused comparison of notes on the subject often added a mild spice to his colloquies with Maud Blandy. They knew, the young pair, as they considered, many secrets, but they liked to think

that they knew none quite so scandalous as the way that, to put
it roughly, this distinguished person maintained his distinction.

It was known certainly to all who had to do with the Papers,
a brotherhood, a sisterhood of course interested – for what was
it, in the last resort, but the interest of their bread and butter? –
in shrouding the approaches to the oracle, in not telling tales
out of school. They all lived alike on the solemnity, the sanctity
of the oracle, and the comings and goings, the doings and
undoings, the intentions and retractations of Sir A. B. C.
Beadel-Muffet K.C.B., M.P., were in their degree a part of
that solemnity. The Papers, taken together the glory of the age,
were, though superficially multifold, fundamentally one, so
that any revelation of their being procured or procurable to
float an object not intrinsically buoyant would very logically
convey discredit from the circumference – where the revelation
would be likely to be made – to the centre. Of so much as this
our grim neophytes, in common with a thousand others, were
perfectly aware; but something in the nature of their wit, such
as it was, or in the condition of their nerves, such as it easily
might become, sharpened almost to acerbity their relish of so
artful an imitation of the voice of fame. The fame was *all* voice,
as they could guarantee who had an ear always glued to the
speaking-tube; the items that made the sum were individually
of the last vulgarity, but the accumulation was a triumph –
one of the greatest the age could show – of industry and vigilance. It was after all not true that a man had done nothing who
for ten years had so fed, so dyked and directed and distributed
the fitful sources of publicity. He had laboured, in his way, like a
navvy with a spade; he might be said to have earned by each
night's work the reward, each morning, of his small spurt
of glory. Even for such a matter as its not being true that Sir
A. B. C. Beadel-Muffet K.C.B., M.P., was to start on his visit
to the Sultan of Samarcand on the 23rd, *but* being true that he
was to start on the 29th, the personal attention required was no
small affair, taking the legend with the fact, the myth with the
meaning, the original artless error with the subsequent earnest
truth – allowing in fine for the statement still to come that the
visit would have to be relinquished in consequence of the

visitor's other pressing engagements, and bearing in mind the countless channels to be successively watered. Our young man, one December afternoon, pushed an evening paper across to his companion, keeping his thumb on a paragraph at which she glanced without eagerness. She might, from her manner, have known by instinct what it would be, and her exclamation had the note of satiety. 'Oh, he's working *them* now?'

'If he has begun he'll work them hard. By the time that has gone round the world there'll be something else to say. "We are authorised to state that the marriage of Miss Miranda Beadel-Muffet to Captain Guy Devereux, of the Fiftieth Rifles, will not take place." Authorised to state – rather! when every wire in the machine has been pulled over and over. They're authorised to state something every day in the year, and the authorisation is not difficult to get. Only his daughters, now that they're coming on, poor things – and I believe there are many – will have to be chucked into the pot and produced on occasions when other matter fails. How pleasant for them to find themselves hurtling through the air, clubbed by the paternal hand, like golf-balls in a suburb! Not that I suppose they don't like it – why should one suppose anything of the sort?' Howard Bight's impression of the general appetite appeared to-day to be especially vivid, and he and his companion were alike prompted to one of those slightly violent returns on themselves and the work they were doing which none but the vulgar-minded altogether avoid. 'People – as I see them – would almost rather be jabbered about unpleasantly than not be jabbered about at all: whenever you try them – whenever, at least, I do – I'm confirmed in that conviction. It isn't only that if one holds out the mere tip of the perch they jump at it like starving fish; it is that they leap straight out of the water themselves, leap in their thousands and come flopping, open-mouthed and goggle-eyed, to one's very door. What is the sense of the French expression about a person's making *des yeux de carpe*? It suggests the eyes that a young newspaper-man seems to see all round him, and I declare I sometimes feel that, if one has the courage not to blink at the show, the gilt is a good deal rubbed off the gingerbread of one's early illusions. They all do it, as the song is at the music-halls, and it's some of one's surprises that tell one most. You've thought there were some high souls that didn't do it – that wouldn't, I mean, to work the oracle, lift a little finger of their own. But, Lord bless you, give them a chance – you'll find some of the greatest the greediest. I give you my word for it, I haven't a scrap of faith left in a single human creature. Except, of course,' the young man added, 'the grand creature that *you* are, and the cold, calm, comprehensive one whom you thus admit to your familiarity. *We* face the music. We see, we understand; we know we've got to live, and how we do it. But at least, like this, alone together, we take our intellectual revenge, we escape the indignity of being fools dealing with fools. I don't say we shouldn't enjoy it more if we *were*. But it can't be helped; we haven't the gift – the gift, I mean, of not seeing. We do the worst we can for the money.'

'*You* certainly do the worst you can,' Maud Blandy soon replied, 'when you sit there, with your wanton wiles, and take the spirit out of me. I require a working faith, you know. If one isn't a fool, in our world, where *is* one?'

'Oh, I say!' her companion groaned without alarm. 'Don't you fail *me*, mind you.'

They looked at each other across their clean platters, and, little as the light of romance seemed superficially to shine in them or about them, the sense was visibly enough in each of being involved in the other. He would have been sharply alone, the softly sardonic young man, if the somewhat dry young woman hadn't affected him, in a way he was even too nervous to put to the test, as saving herself up for him; and the consciousness of absent resources that was on her own side quite compatible with this economy grew a shade or two less dismal with the imagination of his somehow being at costs for her. It wasn't an expense of shillings – there was not much question of that; what it came to was perhaps nothing more than that, being, as he declared himself, 'in the know', he kept pulling her in too, as if there had been room for them both. He told her everything, all his secrets. He talked and talked, often making her think of herself as a lean, stiff person, destitute of skill or art, but with ear enough to be performed to, sometimes strangely touched, at moments completely ravished, by a fine violinist. He was her fiddler and genius; she was sure neither of her taste nor of his tunes, but if she could do nothing else for him she could hold the case while he handled the instrument. It had never passed between them that they could draw nearer, for they seemed near, near verily for pleasure, when each, in a decent young life, was so much nearer to the other than to anything else. There was no pleasure known to either that wasn't further off. What held them together was in short that they were in the same boat, a cockle-shell in a great rough sea, and that the movements required for keeping it afloat not only were what the situation safely permitted, but also made for reciprocity and intimacy. These talks over greasy white slabs, repeatedly mopped with moist grey cloths by young women in black uniforms, with inexorable braided 'buns' in the nape of weak necks, these sessions, sometimes prolonged, in halls of oilcloth, among penal-looking tariffs and pyramids of scones, enabled them to rest on their oars; the more that they were on terms with the whole families, chartered companies, of food-stations, each a race of innumerable and indistinguishable members, and had mastered those hours of comparative elegance, the earlier and the later, when the little weary ministrants were limply sitting down and the occupants of the red benches bleakly interspaced. So it was, that, at times, they renewed their understanding, and by signs, mannerless and meagre, that would have escaped the notice of witnesses. Maud Blandy had no need to kiss her hand across to him to show she felt what he meant; she had moreover never in her life kissed her hand to anyone, and her companion couldn't have imagined it of her. His romance was so grey that it wasn't romance at all; it was a reality arrived at without stages, shades, forms. If he had been ill or stricken she would have taken him – other resources failing – into her lap; but would that, which would scarce even have been motherly, have been romantic? She nevertheless at this moment put in her plea for the general element. 'I can't help it, about Beadel-Muffet; it's too magnificent – it appeals to me. And then I've a particular feeling about him – I'm waiting to see what will happen. It *is* genius, you know, to get yourself so celebrated for nothing – to carry out your idea in the face of everything. I mean your idea of *being* celebrated. It isn't as if he had done even one little thing. What *has* he done when you come to look?'

'Why, my dear chap, he has done everything. He has missed nothing. He has been in everything, *of* everything, *at* everything, *over* everything, *under* everything, that has taken place for the last twenty years. He's *always* present, and, though he never makes a speech, he never fails to get alluded to in the speeches of others. That's doing it cheaper than anyone else does it, but it's thoroughly doing it – which is what we're talking about. And so far,' the young man contended, 'from its being "in the face" of anything, it's positively with the help of everything, since the Papers are everything and more. They're made for such people, though no doubt he's the person who has known best how to use them. I've gone through one of the biggest sometimes, from beginning to end – it's quite a thrilling little game – to catch him once out. It has happened to me to think I was near it when, on the last column of the last page – I count "advertisements", heaven help us, out! – I've found him as large as life and as true as the needle to the pole. But at last, in a way, it goes, it can't help going, of itself. He comes in, he breaks out, of himself; the letters, under the compositor's hand, form themselves, from the force of habit, into his name – any connection for it, any context, being as good as any other, and the wind, which he has originally "raised", but which continues to blow, setting perpetually in his favour. The thing would really be now, don't you see, for him to keep himself out. That would be, on my honour, it strikes me – his *getting* himself out – the biggest fact in his record.'

The girl's attention, as her friend developed the picture, had become more present. 'He *can't* get himself out. There he is.' She had a pause; she had been thinking. 'That's just my idea.'

'Your idea? Well, an idea's always a blessing. What do you want for it?'

She continued to turn it over as if weighing its value. 'Something perhaps *could* be done with it – only it would take imagination.'

He wondered, and she seemed to wonder that he didn't see. 'Is it a situation for a "ply"?'

'No, it's too good for a ply – yet it isn't quite good enough for a short story.'

'It would do then for a novel?'

'Well, I seem to see it,' Maud said – 'and with a lot *in* it to be got out. But I seem to see it as a question not of what you or I might be able to do with it, but of what the poor man himself may. That's what I meant just now,' she explained, 'by my having a creepy sense of what may happen for him. It has already more than once occurred to me. *Then*,' she wound up, 'we shall have real life, the case itself.'

'Do you know *you've* got imagination?' Her friend, rather interested, appeared by this time to have seized her thought.

'I see him having for some reason, very imperative, to seek retirement, lie low, to hide, in fact, like a man "wanted", but pursued all the while by the lurid glare that he has himself so started and kept up, and at last literally devoured ("like Frankenstein", of course!) by the monster he has created.'

'I say, you *have* got it!' – and the young man flushed, visibly, artistically, with the recognition of elements which his eyes had for a minute earnestly fixed. 'But it will take a lot of doing.'

'Oh,' said Maud, '*we* shan't have to do it. He'll do it himself.'

'I wonder.' Howard Bight really wondered. 'The fun would be for him to do it *for* us. I mean for him to want us to help him somehow to get out.'

'Oh, "us"!' the girl mournfully sighed.

'Why not, when he comes to us to get in?'

Maud Blandy stared. 'Do you mean to you personally? You surely know by this time that no one ever "comes" to me.'

'Why, I went to him in the first instance; I made up to him straight, I did him "at home", somewhere, as I've surely mentioned to you before, three years ago. He liked, I believe – for he's really a delightful old ass – the way I did it; he knows my name and has my address, and has written me three or four times since, with his own hand, a request to be so good as to

make use of my (he hopes) still close connection with the daily
Press to rectify the rumour that he has reconsidered his opinion
on the subject of the blankets supplied to the Upper Tooting
Workhouse Infirmary. He has reconsidered his opinion on no
subject whatever – which he mentions, in the interest of
historic truth, without further intrusion on my valuable time.
And he regards that sort of thing as a commodity that I can
dispose of – thanks to my "close connection" – for several
shillings.'

'And can you?'

'Not for several pence. They're all tariffed, but he's tariffed
low – having a value, apparently, that money doesn't represent.
He's always welcome, but he isn't always paid for. The beauty,
however, is in his marvellous memory, his keeping us all so
apart and not muddling the fellow to whom he has written
that he hasn't done this, that or the other with the fellow to
whom he has written that he has. He'll write to me again some
day about something else – about his alleged position on the
date of the next school-treat of the Chelsea Cabmen's Orphan-
age. I shall seek a market for the precious item, and that will
keep us in touch; so that if the complication you have the sense
of in your bones does come into play – the thought's too
beautiful! – he may once more remember me. Fancy his coming
to one with a "What can you do for me *now*?"' Bight lost
himself in the happy vision; it gratified so his cherished consciousness of the 'irony of fate' – a consciousness so cherished
that he never could write ten lines without use of the words.

Maud showed however at this point a reserve which
appeared to have grown as the possibility opened out. 'I believe
in it – it must come. It can't not. It's the only end. He doesn't
know; nobody knows – the simple-minded all: only you and
I know. But it won't be nice, remember.'

'It won't be funny?'

'It will be pitiful. There'll have to be a reason.'

'For his turning round?' the young man nursed the vision.
'More or less – I see what you mean. But except for a "ply" will
that so much matter? His reason will concern himself. What
will concern us will be his funk and his helplessness, his having

to stand there in the blaze, with nothing and nobody to put it out. We shall see him, shrieking for a bucket of water, wither up in the central flame.'

Her look had turned sombre. 'It makes one cruel. That is it makes *you*. I mean our trade does.'

'I daresay – I see too much. But I'm willing to chuck it.'

'Well,' she presently replied, 'I'm not willing to, but it seems pretty well on the cards that I shall have to. *I* don't see too much. I don't see enough. So, for all the good it does me—!'

She had pushed back her chair and was looking round for her umbrella. 'Why, what's the matter?' Howard Bight too blankly inquired.

She met his eyes while she pulled on her rusty old gloves. 'Well, I'll tell you another time.'

He kept his place, still lounging, contented where she had again become restless. 'Don't you call it seeing enough to see – to have had so luridly revealed to you – the doom of Beadel-Muffet?'

'Oh, he's not my business, he's yours. You're his man, or one of his men – he'll come back to you. Besides, he's a special case, and, as I say, I'm too sorry for him.'

'That's a proof then of what you do see.'

Her silence for a moment admitted it, though evidently she was making, for herself, a distinction, which she didn't express. 'I don't then see what I want, what I require. And *he*,' she added, 'if he does have some reason, will have to have an awfully strong one. To be strong enough it will have to be awful.'

'You mean he'll have done something?'

'Yes, that may remain undiscovered if he can only drop out of the papers, sit for a while in darkness. You'll know what it is; you'll not be able to help yourself. But I shan't want to, for anything.'

She had got up as she said it, and he sat looking at her, thanks to her odd emphasis, with an interest that, as he also rose, passed itself off as a joke. 'Ah, then, you sweet sensitive thing, I promise to keep it from you.'

II

THEY met again a few days later, and it seemed the law of their meetings that these should take place mainly within moderate eastward range of Charing Cross. An afternoon performance of a play translated from the Finnish, already several times given, on a series of Saturdays, had held Maud for an hour in a small, hot, dusty theatre where the air hung as heavy about the great 'trimmed' and plumed hats of the ladies as over the flora and fauna of a tropical forest; at the end of which she edged out of her stall in the last row, to join a small band of unattached critics and correspondents, spectators with ulterior views and pencilled shirtcuffs, who, coming together in the lobby for an exchange of ideas, were ranging from 'Awful rot' to 'Rather jolly'. Ideas, of this calibre, rumbled and flashed, so that, lost in the discussion, our young woman failed at first to make out that a gentleman on the other side of the group, but standing a little off, had his eyes on her for some extravagant, though apparently quite respectable, purpose. He had been waiting for her to recognise him, and as soon as he had caught her attention he came round to her with an eager bow. She had by this time entirely placed him – placed him as the smoothest and most shining subject with which, in the exercise of her profession, she had yet experimented; but her recognition was accompanied with a pang that his amiable address made but the sharper. She had her reason for awkwardness in the presence of a rosy, glossy, kindly, but discernibly troubled personage whom she had waited on 'at home' at her own suggestion – promptly welcomed – and the sympathetic element in whose 'personality', the Chippendale, the photographic, the autographic elements in whose flat in the Earl's Court Road, she had commemorated in the liveliest prose of which she was capable. She had described with humour his favourite pug, she had revealed with permission his favourite make of Kodak, she had touched upon his favourite manner of spending his Sundays and had extorted from him the shy confession that he preferred after all the novel of adventure to the novel of subtlety. Her embarrassment was therefore now the greater as, touching to behold, he so clearly had approached her with no intention of asperity, not even at first referring at all to the matter that couldn't have been gracefully explained.

She had seen him originally – had had the instinct of it in making up to him – as one of the happy of the earth, and the impression of him 'at home', on his proving so good-natured about the interview, had begotten in her a sharper envy, a hungrier sense of the invidious distinctions of fate, than any her literary conscience, which she deemed rigid, had yet had to reckon with. He must have been rich, rich by such estimates as hers; he at any rate had everything, while she had nothing – nothing but the vulgar need of offering him to brag, on his behalf, for money, if she could get it, about his luck. She hadn't in fact got money, hadn't so much as managed to work in her stuff anywhere; a practical comment sharp enough on her having represented to him – with wasted pathos, she was indeed soon to perceive – how 'important' it was to her that people should let her get at them. This dim celebrity had not needed that argument; he had not only, with his alacrity, allowed her, as she had said, to try her hand, but had tried *with* her, quite feverishly, and all to the upshot of showing her that there were even greater outsiders than herself. He could have put down money, could have published, as the phrase was – a bare two columns – at his own expense; but it was just a part of his rather irritating luxury that he had a scruple about that, wanted intensely to taste the sweet, but didn't want to owe it to any wire-pulling. He wanted the golden apple straight from the tree, where it yet seemed so unable to grow for him by any exuberance of its own. He had breathed to her his real secret – that to be inspired, to work with effect, he had to feel he was appreciated, to have it all somehow come back to him. The artist, necessarily sensitive, lived on encouragement, on knowing and being reminded that people cared for him a little, cared even just enough to flatter him a wee bit. They had talked that over, and he had really, as he called it, quite put himself in her power. He had whispered in her ear that it might be very weak and silly, but that positively to be himself, to do anything, certainly to do his best, he required the breath of sympathy.

He did love notice, let alone praise – there it was. To be systemically ignored – well, blighted him at the root. He was afraid she would think he had said too much, but she left him with his leave, none the less, to repeat a part of it. They had agreed that she was to bring in prettily, somehow, that he did love praise; for just the right way he was sure he could trust to her taste.

She had promised to send him the interview in proof, but she had been able, after all, to send it but in type-copy. If *she*, after all, had had a flat adorned – as to the drawing-room alone – with eighty-three photographs, and all in plush frames; if she had lived in the Earl's Court Road, had been rosy and glossy and well filled out; and if she had looked withal, as she always made a point of calling it when she wished to refer without vulgarity to the right place in the social scale, 'unmistakeably gentle' – if she had achieved these things she would have snapped her fingers at all other sweets, have sat as tight as possible and let the world wag, have spent her Sundays in silently thanking her stars, and not have cared to know one Kodak, or even one novelist's 'methods', from another. Except for his unholy itch he was in short so just the person she would have liked to be that the last consecration was given for her to his character by his speaking quite as if he had accosted her only to secure her view of the strange Finnish 'soul'. He had come each time – there had been four Saturdays; whereas Maud herself had had to wait till to-day, though her bread depended on it, for the roundabout charity of her publicly bad seat. It didn't matter *why* he had come – so that he might see it somewhere printed of him that he was 'a conspicuously faithful attendant' at the interesting series; it only mattered that he was letting her off so easily, and yet that there was a restless hunger, odd on the part of one of the filled-out, in his appealing eye, which she now saw not to be a bit intelligent, though that didn't matter either. Howard Bight came into view while she dealt with these impressions, whereupon she found herself edging a little away from her patron. Her other friend, who had but just arrived and was apparently waiting to speak to her, would be a pretext for a break before the poor gentleman should begin to accuse her of having failed him. She had failed herself so much more that she would have been ready to reply to him that *he* was scarce the one to complain; fortunately, however, the bell sounded the end of the interval and her tension was relaxed. They all flocked back to their places, and her *camarade* – she knew enough often so to designate him – was enabled, thanks to some shifting of other spectators, to occupy a seat beside her. He had brought with him the breath of business; hurrying from one appointment to another he might have time but for a single act. He had seen each of the others by itself, and the way he now crammed in the third, after having previously snatched the fourth, brought home again to the girl that he was leading the real life. Her own was a dull imitation of it. Yet it happened at the same time that before the curtain rose again he had, with a 'Who's your fat friend?' professed to have caught her in the act of making her own brighter.

'"Mortimer Marshal"?' he echoed after she had, a trifle dryly, satisfied him. 'Never heard of him.'

'Well, I shan't tell him that. But you *have*,' she said; 'you've only forgotten. I told you after I had been to him.'

Her friend thought – it came back to him. 'Oh yes, and showed me what you had made of it. I remember your stuff was charming.'

'I see you remember nothing,' Maud a little more dryly said. 'I didn't show you what I had made of it. I've never made anything. You've not seen my stuff, and nobody has. They won't have it.'

She spoke with a smothered vibration, but, as they were still waiting, it had made him look at her; by which she was slightly the more disconcerted. 'Who won't?'

'Everyone, everything won't. Nobody, nothing will. He's hopeless, or rather *I* am. I'm no good. And he knows it.'

'O – oh!' the young man kindly but vaguely protested. 'Has he been making that remark to you?'

'No – that's the worst of it. He's too dreadfully civil. He thinks I can do something.'

'Then why do you say he knows you can't?'

She was impatient; she gave it up. 'Well, I don't know what he knows – except that he does want to be loved.'

'Do you mean he has proposed to you to love him?'

'Loved by the great heart of the public – speaking through its natural organ. He wants to be – well, where Beadel-Muffet is.'

'Oh, I hope not!' said Bight with grim amusement.

His friend was struck with his tone. 'Do you mean it's coming on for Beadel-Muffet – what we talked about?' And then as he looked at her so queerly that her curiosity took a jump: 'It really and truly *is*? Has anything happened?'

'The rummest thing in the world – since I last saw you. We're wonderful, you know, you and I together – we *see*. And what we see always takes place, usually within the week. It wouldn't be believed. But it will do for *us*. At any rate it's high sport.'

'Do you mean,' she asked, 'that his scare has literally begun?'

He meant, clearly, quite as much as he said. 'He has written to me again he wants to see me, and we've an appointment for Monday.'

'Then why isn't it the old game?'

'Because it isn't. He wants to gather from me, as I *have* served him before, if something can't be done. *On a souvent besoin d'un plus petit que soi*. Keep quiet, and we shall see something.'

This was very well; only his manner visibly had for her the effect of a chill in the air. 'I hope,' she said, 'you're going at least to be decent to him.'

'Well, you'll judge. Nothing at all can be done – it's too ridiculously late. And it serves him right. I shan't deceive him, certainly, but I might as well enjoy him.'

The fiddles were still going, and Maud had a pause. 'Well, you know you've more or less lived on him. I mean it's the kind of thing you *are* living on.'

'Precisely – that's just why I loathe it.'

Again she hesitated. 'You mustn't quarrel, you know, with your bread and butter.'

He looked straight before him, as if she had been consciously, and the least bit disagreeably, sententious. 'What in the world's that but what I shall just be *not* doing? If our bread

and butter is the universal push I consult our interest by not
letting it trifle with us. They're not to blow hot and cold – it
won't do. There he is – let him get out himself. What I call sport
is to see if he can.'

'And not – poor wretch – to help him?'

But Bight was ominously lucid. 'The devil is that he can't *be*
helped. His one idea of help, from the day he opened his eyes,
has been to be prominently – damn the word! – mentioned: it's
the only kind of help that exists in connection with him. What
therefore is a fellow to do when he happens to want it to stop –
wants a special sort of prominence that will work like a trap in a
pantomime and enable him to vanish when the situation
requires it? Is one to mention that he wants *not* to be mentioned
– never, never, please, any more? Do you see the success of that,
all over the place, do you see the headlines in the American
papers? No, he must die as he has lived – the Principal Public
Person of his time.'

'Well,' she sighed, 'it's all horrible.' And then without a
transition: 'What do you suppose has happened to him?'

'The dreadfulness I wasn't to tell you?'

'I only mean if you suppose him in a really bad hole.'

The young man considered. 'It can't certainly be that he has
had a change of heart – never. It may be nothing worse than that
the woman he wants to marry has turned against it.'

'But I supposed him – with his children all so boomed – to *be*
married.'

'Naturally; else he couldn't have got such a boom from the
poor lady's illness, death and burial. Don't you remember two
years ago? – "We are given to understand that Sir A. B. C.
Beadel-Muffet K.C.B., M.P., particularly desires that no flowers be sent for the late Hon. Lady Beadel-Muffet's funeral."
And then, the next day: "We are authorised to state that the
impression, so generally prevailing, that Sir A. B. C. Beadel-
Muffet has expressed an objection to flowers in connection
with the late Hon. Lady Beadel-Muffet's obsequies, rests on a
misapprehension of Sir A. B. C. Beadel-Muffet's markedly
individual views. The floral tributes already delivered in
Queen's Gate Gardens, and remarkable for number and

variety, have been the source of such gratification to the bereaved gentleman as his situation permits.'' With a wind-up of course for the following week – the inevitable few heads of remark, on the part of the bereaved gentleman, on the general subject of Flowers at Funerals as a Fashion, vouchsafed, under pressure possibly indiscreet, to a rising young journalist always thirsting for the authentic word.'

'I guess now,' said Maud, after an instant, 'the rising young journalist. You egged him on.'

'Dear, no. I panted in his rear.'

'It makes you,' she added, 'more than cynical.'

'And what do you call "more than" cynical?'

'It makes you sardonic. Wicked,' she continued; 'devilish.'

'That's it – that *is* cynical. Enough's as good as a feast.' But he came back to the ground they had quitted. 'What were you going to say *he's* prominent for, Mortimer Marshal?'

She wouldn't, however, follow him there yet, her curiosity on the other issue not being spent. 'Do you know then as a fact, that he's marrying again, the bereaved gentleman?'

Her friend, at this, showed impatience. 'My dear fellow, do you *see* nothing? We had it all, didn't we, three months ago, and then we didn't have it, and then we had it again; and goodness knows where we are. But I throw out the possibility. I forget her bloated name, but she may be rich, and she may be decent. She may make it a condition that he keeps out – out, I mean, of the only things he has really ever been "in". '

'The Papers?'

'The dreadful, nasty, vulgar Papers. She may put it to him – I see it dimly and queerly, but I see it – that he must get out first, and then they'll talk; then she'll say yes, then he'll have the money. I see it – and much more sharply – that he *wants* the money, needs it, I mean, badly, desperately, so that this necessity may very well make the hole in which he finds himself. Therefore he must do something – what he's trying to do. It supplies the motive that our picture, the other day, rather missed.'

Maud Blandy took this in, but it seemed to fail to satisfy her. 'It must be something worse. You make it out *that*, so that your practical want of mercy, which you'll not be able to conceal from me, shall affect me as less inhuman.'

'I don't make it out anything, and I don't care what it is; the queerness, the grand "irony" of the case is itself enough for me. You, on your side, however, I think, make it out what you call "something worse", because of the romantic bias of your mind. You "see red". Yet isn't it, after all, sufficiently lurid that he shall lose his blooming bride?'

'You're sure,' Maud appealed, 'that he'll lose her?'

'Poetic justice screams for it; and my whole interest in the matter is staked on it.'

But the girl continued to brood. 'I thought you contend that nobody's half "decent". Where do you find a woman to make such a condition?'

'Not easily, I admit.' The young man thought. 'It will be *his* luck to have found her. That's his tragedy, say, that she can financially save him, but that she happens to be just the one freak, the creature whose stomach has turned. The spark – I mean of decency – has got, after all, somehow to be kept alive; and it may be lodged in this particular female form.'

'I see. But why should a female form that's so particular confess to an affinity with a male form that's so fearfully general? As he's *all* self-advertisement, why isn't it much more natural to her simply to loathe him?'

'Well, because, oddly enough, it seems that people don't.'

'*You* do,' Maud declared. 'You'll kill him.'

He just turned a flushed cheek to her, and she saw that she had touched something that lived in him. 'We *can*,' he consciously smiled, 'deal death. And the beauty is that it's in a perfectly straight way. We can lead them on. But have you ever seen Beadel-Muffet for yourself?' he continued.

'No. How often, please, need I tell you that I've seen nobody and nothing?'

'Well, if you had you'd understand.'

'You mean he's so fetching?'

'Oh, he's great. He's not "all" self-advertisement – or at least he doesn't seem to be: that's his pull. But I see, you female humbug,' Bight pursued, 'how much you'd like him yourself.'

'I want, while I'm about it, to pity him in sufficient quantity.'

'Precisely. Which means, for a woman, with extravagance and to the point of immorality.'

'I ain't a woman,' Maud Blandy sighed. 'I wish I were!'

'Well, about the pity,' he went on; 'you shall be immoral, I promise you, before you've done. Doesn't Mortimer Marshal,' he asked, 'take you for a woman?'

'You'll have to ask him. How,' she demanded, 'does one know those things?' And she stuck to her Beadel-Muffet. 'If you're to see him on Monday shan't you then get to the bottom of it?'

'Oh, I don't conceal from you that I promise myself larks, but I won't tell you, positively I won't,' Bight said, 'what I see. You're morbid. If it's only bad enough – I mean his motive – you'll want to save him.'

'Well, isn't that what you're to profess to him that *you* want?'

'Ah,' the young man returned, 'I believe you'd really invent a way.'

'I would if I could.' And with that she dropped it. 'There's my fat friend,' she presently added, as the entr'acte still hung heavy and Mortimer Marshal, from a row much in advance of them, screwed himself round in his tight place apparently to keep her in his eye.

'He does then,' said her companion, 'take you for a woman. I seem to guess he's "littery".'

'That's it; so badly that he wrote that "littery" ply *Corisanda*, you must remember, with Beatrice Beaumont in the principal part, which was given at three matinées in this very place and which hadn't even the luck of being slated. Every creature connected with the production, from the man himself and Beatrice *her*self down to the mothers and grandmothers of the sixpenny young women, the young women of the programmes, was interviewed both before and after, and he promptly published the piece, pleading guilty to the "littery" charge – which is the great stand he takes and the subject of the discussion.'

Bight had wonderingly followed. 'Of what discussion?'

'Why, the one he thinks there ought to have been. There hasn't been any, of course, but he wants it, dreadfully misses it.

People won't keep it up – whatever they *did* do, though I don't myself make out that they did anything. His state of mind requires something to start with, which has got somehow to be provided. There must have been a noise made, don't you see? to make him prominent; and in order to remain prominent he has got to go for his enemies. The hostility to his ply, and all *because* it's "littery", we can do nothing without that; but it's uphill work to come across it. We sit up nights trying, but we seem to get no for'arder. The public attention would seem to abhor the whole matter even as nature abhors a vacuum. We've nothing to go upon, otherwise we might go far. But there we are.'

'I see,' Bight commented. 'You're nowhere at all.'

'No; it isn't even that, for we're just where *Corisanda*, on the stage and in the closet, put us at a stroke. Only there we stick fast – nothing seems to happen, nothing seems to come or to be capable of being made to come. We wait.'

'Oh, if he waits with *you*!' Bight amicably jibed.

'He may wait for ever?'

'No, but resignedly. You'll make him forget his wrongs.'

'Ah, I'm not of that sort, and I could only do it by making him come into his rights. And I recognise now that that's impossible. There are different cases, you see, whole different classes of them, and his is the opposite to Beadel-Muffet's.'

Howard Bight gave a grunt. 'Why the opposite if you also pity him? I'll be hanged,' he added, 'if you won't save *him* too.'

But she shook her head. She knew. 'No; but it's nearly, in its way, as lurid. Do you know,' she asked, 'what he has done?'

'Why, the difficulty appears to be that he can't have done anything. He should strike once more – hard, and in the same place. He should bring out another ply.'

'Why so? You can't be more than prominent, and he *is* prominent. You can't do more than subscribe, in your prominence, to thirty-seven "press-cutting" agencies in England and America, and, having done so, you can't do more than sit at home with your ear on the postman's knock, looking out for results. *There* comes in the tragedy – there are no results. Mortimer Marshall's postman doesn't knock; the press-cutting agencies can't find anything to cut. With thirty-seven, in the whole English-speaking world, scouring millions of papers for him in vain, and with a big slice of his private income all the while going to it, the "irony" is too cruel, and the way he looks at one, as in one's degree responsible, does make one wince. He expected, naturally, most from the Americans, but it's they who have failed him worst. Their silence is that of the tomb, and it seems to grow, if the silence of the tomb *can* grow. He won't admit that the thirty-seven look far enough or long enough, and he writes them, I infer, angry letters, wanting to know what the deuce they suppose he has paid them for. But what are they either, poor things, to do?'

'Do? They can print his angry letters. That, at least, will break the silence, and he'll like it better than nothing.'

This appeared to strike our young woman. 'Upon my word, I really believe he would.' Then she thought better of it. 'But they'd be afraid, for they do guarantee, you know, that there's something for everyone. They claim it's their strength – that there's enough to go round. They won't want to show that they break down.'

'Oh, well,' said the young man, 'if he can't manage to smash a pane of glass somewhere—!'

'That's what he thought *I* would do. And it's what *I* thought I might,' Maud added; 'otherwise I wouldn't have approached him. I did it on spec, but I'm no use. I'm a fatal influence. I'm a non-conductor.'

She said it with such plain sincerity that it quickly took her companion's attention. 'I *say*!' he covertly murmured. 'Have you a secret sorrow?'

'Of course I've a secret sorrow.' And she stared at it, stiff and a little sombre, not wanting it to be too freely handled, while the curtain at last rose to the lighted stage.

III

SHE was later on more open about it, sundry other things, not wholly alien, having meanwhile happened. One of these had been that her friend had waited with her to the end of the

Finnish performance and that it had then, in the lobby, as they
went out, not been possible for her not to make him acquainted
with Mr Mortimer Marshal. This gentleman had clearly way-
laid her and had also clearly divined that her companion was of
the Papers – papery all through; which doubtless had something to do with his having handsomely proposed to them to
accompany him somewhere to tea. They hadn't seen why they
shouldn't, it being an adventure, all in their line, like another;
and he had carried them, in a four-wheeler, to a small and
refined club in a region which was as the fringe of the Piccadilly
region, where even their own presence scarce availed to contradict the implication of the exclusive. The whole occasion, they
were further to feel, was essentially a tribute to their professional connection, especially that side of it which flushed and
quavered, which panted and pined in their host's personal
nervousness. Maud Blandy now saw it vain to contend with
his delusion that *she*, underfed and unprinted, who had never
been so conscious as during these bribed moments of her non-
conducting quality, was papery to any purpose – a delusion that
exceeded, by her measure, every other form of pathos. The
decoration of the tea-room was a pale, aesthetic green, the
liquid in the delicate cups a copious potent amber; the bread
and butter was thin and golden, the muffins a revelation to her
that she was barbarously hungry. There were ladies at other
tables with other gentlemen – ladies with long feather boas and
hats not of the sailor pattern, and gentlemen whose straight
collars were doubled up much higher than Howard Bight's and
their hair parted far more at the side. The talk was so low, with
pauses somehow so not of embarrassment that it could only
have been earnest, and the air, an air of privilege and privacy to
our young woman's sense, seemed charged with fine things
taken for granted. If it hadn't been for Bight's company she
would have grown almost frightened, so much seemed to be
offered her for something she couldn't do. That word of Bight's
about smashing a window-pane had lingered with her; it had
made her afterwards wonder, while they sat in their stalls, if
there weren't some brittle surface in range of her own elbow.
She had to fall back on the consciousness of how her elbow, in

spite of her type, lacked practical point, and that was just why the terms in which she saw her services now, as she believed, bid for, had the effect of scaring her. They came out most, for that matter, in Mr Mortimer Marshal's dumbly-insistent eyes, which seemed to be perpetually saying: 'You know what I mean when I'm too refined – like everything here, don't you see? – to say it out. You know there ought to be something about me somewhere, and that really, with the opportunities, the facilities you enjoy, it wouldn't be so much out of your way just to – well, reward this little attention.'

The fact that he was probably every day, in just the same anxious flurry and with just the same superlative delicacy, paying little attentions with an eye to little rewards, this fact by itself but scantily eased her, convinced as she was that no luck but her own was as hopeless as his. He squared the clever young wherever he could get at them, but it was the clever young, taking them generally, who fed from his hand and then forgot him. She didn't forget him; she pitied him too much, pitied herself, and was more and more, as she found, now pitying everyone; only she didn't know how to say to him that she could do, after all, nothing for him. She oughtn't to have come, in the first place, and wouldn't if it hadn't been for her companion. Her companion was increasingly sardonic – which was the way in which, at best, she now increasingly saw him; he was shameless in acceptance, since, as she knew, as she felt at his side, he had come only, at bottom, to mislead and to mystify. *He* was, as she wasn't, on the Papers and of them, and their baffled entertainer knew it without either a hint on the subject from herself or a need, on the young man's own lips, of the least vulgar allusion. Nothing was so much as named, the whole connection was sunk; they talked about clubs, muffins, afternoon performances, the effect of the Finnish soul upon the appetite, quite as if they had met in society. Nothing could have been less like society – she innocently supposed at least – than the real spirit of their meeting; yet Bight did nothing that he might do to keep the affair within bounds. When looked at by their friend so hard and so hintingly, he only looked back, just as dumbly, but just as intensely and, as might be said, portentously; ever so impenetrably, in fine, and ever so wick-edly. He didn't smile – as if to cheer – the least little bit; which he might be abstaining from on purpose to make his promises solemn: so, as he tried to smile – she couldn't, it was all too dreadful – she wouldn't meet her friend's eyes, but kept look-ing, heartlessly, at the 'notes' of the place, the hats of the ladies, the tints of the rugs, the intenser Chippendale, here and there, of the chairs and tables, of the very guests, of the very wait-resses. It had come to her early: 'I've done him, poor man, at home, and the obvious thing now will be to do him at his club.' But this inspiration plumped against her fate even as an imprisoned insect against the window-glass. She couldn't do him at his club without decently asking leave; whereby he would know of her feeble feeler, feeble because she was so sure of refusals. She would rather tell him, desperately, what she thought of him than expose him to see again that she was herself nowhere, herself nothing. Her one comfort was that, for the half-hour – it had made the situation quite possible – he seemed fairly hypnotised by her colleague; so that when they took leave he as good as thanked her for what she had this time done for him. It was one of the signs of his infatuated state that he clearly viewed Bight as a mass of helpful cleverness, though the cruel creature, uttering scarce a sound, had only fixed him in a manner that might have been taken for the fascination of deference. He might perfectly have been an idiot for all the poor gentleman knew. But the poor gentleman saw a possible 'leg up' in every bush; and nothing but impertinence would have convinced him that she hadn't brought him, compunctiously as to the past, a master of the proper art. Now, more than ever, how he would listen for the postman!

The whole occasion had broken so, for busy Bight, into matters to be attended to before Fleet Street warmed to its work, that the pair were obliged, outside, to part company on the spot, and it was only on the morrow, a Saturday, that they could taste again of that comparison of notes which made for each the main savour, albeit slightly acrid, of their current consciousness. The air was full, as from afar, of the grand indifference of spring, of which the breath could be felt so much before the face could be seen, and they had bicycled side by side out to Richmond Park as with the impulse to meet it on its way. They kept a Saturday, when possible, sacred to the Suburbs as distinguished from the Papers – when possible being largely when Maud could achieve the use of the somewhat fatigued family machine. Many sisters contended for it, under whose flushed pressure it might have been seen spinning in many different directions. Superficially, at Richmond, our young couple rested – found a quiet corner to lounge deep in the Park, with their machines propped by one side of a great tree and their associated backs sustained by another. But agitation, finer than the finest scorching, was in the air for them; it was made sharp, rather abruptly, by a vivid outbreak from Maud. It was very well, she observed, for her friend to be clever at the expense of the general 'greed'; he saw it in the light of his own jolly luck, and what she saw, as it happened, was nothing but the general art of letting you starve, yourself, in your hole. At the end of five minutes her companion had turned quite pale with having to face the large extent of her confession. It was a confession for the reason that in the first place it evidently cost her an effort that pride had again and again successfully prevented, and because in the second she had thus the air of having lived overmuch on swagger. She could scarce have said at this moment what, for a good while, she had really lived on, and she didn't let him know now to complain either of her privation or of her disappointments. She did it to show why she couldn't go with him when he was so awfully sweeping. There were at any rate apparently, all over, two wholly different sets of people. If everyone rose to his bait no creature had ever risen to hers; and that was the grim truth of her position, which proved at the least that there were two quite different kinds of luck. They told two different stories of human vanity; they couldn't be reconciled. And the poor girl put it in a nutshell. 'There's but one person I've *ever* written to who has so much as noticed my letter.'

He wondered, painfully affected – it rather overwhelmed him; he took hold of it at the easiest point. 'One person—?'

'The misguided man we had tea with. He alone – *he* rose.'

'Well then, you see that when they do rise they *are* misguided. In other words they're donkeys.'

'What I see is that I don't strike the right ones and that I haven't therefore your ferocity; that is my ferocity, if I have any, rests on a different ground. You'll say that I go for the wrong people; but I don't, God knows – witness Mortimer Marshal – fly too high. I picked him out, after prayer and fasting, as just the likeliest of the likely – not anybody a bit grand and yet not quite a nobody; and by an extraordinary chance I was justified. Then I pick out others who seem just as good, I pray and fast, and no sound comes back. But I work through my ferocity too,' she stiffly continued, 'though at first it was great, feeling as I did that when my bread and butter was in it people had no right not to oblige me. It was their duty – what they were prominent *for* – to be interviewed, so as to keep me going; and I did as much for them any day as they would be doing for me.'

Bight heard her, but for a moment said nothing. 'Did you tell them that? I mean say to them it was your little all?'

'Not vulgarly – I know how. There are ways of saying it's "important"; and I hint it just enough to see that the importance fetches them no more than anything else. It isn't important to *them*. And I, in their place,' Maud went on, 'wouldn't answer either; I'll be hanged if ever I would. That's what it comes to, that there *are* two distinct lots, and that my luck, being born so, is always to try the snubbers. You were born to know by instinct the others. But it makes me more tolerant.'

'More tolerant of what?' her friend asked.

'Well, of what you described to me. Of what you rail at.'

'Thank you for *me*!' Bight laughed.

'Why not? Don't you live on it?'

'Not in such luxury – you surely must see for yourself – as the distinction you make seems to imply. It isn't luxury to be ninetenths of the time sick of everything. People moreover are worth to me but tuppence apiece; there are too many, confound them – so many that I don't see really how any can be left over for *your* superior lot. It *is* a chance,' he pursued – 'I've had refusals too – though I confess they've sometimes been of the funniest. Besides, I'm getting out of it,' the young man wound

up. 'God knows I want to. My advice to you,' he added in
the same breath, 'is to sit tight. There are as good fish in the
sea—!'

She waited a moment. 'You're sick of everything and you're
getting out of it; it's not good enough for you, in other words,
but it's still good enough for me. Why am I to sit tight when you
sit so loose?'

'Because what you want will come – can't help coming.
Then, in time, you'll also get out of it. But then you'll have
had it, as I have, and the good of it.'

'But what, really, if it breeds nothing but disgust,' she asked,
'do you *call* the good of it?'

'Well, two things. First the bread and butter, and then the
fun. I repeat it – sit tight.'

'Where's the fun,' she asked again, 'of learning to despise
people?'

'You'll see when it comes. It will all be upon you, it will
change for you any day. Sit tight, sit tight.'

He expressed such confidence that she might for a
minute have been weighing it. 'If you get out of it, what will
you do?'

'Well, imaginative work. This job has made me at least *see*. It
has given me the loveliest tips.'

She had still another pause. 'It has given me – *my* experience
has – a lovely tip too.'

'And what's that?'

'I've told you before – the tip of pity. I'm so much sorrier for
them all – panting and gasping for it like fish out of water – than
I am anything else.'

He wondered. 'But I thought that was what just isn't your
experience.'

'Oh, I mean then,' she said impatiently, 'that my tip is from
yours. It's only a different tip. I want to save them.'

'Well,' the young man replied, and as if the idea had had a
meaning for him, 'saving them may perhaps work out as a
branch. The question is can you be paid for it?'

'Beadel-Muffet would pay me,' Maud suddenly suggested.

'Why, that's just what I'm expecting,' her companion laughed, 'that he will, after to-morrow – directly or indirectly – do *me*.'

'Will you take it from him then only to get him in deeper, as that's what you perfectly know you'll do? You won't save him; you'll lose him.'

'What then would you, in the case,' Bight asked, 'do for your money?'

Well, the girl thought. 'I'd get him to see me – I should have first, I recognise, to catch my hare – and then I'd work up my stuff. Which would be boldly, quite by a masterstroke, a statement of his fix – of the fix, I mean, of his wanting, his supplicating to be dropped. I'd give out that it would really oblige. Then I'd send my copy about, and the rest of the matter would take care of itself. I don't say *you* could do it that way – you'd have a different effect. But I should be able to trust the thing, being mine, not to be looked at, or, if looked at, chucked straight into the basket. I should so have, to that extent, handled the matter, and I should so, by merely touching it, have broken the spell. That's my one line – I stop things off by touching them. There'd never be a word about him more.'

Her friend, with his legs out and his hands locked at the back of his neck, had listened with indulgence. 'Then hadn't I better arrange it for you that Beadel-Muffet shall see you?'

'Oh, not after you've damned him!'

'You want to see him first?'

'It will be the only way – to be of any use to him. You ought to wire him in fact not to open his mouth till he has seen me.'

'Well, I will,' said Bight at last. 'But, you know, we shall lose something very handsome – his struggle, all in vain, with his fate. Noble sport, the sight of it all.' He turned a little, to rest on his elbow, and, cycling suburban young man as he was, he might have been, outstretched under his tree, melancholy Jacques looking off into a forest glade, even as sailor-hatted Maud, in – for elegance – a new cotton blouse and a long-limbed angular attitude, might have prosefully suggested the mannish Rosalind. He raised his face in appeal to her. 'Do you really ask me to sacrifice it?'

'Rather than sacrifice *him*? Of course I do.'

He said for a while nothing more; only, propped on his elbow, lost himself again in the Park. After which he turned back to her. 'Will you have me?' he suddenly asked.

' "Have you"—?'

'Be my bonny bride. For better, for worse. I hadn't, upon my honour,' he explained with obvious sincerity, 'understood you were so down.'

'Well, it isn't so bad as that,' said Maud Blandy.

'So bad as taking up with *me*?'

'It isn't as bad as having let you know – when I didn't want you to.'

He sank back again with his head dropped, putting himself more at his ease. 'You're too proud – that's what's the matter with you. And I'm too stupid.'

'No, you're not,' said Maud grimly. 'Not stupid.'

'Only cruel, cunning, treacherous, cold-blooded, vile?' He drawled the words out softly, as if they sounded fair.

'And I'm not stupid either,' Maud Blandy went on. 'We just, poor creatures – well, we just *know*.'

'Of course we do. So why do you want us to drug ourselves with rot? to go on as if we didn't know?'

She made no answer for a moment; then she said: 'There's good to be known too.'

'Of course, again. There are all sorts of things, and some much better than others. That's why,' the young man added, 'I just put that question to you.'

'Oh no, it isn't. You put it to me because you think I feel I'm no good.'

'How so, since I keep assuring you that you've only to wait? How so, since I keep assuring you that if you do wait it will all come with a rush? But say I *am* sorry for you,' Bight lucidly pursued; 'how does that prove either that my motive is base or that I do you a wrong?'

The girl waived this question, but she presently tried another. 'Is it your idea that we should live on all the people—?'

'The people we catch? Yes, old man, till we can do better.'

'My conviction is,' she soon returned, 'that if I were to marry you I should dish you. I should spoil the business. It would fall off; and, as I can do nothing myself, then where should we be?'

'Well,' said Bight, 'we mightn't be quite so high up in the scale of the morbid.'

'It's you that are morbid,' she answered. 'You've, in your way – like everyone else, for that matter, all over the place – "sport" on the brain.'

'Well,' he demanded, 'what is sport but success? What is success but sport?'

'Bring that out somewhere. If it be true,' she said, 'I'm glad I'm a failure.'

After which, for a longish space, they sat together in silence, a silence finally broken by a word from the young man. 'But about Mortimer Marshal – how do you propose to save *him*?'

It was a change of subject that might, by its so easy introduction of matter irrelevant, have seemed intended to dissipate whatever was left of his proposal of marriage. That proposal, however, had been somehow both too much in the tone of familiarity to linger and too little in that of vulgarity to drop. It had had no form, but the mild air kept perhaps thereby the better the taste of it. This was sensibly moreover in what the girl found to reply. 'I think, you know, that he'd be no such bad friend. I mean that, with his appetite, there would be something to be done. He doesn't half hate me.'

'Ah, my dear,' her friend ejaculated, 'don't, for God's sake, be low.'

But she kept it up. 'He clings to me. You saw. It's hideous, the way he's able to "do" himself.'

Bight lay quiet, then spoke as with a recall of the Chippendale Club. 'Yes, I couldn't "do" you as he could. But if you don't bring it off—?'

'Why then does he cling? Oh, because, all the same, I'm potentially the Papers still. I'm at any rate the nearest he has got to them. And then I'm other things.'

'I see.'

'I'm so awfully attractive,' said Maud Blandy. She got up with this and, shaking out her frock, looked at her resting bicycle, looked at the distances possibly still to be gained. Her companion paused, but at last also rose, and by that time she was awaiting him, a little gaunt and still not quite cool, as an illustration of her last remark. He stood there watching her, and she followed this remark up. 'I do, you know, really pity him.'

It had almost a feminine fineness, and their eyes continued to meet. 'Oh, you'll work it!' And the young man went to his machine.

IV

IT was not till five days later that they again came together, and during these days many things had happened. Maud Blandy had, with high elation, for her own portion, a sharp sense of this; if it had at the time done nothing more intimate for her the Sunday of bitterness just spent with Howard Bight had started, all abruptly, a turn of the tide of her luck. This turn had not in the least been in the young man's having spoken to her of marriage – since she hadn't even, up to the late hour of their parting, so much as answered him straight: she dated the sense of difference much rather from the throb of a happy thought that had come to her while she cycled home to Kilburnia in the darkness. The throb had made her for the few minutes, tired as she was, put on speed, and it had been the cause of still further proceedings for her the first thing the next morning. The active step that was the essence of these proceedings had almost got itself taken before she went to bed; which indeed was what had happened to the extent of her writing, on the spot, a meditated letter. She sat down to it by the light of the guttering candle that awaited her on the dining-room table and in the stale air of family food that only *had* been – a residuum so at the mercy of mere ventilation that she didn't so much as peep into a cupboard; after which she had been on the point of nipping over, as she would have said, to drop it into that opposite pillar-box whose vivid maw, opening out through thick London nights, had received so many of her fruitless little ventures. But she had checked herself and waited, waited to be sure, with the morning, that her fancy wouldn't fade; posting her note in the end, however, with a confident jerk, as soon as she was up. She had, later on, had business, or at least had sought it, among the haunts that she had taught herself to regard as professional; but neither on the Monday nor on either of the days that directly followed had she encountered there the friend whom it would take a difference in more matters than could as yet be dealt with to enable her to regard, with proper assurance or with proper modesty, as a lover. Whatever he was, none the less, it couldn't otherwise have come to her that it was possible to feel lonely in the Strand. That showed, after all, how thick they must constantly have been – which *was* perhaps a thing to begin to think of in a new, in a steadier light. But it showed doubtless still more that her companion was probably up to something rather awful; it made her wonder, holding her breath a little, about Beadel-Muffet, made her certain that he and his affairs would partly account for Bight's whirl of absence.

Ever conscious of empty pockets, she had yet always a penny, or at least a ha'penny, for a paper, and those she now scanned, she quickly assured herself, were edited quite as usual. Sir A. B. C. Beadel-Muffet K. C. B., M. P. had returned on Monday from Undertone, where Lord and Lady Wispers had, from the previous Friday, entertained a very select party; Sir A. B. C. Beadel-Muffet K. C. B., M. P. was to attend on Tuesday the weekly meeting of the society of the Friends of Rest; Sir A. B. C. Beadel-Muffet K. C. B., M. P. had kindly consented to preside on Wednesday, at Samaritan House, at the opening of the Sale of Work of the Middlesex Incurables. These familiar announcements, however, far from appeasing her curiosity, had an effect upon her nerves; she read into them mystic meanings that she had never read before. Her freedom of mind in this direction was indeed at the same time limited, for her own horizon was already, by the Monday night, bristling with new possibilities, and the Tuesday itself – well, what had the Tuesday itself become, with this eruption, from within, of interest amounting really to a revelation, what had the Tuesday itself become but the greatest day yet of her life? Such a description of it would have appeared to apply predominantly to the morning had she not, under the influence, precisely, of the morning's thrill, gone, towards evening, with her design, into the Charing Cross Station. There, at the bookstall, she bought them all, every rag that was hawked; and there, as she unfolded one at a venture, in the crowd and under the lamps, she felt her consciousness further, felt it for the moment quite impressively, enriched. 'Personal Peeps – Number Ninety-Three: a Chat with the New Dramatist' needed neither the 'H. B.' as a terminal signature nor a text spangled, to the exclusion of almost everything else, with Mortimer Marshals that looked as tall as if lettered on posters, to help to account for her young man's use of his time. And yet, as she soon made out, it had been used with an economy that caused her both to wonder and to wince; the 'peep' commemorated being none other than their tea with the artless creature the previous Saturday, and the meagre incidents and pale impressions of that occasion furnishing forth the picture.

Bight had solicited no new interview; he hadn't been such a fool – for she saw, soon enough, with all her intelligence, that this was what he would have been, and that a repetition of contact would have dished him. What he *had* done, she found herself perceiving – and perceiving with an emotion that caused her face to glow – was journalism of the intensest essence; a column concocted of nothing, an omelette made, as it were, without even the breakage of the egg or two that might have been expected to be the price. The poor gentleman's whereabouts at five o'clock was the only egg broken, and this light and delicate crash was the sound in the world that would be sweetest to him. What stuff it had to be, since the writer really knew nothing about him, yet how its being just such stuff made it perfectly serve its purpose! She might have marvelled afresh, with more leisure, at such purposes, but she was lost in the wonder of seeing how, without matter, without thought, without an excuse, without a fact and yet at the same time sufficiently without a fiction, he had managed to be as resonant as if he had beaten a drum on the platform of a booth. And he had not been too personal, not made anything awkward for *her*, had given nothing and nobody away, had tossed the Chippendale Club into the air with such a turn that it had fluttered down

again, like a blown feather, miles from its site. The thirty-seven
agencies would already be posting to their subscriber thirty-
seven copies, and their subscriber, on his side, would be posting, to his acquaintance, many times thirty-seven, and thus at
least getting something for his money; but this didn't tell her
why her friend had taken the trouble – if it had *been* a trouble;
why at all events he had taken the time, pressed as he apparently
was for that commodity. These things she was indeed presently
to learn, but they were meanwhile part of a suspense composed
of more elements than any she had yet tasted. And the suspense
was prolonged, though other affairs too, that were not part of it,
almost equally crowded upon her; the week having almost
waned when relief arrived in the form of a cryptic post-card.
The post-card bore the H. B., like the precious 'Peep', which
had already had a wondrous sequel, and it appointed, for the
tea-hour, a place of meeting familiar to Maud, with the simple
addition of the significant word 'Larks!'

When the time he had indicated came she waited for him, at
their small table, swabbed like the deck of a steam-packet, nose
to nose with a mustard-pot and a price-list, in the consciousness of perhaps after all having as much to tell him as to hear
from him. It appeared indeed at first that this might well be the
case, for the questions that came up between them when he had
taken his place were overwhelmingly those he himself insisted
on putting. 'What has he done, what *has* he, and what will he?' –
that inquiry, not loud but deep, had met him as he sat down;
without however producing the least recognition. Then she as
soon felt that his silence and his manner were enough for her, or
that, if they hadn't been, his wonderful look, the straightest she
had ever had from him, would instantly have made them so. He
looked at her hard, hard, as if he had meant 'I say, mind your
eyes!' and it amounted really to a glimpse, rather fearful, of the
subject. It was no joke, the subject, clearly, and her friend had
fairly gained age, as he had certainly lost weight, in his recent
dealings with it. It struck her even, with everything else, that
this was positively the way she would have liked him to show if
their union had taken the form they hadn't reached the point of
discussing; wearily coming back to her from the thick of things,

wanting to put on his slippers and have his tea, all prepared by her and in their place, and beautifully to be trusted to regale her in his turn. He was excited, disavowedly, and it took more disavowal still after she had opened her budget – which she did, in truth, by saying to him as her first alternative: 'What did you do him *for*, poor Mortimer Marshal? It isn't that he's not in the seventh heaven—!'

'He *is* in the seventh heaven!' Bight quickly broke in. 'He doesn't want my blood?'

'Did you do him,' she asked, 'that he should want it? It's splendid how you could – simply on that show.'

'That show? Why,' said Howard Bight, 'that show was an immensity. That show was volumes, stacks, abysses.'

He said it in such a tone that she was a little at a loss. 'Oh, you don't want abysses.'

'Not much, to knock off such twaddle. There isn't a breath in it of what I saw. What I saw is my own affair. I've got the abysses for myself. They're in my head – it's always something. But the monster,' he demanded, 'has written you?'

'How couldn't he – that night? I got it the next morning, telling me how much he wanted to thank me and asking me where he might see me. So I went,' said Maud, 'to see him.'

'At his own place again?'

'At his own place again. What do I yearn for but to be received at people's own places?'

'Yes, for the stuff. But when you've had – as you had had from him – the stuff?'

'Well, sometimes, you see, I get more. He gives me all I can take.' It was in her head to ask if by chance Bight were jealous, but she gave it another turn. 'We had a big palaver, partly about you. He appreciates.'

'Me?'

'Me – first of all, I think. All the more that I've had – fancy! – a proof of my stuff, the despised and rejected, as originally concocted, and that he has now seen it. I tried it on again with *Brains*, the night of your thing – sent it off with your thing enclosed as a rouser. They took it, by return, like a shot

– you'll see on Wednesday. And if the dear man lives till then, for impatience, I'm to lunch with him that day.'

'I see,' said Bight. 'Well, that was what I did it for. It shows how right I was.'

They faced each other, across their thick crockery, with eyes that said more than their words, and that, above all, said, and asked, other things. So she went on in a moment: 'I don't know what he doesn't expect. And he thinks I can keep it up.'

'Lunch with him *every* Wednesday?'

'Oh, he'd give me my lunch, and more. It was last Sunday that you were right – about my sitting close,' she pursued. 'I'd have been a pretty fool to jump. Suddenly, I see, the music begins. I'm awfully obliged to you.'

'You feel,' he presently asked, 'quite differently – so differently that I've missed my chance? I don't care for *that* serpent, but there's something else that you don't tell me.' The young man, detached and a little spent, with his shoulder against the wall and a hand vaguely playing over the knives, forks and spoons, dropped his succession of sentences without an apparent direction. 'Something else has come up, and you're as pleased as Punch. Or, rather, you're not quite entirely so, because you can't goad me to fury. You can't worry me as much as you'd like. Marry me first, old man, and *then* see if I mind. Why shouldn't you keep it up? – I mean lunching with him?' His questions came as in play that was a little pointless, without his waiting more than a moment for answers; though it was not indeed that she might not have answered even in the moment, had not the pointless play been more what she wanted. 'Was it at the place,' he went on, 'that he took us to?'

'Dear no – at his flat, where I've been before. You'll see, in *Brains*, on Wednesday. I don't think I've muffed it – it's really rather there. But he showed me everything this time – the bathroom, the refrigerator, and the machines for stretching his trousers. He has nine, and in constant use.'

'Nine?' said Bight gravely.

'Nine.'

'Nine trousers?'

'Nine machines. I don't know how many trousers.'

'Ah, my dear,' he said, 'that's a grave omission; the want of the information will be felt and resented. But does it all, at any rate,' he asked, 'sufficiently fetch you?' After which, as she didn't speak, he lapsed into helpless sincerity. 'Is it really, you think, his dream to secure you?'

She replied, on this, as if his tone made it too amusing. 'Quite. There's no mistaking it. He sees me as, most days in the year, pulling the wires and beating the drum somewhere; that is he sees me of course not exactly as writing about "our home" – once I've got one – myself, but as procuring others to do it through my being (as *you've* made him believe) in with the Organs of Public Opinion. He doesn't see, if I'm half decent, why there shouldn't be something about him every day in the week. He's all right, and he's all ready. And who, after all, *can* do him so well as the partner of his flat? It's like making, in one of those big domestic siphons, the luxury of the poor, your own soda-water. It comes cheaper, and it's always on the sideboard. "*Vichy chez soi.*" The interviewer at home.'

Her companion took it in. 'Your place is on *my* sideboard – you're really a first-class fizz! He steps then, at any rate, into Beadel-Muffet's place.'

'That,' Maud assented, 'is what he would like to do.' And she knew more than ever there was something to wait for.

'It's a lovely opening,' Bight returned. But he still said, for the moment, nothing else; as if, charged to the brim though he had originally been, she had rather led his thought away.

'What have you done with poor Beadel?' she consequently asked. 'What is it, in the name of goodness, you're doing *to* him? It's worse than ever.'

'Of course it's worse than ever.'

'He capers,' said Maud, 'on every housetop – he jumps out of every bush.' With which her anxiety really broke out. '*Is* it you that are doing it?'

'If you mean am I seeing him, I certainly am. I'm seeing nobody else. I assure you he's spread thick.'

'But you're acting for him?'

Bight waited. 'Five hundred people are acting for him; but the difficulty is that what he calls the "terrific forces of publicity" – by which he means ten thousand *other* persons – are acting against him. We've all in fact been turned on – to turn everything off, and that's exactly the job that makes the biggest noise. It appears everywhere, in every kind of connection and every kind of type, that Sir A. B. C. Beadel-Muffet K.C.B., M.P. desires to cease to appear *anywhere*; and then it appears that his desiring to cease to appear is observed to conduce directly to his more tremendously appearing, or certainly, and in the most striking manner, to his not in the least *dis*appearing. The workshop of silence roars like the Zoo at dinner-time. He *can't* disappear; he hasn't weight enough to sink; the splash the diver makes, you know, tells where he is. If you ask me what I'm doing,' Bight wound up, 'I'm holding him under water. But we're in the middle of the pond, the banks are thronged with spectators, and I'm expecting from day to day to see stands erected and gate-money taken. There,' he wearily smiled, 'you have it. Besides,' he then added with an odd change of tone, 'I rather think you'll see to-morrow.'

He had made her at last horribly nervous. 'What shall I see?'

'It will all be out.'

'Then why shouldn't you tell me?'

'Well,' the young man said, 'he *has* disappeared. There you are. I mean personally. He's not to be found. But nothing could make more, you see, for ubiquity. The country will ring with it. He vanished on Tuesday night – was then last seen at his club. Since then he has given no sign. How can a man disappear who does *that* sort of thing? It is, as you say, to caper on the house-tops. But it will only be known to-night.'

'Since when, then,' Maud asked, 'have you known it?'

'Since three o'clock to-day. But I've kept it. I *am* – a while longer – keeping it.'

She wondered; she was full of fears. 'What do you expect to get for it?'

'Nothing – if you spoil my market. I seem to make out that you want to.'

She gave this no heed; she had her thought. 'Why then did you three days ago wire me a mystic word?'

'Mystic—?'

'What do you call "Larks"?'

'Oh, I remember. Well, it was because I saw larks coming; because I saw, I mean, what has happened. I was sure it would have to happen.'

'And what the mischief *is* it?'

Bight smiled. 'Why, what I tell you. That he has gone.'

'Gone where?'

'Simply bolted to parts unknown. "Where" is what nobody who belongs to him is able in the least to say, or seems likely to be able.'

'Any more than why?'

'Any more than why.'

'Only *you* are able to say that?'

'Well,' said Bight, 'I can say what has so lately stared me in the face, what he has been thrusting at me in all its grotesqueness: his desire for a greater privacy worked through the Papers themselves. He came to me with it,' the young man presently added. 'I didn't go to *him*.'

'And he trusted you,' Maud replied.

'Well, you see what I have given him – the very flower of my genius. What more do you want? I'm spent, seedy, sore. I'm sick,' Bight declared, 'of his beastly funk.'

Maud's eyes, in spite of it, were still a little hard. 'Is he thoroughly sincere?'

'Good God, no! How *can* he be? Only trying it – as a cat, for a jump, tries too smooth a wall. He drops straight back.'

'Then isn't his funk real?'

'As real as he himself is.'

Maud wondered. 'Isn't his flight—?'

'That's what we shall see!'

'Isn't,' she continued, 'his reason?'

'Ah,' he laughed out, 'there you are again!'

But she had another thought and was not discouraged. 'Mayn't he be, honestly, mad?'

'Mad – oh yes. But not, I think, honestly. He's not honestly anything in the world but the Beadel-Muffet of our delight.'

'Your delight,' Maud observed after a moment, 'revolts me.' And then she said: 'When did you last see him?'

'On Tuesday at six, love. I was one of the last.'

'Decidedly, too, then, I judge, one of the worst.' She gave him her idea. 'You hounded him on.'

'I reported,' said Bight, 'success. Told him how it was going.'

'Oh, I can see you! So that if he's dead—'

'Well?' asked Bight blandly.

'His blood is on your hands.'

He eyed his hands a moment. 'They *are* dirty for him! But now, darling,' he went on, 'be so good as to show me yours.'

'Tell me first,' she objected, 'what you believe. *Is* it suicide?'

'I think that's the thing for us to make it. Till somebody,' he smiled, 'makes it something else.' And he showed how he warmed to the view. 'There are weeks of it, dearest, yet.'

He leaned more toward her, with his elbows on the table, and in this position, moved by her extreme gravity, he lightly flicked her chin with his finger. She threw herself, still grave, back from his touch, but they remained thus a while closely confronted. 'Well,' she at last remarked, 'I shan't pity you.'

'You make it, then, everyone except me?'

'I mean,' she continued, 'if you do have to loathe yourself.'

'Oh, I shan't miss it.' And then as if to show how little, 'I did mean it, you know, at Richmond,' he declared.

'I won't have you if you've killed him,' she presently returned.

'You'll decide in that case for the *nine*?' And as the allusion, with its funny emphasis, left her blank: 'You want to wear *all* the trousers?'

'You deserve,' she said, when light came, 'that I should take him.' And she kept it up. 'It's a lovely flat.'

Well, he could do as much. 'Nine, I suppose, appeals to you as the number of the muses?'

This short passage, remarkably, for all its irony, brought them together again, to the extent at least of leaving Maud's elbows on the table and of keeping her friend, now a little back in his chair, firm while he listened to her. So the girl came out.

'I've seen Mrs Chorner three times. I wrote that night, after our talk at Richmond, asking her to oblige. And I put on cheek as I had never, never put it. I said the public would be so glad to hear from her "on the occasion of her engagement". '

'Do you call that cheek?' Bight looked amused. 'She at any rate rose straight.'

'No, she rose crooked; but she rose. What you had told me there in the Park – well, immediately happened. She did consent to see me, and so far you had been right in keeping me up to it. But what do you think it was for?'

'To show you *her* flat, *her* tub, *her* petticoats?'

'She doesn't live in a flat; she lives in a house of her own, and a jolly good one, in Green Street, Park Lane; though I did, as happened, see her tub, which is a dream – all marble and silver, like a kind of a swagger sarcophagus, a thing for the Wallace Collection; and though her petticoats, as she first shows, seem all that, if you wear petticoats yourself, you can look at. There's no doubt of her money – given her place and her things, and given her appearance too, poor dear, which would take some doing.'

'She squints?' Bight sympathetically asked.

'She's so ugly that she *has* to be rich – she couldn't afford it on less than five thousand a year. As it is, I could well see, she can afford anything – even such a nose. But she's funny and decent; sharp, but a really good sort. And they're *not* engaged.'

'She told you so? Then there you are!'

'It all depends,' Maud went on; 'and you don't know where I am at all. *I* know what it depends on.'

'Then there you are again! It's a mine of gold.'

'Possibly, but not in your sense. She wouldn't give me the first word of an interview – it wasn't for that she received me. It was for something much better.'

Well, Bight easily guessed. 'For *my* job?'

'To see what can be done. She loathes his publicity.'

The young man's face lighted. 'She told you so?'

'She received me on purpose to tell me.'

'Then why do you question my "larks"? What do you want more?'

'I want nothing – with what I have: nothing, I mean, but to help her. We made friends – I like her. And she likes *me*,' said Maud Blandy.

'Like Mortimer Marshal, precisely.'

'No, precisely not like Mortimer Marshal. I caught, on the spot, her idea – *that* was what took her. Her idea is that I can help her – help her to keep them quiet about Beadel: for which purpose I seem to have struck her as falling from the skies, just at the right moment, into her lap.'

Howard Bight followed, yet lingered by the way. 'To keep *whom* quiet—?'

'Why, the beastly Papers – what we've been talking about. She wants him straight out of them – *straight*.'

'She too?' Bight wondered. 'Then *she's* in terror?'

'No, not in terror – or it wasn't that when I last saw her. But in mortal disgust. She feels it has gone too far – which is what she wanted me, as an honest, decent, likely young woman, up to my neck in it, as she supposed, to understand from her. My relation with her is now that I do understand and that if an improvement takes place I shan't have been the worse for it. Therefore you see,' Maud went on, 'you simply cut my throat when you prevent improvement.'

'Well, my dear,' her friend returned, 'I won't let you bleed to death.' And he showed, with this, as confessedly struck. 'She doesn't then, you think, *know*—?'

'Know what?'

'Why, what, about him, there may *be* to be known. Doesn't know of his flight.'

'She didn't – certainly.'

'Nor of anything to make it likely?'

'What you call his queer reason? No – she named it to me no more than you have; though she does mention, distinctly, that he himself hates, or pretends to hate, the exhibition daily made of him.'

'She speaks of it,' Bight asked, 'as pretending—?'

Maud straightened it out. 'She feels him – *that* she practically told me – as rather ridiculous. She honestly has her feeling; and, upon my word, it's what I like her for. Her stomach has turned and she has made it her condition. "Muzzle your Press," she says; "*then* we'll talk." She gives him three months – she'll give him even six. And this, meanwhile – when he comes to *you* – is how you forward the muzzling.'

'The Press, my child,' Bight said, 'is the watchdog of civilisation, and the watchdog happens to be – it can't be helped – in a chronic state of *rabies*. Muzzling is easy talk; one can but keep the animal on the run. Mrs Chorner, however,' he added, 'seems a figure of fable.'

'It's what I told you she would have to be when, some time back, you threw out, as a pure hypothesis, to supply the man with a motive, your exact vision of her. Your motive has come true,' Maud went on – 'with the difference only, if I understand you, that this doesn't appear the whole of it. That doesn't matter' – she frankly paid him a tribute. 'Your forecast was inspiration.'

'A stroke of genius' – he had been the first to feel it. But there were matters less clear. 'When did you see her last?'

'Four days ago. It was the third time.'

'And even then she didn't imagine the truth about him?'

'I don't know, you see,' said Maud, 'what you *call* the truth.'

'Well, that he – quite by that time – didn't know where the deuce to turn. That's truth enough.'

Maud made sure. 'I don't see how she can have known it and not have been upset. She wasn't,' said the girl, 'upset. She *isn't* upset. But she's original.'

'Well, poor thing,' Bight remarked, 'she'll have to be.'

'Original?'

'Upset. Yes, and original too, if she doesn't give up the job.' It had held him an instant – but there were many things. 'She sees the wild ass he is, and yet she's willing—?'

' "Willing" is just what I asked *you* three months ago,' Maud returned, 'how she *could* be.'

He had lost it – he tried to remember. 'What then did I say?'

'Well, practically, that women are idiots. Also, I believe, that he's a dazzling beauty.'

'Ah yes, he *is*, poor wretch, though beauty to-day in distress.'

'Then there you are,' said Maud. They had got up, as at the end of their story, but they stood a moment while he waited for change. 'If it comes out,' the girl dropped, '*that* will save him. If he's dishonoured – as I see her – she'll have him, because then he won't be ridiculous. And I can understand it.'

Bight looked at her in such appreciation that he forgot, as he pocketed it, to glance at his change. 'Oh, you creatures—!'

'Idiots, aren't we?'

Bight let the question pass, but still with his eyes on her, 'You ought to want him to *be* dishonoured.'

'I can't want him, then – if he's to get the good of it – to be dead.'

Still for a little he looked at her. 'And if *you're* to get the good?' But she had turned away, and he went with her to the door, before which, when they had passed out, they had in the side-street, a backwater to the flood of the Strand, a further sharp colloquy. They were alone, the small street for a moment empty, and they felt at first that they had adjourned to a greater privacy, of which, for that matter, he took prompt advantage. 'You're to lunch again with the man of the flat?'

'Wednesday, as I say; 1.45.'

'Then oblige me by stopping away.'

'You don't like it?' Maud asked.

'Oblige me, oblige me,' he repeated.

'And disoblige *him*?'

'Chuck him. We've started him. It's enough.'

Well, the girl but wanted to be fair. 'It's *you* who started him; so I admit you're quits.'

'That then started *you* – made *Brains* repent; so you see what you both owe me. I let the creature off, but I hold you to your debt. There's only one way for you to meet it.' And then as she but looked into the roaring Strand: 'With worship.' It made her, after a minute, meet his eyes, but something just then occurred that stayed any word on the lips of either. A sound reached their ears, as yet unheeded, the sound of newsboys in the great thoroughfare shouting 'extra-specials' and mingling with the shout a catch that startled them. The expression in their eyes quickened as they heard, borne on the air, 'Mysterious Disappearance—!' and then lost it in the hubbub. It was easy to complete the cry, and Bight himself gasped. 'Beadel-Muffet? Confound them!'

'Already?' Maud had turned positively pale.

'They've got it first – be hanged to them!'

Bight gave a laugh – a tribute to their push – but her hand was on his arm for a sign to listen again. It was there, in the raucous throats; it was there, for a penny, under the lamps and in the thick of the stream that stared and passed and left it. They caught the whole thing – 'Prominent Public Man!' And there was something brutal and sinister in the way it was given to the flaring night, to the other competing sounds, to the general hardness of hearing and sight which was yet, on London pavements, compatible with an interest sufficient for cynicism. He had been, poor Beadel, public and prominent, but he had never affected Maud Blandy at least as so marked with this character as while thus loudly committed to extinction. It was horrid – it was tragic; yet her lament for him was dry. 'If he's gone I'm dished.'

'Oh, he's gone – now,' said Bight.

'I mean if he's dead.'

'Well, perhaps he isn't. I see,' Bight added, 'what you do mean. If he's dead you can't kill him.'

'Oh, she wants him alive,' said Maud.

'Otherwise she can't chuck him?'

To which the girl, however, anxious and wondering, made no direct reply. 'Good-bye to Mrs Chorner. And I owe it to *you*.'

'Ah, my love!' he vaguely appealed.

'Yes, it's you who have destroyed him, and it makes up for what you've done *for* me.'

'I've done it, you mean, against you? I didn't know,' he said, 'you'd take it so hard.'

Again, as he spoke, the cries sounded out: 'Mysterious Disappearance of Prominent Public Man!' It seemed to swell as they listened; Maud started with impatience. 'I hate it too much,' she said, and quitted him to join the crowd.

He was quickly at her side, however, and before she reached the Strand he had brought her again to a pause. 'Do you mean you hate it so much you won't have me?'

It had pulled her up short, and her answer was proportionately straight. 'I won't have you if he's dead.'

'Then will you if he's not?'

At this she looked at him hard. 'Do you *know*, first?'

'No – blessed if I do.'

'On your honour?'

'On my honour.'

'Well,' she said after a hesitation, 'if *she* doesn't drop me—'

'It's an understood thing?' he pressed.

But again she hung fire. 'Well, produce him first.'

They stood there striking their bargain, and it was made, by the long look they exchanged, a question of good faith. 'I'll produce him,' said Howard Bight.

V

If it had not been a disaster, Beadel-Muffet's plunge into the obscure, it would have been a huge success; so large a space did the prominent public man occupy, for the next few days, in the Papers, so near did he come, nearer certainly than ever before, to supplanting other topics. The question of his whereabouts, of his antecedents, of his habits, of his possible motives, of his probable, or improbable, embarrassments, fairly raged, from day to day and from hour to hour, making the Strand, for our two young friends, quite fiercely, quite cruelly vociferous. They met again promptly, in the thick of the uproar, and no other eyes could have scanned the current rumours and remarks so eagerly as Maud's unless it had been those of Maud's companion. The rumours and remarks were mostly very wonderful, and all of a nature to sharpen the excitement produced in the comrades by their being already, as they felt, 'in the know'. Even for the girl this sense existed, so that she could smile at wild surmises; she struck herself as knowing much more than she did, especially as, with the alarm once given, she abstained, delicately enough, from worrying, from catechising Bight. She

only looked at him as to say 'See, while the suspense lasts, how
generously I spare you,' and her attitude was not affected by the
interested promise he had made her. She believed he knew
more than he said, though he had sworn as to what he didn't;
she saw him in short as holding some threads but having lost
others, and his state of mind, so far as she could read it,
represented in equal measure assurances unsupported and
anxieties unconfessed. He would have liked to pass for having,
on cynical grounds, and for the mere ironic beauty of it,
believed that the hero of the hour was only, as he had always
been, 'up to' something from which he would emerge more
than ever glorious, or at least conspicuous; but, knowing the
gentleman was more than anything, more than all else, asinine,
he was not deprived of ground in which fear could abundantly
grow. If Beadel, in other words, was ass enough, as was conceivable, to be working the occasion, he was by the same token
ass enough to have lost control of it, to have committed some
folly from which even fools don't rebound. That was the spark
of suspicion lurking in the young man's ease, and that, Maud
knew, explained something else.

The family and friends had but too promptly been
approached, been besieged; yet Bight, in all the promptness,
had markedly withdrawn from the game – had had, one could
easily judge, already too much to do with it. Who but he,
otherwise, would have been so naturally let loose upon the
forsaken home, the bewildered circle, the agitated club,
the friend who had last conversed with the eminent absentee,
the waiter, in exclusive halls, who had served him with five-
o'clock tea, the porter, in august Pall Mall, who had called his
last cab, the cabman, supremely privileged, who had driven
him – where? 'The Last Cab' would, as our young woman
reflected, have been a heading so after her friend's own heart,
and so consonant with his genius, that it took all her discretion
not to ask him how he had resisted it. She didn't ask, she but
herself noted the title for future use – she would have at least got
that, 'The Last Cab', out of the business; and, as the days went
by and the extra-specials swarmed, the situation between them
swelled with all the unspoken. Matters that were grave

depended on it for each – and nothing so much, for instance, as her seeing Mrs Chorner again. To see that lady as things *had* been had meant that the poor woman might have been helped to believe in her. Believing in her she would have paid her, and Maud, disposed as she was, really had felt capable of earning the pay. Whatever, as the case stood, was caused to hang in the air, nothing dangled more free than the profit derivable from muzzling the Press. With the watchdog to whom Bight had compared it barking for dear life, the moment was scarcely adapted for calling afresh upon a person who had offered a reward for silence. The only silence, as we say, was in the girl's not mentioning to her friend how these embarrassments affected her. Mrs Chorner was a person she liked – a connection more to her taste than any she had professionally made, and the thought of her now on the rack, tormented with suspense, might well have brought to her lips a 'See *there* what you've done!'

There was, for that matter, in Bight's face – he couldn't keep it out – precisely the look of seeing it; which was one of her reasons too for not insisting on her wrong. If he couldn't conceal it this was a part of the rest of the unspoken; he didn't allude to the lady lest it might be too sharply said to him that it was on *her* account he should most blush. Last of all he was hushed by the sense of what he had himself said when the news first fell on their ears. His promise to 'produce' the fugitive was still in the air, but with every day that passed the prospect turned less to redemption. Therefore if her own promise, on a different head, depended on it, he was naturally not in a hurry to bring the question to a test. So it was accordingly that they but read the Papers and looked at each other. Maud felt in truth that these organs had never been so worth it, nor either she or her friend – whatever the size of old obligations – so much beholden to them. They helped them to wait, and the better, really, the longer the mystery lasted. It grew of course daily richer, adding to its mass as it went and multiplying its features, looming especially larger through the cloud of correspondence, communication, suggestion, supposition, speculation, with which it was presently suffused. Theories and explanations sprouted at night and bloomed in the morning, to be over-topped at noon by a still thicker crop and to achieve by evening the density of a tropical forest. These, again, were the green glades in which our young friends wandered.

Under the impression of the first night's shock Maud had written to Mortimer Marshal to excuse herself from her engagement to luncheon – a step of which she had promptly advised Bight as a sign of her playing fair. He took it, she could see, for what it was worth, but she could see also how little he now cared. He was thinking of the man with whose strange agitation he had so cleverly and recklessly played, and, in the face of the catastrophe of which they were still so likely to have news, the vanities of smaller fools, the conveniences of first-class flats, the memory of Chippendale teas, ceased to be actual or ceased at any rate to be importunate. Her old inter-view, furbished into freshness, had appeared, on its Wednes-day, in *Brains*, but she had not received in person the renewed homage of its author – she had only, once more, had the vision of his inordinate purchase and diffusion of the precious num-ber. It was a vision, however, at which neither Bight nor she smiled; it was funny on so poor a scale compared with their other show. But it befell that when this latter had, for ten days, kept being funny to the tune that so lengthened their faces, the poor gentleman glorified in *Brains* succeeded in making it clear that he was not easily to be dropped. He wanted now, evidently, as the girl said to herself, to live at concert pitch, and she gathered, from three or four notes, to which, at short intervals, he treated her, that he was watching in anxiety for reverbera-tions not as yet perceptible. His expectation of results from what our young couple had done for him would, as always, have been a thing for pity with a young couple less imbued with the comic sense; though indeed it would also have been a comic thing for a young couple less attentive to a different drama. Disappointed of the girl's company at home the author of *Corisanda* had proposed fresh appointments, which she had desired at the moment, and indeed more each time, not to take up; to the extent even that, catching sight of him, unper-ceived, on one of these occasions, in her inveterate Strand, she checked on the spot a first impulse to make herself apparent. He was before her, in the crowd, and going the same way. He had stopped a little to look at a shop, and it was then that she swerved in time not to pass close to him. She turned and reversed, conscious and convinced that he was, as she mentally put it, on the prowl for her.

She herself, poor creature – as she also mentally put it – she herself was shamelessly on the prowl, but it wasn't, for her self-respect, to get herself puffed, it wasn't to pick up a personal advantage. It was to pick up news of Beadel-Muffet, to be near the extra-specials, and it was, also – as to this she was never blind – to cultivate that nearness by chances of Howard Bight. The blessing of blindness, in truth, at this time, she scantily enjoyed – being perfectly aware of the place occupied, in her present attitude to that young man, by the simple impossibility of not seeing him. She had done with him, certainly, if he *had* killed Beadel, and nothing was now growing so fast as the presumption in favour of some catastrophe, yet shockingly to be revealed, enacted somewhere in desperate darkness – though probably 'on lines', as the Papers said, anticipated by none of the theorists in their own columns, any more than by clever people at the clubs, where the betting was so heavy. She had done with him, indubitably, but she had not – it was equally unmistakeable – done with letting him see how thoroughly she *would* have done; or, to feel about it otherwise, she was laying up treasure in time – as against the privations of the future. She was affected moreover – perhaps but half-consciously – by another consideration; her attitude to Mortimer Marshal had turned a little to fright; she wondered, uneasily, at impressions she might have given him; and she had it, finally, on her mind that, whether or no the vain man believed in them, there must be a limit to the belief she had communicated to her friend. He *was* her friend, after all – whatever should happen; and there were things that, even in that hampered character, she couldn't allow him to suppose. It was a queer business now, in fact, for her to ask herself if she, Maud Blandy, had produced on any sane human sense an effect of flirtation.

She saw herself in this possibility as in some grotesque reflector, a full-length looking-glass of the inferior quality that deforms and discolours. It made her, as a flirt, a figure for frank derision, and she entertained, honest girl, none of the self-pity that would have spared her a shade of this sharpened consciousness, have taken an inch from facial proportion where it would have been missed with advantage, or added one in such other quarters as would have welcomed the gift. She might have counted the hairs of her head, for any wish she could have achieved to remain vague about them, just as she might have rehearsed, disheartened, postures of grace, for any dream she could compass of having ever accidentally struck one. Void, in short, of a personal illusion, exempt with an exemption which left her not less helplessly aware of where her hats and skirts and shoes failed, than of where her nose and mouth and complexion, and, above all, where her poor figure, without a scrap of drawing, did, she blushed to bethink herself that she might have affected her young man as really bragging of a conquest. Her *other* young man's pursuit of her, what was it but rank greed – not in the least for her person, but for the connection of which he had formed so preposterous a view? She was ready now to say to herself that she had swaggered to Bight for the joke – odd indeed though the wish to undeceive him at the moment when he would have been more welcome than ever to think what he liked. The only thing she wished him not to think, as she believed, was that she thought Mortimer Marshal thought her – or anyone on earth thought her – intrinsically charming. She didn't want to put to him 'Do you suppose I suppose that if it came to the point—?' her reasons for such avoidance being easily conceivable. He was not to suppose that, in any such quarter, she struck herself as either casting a spell or submitting to one; only, while their crisis lasted, rectifications were scarce in order. She couldn't remind him even, without a mistake, that she had but wished to worry him; because in the first place that suggested again a pretension in her (so at variance with the image in the mirror) to put forth arts – suggested possibly even that she used similar ones when she lunched, in bristling flats, with the pushing; and because in the second it would have seemed a sort of challenge to him to renew his appeal.

Then, further and most of all, she had a doubt which by itself would have made her wary, as it distinctly, in her present suspended state, made her uncomfortable; she was haunted by the after-sense of having perhaps been fatuous. A spice of conviction, in respect to what was open to her, an element of elation, in her talk to Bight about Marshal, had there not, after all, been? Hadn't she a little liked to think the wretched man *could* cling to her? and hadn't she also a little, for herself, filled out the future, in fancy, with the picture of the droll relation? She had seen it as droll, evidently; but had she seen it as impossible, unthinkable? It had become unthinkable now, and she was not wholly unconscious of how the change had worked. Such workings were queer – but there they were; the foolish man had become odious to her precisely *because* she was hardening her face for Bight. The latter was no foolish man, but this it was that made it the more a pity he should have placed the impassable between them. That was what, as the days went on, she felt herself take in. It was there, the impassable – she couldn't lucidly have said why, couldn't have explained the thing on the real scale of the wrong her comrade had done. It was a wrong, it was a wrong – she couldn't somehow get out of that; which was a proof, no doubt, that she confusedly tried. The author of *Corisanda* was sacrificed in the effort – for ourselves it may come to that. Great to poor Maud Blandy as well, for that matter, great, yet also attaching, were the obscurity and ambiguity in which some impulses lived and moved – the rich gloom of their combinations, contradictions, inconsistencies, surprises. It rested her verily a little from her straightness – the line of a character, she felt, markedly like the line of the Edgware Road and of Maida Vale – that she *could* be queerly inconsistent, and inconsistent in the hustling Strand, where, if anywhere, you had, under pain of hoofs and wheels, to decide whether or no you would cross. She had moments, before shop-windows, into which she looked without seeing, when all the unuttered came over her. She had once told her friend that she pitied everyone, and at these moments, in

sharp unrest, she pitied Bight for their tension, in which nothing was relaxed.

It was all too mixed and too strange – each of them in a
different corner with a different impossibility. There was her
own, in far Kilburnia; and there was her friend's, everywhere –
for where didn't he go? and there was Mrs Chorner's, on the
very edge of Park 'Line', in spite of all petticoats and marble
baths; and there was Beadel-Muffet's, the wretched man, God
only knew where – which was what made the whole show
supremely incoherent: he ready to give his head, if, as seemed
so unlikely, he still *had* a head, to steal into cover and keep
under, out of the glare; he having scoured Europe, it might so
well be guessed, for some hole in which the Papers wouldn't
find him out, and then having – what else was there by this time
to presume? – died, in the hole, as the only way not to see, to
hear, to know, let alone *be* known, heard, seen. Finally, while he
lay there relieved by the only relief, here was poor Mortimer
Marshal, undeterred, undismayed, unperceiving, so hungry to
be paragraphed in something like the same fashion and published on something like the same scale, that, for the very
blindness of it, he couldn't read the lesson that was in the air,
and scrambled, to his utmost, toward the boat itself that ferried
the warning ghost. Just *that*, beyond everything, was the incoherence that made for rather dismal farce, and on which
Bight had put his finger in naming the author of *Corisanda* as
a candidate, in turn, for the comic, the tragic vacancy. It was a
wonderful moment for such an ideal, and the sight was not
really to pass from her till she had seen the whole of the wonder.
A fortnight had elapsed since the night of Beadel's disappearance, and the conditions attending the afternoon performances
of the Finnish drama had in some degree reproduced themselves – to the extent, that is, of the place, the time and several
of the actors involved; the audience, for reasons traceable,
being differently composed. A lady of 'high social position',
desirous still further to elevate that character by the obvious aid
of the theatre, had engaged a playhouse for a series of occasions
on which she was to affront in person whatever volume of
attention she might succeed in collecting. Her success had

not immediately been great, and by the third or the fourth day the public consciousness was so markedly astray that the means taken to recover it penetrated, in the shape of a complimentary ticket, even to our young woman. Maud had communicated with Bight, who could be sure of a ticket, proposing to him that they should go together and offering to await him in the porch of the theatre. He joined her there, but with so queer a face – for her subtlety – that she paused before him, previous to their going in, with a straight 'You *know* something!'

'About that rank idiot?' He shook his head, looking kind enough; but it didn't make him, she felt, more natural. 'My dear, it's all beyond me.'

'I mean,' she said with a shade of uncertainty, 'about poor dear Beadel.'

'So do I. So does everyone. No one now, at any moment, means anything about anyone else. But I've lost intellectual control – of the extraordinary case. I flattered myself I still had a certain amount. But the situation at last escapes me. I break down. Non comprenny? I give it up.'

She continued to look at him hard. 'Then what's the matter with you?'

'Why, just *that*, probably – that I feel like a clever man "done", and that your tone with me adds to the feeling. Or, putting it otherwise, it's perhaps only just one of the ways in which I'm so interesting; that, with the life we lead and the age we live in, there's *always* something the matter with me – there can't help being: some rage, some disgust, some fresh amazement against which one hasn't, for all one's experience, been proof. That sense – of having been sold again – produces emotions that may well, on occasion, be reflected in the countenance. There you are.'

Well, he might say that, 'There you are,' as often as he liked without, at the pass they had come to, making her in the least see where she was. She was only just where she stood, a little apart in the lobby, listening to his words, which she found eminently characteristic of him, struck with an odd impression of his talking against time, and, most of all, tormented to recognise that she could fairly do nothing better, at such a moment, than feel he was awfully nice. The moment – that of his most blandly (she would have said in the case of another most impudently) failing, all round, to satisfy her – was appropriate only to some emotion consonant with her dignity. It was all crowded and covered, hustled and interrupted now; but what really happened in this brief passage, and with her finding no words to reply to him, was that dignity quite appeared to collapse and drop from her, to sink to the floor, under the feet of people visibly bristling with 'paper', where the young man's extravagant offer of an arm, to put an end and help her in, had the effect of an invitation to leave it lying to be trampled on.

Within, once seated, they kept their places through two intervals, but at the end of the third act – there were to be no less than five – they fell in with a movement that carried half the audience to the outer air. Howard Bight desired to smoke, and Maud offered to accompany him, for the purpose, to the portico, where, somehow, for both of them, the sense was immediately strong that *this*, the squalid Strand, damp yet incandescent, ugly yet eloquent, familiar yet fresh, was life, palpable, ponderable, possible, much more than the stuff, neither scenic nor cosmic, they had quitted. The difference came to them, from the street, in a most mild blast, which they simply took in, at first, in a long draught, as more amusing than their play, and which, for the moment, kept them conscious of the voices of the air as of something mixed and vague. The next thing, of course, however, was that they heard the hoarse newsmen, though with the special sense of the sound not standing out – which, so far as it did come, made them exchange a look. There was no hawker just then within call.

'What are they crying?'

'Blessed if I care!' Bight said while he got his light – which he had but just done when they saw themselves closely approached. The Papers had come into sight in the form of a small boy bawling the 'Winner' of something, and at the same moment they recognised their reprieve they recognised also the presence of Mortimer Marshal.

He had no shame about it. 'I fully believed I should find you.'

'But you haven't been,' Bight asked, 'inside?'

'Not at to-day's performance – I only just thought I'd pass. But at each of the others,' Mortimer Marshal confessed.

'Oh, you're a devotee,' said Bight, whose reception of the poor man contended, for Maud's attention, with this extravagance of the poor man's own importunity. Their friend had sat through the piece three times on the chance of her being there for one or other of the acts, and if he had given that up in discouragement he still hovered and waited. Who now, moreover, was to say he wasn't rewarded? To find her companion as well as at last to find herself gave the reward a character that it took, somehow, for her eye, the whole of this misguided person's curiously large and flat, but distinctly bland, sweet, solicitous countenance to express. It came over the girl with horror that here was a material object – the incandescence, on the edge of the street, didn't spare it – which she had had perverse moments of seeing fixed before her for life. She asked herself, in this agitation, what she would have likened it to; more than anything perhaps to a large clean china plate, with a neat 'pattern', suspended, to the exposure of hapless heads, from the centre of the domestic ceiling. Truly she was, as by the education of the strain undergone, learning something every hour – it seemed so to be the case that a strain enlarged the mind, formed the taste, enriched, even, the imagination. Yet in spite of this last fact, it must be added, she continued rather mystified by the actual pitch of her comrade's manner, Bight really behaving as if he enjoyed their visitor's 'note'. He treated him so decently, as they said, that he might suddenly have taken to liking his company; which was an odd appearance till Maud understood it – whereupon it became for her a slightly sinister one. For the effect of the honest gentleman, she by that time saw, was to make her friend nervous and vicious, and the form taken by his irritation was just this dangerous candour, which encouraged the candour of the victim. She had for the latter a residuum of pity, whereas Bight, she felt, had none, and she didn't want him, the poor man, absolutely to pay with his life.

It was clear, however, within a few minutes, that this was what he was bent on doing, and she found herself helpless before his smug insistence. She had taken his measure; he was *made* incorrigibly to try, irredeemably to fail – to be, in short, eternally defeated and eternally unaware. He wouldn't rage – he *couldn't*, for the citadel might, in that case, have been carried by his assault; he would only spend his life in walking round and round it, asking everyone he met how in the name of goodness one did get in. And everyone would make a fool of him – though no one so much as her companion now – and everything would fall from him but the perfection of his temper, of his tailor, of his manners, of his mediocrity. He evidently rejoiced at the happy chance which had presented him again to Bight, and he lost as little time as possible in proposing, the play ended, an adjournment again to tea. The spirit of malice in her comrade, now inordinately excited, met this suggestion with an amendment that fairly made her anxious; Bight threw out, in a word, the idea that he himself surely, this time, should entertain Mr Marshal.

'Only I'm afraid I can take you but to a small pothouse that we poor journalists haunt.'

'They're just the places I delight in – it would be of an extraordinary interest. I sometimes venture into them – feeling awfully strange and wondering, I do assure you, who people are. But to go there with *you*—!' And he looked from Bight to Maud and from Maud back again with such abysses of appreciation that she knew him as lost indeed.

VI

IT was demonic of Bight, who immediately answered that he would tell him with pleasure who everyone was, and she felt this the more when her friend, making light of the rest of the entertainment they had quitted, advised their sacrificing it and proceeding to the other scene. He was really too eager for his victim – she wondered what he wanted to do with him. He could only play him at the most a practical joke – invent appetising identities, once they were at table, for the dull consumers around. No one, at the place they most frequented, had an identity in the least appetising, no one was anyone or anything. It was apparently of the essence of existence on such terms – the terms, at any rate, to which *she* was reduced – that people comprised in it couldn't even minister to each other's curiosity, let alone to envy or awe. She would have wished therefore, for their pursuer, to intervene a little, to warn him against beguilement; but they had moved together along the Strand and then out of it, up a near cross street, without her opening her mouth. Bight, as she felt, was acting to prevent this; his easy talk redoubled, and he led his lamb to the shambles. The talk had jumped to poor Beadel – her friend had startled her by causing it, almost with violence, at a given moment, to take that direction, and he thus quite sufficiently stayed her speech. The people she lived with mightn't make you curious, but there was of course always a sharp exception for *him*. She kept still, in fine, with the wonder of what he wanted; though indeed she might, in the presence of their guest's response, have felt he was already getting it. He was getting, that is – and *she* was, into the bargain – the fullest illustration of the ravage of a passion; so sublimely Marshal rose to the proposition, infernally thrown off, that, in whatever queer box or tight place Beadel might have found himself, it was something, after all, to have so powerfully interested the public. The insidious artless way in which Bight made his point! – 'I don't know that I've ever known the public (and I watch it, as in my trade we have to, day and night) *so* consummately interested.' They had that phenomenon – the present consummate interest – well before them while they sat at their homely meal, served with accessories so different from those of the sweet Chippendale (another chord on which the young man played with just the right effect!), and it would have been hard to say if the guest were, for the first moments, more under the spell of the marvellous 'hold' on the town achieved by the great absentee, or of that of the delicious coarse tablecloth, the extraordinary form of the salt-cellars, and the fact that he had within range of sight, at the other end of the room, in the person of the little quiet man with blue spectacles and an obvious wig, the greatest authority in London about the inner life of the criminal classes. Beadel, none the less, came up again and stayed up – would clearly so have been *kept* up, had there been need, by their host, that the girl couldn't at last fail to see how much it was for herself that his intention worked. What *was* it, all the same – since it couldn't be anything so simple as to expose their hapless visitor? What had she to learn about *him*? – especially at the hour of seeing what there was still to learn about Bight. She ended by deciding – for his appearance bore her out – that his explosion was but the form taken by an inward fever. The fever, on this theory, was the result of the final pang of responsibility. The mystery of Beadel had grown too dark to be borne – which they would presently feel; and he was meanwhile in the phase of bluffing it off, precisely because it was to overwhelm him.

'And do you mean you too would pay with your *life*?' He put the question, agreeably, across the table to his guest; agreeably of course in spite of his eye's dry glitter.

His guest's expression, at this, fairly became beautiful. 'Well, it's an awfully nice point. Certainly one would like to *feel* the great murmur surrounding one's name, to *be* there, more or less, so as not to lose the sense of it, and as I really think, you know, the pleasure; the great city, the great empire, the world itself for the moment, hanging literally on one's personality and giving a start, in its suspense, whenever one is mentioned. Big sensation, you know, that,' Mr Marshal pleadingly smiled, 'and of course if one were dead one wouldn't enjoy it. One would have to come to life for that.'

'Naturally,' Bight rejoined – 'only that's what the dead don't do. You can't eat your cake and have it. The question is,' he good-naturedly explained, 'whether you'd be willing, for the certitude of the great murmur you speak of, to part with your life under circumstances of extraordinary mystery.'

His guest earnestly fixed it. 'Whether *I* would be willing?'

'Mr Marshal wonders,' Maud said to Bight, 'if you are, as a person interested in his reputation, definitely proposing to him some such possibility.'

He looked at her, on this, with mild, round eyes, and she felt, wonderfully, that he didn't quite see her as joking. He smiled – he always smiled, but his anxiety showed, and he turned it again to their companion. 'You mean – a – the knowing how it might be *going* to be felt?'

'Well, yes – call it that. The consciousness of what one's unexplained extinction – given, to start with, one's high position – would mean, wouldn't be able to *help* meaning, for millions and millions of people. The point is – and I admit it's, as you call it, a "nice" one – if you can think of the impression so made as worth the purchase. *Naturally*, naturally, there's but the impression you make. You don't receive any. You can't. You've only your confidence – so far as that's an impression. Oh, it *is* indeed a nice point; and I only put it to you,' Bight wound up, 'because, you know, you do like to be recognised.'

Mr Marshal was bewildered, but he was not so bewildered as not to be able, a trifle coyly, but still quite bravely, to confess to that. Maud, with her eyes on her friend, found herself thinking of him as of some plump, innocent animal, more or less of the pink-eyed rabbit or sleek guinea-pig order, involved in the slow spell of a serpent of shining scales. Bight's scales, truly, had never so shone as this evening, and he used to admiration – which was just a part of the lustre – the right shade of gravity. He was neither so light as to fail of the air of an attractive offer, nor yet so earnest as to betray a gibe. He might conceivably have been, as an undertaker of improvements in defective notorieties, placing before his guest a practical scheme. It was really quite as if he were ready to guarantee the 'murmur' if Mr Marshal was ready to pay the price. And the price wouldn't of course be only Mr Marshal's existence. All this, at least, if Mr Marshal felt moved to take it so. The prodigious thing, next, was that Mr Marshal *was* so moved – though, clearly, as was to be expected, with important qualifications. 'Do you really mean,' he asked, 'that one would excite *this* delightful interest?'

'You allude to the charged state of the air on the subject of Beadel?' Bight considered, looking volumes. 'It would depend a good deal upon who one *is*.'

He turned, Mr Marshal, again to Maud Blandy, and his eyes seemed to suggest to her that she should put his question for him. They forgave her, she judged, for having so oddly forsaken him, but they appealed to her now not to leave him to struggle alone. Her own difficulty was, however, meanwhile, that she feared to serve him as he suggested without too much, by way of return, turning his case to the comic; whereby she only looked at him hard and let him revert to their friend. 'Oh,' he said, with a rich wistfulness from which the comic was not absent, 'of course everyone can't pretend to be Beadel.'

'Perfectly. But we're speaking, after all, of those who do count.'

There was quite a hush, for the minute, while the poor man faltered. 'Should you say that *I* – in any appreciable way – count?'

Howard Bight distilled honey. 'Isn't it a little a question of how much we should find you *did*, or, for that matter, might, as it were, be made to, in the event of a real catastrophe?'

Mr Marshal turned pale, yet he met it too with sweetness. 'I like the way' – and he had a glance for Maud – 'you talk of catastrophes!'

His host did the comment justice. 'Oh, it's only because, you see, we're so peculiarly in the presence of one. Beadel shows so tremendously what a catastrophe does for the right person. His absence, you may say, doubles, quintuples, his presence.'

'I see, I see!' Mr Marshal was all there. 'It's awfully interesting to be so present. And yet it's rather dreadful to be so absent.' It had set him fairly musing; for couldn't the opposites be reconciled? 'If he *is*,' he threw out, 'absent—!'

'Why, he's absent, of course,' said Bight, 'if he's dead.'

'And really dead is what you believe him to be?'

He breathed it with a strange break, as from a mind too full. It was on the one hand a grim vision for his own case, but was on the other a kind of clearance of the field. With Beadel out of the way his own case could live, and he was obviously thinking what it might be to be as dead as that and yet as much alive. What his demand first did, at any rate, was to make Howard Bight look straight at Maud. Her own look met him, but she asked nothing now. She felt him somehow fathomless, and his practice with their infatuated guest created a new suspense. He might indeed have been looking at her to learn how to reply, but even were this the case she had still nothing to answer. So in a moment he had spoken without her. 'I've quite given him up.'

It sank into Marshal, after which it produced something. 'He ought then to come back. I mean,' he explained, 'to see for himself – to *have* the impression.'

'Of the noise he has made? Yes' – Bight weighed it – 'that would be the ideal.'

'And it would, if one must call it "noise", ' Marshal limpidly pursued, 'make – a – more.'

'Oh, but if you *can't*!'

'Can't, you mean, through having already made so much, add to the quantity?'

'Can't' – Bight was a wee bit sharp – 'come back, confound it, at all. Can't return from the dead!'

Poor Marshal had to take it. 'No – not if you *are* dead.'

'Well, that's what we're talking about.'

Maud, at this, for pity, held out a perch. 'Mr Marshal, I think, is talking a little on the basis of the possibility of your not being!' He threw her an instant glance of gratitude, and it gave her a push. 'So long as you're not quite too utterly, you *can* come back.'

'Oh,' said Bight, 'in time for the fuss?'

'Before' – Marshal met it – 'the interest has subsided. It naturally then *wouldn't* – would it? – subside!'

'No,' Bight granted; 'not if it hadn't, through wearing out – I mean your being lost too long – already died out.'

'Oh, of course,' his guest agreed, 'you mustn't be lost *too* long.' A vista had plainly opened to him, and the subject led him on. He had, before its extent, another pause. 'About how long, do you think—?'

Well, Bight *had* to think. 'I should say Beadel had rather overdone it.'

The poor gentleman stared. 'But if he can't help himself—?'

Bight gave a laugh. 'Yes; but in case he could.'

Maud again intervened, and, as her question was for their host, Marshal was all attention. 'Do you consider Beadel has overdone it?'

Well, once more, it took consideration. The issue of Bight's, however, was not of the clearest. 'I don't think we can tell unless he *were* to. I don't think that, without seeing it, and judging by the special case, one can quite know how it would be taken. He might, on the one side, have spoiled, so to speak, his market; and he might, on the other, have scored as never before.'

'It might be,' Maud threw in, 'just the making of him.'

'Surely' – Marshal glowed – 'there's just that chance.'

'What a pity then,' Bight laughed, 'that there isn't someone to take it! For the light it would throw, I mean, on the laws – so mysterious, so curious, so interesting – that govern the great currents of public attention. They're not wholly whimsical – wayward and wild; they have their strange logic, their obscure reason – if one could only get *at* it! The man who does, you see – and who can keep his discovery to himself! – will make his everlasting fortune, as well, no doubt, as that of a few others. It's *our* branch, *our* preoccupation, in fact, Miss Blandy's and mine – this pursuit of the incalculable, this study, to that end, of the great forces of publicity. Only, of course, it must be remembered,' Bight went on, 'that in the case we're speaking of – the man disappearing as Beadel has now disappeared, and supplanting for the time every other topic – must have someone on the spot for him, to keep the pot boiling, someone acting, with real intelligence, in his interest. I mean if he's to get the good of it when he does turn up. It would never do, you see, that *that* should be flat!'

'Oh no, not *flat*, never!' Marshal quailed at the thought. Held as in a vice by his host's high lucidity, he exhaled his interest at every pore. 'It wouldn't be flat for Beadel, would it? – I mean if he *were* to come.'

'Not much! It wouldn't be flat for Beadel – I think I can undertake.' And Bight undertook so well that he threw himself back in his chair with his thumbs in the armholes of his waistcoat and his head very much up. 'The only thing is that for poor Beadel it's a luxury, so to speak, wasted – and so dreadfully, upon my word, that one quite regrets there's no one to step in.'

'To step in?' His visitor hung upon his lips.

'To do the thing better, so to speak – to do it right; to – having raised the whirlwind – really *ride* the storm. To seize the psychological hour.'

Marshal met it, yet he wondered. 'You speak of the reappearance? I see. But the man of the reappearance would have, wouldn't he? – or perhaps I don't follow? – to be the same as the man of the *dis*appearance. It wouldn't do as well – would it? – for *somebody else* to turn up?'

Bight considered him with attention – as if there were fine possibilities. 'No; unless such a person should turn up, say – well, with news of him.'

'But what news?'

'With lights – the more lurid the better – *on* the darkness. With the facts, don't you see, *of* the disappearance.'

Marshal, on his side, threw himself back. 'But he'd have to know them!'

'Oh,' said Bight, with prompt portentousness, 'that could be managed.'

It was too much, by this time, for his victim, who simply turned on Maud a dilated eye and a flushed cheek. 'Mr Marshal,' it made her say – 'Mr Marshal would like to turn up.'

Her hand was on the table, and the effect of her words, combined with this, was to cause him, before responsive speech could come, to cover it respectfully but expressively with his own. 'Do you mean,' he panted to Bight, 'that you have, amid the general collapse of speculation, facts to give?'

'I've always facts to give.'

It begot in the poor man a large hot smile. 'But – how shall I say? – authentic, or as I believe you clever people say, "inspired" ones?'

'If I should undertake such a case as we're supposing, I would of course by that circumstance undertake that my facts should be – well, worthy of it. I would take,' Bight on his own part modestly smiled, 'pains with them.'

It finished the business. 'Would you take pains for *me*?'

Bight looked at him now hard. 'Would you like to appear?'

'Oh, "appear"!' Marshal weakly murmured.

'Is it, Mr Marshal, a real proposal? I mean are you prepared—?'

Wonderment sat in his eyes – an anguish of doubt and desire. 'But wouldn't you prepare me—?'

'Would you prepare *me* – that's the point,' Bight laughed – '*to* prepare you?'

There was a minute's mutual gaze, but Marshal took it in. 'I don't know what you're making me say; I don't know what you're making me *feel*. When one is with people so up in these things—' and he turned to his companions, alternately, a look as of conscious doom lighted with suspicion, a look that was like a cry for mercy – 'one feels a little as if one ought to be saved from one's self. For I daresay one's foolish enough with one's poor little wish—'

'The little wish, my dear sir' – Bight took him up – 'to stand out in the world! Your wish is the wish of all high spirits.'

'It's dear of you to say it.' Mr Marshal was all response. 'I shouldn't want, even if it *were* weak or vain, to have lived wholly unknown. And if what you ask is whether I understand you to speak, as it were, professionally—'

'You *do* understand me?' Bight pushed back his chair.

'Oh, but so well! – when I've already seen what you can do. I need scarcely say, that having seen it, I shan't bargain.'

'Ah, then, *I* shall,' Bight smiled. 'I mean with the Papers. It must be half profits.'

' "Profits"?' His guest was vague.

'Our friend,' Maud explained to Bight, 'simply wants the position.'

Bight threw her a look. 'Ah, he must take what I give him.'

'But what you give me,' their friend handsomely contended, '*is* the position.'

'Yes; but the terms that I shall get! I don't produce you, of course,' Bight went on, 'till I've prepared you. But when I do produce you it will be as a value.'

'You'll get so much for me?' the poor gentleman quavered.

'I shall be able to get, I think, anything I ask. So we divide.' And Bight jumped up.

Marshal did the same, and, while, with his hands on the back of his chair, he steadied himself from the vertiginous view, they faced each other across the table. 'Oh, it's too wonderful!'

'You're not afraid?'

He looked at a card on the wall, framed, suspended and marked with the word 'Soups'. He looked at Maud, who had not moved. 'I don't know; I may be; I must feel. What I *should* fear,' he added, 'would be his coming back.'

'Beadel's? Yes, that would dish you. But since he can't—!'

'I place myself,' said Mortimer Marshal, 'in your hands.'

Maud Blandy still hadn't moved; she stared before her at the cloth. A small sharp sound, unheard, she saw, by the others, had reached her from the street, and with her mind instinctively catching at it, she waited, dissimulating a little, for its repetition or its effect. It was the howl of the Strand, it was news of the absent, and it would have a bearing. She had a hesitation, for she winced even now with the sense of Marshal's intensest look at her. He couldn't be saved from himself, but he might be, still, from Bight; though it hung of course, her chance to warn him, on what the news would be. She thought with concentration, while her friends unhooked their overcoats, and by the time these garments were donned she was on her feet. Then she spoke. 'I don't want you to be "dished".'

He allowed for her alarm. 'But how *can* I be?'

'Something has come.'

'Something—?' The men had both spoken.

They had stopped where they stood; she again caught the sound. 'Listen! They're crying.'

They waited then, and it came – came, of a sudden, with a burst and as if passing the place. A hawker, outside, with his 'extra', called by someone and hurrying, bawled it as he moved. 'Death of Beadel-Muffet – Extraordinary News!'

They all gasped, and Maud, with her eyes on Bight, saw him, to her satisfaction at first, turn pale. But his guest drank it in. 'If it's true then?' – Marshal triumphed at her – 'I'm *not* dished.'

But she only looked hard at Bight, who struck her as having, at the sound, fallen to pieces, and as having above all, on the instant, turned cold for his worried game. 'Is it true?' she austerely asked.

His white face answered. 'It's true.'

VII

THE first thing, on the part of our friends – after each interlocutor, producing a penny, had plunged into the unfolded 'Latest' – was this very evidence of their dispensing with their companion's further attendance on their agitated state, and all the more that Bight was to have still, in spite of agitation, his function with him to accomplish: a result much assisted by the insufflation of wind into Mr Marshal's sails constituted by the fact before them. With Beadel publicly dead this gentleman's opportunity, on the terms just arranged, opened out; it was quite as if they had seen him, then and there, step, with a kind of spiritual splash, into the empty seat of the boat so launched, scarcely even taking time to master the essentials before he gave himself to the breeze. The essentials indeed he was, by their understanding, to receive in full from Bight at their earliest leisure; but nothing could so vividly have marked his confidence in the young man as the promptness with which he appeared now ready to leave him to his inspiration. The news moreover, as yet, was the rich, grim fact – a sharp flare from an Agency, lighting into blood-colour the locked room, finally, with the police present, forced open, of the first hotel at Frankfort-on-the-Oder; but there was enough of it, clearly, to bear scrutiny, the scrutiny represented in our young couple by the act of perusal prolonged, intensified, repeated, so repeated that it was exactly perhaps with this suggestion of doubt that poor Mr Marshal had even also a little lost patience. He vanished, at any rate, while his supporters, still planted in the side-street into which they had lately issued, stood extinguished, as to any facial communion, behind the array of printed columns.

It was only after he had gone that, whether aware or not, the other lowered, on either side, the absorbing page and knew that their eyes had met. A remarkable thing, for Maud Blandy, then happened, a thing quite as remarkable at least as poor Beadel's suicide, which we recall her having so considerably discounted.

Present as they thus were at the tragedy, present in far Frankfort just where they stood, by the door of their stale pothouse and in the thick of London air, the logic of her situation, she was sharply conscious, would have been an immediate rupture with Bight. He was scared at what he had done – he looked his scare so straight out at her that she might almost have seen in it the dismay of his question of how far his responsibility, given the facts, might, if pried into, be held – and not only at the judgment-seat of mere morals – to reach. The dismay was to that degree illuminating that she had had from him no such avowal of responsibility as this amounted to, and the limit to any laxity on her own side had therefore not been set for her with any such sharpness. It put her at last in the right, his scare – quite richly in the right; and as that was naturally but where she had waited to find herself, everything that now silently passed between them had the merit, if it had none other, of simplifying. Their hour had struck, the hour after which she was definitely not to have forgiven him. Yet what occurred, as I say, was that, if, at the end of five minutes, she had moved much further, it proved to be, in spite of logic, not in the sense away from him, but in the sense nearer. He showed to her, at these strange moments, as blood-stained and literally hunted; the yell of the hawkers, repeated and echoing round them, was like a cry for his life; and there was in particular a minute during which, gazing down into the roused Strand, all equipped both with mob and with constables, she asked herself whether she had best get off with him through the crowd, where they would be least noticed, or get him away through quiet Covent Garden, empty at that hour, but with policemen to watch a furtive couple, and with the news, more bawled at their heels in the stillness, acquiring the sound of the very voice of justice. It was this last sudden terror that presently determined her, and determined with it an impulse of protection that had somehow to do with pity without having to do with tenderness. It settled, at all events, the question of leaving him; she couldn't leave him there and so; she must see at least what would have come of his own sense of the shock.

The way he took it, the shock, gave her afresh the measure of how perversely he had played with Marshal – of how he had tried so, on the very edge of his predicament, to cheat his fears and beguile his want of ease. He had insisted to his victim on the truth he had now to reckon with, but had insisted only because he didn't believe it. Beadel, by that attitude, was but lying low; so that he would have no promise really to redeem. At present he had one, indeed, and Maud could ask herself if the redemption of it, with the leading of their wretched friend a further fantastic dance, would be what he depended on to drug the pain of remorse. By the time she had covered as much ground as this, however, she had also, standing before him, taken his special out of his hand and, folding it up carefully with her own and smoothing it down, packed the two together into such a small tight ball as she might toss to a distance without the air, which she dreaded, of having, by any looser proceeding, disowned or evaded the news. Howard Bight, helpless and passive, putting on the matter no governed face, let her do with him as she liked, let her, for the first time in their acquaintance, draw his hand into her arm as if he were an invalid or as if she were a snare. She took with him, thus guided and sustained, their second plunge; led him, with decision, straight to where their shock was shared and amplified, pushed her way, guarding him, across the dense thoroughfare and through the great westward current which fairly seemed to meet and challenge them, and then, by reaching Waterloo Bridge with him and descending the granite steps, set him down at last on the Embankment. It was a fact, none the less, that she had in her eyes, all the while, and too strangely for speech, the vision of the scene in the little German city: the smashed door, the exposed horror, the wondering, insensible group, the English gentleman, in the disordered room, driven to bay among the scattered personal objects that only too floridly announced and emblazoned him, and several of which the Papers were already naming – the poor English gentleman, hunted and hiding, done to death by the thing he yet, for so long, always *would* have, and stretched on the floor with his beautiful little revolver still in his hand and the effusion of his blood, from a wound taken, with rare resolution, full in the face, extraordinary and dreadful.

She went on with her friend, eastward and beside the river, and it was as if they both, for that matter, had, in their silence, the dire material vision. Maud Blandy, however, presently stopped short – one of the connections of the picture so brought her to a stand. It had come over her, with a force she couldn't check, that the catastrophe itself would have been, with all the unfathomed that yet clung to it, just the thing for her companion's professional hand; so that, queerly but absolutely, while she looked at him again in reprobation and pity, it was as much as she could do not to feel it for him as something missed, not to wish he might have been there to snatch his chance, and not, above all, to betray to him this reflection. It had really risen to her lips – 'Why aren't *you*, old man, on the spot?' and indeed the question, had it broken forth, might well have sounded as a provocation to him to start without delay. Such was the effect, in poor Maud, for the moment, of the habit, so confirmed in her, of seeing time marked only by the dial of the Papers. She had admired in Bight the true journalist that she herself was so clearly not – though it was also not what she had *most* admired in him; and she might have felt, at this instant, the charm of putting true journalism to the proof. She might have been on the point of saying: 'Real business, you know, would be for you to start *now*, just as you are, before anyone else, sure as you can so easily be of having the pull'; and she might, after a moment, while they paused, have been looking back, through the river-mist, for a sign of the hour, at the blurred face of Big Ben. That she grazed this danger yet avoided it was partly the result in truth of her seeing for herself quickly enough that the last thing Bight could just then have thought of, even under provocation of the most positive order, was the chance thus failing him, or the train, the boat, the advantage, that the true journalist wouldn't have missed. He quite, under her eyes, while they stood together, ceased to be the true journalist; she saw him, as she felt, put off the character as definitely as she might have seen him remove his coat, his hat, or the contents of his pockets, in order to lay them on the parapet before jumping into the river. Wonderful was the difference that this transformation, marked by no word and supported by no sign, made in the man she had hitherto known. Nothing, again, could have so expressed for her his continued inward dismay. It was as if, for that matter, she couldn't have asked him a question without adding to it; and she didn't wish to add to it, since she was by this time more fully aware that she wished to be generous. When she at last uttered other words it was precisely so that she mightn't press him.

'I think of *her* – poor thing: that's what it makes me do. I think of her there at this moment – just out of the "Line" – with this stuff shrieked at her windows.' With which, having so at once contained and relieved herself, she caused him to walk on.

'Are you talking of Mrs Chorner?' he after a moment asked. And then, when he had had her quick 'Of course – of who else?' he said what she didn't expect. 'Naturally one thinks of her. But she has herself to blame. I mean she drove him—' What he meant, however, Bight suddenly dropped, taken as he was with another idea, which had brought them the next minute to a halt. 'Mightn't you, by the way, see her?'

'See her *now*—?'

' "Now" or never – for the good of it. Now's just your time.'

'But how can it be hers, in the very midst—?'

'*Because* it's in the very midst. She'll tell you things to-night that she'll never tell again. To-night she'll be great.'

Maud gaped almost wildly. 'You want me, at such an hour, to *call*—?'

'And send up your card with the word – oh, of course the right one! – on it.'

'What do you suggest,' Maud asked, 'as the right one?'

'Well, "The world *wants* you" – that usually does. I've seldom known it, even in deeper distress than is, after all, here supposable, to fail. Try it, at any rate.'

The girl, strangely touched, intensely wondered. 'Demand of her, you mean, to let me explain for her?'

'There you are. You catch on. Write *that* – if you like – "Let me explain." She'll want to explain.'

Maud wondered at him more – he had somehow so turned the tables on her. 'But she doesn't. It's exactly *what* she doesn't; she never *has*. And that he, poor wretch, was always wanting to—'

'Was precisely what made her hold off? I grant it.' He had waked up. 'But that was before she had killed him. Trust me, she'll chatter now.'

This, for his companion, simply forced it out. 'It wasn't *she* who killed him. That, my dear, you know.'

'You mean it was I who did? Well then, my child, interview *me*.' And, with his hands in his pockets and his idea apparently genuine, he smiled at her, by the grey river and under the high lamps, with an effect strange and suggestive. '*That* would be a go!'

'You mean' – she jumped at it – 'you'll tell me what you know?'

'Yes, and even what I've done! But – if you'll take it so – for the Papers. Oh, for the Papers only!'

She stared. 'You mean you want me to get it in—?'

'I don't "want" you to do anything, but I'm ready to help you, ready to get it in for you, like a shot, myself, if it's a thing you yourself want.'

'A thing I want – to give you away?'

'Oh,' he laughed, 'I'm just now worth giving! You'd really do it, you know. And, to help you, here I am. It *would* be for you – only judge! – a leg up.'

It would indeed, she really saw; somehow, on the spot, she believed it. But his surrender made her tremble. It wasn't a joke – she *could* give him away; or rather she could sell him for money. Money, thus, was what he offered her, or the value of money, which was the same; it was what he wanted her to have. She was conscious already, however, that she could have it only as he offered it, and she said therefore, but half-heartedly, 'I'll keep your secret.'

He looked at her more gravely. 'Ah, as a secret I can't give it.' Then he hesitated. 'I'll get you a hundred pounds for it.'

'Why don't you,' she asked, 'get them for yourself?'

'Because I don't care for myself. I care only for you.'

She waited again. 'You mean for my taking you?' And then as he but looked at her: 'How should I take you if I had dealt with you that way?'

'What do I lose by it,' he said, 'if, by our understanding of the other day, since things have so turned out, you're not to take me at all? So, at least, on my proposal, you get something else.'

'And what,' Maud returned, 'do you get?'

'I *don't* "get"; I lose. I *have* lost. So I don't matter.' The eyes with which she covered him at this might have signified either that he didn't satisfy her or that his last word – *as* his word – rather imposed itself. Whether or no, at all events, she decided that he still did matter. She presently moved again, and they walked some minutes more. He had made her tremble, and she continued to tremble. So unlike anything that had ever come to her was, if seriously viewed, his proposal. The quality of it, while she walked, grew intenser with each step. It struck her as, when one came to look at it, unlike any offer any man could ever have made or any woman ever have received; and it began accordingly, on the instant, to affect her as almost inconceivably romantic, absolutely, in a manner, and quite out of the blue, *dramatic*; immeasurably more so, for example, than the sort of thing she had come out to hear in the afternoon – the sort of thing that was already so far away. If he was joking it was poor, but if he was serious it was, properly, sublime. And he wasn't joking. He was, however, after an interval, talking again, though, trembling still, she had not been attentive; so that she was unconscious of what he had said until she heard him once more sound Mrs Chorner's name. 'If you don't, you know, someone else will, and someone much worse. You told me she likes you.' She had at first no answer for him, but it presently made her stop again. It was beautiful, if she would, but it was odd – this pressure for *her* to push at the very hour he himself had renounced pushing. A part of the whole sublimity of his attitude, so far as she was concerned, it clearly was; since, obviously, he was not now to profit by anything she might do. She seemed to see that, as the last service he could render, he wished to launch her and leave her. And that came out the more as he kept it up. 'If she likes you, you know, she really wants you. Go to her as a friend.'

'And bruit her abroad as one?' Maud Blandy asked.

'Oh, as a friend *from* the Papers – from them and *for* them, and with just your half-hour to give her before you rush back to them. Take it even – oh, you can safely' – the young man developed – 'a little high with her. That's the way – the real way.' And he spoke the next moment as if almost losing his patience. 'You ought by this time, you know, to understand.'

There was something in her mind that it still charmed – his mastery of the horrid art. He could see, always, the superior way, and it was as if, in spite of herself, she were getting the truth from him. Only she didn't want the truth – at least not that one. 'And if she simply, for my impudence, chucks me out of the window? A short way is easy for them, you know, when one doesn't scream or kick, or hang on to the furniture or the banisters. And I usually, you see' – she said it pensively – 'don't. I've always, from the first, had my retreat prepared for any occasion, and flattered myself that, whatever hand I might, or mightn't, become at getting in, no one would ever be able so beautifully to get out. Like a flash, simply. And if she does, as I say, chuck me, it's *you* who fall to the ground.'

He listened to her without expression, only saying 'If you feel for her, as you insist, it's your duty.' And then later, as if he had made an impression, 'Your duty, I mean, to try. I admit, if you will, that there's a risk, though I don't, with my experience, feel it. Nothing venture, at any rate, nothing have; and it's all, isn't it? at the worst, in the day's work. There's but one thing you can go on, but it's enough. The greatest probability.'

She resisted, but she was taking it in. 'The probability that she will throw herself on my neck?'

'It will be either one thing or the other,' he went on as if he had not heard her. 'She'll not receive you, or she will. But if she does your fortune's made, and you'll be able to look higher than the mere *common* form of donkey.' She recognised the reference to Marshal, but that was a thing she needn't mind now, and he had already continued. 'She'll keep *nothing* back. And you mustn't either.'

'Oh, won't I?' Maud murmured.

'Then you'll break faith with her.'

And, as if to emphasise it, he went on, though without leaving her an infinite time to decide, for he looked at his watch as they proceeded, and when they came, in their spacious walk, abreast of another issue, where the breadth of the avenue, the expanses of stone, the stretch of the river, the dimness of the distance, seemed to isolate them, he appeared, by renewing their halt and looking up afresh toward the town, to desire to speed her on her way. Many things meanwhile had worked within her, but it was not till she had kept him on past the Temple Station of the Underground that she fairly faced her opportunity. Even then too there were still other things, under the assault of which she dropped, for the moment, Mrs Chorner. 'Did you really,' she asked, 'believe he'd turn up alive?'

With his hands in his pockets he continued to gloom at her. 'Up there, just now, with Marshal – what did you take me as believing?'

'I gave you up. And I do give you. You're beyond me. Only,' she added, 'I seem to have made you out since then as really staggered. Though I don't say it,' she ended, 'to bear hard upon you.'

'Don't bear hard,' said Howard Bight very simply.

It moved her, for all she could have said; so that she had for a moment to wonder if it were bearing hard to mention some features of the rest of her thought. If she was to have him, certainly, it couldn't be without knowing, as she said to herself, something – something she might perhaps mitigate a little the solitude of his penance by possessing. 'There were moments when I even imagined that, up to a certain point, you were still in communication with him. Then I seemed to see that you lost touch – though you braved it out for me; that you had begun to be really uneasy and were giving him up. I seemed to see,' she pursued after a hesitation, 'that it was coming home to you that you had worked him up too high – that you were feeling, if

I may say it, that you had better have stopped short. I mean short of *this*.'

'You may say it,' Bight answered. 'I *had* better.'

She looked at him a moment. 'There was more of him than you believed.'

'There was more of him. And now,' Bight added, looking across the river, 'here's *all* of him.'

'Which you feel you have on your heart?'

'I don't know where I have it.' He turned his eyes to her. 'I must wait.'

'For more facts?'

'Well,' he returned after a pause, 'hardly perhaps for "more" if – with what we have – this *is* all. But I've things to think out. I must wait to see how I feel. I did nothing but what he wanted. But we were behind a bolting horse – whom neither of us could have stopped.'

'And *he*,' said Maud, 'is the one dashed to pieces.'

He had his grave eyes on her. 'Would you like it to have been me?'

'Of course not. But you enjoyed it – the bolt; everything up to the smash. Then, with that ahead, you were nervous.'

'I'm nervous still,' said Howard Bight.

Even in his unexpected softness there was something that escaped her, and it made in her, just a little, for irritation. 'What I mean is that you enjoyed his terror. That was what led you on.'

'No doubt – it was so grand a case. But do you call charging me with it,' the young man asked, '*not* bearing hard—?'

'No' – she pulled herself up – 'it *is*. I don't charge you. Only I feel how little – about what has been, all the while, *behind* – you tell me. Nothing explains.'

'Explains what?'

'Why, his act.'

He gave a sign of impatience. 'Isn't the explanation what I offered a moment ago to give you?'

It came, in effect, back to her. 'For use?'

'For use.'

'Only?'

'Only.' It was sharp.

They stood a little, on this, face to face; at the end of which she turned away. 'I'll go to Mrs Chorner.' And she was off while he called after her to take a cab. It was quite as if she were to come upon him, in his strange insistence, for the fare.

VIII

IF she kept to herself, from the morrow on, for three days, her adoption of that course was helped, as she thankfully felt, by the great other circumstance and the great public commotion under cover of which it so little mattered what became of private persons. It was not simply that she had her reasons, but she couldn't during this time have descended again to Fleet Street even had she wished, though she said to herself often enough that her behaviour was rank cowardice. She left her friend alone with what he had to face, since, as she found, she could in absence from him a little recover herself. In his presence, the night of the news, she knew she had gone to pieces, had yielded, all too vulgarly, to a weakness proscribed by her original view. Her original view had been that if poor Beadel, worked up, as she inveterately kept seeing him, *should* embrace the tragic remedy, Howard Bight wouldn't be able not to show as practically compromised. He wouldn't be able not to smell of the wretched man's blood, morally speaking, too strongly for condonations or complacencies. There were other things, truly, that, during their minutes on the Embankment, he *had* been able to do, but they constituted just the sinister subtlety to which it was well that she should not again, yet awhile, be exposed. They were of the order – from the safe summit of Maida Hill she could make it out – that had proved corrosive to the muddled mind of the Frankfort fugitive, deprived, in the midst of them, of any honest issue. Bight, of course, rare youth, had *meant* no harm; but what was precisely queerer, what, when you came to judge, less human, than to be formed for offence, for injury, by the mere inherent play of the spirit of observation, of criticism, by the inextinguishable flame, in fine, of the ironic passion? The ironic passion, in such a world as surrounded one, might assert itself as half the dignity, the decency, of life; yet, none the less, in cases where one had seen it prove gruesomely fatal (and not to one's self, which was nothing, but to others, even the stupid and the vulgar) one was plainly admonished to – well, stand off a little and think.

This was what Maud Blandy, while the Papers roared and resounded more than ever with the new meat flung to them, tried to consider that she was doing; so that the attitude held her fast during the freshness of the event. The event grew, as she had felt it would, with every further fact from Frankfort and with every extra-special, and reached its maximum, inevitably, in the light of comment and correspondence. These features, before the catastrophe, had indubitably, at the last, flagged a little, but they revived so prodigiously, under the well-timed shock, that, for the period we speak of, the poor gentleman seemed, with a continuance, with indeed an enhancement, of his fine old knack, to have the successive editions *all* to himself. They had been always of course, the Papers, very largely about him, but it was not too much to say that at this crisis they were about nothing else worth speaking of; so that our young woman could but groan in spirit at the direful example set to the emulous. She spared an occasional moment to the vision of Mortimer Marshal, saw him drunk, as she might have said, with the mere fragrance of the wine of glory, and asked herself what art Bight would now use to furnish him forth as he had promised. The mystery of Beadel's course loomed, each hour, so much larger and darker that the plan would have to be consummate, or the private knowledge alike beyond cavil and beyond calculation, which should attempt either to sound or to mask the appearances. Strangely enough, none the less, she even now found herself thinking of her rash colleague as attached, for the benefit of his surviving victim, to this idea; she went in fact so far as to imagine him half-upheld, while the public wonder spent itself, by the prospect of the fun he might still have with Marshal. This implied, she was not unconscious, that his notion of fun was infernal, and would of course be especially so were his knowledge as real as she supposed it.

He would inflate their foolish friend with knowledge that was
false and so start him as a balloon for the further gape of the
world. This was the image, in turn, that would yield the last
sport – the droll career of the wretched man as wandering
forever through space under the apprehension, in time duly
gained, that the least touch of earth would involve the smash of
his car. Afraid, thus, to drop, but at the same time equally out of
conceit of the chill air of the upper and increasing solitudes to
which he had soared, he would become such a diminishing
speck, though traceably a prey to wild human gyrations, as
she might conceive Bight to keep in view for future recreation.

It wasn't however the future that was actually so much in
question for them all as the immediately near present, offered
to her as the latter was in the haunting light of the inevitably
unlimited character of any real inquiry. The inquiry of the
Papers, immense and ingenious, had yet for her the saving
quality that she didn't take it as real. It abounded, truly, in
hypotheses, most of them lurid enough, but a certain ease of
mind as to what these might lead to was perhaps one of the
advantages she owed to her constant breathing of Fleet Street
air. She couldn't quite have said why, but she felt it wouldn't be
the Papers that, proceeding from link to link, would arrive
vindictively at Bight's connection with his late client. The
enjoyment of that consummation would rest in another quarter, and if the young man were as uneasy now as she thought he
ought to be even while she hoped he wasn't, it would be from
the fear in his eyes of such justice as was shared with the vulgar.
The Papers held an inquiry, but the Authorities, as they vaguely
figured to her, would hold an inquest; which was a matter –
even when international, complicated and arrangeable,
between Frankfort and London, only on some system
unknown to her – more in tune with possibilities of exposure.
It was not, as need scarce be said, from the exposure of Beadel
that she averted herself; it was from the exposure of the person
who had made of Beadel's danger, Beadel's dread – whatever
these really represented – the use that the occurrence at Frankfort might be shown to certify. It was well before her, at all
events, that if Howard Bight's reflections, so stimulated, kept

pace at all with her own, he would at the worst, or even at the
best, have been glad to meet her again. It was her knowing that
and yet lying low that she privately qualified as cowardice; it
was the instinct of watching and waiting till she should see how
great the danger might become. And she had moreover another
reason, which we shall presently learn. The extra-specials
meanwhile were to be had in Kilburnia almost as soon as in
the Strand; the little ponied and painted carts, tipped at an
extraordinary angle, by which they were disseminated, had for
that matter, she observed, never rattled up the Edgware Road
at so furious a rate. Each evening, it was true, when the flare of
Fleet Street would have begun really to smoke, she had, in
resistance to old habit, a little to hold herself; but for three
successive days she tided over that crisis. It was not till the
fourth night that her reaction suddenly declared itself, determined as it partly was by the latest poster that dangled free at
the door of a small shop just out of her own street. The establishment dealt in buttons, pins, tape, and silver bracelets, but
the branch of its industry she patronised was that of telegrams,
stamps, stationery, and the 'Edinburgh rock' offered to the
appetite of the several small children of her next-door
neighbour but one. 'The Beadel-Muffet Mystery, Startling
Disclosures, Action of the Treasury' – at these words she
anxiously gazed; after which she decided. It was as if from her
hilltop, from her very housetop, to which the window of her
little room was contiguous, she had seen the red light in the
east. It *had*, this time, its colour. She went on, she went far, till
she met a cab, which she hailed, 'regardless', she felt, as she
had hailed one after leaving Bight by the river. 'To Fleet
Street' she simply said, and it took her – that she felt too –
back into life.

Yes, it was life again, bitter, doubtless, but with a taste,
when, having stopped her cab, short of her indication, in Covent Garden, she walked across southward and to the top of the
street in which she and her friend had last parted with Mortimer Marshal. She came down to their favoured pothouse, the
scene of Bight's high compact with that worthy, and here,
hesitating, she paused, uncertain as to where she had best

look out. Her conviction, on her way, had but grown; Howard
Bight would be looking out – *that* to a certainty; something
more, something portentous, had happened (by her evening
paper, scanned in the light of her little shop-window, she had
taken instant possession of it), and this would have made him
know that she couldn't keep up what he would naturally call her
'game'. There were places where they often met, and the
diversity of these – not too far apart, however – would be his
only difficulty. He was on the prowl, in fine, with his hat over
his eyes; and she hadn't known, till this vision of him came,
what seeds of romance were in her soul. Romance, the other
night, by the river, had brushed them with a wing that was like
the blind bump of a bat, but that had been something on *his*
part, whereas this thought of bringing him succour as to a
Russian anarchist, to some victim of society or subject of extradition, was all her own, and was of this special moment. She
saw him with his hat over his eyes; she saw him with his overcoat
collar turned up; she saw him as a hunted hero cleverly drawn
in one of the serialising weeklies or, as they said, in some
popular 'ply', and the effect of it was to open to her on the
spot a sort of happy sense of all her possible immorality. That
was the romantic sense, and everything vanished but the richness of her thrill. She knew little enough what she might have to
do for him, but her hope, as sharp as a pang, was that, if anything, it would put her in danger too. The hope, as it happened
then, was crowned on the very spot; she had never so felt in
danger as when, just now, turning to the glazed door of their
cookshop, she saw a man, within, close behind the glass, still,
stiff and ominous, looking at her hard. The light of the place
was behind him, so that his face, in the dusk of the side-street,
was dark, but it was visible that she showed for him as an object
of interest. The next thing, of course, she had seen more – seen
she could be such an object, in such a degree, only to her friend
himself, and that Bight had been thus sure of her; and the next
thing after that had passed straight in and been met by him, as
he stepped aside to admit her, in silence. He *had* his hat pulled
down and, quite forgetfully, in spite of the warmth within, the
collar of his mackintosh up.

It was his silence that completed the perfection of these things – the perfection that came out most of all, oddly, after he had corrected them by removal and was seated with her, in their common corner, at tea, with the room almost to themselves and no one to consider but Marshal's little man in the obvious wig and the blue spectacles, the great authority on the inner life of the criminal classes. Strangest of all, nearly, was it, that, though now essentially belonging, as Maud felt, to this order, they were not conscious of the danger of his presence. What she had wanted most immediately to learn was how Bight had known; but he made, and scarce to her surprise, short work of that. 'I've known every evening – known, that is, that you've wanted to come; and I've been here every evening, waiting just there till I should see you. It was but a question of time. To-night, however, I was sure – for there's, after all, *something* of me left. Besides, besides—!' He had, in short, another certitude. 'You've been ashamed – I knew, when I saw nothing come, that you would be. But also that that would pass.'

Maud found him, as she would have said, all there. 'I've been ashamed, you mean, of being afraid?'

'You've been ashamed about Mrs Chorner; that is, about *me*. For that you did go to her I know.'

'Have you been then yourself?'

'For what do you take me?' He seemed to wonder. 'What had I to do with her – except *for* you?' And then before she could say: 'Didn't she receive you?'

'Yes, as you said, she "wanted" me.'

'She jumped at you?'

'Jumped at me. She gave me an hour.'

He flushed with an interest that, the next moment, had flared in spite of everything into amusement. 'So that I was right, in my perfect wisdom, up to the hilt?'

'Up to the hilt. She took it from me.'

'That the public wants her?'

'That it won't take a refusal. So she opened up.'

'Overflowed?'

'Prattled.'

'Gushed?'

'Well, recognised and embraced her opportunity. Kept me there till midnight. Told me, as she called it, everything about everything.'

They looked at each other long on it, and it determined in Bight at last a brave clatter of his crockery. 'They're stupendous!'

'It's *you* that are,' Maud replied, 'to have found it out so. You know them down to the ground.'

'Oh, what I've found out—!' But it was more than he could talk of then. 'If I hadn't really felt sure, I wouldn't so have urged you. Only now, if you please, I don't understand your having apparently but kept her in your pocket.'

'Of course you don't,' said Maud Blandy. To which she added, 'And I don't quite myself. I only know that now that I have her there nothing will induce me to take her out.'

'Then you potted her, permit me to say,' he answered, 'on absolutely false pretences.'

'Absolutely; which is precisely why I've been ashamed. I made for home with the whole thing,' she explained, 'and there, that night, in the hours till morning, when, turning it over, I saw all it really was, I knew that I *couldn't* – that I would rather choose *that* shame, that of not doing for her what I had offered, than the hideous honesty of bringing it out. Because, you see,' Maud declared, 'it was – well, it was too much.'

Bight followed her with a sharpness! 'It was so good?'

'Quite beautiful! Awful!'

He wondered. 'Really charming?'

'Charming, interesting, horrible. It was *true* – and it was the whole thing. It was herself – and it was *him*, all of him too. Not a bit made up, but just the poor woman melted and overflowing, yet at the same time raging – like the hot-water tap when it boils. I never saw anything like it; everything, as you guaranteed, came out; it has made me know things. So, to have come down here with it, to have begun to hawk it, either through you, as you kindly proposed, or in my own brazen person, to the highest bidder – well, I felt that I didn't *have* to, after all, if I didn't want to, and that if it's the only way I can get money I would much rather starve.'

'I see.' Howard Bight saw all. 'And that's why you're ashamed?'

She hesitated – she was both so remiss and so firm. 'I knew that by my not coming back to you, you would have guessed, have found me wanting; just, for that matter, as *she* has found me. And I couldn't explain. I can't – I can't to *her*. So that,' the girl went on, 'I shall have done, so far as her attitude to me was to be concerned, something more indelicate, something more indecent, than if I had passed her on. I shall have wormed it all out of her, and then, by not having carried it to market, disappointed and cheated her. She was to have heard it cried like fresh herring.'

Bight was immensely taken. 'Oh, beyond all doubt. You're in a fix. You've played, you see, a most unusual game. The code allows everything *but* that.'

'Precisely. So I must take the consequences. I'm dishonoured, but I shall have to bear it. And I shall bear it by getting *out*. Out, I mean, of the whole thing. I shall chuck them.'

'Chuck the *Papers*?' he asked in his simplicity.

But his wonder, she saw, was overdone – their eyes too frankly met. 'Damn the Papers!' said Maud Blandy.

It produced in his sadness and weariness the sweetest smile that had yet broken through. 'We *shall*, between us, if we keep it up, ruin them! And you make nothing,' he went on, 'of one's having at last so beautifully started you? Your complaint,' he developed, 'was that you couldn't get in. Then suddenly, with a splendid jump, you *are* in. Only, however, to look round you and say with disgust "Oh, *here*?" Where the devil do you *want* to be?'

'Ah, that's another question. At least,' she said, 'I can scrub floors. I can take it out perhaps – my swindle of Mrs Chorner,' she pursued – 'in scrubbing *hers*.'

He only, after this, looked at her a little. 'She has written to you?'

'Oh, in high dudgeon. I was to have attended to the "press-cutting" people as well, and she was to have seen herself, at the furthest, by the second morning (that was day-before-yesterday) all over the place. She wants to know what I mean.'

'And what do you answer?'

'That it's hard, of course, to make her understand, but that I've felt her, since parting with her, simply to be too good.'

'Signifying by it, naturally,' Bight amended, 'that you've felt yourself to be so.'

'Well, that too if you like. But she was exquisite.'

He considered. 'Would she do for a ply?'

'Oh God, no!'

'Then for a tile?'

'Perhaps,' said Maud Blandy at last.

He understood, visibly, the shade, as well as the pause; which, together, held him a moment. But it was of something else he spoke. 'And you who had found they would never bite!'

'Oh, I was wrong,' she simply answered. 'Once they've *tasted* blood—!'

'They want to devour,' her friend laughed, 'not only the bait and the hook, but the line and the rod and the poor fisherman himself? Except,' he continued, 'that poor Mrs Chorner hasn't yet even "tasted". However,' he added, 'she obviously will.'

Maud's assent was full. 'She'll find others. She'll appear.'

He waited a moment – his eye had turned to the door of the street. 'Then she must be quick. These are things of the hour.'

'You hear something?' she asked, his expression having struck her.

He listened again, but it was nothing. 'No – but it's somehow in the air.'

'What is?'

'Well, that she must hurry. She must get in. She must get out.' He had his arms on the table, and, locking his hands and inclining a little, he brought his face nearer to her. 'My sense tonight's of an openness—! I don't know what's the matter. Except, that is, that you're great.'

She looked at him, not drawing back. 'You know everything – so immeasurably more than you admit or than you tell me. You mortally perplex and worry me.'

It made him smile. 'You're great, you're great,' he only repeated. 'You know it's quite awfully swagger, what you've done.'

'What I haven't, you mean; what I never shall. Yes,' she added, but now sinking back – 'of course you see that too. What *don't* you see, and what, with such ways, is to be the end of you?'

'You're great, you're great' – he kept it up. 'And I like you. That's to be the end of me.'

So, for a minute, they left it, while she came to the thing that, for the last half-hour, had most been with her. 'What *is* the "action", announced to-night, of the Treasury?'

'Oh, they've sent somebody out, partly, it would seem, at the request of the German authorities, to take possession.'

'Possession, you mean, of his effects?'

'Yes, and legally, administratively, of the whole matter.'

'Seeing, you mean, that there's still more in it—?'

'Than meets the eye,' said Bight, 'precisely. But it won't be till the case is transferred, as it presently will be, to this country, that they *will* see. Then it will be funny.'

'Funny?' Maud Blandy asked.

'Oh, lovely.'

'Lovely for *you*?'

'Why not? The bigger the whole thing grows, the lovelier.'

'You've odd notions,' she said, 'of loveliness. Do you expect his situation won't be traced to you? Don't you suppose you'll be forced to speak?'

'To "speak"—?'

'Why, if it *is* traced. What do you make, otherwise, of the facts to-night?'

'Do you call them facts?' the young man asked.

'I mean the Astounding Disclosures.'

'Well, do you only read your headlines? "The most astounding disclosures are expected" – *that's* the valuable text. Is *it*,' he went on, 'what fetched you?'

His answer was so little of one that she made her own scant. 'What fetched me is that I can't rest.'

'No more can I,' he returned. 'But in what danger do you think me?'

'In any in which you think yourself. Why not, if I don't mean in danger of hanging?'

He looked at her so that she presently took him for serious at last – which was different from his having been either worried or perverse. 'Of public discredit, you mean – for having so unmercifully baited him? Yes,' he conceded with a straightness that now surprised her, 'I've thought of that. But how can the baiting be proved?'

'If they take possession of his effects won't his effects be partly his papers, and won't they, among them, find letters from you, and won't your letters show it?'

'Well, show what?'

'Why, the frenzy to which you worked him – and thereby your connection.'

'They won't show it to dunderheads.'

'And are they all dunderheads?'

'Every mother's son of them – where anything so beautiful is concerned.'

'Beautiful?' Maud murmured.

'Beautiful, my letters are – gems of the purest ray. I'm covered.'

She let herself go – she looked at him long. 'You're a wonder. But all the same,' she added, 'you don't like it.'

'Well, I'm not sure.' Which clearly meant, however, that he almost *was*, from the way in which, the next moment, he had exchanged the question for another. 'You haven't anything to tell me of Mrs Chorner's explanation?'

Oh, as to this, she had already considered and chosen. 'What do you want of it when you know so much more? So much more, I mean, than even she has known.'

'Then she *hasn't* known—?'

'There you are! What,' asked Maud, 'are you talking about?'

She had made him smile, even though his smile was perceptibly pale; and he continued. 'Of what was behind. Behind any game of mine. Behind everything.'

'So am I then talking of that. No,' said Maud, 'she hasn't known, and she doesn't know I judge, to this hour. Her explanation therefore doesn't bear upon that. It bears upon something else.'

'Well, my dear, on what?'

He was not, however, to find out by simply calling her his dear; for she had not sacrificed the reward of her interview in order to present the fine flower of it, unbribed, even to *him*. 'You know how little you've ever told me, and you see how, at this instant, even while you press me to gratify you, you give me nothing. I give,' she smiled – yet not a little flushed – 'nothing *for* nothing.'

He showed her he felt baffled, but also that she was perverse. 'What you want of me is what, originally, you wouldn't hear of: anything so dreadful, that is, as his predicament must be. You saw that to make him want to keep quiet he must have something to be ashamed of, and that was just what, in pity, you positively objected to learning. You've grown,' Bight smiled, 'more interested since.'

'If I have,' said Maud, 'it's because *you* have. Now, at any rate, I'm not afraid.'

He waited a moment. 'Are you very sure?'

'Yes, for my mystification is greater at last than my delicacy. I don't know till I do know' – and she expressed this even with difficulty – 'what it has been, all the while, that it was a question of, and what, consequently, all the while, we've been talking about.'

'Ah, but why should you know?' the young man inquired. 'I can understand your needing to, or somebody's needing to, if we were in a ply, or even, though in a less degree, if we were in a tile. But since, my poor child, we're only in the delicious muddle of life itself—!'

'You may have all the plums of the pudding, and I nothing but a mouthful of cold suet?' Maud pushed back her chair; she had taken up her old gloves; but while she put them on she kept in view both her friend and her grievance. 'I don't believe,' she at last brought out, 'that there *is*, or that there ever was, anything.'

'Oh, oh, oh!' Bight laughed.

'There's nothing,' she continued, ' "behind". There's no horror.'

'You hold, by that,' said Bight, 'that the poor man's deed is *all* me? That does make it, you see, bad for me.'

She got up and, there before him, finished smoothing her creased gloves. 'Then we *are* – if there's such richness – in a ply.'

'Well, we are not, at all events – so far as we ourselves are concerned – the spectators.' And he also got up. 'The spectators must look out for themselves.'

'Evidently, poor things!' Maud sighed. And as he still stood as if there might be something for him to come from her, she made her attitude clear – which was quite the attitude now of tormenting him a little. 'If you know something about him which she doesn't, and also which *I* don't, she knows something about him – as I do too – which *you* don't.'

'Surely: when it's exactly what I'm trying to get out of you. Are you afraid *I'll* sell it?'

But even this taunt, which she took moreover at its worth, didn't move her. 'You definitely then won't tell me?'

'You mean that if I will you'll tell *me*?'

She thought again. 'Well – yes. But on that condition alone.'

'Then you're safe,' said Howard Bight. 'I *can't*, really, my dear, tell you. Besides, if it's to come out—!'

'I'll wait in that case till it does. But I must warn you,' she added, 'that *my* facts *won't* come out.'

He considered. 'Why not, since the rush at her is probably even now being made? Why not, if she receives others?'

Well, Maud could think too. 'She'll receive them, but they won't receive *her*. Others are like *your* people – dunderheads. Others won't understand, won't count, won't exist.' And she moved to the door. 'There *are* no others.' Opening the door, she had reached the street with it, even while he replied, overtaking her, that there were certainly none such as herself; but they had scarce passed out before her last remark was, to their somewhat disconcerted sense, sharply enough refuted. There was still the other they had forgotten, and that neglected quantity, plainly in search of them and happy in his instinct of the chase, now stayed their steps in the form of Mortimer Marshal.

HE was coming in as they came out; and his 'I *hoped* I might find you,' an exhalation of cool candour that they took full in the face, had the effect, the next moment, of a great soft carpet, all flowers and figures, suddenly unrolled for them to walk upon and before which they felt a scruple. Their ejaculation, Maud was conscious, couldn't have passed for a welcome, and it wasn't till she saw the poor gentleman checked a little, in turn, by their blankness, that she fully perceived how interesting they had just become to themselves. His face, however, while, in their arrest, they neither proposed to re-enter the shop with him nor invited him to proceed with them anywhere else – his face, gaping there, for Bight's promised instructions, like a fair receptacle, shallow but with all the capacity of its flatness, brought back so to our young woman the fond fancy her companion had last excited in him that he profited just a little – and for sympathy in spite of his folly – by her sense that with her too the latter had somehow amused himself. This placed her, for the brief instant, in a strange fellowship with their visitor's plea, under the impulse of which, without more thought, she had turned to Bight. 'Your eager claimant,' she, however, simply said, 'for the opportunity now so beautifully created.'

'I've ventured,' Mr Marshall glowed back, 'to come and remind you that the hours are fleeting.'

Bight had surveyed him with eyes perhaps equivocal. 'You're afraid someone else will step in?'

'Well, with the place so tempting and so empty—!'

Maud made herself again his voice. 'Mr Marshal sees it empty itself perhaps too fast.'

He acknowledged, in his large, bright way, the help afforded him by her easy lightness. 'I do want to get in, you know, before anything happens.'

'And what,' Bight inquired, 'are you afraid *may* happen?'

'Well, to make sure,' he smiled, 'I want myself, don't you see, to happen first.'

Our young woman, at this, fairly fell, for her friend, into his sweetness. '*Do* let him happen!'

'*Do* let me happen!' Mr Marshal followed it up.

They stood there together, where they had paused, in their strange council of three, and their extraordinary tone, in connection with their number, might have marked them, for some passer catching it, as persons not only discussing questions supposedly reserved for the Fates, but absolutely enacting some encounter of these portentous forces. 'Let you – let you?' Bight gravely echoed, while on the sound, for the moment, immensities might have hung. It was as far, however, as he was to have time to speak, for even while his voice was in the air another, at first remote and vague, joined it there on an ominous note and hushed all else to stillness. It came, through the roar of thoroughfares, from the direction of Fleet Street, and it made our interlocutors exchange an altered look. They recognised it, the next thing, as the howl, again, of the Strand, and then but an instant elapsed before it flared into the night. 'Return of Beadel-Muffet! Tremenjous Sensation!'

Tremenjous indeed, so tremenjous that, each really turning as pale with it as they had turned, on the same spot, the other time and with the other news, they stood long enough stricken and still for the cry, multiplied in a flash, again to reach them. They couldn't have said afterwards who first took it up. 'Return—?'

'From the *Dead* – I *say*!' poor Marshal piercingly quavered.

'Then he *hasn't* been—?' Maud gasped it with him at Bight.

But that genius, clearly, was not less deeply affected. 'He's alive?' he breathed in a long, soft wail in which admiration appeared at first to contend with amazement and then the sense of the comic to triumph over both. Howard Bight uncontrollably – it might have struck them as almost hysterically – laughed.

The others could indeed but stare. 'Then who's dead?' piped Mortimer Marshal.

'I'm afraid, Mr Marshal, that *you* are,' the young man returned, more gravely, after a minute. He spoke as if he saw *how* dead.

Poor Marshal was lost. 'But someone was killed—!'

'Someone undoubtedly was, but Beadel somehow has survived it.'

'Has he, then, been playing the game—?' It baffled comprehension.

Yet it wasn't even that what Maud most wondered. 'Have you all the while really known?' she asked of Howard Bight.

He met it with a look that puzzled her for the instant, but that she then saw to mean, half with amusement, half with sadness, that his genius was, after all, simpler. 'I wish I had. I really believed.'

'All along?'

'No; but after Frankfort.'

She remembered things. 'You haven't had a notion this evening?'

'Only from the state of my nerves.'

'Yes, your nerves must be in a state!' And somehow now she had no pity for him. It was almost as if she were, frankly, disappointed. '*I*,' she then boldly said, 'didn't believe.'

'If you had mentioned that then,' Marshal observed to her, 'you would have saved me an awkwardness.'

But Bight took him up. 'She did believe – so that she might punish me.'

'Punish you—?'

Maud raised her hand at her friend. 'He doesn't understand.'

He was indeed, Mr Marshal, fully pathetic now. 'No, I don't understand. Not a wee bit.'

'Well,' said Bight kindly, 'we none of us do. We must give it up.'

'You think *I* really must—?'

'You, sir,' Bight smiled, 'most of all. The places seem so taken.'

His client, however, clung. 'He won't die again—?'

'If he does he'll again come to life. He'll never die. Only *we* shall die. He's immortal.'

He looked up and down, this inquirer; he listened to the howl of the Strand, not yet, as happened, brought nearer to them by one of the hawkers. And yet it was as if, overwhelmed by his lost chance, he knew himself too weak even for *their* fond aid. He still therefore appealed. 'Will *this* be a boom for him?'

'His return? Colossal. For – fancy! – it was exactly what we talked of, you remember, the other day, as the ideal. I mean,' Bight smiled, 'for a man to be lost, and yet at the same time—'

'To be found?' poor Marshal too hungrily mused.

'To be boomed,' Bight continued, 'by his smash and yet never to have been too smashed to know how he was booming.'

It was wonderful for Maud too. 'To have given it all up, and yet to have it all.'

'Oh, better than that,' said her friend: 'to have *more* than all, and more than you gave up. Beadel,' he was careful to explain to their companion, 'will have more.'

Mr Marshal struggled with it. 'More than if he were dead?'

'More,' Bight laughed, 'than if he weren't! It's what *you* would have liked, as I understand you, isn't it? and what you would have got. It's what *I* would have helped you to.'

'But who then,' wailed Marshal, 'helps *him*?'

'Nobody. His star. His genius.'

Mortimer Marshal glared about him as for some sign of such aids in his own sphere. It embraced, his own sphere too, the roaring Strand, yet – mystification and madness! – it was with Beadel the Strand was roaring. A hawker, from afar, at sight of the group, was already scaling the slope. 'Ah, but *how* the devil—?'

Bight pointed to this resource. 'Go and see.'

'But don't *you* want them?' poor Marshal asked as the others retreated.

'The Papers?' They stopped to answer. 'No, never again. We've done with them. We give it up.'

'I mayn't again see you?'

Dismay and a last clutch were in Marshal's face, but Maud, who had taken her friend's meaning in a flash, found the word to meet them. 'We retire from business.'

With which they turned again to move in the other sense, presenting their backs to Fleet Street. They moved together up the rest of the hill, going on in silence, not arrested by another little shrieking boy, not diverted by another extra-special, not pausing again till, at the end of a few minutes, they found themselves in the comparative solitude of Covent Garden, encumbered with the traces of its traffic, but now given over to peace. The howl of the Strand had ceased, their client had vanished forever, and from the centre of the empty space they could look up and see stars. One of these was of course Beadel-Muffet's, and the consciousness of that, for the moment, kept down any arrogance of triumph. He still hung above them, he ruled, immortal, the night; they were far beneath, and he now transcended their world; but a sense of relief, of escape, of the light, still unquenched, of their old irony, made them stand there face to face. There was more between them now than there had ever been, but it had ceased to separate them, it sustained them in fact like a deep water on which they floated closer. Still, however, there was something Maud needed. 'It had been all the while worked?'

'Ah, not, before God – since I lost sight of him – by *me*.'

'Then by himself?'

'I daresay. But there are plenty for him. He's beyond me.'

'But you thought,' she said, 'it *would* be so. You thought,' she declared, 'something.'

Bight hesitated. 'I thought it would be great if he *could*. And *as* he could – why, it *is* great. But all the same I too was sold. I *am* sold. That's why I give up.'

'Then it's why *I* do. We must do something,' she smiled at him, 'that requires less cleverness.'

'We must love each other,' said Howard Bight.

'But can we live by that?'

He thought again; then he decided. 'Yes.'

'Ah,' Maud amended, 'we must be "littery". We've now got stuff.'

'For the dear old ply, for the rattling good tile? Ah, they take better stuff than this – though this too is good.'

'Yes,' she granted on reflection, 'this is good, but it has bad holes. *Who was the dead man in the locked hotel room?*'

'Oh, I don't mean that. *That*,' said Bight, 'he'll splendidly explain.'

'But how?'

'Why, in the Papers. To-morrow.'

Maud wondered. 'So soon?'

'If he returned to-night, and it's not yet ten o'clock, there's plenty of time. It will be in *all* of them – while the universe waits. He'll hold us in the hollow of his hand. His chance is just there. And there,' said the young man, 'will be his greatness.'

'Greater than ever then?'

'Quadrupled.'

She followed; then it made her seize his arm. '*Go* to him!'

Bight frowned. ' "Go"—?'

'This instant. *You* explain!'

He understood, but only to shake his head. 'Never again. I bow to him.'

Well, she after a little understood; but she thought again. 'You mean that the great hole is that he really had no reason, no funk—?'

'I've wondered,' said Howard Bight.

'Whether he *had* done anything to make publicity embarrassing?'

'I've wondered,' the young man repeated.

'But I thought you knew!'

'So did I. But I thought also I knew he was dead. However,' Bight added, 'he'll explain that too.'

'To-morrow?'

'No – as a different branch. Say day after.'

'Ah, then,' said Maud, 'if he explains—!'

'There's no hole? I don't know!' – and it forced from him at last a sigh. He was impatient of it, for he had done with it; it would soon bore him. So fast they lived. 'It will take,' he only dropped, 'much explaining.'

His detachment was logical, but she looked a moment at his sudden weariness. 'There's always, remember, Mrs Chorner.'

'Oh yes, Mrs Chorner; we luckily invented *her*.'

'Well, if she drove him to his death—?'

Bight, with a laugh, caught at it. 'Is that it? *Did* she drive him?'

It pulled her up, and, though she smiled, they stood again, a little, as on their guard. 'Now, at any rate,' Maud simply said at last, 'she'll marry him. So you see how right I was.'

With a preoccupation that had grown in him, however, he had already lost the thread. 'How right—?'

'Not to sell my Talk.'

'Oh yes,' – he remembered. 'Quite right.' But it all came to something else. 'Whom will *you* marry?'

She only, at first, for answer, kept her eyes on him. Then she turned them about the place and saw no hindrance, and then, further, bending with a tenderness in which she felt so transformed, so won to something she had never been before, that she might even, to other eyes, well have looked so, she gravely kissed him. After which, as he took her arm, they walked on together. 'That, at least,' she said, 'we'll put in the Papers.'

FORDHAM CASTLE

SHARP little Madame Massin, who carried on the pleasant pension and who had her small hard eyes everywhere at once, came out to him on the terrace and held up a letter addressed in a manner that he recognised even from afar, held it up with a question in her smile, or a smile, rather a pointed one, in her question – he could scarce have said which. She was looking, while so occupied, at the German group engaged in the garden, near by, with aperitive beer and disputation – the noonday luncheon being now imminent; and the way in which she could show prompt lips while her observation searchingly ranged might have reminded him of the object placed by a spectator at the theatre in the seat he desires to keep during the entr'acte. Conscious of the cross-currents of international passion, she tried, so far as possible, not to mix her sheep and her goats. The view of the bluest end of the Lake of Geneva – she insisted in persuasive circulars that it *was* the bluest – had never, on her high-perched terrace, wanted for admirers, though thus early in the season, during the first days of May, they were not so numerous as she was apt to see them at midsummer. This precisely, Abel Taker could infer, was the reason of a remark she had made him before the claims of the letter had been settled. 'I shall put you next the American lady – the one who arrived yesterday. I know you'll be kind to her; she had to go to bed, as soon as she got here, with a sick-headache brought on by her journey. But she's better. Who isn't better as soon as they get here? She's coming down, and I'm sure she'd like to know you.'

Taker had now the letter in his hand – the letter intended for 'Mr C. P. Addard'; which was not the name inscribed in the two or three books he had left out in his room, any more than it matched the initials, 'A. F. T.' attached to the few pieces of his modest total of luggage. Moreover, since Madame Massin's establishment counted, to his still somewhat bewildered mind, so little for an hotel, as hotels were mainly known to him, he had avoided the act of 'registering', and the missive with which his hostess was practically testing him represented the very first piece of postal matter taken in since his arrival that hadn't been destined to some one else. He had privately blushed for the meagreness of his mail, which made him look unimportant. That however was a detail, an appearance he was used to; indeed the reasons making for such an appearance might never have been so pleasant to him as on this vision of his identity formally and legibly denied. It was denied there in his wife's large straight hand; his eyes, attached to the envelope, took in the failure of any symptom of weakness in her stroke; she at least had the courage of his passing for somebody he wasn't, of his passing rather for nobody at all, and he felt the force of her character more irresistibly than ever as he thus submitted to what she was doing with him. He wasn't used to lying; whatever his faults – and he was used, perfectly, to the idea of his faults – he hadn't made them worse by any perverse theory, any tortuous plea, of innocence; so that probably, with every inch of him giving him away, Madame Massin didn't believe him a bit when he appropriated the letter. He was quite aware he could have made no fight if she had challenged his right to it. That would have come of his making no fight, nowadays, on any ground, with any woman; he had so lost the proper spirit, the necessary confidence. It was true that he had had to do for a long time with no woman in the world but Sue, and of the practice of opposition so far as Sue was concerned the end had been determined early in his career. His hostess fortunately accepted his word, but the way in which her momentary attention bored into his secret like the turn of a gimlet gave him a sense of the quantity of life that passed before her as a dealer with all comers – gave him almost an awe of her power of not wincing. She knew he wasn't, he couldn't be, C. P. Addard, even though she mightn't know, or still less care, who he was; and there was therefore something queer about him if he pretended to be. That was what she didn't mind, there being something queer about him; and what was further present to him was that she would have known when to mind, when really to be on her guard. She attached no importance to his trick; she had doubtless somewhere at the rear, amid the responsive underlings with whom she was sometimes heard volubly, yet so obscurely, to chatter, her clever French amusement about it. He couldn't at all events have said if the whole passage with her most brought home to him the falsity of his position or most glossed it over. On the whole perhaps it rather helped him, since from this moment his masquerade had actively begun.

Taking his place for luncheon, in any case, he found himself next the American lady, as he conceived, spoken of by Madame Massin – in whose appearance he was at first as disappointed as if, a little, though all unconsciously, he had been building on it. Had she loomed into view, on their hostess's hint, as one of the vague alternatives, the possible beguilements, of his leisure – presenting herself solidly where so much else had refused to crystallise? It was certain at least that she presented herself solidly, being a large mild smooth person with a distinct double chin, with grey hair arranged in small flat regular circles, figures of a geometrical perfection; with diamond earrings, with a long-handled eye-glass, with an accumulation of years and of weight and presence, in fine, beyond what his own rather melancholy consciousness acknowledged. He was forty-five, and it took every year of his life, took all he hadn't done with them, to account for his present situation – since you couldn't be, con-clusively, of so little use, of so scant an application, to any mortal career, above all to your own, unless you had been given up and cast aside after a long succession of experiments tried with you. But the American lady with the mathematical hair which reminded him in a manner of the old-fashioned 'work', the weeping willows and mortuary urns represented by the little glazed-over flaxen or auburn or sable or silvered convolutions and tendrils, the capillary flowers, that he had admired in the days of his innocence – the American lady had probably seen her half-century; all the more that before lunch-eon was done she had begun to strike him as having, like himself, slipped slowly down over its stretched and shiny sur-face, an expanse as insecure to fumbling feet as a great cold curved ice-field, into the comparatively warm hollow of resignation and obscurity. She gave him from the first – and he was afterwards to see why – an attaching impression of being, like himself, in exile, and of having like himself learned to butter her bread with a certain acceptance of fate. The only thing that puzzled him on this head was that to parallel his own case she would have had openly to consent to be shelved; which made the difficulty, here, that that was exactly what, as between wife and husband, remained unthinkable on the part of the wife. The necessity for the shelving of one or the other was a case that appeared often to arise, but this wasn't the way he had in general seen it settled. She made him in short, through some influence he couldn't immediately reduce to its elements, vaguely think of her as sacrificed – without blood, as it were; as obligingly and persuadedly passive. Yet this effect, a reflexion of his own state, would doubtless have been better produced for him by a mere melancholy man. She testified unmistakeably to the greater energy of women; for he could think of no manifestation of spirit on his own part that might pass for an equivalent, in the way of resistance, of protest, to the rhythmic though rather wiggy water-waves that broke upon her bald-looking brow as upon a beach bared by a low tide. He had cocked up often enough – and as with the intention of doing it still more under Sue's nose than under his own – the two ends of his half-'sandy' half-grizzled moustache, and he had in fact given these ornaments an extra twist just before coming in to luncheon. That however was but a momentary flourish; the most marked ferocity of which hadn't availed not to land him – well, where he was landed now.

His new friend mentioned that she had come up from Rome and that Madame Massin's establishment had been highly spoken of to her there, and this, slight as it was, straightway contributed in its degree for Abel Taker to the idea that they had something in common. He was in a condition in which he could feel the drift of vague currents, and he knew how highly the place had been spoken of to *him*. There was but a shade of difference in his having had his lesson in Florence. He let his companion know, without reserve, that he too had come up from Italy, after spending three or four months there: though he remembered in time that, being now C. P. Addard, it was only as C. P. Addard he could speak. He tried to think, in order to give himself something to say, what C. P. Addard would have done; but he was doomed to feel always, in the whole connexion, his lack of imagination. He had had many days to come to it and nothing else to do; but he hadn't even yet made up his mind who C. P. Addard was or invested him with any distinguishing marks. He felt like a man who, moving in this, that or the other direction, saw each successively lead him to some danger; so that he began to ask himself why he shouldn't just lie outright, boldly and inventively, and see what that could do for him. There was an excitement, the excitement of personal risk, about it – much the same as would belong for an ordinary man to the first trial of a flying-machine; yet it was exactly such a course as Sue had prescribed on his asking her what he should do. 'Anything in the world you like but talk about *me*: think of some other woman, as bad and bold as you please, and say you're married to *her*.' Those had been literally her words, together with others, again and again repeated, on the subject of his being free to 'kill and bury' her as often as he chose. This was the way she had met his objection to his own death and interment; she had asked him, in her bright hard triumphant way, why he couldn't defend himself by shooting back. The real reason was of course that he was nothing without her, whereas she was everything, could be anything in the wide world she liked, without him. That question precisely had been a part of what was before him while he strolled in the projected green gloom of Madame Massin's plane-trees; he wondered what she *was* choosing to be and how good a time it was helping her to have. He could be sure she was rising to it, on some line or other, and that was what secretly made him say: 'Why shouldn't I get something out of it too, just for the harmless fun –?'

It kept coming back to him, naturally, that he hadn't the breadth of fancy, that he knew himself as he knew the taste of ill-made coffee, that he was the same old Abel Taker he had ever been, in whose aggregation of items it was as vain to feel about for latent heroisms as it was useless to rummage one's trunk for presentable clothes that one didn't possess. But did that absolve him (having so definitely Sue's permission) from seeing to what extent he might temporarily make believe? If he were to flap his wings very hard and crow very loud and take as long a jump as possible at the same time – if he were to do all that perhaps he should achieve for half a minute the sensation of soaring. He knew only one thing Sue couldn't do, from the moment she didn't divorce him: she couldn't get rid of his name, unaccountably, after all, as she hated it; she couldn't get rid of it because she would have always sooner or later to come back to it. She might consider that her being a thing so dreadful as Mrs Abel Taker was a stumbling-block in her social path that nothing but his real, his official, his advertised circulated demise (with 'American papers please copy') would avail to dislodge: she would have none the less to reckon with his continued existence as the drop of bitterness in her cup that seasoned undisguiseably each draught. He might make use of his present opportunity to row out into the lake with his pockets full of stones and there quietly slip overboard; but he could think of no shorter cut for her ceasing to be what her marriage and the law of the land had made her. She was not an inch less Mrs Abel Taker for these days of his sequestration, and the only thing she indeed claimed was that the concealment of the source of her shame, the suppression of the person who had divided with her his inherited absurdity, made the difference of a shade or two for getting honourably, as she called it, 'about'. How she had originally come to incur this awful inconvenience – *that* part of the matter, left to herself, she would undertake to keep vague; and she wasn't really left to herself so long as he too flaunted the dreadful flag.

This was why she had provided him with another and placed him out at board, to constitute, as it were, a permanent *alibi*; telling him she should quarrel with no colours under which he might elect to sail, and promising to take him back when she had got where she wanted. She wouldn't mind so much then – she only wanted a fair start. It wasn't a fair start – *was* it? she asked him frankly – so long as he was always there, so terribly cruelly there, to speak of what she *had* been. She had been nothing worse, to his sense, than a very pretty girl of eighteen out in Peoria, who had seen at that time no one else she wanted more to marry, nor even any one who had been so supremely struck by her. That, absolutely, was the worst that could be said of her. It was so bad at any rate in her own view – it had grown so bad in the widening light of life – that it had fairly become more than she could bear and that something, as she said, had to be done about it. She hadn't known herself originally any more than she had known him – hadn't foreseen how much better she was going to come out, nor how, for her individually, as distinguished from him, there might be the possibility of a big future. He couldn't be explained away – he cried out with all his dreadful presence that she *had* been pleased to marry him; and what they therefore had to do must transcend explaining. It was perhaps now helping her, off there in London, and especially at Fordham Castle – she was staying last at Fordham Castle, Wilts – it was perhaps inspiring her even more than she had expected, that they were able to try together this particular substitute: news of her progress in fact – her progress on from Fordham Castle, if anything could be higher – would not improbably be contained in the unopened letter he had lately pocketed.

There was a given moment at luncheon meanwhile, in his talk with his countrywoman, when he did try that flap of the wing – did throw off, for a flight into the blue, the first falsehood he could think of. 'I stopped in Italy, you see, on my way back from the East, where I had gone – to Constantinople' – he rose actually to Constantinople – 'to visit Mrs Addard's grave.' And after they had all come out to coffee in the rustling shade, with the vociferous German tribe at one end of the terrace, the English family keeping silence with an English accent, as it struck him, in the middle, and his direction taken, by his new friend's side, to the other unoccupied corner, he found himself oppressed with what he had on his hands, the burden of keeping up this expensive fiction. He had never been to Constantinople – it could easily be proved against him; he ought to have thought of something better, have got his effect on easier terms. Yet a funnier thing still than this quick repentance was the quite equally fictive ground on which his companion had affected him – when he came to think of it – as meeting him.

'Why you know that's very much the same errand that took me to Rome. I visited the grave of my daughter – whom I lost there some time ago.'

She had turned her face to him after making this statement, looked at him with an odd blink of her round kind plain eyes, as if to see how he took it. He had taken it on the spot, for this was the only thing to do; but he had felt how much deeper down he was himself sinking as he replied: 'Ah it's a sad pleasure, isn't it? But those are places one doesn't want to neglect.'

'Yes – that's what I feel. I go,' his neighbour had solemnly pursued, 'about every two years.'

With which she had looked away again, leaving him really not able to emulate her. 'Well, I hadn't been before. You see it's a long way.'

'Yes – that's the trying part. It makes you feel you'd have done better –'

'To bring them right home and have it done over there?' he had asked as she let the sad subject go a little. He quite agreed. 'Yes – that's what many do.'

'But it gives of course a peculiar interest.' So they had kept it up. 'I mean in places that mightn't have so *very* much.'

'Places like Rome and Constantinople?' he had rejoined while he noticed the cautious anxious sound of her 'very'. The tone was to come back to him, and it had already made him feel sorry for her, with its suggestion of her being at sea like himself. Unmistakeably, poor lady, she too was trying to float – was striking out in timid convulsive movements. Well, he wouldn't make it difficult for her, and immediately, so as not to appear to cast any ridicule, he observed that, wherever great bereavements might have occurred, there was no place so remarkable as not to gain an association. Such memories made at the least another object for coming. It was after this recognition, on either side, that they adjourned to the garden – Taker having in his ears again the good lady's rather troubled or muddled echo: 'Oh yes, when you come to all the *objects* –!' The grave of one's wife or one's daughter was an object quite as much as all those that one looked up in Baedeker – those of the family of the Castle of Chillon and the Dent du Midi, features of the view to be enjoyed from different parts of Madame Massin's premises. It was very soon, none the less, rather as if these latter presences, diffusing their reality and majesty, had taken the colour out of all other evoked romance; and to that degree that when Abel's fellow-guest happened to lay down on the parapet of the terrace three or four articles she had brought out with her, her fan, a couple of American newspapers and a letter that had obviously come to her by the same post as his own, he availed himself of the accident to jump at a further conclusion. Their coffee, which was 'extra', as he knew and as, in the way of benevolence, he boldly warned her, was brought forth to them, and while she was giving her attention to her demi-tasse he let his eyes rest for three seconds on the super-scription of her letter. His mind was by this time made up, and the beauty of it was that he couldn't have said why: the letter was from her daughter, whom she had been burying for him in Rome, and it would be addressed in a name that was really no more hers than the name his wife had thrust upon him was his. Her daughter had put *her* out at cheap board, pending higher issues, just as Sue had put him – so that there was a logic not other than fine in his notifying her of what coffee every day might let her in for. She was addressed on her envelope as 'Mrs Vanderplank', but he had privately arrived, before she so much as put down her cup, at the conviction that this was a borrowed and lawless title, for all the world as if, poor dear innocent woman, she were a bold bad adventuress. He had acquired furthermore the moral certitude that he was on the track, as he would have said, of her true identity, such as it might be. He couldn't think of it as in itself either very mysterious or very impressive; but, whatever it was, her duplicity had as yet mas-tered no finer art than his own, inasmuch as she had positively not escaped, at table, inadvertently dropping a name which, while it lingered on Abel's ear, gave her quite away. She had spoken, in her solemn sociability and as by the force of old habit, of 'Mr Magaw', and nothing was more to be presumed than that this gentleman was her defunct husband, not so very long defunct, who had permitted her while in life the privilege of association with him, but whose extinction had left her to be worked upon by different ideas.

These ideas would have germed, infallibly, in the brain of the young woman, her only child, under whose rigid rule she now – it was to be detected – drew her breath in pain. Madame Massin would abysmally know, Abel reflected, for he was at the end of a few minutes more intimately satisfied that Mrs Magaw's American newspapers, coming to her straight from the other side and not yet detached from their wrappers, would not be directed to Mrs Vanderplank, and that, this being the case, the poor lady would have had to invent some pretext for a claim to goods likely still perhaps to be lawfully called for. And she wasn't formed for duplicity, the large simple scared foolish fond woman, the vague anxiety in whose otherwise so uninhabited and unreclaimed countenance, as void of all history as an expanse of Western prairie seen from a car-window, testified to her scant aptitude for her part. He was far from the desire to question their hostess, however – for the study of his companion's face on its mere inferred merits had begun to dawn upon him as the possible resource of his ridiculous leisure. He might verily have some fun with her – or he would so have conceived it had he not become aware before they separated, half an hour later, of a kind of fellow-feeling for her that seemed to plead for her being spared. She *wasn't* being, in some quarter still indistinct to him – and so no more was he, and these things were precisely a reason. Her sacrifice, he divined, was an act of devotion, a state not yet disciplined to the state of confidence. She had presently, as from a return of vigilance, gathered in her postal property, shuffling it together at her further side and covering it with her pocket-handkerchief – though this very betrayal indeed but quickened his temporary impulse to break out to her, sympathetically, with a 'Had you the misfortune to *lose* Magaw?' or with the effective production of his own card and a smiling, an inviting, a consoling 'That's who *I* am if you want to know!' He really made out, with the idle human instinct, the crude sense for other people's pains and pleasures that had, on his showing, to his so great humiliation, been found an inadequate outfit for the successful conduct of the coal, the commission, the insurance and, as a last resort, desperate and disgraceful, the book-agency business – he really made out that she didn't want to know, or wouldn't for some little time; that she was decidedly afraid in short, and covertly agitated, and all just because she too, with him, suspected herself dimly in presence of that mysterious 'more' than, in the classic phrase, met the eye. They parted accordingly, as if to relieve, till they could recover themselves, the conscious tension of their being able neither to hang back with grace nor to advance with glory; but flagrantly full, at the same time, both of the recognition that they couldn't in such a place avoid each other even if they had desired it, and of the suggestion that they wouldn't desire it, after such subtlety of communion, even were it to be thought of.

Abel Taker, till dinner-time, turned over his little adventure and extracted, while he hovered and smoked and mused, some refreshment from the impression the subtlety of communion had left with him. Mrs Vanderplank was his senior by several years, and was neither fair nor slim nor 'bright' nor truly, nor even falsely, elegant, nor anything that Sue had taught him, in her wonderful way, to associate with the American woman at the American woman's best – that best than which there was nothing better, as he had so often heard her say, on God's great earth. Sue would have banished her to the wildest waste of the unknowable, would have looked over her head in the manner he had often seen her use – as if she were in an exhibition of pictures, were in front of something bad and negligible that had got itself placed on the line, but that had the real thing, the thing of interest for those who *knew* (and when didn't Sue know?) hung above it. In Mrs Magaw's presence everything would have been of more interest to Sue than Mrs Magaw; but that consciousness failed to prevent his feeling the appeal of this inmate much rather confirmed than weakened when she reappeared for dinner. It was impressed upon him, after they had again seated themselves side by side, that she was reaching out to him indirectly, guardedly, even as he was to her; so that later on, in the garden, where they once more had their coffee together – it *might* have been so free and easy, so wildly foreign, so almost Bohemian – he lost all doubt of the wisdom of his taking his plunge. This act of resolution was not, like the other he had risked in the morning, an upward flutter into fiction, but a straight and possibly dangerous dive into the very depths of truth. Their instinct was unmistakeably to cling to each other, but it was as if they wouldn't know where to take hold till the air had really been cleared. Actually, in fact, they required a light – the aid prepared by him in the shape of a fresh match for his cigarette after he had extracted, under cover of the scented dusk, one of his cards from his pocket-book.

'There I honestly am, you see – Abel F. Taker; which I think you ought to know.' It was relevant to nothing, relevant only to the grope of their talk, broken with sudden silences where they stopped short for fear of mistakes; but as he put the card before her he held out to it the little momentary flame. And this was the way that, after a while and from one thing to another, he himself, in exchange for what he had to give and what he gave freely, heard all about 'Mattie' – Mattie Magaw, Mrs Vander-plank's beautiful and high-spirited daughter, who, as he learned, found her two names, so dreadful even singly, a combination not to be borne, and carried on a quarrel with them no less desperate than Sue's quarrel with – well, with everything. She had, quite as Sue had done, declared her need of a free hand to fight them, and she was, for all the world like Sue again, now fighting them to the death. This similarity of situation was wondrously completed by the fact that the scene of Miss Magaw's struggle was, as her mother explained, none other than that uppermost walk of 'high' English life which formed the present field of Mrs Taker's operations; a circumstance on which Abel presently produced his comment. 'Why if they're after the same thing in the same place, I wonder if we shan't hear of their meeting.'

Mrs Magaw appeared for a moment to wonder too. 'Well, if they do meet I guess we'll hear. I will say for Mattie that she writes me pretty fully. And I presume,' she went on, 'Mrs Taker keeps *you* posted?'

'No,' he had to confess – 'I don't hear from her in much detail. She knows I back her,' Abel smiled, 'and that's enough for her. "You be quiet and I'll let you know when you're wanted" – that's her motto; I'm to wait, wherever I am, till I'm called for. But I guess she won't be in a hurry to call for me' – this reflexion he showed he was familiar with. 'I've stood in her light so long – her "social" light, outside of which everything is for Sue black darkness – that I don't really see the reason she should ever want me back. That at any rate is what I'm doing – I'm just waiting. And I didn't expect the luck of being able to wait in your company. I couldn't suppose – that's the truth,' he added – 'that there was another, anywhere about, with the same ideas or the same strong character. It had never seemed to be possible,' he ruminated, 'that there could be any one like Mrs Taker.'

He was to remember afterwards how his companion had appeared to consider this approximation. 'Another, you mean, like my Mattie?'

'Yes – like my Sue. Any one that really comes up to her. It will be,' he declared, 'the first one I've struck.'

'Well,' said Mrs Vanderplank, 'my Mattie's remarkably handsome.'

'I'm sure –! But Mrs Taker's remarkably handsome too. Oh,' he added, both with humour and with earnestness, 'if it wasn't for that I wouldn't trust her so! Because, for what she wants,' he developed, 'it's a great help to be fine-looking.'

'Ah it's always a help for a lady!' – and Mrs Magaw's sigh fluttered vaguely between the expert and the rueful. 'But what is it,' she asked, 'that Mrs Taker wants?'

'Well, she could tell you herself. I don't think she'd trust me to give an account of it. Still,' he went on, 'she *has* stated it more than once for my benefit, and perhaps that's what it all finally comes to. She wants to get where she truly belongs.'

Mrs Magaw had listened with interest. 'That's just where Mattie wants to get! And she seems to know just where it is.'

'Oh Mrs Taker knows – you can bet your life,' he laughed, 'on that. It seems to be somewhere in London or in the country round, and I daresay it's the same place as your daughter's.

Once she's there, as I understand it, she'll be all right; but she has got to get there – that is to be seen there thoroughly fixed and photographed, and have it in all the papers – first. After she's fixed, she says, we'll talk. We *have* talked a good deal: when Mrs Taker says "We'll talk" I know what she means. But this time we'll have it out.'

There were communities in their fate that made his friend turn pale. 'Do you mean she won't want you to come?'

'Well, for me to "come", don't you see? will be for me to come to life. How can I come to life when I've been as dead as I am now?'

Mrs Vanderplank looked at him with a dim delicacy. 'But surely, sir, I'm not conversing with the remains –!'

'You're conversing with C. P. Addard. *He* may be alive – but even this I don't know yet; I'm just trying him,' he said: 'I'm trying him, Mrs Magaw, on you. Abel Taker's in his grave, but does it strike you that Mr Addard is at all above ground?'

He had smiled for the slightly gruesome joke of it, but she looked away as if it made her uneasy. Then, however, as she came back to him, 'Are you going to wait here?' she asked.

He held her, with some gallantry, in suspense. 'Are you?'

She postponed her answer, visibly not quite comfortable now; but they were inevitably the next day up to their necks again in the question; and then it was that she expressed more of her sense of her situation. 'Certainly I feel as if I must wait – as long as I *have* to wait. Mattie likes this place – I mean she likes it for *me*. It seems the right *sort* of place,' she opined with her perpetual earnest emphasis.

But it made him sound again the note. 'The right sort to pass for dead in?'

'Oh she doesn't want me to pass for *dead*.'

'Then what does she want you to pass for?'

The poor lady cast about. 'Well, only for Mrs Vanderplank.'

'And who or what is Mrs Vanderplank?'

Mrs Magaw considered this personage, but didn't get far. 'She isn't any one in particular, I guess.'

'That means,' Abel returned, 'that she isn't alive.'

'She isn't more than *half* alive,' Mrs Magaw conceded. 'But it isn't what I *am* – it's what I'm passing for. Or rather' – she worked it out – 'what I'm just not. I'm not passing – I don't, can't here, where it doesn't matter, you see – for her mother.'

Abel quite fell in. 'Certainly – she doesn't want to have any mother.'

'She doesn't want to have *me*. She wants me to lay low. If I lay low, she says –'

'Oh I know what she says' – Abel took it straight up. 'It's the very same as what Mrs Taker says. If you lie low she can fly high.'

It kept disconcerting her in a manner, as well as steadying, his free possession of their case. 'I don't feel as if I *was* lying – I mean as low as she wants – when I talk to you so.' She broke it off thus, and again and again, anxiously, responsibly; her sense of responsibility making Taker feel, with his braver projection of humour, quite ironic and sardonic; but as for a week, for a fortnight, for many days more, they kept frequently and intimately meeting, it was natural that the so extraordinary fact of their being, as he put it, in the same sort of box, and of their boxes having so even more remarkably bumped together under Madame Massin's *tilleuls*, shouldn't only make them reach out to each other across their queer coil of communications, cut so sharp off in other quarters, but should prevent their pretending to any real consciousness but that of their ordeal. It was Abel's idea, promptly enough expressed to Mrs Magaw, that they ought to get something out of it; but when he had said that a few times over (the first time she had met it in silence), she finally replied, and in a manner that he thought quite sublime: 'Well, we *shall* – if they do all they want. We shall feel we've helped. And it isn't so *very* much to do.'

'You think it isn't so very much to do – to lie down and die for them?'

'Well, if I don't hate it any worse when I'm really dead –!' She took herself up, however, as if she had skirted the profane. 'I don't say that if I didn't *believe* in Mat –! But I do believe, you see. That's where she *has* me.'

'Oh I see more or less. That's where Sue has *me*.'

Mrs Magaw fixed him with a milder solemnity. 'But what has Mrs Taker against you?'

'It's sweet of you to ask,' he smiled; while it really came to him that he was living with her under ever so much less strain than what he had been feeling for ever so long before from Sue. Wouldn't he have liked it to go on and on – wouldn't that have suited C. P. Addard? He seemed to be finding out who C. P. Addard was – so that it came back again to the way Sue fixed things. She had fixed them so that C. P. Addard could become quite interested in Mrs Vanderplank and quite soothed by her – and so that Mrs Vanderplank as well, wonderful to say, had lost her impatience for Mattie's summons a good deal more, he was sure, than she confessed. It was from this moment none the less that he began, with a strange but distinct little pang, to see that he couldn't be sure of her. Her question had produced in him a vibration of the sensibility that even the long series of mortifications, of publicly proved inaptitudes, springing originally from his lack of business talent, but owing an aggravation of aspect to an absence of nameable 'type' of which he hadn't been left unaware, wasn't to have wholly toughened. Yet it struck him positively as the prettiest word ever spoken to him, so straight a surprise at his wife's dissatisfaction; and he was verily so unused to tributes to his adequacy that this one lingered in the air a moment and seemed almost to create a possibility. He wondered, honestly, what she could see in him, in whom Sue now at last saw really less than nothing; and his fingers instinctively moved to his moustache, a corner of which he twiddled up again, also wondering if it were perhaps only *that* – though Sue had as good as told him that the undue flourish of this feature but brought out to her view the insignificance of all the rest of him. Just to hang in the iridescent ether with Mrs Vanderplank, to whom he wasn't insignificant, just for them to sit on there together, protected, indeed positively ennobled, by their loss of identity, struck him as the foretaste of a kind of felicity that he hadn't in the past known enough about really to miss it. He appeared to have become aware that he should miss it quite sharply, that he would find how he had already learned to, if she should go; and the very sadness of his apprehension quickened his vision of what would work with her. She would want, with all the roundness of her kind, plain eyes, to see Mattie fixed – whereas he'd be hanged if he wasn't willing, on his side, to take Sue's elevation quite on trust. For the instant, however, he said nothing of that; he only followed up a little his acknowledge-ment of her having touched him. 'What you ask me, you know, is just what I myself was going to ask. What has Miss Magaw got against *you*?'

'Well, if you were to see her I guess you'd know.'

'Why I should think she'd like to show you,' said Abel Taker.

'She doesn't so much mind their *seeing* me – when once she has had a look at me first. But she doesn't like them to hear me – though I don't talk so very much. Mattie speaks in the real English style,' Mrs Magaw explained.

'But ain't the real English style not to speak at all?'

'Well, she's having the best kind of time, she writes me – so I presume there must be some talk in which she can shine.'

'Oh I've no doubt at all Miss Magaw *talks*!' – and Abel, in his contemplative way, seemed to have it before him.

'Well, don't you go and believe she talks too much,' his companion rejoined with spirit; and this it was that brought to a head his prevision of his own fate.

'I see what's going to happen. You only want to go to her. You want to get your share, after all. You'll leave me without a pang.'

Mrs Magaw stared. 'But won't you be going too? When Mrs Taker sends for you?'

He shook, as by a rare chance, a competent head. 'Mrs Taker won't send for me. I don't make out the use Mrs Taker can ever have for me again.'

Mrs Magaw looked grave. 'But not to enjoy your seeing –?'

'My seeing where she has come out? Oh that won't be necessary to *her* enjoyment of it. It would be well enough perhaps if I could see without being seen; but the trouble with me – for I'm worse than you,' Abel said – 'is that it doesn't do for me either to be heard *or* seen. I haven't got *any* side –!' But it dropped; it was too old a story.

'Not any possible side at all?' his friend, in her candour, doubtingly echoed. 'Why what do they want over there?'

It made him give a comic pathetic wail. 'Ah to know a person who says such things as that to me, and to have to give her up –!'

She appeared to consider with a certain alarm what this might portend, and she really fell back before it. 'Would you think I'd be able to give up Mattie?'

'Why not – if she's successful? The thing you wouldn't like – *you* wouldn't, I'm sure – would be to give her up if she should find, or if you should find, she wasn't.'

'Well, I guess Mattie will be successful,' said Mrs Magaw.

'Ah you're a worshipper of success!' he groaned. 'I'd give Mrs Taker up, definitely, just to remain C. P. Addard with you.'

She allowed it her thought; but, as he felt, superficially. 'She's your wife, sir, you know, whatever you do.'

' "Mine"? Ah but whose? She isn't C. P. Addard's.'

She rose at this as if they were going too far; yet she showed him, he seemed to see, the first little concession – which was indeed to be the only one – of her inner timidity; something that suggested how she must have preserved as a token, laid away among spotless properties, the visiting-card he had originally handed her. 'Well, I guess the one I feel for is Abel F. Taker!'

This, in the end, however, made no difference; since one of the things that inevitably came up between them was that if Mattie had a quarrel with her name her most workable idea would be to get somebody to give her a better. That, he easily made out, was fundamentally what she was after, and, though, delicately and discreetly, as he felt, he didn't reduce Mrs Vanderplank to so stating the case, he finally found himself believing in Miss Magaw with just as few reserves as those with which he believed in Sue. If it was a question of her 'shining' she would indubitably shine; she was evidently, like the wife by whom he had been, in the early time, too provincially, too primitively accepted, of the great radiating substance, and there were times, here at Madame Massin's, while he strolled to and fro and smoked, when Mrs Taker's distant lustre fairly peeped at him over the opposite mountain-tops, fringing their silhouettes as with the little hard bright rim of a coming day. It was clear that Mattie's mother couldn't be expected not to want to see her married; the shade of doubt bore only on the stage of the business at which Mrs Magaw might safely be let out of the box. Was she to emerge abruptly *as* Mrs Magaw? – or was the lid simply to be tipped back so that, for a good look, she might sit up a little straighter? She had got news at any rate, he inferred, which suggested to her that the term of her suppression was in sight; and she even let it out to him that, yes, certainly, for Mattie to be ready for her – and she did look as if she were going to be ready – she must be right down sure. They had had further lights by this time moreover, lights much more vivid always in Mattie's bulletins than in Sue's; which latter, as Abel insistently imaged it, were really each time, on Mrs Taker's part, as limited as a peep into a death-chamber. The death-chamber was Madame Massin's terrace; and – he completed the image – how could Sue *not* want to know how things were looking for the funeral, which was in any case to be thoroughly 'quiet'? *The* vivid thing seemed to pass before Abel's eyes the day he heard of the bright compatriot, just the person to go round with, a charming handsome witty widow, whom Miss Magaw had met at Fordham Castle, whose ideas were, on all important points, just the same as her own, whose means also (so that they could join forces on an equality) matched beautifully, and whose name in fine was Mrs Sherrington Reeve. 'Mattie has felt the want,' Mrs Magaw explained, 'of some lady, some real lady like that, to go round with: she says she sometimes doesn't find it very pleasant going round alone.'

Abel Taker had listened with interest – this information left him staring. 'By Gosh then, she has struck Sue!'

' "Struck" Mrs Taker –?'

'She isn't Mrs Taker now – she's Mrs Sherrington Reeve.' It had come to him with all its force – as if the glare of her genius were, at a bound, high over the summits. 'Mrs Taker's dead: I thought, you know, all the while, she must be, and this makes me sure. She died at Fordham Castle. So we're both dead.'

His friend, however, with her large blank face, lagged behind. 'At Fordham Castle too – died there?'

'Why she has been as good as *living* there!' Abel Taker emphasised. '"Address Fordham Castle" – that's about all she has written me. But perhaps she died before she went' – he had it before him, he made it out. 'Yes, she must have gone as Mrs Sherrington Reeve. She had to die to go – as it would be for her like going to heaven. Marriages, sometimes, they say, are made up there; and so, sometimes then, apparently, are friendships – that, you see, for instance, of our two shining ones.'

Mrs Magaw's understanding was still in the shade. 'But are you sure –?'

'Why Fordham Castle settles it. If she wanted to get where she truly belongs she has got *there*. She belongs at Fordham Castle.'

The noble mass of this structure seemed to rise at his words, and his companion's grave eyes, he could see, to rest on its towers. 'But how has she become Mrs Sherrington Reeve?'

'By my death. And also after that by her own. I had to die first, you see, for *her* to be able to – that is for her to be sure. It's what she has been looking for, as I told you – to *be* sure. But oh – she was sure from the first. She knew I'd die off, when she had made it all right for me – so she felt no risk. She simply became, the day I became C. P. Addard, something as different as possible from the thing she had always so hated to be. She's what she always would have liked to be – so why shouldn't we rejoice for her? Her baser part, her vulgar part, has ceased to be, and she lives only as an angel.'

It affected his friend, this elucidation, almost with awe; she took it at least, as she took everything, stolidly. 'Do you call Mrs Taker an angel?'

Abel had turned about, as he rose to the high vision, moving, with his hands in his pockets, to and fro. But at Mrs Magaw's question he stopped short – he considered with his head in the air. 'Yes – now!'

'But do you mean it's her idea to marry?'

He thought again. 'Why for all I know she is married.'

'With you, Abel Taker, living?'

'But I ain't living. That's just the point.'

'Oh you're too dreadful' – and she gathered herself up. 'And I won't,' she said as she broke off, 'help to bury you!'

This office, none the less, as she practically had herself to acknowledge, was in a manner, and before many days, forced upon her by further important information from her daughter, in the light of the true inevitability of which they had, for that matter, been living. She was there before him with her telegram, which she simply held out to him as from a heart too full for words. 'Am engaged to Lord Dunderton, and Sue thinks you can come.'

Deep emotion sometimes confounds the mind – and Mrs Magaw quite flamed with excitement. But on the other hand it sometimes illumines, and she could see, it appeared, what Sue meant. 'It's because he's so much in love.'

'So far gone that she's safe?' Abel frankly asked.

'So far gone that she's safe.'

'Well,' he said, 'if Sue feels it –!' He had so much, he showed, to go by. 'Sue *knows*.'

Mrs Magaw visibly yearned, but she could look at all sides. 'I'm bound to say, since you speak of it, that I've an idea Sue has helped. She'll like to have her there.'

'Mattie will like to have Sue?'

'No, Sue will like to have Mattie.' Elation raised to such a point was in fact already so clarifying that Mrs Magaw could come all the way. 'As Lady Dunderton.'

'Well,' Abel smiled, 'one good turn deserves another!' If he meant it, however, in any such sense as that Mattie might be able in due course to render an equivalent of aid, this notion clearly had to reckon with his companion's sense of its strangeness, exhibited in her now at last upheaved countenance. 'Yes,' he accordingly insisted, 'it will work round to that – you see if it doesn't. If that's where they were to come out, and they *have* come – by which I mean if Sue has realised it for Mattie and acted as she acts when she does realise, then she can't neglect it in her own case: she'll just *have* to realise it for herself. And, for that matter, you'll help her too. You'll be able to tell her, you know, that you've seen the last of me.' And on the morrow, when, starting for London, she had taken her place in the train, to which he had accompanied her, he stood by the door of her compartment and repeated this idea. 'Remember, for Mrs Taker, that you've seen the last –!'

'Oh but I hope I haven't, sir.'

'Then you'll come back to me? If you only will, you know, Sue will be delighted to fix it.'

'To fix it – how?'

'Well, she'll tell you how. You've seen how she can fix things, and that will be the way, as I say, you'll help her.'

She stared at him from her corner, and he could see she was sorry for him; but it was as if she had taken refuge behind her large high-shouldered reticule, which she held in her lap, presenting it almost as a bulwark. 'Mr Taker,' she launched at him over it, 'I'm afraid of you.'

'Because I'm dead?'

'Oh sir!' she pleaded, hugging her morocco defence. But even through this alarm her finer thought came out. 'Do you suppose I shall go to Fordham Castle?'

'Well, I guess that's what they're discussing now. You'll know soon enough.'

'If I write you from there,' she asked, 'won't you come?'

'I'll come as the ghost. Don't old castles always have one?'

She looked at him darkly; the train had begun to move. 'I *shall* fear you!' she said.

'Then there you are.' And he moved an instant beside the door. 'You'll be glad, when you get there, to be able to say –' But she got out of hearing, and, turning away, he felt as abandoned as he had known he should – felt left, in his solitude, to the sense of his extinction. He faced it completely now, and to himself at least could express it without fear of protest. 'Why certainly I'm dead.'

JULIA BRIDE

I

SHE had walked with her friend to the top of the wide steps of the Museum, those that descend from the galleries of painting, and then, after the young man had left her, smiling, looking back, waving all gaily and expressively his hat and stick, had watched him, smiling too, but with a different intensity – had kept him in sight till he passed out of the great door. She might have been waiting to see if he would turn there for a last demonstration; which was exactly what he did, renewing his cordial gesture and with his look of glad devotion, the radiance of his young face, reaching her across the great space, as she felt, in undiminished truth. Yes, so she could feel, and she remained a minute even after he was gone; she gazed at the empty air as if he had filled it still, asking herself what more she wanted and what, if it didn't signify glad devotion, his whole air could have represented.

She was at present so anxious that she could wonder if he stepped and smiled like that for mere relief at separation; yet if he wanted in such a degree to break the spell and escape the danger why did he keep coming back to her, and why, for that matter, had she felt safe a moment before in letting him go? She felt safe, felt almost reckless – that was the proof – so long as he was with her; but the chill came as soon as he had gone, when she instantly took the measure of all she yet missed. She might now have been taking it afresh, by the testimony of her charming clouded eyes and of the rigour that had already replaced her beautiful play of expression. Her radiance, for the minute, had 'carried' as far as his, travelling on the light wings of her brilliant prettiness – he on his side not being facially handsome, but only sensitive, clean and eager. Then with its extinction, the sustaining wings dropped and hung.

She wheeled about, however, full of a purpose; she passed back through the pictured rooms, for it pleased her, this idea of a talk with Mr Pitman – as much, that is, as anything could

907

please a young person so troubled. It had happened indeed that when she saw him rise at sight of her from the settee where he had told her five minutes before that she would find him, it was just with her nervousness that his presence seemed, as through an odd suggestion of help, to connect itself. Nothing truly would be quite so odd for her case as aid proceeding from Mr Pitman; unless perhaps the oddity would be even greater for himself – the oddity of her having taken into her head an appeal to him.

She had had to feel alone with a vengeance – inwardly alone and miserably alarmed – to be ready to 'meet', that way, at the first sign from him, the successor to her dim father in her dim father's lifetime, the second of her mother's two divorced husbands. It made a queer relation for her; a relation that struck her at this moment as less edifying, less natural and graceful, than it would have been even for her remarkable mother – and still in spite of this parent's third marriage, her union with Mr Connery, from whom she was informally separated. It was at the back of Julia's head as she approached Mr Pitman, or it was at least somewhere deep within her soul, that if this last of Mrs Connery's withdrawals from the matrimonial yoke had received the sanction of the Court (Julia had always heard, from far back, so much about the 'Court') she herself, as after a fashion, in that event, a party to it, wouldn't have had the cheek to make up – which was how she inwardly phrased what she was doing – to the long lean loose slightly cadaverous gentleman who was a memory, for her, of the period from her twelfth to her seventeenth year. She had got on with him, perversely, much better than her mother had, and the bulging misfit of his duck waistcoat, with his trick of swinging his eye-glass, at the end of an extraordinarily long string, far over the scene, came back to her as positive features of the image of her remoter youth. Her present age – for her later time had seen so many things happen – gave her a perspective.

Fifty things came up as she stood there before him, some of them floating in from the past, others hovering with freshness: how she used to dodge the rotary movement made by his pince-nez while he always awkwardly, and kindly, and often funnily,

talked – it had once hit her rather badly in the eye; how she used
to pull down and straighten his waistcoat, making it set a little
better, a thing of a sort her mother never did; how friendly and
familiar she must have been with him for that, or else a forward
little minx; how she felt almost capable of doing it again now,
just to sound the right note, and how sure she was of the way he
would take it if she did; how much nicer he had clearly been, all
the while, poor dear man, than his wife and the Court had made
it possible for him publicly to appear; how much younger too
he now looked, in spite of his rather melancholy, his mildly-
jaundiced, humorously-determined sallowness and his careless
assumption, everywhere, from his forehead to his exposed and
relaxed blue socks, almost sky-blue, as in past days, of creases
and folds and furrows that would have been perhaps tragic if
they hadn't seemed rather to show, like his whimsical black eyebrows, the vague interrogative arch.

Of course he wasn't wretched if he wasn't more sure of his
wretchedness than that! Julia Bride would have been sure – had
she been through what she supposed *he* had! With his thick
loose black hair, in any case, untouched by a thread of grey, and
his kept gift of a certain big-boyish awkwardness – that of his
taking their encounter, for instance, so amusedly, so crudely,
though, as she was not unaware, so eagerly too – he could by no
means have been so little his wife's junior as it had been that
lady's habit, after the divorce, to represent him. Julia had
remembered him as old, since she had so constantly thought
of her mother as old; which Mrs Connery was indeed now, for
her daughter, with her dozen years of actual seniority to Mr
Pitman and her exquisite hair, the densest, the finest tangle of
arranged silver tendrils that had ever enhanced the effect of a
preserved complexion.

Something in the girl's vision of her quondam stepfather as
still comparatively young – with the confusion, the immense
element of rectification, not to say of rank disproof, that it
introduced into Mrs Connery's favourite picture of her own
injured past – all this worked, even at the moment, to quicken
once more the clearness and harshness of judgement, the retrospective disgust, as she might have called it, that had of late

grown up in her, the sense of all the folly and vanity and vulgarity, the lies, the perversities, the falsification of all life in the interest of who could say what wretched frivolity, what preposterous policy, amid which she had been condemned so ignorantly, so pitifully to sit, to walk, to grope, to flounder, from the very dawn of her consciousness. Didn't poor Mr Pitman just touch the sensitive nerve of it when, taking her in with his facetious, cautious eyes, he spoke to her, right out, of the old, old story, the everlasting little wonder of her beauty?

'Why, you know, you've grown up so lovely – you're the prettiest girl I've ever seen!' Of course she was the prettiest girl he had ever seen; she was the prettiest girl people much more privileged than he had ever seen; since when hadn't she been passing for the prettiest girl any one had ever seen? She had lived in that, from far back, from year to year, from day to day and from hour to hour – she had lived for it and literally *by* it, as who should say; but Mr Pitman was somehow more illuminating than he knew, with the present lurid light that he cast upon old dates, old pleas, old values and old mysteries, not to call them old abysses: it had rolled over her in a swift wave, with the very sight of him, that her mother couldn't possibly have been right about him – as about what in the world had she ever been right? – so that in fact he was simply offered her there as one more of Mrs Connery's lies. She might have thought she knew them all by this time; but he represented for her, coming in just as he did, a fresh discovery, and it was this contribution of freshness that made her somehow feel she liked him. It was she herself who, for so long, with her retained impression, had been right about him; and the rectification he represented had *all* shone out of him, ten minutes before, on his catching her eye while she moved through the room with Mr French. She had never doubted of his probable faults – which her mother had vividly depicted as the basest of vices; since some of them, and the most obvious (not the vices, but the faults) were written on him as he stood there: notably, for instance, the exasperating 'business slackness' of which Mrs Connery had, before the tribunal, made so pathetically much. It might have been, for that matter, the very business slackness that affected Julia as presenting its friendly breast, in the form of a cool loose sociability, to her own actual tension; though it was also true for her, after they had exchanged fifty words, that he had as well his inward fever and that, if he was perhaps wondering what was so particularly the matter with her, she could make out not less than something was the matter with *him*. It had been vague, yet it had been intense, the mute reflexion, 'Yes, I'm going to like him, and he's going somehow to help me!' that had directed her steps so straight to him. She was sure even then of this, that he wouldn't put to her a query about his former wife, that he took to-day no grain of interest in Mrs Connery; that his interest, such as it was – and he couldn't look *quite* like that, to Julia Bride's expert perception, without something in the nature of a new one – would be a thousand times different.

It was as a value of *disproof* that his worth meanwhile so rapidly grew: the good sight of him, the good sound and sense of him, such as they were, demolished at a stroke so blessedly much of the horrid inconvenience of the past that she thought of him, she clutched at him, for a *general* saving use, an application as sanative, as redemptive, as some universal healing wash, precious even to the point of perjury if perjury should be required. That was the terrible thing, that had been the inward pang with which she watched Basil French recede: perjury would have to come in somehow and somewhere – oh so quite certainly! – before the so strange, so rare young man, truly smitten though she believed him, could be made to rise to the occasion, before her measureless prize could be assured. It was present to her, it had been present a hundred times, that if there had only been some one to (as it were) 'deny everything' the situation might yet be saved. She so needed some one to lie for her – ah she so needed some one to lie! Her mother's version of everything, her mother's version of anything, had been at the best, as they said, discounted; and she herself could but show of course for an interested party, however much she might claim to be none the less a decent girl – to whatever point, that is, after all that had both remotely and recently happened, presumptions of anything to be called decency could come in.

After what had recently happened – the two or three indirect but so worrying questions Mr French had put to her – it would only be some thoroughly detached friend or witness who might effectively testify. An odd form of detachment certainly would reside, for Mr Pitman's evidential character, in her mother's having so publicly and so brilliantly – though, thank the powers, all off in North Dakota! – severed their connexion with him; and yet mightn't it do *her* some good, even if the harm it might do her mother were so little ambiguous? The more her mother had got divorced – with her dreadful cheap-and-easy second performance in that line and her present extremity of alienation from Mr Connery, which enfolded beyond doubt the germ of a third petition on one side or the other – the more her mother had distinguished herself in the field of folly the worse for her own prospect with the Frenches, whose minds she had guessed to be accessible, and with such an effect of dissimulated suddenness, to some insidious poison.

It was all unmistakeable, in other words, that the more dismissed and detached Mr Pitman should have come to appear, the more as divorced, or at least as divorcing, his before-time wife would by the same stroke figure – so that it was here poor Julia could but lose herself. The crazy divorces only, or the half-dozen successive and still crazier engagements only – gathered fruit, bitter fruit, of her own incredibly allowed, her own insanely fostered frivolity – either of these two groups of skeletons at the banquet might singly be dealt with; but the combination, the fact of each party's having been so mixed-up with whatever was least presentable for the other, the fact of their having so shockingly amused themselves together, made all present steering resemble the classic middle course between Scylla and Charybdis.

It was not, however, that she felt wholly a fool in having obeyed this impulse to pick up again her kind old friend. *She* at least had never divorced him, and her horrid little filial evidence in Court had been but the chatter of a parrakeet, of precocious plumage and croak, repeating words earnestly taught her and that she could scarce even pronounce. Therefore, as far as steering went, he *must* for the hour take a hand. She might actually have wished in fact that he shouldn't now have seemed so tremendously struck with her; since it was an extraordinary situation for a girl, this crisis of her fortune, this positive wrong that the flagrancy, what she would have been ready to call the very vulgarity, of her good looks might do her at a moment when it was vital she should hang as straight as a picture on the wall. Had it ever yet befallen any young woman in the world to wish with secret intensity that she might have been, for her convenience, a shade less inordinately pretty? She had come to that, to this view of the bane, the primal curse, of their lavishly physical outfit, which had included everything and as to which she lumped herself resentfully with her mother. The only thing was that her mother was, thank goodness, still so much prettier, still so assertively, so publicly, so trashily, so ruinously pretty. Wonderful the small grimness with which Julia Bride put off on this parent the middle-aged maximum of their case and the responsibility of their defect. It cost her so little to recognise in Mrs Connery at forty-seven, and in spite, or perhaps indeed just by reason, of the arranged silver tendrils which were so like some rare bird's-nest in a morning frost, a facile supremacy for the dazzling effect – it cost her so little that her view even rather exaggerated the lustre of the different maternal items. She would have put it *all* off if possible, all off on other shoulders and on other graces and other morals than her own, the burden of physical charm that had made so easy a ground, such a native favouring air, for the aberrations which, apparently inevitable and without far consequences at the time, had yet at this juncture so much better not have been.

She could have worked it out at her leisure, to the last link of the chain, the way their prettiness had set them trap after trap, all along – had foredoomed them to awful ineptitude. When you were as pretty as that you could, by the whole idiotic consensus, be nothing *but* pretty; and when you were nothing 'but' pretty you could get into nothing but tight places, out of which you could then scramble by nothing but masses of fibs. And there was no one, all the while, who wasn't eager to egg you on, eager to make you pay to the last cent the price of your beauty. What creature would ever for a moment help you to behave as if something that dragged in its wake a bit less of a lumbering train would, on the whole, have been better for you? The consequences of being plain were only negative – you failed of this and that; but the consequences of being as *they* were, what were these but endless? though indeed, as far as failing went, your beauty too could let you in for enough of it. Who, at all events, would ever for a moment credit you, in the luxuriance of that beauty, with the study, on your own side, of such truths as these? Julia Bride could, at the point she had reached, positively ask herself this even while lucidly conscious of the inimitable, the triumphant and attested projection, all round her, of her exquisite image. It was only Basil French who had at last, in his doubtless dry but all distinguished way – the way, surely as it was borne in upon her, of all the blood of all the Frenches – stepped out of the vulgar rank. It was only he who, by the trouble she discerned in him, had made her see certain things. It was only for him – and not a bit ridiculously, but just beautifully, almost sublimely – that their being 'nice', her mother and she between them, had *not* seemed to profit by their being so furiously handsome.

This had, ever so grossly and ever so tiresomely, satisfied every one else; since every one had thrust upon them, had imposed upon them as by a great cruel conspiracy, their silliest possibilities; fencing them in to these, and so not only shutting them out from others, but mounting guard at the fence, walking round and round outside it to see they didn't escape, and admiring them, talking to them, through the rails, in mere terms of chaff, terms of chucked cakes and apples – as if they had been antelopes or zebras, or even some superior sort of performing, of dancing, bear. It had been reserved for Basil French to strike her as willing to let go, so to speak, a pound or two of this fatal treasure if he might only have got in exchange for it an ounce or so more of their so much less obvious and less published personal history. Yes, it described him to say that, in addition to all the rest of him, and of *his* personal history, and of his family, and of theirs, in addition to their social posture, as that of a serried phalanx, and to their notoriously enormous wealth and crushing respectability, she might have been ever so much less lovely for him if she had been only – well, a little prepared to answer questions. And it wasn't as if, quiet, cultivated, earnest, public-spirited, brought up in Germany, infinitely travelled, awfully like a high-caste Englishman, and all the other pleasant things, it wasn't as if he didn't love to be with her, to look at her, just as she was; for he loved it exactly as much, so far as that footing simply went, as any free and foolish youth who had ever made the last demonstration of it. It was that marriage was for him – and for them all, the serried Frenches – a great matter, a goal to which a man of intelligence, a real shy beautiful man of the world, didn't hop on one foot, didn't skip and jump, as if he were playing an urchins' game, but toward which he proceeded with a deep and anxious, a noble and highly just deliberation.

For it was one thing to stare at a girl till she was bored at it, it was one thing to take her to the Horse Show and the Opera, and to send her flowers by the stack, and chocolates by the ton, and 'great' novels, the very latest and greatest, by the dozen; but something quite other to hold open for her, with eyes attached to eyes, the gate, moving on such stiff silver hinges, of the grand square forecourt of the palace of wedlock. The state of being 'engaged' represented to him the introduction to this precinct of some young woman with whom his outside parley would have had the duration, distinctly, of his own convenience. That might be cold-blooded if one chose to think so; but nothing of another sort would equal the high ceremony and dignity and decency, above all the grand gallantry and finality, of their then passing in. Poor Julia could have blushed red, before that view, with the memory of the way the forecourt, as she now imagined it, had been dishonoured by her younger romps. She had tumbled over the wall with this, that and the other raw play-mate, and had played 'tag' and leap-frog, as she might say, from corner to corner. That would be the 'history' with which, in case of definite demand, she should be able to supply Mr French: that she had already, again and again, any occasion offering, chattered and scuffled over ground provided, according to his idea, for walking the gravest of minuets. If that then had been all their *kind* of history, hers and her mother's, at least there was plenty of it: it was the superstructure raised on the other group of facts, those of the order of their having been always so perfectly pink and white, so perfectly possessed of clothes, so perfectly splendid, so perfectly idiotic. These things had been the 'points' of antelope and zebra; putting Mrs Connery for the zebra, as the more remarkably striped or spotted. Such were the data Basil French's enquiry would elicit: her own six engagements and her mother's three nullified marriages – nine nice distinct little horrors in all. What on earth was to be done about them?

II

IT was notable, she was afterwards to recognise, that there had been nothing of the famous business slackness in the positive pounce with which Mr Pitman put it to her that, as soon as he had made her out 'for sure', identified her there as old Julia grown-up and gallivanting with a new admirer, a smarter young fellow than ever yet, he had had the inspiration of her being exactly the good girl to help him. She certainly found him strike the hour again with these vulgarities of tone – forms of speech that her mother had anciently described as by themselves, once he had opened the whole battery, sufficient ground for putting him away. Full, however, of the use she should have for him, she wasn't going to mind trifles. What she really gasped at was that, so oddly, he was ahead of her at the start. 'Yes, I want something of you, Julia, and I want it right now: you can do me a turn, and I'm blest if my luck – which has once or twice been pretty good, you know – hasn't sent you to me.' She knew the luck he meant – that of her mother's having so enabled him to get rid of her; but it was the nearest allusion of the merely invidious kind that he would make. It had thus come to our young woman on the spot and by divination: the service he desired of her matched with remarkable closeness what she had so promptly taken into her head to name to himself – to name in her own interest, though deterred as yet from having brought it right out. She had been prevented by his speaking, the first thing, in that way, as if he had known Mr French – which surprised her till he explained that every one in New York knew by appearance a young man of his so quoted wealth ('What did she take them all in New York then *for*?') and of whose marked attention to her he had moreover, for himself, round at clubs and places, lately heard. This had accompanied the inevitable free question 'Was she engaged to *him* now?' – which she had in fact almost welcomed as holding out to her the perch of opportunity. She was waiting to deal with it properly, but meanwhile he had gone on, and to such effect that it took them but three minutes to turn out, on either side, like a pair of pickpockets comparing, under shelter, their day's booty, the treasures of design concealed about their persons.

'I want you to tell the truth for me – as you only can. I want you to say that I was really all right – as right as you know; and that I simply acted like an angel in a story-book, gave myself away to have it over.'

'Why my dear man,' Julia cried, 'you take the wind straight out of my sails! What I'm here to ask of *you* is that you'll confess to having been even a worse fiend than you were shown up for; to having made it impossible mother should *not* take proceedings.' There! – she had brought it out, and with the sense of their situation turning to high excitement for her in the teeth of his droll stare, his strange grin, his characteristic 'Lordy, lordy! What good will that do you?' She was prepared with her clear statement of reasons for her appeal, and feared so he might have better ones for his own that all her story came in a flash. 'Well, Mr Pitman, I want to get married this time, by way of a change; but you see we've been such fools that, when something really good at last comes up, it's too dreadfully awkward. The fools we were capable of being – well, you know better than any one; unless perhaps not quite so well as Mr Connery. It has got to be denied,' said Julia ardently – 'it has got to be denied flat. But I can't get hold of Mr Connery – Mr Connery has gone to China. Besides, if he were here,' she had ruefully to confess, 'he'd be no good – on the contrary. He wouldn't deny anything – he'd only tell more. So thank heaven he's away – there's *that* amount of good! I'm not engaged yet,' she went on – but he had already taken her up.

'You're not engaged to Mr French?' It was all, clearly, a wondrous show for him, but his immediate surprise, oddly, might have been greatest for that.

'No, not to any one – for the seventh time!' She spoke as with her head held well up both over the shame and the pride. 'Yes, the next time I'm engaged I want something to happen. But he's afraid; he's afraid of what may be told him. He's dying to find out, and yet he'd die if he did! He wants to be talked to, but he has got to be talked to right. You could talk to him right, Mr Pitman – if you only *would*! He can't get over mother – that I feel: he loathes and scorns divorces, and we've had first and last too many. So if he could hear from you that you just made her life a hell – why,' Julia concluded, 'it would be too lovely. If she *had* to go in for another – after having already, when I was little, divorced father – it would "sort of" make, don't you see? one less. You'd do the high-toned thing by her: you'd say what a wretch you then were, and that she had had to save her life. In that way he mayn't mind it. Don't you see, you sweet man?' poor Julia pleaded. 'Oh,' she wound up as if his fancy lagged or his scruple looked out, 'of course I want you to *lie* for me!'

It did indeed sufficiently stagger him. 'It's a lovely idea for the moment when I was just saying to myself – as soon as I saw you – that you'd speak the truth for *me*!'

'Ah what's the matter with "you"?' Julia sighed with an impatience not sensibly less sharp for her having so quickly scented some lion in her path.

'Why, do you think there's no one in the world but you who has seen the cup of promised affection, of something really to be depended on, only, at the last moment, by the horrid jostle of your elbow, spilled all over you? I want to provide for my future too as it happens; and my good friend who's to help me to that – the most charming of women this time – disapproves of divorce quite as much as Mr French. Don't you see,' Mr Pitman candidly asked, 'what that by itself must have done toward attaching me to her? *She* has got to be talked to – to be told how little I could help it.'

'Oh lordy, lordy!' the girl emulously groaned. It was such a relieving cry. 'Well, *I* won't talk to her!' she declared.

'You *won't*, Julia?' he pitifully echoed. 'And yet you ask of *me* –!'

His pang, she felt, was sincere, and even more than she had guessed, for the previous quarter of an hour, he had been building up his hope, building it with her aid for a foundation. Yet was he going to see how their testimony, on each side, would, if offered, *have* to conflict? If he was to prove himself for her sake – or, more queerly still, for that of Basil French's high conservatism – a person whom there had been but that one way of handling, how could she prove him, in this other and so different interest, a mere gentle sacrifice to his wife's perversity? She had, before him there, on the instant, all acutely, a sense of rising sickness – a wan glimmer of foresight as to the end of the fond dream. Everything else was against her, everything in her dreadful past – just as if she had been a person represented by some 'emotional actress', some desperate erring lady 'hunted down' in a play; but was that going to be the case too with her own very decency, the fierce little residuum deep within her, for which she was counting, when she came to think, on so little glory or even credit? Was this also going to turn against her and trip her up – just to show she was really, under the touch and the test, as decent as any one; and with no one but herself the wiser for it meanwhile, and no proof to show but that, as a consequence, she should be unmarried to the end? She put it to Mr Pitman quite with resentment: 'Do you mean to say you're going to be married –?'

'Oh my dear, I too must get engaged first!' – he spoke with his inimitable grin. 'But that, you see, is where you come in. I've told her about you. She wants awfully to meet you. The way it happens is too lovely – that I find you just in this place. She's coming,' said Mr Pitman – and as in all the good faith of his eagerness now; 'she's coming in about three minutes.'

'Coming here?'

'Yes, Julia – right here. It's where we usually meet'; and he was wreathed again, this time as if for life, in his large slow smile. 'She loves this place – she's awfully keen on art. Like *you*, Julia, if you haven't changed – I remember how you did love art.' He looked at her quite tenderly, as to keep her up to it. 'You must still of course – from the way you're here. Just let her *feel* that,' the poor man fantastically urged. And then with his kind eyes on her and his good ugly mouth stretched as for delicate emphasis from ear to ear: 'Every little helps!'

He made her wonder for him, ask herself, and with a certain intensity, questions she yet hated the trouble of; as whether he were still as moneyless as in the other time – which was certain indeed, for any fortune he ever would have made. His slackness on that ground stuck out of him almost as much as if he had been of rusty or 'seedy' aspect – which, luckily for him, he wasn't at all: he looked, in his way, like some pleasant eccentric ridiculous but real gentleman, whose taste might be of the queerest, but his credit with his tailor none the less of the best. She wouldn't have been the least ashamed, had their connexion lasted, of going about with him: so that what a fool, again, her mother had been – since Mr Connery, sorry as one might be for him, was irrepressibly vulgar. Julia's quickness was, for the minute, charged with all this; but she had none the less her feeling of the right thing to say and the right way to say it. If he was after a future financially assured, even as she herself so frantically was, she wouldn't cast the stone. But if he had talked about her to strange women she couldn't be less than a little majestic. 'Who then is the person in question for you –?'

'Why such a dear thing, Julia – Mrs David E. Drack. Have you heard of her?' he almost fluted.

New York was vast, and she hadn't had that advantage. 'She's a widow –?'

'Oh yes: she's not –!' He caught himself up in time. 'She's a real one.' It was as near as he came. But it was as if he had been looking at her now so pathetically hard. 'Julia, she has millions.'

Hard, at any rate – whether pathetic or not – was the look she gave him back. 'Well, so has – or so *will* have – Basil French. And more of them than Mrs Drack, I guess,' Julia quavered.

'Oh I know what *they've* got!' He took it from her – with the effect of a vague stir, in his long person, of unwelcome embarrassment. But was she going to give up because he was embarrassed? He should know at least what he was costing

her. It came home to her own spirit more than ever; but meanwhile he had found his footing. 'I don't see how your mother
matters. It isn't a question of his marrying *her*.'

'No; but, constantly together as we've always been, it's a
question of there being so disgustingly much to get over. If we
had, for people like them, but the one ugly spot and the one
weak side; if we had made, between us, but the one vulgar *kind*
of mistake: well, I don't say!' She reflected with a wistfulness of
note that was in itself a touching eloquence. 'To have our
reward in this world we've had too sweet a time. We've had it
all right down here!' said Julia Bride. 'I should have taken the
precaution to have about a dozen fewer lovers.'

'Ah my dear, "lovers" –!' He ever so comically attenuated.

'Well they *were*!' She quite flared up. 'When you've had a
ring from each (three diamonds, two pearls and a rather bad
sapphire: I've kept them all, and they tell my story!) what are
you to call them?'

'Oh rings –!' Mr Pitman didn't call rings anything. 'I've
given Mrs Drack a ring.'

Julia stared. 'Then aren't you her lover?'

'That, dear child,' he humorously wailed, 'is what I want
you to find out! But I'll handle your rings all right,' he more
lucidly added.

'You'll "handle" them?'

'I'll fix your lovers. I'll lie about *them*, if that's all you want.'

'Oh about "them" –!' She turned away with a sombre drop,
seeing so little in it. 'That wouldn't count – from *you*!' She saw
the great shining room, with its mockery of art and 'style' and
security, all the things she was vainly after, and its few scattered
visitors who had left them, Mr Pitman and herself, in their
ample corner, so conveniently at ease. There was only a lady
in one of the far doorways, of whom she took vague note and
who seemed to be looking at them. 'They'd have to lie for
themselves!'

'Do you mean he's capable of putting it to them?'

Mr Pitman's tone threw discredit on that possibility, but she
knew perfectly well what she meant. 'Not of getting at them
directly, not, as mother says, of nosing round himself; but of

listening – and small blame to him! – to the horrible things other people say of me.'

'But what other people?'

'Why Mrs George Maule, to begin with – who intensely loathes us, and who talks to his sisters, so that they may talk to *him*: which they do, all the while, I'm morally sure (hating me as they also must). But it's she who's the real reason – I mean of his holding off. She poisons the air he breathes.'

'Oh well,' said Mr Pitman with easy optimism, 'if Mrs George Maule's a cat –!'

'If she's a cat she has kittens – four little spotlessly white ones, among whom she'd give her head that Mr French should make his pick. He could do it with his eyes shut – you can't tell them apart. But she has every name, every date, as you may say, for my dark "record" – as of course they all call it: she'll be able to give him, if he brings himself to ask her, every fact in its order. And all the while, don't you see? there's no one to speak *for* me.'

It would have touched a harder heart than her loose friend's to note the final flush of clairvoyance witnessing this assertion and under which her eyes shone as with the rush of quick tears. He stared at her, and what this did for the deep charm of her prettiness, as in almost witless admiration. 'But can't you – lovely as you are, you beautiful thing! – speak for yourself?'

'Do you mean can't I tell the lies? No then, I can't – and I wouldn't if I could. I don't lie myself you know – as it happens; and it could represent to him then about the only thing, the only bad one, I don't do. I *did* – "lovely as I am"! – have my regular time; I wasn't so hideous that I couldn't! Besides, do you imagine he'd come and ask me?'

'Gad, I wish he would, Julia!' said Mr Pitman with his kind eyes on her.

'Well then I'd tell him!' And she held her head again high. 'But he won't.'

It fairly distressed her companion. 'Doesn't he want then to know –?'

'He wants *not* to know. He wants to be told without asking – told, I mean, that each of the stories, those that have come to him, is a fraud and a libel. *Qui s'excuse s'accuse*, don't they say? – so that do you see me breaking out to him, unprovoked, with four or five what-do-you-call-'ems, the things mother used to have to prove in Court, a set of neat little "alibis" in a row? How can I get hold of so *many* precious gentlemen, to turn them on? How can *they* want everything fished up?'

She had paused for her climax, in the intensity of these considerations; which gave Mr Pitman a chance to express his honest faith. 'Why, my sweet child, they'd be just glad –!'

It determined in her loveliness almost a sudden glare. 'Glad to swear they never had anything to do with such a creature? Then I'd be glad to swear they had lots!'

His persuasive smile, though confessing to bewilderment, insisted. 'Why, my love, they've got to swear either one thing or the other.'

'They've got to keep out of the way – that's *their* view of it, I guess,' said Julia. 'Where *are* they, please – now that they *may* be wanted? If you'd like to hunt them up for me you're very welcome.' With which, for the moment, over the difficult case, they faced each other helplessly enough. And she added to it now the sharpest ache of her despair. 'He knows about Murray Brush. The others' – and her pretty white-gloved hands and charming pink shoulders gave them up – 'may go hang!'

'Murray Brush –?' It had opened Mr Pitman's eyes.

'Yes – yes; I do mind *him*.'

'Then what's the matter with his at least rallying –?'

'The matter is that, being ashamed of himself, as he well might, he left the country as soon as he could and has stayed away. The matter is that he's in Paris or somewhere, and that if you expect him to come home for me –!' She had already dropped, however, as at Mr Pitman's look.

'Why, you foolish thing, Murray Brush is in New York!' It had quite brightened him up.

'He has come back –?'

'Why sure! I saw him – when was it? Tuesday! – on the Jersey boat.' Mr Pitman rejoiced in his news. '*He's* your man!'

Julia too had been affected by it; it had brought in a rich wave her hot colour back. But she gave the strangest dim smile. 'He *was*!'

'Then get hold of him, and – if he's a gentleman – he'll prove for you, to the hilt, that he wasn't.'

It lighted in her face, the kindled train of this particular sudden suggestion, a glow, a sharpness of interest, that had deepened the next moment, while she gave a slow and sad headshake, to a greater strangeness yet. 'He isn't a gentleman.'

'Ah lordy, lordy!' Mr Pitman again sighed. He struggled out of it but only into the vague. 'Oh then if he's a pig –!'

'You see there are only a few gentlemen – not enough to go round – and that makes them count so!' It had thrust the girl herself, for that matter, into depths; but whether most of memory or of roused purpose he had no time to judge – aware as he suddenly was of a shadow (since he mightn't perhaps too quickly call it a light) across the heaving surface of their question. It fell upon Julia's face, fell with the sound of the voice he so well knew, but which could only be odd to her for all it immediately assumed.

'There are indeed very few – and one mustn't try *them* too much!' Mrs Drack, who had supervened while they talked, stood, in monstrous magnitude – at least to Julia's reimpressed eyes – between them: she was the lady our young woman had descried across the room, and she had drawn near while the interest of their issue so held them. We have seen the act of observation and that of reflexion alike swift in Julia – once her subject was within range – and she had now, with all her perceptions at the acutest, taken in, by a single stare, the strange presence to a happy connexion with which Mr Pitman aspired and which had thus sailed, with placid majesty, into their troubled waters. She was clearly not shy, Mrs David E. Drack, yet neither was she ominously bold; she was bland and 'good', Julia made sure at a glance, and of a large complacency, as the good and the bland are apt to be – a large complacency, a large sentimentality, a large innocent elephantine archness: she fairly rioted in that dimension of size. Habited in an extraordinary quantity of stiff and lustrous black brocade, with enhancements, of every description, that twinkled and tinkled, that rustled and rumbled with her least movement, she presented a huge hideous pleasant face, a featureless desert in a remote quarter of which the disproportionately small eyes might have figured a pair of rash adventurers all but buried in the sand. They reduced themselves when she smiled to barely discernible points – a couple of mere tiny emergent heads – though the foreground of the scene, as if to make up for it, gaped with a vast benevolence. In a word Julia saw – and as if she had needed nothing more; saw Mr Pitman's opportunity, saw her own, saw the exact nature both of Mrs Drack's circumspection and of Mrs Drack's sensibility, saw even, glittering there in letters of gold and as a part of the whole metallic coruscation, the large figure of her income, largest of all her attributes, and (though perhaps a little more as a luminous blur beside all this) the mingled ecstasy and agony of Mr Pitman's hope and Mr Pitman's fear.

He was introducing them, with his pathetic belief in the virtue for every occasion, in the solvent for every trouble, of an extravagant genial professional humour; he was naming her to Mrs Drack as the charming young friend he had told her so much about and who had been as an angel to him in a weary time; he was saying that the loveliest chance in the world, this accident of a meeting in those promiscuous halls, had placed within his reach the pleasure of bringing them together. It didn't indeed matter, Julia felt, what he was saying: he conveyed everything, as far as she was concerned, by a moral pressure as unmistakeable as if, for a symbol of it, he had thrown himself on her neck. Above all, meanwhile, this high consciousness prevailed – that the good lady herself, however huge she loomed, had entered, by the end of a minute, into a condition as of suspended weight and arrested mass, stilled to artless awe by the effect of her vision. Julia had practised almost to lassitude the art of tracing in the people who looked at her the impression promptly sequent; but it was a singular fact that if, in irritation, in depression, she felt that the lighted eyes of men, stupid at their clearest, had given her pretty well all she should ever care for, she could still gather a freshness from the tribute of her own sex, still care to see her reflection in the faces of women. Never, probably, never would that sweet be tasteless – with such a straight grim spoon was it mostly administered, and so flavoured and strengthened by the competence of their eyes. Women knew so much best *how* a woman surpassed – how and where and why, with no touch or torment of it lost on them; so that as it produced mainly and primarily the instinct of aversion, the sense of extracting the recognition, of gouging out the homage, was on the whole the highest crown one's felicity could wear. Once in a way, however, the grimness beautifully dropped, the jealousy failed: the admiration was all there and the poor plain sister handsomely paid it. It had never been so paid, she was presently certain, as by this great generous object of Mr Pitman's flame, who without optical aid, it well might have seemed, nevertheless entirely grasped her – might in fact, all benevolently, have been groping her over as by some huge mild proboscis. She gave Mrs Drack pleasure in short; and who could say of what other pleasures the poor lady hadn't been cheated?

It was somehow a muddled world in which one of her conceivable joys, at this time of day, would be to marry Mr Pitman – to say nothing of a state of things in which this gentleman's own fancy could invest such a union with rapture. That, however, was their own mystery, and Julia, with each instant, was more and more clear about hers: so remarkably primed in fact, at the end of three minutes, that though her friend, and though *his* friend, were both saying things, many things and perhaps quite wonderful things, she had no free attention for them and was only rising and soaring. She was rising to her value, she was soaring *with* it – the value Mr Pitman almost convulsively imputed to her, the value that consisted for her of being so unmistakeably the most dazzling image Mrs Drack had ever beheld. These were the uses, for Julia, in fine, of adversity; the range of Mrs Drack's experience might have been as small as the measure of her presence was large: Julia was at any rate herself in face of the occasion of her life, and, after all her late repudiations and reactions, had perhaps never yet known the quality of this moment's success. She hadn't an idea of what, on either side, had been uttered – beyond Mr Pitman's allusion to her having befriended him of old: she simply held his companion with her radiance and knew she might be, for her effect, as irrelevant as she chose. It was relevant to do what he wanted – it was relevant to dish herself. She did it now with a kind of passion, to say nothing of her knowing, with it, that every word of it added to her beauty. She gave him away in short, up to the hilt, for any use of her own, and should have nothing to clutch at now but the possibility of Murray Brush.

'He says I was good to him, Mrs Drack; and I'm sure I hope I was, since I should be ashamed to be anything else. If I could be good to him now I should be glad – that's just what, a while ago, I rushed up to him here, after so long, to give myself the pleasure of saying. I saw him years ago very particularly, very miserably tried – and I saw the way he took it. I did see it, you dear man,' she sublimely went on – 'I saw it for all you may protest, for all you may hate me to talk about you! I saw you behave like a gentleman – since Mrs Drack agrees with me so charmingly that there are not many to be met. I don't know whether you care, Mrs Drack' – she abounded, she revelled in the name – 'but I've always remembered it of him: that under the most extraordinary provocation he was decent and patient and brave. No appearance of anything different matters, for I speak of what I *know*. Of course I'm nothing and nobody; I'm only a poor frivolous girl, but I was very close to him at the time. That's all my little story – if it *should* interest you at all.' She measured every beat of her wing, she knew how high she was going and paused only when it was quite vertiginous. Here she hung a moment as in the glare of the upper blue; which was but the glare – what else could it be? – of the vast and magnificent attention of both her auditors, hushed, on their side, in the splendour she emitted. She had at last to steady herself, and she scarce knew afterwards at what rate or in what way she had still inimitably come down – her own eyes fixed all the while on the very figure of her achievement. She had sacrificed her mother on the altar – proclaimed her false and cruel; and if that didn't 'fix' Mr Pitman, as he would have said – well, it was all she could do. But the cost of her action already somehow came back to her with increase; the dear gaunt man fairly wavered, to her sight, in the glory of it, as if signalling at her, with wild gleeful arms, from some mount of safety, while the massive lady just spread and spread like a rich fluid a bit helplessly spilt. It was really the outflow of the poor woman's honest response, into which she seemed to melt, and Julia scarce distinguished the two apart even for her taking gracious leave of each. 'Good-bye, Mrs Drack; I'm awfully happy to have met you' – like as not it was for this she had grasped Mr Pitman's hand. And then to him or to her, it didn't matter which, 'Good-bye, dear good Mr Pitman – hasn't it been nice after so long?'

III

JULIA floated even to her own sense swanlike away – she left in her wake their fairly stupefied submission: it was as if she had, by an exquisite authority, now *placed* them, each for each, and they would have nothing to do but be happy together. Never had she so exulted as on this ridiculous occasion in the noted items of her beauty. *Le compte y était*, as they used to say in Paris – every one of them, for her immediate employment, was there; and there was something in it after all. It didn't necessarily, this sum of thumping little figures, imply charm – especially for 'refined' people: nobody knew better than Julia that inexpressible charm and quoteable 'charms' (quoteable like prices, rates, shares, or whatever, the things they dealt in downtown) are two distinct categories; the safest thing for the latter being, on the whole, that it might include the former, and the great strength of the former being that it might perfectly dispense with the latter. Mrs Drack wasn't refined, not the least little bit; but what would be the case with Murray Brush now – after his three years of Europe? He had done so what he liked with her – which had seemed so then just the meaning, hadn't it? of their being 'engaged' – that he had made her not see, while the absurdity lasted (the absurdity of their pretending to believe they could marry without a cent) how little he was of metal without alloy: this had come up for her, remarkably, but after-wards – come up for her as she looked back. Then she had drawn her conclusion, which was one of the many that Basil French had made her draw. It was a queer service Basil was going to have rendered her, this having made everything she had ever done impossible, if he wasn't going to give her a new chance. If he was it was doubtless right enough. On the other hand Murray might have improved, if such a quantity of alloy, as she called it, *were*, in any man, reducible, and if Paris were the place all happily to reduce it. She had her doubts – anxious and aching on the spot, and had expressed them to Mr Pitman: certainly, of old, he had been more open to the quoteable than to the inexpressible, to charms than to charm. If she could try the quoteable, however, and with such a grand result, on Mrs Drack, she couldn't now on Murray – in respect to whom everything had changed. So that if he hadn't a sense for the subtler appeal, the appeal appreciable by people *not* vulgar, on which alone she could depend, what on earth would become of her? She could but yearningly hope, at any rate, as she made up her mind to write to him immediately at his club. It was a question of the right sensibility in him. Perhaps he would have acquired it in Europe.

Two days later indeed – for he had promptly and charmingly replied, keeping with alacrity the appointment she had judged best to propose, a morning hour in a sequestered alley of the Park – two days later she was to be struck well-nigh to alarm by everything he had acquired: so much it seemed to make that it threatened somehow a complication, and her plan, so far as she had arrived at one, dwelt in the desire above all to simplify. She wanted no grain more of extravagance or excess in anything – risking as she had done, none the less, a recall of ancient licence in proposing to Murray such a place of meeting. She had her reasons – she wished intensely to discriminate: Basil French had several times waited on her at her mother's habitation, their horrible flat which was so much too far up and too near the East Side; he had dined there and lunched there and gone with her thence to other places, notably to see pictures, and had in particular adjourned with her twice to the Metropolitan Museum, in which he took a great interest, in which she professed a delight, and their second visit to which had wound up in her encounter with Mr Pitman, after her companion had yielded, at her urgent instance, to an exceptional need of keeping a business engagement. She mightn't in delicacy, in decency, entertain Murray Brush where she had entertained Mr French – she was given over now to these exquisite perceptions and proprieties and bent on devoutly observing them; and Mr French, by good luck, had never been with her in the Park; partly because he had never pressed it, and partly because she would have held off if he had, so haunted were those devious paths and favouring shades by the general echo of her untrammelled past. If he had never suggested their taking a turn there this was because, quite divineably, he held it would commit him further than he had yet gone; and if she on her side had practised a like reserve it was because the place reeked for her, as she inwardly said, with old associations. It reeked with nothing so much perhaps as with the memories evoked by the young man who now awaited her in the nook she had been so competent to indicate; but in what corner of the town, should she look for them, wouldn't those footsteps creak back into muffled life, and to what expedient would she be reduced should she attempt to avoid all such tracks? The Museum was full of tracks, tracks by the hundred – the way really she had knocked about! – but she had to see people somewhere, and she couldn't pretend to dodge every ghost.

All she could do was not to make confusion, make mixtures, of the living; though she asked herself enough what mixture she mightn't find herself to have prepared if Mr French should, not so very impossibly for a restless roaming man – *her* effect on him! – happen to pass while she sat there with the moustachioed personage round whose name Mrs Maule would probably have caused detrimental anecdote most thickly to cluster. There existed, she was sure, a mass of luxuriant legend about the 'lengths' her engagement with Murray Brush had gone; she could herself fairly feel them in the air, these streamers of evil, black flags flown as in warning, the vast redundancy of so cheap and so dingy social bunting, in fine, that flapped over the stations she had successively moved away from and which were empty now, for such an ado, even to grotesqueness. The vivacity of that conviction was what had at present determined her, while it was the way he listened after she had quickly broken ground, while it was the special character of the interested look in his handsome face, hand-somer than ever yet, that represented for her the civilisation he had somehow taken on. Just so it was the quantity of that gain, in its turn, that had at the end of ten minutes begun to affect her as holding up a light to the wide reach of her step. 'There was never anything the least serious between us, not a sign or a scrap, do you mind? of anything beyond the merest pleasant friendly acquaintance; and if you're not ready to go to the stake on it for me you may as well know in time what it is you'll probably cost me.'

She had immediately plunged, measuring her effect and having thought it well over; and what corresponded to her question of his having become a better person to appeal to was the appearance of interest she had so easily created in him. She felt on the spot the difference that made – it was indeed his form of being more civilised: it was the sense in which Europe in general and Paris in particular had made him develop. By every calculation – and her calculations, based on the intimacy of her knowledge, had been many and deep – he would help her the better the more intelligent he should have become; yet she was to recognise later on that the first chill of foreseen disaster had been caught by her as, at a given moment, this greater refinement of his attention seemed to exhale it. It was just what she had wanted – 'if I can only get him interested –!' so that, this proving quite vividly possible, why did the light it lifted strike her as lurid? Was it partly by reason of his inordinate romantic good looks, those of a gallant genial conqueror, but which, involving so glossy a brownness of eye, so many a crispness of curl, so red-lipped a radiance of smile, so natural a bravery of port, prescribed to any response he might facially, might expressively make a sort of florid dis-proportionate amplitude? The explanation, in any case, didn't matter; he was going to mean well – that she could feel, and also that he had meant better in the past, presumably, than he had managed to convince her of his doing at the time: the oddity she hadn't now reckoned with was this fact that from the moment he did advertise an interest it should show almost as what she would have called weird. It made a change in him that didn't go with the rest – as if he had broken his nose or put on spectacles, lost his handsome hair or sacrificed his splendid moustache: her conception, her necessity, as she saw, had been that something should be added to him for her use, but nothing for his own alteration.

He had affirmed himself, and his character, and his temper, and his health, and his appetite, and his ignorance, and his obstinacy, and his whole charming coarse heartless personality, during their engagement, by twenty forms of natural emphasis, but never by emphasis of interest. How in fact could you feel interest unless you should know, within you, some dim stir of imagination? There was nothing in the world of which Murray Brush was less capable than of such a dim stir, because you only began to imagine when you felt some approach to a need to understand. *He* had never felt it; for hadn't he been born, to his personal vision, with that perfect intuition of everything which reduces all the suggested preliminaries of judgement to the impertinence – when it's a question of your entering your house – of a dumpage of bricks at your door? He had had, in short, neither to imagine nor to perceive, because he had, from the first pulse of his intelligence, simply and supremely known: so that, at this hour, face to face with him, it came over her that she had in their old relation dispensed with any such convenience of comprehension on his part even to a degree she had not measured at the time. What therefore must he not have seemed to her as a form of life, a form of avidity and activity, blatantly successful in its own conceit, that he could have dazzled her so against the interest of her very faculties and functions? Strangely and richly historic all that backward mystery, and only leaving for her mind the wonder of such a mixture of possession and detachment as they would clearly to-day both know. For each to be so little at last to the other when, during months together, the idea of all abundance, all quantity, had been, for each, drawn from the other and addressed to the other – what was it monstrously like but some fantastic act of getting rid of a person by going to lock yourself up in the *sanctum sanctorum* of that person's house, amid every evidence of that person's habits and nature? What was going to happen, at any rate, was that Murray would show himself as beautifully and consciously understanding – and it would be prodigious that Europe should have inoculated him with that delicacy. Yes, he wouldn't claim to know now till she had told him – an aid to performance he had surely never before waited for or been indebted to from any one; and then, so knowing, he would charmingly endeavour to 'meet', to oblige and to gratify. He would find it, her case, ever so worthy of his benevolence, and would be literally inspired to reflect that he must hear about it first.

She let him hear then everything, in spite of feeling herself slip, while she did so, to some doom as yet incalculable; she went on very much as she had done for Mr Pitman and Mrs Drack, with the rage of desperation and, as she was afterwards to call it to herself, the fascination of the abyss. She didn't know, couldn't have said at the time, *why* his projected bene-volence should have had most so the virtue to scare her: he would patronise her, as an effect of her vividness, if not of her charm, and would do this with all high intention, finding her case, or rather *their* case, their funny old case, taking on of a sudden such refreshing and edifying life, to the last degree curious and even important; but there were gaps of connexion between this and the intensity of the perception here overtaking her that she shouldn't be able to move in *any* direction without dishing herself. That she couldn't afford it where she had got to – couldn't afford the deplorable vulgarity of having been so many times informally affianced and contracted (putting it only at that, at its being by the new lights and fashions so unpardon-ably vulgar): he took this from her without turning, as she might have said, a hair; except just to indicate, with his new superiority, that he felt the distinguished appeal and notably the pathos of it. He still took it from her that she hoped nothing, as it were, from any other *alibi* – the people to drag into court being too many and too scattered; but that, as it was with him, Murray Brush, she had been *most* vulgar, most everything she had better not have been, so she depended on him for the innocence it was actually vital she should establish. He blushed or frowned or winced no more at that than he did when she

once more fairly emptied her satchel and, quite as if they had
been Nancy and the Artful Dodger, or some nefarious pair of
that sort, talking things over in the manner of 'Oliver Twist',
revealed to him the fondness of her view that, could she but
have produced a cleaner slate, she might by this time have
pulled it off with Mr French. Yes, he let her in that way sacrifice
her honourable connexion with him – all the more honourable
for being so completely at an end – to the crudity of her plan for
not missing another connexion, so much more brilliant than
what he offered, and for bringing another man, with whom she
so invidiously and unflatteringly compared him, into her
greedy life.

There was only a moment during which, by a particular
lustrous look she had never had from him before, he just
made her wonder which turn he was going to take; she felt,
however, as safe as was consistent with her sense of having
probably but added to her danger, when he brought out, the
next instant: 'Don't you seem to take the ground that we were
guilty – that *you* were ever guilty – of something we shouldn't
have been? What did we ever do that was secret, or underhand,
or any way not to be acknowledged? What did we do but
exchange our young vows with the best faith in the world –
publicly, rejoicingly, with the full assent of every one connected
with us? I mean of course,' he said with his grave kind smile, 'till
we broke off so completely because we found that – practically,
financially, on the hard worldly basis – we couldn't work it.
What harm, in the sight of God or man, Julia,' he asked in his
fine rich way, 'did we ever do?'

She gave him back his look, turning pale. 'Am I talking of
that? Am I talking of what *we* know? I'm talking of what others
feel – of what they *have* to feel; of what it's just enough for them
to know not to be able to get over it, once they do really know it.
How do they know what *didn't* pass between us, with all the
opportunities we had? That's none of their business – if we were
idiots enough, on the top of everything! What you may or
mayn't have done doesn't count, for *you*; but there are people
for whom it's loathsome that a girl should have gone on like that
from one person to another and still pretend to be – well, all

that a nice girl is supposed to be. It's as if we had but just waked up, mother and I, to such a remarkable prejudice; and now we have it – when we could do so well without it! – staring us in the face. That mother should have insanely *let* me, should so vulgarly have taken it for my natural, my social career – *that's* the disgusting humiliating thing: with the lovely account it gives of both of us! But mother's view of a delicacy in things!' she went on with scathing grimness; 'mother's measure of anything, with her grand "gained cases" (there'll be another yet, she finds them so easy!) of which she's so publicly proud! You see I've no margin,' said Julia; letting him take it from her flushed face as much as he would that her mother hadn't left her an inch. It was that he should make use of the spade with her for the restoration of a bit of a margin just wide enough to perch on till the tide of peril should have ebbed a little, it was that he should give her *that* lift –!

Well, it was all there from him after these last words; it was before her that he really took hold. 'Oh, my dear child, I can see! Of course there are people – ideas change in our society so fast! – who are not in sympathy with the old American freedom and who read, I daresay, all sorts of uncanny things into it. Naturally you must take them as they are – from the moment,' said Murray Brush, who had lighted, by her leave, a cigarette, 'your life-path does, for weal or for woe, cross with theirs.' He had every now and then such an elegant phrase. 'Awfully interesting, certainly, your case. It's enough for me that it *is* yours – I make it my own. I put myself absolutely in your place; you'll understand from me, without professions, won't you? that I do. Command me in every way! What I do like is the sympathy with which you've inspired *him*. I don't, I'm sorry to say, happen to know him personally' – he smoked away, looking off; 'but of course one knows all about him generally, and I'm sure he's right for you, I'm sure it would be charming, if you yourself think so. Therefore trust me and even – what shall I say? – leave it to me a little, won't you?' He had been watching, as in his fumes, the fine growth of his possibilities; and with this he turned on her the large warmth of his charity. It was like a subscription of a half a million. 'I'll take care of you.'

She found herself for a moment looking up at him from as far below as the point from which the school-child, with round eyes raised to the wall, gazes at the particoloured map of the world. Yes, it was a warmth, it was a special benignity, that had never yet dropped on her from any one; and she wouldn't for the first few moments have known how to describe it or even quite what to do with it. Then as it still rested, his fine improved expression aiding, the sense of what had happened came over her with a rush. She was being, yes, patronised; and that was really as new to her – the freeborn American girl who might, if she had wished, have got engaged and disengaged not six times but sixty – as it would have been to be crowned or crucified. The Frenches themselves didn't do it – the Frenches themselves didn't dare it. It was as strange as one would: she recognised it when it came, but anything might have come rather – and it was coming by (of all people in the world) Murray Brush! It overwhelmed her; still she could speak, with however faint a quaver and however sick a smile. 'You'll lie for me like a gentleman?'

'As far as that goes till I'm black in the face!' And then while he glowed at her and she wondered if he would pointedly look his lies that way, and if, in fine, his florid gallant knowing, almost winking intelligence, *common* as she had never seen the common vivified, would represent his notion of 'blackness': 'See here, Julia; I'll do more.'

' "More" –?'

'Everything. I'll take it right in hand. I'll fling over you –'

'Fling over me –?' she continued to echo as he fascinatingly fixed her.

'Well, the biggest *kind* of rose-coloured mantle!' And this time, oh, he did wink: it *would* be the way he was going to wink (and in the grandest good faith in the world) when indignantly denying, under inquisition, that there had been 'a sign or a scrap' between them. But there was more to come; he decided she should have it all. 'Julia, you've got to know now.' He hung fire but an instant more. 'Julia, I'm going to be married.' His 'Julias' were somehow death to her; she could feel that even *through* all the rest. 'Julia, I announce my engagement.'

'Oh lordy, lordy!' she wailed: it might have been addressed to Mr Pitman.

The force of it had brought her to her feet, but he sat there smiling up as at the natural tribute of her interest. 'I tell you before any one else; it's not to be "out" for a day or two yet. But we want you to know; *she* said that as soon as I mentioned to her that I had heard from you. I mention to her everything, you see!' – and he almost simpered while, still in his seat, he held the end of his cigarette, all delicately and as for a form of gentle emphasis, with the tips of his fine fingers. 'You've not met her, Mary Lindeck, I think: she tells me she hasn't the pleasure of knowing you, but she desires it so much – particularly longs for it. She'll take an interest too,' he went on; 'you must let me immediately bring her to you. She has heard so much about you and she really wants to see you.'

'Oh mercy *me*!' poor Julia gasped again – so strangely did history repeat itself and so did this appear the echo, on Murray Brush's lips, and quite to drollery, of that sympathetic curiosity of Mrs Drack's which Mr Pitman, as they said, voiced. Well, there had played before her the vision of a ledge of safety in face of a rising tide; but this deepened quickly to a sense more forlorn, the cold swish of waters already up to her waist and that would soon be up to her chin. It came really but from the air of her friend, from the perfect benevolence and high unconsciousness with which he kept his posture – as if to show he could patronise her from below upward quite as well as from above down. And as she took it all in, as it spread to a flood, with the great lumps and masses of truth it was floating, she knew inevitable submission, not to say submersion, as she had never known it in her life; going down and down before it, not even putting out her hands to resist or cling by the way, only reading into the young man's very face an immense fatality and, for all his bright nobleness, his absence of rancour or of protesting pride, the great grey blankness of her doom. It was as if the earnest Miss Lindeck, tall and mild, high and lean, with eyeglasses and a big nose, but 'marked' in a noticeable way, elegant and distinguished and refined, as you could see from a mile off, and as graceful, for common despair of imitation, as the curves of the 'copy' set of old by one's writing-master – it was as if this stately well-wisher, whom indeed she had never exchanged a word with, but whom she had recognised and placed and winced at as soon as he spoke of her, figured there beside him now as also in portentous charge of her case.

He had ushered her into it in that way, as if his mere right word sufficed; and Julia could see them throned together, beautifully at one in all the interests they now shared, and regard her as an object of almost tender solicitude. It was positively as if they had become engaged for her good – in such a happy light as it shed. That was the way people you had known, known a bit intimately, looked at you as soon as they took on the high matrimonial propriety that sponged over the more or less wild past to which you belonged and of which, all of a sudden, they were aware only through some suggestion it made them for reminding you definitely that you still had a place. On her having had a day or two before to meet Mrs Drack and to rise to her expectation she had seen and felt herself act, had above all admired herself, and had at any rate known what she said, even though losing, at her altitude, any distinctness in the others. She could have repeated afterwards the detail of her performance – if she hadn't preferred to keep it with her as a mere locked-up, a mere unhandled treasure. At present, however, as everything was for her at first deadened and vague, true to the general effect of sounds and motions in water, she couldn't have said afterwards what words she spoke, what face she showed, what impression she made – at least till she had pulled herself round to precautions. She only knew she had turned away, and that this movement must have sooner or later determined his rising to join her, his deciding to accept it, gracefully and condoningly – condoningly in respect to her natural emotion, her inevitable little pang – for an intimation that they would be better on their feet.

They trod then afresh their ancient paths; and though it pressed upon her hatefully that he must have taken her abruptness for a smothered shock, the flare-up of her old feeling at the breath of his news, she had still to see herself condemned to allow him this, condemned really to encourage him in the mistake of believing her suspicious of feminine spite and doubtful of Miss Lindeck's zeal. She was so far from doubtful that she was but too appalled at it and at the officious mass in which it loomed, and this instinct of dread, before their walk was over, before she had guided him round to one of the smaller gates, there to slip off again by herself, was positively to find on the bosom of her flood a plank under aid of which she kept in a manner and for the time afloat. She took ten minutes to pant, to blow gently, to paddle disguisedly, to accommodate herself, in a word, to the elements she had let loose; but as a reward of her effort at least she then saw how her determined vision accounted for everything. Beside her friend on the bench she had truly felt all his cables cut, truly swallowed down the fact that if he still perceived she was pretty – and *how* pretty! – it had ceased appreciably to matter to him. It had lighted the folly of her preliminary fear, the fear of his even yet, to some effect of confusion or other inconvenience for her, proving more alive to the quoteable in her, as she had called it, than to the inexpressible. She had reckoned with the awkwardness of that possible lapse of his measure of her charm, by which his renewed apprehension of her grosser ornaments, those with which he had most affinity, might too much profit; but she need have concerned herself as little for his sensibility on one head as on the other. She had ceased personally, ceased materially – in respect, as who should say, to any optical or tactile advantage – to exist for him, and the whole office of his manner had been the more piously and gallantly to dress the dead presence with flowers. This was all to his credit and his honour, but what it clearly certified was that their case was at last not even one of spirit reaching out to spirit. *He* had plenty of spirit – had all the spirit required for his having engaged himself to Miss Lindeck; into which result, once she had got her head well up again, she read, as they proceeded, one sharp meaning after another. It was therefore toward the subtler essence of that mature young woman alone that he was occupied in stretching; what was definite to him about Julia Bride being merely, being entirely – which was indeed thereby quite enough – that she *might* end by scaling her worldly height. They would push, they would shove, they would 'boost', they would arch both their straight backs as pedestals for her tiptoe; and at the same time, by some sweet prodigy of mechanics, she would pull them up and up with her.

Wondrous things hovered before her in the course of this walk; her consciousness had become, by an extraordinary turn, a music-box in which, its lid well down, the most remarkable tunes were sounding. It played for her ear alone, and the lid, as she might have figured, was her firm plan of holding out till she got home, of not betraying – to her companion at least – the extent to which she was demoralised. To see him think her demoralised by mistrust of the sincerity of the service to be meddlesomely rendered her by his future wife – she would have hurled herself publicly into the lake there at their side, would have splashed, in her beautiful clothes, among the frightened swans, rather than invite him to that ineptitude. Oh her sincerity, Mary Lindeck's – she would be drenched with her sincerity, and she would be drenched, yes, with *his*; so that, from inward convulsion to convulsion, she had, before they reached their gate, pulled up in the path. There was something her head had been full of these three or four minutes, the intensest little tune of the music-box, and it had made its way to her lips now; belonging – for all the good it could do her! – to the two or three sorts of solicitude she might properly express.

'I hope *she* has a fortune, if you don't mind my speaking of it: I mean some of the money we didn't in *our* time have – and that we missed, after all, in our poor way and for what we then wanted of it, so quite dreadfully.'

She had been able to wreathe it in a grace quite equal to any he himself had employed; and it was to be said for him also that he kept up, on this, the standard. 'Oh she's not, thank goodness, at all badly off, poor dear. We shall do very well. How sweet of you to have thought of it! May I tell her that too?' he splendidly glared. Yes, he glared – how couldn't he, with what his mind was really full of? But, all the same, he came just here, by her vision, nearer than at any other point to being a gentleman. He came quite within an ace of it – with his taking from her thus the prescription of humility of service, his consenting to act in the interest of her avidity, his letting her mount that way, on his bowed shoulders, to the success in which he could suppose she still believed. He couldn't know, he would never know, that she had then and there ceased to believe in it – that she saw as clear as the sun in the sky the exact manner in which, between them, before they had done, the Murray Brushes, all zeal and sincerity, all interest in her interesting case, would dish, would ruin, would utterly destroy her. He wouldn't have needed to go on, for the force and truth of this; but he did go on – he was as crashingly consistent as a motor-car without a brake. He was visibly in love with the idea of what they might do for her and of the rare 'social' opportunity that they would, by the same stroke, embrace. How he had been offhand with it, how he had made it parenthetic, that he didn't happen 'personally' to know Basil French – as if it would have been at all likely he *should* know him, even *im*personally, and as if he could conceal from her the fact that, since she had made him her overture, this gentleman's name supremely baited her hook! Oh they would help Julia Bride if they could – they would do their remarkable best; but they would at any rate have made his acquaintance over it, and she might indeed leave the rest to their thoroughness. He would already have known, he would already have heard; her appeal, she was more and more sure, wouldn't have come to him as a revelation. He had already talked it over with *her*, with Miss Lindeck, to whom the Frenches, in their fortress, had never been accessible, and his whole attitude bristled, to Julia's eyes, with the betrayal of her hand, her voice, her pressure, her calculation. His tone in fact, as he talked, fairly thrust these things into her face. 'But you must see her for yourself. You'll judge her. You'll love her. My dear child' – he brought it all out, and if he spoke of children he might, in his candour, have been himself infantine – 'my dear child, she's the person to do it for you. Make it over to her; but,' he laughed, 'of course see her first! Couldn't you,' he wound up – for they were now near their gate, where she was to leave him – 'couldn't you just simply make us meet him, at tea, say, informally; just *us* alone, as pleasant old friends of whom you'd have so naturally and frankly spoken to him; and then see what we'd *make* of that?'

It was all in his expression; he couldn't keep it undetected, and his shining good looks couldn't: ah, he was so fatally much too handsome for her! So the gap showed just there, in his admirable mask and his admirable eagerness; the yawning little chasm showed where the gentleman fell short. But she took this in, she took everything in, she felt herself do it, she heard herself say, while they paused before separation, that she quite saw the point of the meeting, as he suggested, at her tea. She would propose it to Mr French and would let them know; and he must assuredly bring Miss Lindeck, bring her 'right away', bring her soon, bring *them*, his fiancée and her, together somehow, and as quickly as possible – so that they *should* be old friends before the tea. She would propose it to Mr French, propose it to Mr French: that hummed in her ears as she went – after she had really got away; hummed as if she were repeating it over, giving it out to the passers, to the pavement, to the sky, and all as in wild discord with the intense little concert of her music-box. The extraordinary thing too was that she quite believed she should do it, and fully meant to; desperately, fantastically passive – since she almost reeled with it as she proceeded – she was capable of proposing anything to any one: capable too of thinking it likely Mr French would come, for he had never on her previous proposals declined anything. Yes, she would keep it up to the end, this pretence of owing them salvation, and might even live to take comfort in having done for them what they wanted. What they wanted *couldn't* but be to get at the Frenches, and what Miss Lindeck above all wanted, baffled of it otherwise, with so many others of the baffled, was to get at Mr French – for all Mr French would want of either of them! – still more than Murray did. It wasn't till after she had got home, got straight into her own room and flung herself on her face, that she yielded to the full taste of the bitterness of missing a connexion, missing the man himself, with power to create such a social appetite, such a grab at what might be gained by them. He could make people, even people like these two and whom there were still other people to envy, he could make them push and snatch and scramble like that – and then remain as incapable of taking her from the hands of such patrons as of receiving her straight, say, from those of Mrs Drack. It was a high note, too, of Julia's wonderful composition that, even in the long lonely moan of her conviction of her now certain ruin, all this grim lucidity, the perfect clearance of passion, but made her supremely proud of him.

THE JOLLY CORNER

I

'EVERY one asks me what I "think" of everything,' said Spencer Brydon; 'and I make answer as I can – begging or dodging the question, putting them off with any nonsense. It wouldn't matter to any of them really,' he went on, 'for, even were it possible to meet in that stand-and-deliver way so silly a demand on so big a subject, my "thoughts" would still be almost altogether about something that concerns only myself.' He was talking to Miss Staverton, with whom for a couple of months now he had availed himself of every possible occasion to talk; this disposition and this resource, this comfort and support, as the situation in fact presented itself, having promptly enough taken the first place in the considerable array of rather unattenuated surprises attending his so strangely belated return to America. Everything was somehow a surprise; and that might be natural when one had so long and so consistently neglected everything, taken pains to give surprises so much margin for play. He had given them more than thirty years – thirty-three, to be exact; and they now seemed to him to have organised their performance quite on the scale of that licence. He had been twenty-three on leaving New York – he was fifty-six to-day: unless indeed he were to reckon as he had sometimes, since his repatriation, found himself feeling; in which case he would have lived longer than is often allotted to man. It would have taken a century, he repeatedly said to himself, and said also to Alice Staverton, it would have taken a longer absence and a more averted mind than those even of which he had been guilty, to pile up the differences, the newnesses, the queernesses, above all the bignesses, for the better or the worse, that at present assaulted his vision wherever he looked.

The great fact all the while however had been the incalculability; since he *had* supposed himself, from decade to decade, to be allowing, and in the most liberal and intelligent manner, for brilliancy of change. He actually saw that he had allowed for nothing; he missed what he would have been sure of finding, he found what he would never have imagined. Proportions and values were upside-down; the ugly things he had expected, the ugly things of his far-away youth, when he had too promptly waked up to a sense of the ugly – these uncanny phenomena placed him rather, as it happened, under the charm; whereas the 'swagger' things, the modern, the monstrous, the famous things, those he had more particularly, like thousands of ingenuous enquirers every year, come over to see, were exactly his sources of dismay. They were as so many set traps for displeasure, above all for reaction, of which his restless tread was constantly pressing the spring. It was interesting, doubtless, the whole show, but it would have been too disconcerting hadn't a certain finer truth saved the situation. He had distinctly not, in this steadier light, come over *all* for the monstrosities; he had come, not only in the last analysis but quite on the face of the act, under an impulse with which they had nothing to do. He had come – putting the thing pompously – to look at his 'property', which he had thus for a third of a century not been within four thousand miles of; or, expressing it less sordidly, he had yielded to the humour of seeing again his house on the jolly corner, as he usually, and quite fondly, described it – the one in which he had first seen the light, in which various members of his family had lived and had died, in which the holidays of his overschooled boyhood had been passed and the few social flowers of his chilled adolescence gathered, and which, alienated then for so long a period, had, through the successive deaths of his two brothers and the termination of old arrangements, come wholly into his hands. He was the owner of another, not quite so 'good' – the jolly corner having been, from far back, superlatively extended and consecrated; and the value of the pair represented his main capital, with an income consisting, in these later years, of their respective rents which (thanks precisely to their original excellent type) had never been depressingly low. He could live in 'Europe', as he had been in the habit of living, on the product of these flourishing New York leases, and all the better since, that of the second structure, the mere number in its long row, having within a twelvemonth fallen in, renovation at a high advance had proved beautifully possible.

These were items of property indeed, but he had found himself since his arrival distinguishing more than ever between them. The house within the street, two bristling blocks westward, was already in course of reconstruction as a tall mass of flats; he had acceded, some time before, to overtures for this conversion – in which, now that it was going forward, it had been not the least of his astonishments to find himself able, on the spot, and though without a previous ounce of such experience, to participate with a certain intelligence, almost with a certain authority. He had lived his life with his back so turned to such concerns and his face addressed to those of so different an order that he scarce knew what to make of this lively stir, in a compartment of his mind never yet penetrated, of a capacity for business and a sense for construction. These virtues, so common all round him now, had been dormant in his own organism – where it might be said of them perhaps that they had slept the sleep of the just. At present, in the splendid autumn weather – the autumn at least was a pure boon in the terrible place – he loafed about his 'work' undeterred, secretly agitated; not in the least 'minding' that the whole proposition, as they said, was vulgar and sordid, and ready to climb ladders, to walk the plank, to handle materials and look wise about them, to ask questions, in fine, and challenge explanations and really 'go into' figures.

It amused, it verily quite charmed him; and, by the same stroke, it amused, and even more, Alice Staverton, though perhaps charming her perceptibly less. She wasn't however going to be better-off for it, as *he* was – and so astonishingly much: nothing was now likely, he knew, ever to make her better-off than she found herself, in the afternoon of life, as the delicately frugal possessor and tenant of the small house in Irving Place to which she had subtly managed to cling through her almost unbroken New York career. If he knew the way to it now better than to any other address among the dreadful multiplied numberings which seemed to him to reduce the whole place to some vast ledger-page, overgrown, fantastic, of ruled

and criss-crossed lines and figures – if he had formed, for his
consolation, that habit, it was really not a little because of the
charm of his having encountered and recognised, in the vast
wilderness of the wholesale, breaking through the mere gross
generalisation of wealth and force and success, a small still
scene where items and shades, all delicate things, kept the
sharpness of the notes of a high voice perfectly trained, and
where economy hung about like the scent of a garden. His old
friend lived with one maid and herself dusted her relics and
trimmed her lamps and polished her silver; she stood off, in the
awful modern crush, when she could, but she sallied forth and
did battle when the challenge was really to 'spirit', the spirit she
after all confessed to, proudly and a little shyly, as to that of the
better time, that of *their* common, their quite far-away and
antediluvian social period and order. She made use of the
street-cars when need be, the terrible things that people
scrambled for as the panic-stricken at sea scramble for the
boats; she affronted, inscrutably, under stress, all the public
concussions and ordeals; and yet, with that slim mystifying
grace of her appearance, which defied you to say if she were a
fair young woman who looked older through trouble, or a fine
smooth older one who looked young through successful indifference; with her precious reference, above all, to memories
and histories into which he could enter, she was as exquisite for
him as some pale pressed flower (a rarity to begin with), and,
failing other sweetnesses, she was a sufficient reward of his
effort. They had communities of knowledge, 'their' knowledge
(this discriminating possessive was always on her lips) of presences of the other age, presences all overlaid, in his case, by the
experience of a man and the freedom of a wanderer, overlaid by
pleasure, by infidelity, by passages of life that were strange and
dim to her, just by 'Europe' in short, but still unobscured, still
exposed and cherished, under that pious visitation of the spirit
from which she had never been diverted.

She had come with him one day to see how his 'apartment-
house' was rising; he had helped her over gaps and explained to
her plans, and while they were there had happened to have,
before her, a brief but lively discussion with the man in charge,

the representative of the building-firm that had undertaken his work. He had found himself quite 'standing-up' to this personage over a failure on the latter's part to observe some detail of one of their noted conditions, and had so lucidly argued his case that, besides ever so prettily flushing, at the time, for sympathy in his triumph, she had afterwards said to him (though to a slightly greater effect of irony) that he had clearly for too many years neglected a real gift. If he had but stayed at home he would have anticipated the inventor of the sky-scraper. If he had but stayed at home he would have discovered his genius in time really to start some new variety of awful architectural hare and run it till it burrowed in a gold-mine. He was to remember these words, while the weeks elapsed, for the small silver ring they had sounded over the queerest and deepest of his own lately most disguised and most muffled vibrations.

It had begun to be present to him after the first fortnight, it had broken out with the oddest abruptness, this particular wanton wonderment: it met him there – and this was the image under which he himself judged the matter, or at least, not a little, thrilled and flushed with it – very much as he might have been met by some strange figure, some unexpected occupant, at a turn of one of the dim passages of an empty house. The quaint analogy quite hauntingly remained with him, when he didn't indeed rather improve it by a still intenser form: that of his opening a door behind which he would have made sure of finding nothing, a door into a room shuttered and void, and yet so coming, with a great suppressed start, on some quite erect confronting presence, something planted in the middle of the place and facing him through the dusk. After that visit to the house in construction he walked with his companion to see the other and always so much the better one, which in the eastward direction formed one of the corners, the 'jolly' one precisely, of the street now so generally dishonoured and disfigured in its westward reaches, and of the comparatively conservative Avenue. The Avenue still had pretensions, as Miss Staverton said, to decency; the old people had mostly gone, the old names were unknown, and here and there an old association seemed to stray, all vaguely, like some very aged person, out too late, whom you might meet and feel the impulse to watch or follow, in kindness, for safe restoration to shelter.

They went in together, our friends; he admitted himself with his key, as he kept no one there, he explained, preferring, for his reasons, to leave the place empty, under a simple arrangement with a good woman living in the neighbourhood and who came for a daily hour to open windows and dust and sweep. Spencer Brydon had his reasons and was growingly aware of them; they seemed to him better each time he was there, though he didn't name them all to his companion, any more than he told her as yet how often, how quite absurdly often, he himself came. He only let her see for the present, while they walked through the great blank rooms, that absolute vacancy reigned and that, from top to bottom, there was nothing but Mrs Muldoon's broomstick, in a corner, to tempt the burglar. Mrs Muldoon was then on the premises, and she loquaciously attended the visitors, preceding them from room to room and pushing back shutters and throwing up sashes – all to show them, as she remarked, how little there was to see. There was little indeed to see in the great gaunt shell where the main dispositions and the general apportionment of space, the style of an age of ampler allowances, had nevertheless for its master their honest pleading message, affecting him as some good old servant's, some lifelong retainer's appeal for a character, or even for a retiring-pension; yet it was also a remark of Mrs Muldoon's that, glad as she was to oblige him by her noonday round, there was a request she greatly hoped he would never make of her. If he should wish her for any reason to come in after dark she would just tell him, if he 'plased', that he must ask it of somebody else.

The fact that there was nothing to see didn't militate for the worthy woman against what one *might* see, and she put it frankly to Miss Staverton that no lady could be expected to like, could she? 'craping up to thim top storeys in the ayvil hours'. The gas and the electric light were off in the house, and she fairly evoked a gruesome vision of her march through the great grey rooms – so many of them as there were too! – with her glimmering taper. Miss Staverton met her honest glare with a smile and the profession that she herself certainly would recoil from such an adventure. Spencer Brydon meanwhile held his peace – for the moment; the question of the 'evil' hours in his old home had already become too grave for him. He had begun some time since to 'crape', and he knew just why a packet of candles addressed to that pursuit had been stowed by his own hand, three weeks before, at the back of a drawer of the fine old sideboard that occupied, as a 'fixture', the deep recess in the dining-room. Just now he laughed at his companions – quickly however changing the subject; for the reason that, in the first place, his laugh struck him even at that moment as starting the odd echo, the conscious human resonance (he scarce knew how to qualify it) that sounds made while he was there alone sent back to his ear or his fancy; and that, in the second, he imagined Alice Staverton for the instant on the point of asking him, with a divination, if he ever so prowled. There were divinations he was unprepared for, and he had at all events averted enquiry by the time Mrs Muldoon had left them, passing on to other parts.

There was happily enough to say, on so consecrated a spot, that could be said freely and fairly; so that a whole train of declarations was precipitated by his friend's having herself broken out, after a yearning look round: 'But I hope you don't mean they want you to pull *this* to pieces!' His answer came, promptly, with his reawakened wrath: it was of course exactly what they wanted, and what they were 'at' him for, daily, with the iteration of people who couldn't for their life understand a man's liability to decent feelings. He had found the place, just as it stood and beyond what he could express, an interest and a joy. There were values other than the beastly rent-values, and in short, in short –! But it was thus Miss Staverton took him up. 'In short you're to make so good a thing of your sky-scraper that, living in luxury on *those* ill-gotten gains, you can afford for a while to be sentimental here!' Her smile had for him, with the words, the particular mild irony with which he found half her talk suffused; an irony without bitterness and that came, exactly, from her having so much imagination – not, like the cheap sarcasms with which one heard most people, about the world of 'society', bid for the reputation of cleverness, from nobody's really having any. It was agreeable to him at this very moment to be sure that when he had answered, after a brief demur, 'Well yes: so, precisely, you may put it!' her imagination would still do him justice. He explained that even if never a dollar were to come to him from the other house he would nevertheless cherish this one; and he dwelt, further, while they lingered and wandered, on the fact of the stupefaction he was already exciting, the positive mystification he felt himself create.

He spoke of the value of all he read into it, into the mere sight of the walls, mere shapes of the rooms, mere sound of the floors, mere feel, in his hand, of the old silver-plated knobs of the several mahogany doors, which suggested the pressure of the palms of the dead; the seventy years of the past in fine that these things represented, the annals of nearly three generations, counting his grandfather's, the one that had ended there, and the impalpable ashes of his long-extinct youth, afloat in the very air like microscopic motes. She listened to everything; she was a woman who answered intimately but who utterly didn't chatter. She scattered abroad therefore no cloud of words; she could assent, she could agree, above all she could encourage, without doing that. Only at the last she went a little further than he had done himself. 'And then how do you know? You may still, after all, want to live here.' It rather indeed pulled him up, for it wasn't what he had been thinking, at least in her sense of the words. 'You mean I may decide to stay on for the sake of it?'

'Well, *with* such a home –!' But, quite beautifully, she had too much tact to dot so monstrous an *i*, and it was precisely an illustration of the way she didn't rattle. How could any one – of any wit – insist on any one else's 'wanting' to live in New York? 'Oh,' he said, 'I *might* have lived here (since I had my opportunity early in life); I might have put in here all these years. Then everything would have been different enough – and, I dare say, "funny" enough. But that's another matter. And then the beauty of it – I mean of my perversity, of my refusal to agree to a "deal" – is just in the total absence of a reason. Don't you see that if I had a reason about the matter at all it would *have* to be the other way, and would then be inevitably a reason of dollars? There are no reasons here *but* of dollars. Let us therefore have none whatever – not the ghost of one.'

They were back in the hall then for departure, but from where they stood the vista was large, through an open door, into the great square main saloon, with its almost antique felicity of brave spaces between windows. Her eyes came back from that reach and met his own a moment. 'Are you very sure the "ghost" of one doesn't, much rather, serve –?'

He had a positive sense of turning pale. But it was as near as they were then to come. For he made answer, he believed, between a glare and a grin: 'Oh ghosts – of course the place must swarm with them! I should be ashamed of it if it didn't. Poor Mrs Muldoon's right, and it's why I haven't asked her to do more than look in.'

Miss Staverton's gaze again lost itself, and things she didn't utter, it was clear, came and went in her mind. She might even for the minute, off there in the fine room, have imagined some element dimly gathering. Simplified like the death-mask of a handsome face, it perhaps produced for her just then an effect akin to the stir of an expression in the 'set' commemorative plaster. Yet whatever her impression may have been she produced instead a vague platitude. 'Well, if it were only furnished and lived in –!'

She appeared to imply that in case of its being still furnished he might have been a little less opposed to the idea of a return. But she passed straight into the vestibule, as if to leave her words behind her, and the next moment he had opened the house-door and was standing with her on the steps. He closed the door and, while he re-pocketed his key, looking up and down, they took in the comparatively harsh actuality of the Avenue, which reminded him of the assault of the outer light of the Desert on the traveller emerging from an Egyptian tomb. But he risked before they stepped into the street his gathered answer to her speech. 'For me it *is* lived in. For me it *is* furnished.' At which it was easy for her to sigh 'Ah yes –!' all vaguely and discreetly; since his parents and his favourite sister, to say nothing of other kin, in numbers, had run their course and met their end there. That represented, within the walls, ineffaceable life.

It was a few days after this that, during an hour passed with her again, he had expressed his impatience of the too flattering curiosity – among the people he met – about his appreciation of New York. He had arrived at none at all that was socially producible, and as for that matter of his 'thinking' (thinking the better or the worse of anything there) he was wholly taken up with one subject of thought. It was mere vain egoism, and it was moreover, if she liked, a morbid obsession. He found all things come back to the question of what he personally might have been, how he might have led his life and 'turned out', if he had not so, at the outset, given it up. And confessing for the first time to the intensity within him of this absurd speculation – which but proved also, no doubt, the habit of too selfishly thinking – he affirmed the impotence there of any other source of interest, any other native appeal. 'What would it have made of me, what would it have made of me? I keep for ever wondering, all idiotically; as if I could possibly know! I see what it has made of dozens of others, those I meet, and it positively aches within me, to the point of exasperation, that it would have made something of me as well. Only I can't make out *what*, and the worry of it, the small rage of curiosity never to be satisfied, brings back what I remember to have felt, once or twice, after judging best, for reasons, to burn some important letter unopened. I've been sorry, I've hated it – I've never known what was in the letter. You may of course say it's a trifle –!'

'I don't say it's a trifle,' Miss Staverton gravely interrupted.

She was seated by her fire, and before her, on his feet and restless, he turned to and fro between this intensity of his idea and a fitful and unseeing inspection, through his single eye-glass, of the dear little old objects on her chimney-piece. Her interruption made him for an instant look at her harder. 'I shouldn't care if you did!' he laughed, however; 'and it's only a figure, at any rate, for the way I now feel. *Not* to have followed my perverse young course – and almost in the teeth of my father's curse, as I may say; not to have kept it up, so, "over there", from that day to this, without a doubt or a pang; not, above all, to have liked it, to have loved it, so much, loved it, no doubt, with such an abysmal conceit of my own preference: some variation from *that*, I say, must have produced some different effect for my life and for my "form". I should have stuck here – if it had been possible; and I was too young, at twenty-three, to judge, *pour deux sous*, whether it *were* possible. If I had waited I might have seen it was, and then I might have been, by staying here, something nearer to one of these types who have been hammered so hard and made so keen by their conditions. It isn't that I admire them so much – the question of any charm in them, or of any charm, beyond that of the rank money-passion, exerted by their conditions *for* them, has nothing to do with the matter: it's only a question of what fantastic, yet perfectly possible, development of my own nature I mayn't have missed. It comes over me that I had then a strange *alter ego* deep down somewhere within me, as the full-blown flower is in the small tight bud, and that I just took the course, I just transferred him to the climate, that blighted him for once and for ever.'

'And you wonder about the flower,' Miss Staverton said. 'So do I, if you want to know; and so I've been wondering these several weeks. I believe in the flower,' she continued, 'I feel it would have been quite splendid, quite huge and monstrous.'

'Monstrous above all!' her visitor echoed; 'and I imagine, by the same stroke, quite hideous and offensive.'

'You don't believe that,' she returned; 'if you did you wouldn't wonder. You'd know, and that would be enough for you. What you feel – and what I feel *for* you – is that you'd have had power.'

'You'd have liked me that way?' he asked.

She barely hung fire. 'How should I not have liked you?'

'I see. You'd have liked me, have preferred me, a billionaire!'

'How should I not have liked you?' she simply again asked.

He stood before her still – her question kept him motionless. He took it in, so much there was of it; and indeed his not otherwise meeting it testified to that. 'I know at least what I am,' he simply went on; 'the other side of the medal's clear enough. I've not been edifying – I believe I'm thought in a hundred quarters to have been barely decent. I've followed strange paths and worshipped strange gods; it must have come to you again and again – in fact you've admitted to me as much – that I was leading, at any time these thirty years, a selfish frivolous scandalous life. And you see what it has made of me.'

She just waited, smiling at him. 'You see what it has made of *me*.'

'Oh you're a person whom nothing can have altered. You were born to be what you are, anywhere, anyway: you've the perfection nothing else could have blighted. And don't you see how, without my exile, I shouldn't have been waiting till now –?' But he pulled up for the strange pang.

'The great thing to see,' she presently said, 'seems to me to be that it has spoiled nothing. It hasn't spoiled your being here at last. It hasn't spoiled this. It hasn't spoiled your speaking –' She also however faltered.

He wondered at everything her controlled emotion might mean. 'Do you believe then – too dreadfully! – that I *am* as good as I might ever have been?'

'Oh no! Far from it!' With which she got up from her chair and was nearer to him. 'But I don't care,' she smiled.

'You mean I'm good enough?'

She considered a little. 'Will you believe it if I say so? I mean will you let that settle your question for you?' And then as if making out in his face that he drew back from this, that he had some idea which, however absurd, he couldn't yet bargain away: 'Oh you don't care either – but very differently: you don't care for anything but yourself.'

Spencer Brydon recognised it – it was in fact what he had absolutely professed. Yet he importantly qualified. '*He* isn't myself. He's the just so totally other person. But I do want to see him,' he added. 'And I can. And I shall.'

Their eyes met for a minute while he guessed from something in hers that she divined his strange sense. But neither of them otherwise expressed it, and her apparent understanding, with no protesting shock, no easy derision, touched him more deeply than anything yet, constituting for his stifled perversity, on the spot, an element that was like breathable air. What she said however was unexpected. 'Well, *I've* seen him.'

'You –?'

'I've seen him in a dream.'

'Oh a "dream" –!' It let him down.

'But twice over,' she continued. 'I saw him as I see you now.'

'You've dreamed the same dream –?'

'Twice over,' she repeated. 'The very same.'

This did somehow a little speak to him, as it also gratified him. 'You dream about me at that rate?'

'Ah about *him*!' she smiled.

His eyes again sounded her. 'Then you know all about him.' And as she said nothing more: 'What's the wretch like?'

She hesitated, and it was as if he were pressing her so hard that, resisting for reasons of her own, she had to turn away. 'I'll tell you some other time!'

II

IT was after this that there was most of a virtue for him, most of a cultivated charm, most of a preposterous secret thrill, in the particular form of surrender to his obsession and of address to what he more and more believed to be his privilege. It was what in these weeks he was living for – since he really felt life to begin but after Mrs Muldoon had retired from the scene and, visiting the ample house from attic to cellar, making sure he was alone, he knew himself in safe possession and, as he tacitly expressed it, let himself go. He sometimes came twice in the twenty-four hours; the moments he liked best were those of gathering dusk, of the short autumn twilight; this was the time of which, again and again, he found himself hoping most. Then he could, as seemed to him, most intimately wander and wait, linger and listen, feel his fine attention, never in his life before so fine, on the pulse of the great vague place: he preferred the lampless hour and only wished he might have prolonged each day the deep crepuscular spell. Later – rarely much before midnight, but then for a considerable vigil – he watched with his glimmering light; moving slowly, holding it high, playing it far, rejoicing above all, as much as he might, in open vistas, reaches of communication between rooms and by passages; the long straight chance or show, as he would have called it, for the revelation he pretended to invite. It was a practice he found he could perfectly 'work' without exciting remark; no one was in the least the wiser for it; even Alice Staverton, who was moreover a well of discretion, didn't quite fully imagine.

He let himself in and let himself out with the assurance of calm proprietorship; and accident so far favoured him that, if a fat Avenue 'officer' had happened on occasion to see him entering at eleven-thirty, he had never yet, to the best of his belief, been noticed as emerging at two. He walked there on the crisp November nights, arrived regularly at the evening's end; it was as easy to do this after dining out as to take his way to a club or to his hotel. When he left his club, if he hadn't been dining out, it was ostensibly to go to his hotel; and when he left his hotel, if he had spent a part of the evening there, it was ostensibly to go to his club. Everything was easy in fine; everything conspired and promoted: there was truly even in the strain of his experience something that glossed over, something that salved and simplified, all the rest of consciousness. He circulated, talked, renewed, loosely and pleasantly, old relations – met indeed, so far as he could, new expectations and seemed to make out on the whole that in spite of the career, of such different contacts, which he had spoken of to Miss Staverton as ministering so little, for those who might have watched it, to edification, he was positively rather liked than not. He was a dim secondary social success – and all with people who had truly not an idea of him. It was all mere surface sound, this murmur of their welcome, this popping of their corks – just as his gestures of response were the extravagant shadows, emphatic in proportion as they meant little, of some game of *ombres chinoises*. He projected himself all day, in thought, straight over the bristling line of hard unconscious heads and into the other, the real, the waiting life; the life that, as soon as he had heard behind him the click of his great house-door, began for him, on the jolly corner, as beguilingly as the slow opening bars of some rich music follows the tap of the conductor's wand.

He always caught the first effect of the steel point of his stick on the old marble of the hall pavement, large black-and-white squares that he remembered as the admiration of his childhood and that had then made in him, as he now saw, for the growth of an early conception of style. This effect was the dim reverberating tinkle as of some far-off bell hung who should say where? – in the depths of the house, of the past, of that mystical other world that might have flourished for him had he not, for weal or woe, abandoned it. On this impression he did ever the same thing; he put his stick noiselessly away in a corner – feeling the place once more in the likeness of some great glass bowl, all precious concave crystal, set delicately humming by the play of a moist finger round its edge. The concave crystal held, as it were, this mystical other world, and the indescribably fine murmur of its rim was the sigh there, the scarce audible pathetic wail to his strained ear, of all the old baffled forsworn possibilities. What he did therefore by this appeal of his hushed presence was to wake them into such measure of ghostly life as they might still enjoy. They were shy, all but unappeasably shy, but they weren't really sinister; at least they weren't as he had hitherto felt them – before they had taken the Form he so yearned to make them take, the Form he at moments saw himself in the light of fairly hunting on tiptoe, the points of his evening-shoes, from room to room and from storey to storey.

That was the essence of his vision – which was all rank folly, if one would, while he was out of the house and otherwise occupied, but which took on the last verisimilitude as soon as he was placed and posted. He knew what he meant and what he wanted; it was as clear as the figure on a cheque presented in demand for cash. His *alter ego* 'walked' – that was the note of his image of him, while his image of his motive for his own odd pastime was the desire to waylay him and meet him. He roamed, slowly, warily, but all restlessly, he himself did – Mrs Muldoon had been right, absolutely, with her figure of their 'craping'; and the presence he watched for would roam restlessly too. But it would be as cautious and as shifty; the conviction of its probable, in fact its already quite sensible, quite audible evasion of pursuit grew for him from night to night, laying on him finally a rigour to which nothing in his life had been comparable. It had been the theory of many super-ficially-judging persons, he knew, that he was wasting that life in a surrender to sensations, but he had tasted of no pleasure so fine as his actual tension, had been introduced to no sport that demanded at once the patience and the nerve of this stalking of a creature more subtle, yet at bay perhaps more formidable, than any beast of the forest. The terms, the comparisons, the very practices of the chase positively came again into play; there were even moments when passages of his occasional experience as a sportsman, stirred memories, from his younger time, of moor and mountain and desert, revived for him – and to the increase of his keenness – by the tremendous force of analogy. He found himself at moments – once he had placed his single light on some mantel-shelf or in some recess – step-ping back into shelter or shade, effacing himself behind a door or in an embrasure, as he had sought of old the vantage of rock and tree; he found himself holding his breath and living in the joy of the instant, the supreme suspense created by big game alone.

He wasn't afraid (though putting himself the question as he believed gentlemen on Bengal tiger-shoots or in close quarters with the great bear of the Rockies had been known to confess to having put it); and this indeed – since here at least he might be frank! – because of the impression, so intimate and so strange, that he himself produced as yet a dread, produced certainly a strain, beyond the liveliest he was likely to feel. They fell for him into categories, they fairly became familiar, the signs, for his own perception, of the alarm his presence and his vigilance created; though leaving him always to remark, portentously, on his probably having formed a relation, his probably enjoying a consciousness, unique in the experience of man. People enough, first and last, had been in terror of apparitions, but who had ever before so turned the tables and become himself, in the apparitional world, an incalculable terror? He might have found this sublime had he quite dared to think of it; but he didn't too much insist, truly, on that side of his privilege. With habit and repetition he gained to an extraordinary degree the power to penetrate the dusk of distances and the darkness of corners, to resolve back into their innocence the treacheries of uncertain light, the evil-looking forms taken in the gloom by mere shadows, by accidents of the air, by shifting effects of perspective; putting down his dim luminary he could still wander on without it, pass into other rooms and, only knowing it was there behind him in case of need, see his way about, visually project for his purpose a comparative clearness. It made him feel, this acquired faculty, like some monstrous stealthy cat; he wondered if he would have glared at these moments with large shining yellow eyes, and what it mightn't verily be, for the poor hard-pressed *alter ego*, to be confronted with such a type.

He liked however the open shutters; he opened everywhere those Mrs Muldoon had closed, closing them as carefully afterwards, so that she shouldn't notice: he liked – on this he did like, and above all in the upper rooms! – the sense of the hard silver of the autumn stars through the window-panes, and scarcely less the flare of the street-lamps below, the white electric lustre which it would have taken curtains to keep out. This was human, actual, social; this was of the world he had lived in, and he was more at his ease certainly for the countenance, coldly general and impersonal, that all the while and in spite of his detachment it seemed to give him. He had support, of course, mostly in the rooms at the wide front and the prolonged side; it failed him considerably in the central shades and the parts at the back. But if he sometimes, on his rounds, was glad of his optical reach, so none the less often the rear of the house affected him as the very jungle of his prey. The place was there more subdivided; a large 'extension' in particular, where small rooms for servants had been multiplied, abounded in nooks and corners, in closets and passages, in the ramifications especially of an ample back staircase over which he leaned, many a time, to look far down – not deterred from his gravity even while aware that he might, for a spectator, have figured some solemn simpleton playing at hide-and-seek. Outside, in fact, he might himself make that ironic *rapprochement*; but within the walls, and in spite of the clear windows, his consistency was proof against the cynical light of New York.

It had belonged to that idea of the exasperated consciousness of his victim to become a real test for him; since he had quite put it to himself from the first that, oh distinctly! he could 'cultivate' his whole perception. He had felt it as above all open to cultivation – which indeed was but another name for his manner of spending his time. He was bringing it on, bringing it to perfection, by practice; in consequence of which it had grown so fine that he was now aware of impressions, attestations of his general postulate, that couldn't have broken upon him at once. This was the case more specifically with a phenomenon at last quite frequent for him in the upper rooms, the recognition – absolutely unmistakeable, and by a turn dating from a particular hour, his resumption of his campaign after a diplomatic drop, a calculated absence of three nights – of his being definitely followed, tracked at a distance carefully taken and to the express end that he should the less confidently, less arrogantly, appear to himself merely to pursue. It worried, it finally quite broke him up, for it proved, of all the conceivable impressions, the one least suited to his book. He was kept in sight while remaining himself – as regards the essence of his position – sightless, and his only recourse then was in abrupt turns, rapid recoveries of ground. He wheeled about, retracing his steps, as if he might so catch in his face at least the stirred air of some other quick revolution. It was indeed true that his fully dislocalised thought of these manoeuvres recalled to him Pantaloon, at the Christmas farce, buffeted and tricked from behind by ubiquitous Harlequin; but it left intact the influence of the conditions themselves each time he was re-exposed to them, so that in fact this association, had he suffered it to become constant, would on a certain side have but ministered to his intenser gravity. He had made, as I have said, to create on the premises the baseless sense of a reprieve, his three absences; and the result of the third was to confirm the after-effect of the second.

On his return, that night – the night succeeding his last intermission – he stood in the hall and looked up the staircase with a certainty more intimate than any he had yet known. 'He's *there*, at the top, and waiting – not, as in general, falling back for disappearance. He's holding his ground, and it's the first time – which is a proof, isn't it? that something has happened for him.' So Brydon argued with his hand on the banister and his foot on the lowest stair; in which position he felt as never before the air chilled by his logic. He himself turned cold in it, for he seemed of a sudden to know what now was involved. 'Harder pressed? – yes, he takes it in, with its thus making clear to him that I've come, as they say, "to stay". He finally doesn't like and can't bear it, in the sense, I mean, that his wrath, his menaced interest, now balances with his dread. I've hunted him till he has "turned": that, up there, is what has happened – he's the fanged or the antlered animal brought at last to bay.' There came to him, as I say – but determined by an influence beyond my notation! – the acuteness of this certainty; under which, however, the next moment, he had broken into a sweat that he would as little have consented to attribute to fear as he would have dared immediately to act upon it for enterprise. It marked none the less a prodigious thrill, a thrill that represented sudden dismay, no doubt, but also represented, and with the selfsame throb, the strangest, the most joyous, possibly the next minute almost the proudest, duplication of consciousness.

'He has been dodging, retreating, hiding, but now, worked up to anger, he'll fight!' – this intense impression made a single mouthful, as it were, of terror and applause. But what was wondrous was that the applause, for the felt fact, was so eager, since, if it was his other self he was running to earth, this ineffable identity was thus in the last resort not unworthy of him. It bristled there – somewhere near at hand, however unseen still – as the hunted thing, even as the trodden worm of the adage *must* at last bristle; and Brydon at this instant tasted probably of a sensation more complex than had ever before found itself consistent with sanity. It was as if it would have shamed him that a character so associated with his own should triumphantly succeed in just skulking, should to the end not risk the open; so that the drop of this danger was, on the spot, a great lift of the whole situation. Yet with another rare shift of the same subtlety he was already trying to measure by how much more he himself might now be in peril of fear; so rejoicing that he could, in another form, actively inspire that fear, and simultaneously quaking for the form in which he might passively know it.

The apprehension of knowing it must after a little have grown in him, and the strangest moment of his adventure perhaps, the most memorable or really most interesting, afterwards, of his crisis, was the lapse of certain instants of concentrated conscious *combat*, the sense of a need to hold on to something, even after the manner of a man slipping and slipping on some awful incline; the vivid impulse, above all, to move, to act, to charge, somehow and upon something – to show himself, in a word, that he wasn't afraid. The state of 'holding-on' was thus the state to which he was momentarily reduced; if there had been anything, in the great vacancy, to seize, he would presently have been aware of having clutched it as he might under a shock at home have clutched the nearest chair-back. He had been surprised at any rate – of this he *was* aware – into something unprecedented since his original appropriation of the place; he had closed his eyes, held them tight, for a long minute, as with that instinct of dismay and that terror of vision. When he opened them the room, the other contiguous rooms, extraordinarily, seemed lighter – so light, almost, that at first he took the change for day. He stood firm, however that might be, just where he had paused; his resistance had helped him – it was as if there were something he had tided over. He knew after a little what this was – it had been in the imminent danger of flight. He had stiffened his will against going; without this he would have made for the stairs, and it seemed to him that, still with his eyes closed, he would have descended them, would have known how, straight and swiftly, to the bottom.

Well, as he had held out, here he was – still at the top, among the more intricate upper rooms and with the gauntlet of the others, of all the rest of the house, still to run when it should be his time to go. He would go at his time – only at his time: didn't he go every night very much at the same hour? He took out his watch – there was light for that: it was scarcely a quarter past one, and he had never withdrawn so soon. He reached his lodgings for the most part at two – with his walk of a quarter of an hour. He would wait for the last quarter – he wouldn't stir till then; and he kept his watch there with his eyes on it, reflecting while he held it that this deliberate wait, a wait with an effort, which he recognised, would serve perfectly for the attestation he desired to make. It would prove his courage – unless indeed the latter might most be proved by his budging at last from his place. What he mainly felt now was that, since he hadn't originally scuttled, he had his dignities – which had never in his life seemed so many – all to preserve and to carry aloft. This was before him in truth as a physical image, an image almost worthy of an age of greater romance. That remark indeed glimmered for him only to glow the next instant with a finer light; since what age of romance, after all, could have matched either the state of his mind or, 'objectively', as they said, the wonder of his situation? The only difference would have been that, brandishing his dignities over his head as in a parchment scroll, he might then – that is in the heroic time – have proceeded downstairs with a drawn sword in his other grasp.

At present, really, the light he had set down on the mantel of the next room would have to figure his sword; which utensil, in the course of a minute, he had taken the requisite number of steps to possess himself of. The door between the rooms was open, and from the second another door opened to a third. These rooms, as he remembered, gave all three upon a common corridor as well, but there was a fourth, beyond them, without issue save through the preceding. To have moved, to have heard his step again, was appreciably a help; though even in recognising this he lingered once more a little by the chimney-piece on which his light had rested. When he next moved, just hesitating where to turn, he found himself considering a circumstance that, after his first and comparatively vague apprehension of it, produced in him the start that often attends some pang of recollection, the violent shock of having ceased happily to forget. He had come into sight of the door in which the brief chain of communication ended and which he now surveyed from the nearer threshold, the one not directly facing it. Placed at some distance to the left of this point, it would have admitted him to the last room of the four, the room without other approach or egress, had it not, to his intimate conviction, been closed *since* his former visitation, the matter probably of a quarter of an hour before. He stared with all his eyes at the wonder of the fact, arrested again where he stood and again holding his breath while he sounded its sense. Surely it had been *subsequently* closed – that is, it had been on his previous passage indubitably open!

He took it full in the face that something had happened between – that he couldn't not have noticed before (by which he meant on his original tour of all the rooms that evening) that such a barrier had exceptionally presented itself. He had indeed since that moment undergone an agitation so extraordinary that it might have muddled for him any earlier view; and he tried to convince himself that he might perhaps then have gone into the room and, inadvertently, automatically, on coming out, have drawn the door after him. The difficulty was that this exactly was what he never did; it was against his whole policy, as he might have said, the essence of which was to keep vistas clear. He had them from the first, as he was well aware, quite on the brain: the strange apparition, at the far end of one of them, of his baffled 'prey' (which had become by so sharp an irony so little the term now to apply!) was the form of success his imagination had most cherished, projecting into it always a refinement of beauty. He had known fifty times the start of perception that had afterwards dropped; had fifty times gasped to himself 'There!' under some fond brief hallucination. The house, as the case stood, admirably lent itself; he might wonder at the taste, the native architecture of the particular time, which could rejoice so in the multiplication of doors – the opposite extreme to the modern, the actual almost complete proscription of them; but it had fairly contributed to provoke this obsession of the presence encountered telescopically, as he might say, focused and studied in diminishing perspective and as by a rest for the elbow.

It was with these considerations that his present attention was charged – they perfectly availed to make what he saw portentous. He *couldn't*, by any lapse, have blocked that aperture; and if he hadn't, if it was unthinkable, why what else was clear but that there had been another agent? Another agent? – he had been catching, as he felt, a moment back, the very breath of him; but when had he been so close as in this simple, this logical, this completely personal act? It was so logical, that is, that one might have *taken* it for personal; yet for what did Brydon take it, he asked himself, while, softly panting, he felt his eyes almost leave their sockets. Ah this time at last they *were*, the two, the opposed projections of him, in presence; and this time, as much as one would, the question of danger loomed. With it rose, as not before, the question of courage – for what he knew the blank face of the door to say to him was 'Show us how much you have!' It stared, it glared back at him with that challenge; it put to him the two alternatives: should he just push it open or not? Oh to have this consciousness was to *think* – and to think, Brydon knew, as he stood there, was, with the lapsing moments, not to have acted! Not to have acted – that was the misery and the pang – was even still not to act; was in fact *all* to feel the thing in another, in a new and terrible way. How long did he pause and how long did he debate? There was presently nothing to measure it; for his vibration had already changed – as just by the effect of its intensity. Shut up there, at bay, defiant, and with the prodigy of the thing palpably proveably *done*, thus giving notice like some stark signboard – under that accession of accent the situation itself had turned; and Brydon at last remarkably made up his mind on what it had turned to.

It had turned altogether to a different admonition; to a supreme hint, for him, of the value of Discretion! This slowly dawned, no doubt – for it could take its time; so perfectly, on his threshold, had he been stayed, so little as yet had he either advanced or retreated. It was the strangest of all things that now when, by his taking ten steps and applying his hand to a latch, or even his shoulder and his knee, if necessary, to a panel, all the hunger of his prime need might have been met, his high curiosity crowned, his unrest assuaged – it was amazing, but it was also exquisite and rare, that insistence should have, at a touch, quite dropped from him. Discretion – he jumped at that; and yet not, verily, at such a pitch, because it saved his nerves or his skin, but because, much more valuably, it saved the situation. When I say he 'jumped' at it I feel the consonance of this term with the fact that – at the end indeed of I know not how long – he did move again, he crossed straight to the door. He wouldn't touch it – it seemed now that he might *if* he would: he would only just wait there a little, to show, to prove, that he wouldn't. He had thus another station, close to the thin partition by which revelation was denied him; but with his eyes bent and his hands held off in a mere intensity of stillness. He listened as if there had been something to hear, but this attitude, while it lasted, was his own communication. 'If you won't then – good: I spare you and I give up. You affect me as by the appeal positively for pity: you convince me that for reasons rigid and sublime – what do I know? – we both of us should have suffered. I respect them then, and, though moved and privileged as, I believe, it has never been given to man, I retire, I renounce – never, on my honour, to try again. So rest for ever – and let *me*!'

That, for Brydon, was the deep sense of this last demonstration – solemn, measured, directed, as he felt it to be. He brought it to a close, he turned away; and now verily he knew how deeply he had been stirred. He retraced his steps, taking up his candle, burnt, he observed, well-nigh to the socket, and marking again, lighten it as he would, the distinctness of his footfall; after which, in a moment, he knew himself at the other side of the house. He did here what he had not yet done at these hours – he opened half a casement, one of those in the front, and let in the air of the night; a thing he would have taken at any time previous for a sharp rupture of his spell. His spell was broken now, and it didn't matter – broken by his concession and his surrender, which made it idle henceforth that he should

ever come back. The empty street – its other life so marked even
by the great lamplit vacancy – was within call, within touch; he
stayed there as to be in it again, high above it though he was still
perched; he watched as for some comforting common fact,
some vulgar human note, the passage of a scavenger or a
thief, some night-bird however base. He would have blessed
that sign of life; he would have welcomed positively the slow
approach of his friend the policeman, whom he had hitherto
only sought to avoid, and was not sure that if the patrol
had come into sight he mightn't have felt the impulse to get
into relation with it, to hail it, on some pretext, from his fourth
floor.

The pretext that wouldn't have been too silly or too compromising, the explanation that would have saved his dignity
and kept his name, in such a case, out of the papers, was not
definite to him: he was so occupied with the thought of record-
ing his Discretion – as an effect of the vow he had just uttered to
his intimate adversary – that the importance of this loomed
large and something had overtaken all ironically his sense of
proportion. If there had been a ladder applied to the front of the
house, even one of the vertiginous perpendiculars employed by
painters and roofers and sometimes left standing overnight, he
would have managed somehow, astride of the window-sill, to
compass by outstretched leg and arm that mode of descent. If
there had been some such uncanny thing as he had found in his
room at hotels, a workable fire-escape in the form of notched
cable or a canvas chute, he would have availed himself of it as a
proof – well, of his present delicacy. He nursed that sentiment,
as the question stood, a little in vain, and even – at the end of he
scarce knew, once more, how long – found it, as by the action
on his mind of the failure of response of the outer world, sinking
back to vague anguish. It seemed to him he had waited an age
for some stir of the great grim hush; the life of the town was
itself under a spell – so unnaturally, up and down the whole
prospect of known and rather ugly objects, the blankness and
the silence lasted. Had they ever, he asked himself, the hard-
faced houses, which had begun to look livid in the dim dawn,
had they ever spoken so little to any need of his spirit? Great

builded voids, great crowded stillnesses put on, often, in the heart of cities, for the small hours, a sort of sinister mask, and it was of this large collective negation that Brydon presently became conscious – all the more that the break of day was, almost incredibly, now at hand, proving to him what a night he had made of it.

He looked again at his watch, saw what had become of his time-values (he had taken hours for minutes – not, as in other tense situations, minutes for hours) and the strange air of the streets was but the weak, the sullen flush of a dawn in which everything was still locked up. His choked appeal from his own open window had been the sole note of life, and he could but break off at last as for a worse despair. Yet while so deeply demoralised he was capable again of an impulse denoting – at least by his present measure – extraordinary resolution; of retracing his steps to the spot where he had turned cold with the extinction of his last pulse of doubt as to there being in the place another presence than his own. This required an effort strong enough to sicken him; but he had his reason, which overmastered for the moment everything else. There was the whole of the rest of the house to traverse, and how should he screw himself to that if the door he had seen closed were at present open? He could hold to the idea that the closing had practically been for him an act of mercy, a chance offered him to descend, depart, get off the ground and never again profane it. This conception held together, it worked; but what it meant for him depended now clearly on the amount of forbearance his recent action, or rather his recent inaction, had engendered. The image of the 'presence', whatever it was, waiting there for him to go – this image had not yet been so concrete for his nerves as when he stopped short of the point at which certainty would have come to him. For, with all his resolution, or more exactly with all his dread, he did stop short – he hung back from really seeing. The risk was too great and his fear too definite: it took at this moment an awful specific form.

He knew – yes, as he had never known anything – that, *should* he see the door open, it would all too abjectly be the end of him. It would mean that the agent of his shame – for his shame was the deep abjection – was once more at large and in general possession; and what glared him thus in the face was the act that this would determine for him. It would send him straight about to the window he had left open, and by that window, be long ladder and dangling rope as absent as they would, he saw himself uncontrollably, insanely, fatally take his way to the street. The hideous chance of this he at least could avert; but he could only avert it by recoiling in time from assurance. He had the whole house to deal with, this fact was still there; only he now knew that uncertainty alone could start him. He stole back from where he had checked himself – merely to do so was suddenly like safety – and, making blindly for the greater staircase, left gaping rooms and sounding passages behind. Here was the top of the stairs, with a fine large dim descent and three spacious landings to mark off. His instinct was all for mildness, but his feet were harsh on the floors, and, strangely, when he had in a couple of minutes become aware of this, it counted somehow for help. He couldn't have spoken, the tone of his voice would have scared him, and the common conceit or resource of 'whistling in the dark' (whether literally or figuratively) have appeared basely vulgar; yet he liked none the less to hear himself go, and when he had reached his first landing – taking it all with no rush, but quite steadily – that stage of success drew from him a gasp of relief.

The house, withal, seemed immense, the scale of space again inordinate; the open rooms, to no one of which his eyes deflected, gloomed in their shuttered state like mouths of caverns; only the high skylight that formed the crown of the deep well created for him a medium in which he could advance, but which might have been, for queerness of colour, some watery under-world. He tried to think of something noble, as that his property was really grand, a splendid possession; but this nobleness took the form too of the clear delight with which he was finally to sacrifice it. They might come in now, the builders, the destroyers – they might come as soon as they would. At the end of two flights he had dropped to another zone, and from the middle of the third, with only one more left, he recognised the influence of the lower windows, of half-drawn blinds, of the occasional gleam of street-lamps, of the glazed spaces of the vestibule. This was the bottom of the sea, which showed an illumination of its own and which he even saw paved – when at a given moment he drew up to sink a long look over the banisters – with the marble squares of his childhood. By that time indubitably he felt, as he might have said in a commoner cause, better; it had allowed him to stop and draw breath, and the ease increased with the sight of the old black-and-white slabs. But what he most felt was that now surely, with the element of impunity pulling him as by hard firm hands, the case was settled for what he might have seen above had he dared that last look. The closed door, blessedly remote now, was still closed – and he had only in short to reach that of the house.

He came down further, he crossed the passage forming the access to the last flight; and if here again he stopped an instant it was almost for the sharpness of the thrill of assured escape. It made him shut his eyes – which opened again to the straight slope of the remainder of the stairs. Here was impunity still, but impunity almost excessive; inasmuch as the side-lights and the high fan-tracery of the entrance were glimmering straight into the hall; an appearance produced, he the next instant saw, by the fact that the vestibule gaped wide, that the hinged halves of the inner door had been thrown far back. Out of that again the *question* sprang at him, making his eyes, as he felt, half-start from his head, as they had done, at the top of the house, before the sign of the other door. If he had left that one open, hadn't he left this one closed, and wasn't he now in *most* immediate presence of some inconceivable occult activity? It was as sharp, the question, as a knife in his side, but the answer hung fire still and seemed to lose itself in the vague darkness to which the thin admitted dawn, glimmering archwise over the whole outer door, made a semicircular margin, a cold silvery nimbus that seemed to play a little as he looked – to shift and expand and contract.

It was as if there had been something within it, protected by indistinctness and corresponding in extent with the opaque surface behind, the painted panels of the last barrier to his escape, of which the key was in his pocket. The indistinctness mocked him even while he stared, affected him as somehow shrouding or challenging certitude, so that after faltering an instant on his step he let himself go with the sense that here *was* at last something to meet, to touch, to take, to know – something all unnatural and dreadful, but to advance upon which was the condition for him either of liberation or of supreme defeat. The penumbra, dense and dark, was the virtual screen of a figure which stood in it as still as some image erect in a niche or as some black-vizored sentinel guarding a treasure. Brydon was to know afterwards, was to recall and make out, the particular thing he had believed during the rest of his descent. He saw, in its great grey glimmering margin, the central vagueness diminish, and he felt it to be taking the very form toward which, for so many days, the passion of his curiosity had yearned. It gloomed, it loomed, it was something, it was somebody, the prodigy of a personal presence.

Rigid and conscious, spectral yet human, a man of his own substance and stature waited there to measure himself with his power to dismay. This only could it be – this only till he recognised, with his advance, that what made the face dim was the pair of raised hands that covered it and in which, so far from being offered in defiance, it was buried as for dark deprecation. So Brydon, before him, took him in; with every fact of him now, in the higher light, hard and acute – his planted stillness, his vivid truth, his grizzled bent head and white masking hands, his queer actuality of evening-dress, of dangling double eye-glass, of gleaming silk lappet and white linen, of pearl button and gold watch-guard and polished shoe. No portrait by a great modern master could have presented him with more intensity, thrust him out of his frame with more art, as if there had been 'treatment', of the consummate sort, in his every shade and salience. The revulsion, for our friend, had become, before he knew it, immense – this drop, in the act of apprehension, to the sense of his adversary's inscrutable manoeuvre. That meaning at least, while he gaped, it offered him; for he could but gape at his other self in this other anguish, gape as a proof that *he*, standing there for the achieved, the enjoyed, the triumphant life, couldn't be faced in his triumph. Wasn't the proof in the splendid covering hands, strong and completely spread? – so spread and so intentional that, in spite of a special verity that surpassed every other, the fact that one of these hands had lost two fingers, which were reduced to stumps, as if accidentally shot away, the face was effectually guarded and saved.

'Saved', though, *would* it be? – Brydon breathed his wonder till the very impunity of his attitude and the very insistence of his eyes produced, as he felt, a sudden stir which showed the next instant as a deeper portent, while the head raised itself, the betrayal of a braver purpose. The hands, as he looked, began to move, to open; then, as if deciding in a flash, dropped from the face and left it uncovered and presented. Horror, with the sight, had leaped into Brydon's throat, gasping there in a sound he couldn't utter; for the bared identity was too hideous as *his*, and his glare was the passion of his protest. The face, *that* face, Spencer Brydon's? – he searched it still, but looking away from it in dismay and denial, falling straight from his height of sublimity. It was unknown, inconceivable, awful, disconnected from any possibility –! He had been 'sold', he inwardly moaned, stalking such game as this: the presence before him was a presence, the horror within him a horror, but the waste of his nights had been only grotesque and the success of his adventure an irony. Such an identity fitted his at *no* point, made its alternative monstrous. A thousand times yes, as it came upon him nearer now – the face was the face of a stranger. It came upon him nearer now, quite as one of those expanding fantastic images projected by the magic lantern of childhood; for the stranger, whoever he might be, evil, odious, blatant, vulgar, had advanced as for aggression, and he knew himself give ground. Then harder pressed still, sick with the force of his shock, and falling back as under the hot breath and the roused passion of a life larger than his own, a rage of personality before which his own collapsed, he felt the whole vision turn to darkness and his very feet give way. His head went round; he was going; he had gone.

III

WHAT had next brought him back, clearly – though after how long? – was Mrs Muldoon's voice, coming to him from quite near, from so near that he seemed presently to see her as kneeling on the ground before him while he lay looking up at her; himself not wholly on the ground, but half-raised and upheld – conscious, yes, of tenderness of support and, more particularly, of a head pillowed in extraordinary softness and faintly refreshing fragrance. He considered, he wondered, his wit but half at his service; then another face intervened, bending more directly over him, and he finally knew that Alice Staverton had made her lap an ample and perfect cushion to him, and that she had to this end seated herself on the lowest degree of the staircase, the rest of his long person remaining stretched on his old black-and-white slabs. They were cold, these marble squares of his youth; but *he* somehow was not, in this rich return of consciousness – the most wonderful hour, little by little, that he had ever known, leaving him, as it did, so gratefully, so abysmally passive, and yet as with a treasure of intelligence waiting all round him for quiet appropriation; dissolved, he might call it, in the air of the place and producing the golden glow of a late autumn afternoon. He had come back, yes – come back from further away than any man but himself had ever travelled; but it was strange how with this sense what he had come back *to* seemed really the great thing, and as if his prodigious journey had been all for the sake of it. Slowly but surely his consciousness grew, his vision of his state thus completing itself: he had been miraculously *carried* back – lifted and carefully borne as from where he had been picked up, the uttermost end of an interminable grey passage. Even with this he was suffered to rest, and what had now brought him to knowledge was the break in the long mild motion.

It had brought him to knowledge, to knowledge – yes, this was the beauty of his state; which came to resemble more and more that of a man who has gone to sleep on some news of a great inheritance, and then, after dreaming it away, after profaning it with matters strange to it, has waked up again to serenity of certitude and has only to lie and watch it grow. This was the drift of his patience – that he had only to let it shine on him. He must moreover, with intermissions, still have been lifted and borne; since why and how else should he have known himself, later on, with the afternoon glow intenser, no longer at the foot of his stairs – situated as these now seemed at that dark other end of his tunnel – but on a deep window-bench of his high saloon, over which had been spread, couch-fashion, a mantle of soft stuff lined with grey fur that was familiar to his eyes and that one of his hands kept fondly feeling as for its pledge of truth. Mrs Muldoon's face had gone, but the other, the second he had recognised, hung over him in a way that showed how he was still propped and pillowed. He took it all in, and the more he took it the more it seemed to suffice: he was as much at peace as if he had had food and drink. It was the two women who had found him, on Mrs Muldoon's having plied, at her usual hour, her latch-key – and on her having above all arrived while Miss Staverton still lingered near the house. She had been turning away, all anxiety, from worrying the vain bell-handle – her calculation having been of the hour of the good woman's visit; but the latter, blessedly, had come up while she was still there, and they had entered together. He had then lain, beyond the vestibule, very much as he was lying now – quite, that is, as he appeared to have fallen, but all so wondrously without bruise or gash; only in a depth of stupor. What he most took in, however, at present, with the steadier clearance, was that Alice Staverton had for a long unspeakable moment not doubted he was dead.

'It must have been that I *was*.' He made it out as she held him. 'Yes – I can only have died. You brought me literally to life. Only,' he wondered, his eyes rising to her, 'only, in the name of all the benedictions, how?'

It took her but an instant to bend her face and kiss him, and something in the manner of it, and in the way her hands clasped and locked his head while he felt the cool charity and virtue of her lips, something in all this beatitude somehow answered everything. 'And now I keep you,' she said.

'Oh keep me, keep me!' he pleaded while her face still hung over him: in response to which it dropped again and stayed close, clingingly close. It was the seal of their situation – of which he tasted the impress for a long blissful moment in silence. But he came back. 'Yet how did you know –?'

'I was uneasy. You were to have come, you remember – and you had sent no word.'

'Yes, I remember – I was to have gone to you at one to-day.' It caught on to their 'old' life and relation – which were so near and so far. 'I was still out there in my strange darkness – where was it, what was it? I must have stayed there so long.' He could but wonder at the depth and the duration of his swoon.

'Since last night?' she asked with a shade of fear for her possible indiscretion.

'Since this morning – it must have been: the cold dim dawn of to-day. Where have I been,' he vaguely wailed, 'where have I been?' He felt her hold him close, and it was as if this helped him now to make in all security his mild moan. 'What a long dark day!'

All in her tenderness she had waited a moment. 'In the cold dim dawn?' she quavered.

But he had already gone on piecing together the parts of the whole prodigy. 'As I didn't turn up you came straight –?'

She barely cast about. 'I went first to your hotel – where they told me of your absence. You had dined out last evening and hadn't been back since. But they appeared to know you had been at your club.'

'So you had the idea of *this* –?'

'Of what?' she asked in a moment.

'Well – of what has happened.'

'I believed at least you'd have been here. I've known, all along,' she said, 'that you've been coming.'

' "Known" it –?'

'Well, I've believed it. I said nothing to you after that talk we had a month ago – but I felt sure. I knew you *would*,' she declared.

'That I'd persist, you mean?'

'That you'd see him.'

'Ah but I didn't!' cried Brydon with his long wail. 'There's somebody – an awful beast; whom I brought, too horribly, to bay. But it's not me.'

At this she bent over him again, and her eyes were in his eyes. 'No – it's not you.' And it was as if, while her face hovered, he might have made out in it, hadn't it been so near, some particular meaning blurred by a smile. 'No, thank heaven,' she repeated – 'it's not you! Of course it wasn't to have been.'

'Ah but it *was*,' he gently insisted. And he stared before him now as he had been staring for so many weeks. 'I was to have known myself.'

'You couldn't!' she returned consolingly. And then reverting, and as if to account further for what she had herself done, 'But it wasn't only *that*, that you hadn't been at home,' she went on. 'I waited till the hour at which we had found Mrs Muldoon that day of my going with you; and she arrived, as I've told you, while, failing to bring any one to the door, I lingered in my despair on the steps. After a little, if she hadn't come, by such a mercy, I should have found means to hunt her up. But it wasn't,' said Alice Staverton, as if once more with her fine intention – 'it wasn't only that.'

His eyes, as he lay, turned back to her. 'What more then?'

She met it, the wonder she had stirred. 'In the cold dim dawn, you say? Well, in the cold dim dawn of this morning I too saw you.'

'Saw *me* –?'

'Saw *him*,' said Alice Staverton. 'It must have been at the same moment.'

He lay an instant taking it in – as if he wished to be quite reasonable. 'At the same moment?'

'Yes – in my dream again, the same one I've named to you. He came back to me. Then I knew it for a sign. He had come to you.'

At this Brydon raised himself; he had to see her better. She helped him when she understood his movement, and he sat up, steadying himself beside her there on the window-bench and with his right hand grasping her left. '*He* didn't come to me.'

'You came to yourself,' she beautifully smiled.

'Ah I've come to myself now – thanks to you, dearest. But this brute, with his awful face – this brute's a black stranger. He's none of *me*, even as I *might* have been,' Brydon sturdily declared.

But she kept the clearness that was like the breath of infallibility. 'Isn't the whole point that you'd have been different?'

He almost scowled for it. 'As different as *that* –?'

Her look again was more beautiful to him than the things of this world. 'Haven't you exactly wanted to know *how* different? So this morning,' she said, 'you appeared to me.'

'Like *him*?'

'A black stranger!'

'Then how did you know it was I?'

'Because, as I told you weeks ago, my mind, my imagination, had worked so over what you might, what you mightn't have been – to show you, you see, how I've thought of you. In the midst of that you came to me – that my wonder might be answered. So I knew,' she went on; 'and believed that, since the question held you too so fast, as you told me that day, you too would see for yourself. And when this morning I again saw I knew it would be because you had – and also then, from the first moment, because you somehow wanted me. *He* seemed to tell me of that. So why,' she strangely smiled, 'shouldn't I like him?'

It brought Spencer Brydon to his feet. 'You "like" that horror –?'

'I *could* have liked him. And to me,' she said, 'he was no horror. I had accepted him.'

' "Accepted" –?' Brydon oddly sounded.

'Before, for the interest of his difference – yes. And as *I* didn't disown him, as *I* knew him – which you at last, confronted with him in his difference, so cruelly didn't, my dear – well, he must have been, you see, less dreadful to me. And it may have pleased him that I pitied him.'

She was beside him on her feet, but still holding his hand – still with her arm supporting him. But though it all brought for him thus a dim light, 'You "pitied" him?' he grudgingly, resentfully asked.

'He has been unhappy, he has been ravaged,' she said.

'And haven't I been unhappy? Am not I – you've only to look at me! – ravaged?'

'Ah I don't say I like him *better*,' she granted after a thought. 'But he's grim, he's worn – and things have happened to him. He doesn't make shift, for sight, with your charming monocle.'

'No' – it struck Brydon: 'I couldn't have sported mine "downtown". They'd have guyed me there.'

'His great convex pince-nez – I saw it, I recognised the kind – is for his poor ruined sight. And his poor right hand –!'

'Ah!' Brydon winced – whether for his proved identity or for his lost fingers. Then, 'He has a million a year,' he lucidly added. 'But he hasn't you.'

'And he isn't – no, he isn't – *you*!' she murmured as he drew her to his breast.

CRAPY CORNELIA

I

THREE times within a quarter of an hour – shifting the while his posture on his chair of contemplation – had he looked at his watch as for its final sharp hint that he should decide, that he should get up. His seat was one of a group fairly sequestered, unoccupied save for his own presence, and from where he lingered he looked off at a stretch of lawn freshened by recent April showers and on which sundry small children were at play. The trees, the shrubs, the plants, every stem and twig just ruffled as by the first touch of the light finger of the relenting year, struck him as standing still in the blest hope of more of the same caress; the quarter about him held its breath after the fashion of the child who waits with the rigour of an open mouth and shut eyes for the promised sensible effect of his having been good. So, in the windless, sun-warmed air of the beautiful afternoon, the Park of the winter's end had struck White-Mason as waiting; even New York, under such an impression, was 'good', good enough – for *him*: its very sounds were faint, were almost sweet, as they reached him from so seemingly far beyond the wooded horizon that formed the remoter limit of his large shallow glade. The tones of the frolic infants ceased to be nondescript and harsh, were in fact almost as fresh and decent as the frilled and puckered and ribboned garb of the little girls, which had always a way, in those parts, of so portentously flaunting the daughters of the strange native – that is of the overwhelmingly alien – populace at him.

Not that these things in particular were his matter of meditation now; he had wanted, at the end of his walk, to sit apart a little and think – and had been doing that for twenty minutes, even though as yet to no break in the charm of procrastination. But he had looked without seeing and listened without hearing: all that had been positive for him was that he hadn't failed vaguely to feel. He had felt in the first place, and he continued to feel – yes, at forty-eight quite as much as at any

point of the supposed region of younger intensities – the great
spirit of the air, the fine sense of the season, the supreme appeal
of Nature, he might have said, to his time of life; quite as if she,
easy, indulgent, indifferent, cynical Power, were offering him
the last chance it would rest with his wit or his blood to
embrace. Then with that he had been entertaining, to the
point and with the prolonged consequence of accepted immo-
bilization, the certitude that if he did call on Mrs Worthingham
and find her at home he couldn't in justice to himself not put to
her the question that had lapsed the other time, the last time,
through the irritating and persistent, even if accidental, presence of others. What friends she had – the people who so
stupidly, so wantonly stuck! If they *should*, he and she, come
to an understanding, that would presumably have to include
certain members of her singularly ill-composed circle, in whom
it was incredible to him that he should ever take an interest.
This defeat, to do himself justice – he had bent rather predominantly on *that*, you see; ideal justice to *her*, with her
possible conception of what it should consist of being another
and quite a different matter – he had had the fact of the Sunday
afternoon to thank for; she didn't 'keep' that day for him, since
they hadn't, up to now, quite begun to cultivate the appointment or assignation founded on explicit sacrifices. He might at
any rate look to find this pleasant practical Wednesday – should
he indeed, at his actual rate, stay it before it ebbed – more
liberally and intendingly given him.

The sound he at last most wittingly distinguished in his nook
was the single deep note of half-past five borne to him from
some high-perched public clock. He finally got up with the
sense that the time from then on *ought* at least to be felt as
sacred to him. At this juncture it was – while he stood there
shaking his garments, settling his hat, his necktie, his shirtcuffs, fixing the high polish of his fine shoes as if for some
reflection in it of his straight and spare and grizzled, his refined
and trimmed and dressed, his altogether distinguished person,
that of a gentleman abundantly settled, but of a bachelor markedly nervous – at this crisis it was, doubtless, that he at once
most measured and least resented his predicament. If he should

go he would almost to a certainty find her, and if he should find her he would almost to a certainty come to the point. He wouldn't put it off again – there was that high consideration for him of justice at least to himself. He had never yet denied himself anything so apparently fraught with possibilities as the idea of proposing to Mrs Worthingham – never yet, in other words, denied himself anything he had so distinctly wanted to do; and the results of that wisdom had remained for him precisely the precious parts of experience. Counting only the offers of his honourable hand, these had been on three remembered occasions at least the consequence of an impulse as sharp and a self-respect that hadn't in the least suffered, moreover, from the failure of each appeal. He had been met in the three cases – the only ones he at all compared with his present case – by the frank confession that he didn't somehow, charming as he was, cause himself to be superstitiously believed in; and the lapse of life, afterward, had cleared up many doubts.

It *wouldn't* have done, he eventually, he lucidly saw, each time he had been refused; and the candour of his nature was such that he could live to think of these very passages as a proof of how right he had been – right, that is, to have put himself forward always, by the happiest instinct, only in impossible conditions. He had the happy consciousness of having exposed the important question to the crucial test, and of having escaped, by that persistent logic, a grave mistake. What better proof of his escape than the fact that he was now free to renew the all-interesting inquiry, and should be exactly about to do so in different and better conditions? The conditions were better by as much more – as much more of his career and character, of his situation, his reputation he could even have called it, of his knowledge of life, of his somewhat extended means, of his possibly augmented charm, of his certainly improved mind and temper – as was involved in the actual impending settlement. Once he had got into motion, once he had crossed the Park and passed out of it, entering, with very little space to traverse, one of the short new streets that abutted on its east side, his step became that of a man young enough to find confidence, quite to find felicity, in the sense, in almost any sense, of action. He could still enjoy almost anything, absolutely an unpleasant thing, in default of a better, that might still remind him he wasn't so old. The standing newness of everything about him would, it was true, have weakened this cheer by too much presuming on it; Mrs Worthingham's house, before which he stopped, had that gloss of new money, that glare of a piece fresh from the mint and ringing for the first time on any counter, which seems to claim for it, in any transaction, something more than the 'face' value.

This could but be yet more the case for the impression of the observer introduced and committed. On our friend's part I mean, after his admission and while still in the hall, the sense of the general shining immediacy, of the still unhushed clamour of the shock, was perhaps stronger than he had ever known it. That broke out from every corner as the high pitch of interest, and with a candour that – no, certainly – he had never seen equalled; every particular expensive object shrieking at him in its artless pride that it had just 'come home'. He met the whole vision with something of the grimace produced on persons without goggles by the passage from a shelter to a blinding light; and if he had – by a perfectly possible chance – been 'snap-shotted' on the spot, would have struck you as showing for his first tribute to the temple of Mrs Worthingham's charming presence a scowl almost of anguish. He wasn't constitutionally, it may at once be explained for him, a goggled person; and he was condemned in New York to this frequent violence of transition – having to reckon with it whenever he went out, as who should say, from himself. The high pitch of interest, to his taste, was the pitch of history, the pitch of acquired and earned suggestion, the pitch of association, in a word; so that he lived by preference, incontestably, if not in a rich gloom, which would have been beyond his means and spirits, at least amid objects and images that confessed to the tone of time.

He had ever felt that an indispensable presence – with a need of it moreover that interfered at no point with his gentle habit, not to say his subtle art, of drawing out what was left him of his youth, of thinly and thriftily spreading the rest of that choicest jam-pot of the cupboard of consciousness over the remainder of a slice of life still possibly thick enough to bear it; or in other words of moving the melancholy limits, the significant signs, constantly a little further on, very much as property-marks or staked boundaries are sometimes stealthily shifted at night. He positively cherished in fact, as against the too inveterate gesture of distressfully guarding his eyeballs – so many New York aspects seemed to keep him at it – an ideal of adjusted appreciation, of courageous curiosity, of fairly letting the world about him, a world of constant breathless renewals and merciless substitutions, make its flaring assault on its own inordinate terms. Newness *was* value in the piece – for the acquisitor, or at least sometimes might be, even though the act of 'blowing' hard, the act marking a heated freshness of arrival, or other form of irruption, could never minister to the peace of those already and long on the field; and this if only because maturer tone was after all most appreciable and most consoling when one staggered back to it, wounded, bleeding, blinded, from the riot of the raw – or, to put the whole experience more prettily, no doubt, from excesses of light.

II

IF he went in, however, with something of his more or less inevitable scowl, there were really, at the moment, two rather valid reasons for screened observation; the first of these being that the whole place seemed to reflect as never before the lustre of Mrs Worthingham's own polished and prosperous little person – to smile, it struck him, with her smile, to twinkle not only with the gleam of her lovely teeth, but with that of all her rings and brooches and bangles and other gew-gaws, to curl and spasmodically cluster as in emulation of her charming complicated yellow tresses, to surround the most animated of pink-and-white, of ruffled and ribboned, of frilled and festooned Dresden china shepherdesses with exactly the right system of rococo curves and convolutions and other flourishes, a perfect bower of painted and gilded and moulded conceits. The second ground of this immediate impression of scenic extravagance, almost as if the curtain rose for him to the first

act of some small and expensively mounted comic opera, was
that she hadn't, after all, awaited him in fond singleness, but
had again just a trifle inconsiderately exposed him to the drawback of having to reckon, for whatever design he might amiably
entertain, with the presence of a third and quite superfluous
person, a small black insignificant but none the less oppressive
stranger. It was odd how, on the instant, the little lady engaged
with her did affect him as comparatively black – very much as if
that had absolutely, in such a medium, to be the graceless
appearance of any item not positively of some fresh shade of a
light colour or of some pretty pretension to a charming twist.
Any witness of their meeting, his hostess should surely have
felt, would have been a false note in the whole rosy glow; but
what note so false as that of the dingy little presence that she
might actually, by a refinement of her perhaps always too
visible study of effect, have provided as a positive contrast or
foil? whose name and intervention, moreover, she appeared to
be no more moved to mention and account for than she might
have been to 'present' – whether as stretched at her feet or erect
upon disciplined haunches – some shaggy old domesticated
terrier or poodle.

Extraordinarily, after he had been in the room five minutes –
a space of time during which his fellow-visitor had neither
budged nor uttered a sound – he had made Mrs Worthingham
out as all at once perfectly pleased to see him, completely aware
of what he had most in mind, and singularly serene in face of his
sense of their impediment. It was as if for all the world she
didn't take it for one, the immobility, to say nothing of the
seeming equanimity, of their tactless companion; at whom
meanwhile indeed our friend himself, after his first ruffled
perception, no more adventured a look than if advised by his
constitutional kindness that to notice her in any degree would
perforce be ungraciously to glower. He talked after a fashion
with the woman as to whose power to please and amuse and
serve him, as to whose really quite organised and indicated
fitness for lighting up his autumn afternoon of life his conviction had lately strained itself so clear; but he was all the
while carrying on an intenser exchange with his own spirit

and trying to read into the charming creature's behaviour, as he could only call it, some confirmation of his theory that she also had her inward flutter and anxiously counted on him. He found support, happily for the conviction just named, in the idea, at no moment as yet really repugnant to him, the idea bound up in fact with the finer essence of her appeal, that she had her own vision too of her quality and her price, and that the last appearance she would have liked to bristle with was that of being forewarned and eager.

He had, if he came to think of it, scarce definitely warned her, and he probably wouldn't have taken to her so consciously in the first instance without an appreciative sense that, as she was a little person of twenty superficial graces, so she was also a little person with her secret pride. She might just have planted her mangy lion – not to say her muzzled house-dog – there in his path as a symbol that she wasn't cheap and easy; which would be a thing he couldn't possibly wish his future wife to have shown herself in advance, even if to him alone. That she could make him put himself such questions was precisely part of the attaching play of her iridescent surface, the shimmering interfusion of her various aspects; that of her youth with her independence – her pecuniary perhaps in particular, that of her vivacity with her beauty, that of her facility above all with her odd novelty; the high modernity, as people appeared to have come to call it, that made her so much more 'knowing' in some directions than even he, man of the world as he certainly was, could pretend to be, though all on a basis of the most unconscious and instinctive and luxurious assumption. She was 'up' to everything, aware of everything – if one counted from a short enough time back (from week before last, say, and as if quantities of history had burst upon the world within the fortnight); she was likewise surprised at nothing, and in that direction one might reckon as far ahead as the rest of her lifetime, or at any rate as the rest of his, which was all that would concern him: it was as if the suitability of the future to her personal and rather pampered tastes was what she most took for granted, so that he could see her, for all her Dresden-china shoes and her flutter of wondrous befrilled contemporary skirts, skip by the side of the coming age as over the floor of a ball-room, keeping step with its monstrous stride and prepared for every figure of the dance.

Her outlook took form to him suddenly as a great square sunny window that hung in assured fashion over the immensity of life. There rose toward it as from a vast swarming *plaza* a high tide of motion and sound; yet it was at the same time as if even while he looked her light gemmed hand, flashing on him in addition to those other things the perfect polish of the prettiest pink finger-nails in the world, had touched a spring, the most ingenious of recent devices for instant ease, which dropped half across the scene a soft-coloured mechanical blind, a fluttered fringed awning of charmingly toned silk, such as would make a bath of cool shade for the favoured friend leaning with her there – that is for the happy couple itself – on the balcony. The great view would be the prospect and privilege of the very state he coveted – since didn't he covet it? – the state of being so securely at her side; while the wash of privacy, as one might count it, the broad fine brush dipped into clear umber and passed, full and wet, straight across the strong scheme of colour, would represent the security itself, all the uplifted inner elegance, the condition, so ideal, of being shut out from nothing and yet of having, so gaily and breezily aloft, none of the burden or worry of anything. Thus, as I say, for our friend, the place itself, while his vivid impression lasted, portentously opened and spread, and what was before him took, to his vision, though indeed at so other a crisis, the form of the 'glimmering square' of the poet; yet, for a still more remarkable fact, with an incongruous object usurping at a given instant the privilege of the frame and seeming, even as he looked, to block the view.

The incongruous object was a woman's head, crowned with a little sparsely feathered black hat, an ornament quite unlike those the women mostly noticed by White-Mason were now 'wearing', and that grew and grew, that came nearer and nearer, while it met his eyes, after the manner of images in the cinematograph. It had presently loomed so large that he saw nothing else – not only among the things at a considerable distance, the things Mrs Worthingham would eventually, yet unmistakeably,

introduce him to, but among those of this lady's various attributes and appurtenances as to which he had been in the very act
of cultivating his consciousness. It was in the course of another
minute the most extraordinary thing in the world: everything
had altered, dropped, darkened, disappeared; his imagination
had spread its wings only to feel them flop all grotesquely at its
sides as he recognised in his hostess's quiet companion, the
oppressive alien who hadn't indeed interfered with his fanciful
flight, though she had prevented his immediate declaration and
brought about the thud, not to say the felt violent shock, of his
fall to earth, the perfectly plain identity of Cornelia Rasch. It
was she who had remained there at attention; it was she their
companion hadn't introduced; it was she he had forborne to
face with his fear of incivility. He stared at her – everything else
went.

'Why, it has been *you* all this time?'

Miss Rasch fairly turned pale. 'I was waiting to see if you'd
know me.'

'Ah, my dear Cornelia' – he came straight out with it –
'rather!'

'Well, it isn't,' she returned with a quick change to red now,
'from having taken much time to look at me!'

She smiled, she even laughed, but he could see how she had
felt his unconsciousness, poor thing; the acquaintance, quite
the friend of his youth, as she had been, the associate of his
childhood, of his early manhood, of his middle age in fact, up to
a few years back, not more than ten at the most; the associate
too of so many of his associates and of almost all of his relations,
those of the other time, those who had mainly gone for ever; the
person in short whose noted disappearance, though it might
have seemed final, had been only of recent seasons. She was
present again now, all unexpectedly – he had heard of her
having at last, left alone after successive deaths and with scant
resources, sought economic salvation in Europe, the promised
land of American thrift – she was present as this almost ancient
and this oddly unassertive little rotund figure whom one
seemed no more obliged to address than if she had been a
black satin ottoman 'treated' with buttons and gimp; a class

of object as to which the policy of blindness was imperative. He felt the need of some explanatory plea, and before he could think had uttered one at Mrs Worthingham's expense. 'Why, you see we weren't introduced!'

'No – but I didn't suppose I should have to be named to you.'

'Well, my dear woman, you haven't – do me that justice!' He could at least make this point. 'I felt all the while –!' However it would have taken him long to say what he had been feeling; and he was aware now of the pretty projected light of Mrs Worthingham's wonder. She looked as if, out for a walk with her, he had put her to the inconvenience of his stopping to speak to a strange woman in the street.

'I never supposed you knew her!' – it was to him his hostess excused herself.

This made Miss Rasch spring up, distinctly flushed, distinctly strange to behold, but not vulgarly nettled – Cornelia was incapable of that; only rather funnily bridling and laughing, only showing that this was all she had waited for, only saying just the right thing, the thing she could make so clearly a jest. 'Of course if you *had* you'd have presented him.'

Mrs Worthingham looked while answering at White-Mason. 'I didn't want you to go – which you see you do as soon as he speaks to you. But I never dreamed –!'

'That there was anything between us? Ah, there are no end of things!' He, on his side, though addressing the younger and prettier woman, looked at his fellow-guest; to whom he even continued: 'When did you get back? May I come and see you the very first thing?'

Cornelia gasped and wriggled – she practically giggled; she had lost every atom of her little old, her little young, though always unaccountable, prettiness, which used to peep so, on the bare chance of a shot, from behind indefensible features, that it almost made watching her a form of sport. He had heard vaguely of her, it came back to him (for there had been no letters; their later acquaintance, thank goodness, hadn't involved that), as experimenting, for economy, and then as settling, to the same rather dismal end, somewhere in England, at one of those intensely English places, St Leonards, Cheltenham, Bognor, Dawlish – which, awfully, *was* it? – and she now affected him for all the world as some small, squirming, exclaiming, genteelly conversing old maid of a type vaguely associated with the three-volume novels he used to feed on (besides his so often encountering it in 'real life') during a far-away stay of his own at Brighton. Odder than any element of his ex-gossip's identity itself, however, was the fact that she somehow, with it all, rejoiced his sight. Indeed the supreme oddity was that the manner of her reply to his request for leave to call should have absolutely charmed his attention. She didn't look at him; she only, from under her frumpy, crapy, curiously exotic hat, and with her good little near-sighted insinuating glare, expressed to Mrs Worthingham, while she answered him, wonderful arch things, the overdone things of a shy woman. 'Yes, you may call – but only when this dear lovely lady has done with you!' The moment after which she had gone.

III

FORTY minutes later he was taking his way back from the queer miscarriage of his adventure; taking it, with no conscious positive felicity, through the very spaces that had witnessed shortly before the considerable serenity of his assurance. He had said to himself then, or had as good as said it, that, since he might do perfectly as he liked, it couldn't fail for him that he must soon retrace those steps, humming, to all intents, the first bars of a wedding-march; so beautifully had it cleared up that he was 'going to like' letting Mrs Worthingham accept him. He was to have hummed no wedding-march, as it seemed to be turning out – he had none, up to now, to hum; and yet, extraordinarily, it wasn't in the least because she had refused him. Why then hadn't he liked as much as he had intended to like it putting the pleasant act, the act of not refusing him, in her power? Could it all have come from the awkward minute of his failure to decide sharply, on Cornelia's departure, whether or no he would attend her to the door? He hadn't decided at all – what the deuce had been in him? – but had danced to and fro in the room, thinking better of each impulse and then thinking worse. He had hesitated like an ass erect on absurd hind legs between two bundles of hay; the upshot of which must have been his giving the falsest impression. In what way that was to be for an instant considered had their common past committed him to crazy Cornelia? He repudiated with a whack on the gravel any ghost of an obligation.

What he could get rid of with scanter success, unfortunately, was the peculiar sharpness of his sense that, though mystified by his visible flurry – and yet not mystified enough for a sympathetic question either – his hostess had been, on the whole, even more frankly diverted: which was precisely an example of that newest, freshest, finest freedom in her, the air and the candour of assuming, not 'heartlessly', not viciously, not even very consciously, but with a bright pampered confidence which would probably end by affecting one's nerves as the most impertinent stroke in the world, that every blest thing coming up for her in any connection was somehow matter for her general recreation. There she was again with the innocent egotism, the gilded and overflowing anarchism, really, of her doubtless quite unwitting but none the less rabid modern note. Her grace of ease was perfect, but it was all grace of ease, not a single shred of it grace of uncertainty or of difficulty – which meant, when you came to see, that, for its happy working, not a grain of provision was left by it to mere manners. This was clearly going to be the music of the future – that if people were but rich enough and furnished enough and fed enough, exercised and sanitated and manicured, and generally advised and advertised and made 'knowing' enough, *avertis* enough, as the term appeared to be nowadays in Paris, all they had to do for civility was to take the amused ironic view of those who might be less initiated. In *his* time, when he was young or even when he was only but a little less middle-aged, the best manners had been the best kindness, and the best kindness had mostly been some art of not insisting on one's luxurious differences, of concealing rather, for common humanity, if not for common decency, a part at least of the intensity or the ferocity with which one might be 'in the know'.

Oh, the 'know' – Mrs Worthingham was in it, all instinctively, inevitably and as a matter of course, up to her eyes; which didn't, however, the least little bit prevent her being as ignorant as a fish of everything that really and intimately and fundamentally concerned *him*, poor dear old White-Mason. She didn't, in the first place, so much as know who he was – by which he meant know who and what it was to *be* a White-Mason, even a poor and a dear and old one, 'anyway'. That indeed – he did her perfect justice – was of the very essence of the newness and freshness and beautiful, brave social irresponsibility by which she had originally dazzled him: just exactly that circumstance of her having no instinct for any old quality or quantity or identity, a single historic or social value, as he might say, of the New York of his already almost legendary past; and that additional one of his, on his side, having, so far as this went, cultivated blankness, cultivated positive prudence, as to her own personal background – the vagueness, at the best, with which all honest gentlefolk, the New Yorkers of his approved stock and conservative generation, were content, as for the most part they were indubitably wise, to surround the origins and antecedents and queer unimaginable early influences of persons swimming into their ken from those parts of the country that quite necessarily and naturally figured to their view as 'God-forsaken' and generally impossible.

The few scattered surviving representatives of a society once 'good' – *rari nantes in gurgite vasto* – were liable, at the pass things had come to, to meet, and even amid old shades once sacred, or what was left of such, every form of social impossibility, and, more irresistibly still, to find these apparitions often carry themselves (often at least in the case of the women) with a wondrous wild gallantry, equally imperturbable and inimitable, the sort of thing that reached its maximum in Mrs Worthingham. Beyond that who ever wanted to look up their annals, to reconstruct their steps and stages, to dot their i's in fine, or to 'go behind' anything that was theirs? One wouldn't do that for the world – a rudimentary discretion forbade it; and

yet this check from elementary undiscussable taste quite consorted with a due respect for them, or at any rate with a due
respect for oneself in connection with them; as was just exemplified in what would be his own, what would be poor dear old
White-Mason's, insurmountable aversion to having, on any
pretext, the doubtless very queer spectre of the late Mr
Worthingham presented to him. No question had he asked, or
would he ever ask, should his life – that is should the success of
his courtship – even intimately depend on it, either about that
obscure agent of his mistress's actual affluence or about the
happy headspring itself, and the apparently copious tributaries,
of the golden stream.

From all which marked anomalies, at any rate, what was the
moral to draw? He dropped into a Park chair again with that
question, he lost himself in the wonder of why he had come
away with his homage so very much unpaid. Yet it didn't seem
at all, actually, as if he could say or conclude, as if he could do
anything but keep on worrying – just in conformity with his
being a person who, whether or no familiar with the need to
make his conduct square with his conscience and his taste, was
never wholly exempt from that of making his taste and his
conscience square with his conduct. To this latter occupation
he further abandoned himself, and it didn't release him from
his second brooding session till the sweet spring sunset had
begun to gather and he had more or less cleared up, in the
deepening dusk, the effective relation between the various parts
of his ridiculously agitating experience. There were vital facts
he seemed thus to catch, to seize, with a nervous hand, and the
twilight helping, by their vaguely-whisked tails; unquiet truths
that swarmed out after the fashion of creatures bold only at
eventide, creatures that hovered and circled, that verily
brushed his nose, in spite of their shyness. Yes, he had practically just sat on with his 'mistress' – heaven save the mark! – as if
not to come to the point; as if it had absolutely come up that
there would be something rather vulgar and awful in doing so.
The whole stretch of his stay after Cornelia's withdrawal had
been consumed by his almost ostentatiously treating himself to
the opportunity of which he was to make nothing. It was as if he

had sat and watched himself – that came back to him: Shall I now or shan't I? Will I now or won't I? Say within the next three minutes, say by a quarter past six, or by twenty minutes past, at the furthest – always if nothing more comes up to prevent.

What had already come up to prevent was, in the strangest and drollest, or at least in the most preposterous, way in the world, that not Cornelia's presence, but her very absence, with its distraction of his thoughts, the thoughts that lumbered after her, had made the difference; and without his being the least able to tell why and how. He put it to himself after a fashion by the image that, this distraction once created, his working round to his hostess again, his reverting to the matter of his errand, began suddenly to represent a return from so far. That was simply all – or rather a little less than all; for something else had contributed. 'I never dreamed you knew her,' and 'I never dreamed *you* did,' was inevitably what had been exchanged between them – supplemented by Mrs Worthingham's mere scrap of an explanation: 'Oh, yes – to the small extent you see. Two years ago in Switzerland when I was at a high place for an "aftercure", during twenty days of incessant rain, she was the only person in an hotel of roaring, gorging, smoking Germans with whom I couldn't have a word of talk. She and I were the only speakers of English, and were thrown together like castaways on a desert island and in a raging storm. She was ill besides, and she had no maid, and mine looked after her, and she was very grateful – writing to me later on and saying she should certainly come to see me if she ever returned to New York. She *has* returned, you see – and there she was, poor little creature!' Such was Mrs Worthingham's tribute – to which even his asking her if Miss Rasch had ever happened to speak of him caused her practically to add nothing. Visibly she had never thought again of anyone Miss Rasch had spoken of or anything Miss Rasch had said; right as she was, naturally, about her being a little clever queer creature. This was perfectly true, and yet it was probably – by being *all* she could dream of about her – what had paralysed his proper gallantry. Its effect had been not in what it simply stated, but in what, under his secretly disintegrating criticism, it almost luridly symbolised.

He had quitted his seat in the Louis Quinze drawing-room without having, as he would have described it, done anything but give the lady of the scene a superior chance not to betray a defeated hope – not, that is, to fail of the famous 'pride' mostly supposed to prop even the most infatuated women at such junctures; by which chance, to do her justice, she had thoroughly seemed to profit. But he finally rose from his later station with a feeling of better success. He had by a happy turn of his hand got hold of the most precious, the least obscure of the flitting, circling things that brushed his ears. What he wanted – as justifying for him a little further consideration – was there before him from the moment he could put it that Mrs Worthingham had no data. He almost hugged that word – it suddenly came to mean so much to him. No data, he felt, for a conception of the sort of thing the New York of 'his time' had been in his personal life – the New York so unexpectedly, so vividly, and, as he might say, so perversely called back to all his senses by its identity with that of poor Cornelia's time: since even she had had a time, small show as it was likely to make now, and his time and hers had been the same. Cornelia figured to him while he walked away as by contrast and opposition a massive little bundle of data; his impatience to go to see her sharpened as he thought of this: so certainly should he find out that wherever he might touch her, with a gentle though firm pressure, he would, as the fond visitor of old houses taps and fingers a disfeatured, over-papered wall with the conviction of a wainscot-edge beneath, recognise some small extrusion of history.

IV

THERE would have been a wonder for us meanwhile in his continued use, as it were, of his happy formula – brought out to Cornelia Rasch within ten minutes, or perhaps only within twenty, of his having settled into the quite comfortable chair that, two days later, she indicated to him by her fireside. He had arrived at her address through the fortunate chance of his having noticed her card, as he went out, deposited, in the good old New York fashion, on one of the rococo tables of Mrs Worthingham's hall. His eye had been caught by the pencilled indication that was to affect him, the next instant, as fairly placed there for his sake. This had really been his luck, for he shouldn't have liked to write to Mrs Worthingham for guidance – *that* he felt, though too impatient just now to analyse the reluctance. There was nobody else he could have approached for a clue, and with this reflection he was already aware of how it testified to their rare little position, his and Cornelia's – position as conscious, ironic, pathetic survivors together of a dead and buried society – that there would have been, in all the town, under such stress, not a member of their old circle left to turn to. Mrs Worthingham had practically, even if accidentally, helped him to knowledge; the last nail in the coffin of the poor dear extinct past had been planted for him by his having thus to reach his antique contemporary through perforation of the newest newness. The note of this particular recognition was in fact the more prescribed to him that the ground of Cornelia's return to a scene swept so bare of the associational charm was certainly inconspicuous. What had she then come back for? – he had asked himself that; with the effect of deciding that it probably would have been, a little, to 'look after' her remnant of property. Perhaps she had come to save what little might still remain of that shrivelled interest; perhaps she had been, by those who took care of it for her, further swindled and despoiled, so that she wished to get at the facts. Perhaps on the other hand – it was a more cheerful chance – her invest-ments, decently administered, were making larger returns, so that the rigorous thrift of Bognor could be finally relaxed.

He had little to learn about the attraction of Europe, and rather expected that in the event of his union with Mrs Worthingham he should find himself pleading for it with the competence of one more in the 'know' about Paris and Rome, about Venice and Florence, than even she could be. He could have lived on in *his* New York, that is in the sentimental, the spiritual, the more or less romantic visitation of it; but had it been positive for him that he could live on in hers? – unless indeed the possibility of this had been just (like the famous *vertige de l'abîme*), like the solicitation of danger, or otherwise of the dreadful) the very hinge of his whole dream. However that might be, his curiosity was occupied rather with the conceivable hinge of poor Cornelia's: it was perhaps thinkable that even Mrs Worthingham's New York, once it should have become possible again at all, might have put forth to this lone exile a plea that wouldn't be in the chords of Bognor. For himself, after all, too, the attraction had been much more of the Europe over which one might move at one's ease, and which therefore could but cost, and cost much, right and left, than of the Europe adapted to scrimping. He saw himself on the whole scrimping with more zest even in Mrs Worthingham's New York than under the inspiration of Bognor. Apart from which it was yet again odd, not to say perceptibly pleasing to him, to note where the emphasis of his interest fell in this fumble of fancy over such felt oppositions as the new, the latest, the luridest power of money and the ancient reserves and moderations and mediocrities. These last struck him as showing by contrast the old brown surface and tone as of velvet rubbed and worn, shabby, and even a bit dingy, but all soft and subtle and still velvety – which meant still dignified; whereas the angular facts of current finance were as harsh and metallic and bewildering as some stacked 'exhibit' of ugly patented inventions, things his mediaeval mind forbade his taking in. He had, for instance, the sense of knowing the pleasant little old Rasch fortune – pleasant as far as it went; blurred memories and impressions of what it had been and what it hadn't, of how it had grown and how languished and how melted; they came back to him and put on such vividness that he could almost have figured himself testify for them before a bland and encouraging Board. The idea of taking the field in any manner on the subject of Mrs Worthingham's resources would have affected him on the other hand as an odious ordeal, some glare of embarrassment and exposure in a circle of hard unhelpful attention, of converging, derisive, unsuggestive eyes.

In Cornelia's small and quite cynically modern flat – the house had a grotesque name, 'The Gainsborough', but at least wasn't an awful boarding-house, as he had feared, and she could receive him quite honourably, which was so much to the good – he would have been ready to use at once to her the greatest freedom of friendly allusion: 'Have you still your old "family interest" in those two houses in Seventh Avenue? – one of which was next to a corner grocery, don't you know? and was occupied as to its lower part by a candy-shop where the proportion of the stock of suspectedly stale popcorn to that of rarer and stickier joys betrayed perhaps a modest capital on the part of your father's, your grandfather's or whoever's tenant, but out of which I nevertheless remember once to have come as out of a bath of sweets, with my very garments, and even the separate hairs of my head, glued together. The other of the pair, a tobacconist's, further down, had before it a wonderful huge Indian who thrust out wooden cigars at an indifferent world – you could buy candy cigars too at the popcorn shop, and I greatly preferred them to the wooden; I remember well how I used to gape in fascination at the Indian and wonder if the last of the Mohicans was like him; besides admiring so the resources of a family whose "property" was in such forms. I haven't been round there lately – we must go round together; but don't tell me the forms have utterly perished!' It was after *that* fashion he might easily have been moved, and with almost no transition, to break out to Cornelia – quite as if taking up some old talk, some old community of gossip, just where they had left it; even with the consciousness perhaps of overdoing a little, of putting at its maximum, for the present harmony, recovery, recapture (what should he call it?) the pitch and quantity of what the past had held for them.

He didn't in fact, no doubt, dart straight off to Seventh Avenue, there being too many other old things and much nearer and long subsequent; the point was only that for everything they spoke of after he had fairly begun to lean back and stretch his legs, and after she had let him, above all, light the first of a succession of cigarettes – for everything they spoke of he positively cultivated extravagance and excess, piling up the crackling twigs as on the very altar of memory; and that by the end of half an hour she had lent herself, all gallantly, to their game. It was the game of feeding the beautiful iridescent flame, ruddy and green and gold, blue and pink and amber and silver, with anything they could pick up, anything that would burn and flicker. Thick-strown with such gleanings the occasion seemed indeed, in spite of the truth that they perhaps wouldn't have proved, under cross-examination, to have rubbed shoulders in the other life so very hard. Casual contacts, qualified communities enough, there had doubtless been, but not particular 'passages', nothing that counted, as he might think of it, for their 'very own' together, for nobody's else at all. These shades of historic exactitude didn't signify; the more and the less that there had been made perfect terms – and just by his being there and by her rejoicing in it – with their present need to have *had* all their past could be made to appear to have given them. It was to this tune they proceeded, the least little bit as if they knowingly pretended – he giving her the example and setting her the pace of it, and she, poor dear, after a first inevitable shyness, an uncertainty of wonder, a breathlessness of courage, falling into step and going whatever length he would.

She showed herself ready for it, grasping gladly at the perception of what he must mean; and if she didn't immediately and completely fall in – not in the first half-hour, not even in the three or four others that his visit, even whenever he consulted his watch, still made nothing of – she yet understood enough as soon as she understood that, if their finer economy hadn't so beautifully served, he might have been conveying this, that and the other incoherent and easy thing by the comparatively clumsy method of sound and statement. 'No, I never made love to you; it would in fact have been absurd, and I don't care – though I almost know, in the sense of almost remembering! – who did and who didn't; but you were always about, and so was I, and, little as you may yourself care who *I* did it to, I daresay you remember (in the sense of having known of it!) any old appearances that told. But we can't afford at this time of day not to help each other to have had – well, everything there was, since there's no more of it now, nor any way of coming by it *except so*; and therefore let us *make* together, let us make over and re-create, our lost world; for which we have after all and at the worst such a lot of material. You were in particular my poor dear sisters' friend – they thought you the funniest little brown thing possible; so isn't that again to the good? You were mine only to the extent that you were so much in and out of the house – as how much, if we come to that, wasn't one in and out, south of Thirtieth Street and north of Washington Square, in those days, those spacious, sociable, Arcadian days, that we flattered ourselves we filled with the modern fever, but that were so different from any of *these* arrangements of pretended hourly Time that dash themselves forever to pieces as from the fiftieth floors of sky-scrapers.'

This was the kind of thing that was in the air, whether he said it or not, and that could hang there even with such quite other things as more crudely came out; came in spite of its being perhaps calculated to strike us that these last would have been rather and most the unspoken and the indirect. They were Cornelia's contribution, and as soon as she had begun to talk of Mrs Worthingham – *he* didn't begin it! – they had taken their place bravely in the centre of the circle. There they made, the while, their considerable little figure, but all within the ring formed by fifty other allusions, fitful but really intenser irruptions that hovered and wavered and came and went, joining hands at moments and whirling round as in chorus, only then again to dash at the slightly huddled centre with a free twitch or peck or push or other taken liberty, after the fashion of irregular frolic motions in a country dance or a Christmas game.

'You're so in love with her and want to marry her!' – she said it all sympathetically and yearningly, poor crapy Cornelia; as if it were to be quite taken for granted that she knew all about it. And then when he had asked how she knew – why she took so informed a tone about it; all on the wonder of her seeming so much more 'in' it just at that hour than he himself quite felt he could figure for: 'Ah, how but from the dear lovely thing herself? Don't you suppose *she* knows it?'

'Oh, she absolutely "knows" it, does she?' – he fairly heard himself ask that; and with the oddest sense at once of sharply wanting the certitude and yet of seeing the question, of hearing himself say the words, through several thicknesses of some wrong medium. He came back to it from a distance; as he would have had to come back (this was again vivid to him) should he have got round again to his ripe intention three days before – after his now present but then absent friend, that is, had left him planted before his now absent but then present one for the purpose. 'Do you mean she – at all confidently! – expects?' he went on, not much minding if it couldn't but sound foolish; the time being given it for him meanwhile by the sigh, the wondering gasp, all charged with the unutterable, that the tone of his appeal set in motion. He saw his companion look at him, but it might have been with the eyes of thirty years ago; when – very likely! – he had put her some such question about some girl long since dead. Dimly at first, then more distinctly, didn't it surge back on him for the very strangeness that there had been some such passage as this between them – yes, about Mary Cardew! – in the autumn of '68?

'Why, don't you realise your situation?' Miss Rasch struck him as quite beautifully wailing – above all to such an effect of deep interest, that is, on her own part and in him.

'My situation?' – he echoed, he considered; but reminded afresh, by the note of the detached, the far-projected in it, of what he had last remembered of his sentient state on his once taking ether at the dentist's.

'Yours and hers – the situation of her adoring you. I suppose you at least know it,' Cornelia smiled.

Yes, it was like the other time and yet it wasn't. *She* was like – poor Cornelia was – everything that used to be; that somehow was most definite to him. Still he could quite reply, 'Do you call it – her adoring me – *my* situation?'

'Well, it's a part of yours, surely – if you're in love with her.'

'Am I, ridiculous old person! in love with her?' White-Mason asked.

'I may be a ridiculous old person,' Cornelia returned – 'and, for that matter, of course I *am*! But she's young and lovely and rich and clever: so what could be more natural?'

'Oh, I was applying that opprobrious epithet –!' He didn't finish, though he meant he had applied it to himself. He had got up from his seat; he turned about and, taking in, as his eyes also roamed, several objects in the room, serene and sturdy, not a bit cheap-looking, little old New York objects of '68, he made, with an inner art, as if to recognise them – made so, that is, for himself; had quite the sense for the moment of asking them, of imploring them, to recognise *him*, to be for him things of his own past. Which they truly were, he could have the next instant cried out; for it meant that if three or four of them, small sallow carte-de-visite photographs, faithfully framed but spectrally faded, hadn't in every particular, frames and balloon skirts and false 'property' balustrades of unimaginable terraces and all, the tone of time, the secret for warding and easing off the perpetual imminent ache of one's protective scowl, one would verily but have to let the scowl stiffen or to take up seriously the question of blue goggles, during what might remain of life.

V

WHAT he actually took up from a little old Twelfth-Street table that piously preserved the plain mahogany circle, with never a curl nor a crook nor a hint of a brazen flourish, what he paused there a moment for commerce with, his back presented to crapy Cornelia, who sat taking that view of him, during this opportunity, very protrusively and frankly and fondly, was one of the wasted mementoes just mentioned, over which he both uttered and suppressed a small comprehensive cry. He stood there another minute to look at it, and when he turned about still kept it in his hand, only holding it now a little behind him. 'You *must* have come back to stay – with all your beautiful things. What else does it mean?'

'"Beautiful"?' his old friend commented with her brow all wrinkled and her lips thrust out in expressive dispraise. They might at that rate have been scarce more beautiful than she herself. 'Oh, don't talk so – after Mrs Worthingham's! *They're* wonderful, if you will: such things, such things! But one's own poor relics and odds and ends are one's own at least; and one *has* – yes – come back to them. They're all I have in the world to come back to. They were stored, and what I was paying –!' Miss Rasch woefully added.

He had possession of the small old picture; he hovered there; he put his eyes again to it intently; then again held it a little behind him as if it might have been snatched away or the very feel of it, pressed against him, was good to his palm. 'Mrs Worthingham's things? You think them beautiful?'

Cornelia did now, if ever, show an odd face. 'Why, certainly, prodigious, or whatever. Isn't that conceded?'

'No doubt every horror, at the pass we've come to, is conceded. That's just what I complain of.'

'Do you *complain*?' – she drew it out as for surprise: she couldn't have imagined such a thing.

'To me her things are awful. They're the newest of the new.'

'Ah, but the old forms!'

'Those are the most blatant. I mean the swaggering reproductions.'

'Oh, but,' she pleaded, 'we can't all be *really* old.'

'No, we can't, Cornelia. But *you* can –!' said White-Mason with the frankest appreciation.

She looked up at him from where she sat as he could imagine her looking up at the curate at Bognor. 'Thank you, sir! If that's all you want –!'

'It *is*,' he said, 'all I want – or almost.'

'Then no wonder such a creature as that,' she lightly moralised, 'won't suit you!'

He bent upon her, for all the weight of his question, his smoothest stare. 'You hold she certainly won't suit me?'

'Why, what can I tell about it? Haven't you by this time found out?'

'No, but I think I'm finding.' With which he began again to explore.

Miss Rasch immensely wondered. 'You mean you don't expect to come to an understanding with her?' And then, as even to this straight challenge he made at first no answer: 'Do you mean you give it up?'

He waited some instants more, but not meeting her eyes – only looking again about the room. 'What do you think of my chance?'

'Oh,' his companion cried, 'what has what I think to do with it? How can I think anything but that she must like you?'

'Yes – of course. But how much?'

'Then don't you really know?' Cornelia asked.

He kept up his walk, oddly preoccupied and still not looking at her. 'Do you, my dear?'

She waited a little. 'If you haven't really put it to her I don't suppose she knows.'

This at last arrested him again. 'My dear Cornelia, she doesn't know –!'

He had paused as for the desperate tone, or at least the large emphasis of it, so that she took him up. 'The more reason then to help her to find it out.'

'I mean,' he explained, 'that she doesn't know anything.'

'Anything?'

'Anything else, I mean – even if she does know *that*.'

Cornelia considered of it. 'But what else need she – in particular – know? Isn't that the principal thing?'

'Well' – and he resumed his circuit – 'she doesn't know anything that *we* know. But nothing,' he re-emphasised – 'nothing whatever!'

'Well, can't she do without that?'

'Evidently she can – and evidently she does, beautifully. But the question is whether *I* can!'

He had paused once more with his point – but she glared, poor Cornelia, with her wonder. 'Surely if you know for yourself –!'

'Ah, it doesn't seem enough for me to know for myself! One wants a woman,' he argued – but still, in his prolonged tour, quite without his scowl – 'to know *for* one, to know *with* one. That's what you do now,' he candidly put to her.

It made her again gape. 'Do you mean you want to marry *me*?'

He was so full of what he did mean, however, that he failed even to notice it. 'She doesn't in the least know, for instance, how old I am.'

'That's because you're so young!'

'Ah, there you are!' – and he turned off afresh and as if almost in disgust. It left her visibly perplexed – though even the perplexed Cornelia was still the exceedingly pointed; but he had come to her aid after another turn. 'Remember, please, that I'm pretty well as old as you.'

She had all her point at least, while she bridled and blinked, for this. 'You're exactly a year and ten months older.'

It checked him there for delight. 'You remember my birth-day?'

She twinkled indeed like some far-off light of home. 'I remember everyone's. It's a little way I've always had – and that I've never lost.'

He looked at her accomplishment, across the room, as at some striking, some charming phenomenon. 'Well, *that's* the sort of thing I want!' All the ripe candour of his eyes confirmed it.

What could she do therefore, she seemed to ask him, but repeat her question of a moment before? – which indeed, presently she made up her mind to. 'Do you want to marry *me*?'

It had this time better success – if the term may be felt in any degree to apply. All his candour, or more of it at least, was in his slow, mild, kind, considering head-shake. 'No, Cornelia – not to *marry* you.'

His discrimination was a wonder; but since she was clearly treating him now as if everything about him was, so she could as exquisitely meet it. 'Not at least,' she convulsively smiled, 'until you've honourably tried Mrs Worthingham. Don't you really *mean* to?' she gallantly insisted.

He waited again a little; then he brought out: 'I'll tell you presently.' He came back, and as by still another mere glance over the room, to what seemed to him so much nearer. 'That table *was* old Twelfth-Street?'

'Everything here was.'

'Oh, the pure blessings! With you, ah, with you, I haven't to wear a green shade.' And he had retained meanwhile his small photograph, which he again showed himself. 'Didn't we talk of Mary Cardew?'

'Why, do you remember it?' – she marvelled to extravagance.

'You make me. You connect me with it. You connect it with *me*.' He liked to display to her this excellent use she thus had, the service she rendered. 'There are so many connections – there will *be* so many. I feel how, with you, they must all come up again for me: in fact you're bringing them out already, just while I look at you, as fast as ever you can. The fact that you knew every one –!' he went on; yet as if there were more in that too than he could quite trust himself about.

'Yes, I knew every one,' said Cornelia Rasch; but this time with perfect simplicity. 'I knew, I imagine, more than you do – or more than you did.'

It kept him there, it made him wonder with his eyes on her. 'Things about *them* – our people?'

'Our people. Ours only now.'

Ah, such an interest as he felt in this – taking from her while, so far from scowling, he almost gaped, all it might mean! 'Ours indeed – and it's awfully good they are; or that we're still here for them! Nobody else is – nobody but you: not a cat!'

'Well, I *am* a cat!' Cornelia grinned.

'Do you mean you can tell me things –?' It was too beautiful to believe.

'About what really *was*?' She artfully considered, holding him immensely now. 'Well, unless they've come to you with time; unless you've learned – or found out.'

'Oh,' he reassuringly cried – reassuringly, it most seemed, for himself – 'nothing has come to me with time, everything has gone from me. How I find out now! What creature has an idea –?'

She threw up her hands with the shrug of old days – the sharp little shrug his sisters used to imitate and that she hadn't had to go to Europe for. The only thing was that he blessed her for bringing it back. 'Ah, the ideas of people now –!'

'Yes, their ideas are certainly not about *us*.' But he ruefully faced it. 'We've none the less, however, to live with them.'

'With their ideas –?' Cornelia questioned.

'With *them* – these modern wonders; such as they are!' Then he went on: 'It must have been to help me you've come back.'

She said nothing for an instant about that, only nodding instead at his photograph. 'What has become of yours? I mean of *her*.'

This time it made him turn pale. 'You remember I *have* one?'

She kept her eyes on him. 'In a "pork-pie" hat, with her hair in a long net. That was so "smart" then; especially with one's skirt looped up, over one's hooped magenta petticoat, in little festoons, and a row of very big onyx beads over one's braided velveteen sack – braided quite plain and very broad, don't you know?'

He smiled for her extraordinary possession of these things – she was as prompt as if she had had them before her. 'Oh, rather – "don't I know?" You wore brown velveteen, and, on those remarkably small hands, funny gauntlets – like mine.'

'Oh, do *you* remember? But like yours?' she wondered.

'I mean like hers in my photograph.' But he came back to the present picture. 'This is better, however, for really showing her lovely head.'

'Mary's head was a perfection!' Cornelia testified.

'Yes – it was better than her heart.'

'Ah, don't say that!' she pleaded. 'You weren't fair.'

'Don't you think I was fair?' It interested him immensely – and the more that he indeed mightn't have been; which he seemed somehow almost to hope.

'She didn't think so – to the very end.'

'She didn't?' – ah, the right things Cornelia said to him! But before she could answer he was studying again closely the small faded face. 'No, she doesn't, she doesn't. Oh, her charming sad eyes and the way they *say* that, across the years, straight into mine! But I don't know, I don't know!' White-Mason quite comfortably sighed.

His companion appeared to appreciate this effect. 'That's just the way you used to flirt with her, poor thing. Wouldn't you like to have it?' she asked.

'This – for my very own?' He looked up delighted. 'I really may?'

'Well, if you'll give me yours. We'll exchange.'

'That's a charming idea. We'll exchange. But you must come and get it at my rooms – where you'll see my things.'

For a little she made no answer – as if for some feeling. Then she said: 'You asked me just now why I've come back.'

He stared as for the connection; after which with a smile: 'Not to do *that* –?'

She waited briefly again, but with a queer little look. 'I can do those things now; and – yes! – that's in a manner why. I came,' she then said, 'because I knew of a sudden one day – knew as never before – that I was old.'

'I see. I see.' He quite understood – she had notes that so struck him. 'And how did you like it?'

She hesitated – she decided. 'Well, if I liked it, it was on the principle perhaps on which some people like high game!'

'High game – that's good!' he laughed. 'Ah, my dear, we're "high"!'

She shook her head. 'No – not you – yet. I at any rate didn't want any more adventures,' Cornelia said.

He showed their small relic again with assurance. 'You wanted *us*. Then here we are. Oh, how we can talk! – with all those things you know! You *are* an invention. And you'll see there are things *I* know. I shall turn up here – well, daily.'

She took it in, but after a moment only answered. 'There was something you said just now you'd tell me. Don't you mean to try –?'

'Mrs Worthingham?' He drew from within his coat his pocket-book and carefully found a place in it for Mary Cardew's carte-de-visite, folding it together with deliberation over which he put it back. Finally he spoke. 'No – I've decided. I can't – I don't want to.'

Cornelia marvelled – or looked as if she did. 'Not for all she has?'

'Yes – I know all she has. But I also know all she hasn't. And, as I told you, she herself doesn't – hasn't a glimmer of a suspicion of it; and never will have.'

Cornelia magnanimously thought. 'No – but she knows other things.'

He shook his head as at the portentous heap of them. 'Too many – too many. And other indeed – *so* other. Do you know,' he went on, 'that it's as if *you* – by turning up for me – had brought that home to me?'

'For you,' she candidly considered. 'But what – since you can't marry me! – can you do with me?'

Well, he seemed to have it all. 'Everything. I can live with you – just this way.' To illustrate which he dropped into the other chair by her fire; where, leaning back, he gazed at the flame. 'I can't give you up. It's very curious. It has come over me as it did over you when you renounced Bognor. That's it – I know it at last, and I see one can like it. I'm "high". You needn't deny it. That's my taste. I'm old.' And in spite of the considerable glow there of her little household altar he said it without the scowl.

THE BENCH OF DESOLATION

I

SHE had practically, he believed, conveyed the intimation, the horrid, brutal, vulgar menace, in the course of their last dreadful conversation, when, for whatever was left him of pluck or confidence – confidence in what he would fain have called a little more aggressively the strength of his position – he had judged best not to take it up. But this time there was no question of not understanding, or of pretending he didn't; the ugly, the awful words, ruthlessly formed by her lips, were like the fingers of a hand that she might have thrust into her pocket for extraction of the monstrous object that would serve best for – what should he call it? – a gage of battle.

'If I haven't a very different answer from you within the next three days I shall put the matter into the hands of my solicitor, whom it may interest you to know I've already seen. I shall bring an action for "breach" against you, Herbert Dodd, as sure as my name's Kate Cookham.'

There it was, straight and strong – yet he felt he could say for himself, when once it had come, or even, already just as it was coming, that it turned on, as if she had moved an electric switch, the very brightest light of his own very reasons. There *she* was, in all the grossness of her native indelicacy, in all her essential excess of will and destitution of scruple; and it was the woman capable of that ignoble threat who, his sharper sense of her quality having become so quite deterrent, was now making for him a crime of it that he shouldn't wish to tie himself to her for life. The vivid, lurid thing was the reality, all unmistakeable, of her purpose; she had thought her case well out; had measured its odious, specious presentability; had taken, he might be sure, the very best advice obtainable at Properley, where there was always a first-rate promptitude of everything fourth-rate; it was disgustingly certain, in short, that she'd proceed. She was sharp and adroit, moreover – distinctly in certain ways a master-hand; how otherwise, with her so limited mere attractiveness, should she have entangled him? He couldn't shut his eyes to the very probable truth that if she should try it she'd pull it off. She *knew* she would – precisely; and her assurance was thus the very proof of her cruelty. That she had pretended she loved him was comparatively nothing; other women had pretended it, and other women too had really done it; but that she had pretended he could possibly have been right and safe and blest in loving *her*, a creature of the kind who could sniff that squalor of the law-court, of claimed damages and brazen lies and published kisses, of love-letters read amid obscene guffaws, as a positive tonic to resentment, as a high incentive to her course – this was what put him so beautifully in the right. It was what might signify in a woman all through, he said to himself, the mere imagination of such machinery. Truly what a devilish conception and what an appalling nature!

But there was no doubt, luckily, either, that he *could* plant his feet the firmer for his now intensified sense of these things. He was to live, it appeared, abominably worried, he was to live consciously rueful, he was to live perhaps even what a scoffing world would call abjectly exposed; but at least he was to live saved. In spite of his clutch of which steadying truth, however, and in spite of his declaring to her, with many other angry protests and pleas, that the line of conduct she announced was worthy of a vindictive barmaid, a lurking fear in him, too deep to counsel mere defiance, made him appear to keep open a little, till he could somehow turn round again, the door of possible composition. He had scoffed at her claim, at her threat, at her thinking she could hustle and bully him – 'Such a way, my eye, to call back to life a dead love!' – yet his instinct was ever, prudentially but helplessly, for gaining time, even if time only more woefully to quake, and he gained it now by not absolutely giving for his ultimatum that he wouldn't think of coming round. He didn't in the smallest degree mean to come round, but it was characteristic of him that he could for three or four days breathe a little easier by having left her under the impression that he perhaps might. At the same time he couldn't not have said – what had conduced to bring out, in retort, her own last word, the word on which they had parted – 'Do you mean to say you yourself would now be *willing* to marry and live with a man of whom you could feel, the thing done, that he'd be all the while thinking of you in the light of a hideous coercion?' 'Never you mind about *my* willingness,' Kate had answered; 'you've known what that has been for the last six months. Leave that to me, my willingness – I'll take care of it all right; and just see what conclusion you can come to about your own.'

He was to remember afterward how he had wondered whether, turned upon her in silence while her odious lucidity reigned unchecked, his face had shown her anything like the quantity of hate he felt. Probably not at all; no man's face *could* express that immense amount; especially the fair, refined, intellectual, gentleman-like face which had had – and by her own more than once repeated avowal – so much to do with the enormous fancy she had originally taken to him. 'Which – frankly now – would you personally *rather* I should do,' he had at any rate asked her with an intention of supreme irony: 'just sordidly marry you on top of this, or leave you the pleasure of your lovely appearance in court and of your so assured (since that's how you feel it) big haul of damages? Shan't you be awfully disappointed, in fact, if I don't let you get something better out of me than a poor plain ten-shilling gold ring and the rest of the blasphemous rubbish, as we should make it between us, pronounced at the altar? I take it, of course,' he had swaggered on, 'that your pretension wouldn't be for a moment that I should – after the act of profanity – take up my life with you.'

'It's just as much my dream as it ever was, Herbert Dodd, to take up mine with *you*! Remember for me that I can do with it, my dear, that my idea is for even as much as that of you!' she had cried; 'remember that for me, Herbert Dodd; remember, remember!'

It was on this she had left him – left him frankly under a mortal chill. There might have been the last ring of an appeal or a show of persistent and perverse tenderness in it, however preposterous any such matter; but in point of fact her large, clean, plain brown face – so much too big for her head, he now more than ever felt it to be, just as her head was so much too big for her body, and just as her hats had an irritating way of appearing to decline choice and conformity in respect to *any* of her dimensions – presented itself with about as much expression as his own shop-window when the broad, blank, sallow blind was down. He was fond of his shop-window with some good show on; he had a fancy for a good show and was master of twenty different schemes of taking arrangement for the old books and prints, 'high-class rarities' his modest catalogue called them, in which he dealt and which his maternal uncle, David Geddes, had, as he liked to say, 'handed down' to him. His widowed mother had screwed the whole thing, the stock and the connection and the rather bad little house in the rather bad little street, out of the ancient worthy, shortly before his death, in the name of the youngest and most interesting, the 'delicate' one and the literary of her five scattered and struggling children. He could enjoy his happiest collocations and contrasts and effects, his harmonies and varieties of toned and faded leather and cloth, his sought colour-notes and the high clearnesses, here and there, of his white and beautifully figured price-labels, which pleased him enough in themselves almost to console him for not oftener having to break, on a customer's insistence, into the balanced composition. But the dropped expanse of time-soiled canvas, the thing of Sundays and holidays, with just his name, 'Herbert Dodd, Successor', painted on below his uncle's antique style, the feeble penlike flourishes already quite archaic – this ugly vacant mask, which might so easily be taken for the mask of failure, somehow always gave him a chill.

That had been just the sort of chill – the analogy was complete – of Kate Cookham's last look. He supposed people doing an awfully good and sure and steady business, in whatever line, could see a whole front turned to vacancy that way, and merely think of the hours off represented by it. Only for this – nervously to bear it, in other words, and Herbert Dodd, quite with the literary temperament himself, was capable of that amount of play of fancy, or even of morbid analysis – you had to be on some footing, you had to feel some confidence, pretty different from his own up to now. He had never *not* enjoyed passing his

show on the other side of the street and taking it in thence with a
casual obliquity; but he had never held optical commerce with
the drawn blind for a moment longer than he could help. It
always looked horribly final and as if it never would come up
again. Big and bare, with his name staring at him from the
middle, it thus offered in its grimness a term of comparison
for Miss Cookham's ominous visage. She never wore pretty,
dotty, transparent veils, as Nan Drury did, and the words
'Herbert Dodd' – save that she had sounded them at him
there two or three times more like a Meg Merrilies or the bold
bad woman in one of the melodramas of high life given during
the fine season in the pavilion at the end of Properley Pier –
were dreadfully, were permanently, seated on her lips. *She* was
grim, no mistake.

That evening, alone in the back room above the shop, he saw
so little what he could do that, consciously demoralised for the
hour, he gave way to tears about it. Her taking a stand so
incredibly 'low', that was what he couldn't get over. The particular bitterness of his cup was his having let himself in for a
struggle on such terms – the use, on her side, of the vulgarest
process known to the law: the vulgarest, the vulgarest, he kept
repeating that, clinging to the help rendered him by this
imputation to his terrorist of the vice he sincerely believed he
had ever, among difficulties (for oh, he recognised the difficulties!) sought to keep most alien to him. He knew what he was, in
a dismal, down-trodden sphere enough – the lean young proprietor of an old business that had itself rather shrivelled with
age than ever grown fat, the purchase and sale of second-hand
books and prints, with the back street of a long-fronted south-
coast watering-place (Old Town by good luck) for the dusky
field of his life. But he had gone in for all the education he could
get – his educated customers would often hang about for more
talk by the half-hour at a time, he actually feeling himself, and
almost with a scruple, hold them there; which meant that he
had had (he couldn't be blind to that) natural taste and had
lovingly cultivated and formed it. Thus, from as far back as he
could remember, there had been things all round him that he
suffered from when other people didn't; and he had kept most

of his suffering to himself – which had taught him, in a manner, *how* to suffer, and how almost to like to.

So, at any rate, he had never let go his sense of certain differences, he had done everything he could to keep it up – whereby everything that was vulgar was on the wrong side of his line. He had believed, for a series of strange, oppressed months, that Kate Cookham's manners and tone were on the right side; she had been governess – for young children – in two very good private families, and now had classes in literature and history for bigger girls who were sometimes brought by their mammas; in fact, coming in one day to look over his collection of students' manuals, and drawing it out, as so many did, for the evident sake of his conversation, she had appealed to him that very first time by her apparently pronounced intellectual side – goodness knew she didn't even then by the physical! – which she had artfully kept in view till she had entangled him past undoing. And it had all been but the cheapest of traps – when he came to take the pieces apart a bit – laid over a brazen avidity. What he now collapsed for, none the less – what he sank down on a chair at a table and nursed his weak, scared sobs in his resting arms for – was the fact that, whatever the trap, it held him as with the grip of sharp, murderous steel. There he was, there he was; alone in the brown summer dusk – brown through *his* windows – he cried and he cried. He shouldn't get out without losing a limb. The only question was which of his limbs it should be.

Before he went out, later on – for he at last felt the need to – he could, however, but seek to remove from his face and his betraying eyes, over his wash-stand, the traces of his want of fortitude. He brushed himself up; with which, catching his stricken image a bit spectrally in an old dim toilet-glass, he knew again, in a flash, the glow of righteous resentment. Who should be assured against coarse usage if a man of his really elegant, perhaps in fact a trifle over-refined or 'effete' appearance, his absolutely gentleman-like type, couldn't be? He never went so far as to rate himself, with exaggeration, a gentleman; but he would have maintained against all comers, with perfect candour and as claiming a high advantage, that he was, in spite of that liability to blubber, 'like' one; which he *was* no doubt, for that matter, at several points. Like what lady then, who could ever possibly have been taken for one, was Kate Cookham, and therefore how could one have anything – anything of the intimate and private order – out with her fairly and on the plane, the only possible one, of common equality? He might find himself crippled for life; he believed verily, the more he thought, that that was what was before him. But he ended by seeing this doom in the almost redeeming light of the fact that it would all have been because he was, comparatively, too aristocratic. Yes, a man in his station couldn't afford to carry that so far – it must sooner or later, in one way or another, spell ruin. Never mind – it was the only thing he could be. Of course he should exquisitely suffer – but when hadn't he exquisitely suffered? How was he going to get through life by *any* arrangement without that? No wonder such a woman as Kate Cookham had been keen to annex so rare a value. The right thing would have been that the highest price should be paid for it – by such a different sort of logic from this nightmare of *his* having to pay.

II

WHICH was the way, of course, he talked to Nan Drury – as he had felt the immediate wild need to do; for he should perhaps be able to bear it all somehow or other with *her* – while they sat together, when time and freedom served, on one of the very last, the far westward benches of the interminable sea-front. It wasn't everyone who walked so far, especially at that flat season – the only ghost of a bustle now, save for the gregarious, the obstreperous haunters of the fluttering, far-shining Pier, being reserved for the sunny Parade of midwinter. It wasn't everyone who cared for the sunsets (which you got awfully well from there, and which were a particular strong point of the lower, the more 'sympathetic' as Herbert Dodd liked to call it, Properley horizon) as he had always intensely cared, and as he had found Nan Drury care; to say nothing of his having also observed how little they directly spoke to Miss Cookham. He had taught this oppressive companion to notice them a bit, as he had taught her plenty of other things, but that was a different matter; for the reason that the 'land's end' (stretching a point it carried off that name) had been, and had had to be by their lack of more sequestered resorts and conveniences, the scene of so much of what she styled their wooing-time – or, to put it more properly, of the time during which she had made the straightest and most unabashed love to *him*: just as it could henceforth but render possible, under an equal rigour, that he should enjoy there periods of consolation from beautiful, gentle, tender-souled Nan, to whom he was now at last, after the wonderful way they had helped each other to behave, going to make love, absolutely unreserved and abandoned, absolutely reckless and romantic love, a refuge from poisonous reality, as hard as ever he might.

The league-long, paved, lighted, garden-plotted, seated, and refuged Marina renounced its more or less celebrated attractions to break off short here; and an inward curve of the kindly westward shore almost made a wide-armed bay, with all the ugliness between town and country, and the further casual fringe of the coast, turning, as the day waned, to rich afternoon blooms of grey and brown and distant – it might fairly have been beautiful Hampshire – blue. Here it was that all that blighted summer, with Nan – from the dreadful Mayday on – he gave himself up to the reaction of intimacy with the *kind* of woman, at least, that he liked; even if of everything else that might make life possible he was to be, by what he could make out, forever starved. Here it was that – as well as on whatever other scraps of occasions they could manage – Nan began to take off and fold up and put away in her pocket her pretty, dotty, becoming veil; as under the logic of his having so tremendously ceased, in the shake of his dark storm-gust, to be engaged to another woman. Her removal of that obstacle to a trusted friend's assuring himself whether the peachlike bloom of her finer facial curves bore the test of such further inquiry into their cool sweetness as might reinforce a mere baffled gaze – her momentous, complete surrender of so much of her charm, let us say, both marked the change in the situation of the pair and established the record of their perfect observance of every propriety for so long before. They afterward in fact could have dated it, their full clutch of their freedom and the bliss of their having so little henceforth to consider save their impotence, their poverty, their ruin; dated it from the hour of his recital to her of the – at the first blush – quite appalling upshot of his second and conclusive 'scene of violence' with the mistress of his fortune, when the dire terms of his release had had to be formally, and oh! so abjectly, acceded to. She 'compromised', the cruel brute, for Four Hundred Pounds down – for not a farthing less would she stay her strength from 'proceedings'. No jury in the land but would give her six, on the nail ('Oh, she knew quite where she was, thank you!'), and he might feel lucky to get off with so whole a skin. This was the sum, then, for which he had grovellingly compounded – under an agreement sealed by a supreme exchange of remarks.

' "Where in the name of lifelong ruin are you to *find* Four Hundred?" ' Miss Cookham had mockingly repeated after him while he gasped as from the twist of her grip on his collar. 'That's *your* look-out, and I should have thought you'd have made sure you knew before you decided on your base perfidy.' And then she had mouthed and minced, with ever so false a gentility, her consistent, her sickening conclusion. 'Of course – I may mention again – if you too distinctly object to the trouble of looking, you know where to find *me*.'

'I had rather starve to death than ever go within a mile of you!' Herbert described himself as having sweetly answered; and that was accordingly where *they* devotedly but desperately were – he and she, penniless Nan Drury. Her father, of Drury & Dean, was like so far too many other of the anxious characters who peered through the dull window-glass of dusty offices at Properley, an Estate and House Agent, Surveyor, Valuer and Auctioneer; she was the prettiest of six, with two brothers, neither of the least use, but, thanks to the manner in which their main natural protector appeared to languish under the accumulation of his attributes, they couldn't be said very particularly or positively to live. Their continued collective existence was a good deal of a miracle even to themselves, though they had fallen into the way of not unnecessarily, or too nervously, exchanging remarks upon it, and had even in a sort, from year to year, got used to it. Nan's brooding pinkness when he talked to her, her so very parted lips, considering her pretty teeth, her so very parted eyelids, considering her pretty eyes, all of which might have been those of some waxen image of uncritical faith, cooled the heat of his helplessness very much as if he were laying his head on a tense silk pillow. She had, it was true, forms of speech, familiar watchwords, that affected him as small scratchy perforations of the smooth surface from within; but his pleasure in her and need of her were independent of such things and really almost altogether determined by the fact of the happy, even if all so lonely, forms and instincts in her which claimed kinship with his own. With her natural elegance stamped on her as by a die, with her dim and disinherited individual refinement of grace, which would have made anyone wonder who she was anywhere – hat and veil and feather-boa and smart umbrella-knob and all – with her regular God-given distinction of type, in fine, she couldn't abide vulgarity much more than he could.

Therefore it didn't seem to him, under his stress, to matter particularly, for instance, if she *would* keep on referring so many things to the time, as she called it, when she came into his life – his own great insistence and contention being that she hadn't in the least entered there till his mind was wholly made up to eliminate his other friend. What that methodical fury was so fierce to bring home to him was the falsity to herself involved in the later acquaintance; whereas just his precious right to hold up his head to everything – before himself at least – sprang from the fact that she couldn't make dates fit anyhow. He hadn't so much as heard of his true beauty's existence (she had come back but a few weeks before from her two years with her terrible trying deceased aunt at Swindon, previous to which absence she had been an unnoticeable chit) till days and days, ever so many, upon his honour, after he had struck for freedom by his great first backing-out letter – the precious document, the treat for a British jury, in which, by itself, Miss Cookham's firm instructed her to recognise the prospect of a fortune. The way the ruffians had been 'her' ruffians – it appeared as if she had posted them behind her from the first of her beginning her game! – and the way 'instructions' bounced out, with it, at a touch, larger than life, as if she had arrived with her pocket full of them! The date of the letter, taken with its other connections, and the date of *her* first give-away for himself, his seeing her get out of the Brighton train with Bill Frankle that day he had gone to make the row at the Station parcels' office about the miscarriage of the box from Wales – those were the facts it sufficed him to point to, as he had pointed to them for Nan Drury's benefit, goodness knew, often and often enough. If he didn't seek occasion to do so for anyone else's – in open court as they said – that was his own affair, or at least his and Nan's.

It little mattered, meanwhile, if on their bench of desolation, all that summer – and it may be added for summers and summers, to say nothing of winters, there and elsewhere, to come – she did give way to her artless habit of not contradicting him enough, which led to her often trailing up and down before him, too complacently, the untimely shreds and patches of his own glooms and desperations. 'Well, I'm glad I *am* in your life, terrible as it is, however or whenever I did come in!' and '*Of course* you'd rather have starved – and it seems pretty well as if we shall, doesn't it? – than have bought her off by a false, abhorrent love, wouldn't you?' and 'It isn't as if she hadn't made up to you the way she did before you had so much as looked at her, is it? or as if you hadn't shown her what you felt her really to be before you had so much as looked at *me*, is it either?' and 'Yes, how on earth, pawning the shoes on your feet, you're going to raise another shilling – *that's* what you want to know, poor darling, don't you?'

III

HIS creditor, at the hour it suited her, transferred her base of operations to town, to which impenetrable scene she had also herself retired; and his raising of the first Two Hundred, during five exasperated and miserable months, and then of another Seventy piece-meal, bleedingly, after long delays and under the

epistolary whiplash cracked by the London solicitor in his
wretched ear even to an effect of the very report of Miss
Cookham's tongue – these melancholy efforts formed a
scramble up an arduous steep where steps were planted and
missed, and bared knees were excoriated, and clutches at way-
side tufts succeeded and failed, on a system to which poor Nan
could have intelligently entered only if she had been somehow
less ladylike. She kept putting into his mouth the sick quaver of
where he should find the rest, the always inextinguishable rest,
long after he had in silent rage fallen away from any further
payment at all – at first, he had but too blackly felt, for himself,
to the still quite possible non-exclusion of some penetrating ray
of 'exposure'. He didn't care a tuppenny damn now, and in
point of fact, after he had by hook and by crook succeeded in
being able to unload to the tune of Two-Hundred-and-
Seventy, and then simply returned the newest reminder of his
outstanding obligation unopened, this latter belated but real
sign of fight, the first he had risked, remarkably caused nothing
at all to happen; nothing at least but his being moved to quite
tragically rueful wonder as to whether exactly some such
demonstration mightn't have served his turn at an earlier stage.

He could by this time at any rate measure his ruin – with
three fantastic mortgages on his house, his shop, his stock, and
a burden of interest to carry under which his business simply
stretched itself inanimate, without strength for a protesting
kick, without breath for an appealing groan. Customers lingering for further enjoyment of the tasteful remarks he had cultivated the unobtrusive art of throwing in, would at this crisis
have found plenty to repay them, might his wit have strayed a
little more widely still, toward a circuitous egotistical outbreak,
from the immediate question of the merits of this and that
author or of the condition of this and that volume. He had
come to be conscious through it all of strangely glaring at
people when they tried to haggle – and not, as formerly, with
the glare of derisive comment on their overdone humour, but
with that of fairly idiotised surrender; as if they were much
mistaken in supposing, for the sake of conversation, that he
might take himself for saveable by the difference between

sevenpence and ninepence. He watched everything impossible and deplorable happen, as in an endless prolongation of his nightmare; watched himself proceed, that is, with the finest, richest incoherence to the due preparation of his catastrophe. Everything came to seem *equally* part of this – in complete defiance of proportion; even his final command of detachment, on the bench of desolation (where each successive fact of his dire case regularly cut itself out black, yet of senseless silhouette, against the red west) in respect to poor Nan's flat infelicities, which for the most part kept no pace with the years or with change, but only shook like hard peas in a child's rattle, the same peas always, of course, so long as the rattle didn't split open with usage or from somebody's act of irritation. They represented, or they had long done so, her contribution to the more superficial of the two branches of intimacy – the intellectual alternative, the one that didn't merely consist in her preparing herself for his putting his arm round her waist.

There were to have been moments, nevertheless, all the first couple of years, when she did touch in him, though to his actively dissimulating it, a more or less sensitive nerve – moments as they were too, to do her justice, when she treated him not to his own wisdom, or even folly, served up cold, but to a certain small bitter fruit of her personal, her unnatural, plucking. 'I wonder that since *she* took legal advice so freely, to come down on you, you didn't take it yourself, a little, before being so sure you stood no chance. Perhaps *your* people would have been sure of something quite different – *perhaps*, I only say, you know.' She 'only' said it, but she said it, none the less, in the early time, about once a fortnight. In the later, and especially after their marriage, it had a way of coming up again to the exclusion, as it seemed to him, of almost everything else; in fact during the most dismal years, the three of the loss of their two children, the long stretch of sordid embarrassment ending in her death, he was afterward to think of her as having generally said it several times a day. He was then also to remember that his answer, before she had learnt to discount it, had been inveterately at hand: 'What would any solicitor have done or wanted to do but drag me just into the hideous public arena' –

he had always so put it – 'that it has been at any rate my pride and my honour, the one rag of self-respect covering my nakedness, to have loathed and avoided from every point of view?'

That had disposed of it so long as he cared, and by the time he had ceased to care for anything it had also lost itself in the rest of the vain babble of home. After his wife's death, during his year of mortal solitude, it awoke again as an echo of far-off things – far-off, very far-off, because he felt then not ten but twenty years older. That was by reason simply of the dead weight with which his load of debt had settled – the persistence of his misery dragging itself out. With all that had come and gone the bench of desolation was still there, just as the immortal flush of the westward sky kept hanging its indestructible curtain. He had never got away – everything had left him, but he himself had been able to turn his back on nothing – and now, his day's labour before a dirty desk at the Gas Works ended, he more often than not, almost any season at temperate Properley serving his turn, took his slow, straight way to the Land's End and, collapsing there to rest, sat often for an hour at a time staring before him. He might in these sessions, with his eyes on the grey-green sea, have been counting again and still recounting the beads, almost all worn smooth, of his rosary of pain – which had for the fingers of memory and the recurrences of wonder the same felt break of the smaller ones by the larger that would have aided a pious mumble in some dusky altar-chapel.

If it has been said of him that when once full submersion, as from far back, had visibly begun to await him, he watched himself, in a cold lucidity, *do* punctually and necessarily each of the deplorable things that were inconsistent with his keeping afloat, so at present again he might have been held agaze just by the presented grotesqueness of that vigil. Such ghosts of dead seasons were all he *had* now to watch – such a recaptured sense for instance as that of the dismal unavailing awareness that had attended his act of marriage. He had let submersion final and absolute become the signal for it – a mere minor determinant having been the more or less contemporaneously unfavourable effect on the business of Drury & Dean of the sudden disappearance of Mr Dean with the single small tin box into which the certificates of the firm's credit had been found to be compressible. That had been his only form – or had at any rate seemed his only one. He couldn't not have married, no doubt, just as he couldn't not have suffered the last degree of humiliation and almost of want, or just as his wife and children couldn't not have died of the little he was able, under dire reiterated pinches, to do for them; but it *was* 'rum', for final solitary brooding, that he hadn't appeared to see his way definitely to undertake the support of a family till the last scrap of his little low-browed, high-toned business and the last figment of 'property' in the old tiled and timbered shell that housed it had been sacrificed to creditors mustering six rows deep.

Of course what had counted too in the odd order was that even at the end of the two or three years he had 'allowed' her, Kate Cookham, gorged with his unholy tribute, had become the subject of no successful siege on the part either of Bill Frankle or, by what he could make out, of anyone else. She had judged decent – he could do her that justice – to take herself personally out of his world, as he called it, for good and all, as soon as he had begun regularly to bleed; and, to whatever lucrative practice she might be devoting her great talents in London or elsewhere, he felt his conscious curiosity about her as cold, with time, as the passion of vain protest that she had originally left him to. He could recall but two direct echoes of her in all the bitter years – both communicated by Bill Frankle, disappointed and exposed and at last quite remarkably ingenuous sneak, who had also, from far back, taken to roaming the world, but who, during a period, used fitfully and ruefully to reappear. Herbert Dodd had quickly seen, at their first meeting – everyone met everyone sooner or later at Properley, if meeting it could always be called, either in the glare or the gloom of the explodedly attractive Embankment – that no silver stream of which he himself had been the remoter source could have played over the career of this all but repudiated acquaintance. That hadn't fitted with his first, his quite primitive raw vision of the probabilities, and he had further been puzzled when, much later on, it had come to him in a round-about way that Miss Cookham was supposed to be, or to have been, among them for

a few days 'on the quiet', and that Frankle, who had seen her
and who claimed to know more about it than he said, was cited
as authority for the fact. But he hadn't himself at this juncture
seen Frankle; he had only wondered, and a degree of mystification had even remained.

That memory referred itself to the dark days of old Drury's
smash, the few weeks between his partner's dastardly flight and
Herbert's own comment on it in the form of his standing up
with Nan for the nuptial benediction of the Vicar of St Bernard's on a very cold, bleak December morning and amid a
circle of seven or eight long-faced, red-nosed, and altogether
dowdy persons. Poor Nan herself had come to affect him as
scarce other than red-nosed and dowdy by that time, but this
only added, in his then, and indeed in his lasting view, to his
general and his particular morbid bravery. He had cultivated
ignorance, there were small inward immaterial luxuries he
could scrappily cherish even among other, and the harshest,
destitutions; and one of them was represented by this easy
refusal of his mind to render to certain passages of his
experience, to various ugly images, names, associations, the
homage of continued attention. That served him, that helped
him; but what happened when, a dozen dismal years having
worn themselves away, he sat single and scraped bare again, as
if his long wave of misfortune had washed him far beyond
everything and then conspicuously retreated, was that, thus
stranded by tidal action, deposited in the lonely hollow of his
fate, he felt even sustaining pride turn to nought and heard no
challenge from it when old mystifications, stealing forth in the
dusk of the day's work done, scratched at the door of speculation and hung about, through the idle hours, for irritated
notice.

The evenings of his squalid clerkship were all leisure now,
but there was nothing at all near home, on the other hand, for
his imagination, numb and stiff from its long chill, to begin to
play with. Voices from far off would quaver to him therefore in
the stillness; where he knew for the most recurrent, little by
little, the faint wail of his wife. He had become deaf to it in life,
but at present, after so great an interval, he listened again,

listened and listened, and seemed to hear it sound as by the pressure of some weak broken spring. It phrased for his ear her perpetual question, the one she had come to at the last as under the obsession of a discovered and resented wrong, a wrong withal that had its source much more in his own action than anywhere else. 'That you didn't make *sure* she could have done anything, that you didn't make sure and that you were too afraid!' – this commemoration had ended by playing such a part of Nan's finally quite contracted consciousness as to exclude everything else.

At the time, somehow, he had made his terms with it; he had then more urgent questions to meet than that of the poor creature's taste in worrying pain; but actually it struck him – not the question, but the fact itself of the taste – as the one thing left over from all that had come and gone. So it was; nothing remained to him in the world, on the bench of desolation, but the option of taking up that echo – together with an abundance of free time for doing so. That he hadn't made sure of what might and what mightn't have been done to him, that he had been too afraid – had the proposition a possible bearing on his present apprehension of things? To reply indeed he would have had to be able to say what his present apprehension of things, left to itself, amounted to; an uninspiring effort indeed he judged it, sunk to so poor a pitch was his material of thought – though it might at last have been the feat he sought to perform as he stared at the grey-green sea.

IV

IT was seldom he was disturbed in any form of sequestered speculation, or that at his times of predilection, especially that of the long autumn blankness between the season of trippers and the season of Bath-chairs, there were westward stragglers enough to jar upon his settled sense of priority. For himself his seat, the term of his walk, was consecrated; it had figured to him for years as the last (though there were others, not immediately near it, and differently disposed, that might have aspired to the title); so that he could invidiously distinguish as he approached, make out from a distance any accident of occupation, and never draw nearer while that unpleasantness lasted. What he disliked was to compromise on his tradition, whether for a man, a woman, or a canoodling couple; it was to idiots of this last composition he most objected, he having sat there, in the past, alone, having sat there interminably with Nan, having sat there with – well, with other women when women, at hours of ease, could still care or count for him, but having never shared the place with any shuffling or snuffling strangers.

It was a world of fidgets and starts, however, the world of his present dreariness; he alone possessed in it, he seemed to make out, of the secret of the dignity of sitting still with one's fate; so that if he took a turn about or rested briefly elsewhere even foolish philanderers – though this would never have been his and Nan's way – ended soon by some adjournment as visibly pointless as their sprawl. Then, their backs turned, he would drop down on it, the bench of desolation – which was what he, and he only, made it, by sad adoption; where, for that matter, moreover, once he had settled at his end, it was marked that nobody else ever came to sit. He saw people, along the Marina, take this liberty with other resting presences; but his own struck them perhaps in general as either of too grim or just of too dingy a vicinage. He might have affected the fellow-lounger as a man evil, unsociable, possibly engaged in working out the idea of a crime; or otherwise, more probably – for on the whole he surely looked harmless – devoted to the worship of some absolutely unpractical remorse.

On a certain October Saturday he had got off as usual, early; but the afternoon light, his pilgrimage drawing to its aim, could still show him, at long range, the rare case of an established usurper. His impulse was then, as by custom, to deviate a little and wait, all the more that the occupant of the bench was a lady, and that ladies, when alone, were – at that austere end of the varied frontal stretch – markedly discontinuous; but he kept on at sight of this person's rising, while he was still fifty yards off, and proceeding, her back turned, to the edge of the broad terrace, the outer line of which followed the interspaced succession of seats and was guarded by an iron rail from the abruptly lower level of the beach. Here she stood before the sea, while our friend on his side, recognising no reason to the contrary, sank into the place she had quitted. There were other benches, eastward and off by the course of the drive, for vague ladies. The lady indeed thus thrust upon Herbert's vision might have struck an observer either as not quite vague or as vague with a perverse intensity suggesting design.

Not that our own observer at once thought of these things; he only took in, and with no great interest, that the obtruded presence was a 'real' lady; that she was dressed – he noticed such matters – with a certain elegance of propriety or intention of harmony; and that she remained perfectly still for a good many minutes; so many in fact that he presently ceased to heed her, and that as she wasn't straight before him, but as far to the left as was consistent with his missing her profile, he had turned himself to one of his sunsets again (though it wasn't quite one of his best) and let it hold him for a time that enabled her to alter her attitude and present a fuller view. Without other movement, but her back now to the sea and her face to the odd person who had appropriated her corner, she had taken a sustained look at him before he was aware she had stirred. On that apprehension, however, he became also promptly aware of her direct, her applied observation. As his sense of this quickly increased he wondered who she was and what she wanted – what, as it were, was the matter with her; it suggested to him, the next thing, that she had, under some strange idea, actually been waiting for him. Any idea about him to-day on the part of any one could only be strange.

Yes, she stood there with the ample width of the Marina between them, but turned to him, for all the world, as to show frankly that she was concerned with him. And she *was* – oh, yes – a real lady: a middle-aged person, of good appearance and of the best condition, in quiet but 'handsome' black, save for very fresh white kid gloves, and with a pretty, dotty, becoming veil, predominantly white, adjusted to her countenance; which through it somehow, even to his imperfect sight, showed strong fine black brows and what he would have called on the spot character. But she was pale; her black brows were the blacker behind the flattering tissue; she still kept a hand, for support, on the terrace-rail, while the other, at the end of an extended arm that had an effect of rigidity, clearly pressed hard on the knob of a small and shining umbrella, the lower extremity of whose stick was equally, was sustainingly, firm on the walk. So this mature, qualified, important person stood and looked at the limp, undistinguished – oh, his values of aspect now! – shabby man on the bench.

It was extraordinary, but the fact of her interest, by immensely surprising, by immediately agitating him, blinded him at first to her identity and, for the space of his long stare, diverted him from it; with which even then, when recognition did break, the sense of the shock, striking inward, simply consumed itself in gaping stillness. He sat there motionless and weak, fairly faint with surprise, and there was no instant, in all the succession of so many, at which Kate Cookham could have caught the special sign of his intelligence. Yet that she did catch something he saw – for he saw her steady herself, by her two supported hands, to meet it; while, after she had done so, a very wonderful thing happened, of which he could scarce, later on, have made a clear statement, though he was to think it over again and again. She moved toward him, she reached him, she stood there, she sat down near him, he merely passive and wonderstruck, unresentfully 'impressed', gaping and taking it in – and all as with an open allowance on the part of each, so that they positively and quite intimately met in it, of the impertinence for their case, this case that brought them again, after horrible years, face to face, of the vanity, the profanity, the impossibility, of anything between them but silence.

Nearer to him, beside him at a considerable interval (oh, she was immensely considerate!) she presented him, in the sharp terms of her transformed state – but thus the more amply, formally, ceremoniously – with the reasons that would serve him best for not having precipitately known her. She was simply another and a totally different person, and the exhibition of it to which she had proceeded with this solemn anxiety was all, obviously, for his benefit – once he had, as he appeared to be doing, provisionally accepted her approach. He had remembered her as inclined to the massive and disowned by the graceful; but this was a spare, fine, worn, almost wasted lady – who had repaired waste, it was true, however, with something he could only appreciate as a rich accumulation of manner. She was strangely older, so far as that went – marked by experience and as if many things had happened to her; her face had suffered, to its improvement, contraction and concentration; and if he had granted, of old and from the first, that her eyes were remarkable, had they yet ever had for him this sombre glow? Withal, something said, she had flourished – he felt it, wincing at it, as that; she had had a life, a career, a history, something that her present waiting air and nervous conscious-ness couldn't prevent his noting there as a deeply latent assur-ance. She had flourished, she had flourished – though to learn it after this fashion was somehow at the same time not to feel she flaunted it. It wasn't thus execration that she revived in him; she made in fact, exhibitively, as he could only have put it, the matter of long ago irrelevant, and these extraordinary minutes of their reconstituted relation – how many? how few? – addressed themselves altogether to new possibilities.

Still it after a little awoke in him as with the throb of a touched nerve that his own very attitude was supplying a con-nection; he knew presently that he wouldn't have had her go, *couldn't* have made a sign to her for it – which was what she had been uncertain of – without speaking to him; and that therefore he was, as at the other, the hideous time, passive to whatever she might do. She was even yet, she was always, in possession of him; she had known how and where to find him and had appointed that he should see her, and, though he had never dreamed it was again to happen to him, he was meeting it already as if it might have been the only thing that the least humanly *could*. Yes, he had come back there to flop, by long custom, upon the bench of desolation *as* the man in the whole place, precisely, to whom nothing worth more than tuppence could happen; whereupon, in the grey desert of his conscious-ness, the very earth had suddenly opened and flamed. With this, further, it came over him that he hadn't been prepared and that his wretched appearance must show it. He wasn't fit to receive a visit – any visit; a flush for his felt misery, in the light of her opulence, broke out in his lean cheeks. But if he coloured he sat as he was – she should at least, as a visitor, be satisfied. His eyes only, at last, turned from her and resumed a little their gaze at the sea. That, however, didn't relieve him, and he perpetrated in the course of another moment the odd desperate gesture of raising both his hands to his face and letting them, while he pressed it to them, cover and guard it. It was as he held them there that she at last spoke.

'I'll go away if you wish me to.' And then she waited a moment. 'I mean now – now that you've seen I'm here. I wanted you to know it, and I thought of writing – I was afraid of our meeting accidentally. Then I was afraid that if I wrote you might refuse. So I thought of this way – as I knew you must come out here.' She went on with pauses, giving him a chance to make a sign. 'I've waited several days. But I'll do what you wish. Only I should like in that case to come back.' Again she stopped; but strange was it to him that he wouldn't have made her break off. She held him in boundless wonder. 'I came down – I mean I came from town – on purpose. I'm staying on still, and I've a great patience and will give you time. Only may I say it's important? Now that I do see you,' she brought out in the same way, 'I see how inevitable it was – I mean that I should have wanted to come. But you must feel about it as you can,' she wound up – 'till you get used to the idea.'

She spoke so for accommodation, for discretion, for some ulterior view already expressed in her manner, that, after taking well in, from behind his hands, that this was her very voice – oh, ladylike! – heard, and heard in deprecation of displeasure, after long years again, he uncovered his face and freshly met her eyes. More than ever he couldn't have known her. Less and less remained of the figure all the facts of which had long ago so hardened for him. She was a handsome, grave, authoritative, but refined and, as it were, physically rearranged person – she, the outrageous vulgarity of whose prime assault had kept him shuddering so long as a shudder was in him. That atrocity in her was what everything had been built on, but somehow, all strangely, it was slipping from him; so that, after the oddest fashion conceivable, when he felt he mustn't let her go, it was as if he were putting out his hand to *save* the past, the hideous, real, unalterable past, exactly as she had been the cause of its being and the cause of his undergoing it. He should have been too awfully 'sold' if he wasn't going to have been right about her.

'I don't mind,' he heard himself at last say. Not to mind had seemed for the instant the length he was prepared to go; but he was afterward aware of how soon he must have added: 'You've come on purpose to see me?' He was on the point of putting to her further: 'What then do you want of me?' But he would keep – yes, in time – from appearing to show he cared. If he showed he cared, where then would be his revenge? So he was already, within five minutes, thinking his revenge uncomfortably over instead of just comfortably knowing it. What came to him, at any rate, as they actually fell to talk, was that, with such precautions, considerations, reduplications of consciousness, almost avowed feelings of her way on her own part, and light fingerings of his chords of sensibility, she was understanding, she *had* understood, more things than all the years, up to this strange eventide, had given him an inkling of. They talked, they went on – he hadn't let her retreat, to whatever it committed him and however abjectly it did so; yet keeping off and off, dealing with such surface facts as involved ancient acquaintance but kept abominations at bay. The recognition, the attestation that she *had* come down for him, that there would be reasons, that she had even hovered and watched, assured herself a little of his habits (which she managed to speak of as if, on their present ampler development, they were much to be deferred to), held them long enough to make vivid how, listen as stiffly or as serenely as he might, she sat there in fear, just as she had so stood there at first, and that her fear had really to do with her calculation of some sort of chance with him. What chance could it possibly be? Whatever it might have done, on this prodigious showing, with Kate Cookham, it made the present witness to the state of his fortunes simply exquisite: he ground his teeth secretly together as he saw he should have to take *that*. For what did it mean but that she would have liked to pity him if she could have done it with safety? Ah, however, he must give her no measure of safety!

By the time he had remarked, with that idea, that she probably saw few changes about them there that weren't for the worse – the place was going down, down and down, so fast that goodness knew where it would stop – and had also mentioned that in spite of this he himself remained faithful, with all its faults loving it still; by the time he had, after that fashion, superficially indulged her, adding a few further light and just sufficiently dry reflections on local matters, the disappearance of landmarks and important persons, the frequency of gales, the low policy of the Town Council in playing down to cheap excursionists: by the time he had so acquitted himself, and she had observed, of her own motion, that she was staying at the Royal, which he knew for the time-honoured, the conservative, and exclusive hotel, he had made out for himself one thing at least, the amazing fact that he had been landed by his troubles, at the end of time, in a 'social relation', of all things in the world, and how of that luxury he was now having unprecedented experience. He had but once in his life had his nose in the Royal, on the occasion of his himself delivering a parcel during some hiatus in his succession of impossible small boys and meeting in the hall the lady who had bought of him, in the morning, a set of Crabbe; largely, he flattered himself, under the artful persuasion of his acute remarks on that author, gracefully associated by him, in this colloquy, he remembered, with a glance at Charles Lamb as well, and who went off, in a day or two, without settling, though he received her cheque from London three or four months later.

That hadn't been a social relation; and truly, deep within his appeal to himself to be remarkable, to be imperturbable and impenetrable, to be in fact quite incomparable now, throbbed the intense vision of his drawing out and draining dry the sensation he had begun to taste. He would do it, moreover – that would be the refinement of his art – not only without the betraying anxiety of a single question, but just even by seeing her flounder (since she must, in a vagueness deeply disconcerting to her) as to her real effect on him. She was distinctly floundering by the time he had brought her – it had taken ten minutes – down to a consciousness of absurd and twaddling topics, to the reported precarious state, for instance, of the syndicate running the Bijou Theatre at the Pierhead – all as an admonition that she might want him to want to know why she was thus waiting on him, might want it for all she was worth, before he had ceased to be so remarkable as not to ask her. He didn't – and this assuredly was wondrous enough – want to do anything worse to her than let her flounder; but he was willing to do that so long as it mightn't prevent his seeing at least where *he* was. He seemed still to see where he was even at the minute that followed her final break-off, clearly intended to be resolute, from make-believe talk.

'I wonder if I might prevail on you to come to tea with me to-morrow at five.'

He didn't so much as answer it – though he could scarcely believe his ears. To-morrow was Sunday, and the proposal referred, clearly, to the custom of 'five-o'clock' tea, known to him only by the contemporary novel of manners and the catchy advertisements of table linen. He had never in his life been present at any such luxurious rite, but he was offering practical indifference to it as a false mark of his sense that his social relation had already risen to his chin. 'I gave up my very modest, but rather interesting little old book business, perhaps you know, ever so long ago.'

She floundered so that she could say nothing – meet *that* with no possible word; all the less too that his tone, casual and colourless, wholly defied any apprehension of it as a reverse. Silence only came; but after a moment she returned to her effort. 'If you *can* come I shall be at home. To see you otherwise than thus was, in fact, what, as I tell you, I came down for. But I leave it,' she returned, 'to your feeling.'

He had at this, it struck him, an inspiration; which he required however a minute or two to decide to carry out; a minute or two during which the shake of his foot over his knee became an intensity of fidget. 'Of course I know I still owe you a large sum of money. If it's about *that* you wish to see me,' he went on, 'I may as well tell you just here that I shall be able to meet my full obligation in the future as little as I've met it in the past. I can never,' said Herbert Dodd, 'pay up that balance.'

He had looked at her while he spoke, but on finishing looked off at the sea again and continued to agitate his foot. He knew now what he had done, and why; and the sense of her fixed dark eyes on him during his speech and after didn't alter his small contentment. Yet even when she still said nothing he didn't turn round; he simply kept his corner as if *that* were his point made, should it even be the last word between them. It might have been, for that matter, from the way in which she presently rose, gathering herself, her fine umbrella and her very small smart reticule, in the construction of which shining gilt much figured, well together, and, after standing another instant, moved across to the rail of the terrace as she had done before and remained, as before, with her back to him, though this time, it well might be, under a different fear. A quarter of an hour ago she hadn't tried him, and had had that anxiety; now that she had tried him it wasn't easier – but she was thinking what she still could do. He left her to think – nothing in fact more interesting than the way she might decide had ever happened to him; but it was a part of this also that as she turned round and came nearer again he didn't rise, he gave her no help. If she got any, at least, from his looking up at her only, meeting her fixed eyes once more in silence, that was her own affair. 'You must think,' she said – 'you must take all your time, but I shall be at home.' She left it to him thus – she insisted, with her idea, on leaving him somewhere too. And on her side as well she showed an art – which resulted, after another instant, in his having to rise to his feet. He flushed afresh as he did it – it exposed him so shabbily the more; and now if she took him in, with each of his seedy items, from head to foot, he didn't and couldn't and wouldn't know it, attaching his eyes hard and straight to something quite away from them.

It stuck in his throat to say he'd come, but she had so curious a way with her that he still less could say he wouldn't, and in a moment had taken refuge in something that was neither. 'Are you married?' – he put it to her with that plainness, though it had seemed before he said it to do more for him than while she waited before replying.

'No, I'm not married,' she said: and then had another wait that might have amounted to a question of what this had to do with it.

He surely couldn't have told her; so that he had recourse, a little poorly as he felt, but to an 'Oh!' that still left them opposed. He turned away for it – that is for the poorness, which, lingering in the air, had almost a vulgar platitude; and when he presently again wheeled about she had fallen off as for quitting him, only with a pause, once more, for a last look. It was all a bit awkward, but he had another happy thought, which consisted in his silently raising his hat as for a sign of dignified dismissal. He had cultivated of old, for the occasions of life, the right, the discriminated bow, and now, out of the grey limbo of the time when he could care for such things, this flicker of propriety leaped and worked. She might, for that matter, herself have liked it; since, receding further, only with her white face toward him, she paid it the homage of submission. He remained dignified, and she almost humbly went.

V

NOTHING in the world, on the Sunday afternoon, could have prevented him from going; he was not after all destitute of three or four such articles of clothing as, if they wouldn't particularly grace the occasion, wouldn't positively dishonour it. That deficiency might have kept him away, but no voice of the spirit, no consideration of pride. It sweetened his impatience, in fact – for he fairly felt it a long time to wait – that his pride would really most find its account in his acceptance of these conciliatory steps. From the moment he could put it in that way – that he couldn't refuse to hear what she might have, so very elaborately, to say for herself – he ought certainly to be at his ease; in illustration of which he whistled odd snatches to himself as he hung about on that cloud-dappled autumn Sunday, a mild private minstrelsy that his lips hadn't known since when? The interval of the twenty-four hours, made longer by a night of many more revivals than oblivions, had in fact dragged not a little; in spite of which, however, our extremely brushed-up and trimmed and polished friend knew an unprecedented flutter as he was ushered, at the Royal Hotel, into Miss Cookham's sitting-room. Yes, it was an adventure, and he had never had an adventure in his life; the term, for him, was essentially a term of high appreciation – such as disqualified for that figure, under due criticism, every single passage of his past career.

What struck him at the moment as qualifying in the highest degree this actual passage was the fact that at no great distance from his hostess in the luxurious room, as he apprehended it, in which the close of day had begun to hang a few shadows, sat a gentleman who rose as she rose, and whose name she at once mentioned to him. He had for Herbert Dodd all the air of a swell, the gentleman – rather red-faced and bald-headed, but moustachioed, waistcoated, necktied to the highest pitch, with an effect of chains and rings, of shining teeth in a glassily monocular smile; a wondrous apparition to have been asked to 'meet' him, as in contemporary fiction, or for him to have been asked to meet. 'Captain Roper, Mr Herbert Dodd' – their entertainer introduced them, yes; but with a sequel immediately afterward more disconcerting apparently to Captain Roper himself even than to her second and more breathless visitor; a 'Well then, good-bye till the next time,' with a hand thrust straight out, which allowed the personage so addressed no alternative but to lay aside his teacup, even though Herbert saw there was a good deal left in it, and glare about him for his hat. Miss Cookham had had her tea-tray on a small table before her, she had served Captain Roper while waiting for Mr Dodd; but she simply dismissed him now, with a high sweet unmistakable decision, a knowledge of what she was about, as our hero would have called it, which enlarged at a stroke the latter's view of the number of different things and sorts of things, in the sphere of the manners and ways of those living at their ease, that a social relation would put before one. Captain Roper would have liked to remain, would have liked more tea, but Kate signified in this direct fashion that she had had enough of him. Herbert had seen things, in his walk of life – rough things, plenty; but never things smoothed with that especial smoothness, carried out as it were by the fine form of Captain Roper's own retreat, which included even a bright convulsed leave-taking cognisance of the plain, vague individual, of no lustre at all and with the very low-class guard of an old silver watch buttoned away under an ill-made coat, to whom he was sacrificed.

It came to Herbert as he left the place a shade less remarkable – though there was still wonder enough and to spare – that he had been even publicly and designedly sacrificed; exactly so that, as the door closed behind him, Kate Cookham, standing there to wait for it, could seem to say, across the room, to the friend of her youth, only by the expression of her fine eyes: 'There – see what I do for you!' 'For' him – that was the extraordinary thing, and not less so that he was already, within three minutes, after this fashion, taking it in as by the intensity of a new light; a light that was one somehow with this rich inner air of the plush-draped and much-mirrored hotel, where the firelight and the approach of evening confirmed together the privacy and the loose curtains at the wide window were parted for a command of his old lifelong Parade – the field of life so familiar to him from below and in the wind and the wet, but which he had never in all the long years hung over at this vantage.

'He's an acquaintance, but a bore,' his hostess explained in respect to Captain Roper. 'He turned up yesterday, but I didn't invite him, and I had said to him before you came in that I was expecting a gentleman with whom I should wish to be alone. I go quite straight at my idea that way, as a rule; but you know,' she now strikingly went on, 'how straight I go. And he had had,' she added, 'his tea.'

Dodd had been looking all round – had taken in, with the rest, the brightness, the distinguished elegance, as he supposed it, of the tea-service with which she was dealing and the variously-tinted appeal of certain savoury edibles on plates. 'Oh, but he *hadn't* had his tea!' he heard himself the next moment earnestly reply; which speech had at once betrayed, he was then quickly aware, the candour of his interest, the unsophisticated state that had survived so many troubles. If he was so interested how could he be proud, and if he was proud how could he be so interested?

He had made her at any rate laugh outright, and was further conscious, for this, both that it was the first time of that since their new meeting, and that it didn't affect him as harsh. It affected him, however, as free, for she replied at once, still smiling and as a part of it: 'Oh, I think we shall get on!'

This told him he had made some difference for her, shown her the way, or something like it, that she hadn't been sure of yesterday; which moreover wasn't what he had intended – he had come armed for showing her nothing; so that after she had gone on, with the same gain of gaiety, 'You must at any rate comfortably have yours,' there was but one answer for him to make.

His eyes played again over the tea-things – they seemed strangely to help him; but he didn't sit down. 'I've come, as you see – but I've come, please, to understand; and if you require to be alone with me, and if I break bread with you, it seems to me I should first know exactly where I am and to what you suppose I so commit myself.' He had thought it out and over and over, particularly the turn about breaking bread; though perhaps he didn't give it, in her presence – this was impossible, her presence altered so many things – quite the full sound or the weight he had planned.

But it had none the less come to his aid – it had made her perfectly grave. 'You commit yourself to nothing. You're perfectly free. It's only I who commit myself.'

On which, while she stood there as if all handsomely and deferentially waiting for him to consider and decide, he would have been naturally moved to ask her what she committed herself then *to* – so moved, that is, if he hadn't, before saying it, thought more sharply still of something better. 'Oh, that's another thing.'

'Yes, that's another thing,' Kate Cookham returned. To which she added, 'So *now* won't you sit down?' He sank with deliberation into the seat from which Captain Roper had risen; she went back to her own, and while she did so spoke again.

'I'm *not* free. At least,' she said over her tea-tray, 'I'm free only for this.'

Everything was there before them and around them, everything massive and shining, so that he had instinctively fallen back in his chair as for the wondering, the resigned acceptance of it; where her last words stirred in him a sense of odd depreciation. Only for 'that'? 'That' was everything, at this moment, to his long inanition, and the effect, as if she had suddenly and perversely mocked him, was to press the spring of a protest. 'Isn't "this" then riches?'

'Riches?' she smiled over, handing him his cup – for she had triumphed in having struck from him a question.

'I mean haven't you a lot of money?' He didn't care now that it was out; his cup was in his hand, and what was that but proved interest? He had succumbed to the social relation.

'Yes, I've money. Of course you wonder – but I've wanted you to wonder. It was to make you take that in that I came. So now you know,' she said, leaning back where she faced him, but in a straighter chair and with her arms closely folded, after a fashion characteristic of her, as for some control of her nerves.

'You came to show you've money?'

'That's one of the things. Not a lot – not even very much. But enough,' said Kate Cookham.

'Enough? I should think so!' he again couldn't help a bit crudely exhaling.

'Enough for what I wanted. I don't always live like this – not at all. But I came to the best hotel on purpose. I wanted to show you I could. Now,' she asked, 'do you understand?'

'Understand?' He only gaped.

She threw up her loosed arms, which dropped again beside her. 'I did it *for* you – I did it *for* you!'

' "For" me –?'

'What I did – what I did here of old.'

He stared, trying to see it. 'When you made me pay you?'

'The Two Hundred and Seventy – all I could get from you, as you reminded me yesterday, so that I had to give up the rest. It was my idea,' she went on – 'it was my idea.'

'To bleed me quite to death?' Oh, his ice was broken now!

'To make you raise money – since you could, you *could*. You did, you did – so what better proof?'

His hands fell from what he had touched; he could only stare – her own manner for it was different now too. 'I did. I did indeed –!' And the woeful weak simplicity of it, which seemed somehow all that was left him, fell even on his own ear.

'Well then, here it is – it isn't lost!' she returned with a graver face.

' "Here" it is,' he gasped, 'my poor agonised old money – my blood?'

'Oh, it's *my* blood too, you must know now!' She held up her head as not before – as for her right to speak of the thing to-day most precious to her. 'I took it, but this – my being here this way – is what I've made of it! That was the idea I had!'

Her 'ideas', as things to boast of, staggered him. 'To have everything in the world, like this, at my wretched expense?'

She had folded her arms back again – grasping each elbow she sat firm; she knew he could see, and had known well from the first, what she had wanted to say, difficult, monstrous though it might be. 'No more than at my own – but to do something with your money that you'd never do yourself.'

'Myself, myself?' he wonderingly wailed. 'Do you know – or don't you? – what my life has been?'

She waited, and for an instant, though the light in the room had failed a little more and would soon be mainly that of the flaring lamps on the windy Parade, he caught from her dark eye a silver gleam of impatience. 'You've suffered and you've worked – which, God knows, is what I've done! *Of course* you've suffered,' she said – 'you inevitably had to! We have to,' she went on, 'to do or to be or to get anything.'

'And pray what have I done or been or got?' Herbert Dodd found it almost desolately natural to demand.

It made her cover him again as with all she was thinking of. 'Can you imagine nothing, or can't you conceive –?' And then as her challenge struck deeper in, deeper down than it had yet reached and with the effect of a rush of the blood to his face, 'It was *for* you, it was *for* you!' she again broke out – 'and for what or whom else could it have been?'

He saw things to a tune now that made him answer straight: 'I thought at one time it might be for Bill Frankle.'

'Yes – that was the way you treated me,' Miss Cookham as plainly replied.

But he let this pass; his thought had already got away from it. 'What good then – its having been for me – has that ever done me?'

'Doesn't it do you any good *now*?' his friend returned. To which she added, with another dim play of her tormented brightness, before he could speak: 'But if you won't even have your tea –!'

He had in fact touched nothing, and if he could have explained, would have pleaded very veraciously that his appetite, keen when he came in, had somehow suddenly failed. It was beyond eating or drinking, what she seemed to want him to take from her. So if he looked, before him, over the array, it was to say, very grave and graceless: 'Am I to understand that you offer to repay me?'

'I offer to repay you with interest, Herbert Dodd' – and her emphasis of the great word was wonderful.

It held him in his place a minute, and held his eyes upon her; after which, agitated too sharply to sit still, he pushed back his chair and stood up. It was as if mere distress or dismay at first worked in him, and was in fact a wave of deep and irresistible emotion which made him, on his feet, sway as in a great trouble and then, to correct it, throw himself stiffly toward the window, where he stood and looked out unseeing. The road, the wide terrace beyond, the seats, the eternal sea beyond that, the lighted lamps now flaring in the October night-wind, with the few dispersed people abroad at the tea-hour; these things, meeting and melting into the firelit hospitality at his elbow – or was it that portentous amenity that melted into *them*? – seemed to form round him and to put before him, all together, the strangest of circles and the newest of experiences, in which the unforgettable and the unimaginable were confoundingly mixed. 'Oh, oh, oh!' – he could only almost howl for it.

And then, while a thick blur for some moments mantled everything, he knew she had got up, that she stood watching him, allowing for everything, again all 'cleverly' patient with him, and he heard her speak again as with studied quietness and clearness. 'I wanted to take care of you – it was what I first wanted – and what you first consented to. I'd have done it, oh, I'd have done it, I'd have loved you and helped you and guarded you, and you'd have had no trouble, no bad blighting ruin, in all your easy, yes, just your quite jolly and comfortable life. I showed you and proved to you this – I brought it home to you, as I fondly fancied, and it made me briefly happy. You swore you cared for me, you wrote it and made me believe it – you pledged me your honour and your faith. Then you turned and changed suddenly, from one day to another; everything altered, you broke your vows, you as good as told me you only wanted it off. You faced me with dislike, and in fact tried not to face me at all; you behaved as if you hated me – you had seen a girl, of great beauty, I admit, who made me a fright and a bore.'

This brought him straight round. 'No, Kate Cookham.'

'Yes, Herbert Dodd.' She but shook her head, calmly and nobly, in the now gathered dusk, and her memories and her cause and her character – or was it only her arch-subtlety, her line and her 'idea'? – gave her an extraordinary large assurance.

She had touched, however, the treasure of his own case – his terrible own case that began to live again at once by the force of her talking of hers, and which could always all cluster about his great asseveration. 'No, no, never, never; I had never seen her then and didn't dream of her; so that when you yourself began to be harsh and sharp with me, and to seem to want to quarrel, I could have but one idea – which was an appearance you didn't in the least, as I saw it then, account for or disprove.'

'An appearance –?' Kate desired, as with high astonishment, to know which one.

'How *shouldn't* I have supposed you really to care for Bill Frankle? – as, thoroughly believing the motive of your claim for my money to be its help to your marrying him, since you couldn't marry me. I was only surprised when, time passing, I made out that that hadn't happened; and perhaps,' he added the next instant, with something of a conscious lapse from the finer style, 'hadn't been in question.'

She had listened to this only staring, and she was silent after he had said it, so silent for some instants that while he considered her something seemed to fail him, much as if he had thrown out his foot for a step and not found the place to rest it. He jerked round to the window again, and then she answered, but without passion, unless it was that of her weariness for something stupid and forgiven in him, 'Oh, the blind, the pitiful folly!' – to which, as it might perfectly have applied to her own behaviour, he returned nothing. She had moreover at once gone on. 'Put it then that there wasn't much to do – between your finding that you loathed me for another woman, or discovering only, when it came to the point, that you loathed me quite enough for myself.'

Which, offered him in that immensely effective fashion, he recognised that he must just unprotestingly and not so very awkwardly – not so *very*! – take from her; since, whatever he had thus come to her for, it wasn't to perjure himself with any pretence that, 'another woman' or no other woman, he hadn't, for years and years, abhorred her. Now he was taking tea with her – or rather, literally, seemed not to be; but this made no difference, and he let her express it as she would while he distinguished a man he knew, Charley Coote, outside on the Parade, under favour of the empty hour and one of the flaring lamps, making up to a young woman with whom (it stuck out grotesquely in his manner) he had never before conversed. Dodd's own position was that of acquiescing in this recall of what had so bitterly been – but he hadn't come back to her, of himself, to stir up, to recall or to recriminate, and for *her* it could but be the very lesson of her whole present act that if she touched anything she touched everything. Soon enough she was indeed, and all overwhelmingly, touching everything – with a hand of which the boldness grew.

'But I didn't let *that*, even, make a difference in what I wanted – which was all,' she said, 'and had only and passionately been, to take care of you. I had *no* money whatever – nothing then of my own, not a penny to come by anyhow; so it wasn't with mine I could do it. But I could do it with yours,' she amazingly wound up – 'if I could once get yours out of you.'

He faced straight about again – his eyebrows higher than they had ever been in his life. 'Mine? What penny of it was mine? What scrap beyond a bare, mean little living had I ever pretended to have?'

She held herself still a minute, visibly with force; only her eyes consciously attached to the seat of a chair the back of which her hands, making it tilt toward her a little, grasped as for support. 'You pretended to have enough to marry me – and that was all I afterwards claimed of you when you wouldn't.' He was on the point of retorting that he had absolutely pretended to nothing – least of all to the primary desire that such a way of putting it fastened on him; he was on the point for ten seconds of giving her full in the face: 'I never *had* any such dream till you yourself – infatuated with me as, frankly, you on the whole appeared to be – got round me and muddled me up and made me behave as if in a way that went against the evidence of my senses.' But he was to feel as quickly that, whatever the ugly, the spent, the irrecoverable truth, he might better have bitten his tongue off: there beat on him there this strange and other, this so prodigiously different beautiful and dreadful truth that no far remembrance and no abiding ache of his own could wholly falsify, and that was indeed all out with her next words. 'That – *using* it for you and using you yourself for your own future – was my motive. I've led my life, which has been an affair, I assure you; and, as I've told you without your quite seeming to understand, I've brought everything fivefold back to you.'

The perspiration broke out on his forehead. 'Everything's mine?' he quavered as for the deep piercing pain of it.

'Everything!' said Kate Cookham.

So it told him how she had loved him – but with the tremendous effect at once of its only glaring out at him from the whole thing that it was verily she, a thousand times over, who, in the exposure of his youth and his vanity, had, on the bench of desolation, the scene of yesterday's own renewal, left for him no forward step to take. It hung there for him tragically vivid again, the hour she had first found him sequestered and accessible after making his acquaintance at his shop. And from this, by a succession of links that fairly clicked to his ear as with their perfect fitting, the fate and the pain and the payment of others stood together in a great grim order. Everything there then was *his* – to make him ask what had been Nan's, poor Nan's of the constant question of whether he need have collapsed. She was before him, she was between them, his little dead dissatisfied wife; across all whose final woe and whose lowly grave he was to reach out, it appeared, to take gifts. He saw them too, the gifts; saw them – she bristled with them – in his actual companion's brave and sincere and authoritative figure, her strangest of demonstrations. But the other appearance was intenser, as if their ghost had waved wild arms; so that half a minute hadn't passed before the one poor thing that remained of Nan, and that yet thus became a quite mighty and momentous poor thing, was sitting on his lips as for its sole opportunity.

'Can you give me your word of honour that I mightn't, under decent advice, have defied you?'

It made her turn very white; but now that she had said what she *had* said she could still hold up her head. 'Certainly you might have defied me, Herbert Dodd.'

'They would have told me you had no legal case?'

Well, if she was pale she was bold. 'You talk of decent advice – !' She broke off; there was too much to say, and all needless. What she said instead was: 'They would have told you I had nothing.'

'I didn't so much as ask,' her sad visitor remarked.

'Of course you didn't so much as ask.'

'I couldn't be so outrageously vulgar,' he went on.

'*I* could, by God's help!' said Kate Cookham.

'Thank you.' He had found at his command a tone that made him feel more gentleman-like than he had ever felt in his life or should doubtless ever feel again. It might have been enough – but somehow as they stood there with this immense clearance between them it wasn't. The clearance was like a sudden gap or great bleak opening through which there blew upon them a deadly chill. Too many things had fallen away, too many new rolled up and over him, and they made something within shake him to his base. It upset the full vessel, and though she kept her eyes on him he let that consequence come, bursting into tears, weakly crying there before her even as he had cried to himself in the hour of his youth when she had made him groundlessly fear. She turned away then – *that* she couldn't watch, and had presently flung herself on the sofa and, all responsively wailing, buried her own face on the cushioned arm. So for a minute their smothered sobs only filled the room. But he made out, through this disorder, where he had put down his hat; his stick and his new tan-coloured gloves – they had cost two-and-thruppence and would have represented sacrifices – were on the chair beside it. He picked these articles up and all silently and softly – gasping, that is, but quite on tiptoe – reached the door and let himself out.

VI

OFF there on the bench of desolation a week later she made him a more particular statement, which it had taken the remarkably tense interval to render possible. After leaving her at the hotel that last Sunday he had gone forth in his reaggravated trouble and walked straight before him, in the teeth of the west wind, close to the iron rails of the stretched Marina and with his tell-tale face turned from persons occasionally met and toward the surging sea. At the land's end, even in the confirmed darkness and the perhaps imminent big blow, his immemorial nook, small shelter as it yielded, had again received him; and it was in the course of this heedless session, no doubt, where the agitated air had nothing to add to the commotion within him, that he began to look his extraordinary fortune a bit straighter in the face and see it confess itself at once a fairy-tale and a nightmare. That, visibly, confoundingly, she was still attached to him (attached in fact was a mild word!) and that the unquestionable proof of it was in this offered pecuniary salve, of the thickest composition, for his wounds and sores and shames – these things were the fantastic fable, the tale of money in handfuls, that he seemed to have only to stand there and swallow and digest and feel himself full-fed by; but the whole of the rest was nightmare, and most of all nightmare his having thus to thank one through whom Nan and his little girls had known torture.

He didn't care for himself now, and this unextinguished and apparently inextinguishable charm by which he had held her was a fact incredibly romantic; but he gazed with a longer face than he had ever had for anything in the world at his potential acceptance of a great bouncing benefit from the person he intimately, if even in a manner indirectly, associated with the conditions to which his lovely wife and his little girls (who would have been so lovely too) had pitifully succumbed. He had accepted the social relation – which meant he had taken even that on trial – without knowing what it so dazzlingly masked; for a social relation it had become with a vengeance when it drove him about the place as now at his hours of freedom (and he actually and recklessly took, all demoralised and unstrung and unfit either for work or for anything else, other liberties that would get him into trouble) under this queer torment of irreconcilable things, a bewildered consciousness of tenderness and patience and cruelty, of great evident mystifying facts that were as little to be questioned as to be conceived or explained, and that were yet least, withal, to be lost sight of.

On that Sunday night he had wandered wild, incoherently ranging and throbbing, but this became the law of his next days as well, since he lacked more than ever all other resort or refuge and had nowhere to carry, to deposit, or contractedly let loose and lock up, as it were, his swollen consciousness, which fairly split in twain the raw shell of his sordid little boarding-place. The arch of the sky and the spread of sea and shore alone gave him space; he could roam with himself anywhere, in short, far or near – he could only never take himself back. That certitude – that this was impossible to him even should she wait there among her plushes and bronzes ten years – was the thing he kept closest clutch of; it did wonders for what he would have called his self-respect. Exactly as he had left her so he would stand off – even though at moments when he pulled up sharp somewhere to put himself an intensest question his heart almost stood still. The days of the week went by, and as he had left her she stayed; to the extent, that is, of his having neither sight nor sound of her, and of the failure of every sign. It took nerve, he said, not to return to her, even for curiosity – since how, after all, in the name of wonder, had she invested the fruits of her extortion to such advantage, there being no chapter of all the obscurity of the years to beat that for queerness? But he dropped, tired to death, on benches, half a dozen times an evening – exactly on purpose to recognise that the nerve required was just the nerve he had.

As the days without a token from her multiplied he came in as well for hours – and these indeed mainly on the bench of desolation – of sitting stiff and stark in presence of the probability that he had lost everything for ever. When he passed the Royal he never turned an eyelash, and when he met Captain Roper on the Front, three days after having been introduced to him, he 'cut him dead' – another privileged consequence of a social relation – rather than seem to himself to make the remotest approach to the question of whether Miss Cookham had left Properley. He had cut people in the days of his life before, just as he had come to being himself cut – since there had been no time for him wholly without one or other face of that necessity – but had never affected such a severance as of this rare connection, which helped to give him thus the measure of his really precious sincerity. If he had lost what had hovered before him he had lost it, his only tribute to which proposition was to grind his teeth with one of those 'scrunches', as he would have said, of which the violence fairly reached his ear. It wouldn't make him lift a finger, and in fact if Kate had simply taken herself off on the Tuesday or the Wednesday she would have been reabsorbed again into the darkness from which she had emerged – and no lifting of fingers, the unspeakable chapter closed, would evermore avail. That at any rate was the kind of man he still was – even after all that had come and gone, and even if for a few dazed hours certain things had seemed pleasant. The dazed hours had passed, the surge of the old bitterness had dished him (shouldn't he have been shamed if it hadn't?) and he might sit there as before, as always, with nothing at all on earth to look to. He had therefore wrongfully believed himself to be degraded; and the last word about him would be that he *couldn't* then, it appeared, sink to vulgarity as he had tried to let his miseries make him.

And yet on the next Sunday morning, face to face with him again at the land's end, what she very soon came to was: 'As if I believed you didn't *know* by what cord you hold me!' Absolutely, too, and just that morning in fact, above all, he wouldn't, he quite couldn't have taken his solemn oath that he hadn't a sneaking remnant, as he might have put it to himself – a remnant of faith in tremendous things still to come of their interview. The day was sunny and breezy, the sea of a cold purple; he wouldn't go to church as he mostly went of Sunday mornings, that being in its way too a social relation – and not least when two-and-thruppenny tan-coloured gloves were new; which indeed he had the art of keeping them for ages. Yet he would dress himself as he scarce mustered resources for even to figure on the fringe of Society, local and transient, at St Bernard's, and in this trim he took his way westward; occupied largely, as he went, it might have seemed to any person pursuing the same course and happening to observe him, in a fascinated study of the motions of his shadow, the more or less grotesque shape projected, in front of him and mostly a bit to the right, over the blanched asphalt of the Parade and dangling and dancing at such a rate, shooting out and then contracting, that, viewed in themselves, its eccentricities might have formed the basis of an interesting challenge: 'Find the state of mind, guess the nature of the agitation, possessing the person so remarkably represented!' Herbert Dodd, for that matter, might have been himself attempting to make by the sun's sharp aid some approach to his immediate horoscope.

It had at any rate been thus put before him that the dandling and dancing of his image occasionally gave way to perfect immobility, when he stopped and kept his eyes on it. 'Suppose she should come, suppose she *should*!' it is revealed at least to ourselves that he had at these moments audibly breathed – breathed with the intensity of an arrest between hope and fear. It had glimmered upon him from early, with the look of the day, that, given all else that could happen, this would be rather, as he put it, in her line; and the possibility lived for him, as he proceeded, to the tune of a suspense almost sickening. It was, from one small stage of his pilgrimage to another, the 'For ever, never!' of the sentimental case the playmates of his youth used to pretend to settle by plucking the petals of a daisy. But it came to his truly turning faint – so 'queer' he felt – when, at the gained point of the long stretch from which he could always tell, he arrived within positive sight of his immemorial goal. His seat was taken and she was keeping it for him – it could only be *she* there in possession; whereby it shone out for Herbert Dodd that if he hadn't been quite sure of her recurrence she had at least been quite sure of his. *That* pulled him up to some purpose, where recognition began for them – or to the effect, in other words, of his pausing to judge if he could bear, for the sharpest note of their intercourse, this inveterate demonstration of her making him do what she liked. What settled the question for him then – and just while they avowedly watched each other, over the long interval, before closing, as if, on either side, for the major advantage – what settled it was this very fact that what she liked she liked so terribly. If it were simply to 'use' him, as she had said the last time, and no matter to the profit of which of them she called it, one might let it go for that; since it could make her wait over, day after day, in that fashion, and with such a spending of money, on the hazard of their meeting again. How could she be the least sure he would ever again consent to it after the proved action on him, a week ago, of her last monstrous honesty? It was indeed positively as if he were now himself putting this influence – and for their common edification – to the supreme, to the finest test. He had a sublime, an ideal flight, which lasted about a minute. 'Suppose, now that I see her there and what she has taken so characteristically for granted, suppose I just show her that she *hasn't* only confidently to wait or whistle for me, and that the length of my leash is greater than she measures, and that everything's impossible always? – show it by turning my back on her now and walking straight away. She won't be able not to understand *that*!'

Nothing had passed, across their distance, but the mute apprehension of each on the part of each; the whole expanse, at the church hour, was void of other life (he had scarce met a creature on his way from end to end) and the sun-seasoned gusts kept brushing the air and all the larger prospect clean. It was through this beautiful lucidity that he watched her watch him, as it were – watch him for what he would do. Neither moved at this high tension; Kate Cookham, her face fixed on him, only waited with a stiff appearance of leaving him, not for dignity but – to an effect of even deeper perversity – for kindness, free to choose. It yet somehow affected him at present, this attitude, as a gage of her *knowing too* – knowing, that is, that he wasn't really free, that this was the thinnest of vain parades, the poorest of hollow heroics, that his need, his solitude, his suffered wrong, his exhausted rancour, his foredoomed submission to any shown interest, all hung together too heavy on him to let the weak wings of his pride do more than vaguely tremble. They couldn't, they didn't carry him a single beat further away; according to which he stood rooted, neither retreating nor advancing, but presently correcting his own share of their bleak exchange by looking off at the sea. Deeply conscious of the awkwardness this posture gave him, he yet clung to it as the last shred of his honour, to the clear argument that it was one thing for him to have felt beneath all others, the previous days, that she was to be counted on, but quite a different for her to have felt that *he* was. His checked approach, arriving thus at no term, could in these odd conditions have established that he wasn't only if Kate Cookham had, as either of them might have said, taken it so – if she had given up the game at last by rising, by walking away and adding to the distance between them, and he had then definitely let her vanish into space. It became a fact that when she did finally rise – though after how long our record scarce takes on itself to say – it was not to confirm their separation but to put an end to it; and this by slowly approaching him till she had come within earshot. He had wondered, once aware of it in spite of his averted face, what she would say and on what note, as it were, she would break their week's silence; so that he had to recognise anew, her voice reaching him, that remarkable quality in her which again and again came up for him as her art.

'There are twelve hundred and sixty pounds, to be definite, but I have it all down for you – and you've only to draw.'

They lost themselves, these words, rare and exquisite, in the wide bright genial medium and the Sunday stillness, but even while that occurred and he was gaping for it she was herself there, in her battered ladylike truth, to answer for them, to represent them, and, if a further grace than their simple syllabled beauty were conceivable, almost embarrassingly to cause them to materialise. Yes, she let her smart and tight little reticule hang as if it bulged, beneath its clasp, with the whole portentous sum, and he felt himself glare again at this vividest of her attested claims. She might have been ready, on the spot, to open the store to the plunge of his hand, or, with the situation otherwise conceived, to impose on his pauperised state an acceptance of alms on a scale unprecedented in the annals of street charity. Nothing so much counted for him, however, neither grave numeral nor elegant fraction, as the short, rich, rounded word that the breeze had picked up as it dropped and seemed now to blow about between them. 'To draw – to draw?' Yes, he gaped it as if it had no sense; the fact being that even while he did so he was reading into her use of the term more romance than any word in the language had ever had for him. He, Herbert Dodd, was to live to 'draw', like people, scarce hampered by the conditions of earth, whom he had remotely and circuitously heard about, and in fact when he walked back with her to where she had been sitting it was very much, for his strained nerves, as if the very bench of desolation itself were to be the scene of that exploit and he mightn't really live till he reached it.

When they had sat down together she did press the spring of her reticule, extracting from it, not a handful of gold nor a packet of crisp notes, but an oblong sealed letter, which she had thus waited on him, she remarked, on purpose to deliver, and which would certify, with sundry particulars, to the credit she had opened for him at a London bank. He took it from her without looking at it, and held it, in the same manner, conspicuous and unassimilated, for most of the rest of the immediate time, appearing embarrassed with it, nervously twisting and flapping it, yet thus publicly retaining it even while aware, beneath everything, of the strange, the quite dreadful, wouldn't it be? engagement that such inaction practically stood for. He could accept money to that amount, yes – but not for nothing in return. For what then in return? He kept asking himself for what, while she said other things and made above all, in her high, shrewd, successful way, the point that, no, he needn't pretend that his conviction of her continued personal interest in him wouldn't have tided him over any question besetting him since their separation. She put it to him that the deep instinct of where he should at last find her must confidently have worked for him, since she confessed to her instinct of where she should find *him*; which meant – oh, it came home to him as he fingered his sealed treasure! – neither more nor less than that she had now created between them an equality of experience. He wasn't to have done all the suffering, *she* was to have 'been through' things he couldn't even guess at; and, since he was bargaining away his right ever again to allude to the unforgettable, so much there was of it, what her tacit proposition came to was that they were 'square' and might start afresh.

He didn't take up her charge, as his so compromised 'pride' yet in a manner prompted him, that he had enjoyed all the week all those elements of ease about her; the most he achieved for that was to declare, with an ingenuity contributing to float him no small distance further, that of course he had turned up at their old place of tryst, which had been, through the years, the haunt of his solitude and the goal of his walk any Sunday morning that seemed too beautiful for church; but that he hadn't in the least built on her presence there – since that supposition gave him, she would understand, wouldn't she? the air, disagreeable to him, of having come in search of her. Her quest of himself, once he had been seated there, would have been another matter – but in short, 'Of course after all you did come to me, just now, didn't you?' He felt himself, too, lamely and gracelessly grin, as for the final kick of his honour, in confirmation of the record that he had then yielded but to her humility. Her humility became for him at this hour and to this tune, on the bench of desolation, a quantity more prodigious and even more mysterious than that other guaranteed quantity the finger-tips of his left hand could feel the tap of by the action of his right; though what was in especial extraordinary was the manner in which she could keep making him such allowances and yet meet him again, at some turn, as with her residuum for her clever self so great.

'Come to you, Herbert Dodd?' she imperturbably echoed. 'I've been coming to you for the last ten years!'

There had been for him just before this sixty supreme seconds of intensest aspiration – a minute of his keeping his certificate poised for a sharp thrust back at her, the thrust of the wild freedom of his saying: 'No, no, I *can't* give them up; I can't simply sink them deep down in my soul for ever, with no cross in all my future to mark *that* burial; so that if this is what our arrangement means I must decline to have anything to do with it.' The words none the less hadn't come, and when she had herself, a couple of minutes later, spoken those others, the blood rose to his face as if, given his stiffness and her extravagance, he had just indeed saved himself.

Everything in fact stopped, even his fidget with his paper; she imposed a hush, she imposed at any rate the conscious decent form of one, and he couldn't afterward have told how long, at this juncture, he must have sat simply gazing before him. It was so long, at any rate, that Kate herself got up – and quite indeed, presently, as if her own forms were now at an end. He had returned her nothing – so what was she waiting for? She had been on the two other occasions momentarily at a loss, but never so much so, no doubt, as was thus testified to by her leaving the bench and moving over once more to the rail of the terrace. She could carry it off, in a manner, with her resources, that she was waiting with so little to wait for; she could face him again, after looking off at the sea, as if this slightly stiff delay, not wholly exempt from awkwardness, had been but a fine scruple of her courtesy. She had gathered herself in; after giving him time to appeal she could take it that he had decided and that nothing was left for her to do. 'Well then,' she clearly launched at him across the broad walk – 'well then, good-bye.'

She had come nearer with it, as if he might rise for some show of express separation; but he only leaned back motionless, his eyes on her now – he kept her a moment before him. 'Do you mean that we don't – that we don't –?' But he broke down.

'Do I "mean" –?' She remained as for questions he might ask, but it was well-nigh as if there played through her dotty veil an irrepressible irony for that particular one. 'I've meant, for long years, I think, all I'm capable of meaning. I've meant so much that I can't mean more. So there it is.'

'But if you go,' he appealed – and with a sense as of final flatness, however he arranged it, for his own attitude – 'but if you go shan't I see you again?'

She waited a little and it was strangely for him now as if – though at last so much more gorged with her tribute than she had ever been with his – something still depended on her. 'Do you *like* to see me?' she very simply asked.

At this he did get up; that was easier than to say – at least with responsive simplicity; and again for a little he looked hard and in silence at his letter; which, at last, however, raising his eyes to her own for the act, while he masked their conscious ruefulness, to his utmost, in some air of assurance, he slipped into the inner pocket of his coat, letting it settle there securely. 'You're too wonderful.' But he frowned at her with it as never in his life. 'Where does it all come from?'

'The wonder of poor me?' Kate Cookham said. 'It comes from *you*.'

He shook his head slowly – feeling, with his letter there against his heart, such a new agility, almost such a new range of interest. 'I mean so *much* money – so extraordinarily much.'

Well, she held him a while blank. 'Does it seem to you extraordinarily much – twelve-hundred-and-sixty? Because, you know,' she added, 'it's all.'

'It's enough!' he returned with a slight thoughtful droop of his head to the right and his eyes attached to the far horizon as through a shade of shyness for what he was saying. He felt all her own lingering nearness somehow on his cheek.

'It's enough? Thank you then!' she rather oddly went on.

He shifted a little his posture. 'It was more than a hundred a year – for you to get together.'

'Yes,' she assented, 'that was what year by year I tried for.'

'But that you could live all the while and have that –!' Yes, he was at liberty, as he hadn't been, quite pleasantly to marvel. All his wonderments in life had been hitherto unanswered – and didn't the change mean that here again was the social relation?

'Ah, I didn't live as you saw me the other day.'

'Yes,' he answered – and didn't he the next instant feel he must fairly have smiled with it? – 'the other day you *were* going it!'

'For once in my life,' said Kate Cookham. 'I've left the hotel,' she after a moment added.

'Ah, you're in – a – lodgings?' he found himself inquiring as for positive sociability.

She had apparently a slight shade of hesitation, but in an instant it was all right; as what he showed he wanted to know she seemed mostly to give him. 'Yes – but far of course from here. Up on the hill.' To which, after another instant, 'At The Mount, Castle Terrace,' she subjoined.

'Oh, I *know* The Mount. And Castle Terrace is awfully sunny and nice.'

'Awfully sunny and nice,' Kate Cookham took from him.

'So that if it isn't,' he pursued, 'like the Royal, why, you're at least comfortable.'

'I shall be comfortable anywhere now,' she replied with a certain dryness.

It was astonishing, however, what had become of his own. 'Because I've accepted –?'

'Call it that!' she dimly smiled.

'I hope then at any rate,' he returned, 'you can now thoroughly rest.' He spoke as for a cheerful conclusion and moved again also to smile, though as with a poor grimace, no doubt; since what he seemed most clearly to feel was that since he 'accepted' he mustn't, for his last note, have accepted in sulkiness or gloom. With that, at the same time, he couldn't but know, in all his fibres, that with such a still-watching face as the dotty veil didn't disguise for him there was no possible concluding, at least on his part. On hers, on hers it was – as he had so often for a week had reflectively to pronounce things – another affair. Ah, somehow, both formidably and helpfully, her face concluded – yet in a sense so strangely enshrouded in things she didn't tell him. What *must* she, what mustn't she, have done? What she had said – she had really told him nothing – was no account of her life; in the midst of which conflict of opposed recognitions, at any rate, it was as if, for all he could do, he himself now considerably floundered. 'But I can't think – I can't think –!'

'You can't think I can have made so much money in the time and been honest?'

'Oh, you've been *honest*!' Herbert Dodd distinctly allowed.

It moved her stillness to a gesture – which, however, she had as promptly checked; and she went on the next instant as for further generosity to his failure of thought. 'Everything was possible, under my stress, with my hatred.'

'Your hatred –?' For she had paused as if it were after all too difficult.

'Of what I should for so long have been doing to you.'

With this, for all his failures, a greater light than any yet shone upon him. 'It made you think of ways –?'

'It made me think of everything. It made me work,' said Kate Cookham. She added, however, the next moment: 'But that's my story.'

'And I mayn't hear it?'

'No – because I mayn't hear yours.'

'Oh, mine –!' he said with the strangest, saddest yet after all most resigned sense of surrender of it; which he tried to make sound as if he couldn't have told it, for its splendour of sacrifice and of misery, even if he would.

It seemed to move in her a little, exactly, that sense of the invidious. 'Ah, mine too, I assure you –!'

He rallied at once to the interest. 'Oh, we *can* talk then?'

'Never,' she most oddly replied. 'Never,' said Kate Cookham.

They remained so, face to face; the effect of which for him was that he had after a little understood why. That was fundamental. 'Well, I see.'

Thus confronted they stayed; and then, as he saw with a contentment that came up from deeper still, it was indeed she who, with her worn fine face, would conclude. 'But I can take care of you.'

'You *have*!' he said as with nothing left of him but a beautiful appreciative candour.

'Oh, but you'll want it now in a way –!' she responsibly answered.

He waited a moment, dropping again on the seat. So, while she still stood, he looked up at her; with the sense somehow that there were too many things and that they were all together, terribly, irresistibly, doubtless blessedly, in her eyes and her whole person; which thus affected him for the moment as more than he could bear. He leaned forward, dropping his elbows to his knees and pressing his head on his hands. So he stayed, saying nothing; only, with the sense of her own sustained, renewed and wonderful action, knowing that an arm had passed round him and that he was held. She was beside him on the bench of desolation.

A ROUND OF VISITS

I

HE had been out but once since his arrival, Mark Monteith; that was the next day after – he had disembarked by night on the previous; then everything had come at once, as he would have said, everything had changed. He had got in on Tuesday; he had spent Wednesday for the most part down town, looking into the dismal subject of his anxiety – the anxiety that, under a sudden decision, had brought him across the unfriendly sea at mid-winter, and it was through information reaching him on Wednesday evening that he had measured his loss, measured, above all, his pain. These were two distinct things, he felt, and, though both bad, one much worse than the other. It wasn't till the next three days had pretty well ebbed, in fact, that he knew himself for so badly wounded. He had waked up on Thursday morning, so far as he had slept at all, with the sense, together, of a blinding New York blizzard and of a deep sore inward ache. The great white savage storm would have kept him at the best within doors, but his stricken state was by itself quite reason enough.

He so felt the blow indeed, so gasped, before what had happened to him, at the ugliness, the bitterness, and, beyond these things, the sinister strangeness, that, the matter of his dismay little by little detaching and projecting itself, settling there face to face with him as something he must now live with always, he might have been in charge of some horrid alien thing, some violent, scared, unhappy creature whom there was small joy, of a truth, in remaining with, but whose behaviour wouldn't perhaps bring him under notice, nor otherwise compromise him, so long as he should stay to watch it. A young jibbering ape of one of the more formidable sorts, or an ominous infant panther smuggled into the great gaudy hotel and whom it might yet be important he shouldn't advertise, couldn't have affected him as needing more domestic attention. The great gaudy hotel – The Pocahontas, but carried out largely on 'Du Barry' lines – made all about him, beside, behind, below, above, in blocks and tiers and superpositions, a sufficient defensive hugeness; so that, between the massive labyrinth and the New York weather, life in a lighthouse during a gale would scarce have kept him more apart. Even when, in the course of that worse Thursday, it had occurred to him for vague relief that the odious certified facts couldn't be all his misery, and that, with his throat and a probable temperature, a brush of the epidemic, which was for ever brushing him, accounted for something, even then he couldn't resign himself to bed and broth and dimness, but only circled and prowled the more within his high cage, only watched the more from his tenth storey the rage of the elements.

   In the afternoon he had a doctor – the caravanserai, which supplied everything in quantities, had one for each group of so many rooms – just in order to be assured that he was *grippé* enough for anything. What his visitor, making light of his attack, perversely told him was that he was, much rather, 'blue' enough, and from causes doubtless known to himself – which didn't come to the same thing; but he 'gave him something', prescribed him warmth and quiet and broth and courage, and came back the next day to readminister this last dose. He then pronounced him better, and on Saturday pronounced him well – all the more that the storm had abated and the snow had been dealt with as New York, at a push, knew how to deal with things. Oh, how New York knew how to deal – to deal, that is, with other accumulations lying passive to its hand – was exactly what Mark now ached with his impression of; so that, still threshing about in this consciousness, he had on the Saturday come near to breaking out as to what was the matter with him. The doctor brought in somehow the air of the hotel – which, cheerfully and conscientiously, by his simple philosophy, the good man wished to diffuse; breathing forth all the echoes of other woes and worries and pointing the honest moral that, especially with such a thermometer, there were enough of these to go round. Our sufferer, by that time, would have liked to tell someone; extracting, to the last acid strain of it, the full strength of his sorrow, taking it all in as he could only do by himself, and with the conditions favourable at least to this, had been his natural first need. But now, he supposed, he *must* be better; there was something of his heart's heaviness he wanted so to give out.

He had rummaged forth on the Thursday night half a dozen old photographs stuck into a leather frame, a small show-case that formed part of his usual equipage of travel – he mostly set it up on a table when he stayed anywhere long enough; and in one of the neat gilt-edged squares of this convenient portable array, as familiar as his shaving-glass or the hair-brushes, of backs and monograms now so beautifully toned and wasted, long ago given him by his mother, Phil Bloodgood handsomely faced him. Not contemporaneous, and a little faded, but so saying what it said only the more dreadfully, the image seemed to sit there, at an immemorial window, like some long effective and only at last exposed 'decoy' of fate. It was *because* he was so beautifully good-looking, because he was so charming and clever and frank – besides being one's third cousin, or whatever it was, one's early school-fellow and one's later college classmate – that one had abjectly trusted him. To live thus with his unremoved, undestroyed, engaging, treacherous face, had been, as our traveller desired, to live with all of the felt pang; had been to consume it in such a single hot, sore mouthful as would so far as possible dispose of it and leave but cold dregs. Thus, if the doctor, casting about for pleasantness, had happened to notice him there, salient since he was, and possibly by the same stroke even to know him, as New York – and more or less to its cost now, mightn't one say? – so abundantly and agreeably had, the cup would have overflowed and Monteith, for all he could be sure of the contrary, would have relieved himself positively in tears.

'Oh, *he's* what's the matter with me – that, looking after some of my poor dividends, as he for the ten years of my absence had served me by doing, he has simply jockeyed me out of the whole little collection, such as it was, and taken the opportunity of my return, inevitably at last bewildered and uneasy, to "sail", ten days ago, for parts unknown and as yet unguessable. It isn't the beastly values themselves, however;

that's only awkward and I can still live, though I don't quite know how I shall turn round; it's the horror of *his* having done it, and done it to *me* – without a mitigation or, so to speak, a warning or an excuse.' That, at a hint or a jog, is what he would have brought out – only to feel afterward, no doubt, that he had wasted his impulse and profaned even a little his sincerity. The doctor didn't in the event so much as glance at his cluster of portraits – which fact quite put before our friend the essentially more vivid range of imagery that a pair of eyes transferred from room to room and from one queer case to another, in such a place as that, would mainly be adjusted to. It wasn't for *him* to relieve himself touchingly, strikingly or whatever, to such a man: such a man might much more pertinently – save for professional discretion – have emptied out there his own bag of wonders; prodigies of observation, flowers of oddity, flowers of misery, flowers of the monstrous, gathered in current hotel practice. Countless possibilities, making doctors perfunctory, Mark felt, swarmed and seethed at their doors; it showed for an incalculable world, and at last, on Sunday, he decided to leave his room.

II

EVERYTHING as he passed through the place went on – all the offices of life, the whole bustle of the market, and withal surprisingly scarce less that of the nursery and the playground, the whole sprawl in especial of the great gregarious fireside; it was a complete social scene in itself, on which types might figure and passions rage and plots thicken and dramas develop, without reference to any other sphere, or perhaps even to anything at all outside. The signs of this met him at every turn as he threaded the labyrinth, passing from one extraordinary masquerade of expensive objects, one portentous 'period' of decoration, one violent phase of publicity, to another: the heavy heat, the luxuriance, the extravagance, the quantity, the colour, gave the impression of some wondrous tropical forest, where vociferous, bright-eyed, and feathered creatures, of every variety of size and hue, were half smothered between undergrowths of velvet and tapestry and ramifications of marble and bronze. The fauna and the flora startled him alike, and among them his bruised spirit drew in and folded its wings. But he roamed and rested, exploring and in a manner enjoying the vast rankness – in the depth of which he suddenly encountered Mrs Folliott, whom he had last seen, six months before, in London, and who had spoken to him then, precisely, of Phil Bloodgood, for several years previous her confidential American agent and factotum too, as she might say, but at that time so little in her good books, for the extraordinary things he seemed to be doing, that she was just hurrying home, she had made no scruple of mentioning, to take everything out of his hands.

Mark remembered how uneasy she had made him – how that very talk with her had wound him up to fear, as so acute and intent a little person she affected him; though he had affirmed with all emphasis and flourish his own confidence and defended, to iteration, his old friend. This passage had remained with him for a certain pleasant heat of intimacy, his partner, of the charming appearance, being what she was; he liked to think how they had fraternised over their difference and called each other idiots, or almost, without offence. It was always a link to have scuffled, failing a real scratch, with such a character; and he had at present the flutter of feeling that something of this would abide. *He* hadn't been hurrying home, at the London time, in any case; he was doing nothing then, and had continued to do it; he would want, before showing suspicion – that had been his attitude – to have more, after all, to go upon. Mrs Folliott also, and with a great actual profession of it, remembered and rejoiced; and, also staying in the house as she was, sat with him, under a spreading palm, in a wondrous rococo *salon*, surrounded by the pinkest, that is the fleshiest imitation Boucher panels, and wanted to know if he *now* stood up for his swindler. She would herself have tumbled on a cloud, very passably, in a fleshy Boucher manner, hadn't she been over-dressed for such an exercise; but she was quite realistically aware of what had so naturally happened – she was prompt about Bloodgood's 'flight'.

She had acted with energy, on getting back – she had saved what she could; which hadn't, however, prevented her losing all disgustedly some ten thousand dollars. She was lovely, lively, friendly, interested, she connected Monteith perfectly with their discussion that day during the water-party on the Thames; but, sitting here with him half an hour, she talked only of her peculiar, her cruel sacrifice – since she should never get a penny back. He had felt himself, on their meeting, quite yearningly reach out to her – so decidedly, by the morning's end, and that of his scattered sombre stations, had he been sated with meaningless contacts, with the sense of people all about him intensely, though harmlessly animated, yet at the same time raspingly indifferent. *They* would have, he and she at least, their common pang – through which fact, somehow, he should feel less stranded. It wasn't that he wished to be pitied – he fairly didn't pity himself; he winced, rather, and even to vicarious anguish, as it rose again, for poor shamed Bloodgood's doom-ridden figure. But he wanted, as with a desperate charity, to give some easier turn to the mere ugliness of the main facts; to work off his obsession from them by mixing with it some other blame, some other pity, it scarce mattered what – if it might be some other experience; as an effect of which larger ventilation it would have, after a fashion and for a man of free sensibility, a diluted and less poisonous taste.

By the end of five minutes of Mrs Folliott, however, he felt his dry lips seal themselves to a makeshift simper. She could *take* nothing – no better, no broader perception of anything than fitted her own small faculty; so that though she must have recalled or imagined that he had still, up to lately, had interests at stake, the rapid result of her egotistical little chatter was to make him wish he might rather have conversed with the French waiter dangling in the long vista that showed the oriental *café* as a climax, or with the policeman, outside, the top of whose helmet peeped above the ledge of a window. She bewailed her wretched money to excess – she who, he was sure, had quantities more; she pawed and tossed her bare bone, with her little extraordinarily gemmed and manicured hands, till it acted on his nerves; she rang all the changes on the story, the dire fatality, of her having wavered and muddled, thought of this and but done that, of her stupid failure to have pounced, when she had first meant to, in season. She abused the author of their wrongs – recognising thus too Monteith's right to loathe him – for the desperado he assuredly had proved, but with a vulgarity of analysis and an incapacity for the higher criticism, as her listener felt it to be, which made him determine resentfully, almost grimly, that she shouldn't have the benefit of a grain of *his* vision or *his* version of what had befallen them, and of how, in particular, it had come; and should never dream thereby (though much would she suffer from that!) of how interesting he might have been. She had, in a finer sense, no manners, and to be concerned with her in any retrospect was – since their discourse was of losses – to feel the dignity of history incur the very gravest. It was true that such fantasies, or that any shade of inward irony, would be Greek to Mrs Folliott.

It was also true, however, and not much more strange, when she had presently the comparatively happy thought of 'Lunch with *us*, you poor dear!' and mentioned three or four of her 'crowd' – a new crowd, rather, for her, all great Sunday lunchers there and immense fun, who would in a moment be turning up – that this seemed to him as easy as anything else; so that after a little, deeper in the jungle and while, under the temperature as of high noon, with the crowd complete and 'ordering', he wiped the perspiration from his brow, he felt he was letting himself go. He did that certainly to the extent of leaving far behind any question of Mrs Folliott's manners. They didn't matter there – nobody's did; and if she ceased to lament her ten thousand it was only because, among higher voices, she couldn't make herself heard. Poor Bloodgood didn't have a show, as they might have said, didn't get through at any point; the crowd was so new that – there either having been no hue and cry for him, or having been too many others, for other absconders, in the interval – they had never so much as heard of him and would have no more of Mrs Folliott's true inwardness, on that subject at least, than she had lately cared to have of Monteith's.

There was nothing like a crowd, this unfortunate knew, for making one feel lonely, and he felt so increasingly during the meal; but he got thus at least in a measure away from the terrible little lady; after which, and before the end of the hour, he wanted still more to get away from everyone else. He was in fact about to perform this manoeuvre when he was checked by the jolly young woman he had been having on his left and who had more to say about the hotels, up and down the town, than he had ever known a young woman to have to say on any subject at all; she expressed herself in hotel terms exclusively, the names of those establishments playing through her speech as the *leit-motif* might have recurrently flashed and romped through a piece of profane modern music. She wanted to present him to the pretty girl she had brought with her, and who had apparently signified to her that she must do so.

'I think you know my brother-in-law, Mr Newton Winch,' the pretty girl had immediately said; she moved her head and shoulders together, as by a common spring, the effect of a stiff neck or of something loosened in her back hair; but becoming, queerly enough, all the prettier for doing so. He had seen in the papers, her brother-in-law, Mr Monteith's arrival – Mr Mark P. Monteith, wasn't it? – and where he was, and she had been with him, three days before, at the time; whereupon he had said, 'Hullo, what can have brought old Mark back?' He seemed to have believed – Newton had seemed – that that shirker, as he called him, never *would* come; and she guessed that if she had known she was going to meet such a former friend ('Which he claims you are, sir,' said the pretty girl) he would have asked her to find out what the trouble could be. But the real satisfaction would just be, she went on, if his former friend would himself go and see him and tell him; he had appeared of late so down.

'Oh, I remember him' – Mark didn't repudiate the friendship, placing him easily; only then he wasn't married and the pretty girl's sister must have come in later; which showed, his not knowing such things, how they had lost touch. The pretty girl was sorry to have to say in return to this that her sister wasn't living – had died two years after marrying; so that Newton was up there in Fiftieth Street alone; where (in explanation of his being 'down') he had been shut up for days with bad *grippe*; though now on the mend, or she wouldn't have gone to him, not she, who had had it nineteen times and didn't want to have it again. But the horrid poison just seemed to have entered into poor Newton's soul.

'That's the way it *can* take you, don't you know?' And then as, with her single twist, she just charmingly hunched her eyes at our friend, 'Don't you want to go to see him?'

Mark bethought himself: 'Well, I'm going to see a lady –'

She took the words from his mouth. 'Of course you're going to see a lady – every man in New York is. But Newton isn't a lady, unfortunately for him, to-day; and Sunday afternoon in this place, in this weather, alone –!'

'Yes, isn't it awful?' – he was quite drawn to her.

'Oh, *you've* got your lady!'

'Yes, I've got my lady, thank goodness!' The fervour of which was his sincere tribute to the note he had had on Friday morning from Mrs Ash, the only thing that had a little tempered his gloom.

'Well then, feel for others. Fit him in. Tell him why!'

'Why I've come back? I'm glad I *have* – since it was to see *you*!' Monteith made brave enough answer, promising to do what he could. He liked the pretty girl, with her straight attack and her free awkwardness – also with her difference from the others through something of a sense and a distinction given her by so clearly having Newton on her mind. Yet it was odd to him, and it showed the lapse of the years, that Winch – as he had known him of old – could *be* to that degree on anyone's mind.

III

OUTSIDE in the intensity of the cold – it was a jump from the Tropics to the Pole – he felt afresh the force of what he had just been saying; that if it weren't for the fact of Mrs Ash's good letter of welcome, despatched, characteristically, as soon as she had, like the faithful sufferer in Fiftieth Street, observed his name, in a newspaper, on one of the hotel-lists, he should verily, for want of a connection and an abutment, have scarce dared to face the void and the chill together, but have sneaked back into the jungle and there tried to lose himself. He made, as it was, the opposite effort, resolute to walk, though hovering now and then at vague crossways, radiations of roads to nothing, or taking cold counsel of the long but still sketchy vista, as it struck him, of the northward Avenue, bright and bleak, fresh and harsh, rich and evident somehow, a perspective like a page of florid modern platitudes. He didn't quite know what he had expected for his return – not certainly serenades and deputations; but without Mrs Ash his wail would have quite lacked geniality, and it was as if Phil Bloodgood had gone off not only with so large a slice of his small *peculium*, but with all the broken bits of the past, the loose ends of old relationships, that he had supposed he might pick up again. Well, perhaps he should still pick up a few – by the sweat of his brow; no motion of their own at least, he by this time judged, would send them fluttering into his hand.

Which reflections but quickened his forecast of this charm of the old Paris inveteracy renewed – the so prized custom of nine years before, when he still believed in results from his fond frequentation of the Beaux Arts; that of walking over the river to the Rue de Marignan, precisely, every Sunday without exception, and sitting at her fireside, and often all offensively, no doubt, outstaying every one. How he had used to want those hours then, and how again, after a little, at present, the Rue de Marignan might have been before him! He had gone to her there at that time with his troubles, such as they were, and they had always worked for her amusement – which had been her happy, her clever way of taking them: she couldn't have done anything better for them in that phase, poor innocent things compared with what they might have been, than be amused by them. Perhaps that was what she would still be – with those of his present hour; now too they might inspire her with the touch she best applied and was most instinctive mistress of: this didn't at all events strike him as what he should most resent. It wasn't as if Mrs Folliott, to make up for boring him with her own plaint, for example, had had so much as a gleam of conscious diversion over his.

'I'm *so* delighted to see you, I've such immensities to tell you!' – it began with the highest animation twenty minutes later, the very moment he stood there, the sense of the Rue de Marignan in the charming room and in the things about all reconstituted, regrouped, wonderfully preserved, down to the very sitting-places in the same relations, and down to the faint sweet mustiness of generations of cigarettes; but everything else different, and even vaguely alien, and by a measure still other than that of their own stretched interval and of the dear delightful woman's just a little pathetic alteration of face. He had allowed for the nine years, and so, it was to be hoped, had she; but the last thing, otherwise, that would have been touched, he immediately felt, was the quality, the intensity, of her care to see him. She cared, oh, so visibly and touchingly and almost radiantly – save for her being, yes, distinctly, a little *more* battered than from even a good nine years' worth; nothing could in fact have perched with so crowning an impatience on the heap of what she had to 'tell' as that special shade of revived consciousness of having him in particular to tell it to. It wasn't perhaps much to matter how soon she brought out and caused to ring, as it were, on the little recognised marqueterie table between them (such an anciently envied treasure), the heaviest gold-piece of current history she was to pay him with for having just so felicitously come back: he knew already, without the telling, that intimate domestic tension must lately, within those walls, have reached a climax and that he could serve supremely – oh, how he was going to serve! – as the most sympathetic of all pairs of ears.

The whole thing was upon him, in any case, with the minimum of delay: Bob had had it from her, definitely, the first of the week, and it was absolutely final now, that they must set up avowedly separate lives – without horrible 'proceedings' of any sort, but with her own situation, her independence, secured to her once for all. She had been coming to it, taking her time, and she had gone through – well, so old a friend would guess enough what; but she was at the point, oh, blessedly now, where she meant to stay, he'd see if she didn't; with which, in this wonderful way, he himself had arrived for the cream of it

and she was just selfishly glad. Bob had gone to Washington –
ostensibly on business, but really to recover breath; she had,
speaking vulgarly, knocked the wind out of him and was allowing him time to turn round. Mrs Folliott, moreover, she was
sure, would have gone – was certainly believed to have been
seen there five days ago; and of course his first necessity, for
public use, would be to patch up something with Mrs Folliott.
Mark knew about Mrs Folliott? – who was only, for that matter,
one of a regular 'bevy'. Not that it signified, however, if he
didn't: she would tell him about *her* later.

He took occasion from the first fraction of a break not quite
to know what he knew about Mrs Folliott – though perhaps he
could imagine a little; and it was probably at this minute that,
having definitely settled to a position, and precisely in his very
own tapestry *bergère*, the one with the delicious little spectral
'subjects' on the back and seat, he partly exhaled, and yet
managed partly to keep to himself, the deep resigned sigh of a
general comprehension. He knew what he was 'in' for, he heard
her go on – she said it again and again, seemed constantly to be
saying it while she smiled at him with her peculiar fine charm,
her positive gaiety of sensibility, scarce dimmed: 'I'm just selfishly glad, just selfishly glad!' Well, she was going to have reason
to be; she was going to put the whole case to him, all her
troubles and plans, and each act of the tragi-comedy of her
recent existence, as to the dearest and safest sympathiser in all
the world. There would be no chance for *his* case, though it was
so much for his case he had come; yet there took place within
him but a mild, dumb convulsion, the momentary strain of his
substituting, by the turn of a hand, one prospect of interest for
another.

Squaring himself in his old *bergère*, and with his lips, during
the effort, compressed to the same passive grimace that had an
hour or two before operated for the encouragement of Mrs
Folliott – just as it was to clear the stage completely for the
present more prolonged performance – he shut straight down,
as he even in the act called it to himself, on any personal claim
for social consideration and rendered a perfect little agony of
justice to the grounds of his friend's vividness. For it was all the

justice that could be expected of him that, though, secretly, he wasn't going to be interested in her being interesting, she was yet going to be so, all the same, by the very force of her lovely material (Bob Ash *was* such a pure pearl of a donkey!) and he was going to keep on knowing she was – yes, to the very end. When after the lapse of an hour he rose to go, the rich fact that she *had* been was there between them, and with an effect of the frankly, fearlessly, harmlessly intimate fireside passage for it that went beyond even the best memories of the pleasant past. He hadn't 'amused' her, no, in quite the same way as in the Rue de Marignan time – it had then been he who for the most part took frequent turns, emphatic, explosive, elocutionary, over that wonderful waxed parquet while she laughed as for the young perversity of him from the depths of the second, the matching *bergère*. To-day she herself held and swept the floor, putting him merely to the trouble of his perpetual 'Brava!' But that was all through the change of basis – the amusement, another name only for the thrilled absorption, having been inevitably for *him*: as how could it have failed to be with such a regular 'treat' to his curiosity? With the tea-hour now other callers were turning up, and he got away on the plea of his wanting so to think it all over. He hoped again he hadn't too queer a grin with his assurance to her, as if she would quite know what he meant, that he had been thrilled to the core. But she returned, quite radiantly, that he had carried *her* completely away; and her sincerity was proved by the final frankness of their temporary parting. 'My pleasure of you is selfish, horribly, I admit; so that if *that* doesn't suit you –!' Her faded beauty flushed again as she said it.

IV

IN the street again, as he resumed his walk, he saw how perfectly it would *have* to suit him and how he probably for a long time wouldn't be suited otherwise. Between them and that time, however, what mightn't for him, poor devil, on his new basis, have happened? She wasn't at any rate within any calculable period going to care so much for anything as for the so quaintly droll terms in which her rearrangement with her husband – thanks to that gentleman's inimitable fatuity – would have to be made. This was what it was to own, exactly, her special grace – the brightest gaiety in the finest sensibility; *such* a display of which combination, Mark felt as he went (if he could but have done it still more justice) she must have regaled him with! That exquisite last flush of her fadedness could only remain with him; yet while he presently stopped at a street-corner in a district redeemed from desolation but by a passage just then of a choked trolley-car that howled, as he paused for it, beneath the weight of its human accretions, he seemed to know the inward 'sinking' that has been determined in a hungry man by some extravagant sight of the preparation of somebody else's dinner. Florence Ash was dining, so to speak, off the feast of appreciation, appreciation of what she had to 'tell' him, that he had left her seated at; and she was welcome, assuredly – welcome, welcome, welcome, he musingly, he wistfully, and yet at the same time a trifle mechanically, repeated, stayed as he was a moment longer by the suffering shriek of another public vehicle and a sudden odd automatic return of his mind to the pretty girl, the flower of Mrs Folliott's crowd, who had spoken to him of Newton Winch. It was extraordinarily as if, on the instant, she reminded him, from across the town, that *she* had offered him dinner: it was really quite strangely, while he stood there, as if she had told him where he could go and get it. With which, none the less, it was apparently where he wouldn't find her – and what was there, after all, of nutritive in the image of Newton Winch? He made up his mind in a moment that it owed that property, which the pretty girl had somehow made imputable, to the fact of its simply being just then the one image of anything known to him that the terrible place had to offer. Nothing, he a minute later reflected, could have been so 'rum' as that, sick and sore, of a bleak New York eventide, he should have had nowhere to turn if not to the said Fiftieth Street.

That was the direction he accordingly took, for when he found the number given him by the same remarkable agent of fate also present to his memory he recognised the direct intervention of Providence and how it absolutely required a miracle

to explain his so precipitately taking up this loosest of connections. The miracle indeed soon grew clearer: Providence had,
on some obscure system, chosen this very ridiculous hour to
save him from cultivation of the sin of selfishness, the obsession
of egotism, and was breaking him to its will by constantly
directing his attention to the claims of others. Who could say
what at that critical moment mightn't have become of Mrs
Folliott (otherwise too then so sadly embroiled!) if she hadn't
been enabled to air to him her grievance and her rage? – just as
who could deny that it must have done Florence Ash a world of
good to have put her thoughts about Bob in order by the aid of a
person to whom the vision of Bob in the light of those thoughts
(or in other words to whom *her* vision of Bob and nothing else)
would mean so delightfully much? It was on the same general
lines that poor Newton Winch, bereft, alone, ill, perhaps dying,
and with the drawback of a not very sympathetic personality –
as Mark remembered it at least – to contend against in almost
any conceivable appeal to human furtherance, it was on these
lines, very much, that the luckless case in Fiftieth Street was
offered him as a source of salutary discipline. The moment for
such a lesson might strike him as strange, in view of the quite
special and independent opportunity for exercise that his spirit
had during the last three days enjoyed there in his hotel bedroom; but evidently his languor of charity needed some
admonition finer than any it might trust to chance for, and by
the time he at last, Winch's residence recognised, was duly
elevated to his level and had pressed the electric button at his
door, he felt himself acting indeed as under stimulus of a sharp
poke in the side.

V

WITHIN the apartment to which he had been admitted, moreover, the fine intelligence we have imputed to him was in the
course of three minutes confirmed; since it took him no longer
than that to say to himself, facing his old acquaintance, that he
had never seen anyone so improved. The place, which had the
semblance of a high studio light as well as a general air of other

profusions and amplitudes, might have put him off a little by its several rather glaringly false accents, those of contemporary domestic 'art' striking a little wild. The scene was smaller, but the rich confused complexion of the Pocahontas, showing through Du Barry paint and patches, might have set the example – which had been followed with the costliest candour – so that, clearly, Winch was in these days rich, as most people in New York seemed rich; as, in spite of Bob's depredations, Florence Ash was, as even Mrs Folliott was in spite of Phil Bloodgood's, as even Phil Bloodgood himself must have been for reasons too obvious; as in fine everyone had a secret for being, or for feeling, or for looking, everyone at least but Mark Monteith.

These facts were as nothing, however, in presence of his quick and strong impression that his pale, nervous, smiling, clean-shaven host had undergone since their last meeting some extraordinary process of refinement. He had been ill, unmistakeably, and the effects of a plunge into plain clean living, where any fineness had remained, were often startling, sometimes almost charming. But independently of this, and for a much longer time, some principle of intelligence, some art of life, would discernibly have worked in him. Remembered from college years and from those two or three luckless and faithless ones of the Law School as constitutionally common, as consistently and thereby doubtless even rather powerfully coarse, clever only for uncouth and questionable things, he yet presented himself now as if he had suddenly and mysteriously been educated. There was a charm in his wide, 'drawn', convalescent smile, in the way his fine fingers – had he anything like fine fingers of old? – played, and just fidgeted, over the prompt and perhaps a trifle incoherent offer of cigars, cordials, ash-trays, over the question of his visitor's hat, stick, fur coat, general best accommodation and ease; and how the deuce, accordingly, had charm, for coming out so on top, Mark wondered, 'squared' the other old elements? For the short interval so to have dealt with him what force had it turned on, what patented process, of the portentous New York order in which there were so many, had it skilfully applied? Were these the things New York did when you just gave her *all* her head, and that he himself then had perhaps too complacently missed? Strange almost to the point of putting him positively off at first – quite as an exhibition of the uncanny – this sense of Newton's having all the while neither missed nor muffed anything, and having, as with an eye to the *coup de théâtre* to come, lowered one's expectations, at the start, to that abject pitch. It might have affected one verily as an act of bad faith – really as such a rare stroke of subtlety as could scarce have been achieved by a straight or natural aim.

So much as this at least came and went in Monteith's agitated mind; the oddest intensity of apprehension, admiration, mystification, which the high north-light of the March afternoon and the quite splendidly vulgar appeal of fifty overdone decorative effects somehow fostered and sharpened. Everything had already gone, however, the next moment, for wasn't the man he had come so quite over-intelligently himself to patronise absolutely bowling him over with the extraordinary speech: 'See here, you know – you must be ill, or have had a bad shock, or some beastly upset: are you very sure you ought to have come out?' Yes, he after an instant believed his ears; coarse common Newton Winch, whom he had called on because he could, as a gentleman, after all afford to, coarse common Newton Winch, who had had troubles and been epidemically poisoned, lamentably sick, who bore in his face and in the very tension, quite exactly the 'charm', of his manner, the traces of his late ordeal, and, for that matter, of scarce completed gallant emergence – this astonishing ex-comrade was simply writing himself at a stroke (into our friend's excited imagination at all events) the most distinguished of men. Oh, *he* was going to be interesting, if Florence Ash had been going to be; but Mark felt how, under the law of a lively present difference, that would be an effect of one's having one's self thoroughly rallied. He knew within the minute that the tears stood in his eyes; he stared through them at his friend with a sharp 'Why, how do you know? How *can* you?' To which he added before Winch could speak: 'I met your charming sister-in-law a couple of hours since – at luncheon, at the Pocahontas; and heard from her that you were badly laid up and had spoken of me. So I came to minister to you.'

The object of this design hovered there again, considerably restless, shifting from foot to foot, changing his place, beginning and giving up motions, striking matches for a fresh cigarette, offering them again, redundantly, to his guest and then not lighting himself – but all the while with the smile of another creature than the creature known to Mark; all the while with the history of something that had happened to him ever so handsomely shining out. Mark was conscious within himself from this time on of two quite distinct processes of notation – that of his practically instant surrender to the consequences of the act of perception in his host of which the two women trained supposably in the art of pleasing had been altogether incapable; and that of some other condition on Newton's part that left his own poor power of divination nothing less than shamed. This last was signally the case on the former's saying, ever so responsively, almost radiantly, in answer to his account of how he happened to come: 'Oh, then it's very interesting!' *That* was the astonishing note, after what he had been through: neither Mrs Folliott nor Florence Ash had so much as hinted or breathed to him that *he* might have incurred that praise. No wonder therefore he was now taken – with this fresh party's instant suspicion and imputation of it; though it was indeed for some minutes next as if each tried to see which could accuse the other of the greater miracle of penetration. Mark was so struck, in a word, with the extraordinarily straight guess Winch had had there in reserve for him that, other quick impressions helping, there was nothing for him but to bring out, himself: 'There must be, my dear man, something rather wonderful the matter with you!' The quite more intensely and more irresistibly drawn grin, the quite unmistakeably deeper consciousness in the dark, wide eye, that accompanied the not quite immediate answer to which remark he was afterward to remember.

'How do you know that – or why do you think it?'

'Because there *must* be – for you to see! I shouldn't have expected it.'

'Then you take me for a damned fool?' laughed wonderful Newton Winch.

VI

HE could say nothing that, whether as to the sense of it or as to the way of it, didn't so enrich Mark's vision of him that our friend, after a little, as this effect proceeded, caught himself in the act of almost too curiously gaping. Everything, from moment to moment, fed his curiosity; such a question, for instance, as whether the quite ordinary peepers of the Newton Winch of their earlier youth could have looked under any provocation, either dark or wide; such a question, above all, as how *this* incalculable apparition came by the whole startling power of play of its extravagantly sensitive labial connections – exposed, so to its advantage (he now jumped at one explana- tion) by the removal of what had probably been one of the vulgarest of moustaches. With this, at the same time, the oddity of that particular consequence was vivid to him; the glare of his curiosity fairly lasting while he remembered how he had once noted the very opposite turn of the experiment for Phil Blood- good. He would have said in advance that poor Winch couldn't have afforded to risk showing his 'real' mouth; just as he would have said that in spite of the fine ornament that so considerably muffled it Phil could only have gained by showing his. But to have seen Phil shorn – as he once had done – was earnestly to pray that he might promptly again bristle; beneath Phil's moustache lurked nothing to 'make up' for it in case of removal. While he thought of which things the line of grimace, as he could only have called it, the mobile, interesting, ironic line the great double curve of which connected, in the face before him, the strong nostril with the lower cheek, became the very key to his first idea of Newton's capture of refinement. He had shaved and was happily transfigured. Phil Bloodgood had shaved and been wellnigh lost; though why should one just now too precipitately drag the reminiscence in?

That question too, at the queer touch of association, played up for Mark even under so much proof that the state of his own soul was being with the lapse of every instant registered. Phil Bloodgood had brought about the state of his soul – there was accordingly that amount of connection; only it became further remarkable that from the moment his companion had sounded him, and sounded him, he knew, down to the last truth of things, his disposition, his necessity to talk, the desire that had in the morning broken the spell of his confinement, the impulse that had thrown him so defeatedly into Mrs Folliott's arms and into Florence Ash's, these forces seemed to feel their impatience ebb and their discretion suddenly grow. His companion was talking again, but just then, incongruously, made his need to communicate lose itself. It was as if his personal case had already been touched by some tender hand – and that, after all, was the modest limit of its greed. 'I know now why you came back – did Lottie mention how I had wondered? But sit down, sit down – only let me, nervous beast as I am, take it standing! – and believe me when I tell you that I've now ceased to wonder. My dear chap, I *have* it! It can't but have been for poor Phil Bloodgood. He sticks out of you, the brute – as how, with what he has done to you, shouldn't he? There was a man to see me yesterday – Tim Slater, whom I don't think you know, but who's "on" everything within about two minutes of its happening (I never saw such a fellow!) and who confirmed my supposition, all my own, however, mind you at first, that you're one of the sufferers. So how the devil can you *not* feel knocked? Why *should* you look as if you were having the time of your life? What a hog to have played it on *you*, on *you*, of all his friends!' So Newton Winch continued, and so the air between the two men might have been, for a momentary watcher – which is indeed what I can but invite the reader to become – that of a nervously displayed, but all considerate, as well as most acute, curiosity on the one side, and that on the other, after a little, of an eventually fascinated acceptance of so much free and in especial of so much right attention. 'Do you *mind* my asking you? Because if you do I won't press; but as a man whose own responsibilities, some of 'em at least, don't differ much, I gather, from some of his, one would like to know how he was ever allowed to get to the point – ! But I *do* plough you up?'

Mark sat back in his chair, moved but holding himself, his elbows squared on each arm, his hands a bit convulsively interlocked across him – very much in fact as he had appeared an hour ago in the old tapestry *bergère*; but as his rigour was all then that of the grinding effort to profess and to give, so it was considerably now for the fear of too hysterically gushing. Somehow too – since his wound was to that extent open – he winced at hearing the author of it branded. He hadn't so much minded the epithets Mrs Folliott had applied, for they were to the appropriator of *her* securities. As the appropriator of his own he didn't so much want to brand him as – just more 'amusingly' even, if one would! – to make out, perhaps, with intelligent help, how such a man, in such a relation, *could* come to tread such a path: which was exactly the interesting light that Winch's curiosity and sympathy were there to assist him to. He pleaded at any rate immediately his advertising no grievance. 'I feel sore, I admit, and it's a horrid sort of thing to have had happen; but when you call him a brute and a hog I rather squirm, for brutes and hogs never live, I guess, in the sort of hell in which he now must be.'

Newton Winch, before the fireplace, his hands deep in his pockets, where his guest could see his long fingers beat a tattoo on his thighs, Newton Winch dangled and swung himself, and threw back his head and laughed. 'Well, I must say you take it amazingly! – all the more that to see you again this way is to feel that if, all along, there was a man whose delicacy and confidence and general attitude might have marked him for a particular consideration, you'd have been the man.' And they were more directly face to face again; with Newton smiling and smiling *so* appreciatively; making our friend in fact almost ask himself when before a man had ever grinned from ear to ear to the effect of its so becoming him. What he replied, however, was that Newton described in those flattering terms a client temptingly fatuous; after which, and the exchange of another protest or two in the interest of justice and decency, and another plea or two in that of the still finer contention that even the basest misdeeds had always somewhere or other, could one get at it, their propitiatory side, our hero found himself on his feet again, under the influence of a sudden failure of everything but horror – a horror determined by some turn of their talk and indeed by the very fact of the freedom of it. It was as if a far-borne sound of the hue and cry, a vision of his old friend hunted and at bay, had suddenly broken in – this other friend's, this irresistibly intelligent other companion's, practically vivid projection of that making the worst ugliness real. 'Oh, it's just making my wry face to somebody, and your letting me and caring and wanting to know: that,' Mark said, 'is what does me good; not any other hideous question. I mean I don't take any interest in *my* case – what one wonders about, you see, is what can be done for him. I mean, that is' – for he floundered a little, not knowing at last quite what he did mean, a great rush of mere memories, a great humming sound as of thick, thick echoes, rising now to an assault that he met with his face indeed contorted. If he didn't take care he should howl; so he more or less successfully took care – yet with his host vividly watching him while he shook the danger temporarily off. 'I don't mind – though it's rather *that*; my having felt this morning, after three dismal dumb bad days, that one's friends perhaps would be thinking of one. All I'm conscious of now – I give you my word – is that I'd like to see him.'

'You'd like to see him?'

'Oh, I don't say,' Mark ruefully smiled, 'that I should like him to see *me* –!'

Newton Winch, from where he stood – and they were together now, on the great hearth-rug that was a triumph of modern orientalism – put out one of the noted fine hands and, with an expressive headshake, laid it on his shoulder. 'Don't wish him that, Monteith – don't wish him that!'

'Well, but' – and Mark raised his eyebrows still higher – 'he'd see I bear up pretty well!'

'God forbid he should see, my dear fellow!' Newton cried as for the pang of it.

Mark had for his idea, at any rate, the oddest sense of an exaltation that grew by this use of frankness. 'I'd go to him. Hanged if I wouldn't – anywhere!'

His companion's hand still rested on him. 'You'd go to him?'

Mark stood up to it – though trying to sink solemnity as pretentious. 'I'd go like a shot.' And then he added: 'And it's probably what – when we've turned round – I *shall* do.'

'When "we" have turned round?'

'Well' – he was a trifle disconcerted at the tone – 'I say that because you'll have helped me.'

'Oh, I do nothing but want to help you!' Winch replied – which made it right again; especially as our friend still felt himself reassuringly and sustainingly grasped. But Winch went on: 'You *would* go to him – in kindness?'

'Well – to understand.'

'To understand how he could swindle you?'

'Well,' Mark kept on, 'to try and make out with him how, after such things –!' But he stopped; he couldn't name them.

It was as if his companion knew. 'Such things as you've done for him, of course – such services as you've rendered him.'

'Ah, from far back. If I could tell you,' our friend vainly wailed – 'if I could tell you!'

Newton Winch patted his shoulder. 'Tell me – tell me!'

'The sort of relation, I mean; ever so many things of a kind –!' Again, however, he pulled up; he felt the tremor of his voice.

'Tell me, tell me,' Winch repeated with the same movement.

The tone in it now made their eyes meet again, and with this presentation of the altered face Mark measured as not before, for some reason, the extent of the recent ravage. 'You must have been ill indeed.'

'Pretty bad. But I'm better. And you do me good' – with which the light of convalescence came back.

'I don't awfully bore you?'

Winch shook his head. 'You keep me up – and you see how no one else comes near me.'

Mark's eyes made out that he *was* better – though it wasn't yet that nothing was the matter with him. If there was ever a man with whom there was still something the matter –! Yet one couldn't insist on that, and meanwhile he clearly did want company. 'Then there we are. I myself had no one to go to.'

'You save my life,' Newton renewedly grinned.

VII

'WELL, it's your own fault,' Mark replied to that, 'if you make me take advantage of you.' Winch had withdrawn his hand, which was back, violently shaking keys or money, in his trousers pocket; and in this position he had abruptly a pause, a sensible absence, that might have represented either some odd drop of attention, some turn-off to another thought, or just simply the sudden act of listening. His guest had indeed himself – under suggestion – the impression of a sound. 'Mayn't you perhaps – if you hear something – have a call?'

Mark had said it so lightly, however, that he was the more struck with his host's appearing to turn just paler; and, with it the latter now *was* listening. 'You hear something?'

'I thought *you* did.' Winch himself, on Mark's own pressure of the outside bell, had opened the door of the apartment – an indication then, it sufficiently appeared, that Sunday after-noons were servants', or attendants', or even trained nurses' holidays. It had also marked the stage of his convalescence, and to that extent – after his first flush of surprise – had but smoothed Monteith's way. At present he barely gave further attention; detaching himself as under some odd cross-impulse, he had quitted the spot and then taken, in the wide room, a restless turn – only, however, to revert in a moment to his friend's just-uttered deprecation of the danger boring him. 'If I make you take advantage of me – that is blessedly talk to me – it's exactly what I want to do. Talk to me – talk to me!' He positively waved it on; pulling up again, however, in his own talk, to say with a certain urgency: 'Hadn't you better sit down?'

Mark, who stayed before the fire, couldn't but excuse him-self. 'Thanks – I'm very well so. I think of things and I fidget.'

Winch stood a moment with his eyes on the ground. 'Are you very sure?'

'Quite – I'm all right if you don't mind.'

'Then as you like!' With which, shaking to extravagance again his long legs, Newton had swung off – only with a move-ment that, now his back was turned, affected his visitor as the most whimsical of all the forms of his rather unnatural manner.

He was curiously different with his back shown, as Mark now
for the first time saw it – dangling and somewhat wavering, as
from an excess of uncertainty of gait; and this impression was so
strange, it created in our friend, uneasily and on the spot, such a
need of explanation, that his speech was stayed long enough to
give Winch time to turn round again. The latter had indeed by
this moment reached one of the limits of the place, the wide
studio bay, where he paused, his back to the light and his face
afresh presented, to let his just passingly depressed and quickened eyes take in as much as possible of the large floor, range
over it with such brief freedom of search as the disposition of
the furniture permitted. He was looking for something, though
the betrayed reach of vision was but of an instant. Mark caught
it, however, and with his own sensibility all in vibration, found
himself feeling at once that it meant something and that what it
meant was connected with his entertainer's slightly marked
appeal to him, the appeal of a moment before, not to remain
standing. Winch knew by this time quite easily enough that he
was hanging fire; which meant that they were suddenly facing
each other across the wide space with a new consciousness.

Everything had changed – changed extraordinarily with the
mere turning of that gentleman's back, the treacherous aspect
of which its owner couldn't surely have suspected. If the
question was of the pitch of their sensibility, at all events, it
wouldn't be Mark's that should vibrate to least purpose. Visibly
it had come to his host that something had within the few
instants remarkably happened, but there glimmered on him
an induction that still made him keep his own manner. Newton
himself might now resort to any manner he liked. His eyes had
raked the floor to recover the position of something dropped or
misplaced, and something, above all, awkward or compromising; and he had wanted his companion not to command this
scene from the hearth-rug, the hearth-rug where he had been
just before holding him, hypnotising him to blindness, *because*
the object in question would there be most exposed to sight.
Mark embraced this with a further drop – while the apprehension penetrated – of his power to go on, and with an immense
desire at the same time that his eyes should seem only to look at

his friend; who broke out now, for that matter, with a fresh appeal. 'Aren't you going to take advantage of me, man – aren't you going to *take* it?'

Everything had changed, we have noted, and nothing could more have proved it than the fact that, by the same turn, sincerity of desire had dropped out of Winch's chords, while irritation, sharp and almost imperious, had come in. 'That's because he sees I see something!' Mark said to himself; but he had no need to add that it shouldn't prevent his seeing more – for the simple reason that, in a miraculous fashion, this was exactly what he did do in glaring out the harder. It was beyond explanation, but the very act of blinking thus in an attempt at showy steadiness became one and the same thing with an optical excursion lasting the millionth of a minute and making him aware that the edge of a rug, at the point where an arm-chair, pushed a little out of position, over-straddled it, happened just not wholly to have covered in something small and queer, neat and bright, crooked and compact, in spite of the strong toe-tip surreptitiously applied to giving it the right lift. Our gentleman, from where he hovered, and while looking straight at the master of the scene, yet saw, as by the tiny flash of a reflection from fine metal, *under* the chair. What he recognised, or at least guessed at, as sinister, made him for a moment turn cold, and that chill was on him while Winch again addressed him – as differently as possible from any manner yet used. 'I beg of you in God's name to talk to me – to *talk* to me!'

It had the ring of pure alarm and anguish, but was by this turn at least more human than the dazzling glitter of intelligence to which the poor man had up to now been treating him. 'It's you, my good friend, who are in deep trouble,' Mark was accordingly quick to reply, 'and I ask your pardon for being so taken up with my own sorry business.'

'Of course I'm in deep trouble' – with which Winch came nearer again; 'but turning you on was exactly what I wanted.'

Mark Monteith, at this, couldn't, for all his rising dismay, but laugh out; his sense of the ridiculous so swallowed up, for that brief convulsion, his sense of the sinister. Of such convenience in pain, it seemed, was the fact of another's pain, and of so much worth again disinterested sympathy! 'Your interest was then –?'

'My interest was in your being interesting. For you *are*! And my nerves –!' said Newton Winch with a face from which the mystifying smile had vanished, yet in which distinction, as Mark so persistently appreciated it, still sat in the midst of ravage.

Mark wondered and wondered – he made strange things out. 'Your nerves have needed company.' He could lay his hand on him now, even as shortly before he had felt Winch's own pressure of possession and detention. 'As good for you yourself, that – or still better,' he went on – 'than I and my grievance were to have found you. Talk to *me*, talk to *me*, Newton Winch!' he added with an immense inspiration of charity.

'That's a different matter – that others but too much can do! But I'll say this. If you want to go to Phil Bloodgood –!'

'Well?' said Mark as he stopped. He stopped and Mark had now a hand on each of his shoulders and held him at arm's-length, held him with a fine idea that was not disconnected from the sight of the small neat weapon he had been fingering in the low, luxurious morocco chair – it was of the finest orange colour – and then had laid beside him on the carpet; where, after he had admitted his visitor, his presence of mind coming back to it and suggesting that he couldn't pick it up without making it more conspicuous, he had thought, by some swing of the foot or other casual manoeuvre, to dissimulate its visibility.

They were at close quarters now as not before and Winch perfectly passive, with eyes that somehow had no shadow of a secret left and with the betrayal to the sentient hands that grasped him of an intense, an extraordinary general tremor. To Mark's challenge he opposed afresh a brief silence, but the very quality of it, with his face speaking, was that of a gaping wound. 'Well, you needn't take *that* trouble. You see I'm such another.'

'Such another as Phil –?'

He didn't blink. 'I don't know for sure, but I guess I'm worse.'

'Do you mean you're guilty –?'

'I mean I shall be wanted. Only I've stayed to take it.'

Mark threw back his head, but only tightened his hands. He inexpressibly understood, and nothing in life had ever been so strange and dreadful to him as his thus helping himself by a longer and straighter stretch, as it were, to the monstrous sense of his friend's 'education'. It had been, in its immeasurable action, the education of business, of which the fruits were all around them. Yet prodigious was the interest, for prodigious truly – it seemed to loom before Mark – must have been the system. 'To "take" it?' he echoed; and then, though faltering a little, 'To take what?'

He had scarce spoken when a long sharp sound shrilled in from the outer door, seeming of so high and peremptory a pitch that with the start it gave him his grasp of his host's shoulders relaxed an instant, though to the effect of no movement in *them* but what came from just a sensibly intenser vibration of the whole man. 'For *that*!' said Newton Winch.

'Then you've known –?'

'I've expected. You've helped me to wait.' And then as Mark gave an ironic wail: 'You've tided me over. My condition has *wanted* somebody or something. Therefore, to complete this service, will you be so good as to open the door?'

Deep in the eyes Mark looked him, and still to the detection of no glimmer of the earlier man in the depths. The earlier man had been what he invidiously remembered – yet would *he* had been the whole simpler story! Then he moved his own eyes straight to the chair under which the revolver lay and which was but a couple of yards away. He felt his companion take this consciousness in, and it determined in them another long, mute exchange. 'What do you mean to do?'

'Nothing.'

'On your honour?'

'*My* "honour"?' his host returned with an accent that he felt even as it sounded he should never forget.

It brought to his own face a crimson flush – he dropped his guarding hands. Then as for a last look at him: 'You're wonderful!'

'We *are* wonderful,' said Newton Winch, while, simultaneously with the words, the pressed electric bell again and for a longer time pierced the warm cigaretted air.

Mark turned, threw up his arms, and it was only when he had passed through the vestibule and laid his hand on the doorknob that the horrible noise dropped. The next moment he was face to face with two visitors, a nondescript personage in a high hat and an astrakhan collar and cuffs, and a great belted constable, a splendid massive New York 'officer' of the type he had had occasion to wonder at much again in the course of his walk, the type so by itself – his wide observation quite suggested – among those of the peacemakers of the earth. The pair stepped straight in – no word was said; but as he closed the door behind them Mark heard the infallible crack of a discharged pistol and, so nearly with it as to make all one violence, the sound of a great fall; things the effect of which was to lift him, as it were, with his company, across the threshold of the room in a shorter time than that taken by this record of the fact. But their rush availed little; Newton was stretched on his back before the fire; he had held the weapon horribly to his temple, and his upturned face was disfigured. The emissaries of the law, looking down at him, exhaled simultaneously a gruff imprecation, and then while the worthy in the high hat bent over the subject of their visit the one in the helmet raised a severe pair of eyes to Mark. 'Don't you think, sir, you might have prevented it?'

Mark took a hundred things in, it seemed to him – things of the scene, of the moment, and of all the strange moments before; but one appearance more vividly even than the others stared out at him. 'I really think I must practically have caused it.'

This book is set in PLANTIN, designed by the great French
printer and typographer Christopher Plantin (c. 1520–89),
who began as a bookbinder in Antwerp. Plantin was
instrumental in establishing the pre-eminence
of Flemish printing during the sixteenth
century, although in the elegance
of his fonts he remained
quintessentially
French.